Library of America, a nonprofit organization,
champions our nation's cultural heritage
by publishing America's greatest writing in
authoritative new editions and providing resources
for readers to explore this rich, living legacy.

JOHN UPDIKE

NOVELS 1968-1975

JOHN UPDIKE

NOVELS 1968–1975

Couples
Rabbit Redux
A Month of Sundays

Christopher Carduff, *editor*

THE LIBRARY OF AMERICA

John Updike:
Novels 1968–1975
is published with support from

THE GIORGI FAMILY FOUNDATION

Contents

COUPLES

To Mary

There is a tendency in the average citizen, even if he has a high standing in his profession, to consider the decisions relating to the life of the society to which he belongs as a matter of fate on which he has no influence—like the Roman subjects all over the world in the period of the Roman empire, a mood favorable for the resurgence of religion but unfavorable for the preservation of a living democracy.

—PAUL TILLICH,
The Future of Religions

We love the flesh: its taste, its tones,
Its charnel odor, breathed through Death's jaws. . . .
Are we to blame if your fragile bones
Should crack beneath our heavy, gentle paws?

—ALEXANDER BLOK,
"The Scythians"

Chapters

I

Welcome to Tarbox

"WHAT DID you make of the new couple?"

The Hanemas, Piet and Angela, were undressing. Their bedchamber was a low-ceilinged colonial room whose woodwork was painted the shade of off-white commercially called eggshell. A spring midnight pressed on the cold windows.

"Oh," Angela answered vaguely, "they seemed young." She was a fair soft brown-haired woman, thirty-four, going heavy in her haunches and waist yet with a girl's fine hard ankles and a girl's tentative questing way of moving, as if the pure air were loosely packed with obstructing cloths. Age had touched only the softened line of her jaw and her hands, their stringy backs and reddened fingertips.

"How young, exactly?"

"Oh, I don't know. He's thirty trying to be forty. She's younger. Twenty-eight? Twenty-nine? Are you thinking of taking a census?"

He grudgingly laughed. Piet had red hair and a close-set body; no taller than Angela, he was denser. His flattish Dutch features, inherited, were pricked from underneath by an acquired American something—a guilty humorous greed, a wordless question. His wife's languid unexpectedness, a diffident freshness born of aristocratic self-possession, still fascinated him. He thought of himself as coarse and saw her as fine, so fair and fine her every gesture seemed transparently informed by a graciousness and honesty beyond him. When he had met her, Angela Hamilton, she had been a young woman past first bloom, her radiance growing lazy, with an affecting slow mannerism of looking away, the side of her neck bared, an inexplicably unscarred beauty playing at schoolteaching and living with her parents in Nun's Bay, and he had been laboring for her father, in partnership with an army friend, one of their first jobs, constructing a pergola in view of the ocean and the great chocolate-dark rock that suggested, from a slightly other angle, a female profile and the folds of a wimple. There had

5

been a cliff, an ample green lawn, and bushes trimmed to the flatness of tables. In the house there had been many clocks, grandfather's and ship's clocks, clocks finished in ormolu or black lacquer, fine-spun clocks in silver cases, with four balls as pendulum. Their courtship passed as something instantly forgotten, like an enchantment, or a mistake. Time came unstuck. All the clocks hurried their ticking, hurried them past doubts, around sharp corners and knobbed walnut newels. Her father, a wise-smiling man in a tailored gray suit, failed to disapprove. She had been one of those daughters so favored that spinsterhood alone might dare to claim her. Fertility at all costs. He threw business his son-in-law's way. The Hanemas' first child, a daughter, was born nine months after the wedding night. Nine years later Piet still felt, with Angela, a superior power seeking through her to employ him. He spoke as if in self-defense: "I was just wondering at what stage they are. He seemed rather brittle and detached."

"You're hoping they're at our stage?"

Her cool thin tone, assumed at the moment when he had believed their intimacy, in this well-lit safe room encircled by the April dark, to be gathering poignant force enough to vault them over their inhibitions, angered him. He felt like a fool. He said, "That's right. The seventh circle of bliss."

"Is that what we're in?" She sounded, remotely, ready to believe it.

They each stood before a closet door, on opposite sides of an unused fireplace framed in pine paneling and plaster painted azure. The house was a graceful eighteenth-century farmhouse of eight rooms. A barn and a good square yard and a high lilac hedge came with the property. The previous owners, who had had adolescent boys, had attached a basketball hoop to one side of the barn and laid down a small asphalt court. At another corner of the two acres stood an arc of woods tangent to a neighboring orchard. Beyond this was a dairy farm. Seven miles further along the road, an unseen presence, was the town of Nun's Bay; and twenty miles more, to the north, Boston. Piet was by profession a builder, in love with snug right-angled things, and he had grown to love this house, its rectangular low rooms, its baseboards and chair rails molded and beaded by hand, the slender mullions of the windows whose older panes were flecked with oblong bubbles and tinged with lavender, the swept worn brick of the fireplace hearths like entryways into a sooty upward core of time, the attic he had lined with silver insulation paper so it seemed now a vaulted jewel box or an Aladdin's cave, the solid freshly poured basement that had been a cellar floored with dirt when they had moved in five years ago. He loved how this house welcomed into itself in every season lemony flecked rhomboids of sun whose slow sliding revolved it with the day, like the cabin of a ship on a curving course. All houses, all things that enclosed, pleased Piet, but his modest Dutch sense of how much of the world he was permitted to mark off and hold was precisely satisfied by this flat lot two hundred feet back from the road, a mile from the center of town, four miles distant from the sea.

Angela, descended from piratical New Bedford whaling captains, wanted a property with a view of the Atlantic. She had mourned when the new couple in town, the Whitmans, had bought, through the agency of Gallagher & Hanema, Real Estate and Contracting, a house she had coveted, the old Robinson place, a jerrybuilt summer house in need of total repair. It had a huge view of the salt marshes and a wind exposure that would defy all insulation. She and Piet had gone over it several times in the winter past. It had been built as a one-story cottage around 1900. In the early twenties it had been jacked up on posts and a new first floor built under it, with a long screened porch that darkened the living room. Then new owners had added a servants' wing whose level differed by two steps from the main structure. Piet showed Angela the shabby carpentry, the crumbling gypsum wallboard, the corroded iron plumbing, the antique wiring with its brittle rubber insulation, the rattling sashes chewed by animals and rain. A skylight in the main bedroom leaked. The only heat came from a single round register in the living-room floor, above a manually fed coal furnace in an unwalled clay hole. A full cellar would have to be excavated. Solid interior walls and a complete heating system were essential. The roof must be replaced. Gutters, sashes. Ceilings. The kitchen was quaint, useless; servants had run it, summers only, making lobster salads. On the two windward sides the cedar shingles had been warped and whitened and blown away. Forty thousand the asking price, and twelve more immediately, minimum. It was too much to ask him to take on. Standing at the broad slate sink contemplating the winter view of ditch-traversed marsh and the brambled islands of hawthorn and alder and the steel-blue channel beyond and the rim of dunes white as salt and above all the honed edge of ocean, Angela at last agreed. It was too much.

Now, thinking of this house from whose purchase he had escaped and from whose sale he had realized a partner's share of profit, Piet conservatively rejoiced in the house he had held. He felt its lightly supporting symmetry all around him. He pictured his two round-faced daughters asleep in its shelter. He gloated upon the sight of his wife's body, her fine ripeness.

Having unclasped her party pearls, Angela pulled her dress, the black décolleté knit, over her head. Its soft wool caught in her hairpins. As she struggled, lamplight struck zigzag fire from her slip and static electricity made its nylon adhere to her flank. The slip lifted, exposing stocking-tops and garters. Without her head she was all full form, sweet, solid.

Pricked by love, he accused her: "You're not happy with me."

She disentangled the bunched cloth and obliquely faced him. The lamplight, from a bureau lamp with a pleated linen shade, cut shadows into the line of her jaw. She was aging. A year ago, she would have denied the accusation. "How can I be," she asked, "when you flirt with every woman in sight?"

"In sight? Do I?"

"Of course you do. You know you do. Big or little, old or young, you eat them up. Even the yellow ones, Bernadette Ong. Even poor little soused Bea Guerin, who has enough troubles."

"You seemed happy enough, conferring all night with Freddy Thorne."

"Piet, we can't keep going to parties back to back. I come home feeling dirty. I hate it, this way we live."

"You'd rather we went belly to belly? Tell me"—he had stripped to his waist, and she shied from that shieldlike breadth of taut bare skin with its cruciform blazon of amber hair—"what do you and Freddy find to talk about for hours on end? You huddle in the corner like children playing jacks." He took a step forward, his eyes narrowed and pink, party-chafed. She resisted the urge to step backwards, knowing that this threatening mood of his was supposed to end in sex, was a plea.

Instead she reached under her slip to unfasten her garters. The gesture, so vulnerable, disarmed him; Piet halted before the fireplace, his bare feet chilled by the hearth's smooth bricks.

"He's a jerk," she said carelessly, of Freddy Thorne. Her voice was lowered by the pressure of her chin against her chest; the downward reaching of her arms gathered her breasts to a dark crease. "But he talks about things that interest women. Food. Psychology. Children's teeth."

"What does he say psychological?"

"He was talking tonight about what we all see in each other."

"Who?"

"You know. Us. The couples."

"What Freddy Thorne sees in me is a free drink. What he sees in you is a gorgeous fat ass."

She deflected the compliment. "He thinks we're a circle. A magic circle of heads to keep the night out. He told me he gets frightened if he doesn't see us over a weekend. He thinks we've made a church of each other."

"That's because he doesn't go to a real church."

"Well Piet, you're the only one who does. Not counting the Catholics." The Catholics they knew socially were the Gallaghers and Bernadette Ong. The Constantines had lapsed.

"It's the source," Piet said, "of my amazing virility. A stiffening sense of sin." And in his chalkstripe suit pants he abruptly dove forward, planted his weight on his splayed raw-knuckled hands, and stood upside down. His tensed toes reached for the tip of his conical shadow on the ceiling; the veins in his throat and forearms bulged. Angela looked away. She had seen this too often before. He neatly flipped back to his feet; his wife's silence embarrassed him. "Christ be praised," he said, and clapped, applauding himself.

"Shh. You'll wake the children."

"Why the hell shouldn't I, they're always waking me, the little bloodsuckers." He went down on his knees and toddled to the edge of the bed. "Dadda, Dadda, wake up-up, Dadda. The Sunnay paper's here, guess what? Jackie Kenneny's having a *ba*by!"

"You're so cruel," Angela said, continuing her careful

undressing, parting vague obstacles with her hands. She opened her closet door so that from her husband's angle her body was hidden. Her voice floated free: "Another thing Freddy thinks, he thinks the children are suffering because of it."

"Because of what?"

"Our social life."

"Well I have to have a social life if you won't give me a sex life."

"If you think *that* approach is the way to a lady's heart, you have a lot to learn." He hated her tone; it reminded him of the years before him, when she had instructed children.

He asked her, "Why shouldn't children suffer? They're supposed to suffer. How else can they learn to be good?" For he felt that if only in the matter of suffering he knew more than she, and that without him she would raise their daughters as she had been raised, to live in a world that didn't exist.

She was determined to answer him seriously, until her patience dulled his pricking mood. "That's positive suffering," she said. "What we give them is neglect so subtle they don't even notice it. We aren't abusive, we're just evasive. For instance, Frankie Appleby is a bright child, but he's just going to waste, he's just Jonathan little-Smith's punching bag because their parents are always together."

"Hell. Half the reason we all live in this silly hick town is for the sake of the children."

"But we're the ones who have the fun. The children just get yanked along. They didn't enjoy all those skiing trips last winter, standing in the T-bar line shivering and miserable. The girls wanted all winter to go some Sunday to a museum, a nice warm museum with stuffed birds in it, but we wouldn't take them because we would have had to go as a family and our friends might do something exciting or ghastly without us. Irene Saltz finally took them, bless her, or they'd never have gone. I like Irene; she's the only one of us who has somehow kept her freedom. Her freedom from crap."

"How much did you drink tonight?"

"It's just that Freddy didn't let me talk enough."

"He's a jerk," Piet said and, suffocated by an obscure sense of exclusion, seeking to obtain at least the negotiable asset of a firm rejection, he hopped across the hearth-bricks worn like a passageway in Delft and sharply kicked shut Angela's closet door, nearly striking her. She was naked.

He too was naked. Piet's hands, feet, head, and genitals were those of a larger man, as if his maker, seeing that the cooling body had been left too small, had injected a final surge of plasma which at these extremities had ponderously clotted. Physically he held himself, his tool-toughened palms curved and his acrobat's back a bit bent, as if conscious of a potent burden.

Angela had flinched and now froze, one arm protecting her breasts. A luminous polleny pallor, the shadow of last summer's bathing suit, set off her surprisingly luxuriant pudendum. The slack forward cant of her belly remembered her pregnancies. Her thick-thighed legs were varicose. But her tipped arms seemed, simple and symmetrical, a maiden's; her white feet were high-arched and neither little toe touched the floor. Her throat, wrists, and triangular bush appeared the pivots for some undeniable effort of flight, but like Eve on a portal she crouched in shame, stone. She held rigid. Her blue irises cupped light catlike, shallowly. Her skin breathed hate. He did not dare touch her, though her fairness gathered so close dried his tongue. Their bodies hung upon them as clothes too gaudy. Piet felt the fireplace draft on his ankles and became sensitive to the night beyond her hunched shoulders, an extensiveness pressed tight against the bubbled old panes and the frail mullions, a blackness charged with the ache of first growth and the suspended skeletons of Virgo and Leo and Gemini.

She said, "Bully."

He said, "You're lovely."

"That's too bad. I'm going to put on my nightie."

Sighing, immersed in a clamor of light and paint, the Hanemas dressed and crept to bed, exhausted.

As always after a party Piet was slow to go to sleep. There had not been many parties for him as a child and now they left him overexcited, tumescent. He touched his own self to make himself sleepy. Quickly his wife was dead weight beside him. She claimed she never dreamed. Pityingly he put his hand beneath the cotton nightie transparent to his touch and massaged the massive blandness of her warm back, hoping to stir in the depths of her sleep an eddy, a fluid fable she could tell herself and in the morning remember. She would be a valley and he a sandstorm. He would be a gentle lion bathing in her river. He could not believe she never dreamed. How could one not dream? He always dreamed. He dreamed last night he was an old minister making calls. Walking in the country, he crossed a superhighway and waited a long time on the median strip. Waiting, he looked down into a rural valley where small houses smoked from their chimneys. He must make his calls there. He crossed the rest of the road and was relieved when a policeman pulled up on a motorcycle and, speaking German, arrested him.

The party had been given by the Applebys in honor of the new couple, the what, the Whitmans. Frank had known Ted, or Dan, at Exeter, or Harvard. Exeter, Harvard: it was to Piet like looking up at the greenhouse panes spattered with white-wash to dull the sun. He shut out the greenhouse. He did not wish to remember the greenhouse. It was a cliff.

Stiffly his fingers tired of trying to give his wife a dream: a baby on the river of herself, Moses in the Nile morning found snagged in the rustling papyrus, Egyptian handmaids, willowy flanks, single lotus, easy access. Sex part of nature before Christ. *Bully.* Bitch. Taking up three-quarters of the bed as if duty done. Mouthbreathing with slack lips. Words in and out. Virgins pregnant through the ear. Talk to me psychologee. He touched in preference again himself. Waxen. Wilted camellia petals. In his youth an ivory rod at will. At the thought of a cleft or in class a shaft of sun laid on his thigh: stand to recite: *breathes there a man with soul so dead.* The whole class tittering at him bent over. The girl at the desk next wore lineny blouses so sheer her bra straps peeped and so short-sleeved that her armpits. Showed, shaved. Vojt. Annabelle Vojt. One man, one Vojt. Easy Dutch ways. Married a poultry farmer from outside Grand Rapids. Wonderful tip of her tongue, agile, squarish. Once after a dance French-kissed him parked by the quarry and he shot off behind his fly. Intenser then, the duct narrower, greater velocity. Not his girl but her underpants satiny, distant peaty odor, rustle of crinoline, formal dance. Quick as a wink, her dark tongue saucy under his. His body flashed the news nerve to nerve. Stiff in an instant. Touch. A waxworks petal laid out pillowed in sensitive frizz: wake up. Liquor. Evil dulling stuff. Lazes the blood, saps muscle tone. He turned over, bunched the pillow, lay flat and straight, trying to align himself with an invisible grain, the grain of the world, fate. Relax. Picture the party.

Twisting. Bald Freddy Thorne with a glinting moist smirk put on the record. Chubby. *Huooff: cummawn naioh evvribuddi less* Twist! Therapy, to make them look awful. They were growing old and awful in each other's homes. Only Carol had it of the women, the points of her pelvis making tidy figure eights, hands aloof like gentle knives, weight switching foot to foot, a silent clicking, stocking feet, narrow, hungry, her scrawny kind of high-school beauty, more his social level, the motion, coolly neat, feet forgotten, eyelids elegantly all but shuttered, making a presumed mist of Frank Appleby bouncing opposite, no logic in his hips, teeth outcurved braying, gums bared, brown breath, unpleasant spray. Everybody twisted. Little-Smith's black snickering feet. Georgene's chin set determinedly as if on second serve. Angela, too soft, rather swayed. Gallagher a jerking marionette. John Ong watched sober, silent, smiling, smoking. Turning to Piet he made high friendly noises that seemed in the din all vowels; Piet knew the Korean was worth more than them all together in a jiggling jouncing bunch but he could never understand what he said: *Who never to himself has said.* Bernadette came up, broad flat lady in two dimensions, half-Japanese, the other half Catholic, from Baltimore, and asked Piet, *Twist?* In the crowded shaking room, the Applebys' children's playroom, muraled in pink ducks, Bernadette kept bumping him, whacking him with her silken flatnesses, crucifix hopping in the shallow space between her breasts, thighs, wrists, bumping him, the yellow peril. *Whoofwheeieu. Wow.* Better a foxtrot. Making fools of themselves, working off steam, it's getting too suburban in here. The windows had been painted shut. Walls of books.

Piet felt, brave small Dutch boy, a danger hanging tidal above his friends, in this town where he had been taken in because Angela had been a Hamilton. The men had stopped having careers and the women had stopped having babies. Liquor and love were left. Bea Guerin, as they danced to Connie Francis, her drunken limpness dragging on his side so his leg and neck

ached, her steamy breasts smearing his shirt, seemed to have
asked why he didn't want to fuck her. He wasn't sure she had
said it, it sounded like something in Dutch, *fokker, in de fuik
lopen*, drifting to him from his parents as they talked between
themselves in the back room of the greenhouse. Little Piet,
Amerikander, couldn't understand. But he loved being there
with them, in the overheated warmth, watching his father's
broad stained thumbs packing moss, his mother's pallid needling fingers wrapping pots in foil and stabbing in the green
price spindles. Once more with the eyes of a child Piet saw the
spools of paper ribbon, the boxes holding colored grits and
pebbles for the tiny potted tableaux of cactuses and violets and
china houses and animal figurines with spots of reflection on
their noses, the drawerful of stacked gift cards saying in raised
silver HANEMA, his name, himself, restraining constellated in
its letters all his fate, *me, a man, amen ah*. Beside the back-
room office where Mama did up pots and Papa paid his bills
were the icy dewy doors where cut roses and carnations being
dyed and lovely iris and gladioli leaned, refrigerated, dead. Piet
tensed and changed position and erased the greenhouse with
the party.

The new couple. They looked precious to themselves,
self-cherished, like gladioli. Cambridge transplants, tall and
choice. Newcomers annoyed Piet. Soil here not that rich,
crowding. Ted? Ken. Quick grin yet a sullen languor, a less
than ironical interest in being right. Something in science,
not mathematics like Ong or miniaturization like Saltz. Biochemistry. Papa had distrusted inorganic fertilizer, trucked
chicken dung from poultry farms: *this is my own, my native
land*. She was called oddly Foxy, a maiden name? Fairfox,
Virginia? A southern flavor to her. Tall, oak and honey hair, a
constant blush like windburn or fever. She seemed internally
distressed and had spent two long intervals in the bathroom
upstairs. Descending the second time she had revealed her
stocking-tops to Piet, reclining acrobatically below. Tawny
ashy rims in an upward bell of shadow. She had seen him peek
and stared him down. Such amber eyes. Eyes the brown of
brushed fur backed by gold.

Bea. What did you say? I must be deaf.
Sweet Piet, you heard. I must be very drunk. Forgive me.

You're dancing divinely.

Don't poke fun. I know I can't matter to you, you have Georgene, and I can't compare. She's marvelous. She plays such marvelous tennis.

That's very flattering. You really think I'm seeing Georgene?

It's all right, singingly, gazing into a blurred distance, *don't bother to deny it, but Piet—Piet?*

Yes? I'm here. You haven't changed partners.

You poke fun of me. That's mean, that's not worthy of you, Piet. Piet?

Hello again.

I'd be kind to you. And someday you're going to need somebody to be kind to you because—now don't get cross—you're surrounded by unkind people.

For instance who? Poor Angela?

You're cross. I feel it in your body you're cross.

No, he said, and stood apart from her, so her dragging was no longer upon his body, and she sagged, then pulled herself erect, blinking, injured, as he went on, *it happens every time I try to be nice to a drunk. I wind up getting insulted.*

Oh!—it was a breathless cry as if she had been struck. *And I meant to be so kind.*

Whitewash wore away after two or three rains, but after the war the chemical companies came up with a compound that lasted pretty well until winter. In winter there could not be too much light. The Michigan snows piled in strata around the glass walls and within the greenhouse there was a lullaby sound of dripping and a rasping purring in the pipes rusted to the color of dirt as they snaked along the dirt floor flecked with tiny clover. A child cried out in her sleep. As if being strangled in a dream. From the voice he guessed it had been Nancy. She, who could tie her shoes at the age of three, had lately, now five, begun to suck her thumb and talk about dying. *I will never grow up and I will never ever in my whole life die.* Ruth, her sister, nine last November, hated to hear her. *Yes you will die everybody will die including trees.* Piet wondered if he should go to Nancy's room but the cry was not repeated. Into the vacuum of his listening flowed a rhythmic squeaking insistent as breathing. A needle working in the night. For her birthday he had given Ruth a hamster; the little animal, sack-shaped and russet, slept all day and ran in its exercise wheel all night. Piet vowed to oil the wheel but meanwhile tried to time his breathing with its beat. Too fast; his heart raced, seemed to bulge like a knapsack as into it was abruptly stuffed two thoughts that in the perspective of the night loomed as dreadful: soon he must begin building ranch houses on Indian Hill, and Angela wanted no more children. He would never have a son. *Eek, ik, eeik, ik, eeek.* Relax. Tomorrow is Sunday.

A truck passed on the road and his ears followed it, focused on its vanishing point. As a child he had soothed himself with the sensation of things passing in the night, automobiles and trains, their furry growling sounds approaching and holding fast on a momentary plateau and then receding, leaving him ignored and untouched, passing on to Chicago or Detroit, Kalamazoo or Battle Creek or the other way to the snow, stitched with animal tracks, of the northern peninsula that only boats could reach. A bridge had since been built. He had pictured himself as Superman, with a chest of steel the flanged wheels of the engines could not dent, passing over him. The retreating whistles of those flatland trains had seemed drawn with a pencil sharpened so fine that in reality it broke. No such thing in nature as a point, or a perfect circle, or infinitude, or a hereafter. The truck had vanished. But must be, must. Must. Is somewhere.

Traffic this late in this corner of New England, between Plymouth and Quincy, between Nun's Bay and Lacetown, was sparse, and he waited a long stretch for the next truck to come lull him. Angela stirred, sluggishly avoiding some obstacle to the onflow of her sleep, a dream wanting to be born, and he remembered the last time they had made love, over a week ago, in another season, winter. Though he had skated patiently waiting for her skin to quicken from beneath she had finally despaired of having a climax and asked him simply to take her and be done. Released, she had turned away, and in looping his arm around her chest his fingers brushed an unexpected sad solidity.

Angel, your nipples are hard.

So?

You're excited and could have come too.

I don't think so. It just means I'm chilly.

Let me make you come. With my mouth.
No. I'm all wet down there.
But it's me, it's my wetness.
I want to go to sleep.
But it's so sad, that you liked my making love to you after all.
I don't see that it's that sad. We'll all be here another night.

He lay on his back like a town suspended from a steeple.
He felt delicate on his face a draft from somewhere in his snug
house, a loose storm window, a tear in the attic foil, a murderer
easing open a door. He rolled over on his stomach and the
greenhouse washed over him. The tables like great wooden
trays, the flowers budding and blooming and dropping their
petals and not being bought. As a child he had mourned the
unbought flowers, beseeching the even gray greenhouse light
with their hopeful corollas and tepid perfume. He surveyed
the party for a woman to bring home and picked Bea Guerin.
*Dear Bea, of course I want to fuck you, how could I not, with
your steamy little body so tired and small and kind. Just about
all lilies, aren't you? Now spread your legs. Easy does it. Ah.* The
moisture and light within the greenhouse had been so constant
and strong that even weeds grew; even when bright snow was
heaped against the glass walls like a sliced cross section in a
school book, clover from nowhere flourished around the legs
of the tables and by the rusty pipes, and the dirt floor bore a
mossy patina and was steeped in an odor incomparably quiet
and settled and profound. He saw them, his father and mother,
vader en moeder, moving gently in this receding polyhedral
heart of light carved from dank nature, their bodies transparent, and his mind came to a cliff—a slip, then a skidding downward plunge. Left fist clenched upon himself, he groped in his
mind for the party, but it was no longer there.

God help me, help me, get me out of this. *Eek ik, eeik ik.*
Dear God put me to sleep. Amen.

A golden rooster turned high above Tarbox. The Congregational Church, a Greek temple with a cupola and spire,
shared a ledgy rise, once common pasturage, with a baseball
backstop and a cast-iron band pavilion used only on Memorial
Day, when it sheltered shouted prayers, and in the Christmas
season, when it became a crèche. Three edifices had succeeded

the first meeting-house, a thatched fort, and the last, renovated in 1896 and 1939, lifted well over one hundred feet into
the air a gilded weathercock that had been salvaged from the
previous church and thus dated from colonial times. Its eye
was a copper English penny. Deposed once each generation
by hurricanes, lightning, or repairs, it was always, much bent
and welded, restored. It turned in the wind and flashed in the
sun and served as a landmark to fishermen in Massachusetts
Bay. Children in the town grew up with the sense that the
bird was God. That is, if God were physically present in Tarbox, it was in the form of this unreachable weathercock visible
from everywhere. And if its penny could see, it saw everything,
spread below it like a living map. The central square mile of
Tarbox contained a hosiery mill converted to the manufacture
of plastic toys, three dozen stores, several acres of parking lot,
and hundreds of small-yarded homes. The homes were mixed:
the surviving seventeenth-century saltboxes the original Kim-
balls and Sewells and Tarboxes and Cogswells had set along
the wobbly pasture lanes, quaintly named for the virtues, that
radiated from the green; the peeling Federalist cubes with
widow's-walks; the gingerbread mansions attesting to the
decades of textile prosperity; the tight brick alleys plotted to
house the millworkers imported from Poland; the middle-class
pre-Depression domiciles with stubby porches and narrow
chimneys and composition sidings the colors of mustard and
parsley and graphite and wine; the new developments like even
pastel teeth eating the woods of faraway Indian Hill. Beyond,
there was a veiny weave of roads, an arrowing disused railroad
track, a river whose water was fresh above the yellow waterfall
at the factory and saline below it, a golf course studded with
bean-shapes of sand, some stubborn farms and checkerboard
orchards, a glinting dairy barn on the Nun's Bay Road, a field
containing slowly moving specks that were galloping horses,
level breadths of salt marsh broken by islands and inlets, and,
its curved horizon marred, on days as clear as today, by the
violet smudge that was the tip of Cape Cod, the eastward sea.
Casting the penny of its gaze straight down, the cock could
have observed, in dizzying perspective, the dotlike heads of
church-goers congregating and, hurrying up the gray path, the
red head of Piet Hanema, a latecomer.

The interior of the church was white. Alabaster effects had been skillfully mimicked in wood. Graceful round vaults culminated in a hung plaster ceiling. A balcony with Doric fluting vertically scoring the parapet jutted as if weightless along the sides of the sanctuary and from under the painted Victorian organ in the rear. The joinery of the old box pews was still admirable. Piet seldom entered the church without reflecting that the carpenters who had built it were dead and that none of their quality had been born to replace them. He took his accustomed place in a left back pew, and latched the paneled door, and was alone with a frayed grape-colored pew cushion —a fund drive to replace these worn-out cushions had only half succeeded—and a pair of powder-blue Pilgrim hymnals and a hideous walnut communion-glass rack screwed to the old pine in obedience to a bequest. Piet always sat alone. His friends did not go to church. He adjusted the cushion and selected the less tattered of the two hymnals. The organist, a mauve-haired spinster from Lacetown, rummaged through a Bach prelude. The first hymn was number 195: "All Hail the Power." Piet stood and sang. His voice, timid and off-key, now and then touched his own ears. ". . . on this terrestrial ball . . . let angels prostrate fall . . . and crown him, Lorhord of all . . ." On command, Piet sat and prayed. Prayer was an unsteady state of mind for him. When it worked, he seemed, for intermittent moments, to be in the farthest corner of a deep burrow, a small endearing hairy animal curled up as if to hibernate. In this condition he felt close to a massive warm secret, like the heart of lava at the earth's core. His existence for a second seemed to evade decay. But church was too exciting, too full of light and music, for prayer to take place, and his mind slid from the words being intoned, and skimmed across several pieces of property that concerned him, and grazed the faces and limbs of women he knew, and darted from the image of his daughters to the memory of his parents, so unjustly and continuingly dead.

They had died together, his mother within minutes and his father at the hospital three hours later, in a highway accident the week before the Christmas of 1949, at dusk. They had been driving home to Grand Rapids from a Grange meeting. There was an almost straight stretch of Route 21 that was often icy.

The river flowed near it. It had begun to snow. A Lincoln skidded head-on into them; the driver, a boy from Ionia, survived with lacerations. From the position of the automobiles it was not clear who had skidded, but Piet, who knew how his father drove, as ploddingly as he potted geraniums, one mile after the other, did not doubt that it had been the boy's fault. And yet—the dusk was confusing, his father was aging; perhaps, in an instant without perspective on that deceptive flat land, at the apparition of onrushing headlights, the wheels for a moment slithering, the old man had panicked. Could there have been, in that placid good gardener, with his even false teeth and heavy step and pallid stubby lashes, a fatal reserve of unreason that had burst forth and destroyed two blameless lives? All those accumulated budgets, and hoarded hopes, and seeds patiently brought to fruition? Piet pictured shattered glass strewn across the road and saw snow continue to descend, sparkling in the policemen's whirling lights. He had been a sophomore at Michigan State, studying toward an architect's certificate, and felt unable to continue, on borrowed money and the world's sufferance. There was a shuddering in his head he could not eliminate. He let his brother Johan—Joop—cheaply buy his share of the greenhouses and let himself be drafted. Since this accident, the world wore a slippery surface for Piet; he stood on the skin of things in the posture of a man testing newly formed ice, his head cocked for the warning crack, his spine curved to make himself light.

". . . and we lift our hearts in petition for those who have died, who in the ripening of time have pierced the beyond . . ." Piet bent his thought toward the hope of his parents' immortality, saw them dim and small among clouds, in their workaday greenhouse clothes, and realized that if they were preserved it was as strangers to him, blind to him, more than an ocean removed from the earthly concerns of which he had—infant, child, boy, and beginning man—been but one. *Kijk, daar is je vader. Pas op, Piet, die hond bijt. Naa kum, it makes colder out. Be polite, and don't go with girls you'd be ashamed to marry.* From the odd fact of their deaths his praying mind flicked to the odd certainty of his own, which the white well-joined wood and the lucent tall window beside him airily seemed to deny.

Piet had been raised in a sterner church, the Dutch Reformed, amid varnished oak and dour stained glass where shepherds were paralyzed in webs of lead. He had joined this sister church, a milder daughter of Calvin, as a compromise with Angela, who believed nothing. Piet wondered what barred him from the ranks of those many blessed who believed nothing. Courage, he supposed. His nerve had cracked when his parents died. To break with a faith requires a moment of courage, and courage is a kind of margin within us, and after his parents' swift death Piet had no margin. He lived tight against his skin, and his flattish face wore a look of tension. Also, his European sense of order insisted that he place his children in Christendom. Now his daughter Ruth, with his own flat alert face and her mother's stately unconscious body, sang in the children's choir. At the sight of her submissively moving her lips his blood shouted *Lord* and his death leaned above him like a perfectly clear plate of glass.

The children's choir's singing, an unsteady theft of melody while the organ went on tiptoe, ceased. In silence the ushers continued their collection of rustles and coughs. Attendance was high today, Palm Sunday. Piet held his face forward, smiling, so that his daughter would see him when, as he foresaw, she searched the congregation. She saw him and smiled, blushed and studied her robed knees. Whereas with Nancy his manhood had the power to frighten, with Ruth it could merely embarrass. The ushers marched up the scarlet carpet, out of step. Crossing a bridge. Vibration. The minister extended his angel-wing arms wide to receive them. The golden plates were stacked. The hymn: "We Are Climbing Jacob's Ladder." Amid Yankees trying to sing like slaves, Piet nearly wept, knowing the Dutch Reformed would never have stooped to this Christian attempt. "Sinner, do you love your Jesus?" Abolitionism. Children of light. "Every rung goes higher, higher . . ." Two of the four ushers sidled into the pew in front of Piet and one of them had satyr's ears, the holes tamped with wiry hair. The back of his neck crisscrossed, pock-marked by time. Minutes. Meteors. Bombarding us. The sermon commenced.

Reverend Horace Pedrick was a skeletal ignorant man of sixty. His delusions centered about money. He had never himself had enough. A poor boy from a Maine fishing family, he had entered the ministry after two business bankruptcies brought about by his extreme caution and fear of poverty. Too timid and old to acquire a city church, worn out with five-year stints in skimping New England towns, he imagined his flock to be composed of "practical men," businessmen whose operations had the scope and harshness of natural processes. In the pulpit, his white hair standing erect as the water on it dried, he held himself braced against imagined mockery, and his sermons, with contortions that now and then bent his body double, sought to transpose the desiccated forms of Christianity into financial terms. "The man Jesus"—one of his favorite phrases—"the man Jesus does not ask us to play a long shot. He does not come to us and say, 'Here is a stock for speculation. Buy at eight-and-one-eighth, and in the Promised Land you can sell at one hundred.' No, he offers us *present security*, four-and-a-half per cent compounded every quarter! Now I realize I am speaking to hard-headed men, businessmen whose decisions are far-ranging in the unsentimental world beyond this sanctuary . . ."

Piet wondered if the hair sprouting from the ears in front of him were trimmed. A cut-bush look: an electric razor, quickly. He fingered his own nostrils and the tickling itch spidered through him; he fought a sneeze. He studied the golden altar cross and wondered if Freddy Thorne were right in saying that Jesus was crucified on an X-shaped cross which the church had to falsify because of the immodesty of the position. Christ had a groin. Not much made of His virginity: mentioned in the Bible at all? Not likely, Arab boys by the age of twelve, a rural culture, sodomy, part of nature, easy access, Egyptian lotus. Coupling in Africa right in the fields as they work: a sip of water. Funny how fucking clears a woman's gaze. Christ's groin Arab but the lucent air vaulted by the ceiling of this church His gaze. Piet feared Freddy Thorne, his hyena appetite for dirty truths. Feared him yet had placed himself in bondage to him, had given him a hostage, spread X-shaped, red cleft wet. Freddy's wise glint. The head with cross-etched wrinkles on the back of its barbered neck under Piet's gaze rotated and the ear orifice became a round brown eye. In Pedrick's sermon the palms spread across Jesus's path had become greenbacks and the theft of the colt a troubled disquisition on property rights. Pedrick struggled and was not reconciled. How blithe was God, how carefree: this unexpected implication encouraged Piet to live. "And so, gentlemen, there *is* something above money, believe it or not: a power which treats wealth lightly, which accepts an expensive bottle of ointment and scorns the cost, which dares to overturn the counting tables of respectable bankers and businessmen like yourselves. May we be granted today the light to welcome this power with hosannahs into our hearts. Amen."

They sang "Lift Up Your Heads, Ye Mighty Gates" and sat for prayer. Prayer and masturbation had so long been mingled in Piet's habits that in hearing the benediction he pictured his mistress naked, a reflected sun pooled between her breasts, her prim chin set, her slightly bulging green eyes gazing, cleared. Erotic warmth infused Piet's greetings as he edged down the aisle, through a china-shop clutter of nodding old ladies, into the narthex redolent of damp paper, past Pedrick's clinging horny handshake, into the open.

At the door Piet was given a palm frond by a combed child in corduroy shorts.

Waiting for his daughter to emerge, he leaned by a warm white pillar, the frond in his left hand, a Lark in the right. Outside the sanctuary, the day was surpassingly sentimental: a thin scent of ashes and sap, lacy shadows, leafless trees, the clapboarded houses around the rocky green basking chalkily. The metal pavilion, painted green, sharpened the gay look of a stage set. The sky enamel-blue, layer on layer. Overhead, held motionless against the breeze, its feet tucked up like parallel staples, a gull hung outlined by a black that thickened at the wingtips. Each pebble, tuft, heelmark, and erosion gully in the mud by the church porch had been assigned its precise noon shadow. Piet had been raised to abhor hard soil but in a decade he had grown to love this land. Each acre was a vantage. Gallagher liked to say they didn't sell houses, they sold views. As he gazed downhill toward the business district, whose apex was formed where Divinity Street met Charity Street at Cogswell's Drug Store and made a right-angled turn up the hill, Piet's vision was touched by a piece of white that by some unconscious chime compelled focus. Who? He knew he knew. The figure, moving with averted veiled head, moved with a bride's floating stiffness. The color white was strange this early in the year, when nothing had budded but the silver maples. Perhaps like Piet she came from a part of the country where spring arrives earlier. She carried a black hymnal in a long glove and the pink of her face was high in tone, as if she were blushing. He knew. The new woman. Whitman. Evidently she was an Episcopalian. St. Stephen's Episcopal Church, unsteepled fieldstone, sat lower down the hill. Walking swiftly, Mrs. Whitman walked to a black MG parked at the foot of the green, far from her church. Perhaps like Piet she habitually came late. A subtle scorn. Thinking herself unseen, she entered her car with violent grace, hitching her skirt and sinking backwards into the seat and slamming the door in one motion. The punky sound of the slam carried to Piet a moment after the vivid sight. The distant motor revved. The MG's weight surged onto its outside tires and she rounded the island of rocks downhill from the green and headed out of town toward her house on the marshes. The women Piet knew mostly drove station wagons. Angela drove a Peugeot. He tipped back his head to view again the zenith. The motionless gull was gone. The blue fire above, layer on layer of swallowed starlight, was halved by a dissolving jet trail. He closed his eyes and imagined sap rising in blurred deltas about him. A wash of ashes. A chalky warmth. A nice bridal taste. Shyly, fearing to wake him, his elder daughter's touch came into the palm of his hanging hand, the hand holding the frond welcoming Jesus to Jerusalem.

After what seemed to Foxy far too long a cocktail time, while the men discussed their stocks and their skiing and the new proposal to revive the dead train service by means of a town contract with the MBTA, and Ken who drove to B.U. in his MG sat looking fastidious and bored, with an ankle on his knee, pondering the intricacies of his shoelaces as if a code could be construed there, Bea Guerin as hostess hesitantly invited them to dinner: "Dinner. Please come. Bring your drinks if you like, but there's wine." The Guerins lived in an old saltbox on Prudence Street, the timbers and main fireplace dating at least from 1680. The house had been so expensively and minutely restored it had for Foxy the apprehensive rawness of a new home; Foxy empathized with childless couples who conspire to baby the furniture.

Rising and setting down their drinks, the company moved to the dining room through a low varnished hallway where on a mock cobbler's bench their coats and hats huddled like a heap of the uninvited. It was Foxy's impression that this set of couples—the Guerins, the Applebys, the Smiths, whom everybody called the little-Smiths, and the Thornes—comprised the "nicer" half of the little society that was seeking to enclose her and Ken. To put herself at ease she had drunk far too much. Under the mechanical urging of her inflexibly frowning host she had accepted two martinis and then, with such stupid false girlishness, a third; feeling a squirm of nausea, she had gone to the kitchen seeking a dilution of vermouth and had whispered her secret to her hostess, a drunken girlish thing to do that would have outraged Ken, yet the kind of thing she felt was desired of her in this company. In a breathy rush Bea Guerin had said, laying a quick tremulous hand on Foxy's forearm, *How wonderful of you.* Though up to this moment Bea had seemed vulnerable to Foxy, defensively whimsical and tipsy, wearing a slightly too naked red velvet Empire dress with a floppy bow below the bosom that Foxy would have immediately snipped, she became now the distinctly older woman, expertly slapping the martini down the sink, retaining the lemon peel with a finger, replacing the gin with dry vermouth. *Don't even pretend to drink if you don't want to. The oven is funny, we had it put in a fireplace and the wind down the chimney keeps blowing out the pilot light, that's why the lamb isn't doing and everything is so late.* It appealed to Foxy that Bea, though Roger was so rich his money was a kind of joke to the others, so rich he apparently barely pretended to work and went in to Boston mostly to have lunch and play squash, was her own cook, and so indifferent at it. Janet Appleby had told her that one of the things they and their friends *loved* about Tarbox was that there were no country clubs or servants; it's so *much* more luxurious to live *simply.* Bea opened the oven door and gingerly peeked in and shut it in a kind of playful fright. The flesh of her upper arm bore a purplish oval blue that might have been a bruise. When she laughed an endearing gap showed between her front teeth.

My dear, you're wonderful, I'm so envious. So envious. Now the touch of her hand was wet, from handling the drink. Foxy left the kitchen feeling still unsettled.

April was her second month of pregnancy and she had hoped the primordial queasiness would ebb. It offended her, these sensations of demur and rebuke from within. She had long wanted to be pregnant and, having resented her husband's prudent postponement, his endless education, now wondered, at the age of twenty-eight, if the body of a younger woman would have felt less strain. She had imagined it would be like a flower's unresisted swelling, a crocus pushing through snow.

Candlelight rendered unsteady a long table covered by an embroidered cloth. Foxy held herself at attention; her stomach had lifted as if she were in flight above this steaming miniature city of china and goblets and silver flickering with orange points. Namecards in a neat round hand had been arranged. Roger Guerin seated her with a faintly excessive firmness and precision. She wanted to be handled driftingly and felt instead that a long time ago, in an incident that was admittedly not her fault but for which she was nevertheless held to account, she had offended Roger and made his touch hostile. The cloud of the consommé's warmth enveloped her face and revived her poise. In the liquid a slice of lemon lay at fetal peace. Foxy waited instinctively for grace. Instead there was the tacit refusal that has evolved, a brief bump of silence they all held their breaths through. Then Bea's serene spoon tapped into the soup, the spell was broken, dinner began.

Roger on her right asked Foxy, "Your new house, the Robinson place. Are you happy in it?" Swarthy, his fingernails long and buffed, her host seemed older than his age; his dark knitting eyebrows made constant demands upon the rest of his face. His mouth was the smallest man's mouth she had ever seen, a snail's foot of a mouth.

She answered, "Quite. It's been primitive, and probably very good for us."

The man on her left, the bald dentist Thorne, said, "Primitive? Explain what you mean."

The soup was good, clear yet strong, with a garnish of parsley and a distant horizon of sherry: she wanted to enjoy it, it was lately so rare that she enjoyed food. She said, "I mean primitive. It's an old summer house. It's cold. We've bought some electric heaters for our bedroom and the kitchen but all they really do is roast your ankles. You should see us hop around in the morning; it's like a folk dance. I'm so glad we have no children at this point." The table had fallen silent, listening. She had said more than she had intended. Blushing, she bent her face to the shallow amber depths where the lemon slice like an embryo swayed.

"I understand," Freddy Thorne persisted, "the word 'primitive.' I meant explain why you thought it was good for you."

"Oh, I think any hardship is good for the character. Don't you?"

"Define 'character.'"

"Define 'define.'" She had construed his Socratic nagging as a ploy, a method he had developed with women, to lead them out. After each utterance, there was a fishy inward motion of his lips as if to demonstrate how to take the bait. No teeth showed in his mouth. It waited, a fraction open, for her to come into it. As a mouth, it was neither male nor female, and not quite infantile. His nose was insignificant. His eyes were lost behind concave spectacle lenses that brimmed with tremulous candlelight. His hair once might have been brown, or sandy, but had become a colorless fuzz, an encircling shadow, above his ears; like all bald heads his had a shine that seemed boastful. So repulsive, Freddy assumed the easy intrusiveness of a very attractive man.

Overhearing her rebuff, the man across the table, Smith, said, "Give it to him, girl," adding as if to clarify: "*Donnez le-lui.*" It was evidently a habit, a linguistic tic.

Roger Guerin broke in. Foxy sensed his desire, in this presuming group, to administer a minimal code of manners. He asked her, "Have you hired a contractor yet?"

"No. The only one we know at all is the man who's the partner of the man who sold us the place. Pi-et . . . ?"

"Piet Hanema," the Smith woman called from beyond Freddy Thorne, leaning forward so she could be seen. She was a petite tense brunette with a severe central parting and mobile earrings whose flicker communicated across her face. "Rhymes with sweet."

"With indiscreet," Freddy Thorne said.

Foxy asked, "You all know him?"

The entire table fully laughed.

"He's the biggest neurotic in town," Freddy Thorne explained. "He's an orphan because of a car accident ten years or so ago and he goes around pinching everybody's fanny because he's still arrested. For God's sake, don't hire him. He'll take forever and charge you a fortune. Or rather his shyster partner Gallagher will."

"Freddy," said his wife, who sat across from Foxy. She was a healthy-looking short woman with a firm freckled chin and narrow Donatello nose.

"Freddy, I don't think you're being quite fair," Frank Appleby called from the end of the table, beyond Marcia little-Smith. His large teeth and gums were bared when he talked, and there was a salival spray that sparkled in candlelight. His head was florid and his eyes often bloodshot. He had big well-shaped hands. Foxy liked him, reading an intended kindness into his jokes. "I thought at the last town meeting that the fire chief was voted the most neurotic. If you had another candidate you should have spoken up." Frank explained to Foxy, "His name is Buzz Kappiotis and he's one of these local Greeks whose uncles own the town. His wife runs the Supreme Laundry and she's pretty supreme herself, she's even fatter than Janet." His wife stuck out her tongue at him. "He has a pathological fear of exceeding the speed limit and screams whenever the ladder truck goes around a corner."

Harold little-Smith, whose uptilted nose showed a shiny double inquisitive tip, said, "Also he's afraid of heights, heat, water, and dogs. *L'eau et les chiens.*"

Appleby continued, "The only way you can get your house insured in this town is to give Liberty Mutual even odds."

Little-Smith added, "Whenever the alarm goes off, the kids in town all rush to the spot with marshmallows and popcorn."

Roger Guerin said to Foxy, "It is true, the rates in town are the highest in Plymouth County. But we have so many old wooden houses."

"Yours is beautifully restored," Foxy told him.

"We find it inhibiting as far as furniture goes. Actually, Piet Hanema was the contractor."

Seated between Ken and little-Smith, Janet Appleby, a powdered plump vexed face with charcoal lids and valentine lips, cried, "And that alarm!" Leaning toward Foxy in explanation, she dipped the tops of her breasts creamily into the light. "You can't hear it down on the marsh, but we live just across the river and it's the absolutely worst noise I ever heard anything civic make. The children in town call it the Dying Cow."

"We've become slaves to auctions," Roger Guerin was continuing. From the square shape of his head Foxy guessed he was Swiss rather than French in ancestry.

Her side was nudged and Freddy Thorne told her, "Roger thinks auctions are like Monopoly games. All over New Hampshire and Rhode Island they know him as the Mad Bidder from Tarbox. Highboys, lowboys, bus boys. He's crazy for commodes."

"Freddy exaggerates," Roger said.

"He's very discriminating," Bea called from her end of the table.

"That's not what I'm told they call it," Harold little-Smith was saying to Janet.

"What are you told, dear?" Janet responded.

Harold dipped his fingers into his water goblet and flicked them at her face; three or four drops, each holding a spark of reflection, appeared on her naked shoulders. "*Femme méchante*," he said.

Frank Appleby intervened, telling Ken and Foxy, "The phrase the children use when the alarm goes would translate into decent language as, 'The Deity is releasing gas.'"

Marcia said, "The children bring home scandalous jokes from school. The other day Jonathan came and told me, 'Mother, the governor has two cities in Massachusetts named after him. One is Peabody. What's the other?'"

"Marblehead," Janet said. "Frankie thought that was the funniest thing he'd ever heard."

Bea Guerin and the silent wife of Freddy Thorne rose and took the soup plates away. Foxy had only half-finished. Mrs. Thorne politely hesitated. Foxy rested her spoon and put her hands in her lap. The soup vanished. Oh thank you. Circling the table, Bea said singingly, "My favorite townsperson is the old lady with the *National Geographics*."

Little-Smith, aware that Ken had not spoken a word, turned to him politely; fierily illuminated, the tip of his nose suggested something diabolical, a cleft foot. "Did Frank tell me you were a geographer, or was it geologist?"

"Biochemist," Ken said.

"He should meet Ben Saltz," Janet said.

"The fate worse than death," Freddy said, "if you don't mind my being anti-Semitic."

Foxy asked the candlelit air, "*National Geographics?*"

"She has them all," the little-Smith woman said, leaning not toward Foxy but toward Ken across the table. From Foxy's angle she was in profile, her lower lip saucily retracted and her earring twittering beside her jaw like a tiny machine. Ken abruptly laughed. His laugh was a boy's, sudden and high and disproportionate. In private with her, he rarely laughed.

Encouraged, the others went on. The old lady was the very last of the actual Tarboxes, and she lived in one or two rooms of a big Victorian shell on Divinity Street toward the fire station, crammed in among the shops, diagonally across from the post office and Freddy's office, and her father, who had owned the hosiery mill that now makes plastic ducks for bath tubs, and teething rings, had been a charter subscriber. They were neatly stacked along the walls, twelve issues every year, since 1888.

"The town engineer," Frank Appleby pronounced, "calculates that with the arrival of the issue of November 1984, she will be crushed to death."

"Like a character in Poe," little-Smith said, and determinedly addressed his wife. "Marcia, which? *Not* 'The Pit and the Pendulum.'"

"Harold, you're confused by 'The House of Usher,'" she told him.

"*Non, non,* tu *es confuse,*" he said, and Foxy felt that but for the table between them they would have clawed each other. "There *is* a story, of walls squeezing in."

Janet said, "It happens on television all the time," and went on in general, "What *can* we do about our children watching? Frankie's becoming an absolute zombie."

Frank Appleby said, "It's called 'The Day the Walls Squeezed In.' As told to Jim Bishop."

Ken added, "By I. M. Flat, a survivor in two dimensions," and laughed so hard a candle flame wavered.

Marcia said, "Speaking of television, you know what I just read? By the year 1990 they're going to have one in every room, so everybody can be watched. The article said"—she faltered, then swiftly proceeded—"nobody could commit adultery." An angel passed overhead.

"My God," Frank said. "They'll undermine the institution of marriage."

The laughter, Foxy supposed, was cathartic.

Freddy Thorne murmured to her, "Your husband is quite witty. He's not such a stick as I thought. I. M. Flat in two dimensions. I like it."

Harold little-Smith was not amused. He turned the conversation outward, saying, "Say. Wasn't that a shocker about the *Thresher*?"

"What shocked you about it?" Freddy asked, with that slippery thrusting undertone. So it wasn't just women he used it on.

"I think it's shocking," little-Smith iterated, "that in so-called peacetime we send a hundred young men to be crushed at the bottom of the sea."

Freddy said, "They enlisted. We've all been through it, Harry boy. We took our chances honeymooning with Uncle, and so did they. *Che sarà sarà*, as Dodo Day so shrewdly puts it."

Janet asked Harold, "Why 'so-called'?"

Harold snapped, "We'll be at war with China in five years. We're at war with her now. Kennedy'll up the stakes in Laos just enough to keep the economy humming. What we need in Laos is another Diem."

Janet said, "Harold, that's reactionary shit. I get enough of that from Frank."

Roger Guerin said to Foxy, "Don't take them too seriously. There's nothing romantic or eccentric about Tarbox. The Puritans tried to make it a port but they got silted in. Like everything in New England, it's passé, only more so."

"Roger," Janet protested, "that's a rotten thing for you to be telling this child, what with our lovely churches and old houses and marshes and absolutely grand beach. I think we're the prettiest unself*con*scious town in America." She did not acknowledge that, as she was speaking, Harold little-Smith was blotting, with the tip of his index finger, each of the water drops he had flicked onto her shoulders.

Frank Appleby bellowed, "Do you two want a towel?"

A leg of lamb and a bowl of vegetables were brought in. The host stood and carved. His hands with their long polished nails could have posed for a cookbook diagram: the opening wedge, the lateral cut along the lurking bone, the vertical slices precise as petals, two to a plate. The plates were passed the length of the table to Bea, who added spring peas and baby potatoes and mint jelly. Plain country fare, Foxy thought; she and Ken had lived six years in Cambridge, a region of complicated casseroles and Hungarian goulashes and garlicky salads and mock duck and sautéed sweetbreads. Among these less sophisticated eaters Foxy felt she could be, herself, a delicacy, a princess. Frank Appleby was given two bottles to uncork, local-liquor-store Bordeaux, and went around the table twice, pouring once for the ladies, and then for the men. In Cambridge the Chianti was passed from hand to hand without ceremony.

Freddy Thorne proposed a toast. "For our gallant boys in the *Thresher*."

"Freddy, that's ghoulish!" Marcia little-Smith cried.

"Freddy, really," Janet said.

Freddy shrugged and said, "It came from the heart. Take it or leave it. *Mea culpa, mea culpa*."

Foxy saw that he was used to rejection; he savored it, as if a dark diagnosis had been confirmed. Further she sensed that his being despised served as a unifying purpose for the others, gave them a common identity, as the couples that tolerated Freddy Thorne. Foxy glanced curiously at Thorne's wife. Sensing Foxy's perusal, she glanced up. Her eyes were a startling pale green, slightly protruding, drilled with pupils like the eyes of Roman portrait busts. Foxy thought she must be made of something very hard, not to show a scar from her marriage.

"Freddy, I don't think you meant it at all," Janet went on, "not at all. You're delighted it was them and not you."

"You bet. You too. We're all survivors. A dwindling band of survivors. I took my chances. I did my time for God and Uncle."

"You sat at a steel desk reading Japanese pornography," Harold told him.

Freddy looked astonished, his shapeless mouth inbent. "Didn't everybody? We've all heard often enough about you and your geishas. Poor little underfed girls, for a pack of cigarettes and half of a Hershey bar."

His wife's bottle-green eyes gazed at the man as if he belonged to someone else.

"You wonder what they think," Freddy went on, swimming, trying not to drown in their contempt, his black mouth lifted. "The goddam gauges start spinning, the fucking pipes begin to break, and—what? Mother? The flag? Jesu Cristo? The last piece of ass you had?"

A contemptuous silence welled from the men.

"What I found so touching," Bea Guerin haltingly sang, "was the way the tender—is that what it is?—"

"Submarine tender, yes," her husband said.

"—the way the tender was called *Skylark*. And how all morning it called and circled, in the sea that from underneath must look like a sky, circling and calling, and nobody answered. Poor *Skylark*."

Frank Appleby stood. "Too much of water hast thou, poor Ophelia. I propose a toast, to the new couple, the Whitmans."

"Hear," Roger Guerin said, scowling.

"May you long support our tax rolls, whose rate is high and whose benefits are nil."

"Hear, hear." It was little-Smith. "*Écoutez*."

"Thank you," Foxy said, blushing and feeling a fresh wave of rebuke rising within her. She quickly put down her fork. The lamb was underdone.

Little-Smith tried again with Ken. "What do you do, as a biochemist?"

"I do different things. I think about photosynthesis. I used to slice up starfish extremely thin, to study their metabolism."

Janet Appleby leaned forward again, tipping the creamy tops of her breasts into the warm light, and asked, "And then do they survive, in two dimensions?" Through a lucid curling wave of nausea Foxy saw that her husband was being flirted with.

Ken laughed eagerly. "No, they die. That's the trouble with my field. Life hates being analyzed."

Bea asked, "Is the chemistry very complex?"

"Very. Incredibly. If a clever theologian ever got hold of how complex it is, they'd make us all believe in God again."

Ousted by Bea, Janet turned to them all. "Speaking of that," she said, "what does this old Pope John keep bothering us about? He acts as if we all voted him in."

"I like him," Harold said. "*Je l'adore.*"

Marcia told him, "But you like Khrushchev too."

"I like old men. They can be wonderful bastards because they have nothing to lose. The only people who can be themselves are babies and old bastards."

"Well," Janet said, "I tried to read this *Pacem in Terris* and it's as dull as something from the UN."

"Hey Roger," Freddy called across Foxy, his breath meaty, "how do you like the way U Whosie has bopped Tshombe in the Congo? Takes a nigger to beat a nigger."

"I think it's *lovely*," Bea said emphatically to Ken, touching his sleeve, "that it's so complex. I don't want to be understood."

Ken said, "Luckily, the processes are pretty much the same throughout the kingdom of life. A piece of yeast and you, for example, break down glucose into pyruvic acid by exactly the same eight transformations." This was an aspect of him that Foxy rarely saw any more, the young man who could say "the kingdom of life." Who did he think was king?

Bea said, "Oh dear. Some days I *do* feel moldy."

Freddy persisted, though Roger's tiny mouth had tightened in response. "The trouble with Hammarskjöld," he said, "he was too much like you and me, Roger. Nice guys."

Marcia little-Smith called to her husband, "Darling, who isn't letting you be a wonderful old bastard? Terrible me?"

"Actually, Hass," Frank Appleby said, "I see you as our local Bertrand Russell."

"I put him more as a Schweitzer type," Freddy Thorne said.

"You bastards, I mean it." The tip of his nose lifted under persecution like the flowery nose of a mole. "Look at Kennedy. There's somebody inside that robot trying to get out, but it doesn't dare because he's too young. He'd be crucified."

Janet Appleby said, "*Let's* talk news. We always talk people.

I've been reading the newspaper while Frank reads Shakespeare. *Why* is Egypt merging with those other Arabs? Don't they know they have Israel in between? It's as bad as us and Alaska."

"I love you, Janet," Bea called, across Ken. "You think like I do."

"Those countries aren't countries," Harold said. "They're just branches of Standard Oil. *L'huile étendarde*."

"Tell us some more Shakespeare, Frank," Freddy said.

"We have laughed," Frank said, "to see the sails conceive, and grow big-bellied with the wanton wind. *Midsummer Night's Dream*. Isn't that a grand image? I've been holding it in my mind for days. Grow big-bellied with the wanton wind." He stood and poured more wine around. Foxy put her hand over the mouth of her glass.

Freddy Thorne leaned close to her and said, "You don't have much of an appetite. Tummy trouble?"

"Seriously," Roger Guerin said on her other side, "I'd have no hesitation about calling Hanema and at least getting an estimate. He does very solid work. He's one of the few contractors left, for instance, who puts up honest plaster walls. And his job for us, though it took forever, was really very loving. Restoration is probably his forte."

Bea added, "He's a dear little old-fashioned kind of man."

"You'll be so-orry," Freddy Thorne said.

Frank Appleby called, "And you can get him to build a dike for you so Ken can farm the marsh. There's a fortune to be made in salt hay. It's used to mulch artichokes."

Foxy turned to her tormentor. "Why don't you like him?" She had abruptly remembered who Hanema was. At Frank's party, a short red-haired man clownishly lying at the foot of the stairs had looked up her dress.

"I *do* like him," Freddy Thorne told her. "I love him. I love him like a brother."

"And he you," little-Smith said quickly.

Thorne said, "To tell the truth, I feel homosexually attracted to him."

"Freddy," Thorne's wife said in a level voice hardly intended to be heard.

"He has a lovely wife," Roger said.

"She *is* lovely," Bea Guerin called. "So serene. I envy the wonderful way she *moves*. Don't you, Georgene?"

"Angela's really a robot," Frank Appleby said, "with Jack Kennedy inside her, trying to get out."

"I don't know," Georgene Thorne said, "that she's so perfect. I don't think she gives Piet very much."

"She gives him social aplomb," Harold said.

Freddy said, "I bet she even gives him a bang now and then. She's human. Hell, everybody's human. That's my theory."

Foxy asked him, "What does he do neurotic?"

"You heard Roger describe the way he builds. He's anally neat. Also, he goes to church."

"But *I* go to church. I wouldn't be without it."

"Frank," Freddy called, "I think I've found the fourth." Foxy guessed he meant that she was the fourth most neurotic person in town, behind the fire chief, the Dutch contractor, and the lady doomed to be crushed by magazines.

Foxy came from Maryland and partook of the aggressiveness of southern women. "You *must* tell me what you mean by 'neurotic.'"

Thorne smiled. His sickly mouth by candlelight invited her to come in. "You haven't told me what you mean by 'character.'"

"Perhaps," Foxy said, scornfully bright, "we mean the same thing." She disliked this man, she had never in her memory met a man she disliked more, and she tried to elicit, from the confusion within her body, a clear expression of this.

He leaned against her and whispered, "Eat some of Bea's lamb, just to be polite, even if it is raw." Then he turned from her, as if snubbing a petitioner, and lit Marcia's cigarette. As he did so, his thigh deliberately slid against Foxy's. She was startled, amused, disgusted. This fool imagined he had made a conquest. She felt in him, and then dreaded, a desire to intrude upon, to figure in, her fate. His thigh increased its pressure and in the lulling dull light she experienced an escapist craving for sleep. She glanced about for rescue. Her host, his eyebrows knitted tyrannically above the bridge of his nose, was concentrating on carving more lamb. Across the table her husband, the father of her need for sleep, was laughing between Bea Guerin and Janet Appleby. The daggery shadow in the cleft between Janet's lush breasts changed shape as her hands darted in emphasis of unheard sentences. More wine was poured. Foxy nodded, in assent to a question she thought had been asked her, and snapped her head upright in fear of having dropped asleep. Her thigh was nudged again. No one would speak to her. Roger Guerin was murmuring, administering some sort of consolation, to Georgene Thorne. Ken's high hard laugh rang out, and his face, usually so ascetic, looked pasty and unreal, as if struck by a searchlight. He was having a good time; she was hours from bed.

As they drove home, the night revived her. The fresh air was cool and the sky like a great wave collapsing was crested with stars. Their headlights picked up mailboxes, hedgerows, crusts of dry snow in a ditch. Ken's MG swayed with each turn of the winding beach road. He asked her, "Are you dead?"

"I'm all right now. I wasn't sure I could get through it when we were at the table."

"It *was* pretty ghastly."

"They seemed so excited by each other."

"Funny people." As if guilty, he added, "Poor Fox, sitting there yawning with her big belly."

"Was I too stupid? I told Bea."

"For God's sake, why?"

"I wanted a pretend martini. Are you ashamed of my being pregnant?"

"No, but why broadcast it? It'll show soon enough."

"She won't tell anybody."

"It doesn't matter."

How little, Foxy thought, *does matter to you.* The trees by the roadside fell away, and rushed back in clumps, having revealed in the gaps cold stretches of moonlit marsh. The mailboxes grew fewer. Fewer houselights showed. Foxy tightened around her her coat, a fur-lined gabardine cut in imitation of a Russian general's greatcoat. She foresaw their cold home with its flimsy walls and senile furnace. She said, "We *must* get a contractor. Should we ask this man Hanema to give us an estimate?"

"Thorne says he's a fanny-pincher."

"That's called projection."

"Janet told me he almost bought the house himself. His wife apparently wanted the view."

Janet, is it?

Foxy said, "Did you notice the antagonism between Frank and the little-Smith man?"

"Aren't they both in stocks somehow? Maybe they're competing."

"Ken, you're so work-oriented. I felt it had to do with s-e-x."

"With Janet?"

"Well, she was certainly trying to make some point with her bosom."

He giggled. *Stop it*, she thought, *it isn't you.* "Two points," he said.

"I knew you'd say that," she said.

There was a rise in the road, cratered by frost heaves, from which the sea was first visible. She saw that moonlight lived on the water, silver, steady, sliding with the motion of their car, yet holding furious myriad oscillations, like, she supposed, matter itself. Ken worked down there, where the protons swung from molecule to molecule and elements interlocked in long spiral ladders. A glimpse of dunes: bleached bones. The car sank into a dip. There were four such rises and falls between the deserted, boarded-up ice-cream stand and their driveway. They lived near the end of the road, an outpost in winter. Foxy abruptly craved the lightness, the freedom, of summer.

Ken said, "Your friend Thorne had a very low opinion of Hanema."

"He is *not* my friend. He is an odious man and I don't understand why everybody likes him so much."

"He's a dentist. Everybody needs a dentist. Janet told me he wanted to be a psychiatrist but flunked medical school."

"He's awful, all clammy and cozy and I kept feeling he wanted to get his hands inside me. I cut him short and he thought I was making a pass. He played kneesies with me."

"But he sat beside you."

"Sideways kneesies."

"I suppose it can be done."

"I think his poor opinion should be counted as a plus."

Ken said nothing.

Foxy went on, "Roger Guerin said he was a good contractor. He did their house. With their money they could have afforded anybody."

"Let's think about it. I'd rather get somebody nobody knows. I don't want us to get too involved in this little nest out here."

"I thought one of the reasons we moved was so our friendships wouldn't be so much at the mercy of your professional acquaintance."

"Say that again?"

"You know what I said. I didn't have any friends of my own, just chemical wives."

"Fox, that's what we all are. Chemicals." He knew she didn't believe that, why did he say it? When would he let her out of school?

A mailbox rammed by a snowplow leaned vacantly on the moonlight. The box belonged to summer people and would not be righted for months. Foxy wrapped her greatcoat tighter around her and in the same motion wrapped her body, her own self, around the small sour trouble brewing in her womb, this alien life furtively exploiting her own. She felt ugly and used. She said, "You really *liked* those women, didn't you, with their push-me-up bras and their get-me-out-of-this giggles?" The women they had known in Cambridge had tended to be plain Quaker girls placidly wed to rising grinds, or else women armored in a repellent brilliance of their own, untouchable gypsy beauties with fiery views on Cuban sovereignty and German guilt. Foxy sighed as if in resignation. "Well, they say a man gets his first mistress when his wife becomes pregnant."

He looked over at her too surprised to speak, and she realized that he was incapable of betraying her, and marveled at her own disappointment. She puzzled herself; she had never been in their marriage more dependent upon him, or with more cause for gratitude. Yet a chemistry of unrest had arisen within her body, and she resented his separation from it. For she had always felt and felt now in him a fastidious, unlapsing accountability that shirked the guilt she obscurely felt belonged to life; and thus he left her with a double share.

He said at last, "What are you suggesting? We were invited. We went. We might as well enjoy it. I have nothing against mediocre people, provided I don't have to teach them anything."

Ken was thirty-two. They had met when he was a graduate student instructing in Biology 10 and she was a Radcliffe senior in need of a science credit. Since her sophomore year Foxy had been in love with a fine-arts major, a bearish Jewish boy from Detroit. He had since become a sculptor whose large welded assemblages of junk metal were occasionally pictured in magazines. There had been a clangor about him even then, a snuffly explosive air of self-parody, with his wiglike mop of hair, combed straight forward, and a nose so hooked its tip appeared to point at his lower lip. The curves of his face had been compressed around a certain contemptuousness. His tongue could quickly uncoil. *Eat me up, little shiksa, I'm a dirty old man. I sneeze black snot. I pop my piles with a prophylactic toothbrush.* He scorned any sign of fear from her. He taught her to blow. His prick enormous in her mouth, she felt her love of him as a billowing and gentle tearing of veils inside her. Before he took her up she had felt pale, tall, stiff, cold, unusable. His back was hairy and humpily muscular across the shoulder blades and thickly sown, as if by a curse, with moles.

With a tact more crushing than brute forbidding her parents gradually made her love grotesque and untenable. She did not know how they did it: it was as if her parents and Peter communicated through her, without her knowing what was being said, until the *No* came from both sides, and met beneath her ribs. That schoolgirl ache, and all those cigarettes. Her senior year at Radcliffe, it had snowed and snowed; she remembered the twittering of the bicycles pushed on the paths, the song of unbuckled galoshes, the damp scarf around her neck, the fluttering of crystals, meek as thoughts, at the tall serene windows of the Fogg. She remembered the bleached light that had filled her room each morning before she awoke to the soreness in her chest.

Ken appeared, was taller than she, wanted her, was acceptable and was accepted on all sides; similarly, nagging mathematical problems abruptly crack open. Foxy could find no fault with him, and this challenged her, touched off her stubborn defiant streak. She felt between his handsomeness and intelligence a contradiction that might develop into the convoluted humor of her Jew. Ken looked like a rich boy and worked like a poor one. From Farmington, he was the only son of a Hartford lawyer who never lost a case. Foxy came to imagine his birth as cool and painless, without a tear or outcry. Nothing puzzled him. There were unknowns but no mysteries. After her own degrading miscalculation—for this was what her first romance must have been, it ended in such a flurry of misery—Foxy sought shelter in Ken's weatherproof rightness. She accepted gratefully his simple superiority to other people. He was better-looking, better-thinking, a better machine. He was fallible only if he took her, on the basis of the cool poise her tallness had demanded, for another of the same breed.

She was, Elizabeth Fox from Bethesda, known to herself in terms of suppressed warmth. Applaudingly her adolescent heart had watched itself tug toward stray animals, lost children, forsaken heroines, and toward the bandaged wounded perambulating around the newly built hospital, with its ugly tall rows of windows like zipped zippers. They had moved from east Washington in the spring of 1941, as the hospital was being built. Her father was a career navy man, a lieutenant commander with some knowledge of engineering and an exaggerated sense of lineage. One of his grandfathers had been a Virginia soldier; the other, a New Jersey parson. He felt himself to be a gentleman and told Foxy, when she came to him at the age of twelve inspired to be a nurse, that she was too intelligent, that she would someday go to college. At Radcliffe, looking back, she supposed that her sense of deflected tenderness dated from her father's long absences during World War II; the accident of global war had deprived her of the filial transition to heterosexual relationships free of slavishness, of the expiatory humiliations she goaded Peter to inflict. Now, herself married, milder and less mathematical in her self-analyses, she wondered if the sadness, the something broken and uncompleted in her upbringing, was not older than the war and belonged to the Depression, whose shadowy air of magnificent impotence, of trolley cars and sinusitis, still haunted the official mausoleums of Washington when she visited her mother. Perhaps the trouble had merely been that her mother, though shrewd and once pretty, had not been a gentlewoman, but a Maryland grocer's daughter.

Foxy had no sooner married than her parents had gotten divorced. Her father, his thirty years of service expired, far from retiring, took a lucrative advisory job to the shipbuilding industry, and moved to San Diego. Her mother, as if defiantly showing that she too could navigate in the waters of prosperity, remarried: a wealthy Georgetown widower, a Mr. Roth, who owned a chain of coin-operated laundromats, mostly in Negro neighborhoods. Foxy's mother now made herself up carefully, put on a girdle even to go shopping, kept a poodle, smoked red-tipped filtered cigarettes, was known to their friends as "Connie," and always spoke of her husband as "Roth."

The couple Foxy's parents had been had vanished. The narrow shuttered frame house on Rosedale Street. The unused front porch. The tan shades always drawn against the heat. The electric fan in the kitchen swinging its slow head back and forth like an imbecile scolding in monotone. The staticky Philco conveying Lowell Thomas. The V-mail spurting through the thrilled slot. The once-a-week Negro woman, called Gracelyn, whose apron pockets smelled of orange peels and Tootsie Rolls. Veronica their jittery spayed terrier who was succeeded by Merle, a slavering black-tongued Chow. The parched flowerless shrubbery where Elizabeth would grub for bottlecaps and "clues," the long newspaper-colored ice-cream evenings, the red-checked oilcloth on the kitchen table worn bare at two settings, the way her mother would sit nights at this table, after the news, before putting her daughter to bed, smoking a Chesterfield and smoothing with a jerky automatic motion the skin beneath her staring eyes: these images had vanished everywhere but in Foxy's heart. She went to church to salvage something. Episcopalianism—its rolling baritone hymns to the sea, its pews sparkling with the officers' shoulder-braid—had belonged to the gallant club of Daddy's friends, headed by caped Mr. Roosevelt, that fought and won the war.

She was graduated and married in June of 1956.

Every marriage is a hedged bet. Foxy entered hers expecting that, whatever fate held for them, there were certain kinds of abuse it would never occur to her husband to inflict. He was beyond them, as most American men are beyond eye-gouging and evisceration. She had been right. He had proved not so much gentle as too fastidious to be cruel. She had no just complaints: only the unjust one that the delay while she waited barren for Ken to complete his doctorate had been long. Four intended years of post-graduate work had been stretched into five by the agonies of his dissertation; two more were spent in a post-doctoral fellowship granted by the U.S. Public Health Service; and then Ken squandered another as an instructor in the vicinity of the same magnetic Harvard gods, whose very names Foxy had come to hate. For her, there had been jobs, little research assistantships amid Flemish prints or Mesozoic fern fossils in comfortable dusty Harvard basements, a receptionist's desk at University Hall, an involvement in a tutoring project for mentally disturbed children that had led her to consider and then to run from a career in social work, some random graduate courses, a stab at a master's degree, two terms of life-drawing in Boston, vacations, even flirtations: but nothing fruitful. Seven years is long, counted in months paid for with a punctual tax of blood, in weeks whose pleasure is never free of the belittling apparatus of contraception, longer than a war. She had wanted to bear Ken a child, to brew his excellence in her warmth. This seemed the best gift she could offer him, since she grew to know that there was something of herself she withheld. A child, a binding of their chemistries, would be an honest pledge of her admiration and trust and would remove them for good from the plane where the sufficiency of these feelings could be doubted. Now this gift was permitted. Ken was an assistant professor at the university across the river, where the department of biochemistry was more permeable to rapid advancement. Their reasons for happiness were as sweeping as the view from their new house.

The house had been Ken's choice. She had thought they should live closer to Boston, in Lexington perhaps, among people like themselves. Tarbox was an outer limit, an hour's drive, and yet he, who must do the commuting, seized the house as if all his life he had been waiting for a prospect as vacant and pure as these marshes, those bony far dunes, that rim of sea. Perhaps, Foxy guessed, it was a matter of scale: his microscopic work needed the relief of such a vastness. And it had helped that he and the real-estate man Gallagher had liked each other. Though she had raised all the reasonable objections, Foxy had been pleased to see him, after the long tame stasis of student existence, emerge to want something new, physical, real. That he had within him even the mild strangeness needed to insist on an out-of-the-way impractical house seemed (as if there had been a question of despair) hopeful.

The house tonight was cold, stored with stale chill. Cotton, their cat, padded loudly toward them from the dark living room and, stiff from sleep, stretched. He was a heavy-footed caramel tom that in years of being their only pet had acquired something of a dog's companionableness and something of a baby's conceit. Courteously he bowed before them, his tail an interrogation mark, his front claws planted in the braided rag rug the Robinsons had abandoned in the hall. Cotton pulled his claws free with a dainty unsticking noise and purred in anticipation of Foxy's picking him up. She held him, his throaty motor running, beneath her chin and like a child wished herself magically inside his pelt.

Ken switched on a light in the living room. The bare walls leaped into being, the exposed studs, the intervals of varnish, the crumbling gypsum wallboard, the framed souvenirs of old summers—fan-shaped shell collections and dried arrays of littoral botany—that the Robinsons had left. They had never met them but Foxy saw them as a large sloppy family, full of pranks and nicknames for each other and hobbies, the mother watercoloring (her work was tacked all around upstairs), the older boys sailing in the marsh, the girl moonily collecting records and being teased, the younger boy and the father systematically combing the shore for classifiable examples of life. The room smelled as if summer had been sealed in and yet had leaked out. The French windows giving onto a side garden of roses and peonies were boarded. The shutters were locked over the windows that would have looked onto the porch and the marsh. The sharp-edged Cambridge furniture, half Door Store and half Design Research, looked scattered and sparse; the room was a good size and of a good square shape. It had possibilities. It needed white paint and walls and light and love and style. She said, "We *must* start doing things."

Ken felt the floor register with his hand. "The furnace is dead again."

"Leave it to morning. No warmth gets upstairs anyway."

"I don't like being outsmarted. I'm going to learn how to bank this bastard."

"I'm more worried about dying in my sleep of coal gas."

"No chance of that in this sieve."

"Ken, please call Hanema."

"You call him."

"You're the man of the house."

"I'm not sure he's the right man."

"You like Gallagher."

"They're not twins, they're partners."

"Then find somebody else."

"If you want him, you call him."

"Well I just might."

"Go ahead. Fine." He went to the door that led down into the narrow hole that did for a basement. The register began to clank and release a poisonous smell. Foxy carried Cotton into the kitchen, plugged in the electric heater, and poured two bowls of milk. One she set on the floor for the cat; the other she broke Saltines into, for herself. Cotton sniffed, disdained the offering, and interrogatively mewed. Foxy ignored him and ate greedily with a soup spoon. Crackers and milk had been a childhood treat between news and bedtime; her craving for it had come over her like a sudden release from fever, a gust of health. While the glow of the heater and the begging friction of fur alternated on her legs, she spread butter thickly on spongy white bread, tearing it, overweighting it, three pieces one after the other, too ravenous to bother with toast, compulsive as a drunk. Her fingertips gleamed with butter.

Washing them, she leaned on her slate sink and gazed from the window. The tide was high; moonlight displayed a silver saturation overflowing the linear grid of ditches. Against the sheen was silhouetted a little houseless island of brambles. In the distance, along the far arm of Tarbox Bay, the lights of another town, whose name she had not yet learned, spangled the horizon. A revolving searchlight rhythmically stroked the plane of ocean. Its beam struck her face at uneven intervals. She counted: five, two, five, two. A double beam. Seconds slipping, gone; five, two. She hastily turned and rolled up the cellophane breadwrapper; a voluminous sadness had been carved for her out of the night. It was after midnight. Today was Easter. She must get up for church.

Ken returned from the furnace and laughed at the traces of her hunger—the gouged butter, the clawed crumbs, the empty bowl.

She said, "Yes, and it's the cheap bread I feel starved for, not

Pepperidge Farm. That old-fashioned rubbery kind with all the chemicals."

"Calcium propionate," he said. "Our child will be an agglutinated monster."

"Did you mean it, I should call this Dutchman?"

"Why not? See what he says. He must know the house, if his wife wanted it."

But she heard doubt in his even voice and changed the subject. "You know what bothered me about those people tonight?"

"They were Republicans."

"Don't be silly, I couldn't care less. No what bothered me was they wanted us to love them. They weren't lovable, but that's what they wanted."

He laughed. Why should his laugh grate so? "Maybe that's what *you* wanted," he told her.

They went to bed up a staircase scarred and crayoned by children they had never seen. Foxy assumed that, with the revival of her appetite, she would enjoy a great animal draught of sleep. Ken kissed her shoulder in token of the love they should not in this month make, turned his back, and quickly went still. His breathing was inaudible and he never moved. The stillness of his body established a tension she could not quite sink through, like a needle on the skin of water. Downstairs, Cotton's heavy feet padding back and forth unsatisfied seemed to make the whole house tremble. The moon, so bright it had no face, was framed by the skylight and for an hour of insomnia burned in the center of her forehead like a jewel.

Monday morning: in-and-out. A powdery blue sky the color of a hymnal. Sunshine broken into code by puffs and schooners of cumulus. The Thornes' sunporch—the tarpaper deck-roof of their garage, sheltered from the wind by feathery tall larches, entered by sliding glass doors from the bedroom—cupped warmth. Every year Georgene had the start of a tan before anyone else. Today she looked already freckled, austere and forbidding in her health.

She had spread her plaid blanket in the corner where she had tacked reflecting sheets of aluminum broiling foil to the balustrade. Piet took off his suède apricot windbreaker and sank down. The sun, tepid and breezy to a standing man, burned the skin of his broad face and dyed his retinas red. "Bliss," he said.

She resumed her place on the blanket and her forearm touched his: the touch felt like a fine grade of sandpaper with a little warm sting of friction left. She was in only underwear. He got up on his elbow and kissed her belly, flat and soft and hot, and remembered his mother's ironing board and how she would have him lay his earaches on its comforting heat; he put his ear against Georgene's belly and overheard a secret squirm of digestion. Still attentive to the sun, she fingered his hair and fumblingly measured his shoulders. She said, "You have too many clothes on."

His voice came out plucking and beggarly. "Baby, I don't have time. I should be over on Indian Hill. We're clearing out trees." He listened for the rasp and spurt of his chain saws; the hill was a mile away.

"Please stay a minute. Don't come just to tease me."

"I can't make love. I don't tease. I came to say hello and that I missed you all weekend. We weren't at the same parties. The Gallaghers had us over with the Ongs. Very dreary."

"We talked about you at the Guerins Saturday night. It made me feel quite lovesick." She sat up and began to unbutton his shirt. Her lower lip bent in beneath her tongue. Angela made the same mouth doing up snowsuits. All women, so solemn in their small tasks, it tickled him, it moved him in a surge, seeing suddenly the whole world sliding forward on this female unsmilingness about things physical—unbuttoning, ironing, sunbathing, cooking, lovemaking. The world sewn together by such tasks. He let her fumble and kissed the gauzy sideburn, visible only in sun, in front of her ear. Even here a freckle had found itself. Seed. Among thorns. Fallen. She opened the wings of his shirt and tried to push the cloth back from his shoulders, an exertion bringing against him her bra modestly swollen and the tender wishbone blankness above. The angle of her neck seemed meek. He peeled his shirt off, and his undershirt: weightless as water spiders, reflected motes from the aluminum foil skated the white skin and amber hair of his chest.

Piet pulled Georgene into the purple shadow his shoulders

cast. Her flesh gentle in her underthings possessed a boyish boniness not like Angela's elusive abundance. Touch Angela, she vanished. Touch Georgene, she was there. This simplicity at times made their love feel incestuous to Piet, a connection too direct. Her forbearance enlarged, he suspected, what was already weak and overextended in him. All love is a betrayal, in that it flatters life. The loveless man is best armed. A jealous God. She opened wide her mouth and drew his tongue into a shapeless wet space; fluttering melted into a forgetful encompassing; he felt lost and pulled back, alarmed. Her lips looked blurred and torn. The green of her eyes was deepened by his shadow. He asked her, "What was said?"

Gazing beyond him, she groped. "The Whitmans were wondering—she's with chi-yuld, by the way—the Whitmans were wondering if you should be the contractor for their house. Frank said you were awful, and Roger said you were great."

"Appleby talked me down? That son of a bitch, what have I done to him? I've never slept with Janet."

"Maybe it was Smitty, I forget. It was just one remark, a joke, really."

Her face was guarded in repose, her chin set and the corners of her mouth downdrawn, with such a studied sadness. The shadows of the larch boughs shuffled across them. He guessed it had been her husband and changed the subject. "That tall cool blonde with the pink face is pregnant?"

"She told Bea in the kitchen. I must say, she did seem rude. Freddy was being a puppy dog for her and she froze over the soup. She's from the South. Aren't those women afraid of being raped?"

"I watched her drive away from church a Sunday ago. She burned rubber. There's something cooking in that lady."

"It's called a fetus." Her chin went firm, crinkled. She added, "I don't think as a couple they'll swing. Freddy thinks *he's* a stick. I sat right across the table from *her*, and I must say, her big brown eyes never stopped moving. She didn't miss a thing. It was insulting. Freddy was being his usual self and I could see her wondering what to make of *me*."

"None of us know what to make of you."

Pretending to be offended yet truly offended, Piet felt, by his interest in the Whitman woman, Georgene drew herself from his arms and stretched out again on the blanket. Giving the sun his turn: whore. The reflecting foil decorated her face with parabolic dabs and nebulae and spurts: solar jism. Piet jealously shucked his shoes and socks and trousers, leaving his under-pants, Paisley drawers. He was a secret dandy. He lay down beside her and when she turned to face him reached around and undid her bra, explaining, "Twins," meaning they should both be dressed alike, in only underpants.

Her breasts were smaller than Angela's, with sunken paler nipples, and, uncovered, seemed to cry for protection. He brought his chest against hers for covering and they lay to-gether beneath the whispering trees, Hansel and Gretel aban-doned. Shed needles from the larches had collected in streaks and puddles on the tarpaper and formed rusty ochre drifts along the wooden balustrade and the grooved aluminum base of the sliding glass doors. Piet stroked the uninterrupted curve of her back, his thumb tracing her spine from the knuckle-like bones at the nape of her neck to the strangely prominent coccyx. Georgene had the good start of a tail. She was more bone than Angela. Her presence pressing against him seemed so natural and sisterly he failed to lift, whereas even Angela's foot on his instep was enough, and he wondered, half-crushed beneath the span of sky and treetops and birdsong, which he truly loved.

Before their affair, he had ignored Georgene. She had been hidden from him by his contempt for her husband. His, and Angela's, dislike of Freddy Thorne had been immediate, though in their first years in Tarbox the Thornes as a couple had rather courted them. The Hanemas in response had been so rude as to refuse several invitations without an excuse or even a reply. They had not felt much in need of friends then. Piet, not yet consciously unhappy with Angela, had dimly dreamed of mak-ing love to other women, to Janet or to stately gypsy-haired Terry Gallagher, as one conjures up fantasies to induce sleep. But two summers ago the Ongs built their tennis court and they saw more of Georgene; and when, a summer ago, Piet's dreams without his volition began to transpose themselves into reality, and unbeknownst to himself he had turned from Angela and become an open question, it was Georgene, in a passing touch at a party, in the apparently unplanned sharing of a car to and from tennis, who attempted an answer, who was there. She said she had been waiting for him for years.

"What else?" he asked.

"What else what?" Behind the sunstruck mask of her face her senses had been attending to his hand.

"What else with you? How's Whitney's cold?"

"Poor little Whit. He had a fever yesterday but I sent him off to school in case you decided to come."

"You shouldn't have done that."

"He'll be all right. Everybody has a spring cold."

"You don't."

She carried forward the note of contention. "Piet, what did you mean, a minute ago, when I told you Frank criticized you, you said you had never slept with Janet?"

"I never have. It's been years since I wanted to."

"But do you think—stop your hand for a second, you're beginning just to tickle—that's why Freddy doesn't like you? I lied, you know. It was Freddy who told the Whitmans you were a bad contractor."

"Of course. The jerk."

"You shouldn't hate him."

"It keeps me young."

"But do you think he *does* know, about us? Freddy."

Her curiosity insulted him; he wanted her to dismiss Freddy utterly. He said, "Not as a fact. But maybe by osmosis? Bea Guerin implied to me the other night that everybody knows."

"Did you admit it?"

"Of course not. What's the matter? *Does* he know?"

Her face was hushed. A thin bit of light lay balanced across one eyelid, trembling; a stir of wind was rippling the sheets of foil, creating excited miniature thunder. She said carefully, "He tells me I must have somebody else because I don't want him as much as I used to. He feels threatened. And if he had to write up a list of who it might be, I guess you'd be at the top. But for some reason he doesn't draw the conclusion. Maybe he knows and thinks he's saving it to use later."

This frightened him, altered the tone of his body. She felt this and opened her eyes; their Coke-bottle green was flecked with wilt. Her pupils in the sun were as small as the core of a pencil.

He asked her, "Is it time to break off?"

When challenged, Georgene, the daughter of a Philadelphia banker, would affect a playful immigrant accent, part shopgirl, part vamp. "Dunt be zilly, fella," she said, and sharply inched upward and pressed her pelvis against his, so that through his cotton he felt her silk. She held him as if captive. Her smooth arms were strong; she could beat him at tennis, for a set. He wrestled against her hold and in the struggle her breasts were freed, swung bulbous above him, then spilled flat when, knees on thighs and hands on wrists, he pinned her on her back. Tarpaper. Her glistening skin gazed. Wounded by winning, he bowed his head and with suppliant lips took a nipple, faintly salt and sour, in. Suddenly she felt to be all circles, circles that could be parted to yield more circles. Birds chirped beyond the rainbow rim of the circular wet tangency holding him secure. Her hand, feathery, established another tangency, located his core. If her touch could be believed, his balls were all velvet, his phallus sheer silver.

Politely he asked, "Do we have on too many clothes?"

The politeness was real. Lacking marriage or any contract, they had evolved between them a code of mutual consideration. Their adultery was divided precisely in half. By daring to mention their breaking up, by rebuking her with this possibility, Piet had asked Georgene to cross the line. Now it was her turn to ask, and his to cross. She said, "What about those trees on Indian Hill?"

"They can fall without me," he said. The sun was baking a musty cidery smell from the drift of needles near his face, by the blanket's edge. The tarpaper scintillated. Good quality: Ruberoid Rolled Roofing, mineralized, $4.25 a roll in 1960. He had laid this deck. He added, "I'm not sure you can."

"Oh I'm not so fallen," Georgene said, and quickly sat up, and, kneeling, flauntingly stretched her arms to the corners of the sky. She possessed, this conscientious clubwoman and firm mother, a lovely unexpected gift. Her sexuality was guileless. As formed by the first years of her marriage with Freddy, it had the directness of eating, the ease of running. Her insides were innocent. She had never had an affair before and, though Piet did not understand the virtue she felt in him, he doubted that she would ever take another lover. She had no love of guilt.

In the beginning, deciding upon adultery with her, Piet had prepared himself for terrible sensations of remorse, as a diver in midair anticipates the underwater rush and roar. Instead, the first time—it was September: apples in the kitchen, children off at school, except for Judy, who was asleep—Georgene led him lightly by one finger upstairs to her bed. They deftly undressed, she him, he her. When he worried about contraception, she laughed. Didn't Angela use Enovid yet? *Welcome*, she said, *to the post-pill paradise*, a lighthearted blasphemy that immensely relieved him. With Angela the act of love had become over-laid with memories of his clumsiness and her failure to tolerate clumsiness, with the need for tact and her irritation with the pleadingness implicit in tact, her equal disdain of his pajama-clad courting and his naked rage, his helpless transparence and her opaque disenchantment. Georgene in twenty minutes stripped away these laminations of cross-purpose and showed him something primal. Now she kneeled under the sun and Piet rose to be with her and with extreme care, as if setting the wafery last cogwheels of a watch into place, kissed the glossy point of her left shoulder bone, and then of her right. She was double everywhere but in her mouths. All things double. Without duality, entropy. The universe God's mirror.

She said, "You're in my sun."

"It's too soon to have a tan." Politely: "Would you like to go inside?"

The sliding glass door led off the sun deck through a play-room into their big bedroom, a room adorned with Chinese lanterns and African masks and carved animal horns from sev-eral countries. Their house, a gambrel-roof late-Victorian, with gingerbread eaves and brackets, scrolling lightning rods, un-dulate shingling, zinc spouting, and a roof of rose slates in graduated ranks, was furnished in a style of cheerful bastardy— hulking black Spanish chests, Chippendale highboys veneered in contrasting fruitwoods flaking bit by bit, nondescript slab-and-tube modern, souvenir-shop colonial, Hitchcock chairs with missing rungs, *art nouveau* rockers, Japanese prints, giant corduroy pillows, Philippine carpets woven of rush rosettes. Unbreakable as a brothel, it was a good house for a party. Through his illicit morning visits Piet came to know these rooms in another light, as rooms children lived in and left

littered with breakfast crumbs as they fled down the driveway
to the school bus, the *Globe* still spread open to the funnies on
the floor. Gradually the furniture—the antic lamps, the staring
masks—learned to greet him, the sometimes man of the house.
Proprietorially he would lie on the Thornes' king-size double
bed, his bare toes not touching the footboard, while Georgene
had her preparatory shower. Curiously he would finger and
skim through Thorne's bedside shelf—Henry Miller in tattered Paris editions, Sigmund Freud in Modern Library, *Our
Lady of the Flowers* and *Memoirs of a Woman of Pleasure* fresh
from Grove Press, inspirational psychology by the Menningers,
a dove-gray handbook on hypnosis, *Psychopathia Sexualis* in
textbook format, a delicately tinted and stiff-paged album
smuggled from Kyoto, the poems of Sappho as published by
Peter Pauper, the unexpurgated Arabian Nights in two boxed
volumes, works by Theodor Reik and Wilhelm Reich, various
tawdry paperbacks. Then Georgene would come in steaming
from the bathroom, a purple towel turbaned around her head.

She surprised him by answering, "Let's make it outdoors for
a change."

Piet felt he was still being chastised. "Won't we embarrass
God?"

"Haven't you heard, God's a woman? Nothing embarrasses
Her." She pulled the elastic of his underpants toward her, eased
it down and around. Her gaze became complacent. A cloud
passingly blotted the sun. Sensing and fearing a witness, Piet
looked upward and was awed as if by something inexplicable
by the unperturbed onward motion of the fleet of bluebel-
lied clouds, ships with a single destination. The little eclipsing
cloud burned gold in its tendrilous masts and stern. A cannon discharge of iridescence, and it passed. Passed on safely
above him. Sun was renewed in bold shafts on the cracked
April earth, the sodden autumnal leaves, the new shoots coral
in the birches and mustard on the larch boughs, the dropped
needles drying, the tarpaper, their discarded clothes. Between
the frilled holes her underpants wore a tender honey stain. Between her breasts the sweat was scintillant and salt. He encircled her, fingered and licked her willing slipping tips, the pip
within the slit, wisps. Sun and spittle set a cloudy froth on her
pubic hair: Piet pictured a kitten learning to drink milk from a

saucer. He hurried, seeking her forgiveness, for his love of her, on the verge of discharge, had taken a shadow, had become regretful, foregone. He parted her straight thighs and took her with the simplicity she allowed. A lip of resistance, then an easeful deepness, a slipping by steps. His widening entry slowly startled her eyes. For fear of finding her surrendered face plain, he closed his lids. The whispering of boughs filtered upon them. Distant saws rasped. The breeze teased his squeezing buttocks; he was bothered by hearing birds behind him, Thorne's hired choir, spying.

"Oh, sweet. Oh so sweet," Georgene said. Piet dared peek and saw her rapt lids veined with broken purple and a small saliva bubble welling at one corner of her lips. He suffered a dizzying impression of waste. Though thudding, his heart went mournful. He bit her shoulder, smooth as an orange in sun, and traveled along a muffled parabola whose red warm walls she was and at whose end she also waited. Her face snapped sideways; drenched feathers pulled his tip; oh. So good a girl, to be there for him, no matter how he fumbled, to find her way by herself. In her strange space he leaped, and leaped again. She said, "Oh."

Lavender she lay in his shadow, the corners of her lips flecked. Politely Piet asked her, "Swing?"

"Dollink. Dunt esk."

"I was sort of poor. I'm not used to this outdoor living."

Georgene shrugged under him. Her throat and shoulders were slick. A speck of black construction dust, granular tar from his hair, adhered to her cheek. "You were you. I love you. I love you inside me."

Piet wanted to weep, to drop fat tears onto her deflated breasts. "Did I feel big enough?"

She laughed, displaying perfect teeth, a dentist's wife. "No," she said. "You felt shrimpy." Seeing him ready, in his dilated suspended state, to believe it, she explained solemnly, "You hurt me, you know. I ache afterwards."

"Do I? Do you? How lovely. How lovely of you to say. But you should complain."

"It's in a good cause. Now get off me. Go to Indian Hill."

Discarded beside her, he felt as weak and privileged as a child. Plucking needs agitated his fingers, his mouth. He asked at her side, "What did Freddy say about me that was mean?"

"He said you were expensive and slow."

"Well. I suppose that could be true."

He began dressing. The birds' chirping had become a clock's ticking. Like butter on a bright sill her nakedness was going rancid. She lay as she must often lie, accepting the sun entirely. The bathing-suit boundaries were not distinct on her body, as on Angela's. Her kitten-chin glutinous with jism. The plaid blanket had been rumpled and pulled from under her head, and some larch needles adhered to her hair, black mixed with gray. Because of this young turning of her hair she kept it feather-cut short.

"Baby," he said, to fill up the whispering silence surrounding his dressing, "I don't care about Freddy. I don't want the Whitmans' job. Cut into these old houses you never know what you'll find. Gallagher thinks we've wasted too much time restoring old heaps for our friends and the friends of our friends. He wants three new ranch houses on Indian Hill by fall. The war babies are growing up. That's where the money is."

"Money," she said. "You're beginning to sound like the rest of them."

"Well," he told her. "I can't be a virgin forever. Corruption had to come even to me."

He was dressed. The cool air drew tight around his shoulders and he put on his apricot windbreaker. With the manners that rarely lapsed between them, she escorted him from her house. He admired and yet was slightly scandalized that she could walk so easily, naked, through doors, past her children's toys, her husband's books, down stairs, under a shelf of cleansing agents, into her polished kitchen, to the side door. This side of the house, where the firewood was stacked and a single great elm cast down a gentle net of shade, had about it something rural and mild unlike the barbaric bulk of the house. Here not a brick or stone walk but a path worn through grass, now muddy, led around the corner of the garage, where Piet had hidden his pick-up truck, a dusty olive Chevrolet on whose tailgate a child had written WASH ME. Georgene, barefoot, did not step down from the threshold but leaned silent and smiling in the open doorway, leaving framed in Piet's mind a complex impression: of a domestic animal, of a fucked woman, of a mocking boy, of farewell.

*

Next Sunday, a little past noon, when Foxy had just returned from church and with a sigh had dropped her veiled hat onto the gate-legged table where the telephone sat, it impudently rang. She knew the voice: Piet Hanema. She had been thinking of calling him all week and therefore was prepared, though they had never really spoken, to recognize his voice, more hesitant and respectful than that of the other local men, with a flattish blurred midwestern intonation. He asked to speak to Ken. She went into the kitchen and deliberately didn't listen, because she wanted to.

All week she had been unable against Ken's silent resistance to call the contractor, and now her hands trembled as if guiltily. She poured herself a glass of dry vermouth. Really, church was getting to be, as the weather grew finer, a sacrifice. Magnolia buds swollen by heat leaned in the space of air revealed by the tilted ventilation pane of commemorative stained glass, birds sang in the little late-Victorian cemetery between the church and the river, the sermon dragged, the pews cracked restlessly. Ken came back from the phone saying, "He asked me to play basketball at two o'clock at his place."

Basketball was the one sport Ken had ever cared about; he had played for Exeter and for his Harvard house, which he had told her as a confession, it had been so unfashionable to do. Foxy said, "How funny."

"Apparently he has a basket on his barn wall, with a little asphalt court. He said in the spring, between skiing and tennis, some of the men like to play. They need me to make six, for three on a side."

"Did you say you would?"

"I thought you wanted to go for a walk on the beach."

"We can do that any time. I could walk by myself."

"Don't be a martyr. What is that, dry vermouth?"

"Yes. I developed a taste for it at the Guerins'."

"And then don't forget we have Ned and Gretchen tonight."

"They won't get here until after eight, you know how arrogant Cambridge people are. Call him back and tell him you'll play, it'll do you good."

Ken confessed, "Well, I left it that I might show up."

Foxy laughed, delighted at having been deceived. "Well if you told him yes why are you being so sneaky about it?"

"I shouldn't leave you here alone all afternoon."

Because you're pregnant, the implication was. His oppressive concern betrayed him. They had gone childless too long; he feared this change and added weight. Foxy made herself light, showed herself gay. "Can't I come along and watch? I thought this was a wives' town."

Foxy was the only wife who came to basketball, and Angela Hanema came out of the house to keep her company. The day was agreeable for being outdoors; nothing in the other woman's manner asked for an apology. The two together carried a bench, a weathered moist settee with a spindle-rung back, from beside the barn to a spot on the gravel driveway where simultaneously they could see the men play, have the sun on their faces, and keep an eye on the many children running and hiding in the big square yard and the lacy screen of budding woods beyond.

Foxy asked, "Whose children are all these?"

"Two are ours, two girls. You can see one of them standing by the birdbath sucking her thumb. That's Nancy."

"Is thumb-sucking bad?" It was a question probably naïve, another mother wouldn't have asked it, but Foxy was curious and felt she could hardly embarrass herself with Angela, who seemed so graceful and serenely humorous.

"It's not aesthetic," she said. "She didn't do it as an infant, it just started last winter. She's worried about death. I don't know where she gets it from. Piet insists on taking them to Sunday school and maybe they talk about it there."

"I suppose they feel they should."

"I suppose. The other children you see—the happy loud ones belong to our neighbors who run the dairy farm and the rest came with their proud daddies."

"I don't know all the daddies. I see Harold—why is it *little*-Smith?"

"It's one of those jokes that nobody knows how to get rid of. There were some other Smiths in town once, but they've long left."

"And that big imposing one is our real-estate man."

"Matt Gallagher. My husband's partner. The bouncy one with red hair is my husband."

Foxy thought, how funny that he is. She said, "He was at the Applebys' party for us."

"We all were. The one with the beard and grinning is Ben Saltz. S-a-l-t-z. I think it's been shortened from something."

"He looks very diabolical," Foxy said.

"Not to me. I think the effect is supposed to be rakish but it comes out Amish. It's to cover up pockmarks; when we first moved to town it was bushier but now he cuts it square. It's misleading, because he's a terribly kind, uxorious man. Irene is the moving spirit behind the League and the Fair Housing group and whatever else does good in town. Ben works in one of those plants along 128 that look as though they make ice cream."

"I thought that was a Chinaman."

"Korean. That's John Ong. He's not here. The only things he plays are chess and very poor tennis. His chess is quite good, though, Freddy Thorne tells me. He's a nuclear physicist who works in MIT. *At* MIT? Actually, I think he works *under* MIT, in a huge underground workshop you need a password to get into."

Foxy asked, "With a cyclotron?"

Angela said, "I forget your husband's a scientist too. I have no idea. Neither he nor Ben can ever talk about their work because it's all for the government. It makes everybody else feel terribly excluded. I think a little tiny switch in something that missed the moon was Ben's idea. He miniaturizes. He once showed us some radios that were like fingernails."

"At the party, I tried to talk to—who, Ong?—you all have such funny names."

"But aren't all names funny until you get used to them? Think of Shakespeare and Churchill. Think of Pillsbury."

"Anyway I tried to talk and couldn't understand a word."

"I know. His consonants are not what you expect. He was some kind of booty in the Korean War; I can't believe he defected, he doesn't seem to have that kind of opinion. He was very big with them I guess; for a while he taught at Johns Hopkins and met Bernadette in Baltimore. If they ever dropped an H-bomb on Tarbox it would be because of him. Like the Watertown arsenal. But you're right. He's not sexy."

Her tone implied a disdain of sex mixed with the equanimous recognition that others might choose to steer by it. Studying the other woman's lips, pale in the sunlight, composed around the premeditation of a smile, Foxy felt as if she, Foxy, were looking up toward a luxurious detached realm where observations and impressions drifted nodding by one another like strolling aristocrats. Every marriage tends to consist of an aristocrat and a peasant. Of a teacher and a learner. Foxy, though by more than an inch the taller, felt beneath Angela, as a student, at once sheltered and challenged. Discovering herself blushing, she hastily asked, "Who's the quick one with the ghostly eyes?"

"I guess they are ghostly. I've always thought of them as steely but that's wrong. His name is Eddie Constantine. He's an airline pilot. They just moved a year or so ago into a grim big house on the green. The tall teen-ager who looks like the Apollo Belvedere is a neighbor's boy he brought along in case there weren't six. Piet didn't know if your husband would come or not."

"Oh. Ken has made the sides uneven?"

"Not at all, they're delighted to have another player. Basketball isn't very popular, you can't do it with women. He's very good. Your husband."

Foxy watched. The neighbor boy, graceful even ill at ease, was standing aside while the six grown men panted and heaved, ducked and dribbled. They looked clumsy, crowded on the little piece of asphalt whose edges fell off into mud softened and stamped by sneaker footprints. Ken and Gallagher were the tallest and she saw Ken, whose movements had a certain nice economy she had not seen displayed for years, lift the ball to the level of his forehead and push it off. It swirled around the rim and flew away, missing. This pleased her: why? He had looked so confident, his whole nicely poised body had expressed the confidence, that it would go in. Constantine seized the rebound and dribbled down low, protecting the ball with an outward elbow. Foxy felt he had been raised in a city. His eyes in their ghostly transparence suggested photographic paper now silver, now black, now clear, depending upon in what they were dipped. His sharp features flushed, little-Smith kept slapping his feet as if to create confusion. He had none of the instinctive moves and Foxy wondered why he played. Saltz, whom she was prepared to adore, moved on the fringes cautiously, stooped and smiling as if to admit he was in a boys' game. His backside was broad and instead of sneakers he wore black laced shoes, such as peek from beneath a priest's robe. As she watched, Hanema, abruptly fierce, stole the ball from Constantine, braving his elbow, pushed past Ken in a way that must be illegal, hipped and hopped and shot. When the ball went in he jumped for a joke on Gallagher's back. The Irishman, his jaws so wide his face was pentagonal, sheepishly carried his partner on a jog once around the asphalt.

"Discontinuous," Saltz was protesting.

"And you fouled the new guy," Constantine said. "You are an unscrupulous bastard."

Their voices were adolescently shrill. "All right crybabies, I won't play," Hanema said, and waved the waiting boy into his place. "Shall I call Thorne to come and make four on a side?"

Nobody answered; play had already resumed. Hanema draped a sweater around his neck and came and stood above the watching pair of women. Foxy could not study his face, a circular purple shadow against the sun. A male scent, sweat, flowed from him. His grainy courtly voice asked his wife, "Shall I call Thorne or do you want to? He's your friend."

Angela answered, "It's rude to call him this late, he'll wonder why you didn't call him sooner." Her voice, lifted toward the man, sounded diminished to Foxy, frightened.

He said, "You can't be rude to Thorne. If rudeness bothered him he'd have left town long ago. Anyway everybody knows on Sundays he has a five-martini lunch and couldn't have come earlier."

"Call him then," Angela said. "And say hello to Foxy."

"Pardon me. How are *you*, Mrs. Whitman?"

"Well, thank you, Mr. Hanema." She was determined not to be frightened also, and felt that she was not.

Sun rimmed his skull with rainbow filaments. He remained an upright shadow in front of her, emanating heat, but his voice altered, checked by something in hers. "It's very endearing," he said, and repeated, "en*dear*ing of you to come and be an audience. We need an audience." And his sudden explosion of energy, his bumping of Ken, his leap to Gallagher's back, were lit in retrospect by the fact of her watching. He had done it for her to see.

"You *all* seem very energetic," Foxy said. "I'm impressed."

He asked her, "Would you like to play?"

"I think not," she answered, wondering if he knew that she was pregnant, remembering him looking up her skirt, and guessing that he did. He would make it his business to know.

"In that case I better call Thorne," he said, and went into his house.

Angela, her casual manner restored, told Foxy, "Women sometimes do play. Janet and Georgene are actually not too bad. At least they look to me as if they know what they're doing."

Foxy said, "Field hockey is my only game."

"What position did you play? I was center halfback."

"You played? I was right inner, usually. Sometimes wing."

"It's a lovely game," Angela said. "It was the one time in my life when I enjoyed being aggressive. It's what men must have a lot of the time." There was a flow and an authority in the drifting way she spoke that led Foxy to agree, to nod eagerly, as the sun drifted lower into a salmon overcast. Keeping their pale faces lifted to the pale light, they talked, these two, of hockey ("What I liked about halfback," Angela said, "was you were both offensive and defensive and yet nobody could blame you for anything."); of sports in general ("It's so good," Foxy said, "to see Ken playing at anything. I think being with students all the time makes you unnecessarily old. I felt ancient in Cambridge."); of Ken's profession ("He never talks to me about his work any more," Foxy said. "It used to be starfish and that was sort of fun, we went to Woods Hole one summer; but now it's more to do with chlorophyll and all the breakthroughs recently have been in other fields, DNA and whatnot."); of Piet's house ("He likes it," Angela said, "because everything is square. I loved the house you have now. So many things could be done with it, and the way it floats above the marsh! Piet was worried about mosquitoes. Here we have these terrible horseflies from the dairy. He's from inland, you know. I think the sea intimidates him. He likes to skate but isn't much of a swimmer. He thinks the sea is wasteful. I think *I* prefer things

to be somewhat formless. Piet likes them finished."); and of
the children who now and then emerged from the woods and
brought them a wound, a complaint, a gift:

"Why, Franklin, thank you! What do you think it can be?"

"A coughball," the boy said. "From an owl or a hawk." The
boy was eight or nine, intelligent but slow to form, and thin-
skinned. The coughball lay in Angela's hand, smaller than a golf
ball, a tidy dry accretion visibly holding small curved bones.

"It's beautiful in its way," Angela said. "What would you like
me to do with it?"

"Keep it for me until they take me home. Don't let Ruthie
have it. She says it's hers because it's her woods but I want to
start a collection and I saw it *first* even though she did pick it
up." Making this long statement brought the child close to
tears.

Angela said, "Frankie, go tell Ruth to come see me." He
blinked and turned and ran.

Foxy said, "Isn't that Frankie Appleby? But Frank himself
isn't here."

"Harold brought him. He's friends with their Jonathan."

"I thought the Smith boy was years older."

"He is, but of course they're thrown together."

Of course?

Three children returned from the woods—four, counting
little Nancy Hanema, who hung back near the birdbath and,
thumb in mouth, fanned her fingers as if to hide her face from
Foxy's gaze.

Ruth was a solid tall round-faced girl. Her body jerked and
stamped with indignant energy. "Mother, he says he saw it *first*
but he didn't see it at all until *I* picked it up. Then he said it was
his because he saw it *first*."

The taller boy, with a clever flickering expression, said,
"That's the truth, Mrs. Hanema. Old Franklin Fink here grabs
everything."

Young Appleby, without preamble, broke into sobs. "I
don't," he said, and would have said more, but his throat stuck
shut.

"Boo hoo, Finkie," the Smith boy said.

"Mother," Ruth said, stamping her foot on the gravel to retrieve Angela's attention. "Last *summer* we found a bird's nest

and *Frankie* said it was *his* for a *collection* and grabbed it out of my hand and it all came apart and fell into *nothing*, all because of *him*!" She flounced so hard her straight hair fanned in space.

Jonathan little-Smith said, "Lookie, Finkie's crying again. Boo hoo, oh dear, goodness gracious me oh my oh."

With a guttural whimper the younger boy attacked his friend with rotating fists. Jonathan laughed; his arm snaked out and flipped the frantic red face aside; he contemptuously pushed. Angela rose and parted them, and Foxy thought how graceful yet solid she looked, and imagined her as a hockey player standing abstracted yet impenetrable in the center of the limed field, in blue bloomers. Her body in turning showed a trace of the process that makes middle-aged women, with their thickened torsos and thinned legs, appear to be engaged in a balancing act.

"Now Jonathan," Angela said, holding each boy's hand equally, "Frankie wants to start a collection. Do you want to have a collection too?"

"No I don't give a fart about some old bird's throw-up. It's Ruthie he stole from."

"Ruthie is here all the time and I *know* she can find another in the woods. I want you all to help her. There's an owl hoots every night in that woods and if you find his tree I bet you'll find lots more coughballs. You help too, Nancy."

The child had approached closer. "Mouse died," she said, not removing her thumb.

"Yes," Ruth said, wheeling, her hair lifting winglike, "and if you don't watch out this enormous owl will come and eat you and your thumb will be sticking out from an enormous coughball with eyes on it!"

"Ruth!" Angela called, too late. Ruth had run back to the woods, her long legs flinging beneath her flying skirt. The boys, united by need for pursuit, followed. Nancy came to her mother's lap and was absent-mindedly caressed. "You have all this," Angela said to Foxy, "to look forward to."

Her pregnancy, then, was common knowledge. She discovered she didn't mind. She said, "I'll be glad when it's at that stage. I feel horrible half the time, and useless the rest."

"Later," Angela said, "it's splendid. You're so right with the world. Then this little package arrives, and it's utterly dependent, with these very clear sharp needs that you can *sat*-isfy! You have everything it wants. I loved having babies. But then you have to raise them." The eyes of the child half lying in her lap listened wide open. Her lips around her thumb made a secret, moist noise.

"You're very good with children," Foxy told her.

"I like to teach," Angela said. "It's easier than learning."

With a splashing sound of gravel, a yellow convertible, top down, came into the driveway and stopped not a yard from their bench. The Thorne man was driving; his pink head poked from the metal shell like the flesh of a mollusc. Standing in the back seat were a sickly-looking boy who resembled him and a younger girl, six or so, whose green eyes slightly bulged. Foxy was jarred by the readiness with which Angela rose to greet them. After an hour of sharing a bench and the sun with her, she was jealous. Angela introduced the children: "Whitney and Martha Thorne, say hello to Mrs. Whitman."

"I know you," the boy told her. "You moved in down the road from us into the spook house." His face was pale and his nostrils and ears seemed inflamed. Possibly he had a fever. His sister was definitely fat. She found herself touched by these children and, lifting her eyes to their father, even by him.

"Is it a spook house?" she asked.

"He means," Angela intervened, "because it stood empty so long. The children can see it from the beach."

"All shuttered up," Whitney said, "with smoke coming out of the chimneys."

"The kid hallucinates," his father said. "He chews peyote for breakfast."

Whitney defended himself. "Iggy Kappiotis said he and some guys snuck up on the porch one time and heard voices inside."

"Just a little innocent teen-age fucking," Freddy Thorne said, squinting at the sallow spring sun. By daylight his amorphous softness was less menacing, more pitiable. He wore a fuzzy claret sports shirt with an acid-green foulard and hightop all-weather boots such as children with weak ankles wear.

"Hey, big Freddy," Harold little-Smith called from the basketball court. The thumping and huffing had suspended.

"It's Bob Cousy!" Hanema called from the porch.

"Looks more like Goose Tatum to me," said Gallagher. "You can always tell by de whites ob dare eyes."

"What whites?" Hanema asked. He hurried over and, taking Thorne by the elbow, announced, "This man is living gin."

"Those are not official sneakers," Ben Saltz protested.

"Those are Frankenstein shoes," Eddie Constantine said. He went mock-rigid and tottered the few steps needed to bump into Thorne's chest. He sniffed Thorne's breath, clutched his own throat, and screamed, "Aagh! The fumes! The fumes!"

Thorne smiled and wiped his mouth. "I'll just watch," he said. "You don't need me, you got plenty of people. Why did you call?"

"We *do* need you," Hanema insisted, handling the man's elbow again and seeming to exult in his relative shortness. "Four on a side. You guard me. You belong to Matt, Eddie, and Ben."

"Thanks a holy arse-licking bunch," Constantine said.

"How many points are you spotting us?" Gallagher asked.

"None," Hanema said. "Freddy will be all right. He's an asset. He's loose. Take a practice shot, Freddy." He slammed the ball off the asphalt into Thorne's stomach. "See how loose he is?"

From the stiff-fingered way Thorne handled the ball Foxy saw he was nothing of an athlete; he was so waddly, so flat-footed, she averted her eyes from the sight.

Beside her, Angela said, "I suppose the house may have been broken into by a few young couples. They have so few places to go."

"What were the people like who owned it before?"

"The Robinsons. We hardly knew them. They only used it summers and weekends. A middle-aged couple with pots of children who suddenly got divorced. I used to see her downtown with binoculars around her neck. Quite a handsome woman with hair in a bun and windburn in tweeds. He was an ugly little man with a huge voice, always threatening to sue the town if they widened the road to the beach. But Bernadette Ong, who knew them, says it was *he* who wanted the divorce. Evidently he played the cello and she the violin and they got into a string quartet with some people from Duxbury. They never did a thing for the house."

Foxy blurted, "Would your husband be willing to look at the house for us? And give us an estimate or some notion as to where to begin?"

Angela gazed toward the woods, a linear maze where children's bodies were concealed. "Matt," she said carefully, "wants Piet to concentrate on building new houses."

"Perhaps he could recommend another contractor then. We must make a beginning. Ken seems to like the house as it is but when winter comes it will be impossible."

"Of course it will." The curtness startled Foxy. Gazing toward the trees, Angela went on hesitatingly, as if her choice of words were distracted by a flowering of things unseen. "Your husband—perhaps he and Piet could talk. Not today after basketball. Everybody stays for beer."

"No, fine. We must hurry back, we have some friends coming from Cambridge."

Thus a gentle rift was established between them. The two faced differently, Angela toward the woods full of children and Foxy toward the men's game. Four on a side was too many. The court, now deep in the shadow of the barn, was crowded and Thorne, with his protrusive rear and confused motions, was in everyone's way. Hanema had the ball. Persistently bumped by Thorne in his attempts to dribble amid a clamor of shouts, he passed the ball on the bounce to the Constantines' neighbor's boy; in the same stride he hooked one foot around Thorne's ankle and by a backwards stab of his weight caused the bigger man to fall down. Thorne fell in stages, thrusting out an arm, then rolling face down on the muddy asphalt, his hand under him.

Play stopped. Foxy and Angela ran to the men. Hanema had kneeled to Thorne. The others made a hushed circle around them. Smearily smiling, his claret shirt muddy, Thorne sat up and showed them a trembling hand whose whitened little finger stuck out askew. "Dislocated," he said in a voice from which pain had squeezed all elasticity.

Hanema, kneeling, blurted, "Jesus Freddy, I'm sorry. This is terrible. Sue me."

"It's happened before," Thorne said. He took the injured hand in his good one and grimaced and pulled. A snap softer than a twig breaking, more like a pod popping, shocked the silent circle. Freddy rose and held his hand, the little finger now aligned, before his chest as something tender and disgraced that must not be touched. He asked Angela, "Do you have surgical tape and anything for a splint—a tongue depressor, a popsicle stick? Even a spoon would do."

Rising with him, Hanema asked, "Freddy, will you be able to work?"

Thorne smirked down at the other's anxious face. He was feeling his edge enlarge, Foxy felt; she thought only women used their own pain as a weapon. "Oh," he said, "after a month or so. I can't go into somebody's mouth wearing a plaster cast, can I?"

"Sue me," Hanema said. His face was a strange stretched mixture of freckles and pallor, of the heat of battle and contrition. The other players had divided equally into two sympathizing rings. Freddy Thorne, holding his hand before him, led Angela and Constantine and the neighbor boy and Saltz into the house, in triumph. Yet Foxy's impression remained that he had been, in the minute before exploitation set in, instinctively stoical.

"You didn't do it on purpose," little-Smith told Hanema. Foxy wondered why he, Thorne's friend, had stayed outdoors, with the guilty. The patterns of union were many.

"But I *did*," Piet said. "I deliberately tripped the poor jerk. The way he bumps with his belly gets me mad."

Gallagher said, "He doesn't understand the game." Gallagher would have been handsome but for something narrowed about the mouth, something predetermined and closed expressed by the bracketlike creases emphasizing the corners: prim tucks. Amid the whiskery Sunday chins his jaws were smooth-shaved; he had been to mass.

She said, "I think you're all awfully rough with each other."

"*C'est la guerre*," little-Smith told her.

Ken, in the lull, was practicing shots, perfecting himself. Foxy felt herself submerged in shadows and cross-currents while he was on high, willfully ignorant, hollow and afloat. His dribbling and the quivering rattle of the rim irritated her like any monologue.

Hanema was beside her. Surprisingly, he said, "I hate being a shit and that's how it keeps turning out. I beg him to come play and then I cripple him."

It was part confession, part brag. Foxy was troubled that he would bring her this, as if laying his head in her lap. She shied, speechless, angered that, having felt from an unexpected angle his rumored force, his orphan's needful openness, she had proved timid, like Angela.

The gravel driveway splashed again. An old maroon coupe pulled in, its windshield aswarm with reflected branches and patches of cloud. Janet Appleby got out on the driver's side. She carried two sixpacks of beer. Georgene Thorne pushed from the other door holding in her arms a child of a cumbersome age, so wadded with clothes its legs were spread like the stalks of an H. By the scorched redness of its cheeks the child was an Appleby.

Little-Smith and Hanema quickly went to greet them. Gallagher joined Ken at shooting baskets. Not wishing to eavesdrop, yet believing her sex entitled her to join the women, Foxy walked slowly down the drive to them as little-Smith caperingly described Freddy's unfortunate finger—"*le doigt disloqué.*"

Georgene said, "Well, I've told him not to try sports when he's potted." Her upper lids were pink, as if she had been lying in the sun.

Piet Hanema told her, "But I asked him especially to come, so we could have four on a side." Such a sad broad face, growing old without wisdom, alert and strained.

"Oh, he would have come anyway. You don't think he'd sit around all Sunday afternoon with just *me.*"

"Why not?" Piet said, and Foxy imagined hostility in his eyes as he gazed at her. "Don't you want to go inside and see how he is?"

"He's all right," she said. "Isn't Angela with him? Let them alone. He's happy."

Janet and Harold were conferring urgently, in whispers. Their conversation seemed logistical, involving schedules and placement of cars and children. When the Appleby infant seized a cat on the lawn and tried to lift it by its hindquarters, as if spilling a bag of candy out, it was little-Smith who went and pried it loose, while Janet held her face in this idle moment up to the sun. The cat, calico, with a mildewed eye, ran off and hid in the lilac hedge. Foxy asked Hanema, "Is that yours?"

"The cat or the child?" he asked, as if also aware that the child's parentage seemed in flux.

"The calico cat. We have a cat called Cotton."

"*Do* bring Cotton to the next basketball game," Georgene Thorne said. She added, throwing an athletic arm toward the woods, "I can't see the children for the trees," as if this explained the rudeness of her first remark, with its implied indignation at Foxy's being here at all.

Hanema explained, "She belongs to the dairy down the road but the children sometimes feed it. They let the damn thing into the house full of fleas and now I have them."

Freddy Thorne came out of the house. His little finger was bandaged to a green plastic picnic spoon. The pad of his fingertip rested prettily in the bowl and the curve of the handle made a very dainty fit. That Angela had improvised this strengthened Foxy's sense of illicit affection between these two. Freddy was plainly proud.

"Oh Freddy," Janet said, "it's just gorgeous." She was wearing white slacks so snug they had horizontally wrinkled along her pelvis. The nap of her turquoise velour jersey changed tint as it rounded the curve of her breasts; as she moved her front was an electric shimmer of shadow. The neck was cut to reveal a slash of mauve skin. Her lips had been painted to be a valentine but her chalky face needed sleep. Like her son she was thin-skinned and still being formed.

Freddy said, "The kid did it."

Constantine's young neighbor explained, "At camp last summer we had to take First Aid." His voice emerged reedy and shallow from manhood's form: a mouse on a plinth.

Eddie Constantine said, "He comes over to the house and massages Carol's back."

Freddy asked, "Oh. She has a bad back?"

"Only when I've been home too long."

Ken and Gallagher stopped playing and joined the grown-ups.

The sixpacks were broken open and beer cans were passed around. "I *despise* these new tabs," little-Smith said, yanking.

"Everybody I know has cut thumbs. It's the new stigmata."
Foxy felt him grope for the French for "stigmata."

Janet said, "I can't do it, I'm too weak and hung. Could
you?" She handed her can to—Ken!

All eyes noticed. Harold little-Smith's nose tipped up and his
voice rose nervously. "Freddy Thorne," he taunted. "Spoon-
finger. The man with the plastic digit. *Le doigt plastique*."

"Freddy, honestly, what a nuisance," Georgene said, and
Foxy felt hidden in this an attempt to commiserate.

"No kidding," Constantine said, "how will you get in there?
Those little crevices between their teeth?" He was frankly
curious and his eyes, which Foxy for a moment saw full on,
echoed, in the absence of intelligence, aluminum and the gray
of wind and the pearly width low in the sky at high altitudes.
He had been there, in the metallic vastness above the boiling
clouds, and was curious how Freddy would get to where *he*
had to go.

"With a laser beam," Thorne said, and the green spoon became a death ray that he pointed, saying *zizz* between his teeth,
at Constantine, at Hanema, at herself. "*Zizz*. Die. *Zizz*. You're
dead."

The people nearest him laughed excessively. They were
courtiers, and Freddy was a king, the king of chaos: though
struck dead, Foxy refused to laugh. At her back, Georgene and
Piet, ignoring Freddy, exchanged words puzzling in their grave
simplicity:

"How are you?"

"So-so, dollink."

"You've been on your sunporch."

"Yes."

"How was it? Lovely?"

"Lonely."

Overhearing, Foxy was rapt, as when a child she listened to
her parents bumbling and grunting behind a closed door, intimacy giving their common words an exalted magic.

Ben Saltz's voice overenunciated; his moving lips had an air
of isolation, as if they were powered by a battery concealed in
his beard. He was saying, "All kidding aside, Freddy, they really
can do great things now with nontactile dentistry."

"Whoops," Freddy Thorne said, "that lets tactile types like

me out," and he slapped the biform seat of Janet's tense white pants. She whirled from cozying with Ken to give Freddy a look less of surprise than of warning, a warning, Foxy felt, that had to do less with the pat than with its being witnessed.

Saltz seized the chance to latch on to Ken. "Tell me, if you can spare a minute, have you felt the effects of laser beams in biochemistry yet? I was reading in the *Globe* the other week where they've had some success with cancer in mice."

"Anybody can do miracles with mice," Ken stated, ruefully staring down at Janet's backside. He was not comfortable, Foxy had noticed years ago, talking to Jews; he had competed unsuccessfully against too many.

"Do me a favor," Saltz went on, "and tell me about DNA. How the blazes, is the way my thinking runs, how the blazes could such a complex structure spontaneously arise out of chaos?"

"Matter isn't chaos," Ken said. "It has laws, legislated by what can't happen."

"I can see," Saltz said, "how out in our western states, say, the Grand Canyon is the best example, how a rock could be carved by erosion into the shape of a cathedral. But if I look inside and see a lot of pews arranged in apple-pie order, in rows, I begin to smell a rat, so to speak."

"Maybe," Ken said, "you put those pews there yourself."

Ben Saltz grinned. "I like that," he said. "I like that answer." His grin was a dazzling throwback, a facial sunburst that turned his eyes into twinkling slits, that seized his whole face like the snarl on the face of a lion in an Assyrian bas-relief. "I like that answer a lot. You mean the Cosmic Unconscious. You know, Yahweh was a volcano god originally. I think it's ridiculous for religious people to be afraid of the majesty and power of the universe."

Angela called from the porch, "Is anybody except me chilly? Please come into the house, anybody."

This signaled some to go and some to stay. Eddie Constantine crushed his beer can double and handed it to Janet Appleby. She placed it above her breast, as if it were a tin corsage. He crossed to his Vespa and, passing close to Foxy, tapped her stomach. "Suck in your gut." Those were his words. The neighbors' boy got on the Vespa behind him, clinging possumlike.

Constantine kicked off, and a spray of stones leaped from his
rear wheel as he went down the drive and banked into the
road beyond the lilac hedge, which was losing transparence
to the swelling of buds. The cat raced from the hedge in
terror and ran silently across the lawn, elongating. Children
were emerging from the darkening woods. Half of them were
crying. Really, it was only Frankie Appleby crying. Jonathan
Smith and Whitney Thorne had tied him to a tree with his
own shoelaces and then couldn't undo the knots so they had to
cut them and now he had no shoelaces and it wasn't his *fault*.
His feet stumbled and flopped to illustrate and Harold little-
Smith ran to him while Janet his mother stood cold, plump
and pluming, on the porch gazing to where the sun, a netted
orange, hung in the thin woods. Across the lawn came the rosy
Hanema girls and a beautiful male child like a Gainsborough
in the romantic waning light, curly black hair and a lithe self-
solicitous comportment. With a firm dismissing nod Gallagher
took this luxurious child by the hand and led him to their car,
the gray Mercedes from whose tall clean windows Foxy had
first viewed Tarbox. Saltz and the Thornes moved to go in. In
the narrow farmhouse doorway the two men, one bearded and
one bald, bumped together and Thorne unexpectedly put his
arm, the arm with the crippled green-tipped hand, around the
Jew and solidly hugged him sideways. Saltz flashed upward his
leonine grin and said something to which Thorne replied, "I'm
an indestructible kind of a prick. Let me tell you about dental
hypnosis." The pleasant house accepted them. Foxy and Ken
moved to go.

"Don't all leave," Angela begged. "Wouldn't you like to have
a *real* drink?"

Foxy said, "We must get back," truly sad. She was to experience this sadness many times, this chronic sadness of late
Sunday afternoon, when the couples had exhausted their
game, basketball or beachgoing or tennis or touch football,
and saw an evening weighing upon them, an evening without
a game, an evening spent among flickering lamps and cranky
children and leftover food and the nagging half-read newspaper with its weary portents and atrocities, an evening when
marriages closed in upon themselves like flowers from which
the sun is withdrawn, an evening giving like a smeared window

on Monday and the long week when they must perform again their impersonations of working men, of stockbrokers and dentists and engineers, of mothers and housekeepers, of adults who are not the world's guests but its hosts.

Janet and Harold were arguing in whispers. Janet whirled and proclaimed, "Sweet, we *can't*. We *must* rescue Marcia and Frank, they're probably *deep* in conver*s*ation." She and little-Smith collected their scrambled children and left in her maroon car. As they backed from the driveway, the sinking sun for an instant pierced the windshield and bleached their two faces in sunken detail, like saints under glass.

"Good-bye," Piet Hanema said politely from the porch. Foxy had forgotten him. He seemed so chastened by the finger incident that she called to him, "Cheer up."

Safe in their MG, Ken said, "Zowie, I'm going to be stiff tomorrow."

"But wasn't it fun?"

"It was exercise. Were you terribly bored?"

"No. I *loved* Angela."

"Why?"

"I don't know. She's gracious and careless and above it all at the same time. She doesn't make the *demands* on you the others do."

"She must have been a knockout once."

"But not now? I must say, your painted friend Janet with her hug-my-bottom sailor pants does *not* impress me aesthetically."

"How does she impress you, Fox?"

"She impresses me as less happy than she should be. She was meant to be a jolly fat woman and somehow missed."

"Do you think she's having an affair with Smith?"

Foxy laughed. "Men are so observant. It's so obvious it must be passé. I think she had an affair with Smith some time ago, is having one with Thorne right now, and is sizing you up for the future."

His flattered languid answering laugh annoyed her. "I have a confession," she said.

"You're having an affair with Saltz. God, Jews are ponderous. They *care* so much. The Cosmic Unconscious, Jesus."

"No. But almost as bad. I told Angela we wanted to have her husband look at our house."

His voice withdrew, acquired a judging dispassion. "Did you set a date?"

"No, but I think we should now. You should call. She didn't think he'd be interested anyway."

Ken drove swiftly down the road they already knew by heart, so both leaned a little before the curve was there. "Well," he said after silence, "I hope his basketball isn't a clue as to how he builds houses. He plays a pretty crusty game."

Ruth, standing beside the bed with almost a woman's bulk, was crying and by speaking woke him from a dream in which a tall averted woman in white was waiting for him at the end of a curved corridor. "Daddy, Nancy says the dairy cat got an animal downstairs and the hamster's not in his cage and I'm afraid to look."

Piet remembered the *eek eeik* by which he had learned to lull himself to sleep and slid from the bed with fear lumping in his stomach. Angela sighed moistly but did not stir. The floor and stairs were cold. Nancy, huddled in her pink nightie on the brown living-room sofa in the shadowless early-morning light, removed her thumb from her mouth and told him, "I didn't mean to, I didn't mean to, it was a 'stake!"

His mouth felt crusty. "Mean to what? Where's the animal?"

The child looked at him with eyes so pure and huge a space far bigger than this low-ceilinged room seemed windowed. The furniture itself, surfacing from the unity of darkness, seemed to be sentient, though paralyzed.

He insisted, "Where is the animal you told Ruthie about, Nancy?"

She said, "I didn't mean to," and succumbed to tears; her smooth face disintegrated like a prodigy of embalming suddenly exposed to air, and Piet was numbed by the force that flowed through the hole her face made in the even gray light.

Ruth said, "Crybaby, crybaby, sit-and-wonder-whybaby," and Nancy plugged her face again with her thumb.

The little animal, sack-shaped, lay belly up in the center of the kitchen linoleum. The dairy cat watched at a distance, both cowardly and righteous, behind the rungs of a kitchen chair. Its quick instinctive work had been nicely done. Though scarcely marked, the hamster was dead. Its body yielded with a sodden resilience to the prodding of Piet's finger; its upper lip was lifted to expose teeth like the teeth of a comb and its eyes, with an incongruous human dignity, were closed. A trace of lashes. The four curled feet. The lumpy bald nose.

Ruth asked, though she was standing in the kitchen doorway and could see for herself, "Is it him?"

"Yes. Sweetie, he's dead."

"I know."

The adventure was easy to imagine. Ruth, feeling that her pet needed more room for running, suspecting cruelty in the endless strenuousness of the wheel, not believing with her growing mind that any creature might have wits too dim to resent such captivity, had improvised around his tiny cage a larger cage of window screens she had found stacked in the attic waiting for summer. She had tied the frames together with string and Piet had never kept his promise to make her a stronger cage. Several times the hamster had nosed his way out and gone exploring in her room. Last night he had made it downstairs, discovering in the moon-soaked darkness undreamed-of continents, forests of furniture legs, vast rugs heaving with oceanic odors; toward morning an innocent giant in a nightgown had admitted a lion with a mildewed eye. The hamster had never been given cause for fear and must have felt none until claws sprang from a sudden heaven fragrant with the just-discovered odors of cat and cow and dew.

Angela came downstairs in her blue bathrobe, and Piet could not convey to her why he found the mishap so desolating, the dim-witted little exploration that had ended with such a thunderclap of death. The kitchen linoleum, the color of grass, felt slick beneath him. The day dawning outside looked stale and fruitless and chill, one more of the many with which New England cheats spring. Angela's concern, after a glance at him and Ruth and the body of the hamster, was for Nancy; she carried her from the living room into the relative brightness of the kitchen. Squeamishly Piet enfolded the russet corpse, disturbingly dense and, the reins of blood slackened, unstable, in a newspaper. Nancy asked to see it.

Piet glanced at Angela for permission and unfolded the newspaper. KENNEDY PRAISES STEEL RESTRAINT. Nancy stared and slowly asked, "Won't he wake up?"

Ruth said, her voice forced through tears, "No stupid he will not wake up because he is dead and dead things do not wake up ever ever ever."

"When will he go to Heaven?"

All three looked to Piet for the answer. He said, "I don't know. Maybe he's up there already, going round and round in a wheel." He imitated the squeaking; Ruth laughed, and it had been her he had meant to amuse. Nancy's anxious curiosity searched out something he had buried in himself and he disliked the child for seeking it. Angela, holding her, seemed part of this same attempt, to uncover and unman him, to expose the shameful secret, the childish belief, from which he drew his manhood.

He asked Nancy roughly, "Did you see it happen?"

Angela said, "Don't, Piet. She doesn't want to think about it."

But she did; Nancy said, staring at the empty floor where it had happened, "Kitty and Hamster played and Hamster wanted to quit and Kitty wouldn't let him."

"Did you know the hamster was downstairs when you let Kitty in?"

Nancy's thumb went back into her mouth.

"I'm sure she didn't," Angela said.

"Let me see him once more," Ruth said, and in disclosing to her the compact body like a stiffening heart Piet saw for himself how the pet had possessed the protruding squarish bottom of the male of its species, a hopeful sexual vanity whose final denial seemed to Piet a kind of relief. With Ruth he knew now the strange inner drying, a soft scorching, that follows the worst, when it has undeniably come true. She went off to school, walked down the crunching driveway in her yellow Easter coat to await the yellow school bus, with all her tears behind her, under a cloudy sky that promised no rain.

Piet had promised her a new hamster and a better cage. He buried the old hamster in the edge of the woods, near a scattering of scilla, little lillies of a wideawake blue, where the earth was soft and peaty. One shovelful did for the grave; two made it deep. The trees were beginning to leaf and the undergrowth was sketchy, still mixed, its threads of green, with winter-bleached dead stalks delicate as straws, as bird bones. In a motion of the air, the passionless air which passively flows downhill, spring's terror washed over him. He felt the slow thronging of growth as a tangled hurrying toward death. Timid green tips shaped like tiny weaponry thrust against nothing. His father's green fond touch. The ungrateful earth, receptive. The hamster in an hour of cooling had lost weight and shape to the elements. All that had articulated him into a presence worth mourning, the humanoid feet and the groping trembling nose whose curiosity, when Ruth set him out on her blanket, made her whole bed lightly vibrate, had sunk downward toward a vast absence. The body slid nose down into the shoveled hole. Piet covered him with guilty quickness. In the nearly five years they had lived here a small cemetery had accumulated along this edge of woods: injured birds they had vainly nursed, dime-store turtles that had softened and whitened and died, a kitten slammed in a screen door, a chipmunk torn from throat to belly by some inconclusive predator who had left a spark of life to flicker all one long June afternoon. Last autumn, when the robins were migrating, Nancy had found one with a broken back by the barn, groveling on the asphalt basketball court in its desire to fly, to join the others. Lifted sheerly by the beating of its heart, it propelled itself to the middle of the lawn, where the four Hanemas gathered in expectation of seeing it take wing, healed. But the bird was unhinged, as Piet's own father with his shattered chest and spine would have been unhinged had his lungs let him live; and the children, bored by the bird's poor attempt to become a miracle, wandered away. So only Piet, standing helpless as if beside a party guest who refuses to leave, witnessed the final effort, an asymmetric splaying of the dusty wings and a heave that drove the robin's beak straight down into the sweetish weedy shadowy grass. The bird emitted a minute high cry, a point of noise as small as a star, and relaxed. Only Piet had heard this utterance. Only Piet, as now, attended the burial.

Angela came across the lawn to him where he stood with the shovel. She was dressed in an English-appearing suit of salt-and-pepper tweed; today, Tuesday, was her day to be a teaching parent at Nancy's nursery school. "How unfortunate," she said, "that of all of us it had to be Nancy who saw it happen. Now she wants me to take her to Heaven so she can see for herself that there's room for her, and a little wheel. I really do wonder, Piet, if religion doesn't complicate things worse than they'd have to be. She can see that I don't believe it myself."

He stooped beside the shovel and assumed the manner of an old yeoman. "Ah," he said, "thet's all verra well for a fine leddy like yerself, ma'am, but us peasants like need a touch o' holy water to keep off the rheumatism, and th' evil eye."

"I de*test* imitations, whether you do them, or Georgene Thorne. And I detest being put in the position of trying to sell Heaven to my children."

"But Angel, the rest of us think of you as never having left Heaven."

"Stop trying to get at me and sympathize with the child. She thinks of death all the time. She doesn't understand why she has only two grandparents instead of four like the other children."

"You speak as if you had married a man with only one leg."

"I'm just stating, not complaining. Unlike you, I don't blame you for that accident."

"Ah, thank ye kindly, ma'am, and I'll be makin' a better hamster cage today, and get the poor kid a new hamster."

"It's not Ruth," Angela said, "I'm worried about." These were the lines drawn. Angela's heart sought to enshrine the younger child's innocence; Piet loved more the brave corruption of the older, who sang in the choir and who had brusquely pushed across the sill of fear where Nancy stood wide-eyed.

Angela and Nancy went off to nursery school together. Piet drove the pick-up truck into downtown Tarbox and at Spiros Bros. Builders & Lumber Supply bought five yards of galvanized cage mesh, a three-by-four-piece of ¾″ plywood, twenty feet of 2″ pine quality knotless stock, a half pound of 1½″ finishing nails, and the same quantity of the finer gauge of poultry staples. Jerry Spiros, the younger of the two brothers, told Piet about his chest, which since Christmas had harbored a congestion that ten days in Jamaica did not clear up. "Those fucking blacks'd steal," Jerry said, "the watch right off your wrist," and coughed prolongedly.

"Sounds like you've been sniffing glue," Piet told him, and charged the hamster-cage materials to the Gallagher & Hanema account, and threw them into the back of his truck, and slammed shut the tailgate that said WASH ME, and drove to Indian Hill, taking the long way around. He swung by his office to see if Gallagher's gray Mercedes was there. Their office was a shacklike wing, one-story, upon an asphalt-shingled tenement, mostly unoccupied, on Hope Street, a little spur off Charity, a short cut to the railroad depot. Charity, the main business street, met Divinity at right angles, and Divinity carried up the hill, past Cogswell's Drug Store. The church bulked white on the green.

Huge airy thing. Twenty-four panes in each half window, forty-eight in all, often while Pedrick wrestled he counted them, no symbolism since when it was built there weren't that many states in the Union, Arizona, Oklahoma, Indian Territory. The lumber those people had. To burn. Waste? Gives the town a sense of itself. Dismal enough otherwise. On this heavy loveless day everything looked to need a coat of paint. The salt air corrupts. In Michigan barns stayed red for ages.

The green was hourglass-shaped, cut in two by a footpath, the church's section pinched off from the part holding the backstop and basepaths. Swinging left along the green's waist, Piet looked toward the Constantines' side yard hoping to see Carol hanging out wash with upstretched arms and flattened breasts. At Greek dances, leading the line, hair in spit curls, slippered toe pointed out, the neighbors' boy linked to her by a handkerchief, lithe. Lower classes have that litheness. Generations of hunger. Give me your poor. Marcia brittle, Janet fat. Angela drifty and that Whitman gawky, a subtle stiffness, resisting something, air. Eddie's Vespa but no Ford, Carol's car. He home and she shopping. Buying back liniment. *I ache afterwards.* Funeral home driveway held a Cadillac hearse and a preschool child playing with pebbles. Growing up in odor of embalming oil instead of flowers, corpses in the refrigerator, a greenhouse better, learn to love beauty, yet might make some fears seem silly. Death. Hamster. Shattered glass. He eased up on the accelerator.

Forsythia like a dancing yellow fog was out in backyards and along fences and hedges and garages, the same yellow, continuous, dancing yard to yard, trespassing. Forgive us. Piet drove on down Prudence Street past the Guerins'. Nicely restored, six thou, one of their first jobs in Tarbox, Gallagher not so greedy then, Adams and Comeau did all the finish work, nobody under sixty knows how to hang a door. The whole frame had sagged. Dry rot. The uphill house sill buried in damp earth. They had threaded a reinforcing rod eighteen feet long through the summer beam up through a closet to an ironshod A-brace in the attic. Solid but still a touch off true. *Why don't you want to fuck me?* Good question. Loyalty to Georgene, offshoot loyalty, last year's shoot this year's limb, mistress becomes a wife. Sets. Determined set of Georgene's chin. Not always attractive. Coke-bottle eyes, nude like rancid butter, tarpaper grits, Freddy's spies. Piet's thoughts shied from a green plastic spoon.

Downhill a mailman gently sloped away from the pull of his bag. Blue uniform, regular hours, walk miles, muscles firm, live forever. At the corner two dogs were saying hello. Hello. Olleh.

He drove along Musquenomenee Street, along the river, tidal up to the factory waterfall, low at this moment, black salt mud gleaming in wide scummy puddled flats, the origin of life. Across the river were high-crowned streets of elms and homes with oval windows and leaded fanlights built in the tinkling decades of ice wagons. Knickers, mustaches, celluloid collars: nostalgic for when he had never been. Piet saw no one. No one walked now. The silver maples were budding in reddish florets but the elms in tan tassels. Rips in a lilac sky. Nature, this sad grinding fine, seed and weed.

His spirits slightly lifted as he passed the Protestant cemetery, fan-shaped acres expanding from a Puritan wedge of tilted slate stones adorned with winged skulls and circular lichen. Order reigned. Soon cemeteries and golf courses the last greenswards. Thronging hungry hordes, grain to India. On the golf course he spotted two lonely twosomes. Too early, mud, heavy lies, spikes chew up the green, proprietors greedy for fees, praise restraint, earth itself hungry, he had thrown it a sop. Pet. Pit. He drove through pastel new developments, raw lawns and patchwork façades, and up a muddy set of ruts beside which hydrants and sewer ports were already installed, in obedience to town ordinances, to his site on Indian Hill.

The bulldozer had arrived. This should have pleased him but the machine, a Case Construction King with hydraulic backhoe and front loader, crushed him with its angry weight, its alarming expense. Twenty-five dollars to move it in, twenty-two fifty per hour with the driver, a large coveralled Negro from Mather. Sitting on his jarring throne, he conveyed the impression that the machine's strength was his strength, and that if the gears ceased to mesh he would himself swing down and barehanded tear the stumps from the outraged red earth. By no extension of his imagination could Piet believe that he had helped cause this man and machine to be roaring and churning and chuffing and throttling here, where birds and children used to hide. Yet the Negro hailed him, and his young foreman Leon Jazinski eagerly loped toward him across the gouged mud, and the work was going smoothly. Stumps whose roots were clotted with drying mud and boulders blind for aeons had been heaped into a towering ossuary that must be trucked away. Now the Negro was descending, foot by foot, into the first cellar hole, diagrammed with string and red-tipped stakes. This house would have the best view, overlooking the fan-shaped cemetery toward the town with its pricking steeple and flashing cock. The other two would face more southerly, toward Lacetown, an indeterminate area of gravel pits and back lots and uneconomic woods strangely intense in color, purple infused with copper; and should bring a thousand or two less. Piet saw the first house, the house where he stood, pine siding stained redwood and floor plan C, seeded terrace lawn linked by five fieldstone steps to the hardtopped driveway of the under-kitchen garage, smart flagstone stoop and three-chime front doorbell, baseboard oil-fired forced-hot-water heating and brick patio in the rear for summer dining and possible sunbathing, aluminum combination all-weather sash and rheostated ceiling fixtures set flush, efficient kitchen in Pearl Mist and Thermopane picture window, as bringing $19,900, or at a knockdown eighteen five if Gallagher panicked, a profit above wages paid even to himself, one-fifty weekly, of three or four, depending on how smoothly he dovetailed the subcontractors, which suddenly didn't seem enough, enough to placate Gallagher, enough to justify this raging and rending close at his back, this rape of a haven precious to ornamental shy creatures who needed no house. Builders burying the world God made. The two-headed tractor, the color of a school bus, trampled, grappled, growled, ramped. Blue belches of smoke flew upward from the hole. The mounted Negro, down to his undershirt, a cannibal king on a dragon dripping oil, grinned and shouted to Piet his pleasure that he had not encountered ledge.

"This is the soft side of the hill," Piet shouted, and was not heard. He felt between himself and the colored man a continental gulf, the chasm between a jungle asking no pity and a pampered rectilinear land coaxed from the sea. The Negro was at home here, in this tumult of hoisted rocks, bucking reversals of direction and shifting gears, clangor and fumes, internal combustion, the land of the free. He was Ham and would inherit. Piet tried to picture the young couple who would live in this visualized home and he did not love them. None of his friends would live in such a home. He stooped and picked a bone from its outline in the earth, where the grid of the dozer's tread had pressed it, and showed it curiously to Jazinski.

"Cow bone," Leon said.

"Doesn't it seem too delicate?"

"Deer?"

"Don't they say there was an Indian burying ground somewhere on this south side?"

Jazinski shrugged. "Beats me." Leon was a weedy, hollow-chested young man originally from Nashua, New Hampshire. He was one of the three men that Gallagher & Hanema kept on the payroll all year long. The other two were venerable carpenters, Adams and Comeau, that Piet had inherited from Ed Byrd, an excessively amiable Tarbox contractor who had declared bankruptcy in 1957. Piet had himself singled out Jazinski from a dozen summer laborers two summers ago. Leon had a good eye and a fair head, an eye for the solid angle and the overlooked bind and a sense for the rhythmic mix of bluff and guess whereby a small operator spaces men and equipment and rentals and promises to minimize time, which is money. Gallagher, who discreetly craved the shoddy—vinyl siding versus wood, pressed wallboard panels versus plaster—had intended to lay Jazinski off last winter; Piet had begged him to hold the boy, offering to drop his own salary to one-twenty-five, fearing that something of himself, his younger self, would be lost if they failed to nurture a little longer Leon's uneducated instinct for the solid, the tight, the necessary.

Piet felt that the bone in his hand was human. He asked Leon, "Have you seen any arrowheads turn up? Beads, bits of pot?"

Leon shook his slow slender head. "Just crap," he said. "Mother Earth."

Embarrassed, Piet said, "Well, keep your eyes open. We may be on sacred ground." He let the bone, too small to have been a thigh, perhaps part of an arm, drop. On Leon's face, downcast beneath a blond eave of hair, Piet spied the smudge of a sneer. In his tone that meant business, the warmth withdrawn, Piet asked, "When can we pour? Early next week?"

"Depends." The boy was sulking. "I'm here all by myself, if Adams and Comeau could stop diddling with that garage . . ."

"They're not to be hurried."

"Waterproofing the foundation takes at least a day."

"It has to be done."

"If it wasn't, who'd be the wiser?"

Piet said swiftly, seeing he must pounce now, or the boy would be a cheat forever, "We would. And in a few years when the house settled and the basement leaked everybody would. Let me tell you about houses. Everything outs. Every cheat. Every short cut. I want the foundation damp-proofed, I want polyethylene under the slab, I want lots of gravel under the drain tile as well as over it, I want you to wrap felt around the joints or they'll sure as hell clog. Don't think because you cover something up it isn't there. People have a nose for the rotten and if you're a builder the smell clings. Now let's look at the drawings together."

Leon's avoiding cheek flushed under the discipline. He gazed at the hole growing in the earth and said, "Those old clunkers have been a month on a garage me and two kids could have put up in a week."

Piet's pedagogic spurt was spent. He said wearily, "They're winding up, I'll go over and see if they can't be up here by tomorrow. I'll call for a load of gravel this afternoon and see if we can set up Ready-Mix over in North Mather for next Monday, do the three at once, that'll give you a day each, I'll help myself if we can't squeeze some trade-school kids out of Gallagher." For an hour, using as a table a boulder under the low boughs of a great oak that would overshadow the patio, he and Leon analyzed the blueprints bought by mail from an architectural factory in Chicago. Piet felt the younger mind picking for holes in his, testing, resenting. It grew upon him as they plotted their campaign together that Leon disliked him, had heard enough about his life to consider him a waster, a drinker, an immigrant clown in the town's party crowd, unfaithful to his wife, bored by his business. This appraisal blew coolly on Piet's face as he traced lines and dimensions with his broad thumbnail and penciled in adjustments demanded by this sloping site. Leon nodded, learning, yet did not let up this cool pressure, which seemed part of the truth of these woods, where the young must prey upon the not-so-young, the ambitious upon the preoccupied. Piet was impatient to leave the site.

In parting, he turned for a moment to the Negro, who had retired with a lunch box and thermos bottle to the edge of the excavation. The sliced sides showed a veined logic of stratification. Pages of an unread book. Impacted vegetable lives. Piet asked him, "Do you ever find Indian graves?"

"You see bones."

"What do you do when you see them?"

"Man, I keep movin'."

Piet laughed, feeling released, forgiven, touched and hugged by something human arrived from a great distance, imagining behind the casually spoken words a philosophy, a night life.

But the Negro's lips went aloof, as if to say that laughter would no longer serve as a sop to his race. His shoulder-balls bigger than soccer balls. His upper lip jeweled with sweat. A faint tarry tigerish smell. Piet, downwind, bowed.

Pardon me, Dr. King.

Piet left the two men in the clearing and drove into town, to the far end of Temperance Avenue, where Adams and Comeau were building a garage at the rear of a house lot. Comeau was thin and Adams was fat, but after years of association they moved as matched planets, even at opposite corners of the garage revolving, backs turned, with an unspoken gravitational awareness of the other. Passing to the toolbox, on a board between sawhorses, they crossed paths but did not bump. Neither acknowledged Piet. He stood in the empty rectangle that awaited a track-hung spring-lift garage door; he inhaled the scent of shaved lumber, the sense of space secured. Except for the door, the structure seemed complete. Piet cleared his throat and asked, "When do you gentlemen think we can call it quits here?"

Adams said, "When it's done."

"And when might that be? I don't see a day's work here, just the door to come."

"Odds and ends," Comeau told him. He was applying a plane to the inside of the window sash, though the sash was factory-made. Adams was screwing in L-shaped shelf brackets between two studs. Adams smoked a pipe and wore bibbed overalls with as many pockets as a hardware store has drawers; Comeau's blue shirts were always freshly laundered and cigarettes had stained his fingers orange. He added, "Once we finish up, the widow'll have to manage herself." The property belonged to a young woman whose husband, a soldier, had been killed—knifed—by the German boy friend of his girl friend in Hamburg.

"It ought to be left neat," Adams said.

Piet, inspecting, paused at a detail of the framing. A two-by-four diagonal brace intersected a vertical stud and, though the angle was not an easy one, and this was rough work, the stud had been fitted as precisely as a piece of veneer. Waste. Piet felt as if he had been handed a flower; but had to say, "Leon needs you on the hill to knock together the basement forms."

"Jack be nimble," old Comeau said, shaking out a match. It was their nickname for Jazinski.

"Door isn't come up yet from Mather," Adams said.

Piet said, "I'll call them. If it isn't brought this afternoon, come up to the hill tomorrow morning anyway. This is a beautiful garage for the widow, but at six-fifty an hour enough is enough. She'll have boy friends who can put up shelves for her. I must get back to the hill."

As he walked around the garage to the street, he heard Comeau, who was still planing at the window, say, "Greedy Gally's on his back."

Piet drove home. The square yard and house were welcoming, empty. He carried the wood and wire he had bought into his basement workshop, which he hadn't used all winter. He cut some segments of the 2″ pine but discovered that the warpage of the rolled wire was so strong that a cumbersome system of braces would be needed to hold the sides straight. So he formed in his mind another design, using the warp of the wire as a force, and rooted a parabolic curve of mesh on either side of the plywood with the poultry staples, and then cut an oval of wire to seal the cage shut. But one end had to be a door. He improvised hinges from a coat hanger and fitted sticks for the necessary stiffness. As he worked, his hands shook with excitement, the agitation of creation that since childhood had often spoiled his projects—birdhouses, go-carts, sand castles —in the final trembling touches. The cage, completed, seemed beautiful to him, a transparent hangar shaped by laws discovered within itself, minimal, invented, Piet's own. He foresaw Ruth's pleased surprise, Angela's grudging admiration, Nancy's delight and her insistence on crawling inside this child-sized shelter. He carried the cage upstairs to the kitchen and, needing to share his joy of accomplishment, dialed the Thornes' number. "Is this the Swedish bakery?" It was their formula, to which she could say No.

Georgene laughed. "Hi, Piet. How *are* you?"

"Miserable."

"Why?"

He told her about the hamster and the dismal work on Indian Hill, but could not specifically locate the cause of his depression, his sense of unconnection among phenomena and of falling. The lack of sun and shadows. Angela's aloofness. The Negro's snub. The slowness of spring to come.

Georgene said, "Poor Piet. My poor little lover."

He said, "Not much of a day for the sunporch, is it?"

"I've been in the house cleaning. I'm having the League Board tonight and Irene frightens me, she's so efficient and worthy."

"How's Freddy's finger?"

"Oh, fine. He took it out of the spoon yesterday."

"I felt crummy about that. I don't see why I should want to hurt him since in a way, without knowing it of course, he lets me have you."

"Is that the way you think of it? I thought *I* let you have me."

"You do, you do. Thank you. But why do I have such a hatred of him?"

"I have no idea." Always, over the telephone, there was the strangeness of their not being able to touch, and the revelation that her firm quick voice could be contentious.

He asked politely, "Could I—would you like me to come visit you for a minute? Just to say hello, we don't have time to make love. I must get back to the hill."

Her pause, in which they could not touch, was most strange. "Piet," she said, "I'd love you to—"

"But?"

"But I wonder if it's wise right this noon. I've had something happen to me."

Pregnant. By whom? There was a mirror above the telephone table and in it he saw himself, a pale taut-faced father, the floor tipped under him.

She went on, hesitating, she who had confided everything to him, her girlish loves, her first sex with Freddy, when they made love now, her periods, her mild momentary yearnings toward other men, everything, "I think I've discovered that Freddy is seeing Janet. I found a letter in the pocket of a suit I was taking to the cleaner's."

"How careless of him. Maybe he wanted you to find it. What did it say?"

"Nothing very much. It said, 'Let's break it off, no more phone calls,' et cetera, which might mean anything. It could mean she's putting on pressure for him to divorce me."

"Why would she want to marry Freddy?" He realized this was tactless and tried to disguise it with another question. "You're sure it's her?"

"Quite. She signed it J and anyway her handwriting is unmistakable, big and fat and spilly. You've seen it on her Christmas cards."

"Well. But sweet, it's been in the air for some time, Freddy and Janet. Does it really shock you?"

"I suppose," Georgene said, "there's something called female pride. But more than that. I'm shocked by the idea of divorce. If it comes to that I don't want him to have anything to throw back at me, for the children to read about in the paper. It wouldn't bother Freddy but it would me."

"So what does this do to us?"

"I suppose nothing, except that we must be very careful."

"How careful is careful?"

"Piet. I'm not going to tell you how much you mean to me. I've said that in ways a woman can't fake. I just don't think I could enjoy you today and I don't want to waste you. Also it's too near noon."

"Have you confronted Freddy with your discovery?" The man in the mirror had begun to squint, as his pang of fear relaxed into cunning.

Georgene, growing franker, said, "I'm too chicken. He'll tell Janet, then she'll know *I* know, and until I have some plan of action I'd rather just *know*."

"I'm touched by how much Freddy means to you."

"Vell, honeybunch, he *is* my husband."

"Sure enough. You picked him, he's all yours. Except I don't see why I must be sacrificed because Freddy is naughty."

"Maybe he is because I am. Because we are. Anyway you sound as though you rather *want* to be sacrificed."

"Tell me when I can see you."

"Oh love, anytime, just not today. I'm not myself."

"Sweet Georgene, forgive me. I'm being very stupid and full of threatened egotism."

"I *love* your egotism. Oh hell. Come on over now if you want, she isn't brought back from nursery school until twelve-thirty."

"No, of course not. I don't want it unless you feel right about it. You feel guilty. You feel you've driven poor old God-fearing monogamous Freddy into the arms of this harlot."

"I *like* Janet. I think she's quite funny and gutsy. I think Frank is impossible and she does quite well considering."

Piet liked Frank; he resisted the urge to quarrel. Every new assertion of Georgene's, as she relaxed into the certainty that he would not come, advanced his anger. "Anyway," he said, "I just heard the noon whistle blow. I don't want Judy coming back from school saying, 'Mommy, what's that lump under the covers? It smells like Nancy's daddy.'" Smells: the woods, the earth, the Negro's skin, the planed pine of the garage, the whiskey on Bea Guerin's breath.

"Piet. Am I putting you off? I do want you."

"I know. Please don't apologize. You've been a lovely mistress."

She ignored his tense. "When I found the note, the first thing I wanted to do was call you and—what? Cry on your shoulder. Crawl into bed beside you. It was Monday night, Freddy was at Lions'. Suddenly I was terrified. I was alone in a big ugly house with a piece of paper in my hand that wouldn't go away."

"Don't be terrified. You're a lovely doubles partner and a fine wife for Freddy. Who else could stand him? If he lost you it would be the worst thing that's happened to him since he flunked medical school." Did she notice his unintended equation of her with dentistry—both practical, clean, simple, both a recourse? By this equation was Angela something difficult that he, Piet, had flunked? "Anyway," he went on, "I don't think either Freddy or Janet have it in them these days to give themselves much to anybody."

She said, "It's so sad. You call to be reassured and end up by reassuring me. Oh my Lord. Bernadette's VW is coming up the drive. Nursery school let out early. Is today a holiday?"

"April twenty-third? The paper said Shakespeare's birthday. He's three hundred and ninety-nine years old."

"Piet. I must run. There's a lot we haven't said. Let's see each other soon."

"Let's," Piet said, and her kiss ticked as he had halfway returned his receiver to the cradle. The man in the mirror was hunched, a shadow ready to spring, sunless daylight filtering into the room behind him. He looked, he thought, young, his crow's feet and the puckering under his eyes smoothed into shadow. A fragment came to him of the first conversation he and Georgene had had as lovers. She had been so gay, so sporting, taking him upstairs to her bed that fresh September day, he could hardly believe he was her first lover. Reflected autumnal brilliance had invaded her house and infused with warmth her exotic furniture of bamboo and straw rosettes and batik and unbleached sailcloth. Gaudy Guatemalan pillows heaped against the kingsized headboard had surprised him. *Here? In Freddy's very bed?*

It's my bed too. Would you rather use the floor?

No, no. It's luxurious. Whose books are all these?

Freddy's pornography, it's disgusting. Please pay attention to me.

I am, Jesus. But . . . shouldn't we do something about not making a little baby?

Sweetie. You're so naïeef. You mean Angela doesn't take Enovid yet?

You do? It works?

Of course it works, it's wonderful. Welcome, Georgene said, *to the post-pill paradise.*

Piet remembered, standing alone in his low-ceilinged living room, where the wallpaper mourned its slanting visitor the sun and the spare neat furniture reflected his and Angela's curiously similar austerity of taste, how Georgene's cheeks, freckled from a summer of sunbathing, had dryly creased as she made this joke. Her manner had been a feathery teasing minimizing his heart's clangor, and always until now she had brought to their affair, like a dowry of virginal lace, this lightness, this guiltlessness. If she was now sullied and spoiled because of Freddy's dabbling, where would he find supplied such absolution? That first time, had she bathed? No, it became her habit when he revealed he liked to kiss between her thighs. And had her easy calm gaiety been a manner she had contrived to suit some other crimp in his manner of bestowing love, perhaps an untoward seriousness that threatened her marriage? His praise had amused her; she had always responded that all women liked to make love, that all women were beautiful, like a toilet bowl, when you needed one. But by daylight he had discovered on her rapt Roman face an expression, of peace deeper than an infant's sleep, that the darkness of night had never disclosed on the face of his wife. Furtive husbandly visitant, he had never known Angela as he had often known his lovely easy matter-of-fact morning lay. The line of her narrow high-bridged nose a double arabesque. Her white hairs belying her body's youth. Her bony bit of a tail.

Her receding hollowed the dull noon. Tipped shoots searched for wider light through sunless gray air. The salami he made lunch from was minced death. He went at last to his office. His telephone voice grew husky, defeated. Garage doors of the type needed were out of stock in Mather and were being ordered from Akron. The price of gravel had gone up two dollars a ton and a truckload could not be delivered before Friday. The urban renewal in Boston had sucked the area dry of carpenters and six phone calls turned up only two apprentices from a trade school twenty miles away. Spring building had begun and he had been slow. Gallagher's silences, though his conversation was commiserating, breathed accusation.

Piet had met Matt in the army, in Okinawa, in 1951. There, then, in that riverless flatland of barracks and sand, of beer in blank cans and listless Luchuan prostitutes, where the danger of death in battle was as unreal as the homeland whose commercial music twanged in the canteens, Piet was attracted by Matt's choir-boy prankishness, his grooming, his black hair and eyes, his freedom from the weary vocabulary of dirt and disdain, his confident ability to sell. He had sold Piet on himself as a short cut to architecture and, both discharged, had brought him to New England, into this life. Piet's loyalty was lately strained. He found Matt grown brittle, prim, quick to judge, Jesuitical in finance. He dreamed of corrupting whole hillsides, yet wished to keep himself immaculate. He secured his wife and only child behind a wall of Catholicism. In the little transparent world of couples whose intrigues had permeated and transformed Piet, Matt stood out as opaquely moral.

When the phone on his desk rang, Piet feared it would be Georgene, seeking a reconciliation. He hated paining Matt with his duplicity; he thought of Matt with the same pain as he thought of his father, that ghost patiently circling in the luminous greenhouse gloom, silently expecting Piet to do right, to carry on.

It was not Georgene but Angela. Nancy at nursery school had burst out crying because of the hamster. The child suddenly saw with visionary certainty that its death had been her fault. *Daddy said*, she said. Her hysterics had been uncontrollable. Angela had carried her from the room and, since she was teaching, the class ended early. They did not go home. There was nothing to eat at home but ham. In hopes of distracting Nancy with syrup and ice cream, Angela had taken her to eat at the Pancake House in North Mather. Now the child, sucking her thumb and running a slight fever, had fallen asleep on the sofa.

Piet said, "The kid sure knows how to get herself sympathy."

"But not from her own father, evidently. I didn't call just to touch you with this, though as a matter of fact I do think you handled it stupidly. Stupidly or cruelly. I called to ask you to meet Ruth after school and drive to the pet shop in Lacetown for a new hamster. I think we should do it *in*stantly."

Magic. The new hamster by sleight of hand would become

the old one, the one moldering nose-down underneath the scilla. A religion of genteel pretense. The idea of a hamster persists, eternal. Plato. Piet was an Aristotelian. He said he couldn't possibly do it this afternoon, he had a thousand things to do, the first quarter's accounts to check, he was trying to move the houses on the hill, a million details, the construction trade was going to hell. He was heavily conscious of Gallagher listening. Softer-voiced, he added, "I wasted half the morning making a new cage. Did you notice it in the kitchen?"

Angela said, "Oh is that what it is? We didn't know what it was for. Why is it such a funny shape? Nancy thought it was a little prison you were going to put *her* in."

"Tell the kid I love her lots and to shape up. Good-bye."

The books showed less than the twenty per cent Gallagher liked to clear. Spiros Bros. had attached to their monthly statement a printed threat to stop the account; the balance owed was $1189.24. Gallagher liked to let bills run long, on the theory that money constantly diminished in value. The figures made a gray hazy net around Piet and to compound his claustrophobia the Whitman woman, who had come to basketball uninvited, phoned and asked him to come look at her house. He didn't want the job, he didn't like working for social acquaintances. But in his hopeless mood, to escape the phone and the accounts and Gallagher's binding nearness, he got into the truck whose tailgate said WASH ME and drove down.

The marshes opened up on his right, grand in the dying day. A strip of enameled blue along the horizon of the sea. Colored tiles along a bathtub. The first drops of a half-hearted rain, cold and dry, struck the backs of his hands as he climbed from the truck. The lilacs by the door of the Robinson place were further along than those of Piet's own roadside hedge. More sun by the sea. More life. Tiny wine-colored cones that in weeks would be lavender panicles of bloom. Drenched. Dew. Salt. Breeze. Buttery daffodils trembled by his cuffs, by the bare board fence where they enjoyed reflected warmth. Piet lifted the aluminum latch, salt-corroded, and went in. Even under close clouds, the view was prodigal, a heart-hollowing carpeted span limited by the purity of dunes and ocean. He had been wrong, overcautious. It should be Angela's.

*

Ken Whitman's field of special competence, after his early interest in echinoid metabolism, was photosynthesis; his doctoral thesis had concerned the 7-carbon sugar sedoheptulose, which occupies a momentary place within the immense chain of reactions whereby the five-sixths of the triosephosphate pool that does not form starch is returned to ribulose-5-phosphate. The process was elegant, and few men under forty were more at home than Ken upon the gigantic ladder, forged by light, that carbon dioxide descends to become carbohydrate. At present he was supervising two graduate students in research concerning the transport of glucose molecules through cell walls. By this point in his career Ken had grown impatient with the molecular politics of sugar and longed to approach the mysterious heart of CO_2 fixation—chlorophyll's transformation of visible light into chemical energy. But here, at this ultimate chamber, the lone reaction that counterbalances the vast expenditures of respiration, that reverses decomposition and death, Ken felt himself barred. Biophysics and electronics were in charge. The grana of stacked quantasomes were structured like the crystal lattices in transistors. Photons excited an electron flow in the cloud of particles present in chlorophyll. Though he had ideas —why chlorophyll? why not any number of equally complex compounds? was the atom of magnesium the clue?—he would have to put himself to school again and, at thirty-two, felt too old. He was wedded to the unglamorous carbon cycle while younger men were achieving fame and opulent grants in such fair fields as neurobiology, virology, and the wonderful new wilderness of nucleic acids. He had a wife, a coming child, a house in need of extensive repair. He had overreached. Life, whose graceful secrets he would have unlocked, pressed upon him clumsily.

As if underwater he moved through the final hour of this heavy gray day. An irreversible, constricted future was brewing in the apparatus of his lab—the fantastic glass alphabet of flasks and retorts, the clamps and slides and tubes, the electromagnetic scales sensitive to the hundredth of a milligram, the dead experiments probably duplicated at Berkeley or across the river. Ken worked on the fourth floor of a monumental neo-Greek benefaction, sooty without and obsolete within, dated 1911. The hall window, whose sill held a dreggy Lily cup,

overlooked Boston. Expressways capillariously fed the humped
dense center of brick red where the State House dome pre-
sided, a gold nucleolus. Dusty excavations ravaged the nearer
ground. In the quad directly below, female students in bright
spring dresses—dyed trace elements—slid along the paths between polygons of chlorophyll. Ken looked with a weariness
unconscious of weariness. There had been rain earlier. The
same rain now was falling on Tarbox. The day was so dull the
window was partly a mirror in which his handsomeness, that
strange outrigger to his career, glanced back at him with a
cocked eyebrow, a blurred mouth, and a glint of eye white. Ken
shied from this ghost; for most of his life he had consciously
avoided narcissism. As a child he had vowed to become a saint
of science and his smooth face had developed as his enemy. He
turned and walked to the other end of the hall; here, for lack
of space, the liquid-scintillation counter, though it had cost
the department fifteen thousand, a Packard Tri-Carb, was sit-
uated. At the moment it was working, ticking through a chain
of isotopically labeled solutions, probably Neusner's minced
mice livers. A thick-necked sandy man over forty, Jewish only
in the sleepy lids of his eyes, Neusner comported himself with
the confidence of the energetically second-rate. His lectures
were full of jokes and his papers were full of wishful reasoning. Yet he was liked, and had established forever the spatial
configuration of one enzyme. Ken envied him and was not
sorry to see, at four-thirty, his lab empty. Neusner was a con-
certgoer and winetaster and womanizer and mainstay of the
faculty supper club; he traveled with the Cambridge political
crowd and yesterday had confided to Ken in his hurried emphatic accents the latest Kennedy joke. *One night about three
A.M. Jackie hears Jack coming into the White House and she meets
him on the stairs. His collar is all rumpled and there's lipstick on
his chin and she asks him, Where the hell have you been? and he
tells her, I've been having a conference with Madame Nhu, and
she says, Oh, and doesn't think any more about it until the next
week the same thing happens and this time he says he was sitting
up late arguing ideology with Nina Khrushchev . . .* A sallow
graduate student was tidying up the deserted labs. A heap of
gutted white mice lay like burst grapes on a tray. Pink-eyed
cagefuls alertly awaited annihilation. Neusner loved computers

and statistical theory and his papers were famous for the sheets of numbers that masked the fantasy of his conclusions. Next door old Prichard, the department's prestigious ornament, was pottering with his newest plaything, the detection and analysis of a memory-substance secreted by the brain. Ken envied the old man his childlike lightness, his freedom to dart through forests of evidence after such a bluebird. Neusner, Prichard —they were both free in a way Ken wasn't. Why? Everyone sensed it, the something wrong with Ken, so intelligent and handsome and careful and secure—the very series expressed it, an unstable compound, unnatural. Prichard, a saint, tried to correct the condition, to give Ken of himself, sawing the air with his papery mottled hands, nodding his unsteady gaunt head, whose flat cheeks seemed rouged, spilling his delicate stammer: *The thing of it, the thing of it is, Wh-Whitman, it's just t-tinkering, you mustn't s-s-suppose life, ah, owes us anything, we just g-get what we can out of the b-bitch, eh?* Next to his lab, his narrow office was a hodgepodge encrusted with clippings, cartoons, snapshots of other people's children and grandchildren, with honorary degrees, gilded citations, mounted butterflies and framed tombstone tracings and other such detritus of the old man's countless hobbies. Ken halted at the door of this living scrapbook wistfully, wanting a moment of encouragement, wondering why such a sanctified cell would never be his. The old man was unmarried. In his youth there had been a scandal, a wife who had left him; Ken doubted the story, for how could any woman leave so good a man?

Inspiration came to him: Prichard's virtues might be a product of being left, a metabolic reduction necessary to growth, a fruitful fractionation. Inspiration died: he looked within himself and encountered a surface bafflingly smooth. On Prichard's cluttered desk today's newspaper declared, ERHARD CERTAIN TO SUCCEED ADENAUER.

Morris Stein was waiting for him with a problem, an enzyme that couldn't be crystallized. Then it was after five. He drove home expertly, a shade arrogantly, knifing along the Southeastern Expressway like a man who has solved this formula often, changing lanes as it suited him, Prichard and Neusner and Stein revolving in his head while automobiles of differing makes spun and shuffled, passed and were passed, outside his speeding windows. He wondered about the people in Tarbox, how Hanema could drive that filthy clanking pick-up truck everywhere and the Applebys stick with that old maroon Mercury when they had the money. He wondered why Prichard had never won the Nobel and deduced that his research was like his hobbies, darting this way and that, more enthusiasm than rigor. He thought of photosynthesis and it appeared to him there was a tedious deep flirtatiousness in nature that withheld her secrets while the church burned astronomers and children died of leukemia. That she yielded by whim, wantonly, to those who courted her offhand, with a careless ardor he, Ken, lacked. *The b-b-bitch.*

The smokestacks and gasholders of South Boston yielded to the hickory woods of Nun's Bay Road. He arrived home before dark. Daylight Saving had begun. Alone in the living room Cotton was curved asleep in the sling chair from Design Research. Ken called Foxy's name. She answered faintly from the porch. Someone had torn away the boards that had sealed the French doors. She sat on a wicker chair, a tall gin drink in her hand, looking through rusted porch screens toward the sea. The sky was clearing after the brief rain. Dark-blue clouds thin as playing cards seen edgewise duplicated the line of the horizon. The lighthouse was tipped with an orange drop of final sun. He asked her, "Aren't you cold?"

"No, I'm warm. I'm fat."

He wanted to touch her, for luck, for safety, as when a child in Farmington after a long hide in the weeds shouts *Free!* and touches the home maple. Gazing in the dying light across the greening marsh, she had a tree's packed stillness. Her blond hair and pink skin and brown eyes were all one shade in the darkness of the porch. With a motion almost swift, the light had died. Bending to kiss her, he found her skin strange; she was shivering. Her arms showed goosebumps. He begged her, "Come in the house."

"It's so pretty. Isn't this what we're paying for?"

He thought the expression strange. They had never given much thought to money. Advancement, distinction: these were the real things. As if having overheard his thoughts, she went on, "We all rather live under wraps, don't we? We hardly ever really open ourselves to the loveliness around us. Yet there it is, every day, going on and on, whether we look at it or not. Such a splendid waste, isn't it?"

"I'm going in to make a drink." She followed him in and told him about her day. She had weeded and raked in the side yard. She had decided she wanted roses, white and red mixed, along the blind southern wall of the servants' wing. The Plymouth agency had called and said her car—a secondhand station wagon they had bought for her, since without a vehicle she was virtually a prisoner at this end of the beach road— would be ready Thursday, with license plates and an inspection sticker. Ken had forgotten about this car, though obviously she needed it. In Cambridge they had done so long without any car at all. Just before lunchtime Irene Saltz, with tiny Jeremiah in a papooselike arrangement on her back, had dropped in on her way back from the beach. She was a conservationist and distressed that the winter storms had flattened a number of dunes. Any town but Tarbox would ages ago have put up fences and brush hedges to hold the sand. She asked Foxy to join the League of Women Voters and drank three cups of coffee. With such a monologuist for a husband, you probably have to develop another erotic outlet, but the trouble with people who have poured themselves into good works is they expect you to do the same, pour away, even if they have husbands as handsome, charming, and attentive as, dear, yourself . . . Ken sipped his drink and wondered what she was driving at. In the living-room light she looked pale, her ears and nostrils nipped pink. She was high on something.

What else happened? Oh, yes, in the middle of her nap, and by the way she had gotten to volume two of Painter's life of Proust, which looked to be much the duller, since Proust was no longer having his childhood, Carol Constantine had called, inviting them to a May Day party; it sounded rather orgiastic. And finally she had got up her nerve and called this man Hanema to come look at the house.

"When will he come?"

"Oh, he came."

"And what did he say?"

"Oh he said fifteen thousand, more or less. It depends on how much you want to do. He'd like to see us with a full basement but a crawl space with I think he said plastic film over the earth might do for the kitchen half. He prefers hot-water heat but says hot air would be cheaper since we can put the ducts right in the walls we're going to have to build anyway. You'll have to talk to him yourself. Everything seemed to depend on something else."

"What about the roof and the shingles?"

"New roof. He thinks we can patch the shingles for now."

"Does this fifteen thousand include doing anything to those ugly upstairs dormers and that leaky skylight?"

"We didn't go upstairs. Of course he knows the house already. He thought the big issue was the basement. He was rather quaint and cute. He kept talking about babies crawling around on a nice warm floor and glancing at my tummy."

Ken felt a weight descend but persisted. "And the kitchen?"

"He sees about four thousand there. He wants to knock out the pantry partition and have new everything except the sink. He agreed with me, the slate sink must be kept. But the plumbing should be done over top to bottom. And the wiring. Have some more bourbon, baby."

She took his glass and smoothly, like a sail pushed by wind, moved toward the kitchen. "Very weak," he said, and, when she returned with the drink, said, "Well. But did you like him?"

Foxy stood a moment, her pale mouth shaped as if to hum. "I can manage him. He seemed a little forlorn today. His daughter's pet hamster was eaten by a neighbor's cat." Ken remembered Neusner's tray of gutted mice and wondered how some men still could permit themselves so much sentiment.

"You're the one," Ken said, "who'll have to deal with him."

She again moved with that airy quickness, as if she had considered a possibility and dismissed it. "I don't think he wants the job. He and your friend are building new houses for the population explosion."

"Gallagher's not my friend especially. Did Hanema recommend any other contractor?"

"I asked him to. He said there wasn't anybody he'd trust us with offhand. He was very indecisive. He seemed to feel possessive about this house."

"His wife had wanted it."

"You keep *saying* that." Her reactions had a quickness, her eyes a hard brightness, that was unusual; he felt an unseen factor operating, an unaccounted-for chemical. She had disliked Hanema: this guess, flattering to himself, inevitable in the light of himself, disposed him to the man, and he told her, "I think, why not put him to work? Exert your charm."

She was moving, swiftly, lightly, about the room, taking a kind of inventory perhaps, touching rough surfaces that soon would be smooth, saying goodbye to the ugly mementos, the fan-shaped shell collection, the dried sprigs of beach pea and woolly hudsonia, that had housed her for this while, this pregnant month. She changed the subject. "How was your day?"

He confessed, "I feel bogged down."

She thought, *You need another woman.* She said, "It's too much commuting."

"It's too much mediocre mental grinding. On my part. I should have gone into law. That we can do. The old man has two flat feet for a brain, and everybody in Hartford thinks he's nifty." She laughed, and he looked up startled; his vocabulary became boyish when he thought of Hartford, and he was unconscious of it. He went on sadly, "I was thinking about Prichard today and it made me realize I don't really have it. The flair. It all just looks like a bunch of details to me, which is the way it looks to every boob."

"Prichard's an old man. You're young. Old men have nothing serious to think about." By "serious" she meant the shadow within herself, her child, the dark world of breeding.

"Except death," Ken said, a touching strange thing for him to say. She had pictured him as thinking no more about death than a watch does about running down. She had assumed he from birth had solved it and had worked out her own solution apart from him.

Foxy said eagerly, "Oh no, when you're young you think about that. So when you're old you have nothing to do but be happy for each new day." She drifted to where a scantling shelf horizontal between two studs held a single forgotten amber marble, striped with a swirl of honey-white. She held it in her pink oval palm and tried to see into its center and imagined God as a man so old each day makes Him absolutely happy. She wondered why she could not share God with Ken, it was so innocent, like this marble, meek and small but there. She didn't ask him to believe in more than this. But in his presence she became ashamed, felt guilty of duplicity.

Ken looked up as if awaking. "Who took the boards off the porch doors?"

"He did. Hanema."

"With his bare hands?"

With your bare hands?

Sure. Why not? Why haven't you done this yourselves?

We thought it served some purpose.

It did, but winter's over. Welcome to spring. Now. This should turn, with a little love. Ah, it does. Come on.

Oh. I've hardly ever been on the porch. Are the screens still mendable?

He had taken a loose piece of rusted screening and crumpled it and showed her the orange dust like pollen in his palm. *New screens will be one of the least of your expenses. Alcoa makes nice big panels we can fit into runners along here. And here. Take them down in the fall. In summer this porch is the best room in the house. Grab the breeze.*

But it makes the living room so dark. I was thinking of having it torn away.

Don't tear away free space. You bought the view. Here's where it is.

Do you think we were silly? To buy it.

Not at all. This could be a dandy house. You have the skeleton and the size. All it needs now is money.

It was my husband who fell in love with it. I thought of us living nearer to Boston, in Lexington or Newton.

You know—Instead of finishing, he had jogged up and down on the boards, where the line of the porch sagged, testing.

Yes?

Your porch sill is missing a support. Don't hold any square dances out here.

You started to say something.

Not really.

She had waited.

I was going to say that your view makes me sad, because my wife loved it, and I didn't have the courage to do what your husband has done, take this place on.

Do you think courage is what it took? It may have been more a matter of self-esteem.

Perhaps.

Maybe it's just not your kind of place.

Thank you. I didn't feel it was. I'm not a seaside type. I like to feel lots of land around me, in case of a flood.

I suppose me too. I hate wet feet.

But you're happy here, aren't you? Somebody told me you said you were. It's none of my business, of course.

He had seemed so courtly and embarrassed, so ready to put himself back into the hired-man role, that her tongue hastened to ease his presumption. *Yes, I'm happy enough. I'm a little bored. But I like the town and I like the people I've met.*

You do?

You say that with such surprise.

Don't mean to. I guess I'm past asking myself if I like them or not. They're mine.

And you're theirs?

In a way. Watch out. It can happen to you.

No, Ken and I have always been independent. We've never gotten involved with people. I suppose we're both rather cold.

He had taken out a knife and, having turned his back on her, was prying. *Your window sashes should all be replaced.*

Wouldn't storm windows make that unnecessary?

Some of these frames are too rotten to screw a storm sash into.

I hope—

You hope what?

I was going to say, I hope we can have your wife down, you and your wife, when the house is fixed up. Already I'm frightened she won't approve of what we do to it.

He had laughed—his laugh came from deeper within him than the laugh of most men, was warmer, a bit disconcerting, more invading.

She had tried to defend herself. *I don't know why I should be worried about your wife's approval. She's a lovely person.*

His laugh repeated. *And your husband's a lovely man.*

II

Applesmiths and Other Games

OXY WAS both right and wrong about Janet. Janet had
never actually slept with Freddy Thorne, though she and
Freddy had held earnest discourse about it, and her affair with
Harold little-Smith had proved to be unexpectedly difficult to
untangle and end.

The Applebys and little-Smiths had moved to Tarbox in
the middle Fifties, unknown to each other, though both men
worked in securities on State Street, Harold as a broker, Frank
as a trust officer in a bank. Frank had gone to Harvard, Harold
to Princeton. They belonged to that segment of their generation of the upper middle class which mildly rebelled against
the confinement and discipline whereby wealth maintained
its manners during the upheavals of depression and world
war. Raised secure amid these national trials and introduced
as adults into an indulgent economy, into a business atmosphere strangely blended of crisp youthful imagery and underlying depersonalization, of successful small-scale gambles
carried out against a background of rampant diversification
and the ultimate influence of a government whose taxes and
commissions and appetite for armaments set limits everywhere,
introduced into a nation whose leadership allowed a toothless
moralism to dissemble a certain practiced cunning, into a culture where adolescent passions and homosexual philosophies
were not quite yet triumphant, a climate still *furtively* hedo-
nist, of a country still too overtly threatened from without to
be ruthlessly self-abusive, a climate of time between, of stand-
off and day-by-day, wherein all generalizations, even negative
ones, seemed unintelligent—to this new world the Applebys
and little-Smiths brought a modest determination to be free,
to be flexible and decent. Fenced off from their own parents
by nursemaids and tutors and "help," they would personally
rear large intimate families; they changed diapers with their
own hands, did their own housework and home repairs, gar-
dened and shoveled snow with a sense of strengthened health.

Chauffered, as children, in black Packards and Chryslers, they drove second-hand cars in an assortment of candy colors. Exiled early to boarding schools, they resolved to use and improve the local public schools. Having suffered under their parents' rigid marriages and formalized evasions, they sought to substitute an essential fidelity set in a matrix of easy and open companionship among couples. For the forms of the country club they substituted informal membership in a circle of friends and participation in a cycle of parties and games. They put behind them the stratified summer towns of their upbringings, with their restrictive distinctions, their tedious rounds of politeness, and settled the year round in unthought-of places, in pastoral mill towns like Tarbox, and tried to improvise here a fresh way of life. Duty and work yielded as ideals to truth and fun. Virtue was no longer sought in temple or market place but in the home—one's own home, and then the homes of one's friends.

In their first years in Tarbox, the social life of the Smiths and Applebys was passed among older men and women. Neighboring aunts dutifully called and were politely received and, in the end, resolutely snubbed. "How dreary," Marcia would say, "these horsey people are," and as she and Janet became intimate they coined a term, the "big H," to signify all those people, hopefully put behind them and yet so persistently attentive, who did all the right things, a skein of acquaintance and cousinship that extended from Quogue to Bar Harbor. Discovering each other at a horsey party, in Millbrook or Scituate, that each with a great show of wifely resignation had agreed to attend, Janet and Marcia would, by way of greeting, neigh at one another. Janet's delicate nostrilly snort, accompanied by a hoofing motion of one foot, was very piquant; she was slimmer then. In truth, they rarely declined these invitations, though as they failed to return them their number slowly diminished. For among these mocked people, however nasal and wooden-headed, the Applebys and Smiths were given presence on the strength of their names and parents' names; it was years before Tarbox provided them with a society as flattering and nutritious as the scorned "big H."

The Thornes and the Guerins were in Tarbox already, but there was something uncomfortable about both couples, something unexplained and embarrassed about the men—one a dentist, and the other seemingly not employed at all, though frequently in Boston. Both wives were shy; Bea did not drink so much then, and would sit quiet and tensely smiling for an entire evening. When Roger glared, she would freeze like a rabbit. Harold called them *Barbe Bleue et Fatime*. They all found Freddy Thorne's smirking pretensions and coziness ridiculous. In those days he still had some hair—wavy fine flax grown long and combed across a bald spot. Georgene was plainly another well-trained, well-groomed filly from the Big H, Philadelphia branch. The couples entertained each other with infrequent stiff dinners, and exchanged maternity clothes—except that Bea was never pregnant.

The people who did throw parties were a decade older and seemed rather coarse and blatant—Dan Mills, the bronzed, limping, and alcoholic owner of the abortive Tarbox boatyard; Eddie Warner, the supervisor of a Mather paint plant, a bullet-headed ex-athlete who could still at beery beach picnics float the ball a mile in the gull-gray dusk; Doc Allen; good old Ed Byrd; a few male teachers in the Tarbox schools, defensive plodders; and their wives, twitchy women full of vicarious sex and rock-and-roll lyrics, their children being adolescent. To Janet they seemed desperate people, ignorant and provincial and loud. Their rumored infidelities struck her as pathetic; their evident heavy drinking disgusted her. She herself had just produced a baby, Franklin, Jr.—eight pounds, six ounces. The skin of his temples exquisitely pulsed as he sucked her breasts, so that not only the hoarsely joshing voices and unsweet breaths but the imperfect complexions of the "boatyard crowd," as she and Marcia had christened it, offended her; lepers should not insist on dancing. The boatyard crowd, a postwar squirearchy of combat veterans, locally employed and uncollegiate, knew that it was patronized by these younger cooler couples and suffered no regrets when they chose to form a separate set and to leave them alone with their liquor and bridge games and noisy reminiscences of Anzio and Guadalcanal.

Had they been less uncongenial, Janet would hardly have made social overtures to the Saltzes and the Ongs, who moved to opposite ends of the town in 1957 and who at least were college graduates. John Ong, indeed, was supposedly very brilliant. He worked in Cambridge, mathematically deciphering matter, in a program underwritten by the government. He should have been fascinating but his English was impossible to understand. His wife, Bernadette, was a broad-shouldered half-Japanese from Baltimore, her father an immigrant Portuguese. She was exotic and boisterous and warm and exhausting, as if she were trying to supply by herself enough gregariousness for two. The Saltzes were killingly earnest but Irene could be fun after the third martini, when she did imitations of all the selectmen and town officials her crusading spirit brought her up against. Ben had only one imitation, which he did unconsciously—a rabbi, with scruffy beard and bent stoop, hands clasped behind him, and an air of sorrowing endurance. But it was not until, in 1958, Hanema and Gallagher set up their office on Hope Street that the final ecology of the couples was established. With these two men, the Irishman and Dutchman, shaped together like Don Quixote and Sancho Panza, began the round of sports—touch football, skiing, basketball, sailing, tennis, touch football again—that gave the couples an inexhaustible excuse for gathering: a calendrical wheel of unions to anticipate and remember, of excuses for unplanned parties. And the two new women, Terry and Angela, brought a style with them, an absent-minded amiability from which the other women were able to imitate the only tone, casual and amused, that could make bearable such a burden of hospitality and intermingling. In 1960 the Constantines moved into their sinister big house on the green; Carol painted, and Eddie flew. As a couple, they had an appealingly dangerous air. And now, in 1963, the Whitmans had moved into the old Robinson place.

These years had seen the boatyard crowd go from decay to disintegration. Two couples had been divorced, the schoolteachers had failed to get tenure and had quit or been dismissed, poor alcoholic Danny Mills had lost his boatyard to the bank and gone to Florida without his wife, whose hard stringy legs had been so quick to master the newest dance step. The only remaining contact with the boatyard crowd was by phone, when one called to ask one of their teen-age daughters to babysit. Their existence, which might have been forgotten entirely, was memorialized by a strange vestige, irksome to Harold and Marcia, within the younger group of couples.

There had been, in those first Tarbox years, another couple called Smith, a pair of big-headed, ruddy, humorless social pushers who had since moved to Newton but who were, for a year, present at the same parties the smaller Smiths were invited to. So the modifiers had been coined as a conversational convenience and had outlived the need for any distinction, and become part of Harold and Marcia, though by now few of their friends knew who the big-Smiths had been, or could envision their ponderous, flushed, doll-like faces, always eagerly nodding, like floats in a Shriners parade. It was an annual cause for hilarity when, with that inexorable plodding friendliness that had been their method of attack, the Smiths from faraway Newton Centre favored the Thornes, the Guerins, the Applebys, and their name-twins with a hectographed Christmas letter. In the salutation to Harold and Marcia they unfailingly put "little" in quotes—*to our Tarbox doppelgängers the "little" Smiths.*

The affair among the Applesmiths began—gossip wrongly assumed that Janet initiated things—with Marcia noticing Frank's hands. In turn the beauty of his hands had emerged from their former pudgy look by way of an ulcer diet brought on by the sharp market slump of April and May of 1962. This slump, which more affected Frank's trusts (he had just been promoted from junior officer) than Harold's brokerage business, and which furthermore caught Frank with thousands of his own in electronics and pharmaceuticals, brought the couples closer than usual that spring and summer. It became their custom, Sunday nights, after tennis, to eat together fried clams or lobster fetched in steaming paper bags from a restaurant in North Mather. One night, as they sat on cushions and chairs around the little-Smiths' tesselated coffee table, Marcia became hypnotized by the shapely force with which Frank's fingers, their tips greasily gleaming, manipulated onion rings. His diet had shorn a layer of fat from them, so the length of the fingers, with something especially sculptured about the knuckles and nail sheaths, was revealed as aristocratic; his thumbs were eloquent in every light. Along the fleecy wrists, through the cordlike tributary veins raised on the backs of his hands, down into the tips, a force flowed that could destroy and shape; pruning roses had given Frank's hands little cuts that suggested the

nicks a clammer or sculptor bears, and Marcia lifted her eyes
to his face and found there, beneath the schoolboy plumpness,
the same nicked, used, unconscious look of having done work,
of belonging to an onflowing force whose pressure made his
cheeks florid and his eyes bloodshot. He was a man. He had a
battered look of having been swept forward past obstacles. After this revelation every motion of his altered Marcia's insides
with a slight turning, a purling in the flow within her. She was
a woman. She sensed now in him a treasurable dreadfulness;
and, when they rose to leave and Janet, eight months pregnant, lost her balance and took Frank's quickly offered hand for
support, Marcia, witnessing as if never before the swift sympathetic interaction of the couple, felt outraged: a theft had been
brazenly executed before her eyes.

Née Burnham, Marcia was the daughter of a doctor and
the granddaughter of a bishop. Her detection of a masculine
beauty in Frank Appleby at first took the form of an innocent
glad lightness in the company of the other couple and a corre-
sponding dreariness on weekends when they were not sched-
uled to see them—though she usually managed to call Janet
and arrange for at least a drink together, or a sail with their
boys in the Applebys' catboat. Her possessive and probing
fondness was hardly distinguishable from their old friendship,
though at dances or at parties where they danced she did feel
herself lifted by a willingness to come into Frank's hands. He
had never been a dancer, and Marcia, locked into his bumping
shuffle, aware of her toes being stubbed and her cool lotioned
hand vanishing in the damp adhesion of his grip and his boozy
sighs accumulating on her bare neck like the patch of mist a
child will breathe onto a windowpane, sometimes watched en-
viously her husband and Janet or Carol Constantine waltzing
from corner to corner around the shadowy rim of the room
whose bright dead center she and Frank statically occupied.
Harold was an adroit, even flamboyant, dancer, and sometimes
after a long set with Frank she would make him take her and
whirl her around the floor to relieve the crick in her neck and
the ache, from reaching too high, across her shoulder blades.
But there was a solidity in Frank that Harold lacked. Harold
had never suffered; he merely dodged. Harold read *Barron's* or
Ian Fleming on the commuting train; Frank read Shakespeare.

What Marcia didn't know was that she preceded Shakespeare: for Frank the market slump, the sleepless nights of indigestion, the birth of his second child, and his friend's wife's starry glances and strange meltingness were parts of one experience, an overture to middle age, a prelude to mortality, that he answered, in the manner of his father, an ardent amateur Sinologist, by dipping deep into the past, where peace reigned. *When all aloud the wind doth blow/And coughing drowns the parson's saw/And birds sit brooding in the snow* . . . Those vanished coughs, melted snow, dead birds seemed sealed in amber, in something finer than amber, because movement could occur within it. *I'll have a starling shall be taught to speak/Nothing but "Mortimer," and give it him/To keep his anger still in motion:* in Frank's contemplation of such passion, perfectly preserved, forever safe, his stomach forgot itself. He was not a natural reader, couldn't focus on two lines of Dante or Milton, disliked plays on the stage and novels, and found this soothing quality, of flux confined with all its colors, only in Shakespeare.

"Everything is in him," he told Marcia, flirtatiously, for he talked about Shakespeare with no one, especially not Janet, who took his reading as a rebuke of her, for not finishing college, but marrying him instead, "everything we can hope to have, and it all ends badly."

Marcia asked, "Even the comedies?"

"They end in marriage, and Shakespeare's marriage was unhappy."

"I feel," Marcia said, for she was a tight-wound nervous woman who had to have things clear, "you're trying to tell me *we* would end badly."

"Us? You and me?"

So he hadn't meant at all to tell her his own marriage was unhappy. But she went on, "If we . . . started anything."

"Should we start something? I'll buy that idea. Yes." His large red head seemed to settle heavier on his shoulders as the notion sank in. "What about Harold and Janet? Should we consult them first? Let's not and say we did."

He was so clumsy and ironical, she took offense. "Please forget whatever I said. It's a female fault, to try and sexualize friendship. I want you only as a friend."

"Why? You have Janet as a friend. Please sexualize me. It sounds like a good process. With this sloppy market running, it's probably the best investment left." They were leaning in the summer heat against the maroon fender of the Applebys' Mercury, after tennis, beside the Gallaghers' rather fortresslike brick house on the back road to North Mather. Matt had got permission to use a neighbor's court. Harold was inside the house, drinking; Janet was home nursing the baby. It had been a girl, whom they had named Catharine, after an aunt Frank remembered as a heap of dusty velvet, knobbed with blood-red garnets.

Marcia said to him, but after laughing enjoyably, "You're shocking, with your doubled responsibilities."

"Double, double, toil and trouble. Janet's been a bitch for nine months plus. Let's at least have lunch together in Boston. I need a vacation. How are your Tuesdays?"

"Car-pool day."

"Oh. Wednesdays I usually have lunch with Harold at the Harvard Club. All he does is sniff. Shall I cancel him?"

"No, no. Harold hates any change of routine. Let me see if I can get a sitter for Henrietta for Thursday. Please, Frank. Let's understand each other. This is just to talk."

"Of course. I'll tell you of men whose heads do grow beneath their shoulders."

"Othello?"

"Right."

"Frank, listen. I've become fixated on you, I know it's absurd, and I'm asking for your help. As a friend."

"Pre- or post-sexualization?"

"Please be serious. I've never been more serious. I'm fighting for my life. I know you don't love me and I don't think I love you but I *need* to talk. I need it so much"—and here, half artfully, she lowered her face to hide tears that were, after all, real—"I'm frightened."

"Dear Marcia. Don't be."

They had lunch, and lunch often again, meeting at the corners of new glass buildings or in the doorways of flower shops, a toothy ruddy man with a soft air of having done well at school and a small dark efficient woman looking a little breathless, hunting hand in hand through the marine stenches of the waterfront and the jostling glare of Washington Street for the perfect obscure restaurant, with the corner table, and the fatherly bartender, and the absence of business acquaintances and college friends. They talked, touching toes, quickly brushing hands in admonishment or pity, talked about themselves, about their childhoods spent behind trimmed hedges, about Shakespeare and psychiatry, which Marcia's lovely father had practiced, about Harold and Janet, who, as they obligingly continued to be deceived, were ever more tenderly considered, so that they became almost sacred in their ignorance, wonderful in their fallibility, so richly forgiven for their frigidity, demandingness, obtuseness, and vanity that the liaison between their spouses seemed a conspiracy to praise the absent. There was a cottage north of Boston—and thus extra safe and remote from their real lives—belonging to one of Frank's aunts, who hid the key on a little sill behind one of the fieldstone foundation-pillars. To Frank as a child, groping for this key cached here had seemed a piratical adventure, the pillaging of a deep grotto powerfully smelling of earth and creosote and rodent dung. Now the key seemed pathetically accessible, and he wondered how many others, strangers to the family, had used these same bare mattresses, had borrowed these same rough army blankets from the cedar chest, and had afterwards carefully tipped their cigarette ashes into the cellophane sealer slipped from the pack. In the kitchen there had been a dead mouse in a trap. Dying, it had flipped, and lay belly up, dirty white, like a discarded swab in a doctor's office. Frank and Marcia stole some sherry from the cupboard but had not disturbed the mouse. They were not here. The cottage was used only on weekends. From its security amid pines and pin oaks it overlooked the slender peninsula of Nahant. The seaside smell that leaked through the window sashes was more saline and rank than that of Tarbox Beach, where Janet and the children would be sunning. Marcia had felt to Frank strangely small, more athletic and manageable than Janet, without Janet's troubled tolling resonance but with a pleasing pointed firmness that reminded him, in his passage into her body, of the little mistresses of the French court, of Japanese prostitutes that Harold had once drunkenly described, of slim smooth boys who had been Rosalind and

Kate and Ophelia. There was in Marcia a nervous corruptibility he had never tasted before. Her thin shoulders sparkled in his red arms. Her face, relaxed, seemed, like an open lens, to be full of his face. "I love your hands," she said.

"You've said that before."

"I loved being in them. They're huge."

"Only relatively," he said, and regretted it, for he had brought Harold into bed with them.

Knowing this, knowing they could never be alone, she asked, "Did I feel different than Janet?"

"Yes."

"My breasts are so small."

"You have lovely breasts. Like a Greek statue. Venus always has little breasts. Janet's—Janet's are full of milk right now. It's kind of a mess."

"What does it taste like?"

"What? Janet's milk?"

"You don't have to tell me."

"No, why not? Sweet. Too sweet, really."

"You're such a gentle man," Marcia said. "I'm not used to being loved so gently." Thus she conveyed, weakening them as lovers but strengthening them as confidants, the suggestion to Frank that he had been too gentle, that Harold was rougher, more strenuous and satisfying with, no doubt, a bigger prick. As if hailing a dim stubby figure on a misted shore, Frank mournfully confronted the endomorph in himself. His demanding deep-socketed mistress, ectomorphic, lay relaxed at his side; their skins touched stickily along her length. The neural glitter of her intelligent face was stilled; a dangling earring rested diagonally forward from her ear lobe, parallel to the line of her cheekbone; the severe central parting of her black hair had been carried off by a kind of wind. Was she asleep? He groped beside the bed, among his underclothes, for his wristwatch. He would soon learn, in undressing, to leave it lying discreetly visible. Its silent gold-rimmed face, a tiny banker's face, stated that he had already been out to lunch an hour and forty minutes. A sour burning began to revolve in his stomach.

Their affair went two months undetected. It is not difficult to deceive the first time, for the deceived possesses no antibodies; unvaccinated by suspicion, she overlooks latenesses, accepts absurd excuses, permits the flimsiest patchings to repair great rents in the quotidian. "*Where* have you been?" Janet asked Frank one Saturday.

"At the dump."

"At the dump for two *hours*?"

"Oh, I stopped at the drug store and talked to Buzz Kappiotis about the tax rate and the firemen's four-per-cent increase."

"I thought Buzz was fishing in Maine." Their cleaning lady was a neighbor.

"I don't mean Buzz, I mean Iggy Galanis, I must be losing my mind."

"I'll say. You're so twitchy in bed you give me insomnia."

"It's my blue-eyed baby ulcers."

"I don't see what you're so nervous about lately. The market's happy again, they've reduced the margin rate. And *how* did your clothes get so rumpled?"

He looked down at himself and saw a long black hair from Marcia's head adhering to the fly of his corduroy pants. Glancing there, he felt the little limb behind the cloth as warm and used, softly stinging. Sun had streamed through the dusty windshield glass onto her skin. He pulled the hair off and said, "From handling the trash cans."

But an affair wants to spill, to share its glory with the world. No act is so private it does not seek applause. In public Frank could scarcely contain his proud and protective feeling toward Marcia; the way at the end of an evening he held her coat for her and slipped it around her was as different from the way he would help Georgene Thorne as receiving the Host is from eating an hors d'oeuvre. All the empty pauses and gropings of this simple social action were luxuriously infused with magic: his fingers in adjusting her collar brushed the nape of her neck; her hands pressed her own lapels secure if they were his hands clasped upon her breasts; her eyes rolled Spanishly; and this innocent pantomime of robing was drenched in reminiscence of their nakedness. Their minds and mouths were committed to stability and deception while their bodies were urging eruption, violence, change. At last the little-Smiths, Harold prattling drunkenly, spilled from the lit porch into the night—a parting glance from Marcia, dark as a winter-killed rose—and the door was finally shut. Janet asked Frank, "Are you having an affair with Marcia?"

"Now there's a strange question."

"Never mind the question. What's the answer?"

"Obviously, no."

"You don't sound convincing. Convince me. Please convince me."

He shrugged. "I don't have the time or the stomach for it. She's not my type. She's tiny and jittery and has no tits. Lastly, you're my wife and you're great. Rare Egyptian! Royal wench! The holy priests bless you when you are riggish. Let's go to bed."

"We have to stack the dishwasher first. Anyway, don't think you've sold me. How does she know so much about Shakespeare all of a sudden?"

"I suppose she's been reading him."

"To please you. To get at me somehow."

"How does that get at you?"

"She knows I never read."

"But you find books in running brooks, sermons in stones, and good in everything."

"Ha ha. That busy little bitch, she keeps telling me she has a secret."

"She says this?"

"Her eyes say it. And her bottom. I used to think of her as so stringy and intellectual, but she's been doing a ton of hip-waggling lately."

"Maybe she's having an affair with Freddy Thorne."

"Take that expression off your face."

"What expression?"

"That amused look. Take it off! Take it off, Frank! I hate it!" And suddenly she was at him, after him with her fists, her struggling weight; he squeezed her against him, regretfully conscious even now, as her pinned fists flailed his shoulders and her face crumpled into contorted weeping and the sharp smell of perfume was scalded from her, that the expression, of serene superiority, of a beautiful secret continually tasted, was still on his face.

Harold little-Smith could not immediately identify the woman who called him at his office one morning. He and Janet rarely talked on the telephone; it was Marcia and Janet, or Marcia and Frank, who arranged the many things—the tennis and sailing, the Friday-night plays and Saturday-night concerts

—that the two couples had done together this summer. The woman's voice said, "I've been in town all morning shopping, the damn stores have *nothing*, and I'm hungry and cross and wondered if you'd like to split a lunch with me. *Not* fried clams, thank you." Just in time, he recognized Janet.

"Janet, really? It's a lovely idea, but this is the day I usually have lunch with Frank. Why don't the three of us have lunch together?"

"That's *not* the idea, Harold. Couldn't you call Frank and cancel it? Think of some good excuse. Tell him you have a girl friend. Don't be afraid of Frank, Harold."

"Who said I was?"

"Well, then. Please. I know it seems funny and pushy, but I must talk to you, and this was the only way I could think of. I knew Wednesday is your day with Frank and that you would be free otherwise."

Still Harold hesitated. He enjoyed a certain freedom of speech and thought because his life, from childhood up, had been outwardly orderly and obedient. Life was a kind of marathon you could run as you please as long as you touched all the checkpoints; his weekly lunch with Frank was one of the checkpoints. They discussed stocks and bonds and hardly ever spoke of their domestic life together in Tarbox.

Janet prompted, "You won't have to *pay* for my lunch, just *have* it with me."

This stung him; he considered himself something of a dandy, an old-fashioned elegant. Last spring, in St. Louis, he had given a girl two hundred dollars to spend the night with him. He told Janet the Ritz, upstairs, at one o'clock, and hung up.

It was strange she should have told him not to be afraid of Frank because it was she Harold had always been afraid of. Any vulgarity that could not be paid off and dismissed intimidated him. Meeting the Applebys the first time, he had wondered why Frank had married such a common girl—fine in bed, no doubt, but why marry her? Though she was from a respectable family (her father owned a pharmaceutical manufacturing firm in Buffalo, and her maiden name was on drugstore shelves across the country) Janet was one of the few women of Harold's social acquaintance who could have been, without any change in physical style, a waitress or a girl in a five and ten (in fact she had worked two summers behind a counter, selling men's jewelry, at Flint & Kent) or a dance-hall hostess. She would some day, some day soon, be fat. Already there was a crease at the front of her ankles, and the flesh of her upper arms was loose, and her hips had a girdled hardness. Not that Harold did not find her attractive. He did, and this went with his fright. Her beauty seemed a gift she would abuse, like a boy with a gun, or squander, like a fool with a fortune. She struck him as a bad investor who would buy high and sell after the drop and take everybody she could down with her. So he walked, up Milk, through the thick of Boston's large codger population, along Tremont, through the Common and the Public Garden, in a pinching mood of caution. The sidewalk was so hot it stung through the soles of his thin black Italianate shoes; yet scraps of velour and highlights of satiny white skin skated through his head, and it was somewhat romantic of him not to have taken a cab. Of the four Applesmiths, Harold was sexually the most experienced. He possessed that trivial air, trivial yet assured and complacent, that women feel free to experiment with, and before his marriage he had slept with enough to lose the exact count. After marriage (he had been old: twenty-six) there had been business trips, and call girls, generally doughy and sullen, with whiskeyish breaths and terrible voices; but he had never betrayed Marcia with a social equal.

After her second martini, Janet said, "Harold, it's about Marcia and Frank."

"They seem very amiable lately."

"I should hope so. I *know* they're seeing each other."

"You know? You have evidence? *Evidence?*"

"I don't need evidence, I *know*. There's a tone about them. He's always bringing her up, casually. 'Did Marcia seem irritable to you tonight?' 'What did you think, dear, of Marcia's dress?' What the fuck do I care about Marcia's dress?"

"But you have no evidence? There's been no confession from Frank? He hasn't asked to leave you?"

"Why should he want to leave me? He's happy. He's milking two cows."

"Janet, you don't put things very gracefully."

"I don't *feel* graceful about it. You evidently do. Evidently you're used to your wife sleeping around."

"I am not. The fact is, I don't believe this. I think there is an attraction between Frank and Marcia, yes. It's natural enough, considering how much we see each other. For that matter, there's an attraction between you and me. *Toi et moi.*"

"This is the first I've heard of it."

"Oh, come on. You know what you are. You know how you look to men. I'd love to go to bed with you."

"You don't put things that gracefully yourself."

"Of course, we won't. We're married now and we've had our flings, our *escapades romantiques.* We have others besides ourselves to think about."

"Well it's the others I'm trying to talk about, Marcia and Frank. You keep talking about you and me going to bed. They *are* going to bed. What are you going to do about it, Harold?"

"Bring me some evidence, and I'll confront her with it."

"What kind of evidence do you expect? Dirty pictures? A notarized diaphragm?"

Ringlets of vibration, fine as watch springs, oscillated on the surface of his Gibson as he laughed; there was an unexpected poetry in the woman, face to face across a table for two, the cloth and the softness of her stirred forward by a passionate worry. Through the windows the trees of the Public Garden were hushed cascades, the great copper beech a glittering fall of lava. Janet said, "All right. How is Marcia in bed for you lately? Less or more?"

How common, really, this was; it smacked of midwifery, of witchery, of womanish cures and auguries, of stolen hairpins and menstrual napkins. The waiter, a gray man polished and bent by service like a spoon, came and Harold ordered without consulting Janet *potage à la reine, quiche Lorraine,* salad, a light dry Chablis. "You're putting me on a diet," she said.

He told her, "In answer to your question. I think more."

"See? She's aroused. She's full of it. Screwing."

He laughed; his Gibson glass was empty and no watchsprings materialized. "Come off it, Janet. You expected me to say less, didn't you?"

"Has it been less?"

"No, I was honest. She's been quite loving lately. Your thesis is that women are polygamous; the more they have the more they want?"

"I don't know, Harold. I've never been unfaithful to Frank, isn't that funny? But I would think, as a woman—"

As a woman: this plump soft phrase out of her mouth gave him the pleasure he felt when, after a party, drunkenly showering, to hear Marcia feign shock he would fasten her bra to his skinny wet chest.

"—that she would feel guilty toward you, and wants to prove to herself that this isn't taking away from her marriage, that she has enough for both; and that furthermore she wants to tell you about it, this wonderful thing about herself, about the whole business. I know that Frank has out of the blue started doing things that *I* never taught him."

The thin wedge of a headache entered Harold's right temple. He reflexively reached for his empty glass, uncertain if Marcia had changed or not, for of those conversations of tranced bodies there is little distinct to recall, only the companionable slow ascent to moon-blanched plateaus where pantomimes of eating and killing and dying are enacted, both sides taking all parts. He found Marcia kittenish, then tigerish, then curiously abstract and cool and mechanical, and finally, afterwards, very grateful and tender and talkative and sticky.

Janet smiled, tipping a little from her glass into his. "Poor Harold," she said. "He hates indiscreet conversations. It's too female, it threatens him. But you know," she went on, having realized he would be good to experiment with, "I can't talk to other women comfortably. I could only have said these things to a man." She stated this with an air of having produced a touching confession for him, but he found it presumptuous and offensive. He thought women should properly talk with women, and men with men, and that communication between the sexes should be a courtly and dangerous game, with understood rules, mostly financial, and strict time limits. Ninety minutes was usually quite enough, and this lunch lasted longer than that.

They agreed to have lunch again, next week, to compare notes. Harold went home to a house more transparent; its privacy had been surrendered. While the Applebys lived in town, on a secluded lane on the far side of the Musquenomenee, in an ample white house of nondescript style whose interior comfort was essentially borrowed or inherited, the little-Smiths had built their own, and designed it in every detail, a flat-roofed redwood modern oriented along a little sheltered ridge overlooking the marsh to the south. The foyer was floored in flagstones; on the right an open stairway went down to a basement level where the three children (Jonathan, Julia, Henrietta) slept and the laundry was done and the cars were parked. Above this, on the main level, were the kitchen, the dining room, the master bedroom, a polished hall where hung reproductions of etchings by Rembrandt, Dürer, Piranesi, and Picasso. To the left of the foyer a dramatically long living room opened up, with a shaggy cerulean rug and two facing white sofas and symmetrical hi-fi speakers and a Baldwin grand and at the far end an elevated fireplace with a great copper hood. The house bespoke money in the service of taste. In the summer evenings he would drive back from the station through the livelong light hovering above the tawny marshes, flooded or dry according to the tides, and find his little wife, her black hair freshly combed and parted, waiting on the longer of the sofas, which was not precisely white but rather a rough Iranian wool bleached to the pallor of sand mixed with ash. A record, Glenn Gould or Dinu Lipatti playing Bach or Schumann, would be sending forth clear vines of sound from the invisible root within the hi-fi closet. A pitcher of martinis would have been mixed and held chilled within the refrigerator toward this precious moment of his daily homecoming; the tinge of green in the vermouth was intensified by the leafy green, green upon green, ivy and alder and hemlock and holly, crowding through their walls of sliding plate glass. Outdoors on the sparkling lawn, sparkling in the lowering light as the sun slowly approached the distant radar station—exquisite silver disc, always fidgeting —Jonathan, in bathing trunks and a candy-striped shirt, would be playing catch with Julia or some children of neighboring summer people, tossing a chewed sponge ball, a little pitted moon, back and forth through the revolving liquid branches of the lawn sprinkler. Henrietta, as neat and alert in feature as Marcia herself, in her duckling nightie, bathed, would run toward Harold barefoot through the cerulean rug to be lifted and hugged and twirled, and Marcia would pour two verdant martinis into glasses that would suddenly sweat, and the ball would fall short and lie crescented by sunlight, soaking, while the children noiselessly argued which would retrieve it and get drenched, and his entire household, even the stray milk butterfly perched on the copper fireplace hood, felt about to spring into bliss, like a tightly wound music box.

He detected small change in Marcia. They had met one summer on Long Island and married the next, and things, more or less, had turned out as charmingly as had been predicted. They had both been in their mid-twenties and were considered by their contemporaries a bit intellectual and cool. They discovered each other to be sensual, but allowed this coolness to characterize their marriage. They never quarreled in public, rarely in private; each expected the other to see clearly into the mechanism of their union and to make without comment the allowances and adjustments needed. He excused his occasional call girls as hygienic; he took them as he took, behind the closed bathroom door, without complaint to Marcia, aspirins to relieve his headaches. He could believe that Marcia might be unfaithful to him, but as some kind of service to himself, to save him trouble, to accommodate him with new subtlety. He had married her after most of her friends had married. He had removed her from that crass monied Middle Atlantic society where she had seemed stilted and fragile. He trusted her to be always his. Smiling, she lifted the martini; the gin and her earrings trembled. He sipped; the coolness was delicious.

Without looking it, they were slightly older than most of their friends in Tarbox; Harold was thirty-eight, Marcia was thirty-six.

She did seem, lately, more inventive and solicitous. A ramshackle boardwalk, in need of repair every spring, had come with their land, with the old summer cottage they had torn down. It led out to a small tidal creek too narrow for most powerboats; here, at high tide, between banks tall with reeds, in water warmer than the sea off the beach, they and their friends and their friends' children could swim. At night, now, this summer, when the tide was right, and the children were asleep, Marcia had taken to inviting him, Harold alone, for a swim before bed, without bathing suits. So they would walk down in moonlight through poison ivy and cut-back sumac, treading warily, and out the often-patched boardwalk, its slats of varied wood like the keys of a gigantic piano, and on the splintery soft dock take off their clothes and stand, husband and wife, naked together, gooseflesh rising, for an instant of nerve-gathering before plunging from the expectant summer air into the flat black water alive with reeds. Beside him her flitting breasts, arching arms, upturned face gashed by black licks of her hair bubbled through the blanched foam and slopping clammy slick. The water's million filaments sucked from his nerve ends the flecks of city filth. Our first love, our love of the elements, restored to him his youngest self. Sometimes, at high tide, like a laboring Cyclopean elephant a powerboat would come crowding up the channel with its searchlight and they would squat like aborigines under the dock in the root-riddled mud until the boat passed. And they would dry each other, Harold and Marcia, she toweling even his fumbly dripping genitals, thinking how innocently part of him they seemed, and not a harsh jutting second life parasitic upon him. As she ran ahead up the boardwalk, clutching her clothes to her breasts, her buttocks would be dancy in the steady moon. If in bed they made love, with salty bodies and damp hair, she praised his ardor—"so fierce"—and expertness—"oh, you know me so well"—as if a standard of comparison, someone gentle and clumsy, had appeared. And she would blurt "I love you" with a new emphasis, as if the "you" were darkened by the shadow of an unspoken "nevertheless."

At their next lunch Janet had nothing to offer but complaints about Marcia's constantly calling up and suggesting they do things together, as couples—sail, swim, play tennis, go to meetings. She was even trying to get her interested in the Tarbox Fair Housing Committee, which Irene Saltz and Bernadette Ong were organizing. "I said to her, 'But there isn't a single Negro in town,' and she said, 'That's the point. We're culturally deprived, our children don't know what a Negro looks like,' and I said, 'Don't they watch television?' and then I said, getting really mad, 'It seems to me awfully hard on the Negro, to bring him out here just so your children can look at him. Why don't they instead look at the Ongs on a dark day?' I shouldn't have said that, I think Bernadette's great; but there's something basically snotty about this committee. It's all because other towns have one. Like a drum-and-bugle corps."

Janet seemed old to Harold, though she was years younger than he, old and double-chinned and querulous, vexing herself with what he knew to be Marcia's simple gregariousness, her innocent need to be doing. He changed the subject. "What were you and Piet talking about so earnestly at the Thornes' party?"

Her valentine mouth, its lipstick flaking, frowned. "He was telling me his wife doesn't give him shit. He tells every woman."

"He's never told Marcia."

"She's never told you. Piet's been aching to break out for a long time and I don't know what's holding him back. Georgene's right there waiting."

It was fascinating, seeing his friends through a whole new set of windows. "And Freddy Thorne?" he asked delicately. He had long wondered if Janet had slept with Freddy.

Janet said, "Freddy's my friend. He understands women."

"And that's all you choose to say."

"That's all I have to say. We've never gone to bed, I'm fond of Freddy, he's harmless. Why are you men so mean to him?"

"Because you women are so nice to him."

Amused to discover himself jealous, Harold studied his fingers, which he set parallel to the table silver, and asked, "Do you think the Hanemas will get a divorce?" He liked Angela, one of the few women in town who could speak his language. He loved her upward-searching diffidence, her motherly presiding above their summer-evening gatherings. Everyone rather loved Angela.

"Never," Janet said flatly. "Piet's too tame. He's too thick in the conscience. He'll stick it out with those three, picking up whatever spare ass he can. The bad thing about a cockteaser like Angela is she turns her man loose on the world and lets a lot of other women in for trouble. Piet can be very winning."

"You speak as one who knows. *Elle qui sait.*"

"There've been overtures, nothing drastic. Among his other problems, he's shy."

"Poor Piet," Harold said, uncertain why, though Janet nodded in agreement.

That weekend, he asked Marcia, after a party, when both were drunk, "Do you love me?"

"I love you, Harold, but please not tonight. We're both too drunk and sleepy. Let's have a nap instead sometime tomorrow." Tomorrow was Sunday.

"I didn't mean to make love, I meant, honestly, *après douze années très heureuses,* aren't you pretty bored with me? Don't you ever think of what it would be like with other men?"

"Oh, maybe a little. Not very consciously." She was wearing a chiffon nightie the color of persimmon, and as she crawled into bed her dark limbs looked monkeyish. Getting into bed demanded nimbleness of her because the bed was high; also it was high and hard, because they found such a mattress best for lovemaking. The little-Smiths' bedroom, as they had designed it, was a shrine, a severe sacred space; its furniture consisted of little more than two teak bureaus, a reading lamp built into the headboard, a mirror on a closet door, a philodendron, and for a rug the hide of a zebra that Harold's grandfather had shot on safari with Teddy Roosevelt. When she was settled in, he turned off the light. The darkness was purple, and high in the window the marsh moon amid moving clouds seemed to swing back and forth like the bob of a pendulum.

"Tell me," he said. "You won't hurt my feelings."

"OK. Ask me the men."

"Have you ever wanted to go to bed with Piet Hanema?"

"Not really. He reminds me too much of a fatherly elf. He's too paternal and sympathetic. Once at the Guerins we were left alone in the room with the bigger fireplace and he began to stroke my back and it felt as if he wanted to burp me. I think Piet likes bigger women. Georgene and Bea and I are too small for him."

"Freddy Thorne."

"Never, never. He's so slippery and womanish, I think sex is all talk with him anyway. Janet responds to him better than I do; ask her."

"You know I can't talk to Janet. Her vocabulary puts me off."

"It's getting worse lately, isn't it?"

"And Frank?"

Patterns of light—long lozenges of moonlight laid across the zebra rug and a corner of the bed; a rod of electric light coming from the hallway through the crack their door was left ajar, to comfort the children; a dim bluish smear on the ceiling from a carbon streetlight on the beach road, entering by the foyer transom—welled from the purple darkness as Harold held his breath, waiting for Marcia's answer.

It came very casually, in a voice half asleep. "Oh, Frank's been a friend too long to think about that way. Besides, he has whiskey breath and an ulcer. No, thanks." When, still studying their placid guests of light, he made no reply, she stirred and asked, "Why? Do you want Janet?"

He laughed quite loudly and said, "*Mon Dieu*, no! That girl's pure trouble."

"She's very hostile to me lately."

"I think," Harold said, snaking his arm around her and snuggling his genitals into the curved warmth of her backside, "we should make an effort to see less of the Applebys. Let's have the Guerins over sometime. Maybe with some new people like the Constantines. The wife seems pretty hip."

Marcia made no response, and he nudged her, and she said, "The Guerins are so depressing."

Janet was gayer at their next lunch, and looked five years younger. The day was one of those very hot days toward the end of August when to a woman summer seems a lover leaving, to be embraced with full abandon: appearances are past mattering; love disdains nothing. Sweat mars her makeup and mats her hairdo. Her arms swim freely in air. The steaming city streets crammed with secretaries have the voluptuousness of a seraglio. Janet wore an armless cotton dress printed with upside-down herons on a turquoise ground and swung herself along as if nothing in the natural world, no thrust of sun or thunderclap, could do her harm. Her feet, naked in sandals, were dusty, and Harold wondered, walking along Federal Street beside her in the heat, what it would be like to suck each dirty one of her ten toes clean. He took off his coat and swung it over his shoulder like a tough; they ate in a cafeteria whose glass doors were open at either end like sluice gates. Noise poured through him, backfiring trucks and the clatter of cutlery and the shouting of orders and the words of the girl across from him, with her sweating round face and eroded lipstick. She said, "How was *your* weekend?"

"Fine. You should know. We saw you every minute of it, except when somebody had to go to the bathroom."

"I know, isn't it boring? Frank and Marcia mooning at each other and exchanging ever so teeny-tiny little tender glances."

"You *do* exaggerate that."

"Balls, Harold. Frank absolutely gets choleric when he can't have Marcia as his tennis partner. And when they're across the net from each other, all those cute little pat shots, I could puke. He's always 'swinging by.' 'I'll swing by the Smith's to pick up Frankie.' 'I just swung by Smitty's to drop off the variorum Shakespeare, and they had me in for a drink.' It turns out 'they' was Marcia and you were off at a town Republican meeting. Harold, *why* are you a conservative?—it's such a pose."

He endured this tirade pleasurably, as if it were a massage or a shower. "But you still have nothing definite."

"How definite must definite be? Harold, he knows too much. He knew you were going to Symphony with the Gallaghers Saturday night. He knew Julia sprained her shoulder diving off the dock Thursday. When I talk to Marcia and tell him what she said he doesn't bother to listen because he's heard it all already. He knows you and she go skinny-dipping down by your dock and then fuck."

"Doesn't everybody know that? The dock part of it. The other doesn't invariably follow."

"How would everybody know? You think your friends have nothing better to do than splosh around the marshes with binoculars?"

"Marcia might tell Bea, or Georgene, or even Irene, in passing."

"Well she doesn't tell me and I'm her best friend supposedly. Frank tells me. Frank."

"I asked her the other night if she was having an affair with Frank."

Janet bit into her pastrami-on-a-roll and stared above the bun. "And she said?"

"I forget exactly what she said. We were both sleepy. She said he was too old a friend and had an ulcer."

"Two good reasons for it. Every woman has a nurse complex. And why not sleep with a friend? It's better than sleeping with an enemy. I've never understood why people are so shocked when somebody sleeps with his best friend's wife. Obviously, his best friend's wife is the one he sees most *of*."

"Well, she convinced me." He tried to state his heart's case. "We're not that unhappy, for her to do me dirt."

"Very well. She's as pure as Snow White and the stains in Frank's underpants are accidents of nature. Let's forget them. Let's talk about us. Why don't you like me, Harold? I like you. I like the way your nose comes to two points, like a very pale strawberry. Why don't you take the afternoon off and walk me through the Common over to Newbury Street and look at pictures? You understand pictures. What's this new gimmick of making things look like comic strips?"

She put her hand palm up on the tabletop; it was moist, a creased pink saucer of moisture on the silver-flecked formica. When he put his hand in hers, the gesture, amid the clatter and breeze of the cafeteria, felt hugely inflated: two immense white hands, like the mock-up of a beefburger, advertising love. With the other hand she was mopping up bits of pastrami with the final bite of the roll. "That's a delectable idea," he said, "but I can't. We're taking off Friday for Maine over Labor Day, so I have only one day left at the office. I need this afternoon. It's called Pop Art. It's also called hard-edge."

"So you'll be gone all weekend?" She withdrew her hand to wipe her fingertips, one by one, on a paper napkin. Her face seemed forlorn; her eye shadow had run, making her look theatrically tired.

Harold said, "Yes, and we're staying a few days past the holiday, so I'll miss next week's lunch with you. *Je regrette*."

"Do you?" In parting she told him, this blowzy stacked woman in upside-down herons, with a wave of her shapely swimmer's arm, "Have a *good* time with Marcia," the emphasis insolent. Then they went out of opposite ends of the cafeteria, she toward her maroon car in the Underground Garage, he toward his office on Post Office Square, glad to be released.

The family place in Maine overlooked a mottled blue harbor choked with glinting sails, swinging buoys, and surprising rocks that all jutted from the water at the same angle, testifying to a geological upheaval aeons ago. The largest rocks supported grass and shrubs and were therefore islands. The water was icy-cold and the beaches, far from the endless dunes of Tarbox, were niggardly arcs of shingle and brownish grit strewn with rack. Yet Harold, who visited Tarbox Beach only once or twice a summer, here swam before every breakfast. He was always happy in Maine. He ate the lobster and potato salad his mother set before him and read brittle paperback mysteries and old explorers' accounts in splotched bindings and sailed through the slapping spray and needled his sisters and brothers-in-law and slept soundly, having made love to Marcia like a sailor in from months at sea. She seemed his whore. She crouched and whimpered above him, her nipples teasing his lips. She went down on him purring; she was a minx. This was new, this quality of prostitution, of her frankly servicing him, and taking her own pleasure as a subdivision of his. Her slick firm body was shameless yet did not reveal, as her more virginal intercourse once had done, the inner petals drenched in helpless nectar. She remained slightly tight and dry. He did not wonder from whence this change in her chemistry had been derived, since he found it an improvement: less tact was demanded of him, and less self-control. Perhaps he abused her, for in the second half of their vacation, abruptly beginning on Labor Day night, she refused him. Afterwards she told Frank that suddenly she couldn't stand the confident touch of Harold's all-too-knowing hands. "He seemed a lewd little stranger who acted as if he had bought me." To have him inside her was distasteful: "like food in my mouth I couldn't swallow." Perhaps, in Maine, Marcia had experimented with corruption too successfully. Carrying within her like a contraceptive loop her knowledge of her lover, she had inflicted a stark sensuality upon her husband and then been dismayed by his eager submission to it. She realized she could serve several men in one bed, many men in one night—that this possibility was part of her nature; and she fled into an exclusive love for Frank. Making love to Harold suddenly lost seriousness. What they did with each other's bodies became as trivial as defecation, and it was not until months later, when his form was charged with the tense threat of his leaving her, that the curse of squeamishness was removed from their physical relations.

The little-Smiths returned to Tarbox Thursday night. Harold was conscious of having broken the string of appointments with Janet and doubted, without conscious regret, that there would be any more. Her theory had been wrong and may have never been more than a pretext. Growing up with three sisters had left him with little reverence for female minds. He had seen his sisters turn from comfortably shouting slugging animals into deceptive creatures condemned to assure their survival without overt aggression; their sensibilities were necessarily morbid. Janet was at best a poor reasoner and at worst a paranoid. About to go fat and lose her looks, stuck with a bilious and boring husband, she had turned desperately to a man in no way desperate. Brokers reaped in fair and foul weather, and Marcia had demonstrated a new versatility and violence in her love of him.

He did expect Janet to call him at his office Friday and, when no call came, was annoyed at the extent to which he permitted himself to listen for it. All day, as he rooted through the earthbound stack of waiting mail and obsolete stock fluctuations, a signal from outer space kept tickling his inner ear. He remembered her strange way of wearing cloth, so that it came loose from her body and fluttered in the mind's eye. Perhaps they would see them this weekend. He hoped she wouldn't attempt a scene. Her indignation was so—fluffy. His secretary asked him why he was smiling.

Saturday morning, Marcia drove up to the center of Tarbox to talk to Irene Saltz about the Fair Housing group; Marcia had agreed to be on the education committee, whose chief accomplishment so far had been to give the high-school library a subscription to *Ebony*. "It might take hours, you know how she talks. Can you feed yourself and the children if I don't make it back by noon? There's some pastrami in the freezer you can heat up. The directions are on the package. The important thing is to boil it with the cellophane *on*."

They had been up drinking with the Thornes and the Hanemas the night before, and Harold was content to putter about gingerly, tucking away the props of high summer, folding the collapsed and torn plastic wading pool, coiling hose and detaching the sprinkler. Jonathan rummaged the football from a closet and he and Harold tossed it back and forth until a playmate, pudgy Frankie Appleby, arrived, with his mother. Janet was wearing snug blue denim slacks, an orange-striped boating jersey, and an unbuttoned peach-colored cashmere sweater, hung on her shoulders like a cape. "Where's Marcia?" she asked, when the boys were out of earshot on the lawn.

"In town conferring with Irene. Where's Frank?"

"He told me he was getting a haircut. But he didn't want to take Franklin because he might go to the drugstore and have to talk politics." She snorted, a sardonic equine noise, and stamped her foot. She was caught beneath a bell of radiance; the mistless sharp light of September was spread around them for miles, to the rim of the marshes, to the bungalow-crowded peninsula of East Mather and the ghostly radar dish, cocked toward the north. Janet was hollow-eyed and pale and ripe with nervous agitation, a soft-skinned ripeness careless of itself.

Harold said, "You think he's lying."

"Of course he's lying. Must we stand out here? The sun hurts."

"I thought you were a sun lover. *Une amoureuse du soleil.*"

"Not today. I'm sick at what I have to do."

"To whom?"

"To youm."

Harold opened for her the door that entered from the lawn the lower level of the house, where the children slept and the laundry was done. The laundry room smelled of cement and soap and, this morning, sourly, of unwashed clothes heaped around the dryer. The gardening and carpentry tools and shelves of paint and grass seed and lime were ranged along the other wall, which reeked of gasoline from the power mower. Amid these fragrances Janet took a stance and said, "While you were away in Maine my car broke down, the transmission, so I had to go shopping in Frank's Corvair. I like the Lacetown IGA and on the way back that officious old Lacetown cop, the one with the gold teeth, stopped me for gliding through the stop sign, you know, just this side of the lace-making museum. What made me so mad, I was almost in Tarbox, where they never arrest you. Anyway, in looking through the glove compartment for the registration, underneath all the maps, I found this." She brought from her purse a piece of smudged white paper folded quarto. Harold recognized the indigo rim of Marcia's stationery. The notepaper had been given her as a wedding present, embossed with a monogram of her new initials, by a Southampton aunt, boxes of it; Marcia had laughed, thinking it hideously pretentious, the essence of everything she had married Harold to escape, and used it so seldom, once the thank-you notes were written, that after twelve years it was not used up. Indeed, he wondered if Janet had not somehow stolen a piece, it was so unlike Marcia to write on it. He reached and Janet held the folded paper back from him. "Are you sure you want to read it?"

"Of course."

"It's awfully conclusive."

"Damn you, give it to me."

She yielded it, saying, "You'll hate it."

The handwriting was Marcia's.

Dear Frank, whom I want to call dearest but can't—

Back from the beach, a quick note, for you to have while I'm in Maine. I drove home from our view of Nahant and took the children to the beach and as I lay there the sun baked a smell of you out of my skin and I thought, That's him. I smelled my palms and there you were again and I closed my eyes and pressed myself up against the sun while Irene and Bernadette chattered on and on and the children called from the ocean—there was extraordinary surf today. I feel today left you sad. I'm sorry the phone rang— like icy water being poured over us—and that I teased you to stay longer. I do tease. Forgive me, and believe that I cherish our times together however unsatisfactorily abbreviated, and that you must take me as you can, without worry or self-blame. Love satisfies not only technically. Think of me in Maine, wishing you beside me and happy even in this wish, my "wanton's bird."

In love and haste,
M.

The signature was hers, the angular "M" of three strokes emphatically overstruck; but the body of the letter was written with a flowing smoothness not quite familiar, as if she had been drunk or tranced—it had been years since he had examined her handwriting. He lifted his eyes from the paper, and Janet's face held all the dismay he was still waiting to feel.

"Well," he said, "I've often wondered what women think about while they're sunbathing."

"Oh Harold," she cried, "if you could see your *face*," and she was upon him, had rushed into his unprepared embrace so swiftly he had to pull Marcia's letter free from being crumpled between them. The blue-bordered note fluttered to the cement floor. His senses were forced open, admitting the scouring odors of cement and *Tide*; along the far wall the sunburned lawn flooded the window with golden stitchwork, like a Wyeth. Janet's chest and hips, pillows sodden with grief, pressed him against the enameled edge of the dryer; he was trapped at the confluence of cold tears and hot breath. He kissed her gaping mouth, the rutted powder of her cheeks, the shying trembling bulges of her shut eyes. Her body his height, they dragged each other down, into a heap of unwashed clothes, fluffy ends of shirtsleeves and pajama pants, the hard floor underneath them like a dank bone. Sobbing, she pulled up her sweater and orange-striped jersey and, in a moment of angry straining, uncoupled her bra, so her blue-white breasts came tumbling of their own loose weight, too big to hold, tumbled like laundry from the uplifted basket of herself, nipples buttons, veins seaweed green. He went under. Her cold nails contemplated the tensed sides of his sucking mouth, and sometimes a finger curiously searched out his tongue. Harold opened his eyes to see that the great window giving on the lawn was solidly golden; no child's watching shadow cleft it; voices glinted from a safe distance, the dock. His face was half-pillowed in dirty clothes smelling mildly of his family, of Jonathan and Julia and Henrietta and Marcia. He was lying on ghosts that had innocently sweated. Janet's touch fumbled at his fly and he found the insect teeth of the zipper snug along her side. *Tszzzc:* he tugged and the small neat startled sound awoke them.

"No," she said. "We can't. Not here."

"One more kiss," he begged.

There was a wetness to her mouth, as her breasts overflowed his hands, whose horizon his tongue wished to swim to. She lifted away. "This is crazy." She kneeled on the cement and harnessed her bosom in cups of black lace that reminded him of the doilies in his grandmother's home in Tarrytown. It had been her side of the family that had known Teddy Roosevelt, who had taken Grandpa hunting. "The kids might barge in any second," Janet said, pulling down her jersey. "Marcia might come back."

"Not if she and Frank are copulating out by the dump."

"You think they'd do it to*day*?"

"Why not?" Harold said. "Big reunion, she's back from Maine with the horned monster. *Avec le coucou.* They've set us up for them to be gone for hours. Haircuts. Fair housing."

She adjusted her peach sweater so it again hung like a cape. Standing, she brushed the smudges on the knees of her slacks, from having kneeled. He remained sprawled on the laundry, and she studied him as if he were an acquisition that looks different in the home from in the store. She asked, "You really never suspected her until just now?"

"No. I didn't think she had the guts. When I married her she was a tight little mouse. My little girl is all growed up."

"You're not shocked?"

"I am desolated. But let's talk about you."

She adjusted her clothes with thoughtful firmness. "That was an instinctive thing. Don't count on me for anything."

"But I *do*. I adore you. *Ta poitrine, elle est magnifique.*"

As if the compliment had adhered, she removed a piece of lint from her jersey. "They're pretty saggy now. You should have known me when I was nineteen."

"They're grand. *Please* come upstairs with me." He felt it was correct, in asking her, to stand; and thus their moment of love was reduced to a flattened heap of laundry. Having surrendered all evidence, he was at her mercy.

Janet said, "It's impossible. The children." Lamely her hands sketched multiple considerations.

"Can't we ever get together?"

"What about Marcia and Frank?"

"What about them? Are they hurting us? Can we give them, honestly, what they give each other?"

"Harold, I'm not that cool. I have a very jealous moralistic nature. I want them to be punished."

"We'll all be punished no matter how it goes. That's a rule of life, people are punished. They're punished for being good, they're punished for being bad. A man in our office, been taking vitamin pills all his life, dropped dead in the elevator two weeks ago. He was surrounded by healthy drunks. People are even punished for doing nothing. Nuns get cancer of the uterus because they don't screw. What are you doing to me? I thought you were offering me something."

"I was, I did, but—"

"I accept."

"I felt sorry for you, I don't know what it was. Harold, it's too corrupt. What do we do? Tell them and make a schedule of swap nights?"

"You *do* de-romanticize. Why tell them anything? Let's get something to tell first. Let's see each other and see how it goes. Aren't you curious? You've *made* me want you, you know; it was you who chased me through all those hot Boston streets in your sexy summer dresses. Janet, don't you want me at all for myself? Am I only a way of getting back at Frank?" He glided the back of his hand down the slope of her left breast, then of the right. From the change in the set of her face he saw that this was the way. Touch her, keep touching her. Her breasts are saggy and want to be touched. Don't give her time to doubt, she hates what she knows and doesn't want the time. Don't pause.

She spoke slowly, testing the roof of her mouth with the tip of her tongue and fingering each button on the way down his shirt. "Frank," she told him, "is going to New York the first part of next week."

"*Quelle coïncidence!* Also next week Marcia was talking about going to Symphony Tuesday night and doing Junior League good deeds Wednesday morning and maybe spending the night in town. I think she should be encouraged to, don't you? Poor saint, that long hour in and out."

Janet gazed over his shoulder; her mouth, whose long out-turned upper lip was such a piquant mismatch with her brief plump lower, tightened sadly. "Has it really come to that? They spend whole nights together?"

"Don't bridle," he said, telling himself, *Don't pause.* "It's a luxury, to fall asleep beside the beloved. *Un luxe.* Don't begrudge them." He continued stroking.

"You know," Janet said, "I *like* Marcia. She's always cheerful, always has something to say; she's often got me out of the dumps. What I think I must mind is not Frank so much—we haven't been that great in bed for years, poor guy, let him run —as that *she* would do this to me."

"Did you hear what I said about Tuesday night?"

"I heard."

"Which of us should get the babysitter?"

So that fall Harold and Janet slept together without Frank and Marcia's knowing. Harold at first found his mistress to be slow; his climax, unmanageably urged by the visual wealth of her, was always premature. Not until their sixth time together, an hour stolen in the Applebys' guest room, beneath a shelf of Chinese-temple paraphernalia and scrolls inherited from Frank's father, did Janet come, pulling in her momentous turning Harold virtually loose from his roots, so that he laughed at the end in relief at having survived, having felt himself to be, for a perilous instant, nothing but a single thunderous heartbeat lost in her. He loved looking at her, her nude unity of so many shades of cream and pink and lilac, the soles of her feet yellow and her veins seaweed-green and her belly alabaster. He found an unexpected modesty and elusiveness in her, which nourished his affection, for he enjoyed the role of teacher, of connoisseur. It pleased him to sit beside her and study her body until, weary of cringing, she accepted his gaze serenely as an artist's model. He was instructing her, he felt, in her beauty, which she had grown to disparage, though her bluntness and forwardness had clearly once assumed it, her beauty of fifteen years ago, when she had been the age of his St. Louis mulatto. Harold believed that beauty was what happened between people, was in a sense the trace of what had happened, so he in truth found her, though minutely creased and puckered and sagging, more beautiful than the unused girl whose ruins she thought of herself as inhabiting. Such generosity of perception returned upon himself; as he lay with Janet, lost in praise, Harold felt as if a glowing tumor of eternal life were consuming the cells of his mortality.

The autumn of 1962, the two couples were ecstatically, scandalously close. Frank and Marcia were delighted to be thrown together so often without seeking it. Janet and Harold in private joked about the now transparent stratagems of the other two lovers. These jokes began to leak out into their four-sided conversations. To the Sunday-night ritual of fetched-in food had been added weekday parties, drinks prolonged into scrambled dinners, arranged on the pretext of driving the children (Frankie Jr. and Jonathan detested each other; Catharine was too much of a baby to respond to Julia's and Henrietta's clumsy mothering) back and forth to each other's houses. While the women cooked and fussed and preened around them, Frank and Harold with bottomless boozy searchingness would discuss Shakespeare, history, music, the bitchy market, monopolies, the tacit merger of business and government, the ubiquity of the federal government, Kennedy's fumblings with Cuba and steel, the similarity of JFK's background to their own, the differences, their pasts, their fathers, their resentment and eventual appreciation and final love of their fathers, their dislike and dread of their mothers, sex, their view of the world as a place where foolish work must be done to support fleeting pleasures. "Ripeness is all," Frank would sometimes say when silence would at last unfold its wings above the four spinning heads intoxicated by an intensity of friendship not known since childhood.

Or Janet would say, knowing they expected something outrageous from her, "I don't see what's so very wrong about incest. Why does everybody have a tabu about it? I often wanted to sleep with my brother and I'm sure he wouldn't have minded with me. We used to take baths together and I'd watch him get a hard on. He did something on my belly I thought was urination. Now he runs my father's antibiotic labs in Buffalo, and we can't."

"Sweetheart," Harold said to her, leaning forward above the round leather coffee table in the Applebys' lantern-hung living room, "that's the reason. That's why it's so tabu. Because everybody wants to do it. Except me. I had three sisters, and two of them would have stood there criticizing. *Trois sœurs est trop beaucoup.*"

Marcia sat up sharply, sensing a cause, and said, "I was just reading that the Ptolemies, you know, those pharaoh types, married brothers and sisters right and left and there were no pinheads produced. So I think all this fear of inbreeding is Puritanism." Her earrings scintillated.

"Cats do it," Frank said. "Sibling cats are always fucking."

"But are fucking cats," Janet asked, "always sibling?"

"I once talked," Harold said, determined to quarrel with Marcia, "to a banker who did a lot of financing for the Amish around Lancaster P-A, and he told me they're tiny. *Très, très petits*. They get smaller every generation. There's inbreeding for you, Marcia. They're no bigger than you are."

"She's a nice size," Frank said.

Marcia said to Janet, "I agree with *you*. I have a dreamy younger brother, he played the oboe and was a pacifist, and it would be *so* nice to be married to him and not have to explain all the time why you are the way you are, somebody who knew all the family jokes and would be sensitive to your *phases*. Not like these two clods."

"Vice versa," Harold persisted, "do you know why Americans are getting bigger at such a phenomenal rate? Nutrition doesn't explain it. Exogamy. People marry outside the village. They fly clear across the continent, to Denver, to St. Louis, to marry."

Marcia asked, "Why on earth St. Louis? Denver I can see."

Harold continued, flushing at his slip (neither of the women knew of the mulatto, but Frank did), "The genes are fresh. It's cross-fertilization. So the advice 'Love thy neighbor' is terrible advice, biologically. Like so much of that Man's advice."

"He said love, He didn't say lay your neighbor," Janet said.

"I want my dreamy brother," Marcia said, pouring herself some more bourbon and twitteringly pretending to cry.

"Ripeness is all," Frank said, after a silence.

Or else they would sit around the rectangular tesselated coffee table in the little-Smiths' living room with its concealed rheostated lighting and watch Harold, bare-handed, gesticulating, conduct sides of Wagner's *Tristan*, or Mozart's *Magic Flute*, or Britten's *War Requiem*. Frank Appleby liked only baroque music and would sit stupefied, his eyeballs reddening and his aching belly protruding, while Harold, whirling like a Japanese traffic cop, plucked the *ting* of a triangle from the rear of the orchestra or with giant motions of embrace signaled in heaving oceans of strings. Janet hypnotically watched Harold do this and Marcia watched Janet curiously. What could she be seeing in this manic performance? How could a woman who nightly shared Frank's bed be even faintly amused by Harold's pathetic wish-fulfillment? One night, when the Applebys had gone, she asked Harold, "Are you sleeping with Janet?"

"Why? Are you sleeping with Frank?"

"Of course not."

"In that case, I'm not sleeping with Janet."

She tried a new tack. "Aren't you awfully tired of the Applebys? What ever happened to our other friends?"

"The big-Smiths moved to Newton."

"They were never our friends. I mean the Thornes and the Guerins and the Saltzes and the Gallaghers and the Hanemas. You know what Georgene told me the other day? She said Matt has had a nibble on the Robinson place, that Angela had wanted. A couple from Cambridge."

"How does Georgene come by all her information? She's become a real expert on the Hanemas. *Un spécialiste vrai.*"

"Don't you think Freddy and Angela are fond of each other?"

"*Tu es comique,*" Harold said. "Angela will be the last lady in town to fall. Next to yourself, of course."

"You think Georgene has Piet?"

"Well. She has a very indulgent smile on her face when she looks at him."

"You mean like Janet has when she looks at you?"

"*Tu es trop comique.* She's twice my size."

"Oh, you have big—"

"Parts?"

"Ideas of yourself, I was going to say."

The other couples began to call them the Applesmiths. Angela Hanema, who never dreamed, dreamed she went to the Applebys' house carrying a cake. On the front porch, with its six-sided stained-glass welcoming light, she realized she couldn't get in the front door because the house was full of wedding invitations. Marcia little-Smith came around the side of the house, in shorts and swinging a red croquet mallet, and said, "It's all right, my dear, we're going to be very happy." Then they were all, a crowd of them, walking along a country path, in some ways the path down to the dock, Angela still carrying the cake on upraised palms before her, and she said to Frank Appleby, "But can you get the insurance policies straightened out?" which was strange, because in waking life Angela never gave a thought to insurance. With a gargantuan wink he assured her, "I'm floating a bond issue," and that was all she could remember, except that both sides of the path were heavily banked with violets, hyacinth, and little blue lilies.

She had coffee with Georgene the next morning after nursery school, and, feeling uneasy with Georgene lately, in nervousness told her the dream. Georgene told Bea and Irene, while Piet, who had heard the dream at breakfast, was telling Matt Gallagher at the office. So Bernadette Ong heard the dream from two directions, from Irene at a Fair Housing executive meeting and from Terry Gallagher after a rehearsal of the Tarbox–North Mather–Lacetown Choral Society; the thirsty singers commonly went back to the Ongs afterwards for a beer.

But it was Bea, Bea whose malice was inseparable from her flirtatiousness, in turn inseparable from her sterility and her tipsiness, Bea who told Marcia. Marcia was puzzled and not amused. She did not for a moment believe that Janet and Harold were sleeping together. She did not think Harold was up to it; a certain awe of Janet, as of all big women, had been heightened by falling in love with this woman's husband. She had not suspected that from outside the couples might appear equal in complicity. She was shocked, frightened. She told Harold; he laughed. They told the Applebys together, and it was Janet who laughed, Frank who showed annoyance. "Why can't people mind their own dirty business?"

"Instead of our dirty business?" Harold said gaily, the double tip of his nose lifted, Marcia thought, like a bee's behind.

"Our language!" she said, nettled.

"Come on, *mon petit chou*," he said to her, "Angela can't help what she dreams. She's the most sublimated woman we know. Bea can't help it that she had to tease you with it. Her husband beats her, she can't have children, she has to make her mark somehow."

Janet was in a lazy mood. "She must ask to be beaten," she said. "She picked Roger so he must have been what she wanted."

"But that's true of all of us," Harold said. "*Tout le monde.* We get what we unconsciously want."

Marcia protested, "But they must think we do *every*thing, which seems to me so sick of *them*, that they can't imagine simple friendship."

"It *is* hard to imagine," Harold said, wondering if to smile would be too much. They were all on the verge. He looked at Janet, sleepily leaning with a cigarette in the Applebys' yellow wing chair, her silk blouse veined by its shimmer and her skirt negligently exposing her stocking-tops and fasteners and bland known flesh, and thought how easy, how right, it would be to take her upstairs now, while these other two cleared away the glasses and went to their own bed.

Frank said, "They're starved. Their marriages have gone stale and anything that tickles their nose they think is champagne. We enjoy relaxing with each other and musn't let them make us self-conscious about it." He cleared his throat to quote. "The mutable, rank-scented many."

This speech conjured a malicious night all about them. Marcia's eyes, watching Frank, were dark, dark like stars too dense to let light escape, and she felt her being as a pit formed to receive this blood-slow soft-handed man whose own speech, more and more as she was his mistress, was acquiring Shakespearian color and dignity. *Tickles their nose is champagne.* He had called them back from the verge. The little-Smiths left at one-thirty and drove through the town whose burning lights, bared in November, seemed to be gossiping about them. From their bedroom window the marsh, rutted and tufted along the ebbed canals, appeared a surface of the moon and the onlooking moon an earth entire in space. Restless, apologetic, they made love, while miles away across the leafless town the other couple, also naked, mirrored them.

Full confession waited until winter. Snow fell early in New Hampshire, and during Christmas vacation the Hanemas, the Applebys, the Thornes, the Gallaghers, and the little-Smiths went north to ski with their older children. The lodge bulletin board was tacked thick with pictures of itself in summer, of canoes and couples pitching quoits and porch rails draped with wet bathing suits. Now packed snow squeaked on the porch steps, a sign forbade ski boots in the dining hall, the dinner was pea soup and baked ham and deep-dish apple pie, the children afterwards thumped and raced in the long hall upstairs, between the girls' bunk room and the boys', and downstairs their parents basked by the fireplace in the afterglow of exercise. Whiskey hurried to replace the calories fresh air had burned from their bodies. Georgene methodically turned the pages of *Ski*. Freddy murmured on the sofa to Janet, who looked discontented. Frank played Concentration with his son and Jonathan little-Smith, and was losing, because he was concentrating upon a rotating inner discomfort, perhaps the ham, which had had a thick raisin sauce. Gaily rattling ice cubes, Harold was mixing a drink for Angela, whose fine complexion had acquired on the bitter slopes an unearthly glow, had reached an altitude beyond decay; she looked more twenty-two than thirty-four. Marcia was listening to Matt Gallagher explain the Vatican's likely verdict, now that the ecumenical council was adjourned, on artificial birth control: "Nix. They won't give us sex, but they may give us meat on Fridays." Marcia nodded understandingly—having a lover deepened her understanding of everything, even of Matt Gallagher's adherence to the letter of an unloving church— and glanced toward Terry. Terry, sitting cross-legged on the floor in black stretch pants, carefully picked through a chord sequence on her lute; it was a gourd-shaped, sumptuous instrument, whose eight strings produced a threadbare distant tone. Matt had bought it for her for Christmas, in line with the policy of conspicuous consumption that had led to the Mercedes, and perhaps with a more symbolic intent, for its blond lustre and inlaid elegance seemed sacramental, like their marriage. Piet lay beside her on the rug gazing at the taut cloth of her crotch. The seam had lost one stitch. Conscious of Georgene sulking at his back, he rolled over and did a bicycling exercise in air, wondering if with Catholics it was different, remembering his long-ago love for Terry, unconsummated, when he and Matt were newly partners. Whitney and Martha Thorne, Ruth Hanema, Tommy Gallagher with his Gainsborough fragility, and Julia Smith in raven pigtails watched a World War II movie starring Brian Donlevy. The channel, from Manchester, was weakly received. The game of Concentration broke up. Frank needed more bourbon to soothe his stomach. In twos and threes the children were led upstairs or out to the gas-heated cottages beneath the bone-white birches. A bridge game among strangers beside the fireplace broke up. Georgene Thorne, a tidy woman with feather-cut graying hair and a boyish Donatello profile, nodded while leafing through *House & Garden* and followed her children out to their cabin to sleep. Freddy blew her a smirking kiss. Walking down the squeaking path alone, she thought angrily of Piet—his flirting, his acrobatics—yet knew it was in the bargain, she had got what she wanted. Her breath was white in the black air. The unseen lake gave a groan and crack, freezing harder. The black birch twigs rattled. Harold and Marcia tried to organize word games—Botticelli, Ghosts —but everyone was too suffused with physical sensations to play. The television set, unwatched, excited itself with eleven-o'clock news about UN military action in the Katanga province of the Congo; and was switched off. Piet begged Terry Gallagher to give them a concert, and so she, watching as if from beyond her own will her white bewitched fingers assume each position on the frets, played the one melody she had mastered, "Greensleeves." They tried to sing with her but had forgotten the words. Her head was tilted; her long black hair fell straight from one side. She finished; Matt, with a military swiftness, stood; and the Gallaghers went outdoors to their cabin. In the momentary opening of the door, all heard a snowplow scraping along the upper road. High in a dusty corner a cuckoo clock, late, sounded eleven. Angela, stately, her fair cheeks flaming, now stood, and Piet, muscled like a loose-skinned dog that loves to be scratched, followed her upstairs to their room. This left the Applesmiths and Freddy Thorne.

The elderly young couple that ran the lodge came in from doing a mountain of dinner dishes and thriftily turned off all the lights but one and separated the fireplace logs so that the fire would die. Their smiles of good will as they faced their guests were wretchedly enfeebled by contempt. "Good night now."

"Good night."

"Night."

"*Bonne nuit.*"

Yet for an hour more, in semidarkness and the growing cold, Freddy held forth, unable to let go of a beauty he had felt, of a goodness the couples created simply by assembling. "You're all such beautiful women. Marcia, why do you laugh? Jesus Christ, every time I try to tell people something nice to their face they laugh. People hate love. It threatens them. It's like tooth decay, it smells and it hurts. I'm the only man alive it doesn't threaten, I wade right in with pick and mirror. I love you, all of you, men, women, neurotic children, crippled dogs, mangy cats, cockroaches. People are the only thing people have left since God packed up. By people I mean sex. Fucking. Hip, hip, hooray. Frank, do you believe in the difference between tragedy and comedy? Tell me, for fuck's sweet sake. This is a serious question."

Frank said carefully, rumbling from the slumped position that seemed to ease his stomach, "I believe in it as a formal distinction Shakespeare believed in. I wouldn't make anything absolute of it."

"Frankfurt, that is beautiful. That's just where any medium intelligent man of the world would come down. That's where you and I differ. Because I do. I believe there are tragic things and comic things. The trouble is, damn near everything, from the yellow stars on in to the yummy little saprophytes subdividing inside your mouth, are tragic. Now look at that fire our penny-pinching hosts broke up to save a nickel. Tragic. Listen to the wind. Very tragic. OK, so what's not tragic? In the western world there are only two comical things: the Christian church and naked women. We don't have Lenin so that's it. Everything else tells us we're dead. Think about it; think about those two boobies bounding up and down. Makes you want to laugh, doesn't it? Smile at least? Think of poor Marilyn Moronrow; her only good pictures were comedies, for Chrissake."

"And the Christian church?" Marcia asked, glancing sideways at Frank as if nervously to gauge his pain.

"Christ, I'd love to believe it," Freddy said. "Any of it. Just the littlest bit of it. Just one lousy barrel of water turned into wine. Just half a barrel. A quart. I'll even settle for a pint."

"Go ahead," Janet told him, lazily. "Believe it."

"I *can't*. Marcia, stop checking on Frank. He's hyperalgesic, he'll live. Come on, this is a real gut talk. This is what people are for. The great game of truth. Take you and that fuzzy big-throated purply sweater; you're terrific. You look like a tinted poodle, all nerves and toenails, a *champeen*, for Chrissake. If your grandfather hadn't been the Bishop of East Egg you'd have made a terrific whore. Janet, you're a funny case. Sometimes you have it, right up the alley, all ten pins, and other times you just miss. Something pruney happens around your mouth. Tonight, you're really on. You're sore as hell about some silly thing, maybe Harold's snubbing you, maybe you have the red flag out, but you're right there. You're not always right there. Where would you rather be? Jesus, you're in every drugstore, and people tell me it's a hell of a good laxative, though I've never needed one myself, frankly."

"We've diversified," Janet told him. "We do a lot with antibiotics now. Anyway it wasn't a laxative, it was mineral oil."

"More power to it. You've lost some weight, that's a shrewd move. For a while there you had something bunchy happening under your chin. You know, honey, you're a fantastic piece—I say this as a disinterested party, girl to girl—and you don't have to wear all those flashy clothes to prove anything. Just you, fat or skinny, Janet Applesauce, that's all we want for dessert; we *love* you, stop worrying. As I say, you're all gorgeous women. It killed me tonight, it really tumefied me, seeing old Terry Tightcunt sitting there with her legs spread and her hair down jerking off that poor melon. Have you ever noticed her mouth? It's enormous. Her tongue is as big as a bed. Every time I work on her molars I want to curl up in there and go to sleep."

"Freddy, you're drunk," Marcia said.

"Let him alone, I like it," Harold said. "*Je l'aime*. Freddy's aria."

"Oh God," Frank said, "that men should put an enemy in their mouths to steal away their brains."

Janet said, "Freddy, enough of us. Tell us about Angela and Georgene."

"Beautiful girls. Beautiful. I'm not kidding. You all knock Angela—"

"We *don't*," Marcia protested.

"You all knock that saint, but she has absolutely the most eloquent ass I've ever seen except on an ostrich."

"Giraffes have beautiful behinds," Harold said.

"Out of your class, I would think," Frank told him.

Harold turned, nose upturned, and said, "You hippopotamus. You ox."

Janet said, "Boys."

Freddy went on, "And *didn't* she look lovely tonight? Angela."

Harold, who had a nasal bass voice of which he was proud, imitated the singing of an aria: "And didn't she, di-hi-hidn't she, look lovely, luh-hu-hovilee tonight. A-aaaaangela, lala!"

Freddy appealed to the two women. "Tell me straight. You're women. You have nice clear Lesbian eyes. Didn't she look about twenty, a virginal twenty, those eyes full of sky, that fantastic skin all rosy, Jesus. I mean, you're both beauties, I'm telling you straight, but she's my ideal. I idolize her. I look at that ass and I think Heaven. Twenty miles of bluebirds and strawberry whip."

The two couples laughed in astonishment. Freddy blinked for orientation; the whiskey in his glass had magically replenished itself. Marcia said, "Freddy, and Georgene? You haven't mentioned your wife."

"A healthy child," Freddy said. "She cooks well, she plays tennis well. In bed"—he squinted estimatingly and wiggle-waggled his hand—"so-so. *Comme ci comme ça.* I like it to be long, to take forever, have a little wine, have some more wine, fool around, try it on backwards, you know, let it be a *human* thing. She comes too quick. She comes so she can get on with the housework. I gave her the *Kama Sutra* for Christmas and she wouldn't even look at the pictures. The bitch won't blow unless she's really looped. What did the Bard say? To fuck is human; to be blown, divine."

Freddy, as usual, had gone beyond all bounds of order; the Smiths and Applebys made restless motions of escape. Janet stood and tossed the contents of her ashtray into the smoldering fireplace. Frank collected the cards scattered by Concentration. Harold rested his ankles on the sofa arm and elaborately feigned sleep. Only Marcia, twiddling one of her earrings, retained an appearance of interest.

Freddy was staring at the far high corner of the lodge, where above the cuckoo clock hung a dusty mass of cobwebs with the spectral air of an inverted reflection in water. He said, "I've seen the light. You know why we're all put here on earth?"

From the depths of his spurious sleep, Harold asked, "Why?"

"It just came to me. A vision. We're all put here to *humanize* each other."

"Freddy, you're so stupid," Marcia said, "but you *do* care, don't you? That *is* your charm. You care."

"We're a subversive cell," Freddy went on. "Like in the catacombs. Only they were trying to break out of hedonism. We're trying to break back into it. It's not easy."

Janet giggled and put her hand across Frank's lips before they could pronounce, as they were going to, "Ripeness is all."

Then fatigue and defeat were among them unannounced. The room was cold. Silence stood sentry. Freddy rose sluggishly, said, "See you on the slopes," and took himself outdoors to his cabin. The black lake beyond the chalky birches seemed an open mouth waiting for attention. The liquorish sweat of his chest froze into a carapace; his bare scalp contracted. He hastened along the squeaking path to Georgene, her forgiveness a dismissal.

Still the two couples were slow to go upstairs. Freddy's sad lewdness had stirred them. Marcia and Janet rotated, picking up glasses and aligning magazines, and sat down again. Frank cleared his throat; his eyes burned red. Harold crossed and recrossed his legs, dartlike in stretch pants, and said, as if on Frank's behalf, "Freddy is very sick. *Très malade.*" Behind the fire screen the embers of the parted logs formed a constellation that seemed to be receding. The silence grew adhesive, impossible. Marcia pushed herself up from the sofa, and Janet, moving in her peach sweater and white slacks like a dancer intently gliding out of the wings toward her initial spring and pirouette, followed her to the stairs, and up. Both couples had rooms upstairs in the lodge. Frank and Harold listened below to the gush and shudder of activated plumbing, and switched off the remaining light. Again Frank cleared his throat, but said nothing.

In the upstairs hall, with its row of sleeping doors, Harold felt his arm touched. He had been expecting it. Frank whispered, mortified and hoarse, "Do you think we have the right rooms?"

Harold quickly said, "We're in nine, you're in eleven."

"I mean, do you think you and I should switch?"

From the elevation of his superior knowledge, Harold was tempted to pity this clumsy man groveling in lust. Daintily he considered, and proposed: "Shouldn't the ladies be consulted? I doubt if they'll concur."

A single bulb burned in the hallway and by this all-night light Frank's forward-thrust head looked loaded to bursting as he tried not to blurt. He wetly whispered, "It'll be all right.

Janet's often said she's attracted to you. Take her. My blessing. What the hell. Let copulation thrive."

Harold feigned arch bemusement. "And Marcia? Does she want you?"

The other man nodded miserably, hastily. "It'll be all right."

The doors each of Rooms 9 and 11 were open a crack.

Harold remembered Janet's naked arms swinging moist along the gritty mica-starred streets of summer Boston, and could not resist tormenting his rival a moment longer. "Uh —do you and Janet work this"—he rotated his hands so the fingers and thumb reversed positions in air—"often?"

"Never. Never before. Come on, yes or no. Don't make a production of it. I'm sleepy and my stomach hurts."

In Frank's inflection there was a rising note of the bigger man whom Harold feared. There was also this, that from his desk at the bank Frank had thrown Harold, as broker, a wealth of commissions. The deposit of secrets Harold held in his head felt tenuous, no longer negotiable. Frank's big horned head was down. The two doors waited ajar. Behind one lay Marcia, with whom stretched side by side he shared every weary night; behind the other, Janet, whose body was a casket of perfume. He saw that the deceit he had worked with her would now lose all value. But there is always a time to sell; the trick of the market is to know when. Janet waited like a stack of certain profit. He carefully shrugged. "Why not? *Pourquoi non?* I'd love to. But be gentle." This last was strange to add, but here in the fragile wallboard and linoleum hall he had felt, as Frank's lifted head released a blast of muggy breath, the man's rank heaviness. Harold feared that his nervous lithe wife could not support such a burden; then remembered that she had sought it many times. The sight of Frank—his donkeyish outcurved teeth, his eyeballs packed with red fuses—became an affront; Harold turned to the door of Room 11, and touched it, and it swung open as if the darkness were expectant.

The latch clicked. A light from beyond the snow-heaped porch roof broke along the walls confusedly. Janet sat up in bed and her words, monosyllabic, seemed matches struck in a perilous inner space. "You. Why? Why now? Harold, it's wrong!"

He groped to the bed and sat on the edge and discovered she was wearing a sweater over her nightgown. "It was your husband's idea. I merely gave in. They'll think this is our first time."

"But now they'll *know*. They'll watch us. Don't you *see*? You should have acted shocked and said you wouldn't dream of any such thing. Frank knows when he's drunk, he wouldn't have minded. I'm sure it's what he expected. Oh God, Harold." She huddled tight against him sexlessly. His arms encircled her rounded back, sweatered like an invalid's.

"But I wanted you, Janet."

"But you can have me anytime."

"No, not anytime. When else could I be with you all night?"

"But how can you enjoy it, with those two a door away?"

"They're not hurting me. I like them both. Let them have what happiness they can."

"I can't stand it. I'm not as cool as you are, Harold. I'm going right in there and break it up."

"No."

"Don't take that bossy tone. Don't try to be my father. I'm all agitated."

"Just lie in my arms. We don't have to make love. Just lie in my arms and go to sleep."

"Don't you feel it? It's so *wrong*. Now we're really corrupt. All of us."

He lay down beside her, on top of the covers. The snow at the window had brightened. "Do you think it matters," he asked, "on the moon?"

"Somehow," Janet said, "it's *her*. She'll have this on me now."

"Marcia? No more than you have on her."

"But she completed college and I didn't."

He laughed in surprise. "I see. She completed college, therefore she knows more about erotic technique than you, therefore she's getting more out of Frank than you could get out of me. Right now she's doing the Fish Bite, followed by the astraddle position as recommended by the Bryn Mawr hygiene department."

Janet put her arms back beneath the covers and sniffed. "That's not it at all. But it seems to be what *you* think."

He supposed that, in his irritation at her lack of ardor, he had hopelessly offended her. All lost, he sighed through his nose.

After a pause she asked him, in the diffident voice of a sales-girl faced with an indecisive customer, "Why don't you get under the covers?"

So he did then travel through a palace of cloth and slid-ing stairways toward the casket of perfume that she spilled upon him from a dozen angles, all radiant. The radiator by the washstand purred in its seven parallel throats. She was, Janet, opaque, pale, powdery, heavy, sweet, cuffing, motherly; she roughly bid him rest with his narrow face between her breasts, his tongue outthrust like a paralyzed lizard's.

While for Frank, a space away, Marcia was transparent, glid-ing, elusive, one with the shadows of the room; he enlarged, enlarged until she vanished quite and the darkness was solid with himself, then receded, admitting her silvery breathless voice saying lightly, "How lovely. Oh. Fuck. How lovely. Fuck. Fuck."

Between the couples, in Room 10, Piet and Angela Hanema slept back to back, oblivious, Piet dreaming of mortised ten-ons unpleasantly confused with the interlocking leap and slide and dipped shoulder of a ski lesson he had had that afternoon, Angela dreaming of nothing, skippingly, of children without names, of snow falling in a mountainous place where she knew she had never been, of a great lion-legged table supporting an empty but perfect blue vase of *mei ping* form—dreams when she awoke she would not remember.

Harold would not forget the cool grandeur of Janet that night, or the crescent of light on her fat shoulders above him, or the graciousness of her submission to the long work of his second climax. Fatigue, and the distracting question posed by their open privacy, made him uncharacteristically slow. She lay beneath him with the passiveness of the slaughtered, her throat elongated, her shoulders in shadow.

"I'm sorry," he said. "I'm taking forever."

"It's all right. I like it."

"Shall I stop?"

"Oh no. No."

The mournful tranquillity of her voice so moved him he attained the edge, fell from suspense, and released her from bondage. She turned and slept. As if he and she were on a seesaw, her dead weight lifted him into insomnia. The snow beyond the window was insistently brilliant, a piece of over-exposed film. The pillow supporting her tangled hair seemed a second snow. Each time Harold closed his eyes he saw again the mountainside, the stunted ice-burdened pines at the top beside the lift shed, the troughs of ice, the slewing powder, the moguls packed by many turnings; and felt tense effort twitch his legs. His shins ached. Music, translucent sheets of it as in Debussy, was trying to break through to him, in the gaps between her breaths. He turned and fitted his body to hers. With a child's voice she sighed, "Oh no, lover, not again."

Dozing, he woke toward dawn. A footstep snapped in the hall. Marcia. His forsaken wife, abused and near madness, was seeking him. Janet's unfamiliar corpulence curled unconscious beside him, making him sweat. Like a spy unsticking an enve-lope, he removed himself carefully from her bed. The fabric of the night itself was showing fragility, crumbling into the brown particles of distinct visual detail—dashes of dirt embedded in the floorcracks, his own narrow feet chafed across the instep by his ski boots, Janet's silk glove liners drying on the radiator like tiny octopi, a jar of hand lotion on her bare pine bureau cupping moonglow. Of the clothes he had entered this room in, he took time to put only his pants and sweater back on. The hall creaked again, nearer this door. He lightly pulled it open, his face a mask of tenderness.

There was Frank, coming from the lavatory, bug-eyed and mottled beneath the all-night bulb. At the sight of Harold his eyes underwent a painful metamorphosis, becoming evasive and yet defiant and yet ashamed and defenseless in sickness.

Harold whispered, "What's up?"

"Stomach. Too much booze."

"Et ma femme? Dort-elle?"

"Like a rock. How about Jan-Jan?"

"La même."

Frank pondered, revolving his condition through his mind. "It's like a ball of tar in there I can't break up. I finally threw up. It feels better. Maybe I'm nervous."

"Do you want to go back to your own room?"

"I suppose we should. The kids will soon be up and might come in."

"Good night, sweet prince. May flights of angels, et cetera."

"Thanks. See you on the slopes."

"*Oui*. See you on the slopes." Harold tried to think of the French for "slopes," couldn't, and laughed as if an irony had been belatedly uncloaked.

Janet had been stirred awake by Harold's leaving and the whispering in the hall and knew it was Frank returning to her bed, though she feigned sleep. Perhaps in this moment began her irritated certainty of being wronged. Janet was a woman in whom early beauty had bred high expectations. Their disappointment brought with it a soured idealism, an idealism capable only of finding the world faulty. She decided that with Harold's acquiescence in the end of deception she had been betrayed. Marcia had entered adultery freely whereas Janet had thrown herself upon Harold to assuage their despair. A cynical ménage cheated her of such justification. Each liaison with Harold had been an installment of vengeance; a pattern of justice was being traced in the dark. But her affair had proved to be not a revenge but a convenience, and Janet's idealism asked of life more than a rectangular administration of reassurance and sex. Deeper than her moral reservations lurked the suspicion that Marcia was more sensual than she, better in bed. Janet did not see why she should submit to two inadequate and annoying men so that Marcia could respectably be a nymphomaniac. The woman, whom Janet had always considered dry and dowdy, was really diabolical, and it irked Janet to know that, in the likely event of a scandal, she would get all the sympathy, and Janet all the blame.

The inadequacy and annoyingness of the men emerged as soon as Janet made resistance. They were sitting, the weekend after their swap, in the Applebys' living room, with its round leather coffee table and its shelves of inherited uniform sets: red Balzac, ochre Scott, D'Annunzio in gold-stamped white calfskin, Mann in the black Knopf editions, green Shaw by Dodd, Mead. This wall of books, never touched, absorbed their smoke and conversation. Snow, the first storm to visit Tarbox that winter, was sealing them in. Frank had made a hot rum punch and they were drunk. He said at midnight, "Let's go upstairs."

"No," Janet said.

"I don't mean with *me*," Frank explained. "You can have *him*."

"I find both of you distinctly resistible."

"Janet!" Harold said, not so surprised, since she had slept with him Wednesday and afterwards told him her feelings.

"I think it's too corrupt," she said. "Don't you, Marcia?"

Marcia pinched her left earring, as if it had chimed. "Not if we all respect each other."

"I'm sorry," Janet said. "I can't respect any of you. I especially can't respect a woman who has to have so many men."

"Only two," Frank protested.

"I'm sorry, Marcia. I honestly think you should put yourself in the hands of a doctor."

"That'll make *three* men," Harold said. He was inwardly betting that Janet's resistance was a kind of mist that seemed solid from a distance but proved negotiable as you moved into it: like golf in the fog.

"You're suggesting I should be *fixed*?" Marcia asked.

"I don't mean a physical doctor, I mean a therapist. An analyst. Frank has told me everything about your affair and I think the way you went after him was scarcely normal. I'm not speaking as the injured wife, I'd say the same if it was any man. In fact it probably could have *been* any man."

"Darling Janet," Marcia said, "I love your concern. But I didn't go after Frank. We came together because you were making him miserable. You were giving him an ulcer."

"His stomach has gotten ten times worse in these last months."

"So, I imagine, have you. From Harold's description of your strip-tease in the laundry room I'm amazed to discover you're so fastidious."

Janet turned to Harold. "You told her?"

He shrugged and touched his left earlobe. "She told *me* everything. I didn't want her to feel guilty."

Janet began to cry, stonily, without any concessive motions of her arms or hands.

Marcia lit a cigarette and stared at the other woman dry-eyed.

"Don't you worry," she said. "I wouldn't take Frank if you begged me. Tonight or any night. I want you to have him until you've ground him down to nothing. I've been keeping him afloat for half a year and frankly I'm tired to death of it. The *last* thing I expect is thanks from *you*."

Janet said nothing and both men pleaded for her.

"It was the bear market gave me the ulcer," Frank said, "not anything Jan-Jan did."

"She's *nice* in bed," Harold told his wife. "*Belle en lit.*"

Marcia told Frank, "Fuck her, then. Take her upstairs and fuck her and don't come creeping to me with your third-rate Shakespeare bits. I'm sick to tears of these big dumb women that don't do a damn thing except let the world lick their lovely derrières. Divorce me," she said to Harold. "Divorce me and marry her if she has such hot tits. Let me not to the blah blah blah admit impediments, isn't that it, Frank? This is the end. You, me, the whole rotten works." She stood, gauging the dismay in the faces suddenly beneath her.

"Marcia," Harold said. "Stop bullying Janet with your foul language."

"She's not bullying me," Janet said. "I agree with her."

"I'll heat up the punch," Frank said. "Or would anybody like a beer?"

"Frank, you're a prince," Harold said. "But if we're not going to bed I really could use the sleep. We have one of the Mills girls babysitting and she's having midyears at B.U."

Frank said, "That Exeter friend of mine who's buying the Robinson place teaches at B.U."

"I hear he's handsome," Janet said.

Marcia, feeling her scene slide away from her, said, "I can't stand any of you and I hate this dreary house." She went to the front hall for her coat, which was mousy and old. Harold followed, knowing that she had brought a diaphragm in her purse and wondering if now she would use it at home. But the little-Smiths had waited too long to leave and both the Applebys, first Frank and then Janet too, had to wade through the snow and push Harold's Porsche to get it started down the driveway. The taillights slithered back and forth insolently in escaping and Janet said, "I hope that's the last we ever see of them. They're little and, I know they can't help it, they're poisonous.

Isn't it a lovely night, Frank? I don't think I've noticed the weather once since we got involved with those people." In the spaces between the trees, dimly lit by their distant porchlight, flakes were hurrying to touch them, lightly, lightly, dying as they did. But in the hot front hall, as she bent over to tug off her galoshes, Frank patted her and she straightened, fierce, and said to him, "Don't you *dare* touch me. It's her you want. You go to her. Just go. *Go.*"

Janet wished powerfully not to be frigid. All her informal education, from Disney's *Snow White* to last week's *Life*, had taught her to place the highest value on love. Nothing but a kiss undid the wicked apple. We move from birth to death amid a crowd of others and the name of the parade is love. However unideal it was, she dreaded being left behind. Hence she could not stop flirting, could not stop reaching out, though something distrustful within her, a bitterness like a residue from her father's medicinal factory, had to be circumvented by each motion of her heart. Liquor aided the maneuver.

For some weeks the Applebys and little-Smiths stayed apart. Marcia and Janet each let it be known there had been a fight. The other couples tactfully did not invite them to parties together. When Harold phoned Janet she said, "I'm sorry, Harold, I loved being with you, person to person, man and woman, you really know how to make a woman feel it. But I think doing it with couples is terribly messy, and I'll have to hang up the next time you call. Think of the children if of nobody else." When Frank called Marcia, she said, "I do want to be with you, Frank, just *with* you, anywhere. I want it worse than any man can imagine. But I'm not, simply *not*, going to give Janet any more ammunition. If I felt you loved me that would be one thing; but I realized that night in the lodge when you left my bed how committed you still are to her, and I must think now about protecting myself. She'd destroy me if she could. I don't mean to be melodramatic; that's her style, not mine. I'm not saying good-bye to you. When you and she get yourselves straightened out, I'd *adore* to see you again. You're the love of my life, unfortunately." Frank could not escape the impression that she was asking him to get a divorce. Meanwhile, our advisory capacity in Vietnam was beginning to stink and the market was frightened, frightened yet excited by the chance of expanding war. Basically business was uneasy with Kennedy; there was something unconvincing about him.

One January Saturday all the Tarbox couples went into Boston for dinner at the Athens Olympia and to see a hockey game: Bruins vs. Red Wings. Both the little-Smiths and Applebys declined to go, under the mistaken impression that the other couple was going. This left them alone in Tarbox together, and it naturally followed that since Jonathan and Frank Jr. had Saturday ski lessons together at the hill in East Mather, under the radar station, the fathers arrange for Frank Sr. to bring them both back at four-thirty; and that, once at the little-Smiths, he accept the offer of a drink, and then another, and then at six, egged on by the giggling little-Smiths, he call Janet at home with the suggestion that she get a sitter and pick up some pizza and come on down. For much of what they took to be morality proved to be merely consciousness of the other couples watching them.

Janet called back in ten minutes saying she couldn't find a sitter; the hockey expedition had taken them all. Harold got on the phone and told her to bring Catharine with her and they would put her to sleep on the cot in Henrietta's room.

Holding the bulky baby in one arm and a steaming paper bag in the other, Janet arrived at seven-thirty. She wore a knee-length mink coat, a coat she had owned since early marriage but that, pretentious and even comical in Tarbox, usually hung idle in a mothproofed bag. Beneath the coat, she was wonderfully dressed: in a poppy-orange silk blouse and blue jeans shrunk and splotch-bleached like a teen-ager's and white calf-length boots she pulled off to reveal bare feet. Seeing her pose thus clothed in his long living room (on the shaggy cerulean rug her toes were rosy from the cold, the insteps and sides of her feet lilac white, her heels and the joints of her toes dusted with pollen), Harold felt his entire frame relax and sweeten. Even Marcia was moved, to think her husband had once possessed such a splendid mistress. Frank stepped toward her solicitously, as if toward an invalid, or a genie that might disappear.

From seven to eight they drank. Between eight and nine they put the children to bed. Franklin Jr., secretly afraid he would wet the sheets, refused to sleep in the same bed with scornful Jonathan. They gave him instead the cot in Henrietta's room.

This left Catharine Appleby, her cheeks as red as permeated wineskins, to go into the great high square sacred marital bed, on top of a rubber sheet. Janet lay down and crooned to the baby while Marcia put the cooled-off pizzas in the oven. Harold read Frankie Junior a Little Golden Book entitled *Minerals*, while Frank watched Jonathan contemptuously settle himself under the covers with a Junior Detective Novel entitled *The Unwanted Visitor*. From nine to ten the grown-ups ate, from ten to eleven they talked, from eleven to midnight they danced. Harold put an old Ella record on their hi-fi and to the tunes of "These Foolish Things" and "You're the Top" and "I've Been Around the World" the pair of couples rotated, Harold and Janet sliding smoothly around the edges, Frank and Marcia holding to the center of the derugged floor. The sliding glass doors giving on the view of the marsh doubled their images, so that a symmetrical party seemed in progress, the two linked couples approaching and withdrawing from two others like blots on a folded paper, or like visitors to a violet aquarium who, seeing no fish, move closer to the glass and discover the watery shadows of women and men.

Marcia, almost motionless, watched Harold's hand confidently cup Janet's derrière as he waltzed her from corner to corner; Janet, whirling, glimpsed Marcia bending closer into Frank's static embrace as he rumbled at her ear. His face was glossy, suffused with drink. The hand of his not on her back was tucked in between her chin and his chest and Janet knew, while Harold's thighs slithered on her thighs, that a single finger of Frank's was hypnotically stroking the base of Marcia's throat, down to the tops of her breasts. It was a trick he had, one of the few. She whirled, and the hand of Frank's not at her throat was unzipping the back of Marcia's dowdy black dress. Then from another angle Janet saw held between Marcia's lips like a cigarette the slitted drag of cruelty that came to her face, Janet had noticed, whenever she was very tired or very much at ease. To Marcia, Janet's eyes staring from across the room seemed immense, so dilated they contained the room in their circle of vision as a metal lawn ball contains, distorted and compressed, an entire neighborhood. Frank's delicate hand uncoupled her bra snaps; his single finger slipped further down her breasts. Her body slightly dissolved. She felt herself grow. "I've flown around the world in a plane," Ella, purple spirit, sang, "I've settled rev-o-lutions in Spain." Janet, dizzy from being whirled, felt tipped back by an insistent pressure, knoblike and zippered, amid a lizardly slithering, and thought it sad that Harold should appear a fool before these cruel two other people when she, alone with him, in an ideal seclusion, could have forgiven so well his conceited probing and insinuations of skin. As her image of herself expanded, milk and pollen and poppies, up to the parallel redwood boards of the ceiling inset with small round flush lights rheostated dim, it seemed to Janet that mothering had always been her specialty.

So it was she, when the music stopped, who said, "I'm sleepy and dizzy. Who's going to take me to bed?" Frank in the center of the room made no move, and Harold stayed at her side.

To make space for themselves the two couples had to rearrange the children. Catharine Appleby, her heavy flushed head lolling, was moved into bed with dainty six-year-old Julia Smith; and the door to Jonathan's room (he had fallen asleep with the light on and *The Unwanted Visitor* face down on the blanket) was closed, so no noise from the master bedroom would wake him. The two white sofas were pushed together to make a second bed. It seemed very strange to Janet, as strange as a visit to Sikkim or high Peru, to journey forth, between three and four that morning, toward their own home; to bundle their two oblivious children in borrowed blankets and carry them across the little-Smiths' stone-hard lawn to their two dark cars; to hiss farewells and exchange last caresses through clothes that upon resumption felt like fake and stiff and makeshift costumes; to drive behind Frank's steady taillights through a threadbare landscape patched with pieces of dry half-melted snow; to enter a deserted house carrying children like thieves with sacks of booty; to fall asleep beside an unfamiliar gross man who was also her husband; to feel the semen of another man still moist between her thighs; to awaken and find it morning and the strangeness banished with no traces save a congested evasive something in Frank's grateful eyes and a painful jarring, perhaps inaccurate overlay printing, in the colors of the Sunday comics section.

This pattern, of quarrel and reunion, of revulsion and surrender, was repeated three or four times that winter, while airplanes collided in Turkey, and coups transpired in Iraq and Togo, and earthquakes in Libya, and a stampede in the Canary Islands, and in Ecuador a chapel collapsed, killing a hundred twenty girls and nuns. Janet had taken to reading the newspaper, as if this smudgy peek into other lives might show her the way out of her own. Why was she not content? The other three were, and there was little in her religious background—feebly Presbyterian; her father, though a generous pledger, had been rather too rich to go to church, like a man who would have embarrassed his servants by appearing at their party—to account for her inconvenient sense of evil. She suspected that Marcia and Harold and Frank, having completed college, knew secrets, and used her. She felt her flesh prized by them. She was their sullen treasure. Once, serving them scrambled eggs in her home after midnight, wearing a bathrobe over a nightie (she had gone to bed with a headache and a temper and had come back downstairs again after an hour of listening to their three-cornered laughter), Janet had leaned over the kitchen table with the frying pan and Frank had stroked her from one side and Harold from the other and Marcia, watching, had smiled. She had become their pet, their topic. They could not understand her claustrophobia and indignation, and discussed her "problem" with her as if it might lie anywhere but with them, the three of them.

"Did you ever see," Harold asked, as they sat around the round grease-stained leather table, "your parents making love?"

"Never. The nearest thing to it, some Sunday mornings the door to their bedroom would be locked."

"Dear Janet," Marcia said. "Poor dear Janet. Tiptoeing in her Sunday-school dress down that long silent hall and pushing, pushing at that locked door."

"Shit," Janet said. "I never pushed at anything. Speak for yourself."

"Dear me," Marcia said. "I suppose that should hurt."

"Bad girl, Janet," Harold said. "You pushed me into the laundry."

"Because you looked so *mis*erable." Janet tried not to cry, which she knew would encourage them.

"Let Jan-Jan alone," Frank said. "She's a lovely broad and the mother of my heirs."

"There's Frank," Marcia said to her husband, "giving himself heirs again." Their intimacy had forced upon each a rôle, and Marcia had taken it upon herself to be dry and witty, when in fact, Janet knew, she was earnest and conscientious, with humorless keen emotions. Janet looked at her and saw a nervous child innocently malicious.

"You don't have to defend Janet to me," Harold told Frank. "I love her."

"You desire her," Marcia corrected. "You've cathected in her direction."

Harold continued, shinily drunk, his twin-tipped nose glinting, "She is the loveliest goddam p—"

"Piece," Marcia completed, and scrabbled in her bent pack of Newports for a cigarette.

"*Pièce de non-résistance* I've ever had," Harold finished. He added, "Out of wedlock."

"The horn, the horn, the lusty horn," Frank said, "is not a thing to laugh to scorn," and Janet saw that the conversation was depressing him also.

Harold went on with Janet, "Were your first experiences with boys under bushes interesting or disagreeable? *Intéressant ou désagréable?*"

"Buffalo boys didn't take me under bushes," Janet said. "I was too fat and rich."

Marcia said, "*We* were never really *rich*. Just respectable. I thought of my father as a holy man."

"Saint Couch," Harold said, and then repronounced it, "*San' Coosh!*"

"I thought of mine," Janet said, growing interested, beginning to hope they could teach her something, "as a kind of pushover. I thought my mother pushed him around. She had been very beautiful and never bothered to watch her weight and even after she got quite large still thought of herself as beautiful. She called me her ugly duckling. She used to say to me, 'I can't understand you. Your father's such a handsome man.'"

"You should tell it to a psychiatrist," Marcia said, unintended sympathy lighting up her face.

"No need, with us here," Harold said. "*Pas de besoin, avec nous ici.* Clearly she was never allowed to work through homosexual mother-love into normal heterosexuality. Our first love-object is the mother's breast. Our first gifts to the beloved are turds, a baby's turds. Her father manufactures laxatives. Oh Janet, it's so obvious why you won't sleep with us."

"She sleeps with me," Frank said.

"Don't brag," Marcia said, and her plain warm caring, beneath the dryness, improved Frank's value in Janet's eyes. She saw him, across the small round raft crowded with empty glasses and decanters, as a fellow survivor, scorched by the sun and crazed by drinking salt water.

"Why must you ruin everything?" he suddenly called to her. "Can't you understand, we all love you?"

"I don't like messy games," Janet said.

"As a child," Harold asked, "did they let you play in the buffalo mud or did you have an anal nanny?"

"Anal nanny," Marcia said. "It sounds like a musical comedy."

"What's the harm?" Frank asked Janet, and his boozy dishevelment, his blood-red eyes and ponderous head rather frightened her, though she had lulled him to sleep, her Minotaur, for ten years' worth of nights. He shouted to all of them, "Let's do it! Let's do it all in the same room! Tup my white ewe, I want to see her whinny!"

Harold sighed daintily through his nose. "See," he told Janet. "You've driven your husband mad with your frigidity. I'm getting a headache."

"Let's humanize each other," Frank pleaded.

Marcia turned on him, possessive of his mind. "Frank, don't quote Freddy Thorne. I'd think you'd have more intellectual self-respect."

Yet it was Freddy Thorne who sensed the trouble, and who tried to turn it to his own advantage. "I hear there's a snake in Applesmithsville," he said to Janet.

"Where's that?" They were in her house, at the April party given to welcome the Whitmans to town. Janet was distracted by her duties as hostess; she imagined that people and couples needed her everywhere. Piet Hanema was lying all over the stairs and down came Foxy Whitman from the bathroom, with him looking up her skirt. She must take Foxy aside and explain about Piet.

"Oh," Freddy answered, demanding her attention, "here and there, everywhere. All the world is Applesmithsville." In the corner, by the wall of uniform sets, John Ong, his ageless face strained and courteous, was listening to Ben Saltz painstakingly jabber; Janet thought that a woman should go over and interpose herself, but with this alternative she turned herself a little closer into Freddy Thorne's murmur. Why does his mouth, she wondered, if he's himself such a dentist, look so toothless? "They're feasting off you, Jan-Jan," he told her. "You're serving two studs and Marcia's in the saddle."

"Spare me your vulgar fantasies, Freddy," Janet said, imitating Marcia. "Contrary to what seems to be the popular impression, Harold and I have never slept together. The possibility has been mentioned; but we decided it would be too messy."

"You're beautiful," Freddy told her. "The way you look me right in the eye handing out this crap is beautiful. Something you don't realize about yourself, you really have it. Not like these other cunts. Marcia doesn't have it, she's trying to jiggle herself into having it. Bea's trying to drink herself into it. Angela's trying to rise above it. You're right there. Do me a favor though and don't fib to jolly old Freddy."

Janet laughed; his words were like the candyish mouthwash by his porcelain dental chair—unswallowable but delicious. She asked, "And Georgene? Does she have it?"

"She's OK in a tennis dress, don't knock the kid. She fucks and she can cook, so what the hell. I'm not proposing marriage."

"Freddy, don't make me hurt your feelings."

"You want out, right?"

"In a way, in a way not. I'm, what's the word, not ambidextrous?"

"Ambivalent. Androgynous. Androdextrorogerogynous."

"We have *fun* with the Smiths, just sitting and talking, neither Frank or I have ever had really close friends before. You can't imagine just friendship, can you?"

He patted his bright bald head and in sudden exultation vigorously rubbed it. "Between you and me, yes. It's what a fish feels for the fish he's eating. You want out, I can get you out. Have a little affair with me and that circus you're supporting will pack up and leave town. You can be your own girl again."

"How little is little?"

"Oh"—his hands did one squeeze of an invisible accordion —"as much as suits. No tickee, no washee. If it doesn't take, it doesn't take. No deposit on the bottle, Myrtle."

"Why do you propose this? You aren't very fond of me. It's Angela you want."

"A, I don't, and B, I am, and C, I like to help people. I think you're about to panic and I hate to see it. You're too *schnapps* for that. You wear clothes too well. Terrific dress you have on, by the way. Are you pregnant?"

"Don't be silly. It's an Empire line."

"Now wouldn't it be awful to get knocked up and not know which was the father? Hey. Are you on the pills?"

"Freddy, I'm beginning to hate this conversation."

"Okey-doak-doak. Let it simmer. As Khrushchev said when he put the missiles on Cuba, nothing ventured, nothing gainski. I'm there if you think you can use me."

"Thank you, Freddy. You're a nice man." Janet's conscience pricked her; she added, "Yes."

"Yes how?"

"Yes, in answer to your question, I am on the pills. Marcia isn't yet. She's afraid of cancer."

Freddy smirked and made a ring with his thumb and forefinger. "You're golden," he told her. "You're the last of the golden girls." He put the ring to his mouth and fluttered his tongue through it.

Janet considered his offer seriously. As she picked her way through the tangle of her party it seemed not so implausible. Freddy would know his way around a woman. Marcia and Frank and Harold would be horrified. Harold's vanity would be unforgivably piqued. Love ousts love. These things happen. Piet was making out with poor little Bea Guerin. Frank was grotesquely Twisting (his digestion!) opposite Carol Constantine. Eddie on the sofa was demonstrating with his circling hands to Bernadette Ong the holding pattern of air traffic over LaGuardia and Idlewild, and why the turboprops and private planes were brought down sooner than the pure jets, the beautiful new 707s and DC-8s, and why with every new type of commercial aircraft several hundred passengers will die through pilot error, and why the starlings and gulls at Logan are a special menace; and finally he brought his narrow curly-haired head down safely onto her silk shoulder and appeared to sleep. The guests of honor felt out of it. Foxy queasy, the Whitmans left early. When everyone had left except the little-Smiths, and they were sitting around the table having the dregs of the liqueurs, Janet asked Marcia, "Did Freddy Thorne seem attractive to you tonight?"

Marcia laughed; the glitter of her earrings clashed on the surface of her face. "Heavens, no. He asked me if I was happy in Applesmithsville."

"What did you say?"

"I was very frosty. He went away. Poor Georgene."

"He asked me, too. In fact"—Janet was not sure if this was a tactic, but the Benedictine made it seem one—"he offered to have an affair with me."

"He really is a fantastic oaf," Frank said. Brandy was the worst thing for him, and he was on his third glass.

Harold swirled his Grand Marnier thoughtfully. "Why are you telling us this?"

"I don't know. I was so surprised at myself, that it didn't seem like such a bad idea. Since he's lost all of his hair, he's rather handsome, in a sinister way."

"In a mealy-mouthed way," Marcia said. She sipped anisette.

"Janet, you disgust me," Harold said. "How can you unload this *merde* on three people who adore you?"

"I half-adore her," Marcia said.

"Two point five people who adore you," Harold said. "*Deux point cinq.*"

"I don't know," Janet said. "I guess I want to be talked out of it. I don't see why you men look so offended. It might bring Georgene in and don't we need some new blood? It seems to me we've said everything we have to say about sixty times. We know all about Frank's ulcer and Frank's father who avoided getting an ulcer by learning all about China and how Shakespeare doesn't work as well as China, maybe he's more acid; I *do* advise Maalox. We know all about what saints her father and grandfather the bishop were from Marcia, and how she hated

Long Island and loves it up here away from all those dreary clubby types who kept playing badminton with martini olives. We know all about Harold's prostitutes, and the little colored girl in St. Louis, and how neither of us are quite as good . . ."

"Any funny business with Freddy," Frank said, bloating with menace, "and it's get thee to a nunnery. I'll divorce you."

"But then," Janet told him, "I'd have to drag all of us out into the open, and we'd look so funny in the newspapers. Things are so hard to explain that are perfectly obvious to friends."

"It's obvious to me," Freddy Thorne said to her the following weekend, when they were alone in the kitchen late at a dinner party given by the Guerins, "you never were in love with Harold, you went after him to even the score with Marcia." In the intervening week she had had a dental appointment, and in the gaps of prophylaxis he had wheedled from her her version of the full story.

"Freddy, how can you judge?" She helped herself to a piece of cream-cheese-laden celery left over from the hors d'oeuvres. "How can you hope to get inside people's lives this way? Harold when he and I are alone is something you can't imagine. He can be irresistible."

"We all can," was the answer. "Resistibility is a direct function of the female decision to resist or not to." He seemed to be sweating behind the thick eyeglasses that kept misplacing his eyes. Freddy had trouble seeing. He had recently installed a new drill with a water-spray attachment, and during her appointment his glasses had often needed to be wiped.

"Freddy," she told him, "I don't like being pried and poked at. You must make a woman your friend first."

"I've been your friend since you moved to town." He stroked her arm, left bare by the black-lace blouse. Candlelight shuddered in the other room, where the others were chattering. "On second thought," Freddy murmured on, "I think you took Harold on not to hurt the other two but to oblige them, to win their affection. For a magnificent piece who's also rich, you're damn unsure of yourself."

"For a near-sighted boob who's also a dentist, you're damn sure of yourself. Speaking of which, stop trying to make the Whitman girl. She's pregnant."

"Praise be. More men to man America's submarines. She doesn't know it yet, but she's a swinger. Women with that super-heated skin are usually fantastic in the sack. Their hearts beat harder."

"You're such a bastard," said Janet, whose skin, though strikingly pale, was rather grainy and opaque.

Freddy was right, she later reflected, in that obligingness had become a part of it; they had reached, the Applesmiths, the boundary of a condition wherein their needs were merged, and a general courtesy replaced individual desire. The women would sleep with the men out of pity, and each would permit the other her man out of an attenuated and hopeless graciousness. Already a ramifying tact and crossweave of concern were giving their homes an unhealthy hospital air. Frank and Harold had become paralyzed by the habit of lust; she and Marcia, between blow-ups, were as guarded and considerate with one another as two defaced patients in an accident ward.

In the following week she had a porcelain filling replaced, and Freddy called her on the phone every noon, always inviting her to sleep with him. But he never named a place where they could go, never suggested a definite time; and it dawned upon her that he had no serious physical intention: the verbal intimacy of gossip satisfied him. Meanwhile Harold, begging her to resume with him, had gone to the trouble of acquiring the key to a Beacon Street bachelors' apartment that was empty all day. Curious as to how bachelors live, she went there with him the Friday before the Sunday when Piet broke Freddy's little finger. At a glance she gathered that the inhabitants were homosexuals. The furnishings too beautifully harmonized; bent wicker and orange velvet prevailed. One of the men painted, or, rather, did collages juxtaposing magazine advertisements and war headlines, deodorized nudes with nacreous armpits and bombed peasants flecked with blood, green stamps and Robert McNamara and enraptured models in striated girdles, comic-strip cannons pasted at the crotch. It was quite ugly and malicious, yet the room was impossible to shock and the magnolias on the south of Beacon were about to flower. Harold was polite, timid, fatherly, reminiscent, touching. She allowed him to slide her from her clothes and, rising quickly, came with him and then, after a cigarette and wine, let him come again, let him gather himself into his groin and hurl himself painlessly into the dilated middle amplitudes of herself. Trembling as if whipped, he licked her eyelids and sucked her toes, one by one. The sensation felt hysterically funny. The next day, Saturday, she wrote Freddy a letter:

Freddy dear—

I am grateful for your caring. Truly. But my future, I am more than ever convinced, lies with Frank. So your phone calls must stop. After today I will hang up on your voice. May we continue to be pleasant, and friends? Please, I don't want to change dentists, you have all my records.

Fondly,
J.

She mailed it to his cottagelike office on Divinity Street. He received it Monday, read it smiling, was not disappointed, considered burning it on the gas flame in his lab but, the amorous keepsakes of his life having been few, instead crumpled the envelope into the wastebasket and tucked the letter into his coat pocket, where Georgene found it that evening, while he was at Lions. The next day she confessed her terror to Piet, and irrevocably offended him.

So Foxy was both right and wrong about Janet. She overestimated Janet's freedom, and had mistaken the quality of Freddy Thorne's sexuality. Though he seemed aggressive toward women, he really sought to make alliance with them. But then summer overwhelmed Foxy's speculations about the love life of others, and swept her as if out to sea, to a vantage where the couples on the shore of Tarbox looked like a string of colored beads.

Piet Hanema was sent out of the room and they decided he was Ho Chi Minh. Frank Appleby wanted him to be Casanova but Irene said the person couldn't be fictional. Frank told Irene that Casanova had been as real as you and I but everyone agreed they had no feeling for him. Irene suggested Vice-President Johnson. Everyone protested that he was much too dreary. Terry Gallagher came up with Ho Chi Minh and it seemed perfect. Good for Terry: ever since getting her lute, she was much more with it. More human. All spring she had been taking lute lessons from an old woman in Norwell. She had let her long black hair down; her wide lips were tucked up at the corners as if she were holding a coin or candy in her mouth. Looking at Terry, Eddie Constantine suggested that Piet be Joan Baez, but the rest voted to stick with Ho Chi Minh, and Georgene went to the foot of the Saltzes' stairs to call Piet down.

It was the last Sunday night in June. The tight wine-colored cones of the lilacs that Piet had noticed as he hesitated by Foxy Whitman's gate had loosened and expanded with the first hot week of May into papal miters of bloom, first the lavender and then the taller, holier, more ascetic white, ensconced amid heart-shaped leaves whose green was suddenly cheap. The lilacs faded and dried, and bridal wreath drooped, gathering dust, by every garage door and drive. Sagitta, most exquisite of constellations, flew unmoving between the Swan and Eagle, giant jeweled airplanes whose pilots are Deneb and Altair; the Milky Way wandered like a line of wash in the heat-bleached sky. Desultory parties, hardly organized, social weeds, sprang up to fill the pale nights bloated by Daylight Saving, parties mixed of tennis leftovers and sunburned half-couples and cold salami and fetched pizza and Bitter Lemon and sandy stray forgotten children lulled asleep by television's blue flicker. *President Kennedy's triumphal tour of Western Europe today subsided to quiet talks in Sussex, England* . . .

The Saltzes, great birdwatchers and walkers, as if Nature were a course they were cramming, had gone down late to the beach, to see the sandpipers and to swim. Irene suffered from sun poisoning and ventured out at midday protected in floppy hats and long-sleeved jerseys, and went swimming only toward evening. Up by the far rocks she and Ben had found the Hanemas, all four of them, with the Whitmans, the two of them. Ken liked to snorkel, and the Hanema children had been fascinated by his equipment. The beach here by the rocks dropped off steeply enough for diving. Piet was giving Ruth, in face mask and foot fins, a lesson while Nancy, anxious for her sister and envious, cried. Ken and Angela stood together, an almost godlike couple, untroubled, invulnerable, gazing at the horizon, where a sailboat race was suspended, gaudy spinnakers bellied. Foxy, in a skirted lemon-yellow maternity swimsuit, lay supine on a smooth rock, eyes shut, smiling. Irene was envious of everyone's happiness and ease beneath the same sun that gave her a painful rash. They had all been here since noon. Impulsively, yet with some small hope of inducing the Whitman woman, so complacently uncommitted, to work on one of her causes (pre-primary education, fair housing, soil conservation), she invited them back for a drink. The Saltzes lived near the green, in a narrow asbestos-shingled house visible from the Constantines. The Constantines saw the cars and came over. They brought Terry Gallagher with them. Carol, who had taken ballet and who sewed and wove and painted, also played the guitar, and that summer the two women sometimes met for duets. At Eddie's prompting, Ben Saltz phoned the Applebys, who were having the little-Smiths and Thornes over for a pick-up meal, and half of this party showed up—Frank, Marcia, and Georgene. By now it was after eight. Before the light died, Eddie took Angela, of all people, on his Vespa to the Italian place on Route 123 and they brought back five pizzas. Reëntering the Saltzes' narrow living room, Angela looked glorious, flushed from the wind and the fear and the effort of balancing the cardboard boxes. She wore a damp towel tucked around the waist of a wet black bathing suit, and when she bent forward to bite a point of pizza slice Piet could see her nipples. His wife. Where he had sucked. Not thinking it would be so long a party, they had brought their children along. Ruth, her wide eyes watering, watched streams of television with the older Saltz boy Bernard, and Nancy fell asleep in little Jeremiah's room. Irene loved word games. By eleven-thirty, when Ken Whitman was studying the laces of his sneakers and Frank Appleby's eyes had rolled inward upon his digestion and Janet had phoned twice to make sure that he and Marcia had not gone off alone somewhere and to ask him how ever were they supposed to get Freddy Thorne out of the house, the crowd at the Saltzes' had played four games of Ghosts, two of Truth, and three of Botticelli. This left Impressions. Eddie Constantine had gone out first and with only one wrong guess, Burl Ives, identified himself as the late Pope John. It took Georgene somewhat longer to discover that she was Althea Gibson. Then Piet volunteered because he wanted to go to the john and to check on Nancy

(*I will never grow up and will never ever in my whole life die.*
Her hair was tangled and stiff; her aqua bathing suit, riding
up in sleep, had exposed of her bottom half-moons sparkling
with sand. Piet mourned the child's body but the tug of bright
life downstairs held him helpless here. *Sleep. Forgive us in your
sleep.*) and they made him Ho Chi Minh.

At the foot of the stairs he tapped Georgene's flank with the
side of his hand for old time's sake while gazing straight ahead.
He came into the living room; he wore a sweater and plaid
bathing trunks; his bare feet looked knobbed and splayed on
the floor and in Foxy's eyes his naked legs wore a pale fur halo.
"What kind of landscape am I?" he asked.

"Jungle," Georgene said.

"Rice paddies," said Marcia little-Smith.

Terry Gallagher said, "Torn."

Piet asked, "A torn landscape?"

"Maybe I mean pacified."

Angela closed her eyes. "I see a temple, with reddish pillars,
and an idol with its head knocked off, overgrown with vines,
and someone has been doing mathematical calculations with
chalk on the broad part of one thigh."

"Sexy," Eddie Constantine said.

Georgene said, her chin hardening, "No fair couples using
ESP."

Piet asked, "Anybody else? Foxy? Ken?"

Ken said, "I get Indiana, I don't know why."

Everyone laughed, except Foxy, who nodded. "He's right.
Something quiet and gray and ordinary," she said. "Oregon?
South Dakota?"

Frank Appleby said, "You mean North Dakota."

"No hints," Carol Constantine protested. She was sitting on
the floor in the position of one weaving, or praying, or playing Monopoly. Her legs were folded under a green lily pad of
a ballerina's skirt from which her torso rose like a stem. Her
waist was remarkably thin and pliant and her nostrils, long slits,
seemed always to be inhaling.

Piet asked, "What flower?"

"Poppy."

"Poppy."

"Nodding pogonia," Irene Saltz said. "Or maybe a fringed
orchis."

"A fringed orchis in the shade of an enormous Chinese tulip tree," Frank Appleby said.

Carol said to Marcia, "I don't think Frank understands the game. He hints."

Foxy Whitman said, "I see something gray. Mistletoe."

"I keep getting gray out of you," Piet said to her, with strange edge, and asked Angela, "Flower? Ken?"

"Daisy fleabane," Ken said, perhaps antagonistically, staring at his feet. Did he mean it?

Angela said, "No flower or any flower. A single lily presented by a child to the major's wife on a fête day."

"A wilted gardenia in a busboy's lapel," Terry Gallagher said, and smiled broadly when they all burst into compliments. They felt her developing, coming to bloom.

Georgene said, "A thistle. From an official point of view."

Piet complained, "I can't even tell if you like this person or not."

"What sex are you getting?" Carol asked him. Her face, though composed and smooth, held contentious points of shadow—at the nostril wings, at the corners of her mouth, beneath her pouting lower lip, where there seemed to be a smudge. Piet saw that she lengthened the line of her lids with eye shadow, and realized that her eyes were small and rather close together, so close together that in certain flitting lights her stilted dignity of stance appeared that of a cross-eyed person. He felt better about her, less fascinated. Her hair was a dull brown nothing color done up in a pony tail she was too old for.

"Male," he answered. "But it doesn't seem to matter. His maleness isn't his claim to fame."

"Unlike who?" Carol coolly asked.

Piet obligingly blushed. "What—what period of painting?"

"Art Nouveau," Angela said promptly.

"Spanish cave," Foxy said, also prompt.

Frank Appleby rolled his eyes inward and groaned. "All I get is what Carol doesn't want me to get."

"What's that?" Carol asked.

"Soviet posters."

"No," Carol said, "I don't mind that. It's not very good, but I don't mind it."

Irene Saltz asked her, "Who appointed you referee?"

"Medical-textbook illustrations," Ken Whitman said firmly, "with a rice-paper overlay leaf."

"Good," someone said politely, after a pause.

"Terry and the Pirates," Eddie Constantine said.

Carol said, "I'm sorry, I think you're all horrible. He's definitely Yves Tanguy. And maybe Arshile Gorky."

"He's a playwright," Frank told her.

"That's Maxim," she told him.

Ken, remembering the success of some of his other puns, asked innocently, "Who was Maxim Ize?"

Foxy winced.

"A Jewish expansionist," Eddie said. "Whoops, no offense intended, Ben."

Patiently Piet asked, "Any other painters or periods of painting?"

"I don't think," Marcia said, "they ever work out very well. They're too literal. Stretch our minds, Piet."

Into this Piet read Frank's becoming bored, and asked him, "Frank, what play by Shakespeare am I?"

Frank revolved the question uncomfortably inside him, and after a swallow of brandy pronounced, "*Anthony and Cleopatra*, from the viewpoint of Octavius."

Marcia in a helpful wifely way prompted, "What about *Titus Andronicus*?"

"Too messy," Frank said. "This man is efficient."

Foxy Whitman—she had stopped off at her house to change from her tentlike maternity bathing suit into a more flattering shift, a canary-yellow muu-muu that tapped and hugged her hidden shape—was fighting for attention. "What about an *Othello* in which Iago is right?"

Frank said, "He's always right," and brayed.

Ben Saltz, looking tired, got to his feet and asked, "Who wants some more beer? Brandy? We have lots of gin but we're out of Bitter Lemon."

Georgene said, "Piet, you're taking much too long. We've given you beautiful answers and you spurn us."

"You've confused me, you're all so beautiful. I keep thinking about Ken's medical textbook."

"Ignore it," Foxy said.

"All right: what beverage?"

"Tea."

"Tea."

"Souchong more than orange pekoe."

"Tea with nutmeg," Angela said.

"Angela, you really like this person, don't you?" It was Terry asking.

"I have to, he's my husband."

"I hate tea," Piet said. "I hate tea with nutmeg."

"You've never had it," Angela told him.

"Don't be too sure." The others hushed, to give them space to quarrel. Piet hastily moved on: "What kind of food?"

"Rice."

"Rice, but you want more," Ben said, returning with beer in two brown nonreturnable bottles.

Piet asked, "Boiled or fried?"

Angela said, "Boiled. It's purer."

Marcia said, "Delicately fried."

Terry closed her eyes and said, "A BLT on burnt toast."

Frank Appleby said, "To hell with you all. I'll say what comes to me. A monk barbecue."

Carol cried, all her lithe lines electric, her feet thrusting from under her skirt, "Frank, you're a pig! You've given it to him!"

Piet said in great relief, "I'm No-go Diem."

The voices of the others flocked: "Ngo, you're not." "Close, but no sitar." "Close? He couldn't be wronger." "Right church, wrong side of the aisle." This last was Georgene, reaching out to him; her help was accepted while she was spurned.

Piet arrived: "Ho Chi Minh." In a glad clatter the game collapsed. The beer went around. Terry Gallagher and Ken Whitman stood with one motion and looked at each other, surprised by unison.

"It's treasonous," Piet was saying, "how affectionate your impressions were. This enemy of our democracy, all those flowers and delicate grays." His complaint was directed, Georgene felt, toward Angela and Foxy.

"*You* asked flowers."

"You never asked animals. A whiskery weasel."

"A very thin panda."

"Why hate him? He's what they want." This was Irene, who had been uncharacteristically silent.

"*Chacun à son goût*, as Harold would say if he were here," Marcia said with quaint loyalty.

"I thought that was good of me to remember him being a busboy in Paris," Terry said. "Thanks, people, but I must go. We went to early mass this morning and poor Matt's been showing houses all afternoon."

"I second that," Ken said. "Fox, come."

But the momentary impression, of Terry and Ken standing together as a handsome couple, tall and dark-haired and grave, led the others to tease Foxy.

"Oh please," Carol begged. "Stay for one more."

"We'll let Foxy be it."

"Foxy's it. It, Foxy."

"All pregnant women leave the room."

Foxy looked toward Ken; he read on her face a touching indecision. This boozy catty crowd tempted her; their own house was full of mosquitoes and uncompleted carpentry. Yet she was tired, and his wife, and faithful. She said, "No, I'd just be stupid. I don't really understand the game."

"Oh, but you do, you do."

"The game is to be yourself."

"Your impressions are lovely."

"We'll pick somebody simple. Margaret Truman. *Not* Jackie. It'll take ten minutes."

She wavered, and Ken spoke to her across the calling heads with perfect kindness, yet his voice frightened her; his appearance had no roundness. An immaculate cutout seemed wired for sound. "I'm dead, Fox, but you stay and play. Marcia can drop you off."

"Oh," she said, "but that's not right. Marcia has Harold to worry about. I'll go with you."

They all said, "You can't. You're it. Stay."

"Stay," Ken told her, and turned to leave, and she felt herself cut off, her roundness rejected; her shape offended him. She had asked him to rescue her from indecision and he had petulantly set her adrift. Angered, she agreed to stay, and went upstairs, where Piet had been. He had left no clues.

It did not take them long to decide, June having been so fertile of news: Pope John had died, Quang Duc had immolated himself, Valentina Tereshkova had become the first woman in space, John Profumo had resigned, the Lord's Prayer had been banned in the American public schools. Soon Georgene was at the foot of the stairs, calling, "E-liz-a-beth! Elizabeth Fox Whitman, come right down here!" It was the voice of her Wilmington aunt.

Like a rebuked child Foxy entered the living room; its human brightness seemed savage. The darkened rooms upstairs, rooms of pinned-up maps and scattered toy tracks, of silently sleeping children and docile plumbing fixtures, had been a better world. She thought of her bedroom and the moon that shared her insomnia. The blank pillow beside Ken's head was her. Here, Ken and Terry Gallagher were gone. Frank Appleby was asleep, his feet in sandals cocked up on the Saltzes' fake-colonial coffee table, his mouth ajar and raggedly snoring. Foxy also heard whispering in the kitchen and counted Eddie Constantine and Irene missing. The six survivors, four of them women, looked weary and forbearing and she realized she should have gone home with Ken. The game was exhausted, they were merely being polite, to make her feel loved and part of them. She must quickly guess and go.

"What—what kind of ocean am I?" Foxy wasn't sure if the rules forbad using associations others had used, and she wanted to be creative, sensitive, unique. On the nubbly sofa next to his wife, Piet Hanema gazed down into his glass.

"What kind of ocean?" Carol echoed. "How odd. Choppy, I guess."

"Sometimes choppy," Marcia said. "Sometimes very still and tranced. Sometimes even a big wave."

"Untracked," Piet said.

"Untracked?"

"Ships go back and forth across you and leave no trace. You accept them all. They don't impress you."

"A piece of ocean," Ben said, grinning, "with a mermaid in it."

Carol said, "No direct hints."

Suddenly immersed in timidity, Foxy asked, "Angela? Any ocean?"

"Not an ocean," Angela said. "A sad little pond."

"Sad?"

"Kind of scummy," Georgene said: a startling flat insult, but everyone, especially the men, laughed, agreeing.

"Well. What time of day?"

"Two in the morning."

"Eleven A.M., with rumpled sheets."

"Any time. All day."

Again, this unkind laughter. A slow blush caked Foxy's face. She wanted to like this person she was, in spite of them.

Angela tried to rescue her. "I see this person around nine at night, going out, into the city lights, kind of happy and brainless."

"Or maybe even," Marcia added, "at four-thirty in the afternoon, walking in a park, without a hat, smiling at the old men and the squirrels and the babies."

"And the bobbies," Piet said.

Carol sang, "We're getting too spe-ci-fic," and glanced toward the whispering kitchen with that abrupt head turn ballerinas use in pirouettes.

English, Piet's implication was. Queen Elizabeth, scummy? Virginia Woolf? *The Waves*. But those rumpled sheets. Perhaps an effeminate seedy man. Cecil Beaton. Alec Guinness, Piet's saying back and forth across an ocean, an actor's parts. But a scummy pond? How stupid she was being. Afraid to guess wrong, self-conscious, stuck. The furnishings of the Saltzes' living room pressed in upon her emptiness: velvety dark easy chairs wearing doilies on their forearms, maple magazine racks of *Scientific American* and *Newsweek* and *Look*, inquisitive bridge lamps leaning over the chairs' left shoulders, Van Gogh sunning on the walls, wedding pictures frozen on the top of an upright piano with yellow teeth, an evil-footed coat rack and speckled oblong mirror in the dark foyer, narrow stairs plunging upward perilously, children climbing each night in a fight with fear. Her mother's Delaware second cousins had lived in such houses, built narrow to the street and lined with hydrangea bushes where a child could urinate or hide from her third cousins. The Jews have inherited the middle class—nobody else wants it. "What social class?" Foxy asked.

"Too direct," Carol said.

"Lower," Georgene said.

"Middle lower," Piet said. "Some airs and graces."

"Transcending all classes," Angela told her. "Lower than low, higher than high."

"You sound," Ben Saltz said to Angela with a pedantic mannered twinkle, "like a Gnostic devotee."

"What a nosty suggestion," Marcia said.

"Oh, I *don't* understand how we *know* about this person, she seems so *common!*" Foxy cried.

"She has hidden talents," Piet said.

"He or she," Carol corrected.

Foxy asked, "What bird am I?"

"Of paradise," Angela said.

"Sparrow."

"Soiled dove."

"Soiled dove is good."

"I envision," Piet said, "a rather tall bird, with a shimmer on its breast. A cockatoo?"

"You're a cowbird," Georgene told Foxy.

Piet turned on Georgene. "How unfair!"

Georgene shrugged. "Using other people's nests."

It was like, Foxy felt, being naked and not knowing it, like being dead on the autopsy table and yet overhearing the remarks, the cold ribaldry. She wanted to be with Ken, to take the wakening presence within her and flee; she had sinned. "What figure am I in the Bible? I know you're going to say Delilah."

"No," Piet said, "you're too hard on yourself. Maybe you're Hagar."

"No," Ben said, "she's Abishag. Abishag was the girl who they brought in to David, when he was dying, to give him some heat. *Vecham leadoni hamelekh*, in the Hebrew."

"And what happened?" Marcia asked.

"*Vehamelekh loh yada-ah.* The king knew her not."

"Ben," Marcia said, "I think it's marvelous, the way you can rattle it off. Hebrew."

"I studied it for ten years. We were conservative."

"Even those little skullcaps?"

"Yarmulkes." His grin was leonine, thrilling, his teeth brilliant within his beard. "Summers I was sent to Camp Ramah."

Foxy asked, "Georgene?"

"I don't know the Bible. I would have said Delilah. Or Magdalen, except that seems presumptuous."

"I see her as one of those Jerusalemites who never got into the Bible," Angela said. "She just couldn't be bothered. She was flirting with a Roman soldier when the Cross went by."

"What a terrible woman," Foxy said. "A scummy pond, a cowbird."

"You've been listening only to Georgene," Piet said. "Georgene's being moralistic tonight."

"You don't like her either. Angela and Ben are the only ones who like her." Saying this made Foxy jealous, for she did not want Ben and Angela to be linked, she vaguely wanted Ben —not the real Ben, but the echoes he evoked—to be her own Jew.

The whispering from the kitchen had ceased.

"This is going on too long," Carol said, and stood up, stiff from long sitting, her throat and wrists stringy, tense. She did not quite dare go into the kitchen; she took a step toward the open doorway and sharply called, "Come help us, you two. She's stuck."

"I quit," Foxy said. "Who am I? I'm sure I've never heard of myself."

"You have, you have," Piet urged; he wanted her to do well, he was embarrassed for her.

"I'm some dreary little starlet and I never notice their names."

"At the moment," Piet told her, "you're a star."

"At the moment. Julie Andrews. Liz Taylor."

"No. You're on the wrong track."

"Phooey," Foxy said. "I was so proud of those. They're both English. I'm not Dame May Whitty?"

"You're being silly," Carol told her.

"Think big," Piet said. "Think world."

Ben said, "Ask some more questions."

They were all prompting, hissing at the balky child in the Christmas recitation. Georgene's hard eyes were plainly pleased. Marcia said, "Ask Frank what Shakespeare play you are. I'll wake him up." Marcia glided to where Frank lay deflated and sunk in the corner of the fat sofa and, wifely, whispered into his ear until his lids parted and his eyes, open, stared sorely ahead. Foxy felt his eyes, in mid-dream, gaze through her.

"Frank, help," she said. "What Shakespearian play am I?"

"*Troilus*," he said, and his eyes closed.

"I've never read it," Foxy said.

"I think you're the sonnets," Marcia said.

"In Russian and English *en face*," Piet said, and everybody, everybody, laughed.

"Oh, you're all too clever," Foxy told them. "I'm totally lost now. I was working on Princess Margaret." Their laughter renewed itself; she said, "I hate you all. I want to go home. I want to give up."

"Don't give up," Piet said. "I know you know it. You're trying too hard."

Ben asked her, "What's the opposite of a princess?"

"A ragpicker. Oh. A flowergirl. Eliza Doolittle. But I thought you couldn't use fictional people."

"You can't. You're not Eliza," Georgene told her. "What's the opposite of a virgin?"

Angela said, "I think Foxy should give up if she wants to."

"She's too close to give up," Carol said.

Irene Saltz, smoothing back her hair, returned to the living room. Her black eyebrows were shapely as wingbeats. She told Carol, "Eddie said to tell you he's gone home. He has to fly tomorrow and went out through the kitchen door."

"Typical," Carol said, and brightened. Her spine as she sat on the floor became again a flower stem, slender, erect. She begged Foxy, "Try one more impression."

With a surrendering sigh, Foxy asked, "What flower?"

The answers were elaborate, since they wanted her now to guess, to know.

"A tiger lily," Carol said, "transplanted from a village garden to a city street."

"Why would anyone bother to do that?" Georgene asked. "I see something coarse but showy. A poppy."

"But Ho Chi Minh was a poppy," Piet told her.

"Yes. There may be an affinity," Georgene said, and turned on him those slightly bulging indignant eyes which, with her cultivated tan and graying hair, belonged to the caustic middle-aged woman she would become. Foxy remembered Georgene's silence during the candlelit dinner at the Guerins, a secretive and contented silence which had seemed, that uncomfortable night, to share, to be of the same chemical nature as, Foxy's pregnancy. Since then this woman had aged unkindly.

Irene said, "I don't know who it is." When Carol whispered the name into her ear, she snapped: "Eglantine."

"In Japan," Angela said, "after our bombs, wasn't there a flower that came out of nowhere and flourished in the radio-active area? I see this person like that, as turning our modern poison into a kind of sweetness."

Foxy said gratefully, "Angela, that's nice. I don't feel so badly now about being this person."

"Devil's paintbrush," Marcia said. "Or something hothousy."

"You know how sometimes," Ben Saltz said, "in weeding around the house, you come to a plant, such as Queen Anne's lace or those spindly wild asters, that is obviously a weed but you don't have the heart to pull because for the time being it's very ornamental?"

Angela said, "We're all like that."

Georgene said, "Speak for yourself, dollink."

"A geranium that's moved from sill to sill to catch the sun," Piet said. "A hyacinth that's sold in a plastic pot. Sometimes a Lady Palmerston rose. Foxy, have you ever noticed, in a greenhouse, how they put cut carnations in a bucket of ink to dye them? That's how they make those green ones for St. Patrick's Day. I think you're a yellow carnation they made drink purple ink, so you're this incredible black, and people keep touching you, thinking you must be artificial, and are amazed that you're an actual flower. As you die, you'll bleed back to yellow again." His flat taut-featured face became this much-touched flower fading.

Carol said, "There's a carefree toughness we're not suggesting."

"Let's do books," Marcia said, impatient. "*Moll Flanders*, by Ian Fleming."

"*Phineas Finn*," Angela said, "abridged for *Playboy*."

"*Little Red Riding Hood*," Ben said, "by the Marquis de Sade."

"*Stop*," Foxy begged. "I give up. I'm very stupid. Angela. Tell me."

"You're Christine Keeler," Piet told her.

In the silence, Foxy's stomach growled.

"That . . . tart? I am? Oh. I'm so *sorry*." Without willing it, without wanting it, not knowing at what instant she passed, averting her head, into tears, Foxy began in fatigue and confusion to cry; and it was clear to all of them, except Angela and Ben, that as they had suspected she was seeing Piet.

III

Thin Ice

As in sleep we need to dream, so while waking we need to touch and talk, to be touched and talked to. *Foxy?*

Yes, Piet? Their simple names had a magic, the magic of a caress that searches out the something monstrous and tender in the genitals of another.

Do you think we're wrong?

Wrong? The concept seemed to swim toward her out of another cosmos of consideration. *I don't know. I don't think so.*

How good of you!

Not to think so?

Yes, yes, yes. Yes. Don't ever think so. Make it right for me. Hey. I dreamed about you last night. I never have before. It's funny, the people you dream about. It's a club with the stupidest rules. I'm always dreaming about Freddy Thorne and I can't stand him.

What did I do in your dream? Was I erotic?

Very chaste. It was in a department store, with a huge skylight overhead. You were a salesgirl. I stopped in front of your counter, without knowing what I wanted.

A salesgirl, am I? She had this mode, of contentious teasing, to vent a touchy pride. *And what do you suppose I am selling?*

It wasn't that atmosphere at all. You were very prim and distant and noncommittal, the way you can be; even though I couldn't say anything, you bent down behind the counter, out of sight, as if to find something, and I woke up with a killing erection.

Sometimes insomniac that summer, Piet, lying in bed beside sleeping Angela, would lift his hand and study its shape stamped black on the window of light-blue panes framed by cruciform mullions. His hand seemed one lifted out of the water in the instant before the final sinking. Angela's heedless slow breathing seemed a tide on the skin of the depths to which he could sink. He missed the squeaking, like glints of light, of the hamster's wheel. He had been shy and circumspect with Foxy, a hired man in her house, and had not intended to desire her. But she had moved with him through the redesign of this old wreck, outdoors to indoors, detail to detail, with a flirting breezy eagerness that had oddly confounded him with the naked wood, where she touched it.

Here there could be shelves.

Or cabinets.

Don't you like open shelves better? Doors are so self-righteous. Then they stick or stop shutting.

They make magnetic catches now that are pretty foolproof. Open shelves are a temptation. You have a cat, you're going to have children. You need spaces you can close. I have two old finish carpenters whose cabinets can be quite handsome.

Did they come from Finland together?

One "n" finish. Their names are Adams and Comeau.

And you want to make work for them.

Piet was taken aback; this woman seemed, as she moved this way and that in her antique kitchen, in her tapping billowing maternity smock, lighter than other women, quicker in exploring him, as if he appeared before her not as himself but as another, whom she had once known well, and still directed some emotion toward. He told her guardedly, *They care, I like them to do work for people who care.*

She turned and held up her arms to the view as if to an ikon and turned again and said urgently, *I want open shelves, and open doorways, and everything open to the sea and the sea air. I've lived my whole life in clever little rooms that were always saving space*, and swept from her narrow kitchen with her lemon-colored smock swinging coolly about her, the high fair color of her face burning. Piet saw she was going to be trouble.

Georgene asked him, "Why have you taken the job? You told me you had to build ranch houses."

They were beside the Ongs' tennis court on Sunday morning. Piet had given up church so that Angela could accept a challenge teasingly given by Freddy Thorne. Piet missed that hour of seated mulling and standing song. Also his head was pinched in tightened icy bands of last night's gin. The challenge, delivered loudly by Freddy at the Constantines' last night, had been for Angela to play him at singles; but then this morning Bernadette was already returning with her three sons from early mass, so the Ongs had to be invited to play, on their own court. The court had been carved from a sloping field adjoining their newly built house. The exotic and expensive house, all flat eaves and flagstones and suspended stairways, designed by an architect John knew in Cambridge, an associate of I. M. Pei, was a puzzling reminder, for the self-important young couples of Tarbox, of John Ong's incongruous prestige. John himself, a small bony butternut-colored man, in love with everything American from bubble chambers to filtered cigarettes, was a tennis enthusiast without aptitude; he invariably played in freshly pressed whites, complete to the wrist band, and a green eyeshade. His dainty popping strokes, accompanied by himself with a running comment of encouraging cries and disappointed coos, were rudely smashed away by his Occidental friends. Bernadette, however, was a walloper. She and Freddy, who stood comically flatfooted and served patball like a child, opposed John and Angela, whose game was graceful and well schooled and even, except at the net, where she had no sense of kill. Piet and Georgene, watching, talked. They spoke at what seemed normal pitch but took care not to be overheard.

He answered her, "Ranch houses are so boring. They all look alike."

There was in Georgene a store of clubwomanly indignation. "So do teeth," she said. "Teeth all look alike. Stocks and bonds all look alike. Every man works with things that look alike; what's so special about you? What makes you such a playboy? You don't even have any money."

Ever since childhood, being scolded had given Piet cerebral cramps; that the world was capable at any point of its immense surface of not loving him seemed a mathematical paradox it was torture to contemplate. He said, "The rest of you have money for me."

"That *is* your style, isn't it? You take. You take, and bow, and leave." Her face was in profile, one-eyed and prim, like the Jack of Diamonds. Sun-glisten salted her chin.

"It was *you*," he told her, having waited until a flurry of strokes and exclamations from the game concealed his voice, "who said we must be careful. Because of Janet's letter, re-member? I needed you that day and you shut me out."

"That was months ago. I said to be careful, not to call it off."

"I don't like being told to be careful."

"No, of course you don't, you don't have to be. Angela knows damn well what you're up to but prefers not to see it."

Angela, hearing her name, turned her head. Piet called to her, "Georgene's admiring your style." To Georgene he said, smiling as if chatting, "And what about you and yours? Did you ever confront him with the letter?"

"Yes. Eventually."

"And what did the dear man say?"

She turned her tennis racket between her knees and studied the strings. Rough and smooth. Rough, smooth. "I forget. He wriggled out of it somehow. He said it was a purely paternal thing, that he had been trying to help Janet get out of the Applesmith mess, and she was too neurotic, she had turned on him. It was pretty plausible, from the way her note was worded."

"And then in relief you went to bed with him."

"Yes, as a matter of fact."

"And it was splendid."

"Not bad."

"You each had seven orgasms and read Henry Miller to each other between times."

"You see it very clearly."

"Working from your many vivid descriptions."

"Piet. Stop being a bastard. I'm tired of being a bitch. Come see me. Just for coffee."

"Just for coffee is as bad as for screwing if we're caught."

"I miss you."

"Here I am."

"You have somebody else, that's it, isn't it?"

"Dollink," he said, "you know me better than that."

"I can't believe it's that Whitman girl. She's just too stiff and pretty-pretty for you. She's not your type."

"You're right. It's not her. It's Julia little-Smith."

"Foxy's too tall for you, Piet. You make yourself ridiculous."

"Not only am I poor, I'm a midget. How did a high-class chick like you ever get mixed up with me?"

Georgene contemplated him coldly. Beyond her green eyes and high-bridged nose, wire mesh of the tennis court; beyond, the slope of summer grass whitening where wind touched it. Waves. Lattices. Combine and recombine. Dissolution. She whispered. "I wonder. It must have been purely chemical." The sadness of lust swept numbly up from below Piet's belt. They had come together. Time and again. Larches, tarpaper. Her purple turban.

A final point, and the game was over. Angela and John Ong, winners, walked to the sidelines shining with sweat. John spoke, and Piet didn't understand what he was saying; the vowels, all flattened toward "a," were strung together with clattering consonants. Piet, squinting upward, felt intelligence wildly straining toward him from behind that smooth golden mask. "He says he has no wind any more," Bernadette said for him. She was broad in the shoulders and pelvis and her face had the breadth of a smile even when she was not smiling. Piet loved the Ongs: they let him use their tennis court, they never patronized him, their presence in Tarbox was as contingent as his own. John lit a cigarette and suffered a fit of dry coughing, and Piet was surprised that the coughs were intelligible. An elemental vocabulary among all men. The cough, the laugh, the sob, the scream, the fart, the sigh. Amen.

John said, bent double by coughing, "Oo two now," meaning the other two couples must play. The Ongs walked together toward their house, amid their trio of petitioning boys.

The Hanemas faced the Thornes. Georgene had put on sunglasses; the rest of her face looked chiseled. The sun was high. Sheen skated on the green composition court. Angela served; her serves, though accurate, lacked pace and sat up pleasantly fat to hit. Georgene's return, one of her determined firm forehands, streaked toward Piet as he crouched at the net; anger had hurried her stroke slightly and the ball whacked the net at the height of his groin and fell dead on her side.

"Fifteen love," Angela called, and prepared, on tiptoe, to serve again.

Piet changed courts. Opposite him Freddy Thorne wore loud plaid shorts, a fairyish pink shirt, a duck bill hat for his bald head, fallen blue socks, and rubbery basketball sneakers that seemed too large. Freddy pointed his feet outward clownishly and hoisted his racket to his shoulder like a baseball bat. Angela, having laughed and lost rhythm, double-faulted.

"Fifteen all," she called, and Piet faced Georgene again. A fluid treacherous game. Advantages so swiftly shifted. Love became hate. *You give me my shape.* Georgene, eyeless, braced for the serve, gauged it for her forehand, took back the racket, set her chin, stepped forward, and Piet, gripping his handle so hard it sweated, bit down on a shout for mercy.

"Daddy. Am I pretty?"

Piet's jaw ached with a suppressed yawn. He had thought his job was done. He had watched Nancy brush her teeth and read with her for the twentieth time *Where the Wild Things Are* and recited with her, what they did more and more rarely, a good-night prayer, a little litany of blessings into which Piet never knew whether or not to insert the names of his parents. He felt that they too, along with her maternal grandparents, should be remembered by the child; but their unalterable deadness disturbed her. So usually Jacobus and Marte Hanema went unblessed, and their unwatered ghosts in Heaven further withered. "Yes, Nancy, you are very pretty. When you grow up you will be as pretty as Mommy."

"Am I pretty now?"

"Aren't you being a silly? You are very pretty now."

"Are other girls pretty?"

"What other girls?"

"Martha and Julia." Topless little females shrieking in the icy water of Tarbox Bay. Round limbs sugared with sand. Squatting in sunset glaze to dam the tide.

Piet asked her, "What do *you* think?"

"They're ugly."

"They're pretty in their way and you're pretty in your way. Martha is pretty in a Thorne way and Julia is pretty in what way?"

"Smith way."

"Right. And Catharine in what way?"

"In an Applebay."

"In an Appleby way. And when Mrs. Whitman has her baby it will be pretty in a Whitman way." It was wrong to use the innocent ears of a child, but it gave Piet pleasure to say Foxy's name, to hold it in his mouth and feel his body suffused with remembrance of her. Angela, sensitive beyond her conscious understanding, showed irritation with his talk, so carefully casual, of the Whitmans, and the name had become subliminally forbidden in the house.

Nancy understood the game now. Her round face gleeful in the pillow, she said, "And when Jackie Kenneny has her baby it will be pretty in a Kenneny way."

"*Right.* Now go to sleep, pretty Nancy, or you will be grumpy and lumpy in the morning."

But there was in this child, more than in her blunt Dutch-blooded sister Ruth, that thing female which does not let go. "But am I the prettiest?"

"Baby, we just said, everybody is pretty in her own way and nobody wants them to change because then everybody would be alike. Like turnips." He had left a martini-on-the-rocks beside his chair downstairs and the ice would be melting, spinning water into the jewel-clear gin.

Nancy's face was distorted by the effort not to cry. "But I'll *die*," she explained.

He groped for her thought. "You think if you're the prettiest God won't let you die?"

She wordlessly nodded. Her thumb had found its way to her mouth and her eyes darkened as if she were sucking from it ink.

"But pretty people must die too," Piet told her. "It wouldn't be fair to let only ugly ones die. And nobody looks ugly to people who love them."

"Like mommies and daddies," she said, removing and replacing her thumb in an instant.

"Right."

"And boy friends and girl friends."

"I suppose."

"I know your girl friend, Daddy."

"You do! Who?"

"Mommy."

Piet laughed. "And who's Mommy's boy friend?" Symmetry. The child said, "Martha's daddy."

"That awful man?"

"He's funny," Nancy explained. "He says poo."

"You mean if I said poo I'd be funny too?"

She laughed: the noise was pulled bubbling from deep near the door to the kingdom of sleep. "You said poo," she said. "Shame on Daddy."

A silence fell between them. The lilac leaves, flourishing, flowerless, had reached to the height of Nancy's window and, heart-shaped, brushed her screen. Fear tapped, scraped. Piet did not dare leave. "Are you really worried about dying, baby?"

Solemnly Nancy nodded. "Mommy says I'll get to be an old, old lady, and then die."

"Isn't that nice? When you're a very old lady you can sit in your rocking chair and tell all your great-great-grandchildren how once you had a daddy who said poo."

The desired laugh rose toward the surface of the child's shadowed face, and without a sound submerged. She was gazing into the horror he had conjured up. "I don't want to be an old lady! I don't want to be big!"

"But already you're bigger than you were. Once you were no bigger than my two hands. You don't want to be that small again. You couldn't talk or walk or anything."

"I do too, Daddy. Go away, send Mommy."

"Nancy, listen. You won't die. That little thing inside you that says 'Nancy' won't ever ever die. God never lets anybody die; he lifts them up and takes them into Heaven. That old thing they put in the ground isn't you at all."

"I want Mommy!"

Piet, sickened, saw that Angela, in her simplicity, had made this doctrine of hope, the only hope, strange and frightful to the child. "Mommy's doing the dishes downstairs."

"I want her."

"She'll come and give you a kiss when you're fast asleep."

"I want her now."

"And you don't want Daddy?"

"*No.*"

Sometimes in these warm pale nights, as the air cooled and the cars on the road beyond the lilac hedge swished toward Nun's Bay trailing a phosphorescence of radio music, Angela would turn to Piet while he lay willing to yield himself to fatigue. It seemed crucial that he make no motion of desire toward her; then, speaking no word, as if a visitant from space had usurped his wife's body, Angela would press herself against him and with curved fingers curiously trace his sides and spine. Unspeaking also, lest the spell break, he would dare mirror her caress, discovering her nightgown, usually an opaque and entangling obstacle, transparent, rotten, sliding and falling from her flesh like deteriorated burial cloth from a body resurrected in its strength. She showed behind and between her legs a wealth of listening curves and damps. She tugged her gown to her throat and the bones of her fingers confided a glimmering breast to his mouth, shaped by an *ah* of apprehension; when with insistent symmetry she rolled onto her back to have him use the other, his hand discovered her mons Veneris swollen high, her whole fair floating flesh dilated outward toward a deity, an anyoneness, it was Piet's fortune to have localized, to have seized captive in his own dark form. The woman's beauty caressed the skin of his eyes; his shaggy head sank toward the ancient alleyway where, foul proud queen, she frothed most. His tongue searched her sour labia until it found them sweet. She pulled his hair, *Come up.* "Come inside me?" He realized, amazed, he who had entered Foxy Whitman the afternoon before, that there was no cunt like Angela's, none so liquorish and replete. He lost himself to the hilt unresisted. The keenness of her chemistry made him whimper. Always the problem with their sex had been that he found her too rich to manipulate. She touched his matted chest, *wait*, and touched her own self, and, mixed with her fluttering fingers, coming like a comet's dribble, he waited until her hand flew to his buttocks and, urging him to kill her, she gasped and absolved herself from tension.

He said, "My dear wife. What a nice surprise."

She shrugged, flat on her back on the sweated sheet, her bare shoulders polished by starlight. "I get hot too. Just like your other women."

"I have no other women." He stroked and smoothed the outflowing corona of her hair. "Your cunt is heavenly."

Angela motioned him off and rolled away to sleep; it was their custom since the start of their marriage to sleep nude after making love. "I'm sure," she said, "we're all alike down there."

"That's not true," Piet told her, "not true at all." She ignored his confession.

*

He had been shy and circumspect with Foxy and had not wanted to desire her. He would spend most of each day on Indian Hill with the three ranch houses, which rose in quick frames from the concrete foundations: an alphabet of two-by-fours, N and T and M and H, interlocked footings and girders and joists and flooring and studs and plates and sills. Piet, hammer in hand, liked to feel the bite taken into gravity. The upright weight-bearing was a thing his eye would see, and a house never looked as pretty again to him as it did in the framing, before bastard materials and bastard crafts eclipsed honest carpentry, and work was replaced by delays and finagling with subcontractors—electricians like weasels, grubby plumbers, obdurate motionless masons.

So, many days, it was not until three or four o'clock that he rattled down the beach road to the Robinson place. The worst problem, the lack of a basement, had been solved first. The servants' wing, four skimpy dormered bedrooms and a defunct kitchenette, had been torn down, enabling a backhoe to dig a hole ten feet deep to the edge of the kitchen, in two days. Four college boys with hand shovels had taken a week to dig under the length of the kitchen and hallway area and break through to the existing furnace hole beneath the living room. For a few days, while concrete was poured and spread (the operation co-incided with an early-June heat wave; the scene in the cave beneath the house, boys stripped to the waist and ankle-deep in sludge, was infernal), half of Foxy's home rested on a few cedar posts and Lally columns footed on cinder block. Then, above the basement where the wing had been, Piet built a modified annex of one story, two rooms one of which could be a nursery and one a playroom, with a screened-in sunporch overlooking the marsh, connected to the kitchen by a passageway where gardening tools could be kept. Before June's end Foxy had ordered six rose bushes from Vos & Sons' greenhouses, and had had them set along the butt end of the new wing, and was trying with Bovung and peat moss to nurse them to health in a clayey earth still littered with splinters and scarred by tractor-tire tracks.

In five July days, a roofer's crew stripped the lumpy leaky accumulation of shingles and hammered down a flat snug roof.

The old sagging porch was torn away. Light flooded the living room, whose walls, as the hot-air ducts from the new

furnace were installed, were covered with wire lath and plas-
tered by an old Czech from Lacetown, with his crippled
nephew: the last plasterers south of Mather. These major renovations, substantially completed by August, cost Ken Whitman
eleven thousand dollars, of which only twenty-eight hundred
came to Piet's firm, and only a few hundred adhered as profit.
The rest went for material, for rough labor, for the skilled labor
of Adams and Comeau, to the heating contractor, the concrete
supplier, the plumbing subcontractor. Kitchen improvement
—new appliances, additional plumbing, cabinets, linoleum—
came to another three thousand, and Piet, pitying Whitman
(who never asked for pity, who comprehended the necessities
and expenses with a series of remote nods, as the house at each
transformation became less his and more Foxy's), held his own
charges close to cost. As everyone, especially Gallagher, had
foreseen, the job was a loser.

But it gave Piet pleasure to see Foxy, pregnant, reading a
letter beside a wall of virgin plaster, her shadow subtly golden.
And he wanted her to be pleased by his work. Each change
he wrought established more firmly an essential propriety. At
night, and in the long daytime hours when he was not yet
with her, he envisioned her as protected and claimed by sentinels he had posted: steel columns standing slim and strong
in the basement, plaster surfaces of a staring blankness, alert
doors cleverly planed to hang lightly in old frames slumped
from plumb, a resecured skylight, now of double thickness and
freshly flashed, above her sleeping head. He saw her as always
sleeping when he was not there, her long body latent, ripening in unconsciousness. Sometimes, when he came in mid-
afternoon, she would be having a nap. The sea sparkled dark
in the twisting channels. Lacetown lighthouse trembled in the
distance and heat. High summer's hay smell lay thick upon the
slope, full of goldenrod and field mice, down to the marsh. Beside the doorway there were lilac stumps. No workmen's cars
were parked in the driveway, only her secondhand Plymouth
station wagon, hymnal blue.

He lifted the aluminum gate latch. He examined the unfinished framing of the annex, noted two misnailed and split
pieces of cross-bridging between joists, walked around the front
of the house where the porch had been and an unconcluded

rubble of mud and hardened concrete splotches and dusty hundredweight paper bags and scraps of polyethylene film and insulation wool now was, and, continuing, tapped on the side door, a door that seemed to press outward with the silence it contained. Within, something made the house slightly tremble. It was Cotton, the Whitmans' heavy-footed caramel tom. Piet entered, and the cat, bowing and stretching and purring in anticipation of being picked up, greeted him amid the holy odor of shavings.

Foxy was above him. With a stealth meant to wake her slowly, Piet moved through the unfinished rooms, testing joints with his pocket knife, opening and shutting cabinet doors that closed with a delicate magnetic suck. Above him, a footstep heavier than a cat's sounded. Furiously Piet focused on the details of the copper plumbing installed beneath the old slate sink, suspended in mid-connection, where the plumbers had left it, open like a cry. She was beside him, wearing a loosely tied bathrobe over a slip, her face blurred by sleep, her blond hair moist on the pillowed side of her head. *They said they'd be back.*

I was trying to figure out why they had quit.

They explained it to me. Something about a male threader and a coupling.

Plumbers are the banes of this business. Plumbers and masons.

They're a vanishing breed?

Even vanishing they do slowly. You and Ken must be tired to death of living in the middle of a mess.

Oh, Ken's never here in the day and it's fun for me, to have men bringing me presents all day long. Adams and Comeau and I sit around the coffee table talking about the good old days in Tarbox.

What good old days?

Apparently it's always been a salty town. Look, would you like something to drink? I've woken up with a terrible thirst, I could make lemonade. That only needs cold water.

I ought to get back to the office and give the plumbers a blast.

They promised they'd be back so I'd have hot water. Do you mind if it's pink?

Pink lemonade? I prefer it. My mother used to make it. With strawberries.

In the good old days, Adams and Comeau tell me, the trolley car ran along Divinity Street and all the drunks would pile out because this was the only un-dry town between Boston and Plymouth. Even in the middle of a blizzard this would happen.

Funny about the trolley cars. How they came and went.

They used to make me sick. That awful smell, and the motorman's cigars.

Speaking of messes, what about where your porch was? Do you see that as lawn, or a patio, or what?

I'd love a grape arbor. Why is that funny?

You'd lose all the light you've gained. You'd lose your view from those windows.

The view bores me. The view is Ken's thing. He's always looking outward. Let me tell you about grape arbors.

Tell me.

When I was growing up one summer, the summer before Pearl Harbor, my parents wanted to get out of Bethesda and for a month we rented a brick house in Virginia with an enormous grape arbor over bricks where the ants made little hills. I must have been, what? '41, seven. Forgive me, I'm not usually so talkative.

I know.

I remember the little offshoots of the vines had letters in them, formed letters, you know. She made an A with her fingers. *I tried to make a complete collection. From A to Z.*

How far did you get?

I think to D. I never could find a perfect E. You'd think in all those vines there would have been one.

You should have skipped to F.

I was superstitious and I thought I couldn't. I inhibited myself all the time.

Piet grimaced and considered. The lemonade needed sugar. *It seems to be going out. Inhibition. In a way, I miss it.*

What a sad thing to say. Why? I don't miss it at all. Ever since I got pregnant I've become a real slob. Look at me, in a bathrobe. I love it. Her lips, in her clear pink complexion, looked whitish, as if rubbed with a chapstick. *Shall I tell you a secret?*

Better not. Tell me, what shade of white do you want your living-room woodwork? Flat white, glossy, ivory, or eggshell?

My secret is really so innocent. For years I wanted to be pregnant, but also I was afraid of it. Not just losing my figure, which

*was too skinny to care about anyway, but my body being somehow
an embarrassment to other people. For months I didn't tell anybody except Bea Guerin.*

Who told everybody else.

*Yes, and I'm glad. Because it turns out not to matter. People
just don't care. I was so conceited to think that people would care.
In fact they like you a little better if you look beat-up. If you look
used.*

You don't look very used to me.

Or you to me.

Do men get used? They just use.

*Oh, you're so wrong. We use you all the time. It's all we know
how to do. But your saying that fits with your missing inhibition. You're very Puritan. You're quite hard on yourself. At first
I thought you fell down stairs and did acrobatics to show off. But
really you do it to hurt yourself. In the hope that you will. Now
why are you laughing?*

Because you're so clever.

*I'm not. Tell me about your childhood. Mine was dreary. My
parents finally got a divorce. I was amazed.*

*We had a greenhouse. My parents had Dutch accents I've
worked quite hard not to inherit. They were both killed years ago
in an automobile accident.*

Yes, of course. Freddy Thorne calls you our orphan.

How much do you see of Freddy Thorne?

No more than I must. He comes up to me at parties.

He comes up to everybody at parties.

I know that. You don't have to tell me.

*Sorry. I don't mean to tell you anything. I'm sure you know
quite enough. I just want to get this job done for you so you and
your baby can be comfortable this winter.*

Her lips, stunned a moment, froze, bloodless, measuring a
space of air like calipers. She said, *It's not even July.*

Time flies, he said. It was not even July, and he had never
touched her, except in the conventions of greeting and while
dancing. In dancing, though at least his height, she had proved
submissive to his lead, her arm weightless on his back, her
hard belly softly bumping. He felt her now expectant, sitting
composed in a careless bathrobe on a kitchen chair, aggressive

even, unattractive, so full of the gassy waitingness and pallor of pregnancy.

He said casually, *Good lemonade*, in the same moment as she sharply asked, *Why do you go to church?*

Well, why do you?

I asked first.

The usual reasons. I'm a coward. I'm a conservative. Republican, religious. My parents' ghosts are there, and my older girl sings in the choir. She's so brave.

I'm sorry you're a Republican. My parents worshipped Roosevelt.

Mine were offended because he was Dutch, they didn't think the Dutch had any business trying to run the country. I think they thought power was sin. I don't have any serious opinions. No, I do have one. I think America now is like an unloved child smothered in candy. Like a middle-aged wife whose husband brings home a present after every trip because he's been unfaithful to her. When they were newly married he never had to give presents.

Who is this husband?

God. Obviously. God doesn't love us any more. He loves Russia. He loves Uganda. We're fat and full of pimples and always whining for more candy. We've fallen from grace.

You think a lot about love, don't you?

More than other people?

I think so.

Actually, I never think about love. I've left that to your friend Freddy Thorne.

Would you like to kiss me?

Very much, yes.

Why don't you?

It doesn't seem right. I don't have the nerve. You're carrying another man's child.

Foxy impatiently stood, exclaiming, *Ken's frightened of my baby. I frighten him. I frighten you.* Piet had risen from his chair and she stood beside him, asking in a voice as small as the distance between them, *Aren't we in our house? Aren't you building this house for me?*

Before kissing her, yet after all alternatives had been closed to him, Piet saw her face to be perfectly steady and clean of feeling, like a candleflame motionless in a dying of wind, or a road straight without strategies, like the roads of his native state, or the canals of Holland, and his hands on her body beneath the loose robe found this same quality, a texture almost wooden yet alive and already his; so quickly familiar did her body feel that there was no question, no necessity, of his taking her that afternoon—as a husband and wife, embracing in the kitchen, will back off because they will soon have an entire night, when the children are asleep, and no mailman can knock.

Outdoors again, amid the tracked clay, the splinters, the stacked bundles of raw shingles, the lilac stumps, Piet remembered how her hair, made more golden by the Tarbox sun, had been matted, a few damp strands, to her temple. She had averted her blushing face from his kiss as if to breathe, exhaling a sigh and gazing past his shoulder at a far corner of the unfinished room. Her lips, visually thin, had felt wide and warm and slippery; the memory, outdoors, as if chemically transformed by contact with oxygen, drugged Piet with a penetrating dullness.

His life with Angela suffered under a languor, a numbness that Georgene had never imposed. His blood brooded on Foxy; he dwelled endlessly upon the bits of her revealed to him—her delicate pubic fleece, her high-pitched coital cries, the prolonged and tender and unhoped-for meditations of her mouth upon his phallus. He became an obsessed inward housekeeper, a secret gardener.

I didn't know you'd be blond here too.

What would I be? You're red.

But you're so delicate. Transparent. Like the fuzz on a rose.

She laughed. *Well I've learned to live with it, and so must you.*

He lived dimly, groping, between those brilliant glimpses when they quickly slipped each other from their clothes and she lay down beside him, her stretched belly shining, and like a lens he opened, and like a blinded skier lost himself on the slopes of her presence. July was her fifth month; her condition forced upon their intercourse homely accommodations. Since bending was awkward, she would slide down in the bed to kiss him. *Do you really like that?*

Love it.

Is there a taste?

A good taste. Salty and strong. A bit of something bitter, like lemon.

I'm afraid of abusing you.

Don't be. Do.

She never came. However gladly she greeted him, and with however much skill he turned her body on the lathe of the light, shaping her with his hands and tongue, finally they skidded separate ways. *Come in me.*

Are you ready?

I want you in me.

He felt her inner music stall. Her cunt was young, snug. A kind of exasperation swept him forward toward the edge, and as she whimpered he ejaculated, and sighing she receded. But in her forgiving him and his forgiving her, in her blaming herself and his disagreeing, in their accepting the blame together, their love had exercise and grew larger. Her brown eyes, gazing, each held in miniature the square skylight above him. She apologized, *I'm sorry. I can't quite forget that it's you.*

Who should I be?

Nobody. Just a man. I think of your personality and it throws me off the track.

Does this happen with Ken?

No. Sometimes I come first. We've known each other so long we're rather detached, and just use each other. Anyway, as I guess I've told you, we don't make much love since I've gotten big.

That seems strange. You're lovely this way. Your skin is glossy, even your shape seems right. I can't imagine making love to you with a flat tummy. It wouldn't be you. You'd lack grandeur.

Ken is strange. He wants sex to stay in a compartment. He married me, and that solved the problem, as far as he was concerned. He never wanted me to have a baby. We had enough money, it was just his selfishness. I was never his wife, I was his once-a-week whore for all those years.

I'm jealous.

Don't be. Piet, don't feel bad about my not coming. I feel love too much with you, is the problem.

You're kind, but I honestly fear I'm second-rate at this. Like my skiing and my golf. I began too late.

Horrible man. I hate you when you fish for compliments. As all the ladies must tell you, you're incredible. You're incredibly affectionate.

Any man you took to bed with all his clothes off would be affectionate.

No. At least, I've only known three men, and the other two weren't especially.

Not the Jew? She had told him about the Jew.

He laughed at me. Sometimes he hurt me. But then I had been a virgin and probably he couldn't help hurting me. Probably he wouldn't hurt me now.

Do you want him now?

I have him now. Is that awful to say? I have him in you, and you besides. It's better. He was perverse, Piet.

But you're perverse too.

Her brown eyes childishly widened. *How? You mean*—her fingertips touched her lips, then his penis—*that? But why is that perverse? Don't you like it?*

I love it. It binds us so close, though, I'm frightened.

Are you? I'm glad. I was afraid only I was. Piet. What will the world do to us?

Is it God or the world you care about?

You think of them as different? I think of them as the same.

Maybe that's what I mean when I say you're perverse. Her face so close to his seemed a paradigm, a pattern of all the female faces that had ever been close to him. Her blank brow, her breathing might have belonged to Angela; then Foxy turned her head on the pillow so her pink face took the light from above, the cold blue light of the sky, and was clearly not Angela, was the Whitman woman, the young adulteress.

She was frightened, brazen, timid, wanton, appalled by herself, unrepentant. Adultery lit her from within, like the ashen mantle of a lamp, or as if an entire house of gauzy hangings and partitions were ignited but refused to be consumed and, rather, billowed and glowed, its structure incandescent. That she had courted him; that she was simultaneously proud and careless of her pregnancy; that she would sleep with him; that her father had been an inflexible family-proud minor navy deskman; that her mother had married a laundromat entrepreneur; that by both birth and marriage she was above him in the social scale; that she would take his blood-stuffed prick into the floral surfaces of her mouth; that there had been a Jew she had refound in him; that her mind in the midst of love's throes could be as dry and straight-seeking as a man's; that her fabric was delicate and fragile and burned with another life; that she was his slave; that he was her hired man; that she was frightened—compared to these shifting and luminous transparencies, Angela was a lump, a barrier, a boarded door. Her ignorance of the affair, though all the other couples guessed it, was the core of her maddening opacity. She did not share what had become the central issue of their lives. She was maimed, mute; and in the eggshell-painted rooms of their graceful colonial house she blundered and rasped against Piet's taut nerves. He was so full of Foxy, so pregnant with her body and body scents and her cries and remorses and retreats and fragrant returnings, so full of their love, that his mind felt like thin ice. He begged Angela to guess, and her refusal seemed willful, and his gratitude to her for permitting herself to be deceived turned, as his secret churned in sealed darkness, to a rage that would burst forth irrationally.

"Wake up!"

She had been sitting reading a book in lamplight, and blinked. Her eyes, lifted from the bright page, could not see him. "I am awake."

"You're *not*. You're drifting through life in a trance. Don't you feel what's happening to us?"

"I feel you getting meaner every day."

Bruised moths bumped and clung to the lampshade above her shoulder. "I'm upset," he said.

"What about?"

"About everything. About that pinchy-mouthed gouger Gallagher. About the crappy ranch houses on the hill. About Jazinski: he thinks I'm a drunk. About the Whitman job. I'm losing my shirt for the bastard and he isn't even grateful."

"I thought you enjoyed it, tripping down there every day to visit the little princess."

He laughed gratefully. "Is that what you think of her?"

"I think she's young. I also think she's arrogant. I think she'll be mellowed eventually, I think having a baby will do her good. I don't think she needs your paternal attentions especially."

"Why do you think my attentions are paternal?"

"Whatever they are. Can I go back to my book? I don't find Foxy Whitman or this conversation that interesting."

"God, you are smug. You are so fantastically above it all you stink."

"Listen, I promise I'll make love to you tonight, just let me get to the end of this chapter."

"Finish the fucking book for all I care. Stuff it. Give yourself a real literary thrill."

She heard the appeal in his violence and tried to lift her head, but the hooked print held her gaze. Absent-mindedly she asked, "Can't you relax ten minutes? I have five more pages."

He jumped to his feet, strode two steps to the mirror above the telephone, strode back. "I need to go out. I need a party. I wonder what the Applesmiths are doing. Or the Saltines."

"It's eleven o'clock. Please hush."

"I'm dying. I'm a thirty-four-year-old fly-by-night contractor. I have no sons, my wife snubs me, my employees despise me, my friends are all my wife's friends, I'm an orphan, a pariah."

"You're a caged animal."

"Yes." He took an aggressive stance, presenting himself before her with fists on hips, a bouncy close-set red-haired man whose rolled-up shirtsleeves revealed forearms dipped in freckles. "But Angel, who made the cage, huh? Who? *Who?*"

He meant her to fling him open and discover his secret, to be awed and enchanted by it, to decipher and nurture with him its intricate life. But, enclosed in the alternative world—a world exotic yet strict, mixing a lover's shamelessness and a father's compassion—arising from her lap, she did not respond. The book was an old college text, little appreciated at the time, stained by girlish annotations and translucent blots of the oil she and her roommates had used under their sunlamp, the Modern Library edition of *The Interpretation of Dreams.*

Janet Appleby had confessed to Angela on the beach that she was seeing a psychiatrist. Angela explained it to Piet: "It's just twice a week, for therapy, as opposed to real analysis. Frank's all for it, though it was her idea. She described coming home about three A.M. from the little-Smiths after a terrible scene with Marcia and suddenly knowing that she needed help, help from somebody who isn't a friend or a lover or has any reason to care about her at all. She's only been a few times but already she's convinced she doesn't know why she does what she does. She never loved Harold, so why did she go to bed with him? She told herself it was because she felt sorry for him but he didn't feel sorry for himself especially so who was she kidding? And why now, even though they've all stopped sleeping with each other, or at least she and Harold have, can't they stay away from the other couple every weekend? She says now they've somehow acquired the Thornes, too, especially Freddy—"

"That jerk," Piet said.

"—and it's a real mess. Onion rings and gin. The Thornes never go home, apparently. Georgene just sits and drinks, which she never used to do, and Freddy writes an endless pornographic play on his knee."

"So Janet has to go to a psychiatrist because Georgene drinks?"

"Of course not. Because she thinks she, Janet, is neurotic."

"Define neurotic."

Janet had a variety of bikinis and semi-bikinis and Piet pictured her making her confession while lying belly down on the sand, her top untied to give her back an unbroken tan, her cheek pillowed on a folded towel, her breasts showing white when she lifted up on her elbows to explain better or to survey her children.

Angela said, "You know what neurotic is. You do things you know not why. You sleep with women when you're really trying to murder your mother."

"Suppose your mother's already been murdered?"

"Then maybe you're trying to bring her back to life. The ego tries to mediate between external reality and the id, which is our appetites. The ego carries all this bad news back and forth, but the id refuses to listen, and keeps trying to do whatever it wanted to do, even though the ego has turned its back. I don't explain it very well, because I don't understand it, but dreams are a way of letting out these suppressions, which mostly have to do with sex, which mostly has to do with your parents, who have become a superego and keep tormenting the ego from the *other* side. You know all this, everybody does."

"Well, do you see anything unnatural about Janet sleeping

with Harold now and then? Frank can be a real boor; would
you like to go to bed with him for the rest of your life, night
after night?"

"It's not a question of natural or unnatural or right or wrong.
It's understanding why you do things so you can stop doing
them. Or enjoy doing them. Certainly Janet does not make
herself happy. I don't think she enjoys her children very much,
or sex, or even her money. She could be great, you know. She
has everything."

"But it's just those people who are unhappy. The people
with everything are the ones who panic. The rest of us are too
busy scrambling."

"Piet, that's a very primitive attitude. You're saying the rich
can't get through the needle's eye. The first shall be last."

"Don't poke fun of the Bible. What's your stake in all this
hocus-pocus with egos and ids? Why are you so defensive? I
suppose you want to go to a psychiatrist too."

"Yes."

"The hell you will. Not as long as you're my wife."

"Oh? You're thinking of getting another wife."

"Of course not. But it's very insulting. It implies I don't give
you enough sex."

"There is no such implication."

"I give you more than you want."

"Exactly. Maybe a psychiatrist could tell me why I don't
want more. I do and I don't. I hate myself the way I am. It's
doing awful things to both of us."

Piet was taken aback; he had inwardly assumed that Angela
knew best, that the amount of sex she permitted was the proper
amount, and the surplus was his own problem, his own fault.
He asked her, "You don't think our sex life is right?"

"It's awful. Dreadful. You know that."

He tried to pin this estimate down. "How would you rate it
on a scale of one to ten?"

"Two."

"Oh come *on*, it's not *that* bad. You can be gorgeous."

"But so rarely. And I don't use my hands or mouth or
anything. I'm sick. I need help, Piet. I'm turning you into
a bully and a cheat and myself into one of those old maids
everybody says you wouldn't believe how beautiful she once

was." Blue-eyed, she began to cry. When she cried, it made her face look fat, like Nancy's. Piet was touched. They were in the kitchen, she with vermouth and he with gin-and-Bitter-Lemon, after putting the girls to bed. Against the tiny red florets of the kitchen wallpaper Angela's head, nicely oval, with summer braids and bun, did have a noble neatness that was maidenly. He then realized that in a sociable way she was preparing him for another night without lovemaking. Confessing her frigidity sanctioned it.

He protested, "But everybody loves you. Any man in town would love to go to bed with you. Even Eddie Constantine flirts with you. Even John Ong adores you, if you could understand him."

"I know. But I don't en*joy* knowing it. I don't want to go to bed with *any*body. I don't feel I'm a woman really. I'm a kind of cheerful neuter with this sex appeal tacked on as a kind of joke."

"My poor Angel. Like having Kick Me on your back."

"Exactly. I really thought, listening to Janet, how much we're alike. A lot of coziness and being nice to creeps and this disgusted emptiness at heart. We both come from good families and have big bottoms and try to be witty and get pushed around. Do you know she keeps sleeping pills by her bed and some nights doesn't bother to count how many she takes?"

"Well you don't do that."

"But I could. It sounded very familiar, the way she described it. I love sleep, just delicious nothing sleep. I'd love not to wake up."

"Angela! That's sinful."

"The big difference between Janet and me is, I repress and she tries to express. No?"

"Don't ask *me*."

"I'm sure you've had an affair with her and know just what I mean. Tell me about us, Piet."

"You are a scandalous wife. I have never slept with Janet."

"In a way, I want you to. In a Lesbian way. I felt very drawn, lying beside her on the beach. I think I must be Sapphic. I'd love to have a girls' school, where we'd all wear chitons and play field hockey and sit around listening to poetry after warm baths."

"If you have it all analyzed, you don't need an analyst."

"I don't. I'm just guessing. He'd probably say the reverse was true. I can't stand being touched by other women, for instance. Carol Constantine is always patting, and so does Bea. He might say I'm *too* heterosexual, for America the way it is now. Why did nobody marry me, for example, until you came along? I must have frightened them away."

"Or your father frightened them away."

"Do you want to know something else sick? Can you take it?"

"I'll try."

"I masturbate."

"Sweetie. When?"

"More in the summer than in the winter. I wake up some mornings between four and five, when the birds are just beginning, or a trailer truck goes by on the road, and the sheets feel terribly sensitive on my skin, and I do it to myself."

"That sounds pretty normal. Do you imagine anybody, any particular man?"

"Not very clearly. It's mostly sensation. You're the only man I've ever known, so if I picture anyone it's you. Now why don't I wake the real you up?"

"You're too considerate and shy."

"Oh balls, Piet. Just balls."

"You must stop talking to Freddy Thorne at parties. Your language is deteriorating."

"*I'm* deteriorating. I don't know how to act in this sexpot."

"Sexpot?"

"Tarbox."

"A sexpot is a person, not a place."

"This one's a place. Get me out or get me to a doctor."

"Don't be silly. The town is like every other town in the country. What you're saying is you're too good for this world. You're too fucking good for any of us."

"Don't raise your voice. I hate that high voice you put on."

"Of course you hate it, you're supposed to hate it. You hate me, why not hate my voice?"

"I don't hate you."

"You must, because I'm beginning to hate you."

"Ah. Now you're saying it."

"Well, I don't quite mean it. You're gorgeous. But you're *so* self-centered. You have no idea what I'm like inside—"

"You mean you're having an affair and you want me to guess the woman?"

"No I don't mean that."

"Foxy Whitman."

"Don't be grotesque. She's pregnant and adores her icy husband and gives me a professional pain in the neck besides."

"Of course—but why do I imagine it? I know it's neurotic but every time you go down there and come back so affectionate to me and the children I think you've been sleeping with her. I watch her face and feel she has a secret. She's so tender and gay talking to me. She knows me all too well, they've only been in town since March."

"She likes you. Maybe she's a Lesbian too."

"And it's not just Foxy, it can be Janet or Marcia or even Georgene—I'm madly jealous. And the more jealous I get the less I can bring myself to make love to you. It's sad. It's miserable. Your telephone was busy for half an hour yesterday and I made myself a martini at eleven in the morning, imagining it was some woman."

Her oval face yearned to cry some more but a sophisticated mechanism produced a half-laugh instead. Painfully Piet looked toward the floor, at her bare feet; neither of her little toes touched the linoleum. His dear poor blind betrayed Angel: by what right had he torn her from her omnipotent father? Each afternoon, an hour before quitting, old man Hamilton would walk down his lawn between his tabletop hedges, trailing pipesmoke, bringing a quart bottle of Heineken's and Dixie cups for the workmen. Piet told her, "I don't have Appleby's money. I can't afford it."

She asked, "Isn't there some way I can earn it? I could go into Boston this fall and get enough education credits to teach at least at a private school. Nancy will be away all day in the first grade; I must do *some*thing with my time. I can begin therapy, just twice a week, with the education courses. Oh, Piet, I'll be a wonderful wife; I'll know *every*thing."

It grieved Piet to see her beg, to see her plan ahead. She was considering herself as useful, still useful to him, exploring herself bravely toward a new exploitation when to him she was exhausted, a stale labyrinth whose turnings must be ne-gotiated to reach fresh air and Foxy. Foxy asleep, moonlight lying light along her bones and diagonally stroking the down of her brow: at this vision his stomach slipped, his skin moist-ened, numbness stung his fingertips and tongue. There was a silver path beneath the stars. Obliviously Angela barred his way. "No," broke from him, panicked as he felt time sliding, houses, trees, lifetimes dumped like rubble, chances lost, neb-ulae turning, "*no*; sweetie, don't you see what you're doing to me? Let me *go*!"

At his high voice her face paled; its eager flush and the offer of its eyes withdrew. "Very well," she said, "go. What are you going to, may I ask?"

Piet opened his mouth to tell her, but the ice shelling his secret held.

Angela diffidently turned her back. "Your routines," she told him, "are getting less and less funny."

"Daddy, wake up! Jackie Kenneny's baby died because it was born too tiny!"

Nancy's face was a moon risen on the horizon of his sleep. Her eyes were greatly clear, skyey in astonishment. Red tear ducts the tone of a chicken's wattle. Slaughter. The premature Kennedy had been near death for two days. Nancy must have heard the news over television. "I'm sorry," he said. His voice was thick, stuffed and cracked. August was Piet's hay-fever sea-son. Strange, he thought, how pain seeks that couple out. Not wealth nor beauty nor homage shelters them. Suffering tug-ging at a king's robe. Our fragile gods.

"Daddy?"

"Mm."

"Was the baby scared?" Fear, a scent penetrating as cat musk, radiated through the flannel perfume of her infant skin. He had been dreaming. His brother. His brother frozen un-der glass, a Pope's remains, Piet apologetic about not having stayed and helped him, been his partner, in the greenhouse. *Is het koud, Joop?* Frozen by overwork, gathering edelweiss. He turned and explained, to the others, *Mijn broeder is dood.* Yet also Foxy was in the dream, though not visibly; her presence, like the onflow of grace, like a buried stream singing from well to well, ran beneath the skin of dreaming as beneath reality, a living fragility continually threatened.

"The baby was too little to be scared. The baby never knew anything, Nancy. It had no mind yet."

"He wants his mommy!" Nancy said, stamping her foot. "He cries and he cries and nobody listens. Everybody is *happy* he hurt hisself."

"Nobody is happy," Piet told her, returning his cheek to the pillow, knowing the child was right, nobody listens. The window against whose panes his upheld hand was silhouetted at night as a monstrous many-horned shape now, at dawn, gave on the plain sweet green of leaves, heart-shaped lilac and feathery, distant elm. Space, it seemed, redeems. Piet reached outwards and pulled Nancy toward him, into the mediating warmth that remained of his sleep. She fought his embrace, feeling its attempt to dissolve and smother the problem. Her wide face studied him angrily, cheated. Freckles small as flyspecks had come to her nose this summer, though they had thought she had inherited her mother's oily brunette skin. Angela's serene form pricked by his own uneasy nature. Flecks of lead in the condensed blue smoke of her irises. Sea creatures. Vague light becomes form becomes thought becomes soul and dies. The retina retains nothing. Piet asked, "Where's Mommy?"

"Up. Get up, Daddy."

"Go talk to Mommy about the Kennedy baby while Daddy gets dressed." Last night he had attempted to make love and though Angela had refused him he had slept nude. He did not wish his body to frighten the child. "Go downstairs," he said. "Daddy feels funny."

"Are you drunk?" She had learned the word and felt threatened by it; once Frank Appleby had crawled into her playpen and shattered a plastic floating duck, and the next day they had explained to her that he had been drunk.

"No. I *was* drunk, and now I wish I hadn't been. My head hurts. I feel sad about the Kennedy baby."

"Mommy said I would never die until I was an old old lady wearing earrings."

"That's absolutely right."

But— It was unspoken. Impatiently needing to urinate, he threw back the covers; his body filled her eyes and they overflowed into tears. He said, "But the little baby was even smaller than you?"

She nodded helplessly.

Piet kneeled and hugged her and recognized in his arms the mute tepid timbre he had often struck from Angela's larger form. He said urgently, "But the baby came out too soon, it was a mistake, God never meant it to live, like a big strong chubby girl like you." His nakedness in air, the stir of her skin in his arms, was gently leading his penis to lift. A cleft or shaft of sun.

Nancy pulled from his arms and shouted from the head of the stairs, "God should have teached the baby not to come out!"

Angela called, "Piet, are you up?"

"Be down in three minutes," he answered. He half dressed and shaved and finished dressing. Today was to be a desk-work day. From the bedroom windows his square lawn looked parched. A droughty summer. Prevailing winds shifting. Ice-caps melting. The great forests thinning. On Indian Hill clouds of dust coated the constructions, seeped into the unfinished frames cluttered by leaning plywood and loose electric cable. Here and there in the woods a starved maple turning early. The crickets louder at night. But from Foxy Whitman's windows the marshes, needing no rain, sucking water from the mother sea, spread lush and young, green as spring and carved like plush by the salt creeks' windings. Some afternoons, the tide high, the marshes were all but submerged, and Piet felt the earth reaching for the moon. Atlantis. Ararat.

The narrow farmhouse stairs descended through two landings and stopped a step from the front door, in a hall so cramped the opening door banged the newel post. On Piet's right, in a living room which the crowding lilacs left rather dark and where like sentinels in castellar gloom the empty glasses used last night by the little-Smiths and Saltzes and Guerins were still posted on arms and edges of furniture, Nancy and Ruth were watching television. A British postal official, relayed by satellite, supercilious and blurred, was discussing yesterday's seven-million-dollar robbery of a London mail train, the biggest haul in history—"not counting, of course, raids and confiscations which should properly be termed political acts, if you follow me. As far as we can determine, there was nothing political about these chaps." Television brought them the outer world. The little screen's icy brilliance implied a universe of profound cold beyond the warm encirclement of Tarbox, friends, and family. Mirrors established in New York and Los Angeles observed the uninhabitable surface between them and beamed reports that bathed the children's faces in a poisonous, flickering blue. This poison was their national life. Not since Korea had Piet cared about news. News happened to other people.

On his left, in the already sun-flooded kitchen, Angela laid out breakfast plates on four rectangular mats. Dish, glass, spoon, knife. Her nipples darkly tapped her nightie from within. Her hair was down, swung in sun as she moved, blithe. She seemed to Piet to be growing ever more beautiful, to be receding from him into abstract realms of beauty.

He said to her, "Poor Nancy. She's all shook up."

Angela said, "She asked me if the Kennedy baby was up in Heaven with the hamster going round and round in the wheel. Honestly I wonder, Piet, if religion's worth it, if it wouldn't be healthier to tell them the truth, we go into the ground and don't know anything and come back as grass."

"And are eaten by cows. I don't know why all you stoics think death is so damn healthy. Next thing you'll get into a warm bath with your wrists slit to prove it."

"Oh, you do like that idea."

Nancy came into the kitchen sobbing. "Ruthie says—Ruthie says—"

Ruth followed, flouncing. "I said God is retarded." She sneered at Nancy, "*Baaby.*"

"Ruth!" Angela said.

"Retarded?" Piet asked. It was an adjective her generation applied to everything uncooperative. *The retarded teacher kept us all after class. This retarded pen won't write. Frankie is a re-tard.*

"Well He is," Ruth said. "He lets little babies die and He makes cats eat birds and all that stuff. I don't want to sing in the choir next fall."

"I'm sure that'll make God shape up," Piet said.

"I don't see why the child should be forced to sing in the

choir every Sunday," Angela told him, standing bent as Nancy cried into her lap. Her hair overhung the child. Mothering. Seeking the smothering she had fled from in Piet. Loves her more than me. Each to each. Symbiosis.

"For the same fucking reason," Piet told Angela, "that I must spend my life surrounded by complaining females." He ate breakfast surrounded by wounded silence. He felt nevertheless he had done a good deed, had rescued Nancy from the grip of death. Better anger than fear. Better kill than be killed.

He drove to the office, rattling down Charity, parking on Hope. A space today, lately often not. Talk of the need for a stoplight at the corner where Divinity turned. Confusing to out-of-towners. Too many cars. Too many people. Homosexuality the answer? The pill. Gallagher was talking on his phone, Irish accent emergent. "We've got thirty-three rooms, Sister, and removing a lone partition would give us a grand refectory." Piet heated water on their electric coil and made instant coffee. Maxwell. Faraday. He settled at his desk to concentrate on deskwork. Lumber $769.82, total, overdue, if has escaped your previous notice please remit, since a sound credit rating, etc. His nasal passages itched and his eyes watered. Another scratchy August day. Foxy far. Hours away. Her laughter, her fur. *To visit the little princess. Too pretty-pretty for you.* His own phone rang.

"Allo, dollink." It had been a month since they had talked.

"Hello." He used his flat contractor's voice.

"Are you surrounded? Is Matt there?"

"No. Yes." They had recently installed in their crowded space a corrugated-glass divider (ASG mfg., 1″ thickness overall) which set Gallagher apart and made him appear, subtly, the head of the office. But the partition was thin and without a client in his cubbyhole Gallagher kept the door open, to create a breeze. He needed a breeze, or his shirt would wrinkle. He had walled himself in without a window. In there with him were an electric clock, a Ford-agency calendar, a colored zoning map of Tarbox, an aerial photograph of the downtown and beach area, an overall map of Plymouth County, a Mandarin-orange street directory of Tarbox, the pale-blue annual town reports back to 1958, a thin red textbook entitled *Property Valuation*, a thumbed fat squat black missal. While Piet worked, when he did, at a yellow oak desk salvaged from a high school and littered with molding samples and manufacturers' catalogs, Gallagher's desk was military gray steel and clean except for a pen set socketed in polished serpentine, a blotter, framed photographs of Terry and Tommy, and two telephones. Behind his head hung framed his license from the Board of Registration of Real Estate Brokers and Salesmen. He had just purchased for their firm the fifty-odd acres and the thirty-odd rooms of an estate in Lacetown with iron deer on the lawn. He had intended to develop the grounds piecemeal but had since got wind of an order of nuns who were seeking to relocate a novitiate. As he exultantly told Piet, the Church doesn't haggle. In the meantime their tiny office supported among its debts a hundred-thousand-dollar mortgage; it felt precarious. But gambling was Gallagher's meat, and having dared the deal increased the amount of psychic space he occupied. Piet feared Georgene's voice was coming through too strong; he huddled the receiver tight against his ear.

"Don't worry, I'll hang up in a minute," she said. "I just had a crazy impulse to call and find out how you were doing. Is that presumptuous? I still have some rights, don't I? I mean you and me, we *were* something real, weren't we?

"I understand you," Piet said.

"You can't really talk, can you?"

"That sounds correct."

"Well, if you'd call me once in a while this wouldn't happen. We hear you had a little party last night and I felt very hurt we weren't invited. The way Irene let it slip out was positively malicious."

"The orders," Piet said uncertainly, "are slow coming through this time of year. The government's buying up a lot of west-coast fir."

"Piet, I miss you so much, it's killing me. Couldn't you just come for coffee on your way to somewhere else sometime? Like this morning? It's perfectly safe. Whitney's off at camp and Irene took Martha and Judy down to the beach. I told her I had a plumber coming. It's true, our pressure's down to nothing. Don't ever live on a hill. Can't you come, please? Just to talk a *little* bit? I promise I won't be pushy. I was *such* a bitch at the Ongs'."

"The estimate looks discouraging."

"I'm *mis*erable, Piet. I can't stand living with that man much longer. He gets worse and worse. I'm losing all sense of myself as a woman."

"I thought he did good work."

Georgene laughed, a brisk, slightly formal noise. "I'm sure Matt isn't fooled at all. The games you two play down there. No, if you must know, he does lousy work. Freddy's lousy in bed, that's what you want to hear, isn't it? That's what you always wanted to hear. I lied to you. I protected him. He can't manage anything until he's drunk and then he's sloppy and falls asleep. He wilts. Do you understand what I'm saying?"

"We're speaking of upright supports."

"It's *so* sad. It makes me so *ashamed*. I have no self-confidence at anything any more, Terry and I lost six-two, six-three to Bernadette and Angela yesterday, I suppose she told you, crowing about it."

"No."

"*Please* come over. I'm *so* blue, so *blue*. I won't pry, I promise. I know you have somebody else but I don't care any more. Was I ever that demanding? Was I? Didn't I just take you as you came?"

"Yes." Gallagher loudly rustled papers and tapped shut a steel desk drawer.

"God, I hate the sound of my voice. I hate it, Piet. I hate to beg. It's taken me weeks to bring myself to make this call. You don't have to go to bed with me, I promise. I just need to have you to myself for half an hour. For fifteen minutes."

"We're behind schedule now, I'm afraid."

"Come, or I'll tell Freddy about us. I'll tell Freddy and Angela everything. No. Forget Angela. I'll tell Foxy. I'll waltz right down there and plump myself down and tell her the kind of bastard she's mixed herself up with."

"Let me call you back. I'll look at my schedule again."

She began to cry; Georgene's crying, rare, was an unlovely and unintelligent sound, and Piet feared it would fill the little office as it filled his skull. "I didn't know," she sobbed, "I'd miss you this much, I didn't know . . . you were into me . . . so deep. You knew. You knew just what you were doing to me, you bastard, you marvelous poor bastard. You're making me suffer because your parents were killed. Piet, I didn't kill your parents. I was in Philadelphia when it happened, I didn't know them, I didn't *know* you . . . oh, forgive me, I have no idea what I'm saying . . ."

"In the meantime," Piet said, "watch out for seepage," and hung up.

There was an inquisitive silence behind him. He responded, "Bea Guerin. She thinks her house might be settling. She doesn't trust those cedar posts I put in because we used metal in the Whitman renovation. I think she's hysterical. It's too bad, all she needs is a baby. Which reminds me, Matt, something I wanted your opinion on. Angela thinks she needs to go to a psychiatrist."

As Piet had hoped, the second statement caught Matt's attention; the truth is always more interesting than the lie. "Angela's the sanest woman I know," Matt said.

"Ah, Matt," Piet answered, "in this fallen world, being sane and being well aren't the same thing." Gallagher uncomfortably frowned; it was part of his Catholicism to believe that all theological references in private conversation must be facetious. Piet had developed with Gallagher a kidding pose, a blarneyish tone, useful in both acknowledging and somewhat bridging the widening gap between them. Gradually they were finding each other impossible. Without an act, a routine, Piet would hardly have been able to talk to Gallagher at all. "And surely she's no saner than Terry," he said.

"Terry. She's gone gaga over the lute. She's in Norwell twice a week and now she wants to take pottery lessons from the woman's husband."

"Terry is very creative."

"I suppose. She won't play for *me*. I don't know how to treat Terry these days."

Piet abruptly volunteered, "Actually, what Angela needs is a lover, not a psychiatrist."

Matt's brittle face, his jaw so smooth-shaven it seemed burnished, hardened at this; his mouth tightened. He felt in Piet's train of association possible news for himself. Yet he was curious; he was human, Freddy Thorne would have pointed out. He asked, "You'd let her?"

"Well, I'd expect her out of decency to try to conceal it. I'd simply not pry. If it came into the open, I'd of course have to be sore."

They were talking through the doorway; Matt was framed by corrugated glass. The office was so small there was no need to raise their voices. Matt said, "Piet, if I may say so—"

"You may, my good fellow. An honest man's the noblest work of God."

"You seem quite jealous of her. Terry and I have always been struck by you two as a couple, how protective and fond you are of each other, while pretending the opposite."

"Do we pretend the opposite?" Piet was offended, but Matt was too intent to notice.

"Terry and I," he said, "don't have your room for maneuver. Fidelity can't be a question. Do you know that, in the view of the Church, marriage is a sacrament administered by the couple themselves?"

"Maybe some of the sacrament should be giving the other some freedom. Why all this fuss about bodies?" Piet asked. "In fifty years we'll all be grass. You know what would seem like a sacrament to me? Angela and another man screwing and me standing above them sprinkling rose petals on his back." Piet held up his hand and rubbed thumb and forefinger. "Sprinkling blessings on his hairy back."

Gallagher said, "Mother and father."

"Whose?"

"Yours. As you described that I pictured a child beside his parents' bed. He loves his mother but knows he can't handle her so he lets the old man do the banging while he does the blessing."

Again offended, Piet said, "Everybody's so damn psychoanalytical all of a sudden. Let me ask you something. Suppose you discovered Terry wasn't going off for music lessons."

"I'd refuse to discover it," Gallagher answered with catechetical swiftness, and smiled. The smiles of the Irish never fail to strike a spark; they have the bite in their eyes of the long oppressed. The flint of irony. He told Piet, "You have a kind of freedom I don't have. You can be an adventurer where I can't. I have to have my adventures here." He laid his hand flat on the steel desk. His hand was hair-backed. Big pores. Coarse dogma.

Piet said, "And they make me damn nervous. What the hell are we going to do with that rotten old castle in Lacetown? That partition you were telling the sister about can't just be knocked out. It's weight-bearing."

Matt told him, "You shouldn't be in this business, you're too conservative. You don't have the nerves for it. What you got to realize, Piet, is that land can't lose. There's only so much of it, and there are more and more people."

"Thanks to the Pope."

"You have more children than I do."

"I don't know how you do it, it's a miracle."

"Self-control. Try it."

This was Piet's day to fight. That Gallagher, with his wife off with some old potter, felt able to deliver instruction so angered Piet that he rose from his creaky swivel chair and said, "Which reminds me, I better get over to the hill and see if they're using wood on the houses or cardboard like you tell them to."

Matt's face was a crystal widening toward the points of the jaws, his shaved cheeks and flat temples facets. He said, "And check on Mrs. Whitman while you're at it."

"Thanks for reminding me. I will."

Stepping outdoors onto treeless Hope Street, Piet was struck by the summer light so hard that his eyes winced and the world looked liquid. It was all, he saw, television aerials and curbstone grits, abortive—friendships, marriages, conversations, all aborted, all blasted by seeking the light too soon.

On Indian Hill the three ranch houses had reached a dismal state of incompletion. The frames, sheathed in four-by-eight sheets of plywood, were complete but the rooms within were waiting for electricians and plumbers and plasterers. Cedar shingles lay on the damp earth in costly unbroken stacks. Jazinski was watching two trade-school boys nail shingles and Piet was annoyed by his idle supervision. He told him, "Get a hammer," and spent the morning beside him, aligning and nailing cedar shingles over insulating foil. The cedar had an ancient fragrance; the method of aligning the shingles, by snapping a string rubbed with chalk, was agreeably primitive. Sun baked Piet's shoulders and steamed worry from him. It was good to work, to make weatherproof, to fashion overlapping fishscales. He was Noah; the skinny-armed young Polack swinging his hammer in unison beside him perhaps was a son. Piet tried to converse with Leon, but between hammer blows the boy responded with pronouncements that, sullen yet definite, were complete in themselves, and led nowhere.

On the death of the Kennedy baby: "That crowd has everything but luck. Old Joe can't buy them luck." On the Catholic religion: "I believe in some kind of Supreme Being but none of the rest of it. My wife agrees, I was surprised." On the progress of the job: "It's waiting on the plumbers now. I guess two have been already sold. The families want to move in by the start of school. Do you want to give the plumbers a ring, or shall I?" On the colored Construction King operator, whom Piet remembered fondly, for having shown him cheerfulness on a day of death: "I feel this way about it. If they measure up they should be treated like everybody else. That don't mean I want to live next door to them." On the future: "I may not be here next summer. I'm looking around. I have responsibilities to myself."

"Well, Leon, maybe next summer I won't be here, and you can be me."

The boy said nothing, and Piet, glancing over, wondered how his arms could remain so stringy and pale, like those of a desk-worker, though he worked all summer in the sun.

In the rhythmic silence Piet began to talk with Foxy in his head. He would take her a flower from the roadside—a stalk of chicory, with flowers as blue as the eyes of a nymphomaniac. *For me?*

Who else?

You're so tender. When you're not with me I remember the passion but I forget the affection.

He would laugh. *How could I not be affectionate?*

Other men could. I guess. I've not had much experience.

You've had enough, I'd say.

What can you see in me? I'm getting huge, and I never come for you, and I'm not good, or witty, like Angela.

I find you quite witty.

Should we go up to bed?

Just for a moment. To rest.

Yes. To rest.

I love your maternity clothes. The way they billow and float. I love the way your belly is so hard and pushes at me. In another month it'll start kicking.

Do you really like me this way? Look, I'm getting veins in my legs.

Beautiful blue. Blue blond furry rosy Foxy.

Oh Piet. Take these awful Paisley things off. I want to kiss you. As you like.

Leonine he would lie back. Eyelids lowered, her dusty-rose cheek dented by the forcing apart of her jaws, her sleeping face would eclipse that gnarled choked part of him a Calvinist whisper by his cradle had taught him to consider vile. Touch of teeth like glints of light. Her fluttered tongue and lips' encirclement. Her hair spun air between his lifted thighs, nipples and fingernails, muddled echoes of blood. He would seek the light with one thrust and she would gag; penitent he would beg *Come up* and her tranced drained face swim to his and her cold limp lips as he kissed them wear a moony melted stale smell whose vileness she had taken into herself. All innocent they would lock loins, her belly gleaming great upon his, and though short of breath and self-forsaken she would not quite come; this had happened and would happen again that summer of the solar eclipse.

Three weeks ago, it had been ninety per cent at their latitude. An invisible eater moved through the sun's disc amid a struggle of witnessing clouds. The dapples of light beneath the elm became crescent-shaped; the birds sang as in the evening. Seen through smoked glass the sun was a shaving, a sideways eyebrow, a kindergarten boat riding a tumult of contorted cumulus. The false dusk reversed; the horns of the crescents beneath the trees pointed in the opposite direction; the birds sang to greet the day. Not a month before, he had first slept with Foxy.

Only one other time had been so ominous: the Wednesday in October of 1962 when Kennedy had faced Khrushchev over Cuba. Piet had had a golf date with Roger Guerin. They agreed not to cancel. "As good a way to go as any," Roger had said over the phone. Stern occasions suited him. As Piet drove north to the course, the Bay View, he heard on the radio that the first Russian ship was approaching the blockade. They teed off into an utterly clear afternoon and between shots glanced at the sky for the Russian bombers. Chicago and Detroit would go first and probably there would be shouts from the clubhouse when the bulletins began coming in. There was almost nobody else on the course. It felt like the great rolling green deck of a ship, sunshine glinting on the turning foliage. As Americans they had enjoyed their nation's luxurious ride and now they shared the privilege of going down with her. Roger, with his tight angry swing, concentrating with knit brows on every shot, finished the day under ninety. Piet had played less well. He had been too happy. He played best, swung easiest, with a hangover or a cold. He had been distracted by the heavensent glisten of things—of fairway grass and fallen leaves and leaning flags—seen against the onyx immanence of death, against the vivid transparence of the sky in which planes might materialize. Swinging, he gave thanks that, a month earlier, he had ceased to be faithful to Angela and had slept with Georgene. It had been a going from indoors to outdoors; they met at beaches, on porches, beneath translucent trees. Happy remembering her, picturing her straight limbs, Piet sprayed shots, three-putted, played each hole on the edge of an imaginary cliff. Driving home, he heard on the car radio that the Russians had submitted to inspection and been allowed to pass. He had felt dismay, knowing that they must go on, all of them, Georgene and Angela and Freddy and himself, toward an untangling less involuntary and fateful. He had been fresh in love then.

Leon said: "That sun is brutal. I like winter myself. My wife and I thought we'd try skiing this year."

Noon passed, and one. The connective skin between thumb and palm, where the hammer rubbed, smarted as if to blister. Piet left Leon and drove into town, through town, on down the beach road. Dusty flowers, chicory and goldenrod, a stand of late daisies, flickered at the roadside, but he was in too much of a hurry to stop. *I wanted to bring you a flower but it seemed too urgent so I just brought you myself.*

Of course. What a nice present.

Her house was empty. No Plymouth station wagon, no workman's truck, was in the driveway. The door was unlocked.

The hall rug awry. Cotton slept in the blue sling chair. The
work was nearly done, the plastering completed even to the
sweeping up. A round thermostat and square light switch on
the smooth wall side by side. Rough edges. Books of wallpaper
samples lay face up on the sanded and sealed floor. A folder
of paint shades was propped against a pine baseboard. In the
kitchen all that was needed was white paint and for the dishwasher on order to arrive. Sawdust and earth smells still lived in
the house. Salt air would wipe them away. She had promised to
invite Piet and Angela down when the house was finished. The
wallpaper books were open to samples that were not Angela's
taste. Big pastel splashes. Vulgar passion.

Where was she? She never shopped at this hour, her nap
hour. Had he only dreamed of possessing her? The tide was
low and the channels seen from the kitchen windows were ribbons glittering deep between banks of velvet clay. Three red
deer were bounding across the dry marsh to the uninhabited
shrub island. The days to hunting season were finite. The crystalline sky showed streaks of cirrus wispy at one end, like the
marks of skates braking. Miscarriage. Doctors, workmen returning. Without her here he felt the house hostile, the walls of
their own will rejecting him. Too soon, too soon. He became
anxious to leave and, driving back toward town, turned on an
impulse up the Thornes' long driveway.

The Saltzes and the Constantines, maliciously called the
Saltines by the other couples, had jointly bought a boat, the
Applebys' catboat, with a six-horsepower motor, and after a
Saturday or Sunday of sailing would drink beer and California
sauterne in their damp bathing suits and have other couples
over. The Sunday night before Labor Day a crowd collected
in the Constantines' messy Victorian manse. The couples
were excited and wearied by tennis; this was the weekend
of the North Mather Court Club Open Tournament. Annually
the North Mather men, rangy automobile salesmen and insurance claims agents who exerted themselves all winter long on
two domed courts grassed with plastic fiber, easily eliminated
even the best of the Tarbox men, such as Matt Gallagher; but,
contrariwise, the North Mather wives wilted under the assault
of their Tarbox counterparts. Invariably Georgene and Angela,

Terry and Bernadette dominated the female finals, and for weeks before Labor Day their telephones jangled as the men of North Mather, centaurs in search of Amazons, beseeched the fabulous Tarbox women to be their partners in mixed doubles.

None of the Saltines played. A delicate social line had early hardened and not been crossed. Instead, today they had taken Freddy Thorne, who played terribly, out into the Bay for skin diving. It amused him to keep his wetsuit on. His appearance in the tight shiny skin of black rubber was disturbingly androgynous: he was revealed to have hips soft as a woman's and with the obscene delicacy of a hydra's predatory petals his long hands flitted bare from his sleeves' flexible carapace. This curvaceous rubber man had arisen from another element. Like a giant monocle his Cyclopean snorkeling mask jutted from his naked skull, and his spatulate foot flippers flopped grotesquely on the Constantines' threadbare Oriental rugs. When he sat in a doilied armchair and, twiddling a cigarette, jauntily crossed his legs, the effect was so outrageous and droll, monstrous and regal that even Piet Hanema laughed, feeling in Freddy's act life's bad dreams subdued.

"Read us your play," Carol Constantine begged him. She wore a man's shirt over an orange bikini. Something had nerved her up tonight; a week ago, she had dyed her hair orange. "Let's all take parts."

All summer it had been rumored that Freddy was writing a pornographic play. Now he pretended not to understand. "What play?" he asked. Beneath the misted snorkel mask he missed his customary spectacles. His eyes were blind and furry; his lipless mouth bent in upon itself in a pleased yet baffled way.

"Freddy, I've *seen* it," Janet Appleby said. "I've seen the cast of characters."

With the dignity of a senile monarch Freddy slowly stared toward her. "Who are you? Oh, I know. You're Jan-Jan Applesauce. I didn't recognize you out of context. Where are your little friends?"

"They're in Maine, thank God."

"Don't be your usual shitty self, Freddy," Carol said, sitting on the arm of the chair and draping her gaunt arms around his rubber shoulders. The action tugged open her shirt. Piet, sitting cross-legged on the floor, saw her navel: a thick-lidded eye. Carol caressed Freddy's air hose, hung loose around his neck. "We want to do your play," she insisted.

"We can make a movie of it," Eddie Constantine said. He flew in spells; he had been home three days. His growth of beard suggested a commando, cruel and sleepless. He held a beer can in each hand. Seeing his wife draped across Freddy, he had forgotten who he was fetching them for, his vacant eyes the tone of the same aluminum. Abruptly, as if tossing a grenade, he handed a can to Ben Saltz, who sat in the corner.

"I want to be the one who answers the door," Carol said. "Don't all dirty movies begin with a woman answering the door?"

Ben sat staring, his dark eyes moist with disquiet. He had recently shaved, and looked enfeebled, slack-chinned, mockingly costumed in sailing clothes—a boat-neck jersey, a windbreaker, a white officer's cap, and suntans cut down to make shorts, fringed with loose threads. Ben's calves were heavily, mournfully hairy. Piet glimpsed himself in that old-fashioned male shagginess but his own body hair was reddish, lighter, gayer, springy. Ben's lank hairs ran together to make black seams, like sores down-running into the tops of his comically new topsiders, cup-soled, spandy-bright. Except for his sunburned nose, Ben's skin was pasty and nauseated. He had pockmarks. His wounded love of Carol weighed on the air of the room and gave the couples an agitated importance, like children in safe from a thunderstorm.

"What's a dirty movie?" Freddy asked, blinking, pretending to be confused.

"*Tom Jones*," Terry Gallagher said.

Angela rose up unexpectedly and said, "Come on Carol, let's undress him. I know he has the play in his pocket."

"You think he takes it underwater with him?" Piet asked mildly, exchanging with Foxy a quizzical look over Angela's uncharacteristic display of flirtatious energy. They had become, these two, the parents of their spouses, whose faults they forgave and whose helplessness they cherished from the omniscient height of their adultery.

Foxy had come to the party without Ken, but with Terry

Gallagher. Ken and Matt, having been easily beaten in North Mather, had played consolation singles together all afternoon on the Ongs' court. The two men, uncomfortable among the couples, were comfortable with each other. Foxy and Terry shared tallness and an elusive quality of reluctance, of faintly forbidding enchantment, reflected, perhaps, from their similar husbands. But Foxy was Snow White and Terry Rose Red—something Celtic strummed her full lips, her musical hands, the big muscles knitting her hips to her thighs. She stood tall and joined in the rape, asking Janet, "Where are his pants? You told me he always carries it in his pants."

"Upstairs," Carol said brokenly, wrestling with Freddy's flailing arms, struggling to undo his jacket's rusty snaps. "In Kevin's room. Don't wake him up."

Janet, who had been in therapy two months now, watched the struggle and pronounced, "This is childish."

Angela tried to pin Freddy's ankles as he slid from the chair. One of his flippers kicked over a tabouret holding a crammed ashtray and a small vase of asters. Angela brushed up the ashes and butts with two copies of *Art News*, Eddie carefully poured beer over Freddy's head, and Ben Saltz sat dazed by the sight of Carol, her hair a color no hair in nature ever was, writhing nearly nude in the man's black embrace. The rubber of his suit squeaked as her bare skin slid across his lap. Her shirt had ridden up to her armpits; her orange top twisted, and a slim breast flipped free. Crouching on the carpet, Carol quickly readjusted herself, but kneeled a while panting, daring to look nowhere. All these people had seen her nipple. It had been orangish.

In the front parlor, reached through a doorway hung with a beaded curtain, Irene Saltz's voice was saying, "I can't believe you know what you're saying. Frank, I *know* you, and I *know* that you're a human being." She was drunk.

His voice responded, heated and pained. "It's *you* who want to keep them down, to give them on a platter everything everybody else in this country has had to work for."

"Work! What honest work have you ever done?"

Janet Appleby shouted toward them, "He's worked himself into an ulcer, Irene. Come on in here and take your husband home, he looks sick."

The Constantines' house was large, but much of its space

was consumed by magniloquent oak stairways and wide halls and cavernous closets, so that no single room was big enough to hold a party, which then overflowed into several, creating problems of traffic and acoustics. Janet was not heard, but Frank's voice came to them from the parlor clearly. "The federal government was never meant to be a big mama every crybaby could run to. Minimal government was the founders' ideal. States' rights. Individual rights."

Irene's voice in argument was slurred and even affectionate. "Frank, suppose you were Mrs. Medgar Evers. Would you want to cry or not?"

"Ask any intelligent Negro what the welfare check has done to his race. They hate it. It castrates. I agree with Malcolm X."

"You're not answering me, Frank. What about Medgar Evers? What about the six Birmingham Sunday-school children?"

"They should have the protection of the law like everybody else, like everybody else," Frank said, "no more and no less. I don't approve of discriminatory legislation and that's what the Massachusetts Fair Housing Bill is. It deprives the homeowner of his right to choose. The constitution, my dear Irene, tries to guarantee equality of *opportunity*, not equality of status."

Irene said, "Status and opportunity are inseparable."

"Can't we shut them up?" Eddie Constantine asked.

"It's sex for Irene," Carol told him, standing and buttoning her shirt. "Irene loves arguing with right-wing men. She thinks they have bigger pricks."

Janet's lips opened but, eyes flicking from Carol to Freddy to Ben, she said nothing. Self-knowledge was turning her into a watcher, a hesitater.

Terry Gallagher came down the Constantines' grand staircase holding a single often-folded sheet of paper. "It's nothing," she said. "It's not even begun. It's a cast of characters. Freddy, you're a fake."

Freddy protested, "But they're beautiful characters."

Amid laughter and beer and white wine, through the odors of brine and tennis sweat, the play was passed around. It bore no title. The writing, beginning at the top as a careful ornamental print, degenerated into Freddy's formless hand, with no decided slant and a tendency for the terminal strokes to swing down depressively.

DRAMATIS PERSONÆ

Eric Shun, *hero*
Ora Fiss, *heroine*

Cunny Lingus, *a tricksome Irish lass*
Testy Cull, *a cranky old discard*

Anna L. Violation ⎫
Ona Nism   ⎬ *nymphs*
Labia Minoris   ⎭

Auntie Climax, *a rich and meaningful relation*

ACT I

Eric (*entering*): !
Ora (*entered*): O!

"That's not fair," Janet said. "Nobody is really called Ora or Ona."

"Maybe the problem," Piet said, "is that Eric enters too soon."

"I was saving Auntie Climax for the third act," Freddy said.

Terry said, "I'm so glad Matt isn't here."

Foxy said, "Ken loves word games."

"Good job, Freddy," Eddie Constantine said. "I'll buy it." He clapped Ben Saltz on the back and held the paper in front of Ben's eyes. Ben's face had become white, whiter than his wife's sun-sensitive skin. Foxy went and, awkwardly pregnant, knelt beside him, tent-shaped, whispering.

Piet was busy improvising. The crude energy the others loved in him had been summoned. "We need more plot," he said. "Maybe Ora Fiss should have a half-brother, P. Niss. Peter Niss. They did filthy things in the cradle together, and now he's returned from overseas."

"From Titty City," Eddie said. He was of all the men the least educated, the least removed in mentality from elementary school. Yet he had lifted and hurled thousands of lives safely across the continent. They accepted him.

Janet said, "You're all fantastically disgusting. What infuriates me, I'm going to have to waste a whole twenty-dollar session on this grotesque evening."

"Leave," Carol told her.

Piet was continuing, gesturing expansively, red hair spinning from his broad arms. "Ora is frightened by his return. Will the old magic still be there? Dear God, pray not! She takes one look. Alas! It is. 'Ora!' he ejaculates. 'Mrs. Nism now,' she responds coldly, yet trembling within."

"You're mixing up my beautiful characters," Freddy complained.

"Let's play some new game," Carol said; she squatted down to gather the residue of the spilled ashes. Her slim breasts swung loose in Piet's eyes. Welcome to Titty, somber city of unmockable suckableness: his heart surged forward and swamped Carol as she squatted. Love for her licked the serial bumps of her diapered crotch. Her bare feet, long-toed, stank like razor clams. Her painted hair downhung sticking drifting to her mouth. She stood, ashes and aster petals in her lily palm, and glared toward the corner where, beneath a Miró print, Foxy was ministering with words to the immobilized Ben Saltz.

"Let's not," Freddy Thorne said to her. "It's good. It's good for people to act out their fantasies."

Angela leaped up, warm with wine, calling Freddy's bluff, and announced, "I want to take off all my clothes!"

"Good, good," Freddy said, nodding calmly. He stubbed out his cigarette on his own forehead, on the Cyclopean glass mask. It sizzled. His wise old woman's face with its inbent lips streamed with sweat.

Piet asked him, "Shouldn't you take that outfit off? Don't you eventually die if the skin can't breathe?"

"It's me. Piet baby, this suit *is* my skin. I'm a monster from the deep."

Angela's hand had halted halfway down the zipper at the back of her pleated white tennis dress. "No one is watching," she said. Piet touched her hand and redid the zipper, which made a quick kissing sound.

"Let her go, it's good," Freddy said. "She wants to share the glory. I've always wanted to see Angela undressed."

"She's beautiful," Piet told him.

"Jesu, I don't doubt it for a sec. Let her strip. She wants to, you don't understand your own wife. She's an exhibitionist. She's not this shy violet you think you're stuck with."

"He's sick," Foxy told Carol, of Ben, in self-defense.

"Maybe," Carol said, "he'd like to be left alone."

"He says you all gave him lobster and rum for supper."

Ben groaned. "Don't mention." Piet recognized a maneuvering for attention, an economical use of misery. But Ben would play the game, Piet saw, too hard in his desire to succeed, and the game would end by playing him. The Jew's fierce face was waxen: dead Esau. Where his beard had been it was doubly pale.

"Shellfish," Eddie explained to all of them. "Not kosher."

Carol said sharply, "Foxy, let him sit it out. He can go upstairs to a bed if he has to."

"Does he know where the beds are?" Freddy asked.

"Freddy, why don't you put that mask over your mouth?" Carol's skin was shivering as if each nerve were irritated. The holiday eve was turning chilly and the furnace had been shut off for the summer. Her lips were forced apart over clenched teeth like a child's after swimming and, touched and needing to touch her, Piet asked, "Why are you being such a bitch tonight?"

"Because Braque just died." Her walls were full of paintings, classic prints and her own humorless mediocre canvases, coarse in their coloring, modishly broad in their brushwork, showing her children on chairs, the Tarbox wharf and boatyard, Eddie in a turtleneck shirt, the graceless back view of the Congregational Church, houses, and trees seen from her studio windows and made garish, unreal, petulant. Cézanne and John Marin, Utrillo and Ben Shahn—her styles muddled theirs, and Piet thought how provincial, how mediocre and lost we all are.

Carol sensed that he thought this and turned on him. "There's something I've been meaning to ask you for a long time, Piet, and now I've had just enough wine to do it. Why do you build such ugly houses? You're clever enough, you wouldn't have to."

His eyes sought Foxy's seeking his. She would know that, hurt, he would seek her eyes. Their glances met, locked, burned, unlocked. He answered Carol, "They're not ugly. They're just ordinary."

"They're hideous. I think what you're doing to Indian Hill is a disgrace."

She had, slim Carol, deliberately formed around her a ring of astonishment. For one of their unspoken rules was that professions were not criticized; one's job was a pact with the meaningless world beyond the ring of couples.

Terry Gallagher said, "He builds what he and Matt think people want to buy."

Freddy said, "I *like* Piet's houses. They have a Dutch something, a fittingness. They remind me of teeth. Don't laugh, everybody, I mean it. Piet and I are spiritual brothers. I put silver in my cavities, he puts people in his. Jesus, you try to be serious in this crowd, everybody laughs."

Angela said, "Carol, you're absurd."

Piet said, "No, she's right. I hate my houses. God, I hate them."

Janet Appleby said, "Somebody else died last month. A poet, Marcia was very upset. She said he was America's greatest, and not that old."

"Frost died last January," Terry said.

"*Not* Frost. A German name. *Oh.* Marcia and Harold would know it. None of us *know* anything."

"I thought you'd start to miss them," Freddy said to her.

Janet, sitting on the floor, sleepily rested her head on a hassock. She had switched from twice-a-week therapy to analysis, and drove into Brookline at seven-thirty every weekday morning. It was rumored that Frank had commenced therapy. "We need a new game," she said.

"Freddy, let's play Impressions," Terry said.

"Let's think up more names for my play," he said. "They don't have to be dirty." He squinted blindly into space, and came up with, "Donovan U. Era."

"You had that prepared," Janet said. "But Harold the other night did think of a good one. What was it, Frank?" With a rattle of wooden beads, the couple had returned from the political parlor. Frank looked sheepish, Irene's eyebrows and lips seemed heavily inked.

"León MacDouffe," Frank pronounced, glancing toward Janet, wanting to go home.

Carol said, in the tone of a greatly removed observer, "Irene, your husband looks less and less well. I think he should go upstairs but nobody else has bothered to agree. It makes no difference to me but we can't afford to have our rug ruined."

Irene's expression as she studied Ben was strange. Maternal concern had become impatient and offended. Delilah gazed upon the Samson she had shorn. In the room's center Eddie Constantine, a small effective man without religion or second thoughts, wiry and tanned and neatly muscled, vied in his health for her attention; a beer can glinted in his hand and his gray eyes could find the path through boiling Himalayas of cloud. As he gazed at her it dawned on the room that she was worth destroying for. Though pale and heavy, she had a dove's breasted grace. Irene asked, "Why can't he go upstairs in his own house a few doors away?"

"I'll take him," Eddie said and, going and thrusting his head under Ben's arm, expertly hoisted him up from the chair.

The sudden motion, like a loud noise to the sleeping, led Ben's conversational faculty to roll over. "I'm very interested in this," he said distinctly. "What should the aesthetics of modern housing be? Should there be any beyond utility and cost?"

Gleefully Freddy Thorne chimed in, "Did the peasants who put up thatched huts worry about aesthetics? Yet now we all love the Christ out of thatched huts."

"Exactly," Ben said. He sounded like himself, and was reasoning well, but the sounds floated from his ghostly mouth at half-speed. "But perhaps a more oral and sacramental culture has an instinctive sense of beauty that capitalism with its assembly-line method of operation destroys. *Commentary* this month has a fascinating—"

"Greed," Carol said vehemently, "modern houses stink of greed, greed and shame and plumbing. Why should the bathroom be a dirty secret? We all do it. I'd as soon take a crap in front of all of you as not."

"Carol!" Angela said. "That's even more wonderful than my wanting to take off my clothes."

"Let's play Wonderful," Freddy Thorne announced, adding, "I'm dying in this fucking suit. Can't I take it off?"

"Wear it," Piet told him. "It's you."

Foxy asked, "How do you play Wonderful?"

"You," Freddy told her, "you don't even have to try."

Terry asked, "Is it at all like Impressions?"

Ben said, his weight full on Eddie now, his colorless face turned to the floor, "I'd like to discuss this seriously some time. Super-cities, for example, and the desalinization of seawater. I think the construction industry in this country is badly missing the boat."

"Toot, toot," Eddie said, pulling on an imaginary whistle cord and hauling Ben toward the doorway.

Irene asked, "Shall I come along?" Her expression was again indecisive. To be with her husband was to be with her lover. The romantic Semitic shadowiness of her lower lids contended with pragmatic points in her eyes and lips seeking their good opinion, these heirs of the Puritans.

Eddie looked at her acutely, estimated her ripeness, chose his path, and said decisively, "Yes. I'll get him over there and you put him to bed." So all three made exodus from the musty room, through the huge space-wasting hallway smelling in all weathers of old umbrellas, into the leaf-crowded night splashed by blue streetlamps.

Carol swung her arms, relieved and seething. The Applebys exchanged solicitous confidences—Frank's stomach, Janet's head—and also left, reluctantly; their manner of leaving suggested that this was an end, an end to this summer of many games, that they were conscious of entering now an autumn of responsibilities, of sobered mutuality and duty. Only Freddy Thorne begged them not to go. He had peeled himself out of his skin-diving suit and stood revealed in a soaked T-shirt and crumpled bathing trunks. The skin of his legs and arms had been softened and creased by long enclosure like a washerwoman's palms. The Applebys' leaving left Freddy and Piet alone with many women.

Foxy rose, stately in yards of ivory linen, seven months gone, and said, "I should go too."

"Sweetheart, you can't," Freddy told her. "We're going to play Wonderful."

Foxy glanced at Piet's face and he knew that whatever was written there she would read, *Don't go*. He said, "Don't go."

Terry asked Freddy, "How do you play?" Piet pictured Gallagher, grim as a mother, waiting up for her, and wondered how she dare not go, dare sit there serene. Women have no conscience. Never their fault. The serpent beguiled me.

Freddy licked his lips, then answered weakly, "Each of us names the most wonderful thing he or she can think of. Carol, where's the fucking furnace? I'm freezing."

She fetched from another room an Afghan blanket; he wrapped it around himself like a shawl. "Freddy," she said, "you're getting old."

"Thank you. Now please sit down and stop swishing, Carollino. Eddie and Irene are just putting Ben to bed. They'll be back in a minute. And what if they aren't? The world won't stop grinding. Imagine Eddie's off on a flight to Miami. *Che sarà, sarà,* I keep telling everybody."

"Explain," Terry said, "the point of Wonderful."

"The point is, Terrycloth, at the end of the game we'll all know each other better."

Angela said, "I don't *want* to know any of you better."

Foxy said, "I don't want any of you to know *me* better."

Piet asked, "Where's the competitive element? How can you win or lose?"

Freddy answered Piet with oracular care. He still wore the giant monocle and was drunk, drunker than anyone except Angela, white-wine-drunk, a translucent warm drunkenness whose truth lifts the mind. "You can't lose, Piet. I'd think you'd like that for a change. You know, Peterkins—may I speak my heart?—"

"Oh do, brother, do!" Piet holy-rolled on the floor. "Say it, brother, say it!"

Freddy spoke solemnly, trying to be precise. "You are a paradox. You're a funny fellow. A long time ago, when I was a little boy studying my mommy and my daddy, I decided there are two kinds of people in the world: A, those who fuck, and, B, those who get fucked. Now the funny thing about you, Petrov, is you think you're A but you're really B."

"And the funny thing about you," Piet said, "is you're really neither."

Before he began sleeping with Foxy, when Freddy, however unknowingly, held Georgene as hostage, Piet would not have been so quick to answer, so defiant. Freddy blinked, baffled by feeling Piet free, and more openly an enemy.

"If you two prima donnas," Terry said, "would stop being hateful to each other, we could play Wonderful."

"I think more wine would be wonderful," Carol said. "Who else?"

"Me," Angela said, extending a shapely arm and an empty glass. "I must face Georgene in the finals tomorrow."

"Where *is* Georgene?" Piet asked Freddy politely, afraid he had overstepped a moment before, saying "neither."

"Resting up for the big match," Freddy answered, apparently forgiving.

"We really must go soon," Foxy said to Terry.

"Us too," Piet told Angela. In her rare moods of liberation she held for him the danger that she would disclose great riches within herself, showing him the depths of loss frozen over by their marriage.

Carol poured from the Almadén jug, making of it a dancer's routine. Six glasses were refilled. "OK," Freddy said. "Carol has begun by saying that more wine is wonderful."

"I didn't say it was the most wonderful thing I could think of. I still have my turn."

"All reet-o, take it. You're the hostess; begin."

"Must I start?"

All agreed yes, she must, she must. As Carol stood barefoot in silence, Angela asked of the air, "Isn't this exciting?"

Carol decided, "A baby's fingernails."

Gasps, *ah*, awed, then parodies of gasps, *aaah*, greeted this.

Freddy had provided himself with a pencil and wrote on a small piece of paper, the back of his folded play. "A baby's fingernails. Very well. Please explain."

"I must explain?"

"Well. I mean the whole process, all the chemistry. I don't understand it, which may be why it seems wonderful. You know," she went on, speaking to Foxy, who alone of the women did not absolutely know, "the way it produces out of nothing, no matter almost what we do, smoke or drink or fall downstairs, even when we don't want it, this living *baby*, with perfect little fingernails. I mean," she went on, having scanned all their faces and guessed she was not giving enough, "what a lot of *work*, somehow, ingenuity, *love* even, goes into making each one of us, no matter what a lousy job we make of it afterwards."

Piet said, "Carol, how sweet you are. How can anyone so sweet hate me and my nice little houses?" He felt she had taken the opportunity to repair her image; she was aware of having appeared a hennaed bitch and, deserted by the Saltzes and her husband, needed love from those left around her, and perhaps especially from him, who like her had been born lower in the middle class than these others.

She said, "I *don't* hate you. On the contrary, I think you have too much to give people to waste it the way you do."

After a mild silence Angela said, "I can't tell if that's an insult or a come-on."

"We have a baby's fingernails," Freddy Thorne said. "Who's next?"

"Let's have a man," Terry Gallagher said.

Piet felt singled out, touched, by her saying this. Let's. She reposed on the floor, a tall woman, legs bent under her broadened haunches and the knit of her hips. Her lips held a coin. Her dark hair's harp-curve hung down. Once he loved her, too shy then to know they are waiting. Vessels shaped before they are filled. He drank more of the wine of a whiteness like that of the sun seen through fog, a perfect circle smaller than the moon. The eclipse. Love doomed? Foxy was watching him sip, her pink face framed by pale hair fluffed wide by seabathing. Sometimes her belly tasted of salt. Bright drum taut as the curve of the ocean above the massed watchsprings of blond hair. Her navel inverted. Their lovemaking lunar, revolving frictionless around the planet of her womb. The crescent bits of ass his tongue could touch below her cunt's petals. Her far-off cries, eclipsed.

"Piet, you go," Angela said.

His mind skimmed the world, cities and fields and steeples and seas, mud and money, cut timbers, sweet shavings, blue hymnals, and the fuzz on a rose. Ass. His mind plunged unresisted into this truth: nothing matters but ass. Nothing is so good. He said, "A sleeping woman." Why sleeping? "Because when she is sleeping," he added, "she becomes all women."

"Piet, you're drunk," Carol said, and he guessed he had spoken too simply from himself, had offended her. The world hates the light.

Freddy's mouth and eyes slitted. "Maybe sleeping," he said, "because awake she threatens you."

"Speak for yourself," Piet said, abruptly bored with this game and wanting to be with his sleeping children; maybe they, Ruth and Nancy, were the women he meant, drenched and heavy with sleep like lumps of Turkish delight drenched in sugar. "A sleeping woman," he insisted.

"Containing a baby's fingernails," Freddy Thorne added. "My, we're certainly very domestic. Horizonwise, that is. Terry?"

She was ready, had been ever since her smile became complacent. "The works of J. S. Bach."

Piet asked jealously, "Arranged for the lute?"

"Arranged for anything. Played anyhow. That's what's so wonderful about Bach. He didn't know how great he was. He was just trying to support his seventeen children with an honest day's work."

"More domesticity," Angela murmured.

"Don't you believe it," Piet told Terry. "He wanted to be great. He was mad to be immortal." In saying this he was still involved with Carol, arguing about his houses, her paintings, apologizing, confessing to despair.

Terry said serenely, "He feels very unself-conscious and—ordinary to me. Full of plain daylight. It's wonderful to have him in your fingers."

"Keep it clean," Freddy said, writing. "The works of J. S. Bach, not necessarily for stringed instruments. Angela."

"I'm about to cry," Angela said, "you're all so sure of what's good. I can't think of anything wonderful enough to name. The children, I suppose, but do I mean *my* children or the fact of having children, which is what Carol already said? Please come back to me, Freddy. Please. I'm not ready."

Foxy said, "The Eucharist. I can't explain."

"Now it's Freddy's turn," Piet said. It had been a double rescue: Foxy Angela, he Foxy. Exposure was, in the games Freddy invented, the danger. The danger and the fruit.

Freddy rested his pencil and with a groping mouth, as if the words were being read from a magic text materializing in air, said, "The most wonderful thing I know is the human capacity for self-deception. It keeps everything else going."

"Only in the human world," Carol interjected. "Which is just a conceited little crust on the real world. Animals don't deceive themselves. Stones don't."

Angela sat up: "Oh! You mean the world is *everything*? Then I say the stars. Of course. The stars."

Surprised, frightened—he seemed to sink in the spaces of her clear face—Piet asked her, "Why?"

She shrugged: "Oh. They're so fixed. So above it all. As if somebody threw a handful of salt and that's how it stays for billions of years. I know they move but not relative to us, we're too small. We die too soon. Also, they *are* beautiful—Vega on a summer night, Sirius in winter. Am I the only person who ever looks at them any more? One of my uncles was an astronomer, on my mother's side, Lansing Gibbs. I think there's an effect named after him—the Gibbs effect. Maybe it's a galaxy. Imagine a galaxy, all those worlds and suns, named after one man. He was very short, some childhood disease, with pointed teeth and bow legs. He liked me, even when I got taller than him. He taught me the first-magnitude stars—Vega, Deneb, Antares, Arcturus . . . I've forgotten some. As a girl I'd lie on the porch of our summer place in Vermont and imagine myself wandering among them, from life to life, forever. They're wonderful."

"Angela," Foxy said. "You're lovely."

"Angela can be lovely," Piet admitted to them all, and sighed. It was past time to go.

"Freddy, tell us about self-deception," Terry said. Freddy looked elderly and absurd, huddled in his shawl. In the slots of his flippers his toenails were hideous: ingrown, gangrenous, twisted toward each other by the daily constriction of shoes.

Freddy told them, "People come to me all the time with teeth past saving, with abscesses they've been telling themselves are neuralgia. The pain has clearly been terrific. They've been going around with it for months, unable to chew or even close their jaws, because subconsciously they don't want to lose a tooth. Losing a tooth means death to people; it's a classic castration symbol. They'd rather have a prick that hurts than no prick at all. They're scared to death of me because I might tell the truth. When they get their dentures, I tell 'em it looks better than ever, and they fall all over me believing it. It's horseshit. You never get your own smile back when you lose your teeth. Imagine the horseshit a doctor handling cancer has to hand out. Jesus, the year I was in med school, I saw skeletons talking about getting better. I saw women without faces putting their hair up in curlers. The funny fact is, you don't get better, and nobody gives a cruddy crap in hell. You're born to get laid and die, and the sooner the better. Carol, you're right about that nifty machine we begin with; the trouble is, it runs only one way. Downhill."

Foxy asked, "Isn't there something we gain? Compassion? Wisdom?"

"If we didn't rot," Freddy said, "who'd need wisdom? Wisdom is what you use to wave the smell away."

"Freddy," Piet said, tenderly, wanting to save something of himself, for he felt Freddy as a vortex sucking them all down with him, "I think you're professionally obsessed with decay. Things grow as well as rot. Life isn't downhill; it has ups and downs. Maybe the last second is up. Imagine being inside the womb—you couldn't imagine this world. Isn't anything's existing wonderfully strange? What impresses me isn't so much human self-deception as human ingenuity in creating unhappiness. We believe in it. Unhappiness is us. From Eden on, we've voted for it. We manufacture misery, and feed ourselves on poison. That doesn't mean the world isn't wonderful."

Freddy said, "Stop fighting it, Piet baby. We're losers. To live is to lose." He passed the sheet of paper over. "Here it is. Here is your wonderful world." The list read:

> Baby's fingernails
> woman (zzzz)
> Bach
> Euch.
> ☆ ☆ ☆
> capac. for self-decep.

Foxy said sharply, "I won't believe it. Everything people have ever built up, Freddy, you'd let slide and fall apart."

"I do my job," he answered. "It's not the job I would have chosen, but every day I put on that white coat and do it."

White coat. The antiseptic truth. He has learned to live in it. I have not. Better man than I. Piet felt himself falling in a frozen ridged abyss, Freddy's mind. Foxy silently held out her hand toward him; Terry turned to him and recited, "Hope isn't something you reason yourself into. It's a virtue, like obedience. It's given. We're free only to accept or reject."

Angela stood and said, "I think we're all pretty much alike, no matter what we think we believe. Husband, I'm drunk. Take me home."

In the hall, with its elephantine scent of umbrellas, Piet playfully poked Freddy in the stomach and said, "Tell Georgene we missed her."

Freddy's response was not playful; his blurred face menacingly bloated beneath the glare of his subaqueous mask. "She chose not to come. You have any message for her?" The cold fact of his knowing seemed to flow across Piet's face.

"No, just give her all our loves," Piet said nimbly, able to skim and dodge at this level, where actions counted, and no submission to death was asked. He doubted that Freddy knew anything. Georgene had wept after sleeping with him again after her long hiatus of innocence, but Piet had tested her strength before and knew she could withstand all pressure of grief, all temptation to confess. Freddy's tone of menace was a bluff, a typical groping gesture in the murk. His element. Piet jabbed again: "Shouldn't you be going home to her now?" Freddy was making no show of leaving with the four others.

"She's asleep," he said. A woman asleep. As ominous as wonderful. Rather than come to a gathering where her lover might be, she had chosen to sleep. Nursing her misery. Piet felt her captive within the murk of this man, her husband, and regretted having visited her again.

Carol had fallen silent, listening for Eddie's return. Now she roused herself to say good night. She and Freddy, both dressed to swim, waved together from the sallowly lit side porch. Down the side street the Saltzes' narrow house was dark but for a bulb left burning at the rear of the downstairs. Tarbox was settled to sleep. The waterfall by the toy factory faintly roared. A car screeched its tires by the rocks at the base of the green. A jet rattled invisibly among the stars. Its sound was a scratch on glass. A final flurry of good nights. Terry and Foxy, limping shadows on the blue September street, went to the Gallaghers' Mercedes. Without glancing backward she twiddled the fingers of her left hand: farewell until I touch you. Angela said softly,

"Poor Foxy, why didn't Terry have the sense to take her home hours ago?"

Insulted, Piet asked, "You thought she wanted to go?"

"Of course, she was exhausted. Isn't she due next month?"

"Don't ask me. How should I know?"

"Once in the middle of that endless game—and by the way you and Freddy should *not* work out your private difficulties in front of us ladies; it's *not* that fascinating or delightful—I happened to glance over at her and she looked completely desolated."

"I didn't notice."

"She was so beautiful when she came to this town and we're turning her into a hag."

The shade of the brick pavement under the streetlamps was the purple of wine dregs. Piet noticed a small round bug scurrying along in a crevice: a citizen out late, seen from a steeple. No voice to call him home. Motherless, fatherless. *Onvoldaan.* Too much wine had unfocused the camera of Piet's head; he lifted his eyes and saw beyond the backstop screen his church bulking great, broad and featureless from the rear, a stately hollow blur.

Piet heard about Ben's losing his job from three directions. Angela was told after nursery school, where she had agreed to teach Tuesdays and Fridays, though Nancy now went to the public first grade. Irene herself told her; it came out flat, handed to Angela in a voice like a printed card. "I suppose you've already heard. Ben's changing jobs."

"No! I hadn't heard at all. How exciting! Where is his new job? I hope it won't mean you're leaving Tarbox."

"Well, that part of it is still a bit up in the air. But he has definitely given them his resignation."

"Good for him," Angela said, having been forced into inanity by the constraint of Irene's manner; the impulse of condolence had to be forcefully suppressed. Angela told Piet, "She looked ghastly. Ravished. All of a sudden, you know how pretty she's been looking this summer, she was a weighed-down Jewish middle-aged woman. Her eyes were absolutely black telling me and, you know, *too* steady. Quite hard. I felt she was *bargaining* with me."

"I never knew," Piet said, unable to feign much surprise, for he had already been told the news, "exactly what Ben did anyway."

"He miniaturized, sweetie. For the space program. It was secret exactly what." She was setting out the places for the girls' supper; she was at her most companionable while making meals. They themselves were to have dinner at the Guerins tonight.

"I meant," Piet said, "how good was he at it? Was he just a technician, or was his work more theoretical?"

"He loves theory in conversation."

"Which makes me wonder. From what Irene used to imply, the whole Mariner Venus probe belonged to Ben. At the least he was in the same league with John Ong. Now it turns out his company can can him virtually the minute the poor bastard wanders from the straight and narrow."

"Oh, you think the Saltine business had something to do with it?"

"Obviously. Everything to do with it. The Constantines ran him ragged. Neither one of them ever sleeps and Eddie only flies forty hours a month, by regulation. Even Irene was letting slip that Ben was missing the early train." Piet was putting forward as conjecture what Georgene had passed on to him as fact, as reported by Freddy.

"I can't believe it was that bad."

"You're so *god*dam innocent, Angel. You can't believe that anybody has more sexual energy than you. These four would stay up all night swapping off. Carol loves having two men at the same time; before Ben she was sleeping with that kid Eddie used to bring to basketball."

"How do you know all this?"

He said quickly, "Everybody knows it."

Angela thought, pausing in ladling chicken soup into two chaste bowls. "But would she *take* both at once?—I mean, is there room? And where would it happen? In her studio, with all those messy tubes of paint? What would Irene do while this acrobatic act was going on?" Her blue eyes flickered with the attempted vision; Piet was pleased to see her interested. But he could not locate, among all the males they knew, the man

with whom he would share her. Thorne was too awful, and
Whitman too pure.

The next Tuesday, Angela came back from nursery school
late, the sky of her eyes scintillating, and said, "You were
right. It was the Constantines. Irene took me home for a
cup of tea, only it turned out to be bourbon, and told me
everything. She's extremely bitter about it. She refuses to see
the Constantines at all, though Carol keeps coming over and
wants to talk it out. Irene admits it was partly her fault, and
Ben should have known enough to control it himself, but
she says it was just terribly exciting for them, they had always
been so serious about everything, and had never really been
close friends with another couple before. She and Ben just
thought it was *wonderful*, the way the Constantines lived by
a wholly different philosophy, and were always so relaxed and
game for everything, and ate whenever it occurred to them,
and would stay up all night if they felt like it. She says, to
give them credit, that Carol and Eddie can be terribly charming, and in a way they're not to blame, it's how they are,
amoral. In a way, she says, she's even grateful for the summer,
it was an experience she's glad she's had, even though it nearly
wrecked her marriage and they apparently are really strapped
for money now. She admitted she lied to me about changing
jobs. Ben has no other job."

"Of course not. Did she go into the mechanics of it at all? I
mean, what was the effect on Ben so bad they had to fire him?"

"She didn't really, except to admit he wasn't merely late, some
days evidently he wouldn't go in at all, especially after they got
the boat, when they'd go for these long all-day cruises. Once
they actually made it to Provincetown, can you imagine, in
this old catboat made for playing around the marshes in. Irene
said she was terrified half the time, but Eddie apparently is a
very clever sailor. I love the picture—Irene in that huge floppy
purple hat and long-sleeved blouse, and Ben fighting seasick-
ness all the way. Like two owls and two pussycats in a beautiful
pea-green boat. To Provincetown! My father and uncle used to
take a crew of six, and even then the children weren't allowed
along. And of course Ben doesn't really have any stomach for
alcohol either, so even when he did go in to work he'd be too

sick to work often, and he doesn't have a private office, just a glass cubicle, so there was no hiding it."

"What about the sex? Did she go into that?"

"She got very cagey, and I didn't want to press her; I felt so flattered and bewildered by it all, just sitting there and getting this torrent. I wonder why she decided to tell *me*?"

"You're our town conscience. Everybody must placate you."

"Don't be sarcastic. She did imply it wasn't what I may have heard from other sources. She said that Eddie could be very appealing—as if she had felt this appeal but hadn't of course succumbed. If you've succumbed, it's no longer an appeal, is it?"

"You're the expert," Piet told her. He was offended by how fully vicarious experience seemed to satisfy her.

"The evenings they all spent together she described as being all *talk*. Freddy Thorne and sometimes Terry were there. She went out of her way, I thought, to let me know that the night she and Eddie put Ben to bed and all the lights in their house looked out she and Eddie were really in the kitchen talking about Ben's job; even by then he had gotten a pretty drastic warning."

"But no sex. Booze and boats undid him."

"Irene didn't precisely *say*, but the suggestion was certainly *not*. She even—I was dumbfounded, it coming from Irene— called Carol a cockteaser. As if she *should* have gone to bed with Ben, and didn't, or didn't often enough, I don't know. It's pretty messy and sad. When you think of the children especially. Most of it apparently happened at the Constantines' house because it was easier for the Saltzes to leave Bernard, who stays up forever reading anyway, to sit for his brother, but after midnight Irene would sometimes feel guilty enough to go home, leaving Ben talking with Eddie. They would talk everything— space, computers, public versus private schools, religion. Eddie is so lapsed he begins to scream whenever he thinks at all about the Church."

"And then Carol would lay them both."

"Piet, I don't want to diminish your high estimate of Carol but I really think that's unlikely. Maybe in Okinawa whorehouses, but in somebody's home who we know . . . it's grotesque."

"Love, she's human. She could take one in her mouth."

The sky of Angela's eyes flashed. "That's what you want me to do, isn't it?"

"No, no, no," he said. "Good heavens, no. That's sodomy."

Foxy had a rather different story, Carol's as confided to Terry Gallagher. Terry and Carol shared music; Foxy and Carol once in a while drew together, with one of the exquisite Constantine girls, Laura or Patrice, posing in leotards. "She says," she said, "that the Saltzes just moved in on them. That they were outcasts in the town, and terribly lonely, and when they saw that she and Eddie would accept them, there was just no moderation. That Ben had had a *very* sheltered and old-fashioned upbringing, in a Hebrew ghetto in Brooklyn—"

Piet laughed. "I can just see Carol saying 'Hebrew.'" Foxy was a fair mimic and unconsciously colored her retellings with something of the lilt of the telling. Piet's head lay on her lap, and the heartbeat of her unborn infant was next to his ear.

"—a Hebrew ghetto, and was just *starved* for, well, a little swinging. Carol's point, and she's very convinced about this, is that until the Constantines came to town the Saltzes had been excluded by the 'nice' couples, the Guerins who live just a block away on Prudence Street, and the darling Thornes, and the extremely lovely Applesmiths, and the ever-fashionable Hanemas, not to mention the delightfully up-and-coming Gall—"

"Not true. We always asked Ben to basketball. They don't ski or play tennis, whose fault is that? They were always at large parties. The Dutch are more of a minority in this town than Jews."

"Well, this is what Carol's impression was, presumably from Irene." Absent-mindedly as she talked Foxy was stroking Piet's hair. "Your hair is quite unsmoothable."

"Is it thinning out? Will I get bald like Freddy? Red-haired men do. It's Jehovah's rebuke to our vigor. Don't stop. I am *very* hurt that Irene, whom I've always adored, thought we were all anti-Semitic."

"Well evidently she did. Does. She was furious when the elementary school put Bernard in a Christmas pageant. As Joseph yet. According to Terry, Carol is positive that Irene was the real moving spirit behind the couples' getting together. The

Saltzes' marriage has been on the rocks for years. They were staying together because of Bernard, and then Jeremiah was a mistake. Irene had a kind of nervous breakdown over it."

"I remember her as so lovely, pregnant. I do love pregnant women."

"So I see."

"According to Carol according to Terry, what is or was Irene's complaint about Ben?"

"She feels he has no ambition, no drive. Her father came up the hard way in the garment business. Anyway, Piet, who knows why women like some men and don't like others? Chemistry? Carol's story is that Irene took a fancy to Eddie and lit out after him the way she lights into everything—Fair Housing, or the nursery school, or conservation. He became a cause."

"I love the way you say 'cozz.' Honeh chile, ah loves it."

"How do you say it? Cawss. Like the way you say 'haas' for 'house.'"

"OK, I'm an immigrant. Anyway, your description sounds more like Terry than Carol. Carol would say 'She wanted him' or something with the same awesome simplicity and then look daggers. 'She vowed to *have* him.' 'She thenceforth consecrated herself to sharing his pallet.'"

"She wouldn't at all. She'd say, 'The bitch went into heat and got herself screwed.'"

"Oh, my mistress. Your language. Skeerooed."

"Don't jiggle your head like that. You'll induce me."

"It's true, Irene has been promoted by all this to full-fledged bitch status. She used to be somebody you talked to early at cocktail parties to get her out of the way."

"Carol says she and Eddie used to sit after the Saltzes had left and laugh, Irene was being so blatant."

"Then he'd go down the street and laugh out of the other side of his mouth. I love the idea of Eddie Constantine being a worthy project like school integration or the whooping crane. The most worthless man I know. To think we all entrust our lives to him. What did Carol say she and Ben did to combat this assault on the young aviator's virtue?"

"She says she pitied Ben but, frankly, never found him attractive."

"She excluded him. One more Wasp."

"Yes," Foxy said, "she did mention that, that she was the only Wasp in the ménage. Eddie apparently hates Wasps, and is always testing her. Scaring her when he drives the car, and things like that."

"I thought she was a lapsed R.C."

"*He* is. *She* was a Presbyterian." Her fingers had trespassed from his hair to the sensitive terrain of his face, taut planes she explored as if blind. "Furthermore," she said, in a voice whose musical shadows and steeps had become, like the flowing sight of her and her perfumed weight, a body his love inhabited, "furthermore, and stop looking at me like that, she doesn't think what he did with them has anything to do with Ben's losing his job. Carol thinks he was just poor at it, which in a way I can believe, since the times he's talked to Ken—"

"Ken and Ben, they don't know when," Piet said.

"—the times he talked to Ken, after expressing all this interest in biochemistry, and the secret of life and whatnot, Ken says he shows no real comprehension or much interest beyond the superficial sort of thing that appears in *Newsweek*. He's really looking for religious significance, and nothing could bore Ken more. What was his word?—eclectic. Ben has a thoroughly eclectic mind."

"*My* theory is," Piet said, closing his eyes the more keenly to sense Foxy's circumambient presence, her belly beside his ear, her fingers on his brow, her thighs pillowing his skull, "that the Saltzes went into it so Ben could learn about aviation from Eddie and improve his job in the aerospace complex. That once they got into that smelly old house, Carol being a nymphomaniac, she had to get laid, and rather than stand around watching, Eddie gave Irene a bang, and she said to herself, 'What the hell! This is fun!'"

"Well, without everything being spelled out, that's more or less Carol's story too."

"Carol and I, we think alike."

"Oh, don't *say* that!" Foxy urgently begged, touching his lips, recalling them to the incomparable solemnity of their sin.

Angela brought home new refinements of Irene's version. "She took me aside after nursery school almost in tears and said Carol's been spreading around the story that she, Irene, felt ostracized in town because she was Jewish. She wanted me to know this was perfectly untrue, that she and Ben agree they've always been very warmly treated, and they'd be very upset to have their friends think they thought otherwise. She says Carol is *extremely* neurotic, that Kevin is the way he is because of how she's treated him. Whenever she wants to paint she locks him in his room and some mornings he screams so much the neighbors have complained. Irene also said her point about Bernard's being in the Christmas play has been deliberately misunderstood. She never said they shouldn't put on a Christmas pageant; she just thinks to be fair they should have some kind of Hanukkah observance too."

"Yeah," Piet said, "and why not make the kids celebrate Ramadan by not eating their box lunches?"

Angela, who had been considering Irene's cause seriously, from the standpoint of an hereditary liberal, told Piet, "I don't know why you bother to go to church, it seems to do you less and less good."

Georgene threw a lurid borrowed light upon the mystery. Over the phone, she told Piet, "Freddy's been talking to Eddie—"

"Freddy and Eddie, they're always ready," Piet said. Gallagher was off talking to the nuns who were about to buy the mortgaged estate in Lacetown, and Piet was alone in the office.

"Don't interrupt. Eddie told him that Ben late at night used to talk about the work he was doing on these rockets—is there a thing called the Titan?—and the ridiculous waste and backbiting between the different departments and government representatives, and some of the ideas they were working on with solid propellants and self-correcting guidance systems, which I guess Ben helped with, and Eddie was shocked, that Ben would be telling him all this. He thinks if he told *him* he must have told others, and the government got wind of it, and had him released."

"Don't you think Ben would put any spy to sleep that tried to listen to him?"

"Freddy thinks that Eddie might have been the one to turn Ben in. I mean, he *is* in aeronautics, so he would know who to report him to."

"Why would he want to ruin his wife's lover? You think Eddie minds?"

"Of course he minds. That woman has put him through hell. She's insane. She's an utter egotist."

"More hell than vice versa?"

"Oh, much more. Eddie's just a little boy who likes to play with engines."

"Huh. I distrust all little-boy theories of male behavior. They rob us of our sinful dignity."

"Hey. When are you coming to see me again?"

"I just did."

"That was a month ago."

"Time flies."

"God this is humiliating. The hell with you, Piet Hanema."

"What have I done?"

"Nothing. Forget it. Good-bye. I'll see you at parties."

"Wait."

She had hung up.

The next day she called again, imitating a secretary. "I just wanted to report, sir, in regard to our conversation as of yesterday A.M., that two men in suits and hats were seen surveying and then entering the Saltz residence on West Prudence Street, Tarbox."

"Who told you this?"

"A patient of Freddy's told him, very excited. Who would wear hats in Tarbox but FBI agents? Apparently the entire town knows about Ben."

"Do you think he'll be electrocuted like the Greenbergs or traded to Russia for Gary Powers?"

"Ha ha. Ever since you've been sleeping with Foxy you've been high as a kite. You're riding for a fall, Piet. This time I am *not* going to catch you."

"I have not been sleeping with that extremely pregnant and very chaste lady. Hey. I dreamed about you last night."

"Oh. A nice dream?"

"Not bad. It was in a kind of wine cellar. Freddy was running for selectman this fall and you took me down into the cellar to show me the champagne you were going to use if he won. Then down there, surrounded by old wicker furniture, you asked me to smell the new perfume you were wearing behind the ear. You said, very proudly, you had bought it at Cogswell's Drug Store. I put my face deep into your hair and you gently put your arms around me and I realized you wanted to make love and woke up. Somehow you had much longer hair than yours. You had dyed it red."

"It wasn't me at all. You bastard."

"It was, Georgene. You talked just like yourself, in that reedy indifferent voice, about Freddy's chances of winning."

"Come see me, Piet."

"Soon," he promised.

That evening, Angela said, "Irene was almost funny today. She said that Ben with nothing to do keeps entertaining these two young Mormons. They think they're a lost tribe of Israel, so it's really like a family reunion with Ben."

"What Mormons?"

"You must have noticed them walking around town, what do you *do* all day? Two young men with suits and broad-brimmed Western-style hats on. Apparently it's part of every Mormon's life to go out and proselytize some benighted area. That's us. We're Hottentots as far as they're concerned."

"I heard they were FBI men."

"Irene says that's what everybody thinks. She says Carol has been spreading it all around that Ben betrayed government secrets."

"That woman is losing her marbles. Carol."

"I saw her in the A & P today and she couldn't have been sweeter. She said Eddie wants to take me for another ride on his Vespa."

At the center of this storm of gossip, the destroyed man raked leaves, made repairs and painted within his house, took his sons to the beach on clear weekend afternoons. Summer over, the beach was restored to the natives, who ran their dogs along the running surf and tried to raise kites above the sea of dunes. The clouds changed quality, changed from the puffy schooners of hot weather to grayer, longer bodies, with more metal in them. The horse trailers of North Mather stables parked in the Tarbox lot and teen-age girls galloped across the dun-colored flats of low tide. Here one Sunday morning in mid-October, Piet, walking with Ruth—since he had not gone to church today she had not sung in the choir—saw Ben Saltz at a distance, holding little Jeremiah by the hand, stopping with Bernard to examine shells and instructive rubbish in the wrack. Piet wanted to approach Ben, to express fellow-feeling, but he dreaded the man as he dreaded the mortally diseased. His own life felt too precarious to be drawn into proximity with a life that had truly broken through. Angela thought they should have the Saltzes over, just the two couples, for a relaxed dinner. Piet resisted, then consented; but Irene coolly refused. She and Ben had agreed that, since they were not in a financial position to repay hospitality, they would not accept any. By tacit agreement among the other couples the Saltzes were no longer invited to parties, which would have been painful for them and have embarrassed the Constantines. Still Piet yearned to peer into the chasm, to spy out the face of catastrophe. He went out of his way at all hours to drive by their house. The Saltzes' lights went dark early at night; the Constantines' defiantly blazed. They were seeing a lot of the Guerins, the Thornes, and the Gallaghers. In the mornings, the older children—Bernard, Laura—of each household set off to school along parallel paths across the much-traversed green; before evening they returned together, talking more seriously than children should have to.

One windy weekday afternoon Piet, rounding the green in his pick-up truck, saw Ben putting up storm windows. They were stacked, a leaning deck of great glass cards, at the side of the house, and Ben was puzzling over the numbers. Wanting to hail him, yet afraid to slow down and be caught, Piet gave himself only a glimpse; but it was a glimpse, shockingly, of happiness. Ben was letting his beard grow back. His archaic profile as it bent to the Roman numerals chiseled on the upper edges of the storm windows seemed asleep and smiling. His air was of a man who deserved a holiday like any other, who had done something necessary and was now busy surviving, who—Piet's impression was—had touched bottom and found himself at rest, safe.

Piet dreamed, at this same time of his life, that he was in an airplane, a big new jet. The appointments, in beige and aqua, of the immense tubular interior were vivid to his eyes, though he had never ridden in such a plane. Since the army, he had flown rarely; the last time had been two years ago, to visit his brother in Michigan. The plane to Detroit had been a sooty-engined Electra, shivering in flight like an old hound. Now the luxurious plane of his dream was gliding as if motionless through the sky; the backs of heads and hands receded tranquilly down the length of aqua-carpeted aisle. The pilot's voice, too musical and southern to be Eddie Constantine's, jubilantly announced over the loudspeaking system, "I think we've slipped it, folks!" and through his little rubber-sealed porthole Piet saw a wall of gray cloud, tendrilous and writhing, slowly drift backward, revealing blue sky. They had evaded a storm. Then the plane rocked and jerked in the bumpy air currents; it sank flatly through a gap in atmosphere, grabbed for something, missed, slipped, and tilted. The angle of tilt increased; the plane began to plunge. The huge hull rushed toward the earth. The delicately engineered details—the luminous stenciled seat numbers, the chrome rivets holding the tinted head napkins—stayed weirdly static amid the rising scream of the dive. Far down the aisle, a stewardess, her ginger hair in a high stiff coiffure, gripped the seats for support, and the curtains hiding the first-class section billowed. Otherwise there was no acknowledgment of the horror, no outcry. Piet thought, *The waste.* Such ingenious fragility utterly betrayed. The cost. The plane streamed straight down. The liquid in Piet's inner ear surged, froze. He knew there could be no pulling from this dive and awoke in darkness, convinced of his death.

Angela's breathing was moist and regular beside him. Her body tilted the mattress toward the middle. Her honeyish pungent female smell monopolized the warm bed. Vague light limned the ridges of the pleated linen shade of the lamp on the bureau by the window. His house. A trim ship motionless on the swell of the night. He raised his hand from beside his cheek. Its black silhouette showed cornute against the cruciform mullions and blue panes. His hand. He made the fingers twiddle. He was alive. Yet, having faced the full plausibility of his death—the screaming air of the dream had been so willing to swallow him, so voraciously passive—he was unable to reënter the illusion of security that is life's antechamber. Heavy as lead he lay on the thinnest of ice. He began to sweat. A ponderous creeping moisture coated his skin and, like a loose chain dangling from his stomach, nausea, the clumsy adrenal nausea of panic, threatened to wrench him inside out. Nimbly he turned and lay on his back.

He had experienced this panic before. Antidotes existed. Picture snow. Picture a curved tent secure against the rain. Pretend the blankets are shelter. Think of skin. Piet tried to lull himself with bodies of women he knew. Foxy's powdery armpits and petaled cleft simpler than a rose. The freckled boniness below Georgene's throat. Her factual nakedness and feather-cut hair full of gray, dulled his lust to see it, perhaps loveless-ness let them come always together. Unlike Angela's ambrosial unsearchable. Carol's lissome waist and nerved-up dancer's legs. Bea Guerin's swarmy drunken breasts, nectar sweat be-tween. The rank elastic crotch of the step-ins of Annabelle Vojt who, though both were virgins, would allow him, in that rain-pattered cavity of a car parked amid nodding weedy hay, to kiss there, and exploringly tongue, applying mind to matter, his face upside-down between her thighs, his broad back aching, crickets trilling, her tranced fingers combing his uncombable hair. Of pious family, in the hamburger heat, the radio down but glowing, she would sometimes wordlessly remove the se-cret wall of silk, heaving with a motion that disturbed him by being expert her pelvis up free from the car seat and tugging her pants down from behind; to that mute silver flicking and heave, leaping arched from memory like a fish, he held tight a second, then it too, with the other pale bodies, proved too slip-pery to ride into sleep. He was too agitated to sink. Nerves and atoms whirled and scintillated within him. Hollow-boned like a bird, he would forever hover, retasting the same sourness.

Angela's even breathing broke pace; she turned with a slith-ering turmoil of sheets, and the stride of her unconscious sigh-ing resumed.

Horribly awake, Piet tried to pray. His up-pouring thoughts touched nothing. An onyx dust of gas above his face. Some-thing once solid had been atomized. *Thou shalt not covet. Who-soever lusteth in his heart.* Pedrick's foolish twisting. A dour desert tribe: Dead Sea. Pots broken by a shepherd boy. Orange dust. One more dismal sect. Mormons. Salt Lake. Hymnals unopened all week stink of moldy paper: unwrapping a fish. Forgive me. Reach down and touch. He had patronized his faith and lost it. God will not be used. Death stretched endless under him. Life a scum, consciousness its scum. Piet lay as a shimmering upon an unfounded mineral imperviousness. His parents were twin flecks of mica squeezed in granite. No light touched them into light. The eternal loss of light: in the plane's plunge, not knowing he was dreaming, honest to his bones, he had phrased it so to himself, like any unchurched commuter whose day takes a bad turn. Why tease God longer? Busy old fellow has widows and orphans to interview, grieving Tehranese, still benighted. Bite down on death. Bite down. No screaming within the plane. All still in falling. Stoic grace learned from movies. Hope of heaven drains the sky. No Hottentot he. Away with the blindfold. Matter mostly nothing, a titter skinning a vacuum. Angela sleeps in the cradle of the stars, her uncle's web. Nothing sacred. Triune like cock and balls: Freddy Thorne. Oh Lord, this steepness of sickness, this sliding. Patient parents thumbing home seeds in peat had planted a tree whose fruit he had fed to women. The voracious despair of women had swallowed God.

From his height of fear Piet saw his life dwindled small, distinct. The three new houses, sold, on Indian Hill as from a helicopter. Now Gallagher wanted acres more, saw himself a developer, a builder of cities. Gallagherville. Terrytown. Hanema Plaza. Angela Place. Maps, prospecti, underground garages, a grateful Commonwealth votes its thanks. Sir Matthew Galleyslave, having given employment to thousands, true prince of the Church, dinner at the White House starring Pablo Casals and Ruby Newman. *And Mr. President, this is my partner.* That flinty Irish smile, stiff-backed, wall-eyed. Jack: *This cunning little fellow? May I pet him?* Another voice, more musical: *Does he bite?*

Feeling his thoughts expand into nonsense, Piet went tense with gratitude, with eager anticipation of sleeping, and snapped wide awake again, his heart churning. He needed to touch something. He could never rise with Gallagher because he needed to touch a tool. Grab the earth. The plane had plunged and he had been without resources, unchurched, unmanned. He needed to touch Foxy, her nipples, her belly, in oblique moonlight. Her head was full of braid and crosses. She believed. She adored his prick. With billowing gauzy width she had flung herself onto him, was his, his woman given to him.

Angela obliviously stirred, faintly moaned. Piet got out of bed and went downstairs for a glass of milk. Whenever he was most lovesick for Foxy, that summer, he would go to the refrigerator, the cool pale box full of illuminated food, and feed something to the void within. He leaned his cheek against the machine's cold cheek and thought of her voice, its southern shadows, its playful dryness, its musical remembrance of his genitals. He spelled her name with the magnetized alphabet the girls played with on the tall blank door. FOXY. PIET L VES FOXY. He scrambled the letters and traveled to bed again through a house whose familiar furniture and wallpaper were runes charged with malevolent magic. Beside Angela, he thought that if he were beside Foxy he could fall asleep on broken glass. Insomnia a failure of alignment. A rumbling truck passed, vanishing.

The weight of this stagnant night. Fear scurried inside him, seeking a place to stop. How Annabelle would spread her legs as if imperiously to seize his entire face in the lips of her young swamp. Foxy's delicately questioning sideways glint: a dry mind that sized him up through veils of rapture. His daughters' anxious great eyes: in a sense what a mercy to die and no longer torment his children with the apparition of their father. The death of another always a secret relief. Tides of life swing up to God for slaughter. Slum clearance. Dearest Lord do shelter Foxy my shyest candleflame from this holocaust Thy breath. Amen. Revolving terror scooped the shell of him thin. A translucent husk emptied of seed, Piet waited to be shattered.

The Chinese knife across the eye. The electric chair dustless in the tiled room. The earthquake that snaps cathedral rafters. The engorged mineral ocean. The knotted silk cord. The commando's piano wire. The crab in the intestine. The chicken bone in the windpipe. The slippery winter road. The misread altimeter. The firing squad crushing out its Spanish cigarettes in the baked clay courtyard, another dull dawn, exhaling philosophically. The boy from Ionia. The limp-limbed infant smothered in his crib. The rotting kidney turning the skin golden. The shotgun blast purging the skull of brains. The massive coronary. The guillotine. The frayed elevator cable. The booming crack and quick collapse of ice: in Michigan on the lakes the fishermen would ride their jalopies to the bottom in the air bubble and with held breaths ascend to the jagged light. The threshing machine. The random shark. Puffy-tongued dehydration. Black-faced asphyxia. Gentle leprosy. Crucifixion. Disembowelment. Fire. Gas in the shower room. The scalper's hurried adze. The torturer's intent watchmaker's face. The pull of the rack. The suck of the sea. The lion's kittenish gnawing. The loose rock, the slipping boot, the dreamlike fall. The anger of kings. The bullet, the bomb, the plague, the wreck, the neglected infection, the mistaken reaction. The splintered windshield. The drunken doctor's blunder shrugged away. The shadow of fragility on the ice, beneath the implacably frozen stars: the muffled collapse, the opaque gasp, the unresisted plunge.

"Angela?" His voice sounded alien, dragged from a distance. "Could you wake up a little and put your arm round me? I've had a nightmare."

She half-woke and half-obeyed, turning toward him but sinking into sleep again on her stomach; her arm tried to reach him but lapsed at her side. He listened for the glinting of the hamster's wheel and instead heard the refrigerator shudder and break into purring.

Dear Piet—

The tide is coming in high and so blue it seems ink. A little boy in a red shirt has been anchored in a rowboat off the island ever since my second cup of coffee. I have been thinking about us and there seems a lot to say until I sit down and try to write it. When we were together yesterday I tried to explain about Ken and me and "coming" but you chose to be haughty and hurt—my lover, don't be. How timid I feel writing that odd word "lover." And ridiculous too. But you must have a name and what else are you of mine?

Ken is my husband. I love him as such. I feel right, *is what I tried to say, making love to him. There is no barrier between us except boredom which is not so serious since life is such a daily thing anyway. With you there are many barriers—my guilt of course, a true shyness and fear of seeming inadequate compared with the other women you've had, our fear of being discovered, a sometimes (I suggest) needless impatience and hurry in you, your annoying habit of mocking yourself and waiting to be contradicted, and even your extreme lovingness toward me, which I find sometimes dismaying, let me confess. To all this add the libidinous vagaries of the pregnant state. These barriers are piled high, so my not coming, dear Piet, does not mean I do not go high with you. I go very high. Do not ask me to say more. Do not ask me to deny my pledge to Ken—which I felt at the time and still feel is sacred above and beyond all discomfort and discontent—or try to compete. There is no competition. I do not understand why I have taken you into my life at this time of all times but the place you occupy is one you have created and you must not be insecure in it.*

I have brought this letter outside to the sun, me in my underwear, casually enough, since none of my bathing suits fit. I trust the plumbers not to suddenly arrive. The boy in red has gone away. I don't think he caught anything. Rereading this, it seems so poorly expressed, so self-protective and hedgy, I wonder if I will give it to you. Your sleepy but fond

Foxy

Undated and not always signed, Foxy's letters accumulated in the back of a Gallagher & Hanema office filing cabinet, under the carbon paper, where Gallagher would never look. They were of varying shapes and sizes. Some consisted of as many as four sheets smoothly covered on both sides with a swift upright script. Others, holding a few hurried words, were mere scraps passed wadded into Piet's hand at parties. Orderly, superstitious, Piet saved them all, and fitfully read them through in the numb days following his night of dread. He read them as an insignificant person seeks himself in a fable whose hero is a remote ancestor.

My lover!—

My whole house breathes of you—the smell of planed wood is you, and the salt wind is you, and the rumpled sheets whose scent is sweetest and subtlest—of us—is you. I have been all open windows and blowing curtains and blue view these last hours—so much yours I must write and tell you, though Ken is downstairs waiting to go to the little-Smiths. In a few minutes I will see you. But surrounded by others. Accept this kiss.

Other letters were more expansive and discursive, even didactic. Piet felt in them an itch to shape him, to rectify and justify.

Holy Firecracker Day

My dear lover—

I have gone far down the beach, the public end, past the holiday crowds (Italian grandmothers with aluminum chairs sitting right in the surf, skirts up to their knees and knitting in their laps) to where none of our mutual friends might ambush me. It is curiously different down here, cliffy and pebbly, and windier and the water choppier than the sheltered stretch where our lovely Tarbox matrons and their offspring dabble. Lacetown lighthouse seems very close in the haze. Now and then a pair of Boston or Cape fairies go by in their skimpy trunks—Freddy calls them ballhuggers—holding hands. Otherwise I am alone, a pregnant and therefore pass-proof lass with a crinkled New Yorker on her knees for a writing pad, coining funny phrases for her lover, who thinks he is a Jew.

I explained badly about Peter. You are not he, the coincidence of your names notwithstanding. For years he has ceased to be a name for me, just a shadow, a shadow between me and my parents, between me and Ken. He didn't love me—I amused him, awkward and innocent shiksa as I was. I was a toy for him (toy/ goy), and the frightening thing I discovered, I liked it. I loved being used/abused. There was nothing he could do that did not intensify my love for him, even his terrible mood of coldness, the scorn that wished me away. He needed to be alone more than I could let him be alone. It was all very young and uncontrolled and must have been influenced for each of us by how our parents had behaved. My father's absences had been cruel for my mother and as long as Peter was not absent from me, even if his language was foul, I was grateful. Or perhaps I was attracted to just that pride, a kind of mechanical selfishness, in which he resembled my father. Do you know, he has become famous? His picture was in Time a year or so ago, with a junk sculpture he had welded. He still lives in Detroit. With his mother, unmarried. So I had years when I could have flown to him, years of being childless with Ken, and I didn't. It would have been like eating chocolate sundaes again.

You and I are different, surely. With you I feel for the first time what it is like not *to be young. With you I feel that I at last have exercised my right of choice—free of habit or command or compulsion. In a sense you are my first* companion. *Our sweet sin is strangely mixed with the sweetness of pregnancy—perhaps Ken waited too long to make me pregnant and now that it is here I have turned toward someone else with the gratitude. I trust you and fear you. I feared Peter, and trust Ken. The conjunction is uniquely yours.*

Am I proposing marriage? Scheming woman!! Nothing of the kind—I am so securely tied to Ken I dare open myself to you as I might to a stranger in a dream, knowing I was all the time securely asleep beside my husband. Please do not fear I will try to take you from Angela. I know even better than you how precious she is to you, she and the home you have made together, how well, truly, you are wed. Isn't it our utter captivity that makes us, in our few stolen afternoons together, so free? My hand is tired and shakes. Please don't leave me yet. My flying Dutchman —contradiction in terms?

Later.

I went down to swim—delicious, like being inside a diamond, the water at Woods Hole was much warmer—and examined the pebbles. Did you know, I once took a term of geology? I recognized basalt and quartz, the easy ones, black and white, God and the Devil, and then a lot of speckly candyish stones I mentally lumped as "granite." So much variety! And what a wealth of time we hold in our hands in the smoothness of these stones! I wanted to kiss them. Remembering your smoothness. I do love the beach. I wonder if I was ever myself until Ken moved me into sight of the sea.

Then, *to my horror, who should come along but Janet and Harold! Damn!! It was I who was embarrassed, and they who should have been. They were brazen as always—they had left Frank and Marcia back with the children and what was I doing way up here in Fairyland? I told them the walk was necessary exercise and that I wanted to sketch the Lacetown lighthouse. They noticed that I had been writing a letter and were very twinkly and jolly and I think genuinely like me but seemed depressingly corrupt. Who am I to pass judgment? Yet I seem very righteous within myself still and virtually cried, as you saw, when I turned out to be Christine Keeler.*

Still later.

I fell asleep. So strange to wake in floods of light, mouth bloated and hair full of sand. I must go home. Ken is tennising with Gallagher and Guerin and I don't know who the fourth is. You? Answer to a riddle: the fourth of July.

Piet, have I explained anything? I think I wanted somehow to untangle us from those others, to spare you that woeful wild look that comes into your eye when it's time to be back on the job or you imagine the phone in your office ringing. In a way, because you suspect a Heaven somewhere else (like Harold's French: a constant appeal to above), you live in Hell, and I have become one of the demons. I don't want this, I want to be healing—to be white and anonymous and wisecracking for you, the nurse I suppose my father said I was too good to be. I worry that you'll do something extravagant and wasteful to please your funny prickly conscience. Don't. Have me without remorse. Remorse is boring to women. Your seducing me is fine. I wouldn't have missed it for the world. Better you than Freddy Thorne.

Which is a way of concealing that falling asleep on the sand has sexed me up. I crave your strength and length, and remain,

Your mistress

Oh blessed, blessed Piet—

How tactless, how worse than tactless wrong *I was to use you today as an audience for my feelings about Ken. How comic your anger was—you seemed amazed that I had feelings about him —and how sad, in the end, your effort to turn your anger into a joke. It is one of your charms that you make both too much and too little of yourself, with a swiftness of alternation that is quite hypnotic. But your departure left me depressed and with a need to try again.*

When I said that he and I had been married seven years whereas you and I had known each other a few months it was not a criticism—clearly your newness in many ways works to your advantage. But in the mysterious (as much to me as to anyone) matter of my sexual response, it is an advantage in Stage I, a dis- in Stage II. Maybe men like new women while women perform best with men they know. There is something of trust in this—there really is, whenever you spread your legs, the flitting fear you are going to be hurt—*and something of the sad (why do*

*I find it sad?) fact that with women personality counts for less in
sex than with men. In actual sex as opposed to all the preamble. A
dull familiar trustworthy tool is all we ask. Female genitalia are
extremely* stupid, *which gets us into many a fix our heads would
get us out of.*

*Why must I apologize to you for continuing to enjoy my hus-
band? You have woken me from my seven years' sleep and Ken
benefits. Isn't it enough for your ego to promise you that you exist
in dimensions where Ken is blank? And that his ignorance of
our affair, of what consumes my inner life, makes him seem a
child, a child behind glass, a child* willfully *behind glass. He has
never been very curious about life, above the molecular level. He
is a masked man who climbs a balcony to be with me at night.
I discover in myself a deep coldness toward him. In this coldness
I manipulate our bodies and release the tension you have built
in me.*

Yet do *let me love him as I can. He is my man, after all.
Whereas you are only* a *man. Maybe* the *man. But not mine.*

*I suppose I am confused. Having decided, long before we slept
together, to have you, I determined to keep you each in place, in
watertight compartments. Instead, the two of you are using my
body to hold a conversation in. I want to tell you each about the
other. I live in fear of calling out the wrong name. I want to confide you to Ken, and Ken to you—he is unhappy about his career,
and apprehensive about our unborn child, and turns to me more
often now than since our first year of marriage. Of course, I am
so safe. He pierces me saying, You can't impregnate the pregnant.
You can't kill the dead. Compared to you it is mechanical but
then Ken's career is to demonstrate how mechanical life is.*

*Yours is to build and blessed lover you have built wonderfully
in me. I breathe your name and in writing this I miss your voice,
your helpful face. Do you really think we bore God? You once told
me God was bored with America. Sometimes I think you under-
estimate God—which is to say, you despise the faith your fear of
death thrusts upon you. You have struck a bad bargain and keep
whittling away at your half. You should be a woman. The woman
in the newspaper holding a dead child in her arms knows God has
struck her. I feel Him as above me and around me and in you
and in spite of you and because of you. Life is a game of lost and
found. I must start Ken's supper. Unapologetic love. Love.*

Piet turned with relief from these narcissistic long letters to a small scrap asking: *Are you still sleeping with Georgene?*

After she had told him about the Jew, he had told her about Georgene. In September her instinct, or gossip, informed her that he had resumed. In truth, there had been the unplanned lapse on the day the Kennedy infant died, and in the month and a half since, only three visits, and these largely spent in tentative exploration of the new way out. He found Georgene sulky, passive, flat-stomached, and sexually unadventurous. Whether in Freddy's bed or outdoors under the sun, Piet was so nervous and watchful he had difficulty maintaining an erection. Foxy's note seemed a warning, a loud snap in the dark. He saw Georgene once more, early in October: the shedding larch needles pattered steadily on the tarpaper, the sun was wan, her chin trembled, her eyes in tears refused to confront his. He left her with no doubt that he would not come soon again, blaming Angela's suspiciously *gemütlich* intimacy with Freddy, Freddy's threatening manner lately, Piet's strained relations with Gallagher and increased work load, Georgene's own well-being—surely the essence of an affair was mutual independence, and Georgene had sinned, endangering herself, by becoming dependent. Her firm chin nodded but still her green eyes, though he seized her naked shoulders in his hands, refused to gaze into his. To Foxy's question he answered No, he had not slept with Georgene since soon after the Whitmans came to town and he had first glimpsed Foxy slamming her car door after church. He retrospectively dated his love from this glimpse. He admitted that Georgene remained his friend, and—with such a husband, who could blame her?—now and then called him at his office; Piet admitted this on the chance that Foxy already knew, via Matt and Terry. Thus, in being deceived, Foxy closer approached the condition of a wife.

RIDDLES

1. *What is five feet nine, Episcopalian, and about to burst?*
2. *What is smaller than a boxcar but bigger than mortality?*
3. *What is five feet ?, clever with its hands, has red hair, big feet, and foreign origins?*

4. *What is smaller than a breadbox but gives satisfaction anyway?*

4. *Right. Where are you, lover?*
3. *An auburn kangaroo doing needlepoint. Hah!*
2. *A bed.*
1. *Foxy Whitman.*

As they aged in their affair her notes became briefer and more playful; as fall progressed he was able to see her less. The renovations within her home were completed, and Gallagher had obtained a lucrative rush contract, the enlargement of a local restaurant in antique style. So Piet was compelled to spend long days rough-hewing factory-planed beams and fabricating seventeenth-century effects in green lumber. The owners of the Tarbox Inne, a pair of pushing Greek brothers, wanted the new wing ready for operation by November. The trips were tedious and frequent to Mather for old bricks, to Brockton for hand-wrought iron, to Plymouth for research into details of colonial carpentry: *the side bearers for the second story being to be loaden with corne, &tc., must not be pinned on, but rather eyther lett in to the studds, or borne up with false studds, & soe tenented in at the ends. In this story over the first, I would have a particion, whether in the middest or over the particion vnder, I leave it to the carpenters. I desire to have the sparrs reach downe pretty deep at the eves to preserve the walls the better from the wether. I would have the howse strong in timber, though plaine & well brased. I would have it covered with very good oake-hart inch board . . .* Trying to turn these ethical old specifications into modern quaintness demoralized Piet. The fraudulent antiquation of the job seemed prophetic of the architectural embalming destined for his beloved unself-conscious town, whose beauty had been a by-product of neglect. Maddeningly, he could not get to Foxy, and absurdly he hoped for her unmistakable silhouette to bloom on the streets of strange towns, in the drab alleyways leading to construction-supply yards. Every blue station wagon stopped his heart; every blond blur in a window became a broken promise. Now and then they did meet in spots away from Tarbox—in a Mather bar where fluorescent beer advertisements described repetitive parabolas, in a forest preserve west of Lacetown where huge mosquitoes clustered thick as hair on her arms whenever they paused in walking to embrace, on a wild beach north of Duxbury where the unsoftened Atlantic surf pounded wrathfully and the high dunes were littered with rusting cans, shards of green glass, and abandoned underpants. The danger of being discovered seemed greater out of town than in it, within the maze of routines and visiting patterns they could predict; and as Foxy's time drew near she became reluctant to drive far. Outside of Tarbox they seemed to themselves merely another furtive illicit couple, compelled toward shabby seclusion, her pregnancy grotesque. Within her breezy home they seemed glorious nudes, symphonic vessels of passion. Their dream was of a night together.

Piet—Ken has to go to a conference—in New York, Columbia —this Tuesday/Thursday. Could you possibly get free to see me, or shall I go to Cambridge and stay with friends—with Ned and Gretchen—for these days? Ken wants the latter—doesn't want me left alone—but I can argue him down if there's a reason—is there? I ache and need to be praised by you. My bigness is either horrible or a new form of beauty—which?

He could not get free. The restaurant wing was in the finish stage and he and Adams and Comeau had to be there ten hours a day. And now that the foliage was down, the beach road seemed transparent. He was timid of driving his truck past the Thornes' watching hill to the Whitmans' house, visible in fall from the little-Smiths'. At night, also, he was barred from seeing her, by a new turn in their social life: Angela in her fascination with psychiatry had taken up with the Applebys and Freddy Thorne, which involved both the Thornes. Georgene's brittle, slightly hyperthyroid eyes, when it emerged in conversation that Ken Whitman was going to be away, flicked toward Piet with the narrowing that appeared on her face when set point was deuced. Piet told Foxy to go to Cambridge, to place herself above gossip and to remove his temptation to do something desperate, revealing, and fatal.

Damn! My mother has decided to come hold my hand through "the adventure" so she will be in the house from Monday on. Could you go to church tomorrow?

After church, on the hill, beneath the penny eye of the weathercock, Piet walked down the gray path past the iron pavilion toward the reddish rocks by which Foxy had parked. Standing waiting with an alert appearance of politeness, she was vast, a full sail in pale wool, one of the high tight turbans fashionable that fall covering her hair and making her face appear stripped and sleek. He felt pulled into her orbit; he yearned to embrace, to possess forever, this luxurious ball, this swollen woman whose apparition here recalled his first impression, of wealth and an arrogant return home.

"Hi."

"Hi. Why the solemn face?"

"You look so good. You look grand."

"So do you, Mr. Hanema. Is that a new suit?"

"New last fall. You didn't know me then. Is that a new hat?"

"It's called 'a hat to meet your mother at the airport in, to show her you're doing all right.'"

"It's very successful."

"Is it too severe? I'd take it off but it's pinned."

"It's great. It brings out the pampered pink of your face."

"God, you're hostile."

"I may be hostile, but I adore you. Let's go to bed."

"Wouldn't that be a relief? Do you know how many days it's been since we made love?"

"Many."

"Nineteen. Two Tuesdays ago."

"Can we elude your mother?" Piet's palms and the area of his lips had gone cold; he felt here at the town's center that he was leaning inwards like a man on the edge of a carrousel.

Foxy said, "I can if you can get away from Angela and Gallagher."

"They're a vigilant pair these days. Jesus, I hate not seeing you. I find myself—"

"Say it." Perhaps she thought he was going to confess another woman.

"Terrified of death lately."

"Oh, Piet. Why? Are you sick?"

"It's not practical death I'm worried about, it's death anytime, at all, ever."

She asked, "Does it have to do with me?"

He had not thought so, but now he said, "Maybe. Maybe I'm frightened of you having your baby and everything changing."

"Why should it?"

He shrugged. "You'll be a mother. It won't be my child. It just won't work, you'll be too torn."

She was blank, still. Sunday was gathered around them, the sky a rung bell, cars in all colors hurrying home. Against her silence he suddenly pleaded, "I need to see you, woman. I need to see your belly."

They were exposed in sunlight and traffic, and she decided to turn to her car. "Call me," she said. "Can you call tomorrow before nine? Mother's plane comes in at ten-thirty." She thought. "No. You can't. Ken is going into Boston with me, so he'll be at the house." She thought again. "I'll try to call your office when I go shopping in the afternoon. But you'll be at the Inne." She paused a third time, having been listening to herself. "Damn, this is shitty," she said. "I *want* you to see me. I want to be with you all the time. I want to own you."

As if this last admission had confirmed and justified him in his sense of certain loss, Piet waved his hand generously, meaning it couldn't be helped. "Your wanting it," he told her, "is what matters to me. We'll keep in touch. Be nice to your Mom."

Her white-gloved hand appeared to flinch on the car-door handle. "I must go," broke from her. In full view of the town, he comically bowed, and saw she was wearing, for the good of her legs, elastic stockings dusty rose in color.

"Charrming," he said, "to be seeing ye sae fair on so fair a morrning, Mrs. Whitman."

"Likewise, I'm sure, Mr. Hanema," she replied, her brown eyes alive in the trap of their plight.

The brilliant October days brimmed for him with her absence. On the evenings when there was no party, no gathering, Piet and Angela sat at home in the stifling atmosphere of his longing. "Stop sighing."

Piet looked up surprised from a page of *Life:* saffron-robed monks protesting. "I'm not, am I?"

"Well, your breathing is unpleasant."

"Sorry. I'll try to stop breathing."

"What's bothering you? The Tarbox Inne?"

"Nothing. I just feel restless. What's in the refrigerator?"

"You've already looked. You'll get fat, the way you nibble. Why don't you go out and look at the stars? I can't stand that sighing."

"Will you come out with me?"

"In a minute." She was absorbed in her book, the new Salinger, with an endless title and a mustard jacket whose front and back were identical. "They're about to have a revelation." At what point in their courtship was it, years ago, on the Nun's Bay cliffs, that she had astonished him by knowing the stars, her uncle having been an astronomer? Her cheek to his so he could follow her pointing hand, she had taught him. Find the bright stars first. Then travel between them. Imagine straight lines. The dew touching them through the blanket. Her father's windowlights marching across the grass but dying among the shrubs trimmed like table tops. Her warm breath telling of legends above them.

He left her beneath the lamp and ventured across the crunching driveway into the yard's darkness, green-veined like black marble. The high-pitched thrum of cicadas encircled him. The clear night threatened frost. The rigid cascade of stars had been dealt a sideways blow: Vega the queen of the summer sky no longer reigned at the zenith, having yielded to paler Deneb and to a faint house-shaped constellation. Cepheus. In Andromeda Piet searched for the very dim stir of light that Angela had once pointed out to him as another galaxy altogether, two million light years distant. Through oceans of onyx its light had traveled to him. Mirrorwise his gaze, followed shortly by his death, would travel outward in an eternal straight line. Vertigo afflicted him. Amid these impervious shining multitudes he felt a gigantic slipping; sinking upwards, he gripped the dim earth with his eyes. The leaves of a broken lilac branch, dead and unable to girdle their stems and fall, hung unstirring in windowlight. He pictured Foxy, a vapor, a fur, a memory of powdery armpits, lips dry then wet, the downy small of her back where his thumbs would massage the ache of carrying a child, her erect coral nipples teased by his fingernails, the guarded blur of her gaze. She became formless and undefended beneath the sorrowful confiding of his seed. *I abuse you.*

No. Don't stop.

I'll come.

Do. I can't this time. Do, Piet.

Truly? You like it? She nodded, silent, her mouth full. Her tongue fluttered him into heat; her hand helped. *Oh. Sweet. Swallow me.* She swallowed him.

The leaves of the broken lilac branch, dead and unable to girdle their stems and fall, hung unstirring in windowlight. Behind glass Angela calmly turned a page. Above his square yard the burning dome seemed splintered by a violent fleeing. Give me now her by whom You have fled.

Piet that night fell asleep promptly, but awoke in the early morning, hours before dawn, feeling cheated, having been unable to dream. Angela lay oblivious beside him. He brought her hand to his penis but it slipped away. With his own skilled hand he lightened himself of desire; yet still he could not relax and sink. He remembered from childhood a curling warm darkness he could snuggle backwards into, at the touch of a soft blanket, of a furry toy, of rain overhead, of voices below. Now, at midpoint of his life's arc, this first darkness had receded beyond recovery and the second, the one awaiting him, was not yet comfortable. Sudden faces, totally unknown, malevolent, flicked through his mind as it sought to erase itself into sleep. Detailed drawings of unbuilt buildings, clear in every pinion and cornice, were momentarily laid flat upon his unsteady inner surface. Again and again his racing heart checked his mind's intended dissolution. He itched to thump Angela awake; the desire to confess, to confess his misery, his fornication with Foxy, rose burning in his throat like the premonition of vomit. After many turnings and futile resettlings he crept downstairs, outdoors.

The stars had wheeled out of all recognition. They were as if seen from another earth, beyond the Milky Way, rich in silence and strangeness. Treading lightly upon the rime-whitened grass, ice to his bare soles, he finally located, southward above the barn ridge with its twin scrolled lightning rods, a constellation gigantic and familiar: Orion. The giant of winter, surprised in his bed. So the future is in the sky after all. Everything already exists. Piet returned to his snug house satisfied that a crisis in his love for Foxy had passed, that henceforth he would love her less.

IV

Breakthrough

FOXY FELT that her mother's presence in the house formed a dreadful, heavensent opportunity to confess that she had a lover. No practical benefit could follow from such a confession, and her mother, in the blithe, efficient complacence bestowed upon her by remarriage and middle age, exerted no pressure to confess; rather, she assumed that the marriage she had chosen for her daughter was going all the smoother now that its one blemish, childlessness, was about to be removed. This assumption annoyed Foxy; the world's downward skid seemed to her greased by such assumptions. Confession to the contrary ballooned against the roof of her mouth. Foxy had carried her secret alone too long. Her two hidden burdens had grown parallel, and now the guilty one also demanded to emerge, to show itself, to be satisfied by a wider environment, a sunlit hemisphere of consultation and sympathy.

Yet her mother was in the house two weeks, and Foxy proved awkwardly retentive. Her delicate flush masked an inconvenient toughness. The baby was late. There were jokes, too many, about the possibility of quintuplets like those born in South Dakota the previous month. Ken and Foxy's mother —Constance Price Fox Roth, she begged them to call her Connie—got along all too nicely. They dressed in the same way: in costumes rather than clothes. Ken had outfits for every occasion, for going to work, for being at work, for being at home casually, for being at home less casually, for walking on the beach, for playing tennis, for playing touch football with the other young husbands of Tarbox on fall Sunday afternoons; he owned a closet of suits graded by sobriety, madras and linen and tweedy sports jackets, sweaters of many weights, chinos and jeans in all degrees of wear, several types of sneakers, even a foulard and a smoking jacket for the at-home occasion pitched to just this formality. In the same style, Foxy's mother, now wealthy, changed at every turn of the day. Between five-thirty and six, when the two women could make themselves a drink and settle to waiting for Ken's arrival from Boston, Connie would slip into one of her quieter cocktail dresses and Foxy in her exhausted maternity tent would be obliged to covet her mother's figure; though thickening at the waist and shrinking at the hips, it was still more compact and orthodoxly sexy than Foxy's languorous, flat-footed, overtall own. Too keenly Connie would await Ken. He had grown handsomer in the years since Foxy's parents had approved him, the same years in which Foxy had grown numb to his handsomeness. The elegant height held so uprightly, the shapely long skull now becomingly touched at the temples with gray, the gray gaze bold as a child's. Connie was impressed by Ken's professional distinction, which Foxy had come to see as an anticlimax to their long student wait, a cheat. Mrs. Roth was intrigued by what Foxy dismissed as aspects of Ken's essential coldness—the dash and abruptness with which he performed some actions, such as driving his car, ending a conversation, or acquiring this house. "I *love* the house, Liz," she told her daughter. "The view is *so* New England." Her accent sounded exaggeratedly southern to Foxy; her ceaseless emphases suggested a climacteric society where politeness has absorbed the deeper passions and become a charade. Yet beneath this flossy alien creature with teased and skillfully tinted hair, this second wife chosen to reign over mountains of laundromat quarters, there was the prior woman, the war wife and young mother, with her straggling dull bun, her serge dresses and low-heeled shoes, her scorched ironing board and her varnished Philco crackling with news from both oceans, her air of brave fatigue, her way of suddenly dropping her hands and revealing dread. Foxy thought she could find this woman if she needed her.

Mrs. Roth continued with proprietary enthusiasm: "It's a *castle*. How sweet and ambitious of Ken to have wanted it just for the two of you."

"And the baby."

"Oh, of course, for the baby, *how* could I forget the *ba*by? The cherub is why I'm here!"

Foxy said, of the house, "It was a wreck of an old summer place when we moved in. We got a rather cute local contractor to make it livable. The walls, the porch, the kitchen and the little wing beyond are all new. We had to excavate a cellar."

Foxy's mother, squinting through the smoke of the red-filtered cigarette, the aged skin of her throat betrayed by the lifting of her head, surveyed Piet's work. Foxy's heart felt displaced upward by an inward kicking. "I don't know, Liz. It seems a bit fussy. All this old-fashioned blank plaster just *isn't* you and Ken."

"You need something solid on the marshes," Foxy said defensively, "to keep out the wind."

Wishing to be tactful, and sensing a sudden need for tact, Mrs. Roth said, "I'm sure as you live here you'll make it more cozy," and changed the subject. "Speaking of the wind, Libby, do you know—it's fresh on my mind, my book circle has been reading Greek mythology, it seems to be the literary rage this year—the ancient Greeks and all those people apparently thought women were *fer*tilized by it? The *wind*!"

Foxy laughed. "Do you remember, Mother, in Bethesda, old Miss Ravenel always sitting rocking in her breezeway?" Every day, she steered the conversation to reminiscence of Bethesda.

"*Do* I?" Connie cried. "Of course, That's what she was waiting for, to be fertilized!" The laughter in the big bare-walled room sounded thin; each woman had proved fertile but once.

Ken liked his mother-in-law's presence in the house because it kept Foxy entertained at home, away from the gatherings of the couples he had taken to describing to her as "your friends." When they did go out, it was the three of them together, and Foxy's mother, in crackling purples, with a white silk stole she kept flicking and adjusting, was a social success, half-chaperon, half-fool. Freddy Thorne and she hit it off especially well. After the little-Smiths' Halloween party, held the night after the holiday and without masks, she said to Foxy, "I must say, he seems terribly *up* on things, to be only a *den*tist. He was fascinating on modern psychology and myths. Don't you, among your gay friends, find him one of the most sympatico?"

"Frankly, Mother, no. I find him insidious and odious."

"Truly? Of course, his mouth is unfortunate, but then no man will truly seem handsome set against Ken." She spoke gropingly, for in two weeks she had begun to sense Ken's curious absence, the deadening in Foxy that his presence caused. He was off this morning playing tennis, having served breakfast to himself and set his dishes nicely rinsed, as a kind of rebuke, in the slate sink. "Whom *do* you like?" she asked.

"Well," Foxy said, "mostly the women, sad to say. Terry Gallagher, she's the tall one with straight dark hair who couldn't be coaxed into playing her lute even though she brought it, and in a way Janet Appleby. She's the plump one who toward the end got quite drunk and did the impersonation of her psychiatrist."

"I thought she should be happier than she is."

"She thinks that too. And of the couples, I quite like the Hanemas and don't mind the Guerins. I can't communicate with Roger but Bea, even though she's a show-off about it, I think is genuinely affectionate. *Their* tragedy is, they can't have any children."

"The Hanemas. Not that horrid little redheaded man who ran around slapping everyone's behind and doing handstands?"

"That is Piet, yes. His wife is lovely. Very kind and serene and amused."

"I didn't notice her. But I must say, as a group, you all seemed *very* sympatico with each other. You're fortunate to have found friends you can have *fun* with. Your father and I had no such circle. We were alone; alone with you. It's good, to be able to let off steam."

"Ken thinks we *make* steam. Ken thinks we know each other *too* well. It's true, one man of a couple we know has lost his job because of their involvement with another couple."

"Which was he?"

"They don't come any more. His name was Ben Saltz. They were Jewish." Helplessly, incriminatingly, Foxy blushed.

Her mother gave no sign of remembering, with her, Peter. Rather, she said, tidily dousing her cigarette in her slopped coffee saucer, "It must have been a combination of circumstances."

"The woman he was in love with was there last night. Carol Constantine. Piled red hair with dark roots and a very thin waist. She paints. I've been thinking of buying a painting from her, after your chilling remarks about our bare walls."

"I noticed her. Stunning now, but she'll soon go brassy. She knows it, too. And she can expect precious little mercy from that dandy little husband of hers."

"Eddie? We don't take him very seriously."

"You should. He is a very vain and ruthless young Italian. I told him to his face, I'd be happy to ride in any airplane he was piloting; he was too conceited to crash."

"Mother! Aren't you wicked, flirting with these men young enough to be your sons?"

"I wasn't flirting, I was alarmed. And so is his poor emaciated wife."

"Speaking of couples," Foxy asked, homesick for Washington, "how are the Kennedys?"

"People say, better than they used to be. He used to be notorious, of course."

"She looks less anxious in the newspapers lately. At her Greek beach."

"A *dreadful* misfortune, their premature child. But I suppose being Catholics they have some way of turning it all to the good. One more angel up there, tra la."

"You don't think we Episcopalians have these ways."

"Dear good Elizabeth." Her mother's hand reached tentatively to touch hers, and their wedding rings lightly clashed, gold to gold. "I must confess I've stopped thinking of myself as anything. Roth scorns it all, of course. It was mostly a navy thing with your father."

"Does he still go to church?"

"I've never thought to ask him, and now it's been years since I've seen him. He's in San Diego, I may never see him again. Think of that."

Foxy refused to think of it. Carefully she asked, "Is it true, what everybody said, they almost got divorced?"

"The Kennedys. We don't see many government people, but yes, you do hear that sort of thing. Not divorced, of course; they'd have to buy an annulment, I suppose from Cardinal Spellman. Of course, with his back, he's *not* as active as apparently he was." Mrs. Roth rested her elbows on the table edge and wearily smoothed the skin beneath her eyes. "Why do you ask?"

Foxy said, "I'm curious about divorce." In turning her head to mute this admission she read the banner headline of the newspaper left neatly folded at Ken's empty place: DIEM OVERTHROWN. Diem. *Dies, diei, diei, diem.* "I wonder sometimes if Ken and I shouldn't get one."

The planet turned while Foxy waited to hear which woman would respond, her mother or Mrs. Roth. "Seriously?" Which was it?

Foxy sought cover. "Not very," she said very lightly. "The thought comes and goes. Since coming out here I have too much time to myself. Once the baby arrives I'll be all right."

"Well I *won*der," her mother said. "But if you're not happy why didn't you end things when there was no one else involved? You lived alone with Ken how many years was it? Seven?"

"I didn't *know* I wasn't happy till I moved here. Oh mother, it's such a mess—so *sad*. He's everything I could want but we don't make *con*tact."

"Oh, child. Cry, yes. I'm so sorry."

"He's so good, Mother, he's so goddam *good*. He doesn't *see* me, he doesn't *know* me."

"Are you sure?"

"Oh, yes, yes. I've been seeing another man and Ken doesn't have a clue. A *clue*."

"What other man?" Mrs. Roth asked sharply. "Truly seeing?"

"It doesn't *matter* what other man. A man. Oh, God, yes, seeing to sleep with."

"The child is his?"

"No, Mother, the child is *Ken's*."

This admission was the worst; as Foxy sobbed into crumpled whiteness, sobbed toward her own lap beyond the pinkness of her fingers supporting her face, she saw that this was the worst, that had the child been Piet's there would be a rationale, she would not be so purely beyond the pale.

"Well," the other woman at last found tongue to say, "it must stop."

Foxy felt the power of tears; behind the silver shield of them she advanced against her mother, refusing her an easy victory, demanding to be rescued. "But if I could *stop* I wouldn't have started. It was so wrong in the first place. It wasn't his idea it was *mine*. What I'm most afraid of isn't hurting Ken it's hurting *him*, of using his love for me to make him *marry* me."

"The man, I take it, is married also?"

"Of course he is, we're all married out here."

"Has he expressed a wish to marry you?"

"No. Yes. I don't know. It's not possible."

"Well, my advice is certainly to break it off. But I'd be the last person to say that divorce is always catastrophic."

"Oh, but it would be. He loves his wife."

"He says this?"

"He loves us both. He loves us all. I don't want to be the bitch who took advantage of him."

"Such elevated morality. In my day it was the woman who was taken advantage of. If it's the man I think it is, he'll land on his feet."

"Who do you think it is?"

"The contractor. The tall Irishman, I forget his name, who danced with you last night."

"Matt Gallagher?" Foxy laughed. "He's a good dancer but, Mother, he's just like Ken, only not as bright."

Connie blushed, hearing in her daughter's laugh how wrong her guess had been. She said, weakly, "He's the only one tall enough for you," and then, stronger, having found the right line, "Sweetheart, I don't *want* to know who the man is. If I knew the man, I'd be obliged to tell Ken. I'd rather know what dissatisfies you. To me, Ken seems perfect."

"I know he seems that to you. You've made that clear."

"And he a*dores* you. Is it the sex?"

"The sex is all right."

"You have climaxes?"

"Mother. Of course."

"Don't be so short. I didn't begin to enjoy my body until I was past thirty."

"Well I must say I don't much enjoy my body in this condition. I can't bend in the middle and my legs hurt." She abruptly stood and swept back and forth carrying plates and cups, making her mother call to her on the fly.

"How can this other man have continued with you when you are carrying this child?"

Foxy shrugged. "He never knew me when I wasn't carrying this child. It didn't seem to matter that much. He's very tender about it. His wife has stopped having children. She believes in overpopulation."

"Oh, Liz, he sounds *so* unstable to me. You have *such* unfortunate taste."

"You ask me about Ken. I think what's wrong with him is that I didn't choose him. You chose him. Daddy chose him. Radcliffe and Harvard chose him. All the world agreed he was right for me, and that's why he's not. Nobody *knew* me.

Nobody *cared*. I was just something to be bundled up and got out of the way so you and Daddy could have your wonderful divorce." The accusation was so grave she sat down at the table again. Beneath her crowded heart there was an unaccustomed burning.

Her mother massaged the moist red spaces below her eyes, and answered huskily, "Is that how it looked to you? It wasn't that way, we didn't think, but I'm so sorry, Liz, so sorry. We both loved you so, you had always been so brave for us, all those dull years your bright voice, your prettiness, we were terrified over what you were doing to yourself with Peter."

"But, Mother"—their hands on the table avoided touching, remembering the grotesque click of wedding rings—"I knew that. I knew Peter. I knew it would end of itself, you shouldn't have stepped in. I lost all dignity. This other man and I. I know it will end. He'll leave me. He'll move on. Don't tell Ken about it. Please."

"I never *thought* to tell Ken. He wouldn't know what to do with it; he might panic. You know, Liz, I'm not totally a garish old fool. I can see Ken's limits. He's like your father, he needs a form for everything. But within the rules, I think he's remarkable. He's worth treasuring."

"He is, I do treasure him. It's just so devastating, to have a husband whose job is to probe the secrets of life, and to feel yourself dying beside him, and he doesn't know it or seem to care."

"He cares, I'm sure."

"He cares about his equipment and I'm part of it."

Mrs. Roth came to attention again. "You honestly believe," she said, "that you and this other man can end it? It hasn't gone too far?"

The breakfast debris on the table, orange rinds and eggshells and newspaper, seemed to Foxy to epitomize the contents of the world. Small wonder the child was reluctant to emerge. Its weight within her—the fetus had dropped over a week ago, and its movements, once a faint fluttering, had grown tumultuous —felt leaden, panicked, betrayed. Foxy answered her mother. "It may be ended already. We've hardly talked since you came. We haven't—been together really, for five weeks."

Mrs. Roth's fingertips crept up her face and now stroked,

as if treasuringly, the shape of her eyeballs beneath shut lids. "Dear Libby," she said, not looking. "What I most remember from that terrible Bethesda house was the radio dial glowing, and your lovely flaxen hair, that I combed, and combed."

"Gone, Mother, gone," Foxy airily stated, rising and startling in the small of her back an untypical, musical phrase of pain.

Just ten now, still stocky yet dawningly comely, Ruth was given to placid self-communings in her room, which she kept extremely neat. For her birthday Piet had given her a full-length mirror, a doorway to vanity, a father's doting and perhaps intrusive gift. He had grown shy, wary of intruding on her. When he ventured into Ruth's room, he glanced at the mirror to detect signs of its use and surprised his own sharp reflection, looking pouchy and thievish. Surrounded by her mirror, by the splashy flowers of the wallpaper she had chosen herself, by collections, each to its shelf, of books, seashells, bottlecaps, and the foreign dolls sent to her by Angela's parents from the harbors of their winter cruises, by a turquoise-oceaned map of the world and a green-and-white Tarbox High football banner, by Scotch-taped Brownie snapshots she had taken herself of her parents arm-in-arm, of the hamster who had died, of the lilac hedge in bloom, of her friends at the beach but none of her sister—so surrounded, Ruth would sit at the fold-down desk Piet had built for her and do her homework, or make entries in her laconic diary of weather and excursions, or maintain her scrapbook of figures carefully scissored from *Life* and the *National Geographic*, an assortment including Sophia Loren, Queen Elizabeth II of England, a Russian spacedog, a huge stone Pharaoh threatened with immersion by the Aswan Dam, a naked Nigerian bride, a Pakistani mother bewailing the death of her child by earthquake, Jacqueline Kennedy, a vocal group called the Beatles.

On days like this Monday when Piet returned home before Angela, he felt his daughter busy above him; she was bused back from school by four. The silence behind her closed door, broken when she rearranged objects or crooned to herself hymns learned at choir, intimidated him; he had scrubbed her diapers and warmed her bottles and now his only function was to safeguard her privacy, to make himself unobtrusive. He re-read the newspaper and considered replacing the rotten boards of his own barn and instead made himself an early gin-and-Bitter-Lemon. Now that the tavern addition was completed, and christened with a formal banquet attended by all three selectmen and fire chief Kappiotis, who fell asleep, there was not enough for Piet to do. Gallagher had sold the estate in Lacetown to the nuns, but a Watertown firm whose director's brother was a priest had been awarded the fat reconstruction contract. They were told the bids had been considered blind; all Gallagher's charm with the sisters had been wasted. They were down to a single job, converting the old Tarbox house on Divinity into offices and apartments suitable for rental. Old Gertrude Tarbox, having constructed for herself a paradise of hoarded paper and tin, was in September carted off to a nursing home, at the command of cousins living in Palo Alto, through the agency of a New Bedford bank. Piet's job—replacing clap-boards, removing partitions, sanding floors, dressing up ratty surfaces with decorator panels of vinyl surfaced to counterfeit wood—was scarcely enough to occupy Adams and Comeau and Jazinski, who, being employees paid by the hour, were entitled to work first. So Piet was often idle. He drank deep of the sweetened gin and tried not to think of Foxy; since she had hidden behind her mother she was in his mind like a can-ker that memory's tongue kept touching. The summer seemed dreamlike and distant. She had vanished—the slam of a car door after church. He missed the thrift of a double life, the de-fiant conservation. Faithful, he was going to waste. Attenuated hours spread lifeless around him. He drank to kill time.

Angela came home brimful of Irene. "You know what that woman has done? She's gotten a paying job at the Lacetown Academy for Girls, starting next Monday, today a week, which means I have to do the whole kindergarten by myself."

"Tell her you can't do it."

"Who said I can't? If I can't go to a psychiatrist at least I can run a dozen children by myself, without Irene's kibbutzy theories getting in my way."

"You *want* to do it."

"What's so surprising about that? I don't want to very much. I don't think children this small are my meat really, but I do want to see how teaching after all these years strikes me. I mean, wouldn't you like it if I could bring home a little money?"

"You're afraid I can't support you."

Angela bent and rubbed her cheek against his temple softly, yet hastily, the brush of a wing about to fly. "Of course you can. But I'm a person too. My children are growing up." She whispered: "Nancy goes all morning without sucking her thumb, unless something happens to remind her." She whispered because she had brought the child home, and Nancy was on the stairs, wondering if she dared go bother Ruth.

"What else did Irene say? You've been gone forever. Has Ben found a job yet?"

"No, I'm not even sure he's looking. But she was full of news. She keeps a beady black eye on the Constantines across the way and says they've taken up with the Guerins. Roger and Bea are over there every night, and what Irene thinks, you have to hear it from her to get the humor of it, is that the attraction is between the like halves of the couples." She drew a box in air with her fingers to explain. "Carol and Bea are attracted to each other, and Roger and Eddie."

"Well does she think they're putting this attraction into practice? I'm having another drink. Would you like one?"

"Bourbon, not gin. Piet, summer's over. She doesn't quite dare say so. But she thinks Carol is capable of anything physically and Bea *does* have this very passive streak. She's always been a kind of a woman's woman, in a way; she *flirts* with women, and gives them little pats."

"But it must be a huge step," Piet said, though knowing that heterosexually it was not so, "between that kind of current and taking off your clothes and doing the stuff."

Angela took her musky gold drink from his hand; as she sipped her eyes went bluer, gazing toward scenes she had been told of. "But," she said, "we're none of us getting younger and if it's something you've always wanted aren't the inhibitions less and less? Things keep getting less sacred."

Piet said, pouring lucid gin for himself, "Roger *is* homosexual, sure, but his charm has always been his refusal to admit it. Except in his manner to women, which is either rude or excessively polite."

"I think there's a difference," Angela said, "between being

homosexual and being angry at females. Has Roger ever, on the golf course say, made a pass at you?"

"No. But he *is* very comfortable, and can't *stand* being stuck behind a female foursome. But I think Eddie's the mystery. How can Irene accuse her lover of a few months ago of being a working fairy?"

"Well, for one thing, she didn't exactly, and for another she is quite hurt and bitter. When I sort of asked her this, all she'd say was that Eddie could be very per*sua*sive. I don't know what it meant, but she said it three or four times."

Piet asked her, "Where does your friend Freddy Thorne fit in this new arrangement?"

"Oh, well Freddy's the one who brought them together; the Guerins and Constantines had almost nothing to do with each other until Freddy. I guess he's over there pretty much, stirring the brew."

"Poor Georgene."

Angela asked, alert, her upper lip lifted, her wet teeth aglint, "Why poor Georgene?"

"On general principles. Married to that evil jerk."

"You can't really think he's evil. He just loves a mess. Anyway, Georgene's been *very* frosty to me ever since school started. Once Irene goes, it wouldn't surprise me if Georgene stopped doing her day."

"What else did Irene have on her teeming mind?"

"Let me remember. John Ong is apparently sick. Something with his chest; the doctors have told him to quit smoking and he won't. He can't."

"My Lord. Cancer?"

"Nobody knows. Of course, he's older than any of us, it just hasn't showed, because he's Asiatic."

"Is he in the hospital?"

"Not yet. And, oh yes, of course. This will please you. Foxy Whitman has had her baby."

The air compressed; a sense of suffocation was followed by a carefree falling independent of space. Piet asked, "When?"

"Sometime this weekend. I think on Sunday. You saw her Friday night at the little-Smiths'. Maybe dancing with Matt Gallagher brought it on. He's awfully bouncy."

"Why hasn't anybody told us before?"

"Piet, you're taking it so *per*sonally. You're not exactly the next of kin. I *am* surprised that Matt didn't mention it at work. Terry must have heard, if she's Foxy's best friend."

"Matt and I don't communicate much at work these days. He's sulking because we lost the nunnery. But that's very nice. She had gotten enormous. Boy or girl?"

"Boy. Seven pounds something. Should we send flowers? I like Foxy, but we don't seem quite at the flower-sending stage."

"Oh, send her some. Loosen up. You can't take them with you, Angel. Flowers don't grow in Heaven, they only spring from dung."

Angela grimaced, puzzled by his hostile patter, and left the kitchen, calling, "Ru-uth! Come down and be sociable. Nancy wants to play Fish."

Alone, Piet tried to grasp the happiness distinct yet unsteady within him. She was safe. The child had been a boy. Foxy's luck had held. He wanted to be very close to her, to creep into the antiseptic white room where she lay, deflated and pink, invisibly bleeding, breathing in unconsciousness, her pale mouth askew, her hair adrift. He saw hothouse flowers—lush gladiolas, display dahlias, beribboned hyacinths fragrant of greenhouse earth packed tight by mossy thumbs, red cut roses leaning heavy-headed and coolly rank. He glimpsed the glass of water standing stale-beaded beyond her blurred face, and the cartoon cards of congratulation, and a candy bar concealed half-eaten in an enameled drawer. And in a chamber beyond this possessive daydreaming waited the realization that, in giving birth without notifying him, she had been guilty of an affront and in that guilt promised him freedom. Once, uncoming, she had masturbated against his thigh squeezed between hers. *Is this too awful for you?*

No, of course not, no. Youth must be served.

Don't tease. I'm shy enough with you as is.

With me, your lover? Shy?

Just am.

It's so touching, how hard women must work.

Touch my nipples.

Gladly.

More gently. I'm almost there.

Come. His thigh was beginning to ache and tingle, the circulation hampered. *Oh come. Good. Terrific. Wow.*

On top of the refrigerator was a wooden salad bowl brimming with Halloween candy that Ruth and Nancy had begged. To celebrate, to lend substance to, his happiness Piet took down the bowl and gobbled a handful of imitation corn; he rarely ate candy, out of fear for his teeth.

Though Foxy had made the appointment three weeks ago, while still in the hospital, for this Friday at one, Freddy Thorne seemed startled by her appearance in his office. Until now she had kept her Cambridge dentist, but toward the end of her pregnancy her teeth had begun to twinge, and with the baby nursing her mobility was lessened. No one, not even Piet, denied that Freddy was a competent dentist. Yet she could not escape the feeling, entering his inner office, that by coming to him, in his absurd cottage tucked beside the post office on Divinity Street, when there were other competent dentists in town, she was, emboldened by motherhood, playing the game that Tarbox had taught her, the game of tempting her fate.

He wore a white jacket and, an inch or more in front of his regular glasses, a pair of rectangular magnifying lenses. The sanctum was fanatically clean, from the circular napkin on the swinging tool tray to the scrubbed blush of Freddy's palms, uplifted in surprise or blessing, in front of his backwards white jacket. A square black clock said twelve after one. His first appointment after lunch. She had nibbled around ten; the baby had scattered her habits of sleep and eating. It reassured her that like all normal dentists Freddy ran behind schedule. "Well look who's here!" he said when she entered. "Lovely day," he murmured while he adjusted her into the chair. Now he asked, as her mouth obediently opened, "Which is the area of discomfort?" Three persons had spoken: the first a frivolous prying man she knew, the second a polite bored acquaintance, the third a wholly alien technician.

"Here," she said. She pointed with her finger from outside her cheek and with her tongue from within. Freddy held the pick and mirror crossed at his chest as she explained. "The upper, molar I suppose it is. I get a twinge when I eat candy. And over here, on the other side, I can feel a hole where a filling used to be. Also all the books say, and my mother in*sis*ted, my teeth would fall out because the calcium went into the baby."

"Did you take calcium pills?"

"Iron, I know. I took whatever Doc Allen gave me."

Freddy said, "With a modern diet calcium displacement isn't usually a problem. Primitive women *do* tend to lose their smiles. Shall we have us a look?" His touch with the exploratory picks was delicate. A steel point touched a nerve once, and tactfully feathered off. Mint on his breath masked the odor of whatever he had eaten for lunch, perhaps veal. His perfumed fingers were in her mouth, and, like many things she had abstractly dreaded, like childbirth, like adultery, the reality was more mixed than she had imagined, and not so bad.

"You have strong teeth," he said. He made precise pencil marks on one of those dental charts that to Foxy as a child had seemed a wide-open scream. Curious, his choice of "strong" over "nice" or "good."

She counted the marks and said, "*Four* cavities!" Always in dental chairs she wanted to talk too much, to fend the drill away from her mouth.

"You're in respectable shape," he told her. "Let's begin with the upper right, the one you've been feeling."

He removed an injecting needle from a tray of blue sterilizer. She told him, "I don't usually bother with Novocain."

"I want you to today." His manner was mild and irresistible; where was that sloppy troll she knew from parties? With the secondary lenses in place, his eyes were totally elusive. Freddy became a voice and a touch. He said, "This is a new gadget," and his fingers exposed a spot on her upper gum where, with a tiny hiss, something icy was sprayed. Thus numbed, she did not feel the stab of the needle.

They waited for the Novocain to take effect. Freddy busied himself behind her back. She yawned; Toby had been fed at two and awakened again at five. Her feet on the raised metal tread looked big and flat and pale in ballet slippers. Above her feet a large window curtained in dun sacking framed an abstract view: the slate roof of the Tarbox post office descended in courses of smaller to greater from a ridge of copper flashing set smack, it seemed, against the sky. The day was balmy for this late in November. Small tugging clouds darkened Tarbox with incongruous intensity when they crossed the sun. She wondered why Piet had sent no flowers. Freddy shuffled tinkling metal and his receptionist, a pug-nosed girl with skunk-striped bangs, passed back and forth between the anteroom and a nether room in which Foxy could glimpse a table, a Bunsen burner, a tattered chart dramatizing dental hygiene for children, and the end of a cot. Nearer, on a chest of enameled drawers, a small blond radio played colorless music interrupted now and then by a characterless male voice, a voice without a trace of an accent or an emotion. Foxy wondered where such music originated, whether in men or machines, and who supplied it so inexhaustibly to dentists' offices, hotel lobbies, and landing airplanes. Ken called it toothpaste music.

Freddy cleared his throat and asked, "Is your mother still here? Will she be coming tonight?" The Thornes were giving a black-tie party tonight. To Foxy it meant that after weeks of seclusion she would at last again see Piet.

"No, we put her on a plane Tuesday. At last."

"Did Ken not enjoy having his mother-in-law in the house?"

"He minded it less than I did. I'm used to being a hermit."

"She seemed jolly."

"She is. But I haven't really had much to do with her since college. I'm too old to have a mother."

"She enjoyed the baby." It was not quite a question.

"She made the noises. But people that age, I discover, aren't very flexible, and it took a lot of my energy to keep the baby off of her nerves. She kept changing clothes and trying to reminisce while I wobbled up and down stairs." As the moment for Freddy to use the drill neared, Foxy's mouth watered, fairly bubbled with the wish to tell him everything—the musical first pains, the narrowing intermittences, the dreamlike unconcern of the doctors and nurses, the anesthesia like a rustling roaring wing enfolding her, the newborn infant's astonishingly searching gaze, her wild drugged thought that he more resembled Piet than Ken, and the miraculous present fact that she, slim Foxy, was a good nurser, a tall tree of food.

Freddy said, "She seemed in no hurry to go back to her husband."

"Yes, I wondered about that. She spoke very loyally of 'Roth,' when she thought of him. I think she sees her life as a kind of Cinderella story, rescued at the end, and now that she's living happily ever after, she's bored."

"She found Ken congenial." Again, it was not quite interrogative.

"Very."

Freddy had not expected so curt a response; delicately balked, he licked his lips and volunteered, "She also seemed attracted to me."

"Oh, Freddy, we all are."

The receptionist, who had been tinkling in the corner with the sterilizer, flashed a naughty smile behind Freddy's back. Sensing teasing, he became dryer in manner. "We discussed fertility; did she tell you?" The receptionist left the room.

"Breathlessly. All about myths."

"In part. We concluded, as I remember, that women could as easily be fertilized by the wind as by men, if they believed in it. That all conception is immaculate, on the handiest excuse." That blurred smirk: what was she supposed to imagine it implied?

Foxy said, "How silly. We're obviously helpless."

"Are you?"

"Otherwise why would there be so many only children? I *hated* being an only child. My father just wasn't there. We had plenty of electric fans."

"Did you?" He had lost track of the joke, the wind.

"One in every room. I know I certainly don't intend my child to be only." There it was: just when Foxy had decided for the hundredth time that Freddy was contemptible, she found she had been drawn out.

He asked, "Numb yet?"

She said, "Almost. What's that cot for?" She gestured toward the nether room, to fling the conversation from herself. A small cloud crossed the sun and dipped them into momentary shadow as if into intimacy. The music was mechanically doing "Tea for Two." She was suddenly hungry for English muffins.

"Not what you think," Freddy said.

"I don't think anything. I'm just asking."

"Instead of lunch sometimes I take a nap."

"I've wondered how you keep going with all those parties. But what did you think I thought?" She made silent motions indicating the young receptionist, doing her doll stare and touching her forehead for the skunk bangs, and, folding her hands beside her face, sleep. She formed a kissing mouth to cement her meaning.

"No," Freddy whispered. "That I give abortions."

Shocked, stifled by shock, Foxy wanted to flee the chair. "I *never* thought that."

"Oh, but dentists do. It's a perfect set-up. They have everything, the chair, anesthetic, instruments . . ."

She judged he was saying these things to enlarge himself in her eyes, to inflame with innuendo her idea of him. If he had gone to medical school, he had aspired to power over life and death; having failed, having settled for dentistry, a gingerly meddling at the mouth of life, he still aspired. She put him down: "I don't want to hear about it."

He answered, "You must be numb now," and began to drill. Upside down, his warm cheek close against her head, Freddy resolved into a pair of hairy nostrils, a dance of probing fingers, and glinting crescents of curved glass. His aura was maternal, soapy. Foxy relaxed. Her breasts began to sting and she anticipated release, leaving this office, collecting the baby in his vanilla Carry-Cot at Bea Guerin's, driving down the winding beach road to her empty house, undoing her upper clothes, and giving her accumulated richness over to that tiny blind mouth so avid to suck. He had begun on the right breast this morning, so it would be the left this noon. Twenty minutes, and the Novocain would be wearing off, and she could make a lunch of leftover salad and a tuna sandwich. How innocently life ate the days. How silly she was, how Christianly neurotic, to feel beneath the mild mixed surface of aging and growing, of nursing and eating and sleeping, of love feigned and stolen and actual, a terror, a tipping wrongness, a guilt gathering toward discharge. Poor Freddy, their ringleader, was revealed as a competent dentist. "Lady Be Good" was played. Beneath the red blanket of her closed eyelids Foxy saw that she must soon break with Piet, and felt no pain.

In mid-melody the radio music stopped.

The characterless male voice, winded, hurried, as if called back to the microphone from a distance, pronounced, "A special bulletin. Shots have been heard in Dallas in the vicinity of the Presidential motorcade. We repeat. Gunshots have been reported in Dallas in the vicinity of President Kennedy's motorcade."

There was a second of sharp silence. Then the needle was returned to the groove and the toothpaste music smoothly resumed "Lady Be Good." The black clock said 1:36.

Freddy held the drill away from her mouth. "You hear that?"

She asked him, "What does it mean?"

"Some crazy Texan." He resumed drilling. The pitch of speed lifted impatiently. The star of heat pricked its cloud of spray, and hurt. Freddy sighed mint. "You may spit."

The receptionist, wide-eyed from having overheard the radio, came in from the anteroom to whip the silver and to listen. "Do you think it was Communists?" the girl asked. The music halted again. She signed herself with the cross. On the slates opposite, a small flock of pigeons, having settled near the post office chimney for warmth, clumsily swirled and lifted. The bulletin was repeated, with the additional information that the motorcade had definitely been fired *at*. Three shots had been counted. The pigeons gripped flight in their dirty wings and beat away, out of Foxy's sight. The girl brought a pellet of silver in a chamois pad and set it on the impeccable circular napkin of Freddy's tool tray. Freddy rolled it tighter with his fingertips. The blunder of resuming the music was not repeated. Words spaced by silence filled in the solid truth. The President had been shot at, the President had been hit, he had been hit in the head, his condition was critical, a priest had been summoned, the President was dead. By two o'clock, all of this was known. Amid medicinal whiffs, Freddy had swabbed Foxy's cavity and flanked the tooth with cotton and clamps and pressed the silver filling tight. Foxy had waited in the chair ten additional minutes to hear the worst. Kennedy dead, she left. The nurse was crying, her eyes still held wide, as if like a doll's unable to close unless she lay down. Foxy, grateful to her for showing emotion, patted her hand, a cool tap in passing. Living skin seeks skin. The girl blurted, "We didn't even vote for him, my family, but would have the next time."

Freddy seemed distended and titillated by this confirmation of chaos. Escorting Foxy out through the anteroom, he said in the hall, "This fucks up our party, doesn't it?"

"You must cancel," Foxy told him. She would not see Piet tonight.

"But I've bought all the *booze*," Freddy protested.

Foxy went out into Freddy's tiny front yard, which held a crabapple tree skeletal and spidery without leaves. The post office flag was already at half-mast. Divinity Street was so silent she heard an electric sander working well down the block. Through the plate-glass windows of the pizza shop and the Tarbox *Star* and the shoe-repair haven that was also a bookie joint, she saw shadows huddled around radios. She thought of the little blond radio's embarrassed fall from its empyrean of bland music, of the receptionist's navy-blue eyes lacquered by tears, of Freddy's stupid refusal to mourn, mistaken and contemptible, yet—what was better in herself? She tried to picture the dead man, this young man almost of her generation, with whom she could have slept. A distant husband had died and his death less left an emptiness than revealed one already there. Where grief should have dwelt there was a reflex tenderness, a personal cringing. At Cogswell's corner she glanced up toward the Congregational Church and her heart, blind lamb, beat faster. The Plymouth was parked by the rocks; she must hurry to the baby. Striding uphill through the spotty blowing sunlight, Foxy imagined her son's avid toothless mouth. Her left breast eagerly ached. She tested the right side of her mouth and found it still numb. Would her lopsided smile frighten him? Then it seemed to her that the cocky pouchy-eyed corpse had been Piet and the floor of her stomach fell and the town around her gripped guilt in its dirty white gables and tried to rise, to become a prayer.

The Thornes decided to have their party after all. In the late afternoon, after Oswald had been apprehended and Johnson sworn in, and the engines of national perpetuity had demonstrated their strength, Georgene called all the houses of the invited and explained that the food and liquor had been purchased, that the guests had bought their dresses and had their tuxedos cleaned, that she and Freddy would feel lonely tonight and the children would be *so* disappointed, that on this terrible day she saw nothing wrong in the couples who knew each other feeling terrible together. In a way, Georgene explained to Angela, it would be a wake, an Irish wake, and a formal dinner-dance was very fitting for the dead man, who had had such style. Do come. Please. Freddy will be very hurt, you know how vulnerable he is.

The fashion that fall was for deep décolletage; Piet, arriving at nine, was overwhelmed by bared breasts. He had been reluctant to come. His superstitious nature had groped for some religious observance, some ceremony of acknowledgment to gallant dead Kennedy, though he was a Republican. He knew Freddy would be blasphemous. Further, he felt unwell: his tongue and gums had developed a rash of cankers, and since Foxy had become inaccessible Angela had also ceased to make love to him, and his tuxedo was old, a hand-me-down from his father-in-law, and unfashionably wide-lapelled, and the black shoulders showed his dandruff. Entering the Thornes' living room he saw naked shoulders and flaringly bared bosoms floating through the candlelight, haunting the African masks, the gaudy toss pillows, the wickerwork hassocks and strap-hinged Spanish chests and faded wing chairs. Logs burned in the fieldstone fireplace. The bar table of linen and glasses and bottles formed an undulant field of reflected fire. Janet Appleby wore an acid-green gown whose shoelace straps seemed unequal to the weight squeezed to a sharp dark cleavage like the vertical crease of a frowning brow. Marcia little-Smith, in a braless orange bodice, displayed, as she reached forward, earrings shuddering, to tap a cigarette into a copper ashtray each dent of which was crescental in the candlelight, conical tits hanging in shadow like tubular roots loose in water. Georgene wore white, two filmy breadths of cloth crossed to form an athletic and Attic binder, her breasts flattened boyishly, as if she were on her back. Carol Constantine had stitched herself a blue silk sheath severely narrow at the ankles and chastely high in front but scooped in the back down to her sacral vertebrae. Irene Saltz—for the Saltzes had come, partly renewed confidence brought on by Irene's job, partly impish insistence on Freddy's part—had put on a simple cocktail dress of black velvet; its oval neckline inverted the two startled arcs of her eyebrows as she jealously, anxiously surveyed the room for the whereabouts of Ben and Carol and Eddie. Piet was touched by her. Like him, she felt it was wrong to have come. She had lost weight. Humiliation flattered her.

Bea Guerin drifted toward him with uplifted face; her bosom, sprinkled with sweat, was held forward in a stiff scarlet carapace like two soft sugared buns being offered warm in the metal vessel of their baking. "Oh Piet," she said, "isn't it awful, that we're all here, that we couldn't stay away, couldn't stay home and mourn decently?" With lowered lids he fumbled out a concurrence, hungering for the breasts that had risen to such a roundness their upper rims made a dimpled angle with Bea's chest-wall. *Why don't you want to fuck me?* Her lifted upper lip revealed the little gap between her front teeth; she laid a trembling hand on his arm, for balance, or as a warning. *You're surrounded by unkind people.* Embarrassed, he sipped his martini, and the cankers lining his mouth burned.

He said, "I hear you're seeing a lot of the Constantines."

"They're bores, Piet. Roger enjoys them, but they're self-centered bores. After a while one minds their not having gone to college."

"Who does Roger enjoy most, Eddie or Carol?"

"Don't be wicked, Piet. I don't mind it from these others, but I hate it from you. You're not wicked, why pretend?"

"Answer my question."

"Carol can be fun," Bea said, "but she's *so* cold. Cold and crude. I think—this is terribly sad—I think she was honestly in love with Ben, terribly in love, and never let herself know it, and now she can't admit it, it's too un*dig*nified, and does the *cruelest* imitations of him."

"But Ben is so boring."

"Piet, I don't think they noticed, they're such bores themselves. Oh, it's awful, everybody is so boring. Roger is so ex*treme*ly boring."

"You think I wouldn't be?"

"Not for a while, sweet Piet. Not for a long while. But you don't like short women, it's *so* Napoleonic of you."

Piet laughed and gazed over Bea's head. Where was Foxy? He searched the flickering room in vain. He felt that in her staying away she had achieved over him a moral ascendancy that completed the triumph, the royal disregard, of her giving birth to a son. Pity sucked at him; he felt abandoned, small. He asked Bea, "Where are the Gallaghers?"

"Matt told Georgene they were going with their children to a special mass. She said he was polite over the phone but just barely."

"Matt is getting very independent. And the Ongs?"

"John was too sick."

"How sick is he?"

"Freddy says he's dying," Bea said, the curve of her cheek a Diana's bow in candlelight. Dying. Before coming to the party Piet and his daughters had watched, on television, the casket being hauled from the plane amid the spotlights of the air field: a long gleam on the polished wood as sudden as a bullet, the imagined airless privacy within, the flooding lights without, the widow blanched amid rapid shadows, the eclipsing shoulders of military attachés. The casket had tipped, bumped. Bea said to Piet, "You haven't asked where are the Whitmans."

"Oh, aren't they here?"

"Piet, you're *so* obvious. I have *no* idea where they are, but you've been looking over my head *all* this time. It's not very flattering."

"I was thinking I should get another drink." To quench panic. The refrigerator. The stars.

"Piet," Bea said swiftly, softly, seeing he was pulling away. "I could love you, if you'd let me."

At the drinks table Carol was flirting simultaneously with Harold and Frank. "Frank," she said loudly in a voice that did not quite dare call the party to attention, to make an occasion, "give us a Shakespeare quote. Nobody knows quite what to say."

"Good night, sweet prince?" Angela offered. It startled Piet to see her there, her fine oval skull and throat suspended in the hovering light, shadows fluctuating on her white shoulders, the scalloped neckline, the discreet parabola of pearls.

Frank Appleby, red-eyed, considered and said, "Ambition's debt is paid."

Carol asked, "Is that a quote?"

"From *Julius Caesar*. What a dumb floozy." He gave Carol a crunching shoulder hug that Piet feared would shatter her brittle blue sheath.

"What about"—Harold little-Smith interrupted himself with a giggle—"For Oswald is an honorable man?" Enjoying the laughter of the others, he went on, "I *really* had to laugh, the news came in just as I was having dessert, *gâteau avec des fraises*, with three of my most Republican associates, including, Frank—this will amuse you—young Ed Foster, who as Frank knows thinks Bob Taft was turning pink at the end. *Un peu de rose au fin.* Naturally everybody's first assumption, including the broadcasters, who are all liberals of course—"

Carol interrupted, "Harold, are you *really* a conservative?"

Janet spoke up. "Harold and Frank are different. Frank's a Federalist; he honestly *loves* the Founding Fathers. Harold's an ultramontane; with him it's just a form of swank."

"*Merci pour votre mots très incisifs.* May I please continue? Well, naturally everybody assumed that a *right*-wing crackpot had done it. You remember at first there was a lot of melancholy fill-in about Dallas the Birchers' paradise, et cetera; we were all very pious and tut-tutty."

"Is that French?" Carol asked.

"But then, around two-thirty, when I'd got back to the office and the stuff on Oswald had begun to filter through, young Ed called up absolutely ec*stat*ic and said, 'Did you hear? It wasn't one of ours, it was one of *theirs*!'" Perhaps because all those listening had experienced the same reversal of prejudice, there was less laughter than Harold had expected.

Frank offered, "Ever since McCarthy cracked up, all the real wolves have been on the left."

Freddy said, "One thing I'm absolutely certain of, he wasn't in it alone. There were too many shots. The whole fucking thing was too successful."

He was unanimously pooh-poohed. Janet said, "Freddy, you see conspiracies in everything."

"He thinks," Angela stated, "we're all a conspiracy to protect each other from death."

"To shut out the night, I think I said."

Piet was impressed that Freddy remembered anything of what he said. Shapelessness was growing bones. Feeding on calcium stolen from Piet's own slack and aimless life. Lately Freddy had taken to staring at Piet too hard, meaningfully.

"One conspiracy I'll let you all in on is," Harold little-Smith said, "when the market opens again, buy. Business was *not* happy with Kennedy, and it's going to *love* Johnson. He's just the kind of old bastard business is happy under."

Carol with her long bare back shivered. "That gross sad man. It was like the high-school shot putter accepting the class presidency, all humility and rotten grammar. Freddy, are you going to let us dance?"

"Whatever my guests think is proper. I don't know how to act, frankly. I've never had my President assassinated before. I was a baby when they did Lincoln in. Honest Abyface."

Ben Saltz overheard and came up to them. His face above his beard appeared to Piet shell-white, a grinning fragment from an exploded past. "And yet," he informed Freddy, "this country since 1865 has an unenviable record for political violence. *Four* presidents, plus the attempts on Truman and both Roosevelts—as you know, Teddy was actually wounded, in his unsuccessful campaign in 1912—not to mention Huey Long. There isn't a country west of the Balkans with any kind of the same record. The Prime Ministers of England go everywhere with a single bodyguard."

"We fought for the right to bear arms," Frank said.

Carol was saying, "Ben will dance with me, won't you, Ben? Wouldn't you like to dance with me?"

His carved lion's smile appeared, but his eyes remained dubious, frightened, human. Carol twitchily seized Harold's arm and said, "If Ben's scared to, Harold will, won't you, Harold? Dance with me. After Janet's been so mean about your elegant politics. Freddy, put on music." She turned the chill pallor of her back on Piet.

Ben too, in a trim tuxedo that looked rented, turned his back, and spoke to Angela. Piet heard his wife ask, ". . . like her teaching by now?"

Ben's voice, doleful and clear, responded, ". . . gratifying to me to see her using her mind after all these years, being at least to some extent intellectually challenged."

Georgene was standing in the middle of the room with the air of a hostess undecided between duties. Piet approached her and let her sip his drink. "Carol is terribly high," he said.

"Well, take her to bed. You know where it is."

"I wouldn't dream of it. She'd scratch. But I wonder whose inspiration it was to have the Saltzes and Constantines together."

"Freddy's, of course."

"But you made it stick. Freddy has a lot of ideas that you let wither."

Georgene's righteous clubwoman's temper flared. "Well really Piet, it's too tedious, if people aren't going to have their affairs in private." We were different, she was saying, we were secret, and brave, and better than these corrupt couples. She went on aloud, roughly pushing her fingers through her graying hair, as if combing out larch needles, "I seem to be the only person I know left who has any sense of privacy."

"Oh. That's an interesting remark."

"It's not meant to be."

"Sweet Georgene, what *are* you doing with all this privacy, now that I'm not around?"

"Oh," she said, "men come and go. I can't keep track of them all. They've worn a path through the woods." She asked, "Do you care?"

"Of course. You were wonderful for me."

"What happened then?"

"It began to frighten me. I felt Freddy knew."

"What if he did? I was handling Freddy."

"Maybe I'm not being entirely honest."

"I know you're not," Georgene said, "you never are," and, like a playing card being snapped, showed him her edge and dealt herself away. Let women in, Piet thought, and they never stop lecturing. Pedagogy since the apple. Be as gods.

Roger Guerin came up to him. His brows were knit tight and he was wearing a frilled and pleated dress shirt, with ruby studs and a floppy bow tie in the newest fey fashion. He asked, "Put your golf clubs away yet?"

Piet said, "There may be one more warm weekend."

Eddie Constantine came up to them crouching. "Hey Jesus," he said, "have either of you looked down Marcia's dress yet? She's nose cones down to her navel."

"You've always known they were there," Piet told him.

"Believing isn't seeing. God, we were in the kitchen talking about some cruddy thing, air pollution, and I kept looking down and they kept bobbling around, I got such a hard-on I had to dive in here to level off."

Roger laughed, too loudly out of his tiny mouth, like one who has learned about laughing late in life, and Piet realized he was standing here as an excuse, that the point of Eddie's anecdote had been to amuse and excite Roger. My cock, he had been secretly saying, is big as a fuselage. Women, he had been saying, are dirt.

"How about Janet?" Roger asked him. "Held by those two little shoestrings."

Eddie drew closer, still in his scuttling position, to the other man, stiff-standing. "It looks to me the way they're squeezed she's carrying a second backside, in case the first wears out." The beauty of duality. A universe of twos. "Hey Roger, do you want to know what crazy Carol did the other night? We were . . . you know . . . in my lap . . . up . . . and what does the bitch do but swing her leg way the hell back and stick her foot in my mouth! It was great, I damn near puked. Get Bea to try it."

Piet moved off and gently, by standing expectant, detached Janet from the little-Smiths and Freddy Thorne. The glass in her hand held a few melted ice cubes; he touched it to take it from her. She did not resist, her head was bowed. In the hushed space walled by their bodies Piet asked, "How goes it, Jan-Jan? How's your beautiful shrink?"

"That bastard," she said, without looking up, "that son of a bitch. He won't tell me to stop seeing Harold."

"We all thought you'd stopped seeing Harold ages ago. Ever since your goodness and health regime."

Now she did look up. "You're nice, Piet. Naïve but nice."

He asked her, "Why is it your psychiatrist's job to tell you to stop seeing Harold?"

"That's what *he* says," she said. "Because I love him, that's why. He's a fat old Kraut with a brace on one leg and I love him, he's a total fink but I adore him, and if he gave even the simplest kind of a fart about me he'd tell me to stop sleeping with Harold. But he won't. He doesn't. The old re-tard."

"What *does* the man tell you?"

"I've been going now five months and the only hint he's

ever dropped is that because of the pharmaceutical business every time I take a pill I'm having intercourse with my father, it's his seed. I said to him, What am I supposed to do when I get a headache and need two aspirin, dial a prayer?"

"Dear lovely Janet, don't cry. Tell me instead, should Angela go? Ever since you started, she's wanted to go. What's my duty as a husband?"

"Don't let her. Get her a lover, send her to Yugoslavia, anything but this. God, it's degrading. It'll get her all mixed up and she's so serene. She doesn't know how neurotic she is."

"She's beginning to. She tells me she feels too detached, as if she's already dead."

"Mm, I know that feeling. Angela and I are somewhat alike."

"Yes, that's what she says too. She says you both have big bosoms and it makes you both melancholy."

"Let Angela speak for herself. I'm not sure I like being somebody's twin. Are you going to get me another bourbon or not?"

While Piet was at the drink table, Freddy Thorne sidled up to him and said, "Could we talk a moment? Alone."

"Freddy, how exciting! Just little old me and big old you?"

"Notice I'm not smiling."

"But I can see your skull smiling through, behind those poodgy lips."

"How much have you had to drink?"

"Never ask an Irishman that question at a wake. Eh cup quaffed fer sorree's sake isn't eh cup at all. Stop standing there looking portentous. I have to take Janet her drink. I think I'm falling in love with Janet."

But by his return with the drink, Janet was deep in conversation with Harold, and Piet let himself be led to a corner by Freddy, the corner behind the unstrung harpframe.

"Piet," Freddy said, biting the word short. "I'll give you this cold turkey. I know about you and Georgene."

"Cold turkey? I thought that was how dope addicts broke the habit. Or am I thinking of the day after Thanksgiving?"

"I told you that night at the Constantines to lay off. Remember?"

"Was that the night you were Chiang Kai-shek?"

"And just now I see you and she having a cozy-type talk in the middle of the room. Righty-right?"

"I don't care what they say at the State Department, I think we should let you invade. Unleash Freddy Thorne, I'm always saying, as our many mutual friends will testify."

Freddy said nothing. Piet found the lack of any answer a frightening void. He asked, "How do you think you know this?" When again no answer came, he asked, "What do you think you know?"

"She told me herself. You and she were lovers."

"Georgene?"

"Well, did she lie?"

"She might have, to get back at you for something else. Or you might be lying to me. When is this supposed to have happened?"

"Don't play games. You know when."

"All right. I confess. It happened last summer. We were tennis partners. I lost my head, her pretty white dress and freckles and all, I flung her right down on the service line and we conceded the set six-love. I'm sorry. I'm sorry, I'm sorry, I'm sorry." His mouth felt very dry, though his third martini was light in his hand: empty, flown, the olive a tame green egg.

Freddy tried, with some success, to gather himself into a menacing mass, a squinting cloud, his narrow hairless skull majestic. When he frowned, forked wrinkles spread back on his pate. "I'm going to hurt you," he told Piet, and stalked toward the kitchen, for more ice.

Angela, seeing Piet shaken, left Ben lecturing to air and came to her husband and asked, "What were you and Freddy saying? You're pale as a ghost."

"He was telling me I must have my teeth straightened. Ow. My mouth hurts."

"You won't tell me. Was it about me?"

"Angel, you've got it. He asked me for the honor of your hand. He said he's been in love with you for years."

"Oh, he always says that."

"He does?"

"It's his way of bugging me."

"But you like it. I can tell by your face that you like hearing crap like that."

"Why not? Why are you so mean about Freddy? What has he ever done to you?"

"He threatens my primitive faith," Piet told his wife.

Foxy came into the room with Ken. She wore a strapless silver gown. Her breasts were milk-proud. There was a slow luminous preening of her upper body as she turned, searching for Piet in the mad shadows. The Whitmans' entrance at the front door had disturbed the air of the house, for the candleflames now underwent a struggle and the furniture and walls seemed to stagger and billow. She had come for him. She had abandoned her house and warm baby on this tragic night solely to seek him out, to save him from harm amid this foul crowd. He heard her explain to Georgene, "We had the sitter all lined up and thought we'd come for a little while just to make it worthwhile for her—she's Doc Allen's daughter and we don't want to discourage her when we're just beginning, we've never *needed* sitters before. Then after she came we sat around for the longest while unable to tear ourselves away from the television."

"What's happening now?" Roger's deep voice inquired.

"Oh," Foxy said, "mostly old film clips. What are really heartbreaking are the press conferences. He was so quick and sassy and, I don't know, attentive. He somehow brought back the *fun* in being an American." Piet saw that as she spoke she held close to her husband's arm, sheltering. Ken stood erect and pale in impeccable black. His studs were onyx.

"I loved him," Bea Guerin cried, in a flung voice whose woe seemed distant within it, a woe calling from an underworld, "I could never have voted for him, I really don't believe in all those wishy-washy socialist things he wanted, I think people must be themselves even if it's only to suffer, but I *loved* the way he held himself, and dressed, never wearing a hat or an overcoat, I mean."

"The terrible sadness," Frank Appleby said, "of those strange wall eyes."

Marcia asked, "Were they really wall? I thought it was just he was always reading a Teleprompter."

Music translucently flooded the room. Doris Day, "Stars Fell on Alabama." Freddy loved Doris Day. Freddy was all heart and as American as apple pie and Swapsies.

"Freddy!" Carol cried. "You angel! Where's Roger?" The Thornes' rug of interwoven rush rosettes was rolled to the legs of the satin chaise longue, and Carol and Roger, she lithely, he stiffly, danced. "Oh," she cried, "your hand is icy!"

"From holding a drink," he muttered, scowling, embarrassed, and on the bony stem of her naked back set his hand edgewise, curled in a limp half-fist like a sleeping child's.

The others watched uneasily. In moving to get his wife and himself a drink, Ken Whitman fastidiously skirted the bare floor and, waiting for Freddy to bring ice from the kitchen, talked softly with Janet. Ben Saltz moved to be beside Foxy. Her gestures expressed pleasure at seeing him again, after his long absence from parties; then, in response to words of his, she looked down at her flat soft stomach and obligingly, not displeased, enjoying in his Jewishness the ghost of Peter, blushed. Angela touched Piet's arm and asked, "Shall we dance?"

"Do you want to? It seems blasphemous, waltzing on the poor guy's grave."

"It does, it is, but we must. It's terrible taste, but we can't let Roger and Carol do it alone. They're getting too embarrassed."

She was familiar and thick and pliant in his arms; he had never learned proper steps and in the course of their marriage she had learned to follow his vague stridings lightly, as if they made a pattern, her thighs and pelvis gently cushioned against his. Their heights were equal. She rarely wore perfume, so her hair and skin released a scent unspecific but absolutely good, like water, or life, or existence itself, considered in contrast to the predominant vacuum between the stars.

"Where," he asked her, "are Irene and Eddie?"

"In the kitchen talking about air pollution."

"They are the *smuggest* couple," Piet said. "After all that fuss. I hope you take Irene's injured confidences henceforth with a lick of salt." He meant a saltlick, a large cake such as were mounted in the barnyards of Michigan dairy farms, but it came out sounding like a tiny amount, less than a grain.

"Well Ben," Angela said, "is talking to your ex-pregnant girl friend, so Irene *had* to go back to Eddie."

"That's too complicated," Piet said, trying to match his feet to the change of tempo as "Stars Fell on Alabama" became "Soft as the Starlight." "And the other lady is surely ex-pregnant but she was never my girl friend."

"I was kidding. Don't resist me like that. Relax. Glide."

"I hate this party, frankly. When can we go home?"

"Piet, it's the sort of party you love."

"I feel we're insulting Kennedy."

"Not at all. Yesterday, he was just our President way down in Washington, and now he belongs to all of us. He's right here. Don't you feel him?"

He looked into her blue eyes amazed. There was an enduring strangeness to Angela that continued through all disillusions to enchant him. Perceiving this, he resented his subtle bondage, and burned to tear Foxy from Ben, to trample on his bushy face with boots. Ineptly he stepped on Angela's toe.

Now Ken and Janet joined them on the dance floor, and Freddy and Irene. Above his black shoulder the twin circumflex of her perfect eyebrows seemed a lifted wingbeat. Her hair was parted precisely in the middle. Eddie Constantine came as if to capture her but at the last moment veered off and cut in to dance with Angela. Piet went and asked Georgene, standing gazing by the table of lightened bottles and dirtied glasses.

In his arms she asked him, "Do you think it's too early for the ham? We bought some salmon but no Catholics have come."

He accused her: "You and your noble privacy. Your husband just lowered the boom on me."

"Freddy? What on earth for?"

"For having an affair with you."

"Don't tease. Our times together were very precious, at least to me."

"Tease! He said you yourself told him everything. Postures, dates, phases of the moon."

"That's such a lie. I've *never* admitted anything about us, though he's tried to get me to often enough. It's the way he works. I hope *you* didn't admit anything."

"I didn't, but it was sheer perversity. I assumed he had me cold."

"He talks to Carol and Janet all the time; maybe one of them has made him think he knows something."

"Are you sure he doesn't? Are you sure you didn't tell him some night before dropping off to sleep, figuring I was a lost cause anyway, and needing something to even some score with, like an affair he'd had with Carol."

"Carol? Do you know this?" He loved feeling her experience fear in his arms; there was a dissolution of the bodily knit indistinguishable from sexual willingness.

"No. But he's over there all the time, and Carol's not too fussy. Not," he added hastily, "that Freddy isn't a gorgeous hunk of man."

She ignored his unkind parody of tact, asking instead, "And you? *Are* you a lost cause?"

"Soft as the Starlight" became "It Must Have Been Moonglow." "Well," Piet said carefully, "more and more, as Freddy acts as if he knows."

"Oh, Freddy. He doesn't want to know *any*thing, he just wants people to *think* he knows *every*thing. But if I'm not worth the trouble to you, there's no use talking, is there, Piet?" With her quick athletic firmness she put her hands on his arms and pushed herself out of his embrace. "Only don't come running to *me* the next time you need a little change of ass." Watching her retreat, he realized that all these months, all through Foxy, he had been considering Georgene still his mistress.

Foxy was across the room dancing with Frank Appleby. They moved together placidly, without reference to the beat, silver locked in lead's grip. "Wrap Your Troubles in Dreams" became the song. Marcia was at hand and, slithery quick, she nestled against his damp shirtfront, asking, "Piet, what's happened to you? You're not funny like you used to be."

"I never was trying to be funny."

"You were too. You were so delighted to be with us, at the beach, skiing, anywhere. Now you've stopped caring. You think we're ugly, silly people."

"Marcia, I love you. I bet you were class secretary in school."

"Is it your work? What are you doing now that it's too cold to put up any more cozy little horrors on Indian Hill?"

"We've been saved by the bell. Just the other week we got a big inside job on Divinity. They hauled off Gertrude Tarbox to a nursing home and the bank in New Bedford that held the mortgage is turning the house into offices. We've taken out three truckloads of *National Geographics*." Telling Marcia this troubled him, for he had been working in this house all day, alone, operating a big sander on the floors of what had once

been a chandeliered dining room. Lost in the hypnotic whine
and snarl of the machine, fascinated by the disappearance of
decades of dirt and paint, by this reversal into clean wood,
he had been ignorant of the President's assassination until Jazinski returned at three from a mysteriously long lunch hour.
Deafened by the sander, Piet had let the bullet pass painlessly
through him.

Marcia asked irritably, "Why does anyone need office space
in Tarbox?"

"Oh, you'd be surprised. There's a crying shortage downtown. Insurance companies, chiropractors. AA wants to set up
a branch here. This isn't the idyllic retreat you moved to, Marcia. We're sadly suburban. There's going to be a big shopping
center between here and Lacetown. Isn't Frank on the committee to squeeze more train service out of the poor old New
Haven, or the MBTA, or the Lionel Company, or somebody?"

"Piet, when are you going to get away from Gallagher? Frank
and Harold were talking at lunch in Boston to a man who
knows the South Shore and he expects Gallagher to go bankrupt. The banks own him twice over and he keeps gambling.
If the nuns hadn't bailed him out last summer he couldn't have
met another payment."

"No, sweetie, you don't understand. Matt can't lose. We live
in an expanding universe." To quiet her, to quell her critical
spirit, he dipped his hand to her buttocks; they were narrow
and nipped-in like the responsive little wheels at the front of
a tractor. At a guiding touch from him she brought her body
closer, so close his lips shrank from the cold aura of her dangling earring. He murmured, "How *is* Frank, speaking of the
MBTA?"

"The same. Maybe worse. Simply going to bed doesn't
soothe him any more. He needs to get out from under that
heavy neurotic bitch."

"Oh hell, we all need to get out from under."

"Not me. I need Harold. To hurt me. He's beautifully cruel,
don't you think?"

"Beautifully?"

"And yet gallant, in an old-fashioned way. I'm his, but he re-
spects my independence. I think we're a very nice old-fashioned
couple, don't you?"

"Antique. Victoria and Prince Albert. But let's talk about me. Don't I need to get out from under Angela?"

"Oh Piet," Marcia said impatiently, "without Angela, you'd die."

Struck empty by this, unable to answer, he sang with the gauze-voiced record into the curled cool shell of her ear, "*Cas*-tles may *tum*ble, that's *fate* after *all*, life's really *fun*ny that *way*."

She mistook his mood and flattened her body more sinuously against his. Her fingertips found the small hairs at the back of his neck, her pelvis lifted an inch. This a woman twice spoken for: he glanced around the room for rescue. Ken was still dancing with Janet. His temples looked gray as they circled near a candle. Freddy had replaced Eddie with Angela. Eddie and Irene had gone to stand against the wall, talking. Frank Appleby was making himself another drink. Foxy had fled. Doris Day's song became "Moonglow." Harold, catching Piet's eyes, came over, dug his fingers into Marcia's sleeping arm so cruelly her olive skin leaped white between his nails, and said, "Now on the idiot box they're talking about giving him an eternal flame. *Une flamme éternelle.* For Christ's sake, he wasn't the Unknown Soldier, he was a cleverly manufactured politician who happened to catch a nobody's bullet. *Chérie, es-tu ivre?*"

Marcia said huskily, having slept against Piet's body, now awoken, "Yes."

"Then come with me. *Pardonnez-nous*, Piet."

"Gladly. I'll go catch a bullet." Piet made his fourth martini, silvery. Foxy. Was she in the woods? Where was Ben? Not among the men dancing. Like a moth to flame was she to Jews. Abram over Lot. Ben's fingers, deft from miniaturizing, gliding down the tawny long insides of her stocking-topped thighs to fumble in the nigger-lipped pale fur there. Her clitoris welling through a milky film slowly, ruby rosy, watchsprings in a pansy shape. All shadowy smiling distances, Foxy would stretch and guide. Ben leonine, in the concealing shade of a Thorne-owned bush. Beyond these black windows she had opened to another lover.

Piet turned in pain from the window and it seemed that the couples were gliding on the polished top of Kennedy's casket. An island of light in a mourning nation. "Close Your Eyes."

"Cuhlozzz yur eyeszz": the velvet voice from Hollywood whispered an inch inside Piet's ear. The olive egg in his martini had been abandoned by its mother high and dry. His cankers hurt, especially the one his tongue had to stretch to reach, low and left on the front gum, at the root of his lip. A maze of membranes, never could have evolved from algae unassisted. God gave us a boost. He felt he shouldn't have another drink. No supper, empty stomach. Marcia's slithering had stirred him. Half-mast, subsided, lumpy. His kidneys signaled: the sweetness pealing of a silent bell: relieve me. The Thornes' bathroom. There Georgene would wash herself before and after. Said his jizz ran down her leg, too much of it, should screw Angela more. Hexagonal little floor tiles, robin's-egg toilet paper, posh purple towels. *Welcome to the post-pill . . .* Sashaying from the shower nude, her pussy of a ferny freshness. The grateful lumpiness following love. Well done, thou good and faithful. Turning up the familiar stairs, his black foot firm on the swaying treads, he glanced into the dark side room, where a few obscure heads were watching a weary flickering rerun of the casket's removal from the belly of the airplane. Ben was there, bent forward, his profile silvered as in Sunday-school oleographs, facing Sinai. Roger and Carol, sharing a hassock. Frank sucked a cigar whose smoke was charged with the dartings of light as casket became widow, widow became Johnson, Johnson became commentator. Ghouls. Foxy must be in the kitchen. The paneled bathroom door was closed. Tactfully he tapped. Her musical voice called, "Just a min-ute."

Piet said, "It's me," and pushed. The door gave. She was sitting on the toilet in her uplifted silver gown, startled, a patch of blue paper like a wisp of sky in her hand. The pressure of the oval seat widened her garter-rigged and pallid thighs; she was perched forward; her toes but not her heels touched the hexagonal tiles of the floor. "I love you" was pulled from him like a tooth. The mirror above the basin threw him back at himself. His flat taut face looked flushed and astonished, his mouth agape, his black tie askew.

Foxy said in a whisper reverberant in the bright tiled space, "You're mad to be in here." Then with incongruous deliberation she patted herself, let the paper drop into the oval of water below, and, half-turning on the seat, depressed the silver handle. Sluggishly the toilet flushed: Georgene used to complain about the low water pressure on the hill. Foxy rose from the vortex and smoothed her gown downward. Facing him, she seemed tall, faintly challenging and hostile, her closed lips strangely bleached by pale pink lipstick, newly chic. He made sure the door behind them was shut, and moved past her to urinate standing. With a pang, initially reluctant, his golden arc occurred. "God," he said, "it's a relief to see you alone. When the hell can we meet?"

She spoke hurriedly, above his splashing. "I wasn't sure you wanted to. You've been very distant."

"Ever since you've had the baby I've been frightened to death of you. I assumed it was the end of us."

"That's not true. Unless you want it to be true."

"The fact is, all fall I've been frightened of everything. Death, my work, Gallagher, my children, the stars. It's been hideous." A concluding spurt, somewhat rhetorical, and a dismissive drying shake. He tucked himself in. "My whole life seems just a long falling."

"But it's *not*. You have a good life. Your lovely family, your nice square house, me if you want me. We can't talk here. Call me Monday. I'm alone again."

He flushed, but the water closet had not filled. "Wait. Please. Let me see your breasts."

"They're all milky."

"I know. Just for a moment. Please. I do need it."

They listened for steps on the stairs; there were none. Music below, and the television monologue. Her mouth opened and her tongue, red as sturgeon, touched her upper lip as she reached behind her to undo snaps. Her gown and bra peeled down in a piece. Fruit.

"Oh. God."

She blushed in answer. "I feel so gross."

"So veiny and full. So hard at the tops, here."

"Don't get them started. I must go home in an hour."

"And nurse."

"Yes. What funny sad lines you're getting here, and here. Don't frown, Piet. And gray hairs. They're new."

"Nurse me."

"Oh darling. No."

"Nurse me."

She covered one breast, alarmed, but he had knelt, and his broad mouth fastened on the other. The thick slow flow was at first suck sickeningly sweet. The bright bathroom light burned on his eyelids and seemed to dye his insides a deep flowing rose, down to the pained points of his knees on the icy tile. Foxy's hand lightly cupped the curve of the back of his skull and now guided him closer into the flood of her, now warned by touching his ear that he was giving her pain. He opened his eyes; the nipple of her other breast jutted cherry-red between ivory fingers curled in protection; he closed his eyes. Pulses of stolen food scoured his tongue, his gums; she toyed with his hair, he caressed her clothed buttocks. She was near drowning him in rose.

Knocks struck rocklike at the unlocked door inches behind them. Harsh light flooded him. He saw Foxy's free hand, ringed, grope and cup the sympathetic lactation of the breast jutting unmouthed. She called out, as musically as before, "One moment, please."

Angela's lucid polite voice answered, "Oops, sorry, Foxy. Take your time."

"All ri-ight," Foxy sang back, giving Piet a frantic look of interrogation. Her bare breasts giant circles. A Christian slave stripped to be tortured.

His body thundered with fear. His hands were jerking like puppets on strings but his brain took perspective from the well-lit room in which he was trapped. There was no other door. The shower curtain was translucent glass, two sliding panels; his shape would show. There was a little window. Its sill came up to his chest. Realizing the raising of the sash would make noise, he motioned Foxy to flush the toilet. As she bent to touch the silver handle the shape of her breasts changed, hanging forward, long-tipped udders dripping cloudy drops. He undid the brass catch and shoved up the sash as the water closet again, feebly, drained. Setting one black dancing slipper on the lip of the tub, he hoisted himself into the black square of air headfirst. Trees on this side of the house, elms, but none near enough to grasp. His hands could touch only vertical wood and freezing air pricked by stars. Too late he knew he should have gone feet first; he must drop. This the shady rural side of the house. Soft grass. The toilet had quieted and left no noise to cover the sounds of his scrambling as he changed position. Foxy thought to turn both faucets on full. By logic she must next open the door to Angela. Piet backed out of the window. Foxy was standing by the roaring faucets staring at him and mopping herself with a purple washcloth and resecuring the bodice of her silver gown. He imagined she smiled. No time to think about it. He stood on the slick tub lip and got a leg through the little window and doing a kind of handstand on the radiator cover maneuvered the other leg through also. Button. Caught. Ah. There. He slid out on his chest and dangled his weight by his hands along Thorne's undulate shingles. Loose nails, might catch on a nostril, tear his face like a fish being reamed. Air dangled under his shoes. Ten feet. Eleven, twelve. Old houses, high ceilings. Something feathery brushed his fingers gripping the sill inside the bathroom. Foxy begging him not to dare it? Angela saying it was all right, she knew? Too late. Fall. No apologies. Pushing off lightly from the wall with his slippers and trying to coil himself loosely against the shock, he let go. Falling was first a hum, then concussion: a harpstring in reverse. His heels hit the frost-baked turf; he took a somersault backwards and worried about grass stains on his tuxedo before he thought to praise God for breaking no bones. Above him, a pink face vanished and a golden window whispered shut. They were safe. He was sitting on the brittle grass, his feet in their papery slippers stinging.

The silhouette of the trunk of the elm nearest him wavered; a female voice giggled. "Piet, you're such a show-off," Bea Guerin said.

Ben Saltz's orotund voice pronounced, "That was quite a tumble. I'm impressed."

Piet stood and brushed dirt from his clothes. "What are you two doing out here?"

"Oh," Bea said, and her offhand accents seemed, out of doors, disembodied, "Ben brought me out here to watch a satellite he miniaturized something in go by overhead."

"A tiny component," Ben said. "My old outfit developed it, with maybe one or two of my bright ideas. I thought it might be passing right about now, but all we've seen is a shooting star."

"So lovely," Bea said, and to Piet, still dizzy, the tree was talking, though the scarlet of her dress was growing distinct, "the way it fell, flaring all greeny-blue, like a match being struck, then nothing. I hadn't seen a comet since a child."

"That wasn't a comet," Ben said. "That was a meteor, an inert chunk of matter, of space dust you might say, burning up with friction upon contact with our atmosphere. Comets are incandescent and have elliptical orbits."

"Oh Ben, you're wonderful, you know everything, doesn't he, Piet? But now tell us, whatever were you and Foxy *doing?*"

"Why do you say Foxy?"

"We saw her close the window. Didn't you?"

"Are you sure it was Foxy? I thought it was Angela."

"Angela, poo. Of course it was Foxy, that lovely honey hair. Were you making love? In the bathroom?"

"Boy, that takes nerves of iron," Ben said. "Not to mention pretty well-padded bodies. I've tried it in a boat and it just wasn't my style, very frankly."

"Don't be silly," Piet said. "Of course we weren't. You two are grotesque." Perhaps anger could dissolve this unexpected couple.

"Why is that *silly?*" Bea cried in a soft raising wail, as when she had mourned Kennedy. "Everyone knows about you and Foxy. Your truck is parked down there all the time. We think it's *nice.*"

"My truck hasn't been there for months."

"Well my dear, she's hardly been in a condition to."

"You know," Ben said, "I wonder about that. Forbidding intercourse during pregnancy. I suspect it will turn out to be one more pseudo-medical superstition, like not breast-feeding because it wasn't sanitary, which they sincerely believed in the Thirties. I *made* Irene breast-feed, and she's grateful."

"You're a wonderful husband, Ben," Piet said. "Now you're making her work and she's grateful again."

Bea put her hand, trembling, on his forearm. "Now don't be sarcastic to Ben, just because you yourself are embarrassed. We won't tell anybody we saw you jump. Except Roger and Irene."

"Well, who shall I tell about you and Ben necking out here?"

"You may tell one person," Bea said, "those are the rules, but you mayn't tell Angela, because she'll tell Freddy Thorne, and then everybody will know. I'm freezing."

All three, they went back into the house together. Doris Day was singing "Stardust." Angela was coming downstairs from the bathroom. She asked, "Where have *you* all been?"

Piet told her, "Ben says he made one of the stars out there, but we couldn't find it."

"Why were you looking under the trees? I *won*dered who was mumbling outside; I could hear you from the bathroom." Suspended halfway up the stairs, she shimmered like a chandelier. Now that he had safely rejoined the party, Piet was piqued by Bea's assumption that Angela told Freddy Thorne everything. Wanting to ask his wife if this were true, he asked her instead, "How much have you drunk?"

"Just enough," she answered, descending. Parting an invisible curtain with her hands, she floated past him.

Piet hurried on; he had questions to ask of every woman. He kept tasting cloying milk. Foxy was in the kitchen, talking to Janet, who turned her back, so the lovers could talk. He asked Foxy hoarsely, "Make it OK?"

"Of course," she whispered.

He went on, "Did I imagine it, or were you standing there smiling at me?"

She glanced about to see they were not being overheard. "You were so manic, it was like a silent comedy. I wanted to tell you not to be silly and kill yourself, but we couldn't make any talking noises, and anyway you were clearly in love with the idea of jumping."

"In love! I was terrified, and now my right knee is beginning to hurt."

"You were terrified of Angela. Why? After all, so your husband is in the bathroom with another woman. It's not the end of the world. Maybe you were helping me get something out of my eye."

Piet drew on his impoverished reserves of moral indignation. "I'm shocked," he said, "that you would laugh. With all our love in the balance."

"I tried to catch your hand at the last minute; but you let go." Her smile became artificial, feral. "We better stop talking. Freddy Thorne has a fishy eye on us and here comes Harold Little."

Harold, petitely storming, his slicked-down hair mussed in pinfeathers in back, said, continuing a conversation begun elsewhere, "If I believed in the omnipotent Lord Jesus, I'd say this was punishment for his letting our one staunch ally in Southeast Asia get nailed to please the pansy left in this country. *La gauche efféminée.*"

"Oh Harold," Foxy said, mothering, "in," "don't talk like that, you're imitating somebody else. Cardinal Richelieu. You think we'll think you're cute if you go right-wing. We think you're cute now. Don't we, Piet?"

"Harold," Piet asked, "have you thought of asking the young widow for her hand? You and Madame Nhu would make a lovely couple. You both have a fiery way of expressing yourselves."

"You both speak French," Foxy added.

"The trouble with this *merde*-heap of a country," Harold said, sullenly flattered by their teasing, "there's no respectable way to not be a liberal."

Piet said, "Why, look at me. I'm not a liberal. Look at all your fellow brokers. They swindle the poor and pimp for the rich. Nothing liberal about that."

"They're idiots." In French: "*Idiots.*" Harold told Piet, "You never venture outside of this bucolic paradise, so you don't know what imbeciles there are. They really *care,*" he said, "about the difference between driving a Buick and a Cadillac."

"That's too hideous to believe," Piet said and, seeing Carol alone by the harpframe, went over to her. "What have you been telling that jerk Freddy Thorne?"

"I don't know," she said, "but I'll tell you this, Piet Hanema. He was about the only person who kept coming around when the rest of you were ostracizing Eddie and me because of poor old Irene. Poor old Irene my ass. Did you see her take Eddie into the kitchen as soon as they got here?"

"You beauty. Let's dance." Doris Day was now singing "Under a Blanket of Blue." Carol's back beneath his hand was extensively naked, bony and supple and expressive of the immense ease with which in bed his hairy long arms could encircle and sooth her slender nerved-up dancer's nakedness. His thumb grazed the edge of one shoulder blade; his palm lay moist across her spine's raised ridge; his fingertips knew the fatty beginnings of her sides. Pliant sides that would downslip, gain muscle, and become the world's wide pivot and counterthrusting throne, which in even a brittle woman is ample and strong. With a clothy liquidity Carol was yielding herself up, grazing easily the length of him. The bodies of women are puzzle pieces that can fit or not, as they decide. Imperceptibly Carol shaded the tilt of her pelvis so his penis felt caressed. She rubbed herself lightly from side to side, bent her neck so he could see her breasts, blew into his ear. The music stopped. She backed off, her face frowningly dilated, and sighed. She told him, "You're such a bastard," and walked away, naked from nape to waist. Mermaid. Slip from his hands like a piece of squeezed soap.

Such a bastard. When he had been told, at college, coming in late from a date that had left his mouth dry and his fly wet and his fingertips alive with the low-tide smell of cunt, about his parents' accident, his thought had been that had he been there, been there in Grand Rapids in any capacity, his presence would have altered the combination of events, deflected their confluence, enough to leave his mother and father alive. In the same way, he felt guilty about Kennedy's death, when Jazinski told him of it, in the silence of the sander.

Irene Saltz floated toward him, her eyebrows arched above bright tears, scintillant in candlelight. "Are you happy, Irene?" he asked her.

"I still love him, if that's what you're asking," she said.

"You want to be laughed at," Piet told her, "like me. We're scapegoat-types."

Triumphantly upheld by Freddy flanked by Georgene and Angela, the ham, the warm and fat and glistening ham, scotched and festooned with cloves, was fetched in from the kitchen. Bea Guerin, her washed-out hair, paler than wind, done up loosely in a Psyche knot, followed holding a salad bowl heaped full of oily lettuce, cucumber slices, avocados, tomatoes, parsley, chives, chicory, escarole. Their blessings were beyond counting. With a cruciform clashing of silver Freddy began to sharpen the carving knife. Out of the gathering audience Frank Appleby boomed, "Upon what meat does this our Caesar feed, that he is grown so great?"

Georgene explained, "I had salmon for the Catholics but since none of them came I'll give it to the children for lunch."

Freddy's eyeglasses flickered blindly as he carved; he was expert. Nobody but Freddy could cut slices so thin. "Take, eat," he intoned, laying each slice on a fresh plate a woman held out to him. "This is his body, given for thee."

"Freddy!" Marcia little-Smith cried. "That's disgusting."

"Don't you think," Bea Guerin asked, her voice pure and plaintive and proud of sounding lost, "we should be fasting or something?"

"Fasting or fucking," Freddy Thorne said, with surgical delicacy laying on another slice.

Ken Whitman watched silent from near the wall, beneath an African mask. Ben Saltz, eagerly hunchbacked, fetched radishes and bread to the buffet table. Carol carried two bottles of burgundy black as tar in the candlelight. Piet, being passed a plate, chewed but without saliva; his mouth felt full of ashes that still burned. Suddenly old, he sought a chair. His knee did hurt.

Still limping, he visited Foxy the following Tuesday, when the nation resumed normal life. The three days of omnipresent mourning had passed for these couples of Tarbox as three tranced holidays each alike in pattern. The men each afternoon had played touch football on the field behind the Applebys, by Joy Creek, while the women and children stayed indoors watching television in the library. During dull stretches of the Washington ceremonies or the Dallas postmortems (Piet and his children, just back from church, were watching when Oswald was shot; Ruth calmly turned and asked him, "Was that real?" while Nancy silently stuck her thumb in her mouth) some of the women would come outdoors and arrange themselves in Frank's hay and watch their men race red-faced up and down the hummocky field, shouting for the ball. These days on the verge of winter were autumnally fair, struck through with warmth until the swift lengthening of the shadows. At game's end, that long weekend, the men and children would drink from paper cups the cider someone (the Whitmans, the little-Smiths) had brought from the orchard along the beach road, and then there would be a general drift indoors, to cocktails and a long sitting around the television set while the children grew cranky and raided Janet's supply of crackers, peanut butter, raisins, and apples. Run and rerun as if on the revolving drum of insomnia, Haile Selassie and General

De Gaulle bobbed together down Pennsylvania Avenue, Jack Ruby's stripper drawlingly allowed that his temper could be mean, Lee Oswald, smirking, was led down a crowded corridor toward a lurching hat and wildly tipping cameras. The widow and one of the brothers, passing so near the camera they blurred, bent obliquely over an indeterminate tilted area of earth and flowers. The dome was distant in the southern sunshine. Amid drumrolls, the casket gleamed and was gone. The children came crying, bullied by others. Another drink? It was time to go home, but not yet, not quite yet. It was evening before they packed the children into the cars. The space in the cars as they drove home was stuffy with unasked questions, with the unsayable trouble of a king's murder, a queasy earthquake for little children, a funny stomach-gnawing only sleep eased. School and Tuesday came as a relief.

Piet parked his truck in plain sight in the driveway. The Whitmans' surviving lilacs were leafless and his eyes winced in the unqualified light. Every season has a tone of light we forget each year: a kitchen with frosted windows, a leaf-crowded side porch, the chalky noons of spring, the chill increase, as leaves fall, of neutral clarity. October's orange had ebbed in the marshes; they stretched dun gray to the far rim of sand. The tide was low; the sea lay sunken in the wider channels like iron being cast. Foxy answered his second ring.

Opening the door, she looked delicate, as if recovered from an illness, or as if she had just chastised herself with a severely hot bath. "Oh. You. Wonderful."

"Is it? Are you alone? I've come to see the baby."

"But not me?"

Yet, once inside, on the loop rug, he embraced and held her as if there were no baby, as if there were no one alive in this sunken barren world but themselves. Beneath her coarse house smock, between her lifted breasts and bony pelvis, a defenseless hollow felt placed against his memory of her swollen belly. A snuffling aggrieved sound, less crying than a scratching at some portal of need, arose in the living room. Foxy clung to him in a pose of weeping, and reflexively he bent his head into her hair to kiss the side of her neck, and now her tongue and fingers, as if released from the timidity of long absence, tremblingly attempted to seize him, but blind as bees in a room of smoke they darted to absurd places—his unshaven chin, his jingling pockets, an eye that barely closed in time, a ticklish armpit her ardor could not unlock. He told her, "The baby's crying."

Together they went to where in the living room the baby lay breathing in a bassinet. A pearly quiet blessed its vicinity and the windows giving on the frost-charred marsh seemed to frame images thrown from within, by a magic lantern centered on the infant's untinted soul. Foxy asked, "Do you want to hold him?" and pulled the infant gently up and unceremoniously passed him to Piet's hands. Piet, cupping his broad palms under their sudden unsteady burden, let himself be astounded by, what he had forgotten, the narrowness of the buttocks, the feverish mauve skull. For a second the child appraised him with stern large eyes the color of basalt; then the irises crossed and the muscles in his forehead bulged like elastic levers to squeeze the eyebrows down. The baby began to cry. Fearing his noise would betray their secrecy, Piet returned him to Foxy. Brusquely, she jiggled the bundle against her bosom.

Piet asked, "What is his name?"

"You must know it."

"Angela told me but I've forgotten. An old-fashioned name, I thought. For such a modern couple."

"Tobias."

"That's not the cat?"

"Cotton is the cat. Tobias was Ken's grandfather."

"Why didn't you name him after Ken's father?"

"Ken apparently doesn't like his father."

"I thought his father was perfect, the perfect Hartford lawyer."

"He is. But Ken was very definite, I was surprised."

"Ken is full of surprises, now and then, isn't he? A fascinating fellow."

"Are you trying to sell him to me?"

Piet asked her, "Why are we fencing?"

Foxy said, "I don't know. The baby upsets you."

"I love the baby. I love you as a mother."

"But not as a mistress any more?"

"Well"—embarrassment gnawed his stomach—"you're not ready yet, are you?"

"I shouldn't make love for two more weeks but I think I could stand a little show of affection. Why are you so remote?"

"Am I?" How could he tell her, of the quietness he had found here, the sere marsh filling the windows, the serene room he had carved, its plaster walls spread wide like a wimple, of the pearly aura near the baby, of Foxy's own subdued dry grace, dry as if drained of sleep and self-concern—of this chaste charmed air and his superstitious reluctance to contaminate it? He confessed, "I just wonder if I have any business being here now."

"Why not now? What business did you ever have? I was never your wife. You came here for an extramarital screw, that was fine, I gave it to you, I loved it. Now what? I've made myself dirty by having a baby." Piet felt she too much enjoyed such tough talk, that it was something revived, on the excuse of him, from deeper in her experience. She stood with legs apart, bent forward a bit from the waist, Tobias held tight but unacknowledged in her arms. Her raised voice had lulled him to sleep. Piet loved her maternal clumsiness, her already careless confidence that the child was hers to handle.

He asked her, "How can you want me? You have this marvelous little package. You have Ken who gave it to you."

"He doesn't like it. He doesn't like the baby."

"Impossible."

Foxy began to cry. Her hair, lusterless in the dull late light, hung forward over the child. "It frightens him," she said. "I frighten him. I've always frightened him. I don't blame him, I'm a mess, Piet."

"Nonsense." His inner gnawing was transmuted into a drastic sunk feeling; he had no choice but to go to her, put his arms around her and the child, and say, "You're lovely."

Her sobbing would not stop. Her situation, including his concession and his sheltering arms, seemed to anger her increasingly. "Don't you like talking to me?"

"Of course I do."

"Don't you like talking to me at all? Don't you ever want to do anything with me except go to bed? Can't you wait a few more weeks to have me?"

"Please. Fox. Don't be so silly."

"I was afraid to take ether for fear I'd cry out your name. I go around the house saying 'Piet, Piet' to this innocent baby. I dragged poor Ken to that hideous party just to see you and you risked killing yourself rather than be found with me."

"You exaggerate. There was very little risk. I did it as much to protect you as myself."

"You're still limping from it."

"It was all that football."

"Oh, Piet. I'm beginning to nag. Don't leave me absolutely yet. You're the only thing real I have. Ken is unreal. This marsh is unreal. I'm unreal to myself, I just exist to keep this baby alive, that's all I was put here for, and it makes me *mad*."

"Don't be mad," he begged; but he himself felt anger, to be so pressed and sunk he could not spare breath to explain that for them to keep seeing each other now would be evil, all the more in that it had been good. They had been let into God's playroom, and been happy together on the floor all afternoon, but the time had come to return the toys to their boxes, and put the chairs back against the wall.

Ken came home from work looking more tired than she had seen him since graduate-student days. He carried a sheaf of mimeographed pre-prints and flopped them down on the hall table. "There's been a breakthrough in photosynthesis," he told her. "They've figured out something involving ferredoxin —it seems to be the point of transition between the light and dark reactions."

"What's ferredoxin?"

"A protein. An electron carrier with a very low redox potential."

"Who's figured it out?" He almost never talked to her about his work, so she was anxious to respond fruitfully. For his return she had put on a lemony cocktail dress, celebrative. Their child was six weeks old today.

"Oh," he sighed, "a couple of Japs. Actually, they're good men. Better than me. I've had it." He dropped himself into the armchair, the leather armchair they had steered up and down apartment-house stairs all over Cambridge. Feeling their life slip backwards, she panicked.

"Let *me* see," Foxy said, and went, all wifely bustle and peremptoriness, to the hall table to prove him wrong. The pamphlet on top was titled *Neurophysiological Mechanisms*

Underlying Behavior: Emotions and the Amygdala. The one underneath was *Experimental Phenylketonuria: Pharmacogenetics of Seizures in Mice*. She looked no further.

To our Tarbox doppelgängers the "little" Smiths—
Another Yuletide finds us personally well and prosperous yet naturally saddened by the tragic and shocking events of this November. Man is truly "but as grass." A different sort of sadness entered our household when this September we saw young Tim, our precocious and precious baby of a few short years ago, off for his freshman year at St. Mark's. He has been home for weekends, very much the "young man," but it will be joyous to have him under the manse roof these holidays—even if he has, to our decibel's dismay, taken up the electric guitar. Meanwhile Pat, Audrey, and Gracelyn continue happily in the excellent Newton public schools. Pat, indeed, has been honored with (and that sound you hear is our buttons "popping" with pride)

"God," Marcia said, "the way she crawls right over poor Kennedy to tell us they can afford St. Mark's."

"To our decibel's dismay," Janet said, and both went helpless with laughter.

The evenings before Christmas are gloomy and exciting in downtown Tarbox: the tinfoil stars and wreaths hung from slack wires shivering audibly in the wind, the silent crèche figures kneeling in the iron pavilion, the schoolchildren shrieking home from school in darkness, the after-supper shoppers hurrying head-down as if out on illicit errands and fearful of being seen, the Woolworth's and Western Auto and hardware stores wide-awake with strained hopeful windows and doors that can't help yawning. This year the civic flags were at half-mast and some stores—the old jeweler's, the Swedish bakery—had forsaken the usual displays. In the brilliantly lit and remorselessly caroling five and ten, Piet, shopping with his daughters for their present to Angela, met Bea Guerin at the candle counter. At the sight of her small tipped head, considering, her hair stretched to shining, his heart quickened and his hands, heavily hanging, tingled. She turned and noticed him; her instinctive smile tightened as she gauged his disproportionate gladness at seeing her.

Ruth and Nancy wandered on uncertainly down an aisle of
kitchen gadgets. Their faces looked dirty in the crass light; his
daughters seemed waifs lost and sickened in this wilderness of
trash. Their puzzled greed exasperated Piet. He let them go
down the aisle and knew that they would settle on a package of
cute Pop-pattern dish towels and a red-handled sharpener that
would be lost by New Year's.

Innocent of children, Bea seemed strangely young, unsullied. She wore a green wool cape and elfish suède shoes. She
held a box of long chartreuse tapers. More than young, she
seemed unattached, a puckish interloper meditating theft. Piet
approached her warily, accusing, "Candles?"

"Roger likes them," she said. "I find them eerie, really. I'm
afraid of fire."

"Because you live in a wooden house? We all do."

"He even likes real candles on the tree, because his family
had them. He's such an old fogey." Her face, upturned toward
him in the claustrophobic brightness, was grave, tense, homely,
frightened. Her hairdo pulled her forehead glossily tight. His
parents' house had held prints of Dutch paintings of girls with
such high shining brows.

"Speaking of your house—"

Nancy had returned to him and pulled at his thumb with an
irritating hand tacky from candy. "Daddy, come look with us."

"In a second, sweet."

"Come look with us *now*. Ruthie's teasing me, she won't let
me *say* anything." Her face, round as a cookie, was flyspecked
with freckles.

"I'll be right there," he told her. "You go back and tell
Ruthie I said not to act like a big shot. You each are supposed
to find your own present for Mommy. Maybe you can find
some pretty dish towels."

Against her better judgment Nancy obeyed and wandered
back to her sister. Piet said to Bea, "Poor child, she should be
in bed. Christmas is cruel."

Having no children, she was blind to their domination, and
her eyes expressed admiration of his patience, when in truth he
had slighted an exhausted child. Bea prompted him, "Speaking
of my house—"

"Yes," Piet said, and felt himself begin to blush, to become enormously red in this bath of plastic glare, "I've been wondering, would you mind, some morning or afternoon, if I came around and inspected the restoring job I did for you four years ago? I experimented, hanging the summer beam from an A-brace in the attic, and I'd like to see if it settled. Has your plaster cracked anywhere?"

Something by the side of his nose, some cruelly illuminated imperfection, held her gaze; she said slowly, "I haven't noticed any cracking, but you're welcome to come and look."

"But would you *like* me to?"

Bea's face, its almost lashless lids puffily framing her eyes at a slight slant, became even more of a child's, a child's piqued by Christmas greed yet hesitant, distrustful of gifts.

"Once," he prompted, "you would have liked me to."

"No, I would like you to; it's just"—she groped, and her eyes, a paler blue than Angela's, lifted to his—"a house, you know."

"I know it's a house. A lovely house. Tell me what would be a good morning?"

"Today's Thursday. Let's do it after the weekend. Monday?"

"Tuesday would be better for me. Monday's my catch-up day. Around ten?"

"Not before. I don't know what's the matter with me, I can't seem to get dressed in the mornings any more."

"Daddy. She is *being* a *pesty* crybaby and I am *not* being a *big shot*." Ruth had stormed up to them, trailing tearful Nancy, and Piet was shocked to see that his elder daughter was, though not yet as tall as Bea, of a size that was comparable. While her father had been looking elsewhere she had abandoned the realm of the miniature. In this too strong light he also saw that her heated face, though still a child's, contained the smoky something, the guarded inwardness, of womanhood.

Bea beside him, as if licensed now to know his thoughts, said proprietarily, "She'll be large, like Angela."

At the New Year's Eve party the Hanemas gave, Foxy asked Piet, "Who is she?"

"Who is who?" They were dancing in the trim colonial

living room, which was too small for the purpose. In pushing back the chairs and tables Frank Appleby and Eddie Constantine had scarred the eggshell-white wainscoting. The old pine floorboards creaked under the unaccustomed weight of the swaying couples, and Piet feared they would all be plunged into his cellar. Giving the party had been more Angela's idea than his; lately she, who used to be more aloof from their friends than he, seemed to enjoy them more. She had even persuaded poor Bernadette Ong to come, alone. John was still in the hospital.

"The woman who's taken my place," Foxy said. "Your present mistress."

"Sweet Fox, there isn't any."

"Come off it. I know you. Or has Angela turned into a hot ticket?"

"She *is* more amiable lately. Do you think she has a lover?"

"It's possible, but I'm not interested. The only person in Tarbox who interests me is you. Why don't you call me any more?"

"It's been Christmas. The children have all been home from school."

"Phooey to the children. They didn't bother you all summer."

"There's one more now." He feared he had hurt her, hit out roughly. He petted her wooden back and said teasingly, "Don't you really like any of our friends? You used to love Angela."

"That was on the way to loving you. Now I can't stand her. Why should she own you? She doesn't make you happy."

"You're a hard woman."

"Yes."

Demurely she lowered her lids and danced. Her body, its placid flats and awkward stiffness, was obscurely his, a possession difficult to value now that the bulge, the big jewel, of her belly was gone.

He said at last, "I think we *should* talk. It would be nice to see you." Betrayal upon betrayal. Dovetailing, rising like staging.

"I'm home all the time."

"Is Ken going back to work Monday?"

"He never stops working. He went to Boston every day of his vacation except Christmas."

"Maybe he's seeing a woman."

"I wish he would. I deserve it. But I'm afraid he's seeing a cell. He's beginning modestly."

He laughed and without bringing her visibly closer to him tightened the muscles of his arms for her to feel as an embrace. If Piet had a weakness, it was for feminine irony. "I'm dying to see you," he said, "but I'm afraid of being disappointing. Don't expect too much. We'll just talk."

"Of course, what else? You can't fuck a young mother."

"I think you enjoy misunderstanding me about that. I love your baby."

"I don't doubt it. It's me you don't love."

"But I do, I do, too much I do. I was in you so deep, loved you so terribly, I'm scared of getting back in. I think we were given it once and to do it all over again would be tempting fate. I think we've used up our luck. It's be*cause* I love you, be*cause* I don't want you to be hurt."

"All right, shut up for now. Freddy and Georgene are both looking."

The music, Della Reese, stopped. Piet pushed away from Foxy, relieved to be off, though she did look, standing deserted in a bouffant knee-length dress the milky green of cut flower stems, like the awkward proper girl from Maryland, leggy and young, she had often described to him, and he had never quite believed in.

He heard from the kitchen Bea's clear plaintive voice rising and falling within some anecdote, calling him. But in the narrow front hallway Bernadette Ong's broad shoulders blocked him. "Piet," she said plangently. "When do I get my duty dance?"

He took a grave tone. "Bernadette. How is John doing? When is he coming home?"

She was tipsy, for she took a step and her pelvis bumped him. Her breath smelled brassy. "Who knows? The doctors can't agree. One says soon, the other says maybe. With the government insurance covering, they may keep him there forever."

"How does he feel?"

"He doesn't care. He has his books. He talks to Cambridge on the phone now."

"That's good news, isn't it?" Piet edged toward the stairs.

She stepped again and barred him from touching the newel. "Maybe yes, maybe no. I don't want him back in the house the way he was, up all night fighting for breath and scaring the boys half to death."

"Jesus. Is that how it was?"

Bernadette, her body wrapped in silk, a toy gold cross pasted between her breasts, heard a frug record put on the phonograph and held wide her arms; Piet saw her dying husband in her like a larva in a cocoon. Nervously acrobatic, he slid past her and up a step of the stairs. "I'll be down in two seconds," he said, and needlessly lied, since she would assume he must go to the toilet, "I thought I heard a child cry."

Upstairs, captive to his lie, he turned away from the lit bathroom into the breathing darkness where his daughters lay asleep. Downstairs the voices of Angela and Bea alternated and chimed together. His wife and his mistress. In bed Bea had enraptured him, her skin sugary, granular, the soles of her feet cold, the grip of her vagina liquid and slim, a sly narrowness giving on a vastness where his drumming seed quite sank from sight. Her puffy eyelids shut, she sucked his fingers blindly, and was thus entered twice. She seemed to float on her bed at a level of bliss little altered by his coming and going and thus worked upon him a challenge; at last she confessed he was hurting her and curled one finger around the back of his ear to thank him. She was his smallest woman, his most passive, and his most remote, in these mournful throes, from speech or any question. He had felt himself as all answer. When the time for him to leave at last was acknowledged she wrapped herself quickly in a bathrobe showing, in the split second of standing, that her breasts and buttocks hung like liquid caught in too thin a skin. Ectoplasm.

He crouched where his two daughters' breathing intersected. Nancy's was moist and scarcely audible. Might fall through into silence. The frail web of atoms spinning. The hamster in his heavenly wheel. There. It. Is. Ruth's deeper, renewed itself with assurance, approached the powerful onward drag of an adult. The hauling of a boat upriver. Full steam. Boys soon. Bathroom jokes, Nancy Drew, drawings attempting bosoms: teen-age. The time she was Helen Keller for a school project, bumping through the bright house blindfold, couldn't get her to take it off. Frightening herself. Must do. So brave in choir,

bored. Her breathing stuttered, doubled tempo. A dream. His
leaving. He crouched deeper between their beds and held her
damp square hand. Her breathing eased. Her head changed
position. Sleeping beauty. Poison apple. I am your only lover.
All who follow echo me. Shadows. Sleep. The music downstairs stopped. Frug, nobody could do it yet, too old to learn.
Nancy's breathing eluded his listening. Instead a most gentle of
presences tapped at the window whose mullions were crosses.
Snow. A few dry flakes, a flurry. This winter's shy first. The
greenhouse at home banked deep in snow. A rusty warmth of
happiness suffused him, joy in being rectangularly enclosed,
alive with flowers growing, captive together, his mother at the
far end tying ribbons tight with needling fingers, school vacation on, all need to adventure suspended.

Distantly, a gun was fired. Downstairs, his friends, voice by
voice, launched "Auld Lang Syne." Though his place as host
was with them, Piet remained where he was, crouching above
the ascending din until it subsided, and he could again pick
up the fragile thread of Nancy's breathing, and the witnessing
whisper of the snow.

The visit to Foxy proved disappointing. It was a blowy ear-
achy winter Monday; the truck rattled bitterly as he drove
down the beach road and the radio through its static told of
Pope Paul being nearly trampled in Jerusalem. The house was
cold; Foxy was wearing a heavy sweater and a flannel nightie
and furry slippers. She moved and spoke briskly, angrily, as if to
keep warm. The offending marshes, which permitted the wind
to sweep through the walls he had woven for her, were scarred
by lines of salty gray ice rubble rimming the tidal channels.
Gusts visibly walked on the water. She asked, "Would you like
some hot coffee?"

"Yes, please."

"I'm freezing, aren't you?"

"Is the thermostat up?"

"The furnace is on all the time. Can't you hear it roaring?
I'm scared it's going to explode."

"It won't."

"A friend of Ken's who's built his own house on the Cape
thinks we were crazy not to excavate a full cellar under the
living room."

"It would have meant at least another two thousand."

"It would have been worth it. Look at all the gas I burn buzzing around Tarbox visiting people to keep warm. Janet one day, Carol the next. I know all the dirt."

"What is the dirt?"

"There isn't much. I think we're all tired. Janet was very curious about Ken's boyhood and Carol thinks you're seeing Bea Guerin."

"How sweet of Carol."

"Come into the kitchen for the coffee. It's not so bad there."

"I wonder if wooden-framed storm windows on the marsh side wouldn't help. They have more substance than the aluminum combinations. Or what about shuttering them straight across with the boards that were there?"

"What would happen to Angela's view?"

This humorousness remembered the times she had lain in his arms remarking on her double theft, of Angela's man and Angela's house. In the less chilly kitchen, where the Whitmans had reinstated the electric heater, she said, "You'd laugh to see me at night, Ken on one side and Toby on the other. It's the only way I can keep warm."

Though he knew that her description was intended to pique his jealousy, he did feel jealous, picturing her asleep between her husband and son, her fanning spread of moonlit hair tangent to them both. Knowing that his interest in her child irked her, he asked, "How *is* the young master?"

"Strapping. He's two months old now and looks like Ken's father. That same judicial grimace."

"Two months," Piet said. He was wearing workboots and a lumberjack shirt underneath his apricot windbreaker. She gave him coffee in a mug, without a saucer, as if to a handyman. He felt tongue-tied and coarse, and found her large brown eyes uncomfortably alert. Listening for the phone, another lover? Of course not, she had a child. The mother in her den.

She looked at him intently. The unbiased winter light showed a small sty distorting the shape of her left eyelid. She said, "Two months is more than six weeks."

He groped for the significance of six weeks. "Oh. Terrific. But—do you want to? With me, I mean."

"Do you want to with me, is more the question."

"Of course. Of course I do, I love you. Obviously. But should we? Start everything up again. It frightens me, frankly. Haven't we paid our debt to society? Getting over you once was hard enough."

He feared she might mock him, but she nodded solemnly instead. Foxy's hair was not blond clear through like Bea's but blond in part, of many shades—oak, honey, ash, even amber —and darker with beach weather by. She lifted her head. There was a pink cold sore beneath one nostril. "I frighten you?"

"Not you. It. It would be *wrong* now."

"All right, then go. Go, Piet. Thanks for everything. It's been swell."

"Don't. Don't be hard." In waiting for her to begin to cry, he felt his own eyes warm. The scene must be played.

She seized the high, the haughty, rôle. "I don't know how a dismissed mistress should act. They didn't teach us at Radcliffe. Maybe I took the wrong courses. I'm sure I'll be better at it next time."

"Don't," he begged. Rays were being hurled from her dry eyes, and he hunched to dodge these spears.

"Don't what?" she asked. "Don't make a scene? Don't be a bitch? When all the poor little workingman has done is come into your house and charmed the pants off of you and let you fall in love with him, don't embarrass the poor baby, don't make yourself a nuisance. I won't, Piet love, I won't. Just go. Git. Go to Bea. Go back to Georgene. Go way back to Angela. I couldn't care less."

Her eyes, they wouldn't cry, and he must do something, anything, to smother their icy dry rays, that were annihilating him. He asked, "Can't we lie down together?"

"Oh," she said, and flounced herself, but her sweater and heavy nightie refused, amid the ghosts of summer's billowing, to fling, and the kitchen presences, stove, oven, sink, and windows, retained their precise shape, like unimpressed judges. "You'll make one more stab at it, as a favor. Forget it, I'm not that hard up."

But the integrity of her eyes had cracked, she had been brought to tears. He heard his voice grow wise and warm, reaching into the reserves of darkness he and Foxy had shared. "I want to rub your back, and hear about your baby."

She smoothed the skin beneath her eyes. "I think you're right about us," she confessed. "I just don't want to know exactly when it's happening."

This was, his release, of her many gifts to him the most gracious. In an hour, he knew, in good conscience he would be free. He asked, "Shall we go upstairs? We'll need covers over us."

She said, "We must leave the door open, to hear the baby. He's asleep in the nursery." Piet rejoiced that concern for her child was dovetailing with relinquishment of him.

The upstairs was even colder. In bed she kept her wool nightie on and he his underclothes; he rubbed the smooth planes of her back and backside until she seemed asleep. But when he stopped she rolled to face him, reached down to touch him, in Paisley underpants, and asked as if she could be refused, "Would you like to come inside me?"

"Terribly, actually."

"Gently."

Yes, she had been stretched by the child; the precious virginal tightness had fled. He offered to kiss her breasts, though a stale milky smell disturbed him; her fingers pushed his face away. She must save herself for the baby. Her long body beneath his felt companionable, unsupple, male. His mind moved through images of wood, patient pale widths waiting for the sander, intricate joints finished with steel wool and oil, rounded pieces fitted with dowels, solid yet soft with that placid suspended semblance of life wood retains.

A weight fell on the bed; Piet's heart leaped. Foxy's cheek against his stretched in a smile. It was the cat, Cotton. Purring, the animal nestled complacently into the hollow on top of the blankets between the lovers' spread legs. "I have two lovers," Foxy said softly, but fear had been touched off in Piet, and its flare illuminated the world—the Gallagher & Hanema office on Hope Street, the colonial farmhouse on Nun's Bay Road, the unmistakable pick-up truck blatantly parked in the Whitmans' drive. He must hurry. He asked her, "Can you make it?"

"I don't think so. I've too many emotions."

"Then let me?"

She nodded stiffly and with a few unheeding, gay and forceful strokes he finished it off, holding her pinned through the distracting trembling with which she greeted his coming and which at first he had mistaken for her own climax. He left his lust as if on a chopping block miles within her soft machine. She looked at him with eyes each holding the rectangle of the skylight. "So quick?"

"I know. I'm lousy at love. I must go."

He dressed rapidly, to avoid the discussion and recapitulation he knew she desired. It was good, he thought, that the last time was bad for her. Her slowness to come, he saw now, had always been a kind of greed. As he carefully opened the door behind the lilacs, the baby began to cry in the nursery wing.

Outdoors was as still as a house in that interval after the last subcontractors have left and before the occupants have moved in and the heat is turned on. The woods toward the little-Smiths' house, purple diluted with rime, moved no more under the wind than frost-ferns on glass. No cars passed on the beach road. A single gull knifed across his vision, and he heard behind him Foxy begin to cry. His palms tingling against the wheel, he backed the truck around and headed toward the center of Tarbox. Through the leafless trees peeked a gold weathercock. As the cab warmed, he whistled along with the radio music, exhilarated once again at having not been caught.

Perhaps that day he discovered a treasure of cruelty in himself, for alone with Bea later that week, late in the afternoon, he struck her. She had been above him on all fours, a nursing mammal, her breasts pendulous, with a tulip sheen, and as if to mark an exclamatory limit to happiness he had cuffed her buttocks, her flaccid sides, and, rolling her beneath him, had slapped her face hard enough to leave a blotch. Seeing her eyes incredulous, he had slapped her again, to banish all doubt and establish them firmly on this new frontier. Already he had exploited her passivity in all positions; the slap distracted his penis and he felt he had found a method to prolong the length of time, never long enough, that he could inhabit a woman.

Bea's left eye slitted against a third blow and when it didn't come widened with the surprise of recognition. "That's what Roger does."

"So people say."

"I thought it was because he couldn't make love normally, because I didn't excite him otherwise. But that's not so of you."

"No, it's in you. You invite it. You're a lovely white hole to pour everything into. Jizz, fists, spit." He spat between her breasts and lifted his arm as if to club her.

Her eyes, so washed-out they were scarcely blue, widened in alarm and she turned her head sideways on the shadowy pillow. "It makes me wonder if I'm insane," she said. "That I do this to people. Eddie twists my wrist all the time. Please, Piet, I'd really rather you wouldn't. Use me but don't hurt me if you don't absolutely have to. I don't really like it. Maybe I should."

"Oh I know, I know, you must hate it, forgive me," Piet said, hiding his face in Bea's throat and hair. "Do forgive me." Yet he was pleased, for in abusing her he had strengthened the basis of his love, given his heart leverage to leap. He loved any woman he lay with, that was his strength, his appeal; but with each woman his heart was more intimidated by the counter-thrust of time. Now, with Bea, he had made a ledge of guilt and hurled himself secure into the tranquil pool of her body and bed. High above the sound of children throwing snow-balls as they returned from school in the dusk, Bea sucked his fingers, and her nether mouth widened until he was quite lost, and he experienced orgasm strangely, as a crisisless osmosis, an ebbing of light above the snow-shrouded roofs. Death no longer seemed dreadful.

The phone rang and surprised him by being Foxy. In the month since their unsatisfactory coitus in the cold house, she had not called, and had hardly spoken at parties. She had faded into the tapestry of friends. She asked, "Piet, is Gallagher there?"

"Yes he is," he cheerfully sang.

"Could you go out to a pay phone and call me?"

"Now?"

"Piet. Please. We must talk." Her voice had a distant chafed quality, and he pictured a handkerchief balled in her fingers.

"As you wish." He added a firm, man-to-man "Right." He felt Gallagher listening behind the corrugated glass partition, though his door was closed. Increasingly Gallagher's door was closed. Each morning, coming to his office, Piet found that the walls had been slightly narrowed in the night. Beside his desk hung a calendar, from Spiros Bros. Builders & Lumber Supply, showing a dripping golden retriever mouthing a green-headed mallard; as Piet worked at his desk he could feel the dog's breath pushing on his ear.

He went out into the valentine brightness of plow-heaped snow and entered an aluminum phone booth smelling of galoshes. A single dried-up child's mitten lay on the change shelf, unclaimed. The Whitmans' number rang three, four, five times unanswered. He pictured Foxy lying dead, a suicide, having called him in the clouded last moment of waking and then sinking in coma onto her bed, her long hair spilling, the child crying unheard. The phone was picked up; as if a window had been opened Piet saw, across the street, through the besmirched phone-booth glass, four men rocking a car, trying to push it free.

"Hello." Foxy's voice was cool, impersonal, unfocused.

"It's me. What took you so long to answer the phone?"

Her voice, relieved, collapsed—but not, he felt, all the way. "Oh. Piet. You're so quick to call back."

"You told me to be."

"I was with Toby."

"What's up?"

She hesitated. "I just wondered how you were. I had a spell of missing you, and realized that I'd been resisting calling you just to punish you and you weren't being punished, so what the hell."

He laughed, reassured yet suspicious, for he did not remember her as a waverer. "Well, I *was* being punished, but I figured unless we had something to tell each other it was right we didn't talk. I admired your tact." In her silence he hurried on. "I get your letters out and read them now and then." This was a lie; he had not done this for months; they seemed, all those blue barbs and squiggles, dead thorns the sharper for being dead.

As if sensing this, she laughed. "But I *do* have something to tell you. Good news, you'll be pleased. The house is warm now, and it wasn't your fault. When they installed the furnace the man had put the thermostat too near some hot-water pipes in the wall, so the thermostat thought the house was warm when only *it* was, and kept shutting off. Ken and Frank Appleby figured it out one drunken night. The Applesmiths have been coming over lately."

"Oh, sweet, but it *is* my fault. I was the general contractor, I should have noticed. But I was distracted by making love to you."

"Did you like making love to me? I was never sure, I'm awfully virginal somehow."

"Virginal and whorish together. I adored making love to you. It was somehow it. But don't you feel better now in a way? You can look Angela in the face, and me Ken."

"I never minded Angela. I had a mysterious feeling she approved."

The subject displeased him; he did not like Angela to be dismissed. He felt his mistresses owed it to him to venerate her, since he had taken it upon himself to mock her through their bodies. "And how is Toby? Are you enjoying him?"

"Pretty much. He lifts up his head and seems to listen to what I say. Unlike his father."

"Aren't you enjoying Ken?"

"Not much."

"And this is all you called me for? Got me out here in the snow for?"

"No." The syllable seemed a metallic sound the receiver had made purely by itself. When Foxy's voice resumed, it had collapsed all the way; he felt, listening, that he was skating on a crystal surface, the pure essence of her that God's hands had held before thrusting it into a body, her soul. "Piet. My period is two weeks late. And it would have to be you."

"Me what?" But of course he instantly knew. That cold house, that scared last piece. The chopping block. The hostage.

As she spoke, her voice made soft tearing noises, caused by the skating action of his listening. "It's not just the lateness, it's a whole chemical something, a burny feeling down low that I remember from carrying Toby."

"Would you feel it so soon?"

"It's been a month."

"So soon after giving birth, aren't your insides naturally mixed up?"

"But I had two periods."

"And it can't be Ken?"

"Not really, no." He thought her phrasing strange. She added, "He uses those things."

"Sometimes they break."

"Not Ken's. Anyway, it's not been that often. I depress him since the baby. And he's worried about his work. Not only Jews but now the Japanese are getting ahead of him."

"But *how* often?"

"Twice when it could have been, except for the thing, and once just recently, when I hoped it would bring my period on."

"And you *do* have the burny feeling?"

"Yes. And agitation. Insomnia. Piet, Piet, I'm so sorry, it's so stupid."

"Why did you let me that day, if—"

"I don't know, you didn't act like you were going to do it, and my old diaphragm doesn't fit, and—"

"I assumed you used pills. Everybody else does."

"Oh, *does* everybody else? You've taken a poll."

"Don't be petulant."

"Don't you be. About the pills, not that it matters, Ken doesn't trust them. He thinks it's all too intricate, they may trigger off something."

"Bang," Piet said. "Bang, bang."

Foxy was going on, "And if you must know, if you must know how naïve I am, I thought that I was nursing made me safe." Her tears crackled and rasped in the receiver cold against his ear.

He laughed. "That old wives' tale? I keep forgetting about you, you're a Southern woman, raised on recipes learned at Aunt Jemima's knee."

"Oh," her wet pale voice gasped, "it's good to hear you laugh at me. I've been in hell. I called you this morning to keep from going crazy and then when you called back I was too frightened to answer, and then I lied. I just lie and lie, Piet."

"It's something we all get good at," he said. The receiver was such a little weight in his hand, chill and stiff and hollow, he wondered why he could not hang it up and walk away free, why it was clamped to him as the body is clamped to the soul.

Foxy was asking, "What shall we do?"

In the illusion of giving advice he found some shelter, right angles and stress-beams of sense they could inhabit. "Wait a few more days," he told her. "Take hot baths, as hot as you can stand them. If it still doesn't come on, go to a doctor and take the rabbit test. Then at least we'll know."

"But I *can't* go to Doc Allen. For one thing he'd be shocked that I was pregnant again so soon. He might tell some of his boatyard friends."

"Doctors never tell anything. But didn't you and Ken have a doctor in Cambridge? Go to him if you'd rather. But not quite yet. It might come on still. Angela is sometimes three weeks, sometimes five; she's terribly casual. It's a miracle I haven't knocked her up."

Though he had been serious, Foxy laughed. "Poor Piet and his women," she teased, "picking his way through the phases of the moon. I guess I turned out to be the dud."

"The opposite of dud, I'd say," and he glimpsed in himself amid the terror pleasure that she had proved doubly fertile, that she had shown him capable of bringing more life to bud upon the earth.

She asked, "Will you call me? Please. You won't have to *do* anything, I'll take care of it myself somehow—absolutely; no, don't say anything. But it *is* lonely. Lonely, Piet."

He promised her, "I'll call you tomorrow." A last word felt needed, a blessing to unclamp the receiver from his hand and ear. He stammered in fear of sounding pompous as he unlocked to her all the wisdom he possessed. "Foxy. After years of thought, I have come to this conclusion: there are two kinds of situation in the world, those we can do something about and those we can't, like the stars and death. And I decided it's a great waste, a sin in fact, to worry about what we can't help. So take a hot bath and relax. We're in the hands of Allah."

His not daring saying "God" disgusted him. But Foxy, lulled as if she had not listened, said singsong, "Call me tomorrow, Piet, and I bet it will have gone away like a silly dream, and we can go back to our nice comfortable estrangement."

So "estrangement" was the last word. He hung up and saw that the men had extricated the car from the white gutter, and all of Charity Street, alive with the rasping of shovels, seemed a sacred space, where one could build and run and choose, from which he was estranged.

*

Now began a nightmare of daily phoning, of small false hopes (the burning sensation seemed less distinct today, she had felt a uterine strangeness after this morning's scalding bath, a medical reference book at the Tarbox Library admitted of many postpartum menstrual irregularities) and of cumbersomely advancing certainty. The first rabbit test came back from the lab negative; but the Cambridge doctor explained that this early in the game there was only a ninety per cent accuracy, and implied disapproval of her haste. A curt, hawk-faced man with golfing trophies in his consulting room, he may have diagnosed at a glance her symptoms and recognized the plague, this not uncommon infection of decent society's computations with blind life's long odds, that to Foxy and Piet seemed so isolating. For a whole night of sleeplessness she lay trembling with the good news that she could not deliver to Piet until morning. But the one-in-ten chance dilated fascinatingly as Foxy refused to let go of her microscopic captive and surrender and bleed. Piet battered her over the phone, begged at her with his patience, his refusal to blame her: he had resigned from being her lover, he had lain with her to say good-bye, he was happy with his rare and remote wife, he had been gulled by Foxy's naïveté, she had no claim upon him—none of this he needed to say, it was assumed. She apologized, she ridiculed herself, she offered to take her child, her existing child, and vanish from the town; but for the time being he and he only knew her secret, only he could share with her the ordeal of these days. The sound of his voice was the one thing on earth not alien to her. They agreed to meet, out of pity for each other and a desire, like that of boxers clinching, to draw near to the presence, each to the other, that was giving them pain. In Lacetown there was an IGA whose large parking lot the plows would have cleared; behind the building, where the trucks unloaded, few cars parked. Of their friends only Janet sometimes shopped here. They would be safe.

Friday. A heavy mauve sky. A few dry flakes. His heart leaped at the sight, alone on the asphalt, beneath the close clouds, of the Whitmans' black MG. He parked his truck near the store incinerator barrel and walked across empty parking spaces. Foxy rolled down her window. A flake caught in her left eyebrow. He said, "I thought Ken took this car to Boston."

"He took the train today, because they forecast a storm. Get in."

Inside, having slammed the door, he said, "He's always thinking, Ken."

"Why do you dislike him? This isn't his fault."

"I don't dislike him. I admire him. I envy him. He has a college degree."

"I thought you were going to say he has *me*." They laughed, at her, at themselves, at them all. In leaving the limits of Tarbox they had acquired a perspective; their friends and their houses seemed small behind them. Only they, Foxy and Piet, were life-size. Only they had ceased flirting with life and had permitted themselves to be brought, through biology, to this intensity of definition. Their crisis flattered them like velvet backdrop. She sat awkwardly sideways in the bucket seat behind the wheel, her knees touching the gearshift, her legs long in yellow wool slacks, her hair loose over the shoulders of her Russian general's coat.

He said, "You look pretty good," and patted her thigh. "After our frantic phone conversations I thought you'd look more of a wreck."

She grinned; her nose and chin seemed whittled by the pressure of the coming storm. Snowflakes were making a thin white line along the rubber window sealer. On the loading platform of the IGA a solitary boy in a clerk's apron was stacking cardboard boxes, his breath a commotion of vapor. "Oh," she said, feinting. "We women can keep up appearances."

"I take it there's not much doubt left."

She nodded, as delicately as if a corsage were fastened near her chin. Dances. Girls in cars after dances. It had been a generation since he had sat like this. Foxy said, "Not in my mind. I'm driving in this afternoon to have another rabbit test. I was supposed to. The storm may cancel it."

"Not with you at the wheel." As if rationalizing his laugh, he added, "Funny how that one-in-ten chance didn't go away."

"You always said we'd press our luck too far."

"I'm sorry that the time that did it wasn't better for you."

"I remember it very clearly. How we moved from room to room, the cat jumping on the bed. It's all so silly, isn't it? Adultery. It's so much *trouble*."

He shrugged, reluctant to agree. "It's a way of giving yourself adventures. Of getting out in the world and seeking knowledge."

She asked, "What do we know now, Piet?"

He felt her, in the use of his name, drawing near, making of this desperate meeting an occasion of their being together, a date. He hardened his voice: "We know God is not mocked."

"I was never mocking God."

"No. Your God is right there, between your legs, all shapeless and shy and waiting to be touched. It's all right, Fox. I don't mean to complain. It's partly I suppose that I find you so attractive; I didn't expect to, it makes me crabby. It seems so much beside the point for me to still want you."

She adjusted her legs more comfortably; a knee touched his, and quickly pulled away. "You expected to hate me?"

"A bit. This has been hell, these ten days. Compared to your voice on the phone, you seem happy."

"That's the worst of it. I am happy. I'm happy to be carrying your child. My whole system wants to go ahead and have it."

"You may not have it. May not, may *not*."

"Oh of course. Absolutely. I agree."

But her face had withdrawn into sharpness. A moan caught in his throat; he lurched at her, fumbling, afraid of her face. Her breath was hot, her cheek cold with tears; her body within her massive coat sought to conform to his, but the bucket seats and floor shift prevented them. He backed off and read hastily in her distorted face absolution, permission to scour from her insides all traces of their love. "But how?" he asked. "Sweden? Japan? How do people *do* these things?" Beyond her mussed hair a lane of leafless maples made an embroidered edge upon the snowing sky.

"It's sad, isn't it?" she asked. "We don't seem to know the right people. I know there are abortionists *every*where, waiting for customers, and here am I, and there's no way to get us in touch."

"What about Ken? He knows doctors."

"I can't tell Ken."

"Are you sure? It would make things possible. You could fly to Japan even. He could give a guest lecture."

"He's not that good."

"I was joking."

"I know. Piet, I'll do anything to get rid of this except tell my husband about us. He couldn't handle it. He's too—complacent. And in a way I'm too complacent too. I knuckled under once and I won't again. I won't beg, or apologize for us when we were so *right*. I'd rather risk death. That sounds more arrogant than it is. You could tell Angela you slept with me and the two of you would absorb it, be better for it after a while, but our marriage just isn't built that way. We're not that close. We made a very distinct bargain, one that doesn't allow for either of us making mistakes this big. It would shatter Ken. Am I making any sense?"

He saw that she would not tell her husband, just as months ago she would not install closed cabinets. She was the customer; he must work with her whims. "Well, what about telling him it's his and going ahead and having another little Whitman? It might have red hair but there must be a red-haired gene in one of you."

She spoke with care, after biting the tip of her tongue. Women whose tongues won't stay in their mouths are the sexiest. "It's possible. But it seems to me, if you picture the little child, getting bigger day by day, me watching him as he looks less and less like Ken and more and more like Piet Hanema, as he starts swinging from banisters and nailing pieces of wood together, we'd be giving ourselves a lifetime of hell. I'd rather take the hell in a stronger dose and get it over with."

"My poor Fox." He leaned and kissed her nose. Her red hands lay inert in the lap of her greatcoat; possibly she shrugged.

A maroon Mercury coupe like Janet Appleby's slowly wheeled through the lot. But the driver was unknown, an elderly Lacetown citizen with grizzled jaws and a checked hunter's cap. He stared at them—white-ringed raccoon eyes—and continued his circling arc through the lot and out the other side. The apparition had given them both heartstop, and contaminated their hiding place. The boy stacking boxes was gone from the platform. "We better go," Piet said, "or they'll find us frozen in each other's arms."

*

At home, sheltered from the blizzard amid the sounds of Angela's cooking and his daughters' quarrelsome play, Piet struggled to see his predicament as relative, in any light but the absolute one that showed it to be a disaster identical with death. Pregnancy was life. Nature dangles sex to keep us walking toward the cliff. Slip-ups are genially regarded. Great men have bastards: Grover Cleveland, Charlemagne. Nobody cares, a merry joke, brown beer, the Lord of Norfolk salutes his natural son. One more soul: three billion plus one. Anyway she would probably move to Berkeley or Los Alamos and he'd never see it. Down the drain. Piet Hanema, father of a new nation. To your health. He sipped the double martini and a boiling soughing dread like pigswill welled up to meet the gin. Ken. His dread had to do with Ken's face, the strange trust its faintly rude blankness imposed, the righteousness of the vengeance it would seek. Sickened, slipping, Piet saw that he lived in a moral world of only men, that only men demanded justice, that like a baby held in a nest of pillows from falling he had fallen asleep amid women. He had been dumbstruck to hear Foxy speak slightingly of Ken. In Piet's mind there was no end of Ken, no limit to the ramifying offense of inflicting a child upon Ken's paternity. Paternity a man's cunt. Vulnerable. Gently. His father potting geraniums with stained thumbs, the perspective of the greenhouse implying an infinity of straight lines. He had preferred as a child the dead-ended warm room at the end where his mother sat broad-lapped among looping ribbons. There was a mandate in his father's silences he had shied from. Straight man, his mouth strange from dentures. Ah God, how glad he was that they were gone, all things considered.

All things are relative. As a boy in trouble he would think of something worse. It would be worse than not making the football squad to get polio. It would be worse than not getting invited to Annabelle Vojt's party to accidentally shoot Joop in the eye and have him blind forever. It would be worse to be dead than to be in this box. Would it? In a manner analogous to dying he had trespassed into a large darkness. In Foxy's silken salty loins he had planted seed that bore his face and now he wished to be small and crawl through her slippery corridors and, a murderer, strike. God forgive. No: God do. God who kills so often, with so lordly a lightness, from diatoms to whales, kill once more, obliterate from above, a whip's flick, a finger down her throat, erase this monstrous growth. For Thine is the kingdom.

Ken's face, barely polite. Pale from ambition and study. Piet's guts groveled again; he sipped silver to kill them. The bullet. The sleepy firing squad. The terrible realm where life leaps up from impeccable darkness. God's premeditated deed. Clay mixed with spit. Foxy's sly cunt, coral the petals, more purple within, her eyes like twin bells hung on a tree, tinkled by every wind. Yet she suffered, beneath the woman there was an animal, a man like him, an aged child rather, judging, guessing, hoping, itching. How monstrous to have a thing attach and fester upon you like a fungus. His balls sympathetically crawled. Poor soft Foxy. Erase. Pluck, Lord. Pluck me free.

He drank. The final sweetness of truly falling. Bea. Scared to call, she might guess. She knew some things. Had seen him leap from the window, Foxy's head golden in the bathroom light. In her bed he had left unconfessed only that last drab Monday visit when, trespassing unwittingly upon Ken's paternity, conjuring into the world another responsible soul, he had made himself legally liable. Disgrace, jail, death, incineration, extinction, eternal namelessness. The laughter of their friends. The maledictions of newspapers. He saw Bea smiling, her breasts melted, her body a still pool, his prick suspended in her like a sleeping eel, and knew why he loved her: she was sterile. His semen could dive forever in that white chasm and never snag.

His solitude became desolate. The blizzard crooned mournfully, a thing without existence, a stirring. He emptied his glass and went into the kitchen. His daughters and wife were arranging valentines. He had failed to get Angela one. Ruth and Nancy at school had received fuzzy hearts, mooning cows, giraffes with intertwined necks. Ruth was arranging the best on top of the refrigerator. Reaching up, her figure was strikingly lithe. His coming into the kitchen for more gin intruded upon a triangular female rapport especially precious to little Nancy. She turned her face, shaped like a rounded cartoon heart, upwards toward him, giggled at the approach of her own impudence, and said, "Daddy's ugly."

"No, Daddy not ugly," Ruth said, putting her arm about his waist. "Daddy pwetty."

"He has awful nostrils," Nancy said, moving closer and looking up.

Ruth continued the baby talk in which her impulse of love sought disguise. "Daddy has the beeyeutifullest nostwils," she said, "because he came from Howwand long ago."

Piet had to laugh. "What about my feet?" he asked Nancy.

"Acky feet," she said.

Ruth hugged him tighter and stroked his furry arm. "Loberly feet," she said. "Mommy has silly feet, her little toes don't touch the ground."

"That's considered," Angela said, "a sign of great beauty."

"You know something, Mommy?" Ruth said, abandoning Piet's side and the baby voice. "Mrs. Whitman has *flat* feet, because at the beach this summer Frankie Appleby and Jonathan Smith were being detectives and following people and her footprints had no dent on the inside, you know, where the curvy place, whatever it's called—"

"Arch," Angela said.

"—where the arch is. It was like she was wearing sneakers only with toes." The child glanced over at her father. True, even so unkind an evocation of Foxy gave him pleasure. Slouching flat-footed broad, big with his baby. His tall cockpit.

"How fascinating," Angela said. Her hands busily sparkled amid the leaves of their supper salad. "What else have you noticed about feet?"

"Mr. Thorne has a green toenail," Ruth said.

"Daddy's toes," Nancy said, gazing up impudently from beneath Angela's protection, "are like Halloween teeth," and Piet saw that he represented death to this child: that what menaced and assaulted the fragility of life was being concentrated for her in his towering rank maleness; that this process would bring her in time to Ruth's stage, of daring to admire and tame this strangeness; and at last to Angela's, of seeking to salvage something of herself, her pure self, from the encounter with it. He loved them, his women, spaced around him like the stakes of a trap.

Ruth said, "Mommy, make Nancy stop insulting Daddy. Daddy's handsome, isn't he?"

Piet stooped and picked Nancy up; she shrieked and kicked in mixed pleasure and fear. A peppery whiff of red candy hearts was on her breath. Rotting her fine teeth. Angry, he squeezed her harder; she squealed and tried to fight down, all fear now.

"I don't know if Daddy's exactly *handsome*," Angela was saying. "He's what people call attractive." She added, "And nice, and good." He set Nancy down, pinching her unseen. She stared upward at him, now knowing something she would never forget, and could never express.

Perhaps as a sequitur of the tenderness of their being together with their children and their valentines, perhaps simply excited by their snugness within the blizzard, Angela led him to bed early and, like a warm cloud descending, made love to him sitting astride, in the classic position of Andromache consoling Hector.

Saturday morning their phone rang; Foxy spoke breathily, with her lips against the mouthpiece. "Is Angela right there?"

"No," Piet said, "she's out shoveling with the kids. What would you have said if she had answered?"

"I would have asked her if she was wearing a short or a long dress to the Heart Fund dance."

"It's really risky, you know. She's just beginning to be less suspicious of you."

"I had to talk to you, I'm sorry. I thought you'd be at the Gallaghers last night. Why didn't you come?"

"We weren't invited. Who was there?"

"Everybody. Except you and the Saltzes and the Ongs. There was a new couple who seemed stuffy and young."

"Matt didn't say anything to me. Anyway. What's up with you?"

"The test. It was positive. There's no doubt, Piet."

"Oof." He was fascinated, as he sank into this fact, by the delicacy of his furniture, the maple telephone table with tapering legs, the mirror in its acanthus frame of chipped gilt. These things had been fashioned by men without care, with no weight on their hands. He marveled at himself, that he had ever found the energy, the space, to set two sticks together.

Into his leaden silence she cried, "Oh Piet, I've become such a burden."

"No," he lied. "I still think of you as very light and kind."

"At any rate—hang up if Angela comes in—I think I've hit on something."

"What?"

"Freddy Thorne."

Piet laughed. "Freddy can bore it out of you. That's called an abortion."

"All right. I'll hang up. I won't bother you again. Thanks for everything."

"No. Wait," he shouted, fearing the receiver would already be away from her ear. "Tell me. Don't be so touchy."

"I'm in hell, darling, and I don't like being laughed at."

"That's what hell is like."

"Wait until you know."

He prompted her, "Freddy Thorne."

"Freddy Thorne once told me that dentists commit abortions. They have all the tools, the chair, anesthetic—"

"A likely story. And?"

"And last night at the Gallaghers, you know how he gets you into a corner to be cozy, I brought the subject around, and asked him if he knew any who did it."

"You told him you were pregnant."

"No. Heaven forbid. I told him I knew somebody who was, a perfectly nice girl from Cambridge who was desperate."

"True enough."

"And—are you sure Angela isn't listening?—"

"I'll go to the window and see where she is." He returned and reported, "She's down the driveway shoveling like a woman inspired. She's been in a very up mood lately. She was excited by the storm."

"*I* wasn't. I was driving in and out of Cambridge to donate my urine. Then we had to struggle over to the Gallaghers."

"And Freddy Thorne looked at you with that fuzzy squint and knew fucking damn well it was *you* who were pregnant."

"Yes. He did. But he didn't say so."

"What did he say? He consulted his abortion schedule and gave you an appointment."

"Not exactly. He said a very spooky thing. All this by the way was in the kitchen; the others were in the living room playing a new word game, with a dictionary. He said he'd have to meet the girl and the man."

"That *is* spooky. The girl *and* the man."

"Yes, and since if I'm the girl, he must guess you're the man, I could only conclude he wants to see *you*."

"You're concluding too much. Freddy just isn't that organized. He's playing games. Blind man's bluff."

"I didn't feel that. He seemed quite serious and definite. More his dentist self than his party self."

"You bring out the dentist in Freddy, don't you? I don't want to see him. I don't like him, I don't trust him. I have no intention of putting us at his mercy."

"Whose mercy do you suggest instead?"

The front door was pushed open. Deftly Piet replaced the receiver and faced the hall as if he had been just looking in the mirror. Nancy stood there, swaddled with snowy clothes. Her cheeks were aflame. Wide-eyed she held out to him on one wet leather mitten what he took to be a snowball; but it was half-gray. It was a frozen bird, with a gingery red head and a black spot on its chest, a tree sparrow caught by the blizzard. Crystals adhered to its open eye, round as the head of a hatpin. In a businesslike manner that anticipated his protests, the child explained, "Mommy found it in the snow all stiff and I'm going to put it on the radiator to get warm and come alive again even though I know it won't."

The Heart Fund dance was held annually at the Tarbox Amvets' Club, a gaunt cement-block building off Musquenomenee Street. The club contained a bar and two bowling alleys downstairs and a ballroom and subsidiary bar upstairs. A faceted rotating globe hurled colored dabs of light around and around the walls, speeding at the corners, slowing above the windows, crisscrossing in crazy traffic among the feet of those dancing. No matter how cold the weather, it was always hot in the Amvets'. Whenever the doors opened, steam, tinted pink and blue by neon light, rolled out to mix with the exhaust smoke pluming from parking cars.

This year the dance was indifferently attended by the couples Piet knew. Carol Constantine was a graceful Greek dancer, and while the patriarchs and wives benignly watched from card tables laden with *keftedes* and *dolmathes* and black olives and *baklava*, she would lead lines hand in hand with their sons —grocers, electronic technicians, stockbrokers. Carol had the taut style, the archaic hauteur, to carry it off. But Irene Saltz was on the board of this year's Heart Fund, and the Constantines had gone into Boston with the Thornes and Gallaghers to see the Celtics play. The Hanemas had come mostly out of loyalty to Irene, who had confided to them (don't tell *any*one, es*pec*ially not Terry Gallagher) that these might be their last months in Tarbox, that Ben had been offered a job in Cleveland. The Whitmans were at a table with the Applesmiths, and the Guerins had brought the new couple. Their name was Reinhardt. They looked smooth-faced and socially anxious and Piet barely glanced at them. He only wanted, as the colored dots swirled and the third-generation Greek girls formed their profiled friezes to the Oriental keening of the bouzouki, for the American dancing to begin, so he could dance with Bea. Angela was sluggish from all her shoveling, and Foxy looked rigid with the effort of ignoring him. Only Bea's presence, a circle like the mouth of a white bell of which her overheard voice was the chiming clapper, promised repose. He remembered her as a calm pool in which he could kneel to the depth of his navel. When the teen-aged musicians changed modes, and his arms offered to enclose her, and they had glided beyond earshot of their friends, she said, gazing away, "Piet, you're in some kind of trouble. I can feel it in your body."

"Maybe it's in your body." But she was not drunk, and held a little off from him, whereas he had had three martinis with dinner at the Tarbox Inne, and was sweating. He wanted to smear her breasts against his chest and salve his heart.

"No," she said, singsong, refusing to yield to the questioning pressure of his arms, "it's in you, you've lost your usual bounce. You don't even stand the same. Didn't I once tell you the unkind people would do you in?"

"Nobody's been unkind. You're all too kind. In that same conversation, which I'm surprised you remember, you asked me if I didn't want to—"

"I do remember. Then you did, and didn't come back. Didn't you like it?"

"God, I loved it. I love you. The last time was so lovely. There was no longer any other place to go."

"Is that why you haven't called?"

"I couldn't. You're right, there *is* something in my life right now, a knot, an awful knot. If it ever untangles, will you have me back?"

"Of course. Always." Yet she spoke from a distance; in sorrow he squeezed her against him, pressed her like a poultice against that crusty knot in his chest where betrayal had compounded betrayal. Frank Appleby, dancing with the Reinhardt girl, accidentally caught Piet's eye, and biliously smiled. Lost souls. Hello in hell. Frank, having no mistress pregnant, seemed infinitely fortunate: advantages of an Exeter education. Whitewash.

Bea backed off, broke their embrace, gazing at something over his shoulder. Piet turned, frightened. Foxy had come up behind them. "Bea, it isn't *fair* for you to mon*op*olize this a*dor*able man." She spoke past Piet's face and her touch felt dry and rigid on his arm. Maneuvering him to dance, she said, her voice sharp, her pale mouth bitter, "I've been commissioned by your wife to tell you she's sleepy and wants to go home. But hold me a minute." Yet her body felt angular and uneasy, and they danced as if linked by obligation. She was wearing, uncharacteristically, a cloying perfume, overripe, reminiscent of rotting iris; by the contrast Piet realized Bea's scent had been lemony. She had floated, a ghost, in his arms.

Freddy Thorne's office smelled of eugenol and carpet cleaner and lollypops; holding Nancy by her plump tugging hand, Piet remembered his own childhood dread of that dental odor—the clenched stomach, the awareness of sunlight and freedom outside, the prayer to sleep through the coming half-hour. In Freddy's walnut magazine rack old *Time* and *Newsweek* covers showed Charles De Gaulle and Marina Oswald. Both looked haggard. Freddy's pug-nosed receptionist smiled reassuringly at the nervous child, and Piet's heart, though tracked to run head-on into Freddy, was shunted by a flick of gratitude into love of this girl. A crisp piece, young. Like eating celery, salting each stalk as it parted. Had Freddy ever? He doubted it. He was full of doubt of Freddy; just to picture the man filled him with a hopeless wet heaviness, like wash in a short-circuited machine.

Piet's left palm tingled with shame. He envied little Nancy her fear of merely pain. As he tried to read a much-creased *Look*, his daughter rubbed against him. The wrong way. Two cats. Electricity is fear. Pedrick had once said you could picture

God as electromagnetic waves. He missed the poor devil's struggling, ought to go again. Nancy whispered, and he could not hear. Exasperated by her numb bumping, he said "What?" loudly.

The child cried "Shh!" and her hand darted to his lips. He embarrassed her. She had come to trust only her mother. Angela would normally have taken her to this appointment but today there was a meeting after nursery school and Piet, faced with fate's challenge, reluctantly accepted. *Whose mercy do you suggest instead?* Now indecision and repugnance fluttered in him and only fatigue scaled his dilemma down to something that could be borne. Like waiting outside the principal's office. Old Orff, a fierce Lutheran. Despised the Dutch. Servile Calvinism. Sir, I'm sorry, just awfully sorry, I didn't know—*You didn't know anypody wutt be vatching?* Caught swinging on the banisters in the brick-and-steel stairwell. Nancy whispered more distinctly, "Will he use the busy thing?"

"It's called the drill. Only if you have any cavities."

"Can you see some?" She opened her mouth wide—a huge mouth, his mouth.

"Sweetie, I can't see any, but I'm not a dentist. If you do have any cavities, they will be little ones, because you have such little teeth, because you're such a little girl."

He tickled her, but her body was overheated and preoccupied and did not respond. "Tell him not to do it," she said.

"But he *must*, that's Dr. Thorne's job. If we don't let him fix things now, they will be much worse later." He put his face close to hers. Like a round white blotter she absorbed his refusal to rescue him; and, refusing in turn to cry, she imprinted him with courage. They went together into Freddy's inner office.

Once there, in the robin's-egg-blue reclining chair, with the water chuckling in the bowl beside her ear and Dr. Thorne joking overhead with her father, Nancy somewhat relaxed, and let the dentist pick his way along the reverberating paths of her teeth. "Two," he pronounced at last, and made the marks on his chart, and judged, "Not so bad."

"Two cavavies?" Nancy asked. "Will they hurt?"

"I don't think so," Freddy answered unctuously. "Let us see how quiet you can be. The quieter you are outside, the quieter you are inside, and the quieter you are inside, the less you'll notice the drill."

Piet remembered the dove-gray handbook on hypnotism by Freddy's bed, and would have made a jabbing joke about amateur psychology, but his need for mercy restrained him, and he instead asked humbly, "Should she have Novocain?"

Freddy looked down at him. "They're very little," he said.

Nancy withstood the first drilling in silence; but when Freddy began the second cavity without a pause a guttural protest arose in her throat. Piet moved to the other side of the chair and took her agitated hand in his. He saw into the child's mouth, where between two ridged molars the drill, motionless in its speed, stood upright like a potted flower. Her tongue arched against the point of intrusion and Piet had to restrain her hand from lifting to her mouth. Her guttural complaint struggled into a scream. Her eyes, squared in shape by agony, opened and confronted her father's. Piet burst into sweating; perspiration raced across his chest, armpit to armpit. The coral space of gum between Nancy's lower lip and lower incisors was a gorge of saliva and drill spray. Her back arched. Her free hand groped upwards; Piet caught it and held it, pleading with Freddy, "Let's stop."

Freddy leaned down upon the now convulsive child. His lips thinned, then opened fishily. He said "Ah," and let the drill lift itself away, done with. "There now," he told Nancy, "that wasn't worth all that fuss, was it?"

Her cheeks soaked, she spat into the chuckling bowl and complained, "I wanted only *one*."

"But now," her father told her, "they're both done with and now comes the fun part, when Dr. Thorne puts in the silver!"

"Not fun," Nancy said.

Freddy said, "She's not easily got around, is she? Her mother's daughter." His smirk appeared pleased.

"You shouldn't have plunged in so ruthlessly."

"They were *tiny*. Scratches on the enamel. She frightened herself. Is she apprehensive at home?"

"She has my distrustful nature. The older girl is more stoical, like Angela."

"Angela's not stoical, that's *your* theory. My theory is, she suffers." Freddy's smile implied he enjoyed access to mines of wisdom, to the secret stream running beneath reality. What a sad jerk, really. His skunk-striped assistant came in to spin the silver.

Nancy's ordeal was over. As Freddy inserted and smoothed her fillings, Piet brought himself to ask, "Could we talk afterwards for a moment, in private?"

Freddy looked up. His eyes were monstrously enlarged by the magnifying lenses that supplemented his ordinary glasses. "I'm running behind on my appointments today."

"OK, forget it." Piet was relieved. "It didn't matter. Maybe some other time."

"Now, Handyman. Don't be persnickety. I can fit a minute in."

"It might take two," Piet said, his escape denied.

Freddy said, "Allee allee done free, Nancy. You go with Jeannette and maybe she can find you a lollypop." He ushered Piet into the small side room where his old yellow porcelain chair and equipment were kept for emergency use and cleanings. The window here looked upward over back yards toward the tip of the Congregational Church, a dab of sunstruck gold. Freddy in his sacerdotal white seemed much taller than Piet. Piet blushed. Freddy wiped his glasses and waited; years of malice had enriched that sly congested expression.

"We both know a lady—" Piet began.

"We both know several ladies."

"A tall lady, with long blondish hair and a maiden name that's an animal."

"A lovely lady," Freddy said. "I hear she's wonderful in bed."

"I haven't heard that," Piet said. "However, she and I were talking—"

"Not in bed?"

"I think not. Over the phone, perhaps."

"I find phones, myself, so unsatisfying."

"Have you tried masturbation?"

"Piet my pet, I don't have much time. Spill it. I know what it is, but I want to hear you spill it."

"This lady has told me, or maybe she told somebody else who told me, that you know gentlemen who can perform operations of a nondental nature."

"I might. Or I might not."

"My guess is you might not." Piet made to shoulder past him to the closed door.

Freddy stayed him with a quiet touch, a calibrated technician's touch. "But if I might?"

"But do you? I must trust you. Answer yes or no."

"Try yes."

"Then, sweet Freddy, this lady needs your friendship."

"But old Piet, pious Piet, *friend* Piet, you speak of *her*. What about you and me? Don't *you* need my friendship too?"

"It's possible."

"Probable."

"OK. Probable."

Freddy grinned; one seldom saw Freddy's teeth. They were small and spaced and tartarish.

Piet said, "I hate this game, I'm going. You're bluffing, you bluffed her into getting me to betray us. You stink."

The bigger man stayed him again, holding his arm with injured warmth, as if their years of sarcasm and contempt had given him the rights affection claims. "I'm not bluffing. I can deliver. It's not easy, there's some risk to me, but it would be clean. The man's an idealist, a crackpot. He believes in it. In Boston. I know people who have used him. What month is she in?"

"Second. Just."

"Good."

"It really is possible?" The good news was narcotically spreading through Piet's veins; he felt womanish, submissive, grateful as a dog.

"I said *I* can deliver. Can *you* deliver?"

"You mean money? How much does he ask?"

"Three hundred. Four hundred. Depends."

"No problem."

"For the man, no. What about me?"

"You want money too?" Piet was happy to be again confirmed in his contempt for Freddy. "Help yourself. We'll raise it."

There was a fumbling at the door; Freddy called out, "*Uno momento*, Jeanette."

But it was Nancy's scared voice that answered: "When do we *go*, Daddy?"

Piet said, "One more minute, sweetie-pie. Go into the waiting room and look at a magazine. Dr. Thorne is giving me an X-ray."

Freddy smiled at this. "You've become a very inventive liar."

"It goes with the construction business. We were discussing money."

"No we weren't. Money isn't discussed between old friends like you and me. Surely, old friend, we've gone beyond money as a means of exchange."

"What else can I give you? Love? Tears? Eternal gratitude? How about a new skin-diving suit?"

"Boy, you do make jokes. You play with life and death, and keep making jokes. It must be why women love you. Piet, I'll give it to you cold turkey. There's an unbalanced matter between us: you've had Georgene—right?"

"If she says so. I forget how it was."

"And I, on the other hand, though I've always sincerely admired your bride, have never—"

"Never. She'd never consent. She hates you."

"She doesn't hate me. She's rather attracted to me."

"She thinks you're a jerk."

"Watch it, Handlebar. This is my show and I've had enough of your lip. I want one night. That's very modest. One night with Angela. Work it out, fella. Tell her what you have to. Tell her everything. Confession is good for the soul."

Piet said, "You're asking the impossible. And I'll tell you why you are: you have nothing to deliver. You are a slimy worthless creep."

With crooked forefingers Freddy made gay quick horns at his scalp. "You put 'em there, buddy. You're the expert. I'm just a gullible middle-class grubber who as far as we know hasn't made a career of screwing other men's wives." Freddy's hairless face became very ugly, the underside of some soft eyeless sea creature whose mouth doubles as an anus. "You dug this grave by yourself, Dutch boy."

Again Piet moved toward the door, and this time he was not prevented. He hauled it open, and hopped back, startled; Nancy, having disobeyed, was standing there listening. Her lips were pursed around the stem of a lollypop and her eyes, though she had no words, knew everything.

*

When over the phone Piet told Foxy of Freddy's proposition, she said, "How funny. I had assumed he and Angela did sleep together, or at least *had*."

"On what basis had you assumed this?"

"Oh, how they act together at parties. Very relaxed. Chummy."

"As far as I know, she's never been unfaithful."

"Are you bragging or complaining?"

"You're in a jolly mood. What do you suggest our next step should be?"

"Me. I don't have a next step. It's up to Angela, isn't it?"

"You're kidding. I can't put this to her."

"Why not?" Impatience surmounted fatigue in her voice. "It's not such an enormous deal. Who knows, she might enjoy getting away from you for a night."

He'll hurt her, Piet wanted to explain. Freddy Thorne will hurt Angela. He said, "But it means telling her all about us."

"I don't see why. If she loves you, she'll do it simply because you ask. If you do it right. She's your wife, let her earn it. The rest of us have been keeping you entertained, let her do something for the cause."

"You're tough, aren't you?"

"I'm getting there."

"Please, Fox. Don't make me ask her."

"I'm not *making* you do anything. How can I? It's between you and her. If you're too chicken, or she's too holy, we'll have to work at Freddy some other way, or do without him. I could try throwing myself on the mercy of my Cambridge doctor. He's not a Catholic. I could say I was going to have a nervous breakdown. It might not be a lie."

"You honestly think it's possible for me to ask her? Would you do it, to save Ken?"

"I'd do it to save *me*. In fact, I already offered."

"You offered what? To sleep with Freddy?"

"Don't let your voice get shrill like that. It's unbecoming. Of course I did, more or less. I didn't pull up my skirt; but what else do I have for him? What else do men and women ever talk about? He turned me down. Rather sweetly, I thought. He said I reminded him too much of his mother, and he was afraid of her. But it may have given him the idea of having Angela. I think what he really wants is to get at *you*."

"Because of Georgene?"

"Because you've always scorned him."

"You don't think he just honestly wants *her*?"

"Please don't try to squeeze compliments for your wife out of me. We all know she's magnificent. I have no idea what Freddy honestly wants. All I know is what *I* honestly want. I want this damn thing to stop growing inside of me."

"Don't cry."

"Nature is *so* stupid. It has all my maternal glands working, do you know what that means, Piet? You know what the great thing about being pregnant I found out was? It's something I just couldn't have imagined. You're never alone. When you have a baby inside you you are not *alone*. It's a *person*."

He had already told her not to cry. "You really think . . . she might?"

"Oh for God's sake, she's human like everybody else, I don't know what the hell she'll do or won't do. You still seem to think there's a fate worse than death. She's your divine wife, settle it between yourselves. Just let me know how it comes out, so I can work on something else. I thought I'd done pretty well to get Freddy Thorne for us."

"You did. You're being very brave and resourceful."

"Thank you for the compliment."

Piet told her, "I'll try. You're right. I don't expect it to go. She may ask for a divorce instead, but if it does, Foxy, love—"

"Yes, love."

"If we do get out of this, it has to be the end of our—of us."

"Obviously," Foxy said, and hung up.

A morning later, Nancy described her first dream, the first remembered dream of her life. She and Judy Thorne were on a screened porch, catching ladybugs. Judy caught one with one spot on its back and showed it to Nancy. Nancy caught one with two spots and showed it to Judy. Then Judy caught one with three spots, and Nancy one with four. Because (the child explained) the dots showed how old the ladybugs were!

She had told this dream to her mother, who had her repeat it to her father at breakfast. Piet was moved, beholding his daughter launched into another dimension of life, like school. He was touched by her tiny stock of imagery—the screened porch (neither they nor the Thornes had one; who?), the ladybugs (with turtles the most toylike of creatures), the mysterious power of numbers, that generates space and time. Piet saw down a long amplifying corridor of her dreams, and wanted to hear her tell them, to grow older with her, to shelter her forever. For her sake he must sell Angela.

"Angel?"

"Mm?" They were in the dark, in bed, nearly asleep. They had not made love; Piet had no intention of making love to anyone ever again.

"Would you believe it," he asked, "if I told you I was in deep trouble?"

"Yes," she answered.

Surprised, he asked, "What sort of trouble?"

"You and Gallagher aren't getting along any more."

"True. But that's the least of it. I can work things out with Matt once I get myself straightened out."

"Do you want to talk about it? I'm sleepy but can wake myself up."

"I can't talk about it. Can you accept that?"

"Yes."

"Could you believe it if I told you you could help me greatly by doing a specific thing?"

"Like getting a divorce?"

"No, not that at all. Have you been thinking about that?"

"Off and on. Does that alarm you?"

"Quite. I love my house."

"But that's not the same as loving me."

"I love you too. Obviously." The word echoed dryly and he felt them drifting farther from the point, the question. Perhaps there was a way of making it also seem a drifting, a detail of fate. "No," he said, "the thing you could do for me would only take one night."

"Sleep with Freddy Thorne," she said.

"Why do you say that?"

"Isn't that right?"

In the softness of the dark Piet could find no breath to make an answer; he lay on the bed like a man lying on water, only his eyes and nostrils not immersed. Finally he repeated, "Why do you say that?"

"Because he's always told me he would get into bed with me some day. For years he's been wanting to get a hold over you. Now does he have it?"

Piet answered, "Yes."

"And is that what he wants?"

His silent nodding made the bed slightly shudder.

"Don't be shocked," Angela went on, in a voice soft as the dark, "he's been working on it for years, and would tell me, and I imagined I should laugh. What I always thought strange, was that he never just *asked* me, on his own merits, but assumed it had to be worked by bullying you. I don't love him, of course, but he can be appealing sometimes, and I've been unhappy enough with you so that it might have happened by itself, if he'd just been direct. Do you want to know something sad?"

He nodded again, but this time the trembling of the bed was a theatrical effect, deliberately managed.

She told him, "He's the only man in town who's ever been attracted to me. Eddie Constantine took me for that ride on his Vespa and never followed it up. I'm just not attractive to men. What's wrong with me?"

"Nothing."

"Well something must be. I'm not on anybody's wavelength. Not even the children's, now that Nancy's no longer a baby. I'm very alone, Piet. No. Don't touch me. It sometimes helps but it wouldn't now. I really don't seem to be quite *here*; that's why I meant it about psychiatry. I think I need a rather formal kind of help. I need to go to a school where the subject is myself."

He sensed a bargain forming in the shadows. The far lamps along Nun's Bay Road, the wavy-branched lilacs and vase-shaped elms, leafless, and the reflecting snow made patterns of light along the walls that would never occur in summer. He said, "Why not? If things straighten out."

Angela repeated, "If. One question. I'm incredibly curious, but I'll ask just one. Do you trust Freddy? To keep his end of this bargain."

"I don't know why, I do. He needs to impress me as a man of honor, maybe."

"He wants me only once?"

"That's what he said."

She laughed a syllable and turned her back on him. "I don't seem to arouse very strong passions in men." Her words were muffled but her accent sounded ironical.

He lifted himself on an elbow to hear her better. Was she crying? Would she die?

She answered his lurch, "I'd rather not do it here in town. There are too many cars and children to keep track of. Aren't the Thornes coming on the Washington's Birthday ski weekend?"

"Sure. They never miss anything."

"Well, the children will all be in the bunk rooms and we'll probably be along the same hall. You've slept with Georgene?"

He hesitated, then saw that they had passed into another room of their life altogether, and admitted, "In the past."

"Well then. It's all very neat. No, Piet, don't touch me. I really must go to sleep."

The ski lodge still displayed on its bulletin board photographs of itself in summer, as if to say, *This is me, this soft brown lake, these leafy birches, not the deathlike mask of ice and snow in which you find me.* The defunct cuckoo clock still haunted the high corner misted with cobwebs, the television set crackled with ignored news, the elderly young proprietors came and went with ashtrays and ice trays, trailing an air of disapproval. The rates had been raised. The raisin sauce on the ham was less generous. A quartet of strangers played bridge, and the Tarbox couples played word games on the floor. Whiskey warmed their bodies with a triumphant languor—they were survivors, the fortunate, the employed, the healthy, the free. The slopes today had been brilliant, under the holiday sun that daily looped higher. The conditions had been icy at the top, powdery in the middle of the mountain and along the shaded trails, corny on the broad lower slopes, and slushy by the base lodge, where mud was beginning to wear through. The potent sun, the prickling scintillating showers of dry snow abruptly loosened from the pine branches overhanging the trails, the heavyish conditions, the massive moguls carved by two months of turning and edging all freighted the skiers' bodies with a luxurious lassitude. They began to retire earlier than they had last year, when Freddy Thorne regaled the Applesmiths with his fantasies. Now Jonathan little-Smith, nearly thirteen, was livelier than his parents, and made Frankie Appleby, two years younger and cranky from drowsiness, play one losing game of chess after another. The only way to get him to bed was for Harold and Marcia to go themselves, out to the gas-heated cottage where Julia and Henrietta already were sleeping. The Applebys promptly followed. This year both couples were in cottages—at opposite ends, Janet had insisted, of the row. Then the Guerins, though Freddy huggingly begged Roger to stay for another drink, and Bea cast wise swarming glances of farewell to Piet, went out into the night, barren of a moon, to their hissing cottage. This left the Gallaghers, Hanemas, and Thornes. The Whitmans did not ski. Eddie Constantine, promoted to ever greater responsibilities, was piloting a wonderful new jet, three-engined and hot, the Boeing 727, to San Juan. The Saltzes, who had announced this as the winter when they would take up skiing, were now authoritatively rumored to have accepted the Cleveland offer, to be leaving Tarbox; and instantly they had become pariahs. After some constrained banter Matt Gallagher primly coughed and announced that *he* was going to bed. The emphasis of "he" implied that Terry had been formally given freedom. She, who under circumstances confided only to Carol Constantine had stopped taking pottery lessons, promptly stood and said that so was *she*. When the Hanemas and Thornes were alone, disposed as couples face to face on the two sofas opposed across a maple coffee table stacked with back copies of *Ski* and *Vogue*, Freddy said to Piet, "You and Matt don't seem to have much to say to each other these days."

Piet told him, "He does his end, and I do mine."

Freddy smiled fishily. "Not much doing at your end these days, is there, Handball?"

"There will be soon. As soon as the frost breaks we'll be going back to Indian Hill. Six houses this summer is the plan." A year ago he would not have given Freddy the satisfaction of so full a response, almost an apology.

Angela sat up and parted an invisible drape with her hands. "Well. Is this the night?" Her face looked fevered from sun and windburn, and her eyes had been so steeped in unaccustomed exercise and the beauty of the day that the irises and pupils were indistinguishable. She had changed her ski costume for a looseknit mauve sweater and white pants flared at the ankles; she was barefoot. She had become Janet Appleby.

Georgene stood and said, "I'm not going to listen to this. I'm going to go to bed and lock the door and take a sleeping pill. You three do whatever you want. Don't involve *me*." She stood as if waiting to be argued with.

Freddy said, "But Georgie-pie, you started everything. This is just my tit for your tat. What's sauce for the goose, et cetera."

"You're contemptible. All of you." Her long chin flinty, she crossed through the light of several lamps to the stairs. The day's sun had already become on her face the start of a tan.

While she was still within earshot, Freddy said, "Oh hell. Let's call it off. I was just curious to see your reactions."

Angela said, "No, sir. There's some kind of a bargain and we're going to keep our side. We better go up now because all that fresh air is getting to me and I'll soon fall asleep."

Piet found he could not look at either of them: he felt their faces, blurs in his upper vision, as deformed, so deformed that if he dared to lift his eyes to them he might involuntarily whimper or laugh. He told his stockinged feet, "Let's give Georgene a minute to get into her room. Freddy, should you get your toothbrush or anything?"

Freddy asked, "She's on the pill, isn't she?"

"Of course. Welcome to paradise." Piet stayed sitting on the sofa as they went up. Angela kissed him good night on his cheek; his head refused to move. Her lips had felt weirdly distinct, the parted carved lips of a statue, but a statue warmed by fire. He dared look at her only as she disappeared up the stairs, gazing straight ahead, her gentle hair unbound from the scarlet ear-warmer she wore skiing. Freddy followed, his white hands held lamely at his chest, his mouth open as if to form a bubble.

The upstairs hall was hushed. A single light bulb burned. Georgene's door looked tight shut. The Gallaghers in the room adjacent could be heard murmuring. On silent bare feet Angela led Freddy into her room, and then without their touching excused herself to go back into the hall, to the lavatory. When Freddy in turn returned from the lavatory, she was in her nightie, simple cotton such as a child might wear, a green flower stitched at the neckline. The room's single window over-looked a shallow deck that in summer would be a sunporch; the banister supported baroque shapes of snow sculpted by the melting of the day and the night's refreezing. Within the room there was a double bed with a brass-pipe headboard, a porce-lain washstand stained by the hot-water faucet's tears, a five-and-dime mirror, an old rocking chair painted Chinese red, a pine bureau painted bile green, a black bedside table nicked by alarm-clock legs and holding a paperbound copy of *Beyond the Pleasure Principle* and a gay small lamp whose shade was orange. When Angela, who had been brushing down her hair amid serene explosions of static, bent to turn out this lamp, the light pierced the simple cloth and displayed her silhouetted bulk, the pucker of her belly; her big breasts swayed in the poppy glow like sluggish fish in an aquarium of rosewater. The light snapped off and a ghost replaced her. Her voice out of a frame of fluffed hair asked Freddy, "Don't you want to take off your clothes?"

Snowlight from the window picked out along the rim of her hair those tendrils looped outwards by the vigor of the brushing. She had expanded expectantly. Freddy felt the near presence of her blood-filled body as an animal feels the near-ness of water, of prey, or of a predator. He said, "Love to, but how would you feel about a drink first? You haven't anything in the suitcase, a little Jack Daniel's, say?"

"We brought some bourbon but it's downstairs. Shall I go down and take it from Piet?"

"Jesus, no. Don't go near him."

"Do you really need a drink? I think you've had plenty."

The lining of his mouth felt scratchy, as if he had chewed and swallowed a number of square blocks. This ungainly square-ness had descended, still abrasive, to his stomach. Her long-awaited nearness had crystallized his poisons. He said, "I see you're still reading Freud."

"I love this one. It's very severe and elegant. He says we, all animals, carry our deaths in us—that the organic wants to be returned to the inorganic state. It wants to rest."

"It's been years since I read it. I think I doubted it at the time." Paralyzed, he felt her unbuttoning his shirt. He was immobilized by the vision of a drink—amber, clouded with

ice—and the belief that its smoky golden distillation would
banish his inner kinks. He let her part the halves of his shirt
and fumble at his fly until, irritated at her own inexpertness,
she turned away. She went to the window, glanced out quickly,
peeled off her nightgown, and jackknifed herself, breasts bobbling, into the tightly made bed. "Oh, it's icy," she cried, and
pulled the covers over her face. "Hurry, Freddy": the call came
muffled.

He imagined Piet downstairs with the whiskey bottle, in the
long room golden from the fire, and undressed down to his
underwear, and got into the bed.

"Hey," Angela said. "You're cheating."

"You scared me by saying the bed was so cold."

"Well. Let's warm it up." She touched him in front. "Oh.
You're not excited."

"I'm in shock," Freddy told her, stalling, adjusting the covers. The tightly made sheets had virginally resisted his entry,
and then tangled, exposing him behind.

"Piet never—" Angela stopped. Had she been going to say,
"—is not excited"? She instead said, "I don't move you."

"You stun me. I've always loved you."

"You don't have to say that. I'm nothing special. Sometimes
I look at myself in the mirror Piet gave Ruth and I see this
knotty veiny fat peasant woman's body with tiny red feet and
a dear little oval head that doesn't go with the rest. Piet calls
me a dolphin." She remembered that he called her this in bed,
when she turned her rump upon her husband and, holding
him in herself, exposed her curved back to his smoothing
rough hands.

"How are you and Piet getting along?"

She realized Freddy wanted to talk, and foresaw that talk
would make her sleepy. She tickled the gap between his undershirt and pants elastic while answering, "Better, really. He's
been bothered about something lately, but I think basically
we're more *fun* for each other than we've been for years. I
think it's taken me a year to forgive him for not letting me have
the Robinson place. The Whitman place, I should say. Those
people haven't made much of an impression on me." She lifted
his shirt and snuggled against his bare chest.

"But—how do you reconcile this?" Freddy asked.

"With what?" His dumbstruck silence led her to laugh; fatty warm points, her breasts, shimmered against him, and the jiggled bed complained. "You and me in bed? He told me I should do it. The Hamiltons are always obedient wives. Anyway, I was curious what it would be like. And I must say, Freddy, you're being passive. Take off these insulting clothes."

She managed to lower his elastic waistband—unlike Piet's Paisley, he wore little-boy Jockey briefs. When he was naked, she explored with pinches his sides and the tops of his arms. "Freddy Thorne," she said, "you are pudgy." Her fingers went lower. "And still little," she accused. Delicate and tepid, his genitals lay in her hand like three eggs, boiled and peeled and cooled, she was carrying to the table. The sensation made Angela languorous. She hadn't dreamed men could be this calm with women. She could never have held Piet so long. Even asleep. Their sweetest phase. Not tucked safe inside like women. Committed to venture. More injurable.

Testingly Freddy placed his hand on her back, as if they were dancing. Her skin felt dark to him, oily and Negroid: flat wide muscles glidingly wedged into one another, massive buttocks like moons heaved from an ancient earth. Her body's bland power dismayed him. That Angela, the most aloof of women, whose shy sensitive listening had aroused in his talking tongue the eager art of a drill probing near pulp, should harbor in her clothes the same voracious spread of flesh as other women afflicted Freddy, touching his way across the smooth skin black as lava, with the nausea of disillusion. Her hand under his balls seemed about to claw. He begged, "Let's talk." He longed for her voice to descend from silence, to forgive him.

She asked, "Is there anything you'd like me to do? Anything special?"

"Just talk. Aren't you curious about what the bargain is?"

"No. It feels too scary to me, I don't want to hear it. I feel we've all gone too far to know everything. It's awful of me, but I've never wanted to know about Piet and his women. For me it's no more part of him than his going to the bathroom. You can't realize this, but he's terribly pleasant around the house."

"Tell me about it. I never can picture you and Piet fucking."

"How funny of you, Freddy. You've idealized me or mixed me up with somebody else. Piet and I don't"—she couldn't

manage the word, out of consideration, it seemed, for *him*—
"as often as he'd like, but of course we do. More and more, in
fact."

"Have you ever slept with anyone except Piet?"

"Never. I thought maybe I should."

"Why?"

"So I'd be better at it."

"For *him*. Shit. Let's face it, Angela. You married a bastard.
A bully boy. He's pimping for you. He's got you so intimidated
you'll shack up with anybody he tells you to."

"You're not anybody, Freddy. I more or less trust you. You're
like me. You want to teach."

"I used to. Then I learned the final thing to teach and I
didn't want to learn any more."

"What final thing?"

"We die. We don't die for one second out there in the future,
we die all the time, in every direction. Every meal we eat breaks
down the enamel."

"Hey. You've gotten bigger."

"Death excites me. Death is being screwed by God. It'll be
delicious."

"You don't believe in God."

"I believe in that one, Big Man Death. I smell Him between
people's teeth every day."

He was hoping to keep her at a distance with such violence
of vision but she nudged closer again, crowding him with
formless warmth. Her toes engaged his toes; her chin dug into
his chest, the hard bone to the right of the heart. "Piet's terrified of death," she said, snuggling.

Freddy told her, "It's become his style. He uses it now as
self-justification. He's mad at the world for killing his parents."

"Men are so romantic," Angela said, after waiting for him
to tell her more. "Piet spends all his energy defying death, and
you spend all yours accepting it."

"That's the difference between us. Male versus female."

"You think of yourself as female?"

"Of course. Clearly I'm homosexual. But then, of the men in
town, who isn't, except poor old Piet?"

"Freddy. You're just leading me on, to see what I'll say. Be
sincere."

"I am sincere. Anybody with a little psychology can see I'm right. Think. Frank and Harold. They screw each other's wives because they're too snobbish to screw each other. Janet senses it; she's just their excuse. Take Guerin and Constantine. They're made for each other."

"Of course, Roger—"

"Eddie's worse. He's a suc*cess*ful sadist. Or Gallagher and Whitman. Spoiled priests. Saltz and Ong, maybe not, but one's moving and the other's dying. Anyway, they don't count, they're not Christian. Me, I'm worst of all, I want to be everybody's mother. I want to have breasts so everybody can have a suck. Why do you think I drink so much? To make milk."

Angela said, "You've really thought about this, haven't you?"

"No, I'm making it all up, to distract your attention from my limp prick; but it works, doesn't it? Piet stands alone. No wonder the women in town are tearing him to pieces."

"Is that why you've always hated him?"

"Hated him, hell. I love him. We both love him."

"Freddy, you are not a homosexual and I'm going to prove it." She pushed herself higher in bed, so her breasts swam into starlight and her pelvis was above his. She lifted a thigh so it rested on his hipbone. "Come on. Put it in me."

He had kept a half-measure of firmness, but the slick warmth of her vagina singed him like a finger too slowly passed through a candleflame.

Feeling him grow little again, she asked again, "What can I do?"

He suggested, "Blow me?"

"Do what? I don't know how."

Pitying her, seeing through this confession into a mansion of innocence that the Hanemas, twin closed portals, had concealed, Freddy said, "Skip it. Let's gossip. Tell me if you think Janet still goes to bed with Harold."

"She made a big deal of getting cottages at opposite ends of the row."

"Merely thirty or so yards, not very far even in bare feet, if your heart's in it. My thought about Janet is, being her father's daughter, she really believes in cures. She had the baby, then she took a lover, then she went into analysis; and still she wears that headachy expression."

"I want to go into analysis," Angela told him. Her voice was slow and her weight now rested all on the bed, depressing it in the middle so that Freddy had to resist rolling closer toward her. His voice stroking, his hand on her halo of hair, he talked to her about analysis, about himself, about Marcia and Frank, Irene and Eddie, about John Ong's cancer, about the fate of them all, suspended in this one of those dark ages that visits mankind between millennia, between the death and rebirth of gods, when there is nothing to steer by but sex and stoicism and the stars. Angela, reminded by his tone and rhythm of her parents and uncle talking, of the tireless Gibbs pedantry, the sterile mild preachiness descended from the pilgrims, in which she had been enwombed, and from which Piet had seemed to rescue her, dozed, reawoke, heard Freddy still discoursing, and fell irrevocably asleep. He, having held her at bay and deepened his shame and completed his vengeance, felt himself grow strong and adamant and masturbated toward her belly, taking care not to defile her. Then both, parallel, floated toward dawn, their faces slacker than children's.

Downstairs, Piet, having poured himself one more bourbon, had grown cold beside the dying fire, and bored, and outraged. He tried to use his parka as a blanket but it was too small. He tiptoed up the stairs, listened at his own door, and tapped at Georgene's. He tested the lock. It gave. Georgene, though at first overwhelmingly indignant about being discarded by her lover, betrayed by her husband, and treated like an insignificant counter in this game, accepted Piet into her bed, because there was really nowhere to sit, and it was cold. She vowed to him she would not make love. Piet agreed. But, as he lay meekly beside her, his proximity and the danger of insomnia conspired to render her resolve unreal. He offered to rub her back. She invited him into her body. As always, though many distorting months had intervened, they came together; her face snapped sideways as if slapped, a welling softness merged with his clangor, her thighs flared to take him more fully, and he knew that he had exaggerated his trouble, that fate could be appeased.

V

It's Spring Again

IN BOSTON COMMON there is a somber little pavilion surrounded by uneven brick paving and cement-and-slat
benches for band concerts. Here Piet waited for Foxy to come
down from a dentist's office in a mustard-colored six-story office building on Tremont Street. By this the middle of March
few other idlers were present in the park. Some children in
snowsuits were snuffing caps on the lip of the dry wading pool;
a gray squirrel raced staccato across the dead grass, at intervals
pausing as if to be photographed or to gauge the danger expressed by the muted gunshot sound of the caps. Piet's own
scuffing footsteps sounded loud. There was a mist in which
the neon signs along Tremont and Boylston distinctly burned.
Sooty wet pigeons veered arrogantly close to the heads of
hurrying passersthrough. Trees overhead, serene fountains of
life labeled *Ulmis hollandicis*, dangled into the vaporous air
drooping branchlets dotted with unbroken buds, having survived the blight to greet another year. The wheel turned. Time
seemed to Piet as he waited a magnificent silence: the second
hand of his watch circling the dial daintily, the minute hand
advancing with imperceptible precision. He almost adored the
heartlessness that stretched him here for hours, untouched by
any news. RUBY GUILTY, TO DIE, said a discarded tabloid being mulched by footsteps into the mud and ice bordering the
path. The palm of Piet's left hand tingled thunderously whenever he read the headline, or heard a child shout.

Freddy and Foxy had arranged the matter between them
so efficiently Piet felt excluded. Neither wished to explain the
arrangements to him. Foxy, pale on Charity Street, her nostrils
pinched by wind, a tearing bag of groceries bulky in her arms,
told him, "You don't have to do a thing. I'd rather you didn't
even know when it happens. Just tell me one thing now. Is it
what you want? You want this child destroyed?"

"Yes." His simplicity shocked her; she turned paler still. He
asked, "What are the alternatives?"

357

"You're right," she said coldly, "there are none," and turned away, the bag tearing a bit more in her arms.

She explained the plan to him later, reluctantly, over the phone. Ken had to go to Chicago three days for a biochemical symposium, in the middle of March, beginning on a Wednesday, the eighteenth. Wednesday was also Freddy's day off, so he could take her up to Boston to the idealist who for three hundred fifty dollars would perform the abortion. Freddy would stay with her and drive her back home to Tarbox. Alone in her home at the far end of the beach road, she would need only to feed herself and Tobias, who slept twelve hours a day. Georgene would come by in the mornings and evenings, and Foxy would be free to call her any time. If complications ensued, she could be admitted to the Tarbox hospital as a natural abortion, and Ken would be told the child had been his.

Piet objected to Georgene's knowing.

Foxy said, "She already knows there was some kind of hideous bargain. It's Freddy's decision, and he's entitled to it. If anything were to happen to me, you must realize, he'd be an accessory to murder."

"Nothing will happen to you."

"Let's assume not. Georgene can drop around in a way neither you or Freddy can. Marcia goes up and down that road all day. It is especially important that *you* stay away. Forget I exist." She would not tell him the address of the abortionist until she had talked to Freddy again. "Freddy's afraid you'll do something dramatic and crazy."

"And are you?"

"No." Her tone was not kind.

Freddy called him that afternoon, gave him the address on Tremont, absolutely forbade his coming in with them, and tried to discourage his keeping watch from the Common. "What can you do?" Freddy asked. He answered himself scornfully: "Pray. If she's had it, son, she's had it." The ambiguity of "had it," the suggestion of a finite treasurable "it" that Foxy could enclose and possess, as one says "had him" of sleeping with a man, the faint impression that Foxy was competing for a valuable prize, sent ghosts tumbling and swirling through Piet, the ghosts of all those creatures and celebrities who had already attained the prize. He longed to call it off, to release

Freddy from his bargain and let Foxy swell, but that wouldn't do; he told himself it had gone beyond him, that Freddy and Foxy would push it through regardless: they had become gods moving in the supernature where life is created and destroyed. He replaced the receiver physically sick, his hand swollen like a drowned man's, the brittle Bakelite more alive than he.

Yet last night, playing Concentration with his two daughters, knowing he had set a death in motion, he cared enough to concentrate and win. Piling up cards under Nancy's eyes filling with tears. She had thought the game hers. A little beginner's luck had told her she owned a magic power of selecting pairs. Piet had disillusioned her. A father's duty. But so jubilantly. Ruth had watched his vigorous victory wonderingly.

A snuffly bum approached him, hand out, whiskers like quills. Piet shied from being knifed. The other man confusedly flinched, palm empty. Piet settled to listening; he was being asked for something. Dime. Derelict wanted a dime. His voice retreated behind the whiskers toward the mumbled roots of language. Piet gave him a quarter. "Gahblessyafella." Angel in disguise. Never turn away. Men coming to the door during the Depression. His mother's pies. Bread upon the waters. Takes your coat, give him your cloak. Asks a mile, go twain. Nobody believes. Philanthropy a hoax to avoid Communism. As a child he wondered who would eat wet bread. Tired old tales. Loaves and fishes, litter. Keep your Boston clean. He found himself hungry. A lightness in his limbs, strange sensation, how does it know food? Strange angels, desires. Come from beyond us, inhabit our machines. Piet refused his hunger. If he ran to the cafeteria burning at the corner, Foxy would die. He did without. His mother's beautiful phrase. *Well sen, do wissout.* Her floury arms upreaching to the pantry shelf. Glory. An engine of love ran through him, flattened his gut. Never again. *Moeder is dood.*

Cruel hours passed. The pavilion, the frost-buckled bricks, the squirrels posing for snapshots, the hurtling gangs of hoodlum pigeons, the downhanging twigs glazed with mist to the point of dripping became the one world Piet knew: all the others—the greenhouse, the army, the houses and parties of his friends in Tarbox—seemed phantom precedents, roads skimmed to get here. Hunger questioned his vaporous head, but he went without. Might miss Foxy's moment. The knife. Ask for a dime, give a quarter. Fifteen-cent profit. He was protecting his investment. His being expanded upward in the shape of a cone tapering toward prayer. Undo it. Rid me of her and her of it and us of Freddy. Give me back my quiet place. At an oblique angle she had intersected the plane of his life where daily routines accumulated like dust. Lamplight, breakfast. She had intruded a drastic dimension. He had been innocent amid trees. She had demanded that he know. Straight string of his life, knotted. The knot surely was sin. Piet prayed for it to be undone.

Overhead the elm branches were embedded in a sky of dirty wool: erosion deltas photographed high above the drained land: stained glass. Footsteps returning from lunch scuffed everywhere in the Common distinctly, as if under an enclosing dome. A small reddish bug crawled along an edge of brick. Happened before. When? His head tilted just so. Exactly. His mind sank scrabbling through the abyss of his past searching for when this noticing of an insect had happened before. He lifted his eyes and saw the Park Street church, stately. He looked around him at the grayly streaming passersthrough and all people seemed miraculous, that they could hold behind their glowing faces the knowledge that soon, under the whitewash-spattered sky, they would wither or be cut.

Church. Tolled. Three. He weakened, broke faith with himself, ran for coffee and one, no two, cinnamon doughnuts. When he emerged from the cafeteria the yellow sky between the buildings was full of Foxy. Coffee slopping through the paper cup and burning his fingers, he ran up Tremont, convinced of hopeless guilt. But Freddy's car, his yellow Mercury convertible, the canvas top mildewed from being buttoned up all winter, was still parked, half on the sidewalk, down a narrow alley off the street, near a metal door painted one with the mustard wall yet whose hinges, rubbed down to the bare steel, betrayed that it could be opened. So she was not gone. He went back across Tremont to the pavilion's vicinity and ate.

His feet grew numb. Boston danker than Tarbox: oily harbor lets in the cold sea kiss. More northern. To his dread for Foxy attached a worry that he would be missed at home. Gallagher, Angela, each would think the other had him. The sun slipped lower behind the dome of sky, to where the walls were thinner. Sunshine luminous as tallow tried to set up shadows, touched the tree plaques and dry fountains. In this light Piet saw the far door down the alley open and a dab that must be bald Freddy emerge. Dodging through thickening traffic, Piet's body seemed to float, footless, toward the relief of knowing, as when he would enter the Whitmans' house by the doorway crowded with lilacs and move through the hallway fragrant of freshly planed wood toward the immense sight of the marshes and Foxy's billowing embrace. Freddy Thorne looked up from unlocking his car door, squinting, displeased to see him. Neither man could think to speak. In the gaping steel doorway a Negress in a green nurse's uniform and silver-rim spectacles was standing supporting Foxy.

She was conscious but drugged; her pointed face, half-asleep, was blotched pink and white as if her cheeks had been struck, and struck again. Her eyes paused on Piet, then passed over him. Her hair flowed all on one side, like wheat being winnowed, and the collar of her Russian-general greatcoat, a coat he loved, was up, and buttoned tight beneath her chin like a brace.

Freddy moved rapidly to her side, said "Six steps," and, his mouth grimly lipless, one arm around her waist, the other beneath her elbow, eased her toward the open car door as if at any jarring she might break. The Negress in silence closed the metal door upon herself. She had not stepped into the alley. Piet's running had attracted the curiosity of some pedestrians, who watched from the sidewalk at the alley mouth yet did not step toward them. Freddy lowered Foxy into the passenger's seat, whispering, "Good girl." With the usual punky noise of car doors hers swung shut. She was behind glass. The set of her mouth, the tension above the near corner predicting laughter, appeared imperfectly transported from the past, a shade spoiled, giving her face the mysterious but final deadness of minutely imitated wax effigies. Then two fingertips came up from her lap and smoothed the spaces of skin below her eyes.

Piet vaulted around the front of the car. Freddy was already in the driver's seat; grunting, he rolled his window some inches down. "Well, if it isn't Piet Enema, the well-known purge."

Piet asked, "Is she—?"

"Okey-doak," Freddy said. "Smooth as silk. You're safe again, lover."

"What took so long?"

"She's been lying down, out, what did you think, she'd get up and dance? Get your fucking hand off the door handle."

Perhaps roused by Freddy's fury of tone, Foxy looked over. Her hand touched her lips. "Hi," she said. The voice was warmer, drowsier, than hers. "I know you," she added, attempting, Piet felt, irony and confession at once, the irony acknowledging that she knew very well this intruder whom she could not quite name. Freddy rolled up the window, punched down both door locks, started the motor, gave Piet a blind stare of triumph. Delicately, taking care not to shake his passenger, he eased the car down off the curb into the alley and into the trashy stream of homeward traffic. A condom and candy wrapper lay paired in the exposed gutter.

Not until days later, after Foxy had survived the forty-eight hours alone in the house with Toby and the test of Ken's return from Chicago, did Piet learn, not from Freddy but from her as told to her by Freddy, that at the moment of anesthesia she had panicked; she had tried to strike the Negress pressing the sweet, sweet mask to her face and through the first waves of ether had continued to cry that she should go home, that she was supposed to have this baby, that the child's father was coming to smash the door down with a hammer and would stop them.

After she confessed this to him over the phone on Monday, his silence stretched so long she laughed to break it. "Don't take it upon yourself that you didn't come break down the door. I didn't want you to. It was my subconscious speaking, and only after I had consciously got myself to the point of no return, and I could relax. What we did was right. We couldn't do anything else, could we?"

"I couldn't think of anything else."

"We were very lucky to have brought it off. We ought to thank our, what?—our lucky stars." She laughed again, a perfunctory rustle in the apparatus.

Piet asked her, "Are you depressed?"

"Yes. Of course. Not because I've committed any sin so much, since it was what you asked me to do, what had to be done for everybody's sake, really. But because now I'm faced with it again, *really* faced with it now."

"With what?"

"My life. Ken, this cold house. The loss of your love. Oh, and my milk's dried up, so I have that to feel sorry for myself about. Toby keeps throwing up his formula. And Cotton's gone."

"Cotton."

"My cat. Don't you remember him?"

"Of course. He always greeted me."

"He was here Wednesday morning catching field mice on the edge of the marsh and when I came back that night he was gone. I didn't even notice. Thursday I began to call, but I was too weak to go outdoors much."

Piet said, "He's out courting."

"*No*," Foxy said, "he was fixed," and the receiver was rhythmically scraped by her sobs.

He asked her, "Why didn't you talk to me more, before we did it?"

"I was angry, which I suppose is the same as being frightened. And what did we have to say? We'd said it. You were too chicken to let me have it as if it were Ken's, and I've always known I could never get you away from Angela. No, don't argue."

He was obediently silent.

She said, "But what now, Piet? What shall we expect of each other?"

He answered, after thought, "Not much."

"It's easier for you," she said. "You'll always have somebody else to move on to. Don't deny it. Me, I seem stuck. You want to know something horrible?"

"If you'd like to tell it."

"I can't stand Ken now. I can hardly bear to look at his face, or answer when he talks. I think of it as *him* who made me kill my baby. It's *just* the kind of thing he'd do."

"Sweet, it wasn't him, it was *me*."

Foxy explained to him, what he had heard often before, how Ken, in denying her a child for seven years, had killed in her something only another man could revive. She ended by asking, "Piet, will you ever come talk to me? Just talk?"

"Do you think we should?"

"Should, shouldn't. Of course we shouldn't. But I'm down, lover, I'm just terribly, terribly down." She pronounced these words with a stagy lassitude learned from the movies. The script called for her to hang up, and she did. Losing another dime, he dialed her number from the booth, the booth in front of Poirier's Liquor Mart, where one of their friends might all too likely spot him, a droll corpse upright in a bright aluminum coffin. At Foxy's house, no one answered. Of course he must go to her. Death, once invited in, leaves his muddy bootprints everywhere.

Georgene, faithful to Freddy's orders, came calling on Foxy that Monday, around noon, and was shocked to see Piet's pick-up truck parked in the driveway. She felt a bargain had not been kept. Her understanding had been that the abortion would end Foxy's hold over Piet; she believed that once Foxy was eliminated her own usefulness to Piet would reassert itself. She prided herself, Georgene, on being useful, on keeping her bargains and carrying out the assignments given her, whether it was obtaining a guest speaker for the League of Women Voters, or holding her service in a tennis match, or staying married to Freddy Thorne. She had visited Foxy late Wednesday night, twice on Thursday, and once on Friday. She had carried tea and toast up to the convalescent, changed Toby's spicy orange diapers, and seen two baskets of clothes and sheets through the washer and dryer. On Friday she had spent over an hour vacuuming the downstairs and tidying toward Ken's return. Her feelings toward Foxy altered in these days of domestic conspiracy. Georgene, from her first glimpse, a year ago at the Applebys' party, of this prissy queenly newcomer, had disliked her; when Foxy stole Piet from her this dislike became hatred, with its implication of respect. But with the younger woman at her mercy Georgene allowed herself tenderness. She saw in Foxy a woman destined to dare and to suffer, a younger sister spared any compulsion to settle cheap, whose very mistakes were obscurely enviable. She was impressed with Foxy's dignity. Foxy did not deny that in this painful interregnum she needed help and company, nor did she attempt to twist Georgene's providing it into an occasion for protestation, or scorn, or confession, or self-contempt. Georgene knew from living with Freddy how surely self-contempt becomes contempt for others and was pleased to have her presence in Foxy's house accepted for what it was, an accident. Wednesday night, Foxy dismissed her with the grave tact of a child assuring a parent she is not afraid of the dark. She was weepy and half-drugged and clutched her living baby to her like a doll, yet from a deep reserve of manners thanked Georgene for coming, permitted her bloody bedsheets to be changed, accepted the injunction not to go up and down stairs, nodded gravely when told to call the Thornes' number at any hour, for any reason, even senseless fright. Thursday morning, Georgene found her downstairs, pale from lack of sleep; she had been unable to breast-feed the baby and had had to come downstairs to heat up a bottle. Obedient, she had not attempted the return trip upstairs, and with one blanket had made a bed for them both on the sofa. Imagining those long moon-flooded hours, the telephone offering a tempting release from solitude, Georgene secretly admired the other's courage and pride. She helped her upstairs and felt leaning upon her, naked under its robe and slip, the taller, less supple, rather cool and dry and ungainly body her lover had loved. Imagined love flowed from her. The current was timidly returned. They were silent in unison. They moved together, in these few days, whose weather outside was a humid raw foretaste of spring less comfortable than outright winter, through room upon room of tactful silence. They did not speak of Piet or of Freddy or of the circumstances that had brought them together except as they were implied by Georgene's inquiries into Foxy's physical condition. They discussed health and housework and the weather outside and the needs of the infant. Friday afternoon, the last day Georgene was needed, she brought along little Judy, and in the festive atmosphere of recovery Foxy, now fully clothed, served cookies and vermouth and persuaded Georgene, after her exertions of cleaning, to smoke an unaccustomed cigarette. Awkwardly they lifted their glasses as if to toast one another: two women who had tidied up after a mess.

Georgene had not been asked to return on Monday. But she was curious to know how Foxy had weathered the weekend, had put off Ken. She would ask if Foxy needed any shopping done. Seeing Piet's truck in the driveway, she experienced a compounded jealousy, a multiple destruction within her: the first loss was her tender comradeship with the other woman. Of Piet she expected nothing except that he continue to exist and unwittingly illumine her life. She had willed herself open to him and knew that the chemistry of love was all within her, her doing. Even his power to wound her with neglect was a power she had created and granted; whatever he did he could not escape the province of her freedom, her free decision to love. Whereas between her and Foxy a polity existed: rules, a complex set of assumed concessions, a generous bargain posited upon the presumption of defeat. Georgene seldom visited the middle ground between female submission and sexless mastery, so her negotiated fondness for Foxy was rarer for her, more precious perhaps, than her love for Piet, which was predetermined and unchanging and somewhat stolid. Foxy's betrayal found her vulnerable. She was revealed to herself as not merely helpless but foolish. Helplessness has its sensual consolations; foolishness has none. She pushed through the door without knocking.

Piet and Foxy were sitting well apart, on opposite sides of the coffee table. Piet had not removed the zippered apricot suède windbreaker he wore to jobs, and the stub of a yellow pencil was tucked behind his ear. The morning marsh light struck white fire from the hem of Foxy's frilled nightie and froze into ice her pale hand holding a cigarette from which spiraled smoke sculptural as blue stone. Coffee equipment mixed arcs of china and metal and sun on the low teak table between them. Georgene felt she had entered upon a silence. Her indignation was balked by her failure to surprise them embracing. Nevertheless, Piet was embarrassed, and half rose.

"Don't get up," Georgene told him. "I don't mean to interrupt your cozy tryst."

"It wasn't," he told her.

"Just a meeting of souls. How beautiful." She turned to Foxy. "I came to offer to do your shopping and to see how you were doing. I see you're back to normal and won't be needing me any more. Good."

"Don't take that tone, Georgene. I was just telling Piet, how wonderful you were."

"*He* wasn't telling *you*? I'm hurt."

"Why are you angry? Don't you think Piet and I have a right to talk?"

Piet moved forward on his chair, grunting, "I'll go."

Foxy said, "You certainly will not. You just got here. Georgene, have some coffee. Let's stop playing charades."

Georgene refused to sit. "Please don't imagine," she said, "that I have personal feelings about this. It's none of my business what you two do, or rather it wouldn't be if my husband hadn't saved your necks at the risk of his own. But I *will* say, for your own good, unless you're planning to elope, it is very sloppy to have Piet's pick-up truck out where Marcia could drive by any minute."

"Marcia's at her psychiatrist in Brookline," Foxy said. "She's gone every day from ten to two, or longer, if she has lunch with Frank in town."

Piet said, wanting to have a conversation, a party, "Is Marcia going too? Angela's just started."

Georgene asked him, "How on earth can *you* afford it?"

"I can't," he said. "But Daddy Hamilton can. It's something the two of them cooked up."

"And what were you two cooking up, when I barged in?"

"Nothing," Piet told her. "In fact we were having some trouble finding things to say."

Foxy asked, "Why shouldn't I talk to the father of my child?"

Piet said, "It wasn't a child, it was a little fish, less than a fish. It was nothing, Fox."

"It was *something*, damn you. You weren't carrying it."

Georgene was jealous of their quarrel, their display of proud hearts. She and Freddy rarely quarreled. They went to sleep on one another, and kept going to parties together, and felt dreary all next day, like veteran invalids. Only Piet had brought her word of a world where vegetation was heraldic and every woman was some man's queen. That world was like, she thought, the marsh seen through the windows, where grasses prospered in salty mud that would kill her kind of useful plant. "I honestly think," she heard herself saying, "that one of you ought to move out of Tarbox."

They were amazed, amused. Foxy asked, "Whatever for?"

"For your own good. For everybody's good. You're poisoning the air."

"If any air's been poisoned," Piet told her, "it's your husband that's done it. He's the local gamesmaster."

"Freddy just wants to be human. He knows you all think he's ridiculous so he's adopted that as his act. Anyway, I didn't mean poison. Maybe the rest of us are poisoned and you two upset us with your innocence. Think of just yourselves. Piet, look at her. Why do you want to keep tormenting her with your presence? Make her take her husband back to Cambridge. Quit Gallagher and go somewhere else, go back to Michigan. You'll destroy each other. I was with her at the end of last week. It's not a little thing you put her through."

Foxy cut in dryly. "It was my decision. I'm grateful for your help, Georgene, but I would have gotten through alone. And we would have found a way without Freddy, though that *did* work out. As to Piet and me, we have no intention of sleeping together again. I think you're saying you still want him. Take him."

"That's *not* what I'm saying! Not at all!" There had been some selfless point, some public-spirited truth she had been trying to frame for these two, and they were too corrupt to listen.

Piet said, joking, "I feel I'm being auctioned off. Should we let Angela bid too?"

He was amused. They were both amused. Georgene had entertained them, made them vivid to themselves. Watching her tremblingly try to manage her coffee cup, a clumsy intruder, they were lordly, in perfect control. Having coaxed the abortion from their inferiors, they were quite safe, and would always exist for each other. Their faces were pleasant in sunlight, complacent in the same way, like animals that have eaten.

Georgene took a scalding sip of coffee and replaced the cup in its socket on the saucer and sat primly upright. "I don't know what I'm trying to say," she apologized. "I'm delighted, Foxy, to see you so happy. Frankly, I think you're a very gutsy girl."

"I'm *not* happy," Foxy said, protesting, sensing danger.

"Well, happier. I am too. I'm *so* glad spring is here, it's been a long winter up on my hill. The crocuses, Piet, are up beside the garage. When can we all start playing tennis?" She stood; there was no coat to slow her departure. On all but the coldest days of winter, Georgene wore no more than a skirt and sweater and a collegiate knit scarf. It was warming, on a January afternoon when the sun had slipped through a crack in the sky, to see her downtown dressed as if for a dazzling fall afternoon, leading snowsuited Judy over hummocks of ice, hurrying along full of resolution and inner fire.

Town meeting that spring smelled of whiskey. Piet noticed the odor as soon as he entered the new high-school auditorium, where orange plastic chairs designed to interlock covered the basketball floor solidly between the bleachers and the stage, beneath the high fluorescent emptiness hung with cables and gymnastic riggings. A few feet above the swamp of faces hovered a glimmering miasma of alcohol, of amber whiskey, of martinis hurriedly swallowed between train and dinner, with the babysitter imminent. Piet had never noticed the scent before and wondered if it were the warm night— a thawing fog had rolled in from the sea and suddenly dandelions dotted the football field—or if the town had changed. Each year there were more commuters, more young families with VW buses and Cézanne prints moving into developments miles distant from the heart of historical Tarbox. Each year, in town meeting, more self-assured young men rose to speak, and silent were the voices dominant when Piet and Angela moved to town—droning Yankee druggists, paranoid clammers, potbellied selectmen ponderously fending off antagonisms their fathers had incurred, a nearsighted hound-faced moderator who recognized only his friends and ruled all but deafening dissents into unanimity. At the first meeting Piet had attended, the town employees, a shirtsleeved bloc of ex-athletes who perched in the bleachers apart from their wives, had hooted down the elderly town attorney, Gertrude Tarbox's brother-in-law, until the old man's threadbare voice had torn and the microphone had amplified the whisper of a sob. Now the employees, jacketed, scattered, sat mute and sullen with their wives as year after year another raise was unprotestingly voted them. Now the town attorney was an urbane junior partner in a State Street firm who had taken the job as a hobby, and the moderator a rabbit-eared associate professor of sociology, a

maestro of parliamentary procedure. Only an occasional issue
evocative of the town's rural past—the purchase of an old barn
abutting the public parking lot, or the plea of a farmer, a fabulous creature with frost-burned face and slow tumbling voice,
that he be allowed to reap his winter rye before an S-curve
in the Mather road was straightened—provoked debate. New
schools and new highways, sewer bonds and zoning by-laws
all smoothly slid by, greased by federal grants. Each modern-
ization and restriction presented itself as part of the national
necessity, the overarching honor of an imperial nation. The
last opponents, the phlegmatic pennypinchers and choleric
naysayers who had absurdly blocked the building of this new
school for a decade, had died or ceased to attend, leaving the
business of the town to be carried forward in an edifice whose
glass roof leaked and whose adjustable partitions had ceased
to adjust. There was annual talk now of representative town
meeting, and the quorum had been halved. Among Piet's
friends, Harold little-Smith was on the Finance Committee,
Frank Appleby was chairman of the committee to negotiate
with the Commonwealth for taxpayer-subsidized commuter
service, Irene Saltz was chairlady of the Conservation Commission (and charmingly coupled her report with her resignation,
since she and her husband were with sincere regret moving to
Cleveland), and Matt Gallagher sat on the Board of Zoning
Appeals. Indeed, there was no reason why Matt, if he believed
the hint of the Polish priest, could not be elected selectman;
and Georgene Thorne had narrowly missed—by the margin of
a whiff of scandal—election to the school board.

Politics bored Piet. The Dutch in his home region had been
excluded from, and had disdained, local power. His family had
been Republican under the impression that it was the party
of anarchy; they had felt government to be an illusion the
governed should not encourage. The world of politics had no
more substance for Piet than the film world, and the meeting of which he was a member made him as uncomfortable as
the talent auditions at a country fair, where faces strained by
stolen mannerisms lift in hope toward wholly imagined stars.
Piet went to town meetings to see his friends, but tonight,
though the Hanemas had arrived early, it happened that no
one sat with them. The Applesmiths and Saltzes sat up front

with the politically active. On the stage, as observers, not yet citizens, sat the young Reinhardts, whom Piet detested. The Guerins and Thornes had entered and found seats by the far doors and Piet never managed to catch either woman's eye. Bernadette Ong and Carol Constantine came late, together, without husbands. Most strangely, the Whitmans did not attend at all, though they had now lived in Tarbox long enough to be voting citizens. At Piet's side Angela, who had to rush into Cambridge after nursery school every day and then fight the commuter traffic home, was exhausted, and kept nodding and twitching, yet as a loyal liberal insisted on staying to add her drowsy "Ayes" to the others. The train service proposal, at the annual estimated budget cost of twelve thousand dollars, on the argument that the type of people attracted to Tarbox by creditable commuter service would enrich the community inestimably, unanimously passed. The self-righteous efficiency of the meeting, hazed by booze, so irritated Piet, so threatened his instinct for freedom, that he several times left the unanimous crowd to get a drink of water at the bubbler in the hall, where he imagined that the town building inspector evaded his gaze and refused to return his hello. When the meeting, after eleven, was adjourned, he saw the other couples huddling by an exit, planning a drink at one of their homes. Harold's eager profile jabbered; Bea slowly, dreamily nodded. Angela mocked Piet's premonition of exclusion and said she wanted to go home and sleep. Before psychiatry, she would have equivocated. Piet could only yield. In the car he asked her, "Are you dead?"

"A little. All those right-of-ways and one-foot strips of land gave me a headache. Why can't they just do it in Town Hall and not torment us?"

"How did psychiatry go?"

"Not very excitingly. I felt tired and stupid and didn't know why I was there."

"Don't ask *me* why you're there."

"I wasn't."

"What do the two of you talk about?"

"Just *I'm* supposed to talk. He listens."

"And never says anything?"

"Ideally."

"Do you talk about me? How I made you sleep with Freddy Thorne?"

"We did at first. But now we're on my parents. Daddy mostly. Last Thursday it came out, just popped out of my mouth, that he always undressed in the closet. I hadn't thought about it for years. If I was in their bedroom about something, he'd come out of the closet with his pajamas on. The only way I could see him *really* was by spying on him in the bathroom."

"You spied. Angel."

"I know, it made me blush to remember it. But it made me *mad*, too. Whenever he'd be in there he'd turn on both faucets so we couldn't hear him do anything."

We: Louise, her seldom-seen sister, a smudged carbon copy, two years younger, lived in Vermont, husband teaching at a prep school. Louise married early, not the rare beauty Angela was, smudged mouth and unclear skin, probably better in bed, dirtier. He thought of Joop. His pale blond brother, flaxen hair, watery eyes, younger, purer, had carried on the greenhouse, should have married Angela, the two of them living together in receding light. Leaving him dirty Louise. Piet asked, "Did Louise ever see his penis? Did you and she ever talk about it?"

"Not really. We were terribly inhibited, I suppose, though Mother was always talking about how glorious Nature was, with that funny emphasis, and the house was full of art books. Michelangelo's, the ones on Adam, are terribly darling and limp, with long foreskins, so when I saw you, I thought—"

"What did you think?"

"I'll try to work it out with *him* what I thought."

The Nun's Bay Road was, since it had been widened, unlike the beach road, straight and rather bare, more like a Midwestern road, sparsely populated by a shuttered-up vegetable stand and, high on a knoll, a peeling gingerbread mansion with a single upstairs light burning, where a widower lived. Joop had had more Mama's eyes and mouth. Washed-out, unquestioning, shattered. He felt Angela beginning to doze and said, "I wonder if I ever saw my mother naked. Neither of them ever seemed to take a bath, at least while I was awake. I didn't think they knew a thing about sex and was shocked once when my mother in passing complained about the spots on my sheets.

She wasn't really scolding, it was almost kidding. That must have been what shocked me."

"The one good thing Daddy did," Angela answered, "was to tell us to stand up straight when we began to get breasts. It made him furious to see us hunch over."

"You were ashamed of them?"

"Not ashamed so much, it just feels at first as if you can't *manage* them. They stick out and wobble."

Piet pictured Angela's breasts and told her, "I'm very hurt, that you talk about your father when I thought *I* was your problem. To be sure, he *is* the one paying for it."

"Why does that make you so angry? He has money and we don't."

The wheels of their car, her cream-colored Peugeot, crunched on gravel. They were home. Squares of windowlight transfixed shrubbery in misted crosshatch. The lawn felt muddy underfoot, a loose skin of thaw on winter's body. A maple sapling that had taken root near the porch, in the bulb bed, extended last summer's growth in glistening straight shoots red as thermometer mercury. Beside the black chimney the blurred moon looked warm. Gratefully Piet inhaled the moist night. His year of trouble felt vaporized, dismissed.

Their babysitter was Merissa Mills, the teen-age daughter of the ringleader of the old boatyard crowd, who years ago had divorced his wife and moved to Florida, where he managed a marina and had remarried. Merissa, as often with children of broken homes, was determinedly tranquil and polite and conventional. She said, "There was one call, from a Mr. Whitman. I wrote down the number." On a yellow pad of Gallagher & Hanema receipt forms her round bland hand had penciled Foxy's number.

Piet asked, "*Mr.* Whitman?"

Merissa, gathering her books, gazed at him without curiosity. Her life had witnessed a turmoil of guilt she was determined not to relive. "He said you should call him no matter how late you got back."

"He can't have meant *this* late," Angela told Piet. "You take Merissa home and I'll call Foxy in the morning."

"No!" In sudden focus Piet saw the two women before him as identical—both schooled prematurely in virtue, both secluded behind a willed composure. He knew they were screening him from something out there in the dark that was his, his fate, the fruit of his deeds. His tongue streaked tranced down the narrow path still open. "We may still need Merissa. Let me call Ken before we let her go."

Angela protested, "Merissa has school tomorrow and I'm exhausted." But her voice lacked fiber; he walked through it to the phone, his palms tingling. His movements, as he picked up the receiver and dialed, were as careful as those of a leper whose flesh falls off in silver shards.

Ken answered on the second ring. "Piet," he said. It was not said as a greeting; Ken was giving something a name.

"Ken."

"Foxy and I have had a long talk."

"What about?"

"The two of you."

"Oh?"

"Yes. Do you deny that you and she have been lovers since last summer?"

Ken's silence lengthened. An impatient doctor faced with a procrastinating hope. Piet saw that there was no glimmer, that the truth had escaped and was all about them, like oxygen, like darkness. As a dying man after months of ingenious forestallment turns with relief to the hope of an afterlife, Piet sighed, "No, I don't deny it."

"Good. That's a step forward."

Angela's face, forsaken, pressed wordless against the side of Piet's vision as he listened.

"She also told me that she became pregnant by you this winter and you arranged to have the pregnancy aborted while I was in Chicago."

"Did she though? While you were in the Windy City?" Piet felt before him an adamant flatness upon which his urge was to dance.

"Is that true or false?" Ken persisted.

Piet said, "Tell me the rules of this quiz. Can I win, or only lose?"

Ken paused. Angela's face, as something of what was happening dawned on it, grew pale, and anxiously mouthed the silent syllable, *Who?*

Less disciplinary, a shade concessive, Ken said, "Piet, I think the best thing would be for you and Angela to come over here tonight."

"She's awfully tired."

"Could you put her on the phone, please?"

"No. We'll come over." Hanging up, he faced the rectangle of slightly darker wallpaper where until recently a mirror had hung. Angela had transferred it to Nancy's room because the child expressed jealousy of her father's birthday gift of a mirror to Ruth. He told Angela, "We must go," and asked Merissa, "Can you stay?" Both acquiesced; he had gained, in those few seconds over the phone, the forbidding dignity of those who have no lower to go. His face was a mask while his blood underwent an airy tumult, a boiling alternation of shame and fear momentarily condensing into those small actions—a sticky latch lifted, a pocket-slapping search for car keys, a smile of farewell at Merissa and a promise not to be long—needed to get them out of the house, into the mist, on their way.

By way of Blackberry Lane, a winding link road tenderly corrupted from Nigger Lane, where a solitary escaped slave had lived in the days of Daniel Webster, dying at last of loneliness and pneumonia, the distance from the Hanemas' house to the Whitmans was not great. Often in summer Piet after his afternoon's work would drive his daughters to the beach for a swim and be back by supper. So Piet and Angela had little time to talk; Angela spoke quickly, lightly, skimming the spaces between what she had overheard or guessed. "How long has it been going on?"

"Oh, since the summer. I think her hiring me for the job was a way of seeing if it would happen."

"It occurred to me, but I thought you wouldn't use your work like that, I thought it was beneath your ethics to. Deceive me, yes, but your men, and Gallagher . . ."

"I did a respectable job for her. We didn't sleep together until toward the end. It was after the job was done, when I had no reason to have my truck parked there, that it began to seem not right."

"Oh, it did seem not right?"

"Sure. It became very heavy. Religious, somehow, and sad.

She was so pregnant." It pleased Piet to be able to talk about it, as if under this other form he had been secretly loving Angela, and now could reveal to her the height and depth of his love.

She said, "Yes, that is the surprise. Her being pregnant. It must be very hard for Ken to accept."

Piet shrugged. "It was part of her. I didn't mind it if she didn't. Actually, it made it seem more innocent, as if that much of her was being faithful to Ken no matter what we did with the rest."

"How many times did you sleep with her in all?"

"Oh. Thirty. Forty."

"Forty!"

"You asked." She was crying. He told her, "Don't cry."

"I'm crying because you seemed happier lately and I thought it was *me* and it's been *her*."

"No, it hasn't been her." He felt under him a soft place, a hidden pit, the fact of Bea.

"No? When was the last time?"

The abortion. She mustn't know. But it was too big to hide, like a tree. In its shade the ground was suspiciously bare. He said, "Months ago. We agreed it would be the last time."

"But after the baby had been born?"

"Yes. Six or so weeks after. I was surprised she still wanted me."

"You're so modest." Her tone was empty of irony, dead. A mailbox knocked cockeyed, toppling backwards forever, wheeled through their headlights. Ghosts of mist thronged from the marshes where the road dipped. Angela asked, "Why did you stop?"

Having withheld truth elsewhere, Piet lavished frankness here. "It began to hurt more than it helped. I was becoming cruel to you, and I couldn't *see* the girls; they seemed to be growing up without me. Then, with her baby, it's being a boy, it seemed somehow clear that our time was past." He further explained: "A time to love, and a time to die."

Her crying had dried up but showed in her voice as a worn place, eroded. "You did love her?"

He tried to tread precisely here; their talk had moved from a thick deceptive forest to a desert where every step left a print. He told her, "I'm not sure I understand the term. I enjoyed being with her, yes."

"And you also enjoyed Georgene?"

"Yes. Less complexly. She was less demanding. Foxy was always trying to educate me."

"And any others?"

"No." The lie lasted as they dipped into the last hollow before the Whitmans' little rise.

"And me? Have you ever enjoyed being with me?" The desert had changed; the even sand of her voice had become seared rock, once molten, sharp to the touch.

"Oh," Piet said, "Jesus, yes. Being with you is Heaven." He hurried on, having decided. "One thing you should know, since Ken knows it. At the end, after I figured our affair was over, Foxy got pregnant by me, don't ask me how, it was ridiculous, and we got Freddy Thorne to arrange our abortion for us. His price was that night with you. It sounds awful, but it was the only thing, it was great of you, and it absolutely ended Foxy and me. It's done. It's over. We're just here tonight so I can get reprimanded."

They were at the Whitmans'. With the motor extinguished, Angela's not answering alarmed him. Her voice when it came sounded miniature, dwindled, terminal. "You better take me home."

"Don't be silly," he said. "You *must* come in." He justified his imperious tone: "I don't have the guts to go in without you."

Ken answered their ring. He wore a foulard and smoking jacket: the host. He shook Piet's hand gravely, glancing at him from those shallow gray eyes as if taking a snapshot. He welcomed Angela with a solicitude bordering on flirtation. His man's voice and shoulders filled comfortably spaces where Foxy alone had seemed adrift and forlorn. He took their coats, Angela's blue second-best and Piet's little apricot jacket, and ushered the couple down the rag-rugged hall; Angela stared all about her, fascinated by how the house that should have been hers had been renovated. She murmured to Piet, "Did *you* choose the wallpaper?" Foxy was in the living room, feeding the baby in her lap. Unable to rise or speak in greeting, she grinned. Lit up by her smile, her teary face seemed to Piet a net full of gems; lamplight flowed down her loose hair to the faceless bundle in her lap. The array of bottles on the coffee table glittered. They had been drinking. In the society of Tarbox there was no invitation more flattering than to share, like this, another couple's intimacy, to partake in their humorous déshabille, their open quarrels and implicit griefs. It was hard for these couples this night to break from that informal spell and to confront each other as enemies. Angela took the old leather armchair, and Piet a rush-seat ladderback that Foxy's mother, appalled by how bleak their house seemed, had sent from Maryland. Ken remained standing and tried to run the meeting in an academic manner. Piet's itch was to clown, to seek the clown's traditional invisibility. Angela and Foxy, their crossed legs glossy, fed into the room that nurturing graciousness of female witnessing without which no act since Adam's naming of the beasts has been complete. Women are gentle fruitful presences whose interpolation among us diffuses guilt.

Ken asked them what they would like to drink. The smoking jacket a prop he must live up to. Outrage has no costume. Angela said, "Nothing."

Piet asked for something with gin in it. Since tonic season hadn't begun, perhaps some dry vermouth, about half and half, a European martini. Anything, just so it wasn't whiskey. He described the smell of whiskey at the town meeting, and was disappointed when no one laughed. Irked, he asked, "Ken, what's the first item on your agenda?"

Ken ignored him, asking Angela, "How much did you know of all this?"

"Ah," Piet said. "An oral exam."

Angela said, "I knew as much as you did. Nothing."

"You must have guessed something."

"I make a lot of guesses about Piet, but he's very slippery."

Piet said, "Agile, I would have said."

Ken did not take his eyes from Angela. "But you're in Tarbox all day; I'm away from seven to seven."

Angela shifted her weight forward, so the leather cushion sighed. "What are you suggesting, Ken? That I'm deficient as a wife?"

Foxy said, "One of the things that makes Angela a good wife to Piet, better than I could ever be, is that she lets herself be blind."

"Oh, I don't know about that," Angela said, preoccupied with, what her shifting in the chair had purposed, pouring herself some brandy. It was five-star Cognac but the only glass was a Flintstone jelly tumbler. Foxy's housekeeping had these lapses and loopholes. Admitted to her house late in the afternoon, Piet would see, through the blond rainbow of her embrace, breakfast dishes on the coffee table unwashed, and a book she had marked her place in with a dry bit of bacon. She claimed, when he pointed it out, that she had done it to amuse him; but he had also observed that her underwear was not always clean.

Unable to let Angela's mild demur pass unchallenged, she sat upright, jarring the sleeping bundle in her lap, and argued, "I mean it as a compliment. I think it's a beautiful trait. I could never be that way, the wise overlooking wife. I'm jealous by nature. It used to kill me, at parties, to see you come up with that possessive sweet smile and take Piet home to bed."

Piet winced. The trick was not to make it too real for Ken. Change the subject. A mild man innocently seeking information, he asked the other man, "How did you find out?"

"Somebody told him," Foxy interposed. "A woman. A jealous woman."

"Georgene," Piet said.

"Right," Foxy said.

Ken said, "No, it was Marcia little-Smith. She happened to ask me the other day downtown what work was still being done on the house, that Piet's truck was parked out front so often."

"Don't be ridiculous, that's what the two of them cooked up to say," Foxy told Piet. "Of course it was Georgene. I knew when she found us together last week she was going to do something vicious. She has no love in her life so she can't stand other people having any."

Piet disliked her slashing manner; he felt they owed the couple they had wronged a more chastened bearing. He accused her: "And then you told him everything."

The gems in her face burst their net. "Yes. Yes. Once I got started I couldn't stop. I'm sorry, for you, and then not. You've put me through hell, man."

Angela smiled toward Ken, over brandy. "They're fighting."

He answered, "That's their problem," and Piet, hearing the

unyielding tone, realized that Ken did not view the problem, as he did, as one equally shared, a four-sided encroachment and withdrawal. Ken's effort, he saw, would be to absolve, to precipitate, himself.

Angela, frightened, with Piet, of the other couple's rising hardness, inquired softly, her oval head tilted not quite toward Foxy, "Georgene found you together a week ago? Piet told me it was all over."

Foxy said, "He lied to you, sweet."

"I did *not*." Piet's face baked. "I came down here because you were miserable. We didn't make love, we hardly made conversation. We agreed that the abortion ended what should have been ended long ago. Clearly."

"Was it so clear?" Eyes downcast. Velvety mouth prim. He remembered that certain subtle slidiness of her lips. Her demeanor mixed surrender and defiance. Piet felt her fair body, seized by his eyes, as a plea not to be made to relive the humiliation of Peter.

Ken turned again on Angela. "How much *do* you know? Do you know the night of the Kennedy party they were necking in the upstairs bathroom? Do you know he was having both Georgene and Foxy for a while and that he has another woman now?"

"Who?"

Angela's quick question took both Whitmans aback; they looked at each other for a signal. Piet saw no sign from Foxy. Ken pronounced to Angela's face, "Bea."

"Dear Bea," Angela said, two fingertips circularly lingering on the brass stud second from the top along the outer edge of the left leather arm. Pain so aloofly suffered. The treachery of Lesbians. Dress in chitons and listen to poetry. Touch my arm. Hockey.

Piet interposed, "This is gossip. What evidence do you two have?"

"Never mind, Piet," Angela said aside.

Ken resumed the instructor's role; lamplight showed temples of professorial gray as he leaned over Angela. "You know about the abortion?" His face held a congestion his neat mouth wanted to vent. A pudgy studious boy who had been mocked at recess. *Never tease, Piet, never tease.*

Piet asked Foxy, "Why doesn't he lay off my wife?"

Angela nodded yes and with a graceful wave added, to Ken, "It seems to me they did that as much for you as for themselves. A cynical woman would have had the child and raised it as yours."

"Only if I were totally blind. I know what a Whitman looks like."

"You can tell just by listening," Piet said. "They begin to lecture at birth."

Ken turned to him. "Among the actions I'm considering is bringing criminal charges against Thorne. You'd be an accessory."

"For God's sake, why?" Piet asked. "That was probably the most Christian thing Freddy Thorne ever did. He didn't have to do it, he did it out of pity. Out of love, even."

"Love of who?"

"His *friends*." And Piet pronouncing this felt his heart vibrate with the nervousness of love, as if he and Freddy, the partition between them destroyed, at last comprehended each other with the fullness long desired, as almost had happened one night in the Constantines' dank foyer. Hate and love both seek to know.

Ken said, and something strange, a nasty puffing, an adolescent sneer, was afflicting his upper lip, "He did it because he likes to meddle. But that's neither here nor there. It's been done, and I see no way back through it."

Angela understood him first. She asked, "No way?"

Ken consented to her implication. "I've had it. To be technical: there are reactions that are reversible and those that aren't. This feels irreversible to me. Simple infidelity could be gotten around, even a prolonged affair, but with my *child* in her belly—"

"Oh, don't be so superstitious," Foxy interrupted.

"—and then this monstrous performance with Thorne . . ."

Angela asked him, "How can you judge? As Piet says, in context, it was the most merciful thing."

Piet told him, "She wrote me long letters, all summer, saying how much she loved you." But even as he pleaded he knew it was no use, and took satisfaction in this knowledge, for he was loyal to the God Who mercifully excuses us from pleading,

Who nails His joists of judgment down firm, and roofs the universe with order.

As Ken spoke, still standing above them like a tutor, his voice took on an adolescent hesitancy. "Let me try again. It's clear I don't count for much with any of you. But this has been quite a night for me, and I want to have my say."

"Hear, hear," Piet said. He waited happily to be crushed, and dismissed.

"In a sense," Ken went on, "I feel quite grateful and benevolent, because as a scientist I supposedly seek the truth, and tonight I've gotten it, and I want to be worthy of it. I don't want to shy from it."

Piet poured more gin for himself. Foxy blinked and jostled the baby; Angela sipped brandy and remained on the edge of the huge leather chair.

"In chemistry," Ken told them, "molecules have *bonds*; some compounds have strong bonds, and some have weaker ones, and though now with atomic valences we can explain why, originally it was all pragmatic. Now listening to my wife tonight, not only what she said, the astonishingly cold-blooded deceptions, but the joyful fullness with which she spilled it all out, I had to conclude we don't have much of a bond. We should, I think. We come from the same kind of people, we're both intelligent, we can stick to a plan, she stuck with me through a lot of what she tells me now were pretty dreary years. She told me, Piet, she had forgotten what love was until you came along. Don't say anything. Maybe I'm incapable of love. I've always assumed I loved her, felt what you're supposed to feel. I wanted her to have my child, when we had room for it, I gave her this house—"

Foxy interrupted, "You gave yourself this house."

Piet said, "Foxy."

Ken's hands, long-fingered and younger than his body, had been groping into diagrams on a plane in front of him; now they dropped rebuked to his sides. He turned to Piet and said, "See. No bond. Apparently you and she have it. More power to you."

"*Less* power to them, I would think," Angela interposed.

Ken looked at her surprised. He had thought he had been clear. "I'm divorcing her."

"You're not."

"Is he?"

Angela had spoken to Ken, then Piet to Foxy. She nodded, gems returning to her pink face, burning, eclipsing the attempted gaze of recognition, the confession of hopelessness, toward Piet. He was reminded of Nancy in the instant of equilibrium as she coped with the certain knowledge that she was going to cry, before her face toppled, broke like a vase, exposing the ululant tongue arched in agony on the floor of her mouth.

"If you divorce her, I'll have to marry her." Piet felt the sentence had escaped from him rather than been uttered. Was it a threat, a complaint, a promise?

Dryly Foxy said, "That's the most gracious proposal I've ever heard." But she had named it: a proposal.

"Oh, my God, my God," Angela cried. "I feel sick, sick."

"Stop saying things twice," Piet told her.

"He doesn't love her, he doesn't," Angela told Ken. "He's been trying to ditch her ever since summer."

Ken told Piet, "I don't know what you should do. I just know what *I* should do."

Piet pleaded, "You can't divorce her for something that's over. Look at her. She's repentant. She's confessed. That's your child she's holding. Take her away, beat her, leave Tarbox, go back to Cambridge with her, anything. But no reasonable man—"

Ken said, "I am nothing if not reasonable. I have legal grounds six times over."

"Stop being a lawyer's son for a second. Try to be human. The law is dead."

"The point of it is," Ken said, sitting down at last, "she's not repentant."

"Of *course* she is," Piet said. "*Look* at her. Ask her."

Ken asked gently, as if waking her from sleep, "Fox, are you? Repentant?"

She studied him with bold brown eyes and said, "I'll wash your feet and drink the water every night."

Ken turned to Piet, his experiment successful. "See? She mocks me."

Foxy stood tall, placed the infant on her shoulder, and

rapidly drummed its back. "I can't stand this," she announced, "being treated as a *thing*. Excuse me, Angela. I'm truly sorry for your grief, but these *men*. All this competitive self-pity." She paused by the doorway to retrieve a blanket from a chair, and in the motion of her stooping, in the silence of her leaving, Tobias burped.

At the little salutary hiccup, so portentously audible, Angela's shoulders jerked with laughter. She had hidden her face in her hands. Now she revealed it, as if, her own acolyte, she were reverently unfolding the side wings of a triptych. It was a face, Piet saw, lost to self-consciousness, an arrangement of apertures willing, like a sea anemone, to be fed by whatever washed over it. "I want to go home," she told Ken. "I'm tired, I want a bath. Is everything settled? You're going to divorce Foxy, and Piet's going to divorce me. Do you want to marry me, Ken?"

He responded with a gallantry that confirmed Piet in his suspicion, from infancy on, that the world was populated by people bigger and wiser, more graceful and less greedy, than he. Ken said, "You tempt me. I wish we had met years ago."

"Years ago," Angela said, "we would have been too busy being good children." She asked Piet, "How shall we do? Do you want to move out tonight?"

Piet told her, "Don't dramatize. Nothing is settled. I think we all need to get some daylight on this."

Ken asked, "Then you're already backing out on your offer?"

"What offer?"

Ken said, "Piet, there is something you should know about us, you and me, that for some reason, modern manners I suppose, I don't seem able to express, and that I don't think this discussion has made clear to you, from the way you're sitting there smiling. I hate your guts." It sounded false; he amended it, "I hate what you've done to me, what you've done to Foxy."

Piet thought Angela would defend him, at least vaguely protest; but her silence glided by.

Ken went on, "In less than a year you, you and this sick town, have torn apart everything my wife and I had put together in seven years. Behind all this playfulness you *like* to destroy. You love it. The Red-haired Avenger. You're enjoying this; you've *enjoyed* that girl's pain."

Bored with being chastised, Piet rebelled. He stood to tell Ken, "She's your wife, keep her in your bed. You had lost her before you began. A man with any self-respect wouldn't have married her on the rebound like you did. Don't blame me if flowers didn't grow in this"—at the mouth of the hall, following Angela out, he turned and with whirling arms indicated to Ken his house, the Cambridge furniture, the empty bassinet, mirroring windows, the sum of married years—"test tube." Pleased with his rebuttal, he waited to hear Angela agree but she had already slammed the screen door. Outside, in sudden moist air, he stepped sideways into the pruned lilacs and was stabbed beneath an eye, and wondered if he were drunk, and thus so elated.

The car hurtled through mist. Angela asked, "Was she that much better in bed than me?"

Piet answered, "She was different. She did some things you don't do, I think she values men higher than you do. She's more insecure, I'd say, than you, and probably somewhat masculine. Physically, there's more of *you* everywhere; she's tight and her responsiveness isn't as fully developed. She's young, as you once said."

The completeness of his answer, as if nothing else had convinced her that he had truly known the other woman, outraged Angela; she shrieked, and kneeled on the rubber car floor, and flailed her arms and head in the knobbed and metal-edged space, and tried to smother her own cries in the dusty car upholstery. He braked the Peugeot to a stop and walked around its ticking hood to her side and opened her door. As he pulled her out she felt disjointed, floppy as a drunk or a puppet. "Inhale," he said. The beach road dipped here, low to the marsh, and the mist was thick, suffused with a salinity that smelled eternal. Angela recovered her composure, apologized, tore up some wands of spring grass and pressed them against her eyelids. A pair of headlights slowly trundled toward them in the fog and halted.

A car door opened. Harold little-Smith's penetratingly tipped voice called, "All right there?"

"We're fine, thanks. Just enjoying the sea breeze."

"Oh, Piet. It's you. Who's that with you?"

"Angela."

"Hi," Angela called, to prove it.

Piet called to the others over the glistening car roof, "How was the party?"

Harold guiltily answered, "It wasn't a party, just a beer. *Un peu de bière.* Carol looked for you but you'd gone out the other exit."

"We couldn't have come, thanks anyway," Piet said, and asked, "Who's that with *you*?"

"Marcia. Of course."

"Why of course?"

Marcia's voice piped through the fog. "Cut it out, Piet. You're a dirty old man."

"You're a doll. Good night, all."

"Good night, Hanemas." The pair of red tail lights dwindled, dissolved. In the silence then was the sighing of the sea rising in the marsh channels, causing the salt grass to unbend and rustle and suck. Her shrieks had been animal, less than animal, the noise of a deranged mechanism. Piet could hardly believe that the world—the one-o'clock mist, the familiar geography of Tarbox—could reconstitute itself after such a shattering. But Merissa, as Angela thanked her and told a lie about their going out again ("Their baby was having colic and they panicked; it's their first, you know."), noncommittally gathered together her books, having been reading in the light of television. As Piet drove her home she exuded a perfume of tangerines and talked about the dreadful earthquake in Anchorage. Returning, he found his downstairs lights off and Angela upstairs in the bathtub. The veins in her breasts turquoise, the ghost of a tan distinct on her shoulders and thighs, she was lying all but immersed, idly soaping her pudenda. She scrubbed circularly and then stroked the oozy hair into random peaks and then shifted her body so that the water washed over her and erased the soap. Her breasts slopped and slid with the pearly-dirty water; her hair was pinned up in a psyche knot, exposing tenderly the nape of her neck.

Piet said, "Pardon me, but I must sit down. My stomach is a ball of acid."

"Help yourself. Don't mind me."

He opened himself to the toilet and a burning gush of relief mixed with the fascinating sight of her toes—scalded, rosy, kittenish nubs. Foxy had long prehensile toes; he had seen her one night at the Constantines' hold a pencil in her foot and write *Elizabeth* on the wall. He asked Angela, "How do you feel?"

"Desperate. If you'll pass me the razor, I'll slash my wrists."

"Don't say things like that." A second diarrheic rush, making him gasp, had postponed his answer an instant. Where could so much poison have come from? Did gin kill enzymes?

"Why not?" Angela rolled a quarter-turn. The water sloshed tidally. "That would save you all the nuisance of a divorce. I don't think my father's going to let me be very generous."

"Do you think"—a third, reduced rush—"there's going to be such a thing? I'm scared to death of that woman."

"I heard you propose to her."

"She made it seem that way. Frankly, I'd rather stay married to you."

"Maybe I'd rather not stay married to you."

"But who do you have to go to?"

"Nobody. Myself. Somehow you haven't let me be myself. All these parties you've made me go to and give so you could seduce the wives of all those dreary men."

He loved hearing her talk with such casual even truth; he loved agreeing with her, being her student. "They *are* dreary. I've figured out there are two kinds of jerks in this town, upper-middle-class jerks and lower-middle-class jerks. The upper went to college. My problem is, I'm sort of in the middle."

She asked, "What did you think of Ken?"

"I hated him. A real computer. Put in some data and out comes the verdict."

"I don't know," Angela said, moving her legs gently apart and together and apart in the water. "I think he showed more courage than any of us have."

"Talking about divorce? But he has no intention of divorcing her. All he cares about is frightening her and me and you and protecting his schoolboy honor."

"She didn't seem frightened to me. It's just what she wants. Why else would she tell him so much, all night?"

Now a coldness cut into his voided bowels. He wiped himself and flushed; the odor in the little room, of rotten cinnamon, embarrassed him before his wife. She held a washcloth to her face and moaned through it, "Oh God, oh my God."

He asked her, "Sweet, why?"

"I'll be so alone," she said. "You were the only person who ever tried to batter their way in to me."

"Roll over and I'll scrub your back." Her buttocks were red islands goose-bumped from heat. A slim bit of water between. Her back an animal brown horizontally nicked by the bra strap and starred by three dim scars where moles had been removed. "It won't happen," he told her, smoothly soaping, "it won't happen."

"I shouldn't even let you stay the night."

"Nothing will happen," he told her, making circles around and around her constellation of scars.

"But maybe something should happen," she told him, her voice small in submission to his lulling laving. But when he quit, and she stood in the tub, Angela was colossal: buckets of water fell from the troughs among her breasts and limbs and collapsed back into the tub. Her blue eyes seemed wild, her bare arms flailed with an odd uncoördination. Tears glazed her cheeks while steam fled her skin in the coolness of their eggshell bedroom. "Something *should* happen, Piet. You've abused me horribly. I've asked for it, sure, but that's my weakness and I've been indulging it."

"You're beginning to talk like your own psychiatrist."

"He says I have no self-respect and it's true. And neither do you. We were with two people tonight who have some and they rolled right through us."

"It was his inning. I've had mine."

"Oh, I can't *stand* you when your face gets that stretched look. That's the thing you don't know. How your face looked tonight. When you said you'd have to marry her, there was this incredible, I was stunned, happiness, as if every question ever had been answered for you."

"That can't be true. I don't want to marry her. I'd rather marry Bea Guerin. I'd rather marry Bernadette Ong."

"You've slept with Bernadette."

"Never. But she's bumped me and her husband's dying." He laughed. "Stop it, angel. This is grotesque. I have no desire to marry Foxy, I love you. Compared to you, she's such a bitch."

Her neck had elongated; though exactly her height, he felt he was looking up at her—her thoughtful pout so tense her nostrils were flared, the breasts over which she had defensively flung an arm. "You like bitches," she said. Another thought struck her: "Everybody we know must think I'm an absolute fool."

He calculated he must do something acrobatic. Having removed all his clothes but his Paisley shorts, Piet threw himself on his knees and wrapped his arms around her thighs. The hearth-bricks were cold, her body still steamy; she protestingly pushed down on his head, blocking an amorous rise. Her vulva a roseate brown. Parchment. Egypt. Lotus. "Don't make me leave you," he begged. "You're what guards my soul. I'll be damned eternally."

"It'll do you good," she said, still pushing down on his head. "It'll do Foxy good too. You're right, Ken is not sexually appealing. I tried to get the hots for him tonight and there was nothing, not a spark."

"God, don't joke," he said. "Think of the girls."

"They'll be fine with me."

"They'll suffer."

"You used to say they should suffer. How else can they learn to be good? Stop nibbling me."

Embarrassed, he got to his feet. Standing two feet from her, he removed his undershorts. He was tumescent. "God," he said, "I'd love to clobber you."

She dropped her arm; her breasts swung free, livid and delicate as wounds. "Of course you would," she said, confirmed.

His fist jerked; she flinched and aloofly waited.

Through the April that followed this night, Piet had many conversations, as if the town, sensing he was doomed, were hurrying to have its last say in his ear. Freddy Thorne stopped him one rainy day on Divinity Street, as Piet with hammer and level was leaving the Tarbox Professional Apartments, once Gertrude Tarbox's shuttered hermitage. "Hey," Freddy said, "what have you done to me? I just got a paranoid letter from Ken Whitman about the, you know, the little pelvic orthodonture we performed. He said he had decided not to take legal action at the present time, but, cough, cough, reserved the intention to do so. The whole thing was psychopathically formal. He cited four laws I had broken chapter and verse, with the maximum penalties all neatly typed out. He's anal as hell. Wha' hoppen, Handlebar?"

Piet, who lived now day and night behind glassy walls of fear, clinging each evening to the silence of the telephone and to Angela's stony sufferance, while his children watched wide-eyed and whimpered in their sleep, was pleased to feel that at least he had been redeemed from Freddy Thorne's spell; the old loathing and fascination were gone. Freddy's atheism, his evangelical humanism, no longer threatened Piet; the dentist materialized in the drizzle as a plump fuzzy-minded man with a squint and an old woman's sly mouth. A backwards jacket peeked white under his raincoat. If any emotion, Piet felt fondness, the fondness a woman might feel toward her priest or gynecologist or lover—someone who has accepted her worst. Piet decided not to tell him that Georgene had betrayed them to Ken; he owed the Thornes that much. He said instead, "Foxy broke under the tension and blurted it all out to him the night of town meeting."

And he described briefly the subsequent confrontation of the two couples.

"The old mousetrap play," Freddy said. "She wants you bad, boy."

"Come on, she was hysterical. She couldn't stop crying."

Freddy's lips bit inward wisely. "When that golden-haired swinger has hysterics," he said, "it's because she's punched the release button herself. You've been had, friend. Good luck."

"How worried about Whitman are you?"

"Semi-semi. He's not going to press anything, with Little Miss Vulpes pulling the strings."

"Freddy," Piet said, "you live in a fantasy world of powerful women. I haven't heard from her since. In fact, I'm worried. Could you possibly send Georgene down to see how things are?"

"I think Georgene's errand days are over," Freddy said. "She really blew up after finding you and Foxtrot together; I had a vicious creature on my hands for a few days. The less you and she see each other, the better we'll all be. Keerect?"

"Is that why we're not being invited to parties any more?"

"What parties?"

Georgene phoned him Friday afternoon, while he was leafing through Sweet's Light Construction Catalogue File, looking for flanged sheathing. Two of the houses on Indian Hill had complained about leaks last winter, and Piet wanted to improve the new houses, whose foundations were already being excavated. Gallagher sat listening in his cubbyhole, but Piet let Georgene talk. Her clubwoman's quick enunciation, and the weather outside hinting of tennis and sunporches again, made him sentimental and regretful. He could see larches leaning, remembered the way the inside tendons of her thighs cupped and her pupils contracted as her eyelids widened and how afterwards she would tell him he gave her her shape. "Piet," she said, in syllables from which all roughnesses of love and innuendo had been burred, leaving a smooth brisk sister, "I drove down to the Whitmans today, Freddy mentioned you were worried, and there's nobody there. It doesn't look as if anybody has been there for a while. Four newspapers are bunched up inside the storm door."

"Does Marcia know anything?"

"She says there hasn't been a car in the drive since Tuesday."

"Did you look inside a window?" The open oven. The gobbled sleeping pills. The hallway where a lightbulb has died above a pair of ankles.

"Everything looked neat, as if they had tidied up before going away. I didn't see the bassinet."

"Have you talked to Carol or Terry? Somebody must have the answer. People just don't vanish."

"Easy, dollink, don't panic, you're not God. You can't protect the Whitmans from what they want to do to each other."

"Thanks. Thanks for the pep talk. And thanks a bushel for telling Whitman in the first place."

"I told him almost nothing. I admit I did, more or less maliciously, ask him why your truck was parked down there, but then he jumped all over me with questions, he was really hungry for it. Clearly he had half guessed. I *am* sorry, though. But, Piet—are you listening?—it made me mad the way I came in there that Monday all anxious to be Sue Barton and somehow I was turned into the cleaning lady who invites herself to tea."

He sighed. "OK, forget it. Truth will out, it may be best. You're a good woman. A loyal wife and dutiful mother."

"Piet—I wasn't right for you, was I? I thought we were so good, but we weren't?"

"You were a gorgeous piece of ass," he told her patiently. "You were too good. You made it seem too easy and right for my warped nature. Please forgive me," he added, "if I ever hurt you. I never meant to."

It was Gallagher, of all people, who had the answer. Having overheard this conversation, he called Piet into his inner office, and there, as the late light died in measured segments, without turning on a lamp, so his broad-jawed pentagonal face became a murmuring blur, told Piet of a strange scene. Early Tuesday morning, earlier than the milk, Ken Whitman had appeared at their house. He was soaked and rumpled and sandy; he had spent the night walking the beach in the mist and had taken a cramped nap in his MG. Silent, Piet guiltily remembered how Monday night he had slept warm beside Angela, as soundly as the just, amid irrelevant dreams about flying. Ken explained himself. He had come to the Gallaghers because Matt was the one man in Tarbox he could respect, the only one "uninvolved." Also Terry, he tried to say, could understand Foxy, perhaps. What did he mean? Were they alike? They were both "proud." Here Matt hesitated, caught in private considerations, or debating with himself how much Piet should be told. But having commenced, his Irish blood demanded the tale should continue fully. Piet pictured that early-morning kitchen, the postcard print of Dürer's praying hands framed above the stainless-steel sink, Terry's rough bright tablecloth and the bowls she had clumsily turned, three drowsy mouths sipping coffee, and heard himself being discussed, deplored, blamed. Ken asked them what he should do. Both of course told him to go back to Foxy; he loved her, they had a son now to think of, they were a handsome couple. Everybody, Terry said, lapses—or is tempted to. Piet suspected Matt had added the qualification in his own mind. But they found Ken adamant. Not vindictive. He spoke of the people concerned as of chemical elements, without passion. He had thought it through by the side of the ocean and could make no deduction but divorce. Terry began to cry. Ken ignored her.

What he was curious to know from *them* was whether or not
they thought Piet would divorce Angela to marry Foxy. If they
thought yes, then the sooner the better. If they thought Piet
would be "bastard enough"—Matt tactfully paused before releasing the expressions—to "let her stew," then maybe they at
least should wait, merely separate. He was going to go back
to Cambridge, she should stay in the house. Would they keep
an eye on her? Of course they would. Terry then gave him
a long lecture. She said that he and Foxy had been different
from the rest of them because they had no children, and that
because of this they were freer. That, despite what the Church
said, she did not think a marriage sacred and irrevocable until
the couple produced a third soul, a child. That until then marriage was of no different order than kissing your first boy; it
was an experiment. But when a child was created, it ceased to
be an experiment, it became a fact; like papal infallibility or the
chromatic scale. You must have such facts to build a world on,
even if they appeared arbitrary. Now Ken might still feel free,
he seemed very slow to realize that he had a son—

Piet asked, "She told him that?"

"Yes. She's never liked Whitman much."

"How nice of Terry."

Terry had gone on, Ken might imagine he was free to make
decisions, but Piet certainly wasn't. He loved his children,
he needed Angela, and it would be very wrong of Ken to try
to force him, out of some absurd sense of honor that hasn't
applied to anybody for centuries, to give up everything and
marry Foxy. Piet just wasn't free.

"And how did Ken take all this?"

"Not badly. He nodded and thanked us and left. Later in the
morning Terry went over to see Foxy, since Ken has somehow
chosen us, and she was packing. She was perfectly calm, not a
hair out of place. She was going to take the baby and go to her
mother in Washington, and I assume that's where she is."

"Thank God. I mean, what a relief she's all right. And that
she's out of town."

"You honestly haven't heard from her?"

"Not a whisper."

"And you haven't tried to reach her?"

"Should I have? No matter what I said, that would only have

meant to her that I was still in the game and confused things. What's your advice?"

Matt spoke carefully, picking his words in such a way that Piet saw he was no friend; one did not have to speak so carefully to friends. Matt had grown to dislike him, and why not? —he had grown to dislike Matt, since he had first seen him, in a pressed private's uniform, his black button eyes as shiny as his shoes: an eager beaver. "Terry and I of course have discussed this since, and there is one thing, Piet, we agree you should do. Call his bluff. Let them know, the Whitmans, either by phone to Ken or by letter to Foxy, you surely can find her mother's address, that you will *not* marry her in any case. I think if they know that, they'll get back together."

"But is that necessarily good? Them coming back together to make you and Terry and the Pope comfortable? Georgene just told me I shouldn't try to play God with the Whitmans."

The other man's skull, half-lit, lifted in the gloom, one tightly folded ear and the knot of muscle at the point of the jaw and the concavity of his temple all bluish-white, for beyond the office window the carbon-arc streetlight on Hope Street had come on. Piet knew what had happened and what would: Matt had misjudged the coercive power of his moral superiority and would retreat, threatened by Piet's imperfect docility, into his own impregnable rightness. Matt slammed shut a steel desk drawer. "I don't like involving myself with your affairs. I've given my advice. Take it if you want this mess to have a decent outcome. I don't pretend to know what you're really after."

Piet tried to make peace; the man was his partner and had transmitted precious information. "Matt, frankly, I don't think I'm calling any of the shots any more. All I can do is let things happen, and pray."

"That's all you ever do." Matt spoke without hesitation, as a reflex; it was one of those glimpses, as bizarre as the sight in a three-way clothing-store mirror of your own profile, into how you appear to other people. *The Red-haired Avenger*.

At home Angela had received a phone call. She told him about it during their after-supper coffee while the girls were watching *Gunsmoke*. "I got a long-distance call today, from Washington," she said, beginning.

"Foxy?"

"Yes, how did you know?" She answered herself, "She's been calling you, though she told me she hadn't."

"She hasn't. Gallagher told me today where they both were. Ken apparently went over there Tuesday and told his sad story."

"I thought you knew that. Terry told me days ago."

"Why didn't you say so? I've been worried sick."

"We haven't been speaking." This was true.

"What did the lovely Elizabeth have to say for herself?"

Angela's cool face, slightly thinner these days, tensed, and he knew he had taken the wrong tone. She was becoming a disciplinarian. She said, "She was very self-possessed. She said that she was with her mother and had been thinking, and the more she thought"—Angela crossed her hands on the table-top to control their trembling—"the more she felt that she and Ken should get a divorce now, while the child was still an infant. That she did not want to bring Toby up in the kind of suppressed unhappiness she had known as a child."

"Heaven help us," Piet said. Softly, amid motionless arti-facts, he was sinking.

Angela lifted a finger from the oiled surface of the cherry-wood dining table. "No. Wait. She said she called not to tell me that, but to tell me, and for *me* to tell *you*, that she abso-lutely didn't expect you to leave me. That she"—the finger re-turned, weakening the next word—"loves you, but the divorce is all between her and Ken and isn't because of you really and puts you under no obligation. She said that at least twice."

"And what did you say?"

"What could I? 'Yes, yes, no, thank you,' and hung up. I asked her if there was anything we could do about the house, lock it or check it now and then, and she said no need, Ken would be coming out weekends."

Piet put his palms on the tabletop to push himself up, sigh-ing. "What a mercy," he said. "This has been a nightmare."

"Don't you feel guilty about their divorce?"

"A little. Not much. They were dead on each other and didn't know it. In a way I was a blessing for bringing it to a head."

"Don't wander off, Piet. I didn't have anything to say to Foxy but I do have something to say to you. Could we have some brandy?"

"Aren't you full? That was a lovely dinner, by the way. I don't know why I adore lima beans so. I love bland food."

"Let's have some brandy. Please, quick. *Gunsmoke* is nearly over. I wanted to wait until the children were in bed but I'm all keyed up and I can't. I must have brandy."

He brought it and even as he was pouring her glass she had begun. "I think Foxy's faced her situation and we should face ours. I think you should get out, Piet. Tonight. I don't want to live with you any more."

"Truly?"

"Truly."

"This does need brandy, then. Now tell me why. You know it's all over with Foxy."

"I'm not so sure, but that doesn't matter. I think you still love her, but even if you don't, they mentioned Bea, and if it's not Bea it's going to be somebody else; and I just don't think it's worth it."

"And the girls? It's not worth it for them either?"

"Stop hiding behind the girls. No, actually, I *don't* think it's worth it for them. They're sensitive, they know when we fight, or, even worse I suppose, don't fight. Poor Nancy is plainly disturbed, and I'm not so sure that Ruth, even though she inherited my placid face, is any better."

"I hear your psychiatrist talking."

"Not really. He doesn't approve or disapprove. I try to say what I think, which isn't easy for me, since my father always knew what I should think, and if it bounces back off this other man's silence—I hardly know what he looks like, I'm so scared to look at him—and if it still sounds true, I try to live with it."

"Goddammit, this is all because of that jackass Freddy Thorne."

"Let me finish. And what I think is true is, you do not love me, Piet Hanema. You do not. You do *not*."

"But I do. Obviously I do."

"Stop it, you *don't*. You didn't even get me the house I wanted. You fixed it up for her instead."

"I was paid to. I adore you."

"Yes, that says it. You adore me as a way of getting out of loving me. Oh, you like my bosom and bottom well enough, and you think it's neat the way I'm a professor's niece, and taught you which fork to use, and take you back after every little slumming expedition, and you enjoy making me feel frigid so you'll be free—"

"I adore you. I need you."

"Well then you need the wrong thing. I want out. I'm tired of being bullied."

The brandy hurt, as if his insides were tenderly budding. He asked, "Have I bullied you? I suppose in a way. But only lately. I wanted *in* to you, sweet, and you didn't give it to me."

"You didn't know how to ask."

"Maybe I know now."

"Too late. You know what I think? I think she's just your cup of tea."

"That's meaningless. That's superstition." But saying this was to ask himself what he contrariwise believed, and he believed that there was, behind the screen of couples and houses and days, a Calvinist God Who lifts us up and casts us down in utter freedom, without recourse to our prayers or consultation with our wills. Angela had become the messenger of this God. He fought against her as a raped woman might struggle, to intensify the deed. He said to her, "I'm your husband and always will be. I promise, my philandering is done, not that there was awfully much of it. You imagine there's been gossip, and you're acting out of wounded pride; pride, and the selfishness these fucking psychiatrists give everybody they handle. What does he care about the children, or about your loneliness once I'm gone? The more miserable you are, the deeper he'll get his clutches in. It's a racket, Angel, it's witchcraft, and a hundred years from now people will be amazed that we took it seriously. It'll be like leeches and bleeding."

She said, "Don't expose your ignorance to me any more. I'd like to remember you with some respect."

"I'm not leaving."

"Then I am. Tomorrow morning, Ruthie has dancing class and she was going to have lunch with Betsy Saltz. Nancy's blue dress should be washed and ironed for Martha Thorne's birthday party. Maybe you can get Georgene to come over and do it for you."

"Where could you go?"

"Oh, many places. I could go home and play chess with

Daddy. I could go to New York and see the Matisse exhibit. I could fly to Aspen and ski and sleep with an instructor. There's a lot I can do, Piet, once I get away from you." In her excitement she stood, her ripe body swinging.

The upsurge of music in the dark living room indicated the end of the program. Cactuses. Sunset. Right triumphant. He said, "If you're serious, of course, I'm the one to go. But on an experimental basis. And if I'm asked politely."

Politeness was the final atmosphere. Together they settled the girls in bed, and packed a suitcase for Piet, and shared a final brandy in the kitchen. As he very slowly, so as not to wake the sleeping girls, backed the pick-up truck down the crunching driveway, Angela made a noise from the porch that he thought was to call him back. He braked and she rushed to the side of his cab with a little silver sloshing bottle, a pint of gin. "In case you get insomnia," she explained, and put the bottle dewy in his palm, and put a cool kiss on his cheek, with a faint silver edge that must be her tears. He offered to open the door, but she held the handle from the other side. "Darling Piet, be brave," she said, and raced, with one step loud on the gravel, back into the house, and doused the golden hallway light.

He spent the first weekend in the Gallagher & Hanema office, sleeping under an old army blanket on the imitation-leather sofa, lulling his terror with gin-and-water, the water drawn from the dripping tap in their booth-sized lavatory. The drip, the tick of his wristwatch left lying on the resounding wood desk, the sullen plodding of his heart, the sash-rattling vibration of trucks changing gears as they passed at all hours through downtown Tarbox, and a relentless immanence within the telephone all kept him awake. Sunday he huddled in his underwear as the footsteps of churchgoers shuffled on the sidewalk beside his ear. His skull lined like a thermos bottle with the fragile glass of a hangover, he felt himself sardonically eavesdropping from within his tomb. The commonplace greetings he overheard boomed with a sinister magnificence, intimate and proud as naked bodies. On Monday morning, though Piet had tidied up, Gallagher was shocked to find the office smelling of habitation. That week, as it became clear that Angela was not going to call him back, he moved to the third floor of the professional apartment building he himself had refashioned from the mansion of the last Tarbox. The third floor had been left much as it was, part attic, part servants' quarters. The floor-boards of his room, unsanded, bore leak stains shaped like wet leaves and patches of old linoleum and pale squares where linoleum had been; the oatmeal-colored walls, deformed by the slant of the mansard roof outside, were still hung with careful pastels of wildflowers Gertrude Tarbox had done, as a young single lady of "accomplishments," before the First World War. When it rained, one wall, where the paper had long since curled away, became wet, and in the mornings the heat was slow to come on, via a single radiator ornate as lace and thick as armor. To reach his room Piet had to pass through the plum-carpeted foyer, between the frosted-glass doors of the insurance agency and the chiropractor, up the wide stairs with an aluminum strip edging each tread, around past the doors of an oculist and a lawyer new in town, and then up the secret stair, entered by an unmarked door a slide bolt could lock, to his cave. A man who worked nights, with a stutter so terrible he could hardly manage "Good morning" when he and Piet met on the stairs, lived across the stair landing from Piet; besides these two rooms there was a large empty attic Gallagher still hoped to transform and rent as a ballroom to the dancing school that now rented the Episcopal parish hall, where Ruth took her Saturday morning lessons.

Though work on Indian Hill had begun again, with hopes for six twenty-thousand-dollar houses by Labor Day, Jazinski could manage most problems by himself now. "Everything's under control," Piet was repeatedly told, and more than once he called the lumberyard or the foundation contractors to find that Gallagher or Leon had already spoken with them. So Piet was often downtown with not much to do. On Good Friday, with the stock market closed, Harold little-Smith stopped him on Charity Street, in front of the barber shop.

"Piet, this is terrible. *C'est terrible*. What did the Whitmans pull on you?"

"The Whitmans? Nothing much. It was Angela's idea I move out."

"*La bel ange?* I can't buy that. You've always been the perfect couple. The Whitmans now, the first time I met them I could see they were in trouble. Stiff as boards, both of them. But it makes me and Marcia damn mad they've screwed you up too. Why can't *tout le monde* mind their own business?"

"Well, it's not as if I had been totally—"

"Oh, I know, I know, but that's never really the issue, is it? People use it when they need to, because of our moronic Puritan laws."

"Who used who, do you think, in my case?"

"Why, *clairement*, Foxy used you. How else could she get rid of that zombie? Don't be used, Piet. Go back to your kids and forget that bitch."

"Don't call her a bitch. You don't know the story at all."

"Listen, Piet, I wouldn't be telling you this just on my own account, out of my own reliably untrustworthy neo-fascist opinion. But Marcia and I stayed up till past three last night with the Applebys talking this over and we all agreed: we don't like seeing a couple we love hurt. If I weren't so hung, I'd probably put it more tactfully. *Pas d'offense*, of course."

"Janet agreed too, that Foxy was a bitch and I'd been had?"

"She was the devil's advocate for a while, but we wore her out. Anyway, it doesn't mean a fart in Paradise what we think. The thing is, what are you going to do? Come on, I'm your friend. *Ton frère*. What are you going to do?"

"I'm not doing anything. Angela hasn't called and doesn't seem to need me back."

"You're waiting for her to call? Don't wait, go to her. Women have to be taken, you know that. I thought you were a great lover."

"Who told you? Marcia?" Harold's twin-tipped nose lifted as he scented a remote possibility. Piet laughed, and went on, "Or maybe Janet? A splendid woman. Why I remember when she was a prostitute in St. Louis, the line went clear down the hall into the billiard room. Have you ever noticed, at the moment of truth, how her whole insides kind of *pull*? One time I remember—"

Harold cut in. "Well I'm glad to see your spirits haven't been crushed. Nothing sacred, eh Piet?"

"Nothing sacred. *Pas d'offense*."

"Marcia and I wanted to have you over for a drink sometime, and be serious for a change. She's all in a flap about it. She went over to your house, and Angela was perfectly polite, not a hair out of place, but she wouldn't unbend."

"Is that what Marcia likes, to bend people?"

"Listen, I feel I've expressed myself badly. We care, is the point. Piet, we *care*."

"Je comprends. Merci. Bonjour."

"OK, let's leave it at that," Harold said, miffed, sniffing. "I have to get a haircut." His hair looked perfectly well-trimmed to Piet.

The invitation to a drink at the little-Smiths' never came. Few of the friends he and Angela had shared sought him out. The Saltzes, probably at Angela's urging, had him to dinner by himself, but their furniture was being readied for moving, and the evening depressed Piet. Now that they were leaving, the Saltzes could not stop talking about themselves as Jews, as if during their years in Tarbox they had suppressed their race, and now it could out. Irene's battle with the school authorities over Christmas pageantry was lengthily recounted, her eyebrows palpitating. The fact of local anti-Semitism, even in their tiny enlightened circle of couples, was urgently confided to Piet. The worst offenders were the Constantines. Carol had been raised, you know, in a *very* Presbyterian small-town atmosphere, and Eddie was, of course, an ignorant man. Night after night they had sat over there arguing the most absurd things, like the preponderance of Jewish Communists, and psychoanalysts, and violinists, as if it all were part of a single conspiracy. Terrible to admit, after a couple of drinks they would sit around trading Jewish jokes; and of course the Saltzes knew many more than Eddie and Carol, which was interpreted as their being ashamed of their race, which she, Irene, certainly, certainly was *not*. Piet tried to tell them how he felt, especially in the society of Tarbox, as a sort of Jew at heart; but Irene, as if he had furtively petitioned for membership in the chosen race, shushed him with a torrent of analysis as to why Frank Appleby, that arch-Wasp, always argued with her, yet couldn't resist arguing with her, and sought her out at parties. In fairness, there were two people among their "friends" with whom she had never felt a trace of condescension or fear; and one was Angela. The other was Freddy Thorne. "That miserable bastard," Piet groaned, out of habit, to please; people expected him to hate Freddy. The Saltzes understood his exclamation as a sign that, as all the couples suspected, Freddy and Angela had for ages been lovers.

Piet left early; he missed the silence of his shabby room, the undemandingness of the four walls. Ben put his hand on his shoulder and smiled his slow archaic smile. "You're down now," he told Piet, "and it's a pity you're not a Jew, because the fact is, every Jew expects to be down sometime in his life, and he has a philosophy for it. God is testing him. *Nisayon Elohim.*"

"But I clearly brought this on myself," Piet said.

"Who's to say? If you believe in omnipotence, it doesn't matter. What does matter is to taste your own ashes. Chew 'em. Up or down doesn't matter; *ain ben David ba elle bador shekulo zakkai oh kulo chayyav.* The son of David will not come except to a generation that's wholly good or all bad."

Piet tried to tell them how much he had liked them, how Angela had once said, and he had agreed, that the Saltzes of all the couples they knew were the most free from, well, crap.

Ben kept grinning and persisted with his advice. "Let go, Piet. You'll be OK. It was a helluva lot of fun knowing you."

Irene darted forward and kissed him good-bye, a quick singeing kiss from lips dark red in her pale face, rekindling his desire for women.

Later in the week, after cruising past her house several times a day, he called Bea. He had seen her once downtown, and she had waved from across the street, and disappeared into the jeweler's shop, still decorated with a nodding rabbit, though Easter was over. Her voice on the phone sounded startled, guilty.

"Oh, Piet, how are you? When are you going back to Angela?"

"Am I going back? She seems more herself without me."

"Oh, but at night it must be terrible for her."

"And how is it for you at night?"

"Oh, the same. Nobody goes out to parties any more. All people talk about is their children."

"Would you—would you like to see me? Just for tea, some afternoon?"

"Oh, sweet, I think not. Honestly. I think you have enough women to worry about."

"I don't have any women."

"It's good for you, isn't it?"

"It's not as bad as I would have thought. But what about us? I was in love with you, you know, before the roof fell in."

"You were lovely, so alive. But I think you idealized me. I'm much too lazy in bed for you. Anyway, sweet, all of a sudden, it's rather touching, Roger needs me."

"How do you mean?"

"You won't tell anybody? Everybody's sure you're keeping a nest of girls down there."

"Everybody's wrong. I only liked married women. They reminded me of my mother."

"Don't be uppity. I'm trying to tell you about Roger. He lost a lot of money, one of his awful fairy investment friends in Boston, and he really came crying to me, I loved it."

"So because he's bankrupt I can't go to bed with you."

"Not bankrupt, you *do* idealize everything. But scared, so scared—oh, I must tell somebody, I'm bursting with it!—he's agreed to adopt a child. We've already been to the agency once, and answered a lot of insulting questions about our private life. The odd thing is, white babies are scarce, they have so many more Negroes."

"This is what you've wanted? To adopt a child?"

"Oh, for years. Ever since I knew I couldn't. It wasn't Roger, you know, it was me that couldn't. People poked fun of Roger but it was *me*. Oh, Piet, forgive me, I'm burdening you with this."

"No, it's no burden." Floating, he remembered how she floated, above the sound of children snowballing, as evening fell early, through levels of lavender.

She was sobbing, barely audibly, her voice limp and moist, as her body had been. "It's so rotten, though, that you need me and I must say no when before it was I who needed you, and you came finally."

"Finally. Bea, it's great about the adoption, and Roger's going to the poorhouse."

A laugh skidded through her tears. "I just can't," she said, "when I've been given what I've prayed for. The funny thing is, you helped. Roger was very frightened by you and Angela breaking up. He's become very serious."

"He was always serious."

"Sweet Piet, tell me, I was never very real to you, was I? Isn't it all right, not to? I've been dreading your call so, I thought it would come sooner."

"It should have come sooner," he said, then hastened to add to reassure her with, "No, you were never very real," and added finally, "Kiss."

"Kiss," Bea faintly said. "Kiss kiss kiss kiss kiss."

Sunday, bringing his daughters back from a trip to the Science Museum in Boston, Piet was saddened by the empty basketball court. This was the time of year when the young married men of Tarbox used to scrimmage. Whitman was gone, Saltz had moved, Constantine was flying jets to Lima and Rio, Thorne and little-Smith had always considered the game plebeian. Weeds were threading through a crack in the asphalt and the hoop, netless and aslant, needed to be secured with longer screws. Angela greeted them outdoors; she had been picking up winter-fallen twigs from the lawn, and sprinkling grass seed in the bare spots. Seeing the direction of his eyes, she said, "You should take that hoop down. Or would you like to invite your gentlemen friends to come play? I could tolerate it."

"I have no gentlemen friends, it turns out. They were all your friends. Anyway, it would be artificial and not comfortable, don't you think?"

"I suppose."

"Mightn't Ruth ever want to use the hoop?"

"She's interested right now in being feminine. Maybe later, when they have teams at school; but in the meantime it looks hideous."

"You're too exquisite," he said.

"How was your expedition? Artificial and not comfortable?"

"No, it was fun. Nancy cried in the planetarium, when the machine made the stars whirl around, but for some reason she loved the Transparent Woman."

"It reminded her of me," Angela said.

Piet wondered if this bit of self-disclaiming wit was the prelude to readmitting him into their home. Sneakingly he hoped not. He felt the worst nights of solitude were behind him. In loneliness he was regaining something, an elemental sense of surprise at everything, that he had lost with childhood. Even his visits to Angela in their awkwardness had a freshness that was pleasant. She seemed, with her soft fumbling gestures and unaccountable intervals of distant repose, a timid solid creature formed from his loins and now learning to thrive alone. He asked her, "How have you been?"

"Busy enough. I've had to reacquaint myself with my parents. My mother says that for ten years I snubbed them. I hadn't thought so, but maybe she's right."

"And the girls? They miss me less?"

"A little less. It's worst when something breaks and I can't fix it. Ruth was very cross with me the other day and told me I was stupid to lose their Daddy for them by being so pushy in bed. I guess Jonathan or Frankie at school had told her I was bad in bed, and she thought it must mean I didn't give you enough room. Oh, we had a jolly discussion after that. Woman to woman."

"The poor saint. Two poor saints."

"You look better."

"I'm adjusting. Everybody lets me alone, which in a way is a mercy, since I don't have to play politics. The only people I talk to all day some days are Adams and Comeau; we're doing some cabinets for a new couple toward Lacetown."

"I thought you were on Indian Hill."

"Jazinski and Gallagher seem to be managing that. They're working straight from canned plans that don't fit the slope at all."

"Oh. They had me over, with some North Mather people I hated. Money sort of people. Horsey."

"Matt's on the move."

"Terry seemed very bored."

"She'll be bored from here on in. And you? Bored? Happy? Fighting off propositions from our gentlemen friends?"

"A few feelers," Angela admitted. "But nothing serious. It's a different kettle of fish, a separated woman. It's scarier for them."

"You do think of us as separated?"

Rather than answer him, she looked over his shoulder, toward the corner of woods where scilla was blooming and where he had buried Ruth's hamster and where the girls, in a burst of relief at being released from the confinement of their father's embarrassingly rattly and unwashed pick-up truck, had, still in their Sunday expedition clothes, sought their climbing tree, a low-branching apple stunted among maples. Angela's face was recalled to animation by remembered good news. "Oh Piet, I must tell you. The strangest nicest thing. I've begun to have dreams. Dreams I can remember. It hasn't happened to me for years."

"What kind of dreams?"

"Oh, nothing very exciting yet. I'm in an elevator, and press the button, and nothing happens. So I think, not at all worried, 'I must be on the right floor already.' Or, maybe it's part of the same dream, I'm in a department store, trying to buy Nancy a fur hood, so she can go skiing in it. I know exactly the size, and the kind of lining, and go from counter to counter, and they offer me mittens, earmuffs, galoshes, everything I don't want, but I remain very serene and polite, because I know they have them somewhere, because I bought one for Ruth there."

"What sweet dreams."

"Yes, they're very shy and ordinary. *He* doesn't agree, or disagree, but my idea is my subconscious tried to die, and now it's daring to come back and express things I want. Not for myself yet, but for others."

"He. You're having dreams for *him*. Like a child going wee-wee for her daddy."

She retreated, as he desired, into the enchanted stillness that, in this square yard, this tidy manless house, he liked to visit. "You're such a bully," she told him. "Such a jealous bully. You always dreamed so easily, lying beside you inhibited me, I'm sure."

"Couldn't we have shared them?"

"No, you do it alone. I'm discovering you do everything alone. You know when I used to feel most alone? When we were making love." The quality of the silence that followed demanded she soften this. She asked, "Have you heard from Foxy?"

"Nothing. Not even a postcard of the Washington Monument." His lawn, he saw, beside the well and barn, had been killed in patches where the ice had lingered. Hard winter. The polar cap growing again. The hairy mammoths will be back. "It's kind of a relief," he told Angela.

The girls returned from the woods, their spring coats smirched with bark. "Go now," Nancy said to Piet.

Ruth slapped at her sister. "Nancy! That is *not* very nice."

"I think she's trying to help," Angela explained. "She's telling Daddy it's all right to go now."

"Mommy," Nancy told her, her plump hand whirling with her dizzy upgazing, "the stars went round and round and round."

"And the *ba*by *cried*," Ruth said.

Nancy studied, as if seeking her coördinates, and then sprang at her sister, pummeling Ruth's chest. "Liar! Liar!"

Ruth bit her lower lip and expertly knocked Nancy loose with a sideways swerve of her fist. "*Ba*by *cried*," she repeated, "*Hurt*ing *Dad*dy's *feel*ings, making him *take* us out *ear*ly."

Nancy sobbed against her mother's legs. Her face where Piet would never be again. Convolute cranny, hair and air, ambrosial chalice where seed can cling. "I'm sure it was very exciting," Angela said. "And that's why everybody is tired and cranky. Let's go in and have supper." She looked up, her eyes strained by the effort of refusing to do what was easy and instinctive and ask Piet in too.

Bernadette Ong bumped into Piet on the street, by the door of the book store, which sold mostly magazines. He was entering to buy *Life* and she was leaving with a copy of *Scientific American*. Her body brushing his felt flat, hard, yet deprived of its force; she was sallow, and the Oriental fold of upper-lid skin had sagged so that no lashes showed. She and Piet stood beneath the book-store awning; the April day around them was a refraction of apical summer, the first hot day, beach weather at last, when the high-school students shove down the crusty stiff tops of their convertibles and roar to the dunes in caravans. Above downtown Tarbox the Greek temple on its hill of red rocks was limestone white and the gold rooster blazed in an oven of blueness. Bernadette had thrown off her coat. The fine chain of a crucifix glinted in the neck of a dirty silk blouse. Descending into death, she had grown dingy, like a miner.

He asked her, immediately, guiltily, how John was, and she said, "About as well as we can expect, I guess." From her tone, her expectations had sunk low. "They keep him under drugs and he doesn't talk much English. He used to ask me why nobody visited him but that's stopped now."

"I'm so sorry, I thought of visiting him, but I've had my own troubles. I suppose you've heard Angela and I are separated."

"No, I hadn't heard. That's *terrible*." She pronounced it "tarrible"; all vowels tended in her flat wide mouth toward "a." *Whan do I gat my duty dance?* "You're the last couple I would have thought. John, as you've probably guessed, was always half in love with Angela."

Piet had never guessed any such thing. Impulsively he offered, "Why don't I visit him now? I have the time, and aren't you on your way back to the hospital?"

The Tarbox Veterans' Memorial hospital was two miles from the center of town, on the inland side. Built of swarthy clinker bricks, with a rosy new maternity wing that did not quite harmonize, it sat on a knoll between disused railroad tracks and an outlay of greenhouses (Hendrick Vos & Sons—Flowers, Bulbs, and Shrubs). Behind the hospital was a fine formal garden where no one, neither patients nor nurses, ever walked. The French windows of John Ong's room opened to a view of trimmed privet and a pink crabapple and a green-rusted copper birdbath shaped like a scallop shell, empty of water. Wind loosened petals from the crabapple, and billowed the white drapes at the window, and made the coarse transparent sides of the oxygen tent beside the bed abruptly buckle and snap. John was emaciated and, but for the hectic flushed spots, no larger than half dollars, on each cheekbone, colorless. So thin, he looked taller than Piet had remembered him. He spoke with difficulty, as if from a diminished pocket of air high in his chest, near the base of his throat. Only unaltered was the quick smile with which he masked imperfect comprehension. "Harya Pee? Wam weller mame waller pray terrace, heh?" Bernadette plangently translated: "He says how are you Piet? He says warm weather makes him want to play tennis."

"Soon you'll be out there," Piet said, and tossed up and served an imaginary ball.

"Is emerybonny?"

"He asks how is everybody?"

"Fine. Not bad. It's been a long winter."

"Hanjerer? Kiddies? Feddy's powwow?"

"Angela wants to come see you," Piet said, too loud, calling as if to a receding car. "Freddy Thorne's powwow has been pretty quiet lately. No big parties. Our children are getting too big."

It was the wrong thing to say; there was nothing to say. As the visit grew stilted, John Ong's eyes dulled. His hands, insectlike, their bones on the outside, fiddled on the magazine Bernadette had brought him. Once, he coughed, on and on, an interminable uprooting of a growth with roots too deep. Piet turned his head away, and a robin had come to the lip of the dry birdbath. It became clear that John was drugged; his welcome had been a strenuous leap out of hazed tranquillity. For a moment intelligence would be present in his wasted face like an eager carnivorous power; then he would subside into an inner murmuring, and twice spoke in Korean. He looked toward Bernadette for translation but she shrugged and winked toward Piet. "I only know a few phrases. Sometimes he thinks I'm his sister." Piet rose to leave, but she sharply begged, "Don't go." So he sat fifteen more minutes while Bernadette kept clicking something in her lap and John, forgetting his guest, leafed backwards through *Scientific American*, impatiently skimming, seeking something not there. Rubber-heeled nurses paced the hall. Doctors could be heard loudly flirting. Portentous baskets and pots of flowers crowded the floor by the radiator, and Piet wondered from whom. McNamara. Rusk. The afternoon's first cloud darkened the crabapple, and as if held pinned by the touch of light a scatter of petals exploded toward the ground. The room began to lose warmth. When Piet stood the second time to break away, and took the other man's strengthless fingers into his, and said too loudly, too jokingly, "See you on the tennis court," the drug-dilated eyes, eyes that had verified the chaos of particles on the floor of matter, lifted, and dragged Piet down into omniscience; he saw, plunging, how plausible it was to die, how death, far from invading earth like a meteor, occurs on the same plane as birth and marriage and the arrival of the daily mail.

Bernadette walked him down the waxed hall to the hospital entrance. Outdoors, a breeze dragged a piece of her hair across her eye and a sun-shaped spot on the greenhouses below them glared. Her cross glinted. He felt a sexual stir emanate from her flat-breasted body, her wide shoulders and hips; she had been too long torn from support. She moved inches closer, as if to ask a question, and the nail-bitten fingers rising to tuck back the iridescent black strand whose windblown touch had made her blink seemed to gesture in weak apology for her willingness to live. Her smile was a grimace. Piet told her, "There *are* miracles."

"He rejects them," she said, as simply as if his assertion, so surprising to himself, had merely confirmed for her the existence of the pills she administered daily. A rosary had been clicking.

The adventure of visiting the dying man served to show Piet how much time he had, how free he was to use it. He took long walks on the beach. In this prismatic April the great Bay was never twice the same. Some days, at high tide, under a white sun, muscular waves bluer than tungsten steel pounded the sand into spongy cliffs and hauled driftwood and wrack deep into the dunes where tide-change left skyey isolated pools. Low tide exposed smooth acres that mirrored the mauves and salmons and the momentary green of sunset. At times the sea was steeply purple, stained; at others, under a close warm rain sky, the no-color of dirty wash; choppy rows hurried in from the horizon to be delivered and disposed of in the lick and slide at the shore. Piet stooped to pick up angel wings, razor-clam shells, sand dollars with their infallibly etched star and the considerate airhole for an inhabiting creature Piet could not picture. Wood flecks smoothed like creek pebbles, iron spikes mummified in the orange froth of oxidation, powerfully sunk horseshoe prints, the four-tined traces of racing dog paws, the shallow impress of human couples that had vanished (the female foot bare, with toes and a tender isthmus linking heel and forepad; the male mechanically shod in the waffle intaglio of sneaker soles and apparently dragging a stick), the wandering mollusk trails dim as the contours of a photograph over-developed in the pan of the tide, the perfect circle a blade of beach grass complacently draws around itself—nothing was too ordinary for Piet to notice. The beach felt dreamlike, always renewed in its strangeness. One day, late in an overcast afternoon, with lateral flecks of silver high in the west above the nimbus scud, he emerged from his truck in the empty parking lot and heard a steady musical roaring. Yet approaching the sea he saw it calm as a lake, a sullen muddy green. The tide was very low, and walking on the unscarred ribs of its recent retreat Piet perceived—diagnosed, as if the sustained roaring were a symptom within him—that violent waves were breaking on the sand bar a half mile away and, though little of their motion survived, their blended sound traveled to him upon the tranced water as if upon the taut skin of a drum. This effect, contrived with energies that could power cities, was his alone to witness; the great syllable around him seemed his own note, sustained since his birth, elicited from him now, and given to the air. The air that day was warm, and smelled of ashes.

In his loneliness he detected companionship in the motion of waves, especially those distant waves lifting arms of spray along the bar, hailing him. The world was more Platonic than he had suspected. He found he missed friends less than friendship; what he felt, remembering Foxy, was a nostalgia for adultery itself—its adventure, the acrobatics its deceptions demand, the tension of its hidden strings, the new landscapes it makes us master.

Sometimes, returning to the parking lot by way of the dunes, he saw the Whitmans' house above its grassy slope, with its clay scars of excavation and its pale patches of reshingling. The house did not see him. Windows he had often gazed from, euphoric and apprehensive, glinted blank. Once, driving past it, the old Robinson house, he thought that it was fortunate he and Angela had not bought it, for it had proved to be an unlucky house; then realized that they had shared in its bad luck anyway. In his solitude he was growing absent-minded. He noticed a new woman downtown—that elastic proud gait announcing education, a spirit freed from the peasant shuffle, arms swinging, a sassy ass, trim ankles. Piet hurried along the other side of Charity Street to get a glimpse of her front and found, just before she turned into the savings bank, that the woman was Angela. She was wearing her hair down and a new blue cape that her parents had given her, as consolation.

How strange she had been to be jealous of his dreams, to accuse him of dreaming too easily! Perhaps because each night he dosed himself with much gin, his dreams now were rarely memorable—clouded repetitive images of confusion and ill-fittingness, of building something that would not stay joined or erect. He was a little boy, in fact his own father, walking beside his father, in fact his own grandfather, a faceless man he had never met, one of hundreds of joiners who had migrated from Holland to work in the Grand Rapids furniture factories. His thumbs were hugely callused; the boy felt frightened, holding on. Or he was attending John Ong's funeral, and suddenly the casket opened and John scuttled off, behind the altar, dusty as an insect, and cringing in shame. Such dreams Piet washed away along with the sour-hay taste in his mouth when, before dawn, he would awake, urinate, drink a glass of water, and vow to drink less gin tomorrow. Two dreams were more vivid. In one, he and a son, a child who was both Nancy and Ruth yet male, were walking in a snowstorm up from the baseball diamond near his first home. There was between the playground and his father's lower greenhouses a thin grove of trees, horsechestnut and cherry, where the children would gather and climb in the late afternoon and from which, one Halloween, a stoning raid was launched upon the greenhouses that ended with an accounting in police court and fistfights for Piet all November. In the dream it was winter. A bitter wind blew through the spaced trunks and the path beneath the snow was ice, so that Piet had to take the arm of his child and hold him from slipping. Piet himself walked in the deeper snow beside the tightrope of ice; for if both fell at once it would be death. They reached the alley, crossed it, and there, at the foot of their yard beside the dark greenhouses, Piet's grandmother was waiting for them, standing stooped and apprehensive in a cube of snowlessness. Invisible walls enclosed her. She wore only a cotton dress and her threadbare black sweater, unbuttoned. In the dream Piet wondered how long she had been waiting, and gave thanks to the Lord that they were safe, and anticipated joining her in that strange transparent arbor where he clearly saw green grass, blade by blade. Awake, he wondered that he had dreamed of his grandmother at all, for she had died when he was nine, of pneumonia, and he had felt no sorrow. She had known little English and, a compulsive housecleaner, had sought to bar Piet and Joop not only from the front parlor but from all the downstairs rooms save the kitchen.

The second dream was static. He was standing beneath the

stars trying to change their pattern by an effort of his will. Piet pressed himself upward as a clenched plea for the mingled constellations, the metallic mask of night, to alter position; they remained blazing and inflexible. He thought, *I might strain my heart*, and was awakened by a sharp pain in his chest.

Foxy was back in town. The rumor flew from Marcia little-Smith, who had seen her driving Ken's MG on the Nun's Bay Road, to Harold to Frank to Janet to Bea and Terry in the A & P and from there to Carol and the Thornes, to join with the tributary glimpse Freddy had had of her from his office window as she emerged that afternoon from Cogswell's Drug Store. The rumor branched out and began to meet itself in the phrase, "I know"; Terry, acting within, as she guessed at her duties, the office of confidante that Ken had thrust on the Gallaghers that dawn a month ago, phoned and gingerly told Angela, who took the news politely, as if it could hardly concern her. Perhaps it didn't. The Hanemas had become opaque to the other couples, had betrayed the conspiracy of mutual comprehension. Only Piet, as the delta of gossip interlaced, remained dry; no one told him. But there was no need. He already knew. On Tuesday, in care of Gallagher & Hanema, he had received this letter from Washington:

Dear Piet—

I must come back to New England for a few days and will be in Tarbox April 24th, appropriating furniture. Would you like to meet and talk? Don't be nervous—I have no claims to press.

Love,
F.

After "press" the word "but" had been scratched out. They met first by accident, in the town parking lot, an irregular asphalt wilderness of pebbles and parked metal ringed by back entrances to the stores on Charity Street—the A & P, Poirier's Liquor Mart, Beth's Books and Cards, the Methodist Thrift Shop, even, via an alleyway sparkling with broken glass, the Tarbox Professional Apartments. He discovered himself unprepared for the sight of her—from a distance, the cadence of her, the dip of her tall body bending to put a shopping bag into her lowslung black car, the blond dab of her hair bundled, the sense of the tone of muscle across her abdomen, the vertiginous certainty that it was indeed among the world's billions none other than she. His side hurt; his left palm tingled. He called; she held still in answer, and appeared, closer approached, younger than he had remembered, smoother, more finely made—the silken skin translucent to her blood, the straight-boned nose faintly paler at the bridge, the brown irises warmed by gold and set tilted in the dainty shelving of her lids, quick lenses subtler than clouds, minutely shuttling as she spoke. Her voice dimensional with familiar shadows, the unnumbered curves of her parted, breathing, talking, thinking lips: she was alive. Having lived with frozen fading bits of her, he was not prepared for her to be so alive, so continuous and witty.

"Piet, you look touchingly awful."

"Unlike you."

"Why don't you comb your hair any more?"

"You even have a little tan."

"My stepfather has a swimming pool. It's summer there."

"It's been off and on here. The same old tease. I've been walking on the beach a lot."

"Why aren't you living with Angela?"

"Who says I'm not?"

"She says. She told me over the phone. Before I wrote you I called your house; I was going to say my farewells to you both."

"She never told me you called."

"She probably didn't think it was very important."

"A mysterious woman, my wife."

"She said I was to come and get you."

He laughed. "If she said that, why did you ask why wasn't I living with her?"

"Why aren't you?"

"She doesn't want me to."

"That's only," Foxy said, "half a reason."

With this observation their talk changed key; they became easier, more trivial, as if a decision had been put behind them. Piet asked her, "Where are you taking the groceries?"

"They're for me. I'm living in the house this weekend. Ken's promised to stay in Cambridge."

"You and Ken aren't going to be reconciled?"

"He's happy. He says he works evenings now and thinks he's on to something significant. He's back on starfish."

"And you?"

She shrugged, a pale-haired schoolgirl looking for the answer broad enough to cover her ignorance. "I'm managing."

"Won't it depress you living there alone? Or do you have the kid?"

"I left Toby with Mother. They get along beautifully, they both think I'm untrustworthy, and adore cottage cheese."

He asked her simply, "What shall we do?" adding in explanation, "A pair of orphans."

He carried her bag of groceries up to his room, and they lived the weekend there. Saturday he helped her go through the empty house by the marsh, tagging the tables and chairs she wanted for herself. No one prevented them. The old town catered to their innocence. Foxy confessed to Piet that, foreseeing sleeping with him, she had brought her diaphragm and gone to Cogswell's Drug Store for a new tub of vaginal jelly. As he felt himself under the balm of love grow boyish and wanton, she aged; his first impression of her smoothness and translucence was replaced by the goosebumped roughness of her buttocks, the gray unpleasantness of her shaved armpits, the backs of her knees, the thickness of her waist since she had had the baby. Her flat feet gave her walking movements, on the bare floor of Piet's dirty oatmeal-walled room, a slouched awkwardness quite unlike the casually springy step with which Angela, her little toes not touching the floor, moved through the rectangular farmhouse with eggshell trim. Asleep, she snuffled, and restlessly crowded him toward the edge of the bed, and sometimes struggled against nightmares. The first morning she woke him with her hands on his penis, delicately tugging the foreskin, her face pinched and blanched by desire. She cried out that her being here with him was wrong, wrong, and fought his entrance of her; and then afterwards slyly asked if it had made it more exciting for him, her pretending to resist. She asked him abrupt questions, such as, Did he still consider himself a Christian? He said he didn't know, he doubted it. Foxy said of herself that she did, though a Christian living in a state of sin; and defiantly, rather arrogantly and—his impression was

—prissily, tossed and stroked back her hair, tangled damp from the pillow. She complained that she was hungry. Did he intend just to keep her here screwing until she starved? Her stomach growled.

They ate in the Musquenomenee Luncheonette, sitting in a booth away from the window, through which they spied on Frank Appleby and little Frankie lugging bags of lime and peat moss from the hardware store into the Applebys' old maroon Mercury coupe. They saw but were not seen, as if safe behind a one-way mirror. They discussed Angela and Ken and the abortion, never pausing on one topic long enough to exhaust it, even to explore it; the state of their being together precluded discussion, as if, in the end, everything was either too momentous or too trivial. Piet felt, even when they lay motionless together, that they were skimming, hastening through space, lightly interlocked, yet not essentially mingled. He slept badly beside her. She had difficulty coming with him. Despairing of her own climax, she would give herself to him in slavish postures, as if witnessing in her mouth or between her breasts the tripped unclotting thump of his ejaculation made it her own. She still wore the rings of her marriage and engagement, and, gazing down to where her hand was guiding him into her silken face, her cheek concave as her jaws were forced apart, he noticed the icy octagon of her diamond and suffered the realization that if they married he would not be able to buy her a diamond so big.

She did not seem to be selling herself; rather, she was an easy and frank companion. After the uncomfortable episode of tagging the furniture (he was not tempted to touch her in this house they had often violated; her presence as she breezed from room to room felt ghostly, impervious; and already they had lost that prerogative of lovers which claims all places as theirs) she walked with him Saturday along the beach, along the public end, where they would not be likely to meet friends. She pointed to a spot where once she had written him a long letter that he had doubtless forgotten. He said he had not forgotten it, though in part he had. She suddenly told him that his callousness, his promiscuity, had this advantage for her; with him she could be as whorish as she wanted, that unlike most men he really didn't judge. Piet answered that it was his Calvinism. Only God judged. Anyway he found her totally beautiful. Totally: bumps, pimples, flat feet, snuffles, and all. She laughed to hear herself so described, and the quality of her laugh told him she was vain, that underneath all fending disclaimers she thought of herself as flawless. Piet believed her, believed the claim of her barking laugh, a shout snatched away by the salt wind beside the spring sea, her claim that she was in truth perfect, and he hungered to be again alone with her long body in the stealthy shabby shelter of his room.

Lazily she fellated him while he combed her lovely hair. Oh and lovely also her coral cunt, coral into burgundy, with its pansy-shaped M, or W, of fur: kissing her here, as she unfolded from gateway into chamber, from chamber into universe, was a blind pleasure tasting of infinity until, he biting her, she clawed his back and came. Could break his neck. Forgotten him entirely. All raw self. Machine that makes salt at the bottom of the sea.

Mouths, it came to Piet, are noble. They move in the brain's court. We set our genitals mating down below like peasants, but when the mouth condescends, mind and body marry. To eat another is sacred. *I love thee, Elizabeth, thy petaled rankness, thy priceless casket of nothing lined with slippery buds.* Thus on the Sunday morning, beneath the hanging clangor of bells.

"Oh Piet," Foxy sighed to him, "I've never felt so taken. No one has ever known me like this."

Short of sleep, haggard from a month of fighting panic, he smiled and tried to rise to her praise with praise of her, and fell asleep instead, his broad face feverish, as if still clamped between her thighs.

Sunday afternoon was his time with the children; at Foxy's suggestion the four of them went bowling at the candlepin alleys in North Mather. Ruth and Nancy were wide-eyed at the intrusion of Mrs. Whitman, but Foxy was innocently intent on bowling a good score for herself, and in showing the girls how to grasp the unwieldy ball and keep it out of the gutters. When it went in, Ruth said, "*Merde.*"

Piet asked her, "Where did you learn that word?"

"Jonathan little-Smith says it, to keep from swearing."

"Do you like Jonathan?"

"He's a fink," Ruth said, as Angela had once said of Freddy Thorne, *He's a jerk.*

On the second string Piet bowled only 81 to Foxy's 93. She was competition. The outing ended in ice-cream sodas at a newly reopened roadside ice-cream stand whose proprietor had returned, with a fisherman's squint and a peeling forehead, from his annual five months in Florida. To Piet he said, putting his hand on Ruth's head, "This one is like you, but this little number"—his brown hand splayed on Nancy's blond head—"is your missus here all the way."

Foxy had planned to fly back to Washington late Sunday, but she stayed through the night. "Won't Ken guess where you've been sleeping?"

"Oh, let him. He doesn't give a damn. He has grounds enough already, and anyway the settlement's pretty much ironed out. Ken's not stingy with money, thank God. I've got to admit, he's the least neurotic man I ever met. He's decided this, and he's going to make it stick."

"You sound admiring."

"I always admired him. I just never wanted him."

"And me?"

"Obviously. I want you. Why do you think I came all this way?"

"To divide the furniture."

"Oh who cares about furniture? I don't even know where I'm going to be living."

"Well, I suppose I *am* up for grabs."

"I'm not so sure. Angela may just be giving you a holiday."

"I—"

"Don't try to say anything. If you're there, you're there; if not, not. I must make myself free first. I'll be away for a long time now, Piet. Six weeks, two months. Shall I never come back?"

"Where are you going?"

"I don't know yet. Ken's father thinks it should be a western state, but a friend of ours in Cambridge went to the Virgin Islands and that sounds like more fun than some desert ranch full of Connecticut menopause patients whose husband shacked up with the secretary."

"You're really going to go through with it?"

"Oh," she said, touching his cheek in the dark curiously, as if testing the contour of a child's face, or the glaze on a vase she had bought, "absolutely. I'm a ruined woman."

Later, in that timeless night distended by fatigue, demarcated only by a periodic rising of something within him yet not his, a surge from behind him that in blackness broke beneath him upon her strange forked whiteness, Foxy sighed, "It's good to have enough, isn't it? Really enough."

He said, "Sex is like money; only too much is enough."

"That sounds like Freddy Thorne."

"My mentor and savior."

She hushed his lips with fingers fragrant of low tide. "Oh don't. I can't stand other people, even their names. Let's pretend there's only us. Don't we make a world?"

"Sure. I'm a ticklish question, and you're the tickled answer."

"Oh sweet, I do ache."

"You think I don't? Oooaaoh."

"Piet."

"Oooaauhooaa."

"Stop it. That's a horrible noise."

"I can't help it, love. I'm in the pit. One more fuck, and I'm ready to die. Suck me up. Ououiiiyaa. Ayaa."

Each groan felt to be emptying his chest, creating an inner hollowness answering the hollowness beneath the stars.

She threatened him: "I'll leave you."

"You can't. Try it yourself. Groan. It feels great."

"No. You're disciplining me. You're under no obligation to marry me, I'm not so sure, even, I want to marry you."

"Oh, do. Do. Uuoooiiaaaugh. Oh, mercy. You are tops, Fox."

"Mmmmooh. You're right. It does relax."

He repeated, "Oh, mercy," and, as the wearying wonder of her naked sweated-up fucked-out body being beside his sank in, said with boneless conviction, "Ah, you're mine." She put her blurred cheek against his. The tip of her nose was cold. A sign of health. We are all exiles who need to bathe in the irrational.

Monday morning, sneaking downstairs, they met the other tenant of the third floor returning, a small bespectacled man in

factory grays. Freezing on the narrow stair to let them pass, he
said, "G-g-g-gu-ood mur-mur—"

Outdoors, in the parking lot, beside the glittering MG, Foxy
giggled and said, "Your having a woman scared the poor man
half to death." Piet told her No, the man always talked like that.
The world, he went on, doesn't really care as much about lovers as we imagine. He saw her, said his farewell to her, through
a headachy haze of ubiquitous, bounding sun; her pale brave
face was lost, lightstruck. He saw dimly that her eyes above
their blue hollows had been left soft by their nights, flowers
bloomed from mud. Called upon by their circumstances to
laugh joyfully, or to weep plainly, or to thank her regally for
these three slavish days, or even to be amusingly stoical, he
was nothing, not even polite. She gave him her hand to shake
and he lifted it to his mouth and pressed his tongue into her
palm, and wished her away. He leaned into the car window and
blew on her ear and told her to sleep on the plane. Nothing
had been concluded; nothing wanted to be said. When, after
a puzzled flick of her hand and the sad word "*Ciao*," learned
from movies, her MG swerved out past the automatic car-wash
and was gone, he felt no pang, and this gravel arena of rear
entrances looked papery, like a stage set in daylight.

Loss became real and leaden only later, in the afternoon.
Walking along Divinity Street with an empty skull and aching
loin muscles, he met Eddie Constantine, back from the ends
of the world. Eddie was rarely in town any more, and perhaps
Carol had just filled him in on a month's worth of gossip, for
he gleefully cried in greeting, "Hey, Piet! I hear you got caught
with your hand in the honeypot!"

One Sunday in mid-May Piet took his daughters to the
beach; the crowd there, tender speckled bodies not yet tan,
had herdlike trapped itself between the hot dunes and the cold
water, and formed, with its sunglasses and aluminum chairs,
a living ribbon parallel to the surf's unsteady edge. Nancy
splashed and crowed in the waves with the three Ong boys,
who had come with a grim babysitter; Bernadette's final vigil
had begun. Ruth lay beside Piet unhappily, not quite ready
to bask and beautify herself like a teen-ager, yet too old for
sandcastles. Her face had thinned; the smoky suggestion across

her eyes was intensifying; she would be, unlike her mother, a clouded beauty, with something dark and regretted filtering her true goodness. Piet, abashed, in love with her, could think of no comfort to offer her but time, and closed his eyes upon the corona of curving hairs his lashes could draw from the sun. Distant music enlarged and loomed over him; he saw sandy ankles, a turquoise transistor, young thighs, a bikini bottom allowing a sense of globes. *How many miles must a man . . .* Folk. Rock is out. *. . . the answer, my friends . . .* Love and peace are in. As the music receded he closed his eyes and on the crimson inside of his lids pictured globes parting to admit him. He was thirsty. The wind was from the west, off the land, and tasted of the parched dunes.

Then the supernatural proclaimed itself. A sullen purpling had developed unnoticed in the north. A wall of cold air swept south across the beach; the wind change was so distinct and sudden a unanimous grunt, *Ooh*, rose from the crowd. Single raindrops heavy as hail began to fall, still in sunshine, spears of fire. Then the sun was swallowed. The herd gathered its bright colors and hedonistic machinery and sluggishly funneled toward the boardwalk. Brutal thunderclaps, sequences culminating with a splintering as of cosmic crates, spurred the retreat. The livid sky had already surrounded them; the green horizon of low hills behind which lay downtown Tarbox appeared paler than the dense atmosphere pressing upon it. A luminous crack leaped, many-pronged, into being in the north, over East Mather; calamitous crashing followed. There was a push on the boardwalk; a woman screamed, a child laughed. Towels were tugged tight across huddling shoulders. The temperature had dropped twenty degrees in five minutes. The beach behind Piet and his children was clean except for a few scoffers still lolling on their blankets. The plane of the sea ignited like the filament of a flash bulb.

A moment before Piet and his daughters reached the truck cab, the downpour struck, soaking them; rain slashed at the cab's windows and deafeningly drummed on the metal sides. WASH ME. The windshield had become a waterfall the wipers could not clear. Bits of color scurried through the glass, and shouts punctured the storm's exultant monotone. In their space of shelter his daughters' wet hair gave off an excited doggy smell. Nancy was delighted and terrified, Ruth stoical and amused. At the first slight relenting of the weather's fury, Piet put the truck in gear and made his way from the puddled parking lot, on roads hazardous with fallen boughs, via Blackberry Lane, flooded at one conduit, toward the crunching driveway of Angela's house. In the peril his dominating wish had been to deliver his daughters to their mother before he was overtaken: he must remove his body from proximity with theirs. He refused Angela's offer of tea and headed into the heart of Tarbox, unaware that the year's great event had begun to smolder.

The cloudburst settled to a steady rain. Houses, garages, elms and asphalt submitted to the same gray whispering. Thunder, repulsed, grumbled in retreat. Piet parked behind his building and there was a sudden hooting. The Tarbox fire alarm launched its laborious flatulent bellow. The coded signal was in low numbers; the fire was in the town center. Piet imagined he scented ginger. Quickly he ran upstairs, changed out of his bathing suit, and came down to the front entrance. On Divinity Street people were running. The ladder truck roared by with spinning scarlet light and firemen struggling into slickers, clinging as the truck rounded Cogswell's corner. The fire horn, apocalyptically close, repeated its call. The section of the town leeward from the hill was fogged with yellow smoke. Piet began running with the rest.

Up the hill the crowds and the smoke thickened. Already fire hoses, some slack and tangled, others plump and leaking in graceful upward jets, filled the streets around the green. The Congregational Church was burning. God's own lightning had struck it. The icy rain intensified, and the crowds of people, both old and young, from every quarter, watched in chilled silence.

Smoke, an acrid yellow, was pouring neatly, sheets of rapidly crimping wool, from under the cornice of the left pediment and from the lower edge of the cupola that lifted the gilded weathercock one hundred twenty-five feet into the air. Down among the Doric columns firemen were chasing away the men of the church who had rushed in and already rescued the communion service, the heavy walnut altar and pulpit, the brass cross, the portraits of old divines, stacks of old sermons that were blowing away, and, sodden and blackening in the unrelenting rain, a few pew cushions, new from the last renovation. As a onetime member of the church Piet would have gone forward to help them but the firemen and police had formed a barricade through which only the town dogs, yapping and socializing, could pass. His builder's eye calculated that the bolt had struck the pinnacle, been deflected from the slender lighting-rod cable into the steel rods reinforcing the cupola, and ignited the dry wood where the roofline joined the straight base of the tower. Here, in the hollownesses old builders created for insulation, between the walls, between the roof and the hung plaster ceiling of the sanctuary, in the unventilated spaces behind the dummy tympanum and frieze and architrave of the classic façade, amid the hodgepodge of dusty storage reachable by only a slat ladder behind the disused choir loft, the fire would thrive. Hoses turned upon the steaming exterior surfaces solved nothing. The only answer was immediate axwork, opening up the roof, chopping without pity through the old hand-carved triglyphs and metopes. But the columns themselves were forty feet from porch to capital, and no truck could be worked close enough over the rocks to touch its ladder to the roof, and the wind was blowing the poisonously thickening smoke straight out from the burning side into the throats of the rescuers.

A somewhat ironical cheer arose from the theater of townspeople. Buzz Kappiotis, his swollen silhouette unmistakable, had put on a smoke mask and, ax in hand, was climbing a ladder extended to its fullest to touch the great church's pluming rain gutter. Climbing slower and slower, his crouch manifesting his fear, he froze in a mass of smoke, disappeared, and reappeared inching down. A few teen-agers behind Piet booed, but the crowd, out of noncomprehension or shame, was silent. Another fireman, shiny as a coal in his slicker, climbed to the ladder's tip, swung his ax, produced a violet spurt of trapped gas, so his masked profile gleamed peacock blue, and was forced by the heat to descend.

Now flames, shy flickers of orange, materialized, licking their way up the cupola's base, along the inside edges of the louvered openings constructed to release the sound of the bell. The bell itself, ponderous sorrowing shape, a caged widow, was illumined by a glow from beneath. Jets of water arched high and fell short, crisscrossing. Spirals of whiter smoke curled up the painted cerulean dome of the cupola but did not obscure the weathercock turning in the touches of wind.

The fire signal sounded a third time, and engines from neighboring communities, from Lacetown and Mather, from as far away as Quincy and Plymouth, began to arrive, and the pressure generated by their pumps lifted water to the flickering pinnacle; but by now the tall clear windows along the sides had begun to glow, and the tar shingles of the roof gave off greasy whiffs. The fire had spread under the roof and through the double walls and, even as the alien firemen smashed a hundred diamond panes of glass, ballooned golden in the sanctuary itself. For an instant the Gothic-tipped hymnboards could be seen, still bearing this morning's numerals; the Doric fluting on the balcony rail was raked with amber light; the plush curtain that hid the choir's knees caught and exploded upwards in the empty presbytery like a phoenix. Gone was the pulpit wherein Pedrick had been bent double by his struggle with the Word. The booing teen-agers behind Piet had been replaced by a weeping woman. The crowd, which had initially rushed defenseless and naked to the catastrophe, had sprouted umbrellas and armored itself in raincoats and tarpaulins. There was a smell of circus. Children, outfitted in yellow slickers and visored rainhats, clustered by their parents' legs. Teen-age couples watched from cars cozy with radio music. People crammed the memorial pavilion, clung to the baseball screen. The gathered crowd now stretched far down each street radiating from the green, Divinity and Prudence and Temperance, ashen faces filling even the neon-scrawled shopping section. Rain made dusk premature. The spotlights of the fire trucks searched out a crowd whose extent seemed limitless and whose silence, as the conflagration possessed every section of the church, deepened. Flames, doused in the charred belfry, had climbed higher and now fluttered like pennants from the slim pinnacle supporting the rooster. With yearning parabolas the hoses arched higher. A section of roof collapsed in a whirlwind of sparks. The extreme left column began to smoulder like a snuffed birthday candle. Through the great crowd breathed disbelief that the rain and the fire could persist together, that nature could so war with herself: as if a conflict in God's heart had been bared for them to witness. Piet wondered at the lightness in his own heart, gratitude for having been shown something beyond him, beyond all blaming.

He picked up a soaked pamphlet, a sermon dated 1795. *It is the indispensable duty of all the nations of the earth, to know that the LORD he is God, and to offer unto him sincere and devout thanksgiving and praise. But if there is any nation under heaven, which hath more peculiar and forcible reasons than others, for joining with one heart and voice in offering up to him these grateful sacrifices, the United States of America are that nation.*

Familiar faces began to protrude from the citizenry. Piet spotted the Applebys and little-Smiths and Thornes standing in the broad-leafed shelter of a catalpa tree near the library. The men were laughing; Freddy had brought a beer. Angela was also in the crowd. She had brought the girls, and when they spoke to him it was Ruth, not Nancy, who was weepy, distressed that the man Jesus would destroy His church, where she had always wiped her feet, timid of the holy, and had dutifully, among children who were not her friends, sung His praise, to please her father. Piet pressed her wide face against his chest in apology; but his windbreaker was soaked and cold and Ruth flinched from the unpleasant contact. "This is too damn depressing for them," Angela said, "we're going back." When Nancy begged to stay, she said, "The fire's nearly out, the best part is over," and it was true; visible flames had been chased into the corners of the charred shell.

Nancy pointed upward and said, "The chicken!" The rooster, bright as if above not only the smoke but the rain, was poised motionless atop a narrow pyre. Flames in little gassy points had licked up the pinnacle to the ball of ironwork that supported the vane's pivot; it seemed it all must topple; then a single jet, luminous in the spotlights, hurled itself higher and the flames abruptly vanished. Though the impact made the spindly pinnacle waver, it held. The flashbulbs of accumulating cameras went off like secondary lightning. By their fitful illumination and the hysterical whirling of spotlights, Piet watched his wife walk away, turn once, white, to look back, and walk on, leading their virgin girls.

Pedrick, his wiry old hair disarrayed into a translucent crest, recognized Piet in the crowd, though it had been months since he had been in the congregation. His voice clawed. "You're a man of the world. How much in dollars and cents do you estimate it will take to replace this tragic structure?"

Piet said, "Oh, if the exterior shell can be salvaged, between two and three hundred thousand. From the ground up, maybe half a million. At least. Construction costs increase about eight per cent a year." These figures bent the gaunt clergyman like a weight on his back; Piet added in sympathy, "It *is* tragic. The carpentry in there can never be duplicated."

Pedrick straightened; his eye flashed. He reprimanded Piet: "Christianity isn't dollars and cents. This church isn't that old stump of a building. The church is people, my friend, people. *Hu*man *be*ings." And he waggled a horny finger, and Piet saw that Pedrick too knew of his ouster from his home, his need to be brought into line.

Piet told him in return, "But even if they do save the shell, the walls are going to be so weakened you'll have to tear it down anyway." And as if to bear him out, fresh flames erupted along the wall on the other side and leaped so high, as the hoses were shifted, that a maple sapling, having ventured too close to the church, itself caught fire, and dropping burning twigs on the shoulders of spectators.

The crowd churned to watch this final resurgence of the powers of destruction, and Piet was fetched up against Carol Constantine. She carried an umbrella and invited him under it with her, and two of her children, Laura and Patrice. Her show of sorrow touched him. "Oh Piet," she said, "it's too terrible, isn't it? I loved that church."

"I never saw you in it."

"Of course not, I'm a Presbyterian. But I'd look at it twenty times a day, whenever I was in our yard. I'd really be very religious, if Eddie weren't so anti-everything."

"Where is Eddie? On the road?"

"In the sky. He comes back and tells me how beautifully these Puerto Rican girls lay. It's a joy to see him leave. Why am I telling you all this?"

"Because you're sad to see the church burn."

The gutted walls stood saved. The pillars supported the pediment, and the roof beam held the cupola, but the place of worship was a rubble of timbers and collapsed plaster and charred pews, and the out-of-town firemen were coiling their hose, and Buzz Kappiotis was mentally framing his report, and the crowd gradually dispersing. Carol invited Piet in for a cup of tea. Tea became supper, spaghetti shared with her children. He changed from his wet clothes to a sweater and pants, too tight, of Eddie's. When the children were in bed it developed he would spend the night. He had never before slept with a woman so bony and supple. It was good, after his strenuous experience of Foxy, to have a woman who came quickly, with grateful cries and nimble accommodations, who put a pillow beneath her hips, who let her head hang over the side of the bed, hair trailing, throat arched, and who wrapped her legs around him as if his trunk were a stout trapeze by which she was swinging far out over the abyss of the world. The bedroom, like many rooms in Tarbox that night, smelled of wet char and acidulous smoke. Between swings she talked, told him of her life with Eddie, his perversity and her misery, of her hopes for God and immortality, of the good times she and Eddie had had long ago, before they moved to Tarbox. Piet asked her about their affair with the Saltzes and whether she missed them. Carol seemed to need reminding and finally said, "That was mostly talk by other people. Frankly, she was kind of fun, but he was a bore."

> *Larry & Linda's Guest House*
> *Charlotte Amalie, St. Thomas, V.I.*
> *May 15*

Dearest Piet—

Just to write your name makes me feel soft and collapsing inside. What am I doing here, so far from my husband, or my lover, or my father? I have only Toby, and he, poor small soul, has been sunburned by his idiot mother who, accustomed to the day-by-day onset of the Tarbox summer, has baked both him and herself in the tropical sun, a little white spot directly overhead no bigger than a pea. He cried all night, whenever he tried to roll over. Also, this place, advertised as "an inn in the sleepy tradition of the islands of rum and sun" (I have their leaflet on the desk, the very same one given to me by a Washington travel agent), is in fact two doors up from a steel band nightclub and the slanty little street where blue sewer water runs is alive most of the night with the roar of mufflerless VW's and the catcalls of black adolescents. So I have fits all night and droop all day.

Just then a maid with slithery paper sandals and a downcast lilt I can hardly decipher as English came in. From the way she stared at Toby it might have been a full-grown naked man lying there. I don't suppose too many tourist types bring babies. Maybe they think babies come to us in laundry baskets, all powdered and blue-eyed and ready to give orders.

Peace again. The girl cuddled him at my urging and made the beds and pushed some dust here and there and left and he went back to sleep. Trouble is, his mother is sleepy too. Outside the street is incandescent but in here sun lies slatted like yellow crayon sticks on the gritty green floor—Piet, I think I'm going to love it here, once I stop hurting. On the ride from the airport in I wanted to share it with you—just the way they build their houses, corrugated iron and flattened olive oil cans and driftwood all held together by flowering bougainvillaea, and the softness of the air, stepping from the plane in San Juan, like a kiss after fucking—oh lover, forgive me, I am sleepy.

———————

After her restorative nap, the fair-haired young soon-to-be divorcee swiftly arose, and dressed, taking care not to abrade her sunburned forearms and thighs and (especially touchy) abdomen, and changed her youngling's soiled unmentionables, and hurled herself into the blinding clatter of the tropical ville in a heroic (heroinic?) effort to find food. No counterpart of the Tarbox A & P or Lacetown IGA seems to exist—though I could buy bushels of duty-free Swiss watches and cameras. The restaurants not up on the hills attached to the forbidding swish hotels are either native hamburgeries with chili spilled all over the stools or else "gay" nightclubs that don't open until six. At this time of year most of the non-Negroes seem to be fairies. Their voices are unmistakable and everywhere. I finally found a Hayes-Bickford type of cafeteria, with outrageous island prices, up the street near the open market, which meets my apparently demanding (sweet, I'm such an old maid!) sanitary standards, and gives me milk for Toby's bottle in a reassuring wax paper carton. Larry and Linda aren't much help. They are refugees from New York, would-be actors, *and I have the suspicion she rescued him from being gay. He keeps giving me his profile while she must think her front view is the best, because she keeps coming at me head on, her big brown bubs as scary as approaching headlights on a slick night. I was shocked to learn she's five years younger than me and I could see her tongue make a little determined leap to put me on a first-name basis. They seem waifs, rather. They talk about New York all the time, how horrible it was etc., love-hate as Freddy Thorne would say, and are in a constant flap about their sleepy elusive unintelligible help. Though the evening meals Linda puts on are quite nice and light and French. American plan—they give you breakfast and supper, forage as best you can in between. $18 per diem.*

But it's you, you I think about, and worry about, and wonder about. How grand we were, me as a call girl and you as a gangster in hiding. Did I depress you? You seemed so dazed the last morning, and pleased I was going, I cried all the way into B.U., and let Ken take me to lunch at the faculty club and cried some more, so the tables around us became quite solemn. I think he thought I was crying for him, *which in a way I was, and I could see him fighting down a gentlemanly impulse to offer to call it all off and take me back. He has become so distinguished and courtly without me—his female students must adore him. He had bought a new spring suit, sharkskin, and seemed alarmed that I noticed, as if I were wooing him again or had caught him wooing someone else, when all the time you were flowery between my legs and I was neurotically anxious because we had left Toby in Ken's lab with his technicians and I would go back up the elevator and find him dissected. Horrible! Untrue!! Ken was very cute with the baby, and weighed him in milligrams.*

Days have passed. My letter to you seemed to be going all wrong, chattery and too "fun" and breezy. Rereading I had to laugh at what I did to poor Linda's lovely bosom—she and Larry are really a perfectly sweet phony fragile couple, trying to be parental and sisterly and brotherly all at once to me, rather careful and anxious with each other, almost studiously sensual, and so lazy basically. I wonder if ours was the last generation that will ever have "ambition." These two seem so sure the world will never let them starve, and that life exists to be "enjoyed"—barbarous

*idea. But it is refreshing, after our awful Tarbox friends who
talk only about themselves, to talk to people who care about art
and the theater (they invariably call it, with innocent pomp, "the
stage") and international affairs, if that's what they are. I've
forgotten what else "affair" means. They think LBJ a boor but feel
better under him than Kennedy because K. was too much like the
rest of us semi-educated lovables of the post-Cold War and might
have blown the whole game through some mistaken sense of flair.
Like Lincoln, he lived to become a martyr, a memory. A martyr
to what? To Marina Oswald's sexual rejection of her husband.
Forgive me, I am using my letter to you to argue with Larry in.
But it made me sad, that he thought that somebody like us (if
K. was) wasn't fit to rule us, which is to say, we aren't fit to rule
ourselves, so bring on emperors, demigods, giant robots, what have
you. Larry, incidentally, has let me know, during a merengo at
the Plangent Cat, which is the place down the street, that his sexual ambivalence (AC or DC, he calls it) is definitely on the mend,
but I declined, though he does dance wonderfully, to participate
in the cure. He took the refusal as if his heart hadn't been in it.*

*Which brings us to you. Who are you? Are you weak? This theme,
of your "weakness," cropped up often in the mouths of our mutual
friends, when we all lived together in a magic circle. But I think
they meant to say rather that your strengths weren't sufficiently
used. Your virtues are obsolete. I can imagine you as somebody's
squire, maybe poor prim fanatic Matt's, a splendid redheaded
squire, resourceful, loyal, living off the land, repairing armor
with old hairpins, kidding your way into castles and inns, making
impossible ideals work but needing their impossibility to attach
yourself to. Before I knew you long ago Bea Guerin described you
to me as an old-fashioned man. In a sense if I were to go from
Ken to you it would be a backwards step. Compared to Ken you
are primitive. The future belongs to him or to chaos. But my life
belongs to me now, and I must take a short view. I am not, for all
my vague intellectual poking (about as vague as Freddy's, and
he knew it), good for much—but I know I could be your woman.
As an ambition it is humble but explicit. Even if we never meet
again I am glad to have felt useful, and used. Thank you.*

*The question is, should I (or the next woman, or the next) sub-
due you to marriage? How much more generous it would be to
let you wander, and suffer—there are so few wanderers left. We*

are almost all women now, homebodies and hoarders. You married Angela because your instinct told you she would not possess you. I would. To be mastered by your body I would tame you with my mind. Yet the subconscious spark in me that loves the race wants instead to give you freedom, freedom to rape and flee and to waste yourself, now that the art of building belongs entirely to accountants. Ever since you began to bounce up to my empty house in your dusty pick-up truck and after an hour rattle hastily away, I have felt in you, have loved in you, a genius for loneliness, for seeing yourself as something apart from the world. When you desire to be the world's husband, what right do I have to make you my own?

Toby is crying, and Linda is here. We are taking a picnic to Magens Bay.

Night. The steel band down the street makes me want to go outdoors. What I wrote this afternoon please read understanding that its confusions are gropings toward truth. I am unafraid to seek the truth about us. With Ken I was always afraid. Of coming to the final coldness we shared.

You would have loved it where we went. Coral sand is not like silica sand; it is white and porous and breathes, *and takes deep sharp footprints. My feet look huge and sadly flat. The shells are tiny and various, baby's fingernails for Carol. Remember that night? I was so jealous of Angela. Magens Bay has sea-grape bushes for shade. I am getting a tan. Linda has talked me into a bikini. We roof Toby's basket with mosquito netting and he is turning caramel through it. I have learned to drive on the left-hand side of the road and am mastering my routines. The lawyers are dreadful. You would hate the process. Marriage is something done in the light, at noon, the champagne going flat in the sun, but divorce is done in the dark, where insects scuttle, in faraway places, by lugubrious lawyers. But at the end of the main street where it stops selling watches there is an old square Lutheran church smelling of cedar, with plaques in Danish, where I went Sunday. The congregation was plump colored ladies who sang even the hymns of rejoicing wailingly. The sermon, by a taut young white man, was very intellectual—over my head. I liked it. The Negroes are lovely, softer than the Washington ones I rather dreaded as a child, without that American hardness and shame. I even like the fairies—at least they have made a kind of settlement and aren't tormenting some captive woman. The boats in the harbor are fascinating. Linda has rummaged up a baby carriage and I push Toby a half-mile each way along the quay. My father would tell me about boats and I find I still know a ketch from a yawl. I marvel at the hand-carved tackle on the old fishing boats from the more primitive islands. Not a bit of metal, and they hold together. The clouds are quick, translucent, as if Nature hardly intends them. When it rains in sunlight, they say, the Devil is beating his wife.*

Are you well? Are you there? If you have gone back to Angela, you may show this to her. Think of me fondly, without fear. Your fate need not be mine. I will write again, but not often. There are things to do even here. Linda has put me in charge of the morning help, for a reduction in fee, and has begun to confess to me her love life.   *I am your*

                                                                    Foxy

P.S.: Larry says that man is the sexiest of the animals and the only one that foresees death. I should make a riddle of this.
P.P.S.: At the Plangent Cat down the street I have danced now with Negroes, greatly daring for a Southern girl—the last one who touched me was the nurse in the dentist's office. They are a very silky people, and very innocently assume I want to sleep with them. How sad to instinctively believe your body is worth something. After weeks of chastity I remember lovemaking as an exploration of a sadness so deep people must go in pairs, one cannot go alone.
P.P.P.S.: I seem unable to let this letter go. A bad sign?

John Ong died the same day that France proposed another conference to restore peace to Laos, and Communist China agreed to loan fifteen million dollars to Kenya. Piet was surprised by the length of the obituary in the Globe: born in P'yongyang, political refugee, asylum in 1951, co-discoverer in 1957, with a Finn, of an elementary particle whose life is measured in millionths of a second, list of faculty positions, scientific societies, survived by wife and three sons, Tarbox, Mass. Private services. No flowers. Their friend. Piet walked through the day lightened, excited by this erasure, by John's hidden greatness, imagining the humming of telephone wires among the couples he and John had once known. The same covey of long-haired boys gathered on Cogswell's corner after three, the same blue sky showed through the charred skeleton of the burnt church, topped by an untouched gold rooster.

That same week, on an errand of business, trying to locate Jazinski, who seemed now to hold all of Gallagher's plans and intentions in his head, Piet went to the boy's house, an expanded ranch on Elmcrest Drive, and saw Leon's new golf bag in the garage. Not only were the clubs gleaming new Hogans but the handle of each was socketed in one of those white plastic tubes that were the latest refinement in fussy equipment: pale cannons squarely aimed upward. The bag, black and many-pocketed, was tagged with the ticket of a new thirty-six-hole club, in South Mather, that Piet had never played on. Piet, who played with an originally odd-numbered set filled in with randomly purchased irons whose disparate weights and grips he had come to know like friends, recognized that he must yield to the force expressed by this aspiring bag, mounted on a cart the wheels of which were spoked like the wheels of a sports car. When Leon's pretty wife, her black hair bobbed and sprayed, answered the side door, he read his doom again in her snug cherry slacks, her free-hanging Op-pattern blouse, the bold and equalizing smile that greeted her husband's employer, qualified by something too steady in the eyes, by a curious repressing thoughtful gesture with the tip of her tongue, as if she had often heard Piet unfavorably discussed. Behind her (she did not invite him in; his reputation?) her kitchen, paneled with imitation walnut and hung with copper pâté molds, seemed the snug galley of a ship on its way to warmer waters.

And before May was out Gallagher called Piet in for a serious talk. Matt asked if Piet thought Leon was ready to supervise construction, and Piet answered that he was. Matt asked if Piet didn't feel that over the last year their ends—sales and building —had begun to pull in opposite directions, and Piet responded that he was proud of how promptly the first three houses on Indian Hill had sold. Matt admitted this, but confessed that instead of these half-ass semi-custom-type houses he wanted to go into larger tracts—there was one beyond Lacetown he was bidding for, low clear land swampy only in the spring—and try prefab units, which would be, frankly, a waste of Piet's talents. Personally, he thought Piet's real forte was restoration, and with Tarbox full of old wrecks he would like to see Piet go into business for himself, buying cheap, fixing up, and selling high. Piet thanked him for the idea but said he saw himself more as a squire than a knight. Matt laughed uneasily, hearing another voice or mind emerge from Piet's disturbingly vacant presence. By the time a partnership dissolves, it has dissolved. In consideration for his half of their tangible assets—including a few sticks of office furniture, an inventory of light equipment and carpentry tools and the pick-up truck, a sheaf of mortgages held on faith, and a firm name that sounded like a vaudeville team (here Matt laughed scornfully, as if they had always been a joke)—he offered Piet five thousand, which to be honest was goddam generous. Piet, rebellious as always when confronted with pat solutions, suggested twenty, and settled for seven. He had not imagined himself getting anything, having forfeited, he felt, by his weekend with Foxy, all his rights. To placate his guilt he satisfied himself that Gallagher, who knew the value of their parcels better than he, would have gone higher than seven. They shook on it. The points of Gallagher's jaw flinched. He said earnestly, sellingly, that he wanted Piet to understand that this had nothing to do with Piet's personal difficulties, that he and Terry still believed that he and Angela would be reconciled. Piet was touched by this deceitful assurance for, though Matt had come to relish hard dealing, his conception of himself did not permit him, usually, to lie.

Meanwhile, across the town, Bea Guerin delighted in her adopted baby, its violet toenails, its fearless froggy stare. It was a colored child. "Roger and I have integrated Tarbox!" Bea exclaimed breathlessly over the phone to Carol. "You know we're the last crusaders in the world, it's just that we couldn't bear to wait!" Bernadette Ong awoke to widowhood as if the entire side on which she had been sleeping were torn open, a mouth the length of her, where her church's balm burned like salt; she had respected John's desire to be buried without religion, and was bathed in a recurrent guilt whose scalding was confused with the plucking questioning hands of her children.

"Daddy's gone away. To a place we can't imagine. Yes, they'll speak his language there. Yes, the Pope knows where it is. You'll see him at the end of your lives. Yes, he'll know you, no matter how old you've grown." She had been beside the bed when he died. One moment, there was faint breathing; his mouth was human in shape. The next, it was a black hole —black and deep. The vast difference haunted her, gave the glitter of the mass a holocaustal brilliance. Marcia little-Smith received a shock; having twice invited the Reinhardts to dinner parties and been twice declined, she went to visit Deb Reinhardt, a thin-lipped Vassar graduate with ironed hair, who told her that she and Al, though they quite liked Harold and Marcia in themselves, did not wish to get involved with their friends, with that whole—and here her language slipped unforgivably —"crummy crowd." So the Reinhardts, and the young sociologist who had been elected town moderator, and a charmingly yet unaffectedly bohemian children's book illustrator who had moved from Bleecker Street, and the new Unitarian minister in Tarbox, and their uniformly tranquil wives, formed a distinct social set, that made its own clothes, and held play readings, and kept sex in its place, and experimented with LSD, and espoused liberal causes more militantly than even Irene Saltz. Indignantly the Applesmiths christened them "the Shakers."

Georgene Thorne suffered a brief vision. Heartsick over Piet's collapse, and her final loss of him, and her own rôle in bringing it about, she had turned to her children, and as the weekend weather softened took Whitney and Martha and Judy on long undesired expeditions to museums in the city and wildlife sanctuaries well inland and unfamiliar beaches far down the coast. At one beach she was walking in from the parking area with her children when the laughter of a couple knee-deep in the icy ocean struck her as half familiar. The man was old and bearded and goatish, with knotted yellow legs, skimpy European-style bathing trunks, and a barrel chest coated in gray fur; coarsely hooting, rapacious, he was splashing seawater at a shrieking tall slender woman with tossing dark hair, girlish in a black bikini, Terry Gallagher. The man must be her lute teacher's husband, the potter. Georgene steered her children down the beach past some eclipsing rocks and never breathed a word of this glimpse to anyone, not even to Freddy, not even to Janet Appleby, who, in the course of their confidential out-pourings following the discovery of Janet's note to Freddy, had become her closest friend.

Janet too had her secrets. One Saturday afternoon late in May, driving home from the little-Smiths', she noticed Ken's MG parked in the Whitmans' driveway, and impulsively stopped. She walked around the nursery wing, where Foxy's roses were budding, and found Ken at the front of the house, burning brush. In the light off the flooding marsh his hair was white. At first she talked in pleasantries, but he sensed in her, because he had always liked her, a nervous stalled fullness un-balanced by the beauty of the day. She moved the conversation toward his state of mind, to the loneliness she presumed was his and, unstated beyond that, the shame; and then she offered, not in so many words but with sufficient clarity, to sleep with him, now, in the empty house. After consideration, and with equal tact and clarity, he declined. It was the best possible out-come. "I've been burned, you see; I can't be hurt," had been the basis of her offer; and his refusal was phrased to enhance rather than diminish her notion of her worth: "I think we both need time to generate more self-respect." There was an island of brambles, hawthorn and alder, in the marsh too small to support even a shack, and as they watched, a cloud of star-lings migrating north passingly settled here; even before the last birds of the flock alighted, the leaders lifted and fled. So their encounter, amid the quickening and the grass-smoke and the insect-hum and the tidewater overflowing its rectilinear channels, was sufficient consummation, an exercise for each of freedom. The first breath of adultery is the freest; after it, con-straints aping marriage develop. Janet and Ken were improved for having stood, above the glorious greening marsh, in this scale, fit to live in such an expanding light. Their faces seemed each to each great planetary surfaces of skin and tension, over-flowing dazzlingly at the eyes and mouths. She lowered her gaze; wind unsmoothed his hair. Her offer had been instructive for him; his refusal for her. For years they treasured these min-utes out of all proportion to their circumspection.

The couples, though they had quickly sealed themselves off from Piet's company, from contamination by his failure, were yet haunted and chastened, as if his fall had been sacrificial.

Angela, unattached now, was a threat to each marriage, and, though the various wives continued for a time to call on her politely, to be rebuffed by her coolness and distance, and to return home justified in their antipathy, she was seldom invited to parties. Indeed, parties all but ceased. The children as they grew made increasingly complex and preoccupying demands. The Guerins and Thornes and Applebys and little-Smiths still assembled, but rather sedately; one night, when once Freddy would have organized a deliciously cutting psychological word game, to "humanize" them, they drew up two tables and began to play bridge; and this became their habit. The Gallaghers, without the link of the Hanemas, drifted off to consort with the realtors and money-men of the neighboring towns, and took up horse riding. The Saltzes sent cards to everyone at Christmas. The Jazinskis have moved to an old house near the green and become Unitarians. Doc Allen has learned, the newest thing, how to insert intrauterine loops. Reverend Pedrick, ecstatic, has been overwhelmed by contributions of money, from Catholics as well as Congregationalists, from Lacetown and Mather as well as Tarbox, toward the rebuilding of his church. The fire was well publicized. One national foundation, whose director happened to be reading the *Herald* over breakfast at the Ritz that Monday, has offered to match private contributions dollar for dollar, and reportedly federal funds are available for the restoration of landmarks if certain historical and aesthetic criteria can be met. But the rumor in town is that the new building will be not a restoration but a modern edifice, a parabolic poured-concrete tent-shape peaked like a breaking wave.

The old church proved not only badly gutted but structurally unsound: a miracle it had not collapsed of itself a decade ago. Before the bulldozers and backhoes could munch through the building, the rooster was rescued by a young man riding a steel ball hoisted to the tip of an enormous crane. The elementary-school children were dismissed early to see the sight. Up, up, the young rider went, until he glimmered in the sun like the golden bird, and Piet Hanema, who in his unemployment was watching, and who knew what mistakes crane operators could make, held his breath, afraid. Gently the ball was hoisted and nudged into place; with surprising ease the young man lifted

the gilded silhouette from its pivoted socket and, holding it
in his lap, was swiftly lowered to the earth, as cheers from the
schoolchildren rose. The weathercock measured five feet from
beak to tailfeathers; the copper penny of his eye was tiny. As
the workman walked across the green to present it to Pedrick
and the two deacons waiting with him, the clustering children
made a parade, a dancing flickering field of color as they jostled
and leaped to see better the eye their parents had told them existed. From Piet's distance their mingled cry seemed a jubilant
jeering. The grass of the domed green was vernally lush. The
three stiff delegates of the church accepted the old emblem
and posed for photographs absurdly, cradling the piece of tin
between them; the man on Pedrick's right had hairy ears, the
one on his left was a jeweler. The swarming children encircled
them and touched the dull metal. The sky above was empty
but for two parallel jet trails.

Affected by this scene of joy, seeing that his life in a sense had
ended, Piet turned and realized he was standing where he had
first glimpsed Foxy getting into her car after church, the spot
where later they had met in the shadow of her mother's arrival,
her tall body full, she in her pale turban; and he was glad that
he would marry her, and frightened that he would not.

Is it too severe? I'd take it off but it's pinned.

It's great. It brings out the pampered pink of your face.

God, you're hostile.

I may be hostile, but I adore you. Let's go to bed.

*Wouldn't that be a relief? Do you know how many days it's been
since we made love?*

Many.

Now, though it has not been many years, the town scarcely
remembers Piet, with his rattly pick-up truck full of odd lumber, with his red hair and corduroy hat and eye-catching apricot
windbreaker, he who sat so often and contentedly in Cogswell's
Drug Store nursing a cup of coffee, the stub of a pencil sticking
down from under the sweatband of his hat, his windbreaker
unzippered to reveal an expensive cashmere sweater ruined by
wood dust and shavings, his quick eyes looking as if they had
been rubbed too hard the night before, the skin beneath them
pouched in a little tucked fold, as if his maker in the last instant
had pinched the clay. Angela, who teaches at a girls' school in

Braintree, is still seen around, talking with Freddy Thorne on the street corner, or walking on the beach with a well-tailored wise-smiling small man, her father. She flew to Juárez in July and was divorced in a day. Piet and Foxy were married in September. Her father, pulling strings all the way from San Diego, found a government job for his new son-in-law, as a construction inspector for federal jobs, mostly military barracks, in the Boston-Worcester area. Piet likes the official order and the regular hours. The Hanemas live in Lexington, where, gradually, among people like themselves, they have been accepted, as another couple.

RABBIT REDUX

Chapters

LIEUT. COL. VLADIMIR A. SHATALOV:
I am heading straight for the socket.

LIEUT. COL. BORIS V. VOLYNOV, SOYUZ 5 COMMANDER:
Easy, not so rough.

COLONEL SHATALOV:
It took me quite a while to find you, but now I've got you.

I

Pop/Mom/Moon

M EN EMERGE pale from the little printing plant at four
sharp, ghosts for an instant, blinking, until the outdoor
light overcomes the look of constant indoor light clinging
to them. In winter, Pine Street at this hour is dark, darkness presses down early from the mountain that hangs above
the stagnant city of Brewer; but now in summer the granite
curbs starred with mica and the row houses differentiated by
speckled bastard sidings and the hopeful small porches with
their jigsaw brackets and gray milk-bottle boxes and the sooty
ginkgo trees and the baking curbside cars wince beneath a brilliance like a frozen explosion. The city, attempting to revive
its dying downtown, has torn away blocks of buildings to create parking lots, so that a desolate openness, weedy and rub-
bled, spills through the once-packed streets, exposing church
façades never seen from a distance and generating new perspectives of rear entryways and half-alleys and intensifying the
cruel breadth of the light. The sky is cloudless yet colorless,
hovering blanched humidity, in the way of these Pennsylvania
summers, good for nothing but to make green things grow.
Men don't even tan; filmed by sweat, they turn yellow.

A man and his son, Earl Angstrom and Harry, are among
the printers released from work. The father is near retirement,
a thin man with no excess left to him, his face washed empty by
grievances and caved in above the protruding slippage of bad
false teeth. The son is five inches taller and fatter; his prime is
soft, somehow pale and sour. The small nose and slightly lifted
upper lip that once made the nickname Rabbit fit now seem,
along with the thick waist and cautious stoop bred into him by
a decade of the Linotyper's trade, clues to weakness, a weakness verging on anonymity. Though his height, his bulk, and
a remnant alertness in the way he moves his head continue to
distinguish him on the street, years have passed since anyone
has called him Rabbit.

"Harry, how about a quick one?" his father asks. At the corner where their side street meets Weiser there is a bus stop and a bar, the Phoenix, with a girl nude but for cowboy boots in neon outside and cactuses painted on the dim walls inside. Their buses when they take them go in opposite directions: the old man takes number 16A around the mountain to the town of Mt. Judge, where he has lived his life, and Harry takes number 12 in the opposite direction to Penn Villas, a new development west of the city, ranch houses and quarter-acre lawns contoured as the bulldozer left them and maple saplings tethered to the earth as if otherwise they might fly away. He moved there with Janice and Nelson three years ago. His father still feels the move out of Mt. Judge as a rejection, and so most afternoons they have a drink together to soften the day's parting. Working together ten years, they have grown into the love they would have had in Harry's childhood, had not his mother loomed so large between them.

"Make it a Schlitz," Earl tells the bartender.

"Daiquiri," Harry says. The air-conditioning is turned so far up he unrolls his shirt cuffs and buttons them for warmth. He always wears a white shirt to work and after, as a way of cancelling the ink. Ritually, he asks his father how his mother is.

But his father declines to make a ritual answer. Usually he says, "As good as can be hoped." Today he sidles a conspiratorial inch closer at the bar and says, "Not as good as could be hoped, Harry."

She has had Parkinson's Disease for years now. Harry's mind slides away from picturing her, the way she has become, the loosely fluttering knobbed hands, the shuffling sheepish walk, the eyes that study him with vacant amazement though the doctor says her mind is as good as ever in there, and the mouth that wanders open and forgets to close until saliva reminds it. "At nights, you mean?" The very question offers to hide her in darkness.

Again the old man blocks Rabbit's desire to slide by. "No, the nights are better now. They have her on a new pill and she says she sleeps better now. It's in her mind, more."

"What is, Pop?"

"We don't talk about it, Harry, it isn't in her nature, it isn't the type of thing she and I have ever talked about. Your mother and I have just let a certain type of thing go unsaid, it was the way we were brought up, maybe it would have been better if we hadn't, I don't know. I mean things now they've *put* into her mind."

"Who's this they?" Harry sighs into the Daiquiri foam and thinks, He's going too, they're both going. Neither makes enough sense. As his father pushes closer against him to explain, he becomes one of the hundreds of skinny whining codgers in and around this city, men who have sucked this same brick tit for sixty years and have dried up with it.

"Why, the ones who come to visit her now she spends half the day in bed. Mamie Kellog, for one. Julia Arndt's another. I hate like the Jesus to bother you with it, Harry, but her talk is getting wild and with Mim on the West Coast you're the only one to help me straighten out my own mind. I hate to bother you but her talk is getting so wild she even talks of telephoning Janice."

"Janice! Why would she call Janice?"

"Well." A pull on the Schlitz. A wiping of the wet upper lip with the bony back of the hand, fingers half-clenched in an old man's clutching way. A loose-toothed grimacing getting set to dive in. "Well the talk is *about* Janice."

"*My* Janice?"

"Now Harry, don't blow your lid. Don't blame the bearer of bad tidings. I'm trying to tell you what they say, not what I believe."

"I'm just surprised there's anything to say. I hardly see her any more, now that she's over at Springer's lot all the time."

"Well, that's it. That may be your mistake, Harry. You've taken Janice for granted ever since—the time." The time he left her. The time the baby died. The time she took him back. "Ten years ago," his father needlessly adds. Harry is beginning, here in this cold bar with cactuses in plastic pots on the shelves beneath the mirrors and the little Schlitz spinner doing its polychrome parabola over and over, to feel the world turn. A hopeful coldness inside him grows, grips his wrists inside his cuffs. The news isn't all in, a new combination might break it open, this stale peace.

"Harry, the malice of people surpasses human understanding in my book, and the poor soul has no defenses against it, there she lies and has to listen. Ten years ago, wouldn't she have laid them out? Wouldn't her tongue have cut them down? They've told her that Janice is running around. With one certain man, Harry. Nobody claims she's playing the field."

The coldness spreads up Rabbit's arms to his shoulders, and down the tree of veins toward his stomach. "Do they name the man?"

"Not to my knowledge, Harry. How could they now, when in all likelihood there is no man?"

"Well, if they can make up the idea, they can make up a name."

The bar television is running, with the sound turned off. For the twentieth time that day the rocket blasts off, the numbers pouring backwards in tenths of seconds faster than the eye until zero is reached: then the white boiling beneath the tall kettle, the lifting so slow it seems certain to tip, the swift diminishment into a retreating speck, a jiggling star. The men dark along the bar murmur among themselves. They have not been lifted, they are left here. Harry's father mutters at him, prying. "Has she seemed any different to you lately, Harry? Listen, I know in all probability it's what they call a crock of shit, but—has she seemed any, you know, different lately?"

It offends Rabbit to hear his father swear; he lifts his head fastidiously, as if to watch the television, which has returned to a program where people are trying to guess what sort of prize is hidden behind a curtain and jump and squeal and kiss each other when it turns out to be an eight-foot frozen-food locker. He might be wrong but for a second he could swear this young housewife opens her mouth in mid-kiss and gives the m.c. a taste of her tongue. Anyway, she won't stop kissing. The m.c.'s eyes roll out to the camera for mercy and they cut to a commercial. In silence images of spaghetti and some opera singer riffle past. "I don't know," Rabbit says. "She hits the bottle pretty well sometimes but then so do I."

"Not you," the old man tells him, "you're no drinker, Harry. I've seen drinkers all my life, somebody like Boonie over in engraving, there's a drinker, killing himself with it, and he knows it, he couldn't stop if they told him he'd die tomorrow. You may have a whisky or two in the evening, you're no spring chicken anymore, but you're no drinker." He hides his loose mouth in his beer and Harry taps the bar for another Daiquiri. The old man nuzzles closer. "Now Harry, forgive me for asking if you don't want to talk about it, but how about in bed? That goes along pretty well, does it?"

"No," he answers slowly, disdainful of this prying, "I wouldn't exactly say well. Tell me about Mom. Has she had any of those breathing fits lately?"

"Not a one that I've been woken up for. She sleeps like a baby with those new green pills. This new medicine is a miracle, I must admit—ten more years the only way to kill us'll be to gas us to death, Hitler had the right idea. Already, you know, there aren't any more crazy people: just give 'em a pill morning and evening and they're sensible as Einstein. You wouldn't exactly say it does, go along O.K., is that what I understood you said?"

"Well we've never been that great, Pop, frankly. Does she fall down ever? Mom."

"She may take a tumble or two in the day and not tell me about it. I tell her, I *tell* her, stay in bed and watch the box. She has this theory the longer she can do things the longer she'll stay out of bed for good. I figure she should take care of herself, put herself in deep freeze, and in a year or two in all likelihood they'll develop a pill that'll clear this up simple as a common cold. Already, you know, some of these cortisones; but the doctor tells us they don't know but what the side effects may be worse. You know: the big C. My figuring is, take the chance, they're just about ready to lick cancer anyway and with these transplants pretty soon they can replace your whole insides." The old man hears himself talking too much and slumps to stare into his empty beer, the suds sliding down, but can't help adding, to give it all point, "It's a terrible thing." And when Harry fails to respond: "God she hates not being active."

The rum is beginning to work. Rabbit has ceased to feel cold, his heart is beginning to lift off. The air in here seems thinner, his eyes adjusting to the dark. He asks, "How's her mind? You aren't saying they should start giving her crazy pills."

"In honest truth, I won't lie to you Harry, it's as clear as a bell, when her tongue can find the words. And as I say she's gotten hipped lately on this Janice idea. It would help a lot,

Jesus I hate to bother you but it's the truth, it would help a lot if you and Janice could spare the time to come over tonight. Not seeing you too often her imagination's free to wander. Now I know you've promised Sunday for her birthday, but think of it this way: if you're stuck in bed with nobody but the idiot box and a lot of malicious biddies for company a week can seem a year. If you could make it up there some evening before the weekend, bring Janice along so Mary could look at her—"

"I'd like to, Pop. You know I would."

"I know, Jesus I know. I know more than you think. You're at just the age to realize your old man's not the dope you always thought he was."

"The trouble is, Janice works in the lot office until ten, eleven all the time and I don't like to leave the kid alone in the house. In fact I better be getting back there now just in case." In case it's burned down. In case a madman has moved in. These things happen all the time in the papers. He can read in his father's face—a fishy pinching-in at the corners of the mouth, a tightened veiling of the washed-out eyes—the old man's suspicions confirmed. Rabbit sees red. Meddling old crock. Janice: who'd have that mutt? In love with her father and there she stuck. Happy as a Girl Scout since she began to fill in at the lot, half these summer nights out way past supper, TV dinners, tuck Nelson in alone and wait up for her to breeze in blooming and talkative; he's never known her to be so full of herself, in a way it does his heart good. He resents his father trying to get at him with Janice and hits back with the handiest weapon, Mom. "This doctor you have, does he ever mention a nursing home?"

The old man's mind is slow making the switch back to his own wife. Harry has a thought, a spark like where train wheels run over a track switch. Did Mom ever do it to Pop? Play him false. All this poking around about life in bed hints at some experience. Hard to imagine, not only who with but when, she was always in the house as long as he could remember, nobody ever came to visit but the brush man and the Jehovah's Witnesses, yet the thought excites him, like Pop's rumor chills him, opens up possibilities. Pop is saying, ". . . at the beginning. We want to hold off at least until she's bedridden. If we reach the point where she can't take care of herself before

I'm on retirement and there all day, it's an option we might be forced into. I'd hate to see it, though. Jesus I'd hate to see it."

"Hey Pop—?"

"Here's my forty cents. Plus a dime for the tip." The way the old man's hand clings curlingly to the quarters in offering them betrays that they are real silver to him instead of just cut-copper sandwich-coins that ring flat on the bar top. Old values. The Depression when money was money. Never be sacred again, not even dimes are silver now. Kennedy's face killed half-dollars, took them out of circulation and they've never come back. The metal got sent to the moon. The niggling business of settling their bill delays his question about Mom until they are outdoors and then he sees he can't ask it, he doesn't know his father that well. Out here in the hot light his father has lost all sidling intimacy and looks merely old —liverish scoops below his eyes, broken veins along the sides of his nose, his hair the no-color of cardboard. "What'd you want to ask me?"

"I forget," Harry says, and sneezes. Coming into this heat from that air-conditioning sets off an explosion between his eyes that turns heads around halfway down the block and leaves his nostrils weeping. "No, I remember. The nursing home. How can we afford it?—fifty bucks a day or whatever. It'll suck us right down the drain."

His father laughs, with a sudden snap to retrieve his slipping teeth, and does a little shuffling dance-step, right here on the baking sidewalk, beneath the white-on-red BUS STOP sign that people have scratched and lipsticked to read PUS DROP. "Harry, God in His way hasn't been all bad to your mother and me. Believe it or not there's some advantages to living so long in this day and age. This Sunday she's going to be sixty-five and come under Medicare. I've been paying in since '66, it's like a ton of anxiety rolled off my chest. There's no medical expense can break us now. They called LBJ every name in the book but believe me he did a lot of good for the little man. Wherever he went wrong, it was his big heart betrayed him. These pretty boys in the sky right now, Nixon'll hog the credit but it was the Democrats put 'em there, it's been the same story ever since I can remember, ever since Wilson—the Republicans don't do a thing for the little man."

"Right," Harry says blankly. His bus is coming. "Tell her we'll be over Sunday." He pushes to a clear space at the back where, looking out while hanging onto the bar, he sees his father as one of the "little men." Pop stands whittled by the great American glare, squinting in the manna of blessings that come down from the government, shuffling from side to side in nervous happiness that his day's work is done, that a beer is inside him, that Armstrong is above him, that the U.S. is the crown and stupefaction of human history. Like a piece of grit in the launching pad, he has done his part. Still, he has been the one to keep his health; who would have thought Mom would fail first? Rabbit's mind, as the bus dips into its bag of gears and surges and shudders, noses closer into the image of her he keeps like a dreaded relic: the black hair gone gray, the mannish mouth too clever for her life, the lozenge-shaped nostrils that to him as a child suggested a kind of soreness within, the eyes whose color he had never dared to learn closed bulge-lidded in her failing, the whole long face, slightly shining as if with sweat, lying numbed on the pillow. He can't bear to see her like this is the secret of his seldom visiting, not Janice. The source of his life staring wasted there while she gropes for the words to greet him. And that gentle tawny smell of sickness that doesn't even stay in her room but comes downstairs to meet them in the front hall among the umbrellas and follows them into the kitchen where poor Pop warms their meals. A smell like gas escaping, that used to worry her so when he and Mim were little. He bows his head and curtly prays, *Forgive me, forgive us, make it easy for her. Amen.* He only ever prays on buses. Now this bus has that smell.

The bus has too many Negroes. Rabbit notices them more and more. They've been here all along, as a tiny kid he remembers streets in Brewer you held your breath walking through, though they never hurt you, just looked; but now they're noisier. Instead of bald-looking heads they're bushy. That's O.K., it's more Nature, Nature is what we're running out of. Two of the men in the shop are Negroes, Farnsworth and Buchanan, and after a while you didn't even notice; at least they remember how to laugh. Sad business, being a Negro man, always underpaid, their eyes don't look like our eyes, blood-shot, brown, liquid in them about to quiver out. Read some-where some anthropologist thinks Negroes instead of being more primitive are the latest thing to evolve, the newest men. In some ways tougher, in some ways more delicate. Certainly dumber but then being smart hasn't amounted to so much, the atom bomb and the one-piece aluminum beer can. And you can't say Bill Cosby's stupid.

But against these educated tolerant thoughts leans a certain fear; he doesn't see why they have to be so noisy. The four seated right under him, jabbing and letting their noise come out in big silvery hoops; they know damn well they're bugging the fat Dutchy wives pulling their shopping bags home. Well, that's kids of any color: but strange. They are a strange race. Not only their skins but the way they're put together, loose-jointed like lions, strange about the head, as if their thoughts are a different shape and come out twisted even when they mean no menace. It's as if, all these Afro hair bushes and gold earrings and hoopy noise on buses, seeds of some tropical plant sneaked in by the birds were taking over the garden. His gar-den. Rabbit knows it's his garden and that's why he's put a flag decal on the back window of the Falcon even though Janice says it's corny and fascist. In the papers you read about these houses in Connecticut where the parents are away in the Ba-hamas and the kids come in and smash it up for a party. More and more this country is getting like that. As if it just grew here instead of people laying down their lives to build it.

The bus works its way down Weiser and crosses the Running Horse River and begins to drop people instead of taking them on. The city with its tired five and dimes (that used to be a wonderland, the counters as high as his nose and the Big Lit-tle Books smelling like Christmas) and its Kroll's Department Store (where he once worked knocking apart crates behind the furniture department) and its flowerpotted traffic circle where the trolley tracks used to make a clanging star of intersection and then the empty dusty windows where stores have been starved by the suburban shopping malls and the sad narrow places that come and go called Go-Go or Boutique and the funeral parlors with imitation granite faces and the surplus out-lets and a shoeshine parlor that sells hot roasted peanuts and

Afro newspapers printed in Philly crying MBOYA MARTYRED and a flower shop where they sell numbers and protection and a variety store next to a pipe-rack clothing retailer next to a corner dive called JIMBO'S *Friendly* LOUNGE, cigarette ends of the city snuffed by the bridge—the city gives way, after the flash of open water that in his youth was choked with coal silt (a man once tried to commit suicide from this bridge but stuck there up to his hips until the police pulled him out) but that now has been dredged and supports a flecking of moored pleasure boats, to West Brewer, a gappy imitation of the city, the same domino-thin houses of brick painted red, but spaced here and there by the twirlers of a car lot, the pumps and blazoned overhang of a gas station, the lakelike depth of a supermarket parking lot crammed with shimmering fins. Surging and spitting, the bus, growing lighter, the Negroes vanishing, moves toward a dream of spaciousness, past residential fortresses with sprinkled lawn around all four sides and clipped hydrangeas above newly pointed retaining walls, past a glimpse of the museum whose gardens were always in blossom and where the swans ate the breadcrusts schoolchildren threw them, then a glimpse of the sunstruck windows, pumpkin orange blazing in reflection, of the tall new wing of the County Hospital for the Insane. Closer at hand, the West Brewer Dry Cleaners, a toy store calling itself Hobby Heaven, a Rialto movie house with a stubby marquee: 2001 SPACE OD'SEY. Weiser Street curves, becomes a highway, dips into green suburbs where in the Twenties little knights of industry built half-timbered dreamhouses, pebbled mortar and clinker brick, stucco flaky as pie crust, witch's houses of candy and hardened cookie dough with two-car garages and curved driveways. In Brewer County, but for a few baronial estates ringed by iron fences and moated by miles of lawn, there is nowhere higher to go than these houses; the most successful dentists may get to buy one, the pushiest insurance salesmen, the slickest ophthalmologists. This section even has another name, distinguishing itself from West Brewer: Penn Park. Penn Villas echoes the name hopefully, though it is not incorporated into this borough but sits on the border of Furnace Township, looking in. The township, where once charcoal-fed furnaces had smelted the iron for Revolutionary muskets, is now still mostly farmland, and its few snowplows and single sheriff can hardly cope with this ranch-house village of muddy lawns and potholed macadam and sub-code sewers the developers suddenly left in its care.

Rabbit gets off at a stop in Penn Park and walks down a street of mock Tudor, Emberly Avenue, to where the road surface changes at the township line, and becomes Emberly Drive in Penn Villas. He lives on Vista Crescent, third house from the end. Once there may have been here a vista, a softly sloped valley of red barns and fieldstone farmhouses, but more Penn Villas has been added and now the view from any window is as into a fragmented mirror, of houses like this, telephone wires and television aerials showing where the glass cracked. His house is faced with apple-green aluminum clapboards and is numbered 26. Rabbit steps onto his flagstone porchlet and opens his door with its three baby windows arranged like three steps, echoing the door-chime of three stepped tones.

"Hey Dad," his son calls from the living room, a room on his right the size of what used to be called a parlor, with a fireplace they never use. "They've left earth's orbit! They're forty-three thousand miles away."

"Lucky them," he says. "Your mother here?"

"No. At school they let us all into assembly to see the launch."

"She call at all?"

"Not since I've been here. I just got in a while ago." Nelson, at twelve, is under average height, with his mother's dark complexion, and something finely cut and wary about his face that may come from the Angstroms. His long eyelashes come from nowhere, and his shoulder-length hair is his own idea. Somehow, Rabbit feels, if he were taller it would be all right, to have hair so long. As is, the resemblance to a girl is frightening.

"Whadja do all day?"

The same television program, of people guessing and getting and squealing and kissing the m.c., is still going on.

"Nothing much."

"Go to the playground?"

"For a while."

"Then where?"

"Oh, over to West Brewer, just to hang around Billy's apartment. Hey, Dad?"

"Yeah?"

"*His* father got him a mini-bike for his birthday. It's real cool. With that real long front part so you have to reach up for the handles."

"You rode it?"

"He only let me once. It's all shiny, there isn't a speck of paint on it, it's just metal, with a white banana seat."

"He's older than you, isn't he?"

"By four months. That's all. Just four months, Dad. I'm going to be thirteen in three months."

"Where does he ride it? It's not legal on the street, is it?"

"Their building has a big parking lot he rides it all around. Nobody says anything. It only cost a hundred-eighty dollars, Dad."

"Keep talking, I'm getting a beer."

The house is small enough so that the boy can be heard by his father in the kitchen, his voice mixed with gleeful greedy spurts from the television and the chunky suck of the refrigerator door opening and shutting. "Hey Dad, something I don't understand."

"Shoot."

"I thought the Fosnachts were divorced."

"Separated."

"Then how come his father keeps getting him all this neat junk? You ought to see the hi-fi set he has, that's all his, for his room, not even to share. Four speakers, Dad, and earphones. The earphones are fantastic. It's like you're way in*side* Tiny Tim."

"That's the place to be," Rabbit says, coming into the living room. "Want a sip?"

The boy takes a sip from the can, putting a keyhole width of foam on the fuzz of his upper lip, and makes a bitter face.

Harry explains, "When people get divorced the father doesn't stop liking the kids, he just can't live with them any more. The reason Fosnacht keeps getting Billy all this expensive crap is probably he feels guilty for leaving him."

"Why did they get separated, Dad, do you know?"

"Beats me. The bigger riddle is, why did they ever get married?" Rabbit knew Peggy Fosnacht when she was Peggy Gring, a big-assed walleyed girl in the middle row always waving her hand in the air because she thought she had the answer. Fosnacht he knows less well: a weedy little guy always shrugging his shoulders, used to play the saxophone in prom bands, now a partner in a music store on the upper end of Weiser Street, used to be called Chords 'n' Records, now Fidelity Audio. At the discount Fosnacht got, Billy's hi-fi set must have cost next to nothing. Like these prizes they keep socking into these young shriekers. The one that French-kissed the m.c. is off now and a colored couple is guessing. Pale, but definitely colored. That's O.K., let 'em guess, win, and shriek with the rest of us. Better than that sniping from rooftops. Still, he wonders how that black bride would be. Big lips, suck you right off, the men are slow as Jesus, long as whips, takes everything to get them up, in there forever, that's why white women need them, white men too quick about it, have to get on with the job, making America great. Rabbit loves, on *Laugh-In*, when Teresa does the go-go bit, the way they paint the words in white on her skin. When they watch, Janice and Nelson are always asking him what the words are; since he took up the printer's trade he can read like a flash, upside down, mirror-wise too: he always had good quick eyes, Tothero used to tell him he could see the ball through the holes of his ears, to praise him. A great secret sly praiser, Tothero. Dead now. The game different now, everything the jump shot, big looping hungry blacks lifting and floating there a second while a pink palm long as your forearm launched the ball. He asks Nelson, "Why don't you stay at the playground anymore? When I was your age I'd be playing Horse and Twenty-one all day long."

"Yeah, but you were good. You were tall." Nelson used to be crazy for sports. Little League, intramural. But lately he isn't. Rabbit blames it on a scrapbook his own mother kept, of his basketball days in the early Fifties, when he set some county records: last winter every time they would go visit Mt. Judge Nelson would ask to get it out and lie on the floor with it, those old dry-yellow games, the glue dried so the pages crackle being turned, MT. JUDGE TOPPLES ORIOLE, ANGSTROM HITS FOR 37, just happening for the kid, that happened twenty years ago, light from a star.

"I *got* tall," Rabbit tells him. "At your age I wasn't much taller than you are." A lie, but not really. A few inches. In a world where inches matter. Putts. Fucks. Orbits. Squaring up a form. He feels bad about Nelson's height. His own never did him much good, if he could take five inches off himself and give them to Nelson he would. If it didn't hurt.

"Anyway, Dad, sports are square now. Nobody does it."

"Well, what isn't square now? Besides pill-popping and draft-dodging. And letting your hair grow down into your eyes. Where the hell is your mother? I'm going to call her. Turn the frigging TV down for once in your life."

David Frost has replaced *The Match Game* so Nelson turns it off entirely. Harry regrets the scared look that glimmered across the kid's face: like the look on his father's face when he sneezed on the street. Christ they're even scared to let him sneeze. His son and father seem alike fragile and sad to him. That's the trouble with caring about anybody, you begin to feel overprotective. Then you begin to feel crowded.

The telephone is on the lower of a set of see-through shelves that in theory divides the living room from a kind of alcove they call a breakfast nook. A few cookbooks sit on them but Janice has never to his knowledge looked into them, just dishes up the same fried chicken and tasteless steak and peas and French fries she's always dished up. Harry dials the familiar number and a familiar voice answers. "Springer Motors. Mr. Stavros speaking."

"Charlie, hi. Hey, is Janice around?"

"Sure is, Harry. How's tricks?" Stavros is a salesman and always has to say something.

"Tricky," Rabbit answers.

"Hold on, friend. The good woman's right here." Off-phone, his voice calls, "Pick it up. It's your old man."

Another receiver is lifted. Through the knothole of momentary silence Rabbit sees the office: the gleaming display cars on the showroom floor, old man Springer's frosted-glass door shut, the green-topped counter with the three steel desks behind: Stavros at one, Janice at another, and Mildred Kroust the bookkeeper Springer has had for thirty years at the one in between, except she's usually out sick with some sort of female problem she's developed late in life, so her desk top is empty and bare but for wire baskets and a spindle and a blotter. Rabbit can also see last year's puppy-dog calendar on the wall and the cardboard cutout of the Toyota station wagon on the old coffee-colored safe, behind the Christmas tree. The last time he was at Springer's lot was for their Christmas party. Springer is so tickled to get the Toyota franchise after years of dealing in second-hand he has told Harry he feels "like a kid at Christmas all year round." He tried ten years ago to turn Rabbit into a car salesman but in the end Harry opted to follow his own father into honest work. "Harry sweet," Janice says, and he does hear something new in her voice, a breathy lilt of faint hurry, of a song he has interrupted her singing. "You're going to scold me, aren't you?"

"No, the kid and I were just wondering if and if so when the hell we're going to get a home-cooked meal around here."

"Oh I know," she sings, "I hate it too, it's just that with Mildred out so much we've had to go into her books, and her system is really zilch." Zilch: he hears another voice in hers. "Honestly," she sings on, "if it turns out she's been swindling Daddy of millions none of us will be surprised."

"Yeah. Look, Janice. It sounds like you're having a lot of fun over there—"

"*Fun?* I'm *work*ing, sweetie."

"Sure. Now what the fuck is really going on?"

"What do you mean, *go*ing *on*? Nothing is going on except your wife is trying to bring home a little extra bread." Bread? "'Going on'—really. You may think your seven or whatever dollars an hour you get for sitting in the dark diddling that machine is wonderful money, Harry, but the fact is a hundred dollars doesn't buy anything anymore, it just *goes*."

"Jesus, why am I getting this lecture on inflation? All I want to know is why my wife is never home to cook the fucking supper for me and the fucking kid."

"Harry, has somebody been bugging you about me?"

"Bugging? How would they do that? Janice. Just tell me, shall I put two TV dinners in the oven or what?"

A pause, during which he has a vision: sees her wings fold up, her song suspended: imagines himself soaring, rootless, free. An old premonition, dim. Janice says, with measured words, so he feels as when a child watching his mother levelling tablespoons of sugar into a bowl of batter, "Could you, sweet? Just for tonight? We're in the middle of a little crisis here, frankly. It's too complicated to explain, but we have to get some figures firm or we can't do the paychecks tomorrow."

"Who's this we? Your father there?"

"Oh sure."

"Could I talk to him a second?"

"Why? He's out on the lot."

"I want to know if he got those tickets for the Blasts game. The kid's dying to go."

"Well, actually, I don't see him, I guess he's gone home for supper."

"So it's just you and Charlie there."

"Other people are in and out. We're *des*perately trying to untangle this mess Mildred made. This is the last night, Harry, I promise. I'll be home between eight and nine, and then to-morrow night let's all go to a movie together. That space thing is still in West Brewer, I noticed this morning driving in."

Rabbit is suddenly tired, of this conversation, of everything. Confusing energy surrounds him. A man's appetites diminish, but the world's never. "O.K. Be home when you can. But we got to talk."

"I'd love to talk, Harry." From her tone she assumes "talk" means fuck, when he did mean talk. She hangs up: a satisfied impatient sound.

He opens another beer. The pull-tab breaks, so he has to find the rusty old church key underneath everything in the knife drawer. He heats up two Salisbury steak dinners; while waiting for the oven to preheat to 400°, he reads the ingredients listed on the package: water, beef, peas, dehydrated potato flakes, bread crumbs, mushrooms, flour, butter, margarine, salt, maltodextrin, tomato paste, corn starch, Worcestershire sauce, hydrolyzed vegetable protein, monosodium glutamate, nonfat dry milk, dehydrated onions, flavoring, sugar, caramel color, spice, cysteine and thiamine hydrochloride, gum arabic. There is no clue from the picture on the tinfoil where all this stuff fits in. He always thought gum arabic was something you erased with. Thirty-six years old and he knows less than when he started. With the difference that now he knows how little he'll always know. He'll never know how to talk Chinese or how screwing an African princess feels. The six o'clock news is all about space, all about emptiness: some bald man plays with little toys to show the docking and undocking maneuvers, and then a panel talks about the significance of this for the next five hundred years. They keep mentioning Columbus but as far as Rabbit can see it's the exact opposite: Columbus flew blind and hit something, these guys see exactly where they're aiming and it's a big round nothing. The Salisbury steak tastes of preservative and Nelson eats only a few bites. Rabbit tries to joke him into it: "Can't watch TV without a TV dinner." They channel-hop, trying to find something to hold them, but there is nothing, it all slides past until, after nine, on Carol Burnett, she and Gomer Pyle do an actually pretty funny skit about the Lone Ranger. It takes Rabbit back to when he used to sit in the radio-listening armchair back on Jackson Road, its arms darkened with greasespots from the peanut-butter cracker-sandwiches he used to stack there to listen with. Mom used to have a fit. Every Monday, Wednesday, and Friday night *The Lone Ranger* came on at seven-thirty, and if it was summer you'd come in from kick-the-can or three-stops-or-a-catch and the neighborhood would grow quiet all across the back yards and then at eight the doors would slam and the games begin again, those generous summer days, just enough dark to fit sleep into, a war being fought across oceans so he could spin out his days in such happiness, in such quiet growing. Eating Wheaties, along with Jack Armstrong, and Jell-O, which brought you Jack Benny.

In this skit the Lone Ranger has a wife. She stamps around a cabin saying how she hates housework, hates her lonely life. "You're never home," she says, "you keep disappearing in a cloud of dust with a hearty 'Heigh-ho, Silver.'" The unseen audience laughs, Rabbit laughs. Nelson doesn't see what's so funny. Rabbit tells him, "That's how they always used to introduce the program."

The kid says crossly, "I *know*, Dad," and Rabbit loses the thread of the skit a little, there has been a joke he didn't hear, whose laughter is dying.

Now the Lone Ranger's wife is complaining that Daniel Boone brings his wife beautiful furs, but "What do I ever get from you? A silver bullet." She opens a door and a bushel of silver bullets comes crashing out and floods the floor. For the rest of the skit Carol Burnett and Gomer Pyle and the man who plays Tonto (not Sammy Davis Jr. but another TV Negro) keep slipping and crunching on these bullets, by accident. Rabbit thinks of the millions who are watching, the millions the sponsors are paying, and still nobody took time to realize that this would happen, a mess of silver bullets on the floor.

Tonto tells the Lone Ranger, "Better next time, put-um bullet in gun first."

The wife turns to complaining about Tonto. "*Him*. Why must we always keep having him to dinner? He *never* has *us* back."

Tonto tells her that if she comes to his teepee, she would be kidnapped by seven or eight braves. Instead of being frightened, she is interested. She rolls those big Burnett eyes and says, "Let's go, *que más sabe*."

Nelson asks, "Dad, what's *que más sabe*?"

Rabbit is surprised to have to say, "I don't know. Something like 'good friend' or 'boss,' I suppose." Indeed come to think of it he understands nothing about Tonto. The Lone Ranger is a white man, so law and order on the range will work to his benefit, but what about Tonto? A Judas to his race, the more disinterested and lonely and heroic figure of virtue. When did he get his pay-off? Why was he faithful to the masked stranger? In the days of the war one never asked. Tonto was simply on "the side of right." It seemed a correct dream then, red and white together, red loving white as naturally as stripes in the flag. Where has "the side of right" gone? He has missed several jokes while trying to answer Nelson. The skit is approaching its climax. The wife is telling the Lone Ranger, "You must choose between him or me." Arms folded, she stands fierce.

The Lone Ranger's pause for decision is not long. "Saddle up, Tonto," he says. He puts on the phonograph a record of the *William Tell* Overture and both men leave. The wife tiptoes over, a bullet crunching underfoot, and changes the record to "Indian Love Call." Tonto enters from the other side of the screen. He and she kiss and hug. "I've always been interested," Carol Burnett confides out to the audience, her face getting huge, "in Indian affairs."

There is a laugh from the invisible audience there, and even Rabbit sitting at home in his easy chair laughs, but underneath the laugh this final gag falls flat, maybe because everybody still thinks of Tonto as incorruptible, as above it all, like Jesus and Armstrong. "Bedtime, huh?" Rabbit says. He turns off the show as it unravels into a string of credits. The sudden little star flares, then fades.

Nelson says, "The kids at school say Mr. Fosnacht was having an affair, that's why they got divorced."

"Or maybe he just got tired of not knowing which of his wife's eyes was looking at him."

"Dad, what is an affair exactly?"

"Oh, it's two people going out together when they're married to somebody else."

"Did that ever happen to you and Mom?"

"I wouldn't say so. I took a vacation once, that didn't last very long. You wouldn't remember."

"I do, though. I remember Mom crying a lot, and everybody chasing you at the baby's funeral, and I remember standing in the place on Wilbur Street, with just you in the room beside me, and looking down at the town through the window screen, and knowing Mom was in the hospital."

"Yeah. Those were sad days. This Saturday, if Grandpa Springer has got the tickets he said he would, we'll go to the Blasts game."

"I know," the boy says, unenthusiastic, and drifts toward the stairs. It unsettles Harry, how in the corner of his eye, once or twice a day, he seems to see another woman in the house, a woman who is not Janice; when it is only his long-haired son.

One more beer. He scrapes Nelson's uneaten dinner into the Disposall, which sometimes sweetly stinks because the Penn Villas sewers flow sluggishly, carelessly engineered. He moves through the downstairs collecting glasses for the dishwasher; one of Janice's stunts is to wander around leaving dreggy cups with saucers used as ashtrays and wineglasses coated with vermouth around on whatever ledges occurred to her—the TV top, a windowsill. How can she be helping untangle Mildred's mess? Maybe out of the house she's a whirlwind of efficiency. And a heigh-ho Silver. Indian affairs. Poor Pop and his rumor. Poor Mom lying there prey to poison tongues and nightmares. The two of them, their minds gone dry as haystacks rats slither through. His mind shies away. He looks out the window and sees in dusk the black lines of a TV aerial, an aluminum clothes tree, a basketball hoop on a far garage. How can he get the kid interested in sports? If he's too short for basketball, then baseball. Anything, just to put something there, some bliss, to live on later for a while. If he goes empty now he won't last at all, because we get emptier. Rabbit turns from the window and everywhere in his own house sees a slippery disposable gloss. It glints back at him from the synthetic fabric of the living-room sofa and chair, the synthetic artiness of a lamp Janice bought that has a piece of driftwood weighted and wired as its base, the unnatural-looking natural wood of the shelves empty but for a few ashtrays with the sheen of fairgrounds souvenirs; it glints back at him from the steel sink, the kitchen linoleum with its whorls as of madness, oil in water, things don't mix. The window above the sink is black and as opaque as the orange that paints the asylum windows. He sees mirrored in it his own wet hands. Underwater. He crumples the aluminum beer can he has absentmindedly drained. Its contents feel metallic inside him: corrosive, fattening. Things don't mix. His inability to fasten onto any thought and make something of it must be fatigue. Rabbit lifts himself up the stairs, pushes himself through the underwater motions of undressing and dental care, sinks into bed without bothering to turn out the lights downstairs and in the bathroom. He hears from a mournful smothered radio noise that Nelson is still awake. He thinks he should get up and say good night, give the kid a blessing, but a weight crushes him while light persists into his bedroom, along with the boy's soft knocking noises, opening and shutting doors, looking for something to do. Since infancy Rabbit sleeps best when others are up, upright like nails holding down the world, like lamp-posts, street-signs, dandelion stems, cobwebs . . .

Something big slithers into the bed: Janice. The fluorescent dial on the bureau is saying five of eleven, its two hands merged into one finger. She is warm in her nightie. Skin is warmer than cotton. He was dreaming about a parabolic curve, trying to steer on it, though the thing he was trying to steer was fighting him, like a broken sled.

"Get it untangled?" he asks her.

"Just about. I'm so sorry, Harry. Daddy came back and he just wouldn't let us go."

"Catch a nigger by the toe," he mumbles.

"What sort of evening did you and Nelson have?"

"A kind of nothing sort of evening."

"Anybody call?"

"Nobody."

He senses she is, late as it is, alive, jazzed up, and wants to talk, apologetic, wanting to make it up. Her being in the bed changes its quality, from a resisting raft he is seeking to hold to a curving course to a nest, a laden hollow, itself curved. Her hand seeks him out and he brushes her away with an athlete's old instinct to protect that spot. She turns then her back on him. He accepts this rejection. He nestles against her. Her waist where no bones are nips in like a bird dipping. He had been afraid marrying her she would get fat like her mother but as she ages more and more her skinny little stringy go-getter of a father comes out in her. His hand leaves the dip to stray around in front to her belly, faintly lovably loose from having had two babies. Puppy's neck. Should he have let her have had another to replace the one that died? Maybe that was the mistake. It had all seemed like a pit to him then, her womb and the grave, sex and death, he had fled her cunt like a tiger's mouth. His fingers search lower, touch tendrils, go lower, discover a moistness already there. He thinks of feathering the Linotype keys, of work tomorrow, and is already there.

The Verity Press lives on order forms, tickets to fund-raising dances, political posters in the fall, high-school yearbooks in the spring, throwaway fliers for the supermarkets, junk-mail sales announcements. On its rotary press it prints a weekly, *The Brewer Vat*, which specializes in city scandal since the two dailies handle all the hard local and syndicated national news. Once it also published a German-language journal, *Der Schockelschtuhl*, founded 1830. In Rabbit's time here they had let it die, its circulation thinned down to a few thousand farmers in odd corners of the county and counties around. Rabbit remembers it because it meant the departure from the shop of old Kurt Schrack, one of those dark scowling Germans with whiskers that look tattooed into the skin rather than growing out of it to be shaved. His hair was iron but his jaw was lead as he sat scowling in the corner that belonged only to him; he was paid just to proofread the Pennsylvania Dutch copy and hand-set it in the black-letter fonts no one else was allowed to touch. The borders, and the big ornamental letters used on the inside pages, had been carved of wood, blackened by a century of inky handling. Schrack would concentrate down into his work so hard he would look up at lunchtime and talk in German to Pajasek the Polish foreman, or to one of the two shop Negroes, or to one of the Angstroms. Schrack had been likable in that he had done something scrupulously that others could not do at all. Then one Monday he was let go and his corner was soon walled in for the engravers.

Der Schockelschtuhl has gone and the *Vat* itself keeps threatening to take its custom to one of the big offset plants in Philadelphia. You simply paste it up, ads and photos and type, and send it off. Over Verity hangs a future that belongs to cool processes, to photo-offset and beyond that to photo-composition, computerized television that throws thousands of letters a second onto film with never the kiss of metal, beamed by computers programmed even for hyphenation and runarounds; but just an offset press is upwards of thirty thousand dollars and flatbed letterpress remains the easiest way to do tickets and posters. And the *Vat* might fold up any week. It is certainly a superfluous newspaper.

BREWER FACTORY TOOLS COMPONENT HEADED TOWARD MOON, is this week's front-page story. Rabbit sets, two-column measure, his white fingers feathering, the used matrices dropping back into their channels above his head like rain onto tin.

> **When Brewerites this Sunday gaze up at the moon,**
> **it may look a little bit different to them.**
> **Why?**
> **Because there's going to be a little bit of Brewer on**

No. Widow. He tries to take it back but the line is too tight to close so he settles for the widow.

> **it.**
> **Zigzag Electronic Products Inc., of Seventh and**
> **Locust Streets, City,**

Oops.

Locust Streets, city, revealed to VAT reporters this
week that a crucial electronic switching sequence in
the on-board guidance and nabifiation computer was
the on-board guidance and navigation computer was
manufactured by them here, in the plain brick building, once the cite if Gossamer Ho ˌirey Co, that thou-
ing, once the site of Gossamer Hosiery Co., that thousands of Brewer citizens walk unknowingly by each
day.

If the printed circuits of their switches—half the
size of a postage stamp and weighing less than a sunflower seed—fail to function, astronauts Armstrong,
Aldrin and Collin will drift past the moon and perish
in the infinite vacuum of so-called "deep space."

But there is no danger of that, Zigzag Electronics
general manager Leroy "Spin" Lengel assured the

Jump after twenty lines. Switch to ʹsingle-column lines.

VAT reporter in his highly
modern, light-green office.

"It was just another job to
us," he said. "We do a hundred
like it every week.

"Naturally all of us at Zigzag are proud as punch," Lengel
added. "We're sailinggeatoin
added. "We're sailing on a new
sea."

The machine stands tall and warm above him, mothering,
muttering, a temperamental thousand-parted survival from the
golden age of machinery. The sorts tray is on his right hand;
the Star Quadder and the mold disc and slug tray on his left;
a green-shaded light bulb at the level of his eyes. Above this
sun the machine shoulders into shadow like a thunderhead, its
matrix return rod spiralling idly, all these rustling sighing tons
of intricately keyed mass waiting for the feather-touch of his
intelligence. Behind the mold disc the molten lead waits; sometimes when there is a jam the lead squirts out hot: Harry has
been burned. But the machine is a baby; its demands, though
inflexible, are few, and once these demands are met obedience
automatically follows. There is no problem of fidelity. Do for
it, it does for you. And Harry loves the light here. It is cream

to his eyes, this even bluish light that nowhere casts a shadow, light so calm and fine you can read glinting letters backwards at a glance. It contrasts to the light in his home, where standing at the kitchen sink he casts a shadow that looks like dirt over the dishes, and sitting in the living room he must squint against the bridge lamp Janice uses to read magazines by, and bulbs keep burning out on the stair landing, and the kid complains except when it's totally dark about the reflections on the television screen. In the big room of Verity Press, ceilinged with fluorescent tubes, men move around as spirits, without shadows.

At the ten-thirty coffee break Pop comes over and asks, "Think you can make it over this evening?"

"I don't know. Janice said something last night about taking the kid to a movie. How's Mom?"

"As good as can be hoped."

"She mention Janice again?"

"Not last night, Harry. Not more than in passing at least."

The old man sidles closer, clutching his paper cup of coffee tightly as if it held jewels. "Did you say anything to Janice?" he asks. "Did you search her out any?"

"Search her out, what is she, on trial? I hardly saw her. She was over at Springer's until late." Rabbit winces, in the perfect light seeing his father's lips pinch in, his eyes slide fishily. Harry elaborates: "Old man Springer kept her trying to untangle his books until eleven, ever since he started selling Jap cars he's a slavedriver."

Pop's pupils widen a hairline; his eyebrows lift a pica's width. "I thought he and his missus were in the Poconos."

"The Springers? Who told you that?"

"I guess your mother, I forget who told her, Julia Arndt maybe. Maybe it was last week. Mrs. Springer's legs they say can't take the heat, they swell up. I don't know what to tell you about growing old, Harry; it isn't all it's cracked up to be."

"The Poconos."

"It must have been last week they said. Your mother will be disappointed if you can't come over tonight, what shall I tell her?"

The bell rings, ending the break; Buchanan slouches by, wiping his morning shot of whisky from his lips, and winks. "Daddy knows best," he calls playfully. He is a sleek black seal.

Harry says, "Tell her we'll try after supper but we've promised the kid a movie and probably can't. Maybe Friday." His father's face, disappointed and unaccusing, angers him so he explodes: "Goddammit Pop I have a family of my own to run! I can't do everything." He returns to his machine gratefully. And it fits right around him, purrs while he brushes a word from his mind ("Poconos"), makes loud rain when he touches the keys, is pleased he is back.

Janice is home when he comes back from work. The Falcon is in the garage. The little house is hazed by her cigarette smoke; a half-empty glass of vermouth sits on top of the television set and another on one of the shelves between the living room and the breakfast nook. Rabbit calls, "Janice!" Though the house is small and echoing, so that the click of the television knob, the unstoppering of a bottle, the creaking of Nelson's bedsprings can be heard anywhere, there is no answer. He hears steady tumbling water, climbs the stairs. The upstairs bathroom is packed with steam. Amazing, how hot women can stand water.

"Harry, you've just let a lot of cold air in."

She is shaving her legs in the tub and several small cuts are brightly bleeding. Though Janice was never a knockout, with something sullen and stunted and tight about her face, and a short woman in the decade of the big female balloons Hollywood sent up before it died, she always had nice legs and still does. Taut perky legs with a bony kneecap that Rabbit has always liked; he likes to see the bones in people. His wife is holding one soaped leg up as if for display and he sees through the steam the gray soap-curdled water slopping in and out and around her pussy and belly and bottom as she reaches to shave the ankle, and he is standing at the top of a stairway of the uncountable other baths he has heard her take or seen her have in the thirteen years of their marriage. He can keep count of these years because their marriage is seven months older than their child. He asks, "Where's Nelson?"

"He's gone with Billy Fosnacht to Brewer to look at mini-bikes."

"I don't want him looking at mini-bikes. He'll get killed."

The other child his daughter was killed. The world is quicksand. Find the straight path and stick to it.

"Oh Harry, it won't do any harm to look. Billy has one he rides all the time."

"I can't afford it."

"He's promised to earn half the money himself. I'll give him our half out of *my* money, if you're so uptight." Her money: her father gave her stocks years ago. And she earns money now. Does she need him at all? She asks, "Are you sure you closed the door? There's a terrible draft suddenly. There's not much privacy in this house, is there?"

"Well Jesus how much privacy do you think I owe you?"

"Well you don't have to stand there staring, you've seen me take a bath before."

"Well I haven't seen you with your clothes off since I don't know when. You're O.K."

"I'm just a cunt, Harry. There are billions of us now."

A few years ago she would never have said "cunt." It excites him, touches him like a breath on his cock. The ankle she is reaching to shave starts to bleed, suddenly, brightly, shockingly. "God," he tells her, "you are clumsy."

"Your standing there staring makes me nervous."

"Why're you taking a bath right now anyway?"

"We're going out to supper, remember? If we're going to make the movie at eight o'clock we ought to leave here at six. You should wash off your ink. Want to use my water?"

"It's all full of blood and little hairs."

"Harry, really. You've gotten so uptight in your old age."

Again, "uptight." Not her voice, another voice, another voice in hers.

Janice goes on, "The tank hasn't had time to heat enough for a fresh tub."

"O.K. I'll use yours."

His wife gets out, water spilling on the bathmat, her feet and buttocks steamed rosy. Her breasts sympathetically lift as she lifts her hair from the nape of her neck. "Want to dry my back?"

He can't remember the last time she asked him to do this. As he rubs, her smallness mixes with the absolute bigness naked women have. The curve that sways out from her waist to be swelled by the fat of her flank. Rabbit squats to dry her bottom, goosebumpy red. The backs of her thighs, the stray black hairs, the moss moist between. "O.K.," she says, and steps off. He stands to pat dry the down beneath the sweep of her upheld hair: Nature is full of nests. She asks, "Where do you want to eat?"

"Oh, anywhere. The kid likes the Burger Bliss over on West Weiser."

"I was wondering, there's a new Greek restaurant just across the bridge I'd love to try. Charlie Stavros was talking about it the other day."

"Yeah. Speaking of the other day—"

"He says they have marvellous grape leaf things and shish kebab Nelson would like. If we don't make him do something new he'll be eating at Burger Bliss the rest of his life."

"The movie starts at seven-thirty, you know."

"I *know*," she says, "that's why I took a bath *now*," and, a new Janice, still standing with her back to him, nestles her bottom against his fly, lifting herself on tiptoe and arching her back to make a delicate double damp spreading contact. His mind softens; his prick hardens. "Besides," Janice is going on, edging herself on tiptoes up and down like a child gently chanting to Banbury Cross, "the movie isn't just for Nelson, it's for *me*, for working so hard all week."

There was a question he was about to ask, but her caress erased it. She straightens, saying, "Hurry, Harry. The water will get cold." Two damp spots are left on the front of his suntans. The muggy bathroom has drugged him; when she opens the door to their bedroom, the contrast of cold air cakes him; he sneezes. Yet he leaves the door open while he undresses so he can watch her dress. She is practiced, quick; rapidly as a snake shrugs forward over the sand she has tugged her black pantyhose up over her legs. She nips to the closet for her skirt, to the bureau for her blouse, the frilly silvery one, that he thought was reserved for parties. Testing the tub with his foot (too hot) he remembers.

"Hey Janice. Somebody said today your parents were in the Poconos. Last night you said your father was at the lot."

She halts in the center of their bedroom, staring into the bathroom. Her dark eyes darken the more; she sees his big white body, his spreading slack gut, his uncircumcised member hanging boneless as a rooster comb from its blond roots. She sees her flying athlete grounded, cuckolded. She sees a large white man a knife would slice like lard. The angelic cold strength of his leaving her, the anticlimax of his coming back and clinging: there is something in the combination that she cannot forgive, that justifies her. Her eyes must burn on him, for he turns his back and begins to step into her water: his buttocks merge with her lover's, she thinks how all men look innocent and vulnerable here, reverting to the baby they were. She says firmly, "They were in the Poconos but came back early. Mom always thinks at these resorts she's being snubbed," and without waiting for an answer to her lie runs downstairs.

While soaking in the pool tinged by her hair and blood Rabbit hears Nelson come into the house. Voices rise muffled through the ceiling. "What a crummy mini-bike," the child announces. "It's busted already."

Janice says, "Then aren't you glad it isn't yours?"

"Yeah, but there's a more expensive kind, really neat, a Gioconda, that Grandpa could get at discount for us so it wouldn't cost any more than the cheap one."

"Your father and I agree, two hundred dollars is too much for a toy."

"It's *not* a toy, Mom, it's something I could really learn about engines on. And you can get a license and Daddy could drive it to work some days instead of taking a bus all the time."

"Daddy likes taking the bus."

"I hate it!" Rabbit yells, "it stinks of *Ne*groes," but no voice below in the kitchen acknowledges hearing him.

Throughout the evening he has this sensation of nobody hearing him, of his spirit muffled in pulpy insulation, so he talks all the louder and more insistently. Driving the car (even with his flag decal the Falcon feels more like Janice's car than his, she drives it so much more) back down Emberly to Weiser, past the movie house and across the bridge, he says, "Goddammit I don't see why we have to go back into Brewer to eat, I spend all frigging day in Brewer."

"Nelson agrees with me," Janice says. "It will be an interesting experiment. I've promised him there are lots of things that aren't gooey, it's not like Chinese food."

"We're going to be late for the movie, I'm sure of it."

"Peggy Fosnacht says—" Janice begins.

"That dope," Rabbit says.

"Peggy Fosnacht says the beginning is the most boring part. A lot of stars, and some symphony. Anyway there must be short subjects or at least those things that want you to go out into the lobby and buy more candy."

Nelson says, "I heard the beginning is real neat. There's a lot of cave men eating meat that's really raw, he nearly threw up a guy at school said, and then you see one of them get really zapped with a bone. And they throw the bone up and it turns into a spaceship."

"Thank you, Mr. Spoil-It-All," Janice says. "I feel I've seen it now. Maybe you two should go to the movie and I'll go home to bed."

"The hell," Rabbit says. "You stick right with us and suffer for once."

Janice says, conceding, "Women don't dig science."

Harry likes the sensation, of frightening her, of offering to confront outright this faceless unknown he feels now in their lives, among them like a fourth member of the family. The baby that died? But though Janice's grief was worse at first, though she bent under it like a reed he was afraid might break, in the long years since, he has become sole heir to the grief. Since he refused to get her pregnant again the murder and guilt have become all his. At first he tried to explain how it was, that sex with her had become too dark, too *serious*, too kindred to death, to trust anything that might come out of it. Then he stopped explaining and she seemed to forget: like a cat who sniffs around in corners mewing for the drowned kittens a day or two and then back to lapping milk and napping in the wash basket. Women and Nature forget. Just thinking of the baby, remembering how he had been told of her death over a pay phone in a drugstore, puts a kink in his chest, a kink he still associates, dimly, with God.

At Janice's directions he turns right off the bridge, at JIMBO'S

Friendly LOUNGE, and after a few blocks parks on Quince Street. He locks the car behind them. "This is pretty slummy territory," he complains to Janice. "A lot of rapes lately down here."

"Oh," she says, "the *Vat* prints nothing but rapes. You know what a rape usually is? It's a woman who changed her mind afterward."

"Watch how you talk in front of the kid."

"He knows more now than you ever will. That's nothing personal, Harry, it's just a fact. People are more sophisticated now than when you were a boy."

"How about when you were a girl?"

"I was very dumb and innocent, I admit it."

"But?"

"But nothing."

"I thought you were going to tell us how wise you are now."

"I'm not wise, but at least I've tried to keep my mind open."

Nelson, walking a little ahead of them but hearing too much anyway, points to the great Sunflower Beer clock on Weiser Square, which they can see across slate rooftops and a block of rubble on its way to being yet another parking lot. "It's twenty after six," he says. He adds, not certain his point was made, "At Burger Bliss they serve you right away, it's neat, they keep them warm in a big oven that glows purple."

"No Burger Bliss for you, baby," Harry says. "Try Pizza Paradise."

"Don't be ignorant," Janice says, "pizza is purely Italian." To Nelson she says, "We have plenty of time, there won't be anybody there this early."

"Where *is* it?" he asks.

"Right here," she says; she has led them without error.

The place is a brick row house, its red bricks painted ox-blood red in the Brewer manner. A small un-neon sign advertises it, The Taverna. They walk up sandstone steps to the doorway, and a motherly mustached woman greets them, shows them into what once was a front parlor, now broken through to the room beyond, the kitchen behind swinging doors beyond that. A few center tables. Booths along the two walls. White walls bare but for some picture of an oval-faced yellow woman

and baby with a candle flickering in front of it. Janice slides
into one side of a booth and Nelson into the other and Harry,
forced to choose, slides in beside Nelson, to help him with
the menu, to find something on it enough like a hamburger.
The tablecloth is a red checked cloth and the daisies in a blue
glass vase are real flowers, soft, Harry notices, touching them.
Janice was right. The place is nice. The only music is a radio
playing in the kitchen; the only other customers are a couple
talking so earnestly they now and then touch hands, immersed
in some element where they cannot trust their eyes, the man
red in the face as if choking, the woman stricken pale. They
are Penn Park types, cool in their clothes, beige and pencil-
gray, the right clothes insofar as any clothes can be right in this
muggy river-bottom in the middle of July. Their faces have
an edgy money look: their brows have that frontal clarity the
shambling blurred poor can never duplicate. Though he can
never now be one of them Harry likes their being here, in this
restaurant so chaste it is *chic*. Maybe Brewer isn't as dead on its
feet as it seems.

The menus are in hectographed handwriting. Nelson's face
tightens, studying it. "They don't have any sandwiches," he
says.

"Nelson," Janice says, "if you make a fuss out of this I'll
never take you out anywhere again. Be a big boy."

"It's all in gobbledy-gook."

She explains, "Everything is more or less lamb. *Kebab* is
when it's on a skewer. *Moussaka*, it's mixed with eggplant."

"I *hate* eggplant."

Rabbit asks her, "How do you know all this?"

"Everybody knows that much; Harry, you are so pro*vin*cial.
The two of you, sitting there side by side, determined to be
miserable. Ugly Americans."

"You don't look all that Chinese yourself," Harry says, "even
in your little Lord Fauntleroy blouse." He glances down at his
fingertips and sees there an ochre smudge of pollen, from having touched the daisies.

Nelson asks, "What's *kalamaria*?"

"I don't know," Janice says.

"I want that."

"You don't know what you want. Have the *souvlakia*, it's the simplest. It's pieces of meat on a skewer, very well done, with peppers and onions between."

"I *hate* pepper."

Rabbit tells him, "Not the stuff that makes you sneeze, the green things like hollow tomatoes."

"I know," Nelson says. "I hate them. I know what a *pep*per is, Daddy; my *God*."

"Don't swear like that. When did you ever have them?"

"In a Pepperburger."

"Maybe you should take him to Burger Bliss and leave me here," Janice says.

Rabbit asks, "What are *you* going to have, if you're so fucking smart?"

"Daddy swore."

"Ssh," Janice says, "both of you. There's a nice kind of chicken pie, but I forget what it's called."

"You've been here before," Rabbit tells her.

"I want *melopeta*," Nelson says.

Rabbit sees where the kid's stubby finger (Mom always used to point out, he has those little Springer hands) is stalled on the menu and tells him, "Dope, that's a dessert."

Shouts of greeting announce in the doorway a large family all black hair and smiles, initiates; the waiter greets them as a son and rams a table against a booth to make space for them all. They cackle their language, they giggle, they coo, they swell with the joy of arrival. Their chairs scrape, their children stare demure and big-eyed from under the umbrella of adult noise. Rabbit feels naked in his own threadbare little family. The Penn Park couple very slowly turn around, underwater, at the commotion, and then resume, she now blushing, he pale —contact, touching hands on the tablecloth, groping through the stems of wineglasses. The Greek flock settles to roost but there is one man left over, who must have entered with them but hesitates in the doorway. Rabbit knows him. Janice refuses to turn her head; she keeps her eyes on the menu, frozen so they don't seem to read. Rabbit murmurs to her, "There's Charlie Stavros."

"Oh, really?" she says, yet she still is reluctant to turn her head.

But Nelson turns his and loudly calls out, "Hi, Charlie!" Summers, the kid spends a lot of time over at the lot.

Stavros, who has such bad and sensitive eyes his glasses are tinted lilac, focuses. His face breaks into the smile he must use at the close of a sale, a sly tuck in one corner of his lips making a dimple. He is a squarely marked-off man, Stavros, some inches shorter than Harry, some years younger, but with a natural reserve of potent gravity that gives him the presence and poise of an older person. His hairline is receding. His eyebrows go straight across. He moves deliberately, as if carrying something fragile within him; in his Madras checks and his rectangular thick hornrims and his deep squared sideburns he moves through the world with an air of having chosen it. His not having married, though he is in his thirties, adds to his quality of deliberation. Rabbit, when he sees him, always likes him more than he had intended to. He reminds him of the guys, close-set, slow, and never rattled, who were play-makers on the team. When Stavros, taking thought, moves around the obstacle of momentary indecision toward their booth, it is Harry who says, "Join us," though Janice, face downcast, has already slid over.

Charlie speaks to Janice. "The whole caboodle. Beautiful."

She says, "These two are being horrible."

Rabbit says, "We can't read the menu."

Nelson says, "Charlie, what's *kalamaria*? I want some."

"No you don't. It's little like octopuses cooked in their own ink."

"Ick," Nelson says.

"Nelson," Janice says sharply.

Rabbit says, "Sit yourself down, Charlie."

"I don't want to butt in."

"It'd be a favor. Hell."

"Dad's being grumpy," Nelson confides.

Janice impatiently pats the place beside her; Charlie sits down and asks her, "What *does* the kid like?"

"Hamburgers," Janice moans, theatrically. She's become an actress suddenly, every gesture and intonation charged to carry across an implied distance.

Charlie's squarish intent head is bowed above the menu.

"Let's get him some *keftedes*. O.K., Nelson? Meatballs."

"Not with tomatoey goo on them."

"No goo, just the meat. A little mint. Mint's what's in Life Savers. O.K.?"

"O.K."

"You'll love 'em."

But Rabbit feels the boy has been sold a slushy car. And he feels, with Stavros's broad shoulders next to Janice's, and the man's hands each sporting a chunky gold ring, that the table has taken a turn down a road Rabbit didn't choose. He and Nelson are in the back seat.

Janice says to Stavros, "Charlie, why don't you order for all of us? We don't know what we're doing."

Rabbit says, "*I* know what *I'm* doing. I'll order for myself. I want the"—he picks something off the menu at random—"the *païdakia*."

"*Païdakia*," Stavros says. "I don't think so. It's marinated lamb, you need to order it the day before, for at least six."

Nelson says, "Dad, the movie starts in forty minutes."

Janice explains, "We're trying to get to see this silly space movie."

Stavros nods as if he knows. There is a funny echo Rabbit's ears pick up. Things said between Janice and Stavros sound dead, duplicated. Of course they work together all day. Stavros tells them, "It's lousy."

"Why is it lousy?" Nelson asks anxiously. There is a look his face gets, bloating his lips and slightly sucking his eyes back into their sockets, that hasn't changed since his infancy, when his bottle would go dry.

Stavros relents. "Nellie, for you it'll be great. It's all toys. For me, it just wasn't sexy. I guess I don't find technology that sexy."

"Does everything *have* to be sexy?" Janice asks.

"It doesn't have to be, it tends to be," Stavros tells her. To Rabbit he says, "Have some *souvlakia*. You'll love it, and it's quick." And in an admirable potent little gesture, he moves his hand, palm outward as if his fingers had been snapped, without lifting his elbow from the table, and the motherly woman comes running to them.

"*Yasou*."

"*Kale spera*," she answers.

While Stavros orders in Greek, Harry studies Janice, her

peculiar glow. Time has been gentle to her. As if it felt sorry for her. The something pinched and mean about her mouth, that she had even in her teens, has been relaxed by the appearance of other small wrinkles in her face, and her hair, whose sparseness once annoyed him, as another emblem of his poverty, she now brings down over her ears from a central parting in two smooth wings. She wears no lipstick and in certain lights her face possesses a gypsy severity and the dignity present in newspaper photographs of female guerrilla fighters. The gypsy look she got from her mother, the dignity from the Sixties, which freed her from the need to look fluffy. Plain is beautiful enough. And now she is all circles in happiness, squirming on her round bottom and dancing her hands through arcs of exaggeration quick white in the candlelight. She tells Stavros, "If you hadn't shown up we would have starved."

"No," he says, a reassuring factual man. "They would have taken care of you. These are nice people."

"*These* two," she says, "are so American, they're helpless."

"Yeah," Stavros says to Rabbit, "I see the decal you put on your old Falcon."

"I told Charlie," Janice tells Rabbit, "*I* certainly didn't put it there."

"What's wrong with it?" he asks them both. "It's our flag, isn't it?"

"It's somebody's flag," Stavros says, not liking this trend and softly bouncing his fingertips together under his sheltered bad eyes.

"But not yours, huh?"

"Harry gets fanatical about this," Janice warns.

"I don't get fanatical, I just get a little sad about people who come over here to make a fat buck—"

"I was born here," Stavros quickly says. "So was my father."

"—and then knock the fucking flag," Rabbit continues, "like it's some piece of toilet paper."

"A flag is a flag. It's just a piece of cloth."

"It's more than just a piece of cloth to me."

"What is it to you?"

"It's—"

"The mighty Mississippi."

"It's people not finishing my sentences all the time."

"Just half the time."

"That's better than all the time like they have in China."

"Look. The Mississippi is very broad. The Rocky Mountains really swing. I just can't get too turned-on about cops bopping hippies on the head and the Pentagon playing cowboys and Indians all over the globe. That's what your little sticker means to me. It means screw the blacks and send the CIA into Greece."

"If we don't send somebody in the other side sure as hell will, the Greeks can't seem to manage the show by themselves."

"Harry, don't make yourself ridiculous, they invented civilization," Janice says. To Stavros she says, "See how little and tight his mouth gets when he thinks about politics."

"I don't *think* about politics," Rabbit says. "That's one of my Goddam precious American rights, not to think about politics. I just don't see why we're supposed to walk down the street with our hands tied behind our back and let ourselves be blackjacked by every thug who says he has a revolution going. And it really burns me up to listen to hotshot crap-car salesmen dripping with Vitalis sitting on their plumped-up asses bitching about a country that's been stuffing goodies into their mouth ever since they were born."

Charlie makes to rise. "I better go. This is getting too rich."

"Don't go," Janice begs. "He doesn't know what he's saying. He's sick on the subject."

"Yeah, don't go, Charlie, stick around and humor the madman."

Charlie lowers himself again and states in measured fashion, "I want to follow your reasoning. Tell me about the goodies we've been stuffing into Vietnam."

"Christ, exactly. We'd turn it into another Japan if they'd let us. That's all we want to do, make a happy rich country full of highways and gas stations. Poor old LBJ, Jesus, with tears in his eyes on television, you must have heard him, he just about offered to make North Vietnam the fifty-first fucking state of the damn Union if they'd just stop throwing bombs. We're begging them to rig some elections, any elections, and they'd rather throw bombs. What more can we do? We're trying to give ourselves away, that's all our foreign policy is, is trying to give ourselves away to make little yellow people happy, and guys like you sit around in restaurants moaning, 'Jesus, we're rotten.'"

"I thought it was us and not them throwing the bombs."

"We've stopped; we stopped like all you liberals were marching for and what did it get us?" He leans forward to pronounce the answer clearly. "Not shit."

The whispering couple across the room look over in surprise; the family two booths away have hushed their noise to listen. Nelson is desperately blushing, his eyes sunk hot and hurt in his sockets. "Not shit," Harry repeats more softly. He leans over the tablecloth, beside the trembling daisies. "Now I suppose you're going to say 'napalm.' That frigging magic word. They've been burying village chiefs alive and tossing mortars into hospitals for twenty years, and because of napalm they're candidates for the Albert F. Schweitzer peace prize. S, H, it." He has gotten loud again; it makes him frantic, the thoughts of the treachery and ingratitude befouling the flag, befouling him.

"Harry, you'll get us kicked out," Janice says; but he notices she is still happy, all in circles, a cookie in the oven.

"I'm beginning to dig him," Stavros tells her. "If I get your meaning," he says to Rabbit, "we're the big mama trying to make this unruly kid take some medicine that'll be good for him."

"That's right. You got it. We are. And most of 'em *want* to take the medicine, they're dying for it, and a few madmen in black pajamas would rather bury 'em alive. What's your theory? That we're in it for the rice? The Uncle Ben theory." Rabbit laughs and adds, "Bad old Uncle Ben."

"No," Stavros says, squaring his hands on the checked tablecloth and staring level-browed at the base of Harry's throat —gingerly with him, Harry notices: Why?—"my theory is it's a mistaken power play. It isn't that we want the rice, we don't want *them* to have it. Or the magnesium. Or the coastline. We've been playing chess with the Russians so long we didn't know we were off the board. White faces don't work in yellow countries anymore. Kennedy's advisers who thought they could run the world from the dean's office pushed the button and nothing happened. Then Oswald voted Johnson in who was such a bonehead he thought all it took was a bigger thumb on the button. So the machine overheated, you got inflation and a falling market at one end and college riots at the other and in the middle forty thousand sons of American mothers killed by shit-smeared bamboo. People don't like having Sonny killed in the jungle anymore. Maybe they never liked it, but they used to think it was necessary."

"And it isn't?"

Stavros blinks. "I see. You say war has to be."

"Yeah, and better there than here. Better little wars than big ones."

Stavros says, his hands on edge, ready to chop, "But you *like* it." His hands chop. "Burning up gook babies is right where you're at, friend." The "friend" is weak.

Rabbit asks him, "How did you do your Army bit?"

Stavros shrugs, squares his shoulders. "I was 4-F. Tricky ticker. I hear you sat out the Korean thing in Texas."

"I went where they told me. I'd still go where they told me."

"Bully for you. You're what made America great. A real gun-slinger."

"He's silent majority," Janice says, "but he keeps making noise," looking at Stavros hopefully, for a return on her quip. God, she is dumb, even if her ass has shaped up in middle age.

"He's a normal product," Stavros says. "He's a typical good-hearted imperialist racist." Rabbit knows, from the careful level way this is pronounced, with that little tuck of a sold-car smile, that he is being flirted with, asked—his dim feeling is —for an alliance. But Rabbit is locked into his intuition that to describe any of America's actions as a "power play" is to miss the point. America is beyond power, it acts as in a dream, as a face of God. Wherever America is, there is freedom, and wherever America is not, madness rules with chains and dark-ness strangles millions. Beneath her patient bombers, paradise is possible. He fights back, "I don't follow this racist rap. You can't turn on television now without some black face spitting at you. Everybody from Nixon down is sitting up nights trying to figure out how to make 'em all rich without putting 'em to the trouble of doing any work." His tongue is reckless; but he is defending something infinitely tender, the low flame of loy-alty lit with his birth. "They talk about genocide when *they're* the ones planning it, they're the ones, the Negroes plus the rich kids, who want to pull it all down; not that they can't run squealing for a lawyer whenever some poor cop squints funny at 'em. The Vietnam war in my opinion—anybody want my opinion?—"

"Harry," Janice says, "you're making Nelson miserable."

"My opinion is, you have to fight a war now and then to show you're willing, and it doesn't much matter where it is. The trouble isn't this war, it's this country. We wouldn't fight in Korea now. Christ, we wouldn't fight Hitler now. This country is so zonked out on its own acid, sunk so deep in its own fat and babble and laziness, it would take H-bombs on every city from Detroit to Atlanta to wake us up and even then, we'd probably think we'd just been kissed."

"Harry," Janice asks, "do you want Nelson to die in Vietnam? Go ahead, tell him you do."

Harry turns to their child and says, "Kid, I don't want you to die anyplace. Your mother's the girl that's good at death."

Even he knows how cruel this is; he is grateful to her for not collapsing, for blazing up instead. "*Oh*," she says. "Oh. Tell him why he has no brothers or sisters, Harry. Tell him who refused to have another child."

"This is getting too rich," Stavros says.

"I'm glad you're seeing it," Janice tells him, her eyes sunk deep; Nelson gets that from her.

Mercifully, the food arrives. Nelson balks, discovering the meatballs drenched in gravy. He looks at Rabbit's tidily skewered lamb and says, "That's what I wanted."

"Let's swap then. Shut up and eat," Rabbit says. He looks across to see that Janice and Stavros are having the same thing, a kind of white pie. They are sitting, to his printer's sense, too close, leaving awkward space on either side. To poke them into adjustment he says, "I think it's a swell country."

Janice takes it up, Stavros chewing in silence. "Harry, you've never *been* to any other country."

He addresses himself to Stavros. "Never had the desire to. I see these other countries on TV, they're all running like hell to be like us, and burning our Embassies because they can't make it fast enough. What other countries do *you* get to?"

Stavros interrupts his eating grudgingly to utter, "Jamaica."

"Wow," Rabbit says. "A real explorer. Three hours by jet to the lobby of some Hilton."

"They hate us down there."

"You mean they hate *you*. They never see *me*, I never go. Why do they hate us?"

"Same reason as everywhere. Exploitation. We steal their bauxite."

"Let 'em trade it to the Russkis for potatoes then. Potatoes and missile sites."

"We have missile sites in Turkey," Stavros says, his heart no longer in this.

Janice tries to help. "We've dropped two atom bombs, the Russians haven't dropped any."

"They didn't have any then or they would have. Here the Japanese were all set to commit hari-kari and we saved them from it; now look at 'em, happy as clams and twice as sassy, screwing us right and left. We fight their wars for them while you peaceniks sell their tinny cars."

Stavros pats his mouth with a napkin folded squarely and re-gains his appetite for discussion. "Her point is, we wouldn't be in this Vietnam mess if it was a white country. We wouldn't have gone in. We thought we just had to shout Boo and flash a few jazzy anti-personnel weapons. We thought it was one more Cherokee uprising. The trouble is, the Cherokees outnumber us now."

"Oh those fucking poor Indians," Harry says. "What were we supposed to do, let 'em have the whole continent for a campfire site?" Sorry, Tonto.

"If we had, it'd be in better shape than it is now."

"And we'd be nowhere. They were in the way."

"Fair enough," Stavros says. "Now you're in their way." He adds, "Paleface."

"Let 'em come," Rabbit says, and really is, at this moment, a defiant bastion. The tender blue flame has become cold fire in his eyes. He stares them down. He stares at Janice and she is dark and tense: an Indian squaw. He'd like to massacre her.

Then his son says, his voice strained upward through choked-down tears, "*Dad*, we're going to be *late* for the *mo*vie!"

Rabbit looks at his watch and sees they have four minutes to get there. The kid is right.

Stavros tries to help, fatherly like men who aren't fathers, who think kids can be fooled about essentials. "The opening part's the dullest, Nellie, you won't miss any of the space parts. You got to try some *baklava* for dessert."

"I'll miss the cave men," Nelson says, the choking almost complete, the tears almost risen.

"I guess we should go," Rabbit tells the two other adults.

"That's rude to Charlie," Janice says. "Really rude. Anyway I won't be able to stay awake during this *inter*minable movie without coffee." To Nelson: "*Baklava* is really yummy. It's honey and flakes of thin dough, just the kind of dry thing you love. Try to be considerate, Nelson, your parents so rarely get to eat in a restaurant."

Torn, Rabbit suggests, "Or you could try that other stuff you wanted for the main deal, mellow patties or whatever."

The tears do come; the kid's tense face breaks. "You *prom*-ised," he sobs, unanswerably, and hides his face against the white bare wall.

"Nelson, I am disappointed in you," Janice tells him.

Stavros says to Rabbit, tucking that pencil behind his ear again, "If you want to run now, she could get her coffee and I'll drop her off at the movie house in ten minutes."

"That's a possibility," Janice says slowly, her face opening cautiously, a dull flower.

Rabbit tells Stavros, "O.K., great. Thanks. You're nice to do that. You're nice to put up with us at all, sorry if I said anything too strong. I just can't stand to hear the U.S. knocked, I'm sure it's psychological. Janice, do you have money? Charlie, you tell her how much we owe."

Stavros repeats that masterful small gesture of palm outward, "You owe zilch. On me." There can be no argument. Standing, himself in a hurry to see the cave men (raw meat? a bone turning into a spaceship?), Rabbit experiences, among them here, in this restaurant where the Penn Park couple are paying their bill as if laying a baby to rest, keen family happiness: it prompts him to say to Janice, to cheer Nelson up further, "Remind me tomorrow to call your father about those baseball tickets."

Before Janice can intervene, Stavros says, everybody anxious now to please, "He's in the Poconos."

Janice thought when Charlie calls Harry "paleface" it's the end, from the way Harry looked over at her, his eyes a frightening icy blue, and then when Charlie let that slip about Daddy being away she knew it was; but somehow it isn't. Maybe the movie numbs them. It's so long and then that psychedelic section where he's landing on the planet before turning into a little old man in a white wig makes her head hurt, but she rides home resolved to have it out, to confess and dare him to make his move back, all he can do is run which might be a relief. She has a glass of vermouth in the kitchen to ready herself, but upstairs Nelson is shutting the door to his room and Harry is in the bathroom and when she comes out of the bathroom with the taste of toothpaste on top of the vermouth Harry is lying under the covers with just the top of his head showing. Janice gets in beside him and listens. His breathing is a sleeping tide. So she lies there awake like the moon.

In their ten though it became twenty minutes over the coffee together she had told Charlie she had thought it reckless of him to come to the restaurant when he had known she was bringing them and he said, in that way he has of going onto his dignity, his lips pushing out as if holding a lozenge and the hunch of his shoulders a bit gangsterish, that he thought that's what she wanted, that's why she told him she was going to talk them into it. At the time she thought silently, he doesn't understand women in love, just going to his restaurant, eating food that was him, had been enough an act of love for her, he didn't have to make it dangerous by showing up himself. It even coarsened it. Because once he was physically there all her caution dissolved, if instead of having coffee with her he had asked her to go to his apartment with him she would have done it and was even mentally running through the story she would have told Harry about suddenly feeling sick. But luckily he didn't ask; he finished the coffee and paid the whole bill and dropped her off under the stumpy marquee as promised. Men are strict that way, want to keep their promises to each other, women are beneath it, property. The way while making love Charlie sells her herself, murmuring about her parts, giving them the names Harry uses only in anger, she resisted at first but relaxed seeing for Charlie they were a language of love, his way of keeping himself up, selling her her own cunt. She doesn't panic as with Harry, knowing he can't hold it much longer, Charlie holds back forever, a thick sweet toy she can do anything with, her teddy bear. The fur on the back of his shoulders at first shocked her touch, something freakish, but no, that's the way many men still are. Cave men. Cave bears. Janice smiles in the dark.

In the dark of the car driving over the bridge along Weiser he asked her if Harry guessed anything. She said she thought nothing. Though something had been bugging him the last couple of days, her staying so late supposedly at the office.

"Maybe we should cool it a little."

"Oh, let him stew. His old line on me used to be I was useless, at first he was delighted I got a job. Now he thinks I neglect Nelson. I say to him, 'Give the boy a little room, he's going on thirteen and you're leaning on him worse than your own mother.' He won't even let him get a mini-bike because it's too dangerous supposedly."

Charlie said, "He sure was hostile to me."

"Not really. He's like that about Vietnam with everybody. It's what he really thinks."

"How can he think that crap? We-them, America first. It's dead."

She tried to imagine how. One of the nice things about having a lover, it makes you think about everything anew. The rest of your life becomes a kind of movie, flat and even rather funny. She answered at last, "Something is very real to him about it, I don't know what it is." She went on with difficulty, for a blurring, a halting, comes over her tongue, her head, whenever she tries to think, and one of the many beautiful things about Charlie Stavros is he lets her tumble it out anyway. He has given her not only her body but her voice. "Maybe he came back to me, to Nelson and me, for the old-fashioned reasons, and wants to live an old-fashioned life, but nobody does that anymore, and he feels it. He put his life into rules he feels melting away now. I mean, I know he thinks he's missing something, he's always reading the paper and watching the news."

Charlie laughed. The blue lights of the bridge flickered on the backs of his hands parallel on the steering wheel. "I get it. You're his overseas commitment."

She laughed too, but it seemed a little hard of him to say, to make a joke of the marriage that was, after all, a part of her too. Sometimes Charlie didn't quite listen. Her father was like that: a hurry in their blood, wind in their ears. Getting ahead, you miss what the slow people see.

Stavros sensed the little wound and tried to heal it, patting
her thigh as they arrived at the movie house. "Space odyssey,"
he said. "My idea of a space odyssey would be to get in the
sack with your ass and ball for a week." And right here, with
the light beneath the marquee slanting into the car and the
agitated last late shreds of the audience buying their tickets,
he ran his paw across her breasts and tucked his thumb into
her lap. Heated and ruffled by this touch from him, guilty and
late, she rushed into the movie house—its plum carpeting, its
unnatural coldness, its display-casket of candies—and found
Nelson and Harry down front, where they had had to sit because of her, because she had made them late so she could eat
her lover's food, the great exploding screen close above them,
their hair on fire, their ears translucent red. The backs of their
heads, innocently alike, had sprung a rush of love within her,
like coming, a push of pity that sent her scrambling across the
jagged knees of strangers to the seat her husband and son had
saved.

A car moves on the curved road outside. Rugs of light are
hurled across the ceiling. The refrigerator below speaks to itself, drops its own ice into its own tray. Her body feels tense as a
harp, she wants to be touched. She touches herself: hardly ever
did it as a girl, after marrying Harry it seemed certainly wrong,
marriage should make it never necessary, just turn to the other
person and he would fix it. How sad it was with Harry now, they
had become locked rooms to each other, they could hear each
other cry but couldn't get in, not just the baby though that was
terrible, the most terrible thing ever, but even that had faded,
flattened, until it seemed it hadn't been her in that room but an
image of her, and she had not been alone, there had been some
man in the room with her, he was with her now, not Charlie
but containing Charlie, everything you do is done in front of
this man and how good to have him made flesh. She imagines
it in her, like something you have swallowed. Only big, big.
And slow, slow as sugar melts. Except now that she'd been with
him so many times she could be quick in coming, sometimes
asking him just to pound away and startling herself, coming,
herself her toy, how strange to have to learn to play, they used
to tell her, everybody, the gym teacher, the Episcopal minister,
Mother even one awful embarrassing time, not to make your

body a plaything when that's just what it was, she wonders if
Nelson, his bedsprings creaking, his little jigger waiting for its
hair, poor child, what would he think, what must he think,
such a lonely life, sitting there alone at the TV when she comes
home, his mini-bike, she's lost it. Though she flutters it faster
she's lost it, her heat. How silly. How silly it all is. We're born
and they try to feed us and change our diapers and love us and
we get breasts and menstruate and go boy-crazy and finally
one or two come forward to touch us and we can't wait to get
married and have some babies and then stop having them and
go man-crazy this time without even knowing it until you're in
too deep the flesh grows more serious as we age and then eventually that phase must be over and we ride around in cars in
flowered hats for a while to Tucson or seeing the leaves turn in
New Hampshire and visit our grandchildren and then get into
bed like poor Mrs. Angstrom, Harry is always after her to visit
her but she doesn't see why she should she never had a good
word to say for her when she was healthy, groping for words
while her mouth makes spittle and her eyes trying to pop from
her head trying to hear herself say something malicious, and
then there's the nursing home or the hospital, poor old souls
like when they used to visit her father's older sister, TVs going
all up and down the hall and Christmas decorations dropping
needles on the linoleum, and then we die and it wouldn't have
mattered if we hadn't bothered to be born at all. And all the
time there are wars and riots and history happening but it's
not as important as the newspapers say unless you get caught
in it. Harry seems right to her about that, Vietnam or Korea
or the Philippines nobody cares about them yet they must be
died for, it just is that way, by boys that haven't shaved yet, the
other side has boys Nelson's age. How strange it is of Charlie to care so, to be so angry, as if he's a minority, which of
course he is, her father used to talk of gang fights when he was
in school, us against them, Springer an English name, Daddy
very proud of that, then why, she used to ask herself at school,
was she so dark, olive skin, never sunburned, hair that always
frizzed up and never lay flat in bangs, never knew enough until
recently to let it grow long in front and pin it back, his fucking madonna Charlie calls her blasphemously though there is
an ikon in his bedroom, didn't have enough body in school,

but she forgives those days now, sees she was being shaped, all those years, toward Charlie. His cunt. His rich cunt, though they were never rich just respectable, Daddy gave her a little stock to put away the time Harry was acting so irresponsible, the dividend checks come in, the envelopes with windows, she doesn't like Harry to see them, they make light of his working. Janice wants to weep, thinking of how hard Harry has worked these years. His mother used to say how hard he used to work practicing basketball, dribbling, shooting; whereas she said so spitefully Nelson has no aptitude. This is silly. This thinking is getting nowhere, there is tomorrow to face, must have it out with Harry, Charlie shrugs when she asks what to do, at lunch if Daddy isn't back from the Poconos they can go over to Charlie's apartment, the light used to embarrass her but she likes it best in the day now, you can see everything, men's bottoms so innocent, even the little hole like a purse drawn tight, the hair downy and dark, all the sitting they do, the world isn't natural for them any more: this is silly. Determined to bring herself off, Janice returns her hand and opens her eyes to look at Harry sleeping, all huddled into himself, stupid of him to keep her sex locked up all these years, his fault, all his fault, it was there all along, it was his job to call it out, she does everything for Charlie because he asks her, it feels holy, she doesn't care, you have to live, they put you here you have to live, you were made for one thing, women now try to deny it burning their bras but you were made for one thing, it feels like a falling, a falling away, a deep eye opening, a coming into the deep you, Harry wouldn't know about that, he never did dare dwell on it, racing ahead, he's too fastidious, hates sex really, she was there all along, there she is, oh: not quite. She knows he knows, she opens her eyes, she sees him lying on the edge of the bed, the edge of a precipice, they are on it together, they are about to fall off, she closes her eyes, she is about to fall off: there. Oh. *Oh.* The bed complains.

Janice sinks back. They say, she read somewhere, some doctors measuring your blood pressure when you do it, things taped to your head how can anybody concentrate, it's always best when you do it to yourself. Her causing the bed to shudder has stirred Harry half-awake; he heavily rolls over and loops his arm around her waist, a pale tall man going fat. She strokes his wrist with the fingers that did it. His fault. He is a ghost, white, soft. Tried to make a box for her to put her in like they put Rebecca in when the poor little baby died. The way she held it sopping wet against her chest already dead, she could feel it, and screamed a great red scream as if to make a hole to let life back in. The movie returns upon her, the great wheel turning against the black velvet in time with the glorious symphony that did lift her for all her confusion coming into the theater. Floating now like a ballerina among the sparse planets of her life, Daddy, Harry, Nelson, Charlie, she thinks of her coming without him as a betrayal of her lover, and furtively lifts her fingertips, with their nice smell of swamp, to her lips and kisses them, thinking, *You*.

Next day, Friday, the papers and television are full of the colored riots in York, snipers wounding innocent firemen, simple men on the street, what is the world coming to? The astronauts are nearing the moon's gravitational influence. A quick thunderstorm makes up in the late afternoon over Brewer, pelts shoppers and homebound workmen into the entranceways of shops, soaks Harry's white shirt before he and his father get to huddle in the Phoenix Bar. "We missed you last night," Earl Angstrom says.

"Pop, I *told* you we couldn't make it, we took the kid out to eat and then to a movie."

"O.K., don't bite my head off. I thought you left it more up in the air than that, but never mind, don't kill a man for trying."

"I said we *might*, was all. Did she act disappointed?"

"She didn't let on. Your mother's nature isn't to let on, you know that. She knows you have your problems."

"What problems?"

"How was the movie, Harry?"

"The kid liked it, I don't know, it didn't make much sense to me, but then I felt kind of sick on something I ate. I fell dead asleep soon as we got home."

"How did Janice like it? Did she seem to have a good time?"

"Hell, I don't know. At her age, are you supposed to have a good time?"

"I hope the other day I didn't seem to be poking my nose in where it doesn't belong."

"Mom still raving about it?"

"A little bit. Now Mother, I tell her, now Mother, Harry's a big boy, Harry's a responsible citizen."

"Yeah," Rabbit admits, "maybe that's my problem," and shivers. With his shirt wet, it is cruelly cold in here. He signals for another Daiquiri. The television, sound off, is showing film clips of cops in York stalking the streets in threes and fours, then cuts to a patrol in Vietnam, boys smudged with fear and fatigue, and Harry feels badly, that he isn't there with them. Then the television moves on to the big publicity-mad Norwegian who gave up trying to cross the Atlantic in a paper boat. Even if the TV sound were turned higher what he's saying would be drowned by the noise in the bar: the excitement of the thunderstorm plus its being Friday night.

"Think you could make it over this evening?" his father asks. "It doesn't have to be for long, just fifteen minutes or so. It would mean the world to her, with Mim as good as dead, hardly ever even writing a postcard."

"I'll talk to her about it," Harry says, meaning Janice, though he thinks of Mim whoring around on the West Coast, Mim that he used to take sledding on Jackson Road, snowflakes on her hood. He pictures her at parties, waiting with a face of wax, or lying beside a swimming pool freshly oiled while under the umbrella beside her some suety gangster with a cigar in the center of his face like a secondary prick pulls it from his mouth and snarls. "But don't get her hopes up," he adds, meaning his mother. "We're sure to be over Sunday. I got to run."

The storm has passed. Sun pours through the torn sky, drying the pavement rapidly. Maplike stains: a pulped Kleenex retains an island of wet around it. Overweight bag-luggers and skinny Negro idlers emerge smiling from the shelter of a disused shoe store's entrance. The defaced BUS STOP sign, the wrappers spilled from the KEEP BREWER CLEAN can with its top like a flying saucer, the dimpled and rutted asphalt all glory, glistening, in the deluge having passed. The scattered handkerchiefs and horsetails of inky storm-cloud drift east across the ridge of Mt. Judge and the sky resumes the hazed, engendering, blank look of Pennsylvania humidity. And nervousness, that seeks to condense into anger, regathers in Rabbit.

Janice is not home when he arrives. Neither is Nelson. Coming up the walk he sees that, freshened by rain, their lawn looks greasy with crabgrass, spiky with plantain. The kid supposedly gets his dollar-fifty allowance in part for keeping it mowed but he hasn't since June. The little power mower, that had belonged to the Springers until they got one of those you ride, leans in the garage, a can of 3-in-1 beside one wheel. He oils it and sloshes in the gasoline—amber in the can, colorless in the funnel—and starts it up on the fourth pull. Its swath spits gummy hunks of wet grass, back and forth across the two square patches that form their front lawn. There is a larger lawn behind, where the clothes tree stands and where Nelson and he sometimes play catch with a softball worn down to its strings. It needs mowing too, but he wants Janice to find him out front, to give her a little guilty start to get them going.

But by the time she comes home, swinging down Vista spraying untarred grit and tucking the Falcon into the garage in that infuriating way of hers, just not quite far enough to close the door on the bumper, the blades of grass are mixing long shadows with their cut tips and Rabbit stands by their one tree, a spindly maple tethered to the earth by guy wires, his palm sore from trimming the length of the walk with the hand-clippers.

"Harry," she says, "you're outdoors! How funny of you."

And it is true, Park Villas with its vaunted quarter-acre lots and compulsory barbecue chimneys does not tempt its residents outdoors, even the children in summer: in the snug brick neighborhood of Rabbit's childhood you were always outdoors, hiding in hollowed-out bushes, scuffling in the gravel alleys, secure in the closeness of windows from at least one of which an adult was always watching. Here, there is a prairie sadness, a barren sky raked by slender aerials. A sky poisoned by radio waves. A sewer smell from underground.

"Where the hell have you been?"

"Work, obviously. Daddy always used to say never to cut grass after rain, it's all lying down."

"'Work, obviously.' What's obvious about it?"

"Harry, you're so strange. Daddy came back from the Poconos today and made me stay after six with Mildred's mess."

"I thought he came back from the Poconos days ago. You lied. Why?"

Janice crosses the cut grass and they stand together, he and she and the tree, the spindly planted maple that cannot grow, as if bewildered by the wide raw light. The kerosene scent of someone else's Friday evening barbecue drifts to them. Their neighbors in Penn Villas are strangers, transients—accountants, salesmen, supervisors, adjusters—people whose lives to them are passing cars and the shouts of unseen children. Janice's color heightens. Her body takes on a defiant suppleness. "I forget, it was a silly lie, you were just so angry over the phone I had to say something. It seemed the easiest thing to say, that Daddy was there; you know how I am. You know how confused I get."

"How much other lying do you do to me?"

"None. That I can remember right now. Maybe little things, how much things cost, the sort of things women lie about. Women like to lie, Harry, it makes things more fun." And, flirtatious, unlike her, she flicks her tongue against her upper lip and holds it there, like the spring of a trap.

She steps toward the young tree and touches it where it is taped so the guy wires won't cut into the bark. He asks her, "Where's Nelson?"

"I arranged with Peggy for him to spend the night with Billy, since it's not a school night."

"With those dopes again. They give him ideas."

"At his age he's going to have ideas anyway."

"I half-promised Pop we'd go over tonight and visit Mom."

"I don't see why we should visit her. She's never liked me, she's done nothing but try to poison our marriage."

"Another question."

"Yes?"

"Are you fucking Stavros?"

"I thought women only *got* fucked."

Janice turns and choppily runs into the house, up the three steps, into the house with apple-green aluminum clapboards. Rabbit puts the mower back in the garage and enters by the side door into the kitchen. She is there, slamming pots around, making their dinner. He asks her, "Shall we go out to eat for a change? I know a nifty little Greek restaurant on Quince Street."

"That was just coincidence he showed up. I admit it was Charlie who recommended it, is there anything wrong with that? And you were certainly rude to him. You were incredible."

"I wasn't rude, we had a political discussion. I like Charlie. He's an O.K. guy, for a left-wing mealy-mouthed wop."

"You are really very strange lately, Harry. I think your mother's sickness is getting to you."

"In the restaurant, you seemed to know your way around the menu. Sure he doesn't take you there for lunch? Or on some of those late-work nights? You been working a lot of nights, and don't seem to get much done."

"You know nothing about what has to be done."

"I know your old man and Mildred Kroust used to do it themselves without all this overtime."

"Having the Toyota franchise is a whole new dimension. It's endless bills of lading, import taxes, customs forms." More fending words occur to Janice; it is like when she was little, making snow dams in the gutter. "Anyway, Charlie has lots of girls, he can have girls any time, single girls younger than me. They all go to bed now without even being asked, everybody's on the Pill, they just assume it." One sentence too many.

"How do you know?"

"He tells me."

"So you *are* chummy."

"Not very. Just now and then, when he's hung or needing a little mothering or something."

"Right—maybe he's scared of these hot young tits, maybe he likes older women, *mamma mia* and all that. These slick Mediterranean types need a lot of mothering."

It's fascinating to her, to see him circling in; she fights the rising in her of a wifely wish to collaborate, to help him find the truth that sits so large in her own mind she can hardly choose the words that go around it.

"Anyway," he goes on, "those girls aren't the boss's daughter."

Yes, that is what he'd think, it was what she thought those first times, those first pats as she was standing tangled in a net of numbers she didn't understand, those first sandwich lunches they would arrange when Daddy was out on the lot, those first five-o'clock whisky sours in the Atlas Bar down the street, those first kisses in the car, always a different car, one they had borrowed from the lot, with a smell of new car like a protective skin their touches were burning through. That was what she thought until he convinced her it was her, funny old clumsy her, Janice Angstrom née Springer; it was her flesh being licked like ice cream, her time being stolen in moments compressed as diamonds, her nerves caught up in an exchange of pleasure that oscillated between them in tightening swift circles until it seemed a kind of frenzied sleep, a hypnosis so intense that later in her own bed she could not sleep at all, as if she had napped that afternoon. His apartment, they discovered, was only twelve minutes distant, if you drove the back way, by the old farmers' market that was now just a set of empty tin-roofed sheds.

"What good would my being the boss's daughter do him?"

"It'd make him feel he was climbing. All these Greeks or Polacks or whatever are on the make."

"I'd never realized, Harry, how full of racial prejudice you are."

"Yes or no about you and Stavros."

"No." But lying she felt, as when a child watching the snow dams melt, that the truth must push through, it was too big, too constant: though she was terrified and would scream, it was something she must have, her confession like a baby. She felt so proud.

"You dumb bitch," he says. He hits her not in the face but on the shoulder, like a man trying to knock open a stuck door.

She hits him back, clumsily, on the side of the neck, as high as she can reach. Harry feels a flash of pleasure: sunlight in a tunnel. He hits her three, four, five times, unable to stop, boring his way to that sunlight, not as hard as he can hit, but hard enough for her to whimper; she doubles over so that his last punches are thrown hammerwise down into her neck and back, an angle he doesn't see her from that much—the chalk-white parting, the candle-white nape, the bra strap showing through the fabric of the back of the blouse. Her sobbing arises muffled and, astonished by a beauty in her abasement, by a face that shines through her reduction to this craven faceless posture, he pauses. Janice senses that he will not hit her anymore. She abandons her huddle, flops over to her side, and lets herself cry out loud—high-pitched, a startled noise pinched between sieges of windy gasping. Her face is red, wrinkled, newborn; in curiosity he drops to his knees to examine her. Her black eyes flash at this and she spits up at his face, but misjudges; the saliva falls back into her own face. For him there is only the faintest kiss of spray. Flecked with her own spit Janice cries, "I do, I *do* sleep with Charlie!"

"Ah, shit," Rabbit says softly, "of course you do," and bows his head into her chest, to protect himself from her scratching, while he half-pummels her sides, half-tries to embrace her and lift her.

"I love him. Damn you, Harry. We make love all the time."

"Good," he moans, mourning the receding of that light, that ecstasy of his hitting her, of knocking her open. Now she will become again a cripple he must take care of. "Good for you."

"It's been going on for *months*," she insists, writhing and trying to get free to spit again, furious at his response. He pins her arms, which would claw, at her sides and squeezes her hard. She stares into his face. Her face is wild, still, frozen. She is seeking what will hurt him most. "I do things for him," she says, "I never do for you."

"Sure you do," he murmurs, wanting to have a hand free to stroke her forehead, to re-enclose her. He sees the gloss of her forehead and the gloss of the kitchen linoleum. Her hair wriggles outward into the spilled wriggles of the marbled linoleum pattern, worn where she stands at the sink. A faint rotten smell here, of the sluggish sink tie-in. Janice abandons herself to crying and limp relief, and he has no trouble lifting her and carrying her in to the living-room sofa. He has zombie-strength: his shins shiver, his palm sore from the clipper handles is a stiff crescent.

She sinks lost into the sofa's breadth.

He prompts her, "He makes better love than me," to keep her confession flowing, as a physician moistens a boil.

She bites her tongue, trying to think, surveying her ruins with an eye toward salvage. Impure desires—to save her skin, to be kind, to be exact—pollute her primary fear and anger. "He's different," she says. "I'm more exciting to him than to you. I'm sure it's just mostly our not being married."

"Where do you do it?"

Worlds whirl past and cloud her eyes—car seats, rugs, tree undersides seen through windshields, the beigy-gray carpeting in the narrow space between the three green steel desks and the safe and the Toyota cutout, motel rooms with their cardboard panelling and scratchy bedspreads, his dour bachelor's apartment stuffed with heavy furniture and tinted relatives in silver frames. "Different places."

"Do you want to marry him?"

"No. *No.*" Why does she say this? The possibility opens an abyss. She would not have known this. A gate she had always assumed gave onto a garden gave onto emptiness. She tries to drag Harry down closer to her; she is lying on the sofa, one shoe off, her bruises just beginning to smart, while he kneels on the carpet, having carried her here. He remains stiff when she pulls at him, he is dead, she has killed him.

He asks, "Was I so lousy to you?"

"Oh sweetie, no. You were good to me. You came back. You work in that dirty place. I don't know what got into me, Harry, I honestly don't."

"Whatever it was," he tells her, "it must be still there." He looks like Nelson, saying this, a mulling discontented hurt look, puzzling to pry something open, to get something out. She sees she will have to make love to him. A conflicted tide moves within her—desire for this pale and hairless stranger, abhorrence of this desire, fascination with the levels of betrayal possible.

He shies, afraid of failing her; he falls back from the sofa and sits on the floor and offers to talk, to strike a balance. "Do you remember Ruth?"

"The whore you lived with when you ran away."

"She wasn't a whore exactly."

"Whatever she was, what about her?"

"A couple of years ago, I saw her again."

"Did you sleep with her?"

"Oh God no. She had become very straight. That was the thing. We met on Weiser Street, she was shopping. She had put on so much weight I didn't recognize her, I think she recognized me first, something about the way this woman looked at me; and then it hit me. Ruth. She still had this great head of hair. By then she had gone by, I followed her for a while and then she ducked into Kroll's. I gave it an even chance, I waited there at the side entrance figuring if she came out of that one I'd say hello and if she went out one of the others, O.K. I gave it five minutes. I really wasn't that interested." But in saying this, his beart beats faster, as it had beat then. "Just as I was going away she came out lugging two shopping bags and looked at me and the first thing she said was, 'Let me alone.'"

"She loved you," Janice explains.

"She did and she didn't," he says, and loses her sympathy with this complacence. "I offered to buy her a drink but all she'd let me do is walk her up toward the parking lot where the old Acme used to be. She lived out toward Galilee, she told me. Her husband was a chicken farmer and ran a string of school buses, I got the impression he was some guy older than she was, who'd had a family before. She told me they had three children, a girl and two boys. She showed me their pictures in a wallet. I asked how often she got into town and she said, 'As far as you're concerned, never.'"

"Poor Harry," Janice says. "She sounds awful."

"Well, she was, but still. She'd gotten heavy, as I said, she was sort of lost inside this other person who pretty much blended in with those other fat bag-luggers you see downtown, but at the same time, still, it was *her.*"

"All right. You still love her," Janice says.

"No, I didn't, I don't. You haven't heard the worse thing she did then."

"I can't believe you never tried to get in touch with her after you came back to me. At least to see what she did about her . . . pregnancy."

"I felt I *shouldn't.*" But he sees now, in his wife's dark and judging eyes, that the rules were more complicated, that there were some rules by which he should have. There were rules beneath the surface rules that also mattered. She should have explained this when she took him back.

She asks, "What was the worse thing?"

"I don't know if I should tell you."

"Tell me. Let's tell each other everything, then we'll take off all our clothes." She sounds tired. The shock of having given it all away must be sinking in. He talks to distract, as we joke with a loser at poker.

"You already said it. About the baby. I thought of that and asked her how old the girl was, her oldest child. She wouldn't tell me. I asked to see the wallet pictures again, to see if there was, you know, a resemblance. She wouldn't show them to me. She laughed at me. She was really quite nasty. She said something very strange."

"What?"

"I forget exactly. She looked me over and said I'd gotten fat. This from *her*. Then she said, 'Run along, Rabbit. You've had your day in the cabbage patch.' Or something like that. Nobody ever calls me Rabbit, was what sort of got me. This was two years ago. I think in the fall. I haven't seen her since."

"Tell me the truth now. These ten years, haven't you had any other women?"

He runs his mind backward, encounters a few dark places, a room in a Polish-American Club where Verity was having its annual blast, a skinny flat-chested girl with a cold, she had kept her bra and sweater on; and then a weird episode at the Jersey shore, Janice and Nelson off at the amusement park, him back from the beach in his trunks, a knock at the door of the cabin, a chunky colored girl, two skinny boys escorting her, offering herself for five or seven dollars, depending what he wanted done. He had had trouble understanding her accent, had made her repeat—with downcast eyes, as the boys with her sniggered —"screwin'," "suck-off." Frightened, he had quickly shut the flimsy door on them, locked it as if they had threatened to harm him, and jerked off facing the wall; the wall smelled of damp and salt. He tells Janice, "You know, ever since that happened to Becky, I haven't been that much for sex. It comes on, wanting it, and then something turns it off."

"Let me up."

Janice stands in front of the television set, the screen green ashes, a dead fire. Efficiently she undresses herself. Her dark-tipped breasts droop tubular and sway as she disengages her pantyhose. Her tan stops below her throat. Other summers they used to go to the West Brewer pool some Sundays but the kid became too big to go with his parents so none go now. They haven't gone to the Shore since the Springers discovered the Poconos. Buggy brown lakes imprisoned among dark green trees: Rabbit hates it there and never goes, never goes anywhere, takes his vacation around the house. He used to daydream about going South, Florida or Alabama, to see the cotton fields and the alligators, but that was a boy's dream and died with the baby. He once saw Texas and that has to be enough. Tongue pinched between her lips, naked Janice unbuttons his shirt, fumbling. Numbly he takes over, completes the job. The pants, the shoes last. Socks. Air knows him, air of day still lingering, summer air tingling along the skin that never knows the light. He and Janice have not made love in the light for years. She asks him in the middle of it, "Don't you love *see*ing? I used to be so embarrassed."

In twilight they eat, still naked, salami sandwiches she makes, and drink whisky. Their house stays dark, though the others around them, that mirror it, turn on their lights. These neighboring lights, and the cars that pass along Vista Crescent, throw sliding soft witnesses into their room: the open shelves lunge like parallel swords, the driftwood lamp throws a rhinoceros-shadow, the school portrait of Nelson, in its cardboard frame on the mantel, from beneath the embalming tints of its color wash, smiles. To help them see when darkness comes, Janice turns on the television set without sound, and by the bluish flicker of module models pantomiming flight, of riot troops standing before smashed supermarkets, of a rowboat landing in Florida having crossed the Atlantic, of situation comedies and western melodramas, of great gray momentary faces unstable as quicksilver, they make love again, her body a stretch of powdery sand, her mouth a loose black hole, her eyes holes with sparks in them, his own body a barren landscape lit by bombardment, silently exploding images no gentler than Janice's playful expert touches, that pass through him and do him no harm. She inverts herself and pours out upon him the months of her new knowledge; her appetite frightens him, knowing he cannot fill it, any more than Earth's appetite for death can be satisfied. Her guilt became love; her love becomes rage. The first time was too quick but the second was sweet, with work and sweat in it, and the third time strainingly sweet, a work of the spirit almost purely, and the fourth time, because there was no fourth time, sad; straddling his thighs, her cunt revealed by the flickering touch of the television to be lopsidedly agape, she bows her head, her hair tickling his belly, and drops cold tears, starpricks, upon the slack flesh that has failed her.

"Jesus," he says, "I forgot. We were supposed to go over to Mom's tonight!"

He dreams of driving north with Charlie Stavros, in a little scarlet Toyota. The gear shift is very thin, a mere pencil, and he is afraid of breaking it as he shifts. Also, he is wearing golf shoes, which makes operating the pedals awkward. Stavros sits in the driver's seat and, with that stolid way of muttering, his square ringed hands masterfully gesturing, discusses his problem: Lyndon Johnson has asked him to be his Vice-President. They need a Greek. He would like to accept, but doesn't want to leave Brewer. So they are negotiating to have at least the summer White House moved to Brewer. They have lots of vacant lots they could build it on, Charlie explains. Rabbit is thinking maybe this is his chance to get out of the printing plant and into a white-collar job. Services and software are where the future lies. He tells Stavros hopefully, "I can lick stamps." He shows him his tongue. They are on a super-highway heading north, into the deserted coal regions and, beyond that, the wilds of northern Pennsylvania. Yet here, in this region of woods and lakes, a strange white city materializes beside the highway; hill after hill of tall row houses white as bedsheets, crowding to the horizon, an enormous city, strange it seems to have no name. They part in a suburban region beside a drugstore and Stavros hands him a map; with difficulty Rabbit locates on it where they are. The metropolis, marked with a bull's-eye, is named, simply, The Rise.

The Rise, The Rise . . . the dream is so unpleasant he awakes, with a headache and an erection. His prick feels glassily thin and aches from all that work with Janice. The bed is empty beside him. He remembers they went to bed after two, when the television screen became a buzzing test-signal. He hears the sound of the vacuum cleaner downstairs. She is up.

He dresses in his Saturday clothes, patched chinos and apricot polo shirt, and goes downstairs. Janice is in the living room sweeping, pushing the silver tube back and forth. She glances over at him, looking old. Sex ages us. Priests are boyish, spinsters stay black-haired until after fifty. We others, the demon rots us out. She says, "There's orange juice on the table, and an egg in the pan. Let me finish this room."

From the breakfast table he surveys his house. The kitchen on one side, the living room on the other are visible. The furniture that frames his life looks Martian in the morning light: an armchair covered in synthetic fabric enlivened by a silver thread, a sofa of airfoam slabs, a low table hacked to imitate an antique cobbler's bench, a piece of driftwood that is a lamp, nothing shaped directly for its purpose, gadgets designed to repel repair, nothing straight from a human hand, furniture Rabbit has lived among but has never known, made of substances he cannot name, that has aged as in a department store window, worn out without once conforming to his body. The orange juice tastes acid; it is not even frozen orange juice but some chemical mix tinted orange.

He breaks his egg into the pan, sets the flame low, thinks guiltily of his mother. Janice turns off the vacuum, comes over, pours herself some coffee to sit opposite him with as he eats. Lack of sleep has left purple dents beneath her eyes. He asks her, "Are you going to tell him?"

"I suppose I must."

"Why? Wouldn't you like to keep him?"

"What are you saying, Harry?"

"Keep him, if he makes you happy. I don't seem to, so go ahead, until you've had your fill at least."

"Suppose I never have my fill?"

"Then I guess you should marry him."

"Charlie can never marry anybody."

"Who says?"

"He did once. I asked him why not and he wouldn't say. Maybe it has to do with his heart murmur. That was the only time we ever discussed it."

"What *do* you and he discuss? Except which way to do it next."

She might have risen to this taunt but doesn't. She is very flat, very honest and dry this morning, and this pleases him. A graver woman than he has known reveals herself. We contain chords someone else must strike. "We don't say much. We talk about funny little things, things we see from his windows, things we did as children. He loves to listen to me; when he was a boy they lived in the worst part of Brewer, a town like Mt. Judge looked marvellous to him. He calls me a rich bitch."

"The boss's daughter."

"Don't, Harry. You said that last night. You can't understand. It would sound silly, the things we talk about. He has a gift, Charlie does, of making everything exciting—the way food tastes, the way the sky looks, the customers that come in. Once you get past that defensiveness, that tough guy act, he's quite quick and, *lov*ing, in what he sees. He felt awful last night, after you left, that he had made you say more than you meant to. He hates to argue. He loves life. He really does, Harry. He loves life."

"We all do."

"Not really. I think our generation, the way we were raised, makes it hard for us to love life. Charlie does. It's like—daylight. You want to know something?"

He agrees, "Sure," knowing it will hurt.

"Daylight love—it's the best."

"O.*K*. Relax. I said, keep the son of a bitch."

"I don't believe you."

"Only one thing. Try to keep the kid from knowing. My mother already knows, the people who visit her tell her. It's all over town. Talk about daylight."

"*Let* it be," Janice says. She rises. "Goddam your mother, Harry. The only thing she's ever done for us is try to poison our marriage. Now she's drowning in the poison of her life. She's dying and I'm glad."

"Jesus, don't say that."

"Why not? She would, if it were me. Who did she want you to marry? Tell me, who would have been wonderful enough for you? Who?"

"My sister," he suggests.

"Let me tell you something else. At first with Charlie,

whenever I'd feel guilty, so I couldn't relax, I'd just think of your mother, how she's not only treated me but treated *Nel*son, her own *grand*son, and I'd say to myself, O.K., fella, sock it to me, and I'd just *come*."

"O.K., O.K. Spare me the fine print."

"I'm sick, so sick, of sparing you things. There've been a lot of days"—and this makes her too sad to confess, so that a constraint slips like a net over her face, which goes ugly under the pull—"when I was sorry you came back that time. You were a beautiful brainless guy and I've had to watch that guy die day by day."

"It wasn't so bad last night, was it?"

"No. It was so good I'm angry. I'm all confused."

"You've been confused from birth, kid." He adds, "Any dying I've been doing around here, you've been helping it right along." At the same time, he wants to fuck her again, to see if she can turn inside out again. For some minutes last night she turned all tongue and his mouth was glued to hers as if in an embryo the first cell division had not yet occurred.

The phone rings. Janice plucks it from its carriage on the kitchen wall and says, "Hi, Daddy. How was the Poconos? Good. I knew she would. She just needed to feel appreciated. Of course he's here. Here he is." She holds it out to Rabbit. "For you."

Old man Springer's voice is reedy, coaxing, deferential. "Harry, how's everything?"

"Not bad."

"You still game for the ball game? Janice mentioned you asked about the tickets to the Blasts today. They're in my hand, three right behind first base. The manager's been a client of mine for twenty years."

"Yeah, great. The kid spent the night at the Fosnachts, but I'll get him back. You want to meet at the stadium?"

"Let me pick you up, Harry. I'll be happy to pick you up in my car. That way we'll leave Janice yours." A note in his voice that didn't used to be there, gentle, faintly wheedling: nursing along an invalid. He knows too. The world knows. It'll be in the *Vat* next week. LINOTYPER'S WIFE LAYS LOCAL SALES REP. *Greek Takes Strong Anti-Viet Stand.*

"Tell me, Harry," Springer wheedles on, "how is your mother's health? Rebecca and I are naturally very concerned. *Very* concerned."

"My father says it's about the same. It's a slow process, you know. They have drugs now that make it even slower. I've been meaning this week to get up to Mt. Judge to see her but we haven't managed."

"When you do, Harry, give her our love. Give her our love."

Saying everything twice: he probably swung the Toyota franchise because the Japs could understand him second time around.

"O.K., sure enough. Want Janice back?"

"No, Harry, you can keep her." A joke. "I'll be by twelve-twenty, twelve-thirty."

He hangs up. Janice is gone from the kitchen. He finds her in the living room crying. He goes and kneels beside the sofa and puts his arms around her but these actions feel like stage directions followed woodenly. A button is off on her blouse and the sallow curve of breast into the bra mixes with her hot breath in his ear. She says, "You can't understand, how good he was. Not sexy or funny or anything, just *good*."

"Sure I can. I've known some good people. They make you feel good."

"They make you feel everything you do and are *is* good. He never told me how dumb I am, every hour on the hour like you do, even though he's much smarter than you could ever imagine. He would have gone to college, if he hadn't been a Greek."

"Oh. Don't they let Greeks in now? The nigger quota too big?"

"You say such sick things, Harry."

"It's because nobody tells me how good I am," he says, and stands. The back of her neck is vulnerable beneath him. One good karate chop would do it.

The driveway crackles outside; it's much too early for Springer. He goes to the window. A teal-blue Fury. The passenger door swings open and Nelson gets out. On the other side appears Peggy Gring, wearing sunglasses and a miniskirt that flashes her big thighs like a card dealer's thumbs. Unhappiness —being deserted—has made her brisk, professional. She gives

Rabbit hardly a hello and her sunglasses hide the eyes that he knows from school days look northeast and northwest. The two women go into the kitchen. From the sound of Janice snuffling he guesses a confession is in progress. He goes outside to finish the yard work he began last night. All around him, in the back yards of Vista Crescent, to the horizons of Penn Villas with their barbecue chimneys and aluminum wash trees, other men are out in their yards; the sound of his mower is echoed from house to house, his motions of bending and pushing are carried outwards as if in fragments of mirror suspended from the hot blank sky. These his neighbors, they come with their furniture in vans and leave with the vans. They get together to sign futile petitions for better sewers and quicker fire protection but otherwise do not connect. Nelson comes out and asks him, "What's the matter with Mommy?"

He shuts off the mower. "What's she doing?"

"She's sitting at the table with Mrs. Fosnacht crying her eyes out."

"Still? I don't know, kid; she's upset. One thing you must learn about women, their chemistries are different from ours."

"Mommy almost never cries."

"So maybe it's good for her. Get lots of sleep last night?"

"Some. We watched an old movie about torpedo boats."

"Looking forward to the Blasts game?"

"Sure."

"But not much, huh?"

"I don't like sports as much as you do, Dad. It's all so competitive."

"That's life. Dog eat dog."

"You think? Why can't things just be nice? There's enough stuff for everybody to share."

"You think there is? Why don't you start then by sharing this lawnmowing? You push it for a while."

"You owe me my allowance." As Rabbit hands him a dollar bill and two quarters, the boy says, "I'm saving for a mini-bike."

"Good luck."

"Also, Dad—?"

"Yeah?"

"I think I should get a dollar twenty-five an hour for work. That's still under the federal minimum wage."

"See?" Rabbit tells him. "Dog eat dog."

As he washes up inside, pulling grass bits out of his cuffs and putting a Band-aid on the ball of his thumb (tender place; in high school they used to say you could tell how sexy a girl was by how fat she was here), Janice comes into the bathroom, shuts the door, and says, "I've decided to tell him. While you're at the ball game I'll tell him." Her face looks taut but pretty dried-out; patches of moisture glisten beside her nose. The tile walls amplify her sniffs. Peggy Gring's car roars outside in leaving.

"Tell who what?"

"Tell Charlie. That it's all over. That you know."

"I said, keep him. Don't do anything for today at least. Calm down. Have a drink. See a movie. See that space movie again, you slept through the best parts."

"That's cowardly. No. He and I have always been honest with each other, I must tell him the truth."

"I think you're just looking for an excuse to see him while I'm tucked away at the ball park."

"You would think that."

"Suppose he asks you to sleep with him?"

"He wouldn't."

"Suppose he does, as a graduation present?"

She stares at him boldly: dark gaze tempered in the furnace of betrayal. It comes to him: growth is betrayal. There is no other route. There is no arriving somewhere without leaving somewhere. "I would," she says.

"Where are you going to find him?"

"At the lot. He stays on until six summer Saturdays."

"What reason are you going to give him? For breaking it off."

"Why, the fact that you know."

"Suppose he asks you why you told?"

"It's obvious why I told. I told because I'm your wife."

Tears belly out between her lids and the tension of her face breaks like Nelson's when a hidden anxiety, a D or a petty theft or a headache, is confessed. Harry denies his impulse to put his arm around her; he does not want to feel wooden again. She teeters, keeping her balance while sobbing, sitting on the edge of the bathtub, while the plastic shower curtain rustles at her shoulder.

"Aren't you going to stop me?" she brings out at last.

"Stop you from what?"

"From *see*ing him!"

Given this rich present of her grief, he can afford to be cruel. Coolly he says, "No, see him if you want to. Just as long as *I* don't have to see the bastard." And, avoiding the sight of her face, he sees himself in the cabinet mirror, a big pink pale man going shapeless under the chin, his little lips screwed awry in what wants to be a smile.

The gravel in the driveway crackles again. From the bathroom window he sees the boxy dun top of Springer's spandy new Toyota wagon. To Nelson he calls, "Grandpa's here. Let's go-o." To Janice he murmurs, "Sit tight, kid. Don't commit yourself to anything." To his father-in-law, sliding in beside him, across a spaghetti of nylon safety straps, Rabbit sings, "Buy me some peanuts and crack-er-jack . . ."

The stadium is on the northern side of Brewer, through a big cloverleaf, past the brick hulks of two old hosiery mills, along a three-lane highway where in these last years several roadside restaurants have begun proclaiming themselves as Pennsylvania Dutch, with giant plaster Amishmen and neon hex signs. GENUINE "*Dutch*" COOKING. *Pa. Dutch Smörgåsbord*. Trying to sell what in the old days couldn't be helped. Making a tourist attraction out of fat-fried food and a diet of dough that would give a pig pimples. They pass the country fairgrounds, where every September the same battered gyp stands return, and the farmers bring their stinking livestock, and Serafina the Egyptian Temptress will take off all her clothes for those yokels who put up a dollar extra. The first naked woman he saw was Serafina or her mother. She kept on her high heels and a black mask and bent way backwards; she spread her legs and kept a kind of token shimmy rhythm as she moved in a semi-circle so every straining head (luckily he was tall even then) could see a trace of her cleft, an exciting queasy-making wrinkle shabbily masked by a patch of hair that looked to him pasted-on. Rubbed threadbare? He didn't know. He couldn't imagine.

Springer is shaking his head over the York riots. "Sniper fire four nights in a row, Harry. What is the world coming to? We're so defenseless, is what strikes me, we're so defenseless against the violent few. All our institutions have been based on trust."

Nelson pipes up. "It's the only way they can get justice, Grandpa. Our laws defend property instead of people."

"They're defeating their own purposes, Nellie. Many a white man of good will like myself is being turned against the blacks. Slowly but surely he's being turned against them. It wasn't Vietnam beat Humphrey, it was law and order in the streets. That's the issue that the common man votes upon. Am I right or wrong, Harry? I'm such an old fogey I don't trust my own opinions any more."

One old geezer, Harry is remembering, at the side of the little stage, reached from behind and put his hand up on her pussy, shouting, "Aha!" She stopped her dance and stared out of the black mask. The tent went quiet; the geezer, surprisingly, found enough blood in himself to blush. *Aha.* That cry of triumph, as if he had snared a precious small animal, Harry never forgot. *Aha.* He slouches down and in answer to Springer says, "Things go bad. Food goes bad, people go bad, maybe a whole country goes bad. The blacks now have more than ever, but it feels like less, maybe. We were all brought up to want things and maybe the world isn't big enough for all that wanting. I don't know. I don't know anything."

Old man Springer laughs; he snorts and snarls so his little gray mouse of a mustache merges with his nostril hairs. "Did you hear about Teddy Kennedy this morning?"

"What about him? No."

"Shut your ears, Nellie. I forgot you were in the car or I wouldn't have mentioned it."

"What, Grandpa? What did he do? Did somebody shoot him?"

"Apparently, Harry"—Springer talks out of the side of his mouth, as if to shield Nelson, yet so distinctly the child can easily hear—"he dumped some girl from Pennsylvania into one of those Massachusetts rivers. Murder as plain as my face." Springer's face, from the side, is a carving of pink bone, with rosy splotches where the cheekbones put most pressure, and a bump of red on the point where the nose turns. An anxious sharp face creased all over by a salesman's constant smile. One thing at least about setting type, there's a limit on how much ass you must kiss.

"Did they get him? Is he in jail, Grandpa?"

"Ah, Nellie, they'll never put a Kennedy in jail. Palms will be greased. Evidence will be suppressed. I call it a crying shame."

Rabbit asks, "What do you mean, dumped some girl?"

"They found her in his car upside down in the water beside some bridge, I forget the name, one of those islands they have up there. It happened last night and he didn't go to the police until they were about to nab him. And they call this a democracy, Harry, is the irony of it."

"What would you call it?"

"I'd call it a police state run by the Kennedys, is what I would call it. That family has been out to buy the country since those Brahmins up in Boston snubbed old Joe. And then he put himself in league with Hitler when he was FDR's man in London. Now they've got the young widow to marry a rich Greek in case they run out of American money. Not that she's the goodie-gumdrop the papers say; those two were a match. What's your opinion, Harry? Am I talking out of line? I'm such a back number now I don't trust to hear myself talk." *Aha.*

"I'd say," Harry says, "you're right with it. You should join the kids and buy yourself a bomb to throw."

Springer looks over from driving (the yellow parabolas of a McDonald's flash by; the tinsel spinners of a Mobil station break the noon sun into trinkets) to see if he has oversold. How timid, really, people who live by people must be. Earl Angstrom was right about that at least: better make your deals with things. Springer says, hedgily smiling, showing porcelain teeth beneath the gray blur, "I'll say this for the Kennedys, however, they don't get my dander up like FDR. There was a man, Harry, so mad he died of maggots in the brain. One thing to be said for the Kennedys, they didn't try to turn the economy upside down for the benefit of the poor, they were willing to ride along with the System as it's been handed down."

Nelson says, "Billy Fosnacht says when we grow up we're going to overthrow the System."

Springer can't hear, lost in his vision of executive madness and corruption. "He tried to turn it upside down for the benefit of the black and white trash, and when that didn't work for

eight years he finagled the little Japanese into attacking Pearl
Harbor so he had a war to bail him out of the Depression.
That's why you have these wars, believe it or not, to bail the
Democrats out of their crazy economics. LBJ, now, as soon as
he got his four-year guarantee, went into Vietnam where no-
body wanted us, just to get the coloreds up into the economy.
LBJ, he was an FDR man. Truman, the same thing in Korea.
History bears me out, every time, call me an old fogey if you
want to: what's your angle on it, Nelson?"

"Last night on television," the boy says, "we watched an
old movie about fighting the Japs in the Pacific, this little boat
sank, and the captain or whatever he was swam miles with a
broken back dragging this other guy."

"That was Kennedy," Springer says. "Pure propaganda. They
made that movie because Old Joe owned a lot of those studios.
He sank his money into the movies when all the honest businessmen who'd put this country on the map were losing their
shirts. He was in close league, the story I heard, with those
Jewish Communists out there."

Rabbit tells Nelson, "That's where your Aunt Mim is now,
out there with those Communists."

"She's beautiful," Nelson tells his grandfather. "Have you
ever seen my Aunt Mim?"

"Not as much as I'd have liked to, Nellie. She is a striking
figure, however, I know you're right there. You're right to be
proud of her. Harry, your silence disturbs me. Your silence disturbs me. Maybe I'm way off base—way off. Tell me what *you*
think of the state of the nation. With these riots everywhere,
and this poor Polish girl, she comes from up near Williamsport,
abused and drowned when the future President takes his pleasure. Pregnant, wouldn't surprise me. Nellie, you shouldn't be
hearing any of this."

Harry stretches, cramped in the car, short of sleep. They are
near the stadium, and a little colored boy is waving them into a
lot. "I think," he says, "about America, it's still the only place."

But something has gone wrong. The ball game is boring.
The spaced dance of the men in white fails to enchant, the
code beneath the staccato spurts of distant motion refuses to
yield its meaning. Though basketball was his sport, Rabbit remembers the grandeur of all that grass, the excited perilous

feeling when a high fly was hoisted your way, the homing-in on
the expanding dot, the leathery smack of the catch, the formalized nonchalance of the heads-down trot in toward the bench,
the ritual flips and shrugs and the nervous courtesies of the
batter's box. There was a beauty here bigger than the hurtling
beauty of basketball, a beauty refined from country pastures,
a game of solitariness, of waiting, waiting for the pitcher to
complete his gaze toward first base and throw his lightning,
a game whose very taste, of spit and dust and grass and sweat
and leather and sun, was America. Sitting behind first base
between his son and his father-in-law, the sun resting on his
thighs, the rolled-up program in his hand, Rabbit waits for
this beauty to rise to him, through the cheers and the rhythm
of innings, the traditional national magic, tasting of his youth;
but something is wrong. The crowd is sparse, thinning out
from a cluster behind the infield to fistfuls of boys sprawling
on the green seats sloped up from the outfield. Sparse, loud,
hard: only the drunks, the bookies, the cripples, the senile, and
the delinquents come out to the ball park on a Saturday afternoon. Their catcalls are coarse and unkind. "Ram it down
his throat, Speedy!" "Kill that black bastard!" Rabbit yearns
to protect the game from the crowd; the poetry of space and
inaction is too fine, too slowly spun for them. And for the
players themselves, they seem expert listlessly, each intent on a
private dream of making it, making it into the big leagues and
the big money, the own-your-own-bowling-alley money; they
seem specialists like any other, not men playing a game because
all men are boys time is trying to outsmart. A gallant pretense
has been abandoned. Only the explosions of orange felt on
their uniforms, under the script *Blasts*, evoke the old world of
heraldic local loyalties. Brewer versus Hazleton and who cares?
Not Springer: as he watches, his lips absent-mindedly move as
if sorting out old accounts. Not Nelson: the screen of reality
is too big for the child, he misses television's running commentary, the audacious commercials. His politely unspoken
disappointment nags at Rabbit, prevents the game from rising
and filling the scared hollow Janice's confession has left in him.
The eight-team leagues of his boyhood have vanished with the
forty-eight-star flag. The shortstops never chew tobacco any
more. The game drags on, with a tedious flurry of strategy, of

pinch-hitters and intentional walks, prolonging the end. Ha-zleton wins, 7–3. Old man Springer sighs, getting up as if from a nap in an unnatural position. He wipes a fleck of beer from his mustache. "'Fraid our boys didn't come through for you, Nellie," he says.

"That's O.K., Grampa. It was neat."

To Harry he says, needing to find something to sell, "That young Trexler is a comer though."

Rabbit is cross and groggy from two beers in the sun. He doesn't invite Springer into his house, just thanks him a lot for everything. The house is silent, like outer space. On the kitchen table is a sealed envelope, addressed "Harry." The letter inside, in Janice's half-formed hand, with its unsteady slant and miserly cramping, says

Harry dear—

I must go off a few days to think. Please don't try to find or follow me *please*. It is very important that we all respect each other as people and trust each other now. I was shocked by your idea that I keep a lover since I don't think this would be honest and it made me wonder if I mean anything to you at all. Tell Nelson I've gone to the Poconos with Grandmom. Don't forget to give him lunch money for the playground.

Love,
Jan

"Jan"—her name from the years she used to work at Kroll's selling salted nuts in the smock with *Jan* stitched above the pocket in script. In those days some afternoons they would go to Linda Hammacher's apartment up on Eighth Street. The horizontal rose rays as the sun set behind the great gray gas-holder. The wonder of it as she let him slip off all her clothes. Underwear more substantial then: stocking snaps to undo, the marks of elastic printed on her skin. Jan. That name suspended in her these fifteen years; the notes she left for him around the house were simply signed "J."

"Where's Mom?" Nelson asks.

"She's gone to the Poconos," Rabbit says, pulling the note back toward his chest, in case the boy tries to read it. "She's gone with Mom-mom, her legs were getting worse in this heat.

I know it seems crazy, but that's how things are sometimes. You and I can eat over at Burger Bliss tonight."

The boy's face—freckled, framed by hair that covers his ears, his plump lips buttoned shut and his eyes sunk in fear of making a mistake—goes rapt, seems to listen, as when he was two and flight and death were rustling above him. Perhaps his experience then shapes what he says now. Firmly he tells his father, "She'll be back."

Sunday dawns muggy. The eight-o'clock news says there was scattered shooting again last night in York and the western part of the state. Edgartown police chief Dominick J. Arena is expected today formally to charge Senator Kennedy with leaving the scene of an accident. Apollo Eleven is in lunar orbit and the Eagle is being readied for its historic descent. Rabbit slept badly and turns the box off and walks around the lawn barefoot to shock the headache out of his skull. The houses of Penn Villas are still, with the odd Catholic car roaring off to mass. Nelson comes down around nine, and after making him breakfast Harry goes back to bed with a cup of coffee and the Sunday Brewer *Standard*. Snoopy on the front page of the funny papers is lying dreaming on his doghouse and soon Rabbit falls asleep. The kid looked scared. The boy's face shouts, and a soundless balloon comes out. When he awakes, the electric clock says five of eleven. The second hand sweeps around and around; a wonder the gears don't wear themselves to dust. Rabbit dresses—fresh white shirt out of respect for Sunday—and goes downstairs the second time, his feet still bare, the carpeting fuzzy to his soles, a bachelor feeling. The house feels enormous, all his. He picks up the phone book and searches out

Stavros Chas 1204EisenhwerAv

He doesn't dial, merely gazes at the name and the number as if to see his wife, smaller than a pencil dot, crawling between the letters. He dials a number he knows by heart.

His father answers. "Yes?" A wary voice, ready to hang up on a madman or a salesman.

"Pop, hi; hey, I hope you didn't wait up or anything the other night, we weren't able to make it and I couldn't even get to a phone."

A little pause, not much, just enough to let him know they were indeed disappointed. "No, we figured something came up and went to bed about the usual time. Your mother isn't one to waste herself complaining, as you know."

"Right. Well, look. About today."

His voice goes hoarse to whisper, "Harry, you must come over today. You'll break her heart if you don't."

"I will, I will, but—"

The old man has cupped his mouth against the receiver, urging hoarsely, "This may be her last, you know. Birthday."

"We're coming, Pop. I mean, some of us are. Janice has had to go off."

"Go off how?"

"It's kind of complicated, something about her mother's legs and the Poconos, she decided last night she had to, I don't know. It's nothing to worry about. Everybody's all right, she's just not here. The kid's here though." To illustrate, he calls, "Nelson!"

There is no answer.

"He must be out on his bike, Pop. He's been right around all morning. When would you like us?"

"Whenever it suits you, Harry. Late afternoon or so. Come as early as you can. We're having roast beef. Your mother wanted to bake a cake but the doctor thought it might be too much for her. I bought a nice one over at the Half-A-Loaf. Butterscotch icing, didn't that used to be your favorite?"

"It's her birthday, not mine. What should I get her for a present?"

"Just your simple presence, Harry, is all the present she desires."

"Yeah, O.K. I'll think of something. Explain to her Janice won't be coming."

"As my father, God rest, used to say, It is to be regretted, but it can't be helped."

Once Pop finds that ceremonious vein, he tends to ride it. Rabbit hangs up. The kid's bike—a rusty Schwinn, been meaning to get him a new one, both fenders rub—is not in the garage. Nor is the Falcon. Only the oil cans, the gas can, the lawnmower, the jumbled garden hose (Janice must have used it last), a lawn rake with missing teeth, and the Falcon's snow tires are there. For an hour or so Rabbit swims around the house in a daze, not knowing who to call, not having a car, not wanting to go inside with the television set. He pulls weeds in the border beds where that first excited summer of their own house Janice planted bulbs and set in plants and shrubs. Since then they have done nothing, just watched the azaleas die and accepted the daffodils and iris as they came in and let the phlox and weeds fight as these subsequent summers wore on, nature lost in Nature. He weeds until he begins to see himself as a weed and his hand with its ugly big moons on the fingernails as God's hand choosing and killing, then he goes inside the house and looks into the refrigerator and eats a carrot raw. He looks into the phone directory and looks up Fosnacht, there are a lot of them, and two Olivers, and it takes him a while to figure out M is the one, M for Margaret and just the initial to put off obscene calls, though if he were on that kick he'd soon figure out that initials were unattached women. "Peggy, hi; this is Harry Angstrom." He says his name with faint proud emphasis; they were in school together, and she remembers him when he was somebody. "I was just wondering, is Nelson over there playing with Billy? He went off on his bike a while ago and I'm wondering where to."

Peggy says, "He's not here, Harry. Sorry." Her voice is frosted with all she knows, Janice burbling into her ear yesterday. Then more warmly she asks, "How's everything going?" He reads the equation, Ollie left me; Janice left you: hello.

He says hastily, "Great. Hey, if Nelson comes by tell him I want him. We got to go to his grandmother's."

Her voice cools in saying goodbye, joins the vast glaring ice-face of all those who know. Nelson seems the one person left in the county who doesn't know: this makes him even more precious. Yet, when the boy returns, red-faced and damp-haired from hard pedalling, he tells his father, "I was at the Fosnachts."

Rabbit blinks and says, "O.K. After this, let's keep in better touch. I'm your mother and your father for the time being." They eat lunch, Lebanon baloney on stale rye. They walk up

Emberly to Weiser and catch a 12 bus east into Brewer. It being Sunday, they have to wait twenty minutes under the cloudless colorless sky. At the hospital stop a crowd of visitors gets on, having done their duty, dazed, carrying away dead flowers and read books. Boats, white arrowheads tipping wrinkled wakes, are buzzing in the black river below the bridge. A colored kid leaves his foot in the aisle when Rabbit tries to get off; he steps over it. "Big feet," the boy remarks to his companion.

"Fat lips," Nelson, following, says to the colored boy.

They try to find a store open. His mother was always difficult to buy presents for. Other children had given their mothers cheerful junk: dime-store jewelry, bottles of toilet water, boxes of candy, scarves. For Mom that had been too much, or not enough. Mim always gave her something she had made: a woven pot holder, a hand-illustrated calendar. Rabbit was pretty poor at making things so he gave her himself, his trophies, his headlines. Mom had seemed satisfied: lives more than things concerned her. But now what? What can a dying person desire? Grotesque prosthetic devices—arms, legs, battery-operated hearts—run through Rabbit's head as he and Nelson walk the dazzling, Sunday-stilled downtown of Brewer. Up near Ninth and Weiser they find a drugstore open. Thermos bottles, sunglasses, shaving lotion, Kodak film, plastic baby pants: nothing for his mother. He wants something big, something bright, something to get through to her. Realgirl Liquid Make-Up, Super Plenamins, Non-Smear polish remover, Nudit for the Legs. A rack of shampoo-in hair color, a different smiling cunt on every envelope: Snow Queen Blond, Danish Wheat, Killarney Russet, Parisian Spice, Spanish Black Wine. Nelson plucks him by the sleeve of his white shirt and leads to where a Sunbeam Clipmaster and a Roto-Shine Magnetic Electric Shoe Polisher nestle side by side, glossily packaged. "She doesn't wear shoes any more, just slippers," he says, "and she never cut her hair that I can remember. It used to hang down to her waist." But his attention is drawn on to a humidifier for $12.95. From the picture on the box, it looks like a fat flying saucer. No matter how immobile she gets, it would be there. Around Brewer, though, the summers are as humid as they can be anyway, but maybe in the winter, the radiators dry out the house, the wallpaper peels, the skin cracks; it might help.

It would be there night and day, when he wasn't. He moves on to a Kantleek Water Bottle and a 2½-inch reading glass and dismisses both as morbid. His insides are beginning to feel sickly. The pain of the world is a crater all these syrups and pills a thousandfold would fail to fill. He comes to the Quikease Electric Massager with Scalp Comb. It has the silhouettes of naked women on the box, gracefully touching their shoulders, Lesbians, caressing the backs of their necks, where else the box leaves to the imagination, with what looks like a hair brush on a live wire. $11.95. Bedsores. It might help. It might make her laugh, tickle, buzz: it is life. Life is a massage. And it costs a dollar less than the humidifier. Time is ticking. Nelson tugs at his sleeve and wants a maple walnut ice cream soda. While the kid is eating it, Rabbit buys a birthday card to go with the massager. It shows a rooster crowing, a crimson sun rising, and green letters shouting on the outside *It's Great to Get Up in the A.M.* . . . and on the inside . . . *to Wish You a Happy Birthday, MA!* Ma. Am. God, what a lot of ingenious crap there is in the world. He buys it anyway, because the rooster is bright orange and jubilant enough to get through to her. Her eyes aren't dim necessarily but because her tongue gropes they could be. Play it safe.

The world outside is bright and barren. The two of them, father and son, feel sharply alone, Rabbit gripping his bulky package. Where is everybody? Is there life on Earth? Three blocks down the deserted street of soft asphalt the clock that is the face of a giant flower, the center of the Sunflower Beer sign, says they are approaching four. They wait at the same corner, opposite the Phoenix Bar, where Harry's father customarily waits, and take the 16A bus to Mt. Judge. They are the only passengers; the driver tells them mysteriously, "They're about down." Up they go through the City Park, past the World War II tank and the band-shell and the tennis court, around the shoulder of the mountain. On one side of them, gas stations and a green cliff; on the other, a precipice and, distantly, a viaduct. As the kid stares out of the window, toward the next mountain over, Rabbit asks him, "Where did you go this morning? Tell me the truth."

The boy answers, finally. "Eisenhower Avenue."

"To see if Mommy's car was there?"

"I guess."

"Was it?"

"Yop."

"D'you go in?"

"Nope. Just looked up at the windows awhile."

"Did you know the number to look at?"

"One two oh four."

"You got it."

They get off at Central, beside the granite Baptist church, and walk up Jackson toward his parents' house. The streets haven't changed in his lifetime. They were built too close together for vacant lots and too solidly to tear down, of a reddish brick with purplish bruises in it, with a texture that as a child Rabbit thought of as chapped, like his lips in winter. Maples and horsechestnuts darken the stumpy front lawns, hedged by little wired barricades of barberry and box. The houses are semi-detached and heavy, their roofs are slate and their porches have brick walls and above each door of oak and bevelled glass winks a fanlight of somber churchly colors. As a child Rabbit imagined that fanlight to be a child of the windows above the Lutheran altar and therefore of God, a mauve and golden seeing sentinel posted above where he and Pop and Mom and Mim came and went a dozen times a day. Now, entering with his son, still too much a son himself to knock, he feels his parents' place as stifling. Though the clock on the living-room sideboard says only 4:20, darkness has come: dark carpets, thick drawn drapes, dead wallpaper, potted plants crowding the glass on the side that has the windows. Mom used to complain about how they had the inside half of a corner house; but when the Bolgers, their old neighbors, died, and their half went onto the market, they made no move to inquire after the price, and a young couple from Scranton bought it, the wife pregnant and barefoot and the husband something in one of the new electronics plants out along Route 422; and the Angstroms still live in the dark half. They prefer it. Sunlight fades. They sent him, Harry, out in the world to shine, but hugged their own shadows here. Their neighbor house on the other side, across two cement sidewalks with a strip of grass between them, where lived the old Methodist Mom used to fight with about who would mow the grass strip, has had a FOR SALE sign up for a year. People now want more air and land than those huddled hillside neighborhoods can give them. The house smells to Rabbit of preservative: of odors filming other odors, of layers of time, of wax and aerosol and death; of safety.

A shape, a shade, comes forward from the kitchen. He expects it to be his father, but it is his mother, shuffling, in a bathrobe, yet erect and moving. She leans forward unsmiling to accept his kiss. Her wrinkled cheek is warm; her hand steadying itself on his wrist is knobbed and cold.

"Happy birthday, Mom." He hugs the massager against his chest; it is too early to offer it. She stares at the package as if he has put a shield between them.

"I'm sixty-five," she says, groping for phrases, so that her sentences end in the middle. "When I was twenty. I told my boy friend I wanted to be shot. When I was thirty." It is not so much the strange tremulous attempt of her lips to close upon a thought as the accompanying stare, an unblinking ungathering gaze into space that lifts her eyes out of any flow and frightens Rabbit with a sense of ultimate blindness, of a blackboard from which they will all be wiped clean.

"You told Pop this?"

"Not your dad. Another. I didn't meet your dad till later. This other one, I'm glad. He's not here to see me now."

"You look pretty good to me," Rabbit tells her. "I didn't think you'd be up."

"Nelson. How do I look. To you?" Thus she acknowledges the boy. She has always been testing him, putting him on the defensive. She has never forgiven him for not being another Harry, for having so much Janice in him. *Those little Springer hands.* Now her own hands, held forgotten in front of her bathrobe belt, constantly work in a palsied waggle.

"Nice," Nelson says. He is wary. He has learned that brevity and promptness of response are his best defense.

To take attention off the kid, Rabbit asks her, "*Should* you be up?"

She laughs, an astonishing silent thing; her head tips back, her big nose glints from the facets of its tip and underside, her hand stops waggling. "I know, the way Earl talks. You'd think from the way he wants me in bed. I'm laid out already. The doctor. Wants me up. I had to bake a cake. Earl wanted. One of those tasteless paps from the Half-A-Loaf. Where's Janice?"

"Yeah, about that. She's awfully sorry, she couldn't come. She had to go off with her mother to the Poconos, it took us all by surprise."

"Things can be. Surprising."

From upstairs Earl Angstrom's thin voice calls anxiously, with a wheedler's borrowed triumph, "They're down! Eagle has landed! We're on the moon, boys and girls! Uncle Sam is on the moon!"

"That's just. The place for him," Mom says, and with a rough gesture sweeps her distorted hand back toward her ear, to smooth down a piece of hair that has wandered loose from the bun she still twists up. Funny, the hair as it grays grows more stubborn. They say even inside the grave, it grows. Open coffins of women and find the whole thing stuffed like inside of a mattress. Pubic hair too? Funny it never needs to be cut. Serafina's looked threadbare, mangy. When he touches his mother's arm to help her up the stairs to look at the moon, the flesh above her elbow is disconcerting—loose upon the bone, as on a well-cooked chicken.

The set is in Mom's bedroom at the front of the house. It has the smell their cellar used to have when they had those two cats. He tries to remember their names. Pansy. And Willy. Willy, the tom, got in so many fights his belly began to slosh and he had to be taken to the Animal Rescue. There is no picture of the moon on the tube, just crackling voices while cardboard cutouts simulate what is happening, and electronic letters spell out who in the crackle of men is speaking.

". . . literally thousands of little one and two foot craters around the area," a man is saying in the voice that used to try to sell them Shredded Ralston between episodes of Tom Mix. "We see some angular blocks out several hundred feet in front of us that are probably two feet in size and have angular edges. There is a hill in view just about on the ground track ahead of us. Difficult to estimate, but might be a half a mile or a mile."

A voice identified as Houston says, "Roger, Tranquillity. We copy. Over." The voice has that Texas authority. As if words were invented by them, they speak so lovingly. When Rabbit was stationed at Fort Larson in '53, Texas looked like the moon to him, brown land running from his knees level as a knife, purple rumpled horizon, sky bigger and barer than he could believe, first time away from his damp green Pennsylvania hills, last time too. Everybody's voice was so nice and gritty and loving, even the girls in the whorehouse. *Honeh. You didn't pay to be no two-timer.*

A voice called Columbia says, "Sounds like a lot better than it did yesterday. At that very low sun angle, it looked rough as a cob then." As a what? The electronic letters specify: MIKE COL-LINS SPEAKING FROM COMMAND MODULE ORBITING MOON.

Tranquillity says, "It really was rough, Mike, over the targeted landing area. It was extremely rough, cratered and large numbers of rocks that were probably some many larger than five or ten feet in size." Mom's room has lace curtains aged yellowish and pinned back with tin daisies that to an infant's eyes seemed magical, rose-and-thorns wallpaper curling loose from the wall above where the radiator safety valve steams, a kind of plush armchair that soaks up dust. When he was a child this chair was downstairs and he would sock it to release torrents of swirling motes into the shaft of afternoon sun; these whirling motes seemed to him worlds, each an earth, with him on one of them, unthinkably small, unbearably. Some light used to get into the house in late afternoon, between the maples. Now the same maples have thronged that light solid, made the room cellar-dim. The bedside table supports an erect little company of pill bottles and a Bible. The walls hold tinted photographs of himself and Mim in high school, taken he remembers by a pushy pudgy little blue-jawed crook who called himself a Studio and weaseled his way into the building every spring and made them line up in the auditorium and wet-comb their hair so their parents couldn't resist two weeks later letting them take in to the homeroom the money for an 8 by 10 tinted print and a sheet of wallet-sized grislies of themselves; now this crook by the somersault of time has become a donor of selves otherwise forever lost: Rabbit's skinny head pink in its translucent blond whiffle, his ears out from his head an inch, his eyes unreally blue as marbles, even his lower lids youthfully fleshy; and Miriam's face plump between the shoulder-length shampoo-shining sheaves rolled under in Rita Hayworth style, the scarlet tint of her lipstick pinned like a badge on the starched white of her face. Both children smile out into space, through the crook's smudged lens, from that sweat-scented giggling gym toward their mother bedridden some day.

Columbia jokes, "When in doubt, land long."

Tranquillity says, "Well, we did."

And Houston intervenes, "Tranquillity, Houston. We have a P twenty-two update for you if you're ready to copy. Over."

Columbia jokes again: "At your service, sir."

Houston, unamused, a city of computers working without sleep, answers, "Right, Mike. P one one zero four thirty two eighteen; P two one zero four thirty-seven twenty-eight and that is four miles south. This is based on a targeted landing site. Over."

Columbia repeats the numbers.

Tranquillity says, "Our mission timer is now reading nine zero four thirty-four forty-seven and static."

"Roger, copy. Your mission timer is now static at—say again the time."

"Nine zero four thirty-four forty-seven."

"Roger, copy, Tranquillity. That gravity align looked good. We see you recycling."

"Well, no. I was trying to get time sixteen sixty-five out and somehow it proceeded on the six-twenty-two before I could do a BRP thirty-two enter. I want to log a time here and then I'd like to know whether you want me to proceed on torquing angles or to go back and re-enter again before torquing. Over."

"Rog, Buzz. Stand by."

Nelson and his grandfather listen raptly to these procedures; Mary Angstrom turns impatiently—or is it that her difficulty of motion makes all gestures appear impatient?—and makes her shuffling way out into the landing and down the stairs again. Rabbit, heart trembling in its hollow, follows. She needs no help going down the stairs. In the garishly bright kitchen she asks, "Where did you say. Janice was?"

"In the Poconos with her mother."

"Why should I believe that?"

"Why shouldn't you?"

She stoops over, waveringly, to open the oven and look in, her tangled wire hair making a net of light. She grunts, stands, and states, "Janice. Stays out of my way. These days."

In his frightened, hypnotized condition, Rabbit can only, it seems, ask questions. "Why would she do that?"

His mother stares and stares, only a movement of her tongue between her parted lips betraying that she is trying to speak. "I know too much," she at last brings out, "about her."

Rabbit says, "You know only what a bunch of pathetic old gossips tell you about her. And stop bugging Pop about it, he comes into work and bugs me." Since she does not fight back, he is provoked to go on. "With Mim out turning ten tricks a day in Las Vegas I'd think you'd have more to worry about than poor Janice's private life."

"She was always," his mother brings out, "spoiled."

"Yes and Nelson too I suppose is spoiled. How would you describe me? Just yesterday I was sitting over at the Blasts game thinking how lousy I used to be at baseball. Let's face it. As a human being I'm about C minus. As a husband I'm about zilch. When Verity folds I'll fold with it and have to go on welfare. Some life. Thanks, Mom."

"Hush," she says, expressionless, "you'll make. The cake fall," and like a rusty jackknife she forces herself to bend over and peer into the gas oven.

"Sorry Mom, but Jesus I'm tired lately."

"You'll feel better when. You're my age."

The party is a success. They sit at the kitchen table with the four places worn through the enamel in all those years. It is like it used to be, except that Mom is in a bathrobe and Mim has become Nelson. Pop carves the roast beef and then cuts up Mom's piece in small bits for her; her right hand can hold a fork but cannot use a knife. His teeth slipping down, he proposes a toast in New York State wine to "my Mary, an angel through thick and thin"; Rabbit wonders what the thin was. Maybe this is it. When she unwraps her few presents, she laughs at the massager. "Is this. To keep me hopping?" she asks, and has her husband plug it in, and rests it, vibrating, on the top of Nelson's head. He needs this touch of cheering up. Harry feels Janice's absence gnawing at him. When the cake is cut the kid eats only half a piece, so Rabbit has to eat double so as not to hurt his mother's feelings. Dusk thickens: over in West Brewer the sanitorium windows are burning orange and on this side of the mountain the shadows sneak like burglars into the narrow concrete space between this house and the unsold one. Through the papered walls, from the house of the young barefoot couple, seeps the dull bass percussion of a rock group, making the matched tins (cookies, sugar, flour, coffee) on Mom's shelf tingle in their emptiness. In the living room the glass face of the mahogany sideboard shivers. Nelson's eyes begin to sink, and the buttoned-up cupid-curves of his mouth smile in apology as he slumps forward to rest his head on the cold enamel of the table. His elders talk about old times in the neighborhood, people of the Thirties and Forties, once so alive you saw them every day and never thought to take even a photograph. The old Methodist refusing to mow his half of the grass strip. Before him the Zims with that pretty daughter the mother would shriek at every breakfast and supper. The man down the street who worked nights at the pretzel plant and who shot himself one dawn with nobody to hear it but the horses of the milk wagon. They had milk wagons then. Some streets were still soft dust. Nelson fights sleep. Rabbit asks him, "Want to head home?"

"Negative, Pop." He drowsily grins at his own wit.

Rabbit extends the joke. "The time is twenty-one hours. We better rendezvous with our spacecraft."

But the spacecraft is empty: a long empty box in the blackness of Penn Villas, slowly spinning in the void, its border beds half-weeded. The kid is frightened to go home. So is Rabbit. They sit on Mom's bed and watch television in the dark. They are told the men in the big metal spider sitting on the moon cannot sleep, so the moon-walk has been moved up several hours. Men in studios, brittle and tired from killing time, demonstrate with actual-size mockups what is supposed to happen; on some channels men in space suits are walking around, laying down tinfoil trays as if for a cookout. At last it happens. The real event. Or is it? A television camera on the leg of the module comes on: an abstraction appears on the screen. The announcer explains that the blackness in the top of the screen is the lunar night, the blackness in the lower left corner is the shadow of the spacecraft with its ladder, the whiteness is the surface of the moon. Nelson is asleep, his head on his father's thigh; funny how kids' skulls grow damp when they sleep. Like bulbs underground. Mom's legs are under the blankets; she is propped up on pillows behind him. Pop is asleep in his chair, his breathing a distant sad sea, touching shore and retreating, touching shore and retreating, an old pump that keeps going; lamplight sneaks through a crack in the windowshade and touches the top of his head, his sparse hair mussed into lank feathers. On the bright box something is happening. A snaky shape sneaks down from the upper left corner; it is a man's leg. It grows another leg, eclipses the bright patch that is the surface of the moon. A man in clumsy silhouette has interposed himself among these abstract shadows and glare. An Armstrong, but not Jack. He says something about "steps" that a crackle keeps Rabbit from understanding. Electronic letters travelling sideways spell out MAN IS ON THE MOON. The voice, crackling, tells Houston that the surface is fine and powdery, he can pick it up with his toe, it adheres to his boot like powdered charcoal, that he sinks in only a fraction of an inch, that it's easier to move around than in the simulations on Earth. From behind him, Rabbit's mother's hand with difficulty reaches out, touches the back of his skull, stays there, awkwardly tries to massage his scalp, to ease away thoughts of the trouble she knows he is in. "I don't know, Mom," he abruptly admits. "I know it's happened, but I don't feel anything yet."

II

Jill

"It's different but it's very pretty out here."
—NEIL ARMSTRONG, *July 20, 1969*

Days, pale slices between nights, they blend, not exactly alike, transparencies so lightly tinted that only stacked all together do they darken to a fatal shade. One Saturday in August Buchanan approaches Rabbit during the coffee break. They are part of the half-crew working the half-day; hence perhaps this intimacy. The Negro wipes from his lips the moisture of the morning whisky enjoyed outside in the sunshine of the loading platform, and asks, "How're they treatin' you, Harry?"

"They?" Harry has known the other man by sight and name for years but still is not quite easy, talking to a black; there always seems to be some joke involved, that he doesn't quite get.

"The world, man."

"Not bad."

Buchanan stands there blinking, studying, jiggling up and down on his feet engagingly. Hard to tell how old they are. He might be thirty-five, he might be sixty. On his upper lip he wears the smallest possible black mustache, smaller than a type brush. His color is ashy, without any shine to it, whereas the other shop Negro, Farnsworth, looks shoe-polished and twinkles among the printing machinery, under the steady shadowless light. "But not good, huh?"

"I'm not sleeping so good," Rabbit does confess. He has an itch, these days, to confess, to spill, he is so much alone.

"Your old lady still shackin' up across town?"

Everybody knows. Niggers, coolies, derelicts, morons. Numbers writers, bus conductors, beauty shop operators, the entire brick city of Brewer. VERITY EMPLOYEE NAMED CUCKOLD OF WEEK. *Angstrom Accepts Official Horns from Mayor.* "I'm living alone," Harry admits, adding, "with the kid."

"How about that," Buchanan says, lightly rocking. "How about that?"

528

Rabbit says weakly, "Until things straighten out."

"Gettin' any tail?"

Harry must look startled, for Buchanan hastens to explain, "Man has to have tail. Where's your dad these days?" The question flows from the assertion immediately, though it doesn't seem to follow.

Rabbit says, puzzled, offended, but because Buchanan is a Negro not knowing how to evade him, "He's taking two weeks off so he can drive my mother back and forth to the hospital for some tests."

"Yeass." Buchanan mulls, the two pushed-out cushions of his mouth appearing to commune with each other through a hum; then a new thought darts out through them, making his mustache jig. "Your dad is a real pal to you, that's a wonderful thing. That is a truly wonderful thing. I never had a dad like that, I knew who the man was, he was around town, but he was never my dad in the sense your dad is your dad. He was never my pal like that."

Harry hangs uncertainly, not knowing if he should commiserate or laugh. "Well," he decides to confess, "he's sort of a pal, and sort of a pain in the neck."

Buchanan likes the remark, even though he goes through peppery motions of rejecting it. "Oh, never say that now. You just be grateful you have a dad that cares. You don't know, man, how lucky you have it. Just 'cause your wife's gettin' her ass looked after elsewhere don't mean the whole world is come to some bad end. You should be havin' your tail, is all. You're a big fella."

Distaste and excitement contend in Harry; he feels tall and pale beside Buchanan, and feminine, a tingling target of fun and tenderness and avarice mixed. Talking to Negroes makes him feel itchy, up behind the eyeballs, maybe because theirs look so semi-liquid and yellow in the white and sore. Their whole beings seem lubricated in pain. "I'll manage," he says reluctantly, thinking of Peggy Fosnacht.

The end-of-break bell rings. Buchanan snaps his shoulders into a hunch and out of it as if rendering a verdict. "How about it, Harry, steppin' out with some of the boys tonight," he says. "Come on into Jimbo's Lounge around nine, ten, see what develops. Maybe nothin'. Maybe sumpthin'. You're just turnin' old, the way you're goin' now. Old and fat and finicky, and that's no way for a nice big man to go." He sees that Rabbit's instincts are to refuse; he holds up a quick palm the color of silver polish and says, "Think about it. I like you, man. If you don't show, you don't show. No sweat."

All Saturday the invitation hums in his ears. Something in what Buchanan said. He was lying down to die, had been lying down for years. His body had been telling him to. His eyes blur print in the afternoons, no urge to run walking even that stretch of tempting curved sidewalk home, has to fight sleep before supper and then can't get under at night, can't even get it up to jerk off to relax himself. Awake with the first light every morning regardless, another day scraping his eyes. Without going much of anywhere in his life he has somehow seen everything too often. Trees, weather, the molding trim drying its cracks wider around the front door, he notices every day going out, house made of green wood. No belief in an afterlife, no hope for it, too much more of the same thing, already it seems he's lived twice. When he came back to Janice that began the second time for him; poor kid is having her first time now. Bless that dope. At least she had the drive to get out. Women, fire in their crotch, won't burn out, begin by fighting off pricks, end by going wild hunting for one that still works.

Once last week he called the lot to find out if she and Stavros were reporting for work or just screwing around the clock. Mildred Kroust answered, she put him on to Janice, who whispered, "Harry, Daddy doesn't know about us, don't ever call me here, I'll call you back." And she had called him late that afternoon, at the house, Nelson in the other room watching *Gilligan's Island*, and said cool as you please, he hardly knew her voice, "Harry, I'm sorry for whatever pain this is causing you, truly sorry, but it's very important that at this point in our lives we don't let guilt feelings motivate us. I'm trying to look honestly into myself, to see who I am, and where I should be going. I want us both, Harry, to come to a decision we can live with. It's the year nineteen sixty-nine and there's no reason for two mature people to smother each other to death simply out of inertia. I'm searching for a valid identity and I suggest you do the same." After some more of this, she hung up. Her vocabulary had expanded, maybe she was watching a lot of psychiatric talk shows. The sinners shall be justified. Screw her. Dear Lord, screw her. He is thinking this on the bus.

He thinks, *Screw her*, and at home has a beer and takes a bath and puts on his good summer suit, a light gray sharkskin, and gets Nelson's pajamas out of the dryer and his toothbrush out of the bathroom. The kid and Billy have arranged for him to spend the night. Harry calls up Peggy to check it out. "Oh absolutely," she says, "I'm not going anywhere, why don't you stay and have dinner?"

"I can't I don't think."

"Why not? Something else to do?"

"Sort of." He and the kid go over around six, on an empty bus. Already at this hour Weiser has that weekend up-tempo, cars hurrying faster home to get out again, a very fat man with orange hair standing under an awning savoring a cigar as if angels will shortly descend, an expectant shimmer on the shut storefronts, girls clicking along with heads big as rose-bushes, curlers wrapped in a kerchief. Saturday night. Peggy meets him at the door with an offer of a drink. She and Billy live in an apartment in one of the new eight-story buildings in West Brewer overlooking the river, where there used to be a harness racetrack. From her living room she has a panorama of Brewer, the concrete eagle on the skyscraper Court House flaring his wings above the back of the Owl Pretzels sign. Beyond the flowerpot-red city Mt. Judge hangs smoky-green, one side gashed by a gravel pit like a roast beginning to be carved. The river coal black.

"Maybe just one. I gotta go somewhere."

"You said that. What kind of drink?" She is wearing a clingy palish-purple sort of Paisley mini that shows a lot of heavy leg. One thing Janice always had, was nifty legs. Peggy has a pasty helpless look of white meat behind the knees.

"You have Daiquiri mix?"

"I don't know, Ollie used to keep things like that, but when we moved I think it all stayed with him." She and Ollie Fosnacht had lived in an asbestos-shingled semi-detached some blocks away, not far from the county mental hospital. Ollie lives in the city now, near his music store, and she and the kid have this apartment, with Ollie in their view if they can find him. She is rummaging in a low cabinet below some empty bookcases. "I can't see any, it comes in envelopes. How about gin and something?"

"You have bitter lemon?"

More rummaging. "No, just some tonic."

"Good enough. Want me to make it?"

"If you like." She stands up, heavy-legged, lightly sweating, relieved. Knowing he was coming, Peggy had decided against sunglasses, a sign of trust to leave them off. Her walleyes are naked to him, her face has this helpless look, turned full toward him while both eyes seem fascinated by something in the corners of the ceiling. He knows only one eye is bad but he never can bring himself to figure out which. And all around her eyes this net of white wrinkles the sunglasses usually conceal.

He asks her, "What for you?"

"Oh, anything. The same thing. I drink everything."

While he is cracking an ice tray in the tiny kitchenette, the two boys have snuck out of Billy's bedroom. Rabbit wonders if they have been looking at dirty photographs. The kind of pictures kids used to have to pay an old cripple on Plum Street a dollar apiece for you can buy a whole magazine full of now for seventy-five cents, right downtown. The Supreme Court, old men letting the roof cave in. Billy is a head taller than Nelson, sunburned where Nelson takes a tan after his mother, both of them with hair down over their ears, the Fosnacht boy's blonder and curlier. "Mom, we want to go downstairs and run the mini-bike on the parking lot."

"Come back up in an hour," Peggy tells them, "I'll give you supper."

"Nelson had a peanut-butter sandwich before we left," Rabbit explains.

"Typical male cooking," Peggy says. "Where're you going this evening anyway, all dressed up in a suit?"

"Nowhere much. I told a guy I might meet him." He doesn't say it is a Negro. He should be asking her out, is his sudden frightened feeling. She is dressed to go out; but not so dolled-up it can't appear she plans to stay home tonight. He hands her her g.-and-t. The best defense is to be offensive. "You don't have any mint or limes or anything."

Her plucked eyebrows lift. "No, there are lemons in the fridge, is all. I could run down to the grocery for you." Not entirely ironical: using his complaint to weave coziness.

Rabbit laughs to retract. "Forget it, I'm just used to bars, where they have everything. At home all I ever do is drink beer."

She laughs in answer. She is tense as a schoolteacher facing her first class. To relax them both he sits down in a loose leather armchair that says *pfsshhu*. "Hey, this is nice," he announces, meaning the vista, but he spoke too early, for from this low chair the view is flung out of sight and becomes all sky: a thin bright wash, stripes like fat in bacon.

"You should hear Ollie complain about the rent." Peggy sits down not in another chair but on the flat grille where the radiator breathes beneath the window, opposite and above him, so he sees a lot of her legs—shiny skin stuffed to the point of shapelessness. Still, she is showing him what she has, right up to the triangle of underpants, which is one more benefit of being alive in 1969. Miniskirts and those magazines: well, hell, we've always known women had crotches, why not make it legal? A guy at the shop brought in a magazine that, honestly, was all cunts, in blurred bad four-color but cunts, upside down, backwards, the girls attached to them rolling their tongues in their mouths and fanning their hands on their bellies and otherwise trying to hide how silly they felt. Homely things, really, cunts. Without the Supreme Court that might never have been made clear.

"Hey, how is old Ollie?"

Peggy shrugs. "He calls. Usually to cancel his Sunday with Billy. You know he never was the family man you are."

Rabbit is surprised to be called that. He is getting too tame. He asks her, "How does he spend his time?"

"Oh," Peggy says, and awkwardly turns her body so Rabbit sees pricked out in windowlight the tonic bubbles in her drink, which is surprisingly near drunk, "he rattles around Brewer with a bunch of creeps. Musicians, mostly. They go to Philadelphia a lot, and New York. Last winter he went skiing at Aspen and told me all about it, including the girls. He came back so brown in the face, I cried for days. I could never get him outdoors, when we had the place over on Franklin Street. How do *you* spend *your* time?"

"I work. I mope around the house with the kid. We look at the boob tube and play catch in the back yard."

"Do you mope for *her*, Harry?" With a clumsy shrug of her hip the woman moves off her radiator perch, her wall-eyes staring to either side of him so he thinks he is her target and flinches. But she floats past him and, clattering, refills her drink. "Want another?"

"No thanks, I'm still working on this one. I gotta go in a minute."

"So soon," she croons unseen, as if remembering the beginning of a song in her tiny kitchenette. From far below their windows arises the razzing, coughing sound of the boys on the mini-bike. The noise swoops and swirls, a rude buzzard. Beyond it across the river hangs the murmur of Brewer traffic, constant like the sea; an occasional car toots, a wink of phosphorescence. From the kitchenette, as if she had been baking the thought in the oven, Peggy calls, "She's not worth it." Then her body is at his back, her voice upon his head. "I didn't know," she says, "you loved her so much. I don't think Janice knew it either."

"Well, you get used to somebody. Anyway, it's an insult. With a wop like that. You should hear him run down the U.S. government."

"Harry, you know what I think. I'm sure you know what I think."

He doesn't. He has no idea. She seems to think he's been reading thoughts printed on her underpants.

"I think she's treated you horribly. The last time we had lunch together, I told her so. I said, 'Janice, your attempts to justify yourself do not impress me. You've left a man who came back to you when you needed him, and you've left your son at a point in his development when it's immensely important to have a stable home setting.' I said that right to her face."

"Actually the kid goes over to the lot pretty much and sees her there. She and Stavros take him out to eat. In a way it's like he gained an uncle."

"You're so for*giv*ing, Harry! Ollie would have *strang*led me; he's still immensely jealous. He's always asking me who my boyfriends are."

He doubts she has any, and sips his drink. Although in this

county women with big bottoms usually don't go begging. Dutchmen love bulk. He says, "Well, I don't know if I did such a great job with Janice. She has to live too."

"Well Harry, if that's your reasoning, we *all* have to live." And from the way she stands there in front of him, if he sat up straight her pussy would be exactly at his nose. Hair tickles: he might sneeze. He sips the drink again, and feels the tasteless fluid expand his inner space. He might sit up at any minute, if she doesn't watch out. From the hair on her head probably a thick springy bush, though you can't always tell, some of the cunts in the magazine just had wisps at the base of their bellies, hardy an armpit's worth. Dolls. She moves away saying, "Who'll hold families together, if everybody has to live? Living is a compromise, between doing what *you* want and doing what *oth*er people want."

"What about what poor old God wants?"

The uncalled-for noun jars her from the seductive pose she has assumed, facing out the window, her backside turned to him. The dog position. Tip her over a chair and let her fuss herself with her fingers into coming while he does it from behind. Janice got so she preferred it, more animal, she wasn't distracted by the look on his face, never was one for wet kisses, when they first started going together complained she couldn't breathe, he asked her if she had adenoids. Seriously. No two alike, a billion cunts in the world, snowflakes. Touch them right they melt. What we most protect is where we want to be invaded. Peggy leaves her drink on the sill like a tall jewel and turns to him with her deformed face open. Since the word has been sprung on her, she asks, "Don't you think God is people?"

"No, I think God is everything that isn't people. I guess I think that. I don't think enough to know what I think." In irritation, he stands.

Big against the window, a hot shadow, palish-purple edges catching the light ebbing from the red city, the dim mountain, Peggy exclaims, "Oh, you think with"—and to assist her awkward thought she draws his shape in the air with two hands, having freed them for this gesture—"your whole person."

She looks so helpless and vague there seems nothing for Harry to do but step into the outline of himself she has drawn

and kiss her. Her face, eclipsed, feels large and cool. Her lips
bumble on his, the spongy wax of gumdrops, yet narcotic, not
quite tasteless: as a kid Rabbit loved bland candy like Dots; sitting in the movies he used to plow through three nickel boxes
of them, playing with them with his tongue and teeth, playing,
playing before giving himself the ecstasy of the bite. Up and
down his length she bumps against him, straining against his
height, touching. The strange place on her where nothing is,
the strange place higher where some things are. Her haunches
knot with the effort of keeping on tiptoe. She pushes, pushes:
he is a cunt this one-eyed woman is coldly pushing up into. He
feels her mind gutter out; she has wrapped them in a clumsy
large ball of darkness.

Something scratches on the ball. A key in a lock. Then the
door knocks. Harry and Peggy push apart, she tucks her hair
back around her spread-legged eyes and runs heavily to the
door and lets in the boys. They are red-faced and furious.
"Mom, the fucking thing broke down again," Billy tells his
mother. Nelson looks over at Harry. The boy is near tears.
Since Janice left, he is silent and delicate: an eggshell full of
tears.

"It wasn't my fault," he calls huskily, injustice a sieve in his
throat. "Dad, he says it was my fault."

"You baby, I didn't say that exactly."

"You did. He did, Dad, and it wasn't."

"All I said was he spun out too fast. He always spins out too
fast. He flipped on a loose stone, now the headlight is bent
under and it won't start."

"If it wasn't such a cheap one it wouldn't break all the time."

"It's not a cheap one it's the best one there is almost and
anyway you don't even have any—"

"I wouldn't take one if you gave it to me—"

"So who are you to talk."

"Hey, easy, easy," Harry says. "We'll get it fixed. I'll pay for
it."

"Don't pay for it, Dad. It wasn't anybody's fault. It's just he's
so spoiled."

"You shrimp," Billy says, and hits him, much the same way
that three weeks ago Harry hit Janice, hard but seeking a spot
that could take it. Harry separates them, squeezing Billy's arm

so the kid clams up. This kid is going to be tough some day. Already his arm is stringy.

Peggy is just bringing it all into focus, her insides shifting back from that kiss. "Billy, these things will happen if you insist on playing so dangerously." To Harry she says, "*Damn* Ollie for getting it for him, I think he did it to spite me. He knows I hate machines."

Harry decides Billy is the one to talk to. "Hey. Billy. Shall I take Nelson back home, or do you want him to spend the night anyway?"

And both boys set up a wailing for Nelson to spend the night. "Dad you don't have to come for me or anything, I'll ride my bike home in the morning first thing, I left it here yesterday."

So Rabbit releases Billy's arm and gives Nelson a kiss somewhere around the ear and tries to find the right eye of Peggy's to look into. "Okey-doak. I'll be off."

She says, "Must you? Stay. Can't I give you supper? Another drink? It's early yet."

"This guy's waiting," Rabbit lies, and makes it around her furniture to the door.

Her body chases him. Her vague eyes shine in their tissue-paper sockets, and her lips have that loosened look kissed lips get; he resists the greedy urge to buy another box of Dots. "Harry," she begins, and seems to fall toward him, after a stumble, though they don't touch.

"Yeah?"

"I'm usually here. If—you know."

"I know. Thanks for the g.-and-t. Your view is great." He reaches then and pats, not her ass exactly, the flank at the side of it, too broad, too firm, alive enough under his palm, it turns out, to make him wonder, when her door closes, why he is going down the elevator, and out.

It is too early to meet Buchanan. He walks back through the West Brewer side streets toward Weiser, through the dulling summer light and the sounds of distant games, of dishes rattled in kitchen sinks, of television muffled to a murmur mechanically laced with laughter and applause, of cars driven by teenagers laying rubber and shifting down. Children and old men sit on the porch steps beside the lead-colored milk-bottle boxes.

Some stretches of sidewalk are brick; these neighborhoods, the oldest in West Brewer, close to the river, are cramped, gentle, barren. Between the trees there is a rigid flourishing of hydrants, meters, and signs, some of them—virtual billboards in white on green—directing motorists to superhighways whose number is blazoned on the federal shield or on the commonwealth keystone; from these obscure West Brewer byways, sidewalks and asphalt streets rumpled comfortably as old clothes, one can be arrowed toward Philadelphia, Baltimore, Washington the national capital, New York the headquarters of commerce and fashion. Or in the other direction can find Pittsburgh and Chicago. But beneath these awesome metal insignia of vastness and motion fat men in undershirts loiter, old ladies move between patches of gossip with the rural waddle of egg-gatherers, dogs sleep curled beside the cooling curb, and children with hockey sticks and tape-handled bats diffidently chip at whiffle balls and wads of leather, whittling themselves into the next generation of athletes and astronauts. Rabbit's eyes sting in the dusk, in this smoke of his essence, these harmless neighborhoods that have gone to seed. So much love, too much love, it is our madness, it is rotting us out, exploding us like dandelion polls. He stops at a corner grocery for a candy bar, an Oh Henry, then at the Burger Bliss on Weiser, dazzling in its lake of parking space, for a Lunar Special (double cheeseburger with an American flag stuck into the bun) and a vanilla milkshake, that tastes toward the bottom of chemical sludge.

The interior of Burger Bliss is so bright that his fingernails, with their big mauve moons, gleam and the coins he puts down in payment seem cartwheels of metal. Beyond the lake of light, unfriendly darkness. He ventures out past a dimmed drive-in bank and crosses the bridge. High slender arc lamps on giant flower stems send down a sublunar light by which the hurrying cars all appear purple. There are no other faces but his on the bridge. From the middle, Brewer seems a web, to which glowing droplets adhere. Mt. Judge is one with the night. The luminous smudge of the Pinnacle Hotel hangs like a star.

Gnats bred by the water brush Rabbit's face; Janice's desertion nags him from within, a sore spot in his stomach. Ease off beer and coffee. Alone, he must take care of himself. Sleeping alone, he dreads the bed, watches the late shows, Carson,

Griffin, cocky guys with nothing to sell but their brass. Making millions on sheer gall. American dream: when he first heard the phrase as a kid he pictured God lying sleeping, the quilt-colored map of the U.S. coming out of his head like a cloud. Peggy's embrace drags at his limbs. Suit feels sticky. Jimbo's Friendly Lounge is right off the Brewer end of the bridge, a half-block down from Plum. Inside it, all the people are black.

Black to him is just a political word but these people really are, their faces shine of blackness turning as he enters, a large soft white man in a sticky gray suit. Fear travels up and down his skin, but the music of the great green-and-mauve-glowing jukebox called Moonmood slides on, and the liquid of laughter and tickled muttering resumes flowing; his entrance was merely a snag. Rabbit hangs like a balloon waiting for a dart; then his elbow is jostled and Buchanan is beside him.

"Hey, man, you made it." The Negro has materialized from the smoke. His overtrimmed mustache looks wicked in here.

"You didn't think I would?"

"Doubted it," Buchanan says. "Doubted it severely."

"It was your idea."

"Right. Harry, you are right. I'm not arguing, I am rejoicing. Let's fix you up. You need a drink, right?"

"I don't know, my stomach's getting kind of sensitive."

"You need two drinks. Tell me your poison."

"Maybe a Daiquiri?"

"Never. That is a lady's drink for salad luncheons. Rufe, you old rascal."

"Yazzuh, yazzuh," comes the answer from the bar.

"Do a Stinger for the man."

"Yaz-*zuh*."

Rufe has a bald head like one of the stone hatchets in the Brewer Museum, only better polished. He bows into the marine underglow of the bar and Buchanan leads Rabbit to a booth in the back. The place is deep and more complicated than it appears from the outside. Booths recede and lurk: dark-wood cape-shapes. Along one wall, Rufe and the lowlit bar; behind and above it, not only the usual Pabst and Bud and Miller's gimcracks bobbing and shimmering, but two stuffed small deer-heads, staring with bright brown eyes that will never blink. Gazelles, could they have been gazelles? A space away,

toward a wall but with enough room for a row of booths behind, a baby grand piano, painted silver with one of those spray
cans, silver in circular swirls. In a room obliquely off the main
room, a pool table: colored boys all arms and legs spidering
around the idyllic green felt. The presence of any game reassures Rabbit. Where any game is being played a hedge exists
against fury. "Come meet some soul," Buchanan says. Two
shadows in the booth are a man and a woman. The man wears
silver circular glasses and a little pussy of a goatee and is young.
The woman is old and wrinkled and smokes a yellow cigarette
that requires much sucking in and holding down and closing
of the eyes and sighing. Her brown eyelids are gray, painted
blue. Sweat shines below the base of her throat, on the slant
bone between her breasts, as if she had breasts, which she does
not, though her dress, the blood-color of a rooster's comb,
is cut deep, as if she did. Before they are introduced she says
"Hi" to Harry, but her eyes slit to pin him fast in the sliding
of a dream.

"This man," Buchanan is announcing, "is a co-worker of
mine, he works right beside his daddy at Ver-i-ty Press, an
expert Lino-typist," giving syllables an odd ticking equality, a
put-on or signal of some sort? "But not only that. He is an
ath-e-lete of renown, a basketball player bar none, the Big O
of Brewer in his day."

"Very beautiful," the other dark man says. Round specs tilt,
glint. The shadow of a face they cling to feels thin in the darkness. The voice arises very definite and dry.

"Many years ago," Rabbit says, apologizing for his bulk, his
bloated pallor, his dead fame. He sits down in the booth to
hide.

"He has the hands," the woman states. She is in a trance. She
says, "Give old Babe one of those hands, white boy." A-prickle
with nervousness, wanting to sneeze on the sweetish smoke,
Rabbit lifts his right hand up from his lap and lays it on the
slippery table. Innocent meat. Distorted paw. Reminds him of,
on television, that show with chimpanzees synchronized with
talk and music, the eerie look of having just missed the winning design.

The woman touches it. Her touch reptilian cool. Her eyes
lift, brooding. Above the glistening bone her throat drips

jewels, a napkin of rhinestones or maybe real diamonds; Cadillacs after all, alligator shoes, they can't put their money into real estate like whites; Springer's thrifty Toyotas not to the point. His mind is racing with his pulse. She has a silver sequin pasted beside one eye. Accent the ugly until it becomes gorgeous. Her eyelashes are great false crescents. That she has taken such care of herself leads him to suspect she will not harm him. His pulse slows. Her touch slithers nice as a snake. "Do dig that thumb," she advises the air. She caresses his thumb's curve. Its thin-skinned veined ball. Its colorless moon nail. "That thumb means sweetness and light. It is an indicator of pleasure in Sagittarius and Leo." She gives one knuckle an affectionate pinch.

The Negro not Buchanan (Buchanan has hustled to the bar to check on the Stinger) says, "Not like one of them usual little sawed-off nuggers these devils come at you with, right?"

Babe answers, not yielding her trance, "No, sir. This thumb here is extremely plausible. Under the right signs it would absolutely function. Now these knuckles here, they aren't so good, I don't get much music out of these knuckles." And she presses a chord on them, with fingers startlingly hard and certain. "But this here thumb," she goes back to caressing it, "is a real enough heartbreaker."

"All these Charlies is heartbreakers, right? Just 'cause they don't know how to shake their butterball asses don't mean they don't get Number One in, they gets it in real mean, right? The reason they so mean, they has so much religion, right? That big white God go tells 'em, Screw that black chick, and they really wangs away 'cause God's right there slappin' away at their butterball asses. Cracker spelled backwards is fucker, right?"

Rabbit wonders if this is how the young Negro really talks, wonders if there is a real way. He does not move, does not even bring back his hand from the woman's inspection, her touches chill as teeth. He is among panthers.

Buchanan, that old rascal, bustles back and sets before Rabbit a tall pale glass of poison and shoves in so Rabbit has to shove over opposite the other man. Buchanan's eyes check around the faces and guess it's gotten heavy. Lightly he says, "This man's wife, you know what? That woman, I never had the pleasure of meeting her, not counting those Verity picnics where Farnsworth, you all know Farnsworth now—?"

"Like a father," the young man says, adding, "Right?"

"—gets me so bombed out of my mind on that barrel beer I can't remember anybody by face or name, where was I? Yes, that woman, she just upped and left him the other week, left him flat to go chasing around with some other gentleman, something like an I-talian, didn't you say Harry?"

"A Greek."

Babe clucks. "Honey, now what did he have you didn't? He must of had a thumb long as this badmouth's tongue." She nudges her companion, who retrieves from his lips this shared cigarette, which has grown so short it must burn, and sticks out his tongue. Its whiteness shocks Rabbit; a mouthful of luminous flesh. Though fat and pale, it does not look very long. This man, Rabbit sees, is a boy; the patch of goatee is all he can grow. Harry does not like him. He likes Babe, he thinks, even though she has dried hard, a prune on the bottom of the box. In here they are all on the bottom of the box. This drink, and his hand, are the whitest thing around. Not to think of the other's tongue. He sips. Too sweet, wicked. A thin headache promptly begins.

Buchanan is persisting, "Don't seem right to me, healthy big man living alone with nobody now to comfort him."

The goatee bobs. "Doesn't bother me in the slightest. Gives the man time to think, right? Gets the thought of cunt off his back, right? Chances are he has some hobby he can do, you know, like woodwork." He explains to Babe, "You know, like a lot of these peckerwoods have this clever thing they can do down in their basements, like stamp collecting, right? That's how they keep making it big. Cleverness, right?" He taps his skull, whose narrowness is padded by maybe an inch of tight black wool. The texture reminds Rabbit of his mother's crocheting, if she had used tiny metal thread. Her blue bent hands now helpless. Even in here, family sadness pokes at him, probing sore holes.

"I used to collect baseball cards," he tells them. He hopes to excite enough rudeness from them so he can leave. He remembers the cards' bubble-gum smell, their silken feel from the powdered sugar. He sips the Stinger.

Babe sees him make a face. "You don't have to drink that

piss." She nudges her neighbor again. "Let's have one more stick."

"Woman, you must think I'm made of hay."

"I know you're plenty magical, that's one thing. Off that uptight shit, the ofay here needs a lift and I'm nowhere near spaced enough to pee-form."

"Last drag," he says, and passes her the tiny wet butt.

She crushes it into the Sunflower Beer ashtray. "This roach is hereby dead." And holds her thin hand palm up for a hit.

Buchanan is clucking. "Mother-love, go easy on yourself," he tells Babe.

The other Negro is lighting another cigarette; the paper is twisted at the end and flares, subsides. He passes it to her saying, "Waste is a sin, right?"

"Hush now. This honeyman needs to loosen up, I hate to see 'em sad, I always have, they aren't like us, they don't have the insides to accommodate it. They's like little babies that way, they passes it off to someone else." She is offering Rabbit the cigarette, moist end toward him.

He says, "No thanks, I gave up smoking ten years ago."

Buchanan chuckles, with thumb and forefinger smooths his mustache sharper.

The boy says, "They're going to live forever, right?"

Babe says, "This ain't any of that nicotine shit. This weed is kindness itself."

While Babe is coaxing him, Buchanan and the boy diagonally discuss his immortality. "My daddy used to say, Down home, you never did see a dead white man, any more'n you'd see a dead mule."

"God's on their side, right? God's white, right? He doesn't want no more Charlies up there to cut into his take, he has it just fine the way it is, him and all those black angels out in the cotton."

"Your mouth's gonta hurt you, boy. The man is the lay of the land down here."

"Whose black ass you hustling, hers or yours?"

"You just keep your smack in the heel of your shoe."

Babe is saying, "You suck it in as far as it'll go and hold it down as long as you absolutely can. It needs to mix with *you.*"

Rabbit tries to comply, but coughing undoes every puff. Also he is afraid of getting "hooked," of being suddenly jabbed with a needle, of starting to hallucinate because of something dropped into his Stinger. AUTOPSY ORDERED IN FRIENDLY LOUNGE DEATH. *Coroner Notes Atypical Color of Skin.*

Watching him cough, the boy says, "He *is* beautiful. I didn't know they still came with all those corners. Right out of the crackerbox, right?"

This angers Rabbit enough to keep a drag down. It burns his throat and turns his stomach. He exhales with the relief of vomiting and waits for something to happen. Nothing. He sips the Stinger but now it tastes chemical like the bottom of that milkshake. He wonders how he can get out of here. Is Peggy's offer still open? Just to feel the muggy kiss of summer night on the Brewer streets would be welcome. Nothing feels worse than other people's good times.

Babe asks Buchanan, "What'd you have in mind, Buck?" She is working on the joint now and the smoke includes her eyes.

The fat man's shrug jiggles Rabbit's side. "No big plans," Buchanan mutters. "See what develops. Woman, way you're goin', you won't be able to tell those black keys from the white."

She plumes smoke into his face. "Who owns who?"

The boy cuts in. "Ofay doesn't dig he's a john, right?"

Buchanan, his smoothness jammed, observes, "That mouth again."

Rabbit asks loudly, "What else shall we talk about?" and twiddles his fingers at Babe for the joint. Inhaling still burns, but something is starting to mesh. He feels his height above the others as a good, a lordly, thing.

Buchanan is probing the other two. "Jill in tonight?"

Babe says, "Left her back at the place."

The boy asks, "On a nod, right?"

"You stay away, hear, she got herself clean. She's on no nod, just tired from mental confusion, from fighting her signs."

"Clean," the boy says, "what's clean? White is clean, right? Cunt is clean, right? Shit is clean, right? There's nothin' not clean the law don't go pointing its finger at it, right?"

"Wrong," Babe says. "Hate is not clean. A boy like you with hate in his heart, he needs to wash."

"Wash is what they said to Jesus, right?"

"Who's Jill?" Rabbit asks.

"Wash is what Pilate said he thought he might go do, right? Don't go saying clean to me, Babe, that's one darkie bag they had us in too long."

Buchanan is still delicately prying at Babe. "She coming in?"

The other cuts in, "She'll be in, can't keep that cunt away; put locks on the doors, she'll ooze in the letter slot."

Babe turns to him in mild surprise. "Now you loves little Jill."

"You can love what you don't like, right?"

Babe hangs her head. "That poor baby," she tells the table-top, "just going to hurt herself and anybody standing near."

Buchanan speaks slowly, threading his way. "Just thought, man might like to meet Jill."

The boy sits up. Electricity, reflected from the bar and the streets, spins around his spectacle rims. "Gonna match 'em up," he says, "you're gonna cut yourself in on an all-honky fuck. You can out-devil these devils any day, right? You could of out-niggered Moses on the hill."

He seems to be a static the other two put up with. Buchanan is still prying at Babe across the table. "Just thought," he shrugs, "two birds with one stone."

A tear falls from her creased face to the tabletop. Her hair is done tight back like a schoolgirl's, a red ribbon in back. It must hurt, with kinky hair. "Going to take herself down all the way, it's in her signs, can't slip your signs."

"Who's that voodoo supposed to boogaboo?" the boy asks. "Whitey here got so much science he don't even need to play the numbers, right?"

Rabbit asks, "Is Jill white?"

The boy tells the two others angrily, "Cut the crooning, she'll be here, Christ, where else would she go, right? We're the blood to wash her sins away, right? Clean. Shit, that burns me. There's no dirt made that cunt won't swallow. With a smile on her face, right? Because she's *clean*." There seems to be not only a history but a religion behind his anger. Rabbit sees this much, that the other two are working to fix him up with this approaching cloud, this Jill, who will be pale like the Stinger, and poisonous.

He announces, "I think I'll go soon."

Buchanan swiftly squeezes his forearm. "What you want to do that for, Br'er Rabbit? You haven't achieved your objective, friend."

"My only objective was to be polite." *She'll ooze in the letter slot*: haunted by this image and the smoke inside him, he feels he can lift up from the booth, pass across Buchanan's shoulders like a shawl, and out the door. Nothing can hold him, not Mom, not Janice. He could slip a posse dribbling, Tothero used to flatter him.

"You going to go off half-cocked," Buchanan warns.

"You ain't heard Babe play," the other man says.

He stops rising. "Babe plays?"

She is flustered, stares at her thin ringless hands, fiddles, mumbles. "Let him go. Let the man run. I don't want him to hear."

The boy teases her. "Babe now, what sort of bad black act you putting on? He wants to hear you do your thing. Your darkie thing, right? You did the spooky card-reading bit and now you can do the banjo bit and maybe you can do the hot momma bit afterwards but it doesn't look like it right now, right?"

"Ease off, nigger," she says, face still bent low. "Sometime you going to lean too hard."

Rabbit asks her shyly, "You play the piano?"

"He gives me bad vibes," Babe confesses to the two black men. "Those knuckles of his aren't too good. Bad shadows in there."

Buchanan surprises Harry by reaching and covering her thin bare hands with one of his broadened big pressman's hands, a ring of milk-blue jade on one finger, battered bright copper on another. His other arm reaches around Harry's shoulders, heavy. "Suppose you was him," he says to Babe, "how would that make you feel?"

"Bad," she says. "As bad as I feel anyway."

"Play for me Babe," Rabbit says in the lovingness of pot, and she lifts her eyes to his and lets her lips pull back on long yellow teeth and gums the color of rhubarb stems. "Men," Babe gaily drawls. "They sure can retail the shit." She pushes herself out of the booth, hobbling in her comb-red dress, and crosses through a henscratch of applause to the piano painted as if by children in silver swirls. She signals to the bar for Rufe to turn on the blue spot and bows stiffly, once, grudging the darkness around her a smile and, after a couple of runs to burn away the fog, plays.

What does Babe play? All the good old ones. All show tunes. "Up a Lazy River," "You're the Top," "Thou Swell," "Summertime," you know. There are hundreds, thousands. Men from Indiana wrote them in Manhattan. They flow into each other without edges, flowing under black bridges of chords thumped six, seven times, as if Babe is helping the piano to remember a word it won't say. Or spanking the silence. Or saying, *Here I am, find me, find me.* Her hands, all brown bone, hang on the keyboard hushed like gloves on a table; she gazes up through blue dust to get herself into focus, she lets her hands fall into another tune: "My Funny Valentine," "Smoke Gets in Your Eyes," "I Can't Get Started," starting to hum along with herself now, lyrics born in some distant smoke, decades when Americans moved within the American dream, laughing at it, starving on it, but living it, humming it, the national anthem everywhere. Wise guys and hicks, straw boaters and bib overalls, fast bucks, broken hearts, penthouses in the sky, shacks by the railroad tracks, ups and downs, rich and poor, trolley cars, and the latest news by radio. Rabbit had come in on the end of it, as the world shrank like an apple going bad and America was no longer the wisest hick town within a boat ride of Europe and Broadway forgot the tune, but here it all still was, in the music Babe played, the little stairways she climbed and came tap-dancing down, twinkling in black, and there is no other music, not really, though Babe works in some Beatles songs, "Yesterday" and "Hey Jude," doing it rinky-tink, her own style of ice to rattle in the glass. As Babe plays she takes on swaying and leaning backwards; at her arms' ends the standards go root back into ragtime. Rabbit sees circus tents and fireworks and farmers' wagons and an empty sandy river running so slow the sole motion is catfish sleeping beneath the golden skin.

The boy leans forward and murmurs to Rabbit, "You want ass, right? You can have her. Fifty gets you her all night, all ways you can think up. She knows a lot."

Sunk in her music, Rabbit is lost. He shakes his head and says, "She's too good."

"Good, man; she got to live, right? This place don't pay her shit."

Babe has become a railroad, prune-head bobbing, napkin of jewels flashing blue, music rolling through crazy places, tunnels of dissonance and open stretches of the same tinny thin note bleeding itself into the sky, all sad power and happiness worn into holes like shoe soles. From the dark booths around voices call out in a mutter "Go Babe" and "Do it, do it." The spidery boys in the adjacent room are frozen around the green felt. Into the mike that is there no bigger than a lollipop she begins to sing, sings in a voice that is no woman's voice at all and no man's, is merely human, the words of Ecclesiastes. A time to be born, a time to die. A time to gather up stones, a time to cast stones away. Yes. The Lord's last word. There is no other word, not really. Her singing opens up, grows enormous, frightens Rabbit with its enormous black maw of truth yet makes him overjoyed that he is here; he brims with joy, to be here with these black others, he wants to shout love through the darkness of Babe's noise to the sullen brother in goatee and glasses. He brims with this itch but does not spill. For Babe stops. As if suddenly tired or insulted Babe breaks off the song and shrugs and quits.

That is how Babe plays.

She comes back to the table stooped, trembling, nervous, old.

"That was beautiful, Babe," Rabbit tells her.

"It was," says another voice. A small white girl is standing there prim, in a white dress casual and dirty as smoke.

"Hey. Jill," Buchanan says.

"Hi Buck. Skeeter, hi."

So Skeeter is his name. He scowls and looks at the cigarette of which there is not even butt enough to call a roach.

"Jilly-love," Buchanan says, standing until his thighs scrape the table edge, "allow me to introduce. Harry the Rabbit Angstrom, he works at the printing plant with me, along with his daddy."

"He has a daddy?" Jill asks, still looking at Skeeter, who will not look at her.

"Jilly, you go sit in here where I am," Buchanan says. "I'll go get a chair from Rufe."

"Down, baby," Skeeter says. "I'm splitting." No one offers to argue with him. Perhaps they are all as pleased as Rabbit to see him go.

Buchanan chuckles, he rubs his hands. His eyes keep in touch with all of them, even though Babe seems to be dozing. He says to Jill, "How about a beverage? A 7-Up? Rufe can make a lemonade even."

"Nothing," Jill says. Teaparty manner. Hands in lap. Thin arms. Freckles. Rabbit scents in her the perfume of class. She excites him.

"Maybe she'd like a real drink," he says. With a white woman here he feels more in charge. Negroes, you can't blame them, haven't had his advantages. Slave ships, cabins, sold down the river, Ku Klux Klan, James Earl Ray: Channel 44 keeps having these documentaries all about it.

"I'm under age," Jill tells him politely.

Rabbit says, "Who cares?"

She answers, "The police."

"Not up the street they wouldn't mind so much," Buchanan explains, "if the girl halfway acted the part, but down here they get a touch fussy."

"The fuzz is fussy," Babe says dreamily. "The fuzz is our fussy friends. The fuzzy motherfuckers fuss."

"Don't, Babe," Jill begs. "Don't pretend."

"You let your old black mamma have a buzz on," Babe says. "Don't I take good care of you mostly?"

"How would the police know if this kid has a drink?" Rabbit asks, willing to be indignant.

Buchanan makes his high short wheeze. "Friend Harry, they'd just have to turn their heads."

"There're cops in here?"

"Friend"—and from the way he sidles closer Harry feels he's found another father—"if it weren't for po-lice spies, poor Jimbo's wouldn't sell two beers a night. Po-lice spies are the absolute backbone of local low life. They got so many plants going, that's why they don't dare shoot in riots, for fear of killing one of their own."

"Like over in York."

Jill asks Rabbit, "Hey. You live in Brewer?" He sees that she doesn't like his being white in here, and smiles without answering. Screw you, little girl.

Buchanan answers for him. "Lady, does he live in Brewer? If he lived any more in Brewer he'd be a walking advertisement. He'd be the Owl Pretzel owl. I don't think this fella's ever gotten above Twelfth Street, have you Harry?"

"A few times. I was in Texas in the Army, actually."

"Did you get to fight?" Jill asks. Something scratchy here, but maybe like a kitten it's the way of making contact.

"I was all set to go to Korea," he says. "But they never sent me." Though at the time he was grateful, it has since eaten at him, become the shame of his life. He had never been a fighter but now there is enough death in him so that in a way he wants to kill.

"Now Skeeter," Buchanan is saying, "he's just back from Vietnam."

"That's why he so rude," Babe offers.

"I couldn't tell if he was rude or not," Rabbit confesses.

"That's nice," Buchanan says.

"He was rude," Babe says.

Jill's lemonade arrives. She is still girl enough to look happy when it is set before her: cakes at the teaparty. Her face lights up. A crescent of lime clings to the edge of the glass; she takes it off and sucks and makes a sour face. A child's plumpness has been drained from her before a woman's bones could grow and harden. She is the reddish type of fair; her hair hangs dull, without fire, almost flesh-color, or the color of the flesh of certain soft trees, yews or cedars. Harry feels protective, timidly. In her tension of small bones she reminds him of Nelson. He asks her, "What do you do, Jill?"

"Nothing much," she says. "Hang around." It had been square of him to ask, pushing. The blacks fit around her like shadows.

"Jilly's a poor soul," Babe volunteers, stirring within her buzz. "She's fallen on evil ways." And she pats Rabbit's hand as if to say, *Don't you fall upon these ways.*

"Young Jill," Buchanan clarifies, "has run away from her home up there in Connec-ticut."

Rabbit asks her, "Why would you do that?"

"Why not? Let freedom ring."

"Can I ask how old you are?"

"You can ask."

"I'm asking."

Babe hasn't let go of Rabbit's hand; with the fingernail of her index finger she is toying with the hairs on the back of his fist. It makes his teeth go cold, for her to do that. "Not so old you couldn't be her daddy," Babe says.

He is beginning to get the drift. They are presenting him with this problem. He is the consultant honky. The girl, too, unwilling as she is, is submitting to the interview. She inquires of him, only partly parrying, "How old are *you*?"

"Thirty-six."

"Divide by two."

"Eighteen, huh? How long've you been on the run? Away from your parents."

"Her daddy dead," Buchanan interposes softly.

"Long enough, thank you." Her face pales, her freckles stand out sharply: blood-dots that have dried brown. Her dry little lips tighten; her chin drifts toward him. She is pulling rank. He is Penn Villas, she is Penn Park. Rich kids make all the trouble.

"Long enough for what?"

"Long enough to do some sick things."

"Are you sick?"

"I'm cured."

Buchanan interposes, "Babe helped her out."

"Babe is a beautiful person," Jill says. "I was really a mess when Babe took me in."

"Jilly is my sweetie," Babe says, as suddenly as in playing she moves from one tune to another, "Jilly is my baby-love and I'm her mamma-love," and takes her brown hands away from Harry's to encircle the girl's waist and hug her against the rooster-comb-red of her dress; the two are women, though one is a prune and the other a milkweed. Jill pouts in pleasure. Her mouth is lovable when it moves, Rabbit thinks, the lower lip bumpy and dry as if chapped, though this is not winter but the humid height of summer.

Buchanan is further explaining. "Fact of it is, this girl hasn't got no place regular to go. Couple weeks ago, she comes in here, not knowing I suppose the place was mostly for soul, a little pretty girl like this get in with some of the brothers they would tear her apart limb by sweet limb"—he has to chuckle—"so Babe takes her right away under her wing. Only trouble with that is"—the fat man rustles closer, making the booth a squeeze—"Babe's place is none too big, and anyways . . ."

The child flares up. "Anyways I'm not welcome." Her eyes widen: Rabbit has not seen their color before, they have been shadowy, moving slowly, as if their pink lids are tender or as if, rejecting instruction and inventing her own way of moving through the world, she has lost any vivid idea of what to be looking for. Her eyes are green. The dry tired green, yet one of his favorite colors, of August grass.

"Jilly-love," Babe says, hugging, "you the most welcome little white baby there could be."

Buchanan is talking only to Rabbit, softer and softer. "You know, those things happen over York way, they could happen here, and how could we protect"—the smallest wave of his hand toward the girl lets the sentence gracefully hang; Harry is reminded of Stavros's gestures. Buchanan ends chuckling: "We be so busy keepin' holes out of our own skins. Dependin' where you get caught, being black's a bad ticket both ways!"

Jill snaps, "I'll be all right. You two stop it now. Stop trying to sell me to this creep. I don't want him. He doesn't want me. Nobody wants me. That's all right. I don't want anybody."

"Everybody wants somebody," Babe says. "I don't mind your hangin' around my place, some gentlemen mind, is all."

Rabbit says, "Buchanan minds," and this perception astonishes them; the two blacks break into first shrill, then jingling, laughter, and another Stinger appears on the table between his hands, pale as lemonade.

"Honey, it's just the visibility," Babe then adds sadly. "You make us ever so visible."

A silence grows like the silence when a group of adults is waiting for a child to be polite. Sullenly Jill asks Rabbit, "What do *you* do?"

"Set type," Rabbit tells her. "Watch TV. Babysit."

"Harry here," Buchanan explains, "had a nasty shock the other day. His wife for no good reason upped and left him."

"No reason at all?" Jill asks. Her mouth pouts forward,

vexed and aggressive, yet her spark of interest dies before her breath is finished with the question.

Rabbit thinks. "I think I bored her. Also, we didn't agree politically."

"What about?"

"The Vietnam war. I'm all for it."

Jill snatches in her breath.

Babe says, "I knew those knuckles looked bad."

Buchanan offers to smooth it over. "Everybody at the plant is for it. We think, you don't hold 'em over there, you'll have those black-pajama fellas on the streets over here."

Jill says to Rabbit seriously, "You should talk to Skeeter about it. He says it was a fabulous trip. He loved it."

"I wouldn't know about that. I'm not saying it's pleasant to fight in or be caught in. I just don't like the kids making the criticisms. People say it's a mess so we should get out. If you stayed out of every mess you'd never get into anything."

"Amen," Babe says. "Life is generally shit."

Rabbit goes on, feeling himself get rabid, "I guess I don't much believe in college kids or the Viet Cong. I don't think they have any answers. I think they're minorities trying to bring down everything that halfway works. Halfway isn't all the way but it's better than no way."

Buchanan smooths on frantically. His upper lip is bubbling with sweat under his slit of a mustache. "I agree ninety-nine per cent. Enlightened self-interest is the phrase I like. The way I see, enlightened self-interest's the best deal we're likely to get down here. I don't buy pie in the sky whoever is slicing it. These young ones like Skeeter, they say All power to the people, you look around for the people, the only people around is *them*."

"Because of Toms like you," Jill says.

Buchanan blinks. His voice goes deeper, hurt. "I ain't no Tom, girl. That kind of talk doesn't help any of us. That kind of talk just shows how young you are. What I am is a man trying to get from Point A to Point B, from the cradle to the grave hurting the fewest people I can. Just like Harry here, if you'd ask him. Just like your late daddy, God rest his soul."

Babe says, hugging the stubbornly limp girl, "I just likes Jilly's spunk, she's less afraid what to do with her life than fat old smelly you, sittin' there lickin' yourself like an old cigar end." But while talking she keeps her eyes on Buchanan as if his concurrence is to be desired. Mothers and fathers, they turn up everywhere.

Buchanan explains to Jill with a nice levelness, "So that is the problem. Young Harry here lives in this fancy big house over in the fanciest part of West Brewer, all by himself, and never gets any tail."

Harry protests. "I'm not that alone. I have a kid with me."

"Man has to have tail," Buchanan is continuing.

"Play, Babe," a dark voice shouts from a dark booth. Rufe bobs his head and switches on the blue spot. Babe sighs and offers Jill what is left of Skeeter's joint. Jill shakes her head and gets out of the booth to let Babe out. Rabbit thinks the girl is leaving and discovers himself glad when she sits down again, opposite him. He sips his Stinger and she chews the ice from her lemonade while Babe plays again. This time the boys in the poolroom softly keep at their game. The clicking and the liquor and the music mix and make the space inside him very big, big enough to hold blue light and black faces and "Honeysuckle Rose" and stale smoke sweeter than alfalfa and this apparition across the way, whose wrists and forearms are as it were translucent and belonging to another order of creature; she is not yet grown. Her womanliness is attached to her, it floats from her like a little zeppelin he can almost see. And his inside space expands to include beyond Jimbo's the whole world with its arrowing wars and polychrome races, its continents shaped like ceiling stains, its strings of gravitational attraction attaching it to every star, its glory in space as of a blue marble swirled with clouds; everything is warm, wet, still coming to birth but himself and his home, which remains a strange dry place, dry and cold and emptily spinning in the void of Penn Villas like a cast-off space capsule. He doesn't want to go there but he must. He must. "I must go," he says, rising.

"Hey, hey," Buchanan protests. "The night hasn't even got itself turned around to get started yet."

"I ought to be home in case my kid can't stand the kid he's staying with. I promised I'd visit my parents tomorrow, if they didn't keep my mother in the hospital for more tests."

"Babe will be sad, you sneaking out. She took a shine to you."

"Maybe that other guy she took a shine to will be back. My guess is Babe takes a shine pretty easy."

"Don't you get nasty."

"No, I love her, Jesus. Tell her. She plays like a whiz. This has been a terrific change of pace for me." He tries to stand, but the table edge confines him to a crouch. The booth tilts and he rocks slightly, as if he is already in the slowly turning cold house he is heading toward. Jill stands up with him, obedient as a mirror.

"One of these times," Buchanan continues beneath them, "maybe you can get to know Babe better. She is one good egg."

"I don't doubt it." He tells Jill, "Sit down."

"Aren't you going to take me with you? They want you to."

"Gee. I hadn't thought to."

She sits down.

"Friend Harry, you've hurt the little girl's feelings. Nasty must be your middle name."

Jill says, "Far as creeps like this are concerned, I have no feelings. I've decided he's queer anyway."

"Could be," Buchanan says. "It would explain that wife."

"Come on, let me out of the booth. I'd *like* to take her—"

"Then help yourself, friend. On me."

Babe is playing "Time After Time." *I tell myself that I'm.*

Harry sags. The table edge is killing his thighs. "O.K., kid. Come along."

"I wouldn't dream of it."

"You'll be bored," he feels in honesty obliged to add.

"You've been had," she tells him.

"Jilly now, be gracious for the gentleman." Buchanan hastily pushes out of the booth, lest the combination tumble, and lets Harry slide out and leans against him confidentially. Geezers. His breath rises bad, from under the waxed needles. "Problem is," he explains, the last explaining he will do tonight, "it don't look that good, her being in here, under age and all. The fuzz now, they aren't absolutely unfriendly, but they hold us pretty tight to the line, what with public opinion the way it is. So it's not that healthy for anybody. She's a poor child needs a daddy, is the simple truth of it."

Rabbit asks her, "How'd he die?"

Jill says, "Heart. Dropped dead in a New York theater lobby. He and my mother were seeing *Hair*."

"O.K. Let's shove." To Buchanan Rabbit says, "How much for the drinks? Wow. They're just hitting me."

"On us," is the answer, accompanied by a wave of a palm the color of silver polish. "On the black community." He has to wheeze and chuckle. Struggling for solemnity: "This is real big of you, man. You're a big man."

"See you at work Monday."

"Jilly-love, you be a good girl. We'll keep in touch."

"I bet."

Disturbing, to think that Buchanan works. We all work. Day selves and night selves. The belly hungers, the spirit hungers. Mouths munch, cunts swallow. Monstrous. Soul. He used to try to picture it when a child. A parasite like a tapeworm inside. A sprig of mistletoe hung from our bones, living on air. A jellyfish swaying between our lungs and our liver. Black men have more, bigger. Cocks like eels. Night feeders. Their touching underbelly smell on buses, their dread of those clean dry places where Harry must be. He wonders if he will be sick. Poison in those Stingers, on top of moonburgers.

Babe shifts gears, lays out six chords like six black lead slugs slapping into the tray, and plays, "There's a Small Hotel." *With a wishing well.*

With this Jill, then, Rabbit enters the street. On his right, toward the mountain, Weiser stretches sallow under blue street lights. The Pinnacle Hotel makes a tattered blur, the back of the Sunflower Beer clock shows yellow neon petals; otherwise the great street is dim. He can remember when Weiser with its five movie marquees and its medley of neon outlines appeared as gaudy as a carnival midway. People would stroll, children between them. Now the downtown looks deserted, sucked dry by suburban shopping centers and haunted by rapists. LOCAL HOODS ASSAULT ELDERLY, last week's *Vat* had headlined. In the original version of the head LOCAL had been BLACK.

They turn left, toward the Weiser Street Bridge. River moisture cools his brow. He decides he will not be sick. Never, even as an infant, could stand it; some guys, Ronnie Harrison for one, liked it, throw up after a few beers or before a big game, joke about the corn between their teeth, but Rabbit needed to keep it down, even at the cost of a bellyache. He still carries from sitting in Jimbo's the sense of the world being inside him; he will keep it down. The city night air. The ginger of tar and concrete baked all day, truck traffic lifted from it like a lid. Infrequent headlights stroke this girl, catching her white legs and thin dress as she hangs on the curb hesitant.

She asks, "Where's your car?"

"I don't have any."

"That's impossible."

"My wife took it when she left me."

"You didn't have two?"

"No." This is really a rich kid.

"I have a car," she says.

"Where is it?"

"I don't know."

"How can you not know?"

"I used to leave it on the street up near Babe's place off of Plum, I didn't know it was somebody's garage entrance, and one morning they had taken it away."

"And you didn't go after it?"

"I didn't have the money for any fine. And I'm scared of the police, they might check me out. The staties must have a bulletin on me."

"Wouldn't the simplest thing for you be to go back to Connecticut?"

"Oh, please," she says.

"What didn't you like about it?"

"It was all ego. Sick ego."

"Something pretty egotistical about running away, too. What'd that do to your mother?"

The girl makes no answer, but crosses the street, from Jimbo's to the beginning of the bridge. Rabbit has to follow. "What kind of car was it?"

"A white Porsche."

"Wow."

"My father gave it to me for my sixteenth birthday."

"My father-in-law runs the Toyota agency in town."

They keep arriving at this place, where a certain symmetry snips their exchanges short. Having crossed the bridge, they stand on a little pond of sidewalk squares where in this age of cars few feet tread. The bridge was poured in the Thirties —sidewalks, broad balustrades, and lamp plinths—of reddish rough concrete; above them an original light standard, iron fluted and floral toward the top, looms stately but unlit at the entrance to the bridge, illumined since recently with cold bars of violet on tall aluminum stems rooted in the center of the walkway. Her white dress is unearthly in this light. A man's name is embedded in a bronze plaque, illegible. Jill asks impatiently, "Well, how shall we do?"

He assumes she means transportation. He is too shaky still, too full of smoke and Stinger, to look beyond that. The way to the center of Brewer, where taxis prowl and doze, feels blocked. In the gloom beyond Jimbo's neon nimbus, brown shadows, local hoods, giggle in doorways, watching. Rabbit says, "Let's walk across the bridge and hope for a bus. The last one comes around eleven, maybe on Saturdays it's later. Anyway, if none comes at all, it's not too far to walk to my place. My kid does it all the time."

"I love walking," she says. She touchingly adds, "I'm strong. You mustn't baby me."

The balustrade was poured in an X-pattern echoing rail fences; these Xs click past his legs not rapidly enough. The gritty breadth he keeps touching runs tepid. Flecks as if of rock salt had been mixed into it. Not done that way anymore, not done this color, reddish, the warmth of flesh, her hair also, cut cedar color, lifting as she hurries to keep up.

"What's the rush?"

"Shhh. Dontcha hear 'em?"

Cars thrust by, rolling balls of light before them. An anvil-drop below, to the black floor of the river: white shards, boat shapes. Behind them, pattering feet, the press of pursuit. Rabbit dares stop and peek backwards. Two brown figures are chasing them. Their shadows shorten and multiply and lengthen and simplify again as they fly beneath the successive mauve angles, in and out of strips of light; one man is brandishing something white in his hand. It glitters. Harry's heart jams; he wants to make water. The West Brewer end of the bridge is forever away. LOCAL MAN STABBED DEFENDING OUT-OF-STATE GIRL. *Body Tossed From Historic Bridge.* He squeezes her arm and tries to make her run. Her skin is smooth and narrow yet tepid like the balustrade. She snaps, "Cut it out," and pulls away. He turns and finds, unexpectedly, what he had forgotten was there, courage; his body fits into the hardshell blindness of meeting a threat, rigid, only his eyes soft spots, himself a sufficient shield. *Kill.*

The Negroes halt under the near purple moon and back a step, frightened. They are young, their bodies liquid. He is bigger than they. The white flash in the hand of one is not a knife but a pocketbook of pearls. The bearer shambles forward with it. His eyewhites and the pearls look lavender in the light. "This yours, lady?"

"Oh. Yes."

"Babe sent us after."

"Oh. Thank you. Thank her."

"We scare somebody?"

"Not me. Him."

"Yeah."

"Dude scared us too."

"Sorry about that," Rabbit volunteers. "Spooky bridge."

"O.K."

"O.K." Their mauve eyeballs roll; their purple hands flip as their legs in the stitched skin of Levis seek the rhythm of leaving. They giggle together; and also at this moment two giant trailer trucks pass on the bridge, headed in opposite directions: their rectangles thunderously overlap and, having clapped the air between them, hurtle each on its way, corrosive and rumbling. The bridge trembles. The Negro boys have disappeared. Rabbit walks on with Jill.

The pot and brandy and fear in him enhance the avenue he knows too well. No bus comes. Her dress flutters in the corner of his eye as he tries, his skin stretched and his senses shuffling and circling like a cloud of gnats, to make talk. "Your home was in Connecticut."

"A place called Stonington."

"Near New York?"

"Near enough. Daddy used to go down Mondays and come back Fridays. He loved to sail. He said about Stonington it was the only town in the state that faces the open sea, everything else is on the Sound."

"And he died, you said. My mother—she has Parkinson's Disease."

"Look, do you like to talk this much? Why don't we just walk? I've never been in West Brewer before. It's nice."

"What's nice about it?"

"Everything. It doesn't have a past like the city does. So it's not so disappointed. Look at that, Burger Bliss. Isn't it beautiful, all goldy and plasticky with that purple fire inside?"

"That's where I ate tonight."

"How was the food?"

"Awful. Maybe I taste everything too much, I should start smoking again. My kid loves the place."

"How old did you say he was?"

"Twelve. Thirteen this October. He's small for his age."

"You shouldn't tell him that."

"Yeah. I try not to ride him."

"What would you ride him about?"

"Oh. He's bored by things I used to love. I don't think he's having much fun. He never goes outdoors."

"Hey. What's your name?"

"Harry."

"Hey, big Harry. Would you mind feeding me?"

"Sure, I mean No. At home? I don't know what we have in the icebox. Refrigerator."

"I mean over there, at the burger place."

"Oh, sure. Terrific. I'm sorry. I assumed you ate."

"Maybe I did, I tend to forget material details like that. But I don't think so. All I feel inside is lemonade."

She selects a Cashewburger for 85¢ and a strawberry milkshake. In the withering light she devours the burger, and he orders her another. She smiles apologetically. She has small inturned teeth, roundish and with tiny gaps between them like a printer's hairline spaces. Nice. "Usually I try to rise above eating."

"Why?"

"It's so ugly. Don't you think, it's one of the uglier things we do?"

"It has to be done."

"That's your philosophy, isn't it?" Even in this garishly lit place her face has about it something shadowy and elusive, something that's skipped a stage. Finished, she wipes her fingers one by one on a paper napkin and says decisively, "Thank you very much." He pays. She clutches the purse, but what is in it? Credit cards? Diagrams for the revolution?

He has had coffee, to keep himself awake. Be up all night fucking this poor kid. Upholding the honor of middle-aged squares. Different races. In China, they used to tell you in the Army, the women put razor blades in their cunts in case the Japanese tried rape. Rabbit's scrotum shrivels at the thought. Enjoy the walk. They march down Weiser, the store windows dark but for burglar lights, the Acme parking lot empty but for scattered neckers, the movie marquee changed from 2001 to TRUE GRIT. Short enough to get it all on. They cross the street at a blinking yellow to Emberly Avenue, which then becomes Emberly Drive, which becomes Vista Crescent. The development is dark. "Talk about spooky," she says.

"I think it's the flatness," he says. "The town I grew up in, no two houses were on the same level."

"There's such a smell of plumbing somehow."

"Actually, the plumbing is none too good."

This smoky creature at his side has halved his weight. He floats up the steps to the porchlet, knees vibrating. Her profile by his shoulder is fine and cool as the face on the old dime. The key to the door of three stepped windows nearly flies out of his hand, it feels so magical. Whatever he expects when he flicks on the inside hall light, it is not the same old furniture, the fake cobbler's bench, the sofa and the silverthread chair facing each other like two bulky drunks too tired to go upstairs. The blank TV screen in its box of metal painted with wood grain, the see-through shelves with nothing on them.

"Wow," Jill says. "This is really tacky."

Rabbit apologizes, "We never really picked out the furniture, it just kind of happened. Janice was always going to do different curtains."

Jill asks, "Was she a good wife?"

His answer is nervous; the question plants Janice back in the house, quiet in the kitchen, crouching at the head of the stairs, listening. "Not too bad. Not much on organizational ability, but until she got mixed up with this other guy at least she kept plugging away. She used to drink too much but got that under control. We had a tragedy about ten years ago that sobered her up I guess. Sobered me up too. A baby died."

"How?"

"An accident we caused."

"That's sad. Where do we sleep?"

"Why don't you take the kid's room, I guess he won't be back. The kid he's staying with, he's a real spoiled jerk, I told Nelson if it got too painful he should just come home. I probably should have been here to answer the phone. What time is it? How about a beer?"

Penniless, she is wearing a little wristwatch that must have cost two hundred at least. "Twelve-ten," she says. "Don't you want to sleep with me?"

"Huh? That's not your idea of bliss, is it? Sleeping with a creep?"

"You are a creep, but you just fed me."

"Forget it. On the white community. Ha."

"And you have this sweet funny family side. Always worrying about who needs you."

"Yeah, well it's hard to know sometimes. Probably nobody if I could face up to it. In answer to your question, sure I'd like to sleep with you, if I won't get hauled in for statutory rape."

"You're really scared of the law, aren't you?"

"I try to keep out of its way is all."

"I promise you on a Bible—do you have a Bible?"

"There used to be one somewhere, that Nelson got for going to Sunday school, when he did. We've kind of let all that go. Just promise me."

"I promise you I'm eighteen. I'm legally a woman. I am not bait for a black gang. You will not be mugged or blackmailed. You may fuck me."

"Somehow you're making me almost cry."

"You're awfully scared of me. Let's take a bath together and then see how we feel about it."

He laughs. "By then I guess I'll feel pretty gung-ho about it."

She is serious, a serious small-faced animal sniffing out her new lair. "Where's the bathroom?"

"Take off your clothes here."

The command startles her; her chin dents and her eyes go wide with fright. No reason he should be the only scared person here. Rich bitch calling his living room tacky. Standing on the rug where he and Janice last made love, Jill skins out of her clothes. She kicks off her sandals and strips her dress upward. She is wearing no bra. Her tits tug upward, drop back, give him a headless stare. She is wearing bikini underpants, black lace, in a pattern too fine to read. Not pausing a moment for him to drink her in, she pulls the elastic down with two thumbs, wriggles, and steps out. Where Janice had a springy triangle encroaching on the insides of her thighs when she didn't shave, Jill has scarcely a shadow, amber fuzz dust darkened toward the center to an upright dainty mane. The horns of her pelvis like starved cheekbones. Her belly a child's, childless. Her breasts in some lights as she turns scarcely exist. Being naked elongates her neck: a true ripeness there, in the unhurried curve from base of skull to small of back, and in the legs, which link to the hips with knots of fat and keep a plumpness all the way down. Her ankles are less slim than Janice's. But, hey, she is naked in this room, his room. This really strange creature, too trusting. She bends to pick up her clothes. She treads lightly on his carpet, as if watchful for tacks. She stands an arm's-length from him, her mouth pouting prim, a fleck of dry skin on the lower lip. "And you?"

"Upstairs." He undresses in his bedroom, where he always does; in the bathroom on the other side of the partition, water begins to cry, to sing, to splash. He looks down and has nothing of a hard-on. In the bathroom he finds her bending over to test the temperature mix at the faucet. A tuft between her buttocks. From behind she seems a boy's slim back wedged into the upside-down valentine of a woman's satin rear. He yearns to touch her, to touch the satin symmetry, and does. It stings his fingertips like glass we don't expect is there. Jill doesn't deign to flinch or turn at his touch, testing the water to her satisfaction. His cock stays small but has stopped worrying.

Their bath is all too gentle, silent, liquid, and pure. They are each attentive: he soaps and rinses her breasts as if their utter cleanness challenges him to make them even cleaner; she kneels and kneads his back as if a year of working weariness were in it. She blinds him in drenched cloth; she counts the gray hairs (six) in the hair of his chest. Still even as they stand to dry each other and he looms above her like a Viking he cannot shake the contented impotence of his sensation that they are the ends of spotlight beams thrown on the clouds, that their role is to haunt this house like two bleached creatures on a television set entertaining an empty room.

She glances at his groin. "I don't turn you on exactly, do I?"

"You do, you do. Too much. It's still too strange. I don't even know your last name."

"Pendleton." She drops to her knees on the bathroom rug and takes his penis into her mouth. He backs away as if bitten.

"Wait."

Jill looks up at him crossly, looks up the slope of his slack gut, a cranky puzzled child with none of the answers in the last class of the day, her mouth slick with forbidden candy. He lifts her as he would a child, but she is longer than a child, and her armpits are scratchy and deep; he kisses her on the mouth. No gumdrops, her lips harden and she twists her thin face away, saying into his shoulder, "I don't turn anybody on, much. No tits. My mother has nifty tits, maybe that's my trouble."

"Tell me about your trouble," he says, and leads her by the hand toward the bedroom.

"Oh, Jesus, one of those. Trouble-shooters. From the look of it you're in worse shape than me, you can't even respond when somebody takes off their clothes."

"First times are hard; you need to absorb somebody a little first." He darkens the room and they lie on the bed. She offers to embrace him again, hard mouth and sharp knees anxious to have it done, but he smooths her onto her back and massages her breasts, plumping them up, circling. "These aren't your trouble," he croons. "These are lovely." Down below he feels himself easily stiffening, clotting: cream in the freezer. CLINIC FOR RUNAWAYS OPENED. *Fathers Do Duty On Nights Off.*

Relaxing, Jill grows stringy; tendons and resentments come to the surface. "You should be fucking my mother, she really is good with men, she thinks they're the be-all and end-all. I know she was playing around, even before Daddy died."

"Is that why you ran away?"

"You wouldn't believe if I really told you."

"Tell me."

"A guy I went with tried to get me into heavy drugs."

"That's not so unbelievable."

"Yeah, but his reason was crazy. Look, you don't want to hear this crap. You're up now, why don't you just give it to me?"

"Tell me his reason."

"You see, when I'd trip, I'd see, like, you know—God. He never would. He just saw pieces of like old movies, that didn't add up."

"What kind of stuff did he give you? Pot?"

"Oh, no, listen, pot is just like having a Coke or something. Acid, when he could get it. Strange pills. He'd rob doctors' cars to get their samples and then mix them to see what happened. They have names for all these pills, purple hearts, dollies, I don't know what all. Then after he stole this syringe he'd inject stuff, he wouldn't even know what it was half the time, it was wild. I would never let him break my skin. I figured, anything went in by the mouth, I could throw it up, but anything went in my veins, I had no way to get rid of it, it could kill me. He said that was part of the kick. He was really freaked, but he had this, you know, power over me. I ran."

"Has he tried to follow you?" A freak coming up the stairs. Green teeth, poisonous needles. Rabbit's penis had wilted, listening.

"No, he's not the type. Toward the end I don't think he knew me from Adam really, all he was thinking about was his next fix. Junkies are like that. They get to be bores. You think they're talking to you or making love or whatever, and then you realize they're looking over your shoulder for the next fix. You realize you're nothing. He didn't need me to find God for him, if he met God right on the street he'd've tried to hustle Him for money enough for a couple bags."

"What did He look like?"

"Oh, about five-ten, brown hair down to his shoulders, slightly wavy when he brushed it, a neat build. Even after smack had pulled all the color from him he had a wonderful frame. His back was really marvellous, with long sloping shoulders and all these ripply little ribby bumps behind, you know, here." She touches him but is seeing the other. "He had been a runner in junior high."

"I meant God."

"Oh, God. He changed. He was different every time. But you always knew it was Him. Once I remember something like the inside of a big lily, only magnified a thousand times, a sort of glossy shining funnel that went down and down. I can't talk about it." She rolls over and kisses him on the mouth feverishly. His slowness to respond seems to excite her; she gets up in a crouch and like a raccoon drinking water kisses his chin, his chest, his navel, goes down and stays. Her mouth nibbling is so surprising he fights the urge to laugh; her fingers on the hair of his thighs tickle like the threat of ice on his skin. The hair of her head makes a tent on his belly. He pushes at her but she sticks at it: he might as well relax. The ceiling. The garage light shining upwards shows a stained patch where chimney flashing let the rain in. Must turn the garage light off. Though maybe a good burglar preventive. These junkies around steal anything. He wonders how Nelson made out. Asleep, boy sleeps on his back, mouth open, frightening; skin seems to tighten on the bone like in pictures of Buchenwald. Always tempted to wake him, prove he's O.K. Missed the eleven-o'clock news tonight. Vietnam death count, race riots probably somewhere. Funny man, Buchanan. No plan, exactly, just feeling his way, began by wanting to sell him Babe, maybe that's the way to live. Janice in bed got hot like something cooking but this kid stays cool, a prep-school kid applying what she knows. It works.

"That's nice," she says, stroking the extent of his extended cock, glistening with her spittle.

"You're nice," he tells her, "not to lose faith."

"I like it," she tells him, "making you get big and strong."

"Why bother?" he asks. "I'm a creep."

"Want to come into me?" the girl asks. But when she lies on her back and spreads her legs, her lack of self-consciousness again strikes him as sad, and puts him off, as does the way she winces when he seeks to enter; so that he grows small. Her blurred face widens its holes and says with a rising inflection, "You don't *like* me."

While he fumbles for an answer, she falls asleep. It is the answer to a question he hadn't thought to ask: was she tired? Of course, just as she was hungry. A guilty grief expands his chest muscles and presses on the backs of his eyes. He gets up, covers her with a sheet. The nights are growing cool, August covers the sun's retreat. The cold moon. Scraped wallpaper. Pumice stone under a flash bulb. Footprints stay for a billion years, not a fleck of dust blows. The kitchen linoleum is cold on his feet. He switches off the garage light and spreads peanut butter on six Saltines, making three sandwiches. Since Janice left, he and Nelson shop for what they like, keep themselves stocked in salt and starch. He eats the crackers sitting in the living room, not in the silverthread chair but the old brown mossy one, that they've had since their marriage. He chews and stares at the uninhabited aquarium of the television screen. Ought to smash it, poison, he read somewhere the reason kids today are so crazy they were brought up on television, two minutes of this, two minutes of that. Cracker crumbs adhere to the hair of his chest. Six gray. Must be more than that. What did Janice do for Stavros she didn't do for him? Only so much you can do. Three holes, two hands. Is she happy? He hopes so. Poor mutt, he somehow squelched her potential. Let things bloom. The inside of a great lily. He wonders if Jesus will be waiting for Mom, a man in a nightgown at the end of a glossy chute. He hopes so. He remembers he must work tomorrow, then remembers he mustn't, it is Sunday. Sunday, that dog of a day. Ruth used to mock him and church, in those days he could get himself up for anything. Ruth and her chicken farm, wonders if she can stand it. Hopes so. He pushes himself up from the fat chair, brushes crumbs from his chest hair. Some fall and catch further down. Wonder why it was made so curly there, springy, they could stuff mattresses with it, if people would shave, like nuns and wigs. Upstairs, the body in his bed sinks his heart like a bar of silver. He had forgotten she was on his hands. Bad knuckles. The poor kid, she stirs and tries to make love to him again, gives him a furry-mouthed French kiss and falls asleep at it again. A day's work for a day's lodging. Puritan ethic. He masturbates, picturing Peggy Fosnacht. What will Nelson think?

*

Jill sleeps late. At quarter of ten Rabbit is rinsing his cereal bowl and coffee cup and Nelson is at the kitchen screen door, red-faced from pumping his bicycle. "Hey, Dad!"

"Shh."

"Why?"

"Your noise hurts my head."

"Did you get drunk last night?"

"What sort of talk is that? I never get drunk."

"Mrs. Fosnacht cried after you left."

"Probably because you and Billy are such brats."

"She said you were going to meet somebody in Brewer."

She shouldn't be telling kids things like that. These divorced women, turn their sons into little husbands: cry, shit, and change Tampax right in front of them. "Some guy I work with at Verity. We listened to some colored woman play the piano and then I came home."

"We stayed up past twelve o'clock watching a wicked neat movie about guys landing somewhere in boats that open up in front, some place like Norway—"

"Normandy."

"That's right. Were you there?"

"No, I was your age when it happened."

"You could see the machine gun bullets making the water splash up all in a row, it was a blast."

"Hey, try to keep your voice down."

"Why, Dad? Is Mommy back? Is she?"

"No. Have you had any breakfast?"

"Yeah, she gave us bacon and French toast. I learned how to make it, it's easy, you just smash some eggs and take bread and fry it, I'll make you some sometime."

"Thanks. My mother used to make it."

"I hate her cooking. Everything tastes greasy. Didn't you used to hate her cooking, Dad?"

"I liked it. It was the only cooking I knew."

"Billy Fosnacht says she's dying, is she?"

"She has a disease. But it's very slow. You've seen how she is. She may get better. They have new things for it all the time."

"I hope she does die, Dad."

"No you don't. Don't say that."

"Mrs. Fosnacht tells Billy you should say everything you feel."

"I'm sure she tells him a lot of crap."

"Why do you say crap? I think she's nice, once you get used to her eyes. Don't you like her, Dad? She thinks you don't."

"Peggy's O.K. What's on your schedule? When was the last time you went to Sunday school?"

The boy circles around to place himself in his father's view. "There's a reason I rushed home. Mr. Fosnacht is going to take Billy fishing on the river in a boat some guy he knows owns and Billy asked if I could come along and I said I'd have to ask you. O.K., Dad? I had to come home anyway to get a bathing suit and clean pants, that fucking mini-bike got these all greasy."

All around him, Rabbit hears language collapsing. He says weakly, "I didn't know there was fishing in the river."

"They've cleaned it up, Ollie says. At least above Brewer. He says they stock it with trout up around Eifert's Island."

Ollie, is it? "That's hours from here. You've never fished. Remember how bored you were with the ball game we took you to."

"That was a boring game, Dad. Other people were playing it. This is something you do yourself. Huh, Dad? O.K.? I got to get my bathing suit and I said I'd be back on the bicycle by ten-thirty." The kid is at the foot of the stairs: stop him.

Rabbit calls, "What am I going to do all day, if you go off?"

"You can go visit Mom-mom. She'd rather see just you any-way." The boy takes it that he has secured permission, and pounds upstairs. His scream from the landing freezes his father's stomach. Rabbit moves to the foot of the stairs to receive Nelson in his arms. But the boy, safe on the next-to-bottom step, halts there horrified. "Dad, something moved in your bed!"

"My bed?"

"I looked in and saw it!"

Rabbit offers, "Maybe it was just the air-conditioner fan lifting the sheets."

"*Dad.*" The child's pallor begins to recede as some flaw in the horror of this begins to dawn. "It had long hair, and I saw an arm. Aren't you going to call the police?"

"No, let's let the poor old police rest, it's Sunday. It's O.K., Nelson, I know who it is."

"You do?" The boy's eyes sink upon themselves defensively as his brain assembles what information he has about long-haired creatures in bed. He is trying to relate this contraption of half-facts to the figure of his father looming, a huge riddle in an undershirt, before him. Rabbit offers, "It's a girl who's run away from home and I somehow got stuck with her last night."

"Is she going to live here?"

"Not if you don't want me to," Jill's voice composedly calls from the stairs. She has come down wrapped in a sheet. Sleep has made her more substantial, her eyes are fresh wet grass now. She says to the boy, "I'm Jill. You're Nelson. Your father told me all about you."

She advances toward him in her sheet like a little Roman senator, her hair tucked under behind, her forehead shining. Nelson stands his ground. Rabbit is struck to see that they are nearly the same height. "Hi," the kid says. "He did?"

"Oh, yes," Jill goes on, showing her class, becoming no doubt her own mother, a woman pouring out polite talk in an unfamiliar home, flattering vases, curtains. "You are *very* much on his mind. You're very fortunate, to have such a loving father."

The kid looks over with parted lips. Christmas morning. He doesn't know what it is, but he wants to like it, before it's unwrapped.

Tucking her sheet about her tighter, Jill moves them into the kitchen, towing Nelson along on the thread of her voice. "You're lucky, you're going on a boat. I love boats. Back home we had a twenty-two-foot sloop."

"What's a sloop?"

"It's a sailboat with one mast."

"Some have more?"

"Of course. Schooners and yawls. A schooner has the big mast behind, a yawl has the big one up front. We had a yawl once but it was too much work, you needed another man really."

"You used to sail?"

"All summer until October. Not only that. In the spring we all used to have to scrape it and caulk it and paint it. I liked that almost the best, we all used to work at it together, my parents and me and my brothers."

"How many brothers did you have?"

"Three. The middle one was about your age. Thirteen?"

He nods. "Almost."

"He was my favorite. Is my favorite."

A bird outside hoarsely scolds in sudden agitation. Cat? The refrigerator purrs.

Nelson abruptly volunteers, "I had a sister once but she died."

"What was her name?"

His father has to answer for him. "Rebecca."

Still Jill doesn't look toward him, but concentrates on the boy. "May I eat breakfast, Nelson?"

"Sure."

"I don't want to take the last of your favorite breakfast cereal or anything."

"You won't. I'll show you where we keep them. Don't take the Rice Krispies, they're a thousand years old and taste like floor fluff. The Raisin Bran and Alphabits are O.K., we bought them this week at the Acme."

"Who does the shopping, you or your father?"

"Oh—we share. I meet him on Pine Street after work sometimes."

"When do you see your mother?"

"A lot of times. Weekends sometimes I stay over in Charlie Stavros's apartment. He has a real gun in his bureau. It's O.K., he has a license. I can't go over there this weekend because they've gone to the Shore."

"Where's the shore?"

Delight that she is so dumb creases the corners of Nelson's mouth. "In New Jersey. Everybody calls it just the Shore. We used to go to Wildwood sometimes but Dad hated the traffic too much."

"That's one thing I miss," Jill says, "the smell of the sea. Where I grew up, the town is on a peninsula, with sea on three sides."

"Hey, shall I make you some French toast? I just learned how."

Jealousy, perhaps, makes Rabbit impatient with this scene: his son in spite of his smallness bony and dominating and alert, Jill in her sheet looking like one of those cartoon figures, Justice or Liberty or Mourning Peace. He goes outside to bring in the Sunday *Triumph*, sits reading the funnies in the sunshine on the porchlet steps until the bugs get too bad, comes back into the living room and reads at random about the Egyptians, the Phillies, the Onassises. From the kitchen comes sizzling and giggling and whispering. He is in the Garden Section (*Scorn not the modest goldenrod, dock, and tansy that grow in carefree profusion in fields and roadside throughout these August days; carefully dried and arranged, they will form attractive bouquets to brighten the winter months around the corner*) when the kid comes in with milk on his mustache and, wide-eyed, pressingly, with a new kind of energy, asks, "Hey Dad, can she come along on the boat? I've called up Billy and he says his father won't mind, only we have to hurry up. You can come too."

"Maybe *I* mind."

"*Dad*. Don't." And Harry reads his son's taut face to mean, *She can hear. She's all alone. We must be nice to her, we must be nice to the poor, the weak, the black. Love is here to stay.*

Monday, Rabbit is setting the *Vat* front page. WIDOW, SIXTY-SEVEN, RAPED AND ROBBED. *Three Black Youths Held.*

Police authorities revealed Saturday that they are holding for questioning two black minors and Wendell Phillips, 19, of 42B Plum Street, in connection with the brutal assault of an unidentified sywsfyz kmlhs the brutal assault of an unidentified elderly white woman late Thursday night.

The conscienceless crime, the latest in a series of similar incidents in the Third Ward, aroused residents of the neighborhood to organize a committee of protest which appeared before Friday's City Council session.

Nobody Safe

"Nobody's safe on the st

"Nobody's safe on the streets any more," said committee spokesman Bernard Vogel to VAT reporters.

"Nobody's safe not even in our own homes."

Through the clatter Harry feels a tap on his shoulder and looks around. Pajasek, looking worried. "Angstrom, telephone."

"Who the hell?" He feels obliged to say this, as apology for being called at work, on Verity time.

"A woman," Pajasek says, not placated.

Who? Jill (last night her hair still damp from the boat ride tickled his belly as she managed to make him come) was in trouble. They had kidnapped her—the police, the blacks. Or Peggy Fosnacht was calling up to offer supper again. Or his mother had taken a turn for the worse and with her last heartbeats had dialled this number. He is not surprised she would want to speak to him instead of his father, he has never doubted she loves him most. The phone is in Pajasek's little office, three walls of frosted glass, on the desk with the parts catalogues (these old Mergenthalers are always breaking down) and the spindled dead copy. "Hello?"

"Hi, sweetie. Guess who."

"Janice. How was the Shore?"

"Crowded and muggy. How was it here?"

"Pretty good."

"So I hear. I hear you went out in a boat."

"Yeah, it was the kid's idea, he got me invited by Ollie. We went up the river as far as Eifert's Island. We didn't catch much, the state put some trout in but I guess the river's still too full of coal silt. My nose is so sunburned I can't touch it."

"I hear you had a lot of people in the boat."

"Nine or so. Ollie runs around with this musical crowd. We had a picnic up at the old camp meeting ground, near Stogey's Quarry, you know, where that witch lived so many years. Ollie's friends all got out guitars and played. It was nice."

"I hear *you* brought a guest too."

"Who'd you hear that from?"

"Peggy told me. Billy told her. He was all turned-on about it, he said Nelson brought a girlfriend."

"Beats a mini-bike, huh?"

"Harry, I don't find this amusing. Where did you find this girl?"

"Uh, she's a go-go dancer in here at the shop. For the lunch hour. The union demands it."

"*Where*, Harry?"

Her weary dismissive insistence pleases him. She is growing in confidence, like a child at school. He confesses, "I sort of picked her up in a bar."

"Well. That's being honest. How long is she going to stay?"

"I haven't asked. These kids don't make plans the way we used to, they aren't so scared of starving. Hey, I got to get back to the machine. Pajasek doesn't like our being called here, by the way."

"I don't intend to make a practice of it. I called you at work because I didn't want Nelson to overhear. Harry, now are you listening to me?"

"Sure, to who else?"

"I want that girl out of my home. I don't want Nelson exposed to this sort of thing."

"What sort of thing? You mean the you and Stavros sort of thing?"

"Charlie is a mature man. He has lots of nieces and nephews so he's very understanding with Nelson. This girl sounds like a little animal out of her head with dope."

"That's how Billy described her?"

"After she talked to Billy Peggy called up Ollie for a better description."

"And that was his description. Gee. They got along famously at the time. She was better-looking than those two old crows Ollie had along, I tell ya."

"Harry, you're horrible. I consider this a very negative development. I suppose I have no right to say anything about how you dispose of your sexual needs, but I will not have my son corrupted."

"He's not corrupted, she's got him to help with the dishes, that's more than we could ever do. She's like a sister to him."

"And what is she to you, Harry?" When he is slow to answer, she repeats, her voice taunting, aching, like her mother's, "Harry, what is she to you? A little wifey?"

He thinks and tells her, "Come on back to the house, I'm sure she'll go."

Now Janice thinks. Finally she states: "If I come back to the house, it'll be to take Nelson away."

"Try it," he says, and hangs up.

He sits a minute in Pajasek's chair to give the phone a chance to ring. It does. He picks it up. "Yeah?"

Janice says, near tears, "Harry, I don't like to tell you this, but if you'd been adequate I would never have left. You drove me to it. I didn't know what I was missing but now that I have it I know. I refuse to accept all the blame, I really do."

"O.K. No blame assigned. Let's keep in touch."

"I want that girl away from my son."

"They're getting along fine, relax."

"I'll sue you. I'll take you to court."

"Fine. After the stunts you've been pulling, it'll at least give the judge a laugh."

"That's my house legally. At least half of it is."

"Tell me which my half is, and I'll try to keep Jill in it."

Janice hangs up. Maybe using Jill's name had hurt. He doesn't wait for another ring this time, and leaves the cubicle of frosted glass. The trembling in his hands, which feel frightened and inflated, merges with the clatter of the machines; his body sweat is lost in the smell of oil and ink. He resettles himself at his Mergenthaler and garbles three lines before he can put her phone call in the back of his mind. He supposes Stavros can get her legal advice. But, far from feeling Stavros as one of the enemy camp, he counts on him to keep this madwoman, his wife, under control. Through her body, they have become brothers.

Jill through the succession of nights adjusts Rabbit's body to hers. He cannot overcome his fear of using her body as a woman's—her cunt *stings*, is part of it; he never forces his way into her without remembering those razor blades—but she, beginning the damp-haired night after the boat ride, perfects ways with her fingers and mouth to bring him off. Small curdled puddles of his semen then appear on her skin, and though easily wiped away leave in his imagination a mark like an acid-burn on her shoulders, her throat, the small of her back; he has the vision of her entire slender fair flexible body being eventually covered with these invisible burns, like a napalmed child in the newspapers. And he, on his side, attempting with hands or mouth to reciprocate, is politely dissuaded, pushed away, reassured she has already come, serving him, or merely asked for the mute pressure of a thigh between hers and, after some few minutes during which he can detect no spasm of relief, thanked. The August nights are sticky and close; when they lie on their backs the ceiling of heavy air seems a foot above their faces. A car, loud on the soft tar and loose gravel, slides by. A mile away across the river a police siren bleats, a new sound, more frantic than the old rising and falling cry. Nelson turns on a light, makes water, flushes the toilet, turns out the light with a *snap* close to their ears. Had he been listening? Could he even be watching? Jill's breath saws in her throat. She is asleep.

He finds her when he comes back from work sitting and reading, sitting and sewing, sitting and playing Monopoly with Nelson. Her books are spooky: yoga, psychiatry, zen, plucked from racks at the Acme. Except to shop, she reluctantly goes outdoors, even at night. It is not so much that the police of several states are looking for her—they are looking as well for thousands like her—as that the light of common day, and the sights and streets that have been the food of Rabbit's life, seem to nauseate her. They rarely watch television, since she leaves the room when they turn the set on, though when she's in the kitchen he sometimes sneaks himself a dose of six-o'clock news. Instead, in the evenings, she and Nelson discuss God, beauty, meaning.

"Whatever men make," she says, "what they felt when they made it is there. If it was made to make money, it will smell of money. That's why these houses are so ugly, all the corners they cut to make a profit are still in them. That's why the cathedrals are so lovely; nobles and ladies in velvet and ermine dragged the stones up the ramps. Think of a painter. He stands in front of the canvas with a color on his brush. Whatever he feels when he makes the mark—if he's tired or bored or happy and proud —will be there. The same color, but we'll feel it. Like fingerprints. Like handwriting. Man is a means for turning things into spirit and turning spirit into things."

"What's the point?" Nelson asks.

"The point is ecstasy," she says. "Energy. Anything that is good is in ecstasy. The world is what God made and it doesn't stink of money, it's never tired, too much or too little, it's always exactly full. The second after an earthquake, the stones are calm. Everywhere is *play*, even in thunder or an avalanche.

Out on my father's boat I used to look up at the stars and there seemed to be invisible strings between them, tuned absolutely right, playing thousands of notes I could almost hear."

"Why can't we hear them?" Nelson asks.

"Because our egos make us deaf. Our egos make us blind. Whenever we think about ourselves, it's like putting a piece of dirt in our eye."

"There's that thing in the Bible."

"That's what He meant. Without our egos the universe would be absolutely clean, all the animals and rocks and spiders and moon-rocks and stars and grains of sand absolutely doing their thing, unself-consciously. The only consciousness would be God's. Think of it, Nelson, like this: matter is the mirror of spirit. But it's three-dimensional, like an enormous room, a ballroom. And inside it are these tiny *other* mirrors tilted this way and that and throwing the light back the wrong way. Because to the big face looking in, these little mirrors are just dark spots, where He can't see Himself."

Rabbit is entranced to hear her going on like this. Her voice, laconic and dry normally, moves through her sentences as through a memorized recitation, pitched low, an underground murmur. She and Nelson are sitting on the floor with the Monopoly board between them, houses and hotels and money, the game has been going on for days. Neither gives any sign of knowing he has come into the room and is towering above them. Rabbit asks, "Why doesn't He just do away with the spots then? I take it the spots are us."

Jill looks up, her face blank as a mirror in this instant. Remembering last night, he expects her to look burned around the mouth; it had been like filling a slippery narrow-mouthed pitcher from an uncontrollable faucet. She answers, "I'm not sure He's noticed us yet. The cosmos is so large and our portion of it so small. So small and recent."

"Maybe we'll do the erasing ourselves," Rabbit offers helpfully. He wants to help, to hold his end up. Never too late for education. With Janice and old man Springer you could never have this kind of conversation.

"There is that death-wish," Jill concedes.

Nelson will talk only to her. "Do you believe in life on other planets? I don't."

"Why Nelson, how ungenerous of you! Why not?"

"I don't know, it's silly to say—"

"Say it."

"I was thinking, if there was life on other planets, they would have killed our moon men when they stepped out of the space ship. But they didn't, so there isn't."

"Don't be dumb," Rabbit says. "The moon is right down our block. We're talking about life in systems millions of light years away."

"No, I think the moon was a good test," Jill says. "If nobody bothered to defend it, it proves how little God is content with. Miles and miles of gray dust."

Nelson says, "One guy at school I know says there's people on the moon but they're smaller than atoms, so even when they grind the rocks up they won't find them. He says they have whole cities and everything. We breathe them in through our nostrils and they make us think we see flying saucers. That's what this one guy says."

"I myself," Rabbit says, still offering, drawing upon an old *Vat* feature article he set, "have some hopes for the inside of Jupiter. It's gas, you know, the surface we see. A couple of thousand miles down inside the skin there might be a mix of chemicals that could support a kind of life, something like fish."

"It's your Puritan fear of waste makes you want that," Jill tells him. "You think the other planets must be *used* for something, must be *farmed*. Why? Maybe the planets were put there just to teach men how to count up to seven."

"Why not just give us seven toes on each foot?"

"A kid at school," Nelson volunteers, "was born with an extra finger. The doctor cut it off but you can still see where it was."

"Also," Jill says, "astronomy. Without the planets the night sky would have been one rigid thing, and we would never have guessed at the third dimension."

"Pretty thoughtful of God," Rabbit says, "if we're just some specks in His mirror."

Jill waves his point away blithely. "He does everything," she says, "by the way. Not because it's what He has to do."

She can be blithe. After he told her once she ought to go

outdoors more, she went out and sunbathed in just her bikini underpants, on a blanket beside the barbecue, in the view of a dozen other houses. When a neighbor called up to complain, Jill justified herself, "My tits are so small, I thought they'd think I was a boy." Then after Harry began giving her thirty dollars a week to shop with, she went and redeemed her Porsche from the police. Its garage parking fees had quadrupled the original fine. She gave her address as Vista Crescent and said she was staying the summer with her uncle. "It's a nuisance," she told Rabbit, "but Nelson ought to have a car around, at his age, it's too humiliating not to. Everybody in America has a car except you." So the Porsche came to live by their curb. Its white is dusty and the passenger-side front fender is scraped and one convertible top snap is broken. Nelson loves it so much he nearly cries, finding it there each morning. He washes it. He reads the manual and rotates the tires. That crystalline week before school begins, Jill takes him for drives out into the country, into the farmland and the mountains of Brewer County; she is teaching him how to drive.

Some days they return after Rabbit is home an hour from work. "Dad, it was a blast. We drove way up into this mountain that's a hawk refuge and Jill let me take the wheel on the twisty road coming down, all the way to the highway. Have you ever heard of shifting down?"

"I do it all the time."

"It's when you go into a lower gear instead of braking. It feels neat. Jill's Porsche has about five gears and you can really zoom around curves because the center of gravity is so low."

Rabbit asks Jill, "You sure you're handling this right? The kid might kill somebody. I don't want to be sued."

"He's very competent. And responsible. He must get that from you. I used to stay in the driver's seat and let him just steer but that's more dangerous than giving him control. The mountain was really quite deserted."

"Except for hawks, Dad. They sit on all these pine trees waiting for the guys to put out whole carcasses of cows and things. It's really grungy."

"Well," Rabbit says, "hawks got to live too."

"That's what I keep telling him," Jill says. "God is in the tiger as well as in the lamb."

"Yeah. God really likes to chew himself up."

"You know what you are?" Jill asks, her eyes the green of a meadow, her hair a finespun cedar-colored tangle dissolving into windowlight; a captured idea is fluttering in her head. "You are cynical."

"Just middle-aged. Somebody came up to me and said, 'I'm God,' I'd say, 'Show me your badge.'"

Jill dances forward, on fire with some fun and wickedness the day has left in her, and gives him a hug that dances off, a butterfly hug. "I think you're beautiful. Nelson and I both think so. We often talk about it."

"You do? That's the only thing you can think of to do, talk about me?" He means to be funny, to keep her mood alive, but her face stops, hovers a second; and Nelson's tells him he has struck on something. What they do. In that little car. Well, they don't need much space, much contact: young bodies. The kid's faint mustache, black hairs; her cedar mane. Bodies not sodden yet like his. At that keen age the merest touch. Their brother-sister shyness, touching hands in the flicker of wet glass at the sink. If she'd offer to lay hairy old heavy him the first night, what wouldn't she do to bring the kid along; somebody has to. Why not? Chief question facing these troubled times. Why not.

Though he doesn't pursue this guilt he has startled from her, that night he does make her take him squarely, socks it into her, though she offers her mouth and her cunt is so tight it sears. She is frightened when he doesn't lose his hardness; he makes her sit up on him and pulls her satin hips down, the pelvis bones starved, and she sucks in breath sharply and out of pained astonishment pitched like delight utters, "You're wombing me!" He tries to picture it. A rosy-black floor in her somewhere, never knows where he is, in among kidneys, intestines, liver. His child bride with flesh-colored hair and cloudy innards floats upon him, stings him, sucks him up like a cloud, falls, forgives him. His love of her coats him with distaste and confusion, so that he quickly sleeps, only his first dreams jostled when she gets from bed to go wash, check on Nelson, talk to God, take a pill, whatever else she needs to do to heal the wound where his seared cock was. How sad, how strange. We make companions out of air and hurt them, so they will defy us, completing creation.

*

Harry's father sidles up to him at the coffee break. "How's every little thing, Harry?"

"Not bad."

"I hate like hell to nag like this, you're a grown man with your own miseries, I know that, but I'd be appreciative as hell if you'd come over some evenings and talk to your mother. She hears all sorts of malicious folderol about you and Janice now, and it would help settle her down if you could put her straight. We're no moralists, Harry, you know that; your mother and I tried to live by our own lights and to raise the two children God was good enough to give us by those same lights, but I know damn well it's a different world now, so we're no moralists, me and Mary."

"How is her health, generally?"

"Well, that's another of these problematical things, Harry. They've gone ahead and put her on this new miracle drug, they have some name for it I can never remember, L-dopa, that's right, L-dopa, it's still in the experimental stage I guess, but there's no doubt in a lot of cases it works wonders. Trouble is, also it has these side effects they don't know too much about, depression in your mother's case, some nausea and lack of appetite; and nightmares, Harry, nightmares that wake her up and she wakes me up so I can hear her heart beating, beating like a tom-tom. I never heard that before, Harry, another person's heart in the room as clear as footsteps, but that's what these L-dopa dreams do for her. But there's no doubt, her talk comes easier, and her hands don't shake that way they have so much. It's hard to know what's right, Harry. Sometimes you think, Let Nature take its course, but then you wonder, What's Nature and what isn't? Another side effect"—he draws closer, glancing around and then glancing down as his coffee slops in the paper cup and burns his fingers—"I shouldn't mention it but it tickles me, your mother says this new stuff she's taking, whatever you call it, makes her feel, how shall I say?"—he glances around again, then confides to his son—"lovey-dovey. Here she is, just turned sixty-five, lying in bed half the day, and gets these impulses so bad she says she can hardly stand it, she says she won't watch television, the commercials make it worse. She says she has to laugh at herself. Now isn't that a helluva thing? A good woman like that. I'm sorry to talk your ear off, I live alone with it too much, I suppose, what with Mim on the other side of the country. Christ knows it isn't as if you don't have your problems too."

"I don't have any problems," Rabbit tells him. "Right now I'm just holding my breath to when the kid gets back into school. His state of mind's pretty well stabilized, I'd say. One of the reasons, you know, I don't make it over to Mt. Judge as often as I should, Mom was pretty rough on Nelson when he was little and the kid is still scared of her. On the other hand I don't like to leave him alone in the house, with all these robberies and assaults all over the county, they come out into the suburbs and steal anything they can get their hands on. I was just setting an item, some woman over in Perley Township, they stole her vacuum cleaner and a hundred feet of garden hose while she was upstairs going to the bathroom."

"It's these God, damn, blacks, is what it is." Earl Angstrom lowers his voice so it turns husky, though Buchanan and Farnsworth always take their coffee break outside in the alley, with Boonie and the other drinkers. "I've always called 'em black and they call themselves blacks now and that suits me fine. They can't do a white man's job, except for a few, and take even Buck, he's never made head of makeup though he's been here the longest; so they have to rob and kill, the ones that can't be pimps and prizefighters. They can't cut the mustard and never could. This country should have taken whosever advice it was, George Washington if memory serves, one of the founding fathers, and shipped 'em all back to Africa when we had a chance. Now, Africa wouldn't take 'em. Booze and Cadillacs and white pussy, if you'll pardon my saying so, have spoiled 'em rotten. They're the garbage of the world, Harry. American Negroes are the lowest of the low. They steal and then they have the nerve to say the country owes it to 'em."

"O.K., O.K." To see his father passionate about anything disagrees with Rabbit. He shifts to the most sobering subject they have between them: "Does she mention me much? Mom."

The old man licks spittle from his lips, sighs, slumps confidingly lower, glancing down at the cooled scummed coffee in his hands. "All the time, Harry, every minute of the day. They tell her things about you and she raves against the Springers; oh, how she carries on about that family, especially the women of it. Apparently, the Mrs. is saying you've taken up with a hippie teenager, that's what drove Janice out of the house in the first place."

"No, Janice went first. I keep inviting her back."

"Well, whatever the actualities of the case are, I know you're trying to do the right thing. I'm no moralist, Harry, I know you young people nowadays have more tensions and psychological pressures than a man my age could tolerate. If I'd of had the atomic bomb and these rich-kid revolutionaries to worry about, I'd no doubt just have put a shotgun to my head and let the world roll on without me."

"I'll try to get over. I ought to talk to her," Rabbit says. He looks past his father's shoulder to where the yellow-faced wall clock jumps to within a minute of 11:10, the end of the coffee break. He knows that in all this rolling-on world his mother is the only person who *knows* him. He remembers from the night we touched the moon the nudge delivered out of her dying, but doesn't want to open himself to her until he understands what is happening inside him enough to protect it. She has something happening to her, death and L-dopa, and he has something happening to him, Jill. The girl has been living with them three weeks and is learning to keep house and to give him a wry silent look saying *I know you* when he offers to argue about Communism or kids today or any of the other sore spots where he feels rot beginning and black madness creeping in. A little wry green look that began the night he hurt her upwards and touched her womb.

His father is more with him than he suspects, for the old man draws still closer and says, "One thing it's been on my mind to say, Harry, forgive me talking out of turn, but I hope you're taking all the precautions, knock up one of these minors, the law takes a very dim view. Also, they say they're dirty as weasels and giving everybody the clap." Absurdly, as the clock ticks the last minute and the end-of-break bell rasps, the old man claps.

In his clean crisp after-work shirt he opens the front door of the apple-green house and hears guitar music from above. Guitar chords slowly plucked, and two high small voices moving through a melody. He is drawn upstairs. In Nelson's room, the two are sitting on the bed, Jill up by the pillows in a yoga position that displays the crotch of her black lace underpants. A guitar is cradled across her thighs. Rabbit has never seen the guitar before; it looks new. The pale wood shines like a woman oiled after a bath. Nelson sits beside Jill in Jockey shorts and T-shirt, craning his neck to read from the sheet of music on the bedspread by her ankles. The boy's legs, dangling to the floor, look suddenly sinewy, long, beginning to be shaded with Janice's dark hair, and Rabbit notices that the old posters of Brooks Robinson and Orlando Cepeda and Steve McQueen on a motorcycle have been removed from the boy's walls. Paint has flaked where the Scotch tape was. They are singing, ". . . must a man wa-alk down"; the delicate thread breaks when he enters, though they must have heard his footsteps on the stairs as warning. The kid's being in his underclothes is O.K.: far from dirty as a weasel, Jill has gotten Nelson to take a shower once a day, before his father's homecoming, perhaps because her own father came home to Stonington only on Fridays and deserved a ceremony.

"Hey, Dad," Nelson says, "this is neat. We're singing harmony."

"Where did you get the guitar?"

"We hustled."

Jill nudges the boy with a bare foot, but not quick enough to halt the remark.

Rabbit asks him, "How do you hustle?"

"We stood on streetcorners in Brewer, mostly at Weiser and Seventh, but then we moved over to Cameron when a pig car slowed down to look us over. It was a gas, Dad. Jill would stop these people and tell 'em I was her brother, our mother was dying of cancer and our father had lit out, and we had a baby brother at home. Sometimes she said a baby sister. Some of the people said we should apply to welfare, but enough gave us a dollar or so so finally we had the twenty dollars Ollie promised was all he'd charge us for a forty-four dollar guitar. And he threw in the music free after Jill talked to him in the back room."

"Wasn't that nice of Ollie?"

"Harry, it really was. Don't look like that."

He says to Nelson, "I wonder what they talked about."

"Dad, there was nothing dishonest about it, these people we stopped felt better afterwards, for having got us off their conscience. Anyway, Dad, in a society where power was all to the people money wouldn't exist anyway, you'd just be given what you need."

"Well hell, that's the way your life is now."

"Yeah, but I have to beg for everything, don't I? And I never did get a mini-bike."

"Nelson, you get some clothes on and stay in your room. I want to talk to Jill a second."

"If you hurt her, I'll kill you."

"If you don't shut up, I'll make you live with Mommy and Charlie Stavros."

In their bedroom, Rabbit carefully closes the door and in a soft shaking voice tells Jill, "You're turning my kid into a beggar and a whore just like yourself," and, after waiting a second for her to enter a rebuttal, slaps her thin disdainful face with its prim lips and its green eyes drenched so dark in defiance their shade is as of tree leaves, a shuffling concealing multitude, a microscopic forest he wants to bomb. His slap feels like slapping plastic: stings his fingers, does no good. He slaps her again, gathers the dry flesh of her hair into his hand to hold her face steady, feels cold fury when she buckles and tries to slither away but, after a fist to the side of her neck, lets her drop onto the bed.

Still shielding her face, Jill hisses up at him, strangely hisses out of her little spaced inturned teeth, until her first words come. They are calm and superior. "You know why you did that, you just wanted to hurt me, that's why. You just wanted to have that kick. You don't give a shit about me and Nelson hustling. What do you care about who begs and who doesn't, who steals and who doesn't?"

A blankness in him answers when she asks; but she goes on. "What have the pig laws ever done for you except screw you into a greasy job and turn you into such a gutless creep you can't even keep your idiotic wife?"

He takes her wrist. It is fragile. Chalk. He wants to break it, to feel it snap; he wants to hold her absolutely quiet in his arms for the months while it will heal. "Listen. I earn my money one fucking dollar at a time and you're living on it and if you want to go back bumming off your nigger friends, go. Get out. Leave me and my kid alone."

"You creep," she says, "you baby-killing creep."

"Put another record on," he says. "You sick bitch. You rich kids playing at life make me sick, throwing rocks at the poor dumb cops protecting your daddy's loot. You're just playing, baby. You think you're playing a great game of happy cunt but let me tell you something. My poor dumb mutt of a wife throws a better piece of ass backwards than you can manage frontwards."

"Backwards is right, she can't stand facing you."

He squeezes her chalk wrist tighter, telling her, "You have no juice, baby. You're all sucked out and you're just eighteen. You've tried everything and you're not scared of nothing and you wonder why it's all so dead. You've had it handed to you, sweet baby, that's why it's so dead. Fucking Christ you think you're going to make the world over you don't have a fucking clue what makes people run. Fear. That's what makes us poor bastards run. You don't know what fear is, do you, poor baby? That's why you're so dead." He squeezes her wrist until he can picture the linked curved bones in it bending ghostly as in an X ray; and her eyes widen a fraction, a hairspace of alarm he can see only because he is putting it there.

She tugs her wrist free and rubs it, not lowering her eyes from his. "People've run on fear long enough," Jill says. "Let's try love for a change."

"Then you better find yourself another universe. The moon is cold, baby. Cold and ugly. If you don't want it, the Commies do. They're not so fucking proud."

"What's that noise?"

It is Nelson crying, outside the door, afraid to come in. It had been the same way with him and Janice, their fights: just when they were getting something out of them, the kid would beg them to stop. Maybe he imagined that Becky had been killed in just such a quarrel, that this one would kill him. Rabbit lets him in and explains, "We were talking politics."

Nelson squeezes out in the spaces between his sobs. "Daddy, why do you disagree with everybody?"

"Because I love my country and can't stand to have it knocked."

"If you loved it you'd want it better," Jill says.

"If it was better *I'd* have to be better," he says seriously, and they all laugh, he last.

Thus, through lame laughter—she still rubs her wrists, the hand he hit her with begins to hurt—they seek to reconstitute their family. For supper Jill cooks a filet of sole, lemony, light, simmered in sunshine, skin flaky brown; Nelson gets a hamburger with wheatgerm sprinkled on it to remind him of a Nutburger. Wheatgerm, zucchini, water chestnuts, celery salt, Familia: these are some of the exotic items Jill's shopping brings into the house. Her cooking tastes to him of things he never had: candlelight, saltwater, health fads, wealth, class. Jill's family had a servant, and it takes her some nights to understand that dirtied dishes do not clear and clean themselves by magic, but have to be carried and washed. Rabbit, still, Saturday mornings, is the one to vacuum the rooms, to bundle his shirts and the sheets for the laundry, to sort out Nelson's socks and underwear for the washer in the basement. He can see, what these children cannot, dust accumulate, deterioration advance, chaos seep in, time conquer. But for her cooking he is willing to be her servant, part-time. Her cooking has renewed his taste for life. They have wine now with supper, a California white in a half-gallon jug. And always a salad: salad in Diamond County cuisine tends to be a brother of sauerkraut, fat with creamy dressing, but Jill's hands serve lettuce in an oily film invisible as health. Where Janice would for dessert offer some doughy goodie from the Half-A-Loaf, Jill concocts designs of fruit. And her coffee is black nectar compared to the watery tar Janice used to serve. Contentment makes Harry motionless; he watches the dishes be skimmed from the table, and resettles expansively in the living room. When the dishwashing machine is fed and chugging contentedly, Jill comes into the living room, sits on the tacky carpet, and plays the guitar. What does she play? "Farewell, Angelina, the sky is on fire," and a few others she can get through a stanza of. She has maybe six chords. Her fingers on the frets often tighten on strands of her hanging hair; it must hurt. Her voice is a thin instrument that quickly cracks. "All my tri-als, Lord, soon be o-over," she sings, quitting, looking up for applause.

Nelson applauds. Small hands.

"Great," Rabbit tells her and, mellow on wine, goes on, in apology for his life, "No kidding, I once took that inner light trip and all I did was bruise my surroundings. Revolution, or whatever, is just a way of saying a mess is fun. Well, it *is* fun, for a while, as long as somebody else has laid in the supplies. A mess is a luxury, is all I mean."

Jill has been strumming for him, between sentences, part helping him along, part poking fun. He turns on her. "Now you tell us something. You tell us the story of your life."

"I've had no life," she says, and strums. "No man's daughter, and no man's wife."

"Tell us a story," Nelson begs. From the way she laughs, showing her roundish teeth and letting her thin cheeks go dimply, they see she will comply.

"This is the story of Jill and her lover who was *ill*," she announces, and releases a chord. It's as if, Rabbit thinks, studying the woman-shape of the guitar, the notes are in there already, waiting to fly from the dovecote of that round hole. "Now Jill," Jill goes on, "was a comely lass, raised in the bosom of the middle class. Her dad and mother each owned a car, and on the hood of one was a Mercedes star. I don't know how much longer I can go on rhyming." She strums quizzically.

"Don't try it," Rabbit advises.

"Her upbringing"—emphasis on the "ging"—"was ortho-dox enough—sailing and dancing classes and *français* and all that stuff."

"Keep rhyming, Jill," Nelson begs.

"Menstruation set in at age fourteen, but even with her braces off Jill was no queen. Her knowledge of boys was con-*fined* to boys who played tennis and whose parents with her parents *dined*. Which suited her perfectly *well*, since having observed her parents drinking and chatting and getting and spending she was in no great hurry to become old and fat and *swell*. Ooh, that was a stretch."

"Don't rhyme on my account," Rabbit says. "I'm getting a beer, anybody else want one?"

Nelson calls, "I'll share yours, Dad."

"Get your own. I'll get it for you."

Jill strums to reclaim their attention. "Well, to make a bor-ing story short, one summer"—she searches ahead for a rhyme, then adds, "after her daddy died."

"Uh-oh," Rabbit says, tiptoeing back with two beers.

"She met a boy who became her psycho-physical guide."

Rabbit pulls his tab and tries to hush the *pff.*

"His name was Freddy—"

He sees there is nothing to do but yank it, which he does so quickly the beer foams through the keyhole.

"And the nicest thing about him was that *she* was ready." Strum. "He had nice brown shoulders from being a lifeguard, and his bathing suit held something sometimes soft and sometimes hard. He came from far away, from romantic Rhode Island across Narragansett Bay."

"Hey," Rabbit *olés.*

"The only bad thing was, inside, the nice brown lifeguard had already died. Inside there was an old man with a dreadful need, for pot and hash and LSD and speed." Now her strumming takes a different rhythm, breaking into the middle on the offbeat.

"He was a born loser, though his race was white, and he fucked sweet virgin Jill throughout one sandy night. She fell for him"—*strum*—"and got deep into his bag of being stoned: she freaked out nearly every time the bastard telephoned. She went from popping pills to dropping acid, then"—she halts and leans forward staring at Nelson so hard the boy softly cries, "Yes?"

"He lovingly suggested shooting heroin."

Nelson looks as if he will cry: the way his eyes sink in and his chin develops another bump. He looks, Rabbit thinks, like a sulky girl. He can't see much of himself in the boy, beyond the small straight nose.

The music runs on.

"Poor Jill got scared; the other kids at school would tell her not to be a self-destructive fool. Her mother, still in mourning, was being kept bus-*ee*, by a divorced tax lawyer from nearby Wester-lee. Bad Freddy was promising her Heaven above, when all Jill wanted was his mundane love. She wanted the feel of his prick, not the prick of the needle; but Freddy would beg her, and stroke her, and sweet-talk and wheedle."

And Rabbit begins to wonder if she has done this before, that rhyme was so slick. What *has*n't this kid done before?

"She was afraid to *die*"—strum, strum, pale orange hair thrashing—"he asked her *why*. He said the world was rotten and insane; she said she had no cause to complain. He said racism was rampant, hold out your arm; she said no white man but him had ever done her any harm. He said the first shot will just be beneath the skin; she said okay, lover, put that shit right in." Strum strum *strum*. Face lifted toward them, she is a banshee, totally bled. She speaks the next line. "It was hell."

St-r-r-um. "He kept holding her head and patting her ass, and saying relax, he'd been to life-saving class. He asked her, hadn't he shown her the face of God? She said, *Yes*, thank you, but she would have been happy to settle for *less*. She saw that her lover with his tan skin and white smile was death; she feared him and loved him with every frightened breath. So what did Jill do?"

Silence hangs on the upbeat.

Nelson blurts, "What?"

Jill smiles. "She ran to the Stonington savings bank and generously with*drew*. She hopped inside her Porsche and drove *away*, and that is how come she is living with you two creeps to*day*."

Both father and son applaud. Jill drinks deep of the beer as a reward to herself. In their bedroom, she is still in the mood, artistic elation, to be rewarded. Rabbit says to her, "Great song. But you know what I didn't like about it?"

"What?"

"Nostalgia. You miss it. Getting stoned with Freddy."

"At least," she says, "I wasn't just playing, what did you call it, happy cunt?"

"Sorry I blew my stack."

"Still want me to go?"

Rabbit, having sensed this would come, hangs up his pants, his shirt, puts his underclothes in the hamper. The dress she has dropped on the floor he drapes on a hook in her half of the closet, her dirty panties he puts in the hamper. "No. Stay."

"Beg me."

He turns, a big tired man, slack-muscled, who has to rise and set type in eight hours. "I beg you to stay."

"Take back those slaps."

"How can I?"

"Kiss my feet."

He kneels to comply. Annoyed at such ready compliance, which implies pleasure, she stiffens her feet and kicks so her toenails stab his cheek, dangerously near his eyes. He pins her ankles to continue his kissing. Slightly doughy, matronly ankles. Green veins on her insteps. Nice remembered locker room taste. Vanilla going rancid.

"Your tongue between my toes," she says; her voice cracks timidly, issuing the command. When again he complies, she edges forward on the bed and spreads her legs. "Now here." She knows he enjoys this, but asks it anyway, to see what she can make of him, this alien man. His head, with its stubborn old-fashioned short haircut—the enemy's uniform, athlete and soldier; bone above the ears, dingy blond silk thinning on top —feels large as a boulder between her thighs. The excitement of singing her song, ebbing, unites with the insistent warmth of his tongue lapping. A spark kindles, a green sprig lengthens in the barren space between her legs. "A little higher," Jill says, then, her voice quite softened and crumbling, "Faster. Lovely. *Lovely.*"

One day after work as he and his father are walking down Pine Street toward their before-bus drink at the Phoenix Bar, a dapper thickset man with sideburns and hornrims intercepts them. "Hey, Angstrom." Both father and son halt, blink. In the tunnel of sunshine, after their day of work, they generally feel hidden.

Harry recognizes Stavros. He is wearing a suit of little beige checks on a ground of greenish threads. He looks a touch thinner, more brittle, his composure more of an effort. Maybe he is just tense for this encounter. Harry says, "Dad, I'd like you to meet a friend of mine. Charlie Stavros, Earl Angstrom."

"Pleased to meet you, Earl."

The old man ignores the extended square hand and speaks to Harry. "Not the same that's ruined my daughter-in-law?"

Stavros tries for a quick sale. "Ruined. That's pretty strong. Humored is more how I'd put it." His try for a smile ignored, Stavros turns to Harry. "Can we talk a minute? Maybe have a drink down at the corner. Sorry to butt in like this, Mr. Angstrom."

"Harry, what is your preference? You want to be left alone with this scum or shall we brush him off?"

"Come on, Dad, what's the point?"

"You young people may have your own ways of working things out, but I'm too old to change. I'll get on the next bus. Don't let yourself be talked into anything. This son of a bitch looks slick."

"Give my love to Mom. I'll try to get over this weekend."

"If you can, you can. She keeps dreaming about you and Mim."

"Yeah, some time could you give me Mim's address?"

"She doesn't have an address, just care of some agent in Los Angeles, that's the way they do it now. You were thinking of writing her?"

"Maybe send her a postcard. See you tomorrow."

"Terrible dreams," the old man says, and slopes to the curb to wait for the 16A bus, cheated of his beer, the thin disappointed back of his neck reminding Harry of Nelson.

Inside the Phoenix it is dark and cold; Rabbit feels a sneeze gathering between his eyes. Stavros leads the way to a booth and folds his hands on the Formica tabletop. Hairy hands that have held her breasts. Harry asks, "How is she?"

"She? Oh hell, in fine form."

Rabbit wonders if this means what it seems. The tip of his tongue freezes on his palate, unable to think of a delicate way to probe. He says, "They don't have a waitress in the afternoon. I'll get a Daiquiri for myself, what for you?"

"Just soda water. Lots of ice."

"No hootch?"

"Never touch it." Stavros clears his throat, smooths back the hair above his sideburns with a flat hand that is, nevertheless, slightly trembling. He explains, "The medicos tell me it's a no-no."

Coming back with their drinks, Rabbit asks, "You sick?"

Stavros says, "Nothing new, the same old ticker. Janice must have told you, heart murmur since I was a kid."

What does this guy think, he and Janice sat around discussing him like he was their favorite child? He does remember Janice crying out he couldn't marry, expecting him, Harry, her husband, to sympathize. Oddly, he had. "She mentioned something."

"Rheumatic fever. Thank God they've got those things licked now, when I was a kid I caught every bug they made." Stavros shrugs. "They tell me I can live to be a hundred, if I take care of the physical plant. You know," he says, "these doctors. There's still a lot they don't know."

"I know. They're putting my mother through the wringer right now."

"Jesus, you ought to hear Janice go on about your mother."

"Not so enthusiastic, huh?"

"Not so at all. She needs some gripe, though, to keep herself justified. She's all torn up about the kid."

"She left him with me and there he stays."

"In court, you know, you'd lose him."

"We'd see."

Stavros makes a small chopping motion around his glass full of soda bubbles (poor Peggy Fosnacht; Rabbit should call her) to indicate a new angle in their conversation. "Hell," he says, "I can't take him in. I don't have the room. As it is now, I have to send Janice out to the movies or over to her parents when my family visits. You know I just don't have a mother, I have a *grand*mother. She's ninety-three, speaking of living forever."

Rabbit tries to imagine Stavros's room, which Janice described as full of tinted photographs, and instead imagines Janice nude, tinted, Playmate of the month, posed on a nappy Greek sofa olive green in color, with scrolling arms, her body twisted at the hips just enough to hide her gorgeous big black bush. The crease of the centerfold cuts across her navel and one hand dangles a rose. The vision makes Rabbit for the first time hostile. He asks Stavros, "How do you see this all coming out?"

"That's what I wanted to ask *you*."

Rabbit asks, "She going sour on you?"

"No, Jesus, *au contraire*. She's balling me ragged."

Rabbit sips, swallows that, probes for another nerve. "She miss the kid?"

"Nelson, he comes over to the lot some days and she sees him weekends anyhow, I don't know that she saw much more of him before. I don't know as how motherhood is Janice's best bag anyway. What she doesn't much care for is the idea of her baby just out of diapers shacking up with this hippie."

"She's not a hippie, especially; unless everybody that age is. And I'm the one shacking up."

"How is she at it?"

"She's balling me ragged," Rabbit tells him. He is beginning to get Stavros's measure. At first, meeting him on the street so suddenly, he felt toward him like a friend, met through Janice's body. Then first coming into the Phoenix he felt him as a sick man, a man holding himself together against odds. Now he sees him as a competitor, one of those brainy cute close-set little playmakers. O.K. So Rabbit is competing again. What he has to do is hang loose and let Stavros make the move.

Stavros hunches his square shoulders infinitesimally, has some soda, and asks, "What do you see yourself doing with this hippie?"

"She has a name. Jill."

"What's Jill's big picture, do you know?"

"No. She has a dead father and a mother she doesn't like, I guess she'll go back to Connecticut when her luck runs thin."

"Aren't you being, so to speak, her luck?"

"I'm part of her picture right now, yeah."

"And she of yours. You know, your living with this girl gives Janice an open-and-shut divorce case."

"You don't scare me, somehow."

"Do I understand that you've assured Janice that all she has to do is come back and the girl will go?"

Rabbit begins to feel it, where Stavros is pressing for the opening. The tickle above his nose is beginning up again. "No," he says, praying not to sneeze, "you don't understand that." He sneezes. Six faces at the bar look around; the little Schlitz spinner seems to hesitate. They are giving away refrigerators and ski weekends in Chile on the TV.

"You don't want Janice back now?"

"I don't know."

"You would like a divorce so you can keep living the good life? Or marry the girl, maybe, even? Jill. She'll break your balls, Sport."

"You think too fast. I'm just living day by day, trying to

forget my sorrow. I've been left, don't forget. Some slick-talking kinky-haired peacenik-type Japanese-car salesman lured her away, I forget the son-of-a-bitch's name."

"That isn't exactly the way it was. She came pounding on my door."

"You let her in."

Stavros looks surprised. "What else? She had put herself out on a limb. Where could she go? My taking her in made the least trouble for everybody."

"And now it's trouble?"

Stavros fiddles his fingertips as if cards are in them; if he loses this trick, can he take the rest? "Her staying on with me gives her expectations we can't fulfill. Marriage isn't my thing, sorry. With anybody."

"Don't try to be polite. So now you've tried her in all positions and want to ship her back. Poor old Jan. So dumb."

"I don't find her dumb. I find her—unsure of herself. She wants what every normal chick wants. To be Helen of Troy. There've been hours when I gave her some of that. I can't keep giving it to her. It doesn't hold up." He becomes angry; his square brow darkens. "What do *you* want? You're sitting there twitching your whiskers, so how about it? If I kick her out, will you pick her up?"

"Kick her out and see. She can always go live with her parents."

"Her mother drives her crazy."

"That's what mothers are for." Rabbit pictures his own. His bladder gets a touch of that guilty sweetness it had when as a child he was running to school late, beside the slime-rimmed gutter water that ran down from the ice plant. He tries to explain. "Listen, Stavros. You're the one in the wrong. You're the one screwing another man's wife. If you want to pull out, pull out. Don't try to commit me to one of your fucking coalition governments."

"Back to that," Stavros says.

"Right. You intervened, not me."

"I didn't intervene, I performed a rescue."

"That's what all you hawks say." He is eager to argue about Vietnam, but Stavros keeps to the less passionate subject.

"She was desperate, fella. Christ, hadn't you taken her to bed in ten years?"

"I resent that."

"Go ahead. Resent it."

"She was no worse off than a million wives." A billion cunts, how many wives? Five hundred million? "We had relations. They didn't seem so bad to me."

"All I'm saying is, I didn't cook this up, it was delivered to me hot. I didn't have to talk her into anything, she was pushing all the way. I was the first chance she had. If I'd been a one-legged milkman, I would have done."

"You're too modest."

Stavros shakes his head. "She's some tiger."

"Stop it, you're giving me a hard-on."

Stavros studies him squarely. "You're a funny guy."

"Tell me what it is you don't like about her now."

His merely interested tone relaxes Stavros's shoulders an inch. The man measures off a little cage in front of his lapels. "It's just too—confining. It's weight I don't need. I got to keep light, on an even keel. I got to avoid stress. Between you and me, I'm not going to live forever."

"You just told me you might."

"The odds are not."

"You know, you're just like me, the way I used to be. Everybody now is like the way I used to be."

"She's had her kicks for the summer, let her come back. Tell the hippie to move on, that's what a kid like that wants to hear anyway."

Rabbit sips the dregs of his second Daiquiri. It is delicious, to let this silence lengthen, widen: he will not promise to take Janice back. The game is on ice. He says at last, because continued silence would have been unbearably rude, "Just don't know. Sorry to be so vague."

Stavros takes it up quickly. "She on anything?"

"Who?"

"This nympho of yours."

"On something?"

"You know. Pills. Acid. She can't be on horse or you wouldn't have any furniture left."

"Jill? No, she's kicked that stuff."

"Don't you believe it. They never do. These flower babies, dope is their milk."

"She's fanatic against. She's been there and back. Not that this is any of your business." Rabbit doesn't like the way the game has started to slide; there is a hole he is trying to plug and can't.

Stavros minutely shrugs. "How about Nelson? Is he acting different?"

"He's growing up." The answer sounds evasive. Stavros brushes it aside.

"Drowsy? Nervous? Taking naps at odd times? What do they do all day while you're playing hunt and peck? They must do *some*thing, fella."

"She teaches him how to be polite to scum. Fella. Let me pay for your water."

"So what have I learned?"

"I hope nothing."

But Stavros has sneaked in for that lay-up and the game is in overtime. Rabbit hurries to get home, to see Nelson and Jill, to sniff their breaths, look at their pupils, whatever. He has left his lamb with a viper. But outside the Phoenix, in the hazed sunshine held at its September tilt, traffic is snarled, and the buses are caught along with everything else. A movie is being made. Rabbit remembers it mentioned in the *Vat* (BREWER MIDDLE AMERICA? *Gotham Filmmakers Think So*) that Brewer had been chosen for a location by some new independent outfit; none of the stars' names meant anything to him, he forgot the details. Here they are. An arc of cars and trucks mounted with lights extends halfway into Weiser Street, and a crowd of locals with rolled-up shirtsleeves and bag-lugging grannies and Negro delinquents straggles into the rest of the street to get a closer look, cutting down traffic to one creeping lane. The cops that should be unsnarling the tangle are ringing the show, protecting the moviemakers. So tall, Rabbit gets a glimpse from a curb. One of the boarded-up stores near the old Baghdad that used to show M-G-M but now is given over to skin flicks (*Sepia Follies, Honeymoon in Swapland*) has been done up as a restaurant front; a tall salmon-faced man with taffy hair and a little bronze-haired trick emerge from this pretend-restaurant arm in arm and there is some incident involving a passerby, another painted actor who emerges from the crowd of dusty real people watching, a bumping-into, followed by laughter on the part of the first man and the woman and a slow resuming look that will probably signal when the film is all cut and projected that they are going to fuck. They do this several times. Between takes everybody waits, wisecracks, adjusts lights and wires. The girl, from Rabbit's distance, is impossibly precise: her eyes flash, her hair hurls reflections like a helmet. Even her dress scintillates. When someone, a director or electrician, stands near her, he looks dim. And it makes Rabbit feel dim, dim and guilty, to see how the spotlights carve from the sunlight a yet brighter day, a lurid pastel island of heightened reality around which the rest of us—technicians, policemen, the straggling fascinated spectators including himself—are penumbral ghosts, suppliants ignored.

Local Excavations
Unearth Antiquities

As Brewer renews itself, it discovers more about itself.

The large-scale demolition and reconstruction now taking place in the central city continues uncovering numerous artifacts of the "olden times" which yield interesting insights into our city's past.

An underground speakeasy complete with wall murals emerged to light during the creation of a parking lot at M ing the creation of a parking lot at Muriel and Greeley Streets.

Old-timers remembered the hideaway as the haunt of "Gloves" Naugel and other Prohibition figures, as also the training-ground for musicians like "Red" Wenrich of sliding trombone fame who went on to become household names on a nationwide scale.

Also old sign-boards are common. Ingeniously shaped in the forms of cows,

beehives, boots, mortars, plows, they advertise "dry goods and notions," leath-
erwork, drugs, and medicines, produce
of infinite variety. Preserved underground, most are still easily legible and
date from the nineteenth century.

Amid the old fieldstone foundations,
metal tools and grindstones come to light.

Arrowheads are not uncommon.

Dr. Klaus Schoerner, vice-president of
the Brewer Historical Society, spent a

At the coffee break, Buchanan struts up to Rabbit. "How's little Jilly doing for you?"

"She's holding up."

"She worked out pretty fine for you, didn't she?"

"She's a good girl. Mixed-up like kids are these days, but we've gotten used to her. My boy and me."

Buchanan smiles, his fine little mustache spreading an em, and sways a half-step closer. "Little Jill's still keeping you company?"

Rabbit shrugs, feeling pasty and nervous. He keeps giving hostages to fortune. "She has nowhere else to go."

"Yes, man, she must be working out real fine for you." Still he doesn't walk away, going out to the platform for his whisky. He stays and, still smiling but letting a pensive considerate shadow slowly subdue his face, says, "You know, friend Harry, what with Labor Day coming on, and the kids going back to school, and all this inflation you see everywhere, things get a bit short. In the financial end."

"How many children do you have?" Rabbit asks politely. Working with him all these years, he never thought Buchanan was married.

The plump ash-gray man rocks back and forth on the balls of his feet. "Oh . . . say five, that's been counted. They look to their daddy for support, and Labor Day finds him a little embarrassed. The cards just haven't been falling for old Lester lately."

"I'm sorry," Rabbit says. "Maybe you shouldn't gamble."

"I am just tickled to death little Jilly's worked out to fit your needs," Buchanan says. "I was thinking, twenty would sure help me by Labor Day."

"Twenty dollars?"

"That is all. It is miraculous, Harry, how far I've learned to make a little stretch. Twenty little dollars from a friend to a friend would sure make my holiday go easier all around. Like I say, seeing Jill worked out so good, you must be feeling pretty good. Pretty generous. A man in love, they say, is a friend to all."

But Rabbit has already fished out his wallet and found two tens. "This is just a loan," he says, frightened, knowing he is lying, bothered by that sliding again, that sweet bladder running late to school. The doors will be shut, the principal Mr. Kleist always stands by the front doors, with their rattling chains and push bars rubbed down to the yellow of brass, to snare the tardy and clap them into his airless office, where the records are kept.

"My children bless you," Buchanan says, folding the bills away. "This will buy a world of pencils."

"Hey, whatever happened to Babe?" Rabbit asks. He finds, with his money in Buchanan's pocket, he has new ease; he has bought rights of inquiry.

Buchanan is caught off guard. "She's still around. She's still doing her thing as the young folks say."

"I wondered, you know, if you'd broken off connections."

Because he is short of money. Buchanan studies Rabbit's face, to make certain he knows what he is implying. Pimp. He sees he does, and his mustache broadens. "You want to get into that nice Babe, is that it? Tired of white meat, want a drumstick? Harry, what would your Daddy say?"

"I'm just asking how she was. I liked the way she played."

"She sure took a shine to you, I know. Come up to Jimbo's some time, we'll work something out."

"She said my knuckles were bad." The bell rasps. Rabbit tries to gauge how soon the next touch will be made, how deep this man is into him; Buchanan sees this and playfully, jubilantly slaps the palm of the hand Rabbit had extended, thinking of his knuckles. The slap tingles. Skin.

Buchanan says, "I *like* you, man," and walks away. A plum-pudding-colored roll of fat trembles at the back of his neck. Poor diet, starch. Chitlins, grits.

fascinating hour with the VAT reporter, chatting informally concerning Brewer's easliest days as a trading post with er's earliest days as a trading post with the Indian tribes along the Running Horse River.

He showed us a pint of log huts
He showed us a print of log huts etched when the primitive settlement bore the name of Greenwich, after Greenwich, England, home of the famed observatory.

Also in Dr. Kleist's collection were many fascinating photos of Weiser Street when it held a few rude shops and inns. The most famous of these inns was the Goose and Feathers, where George Washington and his retinue tarried one night on their way west to suppress the Whisky Rebellion in 1720. suppress the Whisky Rebellion in 1799.

The first iron mine in the vicinity was the well-known Oriole Furnace, seven miles south of the city. Dr. Kleist owns a collection of original slag and spoke enthusiastically about the methods whereby these early ironmakers produced a sufficiently powerful draft in

Pajasek comes up behind him. "Angstrom. Telephone." Pajasek is a small tired bald man whose bristling eyebrows increase the look of pressure about his head, as if his forehead is being pressed over his eyes, forming long horizontal folds. "You might tell the party after this you have a home number."

"Sorry, Ed. It's probably my crazy wife."

"Could you get her to be crazy on your private time?"

Crossing from his machine to the relative quiet of the frosted-glass walls is like ascending through supportive water to the sudden vacuum of air. Instantly, he begins to struggle. "Janice, for Christ's sake, I told you not to call me here. Call me at home."

"I don't want to talk to your little answering service. Just the thought of her voice makes me go cold all over."

"Nelson usually answers the phone. She never answers it."

"I don't want to hear her, or see her, or hear about her. I can't describe to you, Harry, the disgust I feel at just the thought of that person."

"Have you been on the bottle again? You sound screwed-up."

"I am sober and sane. And satisfied, thank you. I want to know what you're doing about Nelson's back-to-school clothes. You realize he's grown three inches this summer and nothing will fit."

"Did he, that's terrific. Maybe he won't be such a shrimp after all."

"He will be as big as my father and my father is no shrimp."

"Sorry, I always thought he was."

"Do you want me to hang up right now? Is that what you want?"

"No, I just want you to call me someplace else than at work."

She hangs up. He waits in Pajasek's wooden swivel chair, looking at the calendar, which hasn't been turned yet though this is September, and the August calendar girl, who is holding two ice-cream cones so the scoops cover just where her nipples would be, one strawberry and one chocolate, *Double Dips!* being the caption, until the phone rings.

"What were we saying?" he asks.

"I must take Nelson shopping for school clothes."

"O.K., come around and pick him up any time. Set a day."

"I will not come near that house, Harry, as long as that girl is in it. I won't even go near Penn Villas. I'm sorry, it's an uncontrollable physical revulsion."

"Maybe you're pregnant, if you're so queasy. Have you and Chas been taking precautions?"

"Harry, I don't know you any more. I said to Charlie, I can't believe I lived thirteen years with that man, it's as if it never happened."

"Which reminds me, what shall we get Nelson for his birthday? He's going to be thirteen this fall."

She begins to cry. "You never forgave me for that, did you? For getting pregnant."

"I did, I did. Relax. It worked out great. I'll send Nelson over to your love nest to go shopping. Name the day."

"Send him to the lot Saturday morning. I don't like him coming to the apartment, it seems too terrible when he leaves."

"Does it have to be Saturday? There was some talk of Jill driving us both down to Valley Forge; the kid and I've never seen it."

"Are you poking fun of me? Why do you think this is all so funny, Harry? This is *life*."

"I'm not, we were. Seriously."

"Well, tell her you can't. You two send Nelson over. Only send him with some money, I don't see why I should pay for his clothes."

"Buy everything at Kroll's and charge it."

"Kroll's has gone terribly downhill, you know it has. There's a nice little new shop now up near Perley, past that submarine place that used to be Chinese."

"Open another charge account. Tell him you're Springer Motors and offer a Toyota for security."

"Harry, you mustn't be so hostile. You sent me off myself. You said, that night, I'll never forget it, it was the shock of my life, 'See him if you want to, just so I don't have to see the bastard.' Those were your words."

"Hey, that reminds me, I did see him the other day."

"Who?"

"Chas. Your dark and swarthy lover."

"How?"

"He ambushed me after work. Waiting in the alley with a dagger. *Oog*, I said, you got me, you Commie rat."

"What did he want?"

"Oh, to talk about you."

"What about me? Harry, are you lying, I can't tell any more. *What* about me?"

"Whether or not you were happy."

She makes no comeback, so he goes on, "We concluded you were."

"Right," Janice says, and hangs up.

> **the days before the Bessemer furnace.**
> **Old faded photographs of Weiser**
> **Street show a prosperous-appearing**
> **avenue of tasteful, low brick buildings**
> **with horsedrawn trolly tracks promi-**
> **with horse-drown trolley traks prami-**
> **with horsed-rawn trolleyyyfff etaoin**
> **etaoinshrdlu etaoinshrdlucmfwpvbgkqjet**

He asks her, "What did you and the kid do today?"

"Oh, nothing much. Hung around the house in the morning, took a drive in the afternoon."

"Where to?"

"Up to Mt. Judge."

"The town?"

"The mountain. We had a Coke in the Pinnacle Hotel and watched a softball game in the park for a while."

"Tell me the truth. Do you have the kid smoking pot?"

"Whatever gave you that idea?"

"He's awfully fascinated with you, and I figure it's either pot or sex."

"Or the car. Or the fact that I treat him like a human being instead of a failed little athlete because he's not six feet six. Nelson is a very intelligent sensitive child who is very upset by his mother leaving."

"I know he's intelligent, thanks, I've known the kid for years."

"Harry, do you want me to leave, is that it? I will if that's what you want. I could go back to Babe except she's having a rough time."

"What kind of rough time?"

"She's been busted for possession. The pigs came into the Jimbo the other night and took about ten away, including her and Skeeter. She says they asked for a bigger payoff and the owner balked. The owner is white, by the way."

"So you're still in touch with that crowd."

"You don't want me to be?"

"Suit yourself. It's your life to fuck up."

"Somebody's been bugging you, haven't they?"

"Several people."

"Do whatever you want to with me, Harry. I can't be anything in your real life."

She is standing before him in the living room, in her cutoff jeans and peasant blouse, her hands held at her sides slightly lifted and open, like a servant waiting for a tray. Her fingers are red from washing his dishes. Moved to gallantry, he confesses, "I need your sweet mouth and your pearly ass."

"I think they're beginning to bore you."

He reads this in reverse: he bores her. Always did. He attacks: "O.K., what *about* sex, with you and the kid?"

She looks away. She has a long nose and long chin, and that dry moth mouth that he feels, seeing it in repose, when she is not watching him, as absentmindedly disdainful, as above him and wanting to flutter still higher. Summer has put only a few freckles on her, and these mostly on her forehead, which bulges gently as a milk pitcher. Her hair is twisty from being so much in those little tiny braids hippies make. "He likes me," she answers, except it is no answer.

He tells her. "We can't do that trip to Valley Forge tomorrow. Janice wants Nelson to go shopping with her for school clothes, and I should go see my mother. You can drive me if you want, or I can take the bus."

He thinks he is being obliging, but she gives him her rich-girl sneer and says, "You remind me of my mother sometimes. She thought she owned me too."

Saturday morning, she is gone. But her clothes still hang like rags in the closet. Downstairs on the kitchen table lies a note in green magic marker: *Out all day. Will drop Nelson at the lot.* ⊕ ♡ ✕ ⚲. So he takes the two bus rides all the way across Brewer. The lawns in Mt. Judge, patches of grass between cement walks, are burned; spatterings of leaves here and there in the maples are already turned gold. There is that scent in the air, of going back to school, of beginning again and reconfirming the order that exists. He wants to feel good, he always used to feel good at every turning of the year, every vacation or end of vacation, every new sheet on the calendar: but his adult life has proved to have no seasons, only changes of weather, and the older he gets, the less weather interests him.

The house next to his old house still has the FOR SALE sign up. He tries his front door but it is locked; he rings, and after a prolonged shuffle and rumble within Pop comes to the door. Rabbit asks, "What's this locked door business?"

"Sorry, Harry, there've been so many burglaries in town lately. We had no idea you were coming."

"Didn't I promise?"

"You've promised before. Not that your mother and I can blame you, we know your life is difficult these days."

"It's not so difficult. In some ways it's easier. She upstairs?"

Pop nods. "She's rarely down anymore."

"I thought this new stuff was working."

"It does in a way, but she's so depressed she lacks the will. Nine-tenths of life is will, my father used to say it, and the longer I live the more I see how right he was."

The disinfected scent of the house is still oppressive, but Harry goes up the stairs two at a time; Jill's disappearance has left him vigorous with anger. He bursts into the sickroom, saying, "Mom, tell me your dreams."

She has lost weight. The bones have shed all but the minimum connective tissue; her face is strained over the bones with an expression of far-seeing, expectant sweetness. Her voice emerges from this apparition more strongly than before, with less hesitation between words.

"I'm tormented something cruel at night, Harry. Did Earl tell you?"

"He mentioned bad dreams."

"Yes, bad, but not so bad as not being able to sleep at all. I know this room so well now, every object. At night even that innocent old bureau and that—poor shapeless armchair —they."

"They what?" He sits on the bed to take her hand, and fears the swaying under his weight will jostle and break her bones.

She says, "They want. To suffocate me."

"Those things do?"

"All things—do. They crowd in, in the queerest way, these simple homely bits of furniture I've. Lived with all my life. Dad's asleep in the next room, I can hear him snore. No cars go by. It's just me and the streetlamp. It's like being—under water. I count the seconds I have breath left for. I figure I can go forty, thirty, then it gets down to ten."

"I didn't know breathing was affected by this."

"It isn't. It's all my mind. The things I have in my mind, Hassy, it reminds me of when they clean out a drain. All that hair and sludge mixed up with a rubber comb somebody went and dropped down years ago. Sixty years ago in my case."

"You don't feel that about your life, do you? I think you did a good job."

"A good job at what? You don't even know what you're trying to do, is the humor of it."

"Have a few laughs," he offers. "Have a few babies."

She takes him up on that. "I keep dreaming about you and Mim. Always together. When you haven't been together since you got out of school."

"What do Mim and I do, in these dreams?"

"You look up at me. Sometimes you want to be fed and I can't find the food. Once I remember looking into the icebox and. A man was in it frozen. A man I never knew, just one. Of those total strangers dreams have. Or else the stove won't light. Or I can't locate where Earl put the food when he came home from shopping, I know he. Put it somewhere. Silly things. But they become so important. I wake up screaming at Earl."

"Do Mim and I say anything?"

"No, you just look up like children do. Slightly frightened but sure I'll save. The situation. This is how you look. Even when I can see you're dead."

"Dead?"

"Yes. All powdered and set out in coffins. Only still standing up, still waiting for something from me. You've died because I couldn't get the food on the table. A strange thing about these dreams, come to think of it. Though you look up at me from a child's height. You look the way you do now. Mim all full of lipstick, with one of those shiny miniskirts and boots zippered up to her knee."

"Is that how she looks now?"

"Yes, she sent us a publicity picture."

"Publicity for what?"

"Oh, you know. For herself. You know how they do things now. I didn't understand it myself. It's on the bureau."

The picture, eight by ten, very glossy, with a diagonal crease where the mailman bent it, shows Mim in a halter and bracelets and sultan pants, her head thrown back, one long bare foot—she had big feet as a child, Mom had to make the shoe salesmen go deep into the stockroom—up on a hassock. Her eyes from the way they've reshaped them do not look like Mim at all. Only something about the nose makes it Mim. The kind of lump on the end, and the nostrils: the way as a baby they would tuck in when she started to cry is the way they tuck in now when they tell her to look sexy. He feels in this picture less Mim than the men posing her. Underneath, the message pale in ballpoint pen, she had written, *Miss you all Hope to come East soon Love Mim.* A slanting cramped hand that hadn't gone past high school. Jill's message had been written in splashy upright private-school semi-printing, confident as a poster. Mim never had that.

Rabbit asks, "How old is Mim now?"

Mom says, "You don't want to hear about my dreams."

"Sure I do." He figures it: born when he was six, Mim would be thirty now: she wasn't going anywhere, not even in harem costume. What you haven't done by thirty you're not likely to do. What you have done you'll do lots more. He says to his mother: "Tell me the worst one."

"The house next door has been sold. To some people who want to put up an apartment building. The Scranton pair have gone into partnership with them and then. These two walls go up, so the house doesn't get any light at all, and I'm in a hole looking up. And dirt starts to come down on me, cola cans and cereal boxes, and then. I wake up and know I can't breathe."

He tells her, "Mt. Judge isn't zoned for high-rise."

She doesn't laugh. Her eyes are wide now, fastened on that other half of her life, the night half, the nightmare half that now is rising like water in a bad cellar and is going to engulf her, proving that it was the real half all along, that daylight was an illusion, a cheat. "No," she says, "that's not the worst. The worst is Earl and I go to the hospital for tests. All around us are tables the size of our kitchen table. Only instead of set for meals each has a kind of puddle on it, a red puddle mixed up with crumpled bedsheets so they're shaped like. Children's sandcastles. And connected with tubes to machines with like television patterns on them. And then it dawns on me these are each people. And Earl keeps saying, so proud and pleased he's brainless, 'The government is paying for it all. The government is paying for it.' And he shows me the paper you and Mim signed to make me one of—you know, *them*. Those puddles."

"That's not a dream," her son says. "That's how it is."

And she sits up straighter on the pillows, stiff, scolding. Her mouth gets that unforgiving downward sag he used to fear more than anything—more than vampires, more than polio, more than thunder or God or being late for school. "I'm ashamed of you," she says. "I never thought I'd hear a son of mine so bitter."

"It was a joke, Mom."

"Who has so much to be grateful for," she goes on implacably.

"For what? For exactly what?"

"For Janice's leaving you, for one thing. She was always. A damp washrag."

"And what about Nelson, huh? What happens to him now?" This is her falsity, that she forgets what time creates, she still sees the world with its original four corners, her and Pop and him and Mim sitting at the kitchen table. Her tyrant love would freeze the world.

Mom says, "Nelson isn't my child, you're my child."

"Well, he exists anyway, and I have to worry about him. You just can't dismiss Janice like that."

"She's dismissed you."

"Not really. She calls me up at work all the time. Stavros wants her to come back."

"Don't you let her. She'll. Smother you, Harry."

"What choices do I have?"

"Run. Leave Brewer. I never knew why you came back. There's nothing here any more. Everybody knows it. Ever since the hosiery mills went south. Be like Mim."

"I don't have what Mim has to sell. Anyway she's breaking Pop's heart, whoring around."

"He wants it that way, your father has always been looking. For excuses to put on a long face. Well, he has me now, and I'm excuse enough. Don't say no to life, Hassy. Let the dead bury the dead. Bitterness never helps. I'd rather have a postcard from you happy than. See you sitting there like a lump."

Always these impossible demands and expectations from her. These harsh dreams. "Hassy, do you ever pray?"

"Mostly on buses."

"Pray for rebirth. Pray for your own life."

His cheeks flame; he bows his head. He feels she is asking him to kill Janice, to kill Nelson. Freedom means murder. Rebirth means death. A lump, he silently resists, and she looks aside with the corner of her mouth worse bent. She is still trying to call him forth from her womb, can't she see he is an old man? An old lump whose only use is to stay in place to keep the lumps leaning on him from tumbling.

Pop comes upstairs and tunes in the Phillies game on television. "They're a much sounder team without that Allen," he says. "He was a bad egg, Harry, I say that without prejudice; bad eggs come in all colors."

After a few innings, Rabbit leaves.

"Can't you stay for at least the game, Harry? I believe there's a beer still in the refrigerator, I was going to go down to the kitchen anyway to make Mother some tea."

"Let him go, Earl."

To protect the electrical wires, a lot of the maples along Jackson Road have been mutilated, the center of their crowns cut out. Rabbit hadn't noticed this before, or the new sidewalk squares where they have taken away the little surface gutters that used to trip you roller skating. He had been roller skating when Kenny Leggett, an older boy from across the street, who later became a five-minute miler, a county conference marvel, but that was later, this day he was just a bigger boy who had hit Rabbit with an icy snowball that winter—could have taken out an eye if it had hit higher—this day he just tossed across Jackson Road the shout, "Harry, did you hear on the radio? The President is dead." He said "The President," not "Roosevelt"; there had been no other President for them. The next time this would happen, the President would have a name: as he sat at the deafening tall machine one Friday after lunch his father sneaked up behind him and confided, "Harry, it just came over the radio, engraving had it on. Kennedy's been shot. They think in the head." Both charmers dead of violent headaches. Their smiles fade in the field of stars. We grope on, under bullies and accountants. On the bus, Rabbit prays as his mother told him to do: *Make the L-dopa work, give her pleasanter dreams, keep Nelson more or less pure, don't let Stavros turn too hard on Janice, help Jill find her way home. Keep Pop healthy. Me too. Amen.*

A man in a pink shirt drops down beside him with a stagey sigh, after a stop on the side of the mountain, by the gas station with the Day-Glo spinner. The man's face, turned full, clings to the side of Rabbit's vision; after a while he defiantly returns the stare. The other man's cheeks are like his shirt pink, smooth as a boy's though his hair is gray, and his long worried eyebrows are lifted with an effort of recognition. "I *do* beg your pardon," he says, with an emphasis that curls back into his voice purringly, "but aren't you Harry—?"

"Hey, and you're Eccles. Reverend Eccles."

"Angstrom, yes? Harry Angstrom. How very wonderful. *Really.*" And Eccles takes his hand, in that plump humid grip that feels as if it will never let go. In the clergyman's eyes there is something new, a hardened yet startled something, naked like the pale base of his throat, which lacks a clerical collar. And the shirt, Rabbit sees, is a fancy shirt, with a fine white stitch-stripe and an airy semi-transparent summer weave: he remembers how the man wore not black but a subtly elegant midnight blue. Eccles still has hold of his hand. Harry pulls it free. "*Do* tell me," Eccles says, with that preening emphasis again, which Rabbit doesn't remember from ten years ago, "how things have gone for you. Are you still with—?"

"Janice."

"She didn't seem quite up to you, I can say now, frankly."

"Well, or *vice versa*. We never had another child." That had been Eccles' advice, in those first months of reconciliation, when he and Janice were starting fresh and even going to the Episcopal church together. Then Eccles had been called to a church nearer Philadelphia. They had heard a year or two later, by way of Janice's mother, that he had run into some trouble in his new parish; then nothing. And here he was again, grayer but looking no older: if anything, younger, slimmer through the middle, in self-consciously good condition, hard and tan in a way few in Brewer bother to cultivate, and with that young, startled look to his eyes. His hair is long, and curls at the back of his shirt collar. Rabbit asks him, "And what about things with *you?*" He is wondering where Eccles could have been, to board the bus at the side of the mountain. Nothing there but the gas station, a diner, a view of the viaduct, and some rich men's homes tucked up among the spruces, behind iron fences.

"*Ça va.* It goes. I've been buried; and yet I live. I've parted company with the ministry." And his jaw stays open, propped as if to emit a guffaw, though no sound comes, and those strangely purified eyes remain watchful.

"Why'd you do that?" Rabbit asks.

Eccles' chuckle, which always had something exploratory and quizzical about it, has become impudent, mocking, if not quite unafraid. "A variety of reasons. I was rather invited to, for one. I wanted to, for another."

"You no longer believe it?"

"In my fashion. I'm not sure I believed it then."

"No?" Rabbit is shocked.

"I believed," Eccles tells him, and his voice has taken on an excessive modulation, a self-caressing timbre, "in certain kinds of human interrelation. I still do. If people want to call what happens in certain relationships Christ, I raise no objection. But it's not the word *I* choose to use anymore."

"How'd your father feel about this? Wasn't he a bishop?"

"My father—God rest his, et cetera—was dead when my decision was reached."

"And your wife? She was nifty, I forget her name."

"Lucy. Dear Lucy. She left me, actually. Yes, I've shed many skins." And the mouth of this pale-throated, long-haired man holds open on the possibility of a guffaw, but silently, watchfully.

"She left ya?"

"She fled my indiscretions. She remarried and lives in Wilmington. Her husband's a painfully ordinary fellow, a chemist of some sort. No indiscretions. My girls adore him. You remember my two girls."

"They were cute. Especially the older one. Since we're on the subject, Janice has left me, too."

Eccles' pale active eyebrows arch higher. "Really? Recently?"

"The day before the moon landing."

"She seemed more the left than the leaving type. Look, Harry, we should get together in a more, ah, stationary place

and have a real conversation." In his leaning closer for emphasis, as the bus sways, his arm touches Rabbit's. He always had a
certain surprising muscularity, but Eccles had become burlier,
more himself. His fluffed-up head seems huge.

Rabbit asks him, "Uh, what do you do now?"

Again, the guffaw, the held jaw, the watchfulness. "I live in
Philadelphia, basically. For a while I did youth work with the
Y.M.C.A. I was a camp supervisor three summers in Vermont.
Some winters, I've chosen just to read, to meditate. I think a
very exciting thing is happening in Western consciousness and,
laugh if you will, I'm making notes toward a book about it.
What I think, in essence, is that, at long last, we're coming out
of Plato's cave. How does 'Out from Plato's Cave' strike you
as a title?"

"Kind of spooky, but don't mind me. What brings you back
to this dirty old burg then?"

"Well, it's rather curious, Harry. You don't mind my calling
you Harry? That all is beginning to seem as if it were only yesterday. What curious people we were then! The ghosts we let
bedevil us! Anyhow, you know the little town called Oriole, six
miles south of Brewer?"

"I've been there." With his high-school basketball team, in
his junior year. He had one of his great nights there.

"Well, they have a summer theater, called the Oriole Players."

"Sure. We run their ads."

"That's right—you're a printer. I've heard that."

"Linotyper, actually."

"Good for you. Well, a friend of mine, he's an absurd person, *very* egotistical, but nevertheless a wonderful man, is with
them as co-director, and has talked me into helping with their
P.R. Public relations. It's really being a fund raiser. I was in Mt.
Judge just now seeing this im*poss*ible old Mahlon Younger-
man, that's Sunflower Beer of course, for a donation. He said
he'd think about it. That's code for he *won't* think about it."

"It sounds a little like what you used to do."

Eccles glances at him more sharply; a defensive sleepiness
masks his face. "Pearls before swine, you mean? Pushing
stumbling-blocks at the Gentiles. Yes, a little, but I only do it
eight hours a day. The other sixteen, I can be my own *man*."

Harry doesn't like the hungry way he says *man*, like it means too much. They are jerking and trembling down Weiser Street; Eccles looks past Harry out the window and blinks. "I *must* get off here. Could I ask you to get off with me and have me buy you a drink? There's a bar here on the corner that's not too depressing."

"No, Jesus, thanks. I got to keep riding. I got to get home. I have a kid there alone."

"Nelson."

"Right! What a memory! So thanks a lot. You look great."

"De*light*ful to see you again, Harry. Let's *do* make a more leisurely occasion sometime. Where are you living?"

"Over in Penn Villas, they put it up since you were here. Things are a little vague right now . . ."

"I understand," Eccles says, quickly, for the bus is chuffing and groaning to a stop. Yet he finds time to put his hand on Harry's shoulder, up near the neck. His voice changes quality, beseeches, becomes again a preacher's: "I think these are *mar*vellous times to be alive in, and I'd *love* to share my good news with you at your leisure."

To put distance between them, Rabbit rides the 16A six blocks further, to where it turns up Greely, and gets off there, walking back to the roasted-peanut place on Weiser to catch the bus to Penn Villas. PIG ATROCITIES STIR CAMDEN says a headline on a rack, a radical black paper out of Philly. Harry feels nervous, looking north along Weiser for a pink shirt coming after him. The place on his bare neck where Eccles touched tickles: amazing how that guy wants to cling, after all these years, with both their lives turned upside down. The bus number 12 comes and pulls him across the bridge. The day whines at the windows, a September brightness empty of a future: the lawns smitten flat, the black river listless and stinking. HOBBY HEAVEN. BUTCH CSSDY & KID. He walks down Emberly toward Vista Crescent among sprinklers twirling in unison, under television aerials raking the same four-o'clock garbage from the sky.

The dirty white Porsche is in the driveway, halfway into the garage, the way Janice used to do it, annoyingly. Jill is in the brown armchair, in her slip. From the slumped way she sits he sees she has no underpants on. She answers his questions groggily, with a lag, as if they are coming to her through a packing of dirty cotton, of fuzzy memories accumulated this day.

"Where'd you go so early this morning?"

"Out. Away from creeps like you."

"You drop the kid off?"

"Sure."

"When'd you get back?"

"Just now."

"Where'd you spend all day?"

"Maybe I went to Valley Forge anyway."

"Maybe you didn't."

"I did."

"How was it?"

"Beautiful. A gas, actually. George was a beautiful dude."

"Describe one room."

"You go in a door, and there's a four-poster bed, and a little tasselled pillow, and on it it says, 'George Washington slept here.' On the bedside tables you can still see the pills he took, to make himself sleep, when the redcoats had got him all uptight. The walls have some kind of lineny stuff on them, and all the chairs have ropes across the arms so you can't sit down on them. That's why I'm sitting on this one. Because it didn't. O.K.?"

He hesitates among the many alternatives she seems to be presenting. Laughter, anger, battle, surrender. "O.K. Sounds interesting. I'm sorry we couldn't go."

"Where did you go?"

"I went to visit my mother, after doing the housework around here."

"How is she?"

"She talks better, but seems frailer."

"I'm sorry. I'm sorry she has that disease. I guess I'll never meet your mother, will I?"

"Do you want to? You can see my father any time you want, just be in the Phoenix Bar at four-fifteen. You'd like him, he cares about politics. He thinks the System is shit, just like you do."

"And I'll never meet your wife."

"Why would you want to? What is this?"

"I don't know, I'm interested. Maybe I'm falling for you."

"Jesus, don't do that."

"You don't think much of yourself, do you?"

"Once the basketball stopped, I suppose not. My mother by the way told me I should let Janice screw herself and leave town."

"What'd you say to that?"

"I said I couldn't."

"You're a creep."

Her lack of underpants and his sense that she has already been used today, and his sense of this unique summer, this summer of the moon, slipping away forever, lead him to ask, blushing for the second time this afternoon, "You wouldn't want to make love, would you?"

"Fuck or suck?"

"Whichever. Fuck." For he has come to feel that she gives him the end of her with teeth in it as a way of keeping the other for some man not yet arrived, some man more real to her than himself.

"What about Nelson?" she asks.

"He's off with Janice, she may keep him for supper. He's no threat. But maybe you're too tired. From all that George Washington."

Jill stands and pulls her slip to her shoulder and holds it there, a crumpled bag containing her head, her young body all there below, pale as a candlestick, the breasts hardened drippings. "Fuck me," she says coolly, tossing her slip toward the kitchen, and, when under him and striving, continues, "Harry, I want you to fuck all the shit out of me, all the shit and dreariness of this shit-dreary world, hurt me, clean me out, I want you to be all of my insides, sweetheart, right up to my throat, yes, oh yes, bigger, more, shoot it all out of me, sweet oh sweet sweet creep." Her eyes dilate in surprise. Their green is just a rim, around pupils whose pure black is muddied with his shadow. "You've gotten little."

It is true: all her talk, her wild wanting it, have scared him down to nothing. She is too wet; something has enlarged her. And the waxen solidity of her young body, her buttocks spheres too perfect, feels alien to him: he grasps her across a distance clouded with Mom's dry warm bones and Janice's dark curves, Janice's ribs crescent above where the waist dipped. He senses winds playing through Jill's nerve-ends, feels her moved by something beyond him, of which he is only a shadow, a shadow of white, his chest a radiant shield crushing her. She disengages herself and kneels to tongue his belly. They play with each other in a fog. The furniture dims around them. They are on the scratchy carpet, the television screen a mother-planet above them. Her hair is in his mouth. Her ass is two humps under his eyes. She tries to come against his face but his tongue isn't that strong. She rubs her clitoris against his chin upside down until he hurts. Elsewhere she is nibbling him. He feels gutted, silly, limp. At last he asks her to drag her breasts, the tough little tips, across his genitals, that lie cradled at the join of his legs. In this way he arouses himself, and attempts to satisfy her, and does, though by the time she trembles and comes they are crying over secrets far at their backs, in opposite directions, moonchild and earthman. "I love you," he says, and the fact that he doesn't makes it true. She is sitting on him, still working like some angry mechanic who, having made a difficult fit, keeps testing it.

In the small slipping sound they make he hears their mixed liquids, imagines in the space of her belly a silver machine, spider-shaped, spun from the threads of their secretions, carefully spinning. This links them. He says, surrendering, "Oh cry. Do." He pulls her down to him, puts their cheeks together, so their tears will mix.

Jill asks him, "Why are you crying?"

"Why are you?"

"Because the world is so shitty and I'm part of it."

"Do you think there's a better one?"

"There must be."

"Well," he considers, "why the hell not?"

By the time Nelson comes home, they have both taken baths, their clothes are on, the lights are on. Rabbit is watching the six-o'clock news (the round-up tally on summer riots, the week's kill figures in Vietnam, the estimate of traffic accidents over the coming Labor Day weekend) and Jill is making lentil soup in the kitchen. Nelson spreads over the floor and furniture the unwrapped loot of his day with Janice: snappy new

Jockey shorts, undershirts, stretch socks, two pairs of slacks, four sports shirts, a corduroy jacket, wide neckties, even cufflinks to go with a lavender dress shirt, not to mention new loafers and basketball sneakers.

Jill admires: "Groovy, groovier, grooviest. Nelson, I just pity those eighth-grade girls, they'll be at your mercy."

He looks at her anxiously. "You know it's square. I didn't want to, Mom made me. The stores were disgusting, all full of materialism."

"What stores did she go to?" Rabbit asked. "How the hell did she pay for all this junk?"

"She opened charge accounts everywhere, Dad. She bought herself some clothes too, a really neat thing that looks like pajamas only it's O.K. to wear to parties if you're a woman, and stuff like that. And I got a suit, kind of grayey-green with checks, really cool, that we can pick up in a week when they make the alterations. Doesn't it feel funny when they measure you?"

"Do you remember, who was the name on the accounts? Me or Springer?"

Jill for a joke has put on one of his new shirts and tied her hair in a tail behind with one of his wide new neckties. To show herself off she twirls. Nelson, entranced, can scarcely speak. At her mercy.

"The name on her driver's license, Dad. Isn't that the right one?"

"And the address here? All those bills are going to come here?"

"Whatever's on the driver's license, Dad. Don't go heavy on *me*, I told her I just wanted blue jeans. And a Che Guevara sweatshirt, only there aren't any in Brewer."

Jill laughs. "Nelson, you'll be the best-dressed radical at West Brewer Junior High. Harry, these neckties are *silk*!"

"So it's war with that bitch."

"Dad, *don't*. It wasn't my *fault*."

"I know that. Forget it. You needed the clothes, you're growing."

"And Mom really looked neat in some of the dresses."

He goes to the window, rather than continue to be heavy on the kid. He sees his own car, the faithful Falcon, slowly pull out. He sees for a second the shadow of Janice's head, the way she sits at the wheel hunched over, you'd think she'd be more relaxed with cars, having grown up with them. She had been waiting, for what? For him to come out? Or was she just looking at the house, maybe to spot Jill? Or homesick. By a tug of tension in one cheek he recognizes himself as smiling, seeing that the flag decal is still on the back window, she hasn't let Stavros scrape it off.

III

Skeeter

"We've been raped, we've been raped!"
—BACKGROUND VOICE ABOARD SOYUZ 5

ONE DAY in September Rabbit comes home from work to find another man in the house. The man is a Negro. "What the hell," Rabbit says, standing in the front hall beside the three chime tubes.

"Hell, man, it's revolution, right?" the young black says, not rising from the mossy brown armchair. His glasses flash two silver circles; his goatee is a smudge in shadow. He has let his hair grow out so much, into such a big ball, that Rabbit didn't recognize him at first.

Jill rises, quick as smoke, from the chair with the silver threads. "You remember Skeeter?"

"How could I forget him?" He goes forward a step, his hand lifted ready to be shaken, the palm tingling with fear; but since Skeeter makes no move to rise, he lets it drop back to his side, unsullied.

Skeeter studies the dropped white hand, exhaling smoke from a cigarette. It is a real cigarette, tobacco. "I like it," Skeeter says. "I like your hostility, Chuck. As we used to say in Nam, it is my meat."

"Skeeter and I were just talking," Jill says; her voice has changed, it is more afraid, more adult. "Don't I have any rights?"

Rabbit speaks to Skeeter. "I thought you were in jail or something."

"He is out on bail," Jill says, too hastily.

"Let him speak for himself."

Wearily Skeeter corrects her. "To be precise, I am way out on bail. I have jumped the blessed thing. I am, as they would say, de*sir*ed by the local swine. I have become one hot item, right?"

"It would have been two years," Jill says. "Two years for

620

nothing, for not hurting anybody, not stealing anything, for nothing, Harry."

"Did Babe jump bail too?"

"Babe is a lady," Skeeter goes on in this tone of weary mincing precision. "She makes friends easy, right? I have no friends. I am known far and wide for my lack of sympathetic qualities." His voice changes, becomes falsetto, cringing. "Ah is one *baad* niggeh." He has many voices, Rabbit remembers, and none of them exactly his.

Rabbit tells him, "They'll catch you sooner or later. Jumping bail makes it much worse. Maybe you would have gotten off with a suspended sentence."

"I have one of those. Officialdom gets bored with handing them out, right?"

"How about your being a Vietnam veteran?"

"How *about* it? I am also black and unemployed and surly, right? I seek to undermine the state, and Ol' Massah State, he cottons on."

Rabbit contemplates the set of shadows in the old armchair, trying to feel his way. The chair has been with them ever since their marriage, it comes from the Springers' attic. This nightmare must pass. He says, "You talk a cool game, but I think you panicked, boy."

"Don't boy me."

Rabbit is startled; he had meant it neutrally, one outlaw to another. He tries to amend: "You're just hurting yourself. Go turn yourself in, say you never meant to jump."

Skeeter stretches luxuriously in the chair, yawns, inhales and exhales. "It dawns upon me," he says, "that you have a white gentleman's concept of the police and their exemplary works. There is nothing, let me repeat no thing, that gives them more pleasurable sensations than pulling the wings off of witless poor black men. First the fingernails, then the wings. Truly, they are constituted for that very sacred purpose. To keep me off your back and under your smelly feet, right?"

"This isn't the South," Rabbit says.

"Hee-yah! Friend Chuck, have you ever considered running for po-litical office, there can't be a county clerk left who believes the sweet things you do. The news is, the South is everywhere. We are fifty miles from the Mason-Dixon line where we sit, but way up in Detroit they are shooting nigger boys like catfish in a barrel. The news is, the cotton is in. Lynching season is on. In these Benighted States, everybody's done become a cracker." A brown hand delicately gestures from the shadows, then droops. "Forgive me, Chuck. This is just too simple for me to explain. Read the papers."

"I do. You're crazy."

Jill horns in. "The System is rotten, Harry. The laws are written to protect a tiny elite."

"Like people who own boats in Stonington," he says.

"Score one," Skeeter calls, "right?"

Jill flares. "What of it, I ran away from it, I reject it, I *shit* on it, Harry, where you're still loving it, you're eating it, you're eating my shit. My father's. Everybody's. Don't you see how you're *used*?"

"So now you want to use me. For *him*."

She freezes, white. Her lips thin to nothing. "Yes."

"You're crazy. I'd be risking jail too."

"Harry, just a few nights, until he can hustle up a stake. He has family in Memphis, he'll go there. Skeeter, right?"

"Right, sugar. Oh so right."

"It isn't just the pot bust, the pigs think he's a dealer, they say he pushes, they'll crucify him. Harry. They will."

Skeeter softly croons the start of "That Old Rugged Cross."

"Well, does he? Push."

Skeeter grins under his great ball of hair. "What can I get for you, Chuck? Goof balls, jolly beans, red devils, purple hearts. They have so much Panama Red in Philly right now they're feeding it to cows. Or want to sniff a little scag for a real rush?" From the gloom of the chair he extends his pale palms cupped as if heaped with shining poison.

So he is evil. Rabbit in his childhood used to lift, out of the same curiosity that made him put his finger into his belly-button and then sniff it, the metal waffle-patterned lid on the back yard cesspool, around the corner of the garage from the basketball hoop. Now this black man opens up under him in the same way: a pit of scummed stench impossible to see to the bottom of.

Harry turns and asks Jill, "Why are you doing this to me?"

She turns her head, gives him that long-chinned profile, a dime's worth. "I was stupid," she says, "to think you might trust me. You shouldn't have said you loved me."

Skeeter hums "True Love," the old Crosby–Grace Kelly single.

Rabbit re-asks, "Why?"

Skeeter rises from the chair. "Jesus deliver me from puking uptight honky lovers. She's doing it because I been screwing her all afternoon, right? If I go, she comes with me, hey Jill honey, right?"

She says, again thin-lipped, "Right."

Skeeter tells her, "I wouldn't take you on a bet, you poor cock-happy bitch. Skeeter splits alone." To Rabbit he says, "Toodle-oo, Chuck. Goddam green pickles, but it's been fun to watch you squirm." Standing, Skeeter seems frail, shabby in blue Levis and a colorless little Army windbreaker from which the insignia have been unstitched. His ball of hair has shrunk his face.

"Toodle-oo," Rabbit agrees, with relief in his bowels, and turns his back.

Skeeter declines to go so simply. He steps closer, he smells spicy. He says, "Throw me out. I want you to touch me."

"I don't want to."

"Do it."

"I don't want to fight you."

"I screwed your bitch."

"Her decision."

"And a lousy little cunt she was, too. Like putting your prick in a vise."

"Hear him, Jill?"

"Hey. Rabbit. That's what they used to call you, right? Your mamma's a whore, right? She goes down on old black winos behind the railroad station for fifty cents, right? If they don't have fifty cents she does it free because she likes it, right?"

Remote Mom. The quilty scent of her room, medicine, bed-warmth. Of all those years when she was well he can only remember her big bones bent above the kitchen table with its four worn places; she is not sitting down, she has already eaten, she is feeding him supper, he has come home from practice late, it is after dark, the windows are glazed from within.

"Your daddy's a queer, right? You must be too to take all this shit. Your wife couldn't stand living with a queer, it was like being balled by a mouse, right? You're a mouse down there, hey, ain't that right, gimme a feel." He reaches and Rabbit bats his hand away. Skeeter dances, delighted. "Nothin' there, right? Hey. Rabbit. Jill says you believe in God. I got news for you. Your God's a pansy. Your white God's queerer than the Queen of Spades. He sucks off the Holy Ghost and makes his son watch. Hey. Chuck. Another thing. Ain't no Jesus. He was a faggot crook, right? They bribed the Romans to get his carcass out of the tomb 'cause it smelled so bad, right?"

"All you're showing me," Rabbit says, "is how crazy you are." But a creeping sweetness, rage, is filling him solid. Sunday school images—a dead man whiter than lilies, the lavender rocks where he was betrayed by a kiss—are being revived in him.

Skeeter dances on, he is wearing big creased Army boots. He bumps Harry's shoulder, tugs the sleeve of his white shirt. "Hey. Wanna know how I know? Wanna know? Hey. I'm the real Jesus. I am *the* black Jesus, right? There is none other, no. When I fart, lightning flashes, right? Angels scoop it up in shovels of zillion-carat gold. Right? Kneel down, Chuck. Worship me. I am Jesus. Kiss my balls—they are the sun and the moon, and my pecker's a comet whose head is the white-hot heart of the glory that never does fail!" And, his head rolling like a puppet's, Skeeter unzips his fly and prepares to display this wonder.

Rabbit's time has come. He is packed so solid with anger and fear he is seeing with his pores. He wades toward the boy deliciously and feels his fists vanish, one in the region of the belly, the other below the throat. He is scared of the head, whose glasses might shatter and slash. Skeeter curls up and drops to the floor dry as a scorpion and when Rabbit pries at him he has no opening, just abrasive angles shaking like a sandpaper machine. Rabbit's hands start to hurt. He wants to pry this creature open because there is a soft spot where he can be split and killed; the curved back is too tough, though knuckles slammed at the hole of the ear do produce a garbled whimper.

Jill is screaming and with her whole weight pulling the tail of his shirt and in the ebb of his sweetness Rabbit discovers his hands and forearms somehow clawed. His enemy is cringing on the floor, the carpet that cost them eleven dollars a yard and was supposed to wear longer than the softer loop for fifteen that Janice wanted (she always said it reminded her of the stuff they use in miniature golf courses), cringing expertly, knees tucked under chin and hands over head and head tucked under the sofa as far as it will go. His Levis are rumpled up and it shocks Rabbit to see how skinny his calves and ankles are, iridescent dark spindles. Humans made of a new material. Last longer, wear more evenly. And Jill is sobbing, "Harry, no more, no more," and the door chime is saying its three syllables over and over, a scale that can't get anywhere, that can't get over the top.

The door pops open. Nelson is there, in his spiffy new school clothes, fishbone-striped sport shirt and canary-yellow slacks. Billy Fosnacht is behind him, a hairy head taller. "Hey," Skeeter says from the floor, "it's Babychuck, right?"

"Is he a burglar, Dad?"

"We could hear the furniture being smashed and everything," Billy says. "We didn't know what to do."

Nelson says, "We thought if we kept ringing the bell it would stop."

Jill tells him, "Your father lost all control of himself."

Rabbit asks, "Why should I always be the one to have control of myself?"

Getting up as if from a bin of dust, one careful limb at a time, Skeeter says, "That was to get us acquainted, Chuck. Next time I'll have a gun."

Rabbit taunts, "I thought at least I'd see some nice karate chops from basic training."

"Afraid to use 'em. Break you in two, right?"

"Daddy, who is he?"

"He's a friend of Jill's called Skeeter. He's going to stay here a couple days."

"He is?"

Jill's voice has asked.

Rabbit sifts himself for the reason. Small scraped places smart on his knuckles; overstimulation has left a residue of nausea; he notices through the haze that still softly rotates around him that the end table was upset and that the lamp whose base is driftwood lies on the carpet awry but not smashed. The patient fidelity of these things bewilders him. "Sure," he says. "Why not?"

Skeeter studies him from the sofa, where he sits bent over, nursing the punch to his stomach. "Feeling guilty, huh Chuck? A little tokenism to wash your sins away, right?"

"Skeeter, he's being generous," Jill scolds.

"Get one thing straight, Chuck. No gratitude. Anything you do, do for selfish reasons."

"Right. The kicks I get in pounding you around." But in fact he is terrified at having taken this man in. He will have to sleep with him in the house. The tint of night, Skeeter will sneak to his side with a knife shining like the moon. He will get the gun as he has promised. FUGITIVE FROM JUSTICE HOLDS FAMILY AT GUNPOINT. *Mayor Vows, No Deals.* Why has he invited this danger? To get Janice to rescue him. These thoughts flit by in a flash. Nelson has taken a step toward the black man. His eyes are sunk in their sockets with seriousness. Wait, wait. He is poison, he is murder, he is black.

"Hi," Nelson says, and holds out his hand.

Skeeter puts his skinny fingers, four gray crayons, as thick at the tips as in the middle, in the child's hand and says, "Hi there, Babychuck." He nods over Nelson's shoulder toward Billy Fosnacht. "Who's your gruesome friend?"

And everybody, everybody laughs, even Billy, even Skeeter contributes a cackle, at this unexpected illumination, that Billy *is* gruesome, with his father's skinny neck and big ears and a hint of his mother's mooncalf eyes and the livid festerings of adolescence speckling his cheeks and chin. Their laughter makes a second wave to reassure him they are not laughing at him, they are laughing in relief at the gift of truth, they are rejoicing in brotherhood, at having shared this moment, giggling and cackling; the house is an egg cracking because they are all hatching together.

But in bed, the house dark and Billy gone home, Skeeter breathing exhausted on the sofa downstairs, Rabbit repeats his question to Jill: "Why have you done this to me?"

Jill snuffles, turns over. She is so much lighter than he, she irresistibly rolls down to his side. Often in the morning he wakes to find himself nearly pushed from the bed by this inequality, her sharp little elbows denting his flesh. "He was so pathetic," she explains. "He talks tough but he really has nothing, he really does want to become the black Jesus."

"Is that why you let him screw you this afternoon? Or didn't you?"

"I didn't really."

"He lied?"

Silence. She slides an inch deeper into his side of the bed. "I don't think it counts when you just let somebody do it to you and don't do anything back."

"You don't."

"No, it just happens on the surface, a million miles away."

"And how about with me? Is it the same way, you don't feel anything, it's so far away. So you're really a virgin, aren't you?"

"Shh. Whisper. No, I do feel things with you."

"What?"

She nudges closer and her arm encircles his thick waist. "I feel you're a funny big teddy bear my Daddy has given me. He used to bring home these extravagant Steiff toys from F.A.O. Schwarz's in New York, giraffes six feet high that cost five hundred dollars, you couldn't do anything with them, they'd just stand around taking up space. Mother hated them."

"Thanks a lot." Sluggishly he rolls over to face her.

"Other times, when you're over me, I feel you're an angel. Piercing me with a sword. I feel you're about to announce something, the end of the world, and you say nothing, just pierce me. It's beautiful."

"Do you love me?"

"Please, Harry. Since that God thing I went through I just can't focus that way on anybody."

"Is Skeeter out of focus for you too?"

"He's horrible. He really is. He feels all scaly, he's so bitter."

"Then why in holy hell—?"

She kisses him to stop his voice. "Shh. He'll hear." Sounds travel freely down the stairs, through the house of thin partitions. The rooms are quadrants of one rustling heart. "Because I must, Harry. Because whatever men ask of me, I must give, I'm not interested in holding anything for myself. It all melts together anyway, you see."

"I don't see."

"I think you do. Otherwise why did you let him stay? You had him beaten. You were killing him."

"Yeah, that was nice. I thought I was out of shape worse than I am."

"Yet now he's here." She flattens her body against his; it feels transparent. He can see through her to the blue window beyond, moonlit, giving onto the garage roof, composition shingling manufactured with a strange shadow-line, to give an illusion of thickness. She confesses, in such a whisper it may be only a thought he overhears, "He frightens me."

"Me too."

"Half of me wanted you to kick him out. More than half."

"Well," and he smiles unseen, "if he is the next Jesus, we got to keep on His good side." Her body broadens as if smiling. It has grown plain that the betrayals and excitements of the day must resolve into their making love now. He encloses her skull in his hands, caressing the spinelike ridges behind the sea-shell curve of her ears, palming the broad curve of the whole, this cup, sealed upon a spirit. Knowing her love is coming, he sees very clearly, as we see in the etched hour before snow. He amends, "Also, Janice has been doing some things out of the way, so I have to do things out of the way."

"To pay her back."

"To keep up with her."

The item was narrow-measure:

Sentenced for Possession

Eight local men and one woman were given six-month sentences for possession of marijuana Thursday.

The defendants appearing before Judge Milton F. Schoffer had been apprehended in a police raid on Jimbo's Lounge, Weiser Street, early in the morning of August 24.

The female among them, Miss Beatrice Greene, a well-known local entertainer under her nom de plume of "Babe," had her

sentence suspended, with one
year's probation, as were four
of the men. Two minors were
remanded to juvenile court.

A tenth defendant, Hubert H.
Farnsworth, failed to appear in
court and forfieted bail. A war-
court and forfeited bail. A war-
ant has been issued for his arrest.
ant has been issued for his
arrest.

The proprietor of Jimbo's,
Mr. Timothy Cartney of Penn

Rabbit's ears can sense now when Pajasek is coming up behind him with a phone call. Something weary and menacing in his step, and then his breath has a sarcastic caress. "Angstrom, maybe we should move your Lino into my office. Or install a phone jack out here."

"I'll give her hell, Ed. This is the last time."

"I don't like a man's private life to interfere with his work."

"I don't either. I tell you, I'll tell her."

"Do that, Harry. Do that for good old Verity. We have a team here, we're in a highly competitive game, let's keep up our end, what do you say?"

Behind the frosted walls he says into the phone, "Janice, this is the last time. I won't come to the phone after this."

"I won't be calling you after this, Harry. After this all our communications will be through lawyers."

"How come?"

"How come? How *come*!"

"How come. Come on. Just give me information. I got to get back to the machine."

"Well, for one reason how come, you've let me sit over here without ever once calling me back, and for another you've taken a darkie into the house along with that hippie, you're in*cred*ible, Harry, my mother always said it, 'He means no harm, he just has less moral sense than a skunk,' and she was right."

"He's just there a couple days, it's a funny kind of emergency."

"It must be funny. It must be hilarious. Does your mother know? So help me, I have a mind to call and tell her."

"Who told you, anyway? He never goes out of the house."

He hopes by his reasonable tone to bring hers down; she does unwind a notch. "Peggy Fosnacht. She said Billy came home absolutely bug-eyed. He said the man was on the living-room floor and the first thing he said was to insult Billy."

"It wasn't meant as an insult, it was meant to be pleasant."

"Well I wish *I* could be pleasant. I wish it very much. I've seen a lawyer and we're filing a writ for immediate custody of Nelson. The divorce will follow. As the guilty party you can't remarry for two years. Absolutely, Harry. I'm sorry. I thought we were more mature than this, I *hated* the lawyer, the whole thing is too ugly."

"Yeah, well, the law is. It serves a ruling elite. More power to the people."

"I think you've lost your mind. I honestly do."

"Hey, what did you mean, I let you sit over there? I thought that was what you wanted. Isn't Stavros still doing the sitting with you?"

"You might at least have fought a *little*," she cries, and gasps for breath between sobs. "You're so weak, you're so wishy-washy," she manages to bring out, but then it becomes pure animal sound, a kind of cooing or wheezing, as if all the air is running out of her, so he says, "We'll talk later, call me at home," and hangs up to plug the leak.

> Park, expressed shock and strong disapproval of drug use over the telephone to VAT inquiries.
>
> Cartney was not in the building at the time of the arrests.
>
> Rumors have prevailed for some time concerning the sale of this well-known nightspot and gathering place to a "black capitalist" syndicate.

During the coffee break Buchanan comes over. Rabbit touches his wallet, wondering if the touch will go up. Escalation. Foreign aid. Welfare. He'll refuse if it does. If he asks more than twenty, let them riot in the streets. But Buchanan holds out two ten dollar bills, not the same two, but just as good. "Friend Harry," he says, "never let it be said no black man pays his debts. I'm obliged to you a thousand and one times over, them two sawbucks turned the cards right around. Would you believe two natural full houses in a row? I couldn't believe it myself, nobody could, those fools all stayed the second time like there was no tomorrow." He wads the money into Rabbit's hand, which is slow to close.

"Thanks, uh, Lester. I didn't really—"

"Expect to get it back?"

"Not so soon."

"Well, sometimes one man's in need, sometimes another man is. Spread it around, isn't that what the great ones teach us?"

"I guess they do. I haven't talked to many great ones lately."

Buchanan chuckles politely and rocks back and forth on his heels, estimating, rolling a toothpick in his lips, beneath the mustache no thicker than a toothpick. "I hear tell you're so hard up over at your place you're taking in boarders."

"Oh. That. It's just temporary, it wasn't my idea."

"I believe that."

"Uh—I'd rather it didn't get around."

"That's just what I'd rather."

Change the subject, somehow. "How's Babe now? Back in business?"

"What kind of business you think she's in?"

"You know, singing. I meant after the bust and court sentence. I just set the news item."

"I know what you meant. I know exactly. Come on down to Jimbo's, any night of the week, get better acquainted. Babe's estimation of you has shot way up, I tell you that. Not that she didn't take a shine in the first place."

"Yeah, O.K., great. Maybe I'll get down sometime. If I can get a babysitter." The idea of ever going into Jimbo's again frightens him, as does the idea of leaving Nelson, Jill, and Skeeter alone in the house. He is sinking into an underworld he used to see only from a bus. Buchanan squeezes his arm.

"We'll set something up," the Negro promises. "Oh, yeass." The hand squeezes tighter, as if pressing fingerprints through the screen of Harry's blue workshirt. "Jer-ome asked me to express an especial gratitude."

Jerome?

The yellow-faced clock ticks, the end-of-break buzzer rasps. The last to return to his machine, Farnsworth passes between the brightly lit makeup tables, a man so black he twinkles. He bobs his shaved head, wipes the whisky from his lips, and throws Harry a dazzling grin. Brothers in paternity.

He gets off the bus early, on the other side of the bridge, and walks along the river through the old brick neighborhoods burdened with great green highway signs. Peggy Fosnacht's buzzer buzzes back and when he gets off the elevator she is at the door in a shapeless blue bathrobe. "Oh, *you*," she says. "I thought it would be Billy having lost his key again."

"You alone?"

"Yes, but Harry, he'll be back from school any minute."

"I only need a minute." She leads him in, pulling her bathrobe tighter about her body. He tries to wrap his errand in a little courtesy. "How've you been?"

"I'm managing. How have you been?"

"Managing. Just."

"Would you like a drink?"

"This early in the day?"

"I'm having one."

"No, Peggy, thanks. I can only stay a minute. I got to see what's cooking back at the ranch."

"Quite a lot, I hear."

"That's what I wanted to say something about."

"Please sit down. I'm getting a crick in my neck." Peggy takes a sparkling glass of beaded fluid from the sill of the window that overlooks Brewer, a swamp of brick sunk at the foot of its mountain basking westward in the sun. She sips, and her eyes slide by on either side of his head. "You're offended by my drinking. I just got out of the bathtub. That's often how I spend my afternoons, after spending the morning with the lawyers or walking the streets looking for a job. Everybody wants younger secretaries. They must wonder why I keep my sunglasses on. I come back and take off all my clothes and get into the tub and ever so slowly put a drink inside me and watch the steam melt the ice cubes."

"It sounds nice. What I wanted to say—"

She is standing by the window with one hip pushed out; the belt of her bathrobe is loose and, though she is a shadow against the bright colorless sky, he can feel with his eyes as if with his tongue the hollow between her breasts that would still be dewy from her bath.

She prompts, "What you wanted to say—"

"Was to ask you a favor: could you kind of keep it quiet about the Negro staying with us that Billy saw? Janice called me today and I guess you've already told her, that's O.K. if you could stop it there, I don't want everybody to know. Don't tell Ollie, if you haven't already, I mean. There's a legal angle or I wouldn't bother." He lifts his hands helplessly; it wasn't worth saying, now that he's said it.

Peggy steps toward him, stabbingly, too much liquor or trying to keep the hip out seductively or just the way she sees, two of everything, and tells him, "She must be an awfully good lay, to get you to do this for her."

"The girl? No, actually, she and I aren't usually on the same wavelength."

She brushes back her hair with an approximate flicking motion that lifts the bathrobe lapel and exposes one breast; she is drunk. "Try another wavelength."

"Yeah, I'd love to, but right now, the fact is, I'm running too scared to take on anything else, and anyway Billy's about to come home."

"Sometimes he hangs around Burger Bliss for hours. Ollie thinks he's getting bad habits."

"Yeah, how *is* old Ollie? You and he getting together at all?"

She lets her hand down from her hair; the lapel covers her again. "Sometimes he comes by and fucks me, but it doesn't seem to bring us any closer."

"Probably it does, he just doesn't express it. He's too embarrassed at having hurt you."

"That's how *you* would be, but Ollie isn't like that. It would never enter his head to feel guilty. It's the artist in him, you know he really can play almost any instrument he picks up. But he's a cold little bastard."

"Yeah, I'm kind of cold too." He has stood in alarm, since she has come closer another clumsy step.

Peggy says, "Give me your hands." Her eyes fork upon him, around him. Her face unchanging, she reaches down and lifts his hands from his sides and holds them to her chest. "They're warm." He thinks, *Cold heart.* She inserts his left hand into her bathrobe and presses it around a breast. He thinks of spilling guts, of a cow's stomach tumbling out; elastically she overflows his fingers, her nipple a clot, a gumdrop stuck to his palm. Her eyes are closed—veins in her lids, crow's feet at the corners —and she is intoning, "You're not cold, you're warm, you're a warm man, Harry, a good man. You've been hurt and I want you to heal, I want to help you heal, do whatever you want with me." She is talking as if to herself, rapidly, softly, but has brought him so close he hears it all; her breath beats at the base of his throat. Her heartbeat is sticking to his palm. The skin of her brow is vexed and the piece of her body her bathrobe discloses is lumpy and strange, blind like the brow of an ox, but eased by liquor she has slid into that state where the body of the other is her own body, the body of secretive self-love that the mirror we fill and the bed we warm alone give us back; and he is enclosed in this body of love of hers and against all thought and wish he thickens all over tenderly and the one-eyed rising beneath his waist begins.

He protests "I'm not good" but is also sliding; he relaxes the hand that is holding her breast to give it air to sway in.

She insists "You're good, you're lovely" and fumbles at his fly; with the free hand he pulls aside the lapel of the bathrobe so the other breast is free and the bathrobe belt falls unknotted.

An elevator door sucks shut in the hall. Footsteps swell toward their door. They spring apart; Peggy wraps the robe around herself again. He keeps on his retinas the afterimage of a ferny triangle, broader than his palm, beneath a belly whiter than crystal, with silvery stretch-marks. The footsteps pass on by. The would-be lovers sigh with relief, but the spell has been broken. Peggy turns her back, reknots her belt. "You're keeping in touch with Janice," she says.

"Not really."

"How did you know I told her about the black?"

Funny, everybody else has no trouble saying "black." Or hating the war. Rabbit must be defective. Lobotomy. A pit opens where guilt gnaws, at the edge of his bladder. He must hurry home. "She called me to say a lawyer was starting divorce proceedings."

"Does that upset you?"

"I guess. Sort of. Sure."

"I suppose I'm dumb, I just never understood why you put up with Janice. She was never enough for you, never. I love Janice, but she is about the most childish, least sensitive woman I've ever known."

"You sound like my mother."

"Is that bad?" She whirls around; her hair floats. He has never seen Peggy so suddenly soft, so womanly frontal. Even her eyes he could take. In play, mocking the pressure of Billy impending at his back, he rubs the back of his hand across her nipples. Nibs and Dots.

"Maybe you're right. We should try out our wavelengths."

Peggy flushes, backs off, looks stony, as if an unexpected mirror has shown her herself too harshly. She pulls the blue terrycloth around her so tight her shoulders huddle. "If you want to take me out to dinner some night," she says, "I'm around," adding irritably, "but don't count your chickens."

Hurry, hurry. The 12 bus takes forever to come, the walk down Emberly is endless. Yet his house, third from the end of Vista Crescent, low and new and a sullen apple-green on the quarter-acre of lawn scraggly with plantain, is intact, and all around it the unpopulated stretches of similar houses hold unbroken the intensity of duplication. That the blot of black inside his house is unmirrored fools him into hoping it isn't there. But, once up the three porch steps and through the door of three stepped windows, Rabbit sees, to his right, in the living room, from behind—the sofa having been swung around —a bushy black sphere between Jill's cone of strawberry gold and Nelson's square-cut mass of Janice-dark hair. They are watching television. Skeeter seems to have reinstated the box. The announcer, ghostly pale because the adjustment is too bright and mouthing as rapidly as a vampire because there is too much news between too many commercials, enunciates, ". . . after a five-year exile spent in Communist Cuba, various African states, and Communist China, landed in Detroit today and was instantly taken into custody by waiting FBI men. Elsewhere on the racial front, the U.S. Commission on Civil Rights sharply charged that the Nixon Administration has made quote a major retreat unquote pertaining to school integration in the southern states. In Fayette Mississippi three white Klansmen were arrested for the attempted bombing of the supermarket owned by newly elected black mayor of Fayette, Charles Evers, brother of the slain civil rights leader. In New York City Episcopal spokesmen declined to defend further their controversial decision to grant two hundred thousand dollars toward black church leader James Forman's demand of five hundred million dollars in quote reparations unquote from the Christian churches in America for quote three centuries of indignity and exploitation unquote. In Hartford Connecticut and Camden New Jersey an uneasy peace prevails after last week's disturbances within the black communities of these cities. And now, an important announcement."

"Hello, hello," Rabbit says, ignored.

Nelson turns and says, "Hey Dad. Robert Williams is back in this country."

"Who the hell is Robert Williams?"

Skeeter says, "Chuck baby, he's a man going to fry your ass."

"Another black Jesus. How many of you are there?"

"By many false prophets," Skeeter tells him, "you shall know my coming, right? That's the Good Book, right?"

"It also says He's come and gone."

"Comin' again, Chuck. Gonna fry your ass. You and Nixon's, right?"

"Poor old Nixon, even his own commissions beat on him. What the hell can he do? He can't go into every ghetto and fix the plumbing himself. He can't give every copped-out junkie a million dollars and a Ph.D. Nixon, who's Nixon? He's just a typical flatfooted Chamber of Commerce type who lucked his way into the hot seat and is so dumb he thinks it's good luck. Let the poor bastard alone, he's trying to bore us to death so we won't commit suicide."

"Nixon, shit. That honky was put there by the cracker vote, right? Strom Stormtrooper is his very bag. He is Herod, man, and all us black babies better believe it."

"Black babies, black leaders, Jesus am I sick of the word black. If I said white one-eightieth as often as you say black you'd scream yourself blue. For Chrissake, forget your skin."

"I'll forget it when you forget it, right?"

"Lord I'd love to forget not only your skin but everything inside it. I thought three days ago you said you were getting out in three days."

"Dad, *don't*." The kid's face is tense. Mom was right, too delicate, too nervous. Thinks the world is going to hurt him, so it will. The universal instinct to exterminate the weak.

Jill rises to shield the other two. Three on one: Rabbit is exhilarated. Faking and dodging, he says before she can speak, "Tell the darker of your boyfriends here I thought he promised to pull out when he got a stake. I have twenty bucks here to give him. Which reminds me of something else."

Skeeter interrupts, addressing the air. "I *love* him when he gets like this. He is the Man."

And Jill is saying her piece. "Nelson and I refuse to live with this quarrelling. Tonight after supper we want to have an organized discussion. There's a crying need for education in this household."

"Household," Rabbit says, "I'd call it a refugee camp." He persists in what he has been reminded of. "Hey, Skeeter. Do you have a last name?"

"X," Skeeter tells him. "42X."

"Sure it's not Farnsworth?"

Skeeter's body sheds its shell, hangs there outfeinted a second, before regathering hardness. "That Super Tom," he says definitively, "is not the slightest relation of mine."

"The *Vat* had your last name as Farnsworth."

"The *Vat*," Skeeter pronounces mincingly, "is a Fascist rag."

Having scored, you put your head down and run back up the floor; but with that feeling inside, of having made a mark that can't be rubbed out. "Just wondering," Rabbit smiles. He stretches out his arms as if from wall to wall. "Who wants a beer besides me?"

After supper, Nelson washes the dishes and Skeeter dries. Jill tidies up the living room for their discussion; Rabbit helps her swing the sofa back into place. On the shelves between the living room and the breakfast nook that he and Janice had kept empty Rabbit notices now a stack of tired paperbacks, their spines chafed and biased by handling. *The Selected Writings of W. E. B. Du Bois, The Wretched of the Earth, Soul on Ice, Life and*

Times of Frederick Douglass, others, history, Marx, economics, stuff that makes Rabbit feel sick, as when he thinks about what surgeons do, or all the plumbing and gas lines there are under the street. "Skeeter's books," Jill explains. "I went into Jimbo's today for them, and his clothes. Babe had them."

"Hey Chuck," Skeeter calls from the sink, through the shelves, "know where I got those books? Over in Nam, at the Longbinh base bookstore. They love us to read, that crazy Army of yours. Teach us how to read, shoot, dig pot, sniff scag, black man's best friend, just like they say!" He snaps his towel, *pap!*

Rabbit ignores him and asks Jill, "You went in there? It's full of police, they could easy tail you."

Skeeter shouts from the kitchen, "Don't you worry Chuck, those poor pigs've bigger niggers than me to fry. You know what happened over in York, right? Brewer's gone to make that look like the Ladies Aid ball!" *Pap!*

Nelson washing beside him asks, "Will they shoot every white person?"

"Just the big old ugly ones, mostly. You stay away from that gruesome Billy and stick next to me, Babychuck, you'll be all right."

Rabbit pulls down a book at random and reads,

> Government is for the people's progress and not for the comfort of an aristocracy. The object of industry is the welfare of the workers and not the wealth of the owners. The object of civilization is the cultural progress of the mass of workers and not merely of an intellectual elite.

It frightens him, as museums used to frighten him, when it was part of school to take trips there and to see the mummy rotting in his casket of gold, the elephant tusk filed into a hundred squinting Chinamen. Unthinkably distant lives, abysses of existence, worse than what crawls blind on ocean floors. The book is full of Skeeter's underlinings. He reads,

> Awake, awake, put on thy strength, O Zion! Reject the weakness of missionaries who teach neither love nor brotherhood, but chiefly the virtues of private profit from capital, stolen from your land and labor. Africa, awake! Put on the beautiful robes of Pan-African socialism.

Rabbit replaces the book feeling better. There are no such robes. It is all crap. "What's the discussion about?" he asks, as they settle around the cobbler's bench.

Jill says nervously, blushing, "Skeeter and Nelson and I were talking about it today after school and agreed that since there seems to be such a painful communications problem—"

"Is that what it is?" Rabbit asks. "Maybe we communicate too well."

"—a structured discussion might be helpful and educational."

"Me being the one who needs to be educated," Rabbit says.

"Not necessarily." The care with which Jill speaks makes Rabbit feel pity; *we are too much for her*, he thinks. "You're older than we are and we respect your experience. We all agree, I think, that your problem is that you've never been given a chance to formulate your views. Because of the competitive American context, you've had to convert everything into action too rapidly. Your life has no reflective content; it's all instinct, and when your instincts let you down, you have nothing to trust. That's what makes you cynical. Cynicism, I've seen it said somewhere, is tired pragmatism. Pragmatism suited a certain moment here, the frontier moment; it did the work, very wastefully and ruthlessly, but it did it."

"On behalf of Daniel Boone," Rabbit says, "I thank you."

"It's wrong," Jill goes on gently, "when you say Americans are exploiters, to forget that the first things they exploit are themselves. You," she says, lifting her face, her eyes and freckles and nostrils a constellation, "you've never given yourself a chance to think, except on techniques, basketball and printing, that served a self-exploitative purpose. You carry an old God with you, and an angry old patriotism. And now an old wife." He takes breath to protest, but her hand begs him to let her finish. "You accept these things as sacred not out of love or faith but fear; your thought is frozen because the first moment when your instincts failed, you raced to the conclusion that everything is nothing, that zero is the real answer. That is what we Americans think, it's win or lose, all or nothing, kill or die, because we've never created the leisure in which to take thought. But now, you see, we must, because action is no longer enough, action without thought is violence. As we see in Vietnam."

He at last can speak. "There was violence in Vietnam before we ever heard of the fucking place. You can see by just the way I'm sitting here listening to this crap I'm a pacifist basically." He points at Skeeter. "*He's* the violent son of a bitch."

"But you *see*," Jill says, her voice lulling and nagging, with just a teasing ragged hem showing of the voice she uses in bed, "the reason Skeeter annoys and frightens you is you don't know a thing about his history, I don't mean his personal history so much as the history of his race, how he got to where he is. Things that threaten you like riots and welfare have jumped into the newspapers out of nowhere for you. So for tonight we thought we would just talk a little, have a kind of seminar, about Afro-American history."

"Please, Dad," Nelson says.

"Jesus. O.K. Hit me. We were beastly to the slaves so why do so few American Negroes want to give up their Cadillacs and, excuse the expression, colored televisions and go back to Africa?"

"Dad, *don't*."

Skeeter begins. "Let's forget the slavery, Chuck. It was forever ago, everybody used to do it, it was a country kind of thing, right? Though I must say, the more it began to smell like shit, the more you crackers rolled around in it, right?"

"We had more country."

"Easy, sit back. No arguments, right? You had cotton come along, right? Anybody but black folks die working those cotton swamps, right? Anyhoo, you had this war. You had these crazies up North like Garrison and Brown agitating and down South a bunch of supercrackers like Yancy and Rhett who thought they could fatten their own pie by splitting, funny thing is"— he chuckles, wheezes, Rabbit pictures him with a shaved head and sees Farnsworth—"they didn't, the Confederacy sent 'em away on a ship and elected all play-it-safes to office! Same up North with cats like Sumner. Come to the vote, people scared of the man with the idea, right? Do you know, suppose you don't, dude called Ruffin, bright as could be, invented modern agriculture or next thing to it, hated the Yankees so much he pulled the string on the first cannon at Sumter and shot himself in the head when the South lost? Wild men. Beautiful, right? So any*hoo*, Lincoln got this war, right, and fought it for a bunch of wrong reasons—what's so sacred about a *Union*, just a power trust, right?—and for another wrong reason freed the slaves, and it was done. God bless America, right? So here I begin to get mad."

"Get mad, Skeeter," Rabbit says. "Who wants a beer?"

"Me, Dad."

"Half a one."

Jill says, "I'll split it with him."

Skeeter says, "That stuff rots the soul. Mind if I burn some good Red?"

"It's not legal."

"Right. But everybody does it. All those swish cats over in Penn Park, you think they have a Martini when they come home at night? That's yesterday. They blow grass. Sincerely, it is more in than chewing gum. Over in Nam, it was the fighting boy's candy."

"O.K. Light up. I guess we've gone this far."

"There is far to go," Skeeter says, rolling his joint, from a rubber pouch he produces from within the sofa, where he sleeps, and thin yellow paper, licking it rapidly with that fat pale tongue, and twisting the ends. When he lights it, the twisted end flames. He sucks in hungrily, holds it in as if about to dive very deep, and then releases the sweet used smoke with a belch. He offers the wet end to Rabbit. "Try?"

Rabbit shakes his head, watching Nelson. The kid's eyes are bird-bright, watching Skeeter. Maybe Janice is right, he's letting the kid see too much. Still, he didn't do the leaving. And life is life, God invented it, not him. But he looks at Nelson fearful that his presence in the room will be construed as a blessing. He says to Skeeter, "Get on with your song. Lincoln won the war for the wrong reasons."

"And then he was shot, right?" Skeeter passes the joint to Jill. As she takes it her eyes ask Rabbit, *Is this what you want?* She holds it the way the experts do, not like a tobacco cigarette, something for Fred Astaire to gesture with, but reverently as food, with as many fingers as she can get around it, feeding the wet end to herself like a nipple. Her thin face goes peaceful, puts on the fat of dreams. Skeeter is saying, "So then you had these four million freed slaves without property or jobs in this economy dead on its feet thinking the halleluiah days had

come. Green pastures, right? Forty acres and a mule, right?
Goddam green pickles, Chuck, that was the most pathetic
thing, the way those poor niggers jumped for the bait. They
taught themselves to read, they broke their backs for chicken-
shit, they sent good men to the fuckhead Yoo Ess Senate, they
set up legislatures giving Dixie the first public schools it ever
had, how about that now, there's a fact for your eddi-cayshun,
right? Jill honey, hand that stick back, you gonna blow yourself to the moon, that is uncut Red. And all this here while,
Chuck and Babychuck, the crackers down there were frothing
at the mouth and calling our black heroes baboons. Couldn't
do much else as long as the Northern armies hung around,
right? Baboons, monkeys, apes: these hopeful sweet blacks trying to make men of themselves, thinking they'd been called
to be men at last in these the Benighted States of Amurrika."
Skeeter's face is shedding its shell of scorn and writhing as if
to cry. He has taken his glasses off. He is reaching toward Jill
for the marijuana cigarette, keeping his eyes on Rabbit's face.
Rabbit is frozen, his mind racing. Nelson. Put him to bed.
Seeing too much. His own face as he listens to Skeeter feels
weak, shapeless, slipping. The beer tastes bad, of malt. Skeeter
wants to cry, to yell. He is sitting on the edge of the sofa and
making gestures so brittle his arms might snap off. He is crazy.
"So what did the South do? They said baboon and lynched
and whipped and cheated the black man of what pennies he
had and thanked their white Jesus they didn't have to feed
him anymore. And what did the North do? It copped out. It
pulled out. It had put on all that muscle for the war and now it
was wading into the biggest happiest muck of greed and graft
and exploitation and pollution and slum-building and Indian-
killing this poor old whore of a planet has ever been saddled
with, right? Don't go sleepy on me Chuck, here comes the
interesting part. The Southern assholes got together with the
Northern assholes and said, Let's us do a deal. What's all this
about democracy, let's have here a dollar-cracy. Why'd we ever
care, free versus slave? Capital versus labor, that's where it's at,
right? This poor cunt of a country's the biggest jampot's ever
come along so let's eat it, friend. You screw your black labor
and we'll screw our immigrant honky and Mongolian idiot labor and, *whoo-hee!* Halleluiah, right? So the Freedman's Bureau

was trashed and the military governors were chased back by crackers on horses who were very big on cutting up colored girls with babies inside 'em and Tilden was cheated out of the Presidency in the one bony-fidey swindle election you can find admitted in every honky history book. Look it up, right? And that was the revolution of 1876. Far as the black man goes, that's the '76 that hurt, the one a hundred years before was just a bunch of English gents dodging taxes." Skeeter has put his glasses back on; the glass circles glitter behind a blueness of smoke. His voice has settled for irony again. "So let's all sing America the Beautiful, right? North and West, robber barons and slums. Down South, one big nigger barbecue. Hitler bless his sweet soul leastways tried to keep the ovens out of sight. Down Dixieway, every magnolia had a rope. Man, they passed laws if a nigger sneezed within three miles of a white ass his balls were chewed off by sawtoothed beagles. Some nigger didn't hop off the sidewalk and lick up the tobacco juice whenever the town trash spit, he was tucked into a chain gang and peddled to the sheriff's brother-in-law cheaper than an alligator egg. And if he dared ask for the vote the Fifteenth Amendment had flat-out given him, why, they couldn't think up ways to skin him slowly enough, they couldn't invent enough laws to express their dis-approbation, better for a poor black man to go stick his head up Great-aunt Lily's snatch than try to stick it in a polling booth. Right? Chuck, I got to hand it to you, you had it all ways. The South got slavery back at half the price, it got control of Congress back by counting the black votes that couldn't be cast, the North got the cotton money it needed for capital, and everybody got the fun of shitting on the black man and then holding their noses. You believe any of this?"

"I believe all of it," Rabbit says.

"Do you believe, do you believe I'm so mad just telling this if I had a knife right now I'd poke it down your throat and watch you gargle your life away and would love it, oh, would I love it." Skeeter is weeping. Tears and smoke mix on the skin of his face.

"O.K., O.K.," Rabbit says.

"Skeeter, don't cry," Nelson says.

"Skeeter, it was too rich, I'm going to lose it," Jill says and stands. "I'm dizzy."

But Skeeter will talk only to Harry. "What I want to say to you," he says, "what I want to make ever so clear, Chuck, is you had that chance. You could have gone some better road, right? You took that greedy turn, right? You sold us out, right? You sold yourselves out. Like Lincoln said, you paid in blood, sword for the lash and all that, and you didn't lift us up, we held out our hands, man, we were like faithful dogs waiting for that bone, but you gave us a kick, you put us down, you put us down."

"Skeeter, please don't ever give me any more of that whatever it was, ever, ever," Jill says, drifting away.

Skeeter controls his crying, lifts his face darkened in streaks like ashes wetted down. "It wasn't just us, you sold yourselves out, right? You really had it here, you had it all, and you took that greedy mucky road, man, you made yourself the asshole of the planet. Right? To keep that capitalist thing rolling you let those asshole crackers have their way and now you's all asshole crackers, North and South however you look there's assholes, you lapped up the poison and now it shows, Chuck, you say America to you and you still get bugles and stars but say it to any black or yellow man and you get hate, right? Man the world does hate you, you're the big pig keeping it all down." He jabs blearily with his skinny finger, and hangs his head.

From upstairs, discreet as the noise a cat makes catching a bird, comes a squeezed heaving noise, Jill being sick.

Nelson asks, "Dad, shouldn't you call a doctor?"

"She'll be O.K. Go to bed. You have school tomorrow."

Skeeter looks at Rabbit; his eyeballs are fiery and rheumy. "I said it, right?"

"Trouble with your line," Rabbit tells him, "it's pure self-pity. The real question is, Where do you go from here? We all got here on a bad boat. You talk as if the whole purpose of this country since the start has been to frustrate Negroes. Hell, you're just ten per cent. The fact is most people don't give a damn *what* you do. This is the freest country around, make it if you can, if you can't, die gracefully. But Jesus, stop begging for a free ride."

"Friend, you are wrong. You are white but wrong. We fascinate you, white man. We are in your dreams. We are technology's nightmare. We are all the good satisfied nature you put down in yourselves when you took that mucky greedy turn. We are what has been left *out* of the industrial revolution, so we are the *next* revolution, and don't you know it? You know it. Why else you so scared of me, Rabbit?"

"Because you're a spook with six loose screws. I'm going to bed."

Skeeter rolls his head loosely, touches it dubiously. In the light from the driftwood lamp his round mass of hair is seen as insubstantial, his skull narrow as the bone handle of a knife. He brushes at his forehead as if midges are there. He says, "Sweet dreams. I'm too spaced to sleep right now, I got just to sit here, nursing the miseries. Mind if I play the radio if I keep it low?"

"No."

Upstairs, Jill, a sudden warm wisp in his arms, begs with rapid breath, "Get him out of here, Harry, don't let him stay, he's no good for me, no good for any of us."

"You brought him here." He takes her talk as the exaggerating that children do, to erase their fears by spelling them out; and indeed in five minutes she is dead asleep, motionless. The electric clock burns beyond her head like a small moon's skeleton. Downstairs, a turned-down radio faintly scratches. And shortly Rabbit too is asleep. Strangely, he sleeps soundly, with Skeeter in the house.

"Harry, how about a quick one?" His father tells the bartender, as always, "Let's make it a Schlitz."

"Whisky sour," he says. Summer is over, the air-conditioning in the Phoenix has been turned off. He asks, "How's Mom doing?"

"As good as can be hoped, Harry." He nudges a conspiratorial inch closer. "That new stuff really seems to do the job, she's on her feet for hours at a time now. For my money, though, the sixty-four-thousand-dollar question is what the long-range effects will be. The doctor, he's perfectly honest about it. He says to her when we go on in to the hospital, 'How's my favorite guinea pig?'"

"What's the answer?" Rabbit abruptly asks.

His father is startled. "Her answer?"

"Anybody's."

His father now understands the question and shrugs his narrow shoulders in his faded blue shirt. "Blind faith," he suggests. In a mutter he adds, "One more bastard under the ground."

On the television above the bar men are filing past a casket, but the sound is turned off and Rabbit cannot tell if it is Everett Dirksen's funeral service in Washington, or Ho Chi Minh's ceremonies in Hanoi. Dignitaries look alike, always dressed in mourning. His father clears his throat, breaks the silence. "Janice called your mother last night."

"Boy, I think she's cracking up, she's on the phone all the time. Stavros must be losing his muscle."

"She was very disturbed, she said you'd taken a colored man into your house."

"I didn't exactly take him, he kind of showed up. Nobody's supposed to know about it. I think he's Farnsworth's son."

"That can't be, Jerry's never married to my knowledge."

"They don't marry generally, right? They weren't allowed to as slaves."

This bit of historical information makes Earl Angstrom grimace. He takes, what for him, with his boy, is a tough line. "I must say, Harry, I'm not too happy about it either."

The funeral (the flag on the coffin has stars and stripes, so it must be Dirksen's) vanishes, and flickering in its place are shots of cannons blasting, of trucks moving through the desert, of planes soundlessly batting through the sky, of soldiers waving. He cannot tell if they are Israeli or Egyptian. He asks, "How happy is Mom about it?"

"I must say, she was very short with Janice. Suggested if she wanted to run your household she go back to it. Said she had no right to complain. I don't know what all else. I couldn't bear to listen; when women get to quarrelling, I head for the hills."

"Janice talk about lawyers?"

"Your mother didn't mention it if she did. Between you and me, Harry, she was so upset it scared me. I don't believe she slept more than two, three hours; she took twice the dose of Seconal and still it couldn't knock her out. She's worried and, pardon my crust for horning in where I have no business, Harry, so am I."

"Worried about what?"

"Worried about this new development. I'm no nigger-hater,

I'm happy to work with 'em and I have for twenty years, if needs be I'll live next to 'em though the fact is they haven't cracked Mt. Judge yet, but get any closer than that, you're playing with fire, in my experience."

"What experience?"

"They'll let you down," Pop says. "They don't have any feeling of obligation. I'm not blaming a soul, but that's the fact, they'll let you down and laugh about it afterwards. They're not ethical like white men and there's no use saying they are. You asked me what experience, I don't want to go into stories, though there's plenty I could tell, just remember I was raised in the Third Ward back when it was more white than black, we mixed it up in every sense. I know the people of this county. They're good-natured people. They like to eat and drink and like to have their red-light district and their numbers, they'll elect the scum to political office time and time again; but they don't like seeing their women desecrated."

"Who's being desecrated?"

"Just that menagerie over there, the way you're keeping it, is a desecration. Have you heard from your neighbors what they think about it yet?"

"I don't even know my neighbors."

"That black boy shows his face outside, you'll get to know them; you'll get to know them as sure as I'm sitting here trying to be a friend and not a father. The day when I could whip sense into you is long by, Harry, and anyway you gave us a lot less trouble than Mim. Your mother always says you let people push you around and I always answer her, Harry knows his way around, he lands on his feet; but I'm beginning to see she may be right. Your mother may be all crippled up but she's still hard to fool, ask the man who's tried."

"When did you try?"

But this secret—had Pop played Mom false?—stays dammed behind those loose false teeth the old man's mouth keeps adjusting, pensively sucking. Instead he says, "Do us a favor, Harry, I hate like hell to beg, but do us a favor and come over tonight and talk about it. Your mother stiff-armed Janice but I know when she's been shook."

"Not tonight, I can't. Maybe in a couple of days, things'll clear up."

"Why not, Harry? We promise not to grill you or anything, Lord, I wouldn't ask for myself, it's your mother's state of mind. You know"—and he slides so close their shirt sleeves touch and Rabbit smells the sour fog of his father's breath—"she's having the adventure now we're all going to have to have."

"Stop asking, Pop. I can't right now."

"They've gotcha in their clutches, huh?"

He stands straight, decides one whisky sour will do, and answers, "Right."

That night after supper they discuss slavery. Jill and Skeeter have done the dishes together, Rabbit has helped Nelson with his homework. The kid is into algebra this year but can't quite manage that little flip in his head whereby a polynomial cracks open into two nice equalities of *x*, one minus and one plus. Rabbit had been good at math, it was a game with limits, with orderly movements and a promise of completion at the end. The combination always cracked open. Nelson is tight about it, afraid to let go and swing, a smart kid but tight, afraid of maybe that thing that got his baby sister: afraid it might come back for him. They have half an hour before *Laugh-In*, which they all want to watch. Tonight Skeeter takes the big brown chair and Rabbit the one with silver threads. Jill and Nelson sit on the airfoam sofa. Skeeter has some books; they look childishly bright under his thin brown hands. School days. *Sesame Street*.

Skeeter says to Rabbit, "Chuck, I been thinking I sold out the truth last night when I said your slavery was a country thing. The fact upon reflection appears to be that your style of slavery was uniquely and e-specially bad, about the worst indeed this poor blood-soaked globe has ever seen." Skeeter's voice as he speaks exerts a steady pressure, wind rattling a dead tree. His eyes never deviate to Nelson or Jill.

Rabbit, a game student (in high school he used to get B's), asks, "What was so bad about it?"

"Let me guess what you think. You think it wasn't so bad on the plantations, right? What with banjos and all the fritters you could eat and Ol' Massah up at the big house instead of the Department of Welfare, right? Those niggers were savages anyway, their chuckleheads pure bone, and if they didn't like it, well, why didn't they just up and die in their chains like the noble old redman, right?"

"Yeah. Why didn't they?"

"I love that question. Because I have the answer. The reason is, old Tonto was so primitive farmwork made no sense to him, he was on the moon, right?, and just withered away. Now the black man, he was from West Africa, where they had agriculture. Where they had social organization. How do you think those slaves got to the coast from a thousand miles away? Black men arranged it, they wouldn't cut the white men in, they kept the pie all for themselves. Organization men, right?"

"That's interesting."

"I'm glad you said that. I am grateful for your interest."

"He meant it," Jill intercedes.

"Swallow your tongue," Skeeter says without looking toward her.

"Swallow your tongue yourself," Nelson intervenes. Rabbit would be proud of the boy, but he feels that Nelson's defense of Jill, like Skeeter's attack, are automatic: parts of a pattern the three have developed while he is away working.

"The readings," Jill prompts.

Skeeter explains. "Little Jilly and I, today, been talking, and her idea is, to make cosy nights all together more structured, right? We'd read aloud a few things, otherwise I'm apt to do all the talking, that is until you decide to dump me on the floor again."

"Let me get a beer then."

"Puts pimples on your belly, man. Let me light up some good Tijuana brass and pass it over, old athlete like you shouldn't be getting a beer gut, right?"

Rabbit neither agrees nor moves. He glances at Nelson: the kid's eyes are sunk and shiny, frightened but not to the point of panic. He is learning; he trusts them. He frowns over to stop his father looking at him. Around them the furniture—the fireplace that never holds a fire, the driftwood base like a corpse lying propped on one arm—listens. A quiet rain has begun at the windows, sealing them in. Skeeter holds his lips pinched to seal into himself the first volumes of sweet smoke, then exhales, sighing, and leans back into the chair, vanishing between the brown wings but for the glass-and-silver circles of his spectacles. He says, "He was property, right? From Virginia on, it was profit and capital absolutely. The King of England, all he cared about was tobacco cash, right? Black men just blots on the balance sheet to him. Now the King of Spain, he knew black men from way back; those Moors had run his country and some had been pretty smart. So south of the border a slave was property but he was also other things. King of Spain say, That's my subject, he has legal rights, right? Church say, That's an everlasting immortal soul there: baptize him. Teach him right from wrong. His marriage vows are sacred, right? If he rustles up the bread to buy himself free, you got to sell. This was all written in the law down there. Up here, the law said one thing: no rights. No rights. This is no man, this is one warm piece of animal meat, worth one thousand Yoo Hess Hay coldblooded clams. Can't let it marry, that might mess up selling it when the market is right. Can't let it go and testify in court, that might mess up Whitey's property rights. There was no such thing, *no* such, believe me, as the father of a slave child. That was a legal fact. Now how could the law get that way? Because they did believe a nigger was a piece of shit. And they was scared of their own shit. Man, those crackers were sick and they knew it absolutely. All those years talkin' about happy Rastus chompin' on watermelon they was scared shitless of uprisings, *up*risings, Chuck, when there hadn't been more than two or three the whole hundred years and those not amounted to a bucket of piss. They was scared rigid, right? Scared of blacks learning to read, scared of blacks learning a trade, scared of blacks on the job market, there was no place for a freedman to go, once he *was* freed, all that talk about free soil, the first thing the free-soil convention in Kansas said was we don't want no black faces here, keep 'em away from our eyeballs. The thing about these Benighted States all around is that it was never no place like other places where this happens because that happens, and some men have more luck than others so let's push a little here and give a little here; no, sir, this place was never such a place it was a *dream*, it was a state of mind from those poor fool pilgrims on, right? Some white man see a black man he don't see a man he sees a *symbol*, right? All these people around here are walking around inside their own *heads*, they don't even know if you kick somebody else it *hurts*, Jesus won't even tell 'em because the Jesus they brought over on the boats was the meanest most de-balled Jesus the good Lord ever let run around scaring people. Scared, *scared*. I'm scared of you, you scared of me, Nelson scared of us both, and poor Jilly here so scared of everything she'll run and hide herself in dope again if we don't all act like big daddies to her." He offers the smoking wet-licked reefer around. Rabbit shakes his head no.

"Skeeter," Jill says, "the selections." A prim clubwoman calling the meeting to order. "Thirteen minutes to *Laugh-In*," Nelson says. "I don't want to miss the beginning, it's neat when they introduce themselves."

"Ree-ight," Skeeter says, fumbling at his forehead, at that buzzing that seems sometimes there. "Out of this book here." The book is called *Slavery*; the letters are red, white, and blue. It seems a small carnival under Skeeter's slim hand. "Just for the fun of it, to give us something more solid than my ignorant badmouthing, right? You know, like a happening. Chuck, this gives you pretty much a pain in the ass, right?"

"No, I like it. I like learning stuff. I have an open mind."

"He turns me on, he's so true to life," Skeeter says, handing the book to Jill. "Baby, you begin. Where my finger is, just the part in little type." He announces, "These are old-time speeches, dig?"

Jill sits up straight on the sofa and reads in a voice higher than her natural voice, a nice-girl-school-schooled voice, with riding lessons in it, and airy big white-curtained rooms; territory even higher in the scale than Penn Park.

"*Think*," she reads, "*of the nation's deed, done continually and afresh. God shall hear the voice of your brother's blood, long crying from the ground; His justice asks you even now, 'America, where is thy brother?' This is the answer which America must give: 'Lo, he is there in the rice-swamps of the South, in her fields teeming with cotton and the luxuriant cane. He was weak and I seized him; naked and I bound him; ignorant, poor and savage, and I over-mastered him. I laid on his feebler shoulders my grievous yoke. I have chained him with my fetters; beat him with my whip. Other tyrants had dominion over him, but my finger was on his human flesh. I am fed with his toil; fat, voluptuous on his sweat, and tears, and blood. I stole the father, stole also the sons, and set them to toil; his wife and daughters are a pleasant spoil to me. Behold the children also of thy servant and his handmaidens —sons swarthier than their sire. Askest thou for the African? I have made him a beast. Lo, there Thou hast what is thine."* She hands the book back blushing. Her glance at Rabbit says, *Bear with us. Haven't I loved you?*

Skeeter is cackling. "Green pickles, that turns me on. A pleasant spoil to me, right? And did you dig that beautiful bit about the sons swarthier than their sire? Those old Yankee sticks were really bugged, one respectable fuck would have stopped the abolition movement cold. But they weren't getting it back home in the barn so they sure gave hell to those crackers getting it out in the slave shed. Dark meat is soul meat, right? That was Theodore Parker, here's another, the meanest mouth in the crowd, old William Lloyd. Nellie, you try this. Just where I've marked. Just read the words slow, don't try for any expression."

Gaudy book in hand, the boy looks toward his father for rescue. "I feel stupid."

Rabbit says, "Read, Nelson. I want to hear it."

He turns for help elsewhere. "Skeeter, you promised I wouldn't have to."

"I said we'd see how it *went*. Come on, your daddy likes it. He has an open mind."

"You're just poking fun of everybody."

"Let him off," Rabbit says. "I'm losing interest."

Jill intervenes. "Do it, Nelson, it'll be fun. We won't turn on *Laugh-In* until you do."

The boy plunges in, stumbling, frowning so hard his father wonders if he doesn't need glasses. "*No matter*," he reads, "*though every party should be torn by dis-*, dis—"

Jill looks over his shoulder. "Dissensions."

"*—every sest—*"

"Sect."

"*—every sect dashed into fragments, the national compact dissolved—*"

Jill says, "Good!"

"Let him ride," Skeeter says, his eyes shut, nodding.

Nelson's voice gains confidence. "*—the land filled with the horrors of a civil and a servile war—still, slavery must be buried in the grave of infantry—*"

"Infamy," Jill corrects.

"—*in-fa-my, beyond the possibility of a rez, a razor*—"

"A resurrection."

"*If the State cannot survive the anti-slavery agitation, then let the State perish. If the Church must be cast down by the strugglings of Humanity, then let the Church fall, and its fragments be scattered to the four winds of heaven, never more to curse the earth. If the American Union cannot be maintained, except by immolating*—what's that?"

"Sacrificing," Jill says.

Rabbit says, "I thought it meant burn."

Nelson looks up, uncertain he should continue.

The rain continues at the windows, gently, gently nailing them in, tighter together.

Skeeter's eyes are still closed. "Finish up. Do the last sentence, Babychuck."

"*If the Republic must be blotted out from the roll of nations, by proclaiming liberty to the captives, then let the Republic sink beneath the waves of oblivion, and a shout of joy, louder than the voice of many waters, fill the universe at its extinction.* I don't understand what any of this stuff means."

Skeeter says, "It means, More Power to the People, Death to the Fascist Pigs."

Rabbit says, "To me it means, Throw the baby out with the bath." He remembers a tub of still water, a kind of dust on its dead surface. He relives the shock of reaching down through it to pull the plug. He loops back into the room where they are sitting now, within the rain.

Jill is explaining to Nelson, "He's saying what Skeeter says. If the System, even if it works for most people, has to oppress some of the people, then the whole System should be destroyed."

"Do I say that? No." Skeeter leans forward from the mossy brown wings, reaching a trembling thin hand toward the young people, all parody shaken from his voice. "That'll come anyway. That big boom. It's not the poor blacks setting the bombs, it's the offspring of the white rich. It's not injustice pounding at the door, it's impatience. Put enough rats in a cage the fat ones get more frantic than the skinny ones 'cause they feel more *squeezed*. No. We must look past that, past the violence, into the next stage. That it's gonna blow up we can as*sume*. That's not interesting. What comes next is what's interesting. There's got to be a great *calm*."

"And you're the black Jesus going to bring it in," Rabbit mocks. "From A.D. to A.S. After Skeeter. I should live so long. All Praise Be Skeeter's Name."

He offers to sing but Skeeter is concentrating on the other two, disciples. "People talk revolution all the time but revolution's not interesting, right? Revolution is just one crowd taking power from another and that's bullshit, that's just power, and power is just guns and gangsters, and that's boring bullshit, right? People say to me Free Huey, I say Screw Huey, he's just Agnew in blackface. World forgets gangsters like that before they're dead. No. The problem is really, when the gangsters have knocked each other off, and taken half of everybody else with them, to make use of the *space*. After the Civil War ended, there was space, only they let it fill up with that same old greedy muck, only worse, right? They turned that old dog-eat-dog thing into a divine law."

"That's what we need, Skeeter," Rabbit says. "Some new divine laws. Why doncha go up to the top of Mt. Judge and have 'em handed to you on a tablet?"

Skeeter turns that nicely carved knife-handle of a face to him slowly, says slowly, "I'm no threat to you, Chuck. You're *set*. Only thing I could do to you is kill you and that matters less than you think, right?"

Jill delicately offers to make peace. "Didn't we pick out something for Harry to read?"

"Fuck it," Skeeter says. "That won't swing now. He's giving off ugly vibes, right? He's not ready. He is immature."

Rabbit is hurt, he had only been kidding. "Come on, I'm ready, give me my thing to read."

Skeeter asks Nelson, "What say, Babychuck? Think he's ready?"

Nelson says, "You must read it right, Dad. No poking fun."

"Me? Who'd I ever poke fun of?"

"Mom. All the time you poke fun of Mom. No wonder she left you."

Skeeter gives Harry the book open to a page. "Just a little bit. Just read where I've marked."

Soft red crayon. Those Crayola boxes that used to remind

him of bleachers with every head a different color. This strange return. "*I believe, my friends and fellow citizens,*" Rabbit reads solemnly, "*we are not prepared for this suffrage. But we can learn. Give a man tools and let him commence to use them, and in time he will learn a trade. So it is with voting. We may not understand it at the start, but in time we shall learn to do our duty.*"

The rain makes soft applause.

Skeeter tips his narrow head and smiles at the two children on the sofa. "Makes a pretty good nigger, don't he?"

Nelson says, "Don't, Skeeter. He didn't poke fun so you shouldn't."

"Nothing wrong with what I said, that's what the world needs, pretty good niggers, right?"

To show Nelson how tough he is, Rabbit tells Skeeter, "This is all bleeding-heart stuff. It'd be like me bellyaching that the Swedes were pushed around by the Finns in the year Zilch."

Nelson cries, "We're missing *Laugh-In*!"

They turn it on. The cold small star expands, a torrent of stripes snaps into a picture, Sammy Davis Jr. is being the little dirty old man, tapping along behind the park bench, humming that aimless sad doodling tune. He perks up, seeing there is someone sitting on the bench. It is not Ruth Buzzi but Arte Johnson, the white, the real little dirty old man. They sit side by side and stare at each other. They are like one man looking into a crazy mirror. Nelson laughs. They all laugh: Nelson, Jill, Rabbit, Skeeter. Kindly the rain fastens them in, a dressmaker patting and stitching all around the house, fitting its great wide gown.

Nights with Skeeter, they blend together. Skeeter asks him, "You want to know how a Ne-gro feels?"

"Not much."

"Dad, don't," Nelson says.

Jill, silent, abstracted, passes Rabbit the joint. He takes a tentative puff. Has hardly held a cigarette in ten years, scared to inhale. Nearly sick after the other time, in Jimbo's. You suck and hold it down. Hold it down.

"Ee-magine," Skeeter is saying, "being in a glass box, and

every time you move toward something, your head gets
bumped. Ee-magine being on a bus, and everybody movin'
away, 'cause your whole body's covered with pustulatin' scabs,
and they're scared to get the disease."

Rabbit exhales, lets it out. "That's not how it is. These black
kids on buses are pushy as hell."

"You've set so much type the world is lead, right? You don't
hate nobody, right?"

"Nobody." Serenely. Space is transparent.

"How you feel about those Penn Park people?"

"Which ones?"

"All those ones. All those ones live in those great big piecrust
mock-Two-door houses with His and Hers Caddies parked out
by the hydrangea bushes. How about all those old farts down
at the Mifflin Club with all those iron gates that used to own
the textile mills and now don't own anything but a heap of paper keeps 'em in cigars and girlfriends? How about those? Let
'em settle in before you answer."

Rabbit pictures Penn Park, the timbered gables, the stucco,
the weedless lawns plumped up like pillows. It was on a hill.
He used to imagine it on the top of a hill, a hill he could never
climb, because it wasn't a real hill like Mt. Judge. And he and
Mom and Pop and Mim lived near the foot of this hill, in the
dark next to the Bolgers, and Pop came home from work every
day too tired to play catch in the back yard, and Mom never
had jewelry like other women, and they bought day-old bread
because it was a penny cheaper, and Pop's teeth hurt to keep
money out of the dentist's hands, and now Mom's dying was
a game being played by doctors who drove Caddies and had
homes in Penn Park. "I hate them," he tells Skeeter.

The black man's face lights up, shines. "Deeper."

Rabbit fears the feeling will be fragile and vanish if he looks
at it but it does not; it expands, explodes. Timbered gables,
driveway pebbles, golf clubs fill the sky with debris. He remembers one doctor. He met him early this summer by accident,
coming up on the porch to visit Mom, the doctor hurrying
out, under the fanlight that sees everything, in a swank cream
raincoat though it had just started to sprinkle, that kind of

dude, who produces a raincoat from nowhere when proper, all set up, life licked, tweed trousers knife-sharp over polished strapped shoes, hurrying to his next appointment, anxious to get away from this drizzling tilted street. Pop worrying his teeth like an old woman in the doorway, performing introductions, "our son Harry," pathetic pride. The doctor's irritation at being halted even a second setting a prong of distaste on his upper lip behind the clipped mustache the color of iron. His handshake also metal, arrogant, it pinches Harry's unready hand and says, *I am strong, I twist bodies to my will. I am life, I am death.* "I hate those Penn Park motherfuckers," Harry amplifies, performing for Skeeter, wanting to please him. "If I could push the red button to blow them all to Kingdom Come"—he pushes a button in mid-air—"I would." He pushes the button so hard he can see it there.

"Ka-boom, right?" Skeeter grins, flinging wide his sticklike arms.

"But it is," Rabbit says. "Everybody knows black pussy is beautiful. It's on posters even, now."

Skeeter asks, "How you think all this mammy shit got started? Who you think put all those hog-fat churchified old women at the age of thirty in Harlem?"

"Not me."

"It *was* you. Man, you is just who it was. From those breeding cabins on you made the black girl feel sex was shit, so she hid from it as quick as she could in the mammy bit, right?"

"Well, tell 'em it's not shit."

"They don't believe me, Chuck. They see I don't count. I have no muscle, right? I can't protect my black women, right? 'Cause you don't let me be a man."

"Go ahead. Be one."

Skeeter gets up from the armchair with the silver threads and circles the imitation cobbler's bench with a wary hunchbacked quickness and kisses Jill where she sits on the sofa. Her hands, after a startled jerk, knit together and stay in her lap. Her head does not pull back nor strain forward. Rabbit cannot see, around the eclipsing orb of Skeeter's Afro, Jill's eyes. He can see Nelson's eyes. They are warm watery holes so dark, so stricken that Rabbit would like to stick pins into them, to teach the child there is worse. Skeeter straightens from kissing, wipes the Jill-spit from his mouth. "A pleasant spoil. Chuck, how do you like it?"

"I don't mind. If she doesn't."

Jill has closed her eyes, her mouth open on a small bubble.

"She *does* mind it," Nelson protests. "Dad, don't *let* him!"

Rabbit says to Nelson, "Bedtime, isn't it?"

Physically, Skeeter fascinates Rabbit. The lustrous pallor of the tongue and palms and the soles of the feet, left out of the sun. Or a different kind of skin? White palms never tan either. The peculiar glinting luster of his skin. The something so very finely turned and finished in the face, reflecting light at a dozen polished points: in comparison white faces are blobs: putty still drying. The curious greased grace of his gestures, rapid and watchful as a lizard's motions, free of mammalian fat. Skeeter in his house feels like a finely made electric toy; Harry wants to touch him but is afraid he will get a shock.

"O.K.?"

"Not especially." Jill's voice seems to come from further away than beside him in the bed.

"Why not?"

"I'm scared."

"Of what? Of me?"

"Of you and him together."

"We're not together. We hate each other's guts."

She asks, "When are you kicking him out?"

"They'll put him in jail."

"Good."

The rain is heavy above them, beating everywhere, inserting itself in that chimney flashing that always leaked. He pictures a wide brown stain on the bedroom ceiling. He asks, "What's with you and him?"

She doesn't answer. Her lean cameo profile is lit by a flash. Seconds pass before the thunder arrives.

He asks shyly, "He getting at you?"

"Not that way anymore. He says that's not interesting. He wants me another way now."

"What way can that be?" Poor girl, crazy suspicious.

"He wants me to tell him about God. He says he's going to bring some mesc for me."

The thunder follows the next flash more closely.

"That's crazy." But exciting: maybe she can do it. Maybe he can get music out of her like Babe out of the piano.

"He is crazy," Jill says. "I'll never be hooked again."

"What can I do?" Rabbit feels paralyzed, by the rain, the thunder, by his curiosity, by his hope for a break in the combination, for catastrophe and deliverance.

The girl cries out but thunder comes just then and he has to ask her to repeat it. "All you care about is your *wife*," she shouts upward into the confusion in heaven.

Pajasek comes up behind him and mumbles about the phone. Rabbit drags himself up. Worse than a liquor hangover, must stop, every night. Must get a grip on himself. Get a grip. Get angry. "Janice, for Chrissake—"

"It isn't Janice, Harry. It's me. Peggy."

"Oh. Hi. How's tricks? How's Ollie?"

"Forget Ollie, don't ever mention his name to me. He hasn't been to see Billy in weeks or contributed *any*thing to his keep, and when he finally does show up, you know what he brings? He's a genius, you'll never guess."

"Another mini-bike."

"A puppy. He brought us a Golden Retriever puppy. Now what the hell can we do with a puppy with Billy off in school and me gone from eight to five every day?"

"You got a job. Congratulations. What do you do?"

"I type tape for Brewer Fealty over at Youngquist, they're putting all their records on computer tape and not only is the work so boring you could scream, you don't even know when you've made a mistake, it comes out just holes in this tape, all these premium numbers."

"It sounds nifty. Peggy, speaking of work, they don't appreciate my being called here."

Her voice retreats, puts on dignity. "Pardon *me*. I wanted

to talk to you when Nelson wasn't around. Ollie has promised
Billy to take him fishing next Sunday, not *this* Sunday, and I
wondered, since it doesn't look as if you'll ever ask me, if you'd
like to have dinner Saturday when you bring him over."

Her open bathrobe, that pubic patch, the silver stretchmarks,
don't count your chickens. Meaning do count your chickens.
"That might be great," he says.

"Might be."

"I'll have to see, I'm kind of tied up these days—"

"Hasn't that man gone yet? Kick him out, Harry. He's taking incredible advantage of you. Call the police if he won't go.
Really, Harry, you're much too passive."

"Yeah. Or something." Only after shutting the office door
behind him and starting to walk through the solid brightness
toward his machine does he feel last night's marijuana clutch
at him, drag at his knees like a tide. Never again. Let Jesus find
him another way.

"Tell us about Vietnam, Skeeter." The grass is mixing with
his veins and he feels very close, very close to them all: the
driftwood lamp, Nelson's thatch of hair an anxious tangle,
Jill's bare legs a touch unshaped at the ankles. He loves them.
All. His voice moves in and out behind their eyes. Skeeter's
eyes roll red toward the ceiling. Things are pouring for him
through the ceiling.

"Why you want to be told?" he asks.

"Because I wasn't there."

"Think you should have been there, right?"

"Yes."

"Why would that be?"

"I don't know. Duty. Guilt."

"No sir. You want to have been there because that is where
it was at, right?"

"O.K."

"It was the best place," Skeeter says, not quite as a question.

"Something like that."

Skeeter goes on, gently urging, "It was where you would
have felt not so de-balled, right?"

"I don't know. If you don't want to talk about it, don't. Let's turn on television."

"*Mod Squad* will be on," Nelson says.

Skeeter explains: "If you can't fuck, dirty pictures won't do it for you, right? And then if you can, they don't do it either."

"O.K., don't tell us anything. And try to watch your language in front of Nelson."

At night when Jill turns herself to him in bed he finds the unripe hardness of her young body repels him. The smoke inside him severs his desires from his groin, he is full of flitting desires that prevent him from directly answering her woman's call, a call he helped create in her girl's body. Yet in his mind he sees her mouth defiled by Skeeter's kiss and feels her rotting with his luminous poison. Nor can he forgive her for having been rich. Yet through these nightly denials, these quiet debasements, he feels something unnatural strengthening within him that may be love. On her side she seems, more and more, to cling to him; they have come far from that night when she went down on him like a little girl bobbing for apples.

This fall Nelson has discovered soccer; the junior high school has a team and his small size is no handicap. Afternoons Harry comes home to find the child kicking the ball, sewn of black-and-white pentagons, again and again against the garage door, beneath the unused basketball backboard. The ball bounces by Nelson, Harry picks it up, it feels bizarrely seamed in his hands. He tries a shot at the basket. It misses clean. "The touch is gone," he says. "It's a funny feeling," he tells his son, "when you get old. The brain sends out the order and the body looks the other way."

Nelson resumes kicking the ball, vehemently, with the side of his foot, against a spot on the door already worn paintless. The boy has mastered that trick of trapping the ball to a dead stop under his knees.

"Where are the other two?"

"Inside. Acting funny."

"How funny?"

"You know. The way they act. Dopey. Skeeter's asleep on the sofa. Hey, Dad."

"What?"

Nelson kicks the ball once, twice, hard as he can, until it gets by him and he has worked up nerve to tell. "I hate the kids around here."

"What kids? I never see any. When I was a kid, we were all over the streets."

"They watch television and go to Little League and stuff."

"Why do you hate them?"

Nelson has retrieved the ball and is shuffling it from one foot to the other, his feet clever as hands. "Tommy Frankhauser said we had a nigger living with us and said his father said it was ruining the neighborhood and we'd better watch out."

"What'd you say to that?"

"I said he better watch out himself."

"Did you fight?"

"I wanted to but he's a head taller than me even though we're in the same grade and he just laughed."

"Don't worry about it, you'll shoot up. All us Angstroms are late bloomers."

"I hate them, Dad, I *hate* them!" And he heads the ball so it bounces off the shadow-line shingles of the garage roof.

"Mustn't hate anybody," Harry says, and goes in.

Jill is in the kitchen, crying over a pan of lamb chops. "The flame keeps getting too big," she says. She has the gas turned down so low the little nipples of blue are sputtering. He turns it higher and Jill screams, falls against him, presses her face into his chest, peeks up with eyes amusement has dyed deep green. "You smell of ink," she tells him. "You're all ink, so clean, just like a new newspaper. Every day, a new newspaper comes to the door."

He holds her close; her tears tingle through his shirt. "Has Skeeter been feeding you anything?"

"No, Daddy. I mean lover. We stayed in the house all day and watched the quizzes, Skeeter hates the way they always have Negro couples on now, he says it's tokenism."

He smells her breath and, as she has promised, there is nothing, no liquor, no grass, just a savor of innocence, a faint tinge of sugar, a glimpse of a porch swing and a beaded pitcher. "Tea," he says.

"What an elegant little nose," she says, of his, and pinches it. "That's right. Skeeter and I had iced tea this afternoon." She keeps caressing him, rubbing against him, making him sad. "You're elegant all over," she says. "You're an enormous snowman, twinkling all over, except you don't have a carrot for a nose, you have it here."

"Hey," he says, hopping backwards.

Jill tells him urgently, "I like you there better than Skeeter, I think being circumcised makes men ugly."

"Can you make the supper? Maybe you should go up and lie down."

"I hate you when you're so uptight," she tells him, but without hate, in a voice swinging as a child wandering home swings a basket, "can I cook the supper, I can do anything, I can fly, I can make men satisfied, I can drive a white car, I can count in French up to any number; look!"—she pulls her dress way up above her waist—"I'm a Christmas tree!"

But the supper comes to the table badly cooked. The lamb chops are rubbery and blue near the bone, the beans crunch underdone in the mouth. Skeeter pushes his plate away. "I can't eat this crud. I ain't that primitive, right?"

Nelson says, "It tastes all right, Jill."

But Jill knows, and bows her thin face. Tears fall onto her plate. Strange tears, less signs of grief than chemical condensations: tears she puts forth as a lilac puts forth buds. Skeeter keeps teasing her. "Look at me, woman. Hey you cunt, look me in the eye. What do you see?"

"I see you. All sprinkled with sugar."

"You see Him, right?"

"Wrong."

"Look over at those drapes, honey. Those ugly home-made drapes where they sort of blend into the wallpaper."

"He's not there, Skeeter."

"Look at me. *Look.*"

They all look. Since coming to live with them, Skeeter has aged; his goatee has grown bushy, his skin has taken on a captive's taut glaze. He is not wearing his glasses tonight.

"Skeeter, He's not there."

"Keep looking at me, cunt. What do you see?"

"I see—a chrysalis of mud. I see a black crab. I just thought, an angel is like an insect, they have six legs. Isn't that true? Isn't that what you want me to say?"

Skeeter tells them about Vietnam. He tilts his head back as if the ceiling is a movie screen. He wants to do it justice but is scared to let it back in. "It was where it was coming to an end," he lets out slowly. "There was no roofs to stay under, you stood out in the rain like a beast, you slept in holes in the ground with the roots poking through, and, you know, you could do it. You didn't die of it. That was interesting. It was like you learned there was life on another world. In the middle of a recon action, a little old gook in one of them hats would come out and try to sell you a chicken. There were these little girls pretty as dolls selling you smack along the road in those little cans the press photogs would throw away, right? It was very complicated, there isn't any net"—he lifts his hand—"to grab it all in."

Colored fragments pour down toward him through the hole in the ceiling. Green machines, an ugly green, eating ugly green bushes. Red mud pressed in patterns to an ooze by Amtrac treads. The emerald of rice paddies, each plant set there with its reflection in the water pure as a monogram. The color of human ears a guy from another company had drying under his belt like withered apricots, yellow. The black of the *ao dai* pajamas the delicate little whores wore, so figurine-fine he couldn't believe he could touch them though this clammy guy in a white suit kept pushing, saying, "Black GI, number one, most big pricks, Viet girls like suck." The red, not of blood, but of the Ace of Diamonds a guy in his company wore in his helmet for luck. All that luck-junk: peace-signs of melted lead, love beads, beads spelling LOVE, JESUS, MOTHER, BURY ME DEEP, Ho Chi Minh sandals cut from rubber tires for tiny feet, Tao crosses, Christian crosses, the cross-shaped bombs the Phantoms dropped on the trail up ahead, the X's your laces wore into your boots over the days, the shiny green body bags tied like long mail sacks, sun on red dust, on blue smoke, sun caught in shafts between the canopies of the jungle where dinks with Russian rifles waited quieter than orchids, it all tumbles down on him, he is overwhelmed. He knows he can never make it intelligible to these three ofays that worlds do exist beyond these paper walls.

"Just the sounds," Skeeter says. "When one of them Unfriendly mortar shells hits near your hole it is as if a wall were there that was big and solid, twenty feet thick of noise, and you is just a gushy bug. Feet up there just as soon step on you as not, it doesn't matter to them, right? It does blow your mind. And the dead, the dead are so weird, they are so—*dead*. Like a stiff chewed mouse the cat fetches up on the lawn. I mean, they are so out of it, so peaceful, there is no word for it, this same grunt last night he was telling you about his girl back in Oshkosh, making it so real you had to jack off, and the VC trip a Claymore and his legs go this way and he goes the other. It was bad. They used to say, 'A world of hurt,' and that is what it was."

Nelson asks, "What's a grunt?"

"A grunt is a leg. An eleven bush, right? He is an ordinary drafted soldier who carries a rifle and humps the boonies. The green machine is very clever. They put the draftees out in the bush to get blown and the re-ups sit back at Longbinh tellin' reporters the body count. They put old Charlie Company on some bad hills, but they didn't get me to re-up. I'd had a bushel, right?"

"I thought I was Charlie," Rabbit says.

"I thought the Viet Cong was," Nelson says.

"You are, they are, so was I, everybody is. I was Company C for Charlie, Second Battalion, 28th Infantry, First Division. We messed around all up and down the Dongnai River." Skeeter looks at the blank ceiling and thinks, I'm not doing it, I'm not doing it justice, I'm selling it short. The holy quality is hardest to get. "The thing about Charlie is," he says, "he's everywhere. In Nam, it's all Charlies, right? Every gook's a Charlie, it got so you didn't mind greasing an old lady, a little kid, they might be the ones planted punji stakes at night, they might not, it didn't matter. A lot of things didn't matter. Nam must be the only place in Uncle Sam's world where black-white doesn't matter. Truly. I had white boys die for me. The Army treats a black man truly swell, black body can stop a bullet as well as any other, they put us right up there, and don't think we're not grateful, we are indeed, we hustle to stop those bullets, we're so happy to die alongside Whitey." The white ceiling still is blank, but beginning to buzz, beginning to bend into space; he must let the spirit keep lifting him along these lines. "One boy I remember, *hate* the way you make me bring it back, I'd give one ball to forget this, hit in the dark, VC mortars had been working us over since sunset, we never should have been in that valley, lying there in the dark with his guts spilled out. I couldn't see him, hustling my ass back from the perimeter, I stepped on his insides, felt like stepping on a piece of Jell-O, worse, he screamed out and died right then, he hadn't been dead to then. Another time, four of us out on recon, bunch of their AK-47s opened up, had an entirely different sound from the M-16, more of a cracking sound, dig?, not so punky. We were pinned down. Boy with us, white boy from Tennessee, never shaved in his life and ignorant as Moses, slithered away into the bush and wiped 'em out, when we picked him up bullets had cut him in two, impossible for a man to keep firing like that. It was bad. I wouldn't have believed you could see such bad things and keep your eyeballs. These poor unfriendlies, they'd call in the napalm on 'em just up ahead, silver cans tumbling over and over, and they'd come out of the bush right at you, burning and shooting, spitting bullets and burning like a torch in some parade, come tumbling right into your hole with you, they figured the only place to get away from the napalm was inside our perimeter. You'd shoot 'em to shut off their noise. Little boys with faces like the shoeshine back at base. It got so killing didn't feel so bad, it never felt *good*, just necessary, like taking a piss. Right?"

"I don't much want to hear any more," Nelson says. "It makes me feel sick and we're missing *Samantha*."

Jill tells him, "You must let Skeeter tell it if he wants to. It's good for Skeeter to tell it."

"It happened, Nelson," Rabbit tells him. "If it didn't happen, I wouldn't want you to be bothered with it. But it happened, so we got to take it in. We all got to deal with it somehow."

*

"Schlitz."

"I don't know. I feel lousy. A ginger ale."

"Harry, you're not yourself. How's it going? D'ya hear anything from Janice?"

"Nothing, thank God. How's Mom?"

The old man nudges closer, as if to confide an obscenity. "Frankly, she's better than a month ago anybody would have dared to hope."

Now Skeeter does see something on the ceiling, white on white, but the whites are different and one is pouring out of a hole in the other. "Do you know," he asks, "there are two theories of how the universe was done? One says, there was a Big Bang, just like in the Bible, and we're still riding that, it all came out of nothing all at once, like the Good Book say, right? And the funny thing is, all the evidence backs it up. Now the other, which I prefer, says it only seems that way. Fact is, it says, there is a steady state, and though it is true everything is expanding outwards, it does not thin out to next to nothingness on account of the reason that through strange holes in this nothingness new somethingness comes pouring in from exactly nowhere. Now that to me has the ring of truth."

Rabbit asks, "What does that have to do with Vietnam?"

"It is the local hole. It is where the world is redoing itself. It is the tail of ourselves we are eating. It is the bottom you have to have. It is the well you look into and are frightened by your own face in the dark water down there. It is as they say Number One and Number Ten. It is the end. It is the beginning. It is beautiful, men do beautiful things in that mud. It is where God is pushing through. He's coming, Chuck, and Babychuck, and Ladychuck, let Him in. Pull down, shoot to kill. The sun is burning through. The moon is turning red. The moon is a baby's head bright red between his momma's legs."

Nelson screams and puts his hands over his ears. "I *hate* this, Skeeter. You're scaring me. I don't want God to come, I want Him to stay where He is. I want to grow up like *him*"—his father, Harry, the room's big man—"average and ordinary. I *hate* what you say about the war, it doesn't sound beautiful it sounds horrible."

Skeeter's gaze comes down off the ceiling and tries to focus on the boy. "Right," he says. "You still want to live, they still got you. You're still a slave. Let go. Let go, boy. Don't be a slave. Even *him*, you know, your Daddychuck, is learning. He's learning how to die. He's one slow learner but he takes it a day at a time, right?" He has a mad impulse. He lets it guide him. He goes and kneels before the child where he sits on the sofa beside Jill. Skeeter kneels and says, "Don't keep the Good Lord out, Nellie. One little boy like you put his finger in the dike; take it out. Let it come. Put your hand on my head and promise you won't keep the Good Lord out. Let Him come. Do that for old Skeeter, he's been hurtin' so long."

Nelson puts his hand on Skeeter's orb of hair. His eyes widen, at how far his hand sinks down. He says, "I don't want to hurt you, Skeeter. I don't want anybody to hurt anybody."

"Bless you, boy." Skeeter in his darkness feels blessing flow down through the hand tingling in his hair like sun burning through a cloud. Mustn't mock this child. Softly, stealthily, parting vines of craziness, his heart approaches certainty.

Rabbit's voice explodes. "Shit. It's just a dirty little war that has to be fought. You can't make something religious out of it just because you happened to be there."

Skeeter stands and tries to comprehend this man. "Trouble with you," he sees, "you still cluttered up with common sense. Common sense is bullshit, man. It gets you through the days all right, but it leaves you alone at *night*. It keeps you from *know*ing. You just don't *know*, Chuck. You don't even know that now is all the time there is. What happens to you, is all that happens, right? You are *it*, right? You. Are. It. I've come down" —he points to the ceiling, his finger a brown crayon—"to tell you that, since along these two thousand years somewhere you've done gone and forgotten again, right?"

Rabbit says, "Talk sense. Is our being in Vietnam wrong?"

"Wrong? Man, how can it be wrong when that's the way it is? These poor Benighted States just being themselves, right? Can't stop bein' yourself, somebody has to do it for you, right? Nobody that big around. Uncle Sam wakes up one morning, looks down at his belly, sees he's some cockroach, what can he do? Just keep bein' his cockroach self, is all. Till he gets stepped on. No such shoe right now, right? Just keep doing his cockroach thing. I'm not one of these white lib-er-als like that cracker Fulldull or that Charlie McCarthy a while back gave all the college queers a hard-on, think Vietnam some sort of mistake, we can fix it up once we get the cave men out of office, it is *no* mistake, right, any President comes along falls in love with it, it is lib-er-al-ism's very wang and ding-dong pussy. Those crackers been lickin' their mother's ass so long they forgotten what she looks like frontwards. What is lib-er-alism? Bringin' joy to the world, right? Puttin' enough sugar on dog-eat-dog so it tastes good all over, right? Well now what could be nicer than Vietnam? We is keepin' that coast open. Man, what is we all about if it ain't keepin' things open? How can money and jizz make their way if we don't keep a few cunts like that open? Nam is an act of love, right? Compared to Nam, beatin' Japan was flat-out ugly. We was ugly fuckers then and now we is truly a civilized spot." The ceiling agitates; he feels the gift of tongues descend to him. "We is *the* spot. Few old fools like the late Ho may not know it, we is what the world is begging *for*. Big beat, smack, black cock, big-assed cars and billboards, we is into *it*. Jesus come down, He come down here. These other countries, just bullshit places, right? We got the *ape* shit, right? Bring down Kingdom Come, we'll swamp the world in red-hot real American blue-green ape shit, right?"

"Right," Rabbit says.

Encouraged, Skeeter sees the truth: "Nam," he says, "Nam the spot where our heavenly essence is pustulatin'. Man don't like Vietnam, he don't like America."

"Right," Rabbit says. *"Right."*

The two others, pale freckled faces framed in too much hair, are frightened by this agreement. Jill begs, "Stop. Everything hurts." Skeeter understands. Her skin is peeled, the poor girl is wide open to the stars. This afternoon he got her to drop some mescaline. If she'll eat mesc, she'll snort smack. If she'll snort, she'll shoot. He has her.

Nelson begs, "Let's watch television."

Rabbit asks Skeeter, "How'd you get through your year over there without being hurt?"

These white faces. These holes punched in the perfection of his anger. God is pouring through the white holes of their faces; he cannot stanch the gushing. It gets to his eyes. They had been wicked, when he was a child, to teach him God was a white man. "I *was* hurt," Skeeter says.

BEATITUDES OF SKEETER
(*written down in Jill's confident, rounded, private-school hand, in green felt pen, playfully one night, on a sheet of Nelson's note-book filler*)

> Power is bullshit.
> Love is bullshit.
> Common sense is bullshit.
> Confusion is God's very face.
> Nothing is interesting save eternal sameness.
> There is no salvation, 'cepting through Me.

Also from the same night, some drawings by her, in crayons Nelson found for her; her style was cute, linear, arrested where some sophomore art class had left it, yet the resemblances were clear. Skeeter of course was the spade. Nelson, his dark bangs and side-sheaves exaggerated, the club, on a stem of a neck. Herself, her pale hair crayoned in the same pink as her sharp-chinned face, the heart. And Rabbit, therefore, the diamond. In the center of the diamond, a tiny pink nose. Sleepy small blue eyes with worried eyebrows. An almost invisible mouth, lifted as if to nibble. Around it all, green scribbles she had to identify with an affectionate pointing arrow and a balloon: "in the rough."

One of these afternoons, when Nelson is home from soccer practice and Harry is home from work, they all cram into Jill's Porsche and drive out into the county. Rabbit has to have the front seat; Nelson and Skeeter squeeze into the half-seats behind. Skeeter scuttles blinking from the doorway to the curb and inside the car says, "Man, been so long since I been out in the air, it hurts my lungs." Jill drives urgently, rapidly, with the arrogance of the young; Rabbit keeps slapping his foot on the floor, where there is no brake. Jill's cool profile smiles. Her little foot in a ballet slipper feeds gas halfway through curves, pumps up speed enough just to pinch them past a huge truck

—a raging, belching house on wheels—before another hurtling the other way scissors them into oblivion, on a straight stretch between valleys of red earth and pale corn stubble. The country is beautiful. Fall has lifted that heavy Pennsylvania green, the sky is cleared of the suspended summer milk, the hills edge into shades of amber and flaming orange that in another month will become the locust-husk tint that crackles underfoot in hunting season. A brushfire haze floats in the valleys like fog on a river's skin. Jill stops the car beside a whitewashed fence and an apple tree. They get out into a cloud of the scent of fallen apples, overripe. At their feet apples rot in the long dank grass that banks a trickling ditch, the grass still powerfully green; beyond the fence a meadow has been scraped brown by grazing, but for clumps where burdock fed by cow dung grows high as a man. Nelson picks up an apple and bites on the side away from wormholes. Skeeter protests, "Child, don't put your mouth on that garbage!" Had he never seen a fruit eaten in nature before?

Jill lifts her dress and jumps the ditch to touch one of the rough warm whitewashed slats of the fence and to look between them into the distance, where in the dark shelter of trees a sandstone farmhouse glistens like a sugar cube soaked in tea and the wide gaunt wheel of an old farm wagon, spokes stilled forever, waits beside a rusty upright that must be a pump. She remembers rusty cleats that waited for the prow line of visiting boats on docks in Rhode Island and along the Sound, the whole rusty neglected salt-bleached barnacled look of things built where the sea laps, summer sun on gull-gray wood, docks, sheds, metal creaking with the motion of the water, very distant from this inland overripeness. She says, "Let's go."

And they cram back into the little car, and again there are the trucks, and the gas stations, and the "Dutch" restaurants with neon hex signs, and the wind and the speed of the car drowning out all smells and sounds and thoughts of a possible other world. The open sandstone country south of Brewer, the Amish farms printed on the trimmed fields like magazine covers, becomes the ugly hills and darker valleys north of the city, where the primitive iron industry had its day and where the people built with brick—tall narrow-faced homes with gables and dormers like a buzzard's shoulders, perched on domed lawns behind spiked retaining walls. The soft flowerpot-red of Brewer hardens up here, ten miles to the north, to a red dark like oxblood. Though it is not yet the coal regions, the trees feel darkened by coal dust. Rabbit begins to remember accounts, a series run in the *Vat*, of strange murders, axings and scaldings and stranglings committed in these pinched valleys with their narrow main streets of oxblood churches and banks and Oddfellows' halls, streets that end with, as with a wrung neck, a sharp turn over abandoned railroad tracks into a sunless gorge where a stream the color of tarnished silver is now and then crossed by a damp covered bridge that rattles as it swallows you.

Rabbit and Nelson, Skeeter and Jill, crushed together in the little car, laugh a lot during this drive, laugh at nothing, at the silly expression on the face of a bib-overalled hick as they barrel past, at pigs dignified in their pens, at the names on mailboxes (Hinnershitz, Focht, Schtupnagel), at tractor-riding men so fat nothing less wide than a tractor seat would hold them. They even laugh when the little car, though the gas gauge stands at ½, jerks, struggles, slows, stops as if braked. Jill has time only to bring it to the side of the road, out of traffic. Rabbit gets out to look at the engine; it's in the back, under a tidy slotted hood, a tight machine whose works are not open and tall and transparent as with a Linotype, but are tangled and greasy and closed. The starter churns but the engine will not turn over. The chain of explosions that works by faith is jammed. He leaves the hood up to signal an emergency. Skeeter, crouching down in the back, calls, "Chuck, know what you're doin' with that hood, you're callin' down the fucking fuzz!"

Rabbit tells him, "You better get out of the back. We get hit from behind, you've had it. You too Nelson. Out."

It is the most dangerous type of highway, three-lane. The commuter traffic out from Brewer shudders past in an avalanche of dust and noise and carbon monoxide. No Good Samaritans stop. The Porsche has stalled atop an embankment seeded with that feathery finespun ground-cover the state uses to hold steep soil: crown vetch. Below, swifts are skimming a shorn cornfield. Rabbit and Nelson lean against the fenders and watch the sun, an hour above the horizon, fill the field with stubble-shadows, ridges subtle as those of corduroy. Jill wanders off and gathers a baby bouquet of the tiny daisylike asters that bloom in the fall, on stems so thin they form a cirrus hovering an inch or two above the earth. Jill offers the bouquet to Skeeter, to lure him out. He reaches to bat the flowers from her hand; they scatter and fall in the grit of the roadside. His voice comes muffled from within the Porsche. "You honky cunt, this all a way to turn me in, nothing wrong with this fucking car, right?"

"It won't go," she says; one aster rests on the toe of one ballet slipper. Her face has shed expression.

Skeeter's voice whines and snarls in its metal shell. "Knew I should never come out of that house. Jill honey, I know why. Can't stay off the stuff, right? No will at all, right? Easier than having any will, hand old Skeeter over to the law, hey, right?"

Rabbit asks her, "What's he saying?"

"He's saying he's scared."

Skeeter is shouting, "Get them dumb honkies out of the way, I'm making a run for it. How far down on the other side of that fence?"

Rabbit says, "Smart move, you'll really stick out up here in the boondocks. Talk about a nigger in the woodpile."

"Don't you nigger me, you honky prick. Tell you one thing, you turn me in I'll get you all greased if I have to send to Philly to do it. It's not just me, we're everywhere, hear? Now you fuckers get this car to *go*, hear me? Get it to *go*."

Skeeter issues all this while crouched down between the leather backs of the bucket seats and the rear window. His panic is disgusting and may be contagious. Rabbit lusts to pull him out of his shell into the sunshine, but is afraid to reach in; he might get stung. He slams the Porsche door shut on the churning rasping voice, and at the rear of the car slams down the hood. "You two stay here. Calm him down, keep him in the car. I'll walk to a gas station, there must be one up the road."

He runs for a while, Skeeter's venomous fright making his own bladder burn. After all these nights together betrayal is the Negro's first thought. Maybe natural, three hundred years of it. Rabbit is running, running to keep that black body pinned back there, so it won't panic and flee. Like running late to school. Skeeter has become a duty. Late, late. Then an antique red flying-horse sign suspended above sunset-dyed fields. It is an old-fashioned garage: an unfathomable work space black

with oil, the walls precious with wrenches, fan belts, peen
hammers, parts. An old Coke machine, the kind that dispenses
bottles, purrs beside the hydraulic lift. The mechanic, a weedy
young man with a farmer's drawl and black palms, drives him
in a jolting tow truck back up the highway. The side window is
broken; air whistles there, hungrily gushes.

"Seized up," is the mechanic's verdict. He asks Jill, "When'd
you last put oil in it?"

"Oil? Don't they do it when they put the gas in?"

"Not unless you ask."

"You dumb mutt," Rabbit says to Jill.

Her mouth goes prim and defiant. "Skeeter's been driving
the car too."

Skeeter, while the mechanic was poking around in the engine and pumping the gas pedal, uncurled from behind the
seats and straightened in the air, his glasses orange discs in the
last of the sun. Rabbit asks him, "How far've you been taking
this crate?"

"Oh," the black man says, fastidious in earshot of the mechanic, "here and there. Never recklessly. I wasn't aware," he
minces on, "the automobile was your property."

"It's just," he says lamely, "the waste. The carelessness."

Jill asks the mechanic, "Can you fix it in an hour? My little
brother here has homework to do."

The mechanic speaks only to Rabbit. "The enchine's destroyed. The pistons have fused to the cylinders. The nearest
place to fix a car like this is probably Pottstown."

"Can we leave it with you until we arrange to have somebody come for it?"

"I'll have to charge a dollar a day for the parking."

"Sure. Swell."

"And that'll be twenty for the towing."

He pays. The mechanic tows the Porsche back to the garage. They ride with him, Jill and Harry in the cab ("Careful
now," the mechanic says as Jill slides over, "I don't want to
get grease on that nice white dress"), Skeeter and Nelson in
the little car, dragged backwards at a slant. At the garage, the
mechanic phones for a cab to take them into West Brewer.

Skeeter disappears behind a smudged door and flushes the toilet repeatedly. Nelson settles to watching the mechanic unhitch the car and listens to him talk about "enchines." Jill and Harry walk outside. Crickets are shrilling in the dark cornfields. A quarter-moon, with one sick eye, scuds above the flying-horse sign. The garage's outer lights are switched off. He notices something white on her slipper. The little flower that fell has stuck there. He stoops and hands it to her. She kisses it to thank him, then, silently lays it to rest in a trash barrel full of oil-wiped paper towels and punctured cans. "Don't get your dress greasy." Car tires crackle; an ancient fifties Buick, with those tailfins patterned on B-19s, pulls into their orbit. The taxi driver is fat and chews gum. On the way back to Brewer, his head bulks as a pyramid against the oncoming headlights, motionless but for the rhythm of chewing. Skeeter sits beside him. "Beautiful day," Rabbit calls forward to him.

Jill giggles. Nelson is asleep on her lap. She toys with his hair, winding it around her silent fingers.

"Fair for this time of the year," is the slow answer.

"Beautiful country up here. We hardly ever get north of the city. We were driving around sightseeing."

"Not too many sights to see."

"The engine seized right up on us, I guess the car's a real mess."

"I guess."

"My daughter here forgot to put any oil in it, that's the way young people are these days, ruin one car and on to the next. Material things don't mean a thing to 'em."

"To some, I guess."

Skeeter says sideways to him, "Yo' sho' meets a lot ob nice folks hevin' en acci-dent lahk dis, a lot ob naas folks way up no'th heah."

"Yes, well," the driver says, and that is all he says until he says to Rabbit, having stopped on Vista Crescent, "Eighteen."

"Dollars? For ten miles?"

"Twelve. And I got to go back twelve now."

Rabbit goes to the driver's side to pay, while the others run into the house. The man leans out and asks, "Know what you're doing?"

"Not exactly."

"They'll knife you in the back every time."

"Who?"

The driver leans closer; by street-lamplight Rabbit sees a wide sad face, sallow, a whale's lipless mouth clamped in a melancholy set, a horseshoe-shaped scar on the meat of his nose. His answer is distinct: "Jigaboos."

Embarrassed for him, Rabbit turns away and sees—Nelson is right—a crowd of children. They are standing across the Crescent, some with bicycles, watching this odd car unload. This crowd phenomenon on the bleak terrain of Penn Villas alarms him: as if growths were to fester on the surface of the moon.

The incident emboldens Skeeter. His skin has dared the sun again. Rabbit comes home from work to find him and Nelson shooting baskets in the driveway. Nelson bounces the ball to his father and Rabbit's one-handed set from twenty feet out swishes. Pretty. "Hey," Skeeter crows, so all the homes in Penn Villas can hear, "where'd you get that funky old style of shooting a basketball? You were tryin' to be comical, right?"

"Went in," Nelson tells him loyally.

"Shit, boy, a one-armed dwarf could have blocked it. T'get that shot off you need a screen two men thick, right? You gotta jump and shoot, jump and *shoot*." He demonstrates; his shot misses but looks right: the ball held high, a back-leaning ascent into the air, a soft release that would arch over any defender. Rabbit tries it, but finds his body heavy, the effort of lifting jarring. The ball flies badly. Says Skeeter, "You got a white man's lead gut, but I adore those hands." They scrimmage one on one; Skeeter is quick and slick, slithering by for the layup on the give-and-go to Nelson again and again. Rabbit cannot stop him, his breath begins to ache in his chest, but there are moments when the ball and his muscles and the air overhead and the bodies competing with his all feel taut and unified and defiant of gravity. Then the October chill bites into his sweat and he goes into the house. Jill has been sleeping upstairs. She sleeps more and more lately, a dazed evading sleep that he finds insulting. When she comes downstairs, in that boring white dress, brushing back sticky hair from her cheeks, he asks roughly, "Dja do anything about the car?"

"Sweet, what would I do?"

"You could call your mother."

"I can't. She and Stepdaddy would make a thing. They'd come for me."

"Maybe that's a good idea."

"Stepdaddy's a creep." She moves past him, not focusing, into the kitchen. She looks into the refrigerator. "You didn't shop."

"That's your job."

"Without a car?"

"Christ, you can walk up to the Acme in five minutes."

"People would see Skeeter."

"They see him anyway. He's outside horsing around with Nelson. And evidently you've been letting him drive all around Pennsylvania." His anger recharges itself: *lead gut.* "Goddammit, how can you just run an expensive car like that into the ground and just let it *sit*? There's people in the world could live for ten years on what that car cost."

"Don't, Harry. I'm weak."

"O.K. I'm sorry." He tugs her into his arms. She rocks sadly against him, rubbing her nose on his shirt. But her body when dazed has an absence, an unconnectedness, that feels disagreeable against his skin. He itches to sneeze.

Jill is murmuring, "I think you miss your wife."

"That bitch. Never."

"She's like anybody else, caught in this society. She wants to be alive while she is alive."

"Don't you?"

"Sometimes. But I know it's not enough. It's how they get you. Let me go now. You don't like holding me, I can feel it. I just remembered, some frozen chicken livers behind the ice cream. But they take forever to thaw."

Six-o'clock news. The pale face caught behind the screen, unaware that his head, by some imperfection in reception at 26 Vista Crescent, is flattened, and his chin rubbery and long, sternly says, "Chicago. Two thousand five hundred Illinois National Guardsmen remained on active duty today in the wake of a day of riots staged by members of the extremist faction of the Students for a Democratic Society. Windows were smashed, cars overturned, policemen assaulted by the young militants whose slogan is"—sad, stern pause; the bleached face lifts toward the camera, the chin stretches, the head flattens like an anvil—"Bring the War Home." Film cuts of white-helmeted policemen flailing at nests of arms and legs, of long-haired girls being dragged, of sudden bearded faces shaking fists that want to rocket out through the television screen; then back to clips of policemen swinging clubs, which seems balletlike and soothing to Rabbit. Skeeter, too, likes it. "Right on!" he cries. "Hit that honky snob again!" In the commercial break he turns and explains to Nelson, "It's beautiful, right?"

Nelson asks, "Why? Aren't they protesting the war?"

"Sure as a hen has balls they are. What those crackers protesting is they gotta wait twenty years to get their daddy's share of the pie. They want it *now*."

"What would they do with it?"

"Do, boy? They'd *eat* it, that's what they'd do."

The commercial—an enlarged view of a young woman's mouth—is over. "Meanwhile, within the courtroom, the trial of the Chicago Eight continued on its turbulent course. Presiding Judge Julius J. Hoffman, no relation to Defendant Abbie Hoffman, several times rebuked Defendant Bobby Seale, whose outbursts contained such epithets as"—again, the upward look, the flattened head, the disappointed emphasis —"pig, fascist, and racist." A courtroom sketch of Seale is flashed.

Nelson asks, "Skeeter, do you like *him*?"

"I do not much cotton," Skeeter says, "to establishment niggers."

Rabbit has to laugh. "That's ridiculous. He's as full of hate as you are."

Skeeter switches off the set. His tone is a preacher's, ladylike. "I am by no means full of hate. I am full of love, which is a dynamic force. Hate is a paralyzing force. Hate freezes. Love strikes and liberates. Right? Jesus liberated the moneychangers from the temple. The new Jesus will liberate the new money-changers. The old Jesus brought a sword, right? The new Jesus will also bring a sword. He will be a living flame of love. Chaos is God's body. Order is the Devil's chains. As to

Robert Seale, any black man who has John Kennel Badbreath and Leonard Birdbrain giving him fund-raising cocktail parties is one house nigger in my book. He has gotten into the power bag, he has gotten into the publicity bag, he has debased the coinage of his soul and is thereupon as they say irrelevant. We black men came here without names, we are the future's organic seeds, seeds have no names, right?"

"Right," Rabbit says, a habit he has acquired.

Jill's chicken livers have burned edges and icy centers.

Eleven-o'clock news. A gauzy-bearded boy, his face pressed so hard against the camera the focus cannot be maintained, screams, "Off the pigs! All power to the people!"

An unseen interviewer mellifluously asks him, "How would you describe the goals of your organization?"

"Destruction of existing repressive structures. Social control of the means of production."

"Could you tell our viewing audience what you mean by 'means of production'?"

The camera is being jostled; the living room, darkened otherwise, flickers. "Factories. Wall Street. Technology. All that. A tiny clique of capitalists is forcing pollution down our throats, and the SST and the genocide in Vietnam and in the ghettos. All that."

"I see. Your aim, then, by smashing windows, is to curb a runaway technology and create the basis for a new humanism."

The boy looks off-screen blearily, as the camera struggles to refocus him. "You being funny? You'll be the first up against the wall, you—" And the blip showed that the interview had been taped.

Rabbit says, "Tell me about technology."

"Technology," Skeeter explains with exquisite patience, the tip of his joint glowing red as he drags, "is horseshit. Take that down, Jilly."

But Jill is asleep on the sofa. Her thighs glow, her dress having ridden up to a sad shadowy triangular peep of underpants.

Skeeter goes on, "We are all at work at the mighty labor of forgetting everything we know. We are sewing the apple back on the tree. Now the Romans had technology, right? And the barbarians saved them from it. The barbarians were their saviors. Since we cannot induce the Eskimos to invade us, we have raised a generation of barbarians ourselves, pardon me, *you* have raised them, Whitey has raised them, the white American middle-class and its imitators the world over have found within themselves the divine strength to generate millions of subhuman idiots that in less benighted ages only the inbred aristocracies could produce. Who were those idiot kings?"

"Huh?" says Rabbit.

"Merovingians, right? Slipped my mind. They were dragged about in ox carts gibbering and we are now blessed with motorized gibberers. It is truly written, we shall blow our minds, and dedicate the rest to Chairman Mao. Right?"

Rabbit argues, "That's not quite fair. These kids have some good points. The war aside, what about pollution?"

"I am getting weary," Skeeter says, "of talking with white folk. You are defending your own. These rabid children, as surely as Agnew Dei, desire to preserve the status quo against the divine plan and the divine wrath. They are Antichrist. They perceive God's face in Vietnam and spit upon it. False prophets: by their proliferation you know the time is nigh. Public shamelessness, ingenious armor, idiocy revered, all laws mocked but the laws of bribery and protection: we are Rome. And I am the Christ of the new Dark Age. Or if not me, then someone exactly like me, whom later ages will suppose to have been me. Do you believe?"

"I believe." Rabbit drags on his own joint, and feels his world expand to admit new truths as a woman spreads her legs, as a flower unfolds, as the stars flee one another. "I do believe."

Skeeter likes Rabbit to read to him from the *Life and Times of Frederick Douglass*. "You're just gorgeous, right? You're gone to be our big nigger tonight. As a white man, Chuck, you don't amount to much, but niggerwise you groove." He has marked sections in the book with paper clips and a crayon.

Rabbit reads, "*The reader will have noticed that among the names of slaves that of Esther is mentioned. This was the name of a young woman who possessed that which was ever a curse to the slave girl—namely, personal beauty. She was tall, light-colored, well formed, and made a fine appearance. Esther was courted by*

'Ned Roberts,' the son of a favorite slave of Colonel Lloyd, and who was as fine-looking a young man as Esther was a woman. Some slaveholders would have been glad to have promoted the marriage of two such persons, but for some reason Captain Anthony disapproved of their courtship. He strictly ordered her to quit the society of young Roberts, telling her that he would punish her severely if he ever found her again in his company. But it was impossible to keep this couple apart. Meet they would and meet they did. Then we skip." The red crayon mark resumes at the bottom of the page; Rabbit hears drama entering his voice, early morning mists, a child's fear. "It was early in the morning, when all was still, and before any of the family in the house or kitchen had risen. I was, in fact, awakened by the heart-rendering shrieks and piteous cries of poor Esther. My sleeping-place was on the dirt floor of a little rough closet which opened into the kitchen—"

Skeeter interrupts, "You can smell that closet, right? Dirt, right, and old potatoes, and little bits of grass turning yellow before they can grow an inch, right? Smell that, he *slept* in there."

"Hush," Jill says.

"—and through the cracks in its unplaned boards I could distinctly see and hear what was going on, without being seen. Esther's wrists were firmly tied, and the twisted rope was fastened to a strong iron staple in a heavy wooden beam above, near the fireplace. Here she stood on a bench, her arms tightly drawn above her head. Her back and shoulders were perfectly bare. Behind her stood old master, cowhide in hand, pursuing his barbarous work with all manner of harsh, coarse, and tantalizing epithets. He was cruelly deliberate, and protracted the torture as one who was delighted with the agony of his victim. Again and again he drew the hateful scourge through his hand, adjusting it with a view of dealing the most pain-giving blow his strength and skill could inflict. Poor Esther had never before been severely whipped. Her shoulders were plump and tender. Each blow, vigorously laid on, brought screams from her as well as blood. 'Have mercy! Oh, mercy!' she cried. 'I won't do so no more.' But her piercing cries seemed only to increase his fury." The red mark stops but Rabbit sweeps on to the end of the chapter. "The whole scene, with all its attendant circumstances, was revolting and shocking to the last degree, and when the motives for the brutal castigation are known, language has no power to convey a just sense of its *dreadful criminality. After laying on I dare not say how many stripes, old master untied his suffering victim. When let down she could scarcely stand. From my heart I pitied her, and child as I was, and new to such scenes, the shock was tremendous. I was terrified, hushed, stunned, and bewildered. The scene here described was often repeated, for Edward and Esther continued to meet, notwithstanding all efforts to prevent their meeting."*

Skeeter turns to Jill and slaps her sharply, as a child would, on the chest. "Don't hush me, you cunt."

"I wanted to hear the passage."

"How'd it turn you on, cunt?"

"I liked the way Harry read it. With feeling."

"Fuck your white feelings."

"Hey, easy," Rabbit says, helplessly, seeing that violence is due.

Skeeter is wild. Keeping his one hand on her shoulder as a brace, with the other he reaches to her throat and rips the neck of her white dress forward. The cloth is tough; Jill's head snaps far forward before the rip is heard. She recoils back into the sofa, her eyes expressionless; her little tough-tipped tits bounce in the torn V.

Rabbit's instinct is not to rescue her but to shield Nelson. He drops the book on the cobbler's bench and puts his body between the boy and the sofa. "Go upstairs."

Nelson, stunned, bewildered, has risen to his feet; he moans, "He'll *kill* her, Dad." His cheeks are flushed, his eyes are sunk.

"No he won't. He's just high. She's all right."

"Oh shit, shit," the child repeats in desperation; his face caves into crying.

"Hey there Babychuck," Skeeter calls. "You want to whip me, right?" Skeeter hops up, does a brittle bewitched dance, strips off his shirt so violently one cuff button flies off and strikes the lampshade. His skinny chest, naked, is stunning in its articulation: every muscle sharp in its attachment to the bone. Rabbit has never seen such a chest except on a crucifix. "What's next?" Skeeter shouts. "Wanna whup my bum, right? Here it is!" His hands have undone his fly button and are on his belt, but Nelson has fled the room. His sobbing comes downstairs, diminishing.

"O.K., that's enough," Rabbit says.

"Read a little bitty bit more," Skeeter begs.

"You get carried away."

"That damn child of yours, thinks he owns this cunt."

"Stop calling her a cunt."

"Man, wasn't this Jesus gave her one." Skeeter cackles.

"You're horrible," Jill tells him, drawing the torn cloth together.

He flips one piece aside. "Moo."

"Harry, help me."

"Read the book, Chuck, I'll be good. Read me the next paper clip."

Above them, Nelson's footsteps cross the floor. If he reads, the boy will be safe. "*Alas, that the one?*"

"That'll do. Little Jilly, you love me, right?"

"*Alas, this immense wealth, this gilded splendor, this profusion of luxury, this exemption from toil, this life of ease, this sea of plenty, were not the pearly gates they seemed—*"

"You're my pearly gate, girl."

"*The poor slave, on his hard pine plank, scantily covered with his thin blanket, slept more soundly than the feverish voluptuary who reclined upon his downy pillow. Food to the indolent is poison, not sustenance. Lurking beneath the rich and tempting viands were invisible spirits of evil, which filled the self-deluded gormandizer with aches and pains, passions uncontrollable, fierce tempers, dyspepsia, rheumatism, lumbago, and gout, and of these the Lloyds had a full share.*"

Beyond the edge of the page Skeeter and Jill are wrestling; in gray flashes her underpants, her breasts are exposed. Another flash, Rabbit sees, is her smile. Her small spaced teeth bare in silent laughter; she is liking it, this attack. Seeing him spying, Jill starts, struggles angrily out from under, hugs the rags of her dress around her, and runs from the room. Her footsteps flicker up the stairs. Skeeter blinks at her flight; he resettles the great pillow of his head with a sigh. "Beautiful," is the sigh. "One more, Chuck. Read me the one where he fights back." His carved chest melts into the beige sofa; its airfoam is covered in a plaid of green and tan and red that have rubbed and faded toward a single shade.

"You know, I gotta get up and go to work tomorrow."

"You worried about your little dolly? Don't you worry about

that. The thing about a cunt, man, it's just like a Kleenex, you use it and throw it away." Hearing silence, he says, "I'm just kidding, right? To get your goat, O.K.? Come on, let's put it back together, the next paper clip. Trouble with you, man, you're all the time married. Woman don't like a man who's nothin' but married, they want some soul that keeps 'em guessing, right? Woman stops guessing, she's dead."

Rabbit sits on the silverthread chair to read. "*Whence came the daring spirit necessary to grapple with a man who, eight-and-forty hours before, could, with the slightest word, have made me tremble like a leaf in a storm, I do not know; at any rate, I was resolved to fight, and what was better still, I actually was hard at it. The fighting madness had come upon me, and I found my strong fingers firmly attached to the throat of the tyrant, as heedless of consequences, at the moment, as if we stood equals before the law. The very color of the man was forgotten. I felt supple as a cat, and was ready for him at every turn. Every blow of his was parried, though I dealt no blows in return. I was strictly on the defensive, preventing him from injuring me, rather than trying to injure him. I flung him on the ground several times when he meant to have hurled me there. I held him so firmly by the throat that his blood followed my nails. He held me, and I held him.*"

"Oh I love it, it grabs me, it kills me," Skeeter says, and he gets up on one elbow so his body confronts the other man's. "Do me one more. Just one more bit."

"I gotta get upstairs."

"Skip a couple pages, go to the place I marked with double lines."

"Why doncha read it to yourself?"

"It's not the same, right? Doin' it to yourself. Every school kid knows that, it's not the same. Come on, Chuck. I been pretty good, right? I ain't caused no trouble, I been a faithful Tom, give the Tom a bone, read it like I say. I'm gonna take off all my clothes, I want to hear it with my pores. Sing it, man. Do it. Begin up a little, where it goes *A man without force.*" He prompts again, "*A man without force,*" and is fussing with his belt buckle.

"*A man without force,*" Rabbit intently reads, "*is without the essential dignity of humanity. Human nature is so constituted, that it cannot honor a helpless man, though it can pity him, and even this it cannot do long if signs of power do not arise.*"

"Yes," Skeeter says, and the blur of him is scuffling and slithering, and a patch of white flashes from the sofa, above the white of the printed page.

"*He can only understand*," Rabbit reads, finding the words huge, each one a black barrel his voice echoes in, "*the effect of this combat on my spirit, who has himself incurred something, or hazarded something, in repelling the unjust and cruel aggressions of a tyrant. Covey was a tyrant and a cowardly one withal. After resisting him, I felt as I had never felt before.*"

"Yes," Skeeter's voice calls from the abyss of the unseen beyond the rectangular island of the page.

"*It was a resurrection from the dark and pestiferous tomb of slavery, to the heaven of comparative freedom. I was no longer a servile coward, trembling under the frown of a brother worm of the dust, but my long-cowed spirit was roused to an attitude of independence. I had reached a point at which I was* not afraid to die." Emphasis.

"Oh yes. Yes."

"*This spirit made me a freeman in* fact, *though I still remained a slave in* form. *When a slave cannot be flogged, he is more than half free.*"

"A-men."

"*He has a domain as broad as his own manly heart to defend, and he is really 'a power on earth.'*"

"Say it. Say it."

"*From this time until my escape from slavery, I was never fairly whipped. Several attempts were made, but they were always unsuccessful. Bruised I did get, but the instance I have described was the end of the brutification to which slavery had subjected me.*"

"Oh, you do make one lovely nigger," Skeeter sings.

Lifting his eyes from the page, Rabbit sees there is no longer a patch of white on the sofa, it is solidly dark, only moving in a whispering rhythm that wants to suck him forward. His eyes do not dare follow down to the hand the live line of reflected light lying the length of Skeeter's rhythmic arm. Long as an eel, feeding. Rabbit stands and strides from the room, dropping the book as if hot, though the burning eyes of the stippled Negro on the cover are quick to follow him across the hard carpet, up the varnished stairs, into the white realm where an overhead frosted fixture burns on the landing. His heart is hammering hard.

*

Light from the driftwood lamp downstairs floods the little maple from underneath, its leaves red like your fingers on a flashlight face. Its turning head half-fills their bedroom window. In bed Jill turns to him pale and chill as ice. "Hold me," she says. "Hold me, hold me, hold me," so often it frightens him. Women are crazy, they contain this ancient craziness, he is holding wind in his arms. He feels she wants to be fucked, any way, without pleasure, but to pin her down. He would like to do this for her but he cannot pierce the fright, the disgust between them. She is a mermaid gesturing beneath the skin of the water. He is floating rigid to keep himself from sinking in terror. The book he has read aloud torments him with a vision of bottomless squalor, of dead generations, of buried tortures and lost reasons. Rising, working, there is no reason any more, no reason for anything, no reason why not, nothing to breathe but a sour gas bottled in empty churches, nothing to rise by; he lives in a tight well whose dank sides squeeze and paralyze him, no, it is Jill tight against him, trying to get warm, though the night is hot. He asks her, "Can you sleep?"

"No. Everything is crashing."

"Let's try. It's late. Shall I get another blanket?"

"Don't leave me for even a second. I'll fall through."

"I'll turn my back, then you can hug me."

Downstairs, Skeeter flicks the light off. Outside, the little maple vanishes like a blown-out flame. Within himself, Rabbit completes his motion into darkness, into the rhythmic brown of the sofa. Then terror returns and squeezes him shut like an eyelid.

Her voice sounds tired and wary, answering. "Brewer Fealty, Mrs. Fosnacht. May I help you?"

"Peggy? Hi, it's Harry Angstrom."

"So it is." A new sarcastic note. "I *don't* believe it!" Overexpressive. Too many men.

"Hey, remember you said about Nelson and Billy going fishing this Sunday and inviting me for Saturday dinner?"

"Yes, Harry, I do remember."

"Is it too late? For me to accept?"

"Not at all. What's brought this about?"

"Nothing special. Just thought it might be nice."

"It will be nice. I'll see you Saturday."

"Tomorrow," he clarifies. He would have talked on, it was his lunch hour, but she cuts the conversation short. Press of work. Don't count your chickens.

After work as he walks home from the bus stop on Weiser, two men accost him, at the corner where Emberly Avenue becomes a Drive, beside a red-white-and-blue mailbox. "Mr. Angstrom?"

"Sure."

"Might we talk to you a minute? We're two of your neighbors." The man speaking is between forty and fifty, plump, in a gray suit that has stretched to fit him, with those narrow lapels of five years ago. His face is soft but pained. A hard little hook nose at odds with the puffy patches below his eyes. His chin is two damp knobs set side by side, between them a dimple where the whiskers hide from the razor. He has that yellow Brewer tint and an agile sly white-collar air. An accountant, a schoolteacher. "My name is Mahlon Showalter. I live on the other side of Vista Crescent, the house, you probably noticed, with the new addition in back we added on last summer."

"Oh, yeah." He recalls distant hammering but had not noticed; he really only looks at Penn Villas enough to see that it isn't Mt. Judge: that is, it is nowhere.

"I'm in computers, the hardware end," Showalter says. "Here's my card." As Rabbit glances at the company name on it Showalter says, "We're going to revolutionize business in this town, file that name in your memory. This here is Eddie Brumbach, he lives around the further crescent, Marigold, up from you."

Eddie presents no card. He is black-haired, shorter and younger than Harry. He stands the way guys in the Army used to, all buttoned in, shoulders tucked back, an itch for a fight between their shoulder blades. Only in part because of his brush cut, his head looks flattened on top, like the heads on Rabbit's television set. When he shakes hands, it reminds him of somebody else. Who? One side of Brumbach's face has had a piece of jawbone removed, leaving a dent and an L-shaped red scar. Gray eyes like dulled tool tips. He says with ominous simplicity, "Yessir."

Showalter says, "Eddie works in the assembly shop over at Fessler Steel."

"You guys must have quit work early today," Rabbit says.

Eddie tells him, "I'm on night shift this month."

Showalter has a way of bending, as if dance music is playing far away and he wants to cut in between Rabbit and Eddie. He is saying, "We made a decision to talk to you, we appreciate your patience. This is my car here, would you like to sit in it? It's not too comfortable, standing out like this."

The car is a Toyota; it reminds Harry of his father-in-law and gets a whole set of uneasy feelings sliding. "I'd just as soon stand," he says, "if it won't take long," and leans on the mailbox to make himself less tall above these men.

"It won't take long," Eddie Brumbach promises, hitching his shoulders and coming a crisp step closer.

Showalter dips his shoulder again as if to intervene, looks sadder around the eyes, wipes his soft mouth: "Well no, it needn't. We don't mean to be unfriendly, we just have a few questions."

"Friendly questions," Rabbit clarifies, anxious to help this man, whose careful slow voice is pure Brewer; who seems, like the city, bland and broad and kind, and for the time being depressed.

"Now some of us," Showalter goes on, "were discussing, you know, the neighborhood. Some of the kids have been telling us stories, you know, about what they see in your windows."

"They've been looking in my windows?" The mailbox blue is hot; he stops leaning and stands. Though it is October the sidewalk has a flinty glare and a translucent irritability rests upon the pastel asphalt rooftops, the spindly young trees, the low houses like puzzles assembled of wood and cement and brick and fake-fieldstone siding. He is trying to look through these houses to his own, to protect it.

Brumbach bristles, thrusts himself into Rabbit's attention. "They haven't had to look in any windows, they've had what's going on pushed under their noses. And it don't smell good."

Showalter intervenes, his voice wheedling like a woman's,

buttering over. "No now, that's putting it too strong. But it's true, I guess, there hasn't been any particular secret. They've been coming and going in that little Porsche right along, and I notice now he plays basketball with the boy right out front."

"He?"

"The black fella you have living with you," Showalter says, smiling as if the snag in their conversation has been discovered, and all will be clear sailing now.

"And the white girl," Brumbach adds. "My younger boy came home the other day and said he saw them screwing right on the downstairs rug."

"Well," Rabbit says, stalling. He feels absurdly taller than these men, he feels he might float away while trying to make out the details of what the boy had seen, a little framed rectangle hung in his head like a picture too high on the wall. "That's the kind of thing you see, when you look in other people's windows."

Brumbach steps neatly in front of Showalter, and Rabbit remembers who his handshake had been reminiscent of: the doctor giving Mom the new pills. *I twist bodies to my will. I am life, I am death.* "Listen, brother. We're trying to raise children in this neighborhood."

"Me too."

"And that's something else. What kind of pervert are you bringing up there? I feel sorry for the boy, it's the fact, I do. But what about the rest of us, who are trying to do the best we can? This is a decent white neighborhood," he says, hitting "decent" weakly but gathering strength for, "that's why we live here instead of across the river over in Brewer where they're letting 'em run wild."

"Letting who run wild?"

"You know fucking well who, read the papers, these old ladies can't even go outdoors in broad daylight with a pocketbook."

Showalter, supple, worried, sidles around and intrudes himself. "White neighborhood isn't exactly the point, we'd welcome a self-respecting black family, I went to school with blacks and I'd work right beside one any day of the week, in fact my company has a recruitment program, the trouble is, their own leaders tell them not to bother, tell them it's a sellout, to learn how to make an honest living." This speech has slid further than he had intended; he hauls it back. "If he acts like a man I'll treat him like a man, am I way out of line on that, Eddie?"

Brumbach puffs up so his shirt pocket tightens on his cigarette pack; his forearms bend at his sides as if under the pull of their veins. "I fought beside the colored in Vietnam," he says. "No problems."

"Hey that's funny you're a Viet veteran too, this guy we're kind of talking about—"

"No problems," Brumbach goes on, "because we all knew the rules."

Showalter's hands glide, flutter, touch his narrow lapels in a double downward caress. "It's the girl and the black together," he says quickly, to touch it and get away.

Brumbach says, "Christ those boogs love white ass. You should have seen what went on around the bases."

Rabbit offers, "That was yellow ass, wasn't it? Gook ass?"

Showalter tugs at his arm and takes him aside, some steps from the mailbox. Harry wonders if anybody ever mails a letter in it, he passes it every day and it seems mysterious as a fire hydrant, waiting for its moment that may never come. He never hears it clang. In Mt. Judge people were always mailing Valentines. Brumbach at his little distance stares into space, at TV-aerial level, knowing he's being discussed. Showalter says, "Don't keep riding him."

Rabbit calls over to Brumbach, "I'm not riding you, am I?"

Showalter tugs harder, so Harry has to bend his ear to the man's little beak and soft unhappy mouth. "He's not that stable. He feels very threatened. It wasn't my idea to get after you, I said to him, The man has his rights of privacy."

Rabbit tries to play the game, whispers. "How many more in the neighborhood feel like him?"

"More than you'd think. I was surprised myself. These are reasonable good people, but they have blind spots. I believe if they didn't have children, if this wasn't a children's neighborhood, it'd be more live and let live."

But Rabbit worries they are being rude to Brumbach. He calls over, "Hey, Eddie. I tell you what."

Brumbach is not pleased to be called in; he had wanted Showalter to settle. Rabbit sees the structure: one man is the negotiator, the other is the muscle. Brumbach barks, "What?"

"I'll keep my kid from looking in your windows, and you keep yours from looking in mine."

"We had a name over there for guys like you. Wiseass. Sometimes just by mistake they got fragged."

"I'll tell you what else," Rabbit says. "As a bonus, I'll try to remember to draw the curtains."

"You better do fucking more than pull the fucking curtains," Brumbach tells him, "you better fucking barricade the place."

Out of nowhere a mail truck, red, white, and blue, with a canted windshield like a display case, squeaks to a stop at the curb; hurriedly, not looking at any of them, a small man in gray unlocks the mailbox front and scoops a torrent, hundreds it seems, of letters into a gray sack, locks it shut, and drives away.

Rabbit goes close to Brumbach. "Tell me what you want. You want me to move out of the neighborhood."

"Just move the black out."

"It's him and the girl together you don't like; suppose he stays and the girl goes?"

"The black goes."

"He goes when he stops being my guest. Have a nice supper."

"You've been warned."

Rabbit asks Showalter, "You hear that threat?"

Showalter smiles, he wipes his brow, he is less depressed. He has done what he could. "I told you," he says, "not to ride him. We came to you in all politeness. I want to repeat, it's the circumstances of what's going on, not the color of anybody's skin. There's a house vacant abutting me and I told the realtor, I said as plain as I say to you, 'Any colored family, with a husband in the house, can get up the equity to buy it at the going market price, let them have it by all means. By all means.'"

"It's nice to meet a liberal," Rabbit says, and shakes his hand. "My wife keeps telling me I'm a conservative."

And, because he likes him, because he likes anybody who fought in Vietnam where he himself should have been fighting, had he not been too old, too old and fat and cowardly, he offers to shake Brumbach's hand too.

The cocky little man keeps his arms stiff at his sides. Instead he turns his head, so the ruined jaw shows. The scar is not just a red L, Rabbit sees it is an ampersand, complicated by faint lines where skin was sewn and overlapped to repair a hole that would always be, that would always repel eyes. Rabbit makes himself look at it. Brumbach's voice is less explosive, almost regretful, sad in its steadiness. "I earned this face," he says. "I got it over there so I could have a decent life here. I'm not asking for sympathy, a lot of my buddies made out worse. I'm just letting you know, after what I seen and done, no wiseass is crowding me in my own neighborhood."

Inside the house, it is too quiet. The television isn't going. Nelson is doing homework at the kitchen table. No, he is reading one of Skeeter's books. He has not gotten very far. Rabbit asks, "Where are they?"

"Sleeping. Upstairs."

"Together?"

"I think Jill's on your bed, Skeeter's in mine. He says the sofa stinks. He was awake when I got back from school."

"How did he seem?"

Though the question touches a new vein, Nelson answers promptly. For all the shadows between them, they have lately grown toward each other, father and son. "Jumpy," he answers, into the book. "Said he was getting bad vibes lately and hadn't slept at all last night. I think he had taken some pills or something. He didn't seem to see me, looking over my head, kind of, and kept calling me Chuck instead of Babychuck."

"And how's Jill?"

"Dead asleep. I looked in and said her name and she didn't move. Dad—"

"Spit it out."

"He *gives* her things." The thought is too deep in him to get out easily; his eyes sink in after it, and his father feels him digging, shy, afraid, lacking the right words, not wanting to offend his father.

Harry prompts, "Things."

The boy rushes into it. "She never laughs any more, or takes any interest in anything, just sits around and sleeps. Have you looked at her skin, Dad? She's gotten so pale."

"She's naturally fair."

"Yeah, I know, but it's more than that, she looks *sick*. She doesn't eat hardly anything and throws up sometimes anyway.

Dad, don't let him keep doing it to her, whatever it is. Stop him."

"How can I?"

"You can kick him out."

"Jill's said she'll go with him."

"She won't. She hates him too."

"Don't you like Skeeter?"

"Not really. I know I should. I know you do."

"I do?" Surprised, he promises Nelson, "I'll talk to him. But you know, people aren't property, I can't control what they want to do together. We can't live Jill's life for her."

"We *could*, if you wanted to. If you cared at all." This is as close as Nelson has come to defiance; Rabbit's instinct is to be gentle with this sprouting, to ignore it.

He points out simply, "She's too old to adopt. And you're too young to marry."

The child frowns down into the book, silent.

"Now tell me something."

"O.K." Nelson's face tenses, prepared to close; he expects to be asked about Jill and sex and himself. Rabbit is glad to disappoint him, to give him a little space here.

"Two men stopped me on the way home and said kids had been looking in our windows. Have you heard anything about this?"

"Sure."

"Sure what?"

"Sure they do."

"Who?"

"All of them. Frankhauser, and that slob Jimmy Brumbach, Evelyn Morris and those friends of hers from Penn Park, Mark Showalter and I guess his sister Marilyn though she's awful little—"

"When the hell do they do this?"

"Different times. When they come home from school and I'm at soccer practice, before you get home, they hang around. I guess sometimes they come back after dark."

"They see anything?"

"I guess sometimes."

"They talk to you about it? Do they tease you?"

"I guess. Sometimes."

"You poor kid. What do you tell 'em?"

"I tell 'em to fuck off."

"Hey. Watch your language."

"That's what I tell 'em. You asked."

"And do you have to fight?"

"Not much. Just sometimes when they call me something."

"What?"

"Something. Never mind, Dad."

"Tell me what they call you."

"Nigger Nellie."

"Huh. Nice kids."

"They're just kids, Dad. They don't mean anything. Jill says ignore them, they're ignorant."

"And do they kid you about Jill?"

The boy turns his face away altogether. His hair covers his neck, yet even from the back he would not be mistaken for a girl: the angles in the shoulders, the lack of brushing in the hair. The choked voice is manly: "I don't want to talk about it anymore, Dad."

"O.K. Thanks. Hey. I'm sorry. I'm sorry you have to live in the mess we all make."

The choked voice exclaims, "Gee I wish Mom would come back! I know it can't happen, but I wish it." Nelson thumps the back of the kitchen chair and then rests his forehead where his fist struck; Rabbit ruffles his hair, helplessly, on his way past, to the refrigerator to get a beer.

The nights close in earlier now. After the six-o'clock news there is darkness. Rabbit says to Skeeter, "I met another veteran from Vietnam today."

"Shit, the world's filling up with Nam veterans so fast there won't be nobody else soon, right? Never forget, got into a lighthouse up near Tuy Hoa, white walls all over, everybody been there one time or another and done their drawings. Well, what blew my mind, absolutely, was somebody, Charlie or the unfriendlies, Arvin never been near this place till we handed it to 'em, somebody on that other side had done a whole wall's worth of Uncle Ho himself, Uncle Ho being buggered, Uncle

Ho shitting skulls, Uncle Ho doing this and that, it was down-right disrespectful, right? And I says to myself, those poor dinks being screwed the same as us, we is all in the grip of crazy old men thinkin' they can still make history happen. History isn't going to happen any more, Chuck."

"What is going to happen?" Nelson asks.

"A bad mess," Skeeter answers, "then, most probably, Me."

Nelson's eyes seek his father's, as they do now when Skeeter's craziness shows. "Dad, shouldn't we wake up Jill?"

Harry is into his second beer and his first joint; his stockinged feet are up on the cobbler's bench. "Why? Let her sleep. Don't be so uptight."

"No suh," Skeeter says, "the boy has a good plan there, where is that fucking little Jill? I do feel horny."

Nelson asks, "What's horny?"

"Horny is what I feel," Skeeter answers. "Babychuck, go drag down that no-good cunt. Tell her the menfolk needs their vittles."

"Dad—"

"Come on, Nellie, quit nagging. Do what he asks. Don't you have any homework? Do it upstairs, this is a grown-up evening."

When Nelson is gone, Rabbit can breathe. "Skeeter, one thing I don't understand, how do you feel about the Cong? I mean are they right, or wrong, or what?"

"Man by man, or should I say gook by gook, they are very beautiful, truly. So brave they must be tripping, and a lot of them no older than little Nellie, right? As a bunch, I never could dig what they was all about, except that we was white or black as the case may be, and they was yellow, and had got there first, right? Otherwise I can't say they made a great deal of sense, since the people they most liked to castrate and string up and bury in ditches alive and make that kind of scene with was yellow like them, right? So I would consider them one more facet of the confusion of false prophecy by which you may recognize My coming in this the fullness of time. However. However, I confess that politics being part of this boring power thing do not much turn me on. Things human turn me on, right? You too, right, Chuck? Here she is."

Jill has drifted in. Her skin looks tight on her face.

Rabbit asks her, "Hungry? Make yourself a peanut-butter sandwich. That's what we had to do."

"I'm not hungry."

Trying to be Skeeter, Rabbit goads her. "Christ, you should be. You're skinny as a stick. What the hell kind of piece of ass are you, there's nothing there anymore? Why you think we keep you here?"

She ignores him and speaks to Skeeter. "I'm in need," she tells him.

"Shee-yut, girl, we're all in need, right? The whole world's in need, isn't that what we done agreed on, Chuck? The whole benighted world is in need of Me. And Me, I'm in need of something else. Bring your cunt over here, white girl."

Now she does look toward Rabbit. He cannot help her. She has always been out of his class. She sits down on the sofa beside Skeeter and asks him gently, "What? If I do it, will you do it?"

"Might. Tell you what, Jill honey. Let's do it for the man."

"What man?"

"*The* man. That man. Victor Charlie over there. He wants it. What you think he's keepin' us here for? To *breed*, that's what for. Hey. Friend Harry?"

"I'm listening."

"You like being a nigger, don't ya?"

"I do."

"You want to be a good nigger, right?"

"Right." The sad rustling on the ceiling, of Nelson in his room, feels far distant. Don't come down. Stay up there. The smoke mixes with his veins and his lungs are a branching tree.

"O.K.," Skeeter says. "Now here's how. You is a big black man sittin' right there. You is chained to that chair. And I, I is white as snow. Be-hold." And Skeeter, with that electric scuttling suddenness, stands, and pulls off his shirt. In the room's deep dusk his upper half disappears. Then he scrabbles at himself at belt-level and his lower half disappears. Only his glasses remain, silver circles. His voice, disembodied, is the darkness. Slowly his head, a round cloud, tells against the blue light from the streetlamp at the end of the Crescent. "And this little girl here," he calls, "is black as coal. An ebony virgin torn from the valley of the river Niger, right? Stand up, honey, show us your teeth. Turn clean around." The black shadows of his hands glide into the white blur Jill is, and guide it upward, as a potter guides a lump of clay upward on the humming wheel, into a vase. She keeps rising, smoke from the vase. Her dress is being lifted over her head. "Turn around, honey, show us your rump." A soft slap gilds the darkness, the whiteness revolves. Rabbit's eyes, enlarged, can sift out shades of light and dark, can begin to model the bodies six feet from him, across the cobbler's bench. He can see the dark crack between Jill's buttocks, the faint dent her hip muscle makes, the shadowy mane between her starved hipbones. Her belly looks long. Where her breasts should be, black spiders are fighting: he sorts these out as Skeeter's hands. Skeeter is whispering to Jill, murmuring, while his hands flutter like bats against the moon. He hears her say, in a voice sifted through her hair, a sentence with the word "satisfy" in it.

Skeeter cackles: forked lightning. "Now," he sings, and his voice has become golden hoops spinning forward, an auctioneer who is a juggler, "we will have a demon-stray-shun of o-bee-deeyance, from this little coal-black lady, who has been broken in by expert traders working out of Nashville, Tennessee, and who is guaranteed by them ab-so-lutily to give no trouble in the kitchen, hallway, stable *or* bedroom!" Another soft slap, and the white clay dwindles; Jill is kneeling, while Skeeter still stands. A most delicate slipping silvery sound touches up the silence now; but Rabbit cannot precisely see. He needs to see. The driftwood lamp is behind him. Not turning his head, he gropes and switches it on.

Nice.

What he sees reminds him, in the first flash, of the printing process, an inked plate contiguous at some few points to white paper. As his eyes adjust, he sees Skeeter is not black, he is a gentle brown. These are smooth-skinned children being gently punished, one being made to stand and the other to kneel. Skeeter crouches and reaches down a long hand, fingernails like baby rose petals, to shield Jill's profile from the glare. Her eyelids remain closed, her mouth remains open, her breasts cast no shadow they are so shallow, she is feminine most in the swell of her backside spread on her propping heels and in the white lily of a hand floating beside his balls as if to receive from the air a baton. An inch or two of Skeeter's long cock is un-enclosed by her face, a purplish inch bleached to lilac, below his metallic pubic explosion, the shape and texture of his goatee. Keeping his protective crouch, Skeeter turns his face sheepishly toward the light; his eyeglasses glare opaquely and his upper lip lifts in imitation of pain. "Hey man, what's with that? Cut that light."

"You're beautiful," Rabbit says.

"O.K., strip and get into it, she's full of holes, right?"

"I'm scared to," Rabbit confesses: it is true, they seem not only beautiful but in the same vision an interlocked machine that might pull him apart.

Though the slap of light left her numb, this confession pierces Jill's trance; she turns her head, Skeeter's penis falling free, a bright string of moisture breaking. She looks at Harry, past him; as he reaches to switch off the light mercifully, she screams. In the corner of his vision, he saw it too: a face. At the window. Eyes like two cigarette burns. The lamp is out, the face is vanished. The window is a faintly blue rectangle in a black room. Rabbit runs to the front door and opens it. The night air bites. October. The lawn looks artificial, lifeless, dry, no-color: a snapshot of grass. Vista Crescent stretches empty but for parked cars. The maple is too slender to hide anyone. A child might have made it across the front of the house along the flowerbeds and be now in the garage. The garage door is up. And, if the child is Nelson, a door from the garage leads into the kitchen. Rabbit decides not to look, not to give chase; he feels that there is no space for him to step into, that the vista before him is a flat, stiff, cold photograph. The only thing that moves is the vapor of his breathing. He closes the door. He hears nothing move in the kitchen. He tells the living room, "Nobody."

"Bad," Skeeter says. His prick has quite relaxed, a whip between his legs as he squats. Jill is weeping on the floor; face down, she has curled her naked body into a knot. Her bottom forms the top half of a valentine heart, only white; her flesh-colored hair fans spilled over the sullen green carpet. Rabbit and Skeeter together squat to pick her up. She fights it, she makes herself roll over limply; her hair streams across her face, clouds her mouth, adheres like cobwebs to her chin and throat. A string as of milkweed spittle is on her chin; Rabbit wipes her chin and mouth with his handkerchief and, for weeks afterward, when all is lost, will take out this handkerchief and bury his nose in it, in its scarcely detectable smell of distant ocean.

Jill's lips are moving. She is saying, "You promised. You promised." She is talking to Skeeter. Though Rabbit bends his big face over hers, she has eyes only for the narrow black face beside him. There is no green in her eyes, the black pupils have eclipsed the irises. "It's such dumb hell," she says, with a little whimper, as if to mock her own complaint, a Connecticut housewife who knows she exaggerates. "Oh Christ," she adds in an older voice and shuts her eyes. Rabbit touches her; she is sweating. At his touch, she starts to shiver. He wants to blanket her, to blanket her with his body if there is nothing else, but she will talk only to Skeeter. Rabbit is not there for her, he only thinks he is here.

Skeeter asks down into her, "Who's your Lord Jesus, Jill honey?"

"You are."

"I am, right?"

"Right."

"You love me more'n you love yourself?"

"Much more."

"What do you see when you look at me, Jill honey?"

"I don't know."

"You see a giant lily, right?"

"Right. You promised."

"Love my cock?"

"Yes."

"Love my jism, sweet Jill? Love it in your veins?"

"Yes. Please. Shoot me. You promised."

"I your Savior, right? Right?"

"You promised. You must. Skeeter."

"O.K. Tell me I'm your Savior."

"You are. Hurry. You did promise."

"O.K." Skeeter explains hurriedly. "I'll fix her up. You go upstairs, Chuck. I don't want you to see this."

"I want to see it."

"Not this. It's bad, man. Bad, bad, bad. It's shit. Stay clean, you in deep enough trouble on account of me without being party to this, right? Split. I'm begging, man."

Rabbit understands. They are in country. They have taken a hostage. Everywhere out there, there are unfriendlies. He checks the front door, staying down below the three windows echoing the three chime-tones. He sneaks into the kitchen. Nobody is there. He slips the bolt across, in the door that opens from the garage. Sidling to make his shadow narrow, he climbs upstairs. At Nelson's door he listens for the sound of unconscious breathing. He hears the boy's breath rasp, touching bottom. In his own bedroom, the streetlamp prints negative spatters of the maple leaves on his wallpaper. He gets into bed in his underwear, in case he must rise and run; as a child, in summer, he would have to sleep in his underwear when the wash hadn't dried on the line. Rabbit listens to the noises downstairs—clicking, clucking kitchen noises, of a pan being put on the stove, of a bit of glass clinking, of footsteps across the linoleum, the sounds that have always made him sleepy, of Mom up, of the world being tended to. His thoughts begin to dissolve, though his heart keeps pounding, waves breaking on Jill's white valentine, stamped on his retinas like the sun. Offset versus letterpress, offset never has the bite of the other, looks greasy, the wave of the future. She slips into bed beside him; her valentine nestles cool against his belly and silken limp cock. He has been asleep. He asks her, "Is it late?"

Jill speaks very slowly. "Pretty late."

"How do you feel?"

"Better. For now."

"We got to get you to a doctor."

"It won't help."

He has a better idea, so obvious he cannot imagine why he has never thought of it before. "We got to get you back to your father."

"You forget. He's dead."

"Your mother, then."

"The car's dead."

"We'll get it out of hock."

"It's too late," Jill tells him. "It's too late for you to try to love me."

He wants to answer, but there is a puzzling heavy truth in this that carries him under, his hand caressing the inward dip of her waist, a warm bird dipping toward its nest.

Sunshine, the old clown. So many maple leaves have fallen that morning light slants in baldly. A headache grazes his skull, his dream (Pajasek and he were in a canoe, paddling upstream, through a dark green country; their destination felt to be a distant mountain striped and folded like a tablecloth. "When can I have my silver bullet?" Rabbit asked him. "You promised." "Fool," Pajasek told him. "Stupid." "You know so much more," Rabbit answered, nonsensically, and his heart opened in a flood of light) merges with the night before, both unreal. Jill sleeps dewily beside him; at the base of her throat, along her hairline, sweat has collected and glistens. Delicately, not to disturb her, he takes her wrist and turns it so he can see the inside of her freckled arm. They might be bee-stings. There are not too many. He can talk to Janice. Then he remembers that Janice is not here, and that only Nelson is their child. He eases from the bed, amused to discover himself in underwear, like those times when Mom had left his pajamas on the line to dry.

After breakfast, while Jill and Skeeter sleep, he and Nelson rake and mow the lawn, putting it to bed for the winter. He hopes this will be the last mowing, though in fact the grass, parched in high spots, is vigorously green where a depression holds moisture, and along a line from the kitchen to the street —perhaps the sewer connection is broken and seeping, that is why the earth of Penn Villas has a sweetish stink. And the leaves—he calls to Nelson, who has to shut off the razzing mower to listen, "How the hell does such a skinny little tree produce so many leaves?"

"They aren't all *its* leaves. They blow in from the other trees."

And he looks, and sees that his neighbors have trees, saplings like his, but some already as tall as the housetops. Someday Nelson may come back to this, his childhood neighborhood, and find it strangely dark, buried in shade, the lawns opulent, the homes venerable. Rabbit hears children calling in other yards, and sees across several fences and driveways kids having a Saturday scrimmage, one voice piping, "I'm free, I'm free," and the ball obediently floating. This isn't a bad neighborhood, he thinks, this could be a nice place if you gave it a chance. And around the other houses men with rakes and mowers mirror him. He asks Nelson, before the boy restarts the mower, "Aren't you going to visit your mother today?"

"Tomorrow. Today she and Charlie were driving up to the Poconos, to look at the foliage. They went with some brother of Charlie's and his wife."

"Boy, she's moving right in." A real Springer. He smiles to himself, perversely proud. The legal stationery must be on the way. And then he can join that army of the unattached, of Brewer geezers. Human garbage, Pop used to say. He better enjoy Vista Crescent while he has it. He resumes raking, and listens for the mower's razzing to resume. Instead, there is the lurch and rattle of the starter, repeated, and Nelson's voice calling, "Hey Dad. I think it's out of gas."

A Saturday, then, of small sunlit tasks, acts of caretaking and commerce. He and Nelson stroll with the empty five-gallon can up to Weiser Street and get it filled at the Getty station. Returning, they meet Jill and Skeeter emerging from the house, dressed to kill. Skeeter wears stovepipe pants, alligator shoes, a maroon turtleneck and a peach-colored cardigan. He looks like the newest thing in golf pros. Jill has on her mended white dress and a brown sweater of Harry's; she suggests a cheerleader, off to the noon pep rally before the football game. Her face, though thin, and the skin of it thin and brittle like isinglass, has a pink flush; she seems excited, affectionate. "There's some salami and lettuce in the fridge for you and Nelson to make lunch with if you want. Skeeter and I are going into Brewer to see what we can do about this wretched car. And we thought we might drop in on Babe. We'll be back late this after. Maybe you should visit your mother this afternoon, I feel guilty you never do."

"O.K., I might. You O.K.?" To Skeeter: "You have bus fare?"

In his clothes Skeeter puts on a dandy's accent; he thrusts out his goatee and says between scarcely parted teeth, "Jilly is loaded. And if we run short, your name is good credit, right?" Rabbit tries to recall the naked man of last night, the dangling penis, the jutting heels, the squat as by a jungle fire, and cannot; it was another terrain.

Serious, a daylight man, he scolds: "You better get back before Nelson and I go out around six. I don't want to leave the house empty." He drops his voice so Nelson won't hear. "After last night, I'm kind of spooked."

"What happened last night?" Skeeter asks. "Nothin' spooky that I can remember, we'se all jest folks, livin' out life in these Benighted States." He has put on all his armor, nothing will get to him.

Rabbit tests it: "You're a *baad* nigger."

Skeeter smiles in the sunshine with angelic rows of teeth; his spectacles toss halos higher than the TV aerials. "Now you're singing my song," he says.

Rabbit asks Jill, "You O.K. with this crazyman?"

She says lightly, "He's my sugar daddy," and puts her arm through his, and linked like that they recede down Vista Crescent, and vanish in the shuffle of picture windows.

Rabbit and Nelson finish the lawn. They eat, and toss a football around for a while, and then the boy asks if he can go off and join the scrimmage whose shouts they can hear, he knows some of the kids, the same kids who look into windows but that's O.K., Dad; and really it does feel as though all can be forgiven, all will sink into Saturday's America like rain into earth, like days into time. Rabbit goes into the house and watches the first game of the World Series, Baltimore outclassing the Mets, for a while, and switches to Penn State outclassing West Virginia at football, and, unable to sit still any longer with the bubble of premonition swelling inside him, goes to the phone and calls his home. "Hi Pop, hey. I thought of coming over this after but the kid is outside playing a game and we have to go over to Fosnachts tonight anyhow, so can she wait until tomorrow? Mom. Also I ought to get hot on changing the screens around to storm windows, it felt chilly last night."

"She can wait, Harry. Your mother does a lot of waiting these days."

"Yeah, well." He means it's not his fault, he didn't invent old age. "When is Mim coming in?"

"Any day now, we don't know the exact day. She'll just arrive, is how she left it. Her old room is ready."

"How's Mom sleeping lately? She still having dreams?"

"Strange you should ask, Harry. I always said, you and your mother are almost psychic. Her dreams are getting worse. She dreamed last night we buried her alive. You and me and Mim together. She said only Nelson tried to stop it."

"Gee, maybe she's warming up to Nelson at last."

"And Janice called us this morning."

"What about? I'd hate to have Stavros's phone bill."

"Difficult to say, what about. She had nothing concrete that we could fathom, she just seems to want to keep in touch. I think she's having terrible second thoughts, Harry. She says she's exceedingly worried about you."

"I bet."

"Your mother and I spent a lot of time discussing her call; you know our Mary, she's never one to admit when she's disturbed—"

"Pop, there's somebody at the door. Tell Mom I'll be over tomorrow, absolutely."

There had been nobody at the door. He had suddenly been unable to keep talking to his father, every word of the old man's dragging with reproach. But having lied frightens him now; "nobody" has become an evil presence at the door. Moving through the rooms stealthily, he searches the house for the kit Skeeter must use to fix Jill with. He can picture it from having watched television: the syringe and tourniquet and the long spoon to melt the powder in. The sofa cushions divulge a dollar in change, a bent paperback of *Soul on Ice*, a pearl from an earring or pocketbook. Jill's bureau drawers upstairs conceal nothing under the underwear but a box of Tampax, a packet of hairpins, a half-full card of Enovid pills, a shy little tube of ointment for acne. The last place he thinks to look is the downstairs closet, fitted into an ill-designed corner beside the useless fireplace, along the wall of stained pine where the seascape hangs that Janice bought at Kroll's complete with frame, one piece in fact with its frame, a single shaped sheet of plastic, Rabbit remembers from hanging it on the nail. In this closet, beneath the polyethylene bags holding their winter clothes, including the mink stole old man Springer gave

Janice on her twenty-first birthday, there is a squat black suitcase, smelling new, with a combination lock. Packed so Skeeter could grab it and run from the house in thirty seconds. Rabbit fiddles with the lock, trying combinations at random, trusting to God to make a very minor miracle, then, this failing, going at it by system, beginning 111, 112, 113, 114, and then 211, 212, 213, but never hits it, and the practical infinity of numbers opens under him dizzyingly. Some dust in the closet starts him sneezing. He goes outdoors with the Windex bottle for the storm windows.

This work soothes him. You slide up the aluminum screen, putting the summer behind you, and squirt the inside window with the blue spray, give it those big square swipes to spread it thin, and apply the tighter rubbing to remove the film and with it the dirt; it squeaks, like birdsong. Then slide the winter window down from the slot where it has been waiting since April and repeat the process; and go inside and repeat the process, twice: so that at last four flawless transparencies permit outdoors to come indoors, other houses to enter yours.

Toward five o'clock Skeeter and Jill return, by taxi. They are jubilant; through Babe they found a man willing to give them six hundred dollars for the Porsche. He drove them up-county, he examined the car, and Jill signed the registration over to him.

"What color was he?" Rabbit asks.

"He was green," Skeeter says, showing him ten-dollar bills fanned in his hand.

Rabbit asks Jill, "Why'd you split it with *him*?"

Skeeter says, "I dig hostility. You want your cut, right?" His lips push, his glasses glint.

Jill laughs it off. "Skeeter's my partner in crime," she says.

"You want my advice, what you should do with that money?" Rabbit says. "You should get a train ticket back to Stonington."

"The trains don't run any more. Anyway, I thought I'd buy some new dresses. Aren't you tired of this ratty old white one? I had to pin it up in the front and wear this sweater over it."

"It suits you," he says.

She takes up the challenge in his tone. "Something bugging you?"

"Just your sloppiness. You're throwing your fucking life away."

"Would you like me to leave? I could now."

His arms go numb as if injected: his hands feel heavy, his palms tingly and swollen. Her nibbling mouth, her apple hardness, the sea-fan of her cedar-colored hair on their pillows in the morning light, her white valentine of packed satin. "No," he begs, "don't go yet."

"Why not?"

"You're under my skin." The phrase feels unnatural on his lips, puffs them like a dry wind in passing; it must have been spoken for Skeeter, for Skeeter cackles appreciatively.

"Chuck, you're learning to be a loser. I love it. The Lord loves it. Losers gonna grab the earth, right?"

Nelson returns from the football game with a bruised upper lip, his smile lopsided and happy. "They give you a hard time?" Rabbit asks.

"No, it was fun. Skeeter, you ought to play next Saturday, they asked who you were and I said you used to be a quarterback for Brewer High."

"Quarterback, shit, I was *full* back, I was so small they couldn't find me."

"I don't mind being small, it makes you quicker."

"O.K.," his father says, "see how quick you can take a bath. And for once in your life brush your hair."

Festively Jill and Skeeter see them off to the Fosnachts. Jill straightens Rabbit's tie, Skeeter dusts his shoulders like a Pullman porter. "Just think, honey," Skeeter says to Jill, "our little boy's all growed up, his first date."

"It's just dinner," Rabbit protests. "I'll be back for the eleven-o'clock news."

"That big honky with the sideways eyes, she may have something planned for dessert."

"You stay as late as you want," Jill tells him. "We'll leave the porch light on and won't wait up."

"What're *you* two going to do tonight?"

"Jes' read and knit and sit cozy by the fire," Skeeter tells him.

"Her number's in the book if you need to get ahold of me. Under just M."

"We won't disturb you," Jill tells him.

Nelson unexpectedly says, "Skeeter, lock the doors and don't go outside unless you have to."

The Negro pats the boy's brushed hair. "Wouldn't dream of it, chile. Ol' tarbaby, he just stay right here in his briar patch."

Nelson says suddenly, panicking, "Dad, we shouldn't go."

"Don't be dumb." They go. Orange sunlight stripes with long shadows the spaces of flat lawn between the low houses. As Vista Crescent curves, the sun moves behind them and Rabbit is struck, seeing their elongated shadows side by side, by how much like himself Nelson walks: the same loose lope below, the same faintly tense stillness of the head and shoulders above. In shadow the boy, like himself, is as tall as the giant at the top of the beanstalk, treading the sidewalk on telescoping legs. Rabbit turns to speak. Beside him, the boy's overlong dark hair bounces as he strides to keep up, lugging his pajamas and toothbrush and change of underwear and sweater in a paper grocery bag for tomorrow's boat ride, an early birthday party. Rabbit finds there is nothing to say, just mute love spinning down, love for this extension of himself downward into time when he will be in the grave, love cool as the flame of sunlight burning level among the stick-thin maples and fallen leaves, themselves flames curling.

And from Peggy's windows Brewer glows and dwindles like ashes in a gigantic hearth. The river shines blue long after the shores turn black. There is a puppy in the apartment now, a fuzzy big-pawed Golden that tugs at Rabbit's hand with a slippery nipping mouth; its fur, touched, is as surprising in its softness as ferns. Peggy has remembered he likes Daiquiris; this time she has mix and the electric blender rattles with ice before she brings him his drink, half froth. She has aged a month: a pound or two around her waist, two or three more gray hairs showing at her parting. She has gathered her hair back in a twist, rather than letting it straggle around her face as if she were still in high school. Her face looks pushed-forward, scrubbed, glossy. She tells him wearily, "Ollie and I may be getting back together."

She is wearing a blue dress, secretarial, that suits her more than that paisley that kept riding up her pasty thighs. "That's good, isn't it?"

"It's good for Billy." The boys, once Nelson arrived, went

down the elevator again, to try to repair the mini-bike in the
basement. "In fact, that's mostly the reason; Ollie is worried
about Billy. With me working and not home until dark, he
hangs around with that bad crowd up toward the bridge.
You know, it's not like when we were young, the temptations
they're exposed to. It's not just cigarettes and a little feeling
up. At thirteen now, they're ready to go."

Harry brushes froth from his lips and wishes she would
come away from the window so he could see all of the sky. "I
guess they figure they might be dead at eighteen."

"Janice says you like the war."

"I don't like it; I defend it. I wasn't thinking of that, they
have a lot of ways to die now we didn't have. Anyway, it's nice
about you and Ollie, if it works out. A little sad, too."

"Why sad?"

"Sad for me. I mean, I guess I blew my chance, to—"

"To what?"

"To cash you in."

Bad phrase, too harsh, though it had been an apology. He
has lived with Skeeter too long. But her blankness, the blankness of her silhouette as Peggy stands in her habitual pose
against the windows, suggested it. A blank check. A woman is
blank until you fuck her. Everything is blank until you fuck it.
Us and Vietnam, fucking and being fucked, blood is wisdom.
Must be some better way but it's not in nature. His silence
is leaden with regret. She remains blank some seconds, says
nothing. Then she moves into the space around him, turns on
lamps, lifts a pillow into place, plumps it, stoops and straightens, turns, takes light upon her sides, is rounded into shape. A
lumpy big woman but not a fat one, clumsy but not gross, sad
with evening, with Ollie or not Ollie, with having a lengthening past and less and less future. Three classes behind his,
Peggy Gring had gone to high school with Rabbit and had
seen him when he was good, had sat in those hot bleachers
screaming, when he was a hero, naked and swift and lean. She
has seen him come to nothing. She plumps down in the chair
beside his and says, "I've been cashed in a lot lately."

"You mean with Ollie?"

"Others. Guys I meet at work. Ollie minds. That may be
why he wants back in."

"If Ollie minds, you must be telling him. So you must want him back in too."

She looks into the bottom of her glass; there is nothing there but ice. "And how about you and Janice?"

"Janice who? Let me get you another drink."

"Wow. You've become a gentleman."

"Slightly."

As he puts her gin-and-tonic into her hand, he says, "Tell me about those other guys."

"They're O.K. I'm not that proud of them. They're human. I'm human."

"You do it but don't fall in love?"

"Apparently. Is that terrible?"

"No," he says. "I think it's nice."

"You think a lot of things are nice lately."

"Yeah. I'm not so uptight. Sistah Peggeh, I'se seen de light."

The boys come back upstairs. They complain the new headlight they bought doesn't fit. Peggy feeds them, a casserole of chicken legs and breasts, poor dismembered creatures simmering. Rabbit wonders how many animals have died to keep his life going, how many more will die. A barnyard full, a farmful of thumping hearts, seeing eyes, racing legs, all stuffed squawking into him as into a black sack. No avoiding it: life does want death. To be alive is to kill. Dinner inside them, they stuff themselves on television: Jackie Gleason, *My Three Sons*, *Hogan's Heroes*, *Petticoat Junction*, *Mannix*. An orgy. Nelson is asleep on the floor, radioactive light beating on his closed lids and open mouth. Rabbit carries him into Billy's room, while Peggy tucks her own son in. "Mom, I'm not sleepy." "It's past bedtime." "It's Saturday night." "You have a big day tomorrow." "When is *he* going home?" He must think Harry has no ears. "When he wants to." "What are you going to do?" "Nothing that's any of your business." *"Mom."* "Shall I listen to your prayers?" "When he's not listening." "Then you say them to yourself tonight."

Harry and Peggy return to the living room and watch the week's news roundup. The weekend commentator is fairer-haired and less severe in expression than the weekday one. He says there has been some good news this week. American deaths in Vietnam were reported the lowest in three years, and

one twenty-four-hour period saw no American battle deaths
at all. The Soviet Union made headlines this week, agreeing
with the U.S. to ban atomic weapons from the world's ocean
floors, agreeing with Red China to hold talks concerning their
sometimes bloody border disputes, and launching Soyuz 6, a
linked three-stage space spectacular bringing closer the day of
permanent space stations. In Washington, Hubert Humphrey
endorsed Richard Nixon's handling of the Vietnam war and
Lieutenant General Lewis B. Hershey, crusty and controversial
head for twenty-eight years of this nation's selective service system, was relieved of his post and promoted to four-star general.
In Chicago, riots outside the courtroom and riotous behavior
within continued to characterize the trial of the so-called Chicago Eight. In Belfast, Protestants and British troops clashed.
In Prague, Czechoslovakia's revisionist government, in one of
its sternest moves, banned citizens from foreign travel. And
preparations were under way: for tomorrow's Columbus Day
parades, despite threatened protests from Scandinavian groups
maintaining that Leif Ericson and not Columbus was the dis-
coverer of America, and for Wednesday's Moratorium Day, a
nationwide outpouring of peaceful protest. "Crap," says Rabbit. Sports. Weather. Peggy rises awkwardly from her chair to
turn it off. Rabbit rises, also stiff. "Great supper," he tells her.
"I guess I'll get back to the ranch."

The television off, they stand rimmed by borrowed light:
the bathroom door down the hall left ajar for the boys, the
apartment-house corridor a bright slit beneath the door leading out, the phosphorescence of Brewer through the windows.
Peggy's body, transected and rimmed by those remote fires,
does not quite fit together; her arm jerks up from darkness
and brushes indifferently at her hair and seems to miss. She
shrugs, or shudders, and shadows slip from her. "Wouldn't you
like," she asks, in a voice not quite hers, originating in the dim
charged space between them, and lighter, breathier, "to cash
me in?"

Yes, it turns out, yes he would, and they bump, and fumble,
and unzip, and she is gumdrops everywhere, yet stately as a
statue, planetary in her breadth, a contour map of some snowy
land where he has never been; not since Ruth has he had a
woman this big. Naked, she makes him naked, even kneeling

to unlace his shoes, and then kneeling to him in the pose of
Jill to Skeeter, so he has glided across a gulf, and stands where
last night he stared. He gently unlinks her, lowers her to the
floor, and tastes a salty swamp between her legs. Her thighs
part easily, she grows wet readily, she is sadly unclumsy at this,
she has indeed been to bed with many men. In the knowing
way she handles his prick he feels their presences, feels himself competing, is put off, goes soft. She leaves off and comes
up and presses the gumdrop of her tongue between his lips.
Puddled on the floor, they keep knocking skulls and ankle
bones on the furniture legs. The puppy, hearing their commotion, thinks they want to play and thrusts his cold nose and
scrabbling paws among their sensitive flesh; his fern-furry busy
bustlingness tickles and hurts. This third animal among them
re-excites Rabbit; observing this, Peggy leads him down her
hall, the dark crease between her buttocks snapping tick-tock
with her walk. Holding her rumpled dress in front of her like
a pad, she pauses at the boys' door, listens, and nods. Her hair
has gone loose. The puppy for a while whimpers at their door
and claws the floor as if to dig there; then he is eclipsed by the
inflammation of their senses and falls silent beneath the thunder of their blood. Harry is afraid with this unknown woman,
of timing her wrong, but she tells him, "One sec." Him inside
her, she does something imperceptible, relaxing and tensing
the muscles of her vagina, and announces breathily "Now."
She comes one beat ahead of him, a cool solid thump of a
come that lets him hit home without fear of hurting her: a
fuck innocent of madness. Then slides in that embarrassment
of afterwards—of returning discriminations, of the other re-
emerging from the muddle, of sorting out what was hers and
what was yours. He hides his face in the hot cave at the side of
her neck. "Thank you."

"Thank you yourself," Peggy Fosnacht says, and, what he
doesn't especially like, grabs his bottom to give her one more
deep thrust before he softens. Both Jill and Janice too ladylike
for that. Still, he is at home.

Until she says, "Would you mind rolling off? You're squeezing the breath out of me."

"Am I so heavy?"

"After a while."

"Actually, I better go."

"Why? It's only midnight."

"I'm worried about what they're doing back at the house."

"Nelson's here. The others, what do you care?"

"I don't know. I care."

"Well they don't care about you and you're in bed with someone who does."

He accuses her: "You're taking Ollie back."

"Have any better ideas? He's the father of my child."

"Well that's not my fault."

"No, nothing's your fault," and she tumbles around him, and they make solid sadly skillful love again, and they talk and he dozes a little, and the phone rings. It shrills right beside his ear.

A woman's arm, plump and elastic and warm, reaches across his face to pluck it silent. Peggy Gring's. She listens, and hands it to him with an expression he cannot read. There is a clock beside the telephone; its luminous hands say one-twenty. "Hey. Chuck? Better get your ass over here. It's bad. Bad."

"Skeeter?" His throat hurts, just speaking. Fucking Peggy has left him dry.

The voice at the other end hangs up.

Rabbit kicks out of the bedcovers and hunts in the dark for his clothes. He remembers. The living room. The boys' door opens as he runs down the hall naked. Nelson's astonished face takes in his father's nakedness. He asks, "Was it Mom?"

"Mom?"

"On the phone."

"Skeeter. Something's gone wrong at the house."

"Should I come?"

They are in the living room, Rabbit stooping to gather his clothes scattered over the floor, hopping to get into his underpants, his suit pants. The puppy, awake again, dances and nips at him.

"Better stay."

"What can it be, Dad?"

"No idea. Maybe the cops. Maybe Jill getting sicker."

"Why didn't he talk longer?"

"His voice sounded funny, I'm not sure it was our phone."

"I'm coming with you."

"I told you to stay here."

"I *must*, Dad."

Rabbit looks at him and agrees, "O.K. I guess you must."

Peggy in blue bathrobe is in the hall; more lights are on. Billy is up. His pajamas are stained yellow at the fly, he is pimply and tall. Peggy says, "Shall I get dressed?"

"No. You're great the way you are." Rabbit is having trouble with his tie: his shirt collar has a button in the back that has to be undone to get the tie under. He puts on his coat and stuffs the tie into his pocket. His skin is tingling with the start of sweat and his penis murmuringly aches. He has forgotten to do the laces of his shoes and as he kneels to do them his stomach jams into his throat.

"How will you get there?" Peggy asks.

"Run," Rabbit answers.

"Don't be funny, it's a mile and a half. I'll get dressed and drive you."

She must be told she is not his wife. "I don't want you to come. Whatever it is, I don't want you and Billy to get involved."

"Mo-*om*," Billy protests from the doorway. But he is still in stained pajamas whereas Nelson is dressed, but for bare feet. His sneakers are in his hand.

Peggy yields. "I'll get you my car keys. It's the blue Fury, the fourth slot in the line against the wall. Nelson knows. No, Billy. You and I will stay here." Her voice is factual, secretarial.

Rabbit takes the keys, which come into his hand as cold as if they have been in the refrigerator. "Thanks a lot. Or have I said that before? Sorry about this. Great dinner, Peggy."

"Glad you liked it."

"We'll let you know what's what. It's probably nothing, the son of a bitch is probably just stoned out of his mind."

Nelson has put his socks and sneakers on. "Let's *go*, Dad. Thank you very much, Mrs. Fosnacht."

"You're both very welcome."

"Thank Mr. Fosnacht in case I can't go on the boat tomorrow."

Billy is still trying. "Mo-*om*, let me."

"No."

"Mom, you're a bitch."

Peggy slaps her son: pink leaps up on his cheek in stripes

like fingers, and the child's face hardens beyond further controlling. "Mom, you're a whore. That's what the bridge kids say. You'll lay anybody."

Rabbit says, "You two take it easy," and turns; they flee, father and son, down the hall, down the steel stairwell, not waiting for an elevator, to a basement of parked cars, a polychrome lake caught in a low illumined grotto. Rabbit blinks to realize that even while he and Peggy were heating their little mutual darkness a cold fluorescent world surrounded them in hallways and down stairwells and amid unsleeping pillars upholding their vast building. The universe is unsleeping, neither ants nor stars sleep, to die will be to be forever wide awake. Nelson finds the blue car for him. Its dashlights glow green at ignition. Almost silently the engine comes to life, backs them out, sneaks them along past the stained grotto walls. In a corner by the brickwork of a stairwell the all-chrome mini-bike waits to be repaired. An asphalt exitway becomes a parking lot, becomes a street lined with narrow houses and great green signs bearing numbers, keystones, shields, the names of unattainable cities. They come onto Weiser; the traffic is thin, sinister. The stoplights no longer regulate but merely wink. Burger Bliss is closed, though its purple oven glows within, plus a sallow residue of ceiling tubes to discourage thieves and vandals. A police car nips by, bleating. The Acme lot at this hour has no horizon. Are the few cars still parked on it abandoned? Or lovers? Or ghosts in a world so thick with cars their shadows like leaves settle everywhere? A whirling light, insulting in its brilliance, materializes in Rabbit's rear-view mirror and as it swells acquires the overpowering grief of a siren. The red bulk of a fire engine plunges by, sucking the Fury toward the center of the street, where the trolley-track bed used to be. Nelson cries, "Dad!"

"Dad what?"

"Nothing, I thought you lost control."

"Never. Not your Dad."

The movie marquee, unlit and stubby, is announcing, BACK BY REQST—2001. All these stores along Weiser have burglar lights on and a few, a new defense, wear window grilles.

"Dad, there's a glow in the sky."

"Where?"

"Off to the right."

He says, "That can't be us. Penn Villas is more ahead."

But Emberly Avenue turns right more acutely than he had ever noticed, and the curving streets of Penn Villas do deliver them toward a dome of rose-colored air. People, black shapes, race on silent footsteps, and cars have run to a stop diagonally against the curbs. Down where Emberly meets Vista Crescent, a policeman stands, rhythmically popping into brightness as the twirling fire-engine lights pass over him. Harry parks where he can drive no further and runs down Vista, after Nelson. Fire hoses lie across the asphalt, some deflated like long canvas trouser legs and some fat as cobras, jetting hissingly from their joints. The gutter gnashes with swirling black water and matted leaves; around the sewer drain, a whirlpool widens out from the clogged center. Two houses from their house, they encounter an odor akin to leaf-smoke but more acrid and bitter, holding paint and tar and chemicals; one house away, the density of people stops them. Nelson sinks into the crowd and vanishes. Rabbit shoulders after him, apologizing, "Excuse me, this is my house, pardon me, my house." He says this but does not yet believe it. His house is masked from him by heads, by searchlights and upward waterfalls, by rainbows and shouts, by something magisterial and singular about the event that makes it as hard to see as the sun. People, neighbors, part to let him through. He sees. The garage is gone; the charred studs still stand, but the roof has collapsed and the shingles smolder with spurts of blue-green flame amid the drenched wreckage on the cement floor. The handle of the power mower pokes up intact. The rooms nearest the garage, the kitchen and the bedroom above it, the bedroom that had been his and Janice's and then his and Jill's, flame against the torrents of water. Flame sinks back, then bursts out again, through roof or window, in tongues. The apple-green aluminum clapboards do not themselves burn; rather, they seem to shield the fire from the water. Abrupt gaps in the shifting weave of struggling elements let shreds show through of the upstairs wallpaper, of the kitchen shelves; then these gaps shut at a breath of wind. He scans the upstairs window for Jill's face, but glimpses only the stained ceiling. The roof above, half the roof, is a field of smoke, smoke bubbling up and coming off the shadow-line shingles in serried billows that look combed. Smoke pours out of Nelson's windows, but that half of the house is not yet aflame, and may be saved. Indeed, the house burns spitefully, spitting, stinkingly: the ersatz and synthetic materials grudge combustion its triumph. Once in boyhood Rabbit saw a barn burn in the valley east of Mt. Judge; it was a torch, an explosion of hay outstarring the sky with embers. Here there is no such display.

There is space around him. The spectators, the neighbors, in honor of his role, have backed off. Months ago Rabbit had seen that bright island of moviemakers and now he is at the center of this bright island and still feels peripheral, removed, nostalgic, numb. He scans the firelit faces and does not see Showalter or Brumbach. He sees no one he knows.

The crowd stirs, *ooh*. He expects to see Jill at the window, ready to leap, her white dress translucent around her body. But the windows let only smoke escape, and the drama is on the ground. A policeman is struggling with a slight lithe figure; Harry thinks eagerly, *Skeeter*, but the struggle pivots, and it is Nelson's white face. A fireman helps pin the boy's arms. They bring him away from the house, to his father. Seeing his father, Nelson clamps shut his eyes and draws his lips back in a snarl and struggles so hard to be free that the two men holding his arms seem to be wildly operating pump handles. "She's *in* there, Dad!"

The policeman, breathing hard, explains, "Boy tried to get into the house. Says there's a girl in there."

"I don't know, she must have gotten out. We just got here."

Nelson's eyes are frantic; he screeches everything. "Did Skeeter *say* she was with *him*?"

"No." Harry can hardly get the words out. "He just said things were bad."

In listening, the fireman and policeman loosen their grip, and Nelson breaks away to run for the front door again. Heat must meet him, for he falters at the porchlet steps, and he is seized again, by men whose slickers make them seem beetles. This time, brought back, Nelson screams up at Harry's face: "You fucking asshole, you've let her die. I'll kill you. I'll kill *you*." And, though it is his son, Harry crouches and gets his hands up ready to fight.

But the boy cannot burst the grip of the men; he tells them in a voice less shrill, arguing for his release, "I know she's in there. Let me go, please. Please let me go. Just let me get her out, I know I can. I *know* I can. She'd be upstairs asleep. She'd be easy to lift. Dad, I'm sorry. I'm sorry I swore at you. I didn't mean it. Tell them to let me. Tell them about Jill. Tell them to get her out."

Rabbit asks the firemen, "Wouldn't she have come to the window?"

The fireman, an old rodent of a man, with tufty eyebrows and long yellow teeth, ruminates as he talks. "Girl asleep in there, smoke might get to her before she properly woke up. People don't realize what a deadly poison smoke is. That's what does you in, the smoke not the fire." He asks Nelson, "O.K. to let go, sonny? Act your age now, we'll send men up the ladder."

One beetle-backed fireman chops at the front door. The glass from the three panes shatters and tinkles on the flagstones. Another fireman emerges from the other side of the roof and with his ax picks a hole above the upstairs hall, about where Nelson's door would be. Something invisible sends him staggering back. A violet flame shoots up. A cannonade of water chases him back over the roof ridge.

"They're not doing it right, Dad," Nelson moans. "They're not getting her. I know where she is and they're not *get*ting her, Dad!" And the boy's voice dies in a shuddering wail. When Rabbit reaches toward him he pulls away and hides his face. The back of his head feels soft beneath the hair: an overripe fruit.

Rabbit reassures him, "Skeeter would've gotten her out."

"He *would*n't of, Dad! He wouldn't *care*. All he cared about was *himself*. And all you cared about was *him*. Nobody cared about *Jill*." He writhes in his father's fumbling grasp.

A policeman is beside them. "You Angstrom?" He is one of the new style of cops, collegiate-looking: pointed nose, smooth chin, sideburns cut to a depth Rabbit still thinks of as antisocial.

"Yes."

The cop takes out a notebook. "How many persons were in residence here?"

"Four. Me and the kid—"

"Name?"

"Nelson."

"Any middle initial?"

"F for Frederick." The policeman writes slowly and speaks so softly he is hard to hear against the background of crowd murmur and fire crackle and water being hurled. Harry has to ask, "What?"

The cop repeats, "Name of mother?"

"Janice. She's not living here. She lives over in Brewer."

"Address?"

Harry remembers Stavros's address, but gives instead, "Care of Frederick Springer, 89 Joseph Street, Mt. Judge."

"And who is the girl the boy mentioned?"

"Jill Pendleton, of Stonington, Connecticut. Don't know the street address."

"Age?"

"Eighteen or nineteen."

"Family relationship?"

"None."

It takes the cop a very long time to write this one word. Something is happening to a corner of the roof; the crowd noise is rising, and a ladder is being lowered through an intersection of searchlights.

Rabbit prompts: "The fourth person was a Negro we called Skeeter. *S-k*-double-*e-t-e-r*."

"Black male?"

"Yes."

"Last name?"

"I don't know. Could be Farnsworth."

"Spell please."

Rabbit spells it and offers to explain. "He was just here temporarily."

The cop glances up at the burning ranch house and then over at the owner. "What were you doing here, running a commune?"

"No, Jesus; listen. I'm not for any of that. I voted for Hubert Humphrey."

The cop studies the house. "Any chance this black is in there now?"

"Don't think so. He was the one that called me, it sounded as if from a phone booth."

"Did he say he'd set the fire?"

"No, he didn't even say there was a fire, he just said things were bad. He said the word 'bad' twice."

"Things were bad," the cop writes, and closes his notepad. "We'll want some further interrogation later." Reflected fire-light gleams peach-color off of the badge in his cap. The corner of the house above the bedroom is collapsing; the television aerial, that they twice adjusted and extended to cut down ghosts from their neighbors' sets, tilts in the leap of flame and slowly swings downward like a skeletal tree, still clinging by some wires or brackets to its roots. Water vaults into what had been the bedroom. A lavish cumulus of yellow smoke pours out, golden-gray, rich as icing squeezed from the sugary hands of a pastry cook.

The cop casually allows, "Anybody in there was cooked a half-hour ago."

Two steps away, Nelson is bent over to let vomit spill from his mouth. Rabbit steps to him and the boy allows himself to be touched. He holds him by the shoulders; it feels like trying to hold out of water a heaving fish that wants to go back under, that needs to dive back under or die. His father brings back his hair from his cheeks so it will not be soiled by vomit; with his fist he makes a feminine knot of hair at the back of the boy's hot soft skull. "Nellie, I'm sure she got out. She's far away. She's safe and far away."

The boy shakes his head *No* and retches again; Harry holds him for minutes, one hand clutching his hair, the other around his chest. He is holding him up from sinking into the earth. If Harry were to let go, he would sink too. He feels precariously heavier on his bones; the earth pulls like Jupiter. Policemen, spectators, watch him struggle with Nelson but do not intervene. Finally a cop, not the interrogating one, does approach and in a calm Dutch voice asks, "Shall we have a car take the boy somewhere? Does he have grandparents in the county?"

"Four of them," Rabbit says. "Maybe he should go to his mother."

"*No!*" Nelson says, and breaks loose to face them. "You're not getting me to go until we know where Jill is." His face shines with tears but is sane: he waits out the next hour standing by his father's side.

The flames are slowly smothered, the living-room side of the house is saved. The interior of the kitchen side seems a garden where different tints of smoke sprout; formica, vinyl, nylon, linoleum each burn differently, yield their curdling compounds back to earth and air. Firemen wet down the wreckage and search behind the gutted walls. Now the upstairs windows stare with searchlights, now the lower. A skull full of fireflies. Yet still the crowd waits, held by a pack sense of smell; death is in heat. Intermittently there have been staticky calls over the police radios and one of them has fetched an ambulance; it arrives with a tentative sigh of its siren. Scarlet lights do an offbeat dance on its roof. A strange container, a green rubber bag or sheet, is taken into the house, and brought back by three grim men in slickers. The ambulance receives the shapeless package, is shut with that punky sound only the most expensive automobile doors make, and—again, the tentative sigh of a siren just touched—pulls away. The crowd thins after it. The night overflows with the noise of car motors igniting and revving up.

Nelson says, "Dad."

"Yeah."

"That was her, wasn't it?"

"I don't know. Maybe."

"It was *some*body."

"I guess."

Nelson rubs his eyes; the gesture leaves swipes of ash, Indian markings. The child seems harshly ancient.

"I need to go to bed," he says.

"Want to go back to the Fosnachts?"

"No." As if in apology he explains, "I hate Billy." Further qualifying, he adds, "Unless you do." Unless you want to go back and fuck Mrs. Fosnacht again.

Rabbit asks him, "Want to see your mother?"

"I can't, Dad. She's in the Poconos."

"She should be back by now."

"I don't want to see her now. Take me to Jackson Road."

There is in Rabbit an engine murmuring *Undo, undo,* which wants to take them back to this afternoon, beginning with the moment they left the house, and not do what they did, not leave, and have it all unhappen, and Jill and Skeeter still there, in the house still there. Beneath the noise of this engine the inner admission that it did happen is muffled; he sees Nelson through a gauze of shock and dares ask, "Blame me, huh?"

"Sort of."

"You don't think it was just bad luck?" And though the boy hardly bothers to shrug Harry understands his answer: luck and God are both up there and he has not been raised to believe in anything higher than his father's head. Blame stops for him in the human world, it has nowhere else to go.

The firemen of one truck are coiling their hoses. A policeman, the one who asked after Nelson, comes over. "Angstrom? The chief wants to talk to you where the boy can't hear."

"Dad, ask him if that was Jill."

The cop is tired, stolid, plump, the same physical type as—what was his name?—Showalter. Kindly patient Brewerites. He lets out the information, "It was a cadaver."

"Black or white?" Rabbit asks.

"No telling."

Nelson asks, "Male or female?"

"Female, sonny."

Nelson begins to cry again, to gag as if food is caught in his throat, and Rabbit asks the policeman if his offer is still good, if a cruiser might take the boy to his grandparents' house in Mt. Judge. The boy is led away. He does not resist; Rabbit thought he might, might insist on staying with his father to the end. But the boy, his hair hanging limp and his tears flowing unchecked, seems relieved to be at last in the arms of order, of laws and limits. He doesn't even wave from the window of the silver-blue West Brewer cruiser as it U-turns in Vista Crescent and heads away from the tangle of hoses and puddles and red reflections. The air tastes sulphuric. Rabbit notices that the little maple was scorched on the side toward the house; its twigs smolder like cigarettes.

As the firemen wind up their apparatus, he and the police chief sit in the front of an unmarked car. Harry's knees are crowded by the radio apparatus on the passenger's side. The chief is a short man but doesn't look so short sitting down, with his barrel chest crossed by a black strap and his white hair crew-cut close to his scalp and his nose which was once broken sideways and has accumulated broken veins in the years since. He says, "We have a death now. That makes it a horse of another color."

"Any theories how the fire started?"

"I'll ask the questions. But yes. It was set. In the garage. I notice a power mower in there. Can of gas to go with it?"

"Yeah. We filled the can just this afternoon."

"Tell me where you were this evening."

He tells him. The chief talks on his car radio to the West Brewer headquarters. In less than five minutes they call back. But in the total, unapologetic silence the chief keeps during these minutes, a great lump grows in Rabbit, love of the law. The radio sizzles its words like bacon frying: "Mrs. Fosnacht confirms suspect's story. Also a minor boy in dwelling as additional witness."

"Check," the chief says, and clicks off.

"Why would I burn my own house down?" Rabbit asks.

"Most common arsonist is owner," the chief says. He studies Rabbit thoughtfully; his eyes are almost round, as if somebody took a stitch at the corner of each lid. "Maybe the girl was pregnant by you."

"She was on the Pill."

"Tell me about her."

He tries, though it is hard to make it seem as natural as it felt. Why did he permit Skeeter to move in on him? Well, the question was more, Why not? He tries, "Well, when my wife walked out on me, I kind of lost my bearings. It didn't seem to matter, and anyway he would have taken Jill with him, if I'd kicked him out. I got so I didn't mind him."

"Did he terrorize you?"

He tries to make these answers right. Out of respect for the law. "No. He educated us." Harry begins to get mad. "Some law I don't know about against having people live with you?"

"Law against harboring," the chief tells him, neglecting to write on his pad. "Brewer police report a Hubert Johnson out on default on a possession charge."

Rabbit's silence is not what he wants. He makes it clearer what he wants. "You in ignorance over the existence of this indictment and defiance of court?" He makes it even clearer. "Shall I accept your silence as a profession of ignorance?"

"Yes." It is the only opening. "Yes, I knew nothing about Skeeter, not even his last name."

"His present whereabouts, any ideas?"

"No idea. His call came through from it sounded like a phone booth but I couldn't swear to it."

The cop puts his broad hand over the notebook as if across the listening mouth of a telephone receiver. "Off the record. We've been watching this place. He was a little fish, a punk. We hoped he would lead us to something bigger."

"What bigger? Dope?"

"Civil disturbance. The blacks in Brewer are in touch with Philly, Camden, Newark. We know they have guns. We don't want another York here, now do we?" Again, Rabbit's silence is not what he wants. He repeats, "Now do we?"

"No, of course not. I was just thinking. He talked as if he was beyond revolution; he was kind of religious-crazy, not gun-crazy."

"Any idea why he set this fire?"

"I don't think he did. It isn't his style."

The pencil is back on the notebook. "Never mind about style," the chief says. "I want facts."

"I don't have any more facts than I've told you. Some people in the neighborhood were upset because Skeeter was living with us, two men stopped me on the street yesterday and complained about it, I can give you their names if you want."

The pencil hovers. "They complained. Any specific threats of arson?"

&. Wiseasses get fragged. *You better fucking barricade the whole place.* "Nothing that specific."

The chief makes a notation, it looks like *n.c.*, and turns the notebook page. "The black have sexual relations with the girl?"

"Look, I was off working all day. I'd come back and we'd cook supper and help the kid with his homework and sit around and talk. It was like having two more kids in the house, I don't know what they did every minute. Are you going to arrest me, or what?"

A fatherly type himself, the chief takes a smiling long time answering. Rabbit sees that his nose wasn't broken by accident, somewhere in the alleys of time he had asked for it. His snow-soft hair is cut evenly as a powderpuff, with a pink dent above the ears where the police cap bites. His smile broadens enough to crease his cheek. "Strictly speaking," he says, "this isn't my beat. I'm acting on behalf of my esteemed colleague the sheriff of Furnace Township, who rolled over and went back to sleep. Offhand I'd say we're doing a good enough business in the jails without putting solid citizens like you in there. We'll have some more questions later." He flips the notebook shut and flips the radio on to put out a call, "All cars, Brewer police copy, be on the lookout, Negro, male, height approx five-six, weight approx one-twenty-five, medium dark-skinned, hair Afro, name Skeeter, that is Sally, Katherine, double Easter—" He does not turn his head when Rabbit opens the car door and walks away.

So again in his life the net of law has slipped from him. He knows he is criminal, yet is never caught. Sickness sinks through his body like soot. The firemen wet down the smoking wreckage, the clot of equipment along Vista Crescent breaks up and flows away. The house is left encircled in its disgrace with yellow flashers on trestles warning people off. Rabbit walks around the lawn, so lately a full stage, sodden and pitted by footprints, and surveys the damage.

The burning was worse on the back side: the fixtures of the bedroom bathroom dangle in space from stems of contorted pipe. The wall that took the bed headboard is gone. Patches of night-blue sky show through the roof. He looks in the downstairs windows and sees, by flashing yellow light, as into a hellish fun house, the sofa and the two chairs, salted with fallen plaster, facing each other across the cobbler's bench. The driftwood lamp is still upright. On the shelves giving into the breakfast nook, Skeeter's books squat, soaked and matted. Where the kitchen was, Harry can see out through the garage to an N of charred 2 by 4s. The sky wants to brighten. Birds —birds in Penn Villas, where? there are no trees old enough to hold them—flicker into song. It is cold now, colder than in the heart of the night, when the fire was alive. The sky pales in the east, toward Brewer. Mt. Judge develops an outline in the emulsion of pre-dawn gray. A cloud of birds migrating crosses the suburb southward. The soot is settling on Harry's bones. His eyelids feel like husks. In his weariness he hallucinates; as in the seconds before we sleep, similes seem living organisms. The freshening sky above Mt. Judge is Becky, the child that died, and the sullen sky to the west, the color of a storm sky but flawed by stars, is Nelson, the child that lives. And he, he is the man in the middle.

He walks up to his battered front door, brushes away the glass shards, and sits down on the flagstone porchlet. It is warm, like a hearth. Though none of his neighbors came forward to speak to him, to sparkle on the bright screen of his disaster, the neighborhood presents itself to his gaze unapologetically, naked in the gathering light, the pastel roof shingles moist in patches echoing the pattern of rafters, the back-yard bathing pools and swing sets whitened by dew along with the grass. A half-moon rests cockeyed in the blanched sky like a toy forgotten on a floor. An old man in a noisy green raincoat, a geezer left behind as a watchman, walks over and speaks to him. "This your home, huh?"

"This is it."

"Got some other place to go?"

"I suppose."

"Body a loved one?"

"Not exactly."

"That's good news. Cheer up, young fella. Insurance'll cover most of it."

"Do I have insurance?"

"Had a mortgage?"

Rabbit nods, remembering the little slippery bankbook, imagining it burned.

"Then you had insurance. Damn the banks all you will, they look after their own, you'll never catch them damn Jews short."

This man's presence begins to seem strange. It has been months since anything seemed as strange as this man's presence. Rabbit asks him, "How long you staying here?"

"I'm on duty till eight."

"Why?"

"Fire procedure. Prevent looting." The two of them look wonderingly at the dormant houses and cold lawns of Penn Villas. As they look, a distant alarm rings and an upstairs light comes on, sallow, dutiful. Still, looting these days is everywhere. The geezer asks him, "Anything precious in there, you might want to take along?" Rabbit doesn't move. "You better go get some sleep, young fella."

"What about you?" Rabbit asks.

"Fella my age doesn't need much. Sleep long enough soon enough. Anyway, I like the peacefulness of these hours, have ever since a boy. Always up, my dad, he was a great boozer and a late sleeper, used to wallop the bejesus out of me if I made a stir mornings. Got in the habit of sneaking out to the birds. Anyway, double-hour credit, time outdoors on this shift. Don't always put it in, go over a certain amount, won't get any social security. Kill you with kindness, that's the new technique."

Rabbit stands up, aching; pain moves upward from his shins through his groin and belly to his chest and out. A demon leaving. Smoke, mist rise. He turns to his front door; swollen by water, axed, it resists being opened. The old man tells him, "It's my responsibility to keep any and all persons out of this structure. Any damage you do yourself, you're the party responsible."

"You just told me to take out anything precious."

"You're responsible, that's all I'm saying. I'm turning my back. Fall through the floor, electrocute yourself, don't call for help. Far as I'm concerned, you're not there. See no evil is the way I do it."

"That's the way I do it too." Under pressure the door pops open. Splintered glass on the other side scrapes white arcs into the hall floor finish. Rabbit begins to cry from smoke and the smell. The house is warm, and talks to itself; a swarm of small rustles and snaps arises from the section on his left; settling noises drip from the charred joists and bubble up from the drenched dark rubble where the floor had been. The bed's metal frame has fallen into the kitchen. On his right, the living room is murky but undamaged. The silver threads of the Lustrex chair gleam through an acid mist of fumes; the television set's green blank waits to be turned on. He thinks of taking it, it is the one resaleable item here, but no, it is too heavy to lug, he might drop himself through the floor, and there are millions like it. Janice once said we should drop television sets into the jungle instead of bombs, it would do as much good. He thought at the time the idea was too clever for her; even then Stavros was speaking through her.

She always loved that dumb bench. He remembers her kneeling beside it early in their marriage, rubbing it with linseed oil, short keen strokes, a few inches at a time, it made him feel horny watching. He takes the bench under his arm and, discovering it to be so light, pulls the driftwood lamp loose from its socket and takes that too. The rest the looters and insurance adjusters can have. You never get the smell of smoke out. Like the smell of failure in a life. He remembers the storm windows, Windexing their four sides, and it seems a fable that his life was ever centered on such details. His house slips from him. He is free. Orange light in long stripes, from sun on the side of him opposite from the side the sun was on when he and Nelson walked here a long night ago, stretches between the low strange houses as he walks down Vista Crescent with the table and the lamp tugging under his arms. Peggy's Fury is the only car still parked along the curb: a teal-blue tailfinned boat the ebb has stranded. He opens the door, pushes the seat forward to put the bench in the back, and finds someone there. A Negro. Asleep. "What the hell," Rabbit says.

Skeeter awakes blind and gropes for his glasses on the rubber floor. "Chuck baby," he says, looking up with twin circles of glass. His Afro is flattened on one side. Bad fruit. "All by yourself, right?"

"Yeah." The little car holds a concentration of that smell which in the mornings would spice the living room, give it animal substance, sleep's sweetness made strong.

"How long's it been light?"

"Just started. It's around six. How long've you been here?"

"Since I saw you and Babychuck pull in. I called you from a booth up on Weiser and then watched to see if you'd go by. The car wasn't you but the head was, right, so I snuck along through the back yards and got in after you parked. The old briar patch theory, right? Shit if I didn't fall asleep. Hey get in man, you're lettin' in the air."

Rabbit gets in and sits in the driver's seat, listening without turning his head, trying to talk without moving his mouth. Penn Villas is coming to life; a car just passed. "You ought to know," he says, "they're looking for you. They think you set it."

"Count on the fuzz to fuck up. Why would I go burn my own pad?"

"To destroy evidence. Maybe Jill—what do you call it?—
O.D.'d."

"Not on the scag she was getting from me, that stuff was so
cut sugar water has more flash. Look, Chuck, that up at your
house was honky action. Will you believe the truth, or shall I
save my breath for the pigpen?"

"Let's hear it."

Skeeter's voice, unattached to his face, is deeper than Harry
remembers, with a hypnotic rasping lilt that reminds him of
childhood radio. "Jill sacked out early and I made do with the
sofa, right? Since getting back on the stuff she wasn't putting
out any of her own, and anyway I was pretty spaced and beat,
we went twice around the county unloading that bullshit car.
Right? So I wake up. There was this rattling around. I placed it
coming from the kitchen, right? I was thinkin' it was Jill coming to bug me to shoot her up again, instead there was this
whoosh and soft *woomp*, reminded me of an APM hitting in the
bush up the road, only it wasn't up any road, I say to myself
The war is come home. Next thing there's this slam of a door,
garage door from the rumble of it, and I flip to the window and
see these two honky cats makin' tail across the lawn, across the
street, into between those houses there, and disappear, right?
They had no car I could see. Next thing, I smell smoke."

"How do you know these were white men?"

"Shit, you know how honkies run, like with sticks up their
ass, right?"

"Could you identify them if you saw them again?"

"I ain't identifying Moses around here. My skin is fried in
this county, right?"

"Yeah," Rabbit says. "Something else you should know. Jill
is dead."

The silence from the back seat is not long. "Poor bitch,
doubt if she knows the difference."

"Why didn't you get her out?"

"Hell, man, there was *heat*, right? I thought lynching time
had come, I didn't know there wasn't twelve hundred crackers out there, I was in no shape to take care of some whitey
woman, let Whitey take care of his own."

"But nobody stopped you."

"Basic training, right? I eluded as they say my pursuers."

"They didn't want to hurt you. It was me, they were trying to tell *me* something. People around here don't lynch, don't be crazy."

"Crazy, you've been watching the wrong TV channel. How about those cats in Detroit?"

"How about those dead cops in California? How about all this Off the Pigs crap you brothers have been pushing? I should take you in. The Brewer cops would love to see you, they love to re-educate crazy coons."

Two more cars swish by; from the height of a milk truck the driver looks down curiously. "Let's drive," Skeeter says.

"What's in it for me?"

"Nothing much, right?"

The car starts at a touch. The motor is more silent than their tires swishing in the puddles along Vista Crescent, past the apple-green ruin and the man in the green raincoat dozing on the doorstep. Rabbit heads out the curved streets to where they end, to where they become truck tracks between muddy house foundations. He finds a lost country lane. Tall rows of poplars, a neglected potholed surface. Skeeter sits up. Rabbit waits for the touch of metal on the back of his neck. A gun, a knife, a needle: they always have something. Poison darts. But there is nothing, nothing but the fluctuating warmth of Skeeter's breathing on the back of his neck. "How could you let her die?" he asks.

"Man, you want to talk guilt; we got to go back hundreds of years."

"I wasn't there then. But you were there last night."

"I was severely disadvantaged."

Harry's head is light with lack of sleep; he knows he shouldn't be making decisions. "Tell you what. I'll drive you ten miles south and you take it from there."

"That's cutting it fine, man, but let's say sold. One embarrassment remains. We brothers call it bread."

"You just got six hundred for selling her car."

"My wallet back next to that sofa, every mothering thing, right?"

"How about that black suitcase in the closet?"

"Say. You been snooping, or what?"

"I have maybe thirty dollars," Rabbit says. "You can have that. I'll keep this ride from the cops but then that's quits. Like you said, you've had it in this county."

"I shall return," Skeeter promises, "only in glory."

"When you do, leave me out of it."

Miles pass. A hill, a cluster of sandstone houses, a cement factory, a billboard pointing to a natural cave, another with a huge cutout of a bearded Amishman. Skeeter in yet another of his voices, the one that sounds most like a white man and therefore in Rabbit's ears most human, asks, "How'd Baby-chuck take it, Jill's being wasted?"

"About like you'd expect."

"Broken up, right?"

"Broken up."

"Tell him, there's a ton of cunt in the world."

"I'll let him figure that out himself."

They come to a corner where two narrow roads meet in sunlight. On the far side of a tan cut cornfield a whitewashed stone house sends up smoke. A wooden arrow at the intersection says Galilee 2. Otherwise it could be nowhere. A jet trail smears in the sky. Pennsylvania spreads south silently, through green and brown. A dry stone conduit underlies the road here; a roadside marker is a metal keystone rusted blank. Rabbit empties his wallet into Skeeter's pink palm and chokes off the impulse to apologize for its not being more. He wonders now what would be proper. A Judas kiss? They have scarcely touched since the night they wrestled and Harry won. He holds out his hand to shake farewell. Skeeter studies it as if like Babe he will tell a fortune, takes it into both his slick narrow hands, tips it so the meaty pink creases are skyward, contemplates, and solemnly spits into the center. His saliva being as warm as skin, Harry at first only knows it has happened by seeing: moisture full of bubbles like tiny suns. He chooses to take the gesture as a blessing, and wipes his palm dry on his pants. Skeeter tells him, "Never did figure your angle."

"Probably wasn't one," is the answer.

"Just waiting for the word, right?" Skeeter cackles. When he laughs there is that complexity about his upper lip white men

don't have, a welt in the center, a genial seam reminding Rabbit of the stitch of flesh that holds the head of your cock to the
shaft. As Harry backs Peggy's Fury around in the strait intersection, the young black waits by a bank of brown weed stalks.
In the rearview mirror, Skeeter looks oddly right, blends right
in, even with the glasses and goatee, hanging empty-handed
between fields of stubble where crows settle and shift, gleaning.

COL. EDWIN E. ALDRIN, JR.:
Now you're clear. Over toward me. Straight down, to your left a little bit. Plenty of room. You're lined up nicely. Toward me a little bit. Down. O.K. Now you're clear. You're catching the first hinge. The what hinge? All right, move. Roll to the left. O.K., now you're clear. You're lined up on the platform. Put your left foot to the right a little bit. O.K., that's good. More left. Good.

NEIL ARMSTRONG:
O.K., Houston, I'm on the porch.

IV

Mim

RABBIT is at his machine. His fingers feather, the matrices rattle on high, the molten lead comfortably steams at his side.

ARSON SUSPECTED IN PENN VILLAS BLAZE

Out-of-Stater Perishes

West Brewer police are still collecting testimony from neighbors in connection with the mysterious fire that destroyed the handsome Penn Villas residence of Mr. and Mrs. Harold Angstrom.

A guest in the home, Mill Jiss A guest in the home, Miss Jill Pendleton, 18, of Stonington, Connecticut, perished of smoke inhalation and burns. Rescue attempts by valiant firemen were to no avail.

Miss Pendleton was pronounced dead on arrival at the Sister of Mercy Homeopathic Sisters of Mercy Homeopathic Hospital in Brewer.

A man reported seen in the vicinity of the dwelling, Hubert Johnson last of Plum Street, is being sought for questioning. Mr. Johnson is also known as "Skeeter" and sometimes gives his last name as Farnsworth.

Furnace Township fire chief Raymond "Buddy" Fessler told VAT reporters, "The fire

was set I'm pretty sure, but we
have no evidence of a Molotov
cocktail or anything of that
nature. This was not a bombing
in the ordinary sense."

Neighbors are baffled by the
event, reporting nothing unusual
about the home but the skulking
presence of a black man thought

Pajasek taps him on the shoulder.

"If that's my wife," Rabbit says. "Tell her to bug off. Tell her I'm dead."

"It's nobody on the phone, Harry. I need to have a word with you privately. If I may."

That "if I may" is what puts the chill into Harry's heart. Pajasek is imitating somebody higher up. He shuts his frosted-glass door on the clatter and with a soft thump sits at his desk; he slowly spreads his fingers on the mass of ink-smirched papers there. "More bad news, Harry," he says. "Can you take it?"

"Try me."

"I hate like Jesus to put this into you right on top of your misfortune with your home, but there's no use stalling. Nothing stands still. They've decided up top to make Verity an offset plant. We'll keep an old flatbed for the job work, but the *Vat* said either go offset or have them print in Philly. It's been in the cards for years. This way, we'll be geared up to take other periodicals, there's some new sheets starting up in Brewer, a lot of it filth in my book but people buy it and the law allows it, so there you are." From the way he sighs, he thinks he's made his point. His forehead, seen from above, is global; the worried furrows retreat to the horizon of the skull, where the brass-pale hair begins, wisps brushed straight back.

Rabbit tries to help him. "So no Linotypers, huh?"

Pajasek looks up startled; his eyebrows arch and drop and there is a moment of spherical smoothness, with a long clean highlight from the fluorescent tubes overhead. "I thought I made that point. That's part of the technical picture, that's where the economy comes. Offset, you operate all from film, bypass hot metal entirely. Go to a cathode ray tube, Christ, it delivers two thousand lines a minute, that's the whole *Vat* in seven minutes. We can keep a few men on, retrain them to the computer tape, we've worked the deal out with the union, but this is a sacrifice, Harry, from the management point of view. I'm afraid you're far down the list. Nothing to do with your personal life, understand me—strictly seniority. Your Dad's secure, and Buchanan, Christ, let him go we'd have every do-good outfit in the city on our necks, it's not the way *I'd* do things. If they'd come to me I would have told them, that man is half-soused from eleven o'clock on every morning, they're all like that, I'd just as soon have a moron with mittens on as long he was white—"

"O.K.," Rabbit says. "When do I knock off?"

"Harry, this hurts me like hell. You learned the skill and now the bottom's dropping out. Maybe one of the Brewer dailies can take you on, maybe something in Philly or up in Allentown, though what with papers dropping out or doubling up all over the state there's something of a glut in the trade right now."

"I'll survive. What did Kurt Schrack do?"

"Who he?"

"You know. The *Schockelschtuhl* guy."

"Christ, him. That was back in B.C. As I remember he bought a farm north of here and raises chickens. If he's not dead by now."

"Right. Die I guess would be the convenient thing. From the management point of view."

"Don't talk like that, Harry, it hurts me too much. Give me credit for some feelings. You're a young buck, for Chrissake, you got the best years still ahead of you. You want some fatherly advice? Get the hell out of the county. Leave the mess behind you. Forget that slob you married, no offense."

"No offense. About Janice, you can't blame her, I wasn't that great myself. But I can't go anywhere, I got this kid."

"Kid, schmid. You can't live your life that way. You got to reason outwards from Number One. To you, you're Number One, not the kid."

"That's not how it feels, exactly," Rabbit begins, then sees from the sudden gleaming globe of Pajasek's head bent to study the smirched slips on his desk that the man doesn't really want to talk, he wants Harry to go. So Rabbit asks, "So when do I go?"

Pajasek says, "You'll get two months' pay plus the benefits you've accumulated, but the new press is coming in this weekend, faster than we thought. Everything moves faster nowadays."

"Except me," Rabbit says, and goes. His father, in the bright racket of the shop, swivels away from his machine and gives him the thumbs down sign questioningly. Rabbit nods, thumbs down. As they walk down Pine Street together after work, feeling ghostly in the raw outdoor air after their day's immersion in fluorescence, Pop says, "I've seen the handwriting on the wall all along, whole new philosophy operating at the top now at Verity, one of the partner's sons came back from business school somewhere full of beans and crap. I said to Pajasek, 'Why keep me on, I have less than a year before retirement?' and he says, 'That's the reason.' I said to him, 'Why not let me go and give my place to Harry?' and he says, 'Same reason.' He's running scared himself, of course. The whole economy's scared. Nixon's getting himself set to be the new Hoover, these moratorium doves'll be begging for LBJ to come back before Tricky Dick's got done giving their bank accounts a squeeze!"

Pop talks more than ever now, as if to keep Harry's mind cluttered; he clings to him like sanity. It has been a dreadful three days. All Sunday, on no sleep, he drove back and forth in Peggy's borrowed Fury through Brewer between Mt. Judge and Penn Villas, through the municipal headache of the Columbus Day parade. The monochrome idyll of early morning, Skeeter dwindling to a brown dot in brown fields, became a four-color nightmare of martial music, throbbing exhaustion, bare-thighed girls twirling bolts of lightning, iridescent drummers pounding a tattoo on the taut hollow of Harry's stomach, cars stalled in the side-streets, Knights of Columbus floats, marching veterans, American flags. Between entanglements with this monster celebration, he scavenged in warm ashes and trucked useless stained and soaked furniture, including a charred guitar, to the garage at the back of the Jackson Road place. He found no wallet near the sofa, and no black bag in the closet. Jill's bureau had been along the wall of which only charred 2 by 4s remained, yet he prodded the ashes for a scrap of the six hundred dollars. Back on Jackson Road, insurance investigators were waiting for him, and the sheriff of Furnace Township, a little apple-cheeked old man, in suspenders and a soft felt hat, who was mostly interested in establishing that his failure to be present at the fire could in no way be held against him. He was quite deaf, and every time someone in the room spoke he would twirl around and alertly croak, "Let's put *that* on the record too! I want everything out in the open, everything on the record!"

Worst of all, Harry had to talk to Jill's mother on the telephone. The police had broken the news to her and her tone fluctuated between a polite curiosity about how Jill came to be living in this house and a grieved outrage seeking its ceiling, a bird cramped in a cage of partial comprehension.

"She was staying with me, yes, since before Labor Day," Rabbit told her, over the downstairs phone, in the dark living room, smelling of furniture polish and Mom's medicine. "Before that she had been bumming around in Brewer with a crowd of Negroes who hung out at a restaurant they've closed down since. I thought she'd be better off with me than with them."

"But the police said there *was* a Negro."

"Yeah. He was a friend of hers. He kind of came and went." Each time he was made to tell this story, he reduced the part Skeeter played, beginning with having to lie about driving him south that morning, until the young black man has become in his backwards vision little more substantial than a shadow behind a chair. "The cops say he might have set the fire but I'm sure he didn't."

"How are you sure?"

"I just am. Look, Mrs.—"

"Aldridge." And this, of all things, her second husband's name, set her to crying.

He fought through her sobbing. "Look, it's hard to talk now, I'm dead beat, my kid's in the next room, if we could talk face to face, I could maybe explain—"

The outrage tested a wing. "*Explain!* Can you explain her back to life?"

"No, I guess not."

The politeness returned. "My husband and I are flying to Philadelphia tomorrow morning and renting a car. Perhaps we should meet."

"Yeah. I'd have to take off from work, except for the lunch hour."

"We'll meet at the West Brewer police station," the distant voice said with surprising firmness, a sudden pinch of authority. "At noon."

Rabbit had never been there before. The West Brewer Borough Hall was a brick building with white trim, set diagonally on a plot of grass and flower beds adjacent to the tall madhouse, itself really an addition to the original madhouse, a granite mansion built a century ago by one of Brewer's iron barons. All this land had belonged to that estate. Behind the borough hall stretched a long cement-block shed with a corrugated roof; some doors were open and Rabbit saw trucks, a steamroller, the spidery black machine that tars roads, the giant arm that lifts a man in a basket to trim branches away from electric wires. These appliances of a town's housekeeping seemed to him part of a lost world of blameless activity; he would never be allowed to crawl back into that world. Inside the town hall, there were wickets where people could pay their utilities bills, paneled doors labelled in flaking gold Burgess and Assessor and Clerk. Gold arrows pointed downstairs to the Police Department. Rabbit saw too late that he could have entered this half-basement from the side, saving himself the curious gaze of ten town employees. The cop behind the green-topped counter looked familiar, but it took a minute for the sideburns to register. The collegiate type. Harry was led down a hall past mysterious rooms; one brimmed with radio equipment, another with filing cabinets, a third gave on a cement stairway leading still further down. The dungeon. Jail. Rabbit wanted to run down into this hole and hide but was led into a fourth room, with a dead green table and metal folding chairs. The broken-nosed chief was in here and a woman who, though hollow with exhaustion and slow-spoken with pills, was Connecticut. She had more edge, more salt to her manner, than Pennsylvania women. Her hair was not so much gray as grayed; her suit was black. Jill's pensive thin face must have come from her father, for her mother had quite another kind, a roundish eager face with pushy lips that when she was happy must be greedy. Rabbit flicked away the impression of a peppy little dog: wideset brown eyes, a touch of jowl, a collar of pearls at her throat. *Nifty tits*, Jill had said, but her mother's cupped and braced bosom struck Rabbit in this moment of sexless and sorrowing encounter as a militant prow, part of a uniform's padding. He regretted that he had not enough praised Jill here, her boyish chest with its shallow faint shadows, where she had felt to herself shy and meager and yet had been soft enough in his mouth and hands, quite soft enough, and abundant, as grace is abundant, that we do not measure, but take as a presence, that abounds. In his mist, he heard the chief grunt introductions: Mr. and Mrs. Aldridge. Rabbit remembered in Jill's song the tax lawyer from Westerly, but the man remained blank for him; he had eyes only for the woman, for this wrong-way reincarnation of Jill. She had Jill's composure, less fragilely; even her despairing way of standing with her hands heavy at her sides, at a loss, was Jill's. Rabbit wondered, Has she come from identifying the remains? What was left but blackened bones? Teeth. A bracelet. A flesh-colored swatch of hair. "Hey," he said to her, "I'm sick about this."

"Yes-s." Her bright eyes passed over his head. "Over the phone, I was so stupid, you mentioned explaining."

Had he? What had he wanted to explain? That it was not his fault. Yet Nelson thought it was. For taking her in? But she was unsheltered. For fucking her? But it is all life, sex, fire, breathing, all combination with oxygen, we shimmer at all moments on the verge of conflagration, as the madhouse windows tell us. Rabbit tried to remember. "You had asked about Skeeter, why I was sure he hadn't set the fire."

"Yes. Why were you?"

"He loved her. We all did."

"You all used her?"

"In ways."

"In your case"—strange precision, clubwoman keeping a meeting within channels, the vowels roughened by cigarettes and whisky, weathered in the daily sunslant of cocktails—"as a concubine?"

He guessed at what the word meant. "I never forced it," he said. "I had a house and food. She had herself. We gave what we had."

"You are a beast." Each word was too distinct; the sentence had been lying in her mind and had warped and did not quite fit.

"O.K., sure," he conceded, refusing to let her fly, to let that caged outrage escape her face and scream. Stepdaddy behind her coughed and shifted weight, preparing to be embarrassed. Harry's guts felt suspended and transparent, as before a game. He was matched against this glossy woman in a way he was never matched with Jill. Jill had been too old for him, too wise, having been born so much later. This little pug, her money and rasping clubwoman voice aside, was his generation, he could understand what she wanted. She wanted to stay out of harm's way. She wanted to have some fun and not be blamed. At the end she wanted not to have any apologizing to do to any heavenly committee. Right now she wanted to tame the ravenous miracle of her daughter's being cast out and destroyed. Mrs. Aldridge touched her cheeks in a young gesture, then let her hands hang heavy beside her hips.

"I'm sorry," she said. "There are always . . . circumstances. I wanted to ask, were there any . . . effects."

"Effects?" He was back with blackened bones, patterns of teeth, melted bracelets. He thought of the bracelets girls in high school used to wear, chains with name-tags, Dorene, Margaret, Mary Ann.

"Her brothers asked me . . . some memento . . ."

Brothers? She had said. Three. One Nelson's age.

Mrs. Aldridge stepped forward, bewildered, hoping to be helpful. "There was a car."

"They sold the car," Rabbit said, too loudly. "She ran it without oil and the engine seized up and she sold it for junk."

His loudness alarmed her. He was still indignant, about the waste of that car. She took a step backward, protesting, "She loved the car."

She didn't love the car, she didn't love anything we would have loved, he wanted to tell Mrs. Aldridge, but maybe she knew more than he, she was there when Jill first saw the car, new and white, her father's gift. Rabbit at last found in his mind an "effect." "One thing I did find," he told Mrs. Aldridge, "her guitar. It's pretty well burned, but—"

"Her guitar," the woman repeated, and perhaps having forgotten that her daughter played brought her eyes down, made her round face red and brought the man over to comfort her, a man blank like men in advertisements, his coat impeccable and in the breast pocket a three-folded maroon handkerchief.

"I have *noth*ing," she wailed, "she didn't even leave me a *note* when she *left*." And her voice had shed its sexy roughness, become high and helpless; it was Jill again, begging, *Hold me, help me, I'm all shit inside, everything is crashing in.*

Harry turned from the sight. The chief, leading him out the side door, said, "Rich bitch, if she'd given the girl half a reason to stay home she'd be alive today. I see things like this every week. All our bad checks are being cashed. Keep your nose clean, Angstrom, and take care of your own." A coach's paternal punch on the arm, and Harry was sent back into the world.

"Pop, how about a quick one?"

"Not today, Harry, not today. We have a surprise for you at home. Mim's coming."

"You sure?" The vigil for Mim is months old; she keeps sending postcards, always with a picture of a new hotel on them.

"Yep. She called your mother this morning from New York City, I talked to your mother this noon. I should have told you but you've had so much on your mind I thought, Might as well save it. Things come in bunches, that's the mysterious truth. We get numb and the Lord lets us have it, that's how His mercy works. You lose your wife, you lose your house, you lose your job. Mim comes in the same day your mother couldn't sleep a wink for nightmares, I bet she's been downstairs all day trying to tidy up if it kills her, you wonder what's next." But he has just said it: Mom's death is next. The number 16A bus joggles, sways, smells of exhaust. The Mt. Judge way, there are fewer Negroes than toward West Brewer. Rabbit sits on the aisle; Pop, by the window, suddenly hawks and spits. The spittle runs in a weak blur down the dirty glass. "Goddammit, but that burns me," he explains, and Rabbit sees they have passed a church, the big gray Presbyterian at Weiser and Park: on its steps cluster some women in overcoats, two young men with backwards collars, nuns and schoolchildren carrying signs and unlit candles protesting the war. This is Moratorium Day. "I don't have much use for Tricky Dick and never have," Pop is explaining, "but the poor devil, he's trying to do the decent thing over there, get us out so the roof doesn't fall in until after we leave, and these queer preachers so shortsighted they can't see across the pulpit go organizing these parades that all they do is convince the little yellow Reds over there they're winning. If I were Nixon I'd tax the bejesus out of the churches, it'd take some of the burden off the little man. Old Cushing up there in Boston must be worth a hundred million just by his lonesome."

"Pop, all they're saying is they want the killing to stop."

"They've got you too, have they? Killing's not the worst thing around. Rather shake the hand of a killer than a traitor."

So much passion, where he now feels none, amuses Harry, makes him feel protected, at home. It has been his salvation, to be home again. The same musty teddy-bear smells from the carpet, the same embrace of hot air when you open the cellar door, the same narrow stairs heading up off the living room with the same loose baluster that lost its dowel and has to be renailed again and again, drying out in the ebb of time; the same white-topped kitchen table with the four sets of worn spots where they used to eat. An appetite for boyish foods has returned: for banana slices on cereal, for sugar doughnuts though they come in boxes with cellophane windows now instead of in waxpaper bags, for raw carrots and cocoa, at night. He sleeps late, so he has to be wakened for work; in Penn Villas, in the house where Janice never finished making curtains, he would be the one the sun would usually rouse first. Here in Mt. Judge familiar gloom encloses him. The distortions in Mom's face and speech, which used to distress him during his visits, quickly assimilate to the abiding reality of her presence, which has endured all these years he has been absent and which remains the same half of the sky, sealing him in—like the cellar bulkhead out back, of two heavy halves. As a child he used to crouch on the cement steps beneath them and listen to the rain. The patter above seemed to be pitting his consciousness lovingly and mixing its sound with the brusque scrape and stride of Mom working in the kitchen. She still, for spells, can work in the kitchen. Harry's being home, she claims, is worth a hundred doses of L-dopa.

The one disturbing element, new and defiant of assimilation, is Nelson. Sullen, grieving, strangely large and loutish sprawled on the caneback davenport, his face glazed by some television of remembrance: none of them quite know what to do about him. He is not Harry, he is sadder than Harry ever was, yet he demands the privileges and indulgence of Harry's place. In the worn shadows of the poorly lit half-house on Jackson Road, the Angstroms keep being startled by Nelson's ungrateful presence, keep losing him. "Where's Nellie?" "Where did the kid get to?" "Is the child upstairs or down?" are questions the other three often put to one another. Nelson stays in his temporary room —Mim's old room—for hours of listening to rock-pop-folk turned down to a murmur. He skips meals without explaining or apologizing, and is making a scrapbook of news items the Brewer papers have carried about their fire. Rabbit discovered this scrapbook yesterday, snooping in the boy's room. Around the clippings the boy had drawn with various colors of ball-point flowers, peace signs, Tao crosses, musical notes, psyche-delic rainbows, those open-ended swirling doodles associated with insanity before they became commercial. Also there are two Polaroid snaps of the ruin; Billy took them Monday with a new camera his father had given him. The photos, brownish and curling, show a half-burned house, the burned half dark like a shadow but active in shape, eating the unburned half, the garage studs bent like matchsticks in an ashtray. Looking at the photographs, Rabbit smells ash. The smell is real and not remembered. In Nelson's closet he finds the source, a charred guitar. So that is why it wasn't in the garage when he looked for it, to give to Jill's mother. She is back in Connecticut now, let the poor kid keep it. His father can't reach him, and lives with him in his parents' house as an estranged, because too much older, brother.

He and his father see, walking up Jackson Road, a strange car parked in front of number 303, a white Toronado with orange-on-blue New York plates. His father's lope accelerates; "There's Mim!" he calls, and it is. She is upstairs and comes to the head of the stairs as they enter beneath the fanlight of stained glass; she descends and stands with them in the murky little foyer. It is Mim. It isn't. It has been years since Rabbit has seen her. "Hi," Mim says, and kisses her father dryly, on the cheek. They were never, even when the children were lit-tle, much of a family for kissing. She would kiss her brother the same way, dismissingly, but he holds her, wanting to feel the hundreds of men who have held her before, this his sister whose diapers he changed, who used to hold his thumb when they'd go for Sunday walks along the quarry, who once burst out *oh I love you* sledding with him, the runners whistling on the dark packed slick, the street waxy with snow still falling. Puzzled by his embrace, Mim kisses him again, another peck on the same cheek, and then firmly shrugs his arms away. A competence in that. She feels lean, not an ounce extra but all woman; swimming must do it, in hotel pools, late hours carve the fat away and swimming smooths what's left. She appears to wear no makeup, no lipstick, except for her eyes, which are inhuman, Egyptian, drenched in peacock purple and blue, not merely outlined but re-created, and weighted with lashes he expects to stick fast when she blinks. These marvellously masked eyes force upon her pale mouth all expressiveness; each fractional smile, sardonic crimping, attentive pout, and abrupt broad laugh follows its predecessor so swiftly Harry imagines a coded tape is being fed into her head and producing, rapid as electronic images, this alphabet of expressions. She used to have buck teeth but that has been fixed. Her nose, her one flaw, that kept her off the screen, that perhaps kept her from fame, is still long, with a faceted lump of cartilage at the end, exactly like Mom's nose, but now that Mim is thirty and never going to be a screen beauty seems less a flaw, indeed saves her face from looking like others and gives it, between the peacock eyes and the actressy-fussy mouth, a lenient homeliness. And this, Rabbit guesses, would extend her appeal for men, though now she would get barroom criers, with broken careers and marriages, rather than hard-hearted comers who need an icy showpiece on their arm. In the style of the Sixties her clothes are clownish: bell-bottom slacks striped horizontally as if patched from three kinds of gingham; a pinstripe blouse, mannish but for the puff sleeves; shoes that in color and shape remind him of Donald Duck's bill; and hoop earrings three inches across. Even in high school Mim had liked big earrings; they made her look like a gypsy or Arab then, now, with the tan, Italian. Or Miami Jewish. Her hair is expensively tousled honey-white, which doesn't offend him; not since junior high has she worn it the color it was, the mild brown she once called, while he leaned in her doorway watching her study herself in the mirror, "Protestant rat."

Pop busies his hands, touching her, hanging up his coat, steering her into the dismal living room. "When did you get here? Straight from the West Coast? You fly straight to Idlewild, they do it non-stop now, don't they?"

"Pop, they don't call it Idlewild any more. I flew in a couple days ago, I had some stuff in New York to do before I drove down. Jersey was breathtaking, once you got past the oil tanks. Everything still so green."

"Where'd you get the car, Mim? Rent it from Hertz?" The old man's washed-out eyes sparkle at her daring, at her way with the world.

Mim sighs. "A guy lent it to me." She sits in the caneback rocker and puts her feet up on the very hassock that Rabbit as a child had once dreamed about: he dreamed it was full of dollar bills to solve all their problems. The dream had been so vivid he had tested it; the stitched scar of his incision still shows. The stuffing had been disagreeable fiber deader than straw.

Mim lights a cigarette. She holds it in the exact center of her mouth, exhales twin plumes around it, frowns at the snuffed match.

Pop is enchanted by the routine, struck dumb. Rabbit asks her, "How does Mom seem to you?"

"Good. For someone who's dying."

"She make sense to you?"

"A lot of it. The guy who doesn't make much sense to me is you. She told me what you've been doing. Lately."

"Harry's had a hell of a time lately," Pop chimes in, nodding as if to mesh himself with this spinning wheel, his dazzling daughter. "Today in at Verity, get this, they gave him his notice. They kept me on and canned a man in his prime. I saw the handwriting on the wall but I didn't want it to be me who'd tell him, it was their meatloaf, let them deliver it, bastards, a man gives them his life and gets a boot in the fanny for his pains."

Mim closes her eyes and lets a look of weary age wash over her and says, "Pop, it's fantastic to see you. But don't you want to go up and look in on Mom for a minute? She may need to be led to the pot, I asked her but with me she could be shy still."

Pop rises quickly, obliging; yet then he stands in a tentative crouch, offering to say away her brusqueness. "You two have a language all your own. Mary and I, we used to marvel, I used to say to her, There couldn't ever have been a brother and a sister closer than Harry and Miriam. These other parents used to tell us, you know, about kids fighting, we didn't know what they were talking about, we'd never had an example. I swear to God above we never heard a loud word between the two of you. A lot of boys, all of six when Mim arrived, might have expressed resentment, you know, settled in with things pretty much his own way up to then: not Harry. Right from the start, right from that first summer, we could trust you alone with him, alone in the house, Mary and I off to a movie, about the only way to forget your troubles in those days, go off to a motion picture." He blinks, gropes among these threads for the one to pull it all tight. "I swear to God, we've been lucky," he says, then weakens it by adding, "when you look at some of the things that can happen to people," and goes up; his tears spark as he faces the bulb burning at the head of the stairs, before cautiously returning his eyes to the treads.

Did they ever have a language of their own? Rabbit can't remember it, he just remembers them being here together, in this house season after season, for grade after grade of school, setting off down Jackson Road in the aura of one holiday after another, Hallowe'en, Thanksgiving, Christmas, Valentine's Day, Easter, in the odors and feel of one sports season succeeding another, football, basketball, track; and then him being out and Mim shrunk to a word in his mother's letters; and then him coming back from the Army and finding her grown up, standing in front of the mirror, ready for boys, maybe having had a few, tinting her hair and wearing hoop earrings; and then Janice took him off; and then both of them were off and the house empty of young life; and now both of them are here again. The smoke from her cigarette seems what the room needs, has needed a long time, to chase these old furniture and sickness smells away. He is sitting on the piano stool; he perches forward and reaches toward her. "Gimme a weed."

"I thought you stopped."

"Years ago. I don't inhale. Unless it's grass."

"Grass yet. You've been living it up." She fishes in her purse, a big bright patchy bag that matches her slacks, and tosses him a cigarette. It is menthol, with a complicated filter tip. Death is easily fooled. If the churches don't work, a filter will do.

He says, "I don't know what I've been doing."

"I would say so. Mom talked to me for an hour. The way she is now, that's a lot of talking."

"What d'ya think of Mom now? Now that you have all this perspective."

"She was a great woman. With nowhere to put it."

"Well, is where you put it any better?"

"It involves less make-believe."

"I don't know, you look pretty fantastic to me."

"Thanks."

"What'd she say? Mom."

"Nothing you don't know, except Janice calls her a lot."

"I knew that. She's called a couple times since Sunday, I can't stand it to talk to her."

"Why not?"

"She's too wild. She doesn't make any sense. She says she's getting a divorce but never starts it, she says she'll sue me for burning her house and I tell her I only burned my half. Then she says she'll come get Nelson but never comes, I wish the hell she would."

"What does it mean to you, her being wild like this?"

"I think she's losing her buttons. Probably drinking like a fish."

Mim turns her profile to blunt the cigarette in the saucer serving as an ashtray. "It means she wants back in." Mim knows things, Rabbit realizes proudly. Wherever you go in some directions, Mim has been there. The direction where she hasn't been is the one that has Nelson in it, and the nice hot slap of the slug being made beside your left hand. But these are old directions, people aren't going that way any more. Mim repeats, "She wants you back."

"People keep telling me that," Rabbit says, "but I don't see much evidence. She can find me if she wants to."

Mim crosses her pants legs, aligns the stripes, and lights another cigarette. "She's trapped. Her love for this guy is the biggest thing she has, it's the first step out she's taken since she drowned that baby. Let's face it, Harry. You kids back here in the sticks still believe in ghosts. Before you screw you got to square it with old Jack Frost, or whatever you call him. To square skipping out with herself she has to make it a big deal. So. Remember as kids those candy jars down at Spottsie's you reached inside of to grab the candy and then you couldn't get your fist out? If Janice lets go to pull her hand out she'll have no candy. She wants it out, but she wants the candy too; no, that's not exactly it, she wants the *idea* of what she's made out of the candy in her own mind. So. Somebody has to break the jar for her."

"I don't want her back still in love with this greaseball."

"That's how you have to take her."

"The son of a bitch, he even has the nerve, sitting there in these snappy suits, he must make three times what I do just cheating people, he has the fucking nerve to be a dove. One night we all sat in this restaurant with him and me arguing across the table about Vietnam and them playing touch-ass side by side. You'd like him, actually, he's your type. A gangster."

Patiently Mim is sizing him up: one more potential customer at the bar. "Since when," she asks, "did you become such a war lover? As I remember you, you were damn glad to wriggle out of that Korean thing."

"It's not all war I love," he protests, "it's *this* war. Because nobody else does. Nobody else understands it."

"Explain it to me, Harry."

"It's a, it's a kind of head fake. To keep the other guy off balance. The world the way it is, you got to do something like that once in a while, to keep your options, to keep a little space around you." He is using his arms to show her his crucial concept of space. "Otherwise, he gets so he can read your every move and you're dead."

Mim asks, "You're sure there is this other guy?"

"Sure I'm sure." The other guy is the doctor who shakes your hand so hard it hurts. *I know best.* Madness begins in that pinch.

"You don't think there might just be a lot of little guys trying to get a little more space than the system they're under lets them have?"

"Sure there are these little guys, billions of 'em"—billions, millions, too much of everything—"but then also there's this big guy trying to put them all into a big black bag. He's crazy, so so must we be. A little."

She nods like a type of doctor herself. "That fits," she says. "Be crazy to keep free. The life you been leading lately sounds crazy enough to last you a while."

"What did I do wrong? I was a fucking Good Samaritan. I took in these orphans. Black, white, I said Hop aboard. Irregardless of color or creed, Hop aboard. Free eats. I was the fucking Statue of Liberty."

"And it got you a burned-down house."

"O.K. That's other people. That's their problem, not mine. I did what felt right." He wants to tell her everything, he wants his tongue to keep pace with this love he feels for this his sister; he wants to like her, though he feels a forbidding denseness in her, of too many conclusions reached when he wasn't there. He tells her, "I learned some things."

"Anything worth knowing?"

"I learned I'd rather fuck than be blown."

Mim removes a crumb, as of tobacco but the cigarette is filtered, from her lower lip. "Sounds healthy," she says. "Rather unAmerican, though."

"And we used to read books. Aloud to each other."

"Books about what?"

"I don't know. Slaves. History, sort of."

Mim in her stripey clown costume laughs. "You went back to school," she says. "That's sweet." She used to get better marks than he did, even after she began with boys: A's and B's against his B's and C's. Mom at the time told him girls had to be smarter, just to pull even. Mim asks, "So what'd you learn from these books?"

"I learned"—he gazes at a corner of a room, wanting to get this right: he sees a cobweb above the sideboard, gesturing in some ceiling wind he cannot feel—"this country isn't perfect." Even as he says this he realizes he doesn't believe it, any more than he believes at heart that he will die. He is tired of explaining himself. "Speaking of sweet," he says, "how is *your* life?"

"*Ça va*. That's French for, It goes. *Va bene*."

"Somebody keeping you, or is it a new one every night?"

She looks at him and considers. A glitter of reflexive anger snipes at her mask of eye makeup. Then she exhales and relaxes, seeming to conclude, Well he's my brother. "Neither. I'm a career girl, Harry. I perform a service. I can't describe it to you, the way it is out there. They're not bad people. They have rules. They're not very interesting rules, nothing like Stick your hand in the fire and make it up to Heaven. They're more like, Ride the exercise bicycle the morning after. The men believe in flat stomach muscles and sweating things out. They don't want to carry too much fluid. You could say they're puritans. Gangsters are puritans. They're narrow and hard because off the straight path you don't live. Another rule they have is, Pay for what you get because anything free has a rattlesnake under it. They're survival rules, rules for living in the desert. That's what it is, a desert. Look out for it, Harry. It's coming East."

"It's here. You ought to see the middle of Brewer; it's all parking lots."

"But the things that grow here you can eat, and the sun is still some kind of friend. Out there, we hate it. We live underground. All the hotels are underground with a couple of the windows painted blue. We like it best at night, about three in the morning, when the big money comes to the crap table. Beautiful faces, Harry. Hard and blank as chips. Thousands flow back and forth without any expression. You know what I'm struck by back here, looking at the faces? How soft they are. God they're soft. *You* look so soft to me, Harry. You're soft still standing and Pop's soft curling under. If we don't get Janice propped back under you you're going to curl under too. Come to think of it, Janice is not soft. She's hard as a nut. That's what I never liked about her. I bet I'd like her now. I should go see her."

"Sure. Do. You can swap stories. Maybe you could get her a job on the West Coast. She's pretty old but does great things with her tongue."

"That's quite a hang-up you have there."

"I just said, nobody's perfect. How about you? You have some specialty, or just take what comes?"

She sits up. "She really hurt you, didn't she?" And eases back. She stares at Harry interested. Perhaps she didn't expect in him such reserves of resentful energy. The living room is dark though the noises that reach them from outside say that children are still playing in the sun. "You're all soft," she says, lulling, "like slugs under fallen leaves. Out there, Harry, there are no leaves. People grow these tan shells. I have one, look." She pulls up her pinstripe blouse and her belly is brown. He tries to picture the rest and wonders if her pussy is tinted honey-blond to match the hair on her head. "You never see them out in the sun but they're all tan, with flat stomach muscles. Their one flaw is, they're still soft inside. They're like those chocolates we used to hate, those chocolate creams, remember how we'd pick through the Christmas box they'd give us at the movie theater, taking out only the square ones and the caramels in cellophane? The other ones we hated, those dark brown round ones on the outside, all ooky inside. But that's how people are. It embarrasses everybody but they need to be milked. Men need to be drained. Like boils. Women too for that matter. You asked me my specialty and that's it, I milk people. I let them spill their insides on me. It can be dirty work but usually it's clean. I went out there wanting to be an actress and that's in a way what I got, only I take on the audience one at a time. In some ways it's more of a challenge. So. Tell me some more about your life."

"Well I was nursemaid to this machine but now they've retired the machine. I was nursemaid to Janice but she upped and left."

"We'll get her back."

"Don't bother. Then I was nursemaid to Nelson and he hates me because I let Jill die."

"She let herself die. Speaking of that, that's what I do like about these kids: they're trying to kill it. Even if they kill themselves in the process."

"Kill what?"

"The softness. Sex, love; me, mine. They're doing it in. I have no playmates under thirty, believe it. They're burning it out with dope. They're going to make themselves hard clean through. Like, oh, cockroaches. That's the way to live in the desert. Be a cockroach. It's too late for you, and a little late for me, but once these kids get it together, there'll be no killing them. They'll live on poison."

Mim stands; he follows. For all that she was a tall girl and is enlarged by womanhood and makeup, her forehead comes to his chin. He kisses her forehead. She tilts her face up, slime-blue eyelids shut, to be kissed again. Pop's loose mouth under Mom's chiselled nose. He tells her, "You're a cheerful broad," and pecks her dry cheek. Perfumed stationery. A smile in her cheek pushes his lips. She is himself, with the combination jiggled.

She gives him a sideways hug, patting the fat around his waist. "I swing," Mim confesses. "I'm no showboat like Rabbit Angstrom, but in my quiet way I swing." She tightens the hug, and linked like that they walk to the foot of the stairs, to go up and console their parents.

Next day, Thursday, when Pop and Harry come home, Mim has Mom and Nelson downstairs at the kitchen table, having tea and laughing. "Dad," Nelson says, the first time since Sunday morning he has spoken to his father without first being spoken to, "did you know Aunt Mim worked at Disneyland once? Do Abraham Lincoln for him, please do it again."

Mim stands. Today she wears a knit dress, short and gray; in black tights her legs show skinny and a little knock-kneed, the same legs she had as a kid. She wobbles forward as to a lectern, removes an imaginary piece of paper from a phantom breast pocket, and holds it wavering a little below where her eyes would focus if they could see. Her voice as if on rustling tape within her throat emerges: "Fow-er scow-er and seven yaars ago—"

Nelson is falling off the chair laughing; yet his careful eyes for a split second check his father's face, to see how he takes it. Rabbit laughs, and Pop emits an appreciative snarl, and even Mom: the bewildered foolish glaze on her features becomes intentionally foolish, amused. Her laughter reminds Rabbit of the laughter of a child who laughs not with the joke but to join the laughter of others, to catch up and be human among others. To keep the laughter swelling Mim sets out two more cups and saucers in the jerky trance of a lifesize Disney doll, swaying, nodding, setting one cup not in its saucer but on the top of Nelson's head, even to keep the gag rolling pouring some hot water not in the teacup but onto the table; the water runs, steaming, against Mom's elbow. "Stop, you'll scald her!" Rabbit says, and seizes Mim, and is shocked by the tone of her flesh, which for the skit has become plastic, not hers, flesh that would stay in any position you twisted it to. Frightened, he gives her a little shake, and she becomes human, his efficient sister, wiping up, swishing her lean tail from table to stove, taking care of them all.

Pop asks, "What kind of work did Disney have you do, Mim?"

"I wore a little Colonial get-up and led people through a replica of Mt. Vernon." She curtseys and with both hands in artificial unison points to the old gas stove, with its crusty range and the crazed mica window in the oven door. "The Fa-ther of our Coun-try," she explains in a sweet, clarion, idiot voice, "was himself nev-er a fa-ther."

"Mim, you ever get to meet Disney personally?" Pop asks.

Mim continues her act. "His con-nu-bi-al bed, which we see before us, measures five feet four and three-quarter inches from rail to rail, and from head-board to foot-board is two inch-es under sev-en feet, a gi-ant's bed for those days, when most gentle-men were no bigger than warming pans. Here" —she plucks a plastic fly swatter off the fly-specked wall—"you see a warm-ing pan."

"If you ask me," Pop says to himself, having not been answered, "it was Disney more than FDR kept the country from going under to the Commies in the Depression."

"The ti-ny holes," Mim is explaining, holding up the fly swatter, "are de-signed to let the heat e-scape, so the fa-ther of our coun-try will not suf-fer a chill when he climbs into bed with his be-lov-ed Mar-tha. Here"—Mim gestures with two hands at the Verity Press giveaway calendar on the wall, turned to October, a grinning jack-o-lantern—"is Mar-tha."

Nelson is still laughing, but it is time to let go, and Mim does. She pecks her father on the forehead and asks him, "How's the Prince of Pica today? Remember that, Daddy? When I thought pica was the place where they had the leaning tower."

"North of Brewer somewhere," Nelson tells her, "I forget the exact place, there's some joint that calls itself the Leaning Tower of Pizza." The boy waits to see if this is funny, and though the grown-ups around the table laugh obligingly, he decides that it wasn't, and shuts his mouth. His eyes go wary again. "Can I be excused?"

Rabbit asks sharply, "Where're you going?"

"My room."

"That's Mim's room. When're you going to let her have it?"

"Any time."

"Whyncha go outdoors? Kick the soccer ball around, do something positive, for Chrissake. Get the self-pity out of your system."

"Let. Him alone," Mom brings out.

Mim intercedes. "Nelson, when will you show me your famous mini-bike?"

"It's not much good, it keeps breaking down." He studies her, his possible playmate. "You can't ride it in clothes like that."

"Out West," she says, "everybody rides motorcycles in trendy knits."

"Did you ever ride a motorcycle?"

"All the time, Nelson. I used to be den mother for a pack of Hell's Angels. We'll ride over and look at your bike after supper."

"It's not the kid's bike, it's somebody else's," Rabbit tells her.

"It'll be dark after supper," Nelson tells Mim.

"I love the dark," she says. Reassured, he clumps upstairs, ignoring his father. Rabbit is jealous. Mim has learned, these years out of school, what he has not: how to manage people.

Shakily, Mom lifts her teacup, sips, sets it down. A perilous brave performance. She is proud of something; he can tell by the way she sits, upright, her neck cords stretched. Her hair has been brushed tight about her head. Tight and almost glossy. "Mim," she says, "went calling today."

Rabbit asks, "On who?"

Mim answers. "On Janice. At Springer Motors."

"Well." Rabbit pushes back from the table, his chair legs scraping. "What did the little mutt have to say for herself?"

"Nothing. She wasn't there."

"Where was she?"

"He said seeing a lawyer."

"Old man Springer said that?" Fear slides into his stomach, nibbling. The law. The long white envelope. Yet he likes the idea of Mim going over there and standing in one of her costumes in front of the Toyota cutout, a gaudy knife into the heart of the Springer empire. Mim, their secret weapon.

"No," she tells him, "not old man Springer. Stavros."

"You saw Charlie there? Huh. How does he look? Beat?"

"He took me out to lunch."

"Where?"

"I don't know, some Greek place in the black district."

Rabbit has to laugh. People dead and dying all around him, he has to let it out. "Wait'll he tells her that."

Mim says, "I doubt he will."

Pop is slow to follow. "Who're we talking about, Mim? That slick talker turned Janice's head?"

Mom's face gropes; her eyes stretch as if she is strangling while her mouth struggles to frame a droll thought. In suspense they all fall silent. "Her lover," she pronounces. A sick feeling stabs Rabbit.

Pop says, "Well I've kept my trap shut throughout this mess, don't think Harry there wasn't a temptation to meddle but I kept my peace, but a lover in my book is somebody who loves somebody through thick and thin and from all I hear this smooth operator is just after the ass. The ass and the Springer name. Pardon the expression."

"I think," Mom says, faltering though her face still shines. "It's nice. To know Janice has."

"An ass," Mim finally completes for her. And it seems to Rabbit wicked that these two, Pop and Mim, are corrupting Mom on the edge of the grave. Coldly he asks Mim, "What'd you and Chas talk about?"

"Oh," Mim says, "things." She shrugs her knitted hip off the kitchen table, where she has been perched as on a bar stool. "Did you know, he has a rheumatic heart? He could kick off at any minute."

"Fat chance," Rabbit says.

"That type of operator," Pop says, snarling his teeth back into place, "lives to be a hundred, while they bury all the decent natural Americans. Don't ask me why it works that way, the Lord must have His reasons."

Mim says, "I thought he was sweet. And quite intelligent. And *much* nicer about you all than you are about him. He was very thoughtful about Janice, he's probably the first person in thirty years to give her some serious attention as a *per*son. He sees a lot in her."

"Must use a microscope," Rabbit says.

"And *you*," Mim says, turning, "he thinks you're about the biggest spook he's ever met. He can't understand why if you want Janice back you don't come and get her back."

Rabbit shrugs. "Too proud or lazy. I don't believe in force. I don't like contact sports."

"I did tell him, what a gentle brother you were."

"Never hurt a fly if he could help it, used to worry me," Pop says. "As if we'd had a girl and didn't know it. Isn't that the truth, Mother?"

Mom gets out, "Never. All boy."

"In that case, Charlie says," Mim goes on.

Rabbit interrupts: "'Charlie' yet."

"'In that case,' he said, 'why is he for the war?'"

"Fuck," Rabbit says. He is more tired and impatient than he knew. "Anybody with any sense at all is for the damn war. They want to fight, we *got* to fight. What's the alternative? What?"

Mim tries to ride down her brother's rising anger. "His theory is," she says, "you like any disaster that might spring you free. You liked it when Janice left, you liked it when your house burned down."

"And I'll like it even more," Rabbit says, "when you stop seeing this greasy creep."

Mim gives him the stare that has put a thousand men in their place. "Like you said. He's my type."

"A gangster, right. No wonder you're out there screwing yourself into the morgue. You know where party chicks like you wind up? In coroners' reports, when you take too many sleeping pills when the phone stops ringing, when the gangsters find playmates in not such baggy condition. You're in big trouble, Sis, and the Stavroses of the world are going to be no help. They've put you where you are."

"*Maa*-om," Mim cries, out of old instinct appealing to the frail cripple nodding at the kitchen table. "Tell Harry to lay *off*." And Rabbit remembers, it's a myth they never fought; they often did.

When Pop and Harry return from work the next day, Harry's last day on the job, the Toronado with New York plates is not in front of the house. Mim comes in an hour later, after

Rabbit has put the supper chops in the oven; when he asks her where she's been, she drops her big stripey bag on the old davenport and answers, "Oh, around. Revisiting the scenes of my childhood. The downtown is really sad now, isn't it? All black-topped parking lots and Afro-topped blacks. And linoleum stores. I did one nice thing, though. I stopped at that store on lower Weiser with the lefty newspapers for sale and bought a pound of peanuts. Believe it or not Brewer is the only place left you can get good peanuts in the shell. Still warm." She tosses him the bag, a wild pass; he grabs it left-handed and as they talk in the living room he cracks peanuts. He uses a flowerpot for the shells.

"So," he says. "You see Stavros again?"

"You told me not to."

"Big deal, what I tell you. How was he? Still clutching his heart?"

"He's touching. Just the way he carries himself."

"Boo hoo. You analyze me some more?"

"No, we were selfish, we talked about ourselves. He saw right through me. We were halfway into the first drink and he looks me up and down through those tinted glasses and says, 'You work the field don't you?' Gimme a peanut."

He tosses a fistful overhanded; they pelt her on the chest. She is wearing a twitchy little dress that buttons down the front and whose pattern imitates lizardskin. When she puts her feet up on the hassock he sees clear to the crotch of her pantyhose. She acts lazy and soft; her eyes have relented, though the makeup shines as if freshly applied. "That's all you did?" he asks. "Eat lunch."

"Th-that's all, f-f-folks."

"What're you tryin' to prove? I thought you came East to help Mom."

"To help her help *you*. How can I help *her*, I'm no doctor."

"Well, I really appreciate your help, fucking my wife's boyfriend like this."

Mim laughs at the ceiling, showing Harry the horseshoe curve of her jaw's underside, the shining white jugular bulge. As if cut by a knife the laugh ends. She studies her brother gravely, impudently. "If you had a choice, who would you rather went to bed with him, her or me?"

"Her. Janice, I can always have too, I mean it's possible; but you, never."

"I know," Mim gaily agrees. "Of all the men in the world, you're the only one off bounds. You and Pop."

"And how does that make me seem?"

She focuses hard on him, to get the one-word answer. "Ridiculous."

"That's what I thought. Hey, Jesus. Did you really give Stavros a bang today? Or're you just getting my goat? Where would you go? Wouldn't Janice miss him at the office?"

"Oh—he could say he was out on a sale or something," Mim offers, bored now. "Or he could tell her to mind her own business. That's what European men do." She stands, touches all the buttons in the front of her lizardskin dress to make sure they're done. "Let's go visit Mom." Mim adds, "Don't fret. Years ago, I made it a rule never to be with a guy more than three times. Unless there was some percentage in getting involved."

That night Mim gets them all dressed and out to dinner, at the Dutch smörgåsbord diner north toward the ball park. Though Mom's head waggles and she has some trouble cutting the crust of her apple pie, she manages pretty well and looks happy: how come he and Pop never thought of getting her out of the house? He resents his own stupidity, and tells Mim in the hall, as they go in to their beds—she is back in her old room, Nelson sleeps with him now—"You're just little Miss Fix-It, aren't you?"

"Yes," she snaps, "and you're just big Mister Muddle." She begins undoing her buttons in front of him, and closes her door only after he has turned away.

Saturday morning she takes Nelson in her Toronado over to the Fosnachts; Janice has arranged with Mom that she and Peggy will do something all day with the boys. Though it takes twenty minutes to drive from Mt. Judge to West Brewer, Mim is gone all morning and comes back to the house after two. Rabbit asks her, "How was it?"

"What?"

"No, seriously. Is he that great in the sack, or just about average in your experience? My theory for a while was there must be something wrong with him, otherwise why would he latch on to Janice when he can have all these new birds coming up?"

"Maybe Janice has wonderful qualities."

"Let's talk about him. Relative to your experience." He imagines that all men have been welded into one for her, faces and voices and chests and hands welded into one murmuring pink wall, as once for him the audience at those old basketball games became a single screaming witness that was the world. "To your wide experience," he qualifies.

"Why don't you tend your own garden instead of hopping around nibbling at other people's?" Mim asks. When she turns in that clown outfit, her lower half becomes a gate of horizontal denim stripes.

"I have no garden," he says.

"Because you didn't tend it at all. Everybody else has a life they try to fence in with some rules. You just do what you feel like and then when it blows up or runs down you sit there and pout."

"Christ," he says, "I went to work day after day for ten years."

Mim tosses this off. "You felt like it. It was the easiest thing to do."

"You know, you're beginning to remind me of Janice."

She turns again; the gate opens. "Charlie told me Janice is fantastic. A real wild woman."

Sunday Mim stays home all day. They go for a drive in Pop's old Chevy, out to the quarry, where they used to walk. The fields that used to be dusted white with daisies and then yellow with goldenrod are housing tracts now; of the quarry only the great gray hole in the ground remains. The Oz-like tower of sheds and chutes where the cement was processed is gone, and the mouth of the cave where children used to hide and frighten themselves is sealed shut with bulldozed dirt and rusted sheets of corrugated iron. "Just as well," Mom pronounces. "Awful things. Used to happen there. Men and boys." They eat at the aluminum diner out on Warren Street, with a view of the viaduct, and this meal out is less successful than the last. Mom refuses to eat. "No appetite," she says, yet Rabbit and Mim think

it is because the booths are close and the place is bright and
she doesn't want people to see her fumble. They go to a movie.
The movie page of the *Vat* advertises: *I Am Curious Yellow*,
Midnight Cowboy, a double bill of *Depraved* and *The Circus*
(Girls Never Played Games Like This Before!), a Swedish X-
film titled *Yes*, and *Funny Girl*. *Funny Girl* sounds like more
of the same but it has Barbra Streisand; there will be music.
They make it late to the 6:30 show. Mom falls asleep and Pop
gets up and walks around in the back of the theater and talks
to the usher in a penetrating whine until one of the scattered
audience calls out "*Shh*." On the way out, the lights on, a trio
of hoods give Mim such an eye Rabbit gives them back the
finger. Blinking in the street, Mom says, "That was nice. But
really Fanny. Was very ugly. But stylish. And a gangster. She always knew Nick Arnstein was a gangster. Everybody. Knew it."

"Good for her," Mim says.

"It isn't the gangsters who are doing the country in," Pop
says. "If you ask me it's the industrialists. The monster fortunes. The Mellons and the du Ponts, those are the cookies we
should put in jail."

Rabbit says, "Don't get radical, Pop."

"I'm no radical," the old man assures him, "you got to be
rich to be radical."

Monday, a cloudy day, is Harry's first day out of work. He
is awake at seven but Pop goes off to work alone. Nelson goes
with him; he still goes to school in West Brewer and switches
buses on Weiser. Mim leaves the house around eleven, she
doesn't say where to. Rabbit scans the want ads in the Brewer
Standard. Accountant. Administrative Trainee. Apprentice
Spray Painter. Auto Mechanic. Bartender. The world is full of
jobs, even with Nixon's Depression. He skips down through
Insurance Agents and Programmers to a column of Salesmen
and then turns to the funnies. Goddam *Apartment 3-G*: he
feels he's been living with those girls for years now, when is
he going to see them with their clothes off? The artist keeps
teasing him with bare shoulders in bathrooms, naked legs in
the foreground with the crotch coming just at the panel edge,
glimpses of bra straps being undone. He calculates: after two
months' pay from Verity he has thirty-seven weeks of welfare

and then he can live on Pop's retirement. It is like dying now: they don't let you fall though, they keep you up forever with transfusions, otherwise you'll be an embarrassment to them. He skims the divorce actions and doesn't see himself and goes upstairs to Mom.

She is sitting up in the bed, her hands quiet on the quilted coverlet, an inheritance from her own mother. The television is also quiet. Mom stares out of the window at the maples. They have dropped leaves enough so the light in here seems harsh. The sad smell is more distinct: fleshly staleness mingled with the peppermint of medicine. To spare her the walk down the hall they have put a commode over by the radiator. To add a little bounce to her life, he sits down heavily on the bed. Her eyes with their film of clouding pallor widen; her mouth works but produces only saliva. "What's up?" Harry loudly asks. "How's it going?"

"Bad dreams," she brings out. "L-dopa does things. To the system."

"So does Parkinson's Disease." This wins no response. He tries, "What do you hear from Julia Arndt? And what's-er-name, Mamie Kellog? Don't they still come visiting?"

"I've outlasted. Their interest."

"Don't you miss their gossip?"

"I think. It scared them when. It all came true."

He tries, "Tell me one of your dreams."

"I was picking scabs. All over my body. I got one off and underneath. There were bugs, the same. As when you turn over a rock."

"Wow. Enough to make you stay awake. How do you like Mim's being here?"

"I do."

"Still full of sauce, isn't she?"

"She tries to be. Cheerful."

"Hard as nails, I'd say."

"Inch by inch," Mom says.

"Huh?"

"That was on one. Of the children's programs. Earl leaves the set on and makes me watch. Inch by inch."

"Yeah, go on."

"Life is a cinch. Yard by yard. Life is hard."

He laughs appreciatively, making the bed bounce more. "Where do you think I went wrong?"

"Who says. You did?"

"Mom. No house, no wife, no job. My kid hates me. My sister says I'm ridiculous."

"You're. Growing up."

"Mim says I've never learned any rules."

"You haven't had to."

"Huh. Any decent kind of world, you wouldn't need all these rules."

She has no ready answer for this. He looks out of her windows. There was a time—the year after leaving, even five years after—when this homely street, with its old-fashioned high crown, its sidewalk blocks tugged up and down by maple roots, its retaining walls of sandstone and railings of painted iron and two-family brickfront houses whose siding imitates gray rocks, excited Rabbit with the magic of his own existence. These mundane surfaces had given witness to his life; this cup had held his blood; here the universe had centered, each downtwirling maple seed of more account than galaxies. No more. Jackson Road seems an ordinary street anywhere. Millions of such American streets hold millions of lives, and let them sift through, and neither notice nor mourn, and fall into decay, and do not even mourn their own passing but instead grimace at the wrecking ball with the same gaunt facades that have outweathered all their winters. However steadily Mom communes with these maples—the branches' misty snake-shapes as inflexibly fixed in these two windows as the leading of stained glass—they will not hold back her fate by the space of a breath; nor, if they are cut down tomorrow to widen Jackson Road at last, will her staring, that planted them within herself, halt their vanishing. And the wash of new light will extinguish even her memory of them. Time is our element, not a mistaken invader. How stupid, it has taken him thirty-six years to begin to believe that. Rabbit turns his eyes from the windows and says, to say something, "Having Mim home sure makes Pop happy"; but in his silence Mom, head rolling on the pillow, her nostrils blood-red in contrast with the linen, has fallen asleep.

He goes downstairs and makes himself a peanut-butter sandwich. He pours himself a glass of milk. He feels the whole house as balanced so that his footsteps might shake Mom and tumble her into the pit. He goes into the cellar and finds his old basketball and, more of a miracle still, a pump with the air needle still screwed into the nozzle. In their frailty things keep faith. The backboard is still on the garage but years have rusted the hoop and loosened the bolts, so the first hard shots tilt the rim sideways. Nevertheless he keeps horsing around and his touch begins to come back. Up and soft, up and soft. Imagine it just dropping over the front of the rim, forget it's a circle. The day is very gray so the light is nicely even. He imagines he's on television; funny, watching the pros on the box how you can tell, from just some tone of their bodies as they go up, if the shot will go in. Mim comes out of the house, down the back steps, down the cement walk, to him. She is wearing a plain black suit, with wide boxy lapels, and a black skirt just to the knee. An outfit a Greek would like. Classic widow. He asks her, "That new?"

"I got it at Kroll's. They're outlandishly behind the coasts, but their staid things are half as expensive."

"You see friend Chas?"

Mim puts down her purse and removes her white gloves and signals for the ball. He used to spot her ten points at Twenty-one when he was in high school. As a girl she had speed and a knock-kneed moxie at athletics, and might have done more with it if he hadn't harvested all the glory already. "Friend Janice too," she says, and shoots. It misses but not by much.

He bounces it back. "More arch," he tells her. "Where'd you see Jan?"

"She followed us to the restaurant."

"You fight?"

"Not really. We all had Martinis and *retsina* and got pretty well smashed. She can be quite funny about herself now, which is a new thing." Her grease-laden eyes squint at the basket. "She says she wants to rent an apartment away from Charlie so she can have Nelson." This shot, the ball hits the crotch and every loose bolt shudders looser.

"I'll fight her all the way on that."

"Don't get uptight. It won't come to that."

"Oh it won't. Aren't you a fucking little know-it-all?"

"I try. One more shot." Her breasts jog her black lapels as she shoves the dirty ball into the air. A soft drizzle has started. The ball swishes the net, if the net had been there.

"How could you give Stavros his bang if Janice was there?"

"We sent her back to her father."

He had meant the question to be rude, not for it to be answered. "Poor Janice," he says. "How does she like being out-tarted?"

"I said, don't get uptight. I'm flying back tomorrow. Charlie knows it and so does she."

"Mim. You can't, so soon. What about them?" He gestures at the house. From the back, it has a tenement tallness, a rickety hangdog wood-and-tar-shingle backside mismatched to its solid street face. "You'll break their hearts."

"They know. My life isn't here, it's there."

"You have nothing there but a bunch of horny hoods and a good chance of getting V.D."

"Oh, we're clean. Didn't I tell you? We're all obsessed with cleanliness."

"Yeah. Mim. Tell me something else. Don't you ever get tired of fucking? I mean"—to show the question is sincere, not rude—"I'd think you would."

She understands and is sisterly honest. "Actually, no. I don't. As a girl I would have thought you would but now being a woman I see you really don't. It's what we do. It's what people do. It's a connection. Of course, there are times, but even then, there's something nice. People want to be nice, haven't you noticed? They don't like being shits, that much; but you have to find some way out of it for them. You have to help them."

Her eyes in their lassos of paint seem, outdoors, younger than they have a right to be. "Well, good," he says weakly; he wants to take her hand, to be helped. As her brother, once, he had been afraid she would fall in the quarry if he let go and he had let go and she had fallen and now says it's all right, all things must fall. She laughs and goes on, "Of course I was never squeamish like you. Remember how you hated food that was mixed up, when the pea-juice touched the meat or something? And that time I told you all food had to be mushed like vomit before you could swallow it, you hardly ate for a week."

"I don't remember that. Stavros is really great, huh?"

Mim picks up her white gloves from the grass. "He's nice." She slaps her palm with the gloves, studying her brother. "Also," she says.

"What?" He braces for the worst, the hit that will leave nothing there.

"I bought Nelson a mini-bike. Nobody in this Godforsaken household seems to remember it, but tomorrow is his birthday. He's going to be thirteen, for Cry-eye. *A teenager.*"

"You can't do that, Mim. He'll kill himself. It's not legal on the streets here."

"I'm having it delivered over to the Fosnachts' building. They can share it on the parking lot, but it'll be Nelson's. The poor kid deserves *some*thing for what you put him through."

"You're a super aunt."

"And you're so dumb you don't even know it's raining." In the darkening drizzle she sprints, still knock-kneed and speedy, up the walk through their narrow backyard, up the stairs of their spindly back porch. Harry hugs the ball and follows.

In his parents' house Rabbit not only reverts to peanut-butter sandwiches and cocoa and lazing in bed when the sounds of Pop and Nelson leaving have died; he finds himself faithfully masturbating. The room itself demands it: a small long room he used to imagine as a railway car being dragged through the night. Its single window gives on the sunless passageway between the houses. As a boy in this room he could look across the space of six feet at the drawn shade of the room that used to be little Carolyn Zim's. The Zims were night owls. Some nights, though he was three grades ahead of her, Carolyn would go to bed later than he, and he would strain to see in the chinks of light around her shade the glimmer of her undressing. And by pressing his face to the chill glass by his pillow he could look at a difficult diagonal into Mr. and Mrs. Zim's room and one night glimpsed a pink commotion that may have been intercourse. But nearly every morning the Zims could be heard at breakfast fighting and Mom used to wonder how long they would stay together. People that way plainly wouldn't be having intercourse. In those days this room was full of athletes, mostly baseball players, their pictures came on school tablet covers, Musial and DiMag and Luke Appling and Rudy York. And for a while there had been a stamp collection, weird to remember, the big blue album with padded covers and the waxpaper mounts and the waxpaper envelopes stuffed with a tumble of Montenegro and Sierra Leone cancelleds. He imagined then that he would travel to every country in the world and send Mom a postcard from every one, with these stamps. He was in love with the idea of travelling, with running, with geography, with Parcheesi and Safari and all board games where you roll the dice and move; the sense of a railroad car was so vivid he could almost see his sallow overhead light, tulip-shaped, tremble and sway with the motion. Yet travelling became an offense in the game he got good at.

The tablet covers were pulled from the wall while he was in the Army. The spots their tacks left were painted over. The tulip of frosted glass was replaced by a fluorescent circle that buzzes and flickers. Mom converted his room to her junk room: an old push-treadle Singer, a stack of *Reader's Digest*s and *Family Circle*s, a bridge lamp whose socket hangs broken like a chicken's head by one last tendon, depressing pictures of English woods and Italian palaces where he has never been, the folding cot from Sears on which Nelson slept in his father's room while Mim was here. When Mim left Tuesday, the kid, dazed by his good fortune in owning a mini-bike over in West Brewer, moved back into her room, abandoning Rabbit to memories and fantasies. He always has to imagine somebody, masturbating. As he gets older real people aren't exciting enough. He tried imagining Peggy Fosnacht, because she had been recent, and good, all gumdrops; but remembering her reminds him that he has done nothing for her, has not called her since the fire, has no desire to, left her blue Fury in the basement and had Nelson give her the key, scared to see her, blames her, she seduced him, the low blue flame that made her want to be fucked spread and became the fire. From any thought of the fire his mind darts back singed. Nor can he recall Janice; but for the bird-like dip of her waist under his hand in bed she is all confused mocking darkness where he dare not insert himself. He takes to conjuring up a hefty coarse Negress, fat but not sloppy fat, muscular and masculine, with a trace of a mustache and a chipped front tooth. Usually she is astraddle him like a smiling Buddha, slowly rolling her ass on his thighs, sometimes coming forward so her big cocoa-colored breasts swing into his face like boxing gloves with sensitive tips. He and this massive whore have just shared a joke, in his fantasy; she is laughing and good humor is rippling through his chest; and the room they are in is no ordinary room but a kind of high attic, perhaps a barn, with distant round windows admitting dusty light and rafters from which ropes hang, almost a gallows. Though she is usually above him, and he sometimes begins on his back, imagining his fingers are her lips, for the climax he always rolls over and gives it to the bed in the missionary position. He has never been able to shoot off lying on his back; it feels too explosive, too throbbing, too blasphemous upwards. God is on that side of him, spreading His feathered wings as above a crib. Better turn and pour it into Hell. You nice big purple-lipped black cunt. Gold tooth.

When this good-humored goddess of a Negress refuses, through repeated conjuration, to appear vividly enough, he tries imagining Babe. Mim, during her brief stay, told him offhand, at the end of his story, that what he should have done was sleep with Babe; it had been all set up, and it was what his subconscious wanted. But Babe in his mind has stick fingers cold as ivory, and there is no finding a soft hole in her, she is all shell. And the puckers on her face have been baked there by a wisdom that withers him. He has better luck making a movie that he is not in, imagining two other people, Stavros and Mim. How did they do it? He sees her white Toronado barrelling up the steepness of Eisenhower Avenue, stopping at 1204. The two of them get out, the white doors slam punkily, they go in, go up, Mim first. She would not even turn for a preliminary kiss; she would undress swiftly. She would stand in noon windowlight lithe and casual, her legs touching at the knees, her breasts with their sunken nipples and bumpy aureoles (he has seen her breasts, spying) still girlish and undeveloped, having never nursed a child. Stavros would be slower in undressing, stolid, nursing his heart, folding his pants to keep the crease for when he returns to the lot. His back would be hairy: dark whirlpools on his shoulder blades. His cock would be thick and ropily veined, ponderous but irresistible in rising

under Mim's deft teasing; he hears their wisecracking voices
die; he imagines afternoon clouds dimming the sepia faces of
the ancestral Greeks on the lace-covered tables; he sees the
man's clotted cock with the column of muscle on its underside
swallowed by Mim's rat-furred vagina (no, she is not honey-
blond here), sees her greedy ringless fingers press his balls
deeper up, up into her ravenous stretched cunt; and himself
comes. As a boy, Rabbit had felt it as a space-flight, a squeezed
and weightless toppling over onto his head but now it is a
mundane release as of anger, a series of muffled shouts into
the safe bedsheet, rocks thrown at a boarded window. In the
stillness that follows he hears a tingling, a submerged musical
vibration slowly identifiable as the stereo set of the barefoot
couple next door, in the other half of the house.

One night while he is letting his purged body drift in listening
Jill comes and bends over and caresses him. He turns his head
to kiss her thigh and she is gone. But she has wakened him; it
was her presence, and through this rip in her death a thousand
details are loosed; tendrils of hair, twists of expression, her frail
voice quavering into pitch as she strummed. The minor details
of her person that slightly repelled him, the hairlines between
her teeth, her doughy legs, the apple smoothness of her valentine bottom, the something prim and above-it-all about her
flaky-dry mouth, the unwashed white dress she kept wearing,
now return and become the body of his memory. Times return
when she merged on the bed with moonlight, her young body
just beginning to learn to feel, her nerve endings still curled in
like fernheads in the spring, green, a hardness that repelled him
but was not her fault, the gift of herself was too new to give.
Pensive moments of her face return to hurt him. A daughterly
attentiveness he had bid her hide. Why? He had retreated into
protest and did not wish her to call him out. He was not ready,
he had been affronted. Let black Jesus have her; he had been
converted to a hardness of heart, a billion cunts and only one
him. He tries to picture, what had been so nice, Jill and Skeeter
as he actually saw them once in hard lamplight, but in fantasy
now Rabbit rises from the chair to join them, to be a father and
lover to them, and they fly apart like ink and paper whirling to
touch for an instant on the presses. JILL COMES AGAIN. *Angstrom Senses Presence.* She breathes upon him again as he lies in

his boyhood bed and this time he does not make the mistake of turning his face, he very carefully brings his hand up from his side to touch the ends of her hair where it must hang. Waking to find his hand in empty mid-air he cries; grief rises in him out of a parched stomach, a sore throat, singed eyes; remembering her daughterly blind grass-green looking to him for more than shelter he blinds himself, leaves stains on the linen that need not be wiped, they will be invisible in the morning. Yet she had been here, her very breath and presence. He must tell Nelson in the morning. On this dreamlike resolve he relaxes, lets his room, with hallucinatory shuddering, be coupled to an engine and tugged westward toward the desert, where Mim is now.

"That bitch," Janice said. "How many times did you screw her?"

"Three times," Charlie said. "That ended it. It's one of her rules."

This ghost of conversation haunts Janice this night she cannot sleep. Harry's witch of a sister has gone back to whoring but her influence is left behind in Charlie like a touch of disease. They had it so perfect. Lord they had never told her, not her mother or father or the nurses at school, only the movies had tried to tell her but they couldn't show it, at least not until recently, how perfect it could be. Sometimes she comes just thinking about him and then other times they last forever together, it is beautiful how slow he can be, murmuring all the time to her, selling her herself. They call it a piece of ass and she never understood why until Charlie, it wasn't on her front so much where she used to get mad at Harry because he couldn't make their bones touch or give her the friction she needed long enough so then he ended blaming her for not being with him, it was deeper inside, where the babies happened, where everything happens, she remembers how, was it with Nelson or poor little Becky, they said push and it was embarrassing like forcing it when you haven't been regular, but then the pain made her so panicky she didn't care what came out, and what came out was a little baby, all red-faced and cross as if it had been interrupted doing something else in there inside her. Stuff up your ass, she had hated to hear people say it, what men did to each other in jail or in the Army where the only women are yellow women screaming by the roadside with babies in their arms and squatting to go to the bathroom anywhere, disgusting, but with Charlie it is a piece of ass she is giving him, he is remaking her from the bottom up, the whole base of her feels made new, it's the foundation of life. Yet afterwards, when she tries to say this, how he remakes her, he gives that lovable shrug and pretends it was something anybody could do, a trick like that little trick he does with matches to amuse his nephews, making them always pick the last one up, instead of the sad truth which is that nobody else in the whole wide (Harry was always worrying about how wide the world was, caring about things like how far stars are and the moon shot and the way the Communists wanted to put everybody in a big black bag so he couldn't breathe) world but Charlie could do that for her, she was made for him from the beginning of time without exaggeration. When she tries to describe this to him, how unique they are and sacred, he measures a space of silence with his wonderful hands, just the way his thumbs are put together takes the breath out of her, and slips the question like a cloak from his shoulders.

She asked, "How could you do that to me?"

He shrugged. "I didn't do it to you. I did it to her. I screwed her."

"Why? Why?"

"Why not? Relax. It wasn't that great. She was cute as hell at lunch, but as soon as we got into bed her thermostat switched off. Like handling white rubber."

"Oh, Charlie. Talk to me, Charlie. Tell me why."

"Don't lean on me, tiger."

She had made him make love to her. She had done everything for him. She had worshipped him, she had wanted to cry out her sorrow that there wasn't more she could do, that bodies were so limited. Though she had extracted her lover's semen from him, she failed to extract testimony that his sense of their love was as absolute as her own. Terribly—complainingly, preeningly—she had said, "You know I've given up the world for you."

He had sighed, "You can get it back."

"I've destroyed my husband. He's in all the newspapers."

"He can take it. He's a showboat."

"I've dishonored my parents."

He had turned his back. With Harry it had been usually she who turned her back. Charlie is hard to snuggle against, too broad; it is like clinging to a rock slippery with hair. He had, for him, apologized: "Tiger, I'm bushed. I've felt rotten all day."

"Rotten how?"

"Deep down rotten. Shaky rotten."

And feeling him slip away from her into sleep had so enraged her she had hurled herself naked from bed, shrieked at him the words he had taught her in love, knocked a dead great-aunt from a bureau top, announced that any decent man would at least have *offered* to marry her now knowing she would never accept, did things to the peace of the apartment that now reverberate in her insomnia, so the darkness shudders between pulses of the headlights that tirelessly pass below on Eisenhower Avenue. The view from the back of Charlie's apartment is an unexpected one, of a bend in the Running Horse River like a cut in fabric, of the elephant-colored gas tanks in the boggy land beside the dump, and, around a church with twin blue domes she never knew was there, a little cemetery with iron crosses instead of stones. The traffic out front never ceases. Janice has lived near Brewer all her life but never in it before, and thought all places went to sleep at ten, and was surprised how this city always rumbles with traffic, like her heart which even through dreams keeps pouring out its love.

She awakes. The curtains at the window are silver. The moon is a cold stone above Mt. Judge. The bed is not her bed, then she remembers it has been her bed since, when? July it was. For some reason she sleeps with Charlie on her left; Harry was always on her right. The luminous hands of the electric clock by Charlie's bedside put the time at after two. Charlie is lying face up in the moonlight. She touches his cheek and it is cold. She puts her ear to his mouth and hears no breathing. He is dead. She decides this must be a dream.

Then his eyelids flutter as if at her touch. His eyeballs in the faint cold light seem unseeing, without pupils. Moonlight glints in a dab of water at the far corner of the far eye. He groans, and Janice realizes this is what has waked her. A noise not freely given but torn from some heavy mechanism of restraint deep in his chest. Seeing that she is up on an elbow watching, he says, "Hi, tiger. Jesus it hurts."

"What hurts, love? Where?" Her breath rushes from her throat so fast it burns. All the space in the room, from the corners in, seems a crystal a wrong move from her will shatter.

"Here." He seems to mean to show her but cannot move his arms. Then his whole body moves, arching upward as if twitched by something invisible outside of him. She glances around the room for the unspeaking presence tormenting them, and sees again the lace curtains stamped, interwoven medallions, on the blue of the streetlamp, and against the reflecting blue of the bureau mirroring the square blank silhouettes of framed aunts, uncles, nephews. The groan comes again, and the painful upward arching: a fish hooked deep, in the heart.

"Charlie. Is there any pill?"

He makes words through his teeth. "Little white. Top shelf. Bathroom cabinet."

The crowded room pitches and surges with her panic. The floor tilts beneath her bare feet; the nightie she put on after her disgraceful scene taps her burning skin scoldingly. The bathroom door sticks. One side of the frame strikes her shoulder, hard. She cannot find the light cord, her hand flailing in the darkness; then she strikes it and it leaps from her touch and while she waits for it to swing back down out of the blackness Charlie groans again, the worst yet, the tightest-sounding. The cord finds her fingers and she pulls; the light pounces on her eyes, she feels them shrink so rapidly it hurts yet she doesn't take the time to blink, staring for the little white pills. She confronts in the cabinet a sick man's wealth. All the pills are white. No, one is aspirin; another is yellow and transparent, those capsules that hold a hundred little bombs to go off against hayfever. Here: this one must be it; though the little jar is unlabelled the plastic squeeze lid looks important. There is tiny red lettering on each pill but she can't take the time to read it, her hands shake too much, they must be right; she tilts the little jar into her palm and five hurry out, no, six, and she wonders how she can be wasting time counting and tries to slide some back into the tiny round glass mouth but her whole body is beating so hard her joints have locked to hold her together.

She looks for a glass and sees none and takes the square top of the Water Pik and very stupidly lets the faucet water run to get cold, wetting her palm in turning it off, so the pills there blur and soften and stain the creased skin they are cupped in. She has to hold everything, pills and slopping Water Pik lid, in one hand to free the other to close the bathroom door to keep the light caged away from Charlie. He lifts his large head a painful inch from the pillow and studies the pills melting in her hand and gets out, "Not those. *Little* white." He grimaces as if to laugh. His head sinks back. His throat muscles go rigid. The noise he makes now is up an octave, a woman's noise. Janice sees she does not have time to go back and search again, he is being tuned too high. She sees that they are beyond chemicals; they are pure spirits, she must make a miracle. Her body feels leaden on her bones, she remembers Harry telling her she has the touch of death. But a pressure from behind like a cuff on the back of her head pitches her forward with a keening cry pitched like his own and she presses herself down upon his body that has been so often pressed upon hers; he has become a great hole nothing less large than she wild with love can fill. She wills her heart to pass through the walls of bone and give its rhythm to his. He grits his teeth "Christ" and strains upward against her as if coming and she presses down with great calm, her body a sufficiency, its warmth and wetness and pulse as powerful as it must be to stanch this wound that is an entire man, his length and breadth loved, his level voice loved and his clever square hands loved and his whirlpools of hair loved and his buffed fingernails loved and the dark gooseflesh bag of his manhood loved and the frailty held within him like a threat and lock against her loved. She is a gateway of love gushing from higher ground; she feels herself dissolving piece by piece like a little mud dam in a sluice. She feels his heart kick like pinned prey and keeps it pinned. Though he has become a devil, widening now into a hole wider than a quarry and then gathering into a pain-squeezed upward thrust as cold as an icicle she does not relent; she widens herself to hold his edges in, she softens herself to absorb the spike of his pain. She will not let him leave her. There is a third person in the room, this person has known her all her life and looked down upon her until now; through this other pair of eyes she sees she is weeping, hears herself praying, *Go, Go,* to the devil thrashing inside this her man. "Go!" she utters aloud.

Charlie's body changes tone. He is dead. No, at his mouth she eavesdrops on the whistle of his breathing. Sudden sweat soaks his brow, his shoulders, his chest, her breasts, her cheek where it was pressed against his cheek. His legs relax. He grunts, "O.K." She dares slide from him, tucking the covers, which she had torn down to bare his chest, back up to his chin.

"Shall I get the real pills now?"

"In a minute. Yes. Nitroglycerin. What you brought me was Coricidin. Cold pills."

She sees that his grimace had meant to be laughter, for he does smile now. Harry is right. She is stupid.

To ease the hurt look from her face Stavros tells her, "Rotten feeling. Pressure worse than a fist. You can't breathe, move anything makes it worse, you feel your own heart. Like some animal skipping inside you. Crazy."

"I was scared to leave you."

"You did great. You brought me back."

She knows this is true. The mark upon her as a giver of death has been erased. As in fucking, she has been rendered transparent, then filled solid with peace. As if after fucking, she takes playful inventory of his body, feels the live sweat on his broad skin, traces a finger down the line of his nose.

He repeats, "Crazy," and sits up in bed, cooling himself, gasping safe on the shore. She snuggles at his side and lets her tears out like a child. Absently, still moving his arms gingerly, he fumbles with the ends of her hair as it twitches on his shoulder.

She asks, "Was it me? My throwing that awful fit about Harry's sister? I could have killed you."

"Never." Then he admits, "I need to keep things orderly or they get to me."

"My being here is disorderly," she says.

"Never mind, tiger," he says, not quite denying, and tugs her hair so her head jerks.

Janice gets up and fetches the right pills. They had been there all along, on the top shelf; she had looked on the middle shelf. He takes one and shows her how he puts it under his tongue to dissolve. As it dissolves he makes that mouth she

loves, lips pushed forward as if concealing a lozenge. When she
turns off the light and gets into bed beside him, he rolls on his
side to give her a kiss. She does not respond, she is too full of
peace. Soon the soft rhythm of his unconscious breathing rises
from his side of the bed. On her side, she cannot sleep. Awake
in every nerve she untangles her life. The traffic ebbs down below. She and Charlie float motionless above Brewer; he sleeps
on the wind, his heart hollow. Next time she might not be able
to keep him up. Miracles are granted but we must not lean on
them. This love that has blown through her has been a miracle, the one thing worthy of it remaining is to leave. Spirits are
insatiable but bodies get enough. She has had enough, he has
had enough; more might be too much. She might begin to kill.
He calls her tiger. Toward six the air brightens. She sees his
square broad forehead, the wiry hair in its tidy waves, the nose
so shapely a kind of feminine vanity seems to be bespoken,
the mouth even in sleep slightly pouting, a snail-shine of saliva
released from one corner. Angel, buzzard, floating, Janice sees
that in the vast volume of her love she has renounced the one
possible imperfection, its object. Her own love engulfs her; she
sinks down through its purity swiftly fallen, all feathers.

Mom has the phone by her bed; downstairs Rabbit hears it
ring, then hears it stop, but some time passes before she makes
him understand it is for him. She cannot raise her voice above
a kind of whimper now, but she has a cane, an intimidating
knobby briar Pop brought home one day from the Brewer Salvation Army store. She taps on the floor with it until attention comes up the stairs. She is quite funny with it, waving it
around, thumping. "All my life," she says. "What I wanted. A
cane."

He hears the phone ring twice and then only slowly the tapping of the cane sinks in; he is vacuuming the living-room rug,
trying to get some of the fustiness up. In Mom's room, the
smell is more powerful, the perverse vitality of rot. He has read
somewhere that what we smell are just tiny fragments of the
thing itself tickling a plate in our nose, a subtler smoke. Everything has its cloud, a flower's bigger than a rock's, a dying person's bigger than ours. Mom says, "For you." The pillows she

is propped on have slipped so she sits at a slant. He straightens her and, since the word "Janice" begins with a sound difficult for her throat muscles to form, she is slow to make him understand who it is.

He freezes, reaching for the phone. "I don't want to talk to her."

"Why. Not."

"O.K., O.K." It is confusing, having to talk here, Janice's voice filling his ear while Mom and her rumpled bed fill his vision. Her blue-knuckled hands clasp and unclasp; her eyes, open too wide, rest on him in a helpless stare, the blue irises ringed with a thin white circle like a sucked Life Saver. "Now what?" he says to Janice.

"You could at least not be rude right away," she says.

"O.K., I'll be rude later. Let me guess. You're calling to tell me you've finally gotten around to getting a lawyer."

Janice laughs. It's been long since he heard it, a shy noise that tries to catch itself halfway out, like a snagged yo-yo. "No," she says, "I haven't gotten around to that yet. Is that what you're waiting for?" She is harder to bully now.

"I don't know what I'm waiting for."

"Is your mother there? Or are you downstairs?"

"Yes. Up."

"You sound that way. Harry—Harry, are you there?"

"Sure. Where else?"

"Would you like to meet me anyplace?" She hurries on, to make it business. "The insurance men keep calling me at work, they say you haven't filled out any of the forms. They say we ought to be making some decisions. I mean about the house. Daddy already is trying to sell it for us."

"Typical."

"And then there's Nelson."

"You don't have room for him. You and your greaseball."

His mother looks away, shocked; studies her hands, and by an effort of will stops their idle waggling. Janice has taken a quick high breath. He cannot bump her off the line today. "Harry, that's another thing. I've moved out. It's all decided, everything's fine. I mean, that way. With Charlie and me. I'm calling from Joseph Street, I've spent the last two nights here. Harry?"

"I'm listening. I'm right here. Whatcha think—I'm going to run away?"

"You have before. I was talking to Peggy yesterday on the phone, she and Ollie are back together, and *he* had heard you had gone off to some other state, a newspaper in Baltimore had given you a job."

"Fat chance."

"And Peggy said she hadn't heard from you at all. I think she's hurt."

"Why should she be hurt?"

"She told me why."

"Yeah. She would. Hey. This is a lot of fun chatting, but did you have anything definite you want to say? You want Nelson to come live with the Springers, is that it? I suppose he might as well, he's—" He is going to confess that the boy is unhappy, but his mother is listening and it would hurt her feelings. Considering her condition, she has really put herself out for Nelson this time.

Janice asks, "Would you like to see me? I mean, would it make you too mad, looking at me?"

And he laughs; his own laugh is unfamiliar in his ears. "It might," he says, meaning it might not.

"Oh, let's," she says. "You want to come here? Or shall I come there?" She understands his silence, and confirms, "We need a third place. Maybe this is stupid, but what about the Penn Villas house? We can't go in, but we need to look at it and decide what to do; I mean somebody's offering to buy it, the bank talked to Daddy the other day."

"O.K. I got to make Mom lunch now. How about two?"

"And I want to give you something," Janice is going on, while Mom is signalling her need to be helped to the commode; her blue hand tightens white around the gnarled handle of the cane.

"Don't let her wriggle," is her advice, when he hangs up, "her way. Around you." Sitting on the edge of the bed, Mom thumps the floor with her cane for emphasis, drawing an arc with the tip as illustration.

After putting the lunch dishes in the drainer Harry prepares for a journey. For clothes, he decides on the suntans he is wearing and has worn for two weeks straight, and a fresh white shirt as in his working days, and an old jacket he found in a chest in the attic: his high school athletic jacket. It carries MJ in pistachio green on an ivory shield on the back, and green sleeves emerge from V-striped shoulders. The front zips. Zipped, it binds across his chest and belly, but he begins that way, walking down Jackson Road under the chill maples; when the 12 bus lets him out at Emberly, the warmer air of this lower land lets him unzip, and he walks jauntily flapping along the curving street where the little ranch houses have pumpkins on their porchlets and Indian corn on their doors.

His own house sticks out from way down Vista Crescent: black coal in a row of candies. His station wagon is parked there. The American flag decal is still on the back window. It looks aggressive, fading.

Janice gets out of the driver's seat and stands beside the car looking lumpy and stubborn in a camel-colored loden coat he remembers from winters past. He had forgotten how short she is, how the dark hair has thinned back from the tight forehead, with that oily shine that puts little bumps along the hairline. She has abandoned the madonna hairdo, wears her hair parted way over on one side, unflatteringly. But her mouth seems less tight; her lips have lost the crimp in the corners and seem much readier to laugh, with less to lose, than before. His instinct, crazy, is to reach out and pet her—do something, like tickle behind her ear, that you would do to a dog; but they do nothing. They do not kiss. They do not shake hands. "Where'd you resurrect that corny old jacket? I'd forgotten what awful school colors we had. Ick. Like one of those fake ice creams."

"I found it in an old trunk in my parents' attic. They've kept all that stuff. It still fits."

"Fits who?"

"A lot of my clothes got burned up." This note of apology because he sees she is right, it was an ice-cream world he made his mark in. Yet she too is wearing something too young for her, with a hairdo reverting to adolescence, parted way over like those South American flames of the Forties. Chachacha.

She digs into a side pocket of the loden coat awkwardly. "I said I had a present for you. Here." What she hands him twinkles and dangles. The car keys.

"Don't you need it?"

"Not really. I can drive one of Daddy's. I don't know why I ever thought I did need it, I guess at first I thought we might escape to somewhere. California. Canada. I don't know. We never even considered it."

He asks, "You're gonna stay at your parents'?"

Janice looks up past the jacket to him, seeking his face. "I can't stand it, really. Mother nags so. You can see she's been primed not to say anything to me, but it keeps coming out, she keeps using the phrase 'public opinion.' As if she's a Gallup poll. And Daddy. For the first time, he seems pathetic to me. Somebody is opening a Datsun agency in one of the shopping centers and he feels really personally threatened. I thought," Janice says, her dark eyes resting on his face lightly, ready to fly if what she sees there displeases her, "I might get an apartment somewhere. Maybe in Peggy's building. So Nelson could walk to school in West Brewer again. I'd have Nelson, of course." Her eyes dart away.

Rabbit says, "So the car is sort of a swap."

"More of a peace offering."

He makes the peace sign, then transfers it to his head, as horns. She is too dumb to get it. He tells her, "The kid is pretty miserable, maybe you ought to take him. Assuming you're through with Whatsisname."

"We're through."

"Why?"

Her tongue flicks between her lips, a mannerism that once struck him as falsely sensual but seems inoffensive now, like licking a pencil. "Oh," Janice says. "We'd done all we could together. He was beginning to get jittery. Your sweet sister didn't help, either."

"Yeah. I guess we did a number on him." The "we"—him, her, Mim, Mom; ties of blood, of time and guilt, family ties. He does not ask her for more description. He has never understood exactly about women, why they have to menstruate for instance, or why they feel hot some times and not others, and how close the tip of your prick comes to their womb or whether the womb is a hollow place without a baby in it or what, and instinct disposes him to consign Stavros to that same large area of feminine mystery. He doesn't want to bring back any lovelight into her eyes, that are nice and quick and hard on him, the prey.

Perhaps she had prepared to tell him more, how great her love was and how pure it will remain, for she frowns as if checked by his silence. She says, "You must help me with Nelson. All he'll talk to me about is this terrible mini-bike your sister bought him."

He gestures at the burned green shell. "My clothes weren't the only thing went up in that."

"The girl. Were she and Nelson close?"

"She was sort of a sister. He keeps losing sisters."

"Poor baby boy."

Janice turns and they look together at where they lived. Some agency, the bank or the police or the insurance company, has put up a loose fence of posts and wire around it, but children have freely approached, picking the insides clean, smashing the windows, storm windows and all, in the half that still stands. Some person has taken the trouble to bring a spray can of yellow paint and has hugely written NIGGER on the side. Also the word KILL. The two words don't go together, so it is hard to tell which side the spray can had been on. Maybe there had been two spray cans. Demanding equal time. On the broad stretch of aluminum clapboards below the windows, where in spring daffodils come up and in summer phlox goes wild, yellow letters spell in half-script, *Pig Power = Clean Power*. Also there is a peace sign and a swastika, apparently from the same can. And other people, borrowing charred sticks from the rubble, have come along and tried to edit and add to these slogans and symbols, making Pig into Black and Clean into Cong. It all adds up no better than the cluster of commercials TV stations squeeze into the chinks between programs. A clown with a red spray can has scrawled between two windows TRICK OR TREAT.

Janice asks, "Where was she sleeping?"

"Upstairs. Where we did."

"Did you love her?" For this her eyes leave his face and contemplate the trampled lawn. He remembers that this camel coat has a detachable hood for winter, that snaps on.

He confesses to her, "Not like I should have. She was sort of out of my class." Saying this makes him feel guilty, he imagines how hurt Jill would be hearing it, so to right himself he accuses Janice: "If you'd stayed in there, she'd still be alive somewhere."

Her eyes lift quickly. "No you don't. Don't try to pin *that* rap on me, Harry Angstrom. Whatever happened in there was your trip." Her trip drowns babies; his burns girls. They were made for each other. She offers to bring the truth into neutral. "Peggy says the Negro was doping her, that's what Billy says Nelson told him."

"She wanted it, he said. The Negro."

"Strange he got away."

"Underground Railroad."

"Did you help him? Did you see him after the fire?"

"Slightly. Who says I did?"

"Nelson."

"How did he know?"

"He guessed."

"I drove him south into the county and let him off in a cornfield."

"I hope he's not ever going to come back. I'd call the police, I mean, I would if—" Janice lets the thought die, premature.

Rabbit feels heightened and frozen by this giant need for tact; he and she seem to be slowly revolving, afraid of jarring one another away. "He promised he won't." Only in glory.

Relieved, Janice gestures toward the half-burned house. "It's worth a lot of money," she says. "The insurance company wants to settle for eleven thousand. Some man talked to Daddy and offered nineteen-five as is. I guess the lot is worth eight or nine by itself, this is becoming such a fashionable area."

"I thought Brewer was dying."

"Only in the middle."

"I tell you what. Let's sell the bastard."

"Let's."

They shake hands. He twirls the car keys in front of her face. "Lemme drive you back to your parents'."

"Do we have to go there?"

"You could come to my place and visit Mom. She'd love to see you. She can hardly talk now."

"Let's save that," Janice says. "Couldn't we just drive around?"

"Drive around? I'm not sure I still know how to drive."

"Peggy says you drove her Chrysler."

"Gee. A person doesn't have many secrets in this county."

As they drive east on Weiser toward the city, she asks, "Can your mother manage the afternoon alone?"

"Sure. She's managed a lot of them."

"I'm beginning to like your mother, she's quite nice to me, over the phone, when I can understand what she's saying."

"She's mellowing. Dying I guess does that to you." They cross the bridge and drive up Weiser in the heart of Brewer, past the Wallpaper Boutique, the roasted peanut newsstand, the expanded funeral home, the great stores with the façades where the pale shadow of the neon sign for the last owner underlies the hopeful bright sign the new owners have put up, the new trash disposal cans with tops like flying saucers, the blank marquees of the deserted movie palaces. They pass Pine Street and the Phoenix Bar. He announces, "I ought to be out scouting printshops for a job, maybe move to another city. Baltimore might be a good idea."

Janice says, "You look better since you stopped work. Your color is better. Wouldn't you be happier in an outdoor job?"

"They don't pay. Only morons work outdoors anymore."

"I would keep working at Daddy's. I think I should."

"What does that have to do with me? You're going to get an apartment, remember?"

She doesn't answer again. Weiser is climbing too close to the mountain, to Mt. Judge and their old homes. He turns left on Summer Street. Brick three-stories with fanlights; optometrists' and chiropractors' signs. A limestone church with a round window. He announces, "We could buy a farm."

She makes the connection. "Because Ruth did."

"That's right, I'd forgotten," he lies, "this was her street." Once he ran along this street toward the end and never got there. He ran out of steam after a few blocks and turned around. "Remember Reverend Eccles?" he asks Janice. "I saw him this summer. The Sixties did a number on him, too."

Janice says, "And speaking of Ruth, how did you enjoy Peggy?"

"Yeah, how about that? She's gotten to be quite a girl about town."

"But you didn't go back."

"Couldn't stomach it, frankly. It wasn't her, she was great. But all this fucking, everybody fucking, I don't know, it just makes me too sad. It's what makes everything so hard to run."

"You don't think it's what *makes* things run? Human things."

"There must be something else."

She doesn't answer.

"No? Nothing else?"

Instead of answering, she says, "Ollie is back with her now, but she doesn't seem especially happy."

It is easy in a car; the STOP signs and corner groceries flicker by, brick and sandstone merge into a running screen. At the end of Summer Street he thinks there will be a brook, and then a dirt road and open pastures; but instead the city street broadens into a highway lined with hamburger diners, and drive-in sub shops, and a miniature golf course with big plaster dinosaurs, and food-stamp stores and motels and gas stations that are changing their names, Humble to Getty, Atlantic to Arco. He has been here before.

Janice says, "Want to stop?"

"I ate lunch. Didn't you?"

"Stop at a motel," she says.

"You and me?"

"You don't have to *do* anything, it's just we're wasting gas this way."

"Cheaper to waste gas than pay a motel, for Chrissake. Anyway don't they like you to have luggage?"

"They don't care. Anyway I think I did put a suitcase in the back, just in case."

He turns and looks and there it is, the tatty old brown one still with the hotel label on from the time they went to the Shore, *Wildwood Cabins*. The same suitcase she must have packed to run to Stavros with. "Say," he says. "You're full of sexy tricks now, aren't you?"

"Forget it, Harry. Take me home. I'd forgotten about you."

"These guys who run motels, don't they think it's fishy if you check in before suppertime? What time is it, two-thirty."

"Fishy? What's fishy, Harry? God, you're a prude. Everybody knows people screw. It's how we all got here. When're you going to grow up, even a little bit?"

"Still, to march right in with the sun pounding down—"

"Tell him I'm your wife. Tell him we're exhausted. It's the truth, actually. I didn't sleep two hours last night."

"Wouldn't you rather go to my parents' place? Nelson'll be home in an hour."

"Exactly. Who matters more to you, me or Nelson?"

"Nelson."

"Nelson or your mother?"

"My mother."

"You are a sick man."

"There's a place. Like it?"

Safe Haven Motel the sign says, with slats strung below it claiming

QUEEN SIZE BEDS
ALL COLOR TVS
SHOWER & BATH
TELEPHONES
"MAGIC FINGERS"

A neon VACANCY sign buzzes dull red. The office is a little brick tollbooth; there is a drained swimming pool with a green tarpaulin over it. At the long brick façade bleakly broken by doorways several cars already park; they seem to be feeding, metal cattle at a trough. Janice says, "It looks crummy."

"That's what I like about it," Rabbit says. "They might take us."

But as he says this, they have driven past. Janice asks, "Seriously, haven't you ever done this before?"

He tells her, "I guess I've led a kind of sheltered life."

"Well, it's by now," she says, of the motel.

"I could turn around."

"Then it'd be on the wrong side of the highway."

"Scared?"

"Of what?"

"Me." Racily Rabbit swings into a Garden Supplies parking lot, spewing gravel, brakes just enough to avoid a collision with oncoming traffic, crosses the doubled line, and heads back the way they came. Janice says, "If you want to kill yourself, go ahead, but don't kill me; I'm just getting to like being alive."

"It's too late," he tells her. "You'll be a grandmother in a couple more years."

"Not with you at the wheel."

But they cross the double line again and pull in safely. The VACANCY sign still buzzes. Ignition off. Lever at P. The sun shimmers on the halted asphalt. "You can't just *sit* here," Janice hisses. He gets out of the car. Air. Globes of ether, pure nervousness, slide down his legs. There is a man in the little tollbooth, along with a candy bar machine and a rack of black-tagged keys. He has wet-combed silver hair, a string tie with a horseshoe clasp, and a cold. Placing the registration card in front of Harry, he pats his chafed nostrils with a blue bandana. "Name and address and license plate number," he says. He speaks with a Western twang.

"My wife and I are really bushed," Rabbit volunteers. His ears are burning; the blush spreads downward, his undershirt feels damp, his heart jars his hand as it tries to write, *Mr. and Mrs. Harold Angstrom.* Address? Of course, he must lie. He writes unsteadily, *26 Vista Crescent, Penn Villas, Pa.* Junk mail and bills are being forwarded to him from that address. Wonderful service, the postal. Put yourself in one of those boxes, sorted from sack to sack, finally there you go, *plop*, through the right slot out of millions. A miracle that it works. Young punk revolutionaries, let them try to get the mail through, through rain and sleet and dark of night. The man with the string tie patiently leans on his Formica desk while Rabbit's thoughts race and his hand jerks. "License plate number, that's the one that counts," he peaceably drawls. "Show me a suitcase or pay in advance."

"No kidding, she is my wife."

"Must be on honeymoon straight from haah school."

"Oh, this." Rabbit looks down at his peppermint-and-cream Mt. Judge athletic jacket, and fights the creeping return of his blush. "I haven't worn this for I don't know how many years."

"Looks to almost fit," the man says, tapping the blank space for the plate number. "Ah'm in no hurry if you're not," he says.

Harry goes to the show window of the little house and studies the license plate and signals for Janice to show the suitcase. He lifts an imaginary suitcase up and down by the handle and she doesn't understand. Janice sits in their Falcon, mottled and dimmed by window reflections. He pantomimes unpacking; he draws a rectangle in the air; he exclaims, "God, she's dumb!" and she belatedly understands, reaching back and lifting the bag into view through the layers of glass between them. The man nods; Harry writes his plate number (U20–692) on the card and is given a numbered key (17). "Toward the back," the man says, "more quaat away from the road."

"I don't care if it's quiet, we're just going to sleep," Rabbit says; key in hand, he bursts into friendliness. "Where're you from, Texas? I was stationed there with the Army once, Fort Larson, near Lubbock."

The man inserts the card into a rack, looking through the lower half of his bifocals, and clucks his tongue. "You ever get up around Santa Fe?"

"Nope. Never. Sorry I didn't."

"That's my idea of a *goood* place," the man tells him.

"I'd like to go someday. I really would. Probably never will, though."

"Don't say that, young buck like you, and your cute little lady."

"I'm not so young."

"You're yungg," the man absentmindedly insists, and this is so nice of him, this and handing over the key, people are so nice generally, that Janice asks Harry as he gets back into the car what he's grinning about. "And what took so long?"

"We were talking about Santa Fe. He advised us to go."

The door numbered 17 gives on a room surprisingly long, narrow but long. The carpet is purple, and bits of backlit cardboard here and there undercut the sense of substance, as in a movie lobby. A fantasy world. The bathroom is at the far end, the walls are of cement-block painted rose, imitation oils of the ocean are trying to adorn them, two queen-sized beds look across the narrow room at a television set. Rabbit takes off his shoes and turns on the set and gets on one bed. A band of light appears, expands, jogs itself out of diagonal twitching stripes into *The Dating Game*. A colored girl from Philly is trying to decide which of three men to take her out on a date; one man is black, another is white, the third is yellow. The color is such that the Chinese man is orange and the colored girl looks bluish. The reception has a ghost so that when she laughs there are many, many teeth. Janice turns it off. Like him she is in stocking feet. They are burglars. He protests, "Hey. That was interesting. She couldn't see them behind that screen so she'd have to tell from their voices what color they were. If she cared."

"You *have* your date," Janice tells him.

"We ought to get a color television, the pro football is a lot better."

"Who's this we?"

"Oh—me and Pop and Nelson and Mom. And Mim."

"Why don't you move over on that bed?"

"You *have* your bed. Over there."

She stands there, firm-footed on the wall-to-wall carpet without stockings, nice-ankled. Her dull wool skirt is just short enough to show her knees. They have boxy edges. Nice. She asks, "What is this, a put-down?"

"Who am I to put you down? The swingingest broad on Eisenhower Avenue."

"I'm not so sure I like you anymore."

"I didn't know I had that much to lose."

"Come on. Shove over."

She throws the old camel loden coat over the plastic chair beneath the motel regulations and the fire inspector's certificate. Being puzzled darkens her eyes on him. She pulls off her sweater and as she bends to undo her skirt the bones of her shoulders ripple in long quick glints like a stack of coins being spilled. She hesitates in her slip. "Are you going to get under the covers?"

"We could," Rabbit says, yet his body is as when a fever leaves and the nerves sink down like veins of water into sand. He cannot begin to execute the energetic transitions contemplated: taking off his clothes, walking that long way to the bathroom. He should probably wash in case she wants to go down on him. Then suppose he comes too soon and they are back where they've always been. Much safer to lie here enjoying the sight of her in her slip; he had been lucky to choose a little woman, they keep their shape better than big ones. She looked older than twenty at twenty but doesn't look that much older now, at least angry as she is, black alive in her eyes. "You can get in but don't expect anything, I'm still pretty screwed up." Lately he has lost the ability to masturbate; nothing brings him up, not even the image of a Negress with nipples like dowel-ends and a Hallowe'en pumpkin instead of a head.

"I'll say," Janice says. "Don't expect anything from me either. I just don't want to have to shout between the beds."

With heroic effort Rabbit pushes himself up and walks the length of the rug to the bathroom. Returning naked, he holds his clothes in front of him and ducks into the bed as if into a burrow, being chased. He feels particles of some sort bombarding him. Janice feels skinny, strange, snaky-cool, the way she shivers tight against him immediately; the shock on his skin makes him want to sneeze. She apologizes: "They don't heat these places very well."

"Be November pretty soon."

"Isn't there a thermostat?"

"Yeah. I see it. Way over in the corner. You can go turn it up if you want."

"Thanks. The man should do that."

Neither moves. Harry says, "Hey. Does this remind you of Linda Hammacher's bed?" She was the girl who when they were all working at Kroll's had an apartment in Brewer she let Harry and Janice use.

"Not much. That had a view."

They try to talk, but out of sleepiness and strangeness it only comes in spurts. "So," Janice says after a silence wherein nothing happens. "Who do you think you are?"

"Nobody," he answers. He snuggles down as if to kiss her breasts but doesn't; their presence near his lips drugs him. All sorts of winged presences exert themselves in the air above their covers.

Silence resumes and stretches, a ballerina in the red beneath his eyelids. He abruptly asserts, "The kid really hates me now."

Janice says, "No he doesn't." She contradicts herself promptly, by adding, "He'll get over it." Feminine logic: smother and outlast what won't be wished away. Maybe the only way. He touches her low and there is moss, it doesn't excite him, but it is reassuring, to have that patch there, something to hide in.

Her body irritably shifts; him not kissing her breasts or anything, she puts the cold soles of her feet on the tops of his. He sneezes. The bed heaves. She laughs. To rebuke her, he asks innocently, "You always came with Stavros?"

"Not always."

"You miss him now?"

"No."

"Why not?"

"You're here."

"But don't I seem sad, sort of?"

"You're making me pay, a little. That's all right."

He protests, "I'm a mess," meaning he is sincere: which perhaps is not a meaningful adjustment over what she had said. He feels they are still adjusting in space, slowly twirling in some gorgeous ink that filters through his lids as red. In a space of silence, he can't gauge how much, he feels them drift along sideways deeper into being married, so much that he abruptly volunteers, "We must have Peggy and Ollie over sometime."

"Like hell," she says, jarring him, but softly, an unexpected joggle in space. "You stay away from her now, you had your crack at it."

After a while he asks her—she knows everything, he realizes —"Do you think Vietnam will ever be over?"

"Charlie thought it would, just as soon as the big industrial interests saw that it was unprofitable."

"God, these foreigners are dumb," Rabbit murmurs.

"Meaning Charlie?"

"All of you." He feels, gropingly, he should elaborate. "Skeeter thought it was the doorway into utter confusion. There would be this terrible period, of utter confusion, and then there would be a wonderful stretch of perfect calm, with him ruling, or somebody exactly like him."

"Did you believe it?"

"I would have liked to, but I'm too rational. Confusion is just a local view of things working out in general. That make sense?"

"I'm not sure," Janice says.

"You think Mom ever had any lovers?"

"Ask her."

"I don't dare."

After another while, Janice announces, "If you're not going

to make love, I might as well turn my back and get some sleep. I was up almost all night worrying about this—reunion."

"How do you think it's going?"

"Fair."

The slither of sheets as she rotates her body is a silver music, sheets of pale noise extending outward unresisted by space. There was a grip he used to have on her, his right hand cupping her skull through her hair and his left hand on her breasts gathering them together, so the nipples were an inch apart. The grip is still there. Her ass and legs float away. He asks her, "How do we get out of here?"

"We put on our clothes and walk out the door. But let's have a nap first. You're talking nonsense already."

"It'll be so embarrassing. The guy at the desk'll think we've been up to no good."

"He doesn't care."

"He does, he *does* care. We could stay all night to make him feel better, but nobody else knows where we are. They'll worry."

"Stop it, Harry. We'll go in an hour. Just shut up."

"I feel so guilty."

"About what?"

"About everything."

"Relax. Not everything is your fault."

"I can't accept that."

He lets her breasts go, lets them float away, radiant debris. The space they are in, the motel room long and secret as a burrow, becomes all interior space. He slides down an inch on the cool sheet and fits his microcosmic self limp into the curved crevice between the polleny offered nestling orbs of her ass; he would stiffen but his hand having let her breasts go comes upon the familiar dip of her waist, ribs to hip bone, where no bones are, soft as flight, fat's inward curve, slack, his babies from her belly. He finds this inward curve and slips along it, sleeps. He. She. Sleeps. O.K.?

A MONTH OF SUNDAYS

For Judith Jones

my tongue is the pen of a ready writer
—PSALM 45

This principle of soul, universally and
individually, is the principle of ambiguity.
—PAUL TILLICH

1

Forgive me my denomination and my town; I am a
Christian minister, and an American. I write these pages
at some point in the time of Richard Nixon's unravelling.
Though the yielding is mine, the temptation belongs to others: my keepers have set before me a sheaf of blank sheets—a
month's worth, in their estimation. Sullying them is to be my
sole therapy.

My bishop, bless his miter, has ordered (or, rather, offered as
the alternative to the frolicsome rite of defrocking) me brought
here to the desert, far from the green and crowded land where
my parish, as the French so nicely put it, finds itself. The month
is to be one of recuperation—as I think of it, "retraction," my
condition being officially diagnosed as one of "distraction."
Perhaps the opposite of "dis" is not "re" but the absence of
any prefix, by which construal I am spiritual brother to those
broken-boned athletes who must spend a blank month, amid
white dunes and midnight dosages, in "traction." I doubt (verily, my name *is* Thomas) it will work. In *my* diagnosis I suffer
from nothing less virulent than the human condition, and so
would preach it. Though the malady is magnificent, I should in
honest modesty add that my own case is scarcely feverish, and
pustular only if we cross-examine the bed linen. Masturbation!
Thou saving grace-note upon the baffled chord of self! Paeans
to St. Onan, later.

I feel myself warming to this, which is not my intent. Let
my distraction remain intractable. No old prestidigitator amid
the tilted mirrors of sympathetic counselling will let himself be
pulled squeaking from this glossy, last-resort, false-bottomed
topper.

Particulars!* The motel—I resist calling it a sanatorium, or
halfway house, or detention center—has the shape of an O,
or, more exactly, an omega. The ring of rooms encircling the
pool is fronted by two straight corridors, containing to the left

---

*As Allen Ginsberg intones in one of the cantos of the new Bible waiting for
the winds to unscatter it.

the reception desk, offices, rest rooms sexually distinguished by bovine silhouettes, and a tiny commissary heavy on plastic beadwork and postcards of dinosaur bones but devoid of any magazines or journals that might overexcite the patients—oops, the guests—with topical realities. The other way, along the other foot of the Ω, lie the restaurant and bar. The glass wall of the bar is tinted a chemical purple through which filters a desert vista of diminishing sagebrush and distant, pale, fossiliferous mountains. The restaurant wall, at least at breakfast, wears heavy vanilla curtains out of whose gaps knives of light fall upon the grapefruit and glass of the set tables with an almost audible splintering of brightness. The place seems, if not deserted, less than half full. All middle-aged men, we sit each at our table clearing dry throughts* and suppressing nervous gossip among the silverware. I feel we are a "batch," more or less recently arrived. We are pale. We are stolid. We are dazed. The staff, who peek and move about as if preparatory to an ambush, appear part twanging, leathery Caucasians, their blue eyes bleached to match the alkaline sky and the seat of their jeans, and the rest nubile aborigines whose silent tread and stiff black hair uneasily consort with the frilled pistachio uniforms the waitresses perforce wear. I felt, being served this morning, dealt with reverentially, or dreadfully, as if in avoidance of contamination. A potential topic: touch and the sacred. God as Supreme Disease. *Noli me tangere.* Germs and the altar. The shared chalice versus the disposable paper cuplet: how many hours of my professional life have been chewed to bitter shreds (the apocalyptic antisepticist among the deacons versus the holisticer-than-thou holdouts for the big Grail) by this liturgical debate. Never mind. I am free of that, for a month or forever. Good criddence.†

What can I tell you? I arrived at midnight, disoriented. The airport hellishly clean, a fine dry wind blowing. Little green bus manned by pseudo-cowpoke took us into an enormous hour of

---

*Meant to type "throats," was thinking "thoughts," a happy Freudian, let it stand. The typewriter, which they have provided me after I assured them I was a man of my time, no penman, is new, and races ahead of my fingertips ofttimes. The air is quick.

†Intentional this time: riddance applied to credence.

swallowing desert dark. Met at the glass doors by a large lady, undeformed but unattractive, no doubt chosen for that very quality in this sensitive post. Seemed to be manageress. Named, if my ears, still plugged with jet-hum, deceived me not, Ms. Prynne. Face of a large, white, inexplicably self-congratulating turtle. White neck extended as if to preen or ease a chafing. Snapped rules at us. Us: beefy Irish priest and a third initiate, a slurring shy Tennessean, little hunched man with the hopeful quick smile of a backslider, probably some derelict revivalist who doubled as a duping insurance agent. Rules (as passed on to our hostess by the sponsoring bishoprics and conference boards): meals at eight, twelve-thirty, and seven. Bar open from noon. Commissary closed between two and five. Mornings: write, *ad libitum*. Afternoons: physical exercise, preferably golf, though riding, swimming, tennis facilities do exist. Evenings: board or card games, preferably poker. Many no-nos. No serious discussions, doctrinal or intrapersonal. No reading except escapist: a stock of English detective and humorous fiction from between the two world wars available in the commissary lending library. The Bible above all is banned. No religion, no visitors, no letters in or out. No trips to town (nearest town 40 m. off, named Sandstone) though some field trips would be bussed later in the month.

But you know all this. Who are you, gentle reader?

Who am I?

I go to the mirror. The room still nudges me with its many corners of strangeness, though one night's sleep here has ironed a few rumples smooth. I know where the bathroom is. O, that immaculate, invisibly renewed *sanitas* of rented bathrooms, inviting us to strip off not merely our clothes and excrement and the particles of overspiced flank steak between our teeth but our skin with the dirt and our circumstances with the skin and then to flush every bit down the toilet the loud voracity of whose flushing action so rebukingly contrasts with the clogged languor of the toilets we have left behind at home, already so full of us they can scarcely ebb! The mirror holds a face. I do not recognize it as mine. It no more fits my inner light than the shade of a bridge lamp fits its bulb.

This lampshade. This lopsided lampshade. This lampshade knocked askew. This sallow sack that time has laundered to the tint of recycled paper, inexpungibly speckled and discolored, paper with nevertheless the droop of melting rubber and the erosion of an aerial view, each of its myriad wrinkles a canyon deep enough to hold all the corpses of the last four decades. Not mine. But it winks when I will, *wink*; it occupies, I see by the mirror, the same volume of space wherein the perspectives at which I perceive various projecting edges of the room would intersect, given an ethereal draughtsman. These teeth are mine. Every filling and inlay is a mournful story I could sing. These eyes—holes of a mask. Through which the blue of the sky shows as in one of Magritte's eerily outdoor paintings. God's eyes, my lids.

The Reverend Mr. Thomas Marshfield, 41 this April last, 5′ 10″, 158 pounds, pale and neural, yet with unexpected whirlpools of muscularity here and there—the knees, the padding of the palms, a hard collar of something bullish and taut about the base of the neck and the flaring out of the shoulders. Once a shortstop, once a prancing pony of a halfback. Balding now. Pink on top if I tilt for the light, otherwise a gibbonesque halo of bronze fuzz. Mouse tufts above dead white ears. Something ruddy about the tufts; field mice? Little in the way of eyebrows. Little in the way of lips: my mouth, its two wiggles fitted with a wary set as if ready to dart into an ambiguous flurry of expressions, has never pleased me, though it has allegedly pleased others. Chin a touch too long. Nose also, yet thin enough and sufficiently unsteady in its line of descent to avoid any forceful Hebraism of character. A face still uneasily inhabited, by a tenant waiting for his credit ratings to be checked. In this interregnum neither handsome nor commanding, yet at least with nothing plump about it and, lamplike, a latently incandescent willingness to resist what is current. I have never knowingly failed to honor the supreme, the hidden commandment, which is, Take the Natural World, O Creature Fashioned in Parody of My Own, and Reconvert its Stuff to Spirit; Take Pleasure and Make of it Pain; Chastise Innocence though it Reside within the Gaps of the Atom; Suspect Each Moment, for it is a Thief, Tiptoeing Away with More than it Brings; Question all Questions; Doubt all Doubts; Despise all Precepts which Take their Measure from Man; Remember Me.

I am a conservative dresser. Black, gray, brown let the wearer shine. Though I take care with the knot of my tie, I neglect to polish my shoes.

I believe my penis to be of average size. This belief has not been won through to effortlessly.

My digestion is perversely good, and my other internal units function with the smoothness of subversive cell meetings in a country without a government. A translucent wart on my right buttock should some day be removed, and some nights sleep is forestalled by a neuralgic pain in my left arm, just below the shoulder, that I blame upon a bone bruise suffered in a high-school scrimmage. My appendix is unexcised. I feel it, and my heart, as time bombs.

I love myself and loathe myself more than other men. One of these excesses attracts women, but which?

My voice is really a half-octave too high for the ministry, though in praying aloud I have developed a way of murmuring to the lectern mike that answers to my amplified sense of the soliloquizing ego. My slight stammer keeps, they tell me, the pews from nodding.

What else? My wrists ache.

The state I am in is large and square and holds one refu-gee asthmatic and three drunken Indians in a Ford pickup per square mile. The state I late inhabited, and where I committed my distracted derelictions and underwent my stubborn pangs, has been nibbled by the windings of rivers and deformed by the pull of conflicting territorial claims into an unspecifiable shape, rendered further amorphous by lakes and islands and shelves of urban renewal landfill. A key, Chesterton somewhere says, has no logic to its shape: its only logic is, it turns the lock.

My Lord, this depletes the inner man! Thank Heaven for noon.

2

MS. PRYNNE TELLS me to write (I asked, daring halt her head-long progress down a maroon-muffled and slowly curving hall) about what interests me most.

What interests me most, this morning—the image that hangs most luminous and blue amid the speckled leaves of that far-off, shapeless state where I had a profession, a parish, a marriage, and a parsonage, is of a man with chalk-white legs (myself), clad in naught but the top half of pajamas striped like an untwisted candy cane, treading across a frosty post-Hallowe'en lawn. He climbs a waist-high picket fence, and, gingerly as a kudu dipping his muzzle at the edge of a lion-haunted waterhole, edges his profile, amid bushes, against the glow of the window of a little one-story house, once a parsonage garage. Tom peeps.

A man and a woman are in this house. The outside man, also aware of the flirtatious brushing of Japanese yew needles on his exposed buttocks (he goes to bed without the pajama bottoms for at least a trinity of reasons: to facilitate masturbatory self-access, to avoid belly-bind due to drawstrings or buttons, to send an encouraging signal to the mini-skirted female who, having bitten a poisoned apple at the moment of my father's progenitive orgasm, lies suspended within me), knew this. He knew her car, a rotund black coupe of American vintage. He saw her car, gazing from the window of his bedroom, parked an alley away, visible through the naked branches of trees that (deciduousness! already I mourn for thee) in summer would have concealed its painful placement. The hooked gleam from its scarab back, purple beneath the sulphurous streetlight that brooded above the alley, went straight as steel to his heart. For an hour or more he writhed, this fabulous far-off man (whom I vow will not be forgotten, though all the forces of institutional therapeutics be brought to bear upon me in this diabolical air-conditioned sandbox) trying to worm the harpoon from its lodging in his silvery, idden [*sic*] underside. He masturbated again, imagining for spite some woman remote, a redhead from the attic of his youth, her pubic hair as nicely packed around its treasure as excelsior around an ancestral locket. For a moment, after his poor throttled accomplice had yielded again its potent loot, the bed under him sagged into grateful nonsense and he thought he might slip through the jostle of jealousy into sleep. Then the image of her car under its streetlight returned, and the thought of her cries under caresses, and of her skin under clothes, and of her voice under silence—for there was no doubting, this act of hers addressed itself to *him*. For she was his mistress and that same week had lain with him.

He arose from the bed. His wife adjusted her position within the great gray egg of her unconsciousness. He did not dare test the creak-prone closet door; clad as partially as when he arose he made his way down oaken staircases flayed with moonbeams to a front door whose fanlight held in Byzantine rigidity the ghosts of its Tiffany colors. A-tremble—his whole body one large tremble, only solid seemingly, like solid matter—he pressed his thumb upon the concussive latch, eased the towering giant of a parsonage portal toward his twittering chest, stepped outside, onto granite, and bathed his legs in wintry air.

This is fun! First you whittle the puppets, then you move them around.

The lawn was frosty. The neighborhood was dark. The moon peered crookedly over his shoulder, curious enough to tilt its head. The Reverend Mr. Marshfield avoided stepping on the fragments of a Wiffle Ball his sons had ragefully fragmented, on a can his dog had chewed and savored like a bone, on the glinting pieplate of clothespins his wife, dear sainted sloven, had neglected to bring in from some autumnal drying—the white sheets whipping, the last swirled exodus of starlings peppering the flavorless sky. That was ago. This was now. Once upon a time the secret stars of frost winked out beneath his soles. He foresaw the fence, even remembered the bill (typed with a brown ribbon) from the contractor (a lugubrious cheat, long since bankrupted) who planted it there by vote of the board of deacons (Gerald Harlow, chairman), picked for his tread a spot in the frozen flower border where no old rose clippings might have speared him ("With the help of the thorn in my foot," Kierkegaard wrote, "I spring higher than anyone with sound feet"), and in one smooth parabolic step our ex-athletic cleric and voyeur swung his ungirded loins an airy inch or so above the pointed painted pickets and with cold toes trespassed upon the ill-tended turf of his assistant minister, effeminate, bearded Ned (for Thaddeus, somehow) Bork.

Perfidy, thy name might as well be Bork. The present writer, his nose and eyeballs still stinging from his first afternoon of desert brightness, can scarcely locate what is most signally odious about this far-away young man. His unctuous, melodious, prep-school drawl? His rosy cheeks? His hint of acne? The chestnut curls of his preening beard? His frog-colored eyes? Or was it his limp-wristed theology, a perfectly custardly confection of Jungian-Reichian soma-mysticism swimming in a soupy caramel of Tillichic, Jasperian, Bultmannish blather, all served up in a dime-store dish of his gutless generation's give-away

Gemütlichkeit? His infectious giggle? Or the fact that every-body in the parish, from the puling baptizee to the terminal crone hissing in the oxygen tent, loved him?

Actually, I liked him too.

And wanted him to like me.

He was in there with my carnal love. I crept from window to window, meeting tactile differentiations among the variety of shrubs the local nursery (which piously kept its Puerto Rican peony-pluckers in a state of purposeful peonage) had donated to our holy cause of parsonage improvement. They were in this garage renovated to bachelor's quarters, my organist and my curate, one of each sex, like interlocked earrings in a box too large for such storage. But one dim light shone within Bork's quarters. His rooms, though not many and all on one floor, were arranged with a maddening cleverness; from whatever window I, my nakedness clawed, stealthily scrambled to, the shuffle of partitions eclipsed what I needed to see. The paper cutouts in my hollow Easter egg had fallen all to one side and presented only blurry one-dimensional edges. Yet I could hear, in the gaps between the crackling thunder of my feet and the ponderous surf of my breathing, voices—or, if not quite voices, then the faint rubbed spot on the surface of silence that indi-cates where voices have been erased.

Fearful lest the hypothetical passing patrol car spot me, the ideal bare-bummed burglar, I eased to the alley and peered in the window to the left of the front door; at the other extreme of the tiny house's immense space, by the light of a lamp that seemed to be muffled beneath rose-colored blankets, I beheld a white triangle, quick as a Nikon's shutter, flesh* above the edge of a sofa, and vanish as quickly from view. Too sharp to be a knee, it must have been an elbow. Too fair to be his, it must have been hers. She was above him, in the position of Hera and Zeus, of Shakti and Shiva. More power to the peephole!

The glimpse burned in me like a drop of brandy in the belly of an ostensibly reformed alcoholic. I crept, literally ("upon thy belly shalt thou go"), through the icy grass beneath the sills of the side windows to the window nearest the sofa. With a wariness that made my joints petition against gradualism I

---

*I of course meant to type "flash."

straightened enough to peek in a lower pane. Though dwelling in outer darkness, I might be caught by the flare of a match or by a shouting* star, and anyway felt my face to be burning like a banshee's. I let one bulged eye look on behalf of both.

There, not a man's length away, basking in pinkish glow, lay a bare foot. Hers. Alicia had homely feet, veinous and glazed on the knuckles of some toes as if primed for an appliqué of corns. This was a foot of hers. Irrefutably. And irrefutably naked. I was stunned. I listened for the cries it was her wont wantonly to emit in coitus. But Bork, like so many of his carefree-seeming generation, had a sharp lookout on his own comfort, and had put up his storm windows. Then, before my face, at just the other side of the double installment of glass, there was a commotion of hair, his or hers I couldn't tell, so instantaneous was my flinching, and my subsequent rolling downwards and sideways into the lee of a comradely bush that from the well-oiled prickle of its leaves must have been a holly. Cretinous and cunning as an armadillo, I lay there bathed in mulch chips until I deemed the stillness safe for a dancing retreat—my legs scribbling like chalk on a blackboard—across Bork's moon-hard lawn into the creaky, fusty forgiveness of my fanlighted foyer.

No sirens had arisen in the night to pursue me.

No angels materialized on the staircase.

Moonbeams still lay across it like stripes on the bent brown back of a suppliant slave.

Within myself, under the caked hot crusty sensation that arises to shield us from athletic defeat and direct insult, I felt horror at my visual confirmation of the already evidentially (given the parked car, the house, the hour, the ubiquity of sex, and the infallible Providence that arranges for my discomfort) certain. But, twinned with horror and bedded snugly beside it, a warm body of satisfaction lay detectable within myself. This pleasure, though alloyed, was deep, deeper than the half-believer's masochism, deeper than my truffler's hunger for secrets, of which the bare foot was now one. So deep, indeed, that, gazing down, from within the warm stairwell alive with the ticking of my rent-free radiators,

*O.K. *Cf.* Wm. Blake.

I saw the comfortable carpets and shadow-striped floor of my father's house, also not his own.

But the hands of the motel clock have already moved past the crowing erectitude of noon. Today, I think, a Daiquiri, with an icing of suds atop the soothing rum, and then another.

And first we must move our bare-legged puppet up the stairs and put him to bed. He presses open the bedroom door with a barely perceptible snap that nevertheless, he knows, snaps his wife's eyes open.

"My God. Tom. Where have you been?"

"Checking on the children. Putting out the cat."

He slithers into his vacated place, shoving to one side the warm fragments of herself that she allowed to spill there. She asks, "Why are your feet so cold? And your bottom? You're freezing."

"I was out on the lawn."

"With no pants on?"

"I was looking for UFOs."

"I don't believe it."

"Also the paper said there was going to be a comet. Or some such heavenly portent."

"I don't believe it. You were spying on Ned. That's sick."

"He's in my cure of souls. *Curo, curate, curare.*"

"Tom, that is sick. What are we going to do with you?"

And I thought for an abysmal second she, her hand surveying my coldness, was going to fumble for my penis. But the danger, as do so many, passed.

3

MY FATHER'S house house house hou

Fingers droop above the keys, the shiny print above this desk (a Remingtonesque work depicting a horse, a bush, and a sod hut all basking in a prairie sunset too cerise to be true) develops fascinating details (is that an elbow protruding from one window? is that a fissure or a river off to the left?), and incidents of yesterday's golf match return to me plaguingly. After swinging with a nice clicking freedom from tee to green, in the thin air, in the cactoid terrain, I missed three consecutive putts of less than three feet, indicating either emergent astigmatism or a severe character defect. The sense of that ball, so anxiously tapped, sliding by on the high side and hanging there as obdurately as the fact of pain in the world: it pulls one's insides quite awry. Disbelief warps us so that tears are nearly wrung from our ducts. Red fury rolls in. Perdition! Perdition to the universe of which this hole is the off-center center! All men hate God, Melville says.

My father's house was several houses, as he moved from parish to parish, but the furniture remained the same, and the curved feet, not leonine but paws without claws, without toes, of a mahogany-veneered highboy return large to me, as something that must have engaged my fancy when a crawler. The nap of the Oriental rug, upon whose edge of angular blue flowers these impossibly round feet intruded, was exceptionally lush at the edges, and ominously threadbare where the feet of our family and my father's visitors trod.

They would mumble behind his study door, the visitors. On Saturdays he would type—ejaculations of clatter after long foreplay of silent agony. These sounds of ministerial activity engraved themselves upon a deadly silence. My father and my mother said little. They had few friends to whom he was not a nuncio from a better world. I was the youngest of four children, but the brother nearest me, Stephen, was light-years older than I, and away at school from the time I could toddle. I had been a kind of afterthought, a mistake. My very existence was some sort of jape. I apologized the best I could, by being good. Though the library was lined with books that mingled Heaven with our daily dust, none could explain the riddle of my existence. It lay within my mother. My mother had once been fair; fair, turning sepia with age, her image gazed from the living-room mantel—from the succession of living-room mantels. It was among the treasures I had to claim when she died of lung cancer seven years ago, and I was struck by how small it was, this image, and how conventional, with that high-browed, absent-eyed blur of beauties before World War I. In the end, fashion overcomes personality: all the mistresses of Louis XV look alike. My mother once had a beautiful voice, but by the time I was big enough to stand beside her in church, her voice had been hoarsened by time and chronic bronchitis, and as if in protest she would stand silent beside me, following the words in the hymnal with her eyes, but her mouth softly closed, her silence pealing in my heart. From their bedroom, too, silence, once the mumble of my father's account of their day died, and with it the lighter music, mostly rests, of my mother's responses, and her voluntary canticle of the household, a few chimed facts that primarily, I imagined, concerned me. Then, silence. So my pleasure in verifying that Ned and Alicia were screwing might be, deeply, pleasure in discovering that my parents in their silence were not dead but alive, that my birth had not chilled all love, that the bower of their union continued to flourish above me.

These sentences have come in no special order. Each of them has hurt. Each might have been different, with the same net effect. All facts are equivalently dismal. Any set of circumstances can give rise to a variety of psychological conditions. We acknowledge this when we skip the flashbacks in novels.

Rereading, I see that my mother's singing voice was, for me, her sex; that her hoarseness I transferred in my childish innocence to her lower mouth, which was, as I stood small beside her in the pew, at the level of my mouth; that I equate noise with vitality; that silence, chastity, and death fascinate me with one face; that Alicia's power over the organ keyboards was part of her power over me.

I see that, meaning to write about my father, I have written about my mother instead. Yet she was insignificant, timid, mousily malcontented, immense only in the dimension of time, of constancy. Whereas my father was an impressive, handsome figure, and is so even now, at the age of seventy-seven, sitting senile in a nursing home.

And I notice that I wrote "by being good" when I should have written "by lying low"—for there is a curiously serpentine altitude to not only my infantile impressions but to those received when I had straightened up, even when I had grown to my mother's height. Her hymn book is always above the level of my eyes, and I feel before me the space *under* the pew, with its never-varnished wood and unhemmed edges of velvet held by old-fashioned upholsterer's tacks, their brass heads tarnished to the color of a dried bloodstain. "He who is down," we used to sing, "need fear no fall." "All they that go down to the dust," quoth the Psalmist, "shall bow before Him." Sexually speaking (and why not? school's out) I preferred the inferior position—on top, the woman is so much more supple and knobby and *interested*—and adored "going down." O how Alicia's exclamations, sweeter than honey in the hive, would resound in my ears as they were clamped in the sticky, warm, living vise of her thighs! And down beyond down, those toes, so well described yesterday, what rapture it gave me to kiss them, especially when the smell of sweat and Capezio leather lay secret on their skin or, of a barefooted summer day, sand and salt and the flavor of the innumerable trod particles, from tar-crumb to dead-leaf-flake, that comprise the blessed ground of our being!

The Tillichian pun comes opportunely. For I need still to say, what scrambles the keys to say, that my father's house bred into me a belief in God, which has made my life one long glad feast of inconvenience and unreason.

How did it do this?

How did I manage to gather such a monstrous impression?

That my father, as he pottered about intending to wag the world with the stubby scruffy tail of his stuffy congregation, appeared dim-witted to me, I have already implied. He was not a wise nor, insofar as his public commitment to be exemplary inflicted a mousy tyranny upon his household, a kind man. He was at his best (hel*low* again) in his basement, in the succession of our basements, where he would establish a workbench of phenomenal neatness, the hammers and pliers and calipers placed upon their outlines painted on pegboard, the well-oiled tablesaw (its absolutely level metal top my first vision of rectitude) established on the right, and the cans of paint and putty and solvent shelved on the left, and the jars of nails and screws of progressive and labelled sizes nailed by their lids to a board above; and there my father would spend part of most afternoons, performing, in the warmth of the proximate furnace, small tasks of mending and manufacture that, to my childish sense, were meaningless but for the meaning the shavings breathed, and the cleansing aroma of the turpentine, and the inner peace emanating from my puttering, pipe-smoking, fussy, oblivious father. I would sit on a sawhorse and love my upward view of his cleft chin, his vital nostrils, his wavy gray hair—its brushed luxuriance his one overt vanity.

I did not confuse my father and God. I knew it was not God in that basement, but an underpaid, rather loosely instructed employee. Nor was God in the churches, save rarely, as when a bass organ note left pedalled from the Amen rattled the leading of the apostles' stained-glass haloes and echoed from the darkest, not-even-at-Easter-inhabited rear of the balcony like a waking animal groaning from his burrow. In general the churches, visited by me too often on weekdays—when the custodian was moving the communion table about like a packing case, and sweeping up the chewing-gum wrappers that insolently spangled the sacrosanct reaches of the choir—bore for me the same relation to God that billboards did to Coca-Cola: they promoted thirst without quenching it.

But it was, somehow, and my descriptive zeal flags, in the *furniture* I awoke among, and learned to walk among, and fell asleep amid—it was the moldings of the doorways and the sashes of the windows and the turnings of the balusters —it was the carpets each furry strand of which partook in a pattern and the ceilings whose random cracks and faint discolorations I would never grow to reach, that convinced me, that *told* me, God was, and was here, even as the furnace came on, and breathed gaseous warmth upon my bare, buttonshoed legs. Someone invisible had cared to make these things. There was a mantel clock, with a face of silver scrolls, that ticked and gonged time which would at the last gong end, and the dead would awake, and a new time would begin. Beyond the stairs, there were invisible stairs leading unimaginably upward. There was a sofa where I would, older, lie and eat raisins and read O. Henry and John Tunis and Admiral Byrd and dream; the sofa itself felt to be dreaming; it was stuffed with the substance of the spirit. Though we had moved, following my father's call, from one city of inland America to another, this sofa was a constant island, and the furniture a constant proof of, as it were, a teleologic bias in things, a temporary slant as of an envelope halfway down the darkness inside a mailbox.

Not much of a *point de départ pour le croyant qui souffre*, eh? Not even the grand Argument from Design, for it has taken me forty of my years to begin to transfer my sense of the Divine outdoors. Sunsets, mountaintops, lake surfaces rippling like silk in the wind, all strike me as having the faintly fraudulent splashiness of churches, a forced immanence. Athletic fields and golf courses excepted, the out-of-doors wears an evil aspect, dominated as it is by insects and the brainless proliferation of vegetable forms. Little grits and small fittings are crags and dells enough for my pantheism.

(Pascal dreaded landscapes too. How I do crave the *Pensées*! The squaw at the commissary let me have a John Dickson Carr and a P. G. Wodehouse, but when I gingerly asked if there was any Dorothy Sayers, she blushed as wickedly as if I had asked for the *Summa Theologica*.)

To sum up, and to bring my day's trial to an end, I had no choice but to follow my father into the ministry; the furniture forced me to do it. I became a Barthian, in reaction against his liberalism, a smiling fumbling shadow of German Pietism, of Hegel's and Schleiermacher's and Ritschl's polywebbed attempt to have it all ways, of those doddering Anglican empiricists who contribute the theological articles to the Encyclopaedia Britannica (no mention of Kierkegaard! of Baudelaire! of the Grand Inquisitor! where is the leap! the abyss! the black credibility of the *deus absconditus*! instead, a fine-fingered finicking indistinguishable in texture from the flanking articles on pond biomorphs and macromolecules), which stance in turn had been taken, in defiance of hellfire, out of reaction to his own father, an anti-Darwinian fundamentalist, a barrel-thumping revivalist risen repentant from the swamps of pioneer booze. No doubt these nuances matter less than we in the trade imagine.

And no doubt one Daiquiri less before lunch will do wonders for my sunstruck short putts after. That little Tennessean, a closet sodomist if I read his body-language aright, is deadly from six feet in.

No. Two points arose as I rummaged in the bathroom for the Coppertone. One, I did not become a Barthian in blank recoil, but in positive love of Barth's voice, his wholly masculine, wholly informed, wholly unfrightened prose. In his prose thorns become edible, as for the giraffe. In Barth I heard, at the age of eighteen, the voice my father should have had.

Two, my intuition about objects is thus the exact opposite of that of Robbe-Grillet, who intuits (transcription of a bird call: *in-tu-it, in-too-eeet*) in tables, rooms, corners, knives, etc., an emptiness resounding with the universal nullity. He has only to describe a chair for us to know that God is absent. Whereas for me, puttying a window sash, bending my face close in, awakens a plain suspicion that someone in the immediate vicinity immensely, discreetly cares. God. Since before language dawned I knew what the word meant: all haggling as to this is linguistic sophistry. "Bending my face close in" reminds me (if you care, supposed reader, about this kind of connection) of that redhead some pages and more years ago, "her pubic hair as nicely packed around its treasure as excelsior around an ancestral locket." An attic closeness. I wonder, truly, if "love" (old whore of a word, we'll let you in this once, fumigated by quotation marks) is not a reifying rather than de-reifying process, and "sex object" not the summit of homage.

Away with personhood! Mop up spilt religion! Let us have it in its original stony jars or not at all!

4

I INHERITED HER. Alicia had been hired by my predecessor, a languid gnostic stirred to dynamism only by the numen of church finances. Having ministered to our flock and its fleece during the go-go years, he left me a fat portfolio and lean attendance rolls. I was told, indeed, that the Reverend Morse believed that nothing so became a parishioner's life as the leaving of it, with a valedictory bequest to the building fund. More, *mors*! At any rate the nominal members stayed away from the sabbath pews as from an internal revenue inquisitor, until the word went about in the land that lo! the new parson was not a hunting one, but a hunted. O, shame upon me as I recall those Sundays in the world, my sermons so fetchingly agonized, so fashionably antinomian. I suffered, impaled upon those impossible texts, weeping tears with my refusal to blink at the eschatological, yet happy in my work, pale in my pantomime of holy agitation, self-pleasing in my sleepless sweat, a fevered scapegoat taking upon myself the sins of the prosperous. The blue-suited businessmen regarded me with guarded but approbatory grimace as a curious sort of specialist, while musk arose thicker than incense from between the legs of their seated wives. But enough of such shoptalk. I was sincere, if the word has meaning. Better our own act than another's. The Lord smiled; the cloud of witnesses beneath me grew, while wiring hung inside the pulpit like entrails in a butcher's shop, and my collection of interior pornography improved in technical quality (the early graininess expunged by computer-enhancement from these latest Danish imports), and the organ behind me pertly sliced a premature end to the eloquent anguish of my prayerful pause.

She was pert, short, nearsighted, blonde in the hard ironed style, argumentative, and rather metronomic. My organist at the previous church had been a plump black man who rolled on the bench like a flywheel and set the pews to swaying during collection so freely the plates hopped from hand to hand like the bouncing ball at a sing-along. Sweeping the floors became a franchise, there was so much dropped change. Alicia, why do you keep hiding behind these wisecracks? When you sat down to play, I wondered if the thick soles of your trendy shoes wouldn't keep you from pedalling properly. Chartreuse bell-bottoms peeked from beneath your cassock. Behind your tinted octagonal spectacles, were your red-rimmed rabbit eyes really so shifty? I found out, didn't I?

"Mrs. Crick, did you feel you might have taken 'A Mighty Fortress' a shade fast?" She is divorced, with two small children. Hire the handicapped. Her age on the edge of thirty, as mine is on that of forty. Those ten years up on me, and the contemplative pout of her lips, stiff as a sugar rose, and the impudent monocle-flash of one or the other of her spectacles as she tips her glossy head goad me to add, "'A *Flighty* Fortress,' we should call it. Your tempo left the choir procession stranded halfway down the aisle."

"The children's choir dawdled filing out," is Mrs. Crick's response. And: "You can't drag every hymn just because it's religious."

In retrospect, and no doubt then as well, beneath my risen hackles, I loved her standing up to me. Life, that's what we seek in one another, even with the DNA molecule cracked and our vitality arraigned before us as a tiny Tinkertoy.

"There's such a thing as feeling," I told her.

"And such a thing as feigning," she responded.

Why can't I keep this in the present tense? She recedes in the vaults of the past as, on many a night, the clatter of the choristers having faded in a wash of headlights, she would switch off the organ (a 1920 three-manual electropneumatic, with a thrillingly discordant calliope of mixture stops), gather to her breasts her *Sämtliche Orgelwerke von Dietrich Buxtehude* and *Oeuvres complètes pour Orgue de J. S. Bach annotées et doigtées par Marcel Dupré* and *99 Tabernacle Favorites for Choir & Organ*, and sigh and recede down the dimmed and silenced nave to the lancet doors and the black car parked in the black lot beyond.

"Good-night, Mrs. Crick."

"Good-night, Reverend Marshfield."

The draft from her opening the door arrived at my ankles as the sound of its closing arrived at my ears. I feel my cassock sway in this wind. It is dead winter. Reverend. A chill. Her blonde shimmer receding down the aisle, shifting into murky brunette. Her bottom, in adherent slacks, surprisingly ample and expressive. A touch of sorrow rounding her shoulders. Her dumpy old Chevrolet. I knew little about her life apart from Thursday nights and Sunday mornings. She gave piano lessons in the neighboring suburb. She had two children, who did not come to Sunday school. She must have lovers.

"You are implying," I said above, after her "feigning," "what?" My wariness was not only that of the watcher but that of the watched. For some time, her attention had been upon me: my hackles knew it.

She sat on the arm of a pew and hugged her pastel sheaf of music tighter. In this strained position her knees, bonier than the rest of her, protruded and pressed white edges into the stretchy knit of her tights. Was she about to weep? Her voice was dry. "I'm sorry. I don't know what I was implying. You're a good man. No, you're not. I'm sorry, I don't have any control over what I'm saying. Something else has upset me, not you."

"Would you like to tell me what?" I asked, though it was more about me, her image of me, that I wanted to hear.

"Oh, some man."

"Who won't marry you?"

She looked up, her eyes behind the tinted lenses pink and worn. "That must be it," she said, sarcastically.

"I'm wrong," I offered.

"You're close enough." Her head bowed again. "You just get so tired," she added, of another "you," in weak apology.

Her life, the Gothic carpentry of the church, the night and town outside, the parish and its tired, teeming life all as in an Uccello converged on this sadness; I was in a black center, a mildew-darkened patch on a mural; I was conscious of my white hands, posed anxiously before me as if trying to build a house of cards in the air. Their palms tingled. Her bowed head glowed. To this moment, toward which four decades narrowed, I had never been unfaithful to my wife. There had been temptations as strong, but my will to be tempted had been weaker.

"Tired of what? Tell me."

She lifted her face; her face was behind glass.

What do I mean, writing that? Am I imposing backwards upon the moment the later moment when truly she was behind glass, her foot and her hair, with Ned? Or did my knowledge that a process of seduction was at work, that this face could, if not now, later, be touched, secrete in panic a transparent barrier? Her jaw wore a curious, arrogant, cheap, arrested set, as if about to chew gum. "Of men," she said, interrogatively—"?" The lift in her voice leaving the sentence open was an offering. She clamped it shut after a pause. "You'd be shocked if I told you."

I did not dispute. Dinna press, when swinging a club or parrying with a woman. Let the club do the work. I may have resolved, also, in this pocket of my silence, to make her pay later for this snub of hers; or again this cruel notion may be imposed in retrospect, a later loop of the film overlapping.

"Then tell me about *me*," said I, bold and insouciant, a modern cleric, perching on the arm of a pew opposite. The prim wood nipped my buttocks. "I'm not a good man," I rehearsed my prey. "I feign."

As I had hoped, she became argumentative. "'Good,'" she took up. "I don't understand goodness. The term doesn't have much meaning for me. Things happen, people do things, and that's it. I know you don't believe that. I *do* think you exaggerate yourself as a believing unbeliever, as a man sweating it out on the edge of eternity or whatever; you *tease* the congregation. You shouldn't. Those people out there, they're just dumb; they don't know why they're hurting, or going into bankruptcy, or knocked-up, or lonely, or whatever. You shouldn't act out your personal psychodrama on their time. I mean, this isn't meant to be your show, it's *theirs*."

"I see," I said, lying.

She saw I was. "I mean," she said, and I loved the flush of earnestness stealing that street-wise gum-chewing cool from her features, "don't be so angry, about patterns and obstacles that are all in your head."

"Angry? Am I?"

"I'd say," Alicia said, "you're the angriest *sane* man I've ever met."

So you've met angry insane men? But I didn't ask that; I asked, benevolently, "What do you think I'm angry about?"

"What we're all angry about. You're unhappy."

Still smiling, still stoking my smile with interior vows of revenge, I asked, inevitably, "And what makes me so unhappy?"

I assumed she would answer, *Your theology*. Instead she said, "Your marriage."

"Isn't it perfect?" I asked; the words, inane yet divinely enunciated, arose beyond me, in some dictionary seraphim update.

My dear sexy organist laughed. Her laugh filled the church like golden mud—or do I misquote? "It's *ter*rible," she pronounced,* myopic and merry and her kneecaps thrust into anxious relief by some stress in her perching position. "It's worse than mine even, and that didn't last three years!"

There is a Biblical phrase whose truth I then lived: scales fell from my eyes. She was right. In her helmet of centrally cleft floss this angel had come and with a blazing sword slashed the gray (as cardboard, as brain cells) walls of my prison.

This conversation took place early in Lent; I kissed her in the vestibule the evening of Holy Saturday, between the lancet doors giving inward on the nave and the weatherstripped doors giving outward on the expectant night, gathering her into my arms above the wire rack of Lenten pamphlets and

---

*Let it ride.

appropriate versicles directed at the alcoholic, the lonely, the doubtful, the estranged, gathering into my arms a startling, agitated, conflicted, uneven mix of softnesses and hardnesses, warm spots and cool, her body. After Easter, her veteran Chevrolet Providentially having torn a gasket, she let me drive her home, and took me upstairs to her surprisingly ample bed.

Perhaps the conversation as I have set it down is a medley of several, scattered through a number of post- or pre-rehearsal interludes, in drafty ecclesiastic nooks haunted by whiffs of liquid wax and spilled cider, or on awkward frozen lawns while our gloved hands groped for the handles of differing automobiles (mine a coffee-brown 1971 Dodge Dart, hers a 1963, if memory serves, Bel Air).

Or perhaps these words were never spoken, I made them up, to relieve and rebuke the silence of this officiously chaste room.

5

ALICIA IN BED was a revelation. At last I confronted as in an ecstatic mirror my own sexual demon. In such a hurry we did not always take time to remove socks and necklaces and underthings that clung to us then like shards or epaulettes, we would tumble upon her low square bed, whose headboard was a rectangle of teak and whose bedspread a quiltwork sunburst, and she would push me down and, her right hand splayed on her belly, tugging upward the tarnished gift of her pubic fur so as to make an unwispy fit, would seat herself upon my upraised* phallus, whose mettle she had firmed with fingers and lips, and whimper, and come, and squirm, and come again, her vaginal secretions so copious my once-too-sensitive glans slid through its element calm as a fish, and politely declined to ejaculate, so that she came once more, and her naked joy, witnessed, forced a laugh from my chest. Such laughing was unprecedented for me; under my good wife's administration sex had been a solemn, once-a-week business, ritualized and worrisomely hushed.

---

*The first time, believe it or not, I typed "unpraised"—my uxorious lament in an uninvited consonant.

The minx's breasts were small but smartly tipped, her waist comfortably thick, her feet homely as I have said and well-used-looking, as were her active hands, all muscle and bone, and her pubic patch the curious no-color of tarnish, of gilt dulled to the edge of brown, the high note of her blond head transposed to a seductive minor.

That musical metaphor brought, just now, me to a treacherous pitch—see earlier, the "saving grace note upon the baffled chord of self." I jerked off, lying on the wall-to-wall carpet of goose-turd green, rather than sully my bachelor cot where the Navajo chambermaid might sardonically note the spoor of a wounded paleface. My seed sank into polyester lint and the microscopic desert grits of a hundred transient shoes. I shouldn't have done it, for now my hymn to my mistress will be limp and piecemeal, tapped out half by a hand still tremulous and smelling of venerable slime.

At the join of Alicia's abdomen and thighs you could count the tendrils one by one; they thickened in the center to a virtual beard that, when we showered together ere returning to the scoured world, she would let me shape with soap into a jaunty goatee. She loved her own cunt, handled it and crooned of it as if it were, not the means to a child, but a child itself, tender and tiny and intricate and mischievously willful. "My trouble is," she told me, "I think with my cunt." "I'm kissing my own cunt!" she sighed unforgettably once when I fetched my mouth fresh from below and pressed it wet upon her own. The lover as viaduct. The lover as sky-god, cycling moisture from earth to cloud to earth.

Though she was a fair enough sky herself. We played in each other like children in puddles. Dabbled and stared, dabbled and stared. The mud of her, white and rose and gold, reflected blue zenith.

Play. There was that, in daylight, laughing, after a marriage bed of nighttime solemnity and spilt religion, spilt usually at the wrong angle, at the moment when the cup had been withdrawn. What fun my forgotten old body turned out to be—the toy I should have been given for Christmas, instead of the jack-in-the-box, or the little trapeze artist between his squeezable sticks, or the Lionel locomotive entering and re-entering his papier-mâché tunnel. Thank you, playmate, for such a

light-headed snowy morning, your own body more baubled
than a Christmas tree, with more vistas to it than within a ka-
leidoscope. In holiday truth my wonder did seem to rebound
upon you, merry, merry, and make you chime.

Play, and pain. Her moans, her cries, at first frightened me,
at the very first because I naïvely imagined I was in my new-
found might hurting her ("You're wombing me!" she once
cried, astraddle) and next because I feared such depth of pleasure was not enough my creation, was too much hers, and
could too easily be shifted to the agency of another. There
is this to be said for cold women; they stick. So beneath our
raptures I heard the tearing silk of infidelity, and she heard
the ticking clock that would lift me, from whatever height of
self-forgetfulness, on to the next appointment, and home, to
check the patch of invisible mending on my absence. Alicia
found it hard to let me go, I know. For I was a rare man, in this
latter world of over-experienced men. Her bestowals had not
for some years, I judged, won such gratitude and ardor. So my
swift resumption of my suit of black, even to rubber overshoes
in the post-Paschal season of slush, caused all of her skin, bare
on our bed, to stare amazed. Her clinging to me naked, at the
head of the stairs, is the only embrace it displeases me to recall.
Though the sight of her, then, I turning for one last, upward
glance, the stairs descended, her legs cut off at the ankle and
her propping arms "bled" from the rectangle framing her silhouette, the sight of her, I say, before I turned and pulled open
the barking door to the breezy world, still so moves this abandoning heart that a less tension-loving typist would be driven
again to the ruggy floor of his padded cell.

Play, and pain, and display. Her house was a little peach-
colored one in a row of varicolored but otherwise uniform
houses on a curved street so newly scraped into being that
mud ran red in the gutters when it rained and the only trees
were staked saplings. The upstairs windows were dormered;
her children each had a small room facing front and Alicia had
taken for herself the long room giving on the back yard, with
its brave spindle of an infant beech, and an incipient box hedge,
and her garage, and an alley where an oil truck seemed often
to be idly churning, and the bleak backs of the next street in
the development. Across a tract of purple woods waiting for

their development stood what appeared to be an abandoned gravel pit and, on the crest above it, incongruously, the little spikes and buttons of tombstones in a cemetery, where I had, I believed, a few times, buried souls. I loved this sparse, raw neighborhood, for its impoverished air suggested that Alicia did not have the means to leave me, however often I briskly dressed and left her, and its lack of trees—the opposite of my own heavily oaked and elmed neighborhood of imposing McKinley-vintage manses—let the light in unclouded, nude as ourselves, and like us eternally young. O Alicia, my mistress, my colleague, my adviser, my betrayer, what would I not give—a hand? no, not even a finger, but perhaps the ring from my finger—to see you again mounted at the base of my belly, your shoulders caped with sunshine, your head flung back so your jawbone traced its own omega, your hair on false fire, your breasts hung undefended upon the dainty cage of your ribs and anxious for any mouth to tease them, any hand to touch them, but untouched taking pleasure, it seemed, in their own unresisted swaying, in the wash of light. I lifted my back, the muscles in my thighs pulled, my face was fed, you moaned. We bent a world of curves above the soaked knot where our roots merged.

Alicia was nearsighted, and had to look closely. Else, but for my voice and smell, I was a mist of maleness to her. And I, I borrowed courage from her shamelessness, and looked my fill, and reduced under the caresses of my eyes her pores, striations, wrinkles, wobbles, calluses, and widening flaws—time was making familiar with her, younger than I though she was —to the service of love. That lame word again. I meant to describe "display." Precisely, I worshipped her, adored her flaws as furiously as her perfections, for they were hers; and thus I attained, in the bound of a few spring weeks, a few illicit lays, the attitude which saints bear toward God, and which I in a Christ's lifetime of trying (40 [present age] minus 7 [age of reason] equals 33) had failed to reach, that is, of forgiving Him the pain of infants, the inexorability of disease, the wantonness of fortune, the billions of fossilized deaths, the helplessness of the young, the idiocy of the old, the craftsmanship of torturers, the authority of blunderers, the savagery of accident, the unbreathability of water, and all the other repulsive flecks on the face of Creation.

We preened for each other, posed, danced, socketed every dubious elbow in an avid French kiss of acceptance. You've read it before (I *do* feel someone is reading these pages, though they have the same position on the desk when I return from golf, and my cunning telltales arranged with hairs and paper clips have remained untripped), I know. Skin is an agreeable texture. Penises and vaginas notably so, patent pending. Weaning was an incomplete process. Sex can be fun.

Still, what a relief to have *intelligere* become *esse*. Land ho! She appeared to me during those afternoons of copulation as a promontory on some hitherto sunken continent of light. I had to drive from her town to mine along a highway that, once threaded shadily through fields and pastures, was now straightened, thickened, and jammed with shopping malls, car lots, gas stations, hero sandwich parlors, auto parts paradises, driving ranges, joyless joyrides for the groggy offspring of deranged shoppers, go-go bars windowless as mausoleums (Gay Nite Tuesdays, Cum in Drag), drive-in insurance agencies, the whole gaudy ghastly gasoline-powered consumerish smear, bubbling like tar in the heat of high summer. Yet how washed and constellated it all looked in the aftermath of my sinning! How the fallen world sparkled, now that my faith was decisively lost!

Back from golf (not bad: 94, with only two three-putt greens, and I'm beginning to judge the approach distances better; take two clubs longer than you think, in this deceptive heaven of superair) I feel I should qualify that last rather swanky clause. I brim still, alas, with faith. But Alicia did induce reorientation, of maybe 10°. Imagine me as a circle divided in half, half white and half black. In the white side were such things as my father's furniture, Karl Barth's prose, the fine-grained pliancy and gleeful dependence of my sons* when they were babies, my own crisp hieratic place within the liturgy and sacraments,

---

*"See, the smell of my son is as the smell of a field which the Lord hath blessed"—Genesis.

a secular sense of order within my middle-class life (appointments, meetings, paternity, household and automotive maintenance, falling asleep beside mine *ux.* after the ten o'clock news), certain stray few moments of whiskey and weather, and, on Sundays, the funny papers. This was the Good. I credited God with being on this side. On the other side, the black, which might be labelled the Depressing rather than Evil, lay Mankind (both as a biological species devouring the globe and as those few hundred specimens of it which fell within my ministry—and a cloying, banal, pitiable, mean-spirited, earthbound repetitive lot they were), my own rank body, most institutional and political trends since 1965, the general decadent trend of the globe, time in all its manifestations, pain, food, books, and all the rest of the Sunday newspaper. Well (an itchy word signalling my increasingly vivid anticipations of a shower, a Whiskey Sour, a lulling view of tinted wasteland, and the blameless friction of male chaffing), Alicia, by reclaiming a wedge of mankind for the Good and Beautiful, shifted the axis of the divider 10° (rough estimate) and caused a relabelling of the now-tilted halves: the white was the Live, the black was the Dead. Most of the ingredients were unaffected by the realignment. God, who has His way of siding with the winners, took Life as His element, and continued to audit my prayers and supervise my digestion as before. Everything not-God, indeed, being dead, gave Him a freer hand. But there was one casualty: in the wedge of the circle directly across from Alicia and her peachy cries and floating nipples was an innocuous sector labelled "*ux.*," inhabited by my wife Jane, née Chillingworth. This wedge went dark as an attic window.

6

TODAY IS SUNDAY. Though they try to hide this from us, I can count; I came here on a Monday flight, and this is my sixth morning. I must preach. But without a Bible, without a copious and insipid encyclopedia of sermon aids and Aramaic etymologies, without an organist, without a congregation. So be it. I still have a memory, a soul (let us pray the two not prove at the end of time to be synonymous).

Our text is from the Gospel According to St. John, Chapter 8, verse 11: *Neither do I condemn thee.*

These words are spoken, you will remember, by Jesus to the woman taken in adultery—taken "in the very act," as the posse of Pharisees rather juicily puts it—after none of her accusers has accepted His invitation to cast the first stone. What a beautiful, strange incident this is! Inserted into the narrative, scholars assure us, at a late date, and in a style distinctly unJohannine; and indeed in some manuscripts attached to the second chapter of Luke—a piece of early Christian tradition fluttering hither and thither to find its perch within the canon. As is, the story appears only courtesy of John, the youngest, and least practical, of the Evangelists.

Here, with a gesture unparalleled in the accounts of His life on Earth, Jesus, beset by the brazen importunities of the scribes and Pharisees, stooped down and "with His finger wrote on the ground, as though He heard them not." Nowhere else are we told of His writing. What words He wrote, we are not told, which I take to authenticate the gesture, rather than cast doubt upon it; for why include it, but that it did occur? He wrote idly, irritating His vengeful questioners, and imparting to us yet another impression of our Lord's superb freedom, of the something indolent and abstracted about His earthly career.

Then, the Pharisees dispersed by His magnificent "dare," we read that He rose up, and "saw none but the woman." And He asks her, "Woman, where are those thine accusers?" They are fled. And His aloneness with her reminds us of the later moment when Mary Magdalene, having come to the tomb, and finding only two angels, turns back, and sees Jesus standing, and mistakes Him for the gardener. "Woman, why weepest thou?" He asks her, "Who seekest thou?" and He asks the adulterous woman, "Woman, where are those thine accusers?" and of His own mother, at the age of twelve, when she rebukes Him for deserting her to discourse with the doctors in the temple, He asks, "How is it that ye sought me?"

How many women, indeed, move through these sacred pages seeking Jesus, and with what sublime delicacy and firmness does He deal with them—His mother Mary and the prophetess Anna, and Joanna and Susanna, and Jairus's daughter and Peter's wife's mother, and the woman who touches His gown so that He knows without looking that virtue has gone out of Him, and the woman of many sins who washes His feet with tears and is forgiven because, though she sinned much, also she loved much; and above all Mary and Martha, who receive Him in their home, and anoint His feet with ointment of spikenard, and are rebuked by Judas, and whose brother Lazarus is raised from the dead, though, in Martha's homely warning, "Lord, by this time he stinketh"!

How homely, indeed, how domestic, is this epic of the New Testament! It sings of private hearths and intimate sorrows, not of palaces and battlefields. The underside and periphery of empire serve as stage for this mightiest and most germane of dramas. Each home a temple: what has our Protestant revolution promulgated but this, this truth spelled plain in the houses and days of the Gospel narrative? How crucial, then, to our present happiness are Christ's pronouncements upon those flanking menaces to the fortress of the household—adultery and divorce.

Jesus preached, scholarship tells us, in a time of cosmopolitan laxity in sexual morals. The Jew, indeed, ever had this fault—in contrast to the rigorous fetishist—of a certain humanistic tolerance. Though Leviticus and Deuteronomy excellently specify death for those who break the Seventh Commandment, the great Hebraic scholar John Lightfoot, in his masterwork, *Horae Hebraicae et Talmudicae*, was unable to locate a single instance of the punishment being carried out. Rather, we are told of a bondmaid who, lying with her master, was scourged and not put to death, "because she was not free." Bathsheba, though she betrayed Uriah in adultery with David, became the Queen of Israel and the mother of Solomon. Eve, seduced by the serpent, yet was the mother of mankind. Gomer, the whorish wife of Hosea, is given to him to be loved, in paradigm of the Lord's continuing love of faithless Israel. And in the new dispensation: Joseph, confronted with swelling evidence of Mary's infidelity, found himself not even willing to make her a public example, and mildly was "minded to put her away privily." Of the two adulterous women Christ encounters in the Gospels, as we have seen, one is commended, and the other is not condemned. Indeed this latter woman was brought to Him, we may conjecture, by the Pharisees to trap Him into

asking enforcement of a death penalty universally acknowledged to be absurd. For, as He repeatedly asserts, this is an
"adulterous generation." So Jeremiah had found his generation, and Hosea his; for Israel ever breaks its covenant with the
Lord, and yet the Lord ever loves, and ever forgives.

Adultery, my friends, is our inherent condition: "Ye have
heard that it was said by them of old time, Thou shalt not
commit adultery: But I say unto you, That whosoever looketh
on a woman to lust after her hath committed adultery with her
already in his heart."

But who that has eyes to see cannot so lust? Was not the First
Divine Commandment received by human ears, "Be fruitful,
and multiply"? Adultery is not a choice to be avoided; it is a
circumstance to be embraced. Thus I construe these texts.

But if, dearly beloved, we find our Master abrasively liberal
upon the matter of adultery, we find Him even less comfortably
stringent upon the matter of divorce. The Pharisaical law of His
time was well advanced toward the accommodation of the institution of marriage to the plastic human reality which is never
far, I fear, from the heart of Judaism. Bills of divorcement, as
described in Deuteronomy 24, might be written when the
wife had ceased to find favor in the husband's eyes, "because
of some uncleanness in her." Nor did it stop there. A contemporary of the living Jesus, one Rabbi Hillel, propounded that a
man might divorce his wife if "she cook her husband's food too
much"; and a follower of Hillel, one Rabbi Akiba, offered, with
a purity by whose lights our present divorce laws are seen as the
hypocritic shambles they are, that he might properly divorce
her "if he sees a woman fairer than she."

What does Jesus say to such precepts? That they have been
composed in "hardness of heart." That what "God hath joined
together, let not man put asunder." That "Whosoever shall put
away his wife, and marry another, committeth adultery against
her." I quote, from memory, from Mark, the primal Gospel,
where the words of our Saviour are least diluted by later incur-
sions of Semitic reasonableness and Greek sophistry. Paul, in
Ephesians 5, manfully attempted to mysticize this admittedly
"great mystery," claiming of the married couple that "they two
shall be one flesh," and substituting, as cosmological analogy,
for the covenant between the Lord and Israel the union of

Christ and the Church. He writes, "So ought men to love their wives as their own bodies." But most men dislike their own bodies, and correctly. For what is the body but a swamp in which the spirit drowns? And what is marriage, that supposedly seamless circle, but a deep well up out of which the man and woman stare at the impossible sun, the distant bright disc, of freedom?

Let us turn from Holy Writ to the world that surrounds us. Wherein does the modern American man recover his sense of worth, not as dogged breadwinner and economic integer, but as romantic minister and phallic knight, as personage, embodiment, and hero? In adultery. And wherein does the American woman, coded into mindlessness by household slavery and the stupefying companionship of greedy infants, recover her powers of decision, of daring, of discrimination—her dignity, in short? In adultery. The adulterous man and woman arrive at the place of their tryst stripped of all the false uniforms society has assigned them; they come on no recommendation but their own, possess no credentials but those God has bestowed, that is, insatiable egos and workable genitals. They meet in love, for love, with love; they tremble in a glory that is unpolluted by the wisdom of this world; they are, truly, children of light. Those of you—you whose faces stare mutely up at me as I writhe within this imaginary pulpit—those of you who have shaken off your sleep and committed adultery, will in your hearts acknowledge the truth of my characterization.

The Word is ever a scandal. Do not, I beg you, reflexively spurn the interpretation which my meditation upon these portions of Scripture has urged to my understanding.

Verily, the sacrament of marriage, as instituted in its adamant impossibility by our Saviour, exists but as a precondition for the sacrament of adultery. To the one we bring token reverence, and wooden vows; to the other a vivid reverence bred upon the carnal presence of the forbidden, and vows that rend our hearts as we stammer them. The sheets of the marriage bed are interwoven with the leaden threads of eternity; the cloth of the adulterous couch with the glowing, living filaments of transience, of time itself, our element, our only element, which Christ consecrated by entering history, rather than escaping it, as did Buddha.

Why else, I ask you, did Jesus institute marriage as an eternal hell but to spawn, for each sublimely defiant couple, a galaxy of little paradises? Why so conspicuously forgive the adulterous but to lend the force of covert blessing to the apparent imprecation of "adulterous generation." We *are* an adulterous generation; let us rejoice.

For the ministry of Jesus, the forty months of wandering between His baptism and His crucifixion, are not a supplement to, or an abridgment of, the Law. The Law, under a hundred forms, for a thousand tribes, has always existed, and everywhere more or less satisfactorily promotes social order, which is to say, the order of Caesar. But our Lord came not to serve Caesar, or even, as His contemporary kidnappers would have it, to overthrow Caesar; He came, in His own metaphor, not to debase the coinage current, but to put a totally new currency into circulation. Before Him, reality was monochromatic: its image is the slab, the monolith, the monotonous pasture. After Him, truth is dual, alternating, riddled: its image is the chessboard, tilled fields, Byzantine tessellation, Romanesque zigzag, Siennese striping, and the medieval fool's motley. Christ stands in another light, and His magnificent blitheness, His scorn of all the self-protecting contracts that bind men to the earth, is the shadow of another sun, a shadow brighter than worldly light; by contrast our sunshine burns at His feet blacker than tar.

Amen.

May the peace which passeth all understanding, etc.

7

WE LOOK ALIKE, my wife and I. That is what people meeting us for the first time say, sometimes with evident amusement. We do not, ourselves, feel this; nor, during our courtship, was it anything but our differences that intrigued us. She was serenity and beauty; I, agitation and energy. She was moderate, I extreme. She was liberal and ethical and soft, I Barthian and rather hard. Above all, she was female and fruitful, and I masculine and hungry. My impulse, to *eat* her, to taste, devour, and assimilate, which continues into even this our misery, though my bite has become murderous, began with the first glimpse; she was standing, in pleated tennis garb, in the windy warmth of an April day when tennis had become suddenly possible, beneath a blooming fruit tree, a small apple or a crabapple. Within this dappled shade, her head grazing the petalled limbs, the lowest was so low, Jane's prettily pallid form appeared one with her arbor. There was a piquance in her seeking this delicate shelter, on so delicately bright a day; I later learned she was allergic to the sun.

Both pale, both moderately above median height, both blue-eyed and not a bit fat, tendony rather, with the something tense about us qualified by an aura indifferent and ashen as of stalks of smoke, we make, in public, a twinned impression intensified, of course, by two decades' worth of phrase-swapping, signal-giving, and unconscious facial aping. We have been worn by the same forces into parallel spindles. We lie down in bed together side by side and turn as if on a single lathe. We resort, I sense, to a common expression under stress —an upward tilting of the head and tighter trimming of the mouth that lets our besieger know we have withdrawn into a fastidious and, despite ourselves, shared privacy.

Oh I know, I know, dear unknown reader, that just thinking of this woman tricks my prose into a new ease of fancy and airiness of cadence; I am home. But do not be fooled; this ease and comfort are not palliation, they are the disease.

The Doctor Reverend Wesley Augustus Chillingworth, Jane's father, performed as professor of ethics at the divinity school I attended. A green slanting campus, a lake at the bottom, a great ironstone chapel erected by some industrial (industrious: in dust try us) sinner at the top. A rangy town beyond, with bars and buses for its denizens, while for us there was a screen of elms and ells, and bells, bells pealing the hour, the half-hour, the quarter, until the air seemed permanently liquefied, and spilling everywhere like mercury. Chillingworth was a short, square man whose docile sallow squareness made him seem shorter than he was; he delivered his dry lectures in a virtual whisper, often facing the blackboard or an antique brown globe of the heavens left in his room from an era when natural science and theology were, if not lovers, flirts. The orgy of reading that must have consumed his youth and prime had left him, in his late fifties, wearing a great rake's faintly cocky air of exhaustion; there was a twinkle in his dryness as he led us through the desiccated debates of the Greeks, of the hedonists and the Platonists, the Peripatetics and the Cyrenaics, the Stoics and the Epicureans, over the one immense question, *Is the pleasant the good, or not quite?* His course epitomized everything I hated about academic religion; its safe and complacent faithlessness, its empty difficulty, its transformation of the tombstones of the passionate dead into a set of hurdles for the living to leap on their way to an underpaid antique profession. The old scholar's muttering manner seemed to acknowledge this, as without mercy he dragged us, his pack of pimply postulates, from Hottentot tabus and Eskimo hospitality (fuck my wife, you blubber) on to the tedious Greeks and the neo-Platonists (how can the soul be a form? how can it not be? how can God be a self? what else can He be? what is the good, then, but absorption into God? what is the good *of* it?) and further on to the rollicking saints, knitting their all-weather spacesuits of invisible wool, Augustine and his *concupiscentia*, Bonaventura and his *gratia*, Anselm and his *librum arbitrium*, Aquinas and his *synderesis*, Duns Scotus and his *pondus naturae*, Occam and his razor, and Heaven knows who all else. By spring we had won through to Grotius and his *jus gentium*, and as modern ethics unfolded under Chillingworth's muttering I had the parallel pleasure, as it were in running footnote, of seducing his daughter. We met in the cool British sunshine of Hobbesian realism, hit balls at each other with unbridled egoism, and agreed to play again, as partners. By the time of our next date, Hume was exploding "ought" and "right" and Bentham was attempting to reconstruct hedonism with maximization formulas. Our first kiss came during Spinoza, more *titillatio* than *hilaritas*. Yet I felt my *conatus*, sombre center of my self, beautifully lift from my diaphragm as, in the darkness of my shut lids, her gravity for the first time impinged on mine. As Kant attempted to soften rationalism with categorical imperatives and *Achtung*, Jane let me caress her breast through her sweater. By the time of Hegel's monstrous identification of morality with the demands of the state, my hand was hot in her bra, and my access had been universalized to include her thighs. How solid and smooth this pedant's daughter was! I had expected her to be spun of cobwebs. We were both twenty-two and virgins. The weather loosened; the nights were warm. Schopenhauer exalted will and Nietzsche glorified brutality, cunning, rape, and war. All earlier ethics stood exposed as "slave virtues" and "herd virtues." Jane, in her room atop the great dusty vault of stacked books and learned journals her father called his "study," let me undress her—no, to be honest, undressed herself, with a certain graceful impatience, I having made of her clothing an asymmetric mess of rumples and undone snaps. She flicked away the last morsel of underwear and tucked her hands behind her head in the pose of a napping picnicker and let me look. This was not my first naked female. You will remember the redhead deftly evoked pages ago, and there was a bony fellow-counsellor one summer we may never find the space for. But Jane was as to these as the cut marble is to the melted wax of the preliminary models. No formula, utilitarian or idealist, could quite do justice to the living absoluteness of it. Here was a fact, five foot seven inches long, and of circumferences varying with infinite subtlety from ankles to hips, from waist to skull. The window was open, admitting evening air and light enough to marvel by. Bands of green and salmon glowed behind the spired horizon. Her girlhood room (childish wallpaper of a medallioned cottage alternates with a woolly shepherd, back turned, standing among dogs, and tacked over with collegiate prints of Klee, Miró, and Cézanne) surrounded me like a fog of dream furniture as my eyes in twilight drank. Her father cleared his throat below. Jane made silent offer of a laugh and removed her hands from behind her head; she pulled me down into herself to snuff out my staring. "It's meant to be natural," she whispered, her first reproof, if reproof it was, or the first I remember, the first that shamed me, and that has remained preserved, beetle in amber, in my exuded sense of having—in having taken such awed delight in the sight of her (*Achtung*, indeed)—done something wrong. The British idealists, Green and Bradley, attempted to lift the human self, timeless and unitary, away from the ravening reach of analytical science. Do not think, because we became naked together, we made love. This was the Fifties. There were complications both technical and spiritual, traditional and existential. While Peirce, James, and Dewey, with native American makeshift wit, tried to reverse the divine current and wag the transcendental Dog with the tail of credulity's practical benefits, Jane proved alarmingly adept at dry-fucking (forgive this term among others, Ms. Prynne and whatever vestrymen are in attendance; that which has existence [*ens*] must have a name [*nomen*]). Alarming because her adeptness showed she had done it before. Kneeling or lying sideways, her hands no-nonsensically placed on my buttocks for alignment's and pressure's sake, she would fricate our scratchy contact until one of us, as often she before me as I before her, would trip and come. The laggard would follow suit. What poetry in virginity!—Jane's little gasp at my shoulder, and her glans-crushing push, and the leaps within her unseen, and the wet revelation of my semen, glutinous in her pussy or glistening on her belly like an iota of lunar spit. Penetrant love by comparison comes muffled. The existentialists, beginning with Kierkegaard, who set up a clever roar less unlike Nietzsche's than the tender-minded would wish, did away with essence and connection and left us with an "authenticity" whose relativity is unconfessed. Jane was slow to say she loved me. Of her virginity (a mere wet inch away) she said she should "save herself." For some other? As the logical positivists thought to end human confusion by careful reference to the dictionary (see C. L. Stevenson, *Ethics and Language*, 1944, and the final text Chillingworth assigned), I introduced the word "marriage." Jane nodded, silently. I saw her as "wife"* and went blind with pride.

To what extent, you may well ask, did I seduce this good stately girl as an undermining and refutation of the old polymath's theology, his wry dimness worse than Deism, in which I recognized, carried some steps further by a better mind, my father's terrifying bumbling at the liberal Lord's busywork? Chillingworth would dustily cough beneath us at the oddest moments, so often in synchrony with orgasm as to suggest telepathic discomfort. I was slaying him that the Lord might live.

---

*The word, by the way, is just the Anglo-Saxon *wīf*, for "woman." My wife, *ma femme*, this cunt indentured to me. Sad to say, lib-lubbers.

On his side, I believe, there was nothing so fanciful. He lived in this world. He knew that girls mature and their pelves become butterfly nets for the capture of chromosomes. Jane was the second of three daughters. The first was married, divorced, and crazy—so crazy that, in those years, she opposed Truman's intervention in Korea, and spoke of his dropping the atomic bomb as an atrocity. The younger daughter was chipping away at geology at the University of Colorado. Jane had graduated from Oberlin and had returned home for lack of a better offer; she worked mornings in a local nursery school, and taught Sunday school as well. She played the piano and the flute. She read Victorian novels. But for me, her beaux were older men (an affectedly weedy assistant prof in comp. rel. with extensive nostril-hairs and caustically bad breath from pipe-smoking; a tiny ex-Jesuit with ursine brown eyes and a clangorous stammer to match the manacle of his handshake; a plump pacifist curate with one of the pioneer beards of the fuzzily forming revolution) or members of an accredited minority, a Nigerian here, a Korean there, all of them on the make, ministerially speaking. Jane attracted suitors she could easily shed. Old Chillingworth may even have been pleased when I, with my burrish manners, appeared; my grade in his course had been B+, and my supernatural politics amused him.

"What is it," he would ask me in those not entirely stilted parlor interviews before I would ascend with Jane to the hypothetical study-hall of her room or else take her out to the surrogate paradise of a Chinese meal and a Bogart movie, "that you find so heartening in Barth? Wherein lies this specificity that pleases you?"

And my core of conviction, under his temperate gray-domed gaze, exploded like an overheated Ping-Pong ball.

"You know," he would add, tapping his pipe or a fork or his fountain pen on an ashtray or a plate or the edge of a book, "this type of radical Paulinism is a recurrent strain in the church. Marcion. Bonaventura. Duns Scotus. Occam. Flacius."

I couldn't argue. I didn't want to. I didn't know enough. I liked him. Or do I repeat myself?

Oh, and Jane herself in those years. So charming, patient, calm, abstracted, fearless, healthy, but for her solar allergy. As she walked down a cloistered path toward me it was as if a lone white rose were arriving by telegraph.

Do I regret marrying her? No more can I regret having been born. The question is, having been born, what now?

The answer being, in this place, shave, and go to the bar. Bliss! The afternoon opens before me wide as a fairway split by a straight drive. Graham Greene is right. Gratitude is the way He gets us, when we have gnawed off a leg to escape His other snares.

8

TWO DECADES LATER, Jane has little changed. Two childbearings and a miscarriage and an aeon of standing at the parsonage sink have put a pucker here and a popped vein there, but her way of walking is unchanged, her arms still swing in her strange, conceited, absentminded way, as if with every stride she is burnishing herself brighter still.

In the middle of the golf course, this reminds me, yesterday, in mid-6-iron (I hit it fat and it found a bunker; the sand out here is reprocessed glass), my tireless subconscious flashed on my self-portrait as I so studiously examined Jane naked on her bed and I recognized my pose as that of a housewife bending over a long porcelain sink where a single Brillo pad has been left lying, unmoistened, expectant, abrasive, symbolic of weary worlds of work to come.

This is going to be one of those thick-fingered days. A little fray in the typewriter ribbon moves back and forth like a sentry. A spattering of rain last night, so heavy and sudden I assumed the air-conditioner had gone haywire, has left a legacy of puffy clouds whose occasional shadow, like the shadow of a passing sentry (they guard me on all sides), activates the air of this room ominously.

Jane, two decades later, though the intonation of her person and that of mine have come to be mutual echoes, and the dimple in her cheek has impressed a brother into the center of my chin, and the original russet of my hair and the chestnut of hers have thinned and faded to an interchangeable what's-the-use brown, with gray added to your taste (she is not bald on top, like me, but her forehead has heightened, and when she pulls and flattens her hair back in front of a mirror, something she is inexplicably fond of doing, she looks, as she says, "skinned"), does, by another light—the light, say, of a fireplace as she stirs a Martini with her finger and gazes into the glow, or of the bedroom 60-watt as she darts, headfirst, into her nightie—appear *totaliter aliter*, an Other, a woman, and, as such, marketable. I did seriously hope, amid the pressure-warped improbabilities of my affair with Alicia, to mate Jane with Ned Bork, and thus arrange a happy ending for all but the Pharisees.

For one thing, he was not all that young. He had been in some business—peddling real estate, or making fancy ceramics, or partly managing a ski resort in some Yankee state; or perhaps he ran a pottery shop in a ski lodge that was for sale—before getting the "call," and undergoing, at his family's wise indulgence, divinity school. He was thirty at least.

For another, he reminded me of those thirty-year-olds who had been courting Jane before I carried her off. Ned had the beard of the pacifist, the modest stature and sexual ambiguity of the Jesuit, the pipe and affected drawl of the assistant prof. I always felt I had, in removing Jane from her circle of harmless seminarian misfits, deflected her from her destiny. Here was her chance to reclaim it, to wake from the numb nightmare of marriage to me. I did not, even in my lovelorn madness, imagine that she and Ned would marry; but perhaps they would clasp long enough to permit me to slip out the door with only one bulky armload of guilt.

For a third, they liked each other. They had the same milky human kindness, the same preposterous view of the church as an adjunct of religious studies and social service, the same infuriating politics, a warmed-over McGovernism of smug lamenting: never did they think to see themselves, however heavily their heads nodded, as two luxurious blooms on a stalk fibrous with capital and cops. Of course Jane must have felt in Ned her suitors returned to her; and he, my reasoning was, must see in her a female who, unlike whatever insatiable opposite numbers had scared him away from marriage, would have the grace and wisdom to let the appearance of submission be hers. My acquaintance with the girls of Ned's generation was (at this point) purely scholastic, but I read often enough in the fidasustenative newsletters and quarterlies that pour through a minister's letter slot like urine from a cow's vulva that they (these girls), deprived of shame and given the pill, had created a generation of impotent lads the like of which had not been seen since nannies stopped slicing off masturbators' thumbs. Impotent, I must say, I was (then) never: as ready to stand and ejaculate as to stand and spout the Apostles' Creed. This cause for rejoicing turned out to be, when in the phosphorescent decay of all we held dear old grudges began to twinkle, one of Jane's complaints; if I had not been, her case argued, so eternally upright, she might out of compassion have mastered a dozen lewd tricks and excited herself to a flutter of multiple orgasms in the bargain. So Bork's supposed semipotence became an asset, an added pastel of probability as, on the hectic sketchpad of wishful thinking, I embowered the twain, a silken and limp Adonis and his mellowed, maternal Venus, the blasphemous and opulent couple goaded by remorse toward me (me, the invisible presiding blasphemed, the mutually loved and detested, the y of the triune equation) into one extravagance of penetration after another.

Fuck my wife, you blubber.

Many the night did Bork come for dinner and stay, while I plodded out into the sleet in placation of the telephone, to minister unto a comatose matrix of tubes and medicines that had once been a parishioner or (not often; we were no bolder than we needed to be) to visit Alicia in her airy tract house. Many the night did I return and find them, my mate and my curate, still propped in a daze at the table, or bedded in opposing easy chairs by the fireplace, noogling away at the brandy and beer (they both had the capacities of vats, another auspicious affinity) and gently fumbling for (as far as I could tell) the pacifier of a social cure-all in the tumbled blankets of their minds. What babies they were! I thought they might at least fornicate out of conversational boredom. But they never seemed to weary of talking. My nostrils stuffed with the musky stench of death or sex, my shoulders hoary with sleet and woe, I looked down upon them like an impatient God who, by some crimp in His contract with Noah, cannot destroy. I say "sleet"; it must have been winter. For more seasons than I can correlate the weather of, my prayers that I be betrayed ascended in vain. I prayed, and cried, and tried. I tried the nudge direct:

(In bed, with Mrs. Marshfield and her reek of Cognac) "Do you find Ned sexually attractive?"

"I like his philosophy."

"And his acne?" (constantly at cross-purposes with myself, could bite my tongue)

"I don't mind it."

"What do you think he does, for romance?"

"I have no idea. We never discuss such things. Could I please go to sleep? The whole room is spinning around and I might throw up."

(Not to be dissuaded; the hound of Heaven) "Why *don't* you discuss such things? I'd think you would. Isn't it a little abnormal, that you don't?"

"Tom, there's a whole other world to discuss, besides ego gratification."

"Am I talking about ego gratification?" (she had her father's gift, of enlightening me when I least wanted it)

"That's all you ever talk about, lately."

"You detect a change in me, lately?" (Come on, guess. Alicia's ass sits on my head like an aureole, look. *Guess.* Do *some*thing to get me out of this.)

"Not really. You seem a little less frantic."

"In what sense frantic? When was I ever frantic?" (Me, me, what do you make of me, Mimi?)

"*Please* stop thrashing around. I really might be sick. I wish you wouldn't keep leaving me and Ned alone all the time, it makes us so nervous we both drink too much."

"There's something very beautiful about Ned, don't you think? He doesn't have any of our generation's hang-ups."

"He has hang-ups of his own," mumbled this maddening bed-partner, this flesh of my flesh.

"Oh? Does he leave you kind of titillated but unsatisfied? Want to make love, just to relieve the tension?"

"Isn't tomorrow Sunday?"

"Better yet, to*day* is Sunday. Roll over and tell me about Ned's hang-ups."

A soft snore signals her conquest of liquor, lust, marital heckling, and time. She is beautiful in oblivion. I envy her. She has the style of Grace if not its content. Her goodness keeps defeating me. My hate of her, my love of her, meet at the bottom of our rainbow, a circle.

And the nudge indirect:

"How does Jane seem to you?" Walking Ned home, through the parsonage yard, I take his plump upper arm for steadiness' sake.

"Pleasant, as always. *Très engagée.*" He disengages his arm. Drunkenness doesn't make him unsteady; it merely exaggerates his boarding-school mannerisms.

"Her engagingness doesn't strike you as a cover-up?"

"Not frightfully, really." He senses stressful depths, and has borrowed from me the odious trick of clowning in the face of mystery. "What," he asks, "exactly does my reverend superior mean?"

"Well, I don't know." And I don't. A natural agnostic, converted to right-handedness by a Little League father. "I worry about Jane." This is true. "She's not happy." Is this true? Has she ever been happy since her father stopped clearing his throat under her body? "Not"—I plunge—"ful*filled*, if you can stand the term."

"Here I stand, I can do no other" (drunker than I had thought, and sillier: what callow punks the seminaries are sending us, since the frontier dried up).

I offered him a lesson in practical religion. "Being a minister's wife is curiously isolating, you're always being nice to people as a formality, you forget to *feel*. Now that the boys are breaking away, the only person Jane seems to enjoy talking to is *you*."

"And you, surely."

(Laugh, as memorably bitter as I can make it; etching with acid) "Don't kid. It must be obvious to you, how little she and I communicate."

"Not so. Not obvious. Would never have supposed that to be the case. You even look like one another." He stands at his front door, teetering a touch. Streetlight strikes a gleam from his glassy eyes. His beard makes his face hard to read. The mouth a mere hole, with a sinister drawgate of teeth. Santa Claus as heroin pusher. Even his ears, if they showed, might be a clue to his heart. His centrally parted hair is enough like a woman's to tip my insides toward kissing him good-night. I teeter also. I tug back the abhorrent impulse and yank its leash savagely. All outward composure, I continue (the nudge semi-direct):

"Well I'm very grateful, for your being so sympathetic to Jane. She's in a strange time of her life and needs someone not me she can talk to. You seem to be it."

"My pleasure," quoth he: this speckle-browed dutiful prep-school prick (there must be a better term, Ms. Prynne, but I'm word-weary, my stint is up, the bawdy hand of the dial is now upon the prick of noon).

Mock not my revelations. They are the poor efforts of a decent man to mitigate an indecent bind, an indecently airtight puzzle. Been reading a lot of John Dickson Carr—his many locked rooms. Idea for a funny sermon (funny idea for a sermon?): The Case of the Empty Tomb, solved by an eccentric fat detective, fat, gruff, uncanny, cleanliness-obsessed Ponto Pilato. Who, really, *were* those two "angels"? *Why* did Mary mistake Him for a gardener? Was there a "second Osworld"? Et cet. This room feels pretty airless itself. Those clouds striding the wall. The air-conditioner like the muzzle of a final solution. Get me out of this, as Dutch Schultz (or was it Molly Bloom, or Psalm 22?) said. Anyway, probably already been done, in one of the Dead Sea Scrolls, by Andman Willsin.

I hate this day's pages. The depression grows fangs, this second week.

9

More dialogue, it aërates Hell.

Alicia: "What time *is* it?"

Me: "Time for me to go."

"Couldn't your meeting go on a half-hour longer?"

"Not likely. It's not a meeting. In theory I'm at the hospital, and in fact there *is* one call I must make."

"What would you have been, if you hadn't been a minister?"

"A gigolo? A prison warden? A private detective?" I am dressing, so the answers are preoccupied. The first is immodest, the second is self-rebuke, the third an honest boyhood ambition. "Why do you ask?"

The plump body enjoyed, and dismissed, sits up on the bed, expressing indignation. How frontal she is!—her breasts, her shining knees, her broad mouth and wideset, rubbed-looking, half-blind eyes. "Just wondering if you still think it's your thing."

"Because I keep fucking you? And being a hypocrite?"

"I don't mind the hypocrisy, it's your unhappiness."

"What else can I do?" Than be a minister. Than deceive Jane and keep my appointments. Than be unhappy—I resented, really, being told I was. "Freud speaks," I said, "of normal human unhappiness. Pascal says man's glory is that he knows his misery. I feel pretty good, actually."

"You always feel good," Alicia told me, "when you're with me."

Not precisely true; her saying this engendered queasiness.

But true enough to let it by. Dressed, I kissed her; my clothes were armor against her nakedness. She lifted up onto her knees, the mattress heaving in sympathy, and pressed her body against mine, which had to move a step closer the bed, lest she topple forward. Careful, don't cry, moisture is telltale, and the smell of flesh carries. "It *is* odd," I said, with a bow to Professor Chillingworth, deceased, "that feeling good and being good don't seem to be the same thing."

She snuffled warmly into my dickey. "Are you sure?"

"You want me to leave Jane and the ministry? It'd have to be both. And my children. And my lifetime subscription to *Tidbits for Pulpit Use*."

She laughed through her tears, snorting; I feared a sudden extrusion of phlegm, and backed her face from my chest. Alicia looked up. "Is it so impossible?" she asked and, attempting to study my face an angel's wingbeat longer, answered, "It is." Her spectacles sat brittle on the bedside table; I felt her considering reaching and putting them on, to see me better, and deciding instead to give my waist a tighter squeeze.

I had to counterattack or surrender. "Why do you want me," I asked, "that way? You have me this way."

"I could have anybody this way."

"Then do. Do. You've had lots of others—your musical types, who knows who else, the playground instructor, the man in the oil truck, go ahead."

"O.K., I will," said Alicia, sniffing and licking my belt.

"What would I do, outside the ministry? It's my life. It's my afterlife."

"Be a gigolo or a private detective. Just stop being your own prisoner."

"I'm working on it," I said. "Mostly at night. I can't sleep."

"That's something," she conceded, dropping her arms to release me now.

Now *I* could not quite let go; she was an adhesive complex of interlocking slacknesses and fulcrums, just fucked, in the bald late light of her slanting room, upon the rumpled sunburst of her quilt, whose pattern when we had drunk enough wine I would see as cascading organ notes. "It's hard," I told her.

"It is," she said, soft center of my new world.

To Jane I said, "Have you ever wanted to have an affair?"

We were in bed, her back was to me. "You assume I never have."

"I guess I do."

"Why is that?"

"Because you're a minister's wife."

"What brings this on, anyway?"

"Oh, nothing. Middle age. Angst. It occurs to me I've never really thought enough about you. What *you* want. What *you* feel. Whatever happened to all those boy friends of yours?"

"I didn't have that many."

"Well, you knew how anatomy worked, before I showed up."

"It was just instinct, Tom. Don't be so jealous."

"I am a jealous God. I covet my neighbor's wife's ass."

"Which neighbor? Not that neurotic Harlow woman."

"I love her veils." When I looked down upon Mrs. Harlow in the third pew seat she always took, I thought of beekeepers, purdah, and mourning. However ultramontane my theology strikes you (silent veiled reader out there), in liturgy I lazily gravitate toward low; though I like myself in drag, church is not a costume ball. Jane seemed about to drift into sleep with all my precious questions in her pockets. "Well, have you?"

"Have I what?"

"Wanted other men?"

"Oh, I guess."

"You guess."

"It's too silly to talk about. Sure, in some other world it'd be fun to go to bed with everybody and see what it's like."

"In some other world. I'm touched by your supernaturalism." It was true I was. "Well, who would you begin with? Of the men we know."

"You?"

"Come on. You know I don't satisfy you." I have always admired, in the dialogues of Plato, Socrates' smoothness in attaining his auditors' consent to his premises.

Jane said, "I know no such thing. Are you projecting, or agitating, or what?"

"An ecumenical mixture?" I offered. "Tell me about men. Whatever happened to that pacifist? How do you feel about Ned Bork?"

"He's awfully young."

"All the more vigorous for that. And endlessly sympathetic, don't you find? Don't you love his brand of Jesus? The poor ye have with you not necessarily always. I come to bring not peace but a peace demonstration."

"That is nice."

The gravity of her warm mass pulled me away from Ned. Her phrase, "fun to go to bed with everybody," had packed her with a delectable, permeable substance, many tiny little possible bodies. As I struggled to roll her over, Jane said, sociologically, "It's so un*fair*, women spend their days doing physical work, while men like you who sit at desks or worry about people wind up at night with all this undischarged energy."

"Ah," I said, "but you have two X chromosomes, to my one."

To Ned I said, "That sermon went rather far, I thought."

"How so, sir?" Threatened, he tilted back his head, so his lips showed through his beard, pink and ladylike.

"Do you really believe," I asked him, "that an oligarchy of

blacks and chicanos and college dropouts would come up with a better system, quote unquote, than the corporation board of Exxon?"

"I wouldn't mind seeing it tried. It can't be worse."

"That's where you flower people, in my needless to say humble view, are wrong. It could be a lot worse. Has been, and will be, I expect."

"Does this expectation, in your view, excuse the church from any present proclamation upon the relative improvability of the world?"

"Does this improvability, in *your* view, excuse the church from its task to minister to the world as it finds it? More immediately, does your perception of the businessman in our congregation as an agent of an evil system prevent you from ministering to his immortal soul?"

"Christ said, It is easier for the camel, and so on."

"He also said, Judge not, and so on. Let us sentimentalize neither the rich nor the poor. If their assets were reversed, they would act like one another. The material world, viewed spiritually, is a random grid. Wherever we are placed within it, our task is to witness, to offer a way out of the crush of matter and time. You have been placed here, under me. I wish to hear no more New Left sloganizing from my pulpit."

Ned began, "Simple compassion—"

"Compassion is *not* simple. That is where you so heretically condescend. You give your simple compassion to those you imagine to be simple. Love thy *neighbor*. Love what is near, not what is far. Love the rich, the well off, the white; love the poor suburban burgher who drags in here because he dimly senses another feeble ally in his perilous battle to keep from thieves what other thieves have won for him. If this society strikes you as criminal, remember the criminal on the cross. Forget for a moment this Moloch of social change, and pray to the true God, the God above change, the God who destroyed Rome and Christendom, the God who jealously reserves to His own kingdom the new Jerusalem of perfect equality and justice—pray to Him that, your penitential term with me completed, you may be called to a slum parish, and there sharpen your compassion on another grindstone of circumstance. At all points, Ned, the world presses us toward despair and forgetfulness of God. At no point, perhaps, more than here, in this empty church."

The church was around us. Between the windows stone plaques remembered forgotten pillars; the pipes of the organ played a hugely silent chord. Ned no doubt argued back, there was much to be said on his side; and I responded until weary. My hope was not to convert him, but to alienate him, so he would be eased of guilt, if moved to sleep with my wife.

Mrs. Harlow came to me after a meeting of the Distaff Circle. Without her Sunday veil her face bore the fine reticulations of middle age upon a pretty oval that had not changed since she was seventeen. Her beauty, now fragile, sat upon her nervous as a tremor. And the gray of her eyes had an unsettling purity, as of metal atomized into sky. Some Southern parentage lingered in her accent. Her manner, though unimpeachable, seemed slightly alarmed. She asked, "Reverend Marshfield, do you notice, there seems to be more and more music?"

"Where?"

"In the *ser*vice."

"I hadn't noticed."

"Oh, it's very noticeable from out there. I *do* think Mrs. Crick deserves a great deal of credit, she's performed miracles for the children's choir, my Julie wouldn't miss a time now and we used to have to *bribe* her to go. But that anthem by Praetorius I do believe went on for a good seven minutes. Gerry was taking up the collection and stood so long at the back with the plates he said his arm went utterly to sleep."

"You think the music is overpowering the rest?"

"Not if my pastor doesn't. I was raised to care deeply about the Word, but I realize that was a con*sid*erable time ago." Her eyes never appeared to blink; their fine gray kept coming. She stood some inches closer than necessary, like Europeans and the hard-of-hearing.

"No time at all ago," I said. "A thousand ages in his sight—"

"You *do* flatter. My husband also says some of the elderly deacons are disturbed by the guitars."

"Well, Mrs. Crick is trying—"

"Oh, I *know* Mrs. Crick can do no wrong!" And again I had to observe, of a woman flouncing down the aisle, that her bottom was surprisingly expressive; Mrs. Harlow's was slimmer than some, but exquisitely weighted, a scales shifting balance at each nice, righteous stride.

"Alicia, love."

"Yes, lover."

"Are you conscious of being more ambitious, in the service, than you used to be? How many instrumentalists did that Handel Concerto in F take?"

"Some, but it didn't cost the church anything. They were friends or friends of friends."

"It seemed to me Ned cut his sermon so we wouldn't run long."

"No, he didn't cut it, he planned it short. I told him ahead of time."

"Oh. You two worked it up without telling me."

"Well, if you want to put it that way. Did you mind? Didn't you like the music?"

"I loved it. You have a great touch. I just wonder if the church should become a concert hall."

"Why not? It isn't much else."

"Oh?"

"Except of course a display case for you."

"You feel that, or are you making some other point?"

"You know I feel that, I told you six months ago, before we —were like this." We were in bed. Her hand flicked to indicate our bodies with a certain impatience: her gum-chewing hard self showed. The summer was past. The sky hung dull as pewter in the leafless windows of her bedroom. The oil truck in the alley whined. Her children for much of the summer vacation had been visiting Mr. Crick, who had remarried in Minnesota; they returned from school at 2:30. It was 1:47, stated Alicia's little vanilla-colored bedside electric clock, which had needle-fine, scarcely visible hands, green-tipped for nighttime luminescence, and a chic shy shape, that of a box being squeezed in an invisible press, so its smooth sides bulged. I said, "Time for me to go."

"I suppose," Alicia sighed, and did not cling as I swung my legs from the bed.

I stood and explained, "I told the Distaff Circle I'd help with the hall decorations for the Harvest Supper."

"You don't have to explain."

I put on my underwear snappily and cleared my throat and released what had been on my mind. "From a conversation I had with Mrs. Harlow I got the impression our relationship might not be entirely a thing unseen."

Alicia, propped on a pillow, her small breasts licked by the light, made her wise mouth, looked at me flat as a cat looks at one, and advised, "Screw Mrs. Harlow."

Dear silenced words, your recall makes me fond. Contrary to my preachments to Thaddeus Bork, being far makes these souls, once neighbors of mine, more dear. I hear now, what the roaring of desire and dread in my ears deafened me to at the time, that they each wanted, expected, something from me, from me. In their midst I was powerful. And felt helpless. Here, in this desert routine, I am stripped and anonymous, and feel mighty. The splendor of space and the splendid waste of time enter my self-negation. See Saints, Lives of.

10

I HOPED her black car parked at his brown-and-green cottage was an optical illusion. The naked foot I had classified as a favered* hallucination. I had said nothing to her. We were meeting less frequently, in shorter days pinched mean, pinched black and blue, by our busyness of the fall. Fall, fall, who named thee? The year's graceful aping of our cosmic plunge. How much more congenial, in its daily surrender, to our organic hearts than the gaudy effortful comedy, the backwards-projected travesty, of spring. The diver rises feet first from the pool, the splash seals over where he has been, the board receives him on its tip like a toad's tongue snaring a fly. The

---

*Well, what can this mean? I want to be favored, though fevered? Or my fever has the vanilla flavor of the bedside clock just described at such unexpectedly lovesick length?

stone has been rolled away. O carapace-cracking, rib-pulling halleluiahs! The agony of resurrection, a theme for Unamuno. The agony of dried tubers. See Eliot, Tom. See Tom run. Run, Tom, run.

To work. Our leading character, Tom, miscast as a Protestant clergyman, could not ignore the telltale clue of the black car the second time he saw it. No doubt there were other times when he had not seen it. This time, Tom had been lying awake, listening to noises that a sane man would have dismissed as the normal creak of wood and breathing of somniacs but that he preferred to hear as the step of a murderous intruder, or the half-smothered shuttle of his fate being woven. His wife slept heavily, moaning, *Crucify him, crucify him*. Nixon, of course. Nixema, the noxious salve for liberal sores. O, cursed be the sleep of the just! Barren fig trees, every one. He arose impatiently, went to the window, threw up the sash, and lo! to his wondering eyes did appear . . .

Ignore it. It was just an old black Chevrolet. Sitting a-wink with moonlight and arc light. But, like the cinder of a comet's head, trailing after it a pluming tail of fair skin, gold fuzz, white sheets, undiluted sunshine, radiant intimacy. A tousled pale treasure of flesh and moistened oxygen that had been his. Tom returned to bed but could not sleep. His eyes had sipped poison. Covetousness threatened to burst his skull, ire his spleen, and lust his groin. He twisted, he writhed; the twinned body beside him had ceased to turn on the same lathe. He arose. Learning from frosty experience, and in deference to the Heraclitean river which indeed would be some weeks chiller than when he first stepped into it, for the month had become December and the holy season Advent, he put on not only his trousers but socks (probably mismatched on the dark, though the odds were shortened by the high percentage of his socks that were black), shoes, an overcoat that had gloves in the pockets, and, from the front hall rack (the slavelike, treacherous stairs negotiated), a little wool hat given him ten years earlier by his then-living mother and which, after years of disuse, the hat bearing too comical a suggestion of a Scots gamewarden or a stage detective, he had taken to wearing again. Mother, protect me. 'Gainst hail and cold and doveshit be thou a shield.

The blue night barked as I opened the door. Down, Fido.

An inch of dry snow mottled the brittle lawn. I left tracks. Thinking fast if not well, I did not make straight for the windows baleful with the same mute lamp that had lent substance to the earlier orgy, but held to the brick walk by the parsonage, tripping lightly lest my scuffle stir the Nixonophobe snug above, and left my turf through the gated gap in the hedge provided. Stealthily I approached Ned's house by the pavement, where my steps blended with those of daytime innocents whose hearts had not been pounding like crazy mine. Hark! A far car drew nearer in the ghostly grid of snow-glazed ways. As plain beneath the streetlight as a blot on table linen, I met with no inspiration but to merge with the other blot—that is, to squeeze open the door of Alicia's black Chevrolet, push forward the balky seat, crawl into the back, and crouch on the floor in an attitude that, were I a Moslem and Mecca properly aligned, would have done for prayer.

For minutes I froze there, *motor immotus.* The enveloping aroma of floor mat, haunted by old orange peels and lost M & Ms, was my sufficient universe. At last convinced that my criminal commotion had not alerted the *civitas*, I adjusted my crouch more comfortably, pulled my mothering hat down to my ears, and tried to spare my cheek prolonged acquaintance with the waffly pattern of the rubber mat as it arched across the driveshaft. Sleepiness, long courted, assailed me inconveniently.

At this point an obligation arises (you insatiable ideal reader, you) for an account of my thoughts during my grotesque but somewhat happy vigil. I notice I have slipped into the first person; a Higher Wisdom, it may be, directs my style.

Somewhat happy. I have always been happy, Americanly, in cars. I acquired my license as soon as the law allowed. I became my father's chauffeur. The first piece of furniture I could drive. A car's stale, welded sameness within its purposive speed. Tranquillity in flux. That attic redhead I mentioned (remember?) was undressed and inspected (partially, both) by the submarine glow of a parked car's panel. A generation and the hump of a lifetime later, my dour Dart becomes a hydrofoil skimming above the asphalt waves of the highway of life, severing me from any terrestrial need to be polite, circumspect, wise, reverent, kind, affectionate, entertaining, or instructive. Encapsulation in any form short of the coffin has a charm for me: the cave of wicker porch furniture that children arrange, the journey of a letter from box to sack to sack to slot, the astronaut's fatalistic submission to a web of formulae computers have spun. My position crouched on the floor was in a sense chosen; chances of discovery would only be slightly improved by lying on the rear seat. But being down, empathizing my way along the floor mat's edge, through the crumby detritus of the Crick children's snacks, past a button and chewed pencil stub, into the nether region of the driver's seat, where a square foot of fluff and stray licorice and the red pull-bands of cigarette packs cozily defied purgation and a system of rusty springs inscrutably impinged upon strips of gray felt, pleased me, yea, pleased me not only in its concentrated pose of humiliation but in its potential of springing up, like a child at a surprise party, and startling Alicia into loving laughter.

In fact, after what was a long twenty minutes or a short eternity, my aching back and waffled knees compelled me to sit on the seat, slumped over to avoid decapitation by passing headlight beams. Were the lovers asleep? Was Jane not? I had vowed to return to the parsonage, my boiling rage chilled to a permissive slush, when the light above Ned's door came on. From the sliver of him that for an instant showed he seemed to be wearing a tangled shirt and an unbuttoned beard. Alicia had donned, or redonned, her red dress, in the Christmas spirit, and in her warmed condition hadn't bothered to zip her loden coat. Jaunty, brisk, her car key pre-fished from her purse and ready as a stiletto in her gloved hand, she crossed to her car, my cave, and opened the door. Though I was slumped so the ashy stench of the sidearm ashtray crowded my nostrils, a beam of radiance from Ned's porch lamp fell, à la Latour, upon my face. Alicia never faltered. Her sheaf of hair beclouded the light; she slammed the door, snuggled and shrugged into place behind the wheel, caused the motor (against its better judgment) to start, and set us afloat through the empty rectilinear streets.

I doubted that she had seen me.

But she sniffed and said, after (from the mix of lights and motion in the back seat) some intersections had been passed and corners turned, "Really, Tom. This won't do."

I sat up. "How was it? How is he? I've been telling Jane he was impotent."

"He *said* you'd been pushing Jane at him. That's pathetic, Tom."

"It was just a thought. How else can you and I go off and run the Boro-boro mission school all by ourselves?"

"We can't and won't."

"Agreed. Taxi, take me home."

I didn't like her tone or the tone it was forcing on me. I began to whine, to rage, to wriggle deeper into the loser's comfortable hole. "You bitch. You flaming harlot. How could you do this to me?"

"Take you home?"

"Screw Bork all the time."

"It hasn't been all the time, Tom. Just a few times. I had to do something to break my obsession with you. I need all the help I can get."

"And does Bork give all the help you can take?"

She sat prim at the wheel. Occasional carlights set her hair on false fire. It had been freshly brushed and neatened, I noticed, which made her recent tussle so real I bent forward to pinch off the pain. I gasped. Only her voice could salve that pain. Each potion its own antidote. She pronounced flatly, "I have no intention of describing it to you. I didn't ask you to spy on me."

"Christ," I grunted, "how could I not, you parked your big black cunt of a car right under my nose! The last time it was there I came down and looked in the window and saw your abso*lute*ly naked foot."

Alicia said, "The last time? I don't think we made love that time, we were just talking. I remember. I took off my shoes and put them up because his floor is so cold. Whosever idea was it, to make a place to live in out of a cement-floor garage?"

"Not mine," I said, undeflected. "Not last time, but this time, is that what you're saying?"

"Is it? You spy, you guess."

"Well. How's the beard? Isn't it awfully tickly?"

"Not too."

This made it real again, her giving her body to another, just when my fantasy of Ned's homo- or a-sexuality was inching from the realm of faith into a kind of negative verification; I groaned—involuntarily, for I felt, correctly, that I had used up my groans, and the next one would goad her to anger. Without turning, Alicia pulled out the *Tirade* stop and her voice went up on its hard little pipes. "Well how do you think *I* feel, watching you and Jane make cow eyes back and forth every Sunday, what do you think it does to *me*, having you run in and fuck and hop back into your clothes and traipse off to some adoring deaconess after you've had your

11

"FUN"? "Way with me"? "Kicks for the week"? I forget exactly how she put it. Her complaints went on: my uxoriousness, my pastoral offices, my sense of order and obligation all turned into reproaches, into a young bawd's raillery, and I sat behind her sunk in sadness, sunk deeper each moment as her plaint widened from the justified to the absurd (I even *looked* like my wife; I was planning to seduce Mrs. Harlow; I was going to fire her, Alicia, as soon as she stopped "shelling out"); as she berated me, disclosing all the secret ignominy our affair had visited upon her, and voicing all the shaky hardness that thirty years of being a female in America had produced, a glum ministerial reality overtook my loverly fury and fancies. This woman was a soul in my care. She was crying out, and I must listen—listen not in hope of curing, for our earthly ills elude all earthly ease, but as an act of fraternity amid children descended from, if not one Father, certainly one marriage of molecular accidents. And indeed in some minutes her devils, outpouring, did take up residence in swine, the dark houses flying by, and pass from us. Still controlling the wheel, Alicia sobbed.

I clambed* from the chill back seat to the seat beside her; warmth gushed from the heater onto my legs and face. "I'm sorry," I said, "I'm sorry. It was wrong, our getting each other into this."

"I can't feel that," she said, her syllables prismed by tears.

"Well, something's wrong," I pointed out, "or you wouldn't

---

*I must have meant "climb" or "clambered," but which? Kind of a clamby episode in any case.

be crying and I wouldn't be running around in the middle of the night in my pajamas."

She turned her head, at last, and looked at me, very quickly. "Is that true?"

"Just the top," I conceded. "I took the time this time to put on pants. And even a hat. My mother gave it to me."

"Does it upset you that much? My seeing Ned."

"Seems to. Like I say, I'm sorry. Take it as a compliment."

"What do you want me to do?"

"Nothing. Keep at it. Fuck away."

"You know, you've played this awfully cool. You've never once suggested you might leave Jane. I know you can't, but even so, it would have been nice, to me, if you'd just once said you *wanted* to."

"She had to give me a reason, and she won't. She's just too good."

"Not in bed, evidently."

"That may not be her fault. Women are cellos, fellows the bows. Anyway, you and I wouldn't be that good either, if it were aboveboard and for day after day instead of an hour a week."

"I love you, Tom. Do you love me?"

"I hate the word, but sure. I'm wild about you, to be exact."

"What do you want from me? Tell me."

"Take me home. To my home," in case she misunderstood. She had been driving into the darkened gumbo of commerce between our two towns, and backed around in the lot of a factory-reject shoestore. No pair alike. If it pinch, wear it. If it feel good, cast it out.

"I'm sorry about Ned," she said after silence. "I hope for his sake I didn't do it just to bug you."

"Is the past tense the right one?"

"I don't know." I feared she would cry again. But we were close to the church and parsonage. There was a dead space of asphalt between them. She stopped here, far from any street-light, and I wondered if I was meant to kiss her good-night. It seemed strange, to be kissing right to left, the woman behind the wheel. She dropped her hands to my lap and, as intent as when Buxtehude was challenging her fingers with sixteenth notes, unzipped my fly. Miraculous woman! Not a word was spoken; I roused instantly. She unwedged herself from behind the wheel, maneuvered out of her underpants, made of her crotch a Gothic arch above my lap. Imagine: the thickness of our overcoats, the furtiveness of our flesh, the vaporishness of our breaths, the frosted windows through which the turrets and cupolas and dormers of the neighborhood loomed dim and simplified as wicked castles in a children's book. She was wet (a star winked on as I entered her) and ready; I came quickly as I could, she seemed to come, I rezipped, we kissed, I exited, a patch of ice nearly slipped me up, I recovered balance, her headlights wheeled, my house loomed, my weariness wrapped itself around a dazed and dwindling pleasure.

My porch. My door. My stairs. Again the staircase rose before me, shadow-striped, to suggest the great brown back of a slave; this time the presentiment so forcibly suggested to me my own captivity, within a God I mocked, within a life I abhorred, within a cavernous unnameable sense of misplacement and wrongdoing, that I dragged a body heavy as if wrapped in chains step by step upward. Jane stirred as I entered our bedroom. As I undressed, a strand of belated jism dripped lukewarm onto my thigh. I used the bathroom in the dark and slid into bed as grateful as one of the damned might be when the jaws of eternal night close upon his fearful restlessness. Prayer had become impossible for me. "See any UFOs?" Jane, knowing I had been up, misreading my restlessness and taking pity, rolled over, threw a solid thigh across my hip, fumbled for my penis, found it, and would not let go.

My subsequent attitude toward Ned can fairly be described as morbid. That this pale, slight body (which he insisted on garbing, but for unmistakably ceremonial occasions, in affected imitation of youth's glad rags) had the power of copulating with my beloved's—with the body, forgive the Plotinian language, of my soul—fascinated me; his very skin (not, as I have recorded, his best feature) glowed with the triumph. That he took his triumph casually heightened his corrupt glory in my (admittedly; this therapy must be working) diseased eyes. Here was a young man to whom, in indolent footnote to his vows, fornication was a bodily incident no more crucial than spitting.

His tactile intrusion into, and escape from, the deep vault of my passion gave him a for me Lazarene fascination—he moved in my vision with the unhealthy phosphorescence of a raised corpse. His body, that is, had blindly entered a charmed circle. I was still his superior, and my knowledge of his secret, where he had none of mine, improved my advantage. But the sum of all this was intimacy. Heaven forbid, I began to love him.

Or at least began to listen. His views, which I had earlier dismissed as hopelessly compromised by topical fads, as the very image of the tower of Babel Barth says our merely human religiosity erects, now had some interest for me.

Ned was engaged with not only our parish youth but also that of the town; he dealt with drug users, above whose abysmal severance from our specifically human gifts of volition and organized effort my spirit hung paralyzed and appalled. "You regard them," Ned told me, with a little surprise, "as untouchables."

"Haven't they," I asked, "declared all of us, the society around them, as untouchable?"

"You've made an image in your mind," he told me. "The drug-oriented kid is more enterprising than his peers, in all the old-fashioned work-ethic ways: he hustles, he sets up contacts, the merchandising system is at least as efficient as Sears Roebuck. A drug addict is a busy, busy fellow. He must learn to burgle, to fence, to con the police, to argue in court. The technology some of these kids can use is remarkable. Just to shoot up is a chemistry lesson. Think of it, Tom, as applied chemistry; the chemistry *is* there, we've been putting it there ever since alchemy."

"Exactly. Alchemy, pacts with the devil, shortcuts from lead to gold. Doesn't a certain stink of evil bother you?"

Ned shrugged. "To them it's the highest good. They say, they don't hurt anybody on a nod, it's coming down when the hurt starts. And then it's all their own. Why should we condemn this, when we give Luther his beer and Buddha his *satori* fix underneath the Bo tree?"

"You don't sound as though you're ministering to them, you sound as if you've joined them."

"Well, wasn't it you who was telling me to join the munitions makers?"

"I think I said businessmen."

"Munitions makers are businessmen are munitions makers. The chain from friendly Henry Cog the local watchmaker to napalm has every link in place. Gene Rostow, the only one of Johnson's old gang with the guts to still talk, said it plain in an interview: We went into Vietnam to keep things open, to keep the world open for trade."

"Better open than closed," I offered. "Better Mammon than Stalin." There was beer in my hand, it was a Saturday afternoon in the little house where Alicia had been laid, Kissinger's Houdini-truce had been effected, we were de-vietnamized and could attempt dispassion where the flames of rage and counter-rage had danced. Ned's furniture, I might say, was beanbag and paper ball tattily mixed with Good Will. It made me feel young to be here.

He said, "Some of our parishioners tell me in the late Sixties you refused to join peace marches."

I wondered if it had been a parishioner, or Alicia. "Insofar as a peace march proclaims peace to be nicer than war, it is fatuous, surely. The question is, short of the Second Coming, is war always the worst possible alternative? The Bible says not. I say not. You're right, I hated the peace bandwagon worse than I hated the war; it was nearer. It was a moral form of war profiteering."

"How so?"

"It was a power push. All the fat cats and parasites of the system poor Johnson was sweating to save—the college boys, the bored housewives, the professors and ministers and the princelings of computer technology—thought they could push the bad old hard-goods barons and their cowboys out of office. It was the new rich versus the old rich, and the new rich saw what the old rich didn't, e.g., freedom's just another word for nothin' left to lose. The new rich saw we could do business with the new thugs of collectivism, 1984 was on its way wherever, and thank God Nixon and his knuckleheads won, though I myself couldn't bear to vote for him."

Ned blinked. I was making him tired. "You mean that, including clergymen among the parasites?"

"A man who's had the call," I said, "will cheerfully be a parasite within any monster that lives. Insofar as you and I eat, we serve Mammon. But there may be, there should be, a little something within us that does not eat, that disdains to eat."

"Disdain," he said, "seems behind a lot of what you say. Your political indifference, for instance."

"I'm not indifferent," I protested, "I'm vigorously pro-Caesar. His face is on the coin, look. Render unto him. Do you know who shares the lowest circle of Hell with Judas? Brutus and Cassius. Even there, Caesar outvotes Jesus two to one. Somewhere Barth says, 'What shall the Christian in society *do* but attend to what *God* does.' What God does in the world is Caesar."

"There are no better or worse Caesars?"

"I tend to trust the Caesar that is, as against the Caesar that might be. The Caesar that is, at least has let us live, which the next might not."

"Do you think," Ned asked, sucking on the pipe that went with his drawling, preppy side, "in Stalin's Russia, say, you would have trusted and served *that* Caesar?"

"Probably." I was grateful to him, for seeing this, and stopping me. My head and tongue were whirling with an angry excitement I didn't understand and didn't like.

"You know, this thing with you and Barth," he went on. "They had us read him in seminary. It was impressive, in that he doesn't crawl, like most of the mod-rens." He didn't have to do that, excuse himself from seriousness with gag pronunciations. I could see that in counselling he would still be self-conscious. Irony is the style of our cowardice. "But after a while I began to figure out why," Ned said. "It's atheism. Barth beheads all the liberal, synthesizing theologians with it, and then at the last minute whips away the 'a' and says, 'Presto! *Theism!*' It's sleight of hand, Tom. It sets up a diastasis with nothing over against man except this exultant emptiness. This terrible absolute unknowable other. It panders to despair. I came off of it with more respect for Tillich and Bultmann; it's true, they sell everything short, but after they've had the bargain sale there's something left; they say there's a little *something*, don't you see?"

My love for this man took a submissive form. I wanted him to be wise. I wanted him to grow. There were a dozen ledges in his exposition where one could stage an argument (for instance, the Bible is Barth's *something*), but I went feminine and shrugged: "All I know is when I read Tillich and Bultmann I'm drowning. Reading Barth gives me air I can breathe."

"Well that's what the kids say about pot and smack. You and they have more in common than you know. You both believe there's another world more of a high than this one. And you know where they turn, the ones that kick it, often? They turn to Jesus."

"Lord," I said, half to tease him, half to vent the Barth in me, "I find that depressing."

12

VOICI UNE SCÈNE. Où je ne suis pas. I must make an image in my mind, as Ned just said. It happened well after Christmas, perhaps on St. Valentine's Day. I heard two accounts and must synthesize. Worse, I must create; I must from my lousy fantasies pick the nits of truth. What is truth? My fantasies are what concern you? How you do make me preen, Ms. Prynne.

The parsonage living-room. Morning sunlight streaming, shade-tainted, dust-enlivened, from windows east and south. Snowcrusts from last week's storm visible through them. Car roofs peep above plow-heaped snow worn glassy in spots by childish boots. Also visible through the window: houses with conical roofs, dormers, protrusions, scallop shingling, jigsawed brackets, ovals of stained glass tucked up under eave-peaks like single eyes under a massive gingerbread eyebrow; and hedges and shrubs, and a mailbox painted in patriotic tricolor, a bird-feeder hopping with feathered mendicants, a covetously on-looking squirrel, streetsigns, streetlamps, etc., etc. Within, our eyes, shifting from the dazzle, blink away a sensation of gloomy solidity amid hothouse warmth. The fuel shortage is a winter away. Glass-fronted bookcases. Dark-veneered furniture. Chairs padded and studded. Everything neat: table-runners centered, back issues of magazines arranged in overlapping rows on a half-folded gate-leg table. Various translucent *objets*, senti-mentally given and as sentimentally retained, throw rainbows and loops of light here and there. Dark oaken staircase visible through arched doorway stage left. Knocks offstage. Footsteps.

Enter, chatting, JANE MARSHFIELD, *in austere yet attractive housedress, and* ALICIA CRICK, *bundled in wool, carrying pastel books of music.*

JANE: At least the sun is out.

ALICIA (*tugging off knit cap and fur-trimmed driving-gloves with faintly stagy, excessive, pained exertions*): Is it?

JANE (*hesitantly, aware that this visit is unusual, though not aware yet of its menace*): I don't know exactly where Tom is, I could try—

ALICIA: I just left Tom. At the church.

JANE: Oh.

ALICIA: I came to talk to you. I came, Jane, to ask you to get Tom off my back.

JANE: How—how do you mean?

ALICIA: In about as coarse a sense as you can imagine. I don't know exactly what you and he share, you're a mystery to all of us, but you must have guessed that he and I have—have been together. Have slept together.

JANE (*sitting down, stunned, but in the next heartbeat gathering herself, with an instinctive hauteur perhaps not quite expected by the other, for battle*): No. I had not guessed.

ALICIA: Then I'm sorry to put it to you so bluntly. But I'm desperate. (*She has opted, perhaps because the other's manner has taken some options from her, for a brusque bustly approach, pulling off her scarf, setting down her books, almost stamping her feet, as if to convey a heedless, superior vitality; the effect is rather vulgar, and scatters the plea for sympathy it disguises.*)

JANE (*very gently, after clearing a frog from her throat*): How so?

ALICIA: Your husband is a maddening man. You must know that (*implying, however, that* JANE *doesn't; that she furthermore knows nothing about him* [*me*]).

JANE (*diffidence being her second line of defense*): I don't know, is he really? Around the house, he's been quite cheerful lately.

ALICIA: Now you know why. May I sit down, Jane?

JANE: Please, Alicia, do. Would you like some coffee? Or a little sherry? I know it's still morning, but this seems a rather special occasion.

ALICIA: No, thanks. I can't stay.

JANE: Yet you've taken off your coat. When did this—your—liaison with Tom begin?

ALICIA: After last Easter. Ten months ago.

JANE: And how often did you—usually meet?

ALICIA (*beginning to dislike her responsory role, yet unable to locate where she lost the initiative*): Once a week, more or less. Summer was difficult, with everybody's kids home. When mine were in Minnesota with Fred—my ex-husband—

JANE: I know of Fred.

ALICIA: —Tom and I saw a lot of each other. The rest of the summer, hardly at all. Don't feel sorry for me. There were other consolers.

JANE: Does Tom know this, that there were other men?

ALICIA (*balked almost into angry silence, her anger having to do with* JANE'S *picking up this point so quickly, and with resistance to the agreeable, sliding sensation, not foreseen, of confiding in another woman*): He guesses.

JANE (*considerately seeking to ease her guest's way*): And you wish to end this one of your affairs, the one with Tom?

ALICIA: Why do you say that?

JANE: Why else would you come and tell me? What did you say your object was?—some all-too-vivid phrase, to "get him off your back"? (*discovering irony; the whole situation is roomier than she would have believed*) I suppose I can chain him to the bedpost at night, but in the day, he must be out and about—

ALICIA (*she can't have this*): One thing you don't understand. I love Tom.

JANE: And these others—?

ALICIA: And he loves me. We do something very real for each other. Very real and rare.

JANE: You think it my duty, then, to bow out, to vacate (*hands uplifted, with exasperating delicacy, to indicate the walls and furniture about her*) the parsonage?

ALICIA: I think it *his* duty to shit or get off the pot.

Jane vowed to me those were her exact words; I made her repeat them until we both fell to laughing. Their interview, also, fell apart after this exclamation; Jane's distaste, all the more in that she tried to conceal it, flustered my dear organist with her thick waist and firm hands and cogitative cunt. Having trespassed, having blundered, having failed to gain the violent release from ambiguity she had come for, having even forgotten why she had come, she left, cradling her pastel music with the gloves trimmed in fox fur, almost falling on the icy lower porch step, where the eaves always dripped, in her tear-blind rage at her own mistake, at Jane's gracious obstinacy, at our tough marriage. She had seen we were a pair, but had taken us for a salt and a pepper shaker, not the matched jaws of a heartbreaker.

Jane, Alicia gone, poured herself enough of the offered sherry for the two of them, went upstairs, drew a bath, and thrashed hysterically in the steaming, startled water. But she did not attempt to reach me, at some checkpoint of my tortuous rounds, and she met her own afternoon obligations, which were a luncheon meeting of the local garden club, with slides of Elizabethan gardens; a trip to the orthodontist with Martin, my older son; and the reception at four-thirty, of the piano teacher, who audited my younger son Stephen's sullen hammering of some simplified Bartók. I returned at dusk, having during that long afternoon counselled an impending marriage and an impending divorce, having encouraged the Distaff Circle at their quilt-making and driven thirty miles to visit the hospital room of a carcinoma-riddled parishioner who, with his last surge of vitality, bitterly resented my intrusion. To top it all off, this sundae of junk deeds, I had a beer with Ned.

Supper done and the boys safely stupefied by television, Jane said to me, "I suppose your girl friend told you the news."

"What news?" An unfortunate lag. "What girl friend?"

"Alicia dropped by this morning. We had a pleasant chat but she refused sherry. So I've been drinking sherry all day."

"Did she—?"

"Spill the beans? Yes."

What flashed upon me was, I'll never sleep with her again, never see her riding me in the sunlight again. A radiant abyss, like the divine abyss the Apologists posited to counter the Greek myth of Primal Matter. "Why?" was all I could utter.

"I think to help me know you, and to give us the opportunity to separate. Is that what you want?"

"Lord, no." For all the times I had dreamed of freedom from her, my answer came—nay, was flung—from the heart.

"Why not?" Jane reasonably asked. By the candlelight of the dining-room I perceived that she was shaky, that a sherry bottle had materialized beside her dessert dish. "You can move right in. She has everything you need. A house, a way of supporting herself. It would get you out of the ministry, which would be a relief, wouldn't it? You don't believe any more."

"I do! I believe everything!"

"You should listen to your own sermons sometime." Thus spoke, with easy authority, the daughter of Wesley Chillingworth.

"Did Alicia—did Alicia propose my moving in with her?" It was an enchanted thought, residence in that treeless young development, with its view of the cemetery hill, with my cuddly, gum-chewing wife, who would wear filmy dressing gowns carelessly buttoned and breezy and slippers trimmed with pompons; she would be mine for hour after hour. I would get a job. I would learn to fix cars. I would return to her at sundown with lines of grease in my knuckles and palms. With those same hands I would stroke her willing limbs. Between me and such a vision stood a black wall, utterly solid though utterly transparent: onyx sliced miraculously thin.

"We didn't get that far," Jane said. "We thought it was up to you. She said—" And here her quotation, and my incredulity, and our hilarity, and the vision betrayed. We talked to exhaustion that night; I had a meeting at eight, but returned with haste, for not only was I fascinating to her, as I spilled out the details and near-misses on the other side of the looking glass,* but she to me; for she, too, had ventured, if only mentally, from our nest.

"What did it feel like?" I begged, of her encounter with Alicia, already, not three hours gone since I had denied her (no cock crew), ravenous for the sound of my mistress's name, a glimpse of her gestures even through unfriendly eyes, any morsel of the otherworld in which my supine otherform lay transfigured.

"Oh," Jane said, wanderingly, trying to think back and having had too much sherry to think back through—in my mind's eye we are in our glum and ill-lit bedroom, she is groping for her nightie, a dowdy tent of cotton she must have shopped for in a novel by one of the Alcott sisters—"not so bad. It was like being on stage. She came in with her fists up. I minded it less than I thought I would."

"What was the worst moment?"

"When she said she loved you and you loved her."

"What did you say to that?"

"I said I loved you too. And you loved me."

I cannot imagine her saying it, so I have not put it in. Nor do I remember how, in the vast blur of words we generated that night, I responded to her discomfiting declaration. No more dialogue: I see your blue pencil, Ideal Reader, quivering beneath your blue nose. Jane in deportment was drunk, sad, uncomplaining, rather elegantly rational. Having offered me freedom, she did not cinch my captivity, but left it that I would, when I could get my "priorities arranged" (a dry Chillingworth touch, that), come to a decision, to several decisions. Actually, I had no intention of making any decision that others (read: God) might make for me. I did not even resolve, having decided (or having let God enunciate His decision through me) not to marry Alicia, not to sleep with her; this she decided, as her

---

*FYI: I swear, Alicia's name is real, not contrived to fit Wonderland. And the last "m" wanted to be a "k." "Near-Mrs." occurs to me as a homonym of Alicia's plight.

manner—flat, wry, frosty (her interview with Jane had chastened her rather unbecomingly)—plainly declared, in the subsequent days, as we communicated enough, but no more than enough, to allow our professional relationship to continue. If Alicia, then, took on the minimal, masculine posture of a defensive position, combining the stiffness of one who has miscalculated with that of one who has been wronged, Jane in contrast fluffed up, recurring, many a night, to more sherry and to details of my romance, which, the more it became a farfetched tale of adventure and wonder, made me more and more a hero. That Alicia the unmarried, the free, had liked me as lover was the discreetly unvoiced point of fascination. And when, with the passing of the days, my melancholy reassured her of Alicia's withdrawal, Jane, like a wary kitty slowly satisfied that she has the bowl of milk entirely to herself, began to purr. She confessed, what nineteen uxorious years had not made plain, her body's need for mine. Though I felt my body, in her mind, a kind of shadow of Alicia's, its value enhanced by her secret erotic regard for the other woman (women had just begun to call each other "sister"), I complied. In my darkness there was nothing else. Nothing but this sanctioned rutting. Lying beside her then, my consort sated and snoring, I would panic the panic of the sealed, for the last chink had been closed in the perfect prison of my wife's goodness. She had become "good in bed."

13

AN UNLUCKY NUMBER, but Sunday. Brethren, can it be that another week has gone by, in this fastness, a week of words, mediocre golf (I had the monster on his back, 80 about to break, I swear it, when the lip of a bunker elongated like an elephant's trunk and pulled into its maw a perfectly hit, if underclubbed, 7-iron; I took two to wedge out and three-putted in my craven rage), plenteous drink, and poker games increasingly luminous, as the Demiurge pumices the cards from underneath and renders them transparent to my intuition? Let us repeat together, *Can it be?*

This morning I propose to preach upon the miracles of Christ. Only in the fervor of terror do we dare reach out to touch this most tender flesh of the New Testament. This flesh, bright as a leper's, which modern preaching, as it whores after the sensational, is yet too fastidious to caress. I do not propose to treat of the miracles performed *upon* our Saviour, such as the Bethlehem star, the Voice and Dove that descended on the occasion of His Baptism, the rattling tin sheet and the rheostatted sun backdropping the Crucifixion, or the Miracle of Miracles, that rolled away the rock of His tomb, and as you will remember from last Sunday confronted Mary with the tomb's emptiness, a vacuity smaller than a mustard seed, from which the aeon-spanning branches of this our great church have grown.

For these wonders are the work of God the Father, the Father of all wonders, who parted light from darkness and as easily parted the Red Sea that Moses and his Israelites might pass from Egypt; from the mighty works of this Being, the summit and ground of all being, He who caused the chariot of Apollo to rise from the east for the ancients and who causes the quasars to emit gamma rays for us, we can draw no lesson, but that—a splendid lesson—He is not ourselves. From the solar miracles of the Father let us turn our scorched vision to the lunar miracles of the Son, miracles that impenetrate a mortal, historical course erratically documented some few generations afterwards.

My consideration must proceed from memory. What a paradox it is, dearly beloved, in a nation where every motel room unavailingly offers a Bible for the perusal of travel-worn salesmen, bickering vacationers, and headlong fornicators secluded with eager fornacatrices, that this passel of disgraced and distracted ministers should be uniquely denied the consolation and stimulation of this incredible, most credible book!

For the text of our sermon, let us take the words of Jesus when His mother, anxious that the wedding at Cana go well, importuned Her son, whose unique powers must hitherto have been their guarded domestic secret, to perform His first public miracle. He looked at her astonished and said, "Woman, what have I to do with thee? Mine hour is not yet come."

Mine hour is not yet come. Which well consorts with those of His words recorded in Mark, when, having "sighed deeply in his spirit," He asked the besieging Pharisees, "Why doth this generation seek after a sign? Verily I say unto you, There shall no sign be given unto this generation."

O ye of little faith—this is His cry, for in truth we are insatiable of miracles, and He flees us, as He fled the multitude He had miraculously fed with five barley loaves and two small fishes; yet we of the multitude pursue Him, though He walk on the water to escape us (this according to John), and on the other shore in exasperation He turns, and delivers the accusation, "Ye seek me, not because ye saw the miracles, but because ye did eat of the loaves, and were filled."

And what a fine judgment, by the way, this is of our vaunted American religiosity! From the first Thanksgiving, ours is the piety of the full belly; we pray with our stomachs, while our hands do mischief, and our heads indict the universe.

There once thrived, in that pained and systematic land of Germany, a school of Biblical scholarship that sought to reduce all of the Biblical miracles to natural happenings. The Red Sea's parting was an opportune low tide, and the feeding of the five thousand—the only miracle attested to in each of the four Gospels—was Jesus shaming the multitude into bringing out from under its multitude of cloaks a multitude of box lunches hitherto jealously hoarded. This school of exegetical thought observes that our Lord, before healing the blind man of Bethsaida, spit upon His hands—as if saliva is an attested medication for glaucoma. It notes, with a collusive wink, that the saline density of the Dead Sea is so high that one can virtually "walk" upon it—without noting that Peter, attempting the same maneuver, sank. It whispers the magic word "psychosomatic"—as if Lazarus merely fancied he was dead, the swine spontaneously decided to go for a swim, and the fig tree withered under hypnosis. The absurdities of such naturalism need no belaboring.

Yet a true insight resides in this naturalism. For our Lord produced miracles as naturally as the Earth produces flowers. Miracles fell from Him as drops of water escape between the fingers of a man drinking from his cupped hands. They came in spite of Himself; there is scarcely a one that was not coaxed out of Him—by His mother, by a disciple, by the hunger of a throng, by the unignorable beseeching of an invalid. For Jesus walked in that Roman Palestine upon a sea of suffering. Of the diseases He condescended to cure, there are named blindness, dumbness, dropsy, leprosy, impotence, fever, deformity, issue of blood, madness—a piteous catalogue, and no doubt partial.

It is here, not upon the plausibility of these miracles—they happened as surely as any event in the Gospels happened—but upon their selectivity, that we stumble. If these few, why not *all* the ailing from the beginning of human time? More, of animal time? Why, indeed, institute, with vitality, pain and struggle, disease and parasitism? Reading of the woman with her "issue of blood for twelve years"—twelve years!—who came from behind and touched the hem of His garment, believing, and truly, that this mere touch would make her whole, are we not angry? Angry not at her impudence, but angry that this plucking, this seeking out, this risk of humiliation, was demanded of her, when Omnipotence could have erased her pain as automatically as stony ground lets wither its weeds? Are we not moved to revolt and overthrow this minute and arbitrary aristocracy of the healed, which by chance lived in the three years of our Lord's wandering ministry and by aggression pushed themselves forward into His notice? Do we not cry, with the synagogue at Nazareth, "Whatsoever we have heard done in Capernaum, do also here in thy country"?

And does He not answer, infuriatingly, "Many lepers were in Israel in the time of Eliseus the prophet; and none of them was cleansed, saving Naaman the Syrian"?

And are we not moved, now as then, to rise up, and thrust Him out of the city, and lead Him to the brow of the hill, that we might cast Him down headlong, so that He might taste, with us—us the drowning man, the starving man, the falling man—might taste the implacability of natural laws that do not suspend an atom of their workings however huge and absolute the cry of our appalled spirits?

And, now as then, He passes through our midst invisible, ungraspable, and goes His way.

For His way is not ours.

The hard lesson is borne in upon us, alleviation is not the purpose of His miracles, but demonstration. Their randomness is not their defect, but their essence, as injustice (from our point of view, which is that of children) is essential to a Creation of differentiated particulars. In the primal partition of darkness from light, the potential for better and worse was born, and with it the possibility of envy and pain, process and loss, sin and time. He came not to revoke the Law and Ground of our condition but to demonstrate a Law and Ground beyond.

Let us examine His miracles further. Not all of them heal. Along with the miracles of mercy, which as we see are wrung from Him, not from the strength of His Divinity but from the weakness of His humanity, there are the festive miracles, and, more edifying still, the facetious miracles.

Festivity merges with mercy in the feeding of the thousands, who would otherwise have experienced discomfort. In the turning of the water into wine at the wedding at Cana, and in the miraculous draught of fishes that breaks the net and nearly sinks the boat, festivity acquires a comic note, and prepares us for the comedy of His walking upon the water while Peter sinks, an Abbott and Costello routine at a far stylistic remove from the W. C. Fieldsish blasting of the fig tree and the Chaplinesque ballet of the graceful episode wherein Jesus, queried by his tireless straight man Peter about local taxes, sends the fisher of men to catch a fish and finds in that fish's mouth a coin which is then handed—we can almost see the winsome pursed lips of the cosmic Tramp—to the tax collector!

Let us become Jesus for these moments. Let us seek empathy with the Son of God who, as He was truly man, and who underwent the crucifixion in uncertainty and dread, must have conceived this mad prank, of looking for money in the mouth of a random fish, with some dubiousness; yet it worked. Or imagine yourself Him when, in His first miracle, His powers green and unproven, He bid the servants fill the waterpots with water to the brim and bear them unto the governor of the feast. Suppose the water had not become wine but still proved, in the governor's mouth, water? This would be comedy too, but of another kind; a grim and pratfallen kind—our mortal kind.

When we thus empathize, at what do we marvel? His daring. His faith. "O thou of little faith," He cries to Peter as Peter sinks beneath the waves, and when the disciples, the Evangelist

Matthew tells us a few chapters later, could not cure the lunatic who "falleth into the fire, and oft into the water," Jesus thunders at them, "O faithless and perverse generation, how long shall I be with you?" and tells them, His anger cooled, that "If ye have faith as a grain of mustard seed, ye shall remove mountains; nothing shall be impossible unto you."

Well, are we not such a faithless and perverse generation? A generation of falling men, of starving men, of bleeding women, of drowning Peters? Imagine a man married to goodness, and hating the goodness as darkness hates the light; yet he cannot budge that marriage and his hate by a thumb's-width, and his spirit curses God. Why has the perfect and playful faith that Christ demonstrated in His miracles never come again, though saints have prayed in these two thousand years, and torturers have smiled?

Dearly beloved, let us open ourselves to this lesson. I feel you gathered beneath me, my docile suburban flock, sitting hushed in this sturdy edifice dedicated in the year 1883 and renovated under my canny predecessor in the year 1966. Strong its walls were built; with metal rods and extruded concrete were they reinforced. But let us pray together that its recollected and adamantine walls explode, releasing us to the soft desert air of this Sunday morning a thousand and more miles away. Nay, not explode, but atomize, and vanish noiselessly; nay, not that either, but may its walls and beams and mortar turn to petals, petals of peony and magnolia, carnation and chrysanthemum, and as at one of the infamous feasts of Baal-adoring Heliogabalus collapse in upon us, melting walls of perfume and color and allurement, so that each female among you is graced with a sudden orgasm and each man of you receives at least a hint, a mitigating hint, that the world is not entirely iron and stone and effort and fear. Let us pray for that. Let us confidently expect that. For there must be, in this sea of pinched and scrubbed Sunday faces, a single mustard seed of faith.

There is not. The walls stand. We are damned. I curse you, then, as our Lord cursed the fig tree; may you depart from this place forever sterile; may your generation wither at the roots, and a better be fed by its rot.

Amen.

14

MRS. HARLOW'S fragile, appealing face across my desk from
me. Me trying to keep my thoughts up from her bosom, which
her knit dress is hugging snugly enough to warm a saint. Her
voice floats out and upwards from her face's delicate net, escaping to be drowned in the air from the open window, open
to a bonny slushy day, of false spring, the trappings of winter
melting, March. Another Lent. ". . . and he really loves me so
much, it's quite touching, I feel such a, such a *vill*ainess."

From her pause, I am to say something. As little as possible
at this stage. I am counselling. "I think we should get our feelings out, before we begin censoring them."

This braces her, brings her an inch more upright and nearer
to me. She girds to say the unspeakable. "I *loathe* his touch,"
she tells me. "I'll think of any excuse, a headache, stomach
trouble, I feign sleep"—her vocabulary has about it a touch
of the old-fashioned valentine; her diction is as distinct as her
shape—"and he always understands, and forgives, it's quite ex-
*ac*erbating. I'd rather he'd beat me, leave me, be a *man*—"

My impulse is to reach across the desk and slap her face. She
must sense this, for she halts, her smooth gray eyes alarmed.
"Go on," I say. Into my abrupt boredom the sound of cars
swishing on the melting street pours as if a volume switch had
been turned.

She slumps, surrenders the inch closer she had come. "I can
hardly elaborate further. I don't *really* want him to beat me,
I'd despise him if he did; but it would be an *act*ion, you see, it
would be a—shattering."

"Oh?"

"I beg your pardon?"

"What is it, Mrs. Harlow, that you feel would be shattered?"

With her fine dry skin in her soft knit dress, she senses an
abrasive resistance where I, as minister, should be all divine
compliance, a vacuum where she can expand. It excites her,
my resistance. Her sensing it excites me. Her answer, when she
comes up with it, is good. It has a coin in its mouth. She proclaims, wider-eyed, "Why, our grotesque false peace! I cannot
stand this man, and nobody knows it. Except you."

"I'm not sure I do know that." I shift in my chair. "When did these feelings of distaste begin? Obviously they weren't there when you married."

"Why would that be obvious?" I like her fondness for the subjunctive. We are circumscribed by tangents. She knows that.

"Why would you have married Mr. Harlow otherwise?"

"Because everybody I knew was getting married and I didn't want to be alone!"

"And *are* you alone?"

"I'm more alone *with* him than I would be with*out* him."

"He loves you."

"He doesn't *know* me. How can you love what you don't know? His love is insulting. It's stupid. Reverend Marshfield, I cannot believe love has to be so stupid."

"You can afford to feel insulted," I tell her, "because he protects you." Children returning from school shout in the acoustic wet street. "You and your children," I remind her.

Mrs. Harlow—her first name is Frances, we call her Frankie—comes so swiftly forward in her chair I fear she might hiss. "How can you give me," she asks, her voice brittle and true as rods of glass, "this middle-class moralism? I could get this from my husband."

"Well I don't want to give you what your husband would give you," I say.

"I'm a person," she says. "A soul. Why should I live so dishonestly? Why should I die on my feet just because I've had children?"

"Except a seed dieth," I begin.

"Well I think it's rotten. Tom. I mean that. I think the way I feel I'm just the waste of a human being. And I can't believe the Christian church was instituted to preside over the waste of human beings."

"I can't believe it either," I say, hurriedly, for she has stood up. The snugness of the knit wool about her hips dries my mouth; the sensation is as of an unanatomical emptiness in my chest sucking moisture from my normal cavities, and the emptiness is part (confirmingly, somehow) of a cosmic imbalance.

Her flurry of words races on without me, "And now I have to go home because the damn children are coming home from school, and then the cats need to be fed, and then Gerry comes home from work. Children, cats, Gerry, the dishes, bed. Do you think I should have an affair?"

"Mightn't a part-time job be more constructive?"

"I don't have time for a job! My life is too constructive already!" Her heat embarrasses her; she turns (snug behind as well, in nice balance, liberate Libra) and fluffs herself into her coat, a knee-length mink from more middle-class days. She shoves her smarting pink hands into the pockets and pouts, helpless. I stand, helpless also. My collar bites under the Adam's apple. "Shall I come again?" Her voice lower.

I measure my words. Less a question than a defiance.

"If it helps. You've raised several issues that should be talked through with someone."

"This a good time for you?"

I consult my calendar, suggest that she and her husband might come in together some evening.

"No, goodness," Mrs. Harlow lets out, with a giggle even older than the mink. "He'd kill me if he knew."

She gone, I blink. This interview, like the following, and the preceding (she came to my office, uxoriously troubled, around the time that Alicia staged her scene with Jane), in its shifting transparencies and reflecting opacities, seems an experience so gnostic I am blinded.

O, Ms. Prynne, she was fair and fine and spoiled and open-eyed, the web of time sat like the most delicate purdah upon her face, whereas you are dark and heavyset and militantly competent and uncivil in the hall, which vibrates with your patrolling step: forgive me for tormenting you with fond memories. If I knew what you wanted. If you would leave me a multiple-choice questionnaire as does the Ramada Inn. If you would grant me a sign, disturb the placement of these pages on the dresser top, invert the paper clip I cunningly sandwiched in a northeasterly direction between pages 89 and 90, anything . . . The silence of this room *m'effraie*. It is not one silence but many; the lampshade is silent, the bulb silently burns, the bed in silence waits for my next oblivion, the bathroom mirror silently plays catch with a corner of my bathrobe, the carpeting is a hungry populace of individual acrylic silences, even the air-conditioner, today, is silent. Has the power failed? Has the desert cooled? Has the beautiful last beseeching of the Bible ("Even so, come, Lord Jesus."—Rev. 22.20) been at last answered, and Man's two millennia of Inbetweentimes ended? No, my clock says an hour to noon remains.

How could I leave Jane? How could I make up my betrayal, the lover's perennial betrayal, to Alicia? No way. Any change in circumstances would only have substituted another pang for the pang I felt when, during service, Alicia, looking, in her white surplice over red cassock, remarkably like the sub-teen lads of her choir, but that her hair was a curl longer, bent nearsightedly close above the keyboards of her gorgan* and the beams above us all began to tremble with the whole-note fifths of the *Venite*, or the tripping quarters of the plainsong *Sanctus*, or the preliminary run-through of one of the out-of-the-ordinary hymns she favored, such as "O Master of the Callous Hand" or "Behold a Sower! From Afar" or "Come, Ye Disconsolate, Where'er Ye Languish." I would remember then how in another setting she would bend over me, her hands as tepid and untimid as those of a masseuse, and bring me up to pitch, and the throbbing church would swim in the one sea of love that encircles us, that upholds the mailbox on the corner and the Dow Jones in New York and the starlings on their swiftly portable columns of grace.

I vowed to abjure the word "love," yet write of little else. Let us think of it as the spiritual twin of gravity—no crude force, "exerted" by the planets in their orbits, but somehow simply, Einsteinly there, a mathematical property of space itself. Some people and places just make us feel heavier than others, is all.

In the gaunt and ornate house that Jane and I inhabited until such time as a fresh call would take us away, weightlessness prevailed. Her initial excitation by my adultery and her starring part as Wronged Wife in the post-Christmas pageant had passed; I could feel, now, as the warmer days led me to toss aside the blankets and invite her to attempt a physical attitude airier than the strict vis-à-vis, the moment when remembrance turned her off, when a sensation of being forced into another's

*Thus. My glimpse might turn me to stone?

mold balked her flow and turned our milk-white bodies sour. I minded less than you may think. An anti-sexual wife whom I had the pleasure of arousing guilt in and a mistress whom I had the pleasure of adoring without the inconvenience of managing trysts and shaking off her clinging afterplay comprised not the worst arrangement in this imperfect world. That both women gave me pain seemed a tidy stroke of spiritual economy. Better, St. Paul said, to marry than to burn; better still to marry *and* burn.

Also Mrs. Harlow seemed to be coming along.

Also my father, who in space-time occupied a stark room of a rest home an hour distant, which he furnished with a vigorous and Protean suite of senility's phantoms, was in a genetic dimension unfolding within me, as time advanced, and occupying my body like, as Colette has written to illustrate another phenomenon, a hand being forced into a tight glove. I was reading less Barth and more Tillich, and had taken to puttering pleasurably about the house.

First try, I typed "putting," which shows where my heart lies. Sorry this is such a lumpy issue. Blue Monday. Yesterday's sermon, so close to putrefying into blasphemy, sits ill on my stomach. Perhaps the *consensus gentium* is correct, there should be things called "mysteries," locked up in Latin and forgotten.

15

SHORT, BRIGHT paragraphs today. Yesterday I successfully eliminated, in all but the clutchiest of shots, my excess of backswing. For an at-moments sparkling 82. Amazing, how powerful a short swing (with some hips into it) can be.

Puttering. For instance, a number of broken sash cords hung from the windows, making them sticky to open and yet liable to fall like guillotines upon the numb skull of one attempting to replace storm panes with screens.* I had never taken apart a window before. What an interlocked, multi-deviced yet logical artifact one is! And how exciting, all the screws unscrewed and

* Pains with screams?

stop strips removed, to pull forth from decades of darkness the rusted sashweight, such a solid little prisoner, and fit him with a glossy new noose and feel him, safe once again in his vertical closet, tug like life upon the effortlessly ascendant sash! It is positively sexual, this answering quickening from within the carpentered arcanum of the frame.

Or Jane, whose virtue sought symmetry and enclosure, had been long bothered by the absence of a door leading from the foyer into the living-room. There had once been a door there, hinge-butts testified. But the door itself had vanished. But there were other doors, left over from some renovation of the mercenary Morse, in the cellar, displaced to there from the garage when it was in turn renovated. I found one of them sound and, with some planing, to fit. Finding matching hardware, however, was an ingenious work of salvage, that sent me even into the attic, where a solitary brass strike, of obsolete design, waited loose on a sill to be rendered useful to Man again. Other bits—the other half of the hinges, the latch bar —were painted and riddled with rust, and the idle little work, at my cozy bench beside the furnace, of integrating these components, of cleaning them in coffee cans of seething chemicals and fitting them to the patched and puttied door, which had been hinged oppositely from how I intended to hang it, gave me a pleasure perhaps disproportionate to the benefit achieved. It is true, when at last in place, the residual imperfections of my handiwork struck me more forcibly than its skill, and I had a demonic impulse to splinter the whole thing with the hammer warm in my hand from tapping home the hinge pins. But I desisted, habituation soon assuaged me, and Jane was pleased. That I continued to wish, and continue to wish, to please my wife, I append as a sorry frill upon, as an ulcerated blemish beneath the belt of, these confessions. Perhaps Jane's coo of admiration, wrung by my work from her sainted silence, did for my mother's singing.

It occurs to me, remembering the fabled time when I lived in the world and had my being there, that I was infatuated with completion, with the repair in place, the sermon delivered, the ejaculation achieved, the letter mailed; with the deed done rather than, as a healthy hedonism might fatuously advise, with the doing. As a chid* I would put myself to sleep by imagining objects—pencils, hassocks, teddy bears—sliding over a water-fall. I loved shedding each grade as I ascended through school. Even the purgative sweep of windshield wipers gratifies me. A lifelong drive to disrobe myself of circumstances has brought me stripped to this motel. Remember my compulsive hymn to the toilet bowl? Shall we work on that later? Or flush it?

With Alicia Jane was aloofly correct and, on the occasions when her black Chevrolet, embossed with moonbeams, parked at Ned's house and I suffered, angry on my behalf. "Of *course* she wants you to see, of *course* she wants to hurt you with it," Jane insisted in my ear, when I was lazily inclined to give Alicia the benefit of the doubt and blame my discomfort on a private demon and this visible conjunction on blind chance. After all, I reasoned, she had other lovers, whose houses I did not over-look, so the τελος of her copulation was not to irritate me. Yet when, to rid myself of torment—her appearances at Ned's hav-ing become a virtually unbroken *continuo* under the treble of my fitful dreams—I moved to dismiss my unconscionably mu-sical organist, it was Jane who protested, and Ned who blandly agreed and reinforced my will. But to prolong this paragraph might compromise its shortness and brightness.

My ghostly reader telepathically reminds me that I have written unnaturally little of the two other occupants of the parsonage, my offspring, my blood and seed, my Jacob and Esau, my two sons. To call them "vermin" would convey their sleeplessly greedy activity and the gnawing, gutting effect their quarrels, misadventures, and demands worked upon my brain; but it would confer an undue dynamism upon their position in my plight. As I writhed to escape my life, they were agonizing but inert; they were the two galvanized nails in my palms, the unravelling fringes of my threadbare days, the rumpus upon

*Sic. Yet as a child I was more ignored than chidden. Perhaps wanted more Jahwehian thunder from Dad? More scolding arias from Mom? Or perhaps Freud's stumblebum God does not impart His dark fingerprint to every slip of the tips.

awaking and the headache at bedtime, the unappeasable termites tunnelling to a powdery dust the beams and joists of my time on earth. For are not children exactly that which does not have an ending, which outlasts us, which watches *us* slide over the waterfall, with relief? Society in its conventional wisdom sets a term to childhood; of parenthood there is no riddance. Though the child be a sleek Senator of seventy, and the parent a twisted husk mounted in a wheelchair, the wreck must still grapple with the ponderous sceptre of parenthood.

Martin is sixteen, Stephen fourteen. I have written earlier (find it yourself, you prying Prynne) of a certain tendony sameness Jane and I share; Martin inherited this twofold. Even as an infant in arms he was wiry and would push off from his mother's breast or wriggle from my restraining embrace with the puissance of a wildcat. He excels at all sports, though small, and will amuse us with sudden tricks he has secretly rehearsed, such as kicking a soccer ball with the heel of his foot so it bounces up to his head, or leaping over a broomstick held in his hands, or adroitly catching in midair a button or stack of pennies balanced upon his elbow. Subject to nervous headaches and frighteningly intense stretches of sleep, he is, awake, a jabber, a perfectionist pained to fury by the imperfections around him. No blot sits larger on his horizon than his brother, who is his size, and has been almost from birth. As a fetus Stephen was so ample (ten pounds minus an ounce postpaid) that he frightened Jane away from her plan (which I, with the naïveté of the Fifties, when the global plum pudding, full of dimes and brandy, seemed served up all for Uncle Sam, because he had been so good, shared) of having four children. Our softness, the doughiness of the soul that keeps* us sticking together and mires our essential indignation in the pasty peace of a quiet meal or an evening spent with Bach and a book, has been concentrated in this dear plump child, who would have constructed, for himself, a paradise of model airplanes and collected minerals and introverted musings had not Providence supplied his brother to give evil a physical presence. In toddlerhood, Martin beat upon the offensively large

*The Marshfields mallow?

infant as upon an unresonant drum; as they aged, the older boy outraced and tripped up the younger at every game they played; older still, Martin taunted his brother with a barrage of complaints for which, since they seemed to be forced from him by a demon beyond, I could not hold him culpable. Nor could I but pity my tender son even though, as he grew, he developed from his superior bookishness a hectoring legalism in his own defense. I felt all sides; and could help none. My stomach grinds as, moral gears clashing, I hear them debate at table.

"You're disgusting," Martin abruptly announces to his sibling as he sits opposite in the candleglow of dinner.

"Why? What did I do?" Fear slightly overaccents each syllable; fear, and a determination not to be erased from account.

"Mom!" Martin cries, and in the fine pull of his skin at his temples I feel a headache starting. "First he chews with his mouth open, then he talks so you can see all the mush!"

"No worse than you," Stephen counterclaims. "Coming to the table with hands all roguey from playing basketball in the mud and face all pimply so it looks like a pizza."

"Looks like a pizza, ha, ha, smoothie. For your information I cannot help the skin blemishes induced by adolescent glandular changes but you could learn how to chew properly instead of slobbering like a baby."

"For *your* information my nose is all stuffed up so if I close my mouth I can't breathe. At least I don't ruin everybody else's dinner by talking about it and saying Disgusting and all the stuff we've heard before and is boring anyway."

"My, my," Martin says, in truth a little overwhelmed, sidling his eyes toward me to see if it shows. "Listen to the young fellow expostulate."

"At least," Stephen pursues, "I don't keep disgusting copies of *Penthouse* under my bed and have a face all scabs."

Jane asks, "*Can't* the two of you let each other alone for one meal? I'm ashamed of you both. Tom, say something."

I say, "Where does the kid get *Penthouse*?"

Martin, though the meanness of the vexed will always be his, does not have much aptitude for sin; he has my delight in fittingness, but applied to his own body, and now that he has a driver's license he shames me by always fastening the safety belt, and never exceeding the speed limit.

Stephen, on the other hand, so long bullied into a passive goodness, and for too many years of his life angelic-looking, with his baby complexion and long-lashed eyes, has a backlog of temptations he is anxious to adjust. His inwardness will welcome drugs; his beauty will attract girls; and his years of absorbing abuse will excuse him, I fear, from guilt. This meek one is prepared to inherit the earth. He goes to a private school we can ill afford, and shows no shying away from the life of the rich. I picked him up one midnight after a dance and asked him, in the faintly pregnant silence of the car—he seemed perfumed, and affably dazed—how it was. "O.K.," he said. I asked him to elaborate. He snapped, "Groovy. Hassle-free." My, how this saddened me! Welcome, Buddha. Howdy, Nirvana. Adam did not fall, nor did Christ rise, that the world might be hassle-free.

Martin, by contrast, insisted on going to the local public school, without admitting it was for my sake—to save me money, to make me look community-minded. He is on a team each season and causes our spondaic name to ring from the bleachers. On the anvil of his brother's head he forged himself a backbone. He has aspirations, and expectations; even before my scandal, I embarrassed him, with my overly agonistic sermons, my devious irony, my sense of the priest as fool and scapegoat. He laughs only in triumph—at a goal, a stunt. When the meal is over, he sits at the table tossing crumbs and pellets of paper into empty glasses, and applauds the occasional miracle of ricochet. But it frightens me, the halo of unhappiness around his head. My attempts to talk to him buckle on this fright. My words cease. I remember his kicking out of my arms as a baby. I am timid of touching him, he is too tightly wound, he might break.

Stephen, I might add, with his pliable good looks, was endlessly cuddled, and accepted it, and now stays awake listening to the radio murmur its nothings in darkness; while his older brother, sweating and slack as an unfurled fist, has been dutifully asleep for hours.

*

My two sons. A more fruitful topic than I had supposed. I had meant to go on to my father today, but noon and the desert, liquor and golf, call. Heredity, it occurs to me, works up as well as down. The creatine of golfing passion did not begin shooting in my muscles until I had an athlete for a son. Nor did I become a lover until my second son proved beautiful. A jabber and a taker, a Spartan and a Sybarite: the trunk stands declared in its forking.

16

ONCE A WEEK in theory, less often in practice, I would climb into my clerical brown Dart (if there are Earthgazers in the UFOs, they must see us as a species of mollusc, or perhaps believe that automobiles are our hosts, and we are parasites viable for brief periods of scuttling) and steer a drear hour through America's highway nightmare to the nursing home where my father, seventy-seven years young, was stashed. A rural byway, a crescent of low brick buildings, a euphemistic shingle in gilded woodcraft, *Valleyhead*. Within, an all-denying cleanliness. A stout receptionist, magenta cashmere sweater worn capelike atop nurse's starched bodice, smiles at the kindred arc of my collar; how girls go for a uniform! Down rubber halls hung with *trompe-l'œil*, doorway-sized examples of neo-realism depicting shrivelled staring oldsters waiting for No One between sheets of white. The verisimilitude is breathtaking. The innocent rows of a nursery, of a poultry broodery; each room held a live soul hatching the egg of its rounding, and beckoned me vaporously in, and would have ensnared me in pity and love had I not strode stern, eyes locked against trompery, toward the far cell where sat a magical man who once claimed to be my father.

But no more. His claims had ceased. He confused me with his brother Erasmus, with an old Army mate called Mooney (my father had served in the First World War, not as chaplain but as fighting private, whose battalion disembarked in France in the first week of November 1918, and stayed for six months of riotous peace in the raped villages of Picardy), with several interchangeable m.c.'s who ran daytime television quizzes and exhibitions of middle-class pawkiness, with the obscure power behind and above this slippery establishment in which he found himself, and, obscurer and more ominous still, with some man who, he seemed to believe, threatened to steal my mother from him. My father tended to move through these confusions in the order of my listing; so our interviews went from fraternal cordiality to frightened antagonism. The fright mine, not his: my tolerance for unreality, supernaturalist though I claim to be, turns out to be low. That he looked at me and saw some-one else turned my bones to water. Hung with thoughts no more rooted than mistletoe, his head was still massive and un-like mine (my mother's skimpy genes) still woolly: not only had he lost scarcely a strand to time but his hair, rarely cut by the authorities, had grown richer in wildness, curlier, as dense and candid as a ram's fleece. His mouth, his nose, his nostril-hairs—everything had grown but his eyes, which a swelling in the surrounding flesh had reduced to a beady, ingeniously frantic, rather Mongolian slant. He would be sitting beside his steel bed in an armchair with wooden arms, wearing a plaid bathrobe Jane and I had given him. Jarringly, the cloth of the armchair was virtually the same plaid; it gave his presence an electric penumbra of displacement, like the vibrant aura sur-rounding film actors superimposed upon a background that is in fact another film running.

"Thank the Lord, you've arrived at last!" His great voice, with its mellow country vowels and crisp way of darkening and deepening at the end of a phrase, had survived into senility to give even his most nonsensical utterance the hollow sonorous-ness of sermons I had squirmed through thirty years before. "In the fullness of time," he went on, in a mode more sarcastic, "the bridegroom cometh. We've been waiting by this fool barn an eternity, I thought the shade would turn to vinegar." He heard the tone of a witticism in these words, and his little eyes hardened in expectation of my laughter.

I obliged. "I come whenever I can," I added.

"Then don't make appointments you can't keep," he promptly responded. "Brother's keeper, bet your bottom dol-lar. If our father saw you stealing apples, you'd have a hiding to make your britches glow. Did you bring me any booty?"

"How would this do?" A box of Schrafft chocolates, bought

at a drugstore in a shopping center on the way. His spotted square hands tore at the cellophane like a raccoon's paws; his appetite for food, far from diminishing, as it would in some ordered phasing-out, had grown with the decay of his mind, and aided the illusion that his body was swelling in strength and presence. The backs of his hands were spattered with large moles, ancestors of the moles that had begun to emerge on the backs of mine.

He put a chocolate cherry into his mouth, and followed it too soon with a chewy caramel; excess stained his lips darkly. *You're disgusting*, I thought of telling him. With messy mouth he roguishly told me, "You have a sweet tooth, Ras. Not to mention"—two sugar-coated almonds flew after the caramel, and were crunched—"a sweet lookout for *les filles des villes*"—pronouncing each word disyllabically, with a rhyming *ee-yah*—"*n'est-ce pas*? Tell me true, how was that little filly with the big knockers? Big above, slow below, that's the rule of thumb. Give me a bitty narrow-assed slip of a thing every time, make every man feel a beast, good things in small packages, can you fault me there?"

The baseness of his undressed mind shocked me. My mother had been a small woman.

"Don't sit there slack-jawed as a moron, Mooney, confess your sins with a ready heart. After what we've been through the Lord holds us entitled to a little *plaisir*, a little animal ease-ment. Body and soul, soul and body, the lion and the lamb shall lie down together, and there is no afterlife. Any preacher's son can assure himself of that, just read your molecules. Tell me about the little black-haired twat, might try her myself. *Mam'selle, mam'selle, beaucoup de dollair si vous allez au lit avec moi*, it gets them where they live, losers can't be choosers. What is it these frogs say, *le con est le centre du monde*. You know what my tart told me they call an engagement—a *com-promis*. Hear it? *Com-promis!* A promised cunt! And these were innocent village girls four short years ago. Mooney, you're not laughing. You're homesick."

I told my father, "I'm thinking over the wisdom of your words."

"And well you might, you laggard. Homesick, prick-sick, Mooney, you're sickly, and that's no mistake. Deceit has done you in. That's the trick about sin, it does in the doer. You think you've got on top of me, the hard fact is I've got on top of you. I'm accumulating evidence, and not a court of decency in the commonwealth can fail to uphold me. The vestry concur in this course of action. Even though it may cost a pretty penny, we've agreed to touch the Discretionary Fund." A flicker of suspicion that his scheme—his sensation that a scheme was in motion— might be slipping awry, might indeed have a false bottom the size of perdition, faded from his face at the thought of the Discretionary Fund. He had attained firm ground. He resettled in the chair; the edges where the two nearly matching plaids met vibrated. He crossed his legs, and a long mauve shin showed, rubbed hairless to the height of a man's socks. Betraying the tousled vigor of his head, his ankles looked bloodless. They were a cadaver's denerved stems. My father said, his hands pressed into his lap to suppress their trembling, "The truth of it is, they need me out there. Otherwise, I'd let you have your freezer, and go for the Exxon jackpot with my eyes tight shut against all these ramifications."

"Daddy, who needs you out there? Who do you mean?"

He looked at me fishily, and groped on the bed for his pipe. They had taken it away from him, for burning holes in his blanket. He did not like my calling him "Daddy," nor did I. But he had no other name; "Father" had been our name for God. Squinting obliquely, having turned his head to help grope for the non-existent pipe, he asked me, "Must we always have that vacuous little smile? Is there no surcease from this artificial good humor, this charade of good will?"

"I'm sorry," I said, meaning it, feeling fear grow in me while a prickly righteousness, a kind of invisible hair, began to rise on him.

"Who? You ask me who?" He thought the answer would be obvious, but found it not so; his stare of scorn narrowed to canniness. "Why, all of them. Out there. In Viewerland." He gestured toward the television set, silent and gray-faced behind me. "The meetings," he expatiated, "their many petty concerns as they move from birth to death, and meet their tragedies and difficulties, the disappointments of freedom, the profound fulfillments of the middle way, the ills that flesh is heir to. Its warp and weft comprises the fabric of a parish, and

I am the shuttlecock," he told me, and, pleased with the echo of happiness in this phrase, leaned toward me with heavy confidentiality. "It is not that you do my poor person wrong by this obstructionism; it is that you deprive the many others of what weak wisdom the Gospel of Love might shed."

I was tempted, I fell in with his phantoms. "We all agree, though," I said, "that *this* is the place for your ministry. You have done wonderful work here. Of course, if you *want* to move on, but do you feel that your work is completed?" I gestured at the blank walls, the tightly made bed with its side-rails, the dead television set. The room smelled of ammonia. "Can't you feel it, how you are surrounded by need, and by admiration?"

His head at first had nodded agreement, but by the end of my speech, as my voice flattened against these bare walls, he knew something was amiss. He looked at me with a look a son should never see upon his father's face, the face the father turns away from the home and presents to the enemies outside. "You call it admiration," he growled, "I call it covetousness, and adultery. You and she have wounded me beyond the power of words to express, but I will not be trodden upon. I am no poor worm. I have no such intention, sir. I am disabused, sir. *Damn* your business connections. *Damn* your friends in high places."

I fought down the fear fluttering behind my face; I half-rose, expecting a blow.

With ponderous steadiness, he went on, "I have never liked you, to be frank. You have a cowardly and lecherous smell. I held my nose the moment you came into my house. Though you have powerful allies, I am not powerless. There are legal steps. There is other recourse. Though I never killed, I was once a soldier, and would have killed. I love life too much to be a pacifist. She knows the depth of my feeling. She knows how you used her. You will say she used you in turn. I have heard men say such filthy things. This is how you repay her, with filth."

"Daddy," I said, "I don't know what you're talking about. I'm your son. Mother is dead. She loved only you."

His handsome, heavy face congested; his eyes, smaller than a pig's and cloudy as phlegm, looked through me yet at me with a fury of intent. "Do you want me," he said, and every word trembled with its overburden of passion, "to hurl this sacred book"—the box of chocolates—"right into your face?" I fled.

From outside the room, in the hall, I looked back and saw him, his handsome face mottled, stare at the space where I had been and with an air of absentminded satisfaction take a nougat from the box and pop it, still wrapped in waxpaper, into his mouth.

In the same time of my life as this interview, Mrs. Harlow led me, her hand trembling and the palm damp, down into her den. The Harlows lived on the outskirts of town, where the two-acre building lots were wooded and expensive, in a newly built ranch-house so modernistically glassy there felt to be no corner in its rooms where one might embrace unseen. We had just kissed behind the door, as I tried to leave, my mouth tasting of the coffee with which, irreproachably, she had rewarded my irreproachable call, having to do with the Whitsunday flower display of the Distaff Circle or some such trompery. Her own mouth had been a startling many-petalled bloom of more lips than two and more tongues than one. I melted and froze; the den was down carpeted stairs and floored with maroon rubber and walled with knotty pine and littered with mock-leather furniture and outsize children's toys, billiard tables wide as a lawn and dart boards the height of a man. Giants rumpussed here. She renewed the kiss, producing upward from her throat and the well of her deep being more excited petals of tongue and touch; I felt passive as a sleeper; edges of cloth, silk parting from skin, grazed my fingers; she stood before me naked. She was taller than Alicia and frailer than Jane; the veil of wrinkles upon her face extended no further; her body was as smooth as her gaze. Only something peakèd, an anxious shapely skin-niness in the glossy jut of ilium and clavicle, hinted she was more than girl. I let her undress me as one would a dummy (the stud at the back of my collar a problem as always) and felt exalted holding her nakedness in the arms of mine. But no erection arose. The experience was so new to me I scarcely had the grace to be abashed. Perhaps her jutting, fluttering eagerness left me no space to grow in; her husband's exercise bicycle beside the rack of pool cues didn't help. Harlow was a cherished deacon from my predecessor's go-go days, a stocky gray-jawed bank executive with a formidable way of withholding his smile one judicious second, and then showing even his gold molars in a braying I've-got-you laugh. I was too aware of my car parked visibly outside and Mrs. Harlow felt fragile to me, a fevered child in my care. Unlike Jane and Alicia, she was a believer. She held my limp penis in her hand and called me lovely. Her forgiveness and the pre-Adamic, cave-woman fall of her hair to her bared shoulders broke a capsule inside me. I felt my heart spill, while my penis hung mute. In the house above us, a machine switched itself on. Had it been God's footstep, there was no escaping from this nether zone. I dropped to my knees, a pro at that, and arranged her hands tangent as in prayer in front of her pudenda—a startling dark curly copper, quite unrelated to the hair of her head—and kissed her hands' dry backs and turned them over and kissed their moist palms, their moisture and my immanence of tears mingling; spouting comical vows to come again in glory, I dressed and left. At the foot of the cellar stairs I paused and saw her posed, my lovely Frankie Harlow, a look of expectancy stranded on her face, a gently "hooked" tilt to her head, posed like a bathing savage atop the pale round smear of her reflection sunk in the maroon pool of the floor.

Outside, between rows of wilting peonies, I hurried down the flagstone walk with the same hot, leaden, hunted feeling I had as when fleeing my father's rest home—a feeling of being closely, urgently cherished by a Predator whose success will have something rapturous about it, even for me.

17

THE OLD MAN was right; there was a smell about me now. Women sensed it. They flocked to be counselled. The overweight, the underloved, the brutalized, the female brutes. Some were from other congregations; some were unchurched. Perhaps it was that surreal early summer of the Watergate disclosures; everything sure was coming loose, tumbling. My afternoons were flooded with appointments. My phone would ring at the moment I was dozing off at night, and while I was still dreaming in the morning.

What did they say, these women? In sum, that the world men had made no longer fit them. The chafing for some came in the crotch, for others in the head. Some complained that they loved their husbands more than they were loved in turn. Many had the opposite complaint; indeed a curious image of the race of husbands accumulated, as toothless, spineless, monosyllabically vocal, sticky in texture and tiny in size, deaf and blind—the race of axe-wielding, percentage-calculating giants who managed the nation became infant monkeys upon entering their front doors. Even the physically violent ones —the strikers, the nightgown-rippers—were described as ultimately docile and so foolable, so obtuse in relation to the essential, as to be figures of manipulation and pity. While many women had had lovers, what remained in their minds was not the male lover's prowess or impact but their own, female, magnificently enclosed suffering. Fearful lest I think them frigid, the women, displaying to me incidents of sexual arousal, admitted, rather than credit men, to curious and neutral stimuli—an infant's sucking at the breast, the moment of an airplane's take-off, the vibration of the dishwasher as they leaned against the sink. Other women, even cinematic images of other women—most notably, that summer, the tartish Maria Schneider of *Last Tango*; Brando was despised for protecting his prick* from the camera—were cited, though very few of my middle-class, Jahweh-worshipping ladies had experienced Lesbian sex. But a vague overarching sisterhood of sensitivity and induced guilt and *not being known* was felt, dawning in most cases as dimly and fragmentarily as the New World dawned for Columbus, a continent in the air; and it seemed to me now, watching television, that money, green and golden money which instinctively seeks the light, felt it too, for the commercials, with their invariable feminine heroine, were alone alive, while the sports and "suspense" in between consisted of cursory pap, shovelled out anyhow to male minds of a Merovingian degeneracy.

It generally took four to five interviews to get down to sexual details; the women who came on strong in this respect were most often fronting for some other concern (the death

---

*Prick, pic, truthpic, take it from there, Ms. P.

of a parent, the waywardness of a child). When these details emerged, they circled about the business which the younger generation has graced with the unisex term "giving head." Head and heart, tongue and cunt, mouth and cock—what an astonishing variety of tunes were played on this scale of so few notes. Wives who wanted head from their husbands and didn't get it, wives who got it and hated it, wives who didn't mind getting it if they didn't have to give it, wives who loved giving head so much their clitoris indeed did seem to be, like the freckle-faced blue-movie star, at the back of their throats. Somewhere, amid these juxtapositions and their violent "affect," an American mystery was circumscribed, having to do with *knowing*, with acceptance of body by soul, with recovery of some baggage lost in the Atlantic crossing, with some viral thrill at the indignity of incarnation, with some monstrous and gorgeous otherness the female and male genitals meet in one another. I don't know. Perhaps my own willingness, discussed exhaustively above in connection with the underside of church pews, to "go down" was what my troubled women smelled. Or perhaps the traditional sexual ambiguity of the priest, with his swishing robes and his antistoical proclamation of our pain and sickness and sickly need, excited them. For the scoffers are right, ours is indeed a religion of women and slaves.

And I, what did I say, or dare shout, in this gale of female discontent? That marriage is a sacrament and not a contract of convenience. That a spouse, like the land we are born in and the parents we are born unto, is a given; that our task is to love not what might be but what *is* given. That our faith insists, in the most scandalous and ugliest and least credenced phrase of its creed, that we and our bodies are one; that nothing less galvanic than the resurrection of the dead will deliver our spirits to eternity; that therefore, short of physical pain (and anal violation, about which I have a probably political prejudice), we should not heretically (and what a mighty battle the church fathers gave one another over this!) castigate the body and its dark promptings. That our body looks up at us from a cloudy pool; but it is us, our reflection. That the demand for babies isn't what it once was, though evolutional inertia maintains the orgasm as a bribe. That women's rights cannot be established as a symmetrical copy of men's, nor as an inversion of male wrongs. That communication is often the real problem. That we are all fishers in the dark, in the storm of the senses and mad events, and the tug on the other end of the line must be patiently reeled, with fingertips sensitized by the sandpaper of an abrasive creed. And Heaven knows how much other such not entirely unhelpful stuff.

And I did sleep with a few, by way of being helpful. Fewer, I dare say, than parish rumor or ill-suppressed scandal asserted. But the weeping blotchy-mouthed teenaged bride who had never had an orgasm, and the gaunt divorcee who couldn't stop having them, and the quasi-nun crazy for the liturgy and the Presence and all things dilate with holiness, begged me for a touch, begged though the strength went out of me; and some others seemed, from the description of their private lives, so complimentary to my own secret shape, that we came together as matter-of-factly as two pieces in a jigsaw puzzle. Once the aversion to such use wore off, the church, empty these long afternoons, proved a hushed, capacious treasury of accommodating nooks: the robing room, smelling of clean linen and old paper; the nap mats in the Sunday-school nursery; the ladies' parlor with its Oriental rug and lockable door; my office with its rather sticky and sneeze-inducing horsehair sofa. No partner and I ever tried the nave and its pews; but I was shocked, at first, by how unfussily these seducing women sought out the scrotal concealed in the sacerdotal, how intuitively religious was their view of sex, hasty and improvised though its occasion. Where was their *guilt*? They came to church the next Sunday with clean faces, and listened to the Word intent. There was a continuum for them, where I felt a horrific gap. Bless them all. They brought me out of the wilderness where I did not know that our acts, every one, are homage; only the furniture varies. Churches are spires and domes; we minister now here, now there. There is a grandeur, an onslaught of νούς and of dizzying altitude, in the act of placing a communion wafer between the parted lips of a mouth that, earlier in the very week of which this was the Sabbath day, had received one's throbbingly ejaculated seed.

What else did I learn in this unfallow summer of my ministry? That adultery is not one but several species. The adultery of the freshly married is a gaudy-winged disaster, a phoenix with hot ashes, the revelation that one has mischosen, a life-swallowing mistake has been made. Help, help, it is not too late, the babies scarcely know their father, the wedding presents are still unscarred, the mistake can be unmade, another mate can be chosen and the universe as dragon can be slain.* Murders, abductions, and other fantasies flit into newspaper print from the hectic habitat of this species. The adultery of the hopelessly married, the couples in their thirties with slowly growing children and slowly dwindling mortgages, is a more stolid and more domestic creature, a beast of burden truly, for this adultery serves the purpose of rendering tolerable the unalterable. The flirtation at the benefit dance, the lunch invitation stammered from a company phone, the clock-conscious tryst in the noontime motel, the smuggled letters, the pained and sensible break-up—these are rites of marriage, holidays to the harried, yet, touchingly, not often understood as such by the participants, who flog themselves with blame while they haul each other's bodies into place as sandbags against the swamping of their homes. The adultery of those in their forties recovers a certain lightness, a greyhound skittishness and peacock sheen. Children leave; parents die; money descends; nothing is as difficult as it once seemed. Separation arrives by whim (the last dessert dish broken, the final intolerable cigar-burn on the armchair) or marriages are extended by surrender. The race between freedom and exhaustion is decided. And then, in a religious sense, there is no more adultery, as there is none among schoolchildren, or slaves, or the beyond-all-reckoning rich.

Typing this makes me grieve. I fall, full of grit. Generalizations belong to the Devil; particulars to the Lord. Frankie Harlow's pubic bush was copper and curly and infinitely fun to tease. I would tick my eyelashes against it, seeking to sight the horizon of minimal sensation. I would seem among the copper glints to be among stars. She would whisper, far away, and seek to lull me into length. Having failed in her basement, I thought to have her here, in the loft of the parish hall, where a leaking old skylight made vivid the woody forms of miniature crèches and lifesize mangers, wise kings' crowns and shepherds' crooks, Victorian altar furniture and great padded

*But the universe *is* a dragon, as a glance upward into a clear night sky will show.

Bibles no longer thumped by the virile muckraking parsons of the first Roosevelt's reign, plywood palm trees and temples of gilded cardboard. We stole velvet cushions from a Gothic deacon's bench and a sheet from a stained-glass window ousted by renovation and made a bower for ourselves. Lovely among the cutouts, plastic, alive, she weakened me with wonder. She was too fine. Shutting my lids on the crystalline curls of her shame, I managed stealthily to approach that apoplectic stiffness that inseminates the world, but when I rescrambled my parcel of bones, skin, and guts so our souls could lock eyes and our genitals do their blunt business, the vision of her skylit face (its pale upper lip an arch of expectation, a gem of moisture set where the crevice between her front teeth met her gum) broke upon my heart with a shining humanity, and manliness went from me. We grieved for me, she wished me to succeed, she loved me the more wildly for my failure; and this wish of hers built firmer the barrier I met in this strange seduction.

And, speaking of seduction, gentle reader, I feel your attention wandering; Mrs. Harlow's unravished curls rub your sleepy eyes the wrong way. But that barrier barring my satisfying her was, for the terminal season of my distraction, the one living thing in me. I would weep with her, her unfucked belly became a wailing wall, her forgiving hands would stroke the back of my neck, and I would greet my impotence as the survivor within me of faith, a piece of purity amid all this relativistic concupiscence, this plastic modernity, this adulterate industry, this animated death.

I overreach. Swing easy, I tell myself day after day. The days blend here. The sky at night is lilac. The Milky Way is a dragon. I no longer miss leaves. My indignation ebbs. My characters recede. I know you are praying for me, Ms. Prynne.

18

FALL BRINGS with it in those leafy lake-riddled middle sectors of our rectangular land notions of riddance and beginning anew. Alicia's sulk had infected my side long enough. She rebuked me: "Tom, you barged in with 'God be with you' and broke off the Charpentier before it was halfway through!"

"I did?" I was groggy with counselling and resented feedback from my confusion as a middle-aged woman resents the mirror. "There was a silence," I protested.

"It was a two-beat *rest*," she said, flouncing in her robe, stamping her foot soundlessly on the carpeted aisle. "There was a whole other part of the *Kyrie* to come, with a recorder duet Julie and Sue had worked on for *hours!*"

"Screw," I said, unable in my confused state to resist any semblance of euphony, "Julie and Sue."

"Not them too," Alicia said, making her sour mouth, that recalled to me spoiled sweetness.

I thought this cheap; indeed there was an offensive cheapness to this squat person. Compared to Frankie's silken skin hers was burlap. Her waist was thick; she snuffled. I told her, "I've asked you before, keep the music subliminal. Recorders, trumpet stops, guitars, seven-part Amens, you have it slopping all over the service. Everybody's Sunday roast is charred to a crisp by the time you let us out of your concert."

"Is this you talking, or Mrs. Harlow?"

"Me, thanks."

"Tom. Did it ever occur to you I'm trying to protect you?"

"From what? How?" A tremble of fear waited on her diagnosis; it was indeed diseaselike, her knowing me so well. Our radiant days together had become barium tracers within me.

"By playing so much music. From your making a display of yourself. You're wild these days."

"It's my new evangelical style."

She looked at my chest with glass eyes. "You're heading for a fall, Tom."

"Don't scare me. You sound like my wife."

She blinked, and slightly softened. "That's how we get," she said.

"Who's this we?"

She bit her lips, said, "You know. Us discards," and wantonly the wench let her bunny-pink eyes go teary.

Her tears, here in this church (navish tears), displeased me. *Rejoice in the Lord always: and again I say, Rejoice.* I said in a voice of hypocritic honey, "Maybe you'd be happier playing for another church."

She couldn't stop staring, and couldn't stop her inane weeping; in her white robe she seemed a doctor reading the worst from my fluoroscope and choking on the announcement. "May be," was all that Alicia uttered; she pulled her robe over her head and ran down the aisle somehow pulling, in an illusion fostered by my bone-deep fatigue, the entire church after her—rafters, plaques, pews, carpeting, walls, and windows pulled like a printed scarf through the door after her, into the blue outdoors, to her car, a new scarlet Vega. Her old char-dark chariot had chewed up its own transmission and died—fit punishment for all the nights the sight of it, visible evidence of things invisible, had transmitted torment to me.

Ned Bork and I had been creeping together toward an eerie par. His judgments expanded into every area that appeared to me immaterial: he and the secretary* cooked up the church bulletin every Thursday, he and the youth group held Saturday car-wash parties for the benefit of some North Vietnamese hospital, he was asked by several families to preach the funeral semon† of their departed loved ones, in preference to me. Bork arranged for two families in the parish to adopt black foster children, busloads of ghetto yellers arrived now and then to dabble in our local lake under his apostolic aegis, he was in a court once or twice a week "standing by" some svelte flower child busted for hustling hash or a culturally retrograde beer-oriented lad caught urinating in some policeman's holster. He organized volleyball for the church oddballs and young marrieds (to keep them out of the Oddfellows and Swingers Club respectively) and dominated every game with his bouncy face of hair and his sweatshirt emblazoned (I swear) Jesus Christ Superstar. He organized seances, for all I know. Some salt had appeared in his beard since he had begun to play apprentice to my sorcerer, and even I inwardly registered satisfaction to hear, in his sermons, a diminishment of "you know's" and Jungian

---

*White-haired Miss Froth; excuse me, I assumed you two had met before. She had your efficiency, Ms. Prynne, but not your heft.
†How's that for womb/tomb, life-in-death, etc.? Or maybe I want to say that the corpse, for spurning my steering, is a lemon.

protomyths, a growing chumminess of Word and words, a modulation of his preppy drawl into a penetrating nasal enthusiasm that arrowed forth from his mouth our denomination's curare-tipped formulae; in the silence of the congregation, that protoplasmic vacuum, I detected a spark or two of unwandered attention from my blank bankers and bakers, a tiny willingness to harken. Ned appeared to them as a new creature. Americans have been conditioned to respect newness, whatever it costs them. Ned's queerness, I also thought, was, in the developing pan of his new confidence, becoming less shadowy, emerging as a faintly fussy and rococo edge for his gestures and dress. It was becoming, really: *potens* was becoming *ens*. My own miserably heterosexual example may have helped him here. Alicia's new car, blood-orange by sulphurous lamplight, appeared at his curb, but not so often, and I imagined them talking, shoeless, through veils of that desexing fumigant called grass. What would they be talking about? Me, I imagined, and dropped into sleep like a shoe.

"Ned, you have a minute?"

"But of course, my rector."

"I mean, I don't want to keep you from going down to the jail and bailing out any of your Jesus freaks for healing without a license." It was better, I thought, that we talk thus; the truth with love, St. Paul prescribes, at a mix of 3-to-1 for normal engines.

Ned's narrow teeth bared on the back wall of his beard. "Nor do I," he smiled, "want to hold you from telling any housewife why she shouldn't murder her husband. Or why she should."

I cleared my throat in the presbyterian manner.

"About Alicia. How do you feel?"

The teeth hid. "She's a friend," Ned said.

I said, "I can see that from my bedroom window. But *intra cathedra*, as an integral part of divine service. Would you raise any objection to our letting her go?"

The preppy fink returned, the clergyman momentarily startled out of his frock. "Why would you can such a dear little blonde bimbo?" His eyes, an intricately notched green, began to flicker as he spun calculations of my sexual politics through his brain, and came up with an answer near enough right to make his flip tone regrettable.

I forgave him it. I said, believing, "She's too much at home behind the altar rail. She'd make every Sunday a Bach fest. I've spoken to her, but the fugues keep tumbling on and on. It's not just me. Others have said so. It's a case of"—and even in the throes of perfidy I had to laugh—"bad vibes."

A dim smile winked in answer. His eyes were undergoing calculations again, and a happy answer shot from them. "If you say so," said Ned. "It's your decision."

"I'd naturally prefer to have it *our* decision. Let's put personal considerations aside. Alicia will survive, she gives lessons, another church will surely take her on, her ex-husband sends her something. Our responsibility here is to the congregation that attends in expectation of hearing the word of God."

He said, only gently evasive, "Actually, I've been at services that have done away with music entirely. You recite poetry instead of singing. There're these great dynamic silences. It can really grab the inner man."

"Quakerism's been done. But I repeat, would you object to our giving Alicia notice? I'll break it to her myself, of course."

"Not really," Ned drawled. "I do think the girl was getting stale." The calculations in his eyes had settled; he offered with a clever diffidence, "If you want to think about another organist, I have a friend you should hear."

"Female?"

"Oh, God, no!" Now my Ned took the initiative laughing; where his beard grew sparse his speckled cheeks flushed with the wine of glee. "Male! A *very* serious person. Unmarried. *Very* sensitive."

"That sensitive? How does he feel toward the Church?"

"A*dores* it. In matters of doctrine," Ned said, and it was a pleasure to see him so animated, "Donald is con*sid*erably to the right of our Lord and Saviour Jesus Christ!"

"Ned and I have decided to let Alicia go," I told Jane in passing, by way of refectorial offering, as I innocently arose from the lunch she had given me.

We ate when just the two of us at the kitchen table; she turned from the sink, her face intent and white I assumed from contemplation of the porcelain sink, and, the dish she was drying flashing like a shield, advanced toward me with the tread of an army of women. "You're firing her because she slept with you?"

"Not at all. Because she toots her horn too loud. Her sleeping with me is to her credit as far as I'm concerned. But she doesn't do it any more. She's rather like you in that respect."

"Shit," my good wife said, an expression she had picked up from the children, or from feminist talk shows. "I think I'm doing heroically, just to stay under the same roof with you and put a respectable front on all this."

"All this what?"

"All this *you*!" Jane and I never expressed anger. We had suffered incommodities tacitly since the days of noiseless petting above her father's study; I felt her abandoning our married style, and timorously exulted. "It's too much," she was going on, "you just *won't* do that to this woman, Tom. She's over there in that tacky house trying to keep those kids and herself together and you *can't* do this to her."

"Why can't I?" I simply wanted to be told; as I have said, Jane was good, and goodness knows.

But she took it for arguing. Her words came out at a novel pitch, sharped, and speeded, as if she were hurrying messages over a cable about to break. "Because everyone will wonder why and you can't afford that. Because it's an evil careless selfish thing to do. Because there are going to be some very destructive consequences."

"Such as what?"

"Such as *this*," Jane said, and let fall the plate in her hands; it smashed; from the larger fragments on the linoleum I saw it had been one of Mother's rosy set of Royal Bristol, whose rim pattern of intertwined arabesques I had, during boring grown-up dinners given by my parents, traced and retraced with my eyes until it seemed the very pattern of eternity.

The interview with Alicia was far from painful. Her house, and the afternoon light, had such pleasant associations for me I sang the chime phrase as I rang it and, once inside, stretched in the armchair, overcome by drowsy ease. Her children were not yet home from school. She had greeted me with surprise but led me in willingly; in retrospect I see she might have thought

I had repented, I could not live without her, I was leaving Jane. Alicia had been painting the woodwork in the little girl's room. She was wearing denims worn to thinnest blue on each buttock and a man's (whose?) striped shirt with its tail out and a flecked bandana over her hair; she pushed back a stray arc of hair with the back of a hand whose raising released a dove of turpentine scent. She was slow to shed the pleasant harried self-forgetful manner of women working, their grace all unconscious; ah Lord. Each charming second of her deshabille pressed my brain heavier toward the forgetting of my errand. A thick diagonal shaft of dust stood in the room as witness, anxious with Brownian motion. Alicia offered, uncertain, coffee or sherry. In the days, not forgotten, when I came to make love, Portuguese rosé was served in bed. She had wanted to fatten me, the hopelessly lean. I stretched preeningly in my chair, refusing all beverages, and said, "How would you like to get out of your rut?"

"I might like it," Alicia said, perching near me on a footstool, her kneecaps thrusting nearly through the threadbare cloth.

"Have you noticed," I asked, "that you and I seem to be at odds a lot lately?" Above her head (the bandana eclipsing all but a sunstruck rim of her hair) I could see, at an angle flatter than from her bedroom, through her back yard and its clothes pole and blue-hearted birdbath to her garage and an oil truck idling in the alley.

"I *have* noticed," she said, "and I've decided you may be right; I've been too ambitious. I'll go back to Tabernacle Favorites. It'll be less of a strain on me, too."

How wonderfully she was acting the role, of my organist, with the mistress locked inside, breathless to emerge, if I could but produce the winking key. But, "No," I said, "No," drawling it affectedly as my curate, and stretching my legs again in this absurd sleepy ease, "I think your ambition is great, your touch is great, your music is marvellous, and rather than cramp your style I would like to see you hired by another church."

She shifted on the stool, bringing her knees more primly together, but otherwise gave no sign of injury. "You would," she repeated, her mouth tightened into its slightly sideways, gum-chewing set.

"Isn't that good news? You won't have to watch me teasing the congregation any more. You won't have to put up with a preacher so deaf he butts in whenever there's a two-beat rest. You won't be reminded," I ventured in another voice, "of—us."

"I didn't mind that," she said. "I didn't mind being reminded." She brushed back hair from her temple and faced me. "So I'm fired."

"Ned and I agree it would be best for the church."

"Did Ned agree?" She interrupted my contemplated statements about her bonus pay, about the coming weeks of interim. "And the deacons," she asked. "Mustn't they approve?"

Nod. *My* nod, though it seemed to be floating free of me, and got stuck on the ceiling, where I couldn't stop looking at it. "A formality," I said. "At the next meeting."

Alicia stood up. Chin up. Shirt hanging straight from her breasts' bold shelf. I had to stand too, though I had planned to talk on, to speculate about our futures, to reminisce. My body felt heavy, like an old sun. "Thanks, Tom," my hostess said, and I felt her mind moving back to her upstairs painting, "for telling me yourself. For not putting it into a letter or over the telephone."

I thought she meant this sincerely. I thought it *had* been good of me to come and risk a scene that, praise God, had not transpired. I was as full of illusions as a sunbeam of dust. I wondered if it would be remiss of me not to attempt to kiss her good-bye. Nothing in her stance invited it, so I said instead, stooping (at our old partings she had always been above me), "You *do* see that it's a blessing in disguise, don't you?"

"I'm sure I will," she said, "though right now"—her smile was encouraging—"I can't stop seeing the disguise."

Beyond her shoulder lay a faded loop rug; I wanted to curl up on her warm floor like a cat. Did I make an attempt to? In memory she seems to lift a hand as if to hold me upright. "Just go, Tom. Don't say any more. I'll manage."

Or some such. As I stepped into the outdoors, which was by contrast chill as lake water, her door snapped behind me (locked?) and I felt a premonitory disorientation, like a fairgoer whose wallet has been picked from his hip pocket but who, at first, only subconsciously misses the comradely backpat of its weight.

19

WE THOUGHT a motel might help. All August Frankie had been with her family in some dank resort northward, playing tether ball and canoeing amid lugubrious pines, feeding mosquitoes on the nectar in her veins, admiring Harlow's dragonlike skill at igniting brickets. September was distracted by the return of children to school, October by my flurry with Alicia, and anyway the old happiness diet of narthex necking and sneak sexual snacks had become starvation rations with this new, intimidatingly exquisite love. We needed time if not eternity. We cobbled up a tryst for around All Saints' Day. Since even out of town my face might be recognized (by a buried man's mourner, by a Sunday school student matured, by a renegade Friar Tuck who might hail me from some ecumenical banquet past), Frankie did the distasteful business with the register and the key; she emerged from the red-blinking OFFICE (ORIFICE, I kept reading it as) in her good cloth coat as cool as emergent from matins, having tipped the collection plate. She took the driver's seat of her car (my drab Dart adrift in the twinkling tin sea of a shopping-center parking lot) and drove the little distance, a short chip shot (keep those wrists *stiff*!) to the door with our number on it. Scuttle, scuttle, and don't forget the paper bag containing our lunch, *vin*, and plastic forks and spoons, picnic in the shade, bucolic customs revisited.

The room was unlike this one in accidents rather than essence. Indeed the increment of profit from the tribute we paid then and of the vast drafts of Christian charity supporting my holiday here may eventually trickle to a single bank account, just as a drizzle in Pittsburgh and a flash flood in Casper mingle droplets in the New Orleans delta. The room had a big bed, a bright bathroom, an empty bureau or two, thick curtains that could be drawn, a wastebasket to catch our tangerine peels, a mirror to catch our skins. We had everything; we were as astronauts; we were more than the world.

Frankie, in one of those spatial delusions to which I had been lately prey, seemed to fill our chamber with her delicacy as a spider fills a corner with filaments; she moved here and there, bestowed bags paper and hand, disposed foldingly of her cloth coat, disclosed a black dress so simple and stylish and perfectly chosen for its few moments of motel wear that I wanted to weep, unsnapping it and peeling its softness up, save that it was too early for me to weep, my impotence had yet to be demonstrated. Her high-heeled black shoes, her stockinged feet with their heels flat on the carpet (so childish for all their shapeliness, and childish the pressure of her hands on my head for support as I tugged the smart shoes off; the years dodged away between me and the time when girls at grammar school had pulled my hair, when I had hair, when there was recess, and licorice belts, and paper snowmen glued to the windows, and nobody told us that Jesus had not *really* been born the day after a snowstorm), her feet then bare, bared by my reaching up to her waist to tug down the tights that, so transparent upon her, darkened to a black puddle from which her feet stepped gleaming, every bone a jewel, the toes a stung little pink: lovely, she was lovely at every stage of undress, I could have stopped anywhere and had a creature of paradise, she had so considerately dressed herself for my undressing, lovely in her dress, lovely without it, lovely in the fine-beaten necklace and bracelets and the wristwatch she removed without my asking, lovely even the almost-boy without her bra but still in pants, a topless *mignonette* adequately attired for the beach at St.-Tropez, and, these pants (enhanced with a ribbon of ruffle and a floral weave of watermark delicacy) flippingly shed, lovely in only her fleece and fingernails.

She stood amused, looking over her shoulder at herself in the mirror, waiting for me and my move. More roughly undressing myself, I realized her air, tentative and considerate, of dealing with something fragile, did not have to do with herself and her nakedness, which only my awe lifted out of the ordinary for her, but with me, whether even in this perfect and purchased seclusion I could break through her skein of glory and, in the human way, screw her. And my sensing of this doubt swelled my qualm to its familiar insurmountable dimension.

We lay together, played together, made light of each other; I caressed her and let myself be caressed and finally, my bit part stubbornly shying from the role of hero, gave her a climax with my face between her thighs. How tigressishly, how self-forgetfully, she pushed for those last, breakthrough beats! I was pleased. We ate. The wine had already been half-consumed. Our stolen hours were dwindling. I sought to explain myself.

"I can only think," I said, "it has something to do with your being such a staunch churchwoman."

"But—" She delicately halted.

"The others are too? Jane and Alicia? Jane doesn't believe in God, she believes in the Right Thing. Alicia even less. She likes music and men and that's all she has the spiritual budget for."

"And am I," Frankie asked, shedding shyness, "the only other—?"

"Not exactly." The melancholy and muffled one-shots behind the choir robes I did not want to betray, even to her. Right of therapeutic privacy. "But even if the woman *is* a church member, she doesn't embody faith like you do. You seem really hipped on it. The way you used to look up at me through your veil."

"I'm not veiled now," she precisely said, and bit a Butter Nutter cookie with her smile. "And *am* I"—speaking crumbs, one hand cupped beneath her chin to catch them, lest they make the sheets hurt—"so hipped on it?"

"I think so. Do you believe in God the Father Almighty, maker of Heaven and Earth?"

She blushed and, her voice as modest as possible, answered, "Yes." A fury gathered within me, an amateur plumber's frustrated rage at being unable to dissolve my lump and unclog my ability, my after all hideously common and as they say God-given ability, to deliver myself into this loved woman's loins.

"Say you don't," I commanded.

Frankie didn't understand.

"Say you don't believe in God. Say you think God is an old Israeli fart. Say it."

She wanted to, she even took breath into her lungs to utter something, but couldn't.

Easy stages, I thought. "Say 'fart.'" She did. I gave her more words to say. She passed them through her lips obediently, untastingly, like a child in catechetical class. The corners of her lips curved, pronouncing; she was amused. Our litany excited me; she noticed this, and moved to capitalize; at a new angle I admired the sequence of her vertebrae and the symmetrical flats of her winglike scapulae; I pushed her off, and brought her face up to the level of mine, and held it so hard her cheekbones whitened and her eyes went round. "*How* can you believe, Frankie? How can any sane person?"

"Many do," she told me. Then amended, "Some do."

"It's *so* ridiculous," I said. "It's always been ridiculous. There was this dreadful tribal chauvinism of the Jews. Then some young megalomaniac came along and said, Look at Me. And about a dozen people did. And then . . . We don't know what happened, nobody knows, all we know is that as the Roman Empire went rotten one mystery cult prevailed over the many others. People were as messy then as they are now—it could have been any cult. And the damn thing's still among us. It's an establishment, Frankie love. A racket. Believe me. The words are empty. The bread is just bread. The biggest sales force in the world selling empty calories—Jesus Christ. What is it, Frankie? A detergent? A deodorant? What does it do, Frankie? This invisible odorless thing."

"It lets people live?" The feel of her fragile small jaw struggling to move under my fingers was exciting. My grip had tightened the fine wrinkles from her face.

"It lets them die," I corrected. "It likes them to die. This summer among many delightful distractions I watched a fifteen-year-old boy die of leukemia. He was an ordinary boy, a little duller than most; he couldn't understand why him, and I couldn't either. But he was old enough and bright enough to know what a meaningless foul trick it was; why don't you? Suppose it had been Julie? She's fifteen now, isn't she? Suppose she's struck by a car, while we lie here? How would you feel?"

"Terrible. Sinful." Her eyes, though watering with pain, still searched my face for what I wanted, so she could give it.

I dropped my hands to her throat. A fasces of veins, pumping. I asked her, "If a demon were to enter me and make me strangle you, do you think God would stop it?"

"No." She was frightened, yet tittered; my sudden touch had tickled.

I hit her. First a tap with a cupped hand, then really a hit, with open palm and stiff wrist so our chamber split at the noise, and all the gossamer threads her love had spun were swept away. "You dumb cunt," I said, "how can you be so dumb as to believe in God the Father, God the Son, and God the Holy Ghost? Tell me you really don't. Tell me, so I can fuck you. Tell me you know down deep there's nothing. The dead stink, Frankie; for a while they stink and then they're just bones and then there's not even that. Forever and ever. Isn't that so? Say it."

"I can't."

"Why not, sweet? Why not? Please." I got to my knees and crouched above her, I wanted to lift her away, to safety, away from myself. Paradoxically, I suppose.

"I can't," she cried under me, lightly twisting.

I brushed away the hair agitation had tossed into her eyes. "Why can't you? You know there's nothing. Tell me there's nothing. Tell me it's a fraud, I'm a fraud, it's all right, there's just us and we'll die, there's just your dear cunt, just your dear ass, your tits, your dear mouth, your dear, dear eyes." I touched her eyelids and thought of pressing down.

She bit her lower lip rather than speak.

I crouched lower, urging, clowning. "There is Noboboddy, Frankie, with his faithful dog Nada. There must be nothing. You can't think there's a God. You know you can't. What's your reason? Give me one reason, Frankie."

"You," she said, in a voice half-hostile, and this hostility brought her soul so close I moaned and bowed my head to take my gaze from hers; I saw my own phallus erect up to my navel. She spread her legs quickly, but not quickly enough, for though I entered her, repentant tenderness overtook me; her pelvic bone gnashed against mine as I melted inside her; she came, wide to whatever was, while I couldn't, and it became my time to weep again. She pulled my face down to hers, so roughly I resisted; she thirstily kissed my tears.

"Forgive me," I of course said, "I don't know what happens to me. But at least it was something for you, this time, wasn't it?"

She nodded tremulously, still lapping my tears; her tongue felt so large and strong and single I remembered the kiss when her mouth had seemed to have many petals. She formed words. "You must think of this," she told me, "as holy too."

I rolled from her, her fair body sunk in a trough of sweat. The fresh air on my skin reconstituted the world. "O.K.," I said. "That's good practical theology. I'll try. I think I'll get there next time."

And events did not prove me a false prophet. There was no next time. Distilling my ministry, I find this single flaw: Frankie Harlow never did get to feel my seed inside her, sparkling and burning like a pinch of salt.

I hurried up the brick walk fearful that my motel adventure had consumed more time than even a deathbed might explain away; I need not have worried. In my absence the world had moved beyond any demand for my lies. Ned was there, with Jane; they were sitting in the living-room, in the easy chairs opposing each other by the fireplace, as often when I returned from a night errand in the errant era when I had hoped they might fall in love. Only now there was no fire in the fireplace, the weak daylight of an autumn suppertime bleached romantic shadows from the stage set, and both were sober. As I entered the room, passing beneath the oaken archway with its divinely worked tympanum (cruel as a guillotine if it fell) of knobs and spindles, they both stood, absurdly in unison. I feared the boys might overhear whatever they would say; but from the far end of the house sounded the electric sloshing of television's swill.

Jane glanced at Ned and took a step forward to speak. "Tom, Alicia—"

"Didn't like being canned," Ned interposed, achieving, with a springier step than Jane's, a parallel position on the rug. "So—" He respectfully nodded toward my better half.

"So she went to Gerry Harlow's bank and told him all she knew."

"Which was evidently quite an earful," Ned said, drawling in his vile old style.

After waiting for me to respond, Jane went on, endearingly pained, her forehead looking skinned and her mouth so taut it seemed out of sync, "Not just about you and her, but about—"

"You and everybody," Ned finished, his lustrous beard curling in a thousand smiles.

Jane said, "He was here, for an hour this afternoon, very upset—evidently Frankie wasn't at home or anywhere—and is calling for a meeting of the deacons at his home tonight."

"Very hush-hush," Ned said.

"He of course wants it kept as quiet as possible, a sudden vacation, say, we could say a nervous breakdown or whatever they call it now—"

"Gerry called our good bishop," said Ned, "who told him there was a place even, out West, for cases like yours; evidently cases like yours are the coming thing."

My bishop: a brick-red man in black sitting in a brick-red city rimmed with black industry. To him I was a black pinhead on a map of Christian services—filling stations, refineries, sales offices—within the region. *Prick*, I could be moved. I felt tiny in his eyes and stereoptically huge, a pallid monstrosity beyond the pale, in these two gazes, Ned's warmed by a not unfriendly froggy-green satisfaction, Jane's cooled by goodness and pity and a hopeless blue sense of distance. Without a witness there she would have run into my sooty arms and homogenized with me into one gray one. Ned's presence saved her this. They were waiting for me to speak.

I laughed and asked, "Why do you two remind me of a pair of hi-fi speakers?"

A waste of a question, since they couldn't help it, they were a pair, my instinct had been right, a matched pair of prigs.

20

O, LORD.

Another Sunday is upon us.

Our text shall be taken from Deuteronomy, the thirty-second book: "He found him in a desert place."

Moses is speaking of Jacob, but it might well be of himself, or of a dozen other of the God-chosen men of the Old Testament. The verse continues, if failing memory serves, "He found him in a desert land, and in the waste howling wilderness; he led him about, he instructed him, he kept him as the apple of his eye."

I would propose, my dear brethren, who have deserted the world and been deserted by it, to meditate this morning not upon the loathsome Old Testament God, His vengeful plagues and pestilences and His preposterous obsession with circumcision and with His own name, nor upon those enigmatic brutes, such as Moses and David and Samson, upon whom His favor incorrigibly and unlodgeably rests; but upon the desert, the wilderness as it is more often called, that encircles the world of Bible as parched sand girdles an oasis and bitter black space surrounds our genial and hazy planet.

Though the drama of the Bible is islanded by history, the wilderness is always there, pre-existent and enduring. Adam and Eve are sent forth from their disobedience into it, and our Lord Jesus at the dawn of His ministry retired unto it, to be tempted of Satan. There, as Mark with his characteristic pungence tells us, He "was with the wild beasts; and the angels ministered unto Him." And for each of the forty days of His fast and vigil there, the children of Israel wandered a year of their forty in the wilderness of Sin, or Zĭn, or Sinai, wherein their thirst was often keen, so keen that on at least one occasion the Lord left off His fearsome chiding of His children and led Moses to the Rock of Horeb, and bid him smite, "which turned the rock into a standing water, the flint into a fountain of waters." Our soul, the Psalmist says, *thirsteth* for God —Whose doctrine, we are told elsewhere, drops as the rain, "as the small rain upon the tender herb, and as the showers upon the grass." "He leadeth me beside the still waters; He restoreth my soul"—the special world of God within the Bible is an oasis world; the world beyond, the world of the Lord's wider creation, is a desert.

Now we dwell within the desert. Its air, clean and sweet as mythical ether, astounds our faces as we emerge from the shelter of this benign hostel; we see, on the golf course, the frantic sprinklers doing a dervish dance to keep the heartbeat of green alive; lifting our eyes to the hills, or accompanying our excellent Ms. Prynne on one of her well-shepherded nature walks, we confront a cosmos of fragile silica, rock flaky with long baking and inhospitable as a stove-top to the touch. Seeming lakes prove mirages of shimmer, or else gleaming *playas* paved with salt, not the answer to thirst's prayer but its very mockery. For all the taming clichés of tourism and frequentation that a gross and frivolous empire can impose, but a few quick steps from the beaten path, into the solitude beneath a red rock, serve to convince us that this grandeur is heedless; its breath is a dragon's, its innumerable eyes are blind. Gratefully we return to our haven of cool and shade, and sport in the swimming pool whose water, pumped from deep in the parched earth as greedily as the Bushman in the Kalahari sucks life from the sand through a straw, draws upon the precarious water table and subtly causes the desert to extend itself elsewhere.

For the desert is growing, make no mistake. Pastoral man is more predaceous than the pelted hunter. Entire herdsman nations in Northern Africa have been grazed to desert, where famine now reigns. Many a green landscape where our Saviour walked, and Eden itself, and civilization's very seedbed in Sumeria, have become blanched valleys, home to none but the sheeted Arab. According to geologists, there is more desert now than at any era in the earth's billions of years. Utah was once all a lake. Dinosaurs waded through swamps where now lizards skitter across the boulders of their petrified bones.

And in other senses as well is not the desert also growing? The pavements of our cities are deserted, emptied by fear. In the median strips of our highways, naught blows but trash. In our monotonous suburbs houses space themselves as evenly as creosote bushes, whose roots poison the earth around. The White House itself, intended by its builders to be the center of probity and the symbol of candor, seems instead a burrow wherefrom the scorpion of falsehood emerges only to sting, and sting again, again, and to hide as before.

In the parish hearts it was once our vocation, brethren, to safeguard and nurture, did we not feel a frightful desert, of infertile apathy, of withering scorn, of—to use a strange Greek word suddenly commonplace—*anorexia*, the antithesis of appetite? These barbaric Biblical heroes whom Jahweh appointed the apple of His eye—what sins did they not commit, save this one? Virile bridegrooms lusty for the world, where are they now? Is not even faithlessness, which once assaulted our piety with the vigor of a purer piety, now a desert beyond reclamation, a feeble and featureless wilderness where none but the most degenerate of demonic superstitions—astrology, augury, Hinduism—spring up in the hearts of the young, until they too soon cease to be young, and nurture in their blasted greenness not even these poor occult weeds? What has our technology, that boasted its intention to reconstruct paradise, shown itself to be but an insidious spreader of poisons? Where has it landed us, as its triumph and emblem, but upon the most absolute desert of all, the lunar surface where not even a lichen or a microbe lives?

And yet, and yet . . . For those of us whose heads God has turned, so our very collars are shaped like a pivot, there must always be an "and yet." And yet, how gratefully our lungs inhale this thin desert air! How full, to the acclimated vision, is this landscape devoid of buildings and forests! How luminous the rare rain! How precious the sparse cactus-flowers!

We all know the name Death Valley. How many of us have heard of *La Palma de la Mano de Dios*? So the Spaniards called the harshest basin of the American desert as they knew it. The Palm of God's Hand. Are we not all here, in the palm of God's hand? And do we not see, around us (with the knowledgeable guidance of our dear Ms. Prynne), the Joshua tree lifting its arms awkwardly in prayer, and hear the organ-pipe cactus thundering its transcendent hymn? What a chorale of praise floats free from the invisible teeming of desert life—the peccary and the ocelot, the horned lizard and the blacktailed jack rabbit, the kangaroo rat that needs never to drink water and the century plant that blooms but once in decades. How ingenious and penetrant is life! Living-stone cactuses mimic the stones they push between, whip snakes toss themselves from bush to bush, the mesquite plant can send taproots down a hundred feet, the ocotillo tree sheds its leaves to minimize evaporation and continues photosynthesis through the green of its bark. Birds nest in thorns. Tiny pupfish, transformed from the piscine inhabitants of the once-vast lakes, survive in the salt-saturated pools that remain. More wondrous still, tadpole shrimp hatch, grow, mate, and die all in the few hours of a flash-flood puddle's duration, and with their dried corpses leave eggs to hatch when the next puddle appears in that place many years in the future. The seeds of desert plants wait cunningly; a mere sprinkling does not tempt them to breach their carapaces; only an acid-stirring deluge dissolves. And then the desert is carpeted with primroses and poppies and mallows and zinnias, and the tiny ground daisy and the desert five-spot and sand mat and rock gilia entrust their miniature petals to the glare of the sun, and the Mariposa lily remembers itself, and the sticky yucca blossom invites the yucca moth, and the night-blooming cereus its lunar brother, and the tiny claret-cup cactus holds up its cup to drink. And when the king of the desert dies—when dies the great saguaro cactus—it leaves like a man a skeleton, its soft flesh falling from the woody ribs that held erect its fifteen tons of nobility.

What lesson might we draw from this undaunted profusion? The lesson speaks itself. Live. Live, brothers, though there be naught but shame and failure to furnish forth your living. To those of you who have lost your place, I say that the elf owl makes a home in the pulp of a saguaro. To those upon whom recent events still beat down mercilessly, I say that the coyote waits out the day in the shade. To those who find no faith within themselves, I say no seed is so dry it does not hold the code of life within it, and that except a corn of wheat fall into the ground and die, it abideth alone; but if it die, it bringeth forth much fruit. Blessed, blessed are the poor in spirit.

Brothers, we have come to a tight place. Let us be, then, as the chuckwalla, who, when threatened, *runs* to a tight place, to a crevice in the burning rock of the desert. Once there, does he shrink in shame? No! He puffs himself up, inflates his mortal frame to half again its normal size, fills that crevice as the living soul fills the living body, and cannot be dislodged by the talon or fang of any enemy.

We *are* found in a desert place.

We *are* in God's palm.

We *are* the apple of His eye.

Let us be grateful *here*, and here rejoice. Amen.

21

Do I DETECT an extra whiteness, as of erasure, in the blank space beneath the conclusion of yesterday's sermon? Holding the suspicious spot up to the light, do I not espy the faint linear impress of a pencilled word? There seems to be a capital "N," in a pedestrian school hand—can the word be "Nice"? Ideal Reader, can it be you? If the word was "Nice," why the naughty erasure, the negative second thought, the niggardly

Indian-giving? But bless you, whoever you are, if you are, for this even so tentative intrusion into these pages' solipsism, this pale smudge fainter than the other galaxy that flirts with the naked eye in the constellation of Andromeda.

Three weeks ago today I was put aboard the silver bird, the chariot of fire, that brought me here, by a little windblown party of Jane, my two sons, and Ned—windblown for mid-November had come to our green flat land, and the airport was flatter than flat, so that even the first drifts of snow, thin and bitter as crusts of salt on a dead lake's shore, had no rest, but undulated and scuttled against our hurrying shoes, and my witnesses had no shelter from the whirlwind of my translation. Stephen was crying because of puzzlement, and Martin because he had overheard and understood a bit too much, and Jane because weeping was a wife's right thing, and Ned because of the wind.

Frankie and I had managed our tears (and even here, I could scarcely come, so forgetful of grief did her perfection render me; my ducts barely squeezed forth a drop of ichor each against the pressure of her tailoring and the shimmer of the Courrèges scarf mauve at the throat of her chalkstripe suit and the nicety of her gray-gloved hands, hands whose naked ghosts haunted the bower of our pleached memories—her hands being shoved testily into her pockets of mink in my office, her hand with its moist palm leading me by one of mine into her basement, her lovely hand caressing my limpness, her alert hand cupped to catch crumbs from her mouth in the motel) at some narrow coffee nook in the city we were suburban to. I faltered, "The first time we kissed, you had given me coffee."

"It gives me the shakes," she said.

"Gerry really doesn't know?"

She shook her head silently; her own tears had found, on the glaze of her cheeks, fine channels to follow.

I said, counselling to the end, "Maybe you should tell him. You can't rebuild on sand. On lies."

Frankie, sitting proper across the little Formica table, which was snow-white and ice-slick and held within it a pink blur that was her face reflected, leaned forward an inch and pronounced distinctly, in that garden of a voice whose far corner was shaded by magnolia, words of an alarming vehemence. "I don't want to rebuild, I want to destroy. Everything but us. I don't want that bullying simpleton wallowing around in what you and I had."

"We didn't have much," I pointed out. "I don't mean *you*, of course, I mean—"

She knew what I meant; her gloved hand waved it away. "It would have happened, and been beautiful," my dear devotee avowed.

"Don't destroy," I begged. "You have so much. The house, the furniture—" Perhaps my solicitude for her furniture induced that smile of fine slyness detectable behind her veil —no, she had no veil. Like my reverence for her furniture, a slip. "Think of Julie," I said.

She lifted her wide gray eyes—wide as the local horizon is wide, too wide to be taken in all at once, which is disorienting, which may explain . . . but never mind. As when she had come to me to complain about Alicia's music, her tone seemed alarmed. She said, "I'd come with you, you know."

"You can't. You mustn't. I wouldn't let you. You stay here." Accustomed to ambiguity from me, she lowered her face as if slapped. Then I tried to make myself cry, with the weak results you know.

Alicia stayed unseen in the embarrassed week between her revelation and my departure. She needn't have; the very vulgar thoroughgoingness of this her second betrayal—as contrasted with the wistful muddle of her first—had a happy liberating effect upon me; for until now I had not quite yielded up the hope that she would take me back, on an idle afternoon, into her bed, with its quilted sunburst. It would have been so easy for her, and easy for me, to be rejoined to that triumphant lazy body she called forth from the crypt of my daily existence. Now that she had repaid me in full for my treachery (that is, for my staying with Jane and the cloth and the parsonage), I was quits with my guilt and my hope. Whatever guilt there was, she could shoulder.

Ah, I seem, in that lost vineland, to take the stance of a haughty white hunter who wishes to stroll into the jungle with his hands unburdened; the life I have sorrily described is as a departure point at which I am busy hiring various women as porters for the great train of guilt that is my baggage. Jane carried a load for not adoring me as would a mistress or Mary Magdalene; Frankie bore some for adoring me so much I became with her a desexed angel; and now Alicia, toward whom I had felt heavy for failing to make her my wife when she was so much my woman (see earlier etymology), took on her head the bulky bundle—the struck tent—of my collapsed career. Well, she was thick-waisted and tough and could tote it. Babies and guilt, women are built for lugging.

Time had ceased for my father; whether I was away a month or an hour was the same to him; I was a recurrent apparition that tripped a circuit in his brain. "Ras the rascal," he hailed me fondly, "still up to his mischief. When was it you dipped Lena Horsman's thick braid in the ink well and she shook her head so it spattered across the linen shirt our mother had mended for Sunday wear? Laugh! If ever there was justice done; she told us how you took her dog fashion, *comme les chiens*, her little *derrière* upthrust for demonstration like a double helping of *glace vanille*, eh? Ah, well, we can't be saints all the time, the Lord would get bored. It was a vomitous crossing, and I dread the one back."

"Daddy, please try to listen to what I'm saying."

He looked at me with terrifying minuscule eyes. "What do *you* care," he said, his indignation beginning, "about the capital of Bangladesh? What's it to you, if Bebe Rebozo has a real name? This false hilarity amid so many appliances, whom do you think it fools? I asked for clean walls and a view of the lake, and you give me indecencies in charcoal and curtains drawn tighter than a bear trap. I know some call it art. I call it blasphemy and insubordination; I have a right to my power tools." He leaned forward so anxiously his great woolly head jerked, and I feared it might roll from his shoulders. With these confidences came from his mouth a meaty scent of the lunch he had just consumed. "I have a son," he told me, "whose duty it is to incarcerate fools like you."

"Daddy, *I* am your son. It's me, Tommy. They're sending me away. They say I've disgraced the ministry."

His little eyes blinked as if singed, and seemed to clear. "Well, no doubt you have," he said wearily, in a voice that fit the moment, that had abandoned the effort of filling its many other spheres. "No doubt your mother's blood, it had to tell. She was a tart, you know. I wept to control her, I tried reason and passion, faith and works, but she needed more of the world's goods and pleasure than I could supply, so she turned from my bed to you and your indolent friends, steeped in the muck of inherited wealth."

"No," I pleaded, desperate to hold him to reality, my reality, that only he could forgive. "I am your son. Something's gone wrong. I have no faith. Or, rather, I have faith, but it doesn't seem to apply."

He heard my cry and inside his hollow head struggled to keep his mind from sliding away. "I gave her," he explained to me slowly, his voice doubting the words but unable to frame better, "what comfort I could. Had you not appeared, she would have been contented enough."

He was apologizing to me; I seized this hint of a bond. "What shall we *do*," I asked, "to keep her with us?" I touched his hand, his ancient mole-mottled hand with mine, that was more lightly mottled, and becoming ancient. His skin was cold. "Daddy, I'm frightened. Tell me what to do. What shall I become? I wanted to become better than *you*."

"There's none of that," he said, his voice having entered some sixth realm, beyond indignation; and the thought went through me chillingly—not a brain-thought, but a blood-thought—that he would not live till my return. His hand slid from under mine and got on top of it, and patted absentmindedly. "There's none of that," he reassured me, "until we get to be a little bit older."

At the airport I abruptly squatted down and took my two boys, so quickly they could not shy away, one in each arm. To Martin I said, holding tighter as his wiry body tensed, perhaps angry with me from what he understood of my flight, "Be nice to your brother while I'm away. And take it easy on yourself." To Stephen I said, "Don't get too turned on by anything." His still babyish face looked puzzled and disappointed; I tried to explain. "Don't listen to the radio instead of doing homework. Don't argue with your brother more than you must. When I come back I want you to tell me your month has been hassle-free." And I let them go, and stood up, and kissed Jane. She was pale, and there was a little crust, but it broke through, like a thin mirror breaking, and there was nothing to say, as when one is alone.

Nice?

22

WELL, ANOTHER INTERVIEW from that tiger cage of a claustrophobic week returns to me. Dimly. Too many shimmering cactoid days, too many 8-irons drifting just to the right of the green, too many inside straights that didn't quite fill have intervened. Gerry Harlow came to my office in the church. Our official interview, the one with him barking ultimatums that packed the combined clout of the deaconage and the bishopric (he didn't bark, to be honest; he "issued" them, through clenched teeth or, more exactly still, out of a close-shaved jaw whose masseters kept bulging), had taken place in the parsonage, the night after the night after my motel afternoon. This was days later.

This was different. He wanted something. I had been cleaning up my desk, so Ned as acting minister could have some drawers. I motioned Harlow into the counsellee's chair and sat down myself. He looked like a man who had been out in a wind too long; his face had a sensitive high glaze and in the chair he leaned forward, his lips stretched back from his teeth like a skier on a tight turn. He hoped, as a starter, that I understood he had been acting as a spokesman of the church and parish, rather than in any private capacity.

I said, Of course. I said I had admired his efficiency and clarity of purpose.

There was more stiff and manly palaver. I was glad I was not applying for a loan. This fellow knew how to wear authority's spacesuit. I thought of Frankie's skin against his and felt her shiver. He had the astronaut's lingo, too. Most of

Alicia's allegations had "checked out." (The teenaged bride, especially, had been cheerfully circumstantial, as if her episode with me had been a TV episode she were redescribing. But even the gaunt divorcee had, offhandedly, confessed. As I have preached in these pages, women really don't see much wrong with it. Indeed I was grateful to Harlow for putting me back in touch with some negative directives, from male mission control center.) Since, he said, I had consented to be launched into a leave-of-absence, this "operation" was a "closed book" for the time being as far as he was concerned.

I reeled out six or eight seconds' worth of silence.

But, he said, one thing, frankly, was bothering "the hell" out of him. Harlow deliberated a microsecond over the "hell," but then calculated that, reverend or not, in view of his data, I could take it. The thing was this: Alicia had at first incriminated among the others his own wife, Frankie (as if I didn't know her name. As if orderly procedure dictated we begin from utter scratch). When, Harlow said, he had come back to it in their conversation, Alicia had shied away, become vague, said it was just a guess.

I asked, "What does your wife say about it?"

The wind he was in burned his face a shade pinker. "She denies it."

"You doubt her denial?"

He said, effortfully groping for the truth, he who in his business of giving or withholding loans customarily had the truth neatly pre-stored in the bond box behind his grimace, "The very flatness of it feels wrong—taunting, brazen even. It's as if she doesn't want me to believe her, to be satisfied. It's as if —she hates me."

"Oh no." The promptness of my response was suspect, and odd, considering that she had several times told me just that. But my feminine side quailed at the thought that this provider of the expensive, new, glassy, giant-sized furniture Frankie lived among could be hated. This was her living lord. I said, "In her sessions with me I received very few unambivalent signals that that was the case, though she *is*, and you must know this, at a stage in her life where she should become reacquainted with her own needs, after all these years of other-directed activity—the others of course being primarily yourself and your children."

Besides Julie, slender recorder-playing Julie, there was a boy, Barry, a thirteen-year-old copy of his father, odiously successful at school, a precocious mocker in the choir, a savvy little shark of a boy, a bankling in bud.

Gerry Harlow said, "A neighbor woman told me she saw you coming out of the house one day."

This accusatory fact took me aback, my masculine ego was so effaced in the Christian effort of soothing his doubt and saving his marriage. A witty out occurred to me: "That must have been Jane in slacks," I said. "We look alike, you know."

His answer came straight from space: "Tell me another."

Adopting his metallic tone, I told him then, "There's no reason you should take my word, except that this week you will have noticed I haven't denied anything, and have nothing to lose at this particular point in time. Right?"

"Right."

"So to you I swear, solemnly, that I never"—the word had to be exact—"fucked your good wife."

He waited his judicious second; then a bolt shot back in his brain, his grimace unlocked, his lips retracted, the gold caps of his molars gleamed. I had the loan. He said, "Still, you know her in a way I don't; she's talked freely to you."

How condescending! I had put on skirts in his eyes. I had asked to; yet now itched to tell him the truth, the sexual acts that *had* been, her shameless, slavish acolytism. I said nothing.

He went on, relaxed, winding up details, "What shall I do with her? Should I give her the gate? She kind of wants it, but aside from the children, I'd hate to do it, she's so damn presentable. And we knew each other when. With some other person, you don't have that." I realized that the "neighbor woman" who volunteered her glimpse of me to him must have a reason, and an occasion, to do so. So not even chairmen of boards of deacons were spared the plague, our Dance of Death. He finished. "On the other hand, I don't want to waste the rest of my tour with a woman who hates my guts. There's something of the nun in Frankie, always has been; she can be hard."

I sighed. My desk top, now bare of my papers, my pictures, my paperweights, heaved slightly, as it did on the edge of exhaustion, or when I pondered it preparatory to counselling. "From the little I know of the two of you," I told Harlow, "you are *married*. She's discovered she can say the worst of what she feels and the world does not come to an end. She'll calm down. Who else does she have, but you? Whatever she makes or imagines of some other man or of freedom itself, they are not *serious*, compared to you. She knows this. She is a Christian; she knows where the center is. You are the center. Let her revolve around you, no matter how far out she swings. Love her, listen to her. She loves you—by which I mean merely that you have gravity, and the rest of us don't."

I realized that, in my weariness, I had half-belied, in this final phrase, my carefully framed innocence; but then realized, from the something fervid and conspiratorial and painful in Harlow's parting handclasp, that he had accepted my profession as a technicality, that Frankie had certainly betrayed to him her love for me, that he had been after not an absolution but a working basis, and he had it, and was thanking me. And I felt, sealed by this comradely handshake, a consignment and betrayal of his wife; I had sold her to her husband, when she had begged for flight, for release from gravity, and decency, and duty. It was my duty so to do. How sad I felt, seeing Harlow leave, his shoulders square as those of a young soldier who has just acquitted himself well with an ingenious and more than her trade demands affectionate whore.

Gerry, Frankie, Julie, Barry—how small remoteness has whittled them. They seem dolls I can play with, putting them now in this, now in that obscene position. I put the Frankie doll in a nightie, and lay her in bed, and spread her jointed legs, and set the Gerry doll on top, while the Julie and Barry dolls sleep the dreamless sleep of the safe and the inorganic. I look down upon the copulating dolls by removing a section of the roof no bigger than a chessboard. The Frankie doll's painted eyes stare up at me blindly. I am too big to see. Is it impossible, ideal and severely tested readeress, that, by entering this giant square state from my smaller busier one, I became a giant, among giant dogs and clouds and saguaros; that even letters in the mail sack, crossing the state border, swell into our scale, and that ominous knock beneath my feet in the 707, which for a dip of my heart I took to be the commencement of an inescapable dive, was merely the notch of our transposition, my quantum-jump birth as a Titan?

*

Ms. Prynne, on behalf of all us boys of this peculiar Boys' Town, I want to thank you for the tour yesterday of the dinosaur-bone quarry. The bus trip was most fun, what with the singing and the pranks, but the arrival itself had something of its intended educational impact. Who would have thought the matrix was harder than the bones themselves, and that the process is like drilling away the tooth to leave the filling free. And the scramble of those huge bones!—as hard to decipher as the spaghetti of motive and emotion heaped in our hearts!

Grains of sand, one by one, make an aeon in the end. Yet the solemn and insupportably vast prospect of time opening from the panorama window of these fossils was smudged by the noisy activity of young paleontologists wearing laboratory frocks over jeans. A dime held close to the eye eclipses the sun. No matter in how many ways our lives are demonstrated to be insignificant, we can only live them as if they were not. To the friable thecodont phalanges and the distorted bone crest of the corythosaurus, let me add in the interests of science some bones extricated from this sedimental narrative:

Alicia's patellae thrusting palely, edgily forward when she sat on the arm of the church pew and, again, when she sat on the stool in her living-room.

Frankie's scapulae glinting when in the motel she offered to go down on me.

Ned's humerus, which I momentarily seized in the parsonage yare.*

Gerry's mandible tensing and untensing in my office.

Jane's pubis grinding on mine above her father in his study. ("Let my bones be bedewed with Thy love," I seem to recall from one of St. Augustine's more excited perorations [Pusey translation].)

My father's skull, greater and stranger-brained than a baluchithere's.

My elder son's backbone (figurative).

My own troublesome and mortal "bone," which comes and goes. As what does not, eh Ms. Prynne? O you are the matrix of us all; grain by grain you bring us down, and rightly scoff at the thunder of skyey bluffers such as me.

---

* My first slip in a week of Sundays. My yard of yore?

23

DID NOT SLEEP WELL last night. Homeward thoughts within me burning already? The first week, I slept hardly at all, it seemed; I laid down my head inside a lonely plastic droning that was proceeding west at 550 miles per hour, at a cruising altitude of 34,000 feet. Then, grain by grain, this place stopped moving, it became a *place*, and now the danger is it has become the *only* place. And this accounting the only accounting, and you my reader my only love.

Let me tell you a few golf stories. In the first week of my stay, when the contours of the course had not been sprinkled brightly into my brain (I have been thinking a lot about love, these days, my hatred of the word, my constant recurrence to it, and it occurs to me, one of insomnia's perishable revelations, that before we love something we must make a kind of replica of it, a memory-body of glimpses and moments, which then replaces its external, rather drab existence with a constellatory internalization, oversimplified and highly portable and in the end impervious to reality's crude strip-mining), I played alone, the front nine, as my companions went in to their rooms, their pills, their remorses, and their naps, and on the seventh, as the immense bandshell of desert sky was resonating with muted lilac on one side of the orchestra and on the other side a pink pizzicato of cloud-stipple was tiptoeing toward the cymbal-clash of a fiery sunset (hang on, it's my therapy, not yours), I came down off the hill with a solid but pushed drive and, from an awkward lie, a 5-iron that, in the way of the unexpectedly well-hit shot, went over the flagstick pure and skipped off the green. You remember, of course, how the apron on this side is a little shoulder, glazed on top by a spiked hardpan that invites a scuffed shot every time. But a power greater than myself with my own hands took a 7-iron from the bag, pictured the chip crisply, swung crisply, and watched the ball hop from the clubhead; it jiggled over some worm-castings (the greens committee flies the worms in from Brazil at great expense), hit the pin with a heavenly *thunk*, and dropped in. A birdie three. Joy, for almost the first time since I had beheld Frankie's foot bare on the motel carpeting, unweighted my heart. The next hole, of course, is that very short par-three, a mere 120 yards by

the card; I took an 8-iron and a relaxed little swing, picturing
the ball a-glint by the flagstick. Instead I saw it flutter sideways
into the impenetrable shoulder of sage and creosote bush on
the right. And *the next shot went the same way*. A brand-new
Titleist. I scored myself an X on the hole and dragged back to
the clubhouse. My face felt scorched; I had encountered the
devil. I had brushed up against a terrible truth: it's the sure
shots that do us in.

Or, to put the moral in a more useful form, even a half-hit
demands a shoulder-turn.

And a full intention: lukewarm I spit thee out.

Golf is as it were all bones, an instant chastener and teacher;
lessons glow through, shapely as the graphs of binomial equa-
tions, that would hide forever amid the muffling muscle of
lived life's muddle.

Here is a more human story, and happier for your hero. Last
week we were in our usual foursome—me, Jamie Ray, Amos,
and Woody. Woody and I had on our usual dollar Nassau, and
as usual he was outdriving me by fifteen yards. I don't see how
he ever got those shoulders into a cassock, and don't wonder
the Vatican decided he needed a cooling-off. Every time he
thinks about the de-Latinized Mass his face goes red as a lobster and his claws begin to rattle. He got Jamie Ray as partner
today, which meant he was sure to collect on the team play.
Jamie Ray swings miserably but putts like an angel; I sometimes
wonder if buggery hasn't made the hole look relatively huge to
him. Whereas we poor cunt men keep sliding off to the side,
hunched over as fearful as fetuses who suddenly realize they
can never push their craniums through a three-and-a-half-inch
pelvic opening. Amos must have been a rapist once, for he tries
to hit the back of the cup so hard a miss (and most are) runs
two or three yards past. I know, of course, dear directress, that
Amos's crisis was asexual. We've all spilled our beans, though
forbidden to. He was the pastor of a happy little outer-inner-
city church, wooden colonial, all pillar and pew, annual budget
around thirty thou, two hundred families on the rolls, maybe
fifty active. A cheerfully dying little situation, no strain on a man
of sixty, head bald as an onion, arthritis creeping into the joints,

children off in Teheran and Caracas working for the government or the oil companies, an arthritic evangelical faith kept a little limber by the sprinkling of blacks in the flock and a lot of civic busywork in the "community at large." Suddenly, the church burns down. Faulty wiring? Panther-Muslim vandals from the ghetto one neighborhood away? A loose Jovebolt? No matter, in a great rally of solidarity and if-God-be-on-our-sidism they voted to rebuild, and did, a spiffyish little altar-in-the-round job of cream-colored pressed-garbage bricks, shaped like a hatbox with a hatpin pointing out and upwards. The only trouble was, no one came. The blacks thought the money should have gone into community action, the old faithfuls couldn't stand the new architecture, the younger element took to tripping in one another's basements and calling it devotions, and the rich family that had principally contributed never came anyway, having lived here when this outer-inner city was working pasture at the end of the trolley tracks and still believing that the religious duties of a squirearchy were fully absolved by a Christmastide appearance. Amos's wife and Korean foster-child attended services, and some of the local teenagers who thought they were possessed would break in nights and do things on the altar that left damp spots, and the volleyball and yoga groups thrived upstairs; but it wasn't enough for Amos. The emptiness, the silence, the mortgage payments, the shoddy workmanship and materials of the new building, the funny smell when it rained— they got to him. His custodian found him one Saturday night in the furnace room soaking newspapers in kerosene, and here he is among us.

But you know that story, and I began to tell another. Golf. Golf, gold, good, gods, nods, *nous*, gnus, anus, Amos. Eight strokes, with some cheating and a one-putt. Amos's golf had the peculiarity that, no matter with what club he struck the ball, from driver to wedge, the arc was the same—low and skulled-looking. But he was straight, and could be depended upon for a customary bogey, leaving me free (free! a word to be put into the stocks along with *love:* one an anarchist, the other a fornicator) to go for the pars. Still, against a hot putter and a big hitter, what hope was there? Precious little. A saving remnant. Woody had me three holes up with four to go.

On the fifteenth he hooked his drive into the pond. "*Unum baptisma in remissionem peccatorum*," I said to him, and drove short with an iron for a safe five. Three left and two down. A comfortable cushion, his shoulders implied, my little banderilla of Latin quivering as yet unfelt. Or perhaps felt as an unneeded surge of divine afflatus, for he overswung his fairway wood on the spacious sixteenth fairway and topped it badly; it scuttered into a prairie dog burrow. At least, it vanished, in that band of scruff bordering the arroyo. The four of us circled for ten minutes, like old women gathering fuel in vacant lots you might say, before giving up. "*Qui tollis peccata mundi*," I consoled my priestly opponent, and complacently (I confess it) chipped my own, indifferent but safe wood shot onto the green, for another winning bogey. Jamie Ray had run into trouble in a bunker, and Amos found the dead center of the back of the cup, so we saved some quarters on the team debt as well. Woody felt the world sliding; as we teed up for the par-three seventeenth, I beheld descend upon him for the first time the possibility that his lead might dissolve entirely. He was rattled; he was excited; the Latin had tripped open sluices of *excessus* in him. He surprised me unpleasantly by popping a 6-iron onto the dead center of the green, which slopes toward the sunset, California, and the Sea of Peace that bulges up at the infinite like an unblinkered eyeball. My own 5-iron took a lucky kick and seemed against the glare to creep onto the right edge of the green. Neither was Amos nor Jamie Ray in trouble. Hosannah.

One must walk down steps of orange shale here. The light was so nice, our evening drinks were so close, our match was so amusing—slung among us loosely like a happy infant in a blanket we each held a corner of—that we talked loudly in our joy, and once on the green I, the first to putt, lifted my arms and incanted, "*Pleni sunt coeli et terra gloria tua.*" You may or may not be surprised to know, my ms.terious Ms., that they have licensed me as the clown of the group.

Nothing clownish, however, I pictured the line of my long putt so firmly it became a Platonic Ideal in my mind, as hyper-real as a cubic inch of Sirius would be on Earth, in the second before its weight collapsed the examining table and burned a tidy square tunnel straight to China; and I stroked the lag, and, while it did not go into the cup, it trailed in close enough for a gimme, which is pretty fair from fifty feet. Woody, ruddy with the sunset glow and the remembrance of the Mass spoken as God meant it to be, not unpredictably powered his fifteen-footer half as many feet past on the downhill side, and in sudden consternation putted short coming back, and took a squandered four to my struggled three. One to go, and all even. Our friends were amazed. I was a miracle-worker even if like many another miracle-worker I came to a sad end.

And of course I did not. Pure, floating, purged of all dross, my swing drove the ball a sobbing seventh of a mile toward the edge of the sun; Woody, pressing but not destroyed, was one swale shorter, but straight. He hit (Amos and Jamie Ray poking along beside us like men pushing peanuts with their nose) first, and a cloud momentarily muted my sense of transcendence as I saw that his shot was a beautiful thing, hitting behind the pin so hot it backed up. Yet, out of love for you, Ms. Prynne, among others, I took a 7-iron and gazed from the height of my compact and unhurried backswing at the ball on its crystalline plane of sparkling sand and grass until more suddenly than a melted snowflake it vanished. My divot leaped, which they don't usually do. For a professed lover of down (being, going, staying) I have an odd resistance to *hitting* down; I can't believe the ball will rise of itself. I can't believe the world will go on spinning without me. I can't believe any woman will be happy without me. I can't believe I am not really fifteen billion light-years in diameter and shaped like a saddle, etc.

I let my head lift. Oh, with what a sublime comet's curve was that shot bending gently in, from the half-set sun's edge to the tilted flagstick. I lost the ball in the shimmer of the green, but my glad bones guessed it was inside his. And so it was. Our walking revealed the balls in a line with the cup, his ten feet past, mine five feet short. And still the priestly devil, the minion of the Babylonian mother of harlots, gave battle. His putt, stroked with a Jesuitical fineness, broke away at the last mini-second, as his ally the snivelling Dixie pederast grunted. Whereas my problematical five-footer, too confidently stroked from within my trance of certain grace, would have slid by on the high side had not a benign warp of the divine transparence deflected it; it teetered around half the hole's circumference, but the eventual glottal rattle there could be no denying. My partner, stout Amos, applauded. My opponent looked at me webbily, through the crazed windshield of his shattered faith. "*O salutaris hostia*," I saluted him, and felt myself irradiated by the Lordly joy of having defeated—nay, crushed, obliterated—a foe.

Tomorrow we would all be resurrected, and play again.

24

AGAIN, TROUBLE going to sleep, and fitful waking, between dreams designed and fumbled together by some apprentice subconscious. The body gets into these habits. The bed stretches beneath me tense as a trampoline. I am preparing for some leap. The backwards version of the leap that brought me here?

Yet I like flight; I like the food that is brought without asking, from behind; I like the tinkle of the serving dolly drawing closer, one's saliva tinkling in response; and the giant hum, and the nursery blues and greens of the plastic decor, and the nation's checkered midriff unrolling below. Nothing to do but observe and endure. Between worlds we are free. In *la palma de la mano de Dios*.

It occurs to me that at least three times before in these enforced confessions have I discovered myself above, exalted, *raptus*, looking down as at the golf ball ere smiting it so triumphantly into the heart of the eighteenth green. Once, when returning from a nocturnal mission of mercy to find Ned and Jane fumbling in boozy friendliness beside my fire. Twice, when serving communion to a kneeling recent fellatrice from the height of my priestly role. Thrice, looking down, in my overarching embodiment as author, through the lifted roof at the Harlows' domestic bliss, their house and its inhabitants reduced by reminiscence to a doll-sized seizability. So, perhaps these moments of naked megalojoy show the true face of my grovelling, my comical wriggle in the mud of humiliation. What is a masochist but a sadist whom weakness confines to empathetic satisfactions? And vice versa—the Marquis himself, a careful reading reveals, only wanted to munch excrement in peace. Concentration camp inmates imitated the dress and manner of their SS guards. Captives of pain, all; captives of one category. Freud's darkest truism: opposites are one. Light holds within it the possibility of dark. God is the Devil, dreadfully enough. I, I am all, I am God enthroned on the only ego that exists for me; and I am dust, and like the taste. What is all this reduction I have described, my defrocking myself of dignity, righteousness, respectability, fatherhood, husbandhood, even of an adulterer's furtive pride of performance, but a form of exaltation, an active reaction within a fixed vertical tube? Even my defeat of Woody: is not the heart of its joy nothingness, the nothingness that the annihilator experiences on behalf of the annihilated?

Something crucial in all this, but it skinned away from me as one of your Apache chambermaids went rattling down the hall, humming some fetching snatch of popular electronics. A fetching snatch herself, no doubt.

Did you like yesterday's word golf? Let's play again, let's see if we can get from "love" to "free," those two subversive words so dear to deluded Americans. Love, fove (Webster's preferred spelling for fauve, meaning a tawny beast), foee (an expression of contempt), free. Only three deft shots, a birdie! The words are the same underneath, and free love not a scandal but a tautology.

Transparency. My unseeable theme. The way a golf swing reveals more of a man than decades of mutual conversation. Woody's hearty grunting lunge and the disarmed delicacy of his short shots, which bobble to a premature stop on the apron; Amos's freckled bald head twitching its invariable six inches leftwards as his skulled ball rockets on its defused arc toward a quick reunion with the ground; slithering ashamed little Jamie Ray's redeeming mastery on the greens, the way he tucks his right hip back and tucks his right elbow into it and the back of his gloved left hand moves along toward the hole like a floating guardian above the clubhead and the way his dingy narrow face turns with the follow-through as if he is peeking underneath a porch and then is split by the beginning of a smile as his ball, halfway there, bends knowingly toward the hole, which brims with expectancy, a cup that drinks—we men are spirits naked to one another, on the golf course we move through one another like fish a-swim in one another's veins.

What we know, we move through; it is not opaque; nor an obstacle; nor an enemy; it is us, yet not us. Panovsky points out that the Age of Faith proclaimed *manifestatio*, in its scholastic argumentation and in the visible articulation of its cathedrals. The cross-section of the nave can be read off from the façade, the organization of the structural system from a cross-section of one pier. My father's carpentry opened the furniture of my childhood to me and made it religious; the women who came to me as dark bundles and resistant tangles became transparent in being fucked. I know them; one cannot know and not love.* In this sense the Greeks were not so naïve, in supposing that to know the good was to do the good.

By knowing, we dissolve the world enough to move through it freely. We dispel claustrophobia. Think of the auto mechanic, how greasily graceful his sequential descent into the problem, as opposed to the dumbo (me) who thumps the hood angrily upon the obdurate puzzle of his non-starting engine, and crushes his thumb. By knowing, we dissolve the veneer our animal murk puts upon things, and empathize with God's workmanship.

True of the pathologist who descends daily into the scribbled microforms of malfunction and disease?

True of the pearl-diver who scrapes his breathing-hose and drowns amid the billion lives of coral?

And, worse, isn't there something demonic in such dissolution; can it be the devil urging us into wider and wider transparency, where we no longer see to marvel, and feel nothing but the sticky filaments of our analysis, and have a Void where there had once been a Creation?

Dear Tillich, that great amorous jellyfish, whose faith was a recession of beyonds with these two flecks in one or another pane: a sense of the world as "theonomous," and a sense of

---

* Know, enow, 'nuff, luff.

something "unconditional" within the mind. Kant's saving ledge pared finer than a fingernail. Better Barth, who gives us opacity triumphant, and bids us adore; we do adore, what we also love in the world is its residue of resistance—these motel walls that hold us to this solitude, the woman who resists being rolled over, who is *herself.*

Ms. Prynne, forgive me, I seem to be preaching out of season. I do apologize. As you have seen I am not only a sinner but a somewhat cheerful one, though my clown's costume has been reduced to tatters. A clown, moreover, capable of cruelty, at least toward that side of me in bondage to decency; I have been cruel to Jane.

Doing right is, to too great an extent, a matter of details, of tinkering. That great gush of heavenly *excessus* runs dry in a desert of rivulet distinctions. When is it right for a man to leave his wife? When the sum of his denied life overtops the calculated loss of the children, the grandparents if surviving, the dog, and the dogged *ux.*, known as Fido, residual in himself. When is a war good to fight? When Pearl Harbor is attacked. When does an empire begin to die? When its privileged citizens begin to disdain war. Ethics is plumbing, necessary but dingy. Ethical passion the hobgoblin of trivial minds. What interests us is not the good but the godly. Not living well but living forever.

I distrust these assertions, though I seem to believe them. Truth more likely to grow from small hard perceptions, dicotyledonous in form: the pairing of carpentry and lovemaking, for instance. The musky smell of shavings, the ecstatic *ratio* of disassembly, the concentration among flung limbs, the need for a bench or a bed to work upon, the joiner's pride when it all comes together.

Ms. Prynne, am I trying to seduce you? Help me.

My love of my fellow golfers has helped me to understand Alicia, her flirtations, her many lovers. To be a woman among men is to be surrounded by sexual pressure; the lightest touch invites, the smallest submission releases. The pressing of a key, the pulling of a stop; and what eager tones, what a hungry wind of power! She was making music with us that only she could hear. She was organist, church, and congregation. How superb, to be a woman! At moments, in the bar afterwards, I let the rank maleness of my fellows blow through me, and try to think their wrinkled whiskery jowls, their acrid aromas, their urgent and bad-breathed banalities, into some kind of Stendhalian crystallization. I cannot quite do it, I am less than half queer. But love these fools, tough as I am. And to be a woman, what a constant pleasurable outpouring of forgiveness it must be, to be so surrounded! Like the sensation of sweating on a bonny summer day.

Once I was startled by a glimpse of male beauty. I drove to a school to pick up a sixteen-year-old boy. As he ducked out of the entryway, having spotted my car, he flicked his hair, which continued to bounce as, taller than I remembered him, he loped down the steps; I was seeing him with an unusual perspective, as a young male in the world, severed from me. He was, suddenly, quite without intending it, beautiful. He was my son Martin.

Amos brought a Polaroid along and took photos of us on the eleventh tee one day. I am plainly aware of being photographed, yet also trying honestly to hit the ball. I have just hit it. My head is trying to stay down, though the swing is completed. I see, laughably, the left knee locked, the right foot still illicitly harboring some weight, the arms badly collapsed, my belly, navel showing, thrust with an odd one-eyed earnestness toward the unseen fairway. As I remember, the shot was a massive slice that led to a six. There is a bank of cactus and mesquite behind me, a wedge of sharply shadowed rock above, a triangle of sky. At my feet the horseshoe-shaped tee-markers, and the maddening rubber driving mat, and the confetti of broken tees. I feel in the distance at which I view myself, holding this snapshot, Amos holding the camera, and feel outside the rectangle of the print the silence of our two playing partners, waiting and watching. I see, not quite in focus, a middle-aged, quasi-mesomorphic clergyman doing an ungainly but solemn imitation of an athlete, beneath an alien desert sun, amid the trappings of vacation, in a moment innocuous and lost. I want to laugh, but my throat locks, dried by the realization that this is a picture of me in Paradise.

25

POKER TAKES a larger group, seven and not always the same seven. Woody plays, but the money makes Amos upset, and Jamie Ray prefers the more finesseful microcosm of bridge. Myself, though I hadn't played since college and had to learn the rules of the baroque variations introduced mostly, among us poker-addicted parsons, by Fred, the only minister I have ever met who stutters, and remarkable also for his exhaustively red hair—apricot color on his scalp, bright chestnut in his eyebrows, a washed-out almost custard shade in his lashes. He has a loud voice, stutter and all, and loves to bet. He always gives the pot a kick, he never lets the flywheel of us rest. And I have not been able to discover, without seeming to gossip or pry, what he is here for or what his denomination is.

The transparency of poker of course differs from the pellucid swings and distances of golf: we skate directly upon the glassy surface of the Lord and his dispensations. The encounter, indeed, at first was too turbulent and dizzying, too charged, not only with the psychologies of my fellow-players but with the irrefutable whims of the Bestower of Gifts Himself; so that I, in the dizziness of which beer was a component, became rattled. Being rattled takes two forms: betting losers and folding winners, in boustrophedonic alternation. But, glory be, one's fellows, knowing you to be rattleable, are loathe to fold against you, where a steadier player would convince them, and they would thriftily steal away. So some of the losses return, given that one (as one must, in a mathematically random universe) has the cards sometimes. Thinking you a fool, they do not believe; they stay, and you reap. Credence, so abstract and tenuous in real life, becomes bread and butter in poker. Also, as in international relations, a curious indeterminacy principle obtains: a margin of unpredictability must be maintained around you. So the stupid act becomes obligatory if one is to have a *presence*. When I emerged from my rattled first nights and found I had a poker presence, it was as heartening as discovering, with Alicia, that I had a sexual presence. I have settled to winning some and losing some, trying to keep a card count, trying to curb my Thomistic optimism—give me two fours and in jubilant certainty that the other pair will arrive as a *donum superadditum* I raise. Thus our hero sits on his hardened haunches at an octagonal table from nine to twelve every night in a blissful stupor of Desert Rat Beer and as it were origami eschatology (clitoral eschatology, I want to say, God knows why, something about the way the corners of a deck thrill when rippled), watching the breath of the Lord play across the surface of the cards and the faces and the fortunes of his new-found friends.

Want to hear a poker story, Ms. Prynne? It must be good for you; just as one excursion into the girls' room (no urinals!) is good for every American lad. We were playing a game called Eighty-five. You are dealt five cards, the first face down; then you can buy three, one at a time, each after a round of betting, discarding every time. It is a high-low game: the best possible low is Ace, 2, 3, 4, and 6 of not the same suit. Same suit would be a flush, Ace-2-3-4-5 would be a straight; both high; get it? Though Ace can count as 1 it also tops the King and a pair of Aces is the highest pair. Fred was dealer; I sat to his right. By the third "buy" card the other hands had either folded or were on the face of it committed to going high. I had showing Ace, 2, 4, and 6: a super low, patently. The trouble was, my 6 was paired underneath. The one hand left to draw, Fred's, was nondescript garbage, Jack high. Intuition told me he too was paired. Nevertheless, to be safe, thinking I at least could do better than a pair of 6's low, I threw the down card and drew—*oof*—an Ace, giving me a pair of Aces. Providence had really stretched to discomfort me, for the other two Aces were on the board. Fred, announcing "D-d-d-dealer will take a c-c-card," threw his Jack and got an 8. Not a bad low, now, but mine looked so strong I felt sure I could drive him out. I raised; he raised me back. I raised again, figuring he had been testing, and would fold now. He did not. The third time, then, but with a sinking heart, I raised, and he raised back, which with the raising among the highs (four cards of a flush against a possible full house) made quite a leafy pot. The betting done, I called low, as did Fred, and told him, "Damn you. I'm paired."

"How h-h-h-high?" he asked.

"Aces," I confessed, wondering why he asked.

He had the worst low possible for his hand showing, a pair of eights. Fred had stayed, then, against me when only one card in the deck, the cased Ace, could have made my hand a loser to his. Two truths dawned upon me:

He was crazy.

He had won.

He had raised not on a reasonable faith but on a virtual impossibility; and he had been right. "Y-y-y-you d-didn't feel to me like you h-h-h-h-had it," he told me, raking in.

And I felt his craziness in him like a glowing tumor I longed to touch and heal; I wanted to reach into him, as into a great red-haired chasm, and finger this pulsing marvel of the craziness that made him stay against odds worse than those of Pascal's notorious bet.

I wanted, that is, to minister unto him.

And unto these others; imperceptibly these errant and bankrupt clergymen have replaced the phantoms that chased me here, phantoms it now seems my heart had conjured from its own fevers, had bred like fungi in an unlit dank of self-absorption. This desert sun has baked them away. This desert sun has reduced old bodies to their bones, and given me instead these shaken, hearty, boyish, mortal ministers. In these last days I have heard myself listening to Amos and the tale of his expensive empty church, and advising him that this emptiness is itself eloquent, and a Word, if he but believe that God is not a pathetic dwindling old gentleman but an omnipotence that moves and creates everywhere, that "potently does everything in everything," in the words of Luther, who hailed God's power even in the Turks and Vandals—competing street gangs, it turns out, in Amos's neighborhood. The Church was never meant to be a quantitative success; Christianity is not an industry in competition with other industries. Amos, and so many other colleagues broken and stranded by the ebbing of faith, seem to me racked upon Calvin's curious transition from the absolute majesty and remoteness of God to the possibility that cleverness and thrift in the management of capital is an earthly sign of divine election. It has made our American faith brittle. It has made it crass. Amos's job is to stand and witness, not to pack a room, or operate a "plant." So I try to tell him, with jokes and an implicit fondness.

Woody's rage for Latin, his rage against the bishops and the Berrigans and all who have polluted and distorted and abandoned the sacred fixed forms of the one true faith, I try to suffer in such a way as to bring to his own ears, in the silence of my attention, an echo of undue bitterness, a hint of indignation misplaced from a more personal fear of obsolescence, perhaps a hierarchical envy, an unspeakable suspicion that if such surface adjustments as a translation into the vernacular and the dismissal of St. Christopher and the marriage of some Jesuits can occasion so massive a "falling away," then what was fallen away from had long died, was its husk only, a husk of goldleaf. Woody believes everything because he believes nothing and his anger is terror and his terror is lack of faith.

And to Jamie Ray I have listened even more intently, though smiling at his delicious Southernisms ("asshole slicker than a buttercup" comes to me out of many) and rejecting the sidling fear that any announced homosexual puts into me, trying to detect, for myself and for him, what holy thing it is men see in each other, what fear brings them to cling only to their own sex, though their bodies become, not manly, but mockeries, often fanatically skillful, of the despised feminine. What deep comment on our condition, our ambiguous soul in its palatial but deteriorating prison, is being made here? It seems almost sane, but for an undercurrent of predation and brutality—the use, for instance, of the still sensorily innocent and dumb bodies of boys. What is, old Professor Chillingworth asked through me, the good here mistakenly aspired to? That the mistake occurs deeper than the conscious will, I of course implied to Jamie Ray, and he knew I admired his putting, and he my mid-irons, and so we became a bit less opaque to one another, fumbling and shrugging. I told Jamie Ray, giving myself the pleasure of confession, how, in my despair and bewilderment at being unable to fuck Frankie, I prayed God for the power to have an erection; I begged Him to be my accomplice in adultery, and believe that, had not events intervened, the prayer would have been answered. Our God is a fertility god.

Fred, too, sensing my vivid glimpse of his craziness, and my marvelling at it, has become more relaxed with me, and stutters less.

It is hard, of course, to console or advise professional consolers and advisers; rote phrases, professional sympathy, even an emphatic patience are brusquely shunted aside. At a convention of masseurs no one turns his back. So we learn to say nothing as a way of saying it all. The stately desert silence sets us our example.

As the silence is infecting me, and driving me to short paragraphs.

You ask, what of my own case? A common fall, mine, into the abysmal perplexity of the American female. I feel, however, not merely fallen, but possessed, and such is demonology that the case needs for cure another woman; and the only woman here, on this frontier, is, Ms., you.

26

AVEN* LESS SLEEP than the night before. A churning to get something done. A genuine fear of the return to the world. My left palm tingles, thinking of it; my body at night lies transposed into a graver key; the existential solemnity of my unique ego and fate is borne in upon me as sweatily as death by plague. My defiantly tricksome style of earlier has fallen from me; I limp, lame and fuzzy-brained, from one dim thought to the next.

Spent an hour now rereading, between winces of embarrassment, the pages we (you and I, reader; without you there would be the non-noise of a tree crashing in the inhuman forest) have accumulated. Not, you say, a very edifying or conclusive narrative. A man publicly pledged to goodness and fidelity scorns his wife, betrays one mistress, is ompotent† with another, exploits the trust and unhappiness of some who come to

---

*And a return of auspicious misfingerings. This one hard to read—was going to begin with "Again"? A longing for haven. A half-hope of heaven?

†Dear me. My suggestion of omnipotence in impotence reminds me of Meister Eckhardt, with his cyclical assertions that Everything is God, that all things merge so that everything is nothing, that God is nothing. The triumphant atheism of mysticism. Give me Thomistic degrees instead. There is *something*, dammit. Damn It?

him for guidance, regards his father and his sons as menacing foreign objects, and through it all evinces no distinct guilt but rather a sort of scrabbling restiveness, a sense of events as a field of rubble in which he is empowered to search for some mysterious treasure.

How much, I see backwards, has been left out, even in the zealous matter of sexual detail. The startling hardness of the teenaged bride's breasts, for instance, and the uncomfortable way she liked to have them entirely in my mouth, so my old jaws ached. And the gaunt divorcee, her pubic bush the only bump on her, in profile outthrust like the jaunty pompon of a poodle. Whereas Frankie's hair lay in flat neat circlets, so flat and neat they almost seemed painted on her belly's supple parchment. And many other such details that might have lent plausibility and morally suasive substance to my furtive display of smuggled icons.

Nor is the end clear. I do not expect to find my parish there for me when I return. Ned is in charge; the androgynous homogenizing liberals of the world are in charge, and our American empire obligingly subsides to demonstrate how right they are. The East, the dust between the stars, will prevail. Alicia I do not expect to be there; Ned for his own fey reasons will not have reinstated her, my firing will stick, my plumping for the Word as against pretty liturgy. My last Barthian act. Alicia, I see now, was like those brimming golden afternoons of boyhood, that yet we do not wish to live again, because we do not wish to be again the pint-size, allergy-ridden, powerless person who enjoyed them.

Frankie and Jane are less clear. I aspire within both women as, in some surreal and stippled Doré print, a faunish sufferer struggles to rise within a translucent hellish chute of intricate folds and bannister-like turns. The one all ethics, the other all faith, and I between. No. The formulation does the reality a disservice; there is something gritty, practical, mortised, functional in our lives, something olfactory and mute, which eludes our minds' binomial formulations. I can scarcely believe that either woman waits for me. It is as if the overpopulated green land I left has been blasted to desert by the process that has filled this bare place for me with habits and pleasures, affections and names and flowers of interest.

*

And yet . . . It is a few minutes to noon. A golf game waits, yet not with the innocence and air of abundant escape it had before I wrote days ago those pages bringing it and my companions (not, I fear, entirely convincingly; altruism still tickles my sinuses with a fearful must of futility) into this garbled and saddening audit. In a few days I will leave them. It will be cold at home. My father will greet me under another name, and my children will ask for their presents. Jane—her face is blank. Frankie has moved away, her love for me self-satisfying, self-contemplating, love in love with love.

Last night, dizzy and headsick after a game of poker unrelievedly boring in revenge for my morning's attempt to describe its fascination, I stepped out of this omega-shaped shelter, testing my impending freedom, and looked up at the stars, so close and warmly blue in this atmosphere, yet so immutably fixed in their dome of night; and I felt, for an instant—as if for an instant the earth's revolution had become palpable—that particle or quantity within myself, beyond mind, that makes me a stranger here, in this universe. A quantity no greater than a degree's amount of arc, yet vivid, and mine, my treasure.

God, the sadness of Creation! Is it ours, or Thine?

27

MY BROTHERS: our text today is taken from that Prince of Preachers, the one born out of due time, Saul of Tarsus who became Saint Paul, his epistle to the Corinthians, the fifteenth chapter: "We are of all men most miserable."

We? Who is this we? We who preach the risen Christ: "And if Christ be not risen, then is our preaching vain, and your faith is also vain."

Your? Who is this you? You of Corinth who profess the monstrous new faith, who have received the Gospel, the good news derived from the reports that the dead man Jesus, risen from the tomb, was seen by Cephas, and then of the twelve, and after that of five hundred brethren at once, of whom—Paul says, in that haunting aside that gives this epistle the breath of contemporaneity, the diaphanous urgency of yesterday's newspaper—"the greater part remain unto this present, but some are fallen asleep."

And now all are fallen asleep, and have long been so. Still to this day late in 1973 the rumor lives, that something mitigating has occurred, as if just yesterday, to align, like a magnet passing underneath a paper heaped with filings, the shards of our confusion, our covetousness, our trespasses upon the confusions of others, our sleepless terror and walking corruption. "So when this corruptible shall have put on incorruption, and this mortal shall have put on immortality, then shall be brought to pass the saying that is written, Death is swallowed up in victory."

When? Something has not yet happened. Paul expected it to happen soon: "Behold, I show you a mystery; we shall not all sleep, but we shall all be changed, in a moment, in the twinkling of an eye, at the last trump." The last trump did not sound before Paul slept, nor has it in the long centuries since, centuries crowded with appetite and battle, with lust sowing lives even faster than disease could harvest them, centuries each of which is like a chalice brimming with human tears and blood lifted in homage and oblation to the God above appeal.

Yet still men listen for that last trump; just yesterday, on the delightful bus trip to Sandstone arranged by our capable Ms. Prynne, to prepare us for re-entry into the world, and to buy our children and our wives leathery souvenirs, a tall and gracious youth, the very image of a youthful Jesus save that Jesus was no doubt historically darker and shorter, a third-worlder to his filthy fingernails—this youth handed me a pamphlet illustrated with cartoons of Richard Nixon collapsed beneath a "Shield of Incredibility" and with intricate diagrams of the Sun's perihelion and the comet Kahoutek's orbit in relation to the November ceasefire and the Winter equinox; this pamphlet, produced in Dallas and repulsive in its crazed computations and slangy piety, predicts the end of the world in eighty days, and makes much of the unBiblical slogan, "Around the world in Eighty Days."

May I share with you a paragraph of this cretinous prophecy?

"You see what Jesus show me? Isn't that wonderful how God shows His people! Begins the 12th (November), day after the *Peace, peace* and then on (January) 31st with war, war! Savvy?

—And sudden destruction! You in the *U.S.* have only until *January* to get *out* of the States before some kind of disaster, destruction of judgment of God is to fall because of America's wickedness!"

Well, we recoil from this gibberish, with its devilish savor of astrology and drugged radicalism; but let us ask ourselves, is not the content of this miserable throwaway, promulgated by the most desperate inanity of a desperately inane generation, is not the content, as distinct from the style, the content of our life's call and our heart's deepest pledge?

Consider, again, another pamphlet, pressed upon me by the same weedy Jesus, who singled me out from the giggling pack of you as the one most conspicuously in need of redemption. Under odious purple illustrations, and in a coarse printing aimed at the puerile, we find this travesty of the epic mystery of the Atonement: "God is our great father in Heaven and we are his children on Earth. We've all been naughty and deserve a spanking, haven't we? *But Jesus, our big brother,* loved us and the Father so much that he knew the spanking would hurt us both, so he offered to take it for us!"

Well, even so: yet have we listened to our own Sunday school teachers, or our own singsong children's sermons? Is not our distaste here aesthetic, where aesthetics are an infernal category; is not our love of Christianity an antiquarian and elitist cherishing, a dark and arcane swank, where a living faith for the lowly should obtain? Does not this pornography of faith, like the pornography of copulation printed in the same grimy shop, testify to a needed miracle, a true wonder, a miraculous raw truth which it is one of civilization's conspiracies to suppress? And insofar as we are civilized men, men of courteous disposition and civic conscience, tolerant, sensible, and moderate, are we not members of the conspiracy, distinguishable but distinctly within it, like the few, and extra delicious, black balls within the glass sphere of the Kiwanis gum machine?

"If in this life only we have hope in Christ, we are of all men most miserable." Most miserable, for what to other men is but a hope, added to their lives as a feather to a hat, for us is the hat itself, and more than the hat, the shirt and the pants and the shoes.

We are naked, Paul tells us, if Christ be not raised—"if there be no resurrection of the dead." Yet how heavy, how heavy then and how heavier now, it is to lift the dead in our hearts! How stony and blue they lie on the hospital dollies! How irreversible the progress of demise traced by radiographs and biopsies! And, for the living, how acceptable the death of the dead, how quickly the place seals over where they were, how slyly grateful we are for the little extra space they bequeath us! We would abhor them were they to return. One of our profoundest fears, indeed, is that the dead *will* return; the resurrection of the dead is a horror story. As a child, let me confess, I was terrified that I would pray too well, and out of the darkness Jesus would answer by walking through the door of my room, and that He would demand from me my favorite toy.

And yet, from the other standpoint, that of the infrangible *ego* who cries within us *sum* without ceasing, how much more intelligent is Paul's carnal stipulation than that neo-Platonic afterlife of spirits which survives into our age chiefly as a *mise en scène* for *New Yorker* cartoons. For we do not want to live as angels in ether; our bodies are us, us; and our craving for immortality is, as Death's great philosopher Miguel de Unamuno so correctly and devastatingly remarks, a craving not for transformation into a life beyond imagining but for our *ordinary life*, the mundane life we so driftingly and numbly live, to go on forever and forever. The only Paradise we can imagine is this Earth. The only life we desire is this one. Paul is right in his ghoulish hope, and all those who offer instead some gaseous survival of a personal essence, or one's perpetuation through children or good deeds or masterworks of art, or identification with the race of Man, or the blessedness of final and absolute rest, are tempters and betrayers of the Lord. Is not the situation in our churches indeed that from the pulpit we with our good will and wordy humanism lean out to tempt our poor sheep from those scraps of barbaric doctrine, preserved in the creed like iguanodon footprints in limestone, that alone propel them up from their pleasant beds on a Sunday morning?

Yet the resurrection of the body is impossible.

As impossible, it is fair to say, for Paul and his Corinthians as for us; for though their world had more chemical and astronomical mystery in it than ours, it also had more corpses and more observed death, more putrefying reality.

No man, unless it was Jesus, believes. We can only *profess* to believe. We stand, brethren, where we stand, in our impossible and often mischievously idle jobs, on a boundary of opposing urgencies where there is often not space enough to set one's feet—we so stand as steeples stand, as emblems; it is our station to be visible and to provide men with the opportunity to profess the impossible that makes their lives possible. The Catholic church in this at least was right; a priest is more than a man, and though the man disintegrate within his vestments, and become degraded beyond the laxest of his flock, the priest can continue to perform his functions, as a scarecrow performs his.

My brothers. Your faces, tan from the sun, fat from a month of play and liquor and tacos and tamales, look at me in my imagination, and I know your faces now, as once I knew the faces and veils of my lost suburban parish. Lightning rods for the anxieties of men, left free to roam our communities as rather laughable trouble-shooters, we naturally absorb anxiety and trouble ourselves. Perhaps we are the last salt ere the world definitively loses its savor. Or perhaps—it would be a sin for us to deny the possibility—the Parousia so imminently expected by Paul will now come, and these two millennia between will have been as the absentminded hesitation of a gracious host's hand on the way to ring for dessert, or to strike his wineglass with a knife and bring the table to attention.

In this Inbetweentimes let us take comfort at least from the stiffness of our roles, that still stand though we crumple within them. We do not invent ourselves, and then persuade men to find room for us; rather, men invent our office, and persuade us to fill it.

Soon I must leave you, as you must leave me. We have shared a strange holiday—like nothing so much as the holiday of mourning that Confucian custom imposed upon a Mandarin who, when in the middle of his life a parent died, underwent a retreat in the mountains, far from the claims of responsibility and concubinage. And thus isolate he would compose himself for the remainder of the journey of his life. *Qui m'y a mis?* Who has set me here? The cry arises in a passage of Pascal that impressed me in the days—lost, alas, with so much else!— when I attended seminary and courted the Professor of Ethics' blossom-pale daughter. On the same page where the *Penseur* confesses his fright at the eternal silence of the infinite spaces, he confesses another fear: *je m'effraie et m'étonne de me voir ici plutôt que là, car il n'y a point de raison pourquoi ici plutôt que là, pourquoi à présent plutôt que loin? Qui m'y a mis?*

Qui m'y a mis? Can the mystery, frightening and astonishing, of our existence be more clearly posed? The old mysteries erode; Henri Bergson, that graceful fellow-traveller of our rough faith, spoke of the three creaky hinges, or inexplicable gaps, in the continuum of materialism: between nothing and something, between matter and life, between life and mind. The last two have since silted in with a sludge of atomic information, and even the stark first may, eventually, reveal an anatomy: already radio telescopes have picked up a cosmic hum that apparently originates at the very rim of time.

But what could explicate and trivialize the deepest and simplest mystery, that I find myself here and not there, in the present rather than in the past or future? *Il n'y a point de raison pourquoi*; there is not a particle of reason why. So those of us who live by the irrational may moderate our shame. Who has set us here, in this vocation, at this late date, out of due time? To ask the question is to imply an answer: there is a *qui*, a Who, who has set; we have not accidentally fallen, we have been placed. As of course we already know in our marrow. God bless you. God keep you all. Amen.

[*in pencil, in the slant hand of another:*]
Yes—at last, a sermon that could be preached.

28

YOU SPOKE. You exist. The palm of my left hand tingles like that of a man with an hour to the electric chair. I did not look at my pages last evening, between golf and supper; I confess it, I surreptitiously purchased from the rear of a souvenir-and-junk shop (canvas desert bags, miniature saddles, Stetsons, high-priced foot-lengths of antique barbed wire) a little dusty green book in aid of Sunday school teachers, titled *What Boys and Girls Are Asking*, and was soaking myself in its illicit contents. So I did not see your note until this morning, settling to the typewriter that like a dull wife has grown grudgingly responsive to my touch, above the goose-dung-colored carpet where my twitching feet have worn two fluffy oblongs. The handwriting was yours as I have always imagined it—hurried yet legible, pragmatic yet a shade self-congratulatory in the formation of the capitals.

Do you truly think it a good sign, dear one, that this last sermon, lumpy with quotation and littered with pensée shavings (fact is, even were the sky a neonated 3-D billboard flashing GOD EXISTS twenty-four hours a day we would contrive ways to doubt it) and damply devoid of the neurotic and mocking fire of the others, might be preached in an actual church, with pews, blue hymnals, stained-glass betrayals and departures, and *bona fide* parishioners solidly stuffed with cotton wool? Have you been really preparing me all this time for a return to the world and not translation to a better? Is this the end of therapy, a reshouldering of ambiguity, rote performance, daily grits, hollow vows, stale gratifications, receding illusions?

Yes, is your answer, stern.

And I nod, weakly assenting. I am ready. But for one thing. One rite, one grail stands between me and a renewed reality. You, Ms. Prynne. You with your figure of perfect elegance on a large scale, your dark and abundant hair, your even darker eyes under the eyebrows as pronounced and swift in their curve as two angry strokes of unsharpened charcoal. Can I believe that the graceful extent of your neck and generous curve of your mouth ever reminded me of a turtle, albeit large and white? That I found your manner, always ladylike and dignified, once harsh, even cumbersome and bullying? That the wholly admirable briskness of your manner, fair to all and lucid to all, ever reminded me of an officious, harried, slightly-out-of-her-depth Ho-Jo hostess when the full garlanded membership of two opposed suburban garden clubs simultaneously appear for Tuesday lunch? Forgive me. I swear, I have been in love with you since the moment the jet-hum ceased in my ears. Your infallible courtesy with your redmen factotums, your beautiful glossy bun with the golden pencil stuck in it just so, your rhinestone-starred reading glasses, that so promptly yield to pilot-style shades when your duties compel you to go tap-tap-tapping along the walks of green cement that wind their crumbling

way among the sand and cacti of our garden—your air of mo-
bilized bulk, of girdled purpose that yet never disdains to pause
and briskly flirt with the baby-oiled form of a disgraced cleric
sunning—your delightful way of delegating and describing to
your assistant Mrs. Leonora Givingly, whose crinkly timidity
would in a twinkling jell to tyranny did you not so masterfully
apportion out to her precise daily dopples of instruction—your
slightly tossed and even tragedy-tinted sweeping way of moving along, flattening your hair with a hand tensely bent back
beyond mere flatness, your sable eyes (of the type of darkness
that seems hot) lifted with the heedless, faintly false, put-on
bravery of the woman alone: all this has impressed me. Has
pierced me. Why is there no ring on your left hand? Why have
you been called to manage this desert place, this old world
monastery transposed to the Columbian mode of a Disneyland
junket? *Qui t'y a mis?*

Once, emerging at dusk from the pool, I saw, my eyeballs
chlorinated to match the sunset, you pushily passing through
a double glass door from having chastened a jeaned and rebellious chambermaid, and I thought, of your ass, which had
always before loomed as much beyond me as a mesa, that it was
manageable. That indeed it was, for all its authoritarian majesty
and apparent imperviousness, grabbable, huggable, caressable,
kissable. And knew itself as such. And knew itself as such in my
sunset eyes.

Why do I fancy myself silently, impassively favored? Is it from
any improper acknowledgment on your part of my growing admiration, any downward smile, flirtatious blush, brazen word,
any slackening at all in the taut cable of your management? No.
In case these pages are surreptitiously Xeroxed and forwarded
to your superiors and mine, I insist upon that exonerating negative. You have been inflexible and chaste. Wondrous strength
and generosity of a woman's heart!

Yet, with the same unkillable intuition that leads me to laud
the utterly *absconditus Deus*, I feel there is a place in you for
me. Set aside, indeed, at your first haughty glance. When we
pass in the corridor, there is a curious curvature of time-space
in which our curt greeting billows and dips. When you stand
by my table momently, to make your formal inquest into the
edibility of the chow, I am conscious of your pelvis, presented

I think deliberately at the latitude of my face, though without your stooping your pose could not be otherwise. At night, as I try, with decreasing success (the soporific effect of a strange climate long since dissipated) to sleep, I feel you somewhere on the other side of these many partitions, puzzling your way toward me, hesitating along some inbent circumference of mercy.

How charming you were, Saturday, in Sandstone, when confronted by the drunken Indian! In a suit the black of an ash-smeared stove, he halted you, there on that blinding broad sidewalk lined with bars, ranch suppliers, and vendors of postcards of canyons, as you with your fussy satellite were trying to lead back to the bus your noisy, rubicund, conspicuous pack of faulty ministers. We were too excited to be out, in a highway hamlet that looked like a city, where pickup trucks bespoke a continent of activity and agriculture, and where incongruous, faded, dryly tingling Christmas decorations festooned the hot lampposts. Our commotion had stirred this aborigine, had reached into his trance and caused him to lurch forward dustily, dressed in dirty black. It was as if you, in your dun linen dress, had suddenly grown a shadow. We halted, nonplussed, hushed. From behind me Mrs. Givingly moved toward the head of the line, clucking to herself, wound up to be officious. But with a divinely brisk wave of your hand you halted our motion, and bowed your head—smoothing back the hair on that side with a too-tense palm—to give the Indian's mumbling your ear. In truth, was not his drunkenness a groping up through firewater toward ecstasy and truth (for no other race gets drunk like this), and therefore one more of the American religious dislocations which it is your occupation to repair? He wobbled, in the unique style of drunken Indians, a graceful little stagger with a penumbra of menace to it, and pointed, all the while muttering into your ear. He was pointing at Woody; it was Woody's reactionary pride to wear the priest's bib and collar where the rest of us were in sports shirts; the Indian was offended, or interested; you, to reinforce the distinct English of your explanation, made praying hands to show a holy man, and a large circle to include us all. The Indian understood; he looked up at the sky; he laughed, and his knees suddenly bent, and you reached forward to put a hand beneath his elbow. And

I, watching closely, felt with you your flicker of anticipation, your wish to move him aside so your charges could board the bus, your desire to leave this Indian—your fellow-Westerner—some dignity. Oh, I moved through you, understanding all this and more, and it came to me that love is not an e-motion, an assertive putting out, but a *trans*-motion, a compliant moving *through*.

I saw through you, with you, Ms. Prynne, in your street ministry to that shadow caught in the sun with his cat eyes slitted by drink, and therefore presume to claim you as mine. As my end approaches, everything grows vaporous, my future and my past are the same green cloud, and only you are solid, only you have substance; I fall toward you as a meteorite toward the earth, as a comet toward the sun.

You who were kind to a drunken Indian, be kind to me, poor Wasp stung by the new work-ethic of sufficient sex, sex as the exterior sign of interior grace, as the last sanctuary for violence, conquest, and rapture, in a world as docilely crammed as an elevator ascending after lunchtime.

It occurred to me, sitting on the toilet yesterday at five (ninety swings of a golf club has a salutary loosening effect on the bowels; a second installment is produced, more contemplatively than the morning's urgent and poisoned release), that my situation with my mate Jane, with its obstinate lock of symmetry and lovingkindness, belongs to the province of works purely, and works without faith are constipation. I must cease, it seemed to me, as my happily growling guts sustained their seemingly endless process of emptying, cease regarding any lives other than my own as delivered into my care; they, and mine, are in God's care. Most of what we have is given, not acquired; a gracious acceptance is our task, and a half-conscious following-out of the veins in the circumambient lode.

This century's atrocious evils have stemmed from the previous century's glorification of the Will.

My impotence with Frankie seems now a product of overmanagement, a wish on my part to match the perfection that sat on her as lightly as a cape of feathers. If she had truly loved me, she would have maimed herself. I tried to maim her but lacked the time.

In my insomnia now, between masturbatory spurts of fantasizing about you, Ms. Prynne (your pudenda must be a gleaming heap of coal; there will be a few teasing dark hairs about your nipples), I pray; and my prayers move into the air as ripples on ripples, as a pealing of words on a kind of translucent log-road or supernatural xylophone that moves diagonally upward from me in the manner of smooth breakers, and my words are carried away in the spaces between, and are answered, not steadily, but in gusts of joy that lift me almost out of my ribs and make my early-morning hours of captivity in these gray-green walls too precious to sleep through. Next day, my golf is sloppy, and my poker scatterbrained. Even my tan is slipping away.

But it has been years since I physically felt my prayers being answered. He who is down, Bunyan tells us, need fear no fall. He who is down, says the id, is up.

I look forward respectfully to your comments.

29

NOTHING. Not a word. You read me only on dull Sundays. You are repelled by my advances. You have ceased to exist. I have wasted an hour running my poor lab rat of a mind through the maze of these alternatives, and poking through the old pages looking for words from you I might have missed. Nothing. Not a word.

Today is Tuesday. Thursday I go. Think of me in the sky; think of me as a Sky-god, Uranus to your Gaea, raindrops to your desert, gospel to your despair, prattle to your silence. By what right, you ask, might I expect that you, appointed to this delicate situation because of (among other virtues, abilities, degrees in hotel and hospital management, life-saving courses at the "Y", etc.) your pronounced inseduceability, would condescend to me, a worm, a worm of the sort you process in batches? For all I know, you are chosen for your imperviousness to clergymen, your antipathy toward them, sickly parasites as they are, consuming gasoline and heating fuel in useless missions and rituals, intruding wherever a person is gasping to death or getting married, demanding the right to say grace at the Rotary luncheon, etc. And you see the worst, the flops, a monthly gang of leprous and self-exacerbating failures.

Still, I have this mustard seed. And you have this gap in your armor. There was that air pocket when we pass in the hall. And even the rarity of encouraging helpful comments on my pages takes on a positive erotic significance. You are a gossamer ephemerid treading my edges. You are yet the end, the *intelligens entis*, of my being, insofar as I exist on paper. Give me a body. Otherwise I shall fall through space forever. Stop me.

Something keeps plucking me back from my dreams, and I stay awake for hours, hysterical as a guitar string. Last night I dreamed I was teaching my son to walk. It was not clear which son. He straightened in my arms when I picked him up, fighting to be set down. We walked on red wet tiles, his little feet between mine. Our feet were bare and wet as from the swimming pool; in a curiously adult voice, distinct though high-pitched, he remarked, in gratitude for my instruction, that I had "terrific" legs. I was so pleased I awoke. Elsewhere in the night I crossed a road with a gang of others; we stepped over one of those little guard fences of two cables on stubby posts cut on a bias; we ran down a long grassy bank dotted with daisies and butter-and-eggs; we were back home. The others ran on ahead toward the lake and Frankie waited behind with me; in a soft little gesture she unzipped her jeans and showed me her underpants. They were patterned with flowers, pale yellow and pink. It was something a child might do, for another. They were lovely. The slope of the bank and the sudden impulse of love tipped me forward, so that I awoke.

She was shy; her underpants were the nicest thing I had ever seen; did I have time to tell her so? In my dreams we have all become children, as we must, they say, to enter the kingdom of God.

The things humans do! The little creatures in the UFOs must have figured out the sex by now, and our cars, but the dreaming, and the praying, and the singing . . . How to explain music to them?

*

My most physical religious experience occurred in college, those first nervous years, when my poor adolescent body, just seeking to straighten and throw off its acne and stomach cramps, was cruelly loaded with the wisdom of the ages and the languages of the world. I caught colds; I had insomnia; my teeth ached; I became constitpated.* Days went by; six times a day I would sit on the hopeful porcelain oval and wait; nothing. My over-solicited anus hurt; my lower abdomen became hard as a brick; I tottered from class to class along the leafy walks in a daze of disbelief; my Christianity, never muscular, seemed a febrile useless fancy. Then, one morning, sweating over all my body, I pushed out perhaps an inch of dry compacted turd, knobby as a narwhal's tusk, and stalled; my eyes filled with tears; how could I waddle to class with this extrusion? I bent forward far as my torso would go, driven to homemade yoga in this extremity, and in my soul confessed my desperation to whatever powers there be. And a great force as if manually seized my bowels, and my body, like a magnificent animal escaped from its keeper, savagely and so swiftly the dilation of pain passed in a flash thrust out of itself a great weight of waste. It was a thrust from beyond, a release into *trans*: a true Lutherian experience, and my only. Ever since, through stress and strain, trial and tribulation, I have remained regular, as I think I bragged quite early on in these pages.

I expect my expulsion from this happy place will feel rather like that. Unless you come and love me.

I will treat you real swell, Ms. Prynne. Screwing optional, I swear it; just come and sit, tell me about your job, its difficulties, your life, its plan, the local flora, your impressions of me and the role of organized religion in the next millennium—if the chemistry is there, we'll take it all the way; otherwise, we'll have relaxed for an hour, and been kind to one another. No hassle, really. I just feel we have a potential, there's something between us it would be a sin not to let happen. Have I been a

---

*Thinking of my constitution, or your tit. I have noticed your topload isn't as impressive as your ass, but don't let that inhibit you. Flat-chested women, between us, are some of the best. A breast is like a penis; the excitement has secondarily to do with its size; primarily with the fact that it is *there*. Existence precedes everything; *esse est deus*.

bad guest? Have I complained about the food, tried to smuggle postcards out, attempted to bugger the serving boys, held private Masses in my room, refused to play card games because the Devil speaks in pips, faked fragile health and bribed the doctor to sign my release, pulled sacerdotal rank on you, gone crazy and smashed my typewriter, like some we know? No. I've been a fun boy, faithful to my vows of obedience, full of the right camp spirit, willing to learn, anxious under all my impudence to return to the world as a good exemplar if not a good *exemplum*. I want my merit badge. You, Ms., pynne it on me. At night if you wish, but I'm fresher and more phallic in the morning. Incline unto me, and hear my cry.

I love you because (a) you are there (b) you run this haven ably (c) you never complain (d) you seem to be alone (e) you read what I write.

You love me because (a) I am here (b) I need you.

Oh, never mind. Suddenly it is noon, and the universe has shrunk for me to a single circle of white suds, the cool galactic foam that tops a Daiquiri.

30

THEN DON'T COME, you bitch. You sashaying cunt. I hardly slept a dream's worth, for listening for your step, your fingers on the latch, the rustle of your silk, the little tearful twinned *suck* as you remove the contact lenses it is your vanity to wear when you go out with one of your dreadful square-state "dates." You didn't know I knew that about you, did you? Old Tom Marshfield, he has his spies, to paraphrase Lear.

Seriously. Good-bye. I can write hardly a page today, I have said everything I can think of at least twice concerning my lamentable case, and have wasted the morning in packing and listening for you. Packing, I suppose, on the remote chance, the odds Pascalian, that you will relent and come to me tomorrow morning. The plane isn't until two, there would be time. Time to cheat time.

I am delirious with poor sleeping. It will be a relief to crawl in beside Jane's stony slumber and become a stone myself. Here lieth Thomas and his mate Jane, petrified in the Lord's service, left here as a monument and admonition to passersby.

What else can I imagine about the future? Froggy-eyed Ned sits in the middle of my old lily pad; I expect I will be banished to a remote village parish, where once every Midsummer's Eve the villagers will bring to me a virgin lass as to a Minotaur, and I in turn will perform, every vernal equinox, some miracle, involving a sprinkle of my own blood, to keep the crops coming and their lives innocently merry. So be it. I submit.

The worst thing was cleaning (with a fork snitched from your incandescent dining room with the tall drawn vanilla curtains) all the dirt from the cleats of my golf shoes, so my summer clothes (so spiffily purged and pressed at the Peyote Dry Cleaners) wouldn't be sullied while shivering in the belly of the great aluminum bird. I have used up eleven razor blades and two tubes of toothpaste in this heaping measure of a month's time. In the land of my parish, the shortest day of the year is approaching, and Somebody's birthday, I think, the little fellow who never manages to blow out all of the candles.

Eschatological satisfaction of leaving things behind—two pairs of worn socks, one short-sleeved sports shirt whose seam gave out on an overswung 3-iron, one bottle of Coppertone, bone-dry. Outer darkness. The Superworld's Disposall. Our tenderized consciences wince, but there may be a mercy in it.

Do I want to take *What Boys and Girls Are Asking* back with me? I open it randomly and read,

> In attempting to answer the question, "What can we discover concerning the existence and the nature of God from the life around us?" Doctor Gilkey used for an illustration the example of a shipwrecked sailor who finds a deserted cabin on an island.

> Another question which often perplexes boys and girls was expressed by one boy in this way: "Why did God let Jesus die on the cross?" If a leader has a Christian philosophy of his own with regard to the death of Christ he may lead boys and girls into a helpful consideration of this.

> The bright morning sun beat down on the little Chinese village. For weeks the people had looked hopefully toward the sky for signs of rain. Rain could still save the crops. But no rain fell, and the rice fields withered in the scorching heat.
>
> It was with a heavy heart that the Rev. Mr. Lu Cheng-sun entered the tiny church building.

I guess I must take it. As a souvenir.

The immanence of departure renders this bland room as strange as when I entered it. I leave no trace, no scar. Did I dream this? Meister Eckhardt, if I remember, talks of divinity as "the simple ground, the quiet desert" and of a process, so God can be born in the soul, of *entwerden*, the opposite of becoming, travelling away from oneself. The day after tomorrow, my month may seem a metaphor, a pause briefer than that rest of Alicia's I so reprehensibly interrupted.

Last night after poker I went out under the dome of desert stars and was afraid, not afraid, afraid to be born again.

Even so, come.

31

THE SUITCASES STAND in parade formation by the closet door, their zipped zippers and snapped snaps as disapproving as spinsters' mouths. I am terrified. Up in the air. My life here, like my life from birth, seems all loose ends. Is there really no more sense than this? Flight has already entered my stomach and set it to trembling. I cannot cope. I cannot

Bless you.

What a surprise. Your knock wasn't the knock of doom after all. What remains, at this moment, a moment of this my last hour, was the brave way in which you undressed without comment, disclosing with not the flicker of a plea that you were, not fat, but thick, certainly thick, so that my startled arms, embracing, felt to be encircling the trunk of a solid but warm tree. And the tranquillity of you upon your back! Permitting your breasts to be molded again and again—amazing breasts, so firm they seemed small, the nipples erect upon little mounds of further erectile tissue, so that a cupola upon a dome was evoked, an ascent in several stages, an architectural successiveness. Difficult, from your profile, to guess your pleasure. You seemed lost in thought, only your hand speaking to me, lightly drawing my penis up into its ideal shape, so it could once again lose its ache in the almost—nay, veritably—alarmingly liquid volume of the passage to your womb. The entire process indolent, chronic, tranquil. How many times? I did lose count. I feel drained, light; I have a fever, a light headache. Was I worthy? You have brought me to an edge, a slippery edge. And nothing left for me to do, dear Ideal Reader, but slip and topple off, gratefully.

What is it, this human contact, this blank-browed thing we do for one another? There was a moment, when I entered you, and was big, and you were already wet, when you could not have seen yourself, when your eyes were all for another, looking up into mine, with an expression without a name, of entry and alarm, and of salutation. I pray my own face, a stranger to me, saluted in turn.

APPENDIX

Foreword to
Couples: A Short Story

THE SHORT STORY entitled "Couples" was written in the
spring of 1963; the carbon copy among my papers gives
the completion date as May 16. With it were the notes predat-
ing its composition. A typed scrap reads:

> parties, heading into flowers—remembers moments when
> colors separate—golf, the time with Williamses,
> musselling—the party when all five couples came in a
> blizzard up our hill

On the back of a proof sheet for *The Centaur* I drew in ball-
point pen a square, with the corners labelled M, M, W, W and
with dotted diagonal lines connecting opposite corners. Beside
this is scrawled:

> diagonal lines of attraction when the sides creak and
> break

> _____

> friendships; a woman [illegible] refuses to go when
> a brat [?] offended

> _____

> woman who thought a man comes around in fact
>   homosexually
> attracted to her husband
> fell in love

> _____

> finds self on knees embracing her maternity suit in closet

And there is a chart of the five couples—WILLIAMS MOR-
RIS HORNING GUERIN KROCK—with the names of
the individual marital partners, to keep me from the confusion
of intermingling that overtakes the characters themselves.

The story was written from these notes, submitted to *The New Yorker*, and rejected, though this was a time of frequent acceptances for me. "Couples" is preceded in my stack of papers by the short story "At a Bar in Charlotte Amalie" and followed by my essay on Denis de Rougemont's theories of love, the poem "Report of Health," and the story "The Christian Roommates"—all in due course given space within the pages of that gracious magazine. But my own qualms about "Couples" in the form it had taken reconciled me to its non-publication. It was, above its incidental faults of sentimentality and vagueness, too crowded; its mapping of its garden of two-toned flowers needed the space of the novel which eventually I wrote, some three years later, using the name of the town but surprisingly few of the other names. I don't believe I reread "Couples" before beginning *Couples*.

I did try to salvage from this story a shorter story to be called "Peggy's Clothes" or, after the remark by Nix Morris, "You Voluptuous Piece of Wallpaper You." Neither version was ever printed, and this poor jewel of an image, the voluptuous wallpaper, found its eventual setting in a reminiscence of sorts entitled "When Everyone Was Pregnant" (1971). The simile likening breaking surf to a typewriter carriage was placed, with greater point, in a story written later that summer, "Harv Is Plowing Now." And a number of details first verbalized in "Couples" also made their way into the bedevilled manuscript of a novel called *Marry Me*, whose page proofs I have just yesterday completed reading.

It is fitting that *Marry Me*, as a trade novel, and this short story, in a limited edition, should be published at about the same time. They were among my first attempts to write about suburban adultery, a subject that, if I have not exhausted it, has exhausted me. But I have persisted, as I earlier persisted in describing the drab normalities of a Pennsylvania boyhood, with the conviction that there was something good to say for it, some sad magic that, but for me, might go unobserved. This short story, though it fails to earn the clangor of its last two paragraphs—a passage I find written out in hand on the blank insides of an eviscerated envelope from the Mental Health Association of the North Shore—yet has tendernesses and exactitudes not duplicated in any later manipulation of these themes. The simple party pleasures of the youngly married, the mathematics of a social "set" or "group," the faces around the fire during the blizzard—none of this would return so directly, with such an innocent excitement of presentation. The enchanted moment when the other young couples looked to the narrator like "safeguards, echoes, reinforcements of our happiness" had been overlaid with too many incidents by the time he, in the guise of an author-god lifted above his personae, began to construct the novel that, in honor of its amplitude, was to be called *Couples and Houses and Days.* The lofty and possibly unkind sociological tone of that novel, and the note of personal emotion struck in a number of short stories less clumsy than this one, are here still fused; as it stands (little rewritten for this its first venture into print), "Couples" bares the muffled heart of *Couples,* the theme of friendship—of friendships and their inevitable, never-quite-complete betrayal by, if by nothing else, time.

JOHN UPDIKE
June 11, 1976

Couples
A Short Story

LIVING ALONE, as I do now, I have time to think and remember—more time, in truth, than I need. I remember how, when my wife and I moved to Tarbox almost exactly six years ago (then, as now, the elm trees were furry with buds and yet transparent, brittle as window tracery, in the quiet winter sunlight)—I remember how the other young couples of the town looked to us. They looked like safeguards, echoes, reinforcements of our happiness. Each couple, as our acquaintance widened that first spring, seemed one flower striped or spotted with two colors. It was as if Ann and I had come north from New York City into a large garden where our footsteps began to wear paths and favored patches. Perhaps friendships of the sort we now developed need soil underfoot and fresh air overhead. We had met and married in college, and in the following four years our social life had languished among bachelors, business acquaintances, visitors from the past, and parties of tiresomely exotic strangers. Now we found ourselves transplanted among healthy blooms, and felt health swell our own twinned stalk.

The Hornings and Guerins were living, but not for long, in Tarbox when we arrived; the Williamses moved into their rambling barn-red house on the beach road the very month, April, that we occupied our square gray house on Far Hill (there was a wet snowstorm that week, the first of the many times we found ourselves marooned); the Morrises and Krocks came to town within the year. We were all, all of the couples, except for Billy Horning, in the second half of our twenties, and all the men, except for Dr. Guerin, in some way drew their livelihood, through the rickety siphon of the B & M line, out of Boston. We had come to Tarbox because it was a bit beyond the commuter belt, an ancient colonial settlement turned mill town, somewhat depressed and forgotten, so that even the Poles, who had succeeded the English and French and Greeks here, were old citizens, whose children were the kings and queens of the high school. We were, I suppose, the first curl of a new wave of immigration, the commuter wave, presaged by the Boston rich who for fifty years had summered here within sight of the sea. Unlike them, we stayed all year. The town itself, miles inland, was drab and hodgepodge in its center, rather randomly picturesque in its neighborhoods, and in its environs incomparably furnished with three golf courses, a pond for skating, a river for canoeing, a small hill, with rope tow, for skiing, miles of unspoiled salt marsh, and a magnificently wide, safe beach of white sand. In short it was, for those able to use it, a kind of playground for adults. Nix Morris and I learned golf together, the Krocks cleaned up an abandoned tennis court on their land, the Williamses bought an old dory and an outboard and took us musselling on the flats between the beach and Grace Island (it was not until last winter, however, that Ann and I took up skiing, which is somehow the sport of the desperate). The first fall, the husbands began to play touch football; and by the second summer the wives could always be found in a bunch on the beach, lazily guarding the little colony of babies that in five years was to grow into such a nation of children.

The women were always pregnant—not all of them at once, but some of them all the time. Maternity clothes were swapped back and forth, silhouettes swelled and flattened, our names appeared in boldface in the Births column of the Tarbox weekly, where they looked, to our clannish eyes, like private messages passed to one another. In memory it seems we were playing at being adults, at being fathers and mothers and homeowners. We had all, it chanced, come to it new together, this incredible America where we managed, and controlled, and mattered; we paid taxes and mowed lawns and poured ourselves a deserved drink in the evenings, though in those days only Billy Horning, who was older, and Morton Williams, who was a little unsettled and sullen, really understood the point of drinking. The cocktail parties that at first were just two or three couples diligently making conversation of "topics" mentally clipped from newspapers, and the baby showers that the women quaintly gave each other, and the chance chats in the supermarket that ended with coffee in the diner across the street merged with the long shared hours of sun and exercise to bake us, as it were, into the mold of friendship. Though other couples

moved to town and superficially attached themselves to us—
for instance, the Murketts, of whom he, with his swish black
loafers and Tartan sports jacket, sported a shady record of job-
hopping, and the Eberholzers, of whom she, so young-looking
and bright-eyed, possessed an almost unimaginable history of
mental disturbance and divorce—we six couples jealously retained the corporate identity that our simultaneous initiation
into Tarbox had given us. Any wife of the group, planning a
largish party, automatically began the list with the five other
names, like a tilesetter fitting the easy beginnings of a pattern,
or a mathematician who instantly perceives that if A, B; and, if
A and B, then C, D, and E.

As keenly as a Pilgrim remembering England I remember
the bucolic pleasure, of a weekend night, of driving with Ann
toward one of "our" parties. The darkened streets of the town
seemed to unfold like parted leaves; we seemed to be heading
into the radiance of a flower—a flower spotted, if the party
was to be at the Hornings', with Ruth's nervous gay gold on
the ground of his steady, swarthy maturity; a flower striped,
if the destination was the Morrises', with such quick fineness
that it was impossible to tell, as Nix and Sally yipped and kid-
ded back and forth, which of the couple was contributing the
black and which the white. The Guerins were a more sombre
combination, heavy, like a sunflower of which he was the ponderous, fruitful heart and she the vaguely comic frill of petals;
the Krocks were an iris, fragile, austere, and cool. The limply
curling lips of their slightly overblown hospitality protectively
cloaked the pallor into which their purple edges descended,
a narrow unseen bowl cupping a sickly-sweet scent of money
—their long-stemmed wealth made them seem a little vulnerable and secretive, Anita whose translucent skin was so quickly
kindled into a blush, Fred whose hands, seen sideways, were
freakishly thin. The Williamses, a lush emotional rose blended
of his sullen red and her freckled pink, gave the parties I liked
best of all.

Whichever the house, the porch light would be on. The familiar cars would be parked outside, dented and relaxed and a
little strange, like sleeping faces. Inside, we would be greeted
casually, more pronounced welcomes being saved for those
who were, in fact, less welcome. We would be told to take our

coats upstairs, and there, suspended above the raucous tinkle below by the floor of a bedroom whose hush seemed compounded of the repose of discarded coats and the lingering whispers of past love-making, we might overhear the hostess, in another bedroom, crooning to a baby or reading to a child. We were folded in. Whether separately or together, it didn't matter, Ann and I would descend the stairs to receive our just portion of love; faces and furniture would come toward us, and a kind of voiced applause would go up at our wonderful feat, of simply existing, here.

On our first night out in Tarbox, the second week we were there, we went for dinner to the Hornings', when they lived in the little rented house on Clam Lane, before they bought the seventeenth-century house on the river. We were the only guests. Billy was silent, and Ruth so nervously busy with hors d'oeuvres that she was out of the room half the time. We didn't know them then; Billy's brooding and Ruth's fluttering embarrassed us. During one of the long lulls in the conversation, while Billy studied the glass in his hand with a wry and, we feared, pained expression, the Hornings' little girl, Linda, like a tiny ghost in her long white nightie, appeared at the foot of the stairs and walked a diagonal line across the rug to the window and said, in her tiny, eerily lucid just-beginning-to-talk voice, "See moon?" I have rather loved Linda ever since. The constraint collapsed; we rushed to the window, all four of us, and together partook, as if the night sky beyond the window were a brimming libation, of the child's wonder in the bare bright fact of the moon.

Our first large function was the Heart Fund Dance, in May, at the Polish Veterans' Hall. What I chiefly remember from that are Dr. Guerin's shoes. They were suede boots, thick-soled, coarse-laced, and inappropriate for a dance. He was in manner tense and proper; but his clothes were in defiantly dubious taste, and I wondered if his frilly little wife, with whom he danced only once, were somehow part of the same defiance. Staring at the young doctor's incongruous shoes as, not even tapping his feet, he sat out dance after dance, I had my first premonition of couples as barricades of mystery, as gates closed on sinister catacombs tunnelled through past time.

When the Williamses moved to town, Morton was studying for his Ph.D. in philosophy, and Peggy had just had their first child, John, a month before. They camped in the Bohemian style of students amid a great deal of elegant furniture, and, if Peggy toted gallon jugs of milk from the supermarket to save a few pennies, Morton seemed to have no trouble finding the dollars to buy cases of wine. Their puzzling mixture of thrift and extravagance irritated us. One night, going into Boston for dinner and a play, they left John in our care. It was the sort of favor student couples ask of one another; but Ann and I thought we had moved out of that, into a post-collegiate world where babysitters were hired. Furthermore, we ourselves had an infant son, and, juxtaposed to the rare beauty we read into him, the Williamses' blue-pated pop-eyed baby seemed a repulsive guest. He fretfully squalled all evening. His parents did not return for him until one o'clock. When they did, high and gay, I fear we made our irritation plain, for they never again asked us to keep their child; and I wonder now if in that rebuff was not implicit all the unhappiness we two couples were to cause each other. For the Williamses, in so casually presuming upon a friendship not yet formed, conferred trust upon us, and we, in fastidiously shying from that trust, first tainted the friendship. I don't wish to exaggerate this; it was their parties I enjoyed most, and even Morton—whom I suppose, if a modern man can hate anyone, I do hate—had moments of great charm. He tended, erratically, to be generous, as a host, and as a talker. He was willing, that is, to admit frankly that he was confused. Confused men talk well as long as conversation is understood to be a series of questions; but Morton felt compelled, perhaps by his pedagogic aspirations, to give answers, and in giving answers he was as boring as only the very insecure can be. When he relaxed from his pose as thinker and indulged his real aptitude, which was for doing things—running a boat, digging a garden, mixing a drink—he seemed to me, so contrarily endowed, a delightful man of unequalled (strange, but this is the word) dependability.

I suppose their playing at poverty offended us. To Ann and me, who had been honestly poor, poverty was a solemn business. Also, Ann and Peggy were, in their competing modes, the best-looking women of our six. To see them lying on the beach together always made me feel unreasonably rich; between them, they had every gift—vivacity and poise, life and intelligence. But they seldom lay together on the beach; their beauty served to push them apart, so they were usually in opposite corners of a party and, at volleyball in the sand, on opposed sides of the net. The time the Williamses took us musselling in their boat was uniquely idyllic. I consented to learn from Morton and, though rather squeamish and hydrophobic, dared press my face into the water and tear the clenched purple butterflies from their roots of barnacled rock. Holding with a bleeding hand a kettle of mussels on my head, I waded back to the dory, where Peggy stood, her legs astride the distant sliver of Grace Island, her face confused with a camera held above a grin and beside a squinting eye. They later showed us their slides, and the picture she took shows me—my skin tangerine in the dying light—up to my waist in the water, some underfed half-caste slave, the kettle on my head incandescent where the setting sun was directly reflected. Above my left shoulder, Morton's legs, robed in golden fuzz and shod in sopping tennis sneakers, grip a shelf of slippery rock. Afterwards, they took us into shore, Morton letting me manage the outboard until we hit the surf. We gathered wood and boiled the mussels and fed them to one another. As night grew thick around us, we played word games, Indian-wrestled, finished the wine, and undressed and went swimming. In the whispering black, pierced again and again by the arrow of breaking foam racing down the sand with the regularity of a typewriter carriage, our naked shapes were the chastest of blurs. When we regathered around the fire, Morton and I had put our trousers on over wet legs and the women held towels around their bodies. I had this sharp sense then, filling my eyes with a pressure as if I were confronting an angel, of the four of us, together, amounting to something, some single, complete, and enduring thing—the same feeling, perhaps, that in another form had led the Williamses to assume we would accept their child as our own.

The Morrises came to Tarbox that September, and his beautiful long smooth spirals, flipped often as not with a cigarette dangling from the corner of his mouth, were the heart of the touch football games. The sky on those Sunday afternoons in October and November would be gray and restless with small hurrying clouds, like a heavenly hangover, and as you raced pell-mell over the treacherous stubble of the Guerins' upper field one of Nix's passes would appear in this sky like an oval black omen which would, as your lungs burst, fit, like a nested bird, into your desperately outstretched fingers.

With the arrival of the Krocks, the set softly clicked shut. Their almost elderly reserve, their towering Christmas tree, the shy blessing of their embarrassed money (he was simply "in business") sealed us in. The standards of dinner-party hospitality were subtly elevated. Cigars and brandy appeared after dinner. Any lingering notion, encouraged by the Williamses, that we were cheerfully threadbare Bohemian couples vanished. Our parties took on body. The custom of dancing in a dimmed room was timidly introduced. An evening out became a sparkling river flowing through the spectrum of martinis, prandial wine, brandy, whiskey-and-water, beer, and, after midnight, coffee. Ann and I would return home and the quiet cold living-room, the floorboards we ourselves had sanded, the sleepy baby-sitter fumbling with her purse—she was an old lady active in the Methodist church and the Grange—would afflict us with shame; we would share a glass of milk in the kitchen and search our faces in the bathroom mirror for traces of corruption.

The last burst, the glowing death, of innocence I remember as the birthday party Ann gave for me the third winter. I was twenty-eight. There was a blizzard. The old college friends from Cambridge and Boston that we had invited were unable to come. But, one way or another, the couples of Tarbox slithered their sitters through the mounting snow, left their homes, and climbed our hill on foot. It was just the five couples, and I remember them arriving, red-faced with exertion and shedding snow, in our entryway, which was soon soaked in the wet-wool-and-galoshes smell of a kindergarten cloakroom. How proud and grateful I was, that they should have fought their way through to my birthday, like rescuers to a catastrophe! I even remember their presents: an exquisitely chosen book (*Memento Mori*, by Muriel Spark) from the Hornings; a typically poor-taste joke (a mug with a plastic nude kneeling inside) from the Guerins; a curiously duplex gift—a teddy bear (Peggy?) that unzipped to reveal a pint of

Scotch (Morton?)—from the Williamses; a golf glove from
the Morrises; a touchingly expensive and conservative neck-
tie from the Krocks. Ann gave me a blue sweater, the very
sweater—how the permanence of things mocks us!—that I
am wearing now. The blizzard raged outside, but the food,
liquor, and electricity held out. When at last the electricity
failed, we lit candles, and danced to our own singing—Ruth
Horning, surprisingly, knew the lyrics of all the songs of our
teens, from "Linda" to "Across the Alley from the Alamo."
When the chill of the dead furnace spread through the house,
we sat around the fireplace, our eyes and drinks glittering,
and listened indifferently to our voices and the heavy, patient
protests of the storm outside. In my great love for them all,
I tried to seize my friends with my eyes. Their extended legs
seemed logs about to catch on fire. Doc Guerin and Sally
Morris were murmuring together, his left cheek tucked up
in wrinkles by a drowsy, steady half-smile. Morton Williams'
hand, to emphasize some unheard point, rested on Anita
Krock's long pale forearm and, instead of lifting, thoughtfully travelled on one fingertip down to her wrist, as if he
were testing the finish of a piece of wood. Ann sat beside Nix
Morris and, though both were silent and motionless, gazing
into the fire on parallel beams of vision, from the hunch of
her shoulders and the intent pucker of her lips she seemed to
be enduring an invisible weight. Peggy Williams' voice, which
always flirted with shrillness, grew hysterically high and flung
giggles into the air like sparks up a flue. Ruth Horning, in an
awkward, ostentatious gesture of possession, sighed aloud,
as if exhausted from remembering so many song lyrics, and
rested her bright blond head on Billy's dark shoulder. Fred
Krock, as he drew on his drink, closed his eyes stoically. Georgene Guerin was crying. Yes, those were tears glittering on
the sides of her nose. The colors of the flowers were beginning to separate.

My party was the last of its kind. Through the following
spring and summer, the set began to lose its shape. The Murketts and the Eberholzers intruded more and more successfully, and became inseparable from the Krocks and Williamses,
whose money was beginning to declare itself and to seek its own
level. They bought a bigger boat, and the intimate foursome of

the day we gathered mussels was not repeated. The flat days of idyll were done. In the perspective of personal affinity, some individuals receded and others came into the foreground. What with golf, we saw a good deal more of Nix Morris than of Sally. Grim rumors of Georgene Guerin's mysterious disintegration began to circulate, and the doctor took to appearing at parties alone, or else taking her home early and returning by himself. Ann and I found ourselves more and more with the Hornings, whose increasingly blunt show of marital union, now and then undercut by flashes of girlish acerbity from Ruth, which Billy rebuked with a pained silence, both reassured and bored us. Relationships between couples are squares of which two sides are the marriages and the other two whatever comradely and respectful feelings the persons of the same sex share. It is not enough that affection make connections along all four sides. The square is hollow unless dotted diagonal lines of attraction exist between the opposite corners; it is these illicit lines that hold the square taut. The two diagonals should be roughly equal in strength; my urge to soothe Ruth's jittery blond head was fond rather than fierce, and Ann's feelings toward Billy were, I knew, qualified and mild. Where one diagonal is absent and the other is overpowering, the square collapses. Ann had no use whatsoever for Morton Williams, so we saw them far too seldom.

Among the innumerable items of memory my solitude, like an insatiable card-dealer, forces upon me, there is one that never turns up: the moment when I fell in love with Peggy Williams. There must have been a moment, for my first impression of her was disagreeable—of a shrill, tall, rather silly girl unflatteringly attached to a pretentious, insecure man. She had the demeanor of a secretary and, in those days before the healthy Tarbox summers added womanly weight to her frame, the brittle figure of a tomboy. She seemed defensive generally and hostile especially to me. I seemed to threaten Morton. As she sat in our house the night they had left John in our care, her skirt kept awkwardly riding up over her knees and, as we listened to her husband's absurd opinions on the play they had seen (he thought anything that mentioned death was "existential"), her eyes kept snagging on mine. Her eyes were hot and large; her expression struck me as vapid, dense, and servile. Perhaps my anger is significant. Perhaps I was jealous instantly. But this means that I was in love with Peggy before she appeared in my life, which is impossible. Yet my next memory, as it turns up in the tainted shuffle of time, is of her asking me to dance with her at, I think, a party the Krocks gave. And not only did I react to the invitation with a flare of emotion that has permanently lit the cervine tension of her face, the akimbo position of her arms, the sweep of the neckline of the wheat-yellow gown she wore; but she offered the invitation as if in response to a silent plea I had long been making. So I was in love with her then, and the strange solid fit of her in my arms, the insistent way she held our clasped hands too far out from our bodies, the nervous foot-fumbling as we sought to discover each other's fox-trot styles, were for me like the mental adjustments made when, after many years, we return to a childhood scene and discover that the shed is on our right and not our left, that there are two pear trees instead of one, and that the box hedge is lower than we remembered.

There was no sense of conquest. Each advance she made into me, or I into her, was occupation of territory already, somehow, claimed. Our love was not plotted, but expanded randomly, released by widely spaced accidents. Nix Morris, whom alcohol turned metaphoric, once loudly called across a room to her that she looked like "a voluptuous piece of wallpaper." She was wearing a print dress patterned with big orange flowers. She blushed, and a wild panic tore at my heart, that others could see her beauty, and would steal it from me. I felt no threat from Morton; he was blind to his wife. He took her presence at his side, her queerly tenacious loyalty to him, quite for granted, making her, this splendid upright woman, a weak limb of himself. Perhaps it was Peggy's fate to exist only as a projection of some man. For me, she was like a thought I had always harbored, whose external existence needed the proof of her clothes for me to believe and seize it. Her clothes were the essence of my love. She had a way of wearing anything so that the cloth seemed glad and independently animated. The moon-white towel she wrapped her body in the night we went musselling; the faun jodhpurs, with the oval leather patches sewn inside each thigh, that made her legs look so long; the curious short stiff green jacket, made in Iran and embroidered with looping arabesques of black thread, that she wore shopping in the supermarket; the gray knit suit that hugged her hips at cocktail parties; the paint-deckled dungarees and khaki army shirt, knotted like a diaper above a triangle of bare belly, in which I once discovered her painting their living-room woodwork, the windows wide open, spring in the air; the prim lavender bodice, of velvet, that she wore with a sweeping taffeta skirt to the Mental Health Dance; her chartreuse shorts; her Paisley halter—my heart became a draper's shop. And in the enterprise of love my investment spread to her furniture: to the wing chair covered in beige corduroy, the walnut dining table under the chandelier of wrought copper, the unusually bluish Oriental rug always awry in their hallway, the great gold harp-frame empty of strings, inherited from some grandmother. Whatever touched her, whatever her eyes habitually touched, even the landscapes of Tarbox—the beach, the downtown street—that rhythmically contained her became charged, for me, with an immanence that, though I denied it a name, seemed to be sustaining my life.

While I cannot remember when I fell in love with Peggy, I distinctly remember the moment when I was compelled to admit it to myself. Ann had just borne our third child and lay in the hospital drowsily reading women's magazines. I went directly from visiting her to the Williamses, who were giving a small party. It was much the customary party—there were a few strange faces, and a college boy playing a guitar, but in essence it was the party we couples had been throwing for each other for years. Momentarily a bachelor, I accepted congratulations, talked, ate liver pâté on Onion Thins, and drank. Morton put on records, and there was dancing. When I danced with Peggy, her furniture softly twirled around with us. She seemed sad and pleased to be in my arms; something in her manner suggested that I had returned from a great distance. Because I had to rise with the children, I left at midnight. In my silent house, I paid the sitter and went upstairs, opened a closet door, fell on my knees, and buried my face in the maternity suit, a warm checked tweed, that Peggy had loaned Ann.

Yet another year passed—a full four seasons of sun, touch football, births, blizzards, balky furnaces, and reluctant spring

—before I privately kissed her (public kissings, hello and fare-well, had become part of our parties, as if we had grown into aunts and uncles attending an almost weekly family reunion), and another six months before we made love, and I could add, to the vast wardrobe that sentiment had stolen for me, a black lace brassiere, a tattered white one with recalcitrant snaps, and a pair of silk underpants surprisingly patterned in broad pale flowers, like wallpaper.

The shock of plunging into an affair quickly yielded to de-licious sensations of freedom and elemental acceptance and new knowledge. Opening my eyes, I saw from a startling sub-aqueous perspective the sunny, bobbing world above. The del-icate attentions, for example, that Morton visibly paid to Anita Krock were just an iceberg-eighth of the truth; in fact they had slept together off and on since several summers ago, and beneath the indications of unease I had lately noticed between the two couples there hung frantic four-cornered emotional storms. Reprisals, reconciliations, resumptions lit like light-ning strokes this weird hidden landscape, illuminating an un-expected variety of actors and scenes—Doc Guerin, between appointments, placing persistent telephone calls to Peggy at her home; Billy Horning forcing a French kiss upon her in her own kitchen; Fred Krock stoically climbing into bed with her on a ski weekend because he had nowhere else to sleep; Nix Morris, with whom I had played golf for five summers without the flicker of a confession between us, sitting up with the Wil-liamses until four in the morning outpouring his grief. He and Sally had not had sexual relations in two years. In confessing this, he had burst into tears.

I tended, in the imagery of infatuation, to associate Peggy with the breezy open windows of the afternoon I had found her painting her living-room woodwork, and living within her, as her lover, was like seeing out, for the first time, into the houses of our friends. Windows gave on yet other windows, until in the mixed reflection and refraction no corner remained dark. The flowers turned transparent, each revealing its active green worm, its patch of sour wilt. The Hornings, Billy had confessed to Anita, who relayed it to Morton who had passed it on to his wife, had had, in the guise of a socially notable

Episcopal ceremony, a shotgun wedding; when Peggy told me this I remembered little Linda, at a time when the rest of our children were still babies, walking like a tiny ghostly grown-up across the rug and beginning to talk. The Krocks were held back from a divorce by, of all things, poverty; Fred's attempts to extend the family fortune had failed miserably, and they were, until his father's death, on a tight allowance. Their marriage had been forced by his family, as a medical measure. In college, he had been a homosexual. The Guerins' story was so grim that no one had ever bothered to pursue it beyond the fact that Georgene's unmistakable blue Simca was several times seen (by Mim Eberholzer, drably enough) parked outside a motel in Lynn; and of course even *I* must have noticed the bruises on Georgene's face at the New Year's Eve party. Actually, I hadn't.

Peggy was a splendid window, curtained in her clothes, but even she did not overlook every fact; there were other windows still, as I discovered when, in asking Ann for a divorce, I confessed my months of adultery and she in turn confessed to me that, since two Septembers ago, now and then when I was away overnight on a business trip, Nix Morris would come to the house, shy and serious and full of fondness for me, and make love to her. He was not sure he loved her. She did not love him, and, last winter, during a violent mental crisis that I had accepted as a mysteriously prolonged bout of intestinal flu, she had broken with him. Ann's face was grave and wooden and lovely, like a de Latour, in the restaurant candlelight as she told me this, and her voice assumed a womanly huskiness I had not heard for years. My first reaction was to laugh, in a strange twist of relief. My laugh in memory clangs like a momentarily opened door swinging shut again. For Ann's being my equal in guilt transposed our marriage into a different key without bringing divorce any closer. Indeed, now we had another bond, trivial but tireless: the bond of gossip.

What had happened to us? What was going to happen? I believe, without exaggerating my own importance, that I was, among the six couples, the last innocent, and when I fell, all our furtive woes and suppressed miseries were free to swarm across the social field. We became a ring of confidants. Our parties assumed a feverish intimacy, wherein a third person hesitated to go up to any conversing couple, even a couple as apparently uninvolved as Sally Morris and Billy Horning, for fear of intruding on a tête-à-tête. In groups of three or more, someone would mention a topic culled from the newspaper —Castro, desegregation, rockets, or any of the remote threats that once had so plausibly menaced our happiness—and we would all begin laughing, bubbling with delight at what we knew, and knew that the other people knew, which included knowing that we knew. Uprooted from our rich ground of shared secrets—at, say, dinner in Boston with professional acquaintances—we would become listless and almost physically languish. Back home, in Tarbox, the phone would ring during breakfast, and a new secret, or a slightly fresh slant on an old secret, would begin the day. No newspaper readers were ever more hungry for fresh installments than we. "What's the word?" I would ask Ann as she returned to the table and poured herself coffee.

"Oh, nothing—that was just Georgene calling about the car pool. Ruth can't take Wednesdays any more for some reason."

"What else?"

"Won't you miss your train?"

"I will if you don't tell me what she said."

"It was nothing about you, dear."

"I'm sure. Who was it about?"

"I guess she had an endless talk with Anita yesterday."

"Uh-huh." Anita, the story went, had told Doc Guerin, after some weeks of a flirtation whose growing intensity we had all observed at parties, that she was *not* going to have an affair with him. Doc, with the same stubborn carelessness that allowed him to wear suede shoes and unstriped neckties, had allowed himself to tell Georgene, who became furious, ostensibly because an affair had been contemplated, but really (we thought) because one had not taken place, relieving her of whatever bad conscience she acquired in Lynn motels. She had called Anita that afternoon, said vile drunken things, and disappeared with the children for two nights, during which Anita lived on pills and slept not at all. "Poor old Anita," I added, prompting. I still thought of her as somewhat irislike.

"Well, Georgene's side of it is that poor old Anita was really much more explicit with Doc than she's let on; for example

—you're really going to miss that train—in the playroom at the Morrises'—"

"Ah! Your lover's mansion."

"I beg your pardon."

"Your ex-lover?"

"Nix? He never really seemed like a lover. He was just like he is when you bring him back from golf, except you weren't along."

"I wonder where we'll play this Saturday. The greens at Old Colonial have really been burnt by this drought."

"Will you let me finish?"

"God. You still defend that bastard. He won't leave frigid Sally for you and you still defend him."

"In the Morrises' playroom after he'd beaten her at electric hockey Anita supposedly said to him, 'You arouse me.'"

I finished my coffee. "Anita is just not subtle. Anybody who sleeps with Morton Williams is coarsened for life."

"I think both the Williamses have that effect."

I rose and cried, "Stay! Just the way you are, petulant and beautiful. It's the way I want to remember you, always." I took up my briefcase and left. The day's revelation had been a disappointment to me. I had hoped, with the vagueness of the desperate, that the Guerin incident might somehow shake Anita loose from George, so that Morton might go to her, setting Peggy free, which would bring my own problem half-way to solution.

But no; we were all wedged in. Children, habit, and money blocked every would-be move, and in the atmosphere of increasing restriction, merely psychological events fed the ravenous hunger for gossip that relatively real events had created. Anita Krock, in the wake of her refusal to sleep with the doctor, and as a side effect of her many heart-to-heart talks with Georgene, fell literally in love with the Guerins' children, and would scandalize us all by dragging Teddy Guerin's arithmetic marks and Mitzi Guerin's angelic blue eyes into the sullied air of a party. It was as if, in refusing to sleep with their father, she had betrayed a kind of husband, whose children were also hers.

And then, like a supporting actress given one long solo, Ruth Horning leaped from the wings and announced herself to be in the process of a nervous breakdown. Why, she could not exactly say. The conditions in Tarbox were, of course, unsettling. Billy, apparently, had found himself excessively touched by my wronged wife, and this had triggered in Ruth's blond head the thought that awful things could happen even to them. But this wasn't half of it. Her turmoil had welled up from the deeps of time, and involved a childhood speech impediment, long since corrected, a religious dilemma resolved in adolescence, and a remote quarrel between her parents, who now lived happily in Washington, D.C. She went into her attic and reread her old college papers on Dostoevski. She insisted she was not in love, and never mentioned the shotgun wedding, which was common knowledge. So vivid was her crisis, so remarkable was her feat in producing one without the help of a man, that she magnetically gathered, first one by one and then in little groups, all the wives about her as, tremblingly sipping vermouth, she sang the long song of her childhood, her repressions, her failures as a mother, her grotesque idealization of marriage, her vicious fluctuations of hostility, guilt, and tenderness toward Billy, her sleeplessness, her dreams (she dreamed we were all moving into one another's houses, and the movers were always Southern Negroes), her psychosomatic vomiting, her psychiatrist. She was the first of us (except for Fred Krock in his youth) to enter analysis, and she became, for the month before her parthenogenetic upheaval became tired news, the most dramatic figure in our circle; when she entered a room, radiant-haired, hollow-eyed, Billy hanging behind her like a sheepish shadow, she fetched all eyes. Her ordeal had made her thin, witty, and gallant, and I felt myself in danger of tipping into love with her.

Peggy and I struggled to keep our love, so simple, so naïve, alive under the smothering complication of those around us. After my confession to Ann produced not a divorce but an agreement to hold off everything until the end of summer, Peggy and I met seldom, and always far from Tarbox, in Boston or on an alien beach, and then usually chastely, for the merest touch of our hands reconfirmed the harmony our bodies had enjoyed. At gatherings in Tarbox we were discreet and distant. Nevertheless, in the merciless new atmosphere, everybody knew, except, possibly, Morton. Smiling, squinting, blinking his furry eyelashes, he became the center of fascinated attention as our friends tried to decide if he knew or not. It seemed incredible that he did not know; at times Peggy suspected he did, and then some blind remark would convince her that he did not. His blindness to our love diminished its reality. Summer ended, and I was too weak to abandon my wife and children. In an agonized interview conducted in whispers in the Boston Public Library, Peggy and I broke it off. Here my memory tries to compel me to look at her face as it was that day; and I reject the card. For a month Ann and I avoided parties where the Williamses might be present, and then began attending again. It was autumn.

The scene had grown even more sinister. Sally and Nix were going to a marriage counsellor, Georgene was taking guitar lessons in Lynn, Peggy and both the Krocks were going to psychiatrists. Our unhappiness was the unspoken subject of every word we exchanged, the ground of every game we played. I deliberately tripped Morton Williams at touch football, and he dislocated his finger—I have never seen anything of my own creation as terrible as that finger, the two second joints sticking out at an angle from the empurpled first knuckle. I had sinned. My wronging of Peggy had plunged my love for her into a theological swoon. The fading warmth of the sand on the beach seemed to seep from underneath, the heat of Hell. The infernal gulf between those who knew everything and those who knew nothing restored the six couples to something like their original integrity. A new kind of party replaced the old, a kind that began on Friday night and continued, from house to house, through intervals of sleep and changes of costume, until Monday morning, when the last drugged couples tore themselves away from the cooling fireplaces and flagging self-analyses and headed home, through spitting snow, toward the babysitter and the week's work. Away from each other, we became afraid. Our presences had become mutually narcotic; the drinking of one another's poison had become necessary to our health—frustration, discontent, remorse, drunkenness, laughter, and scandal so thoroughly minced by a multitude of tongues that it had lost all bitter flavor. The ones we loved, or had loved, or had confided in deeply became almost odious, they were so saturated in ourselves; and in the final combination of the couples we gravitated, each of us, toward the relatively empty corners of our set, where the women we had never desired, the man we had always thought a bore, waited with the welcome indifference of a sister or brother. Ann took to having long talks with Fred Krock, whose paper-thin hands had always horrified her. Late one Sunday night she told me, as we climbed into bed sick from our weekend, "Fred thinks he should commit suicide."

"Why he more than any of us?"

"He thinks we all need a sacrifice, and he thinks he'd be good because he can't love women and he can't make money."

"Does his psychiatrist agree?"

"Of course not. Be serious. He was really very frightening."

"I am serious. Do you agree?"

"I don't think he should shoot himself; but I think he's right that something has to happen. It can't go on this way."

"What can't?"

"Any of it. All of it. It's a fantastic mess."

I sighed. "Yes. I'm sorry."

"Sorry for what?"

"For everything. For you. For me. I feel it's my fault, really. Mine and Peggy's."

"Don't be silly. There were things going on before you and Peggy."

"Yes, but somehow we brought it to a boil."

"In a way—but that's over."

"So everybody tells me."

"Has Peggy told you?"

"Many times."

"Do you believe her?"

"No."

We were silent. Ann turned her back, and I curled around her. "I meant I'm sorry that he's right," I said.

"Who? What are you saying? I'm falling asleep."

"Fred. He's right. We need a sacrifice. We're so full of infection we must be bled." Now I was falling asleep; my words tugged at my lips, and unconnected images of surgical tools and cigarettes being lit slipped through my dissolving mind. The bed in darkness developed a tilt to whose smooth downward pull I gave myself as if to a swerve of fate.

But Ann's body had gone tense. "David. What are you thinking?"

"I'm afraid you know," I said.

Two weeks later, dazed with fear and numb with resolution, I went to Morton Williams and asked him for his wife. He was drunk when I arrived. He said he had known since the middle of summer, and gave me the name of a lawyer. Under Morton's guidance, the four of us became as expertly coöperative at obtaining divorces as we had been, years before, at gathering mussels.

Whether my—our—sacrifice has served its purpose, I do not know, for living alone excludes me from the world of couples. The Hornings, the Krocks, and the Morrises have each had me to dinner, but by myself, and in an atmosphere of embarrassed discretion. My impression, truthfully, is that I horrify them, and that they have no appreciation of the dimension in which this thing has been done *for them*. Ann sees them more often than I, but she feels a wall of pity surrounding her, and her attention and energy have turned inward, toward her home, her children, her lawyer, her calculations (she is terrible at arithmetic, but is learning), and the part-time museum job that has been such a boost to her morale. Nix Morris may be sleeping with her again. She hasn't told me and, with an effort, I haven't asked. I am confident, now, that she will survive; the peculiar glancing bloom of a woman alert for a mate is upon her, and her ten years with me, in the end, added as much beauty as they took away. About my children, I am less confident; but the forming mind is a jungle that perhaps inevitably holds a tiger, and my children may be wiser and braver for having seen, so young, the tiger full in the face. I can only hope so. They must live, now, religiously, taking my love for them on faith. I believe at the moment I miss them more than they miss me. Ann is a better, or at least more systematic, mother with me gone. My psychological utility to her had ceased the instant I buried my face in the cloth of Peggy's suit.

Peggy, too, is busy with the doubled duties of her split world. She surprised me—women constantly surprise me—by putting me on a rather formal footing. We do not see each other for days at a time, and our telephone conversations—

those forbidden draughts of old so sweet that after thirty minutes I would feel I had just begun, my wrist aching, to drink from the bottomless electric cup held at my lips—have become guardedly terse and brim on the verge of resentment. In a sad, mutually relieved parley we agreed not to sleep together at least until the court dates are set. I feel little lust for her; her body, in its unintentional masquerade of remembered clothes, seems hard and repellent to me, and when she cries, or complains (the other night she suddenly protested that her children and she would have different last names and burst into tears), an unjust indignation locks my tongue. My love for her is like an exposed film I must carry tightly sealed through these glaring days into the marital darkness where it can be developed. I see, abstractly, that she will be a good wife, a wife much like Ann, who will make my breakfast, and clean our house, and permit me to vent on her white warm body my hopeless seminal rage against mortality. She is a woman, and women are the final guardians of the homocentric illusion Copernicus stripped from the stars; now I live, between wives, without illusions, unless memories count.

A fresh bare world has opened up for me. I eat dinner in luncheonettes, and take long walks where I had only driven in a car before, and have time, mounted on the slow jog of my faithful, neglected legs, to observe trees, porches, and curbstones in their innocent atomic purity. Lying down at night in my rented bed, I do not yearn for either Ann or Peggy, but am instead grateful for their absences; guilt and bewilderment are bedfellows enough. Some evenings I go and help Ann bathe our children and put them to bed. Other evenings I help Peggy with her children. In either case, I come back to my room early, and read, and sleep, and awake after midnight to confront alone the horror of the toothbrush above the bathroom basin. What I find hard to express to either woman, as I drift, sexless and homeless, between them, is how normal I find this life. I have discovered, in passing, the way Nature intends a man to live.

Morton has returned to Boston and has resumed work on his Ph.D. I should explain my hatred of him, since he has been in all this competent, and generous, and rational—which of course is the explanation. He let Peggy go as I let Ann go, and thus revealed, at the very point where there was no retreat, that there had been no advance. The leap that had wrenched every joint in my skeleton had landed me in the same place, only torn from my home and robbed of my children.

Who is the enemy? Who is it against whose threatened invasions we lit our fires and erected our barricades of children, whose subversion we subverted with alcohol, whose propaganda broadcasts we jammed with parties, whose intrigues and fanaticism we counteracted with the intrigues and fanaticism of love; who is the enemy I was delegated to engage alone? He is my friend. I move with ease among his camps, the under-furnished camps of solitude. I have come to admire his methods and Spartan style. His tortures are at bottom benevolent, for they prepare one for death. His tactics are irresistible, for every minute is his ally. Seeing what I have seen, I almost dread returning to my own side. I have no wish to hurry the moment when the doomed axis of couples takes me into itself again. It will not, of course, be exactly the same. Along with the house, the children, and the station wagon, I have given Ann the town. Peggy and I will not live in Tarbox. She shops for houses constantly. But, wherever she finds one, there will be other Hornings, differently tinted, and other Krocks, wearing, perhaps, the Morrises' perfume.

I am a parenthesis—a boat adrift between two continents. At times I remember and foresee the world of couples eagerly, as a garden from which I have been banished but to which I am certain to return. In trying to imagine my domestic life with Peggy, in fondly admiring her tireless touch with furnishings, I have sighted the coast that is not yet christened America. And time, time that knits and unravels all blessings, will pass before this paradise becomes a bewitched armaments factory whose workers, in their frenzy to forge armor for themselves, hammer, burn, and lacerate one another.

"Special Message" to readers of the *Franklin Library's signed limited edition of* Rabbit Redux

WHEN I FINISHED *Rabbit, Run*, very near the end of the Fifties, I did not intend a sequel. But a little over ten years later, as the interminable Sixties were drawing to their end, the idea that Harry Angstrom was still out there and running suddenly excited me. I had spent a year or more reading about the person and Presidency of James Buchanan (1791–1868). After a long and fruitless struggle to make a novel out of resistant historical materials, the perpetual *presentness* of my former hero beckoned as a relief. A number of people had asked me what had happened to Rabbit, who was last seen running along a street of Brewer, Pennsylvania, in no special direction; now I would show them, and throw in all the oppressive, distressing, overstimulating developments of the most dissentious American decade since the Civil War—antiwar protest, black power and rhetoric, teach-ins, middle-class runaways, drugs, and (proceeding eerily to its brilliant technological rendezvous through a turmoil of violence at home and abroad) the moon shot. Having told a number of interviewers I was writing a book about Buchanan, I painted him black and put him in, too. The term "redux" gave some people trouble; I had encountered it in Anthony Trollope's sequel to *Phineas Finn, Phineas Redux*. There is also a poem by Dryden, *Astraea Redux*. The term is Latin, meaning "led back," and is pronounced not with a silent pseudo-French "x" but as a firm spondee: *ray-dooks*.

The novel wrote itself readily; it was good to be back in Brewer. The characters assembled themselves within the numbed orbit of my now paunchy Middle American, and his tolerant curiosity and reluctant education seemed to me the parable that nobody else, in those shrill years, was offering. America and Harry suffered, marvelled, listened, and endured. Not without cost, of course. The cost of the disruption of the social fabric was paid, as in the earlier novel, by a girl. Iphigenia

973

is sacrificed and the fleet sails on, with its quarrelling crew. If Harry seems hard-hearted, "hardness of the heart" was what his original epigraph was about; the rage boiling out of the television set discovers a certain rage in him, too. As much as the ghetto black he hates the whites above them both, in Penn Park, among "the timbered gables, the stucco, the weedless lawns plumped up like pillows." The question that ends the book is not meant to have an easy answer.

J. U.
Georgetown, Massachusetts
1981

CHRONOLOGY

NOTE ON THE TEXTS

NOTES

Chronology

1932   Born John Hoyer Updike on March 18 in Reading Hospital, West Reading, Pennsylvania, the only child of Wesley Russell Updike and Linda Grace Hoyer Updike. (Father, born in 1900 in Trenton, New Jersey, is a former lineman for AT&T accumulating credits toward a state teaching certificate at Albright College, in Reading. Mother, born in 1904 in Plowville, Robeson Township, ten miles south of Reading, is a disciplined and hopeful writer of short fiction, submitting regularly but as yet unsuccessfully to *Collier's*, *The Saturday Evening Post*, and other popular magazines. The couple met in 1919, when both were students at Ursinus College, in Collegeville, Pennsylvania, and were married in Ithaca, New York, in August 1925, shortly after Linda Hoyer earned a master's degree in English from Cornell University. From 1926 through 1931 they traveled together for the phone company, living in hotels and rooming houses in Ohio and western Pennsylvania. In June 1931, after Wesley Updike lost his job in the Great Depression, they accepted Linda's parents' invitation to move in with them.) Called Johnny by his family and "Chonny" by their Pennsylvania Dutch neighbors, he is raised in Shillington (pop. 4,400), a town three miles southwest of Reading (pop. 120,000), the seat of Berks County. He, his parents, and his maternal grandparents live together at 117 Philadelphia Avenue, the home of Grandpa John Franklin Hoyer (b. 1863), a retired schoolteacher and onetime gentleman farmer financially ruined by the Crash, and Grandma Katherine ("Katie") Ziemer Kramer Hoyer (b. 1873), a farmwife made prematurely frail by Parkinson's disease. The two-story house of red brick and flaking cream-colored clapboards—built in 1900 and owned by the Hoyers since 1922—has a side porch, a red brick patio, and over the patio an abundant grape arbor hung with Japanese-beetle traps. At the bottom of the yard is an asbestos-shingled chicken house, a garden growing asparagus to sell at Shillington's Friday market, and, fronting on the back alley, a garage that is rented out to neighbors, as the family has no car. "Our lamps were dim, our carpets worn, our furniture hodgepodge and venerable and damp," Updike will remember. "And yet I never felt that we were poor."

1933   On his first birthday, family plants a dogwood sapling in the side yard. "This tree, I learned quite early, was exactly my age; was, in a sense, me," he will one day write. "The tree was my shadow." In September, mother takes job selling draperies at Pomeroy's department store, in downtown Reading, for fourteen dollars a week, leaving Johnny in the care of Grandma Hoyer.

1934   Through the influence of a Hoyer relative on the regional school board, father, now certified, is hired to teach seventh- and eighth-grade mathematics at Shillington High School (grades 7–12), a job he will hold for the next twenty-eight years. (His starting salary is twelve hundred dollars per school year, with which he supports himself, wife, son, and in-laws. In the summers he will eke out a living by working on town construction crews or as a manual laborer at Carpenter Steel, in Reading.)

1936   Mother quits job at Pomeroy's when, one morning on her way to the trolley stop, Johnny comes down Philadelphia Avenue crying after her.

1937   In September, enters kindergarten at Shillington Elementary School, which he will attend through grade six. There and at home shows a talent for drawing, and is encouraged by mother, who supplies him with paper, pencils, and paints. Working together at the dining table beneath a stained-glass lamp, the two design a cutout puzzle in the shape of a jack-in-the-box, the template for which is then printed in *Children's Activities* magazine, his first experience of "being in print."

1938   An attack of measles in February triggers the onset of psoriasis, a condition also suffered, to a lesser degree, by mother. "Siroil and sunshine and not eating chocolate were our only weapons in our war against the red spots, ripening to silvery scabs, that invaded our skins in the winter," Updike will recall. Because of his skin, he will dismiss all suggestions of his becoming a teacher, doctor, or other "public" professional. "What did that leave? Becoming a craftsman of some sort, closeted and unseen—perhaps a cartoonist or writer." With the anxiety of psoriasis comes another affliction, a stutter: "a distortion of the mouth as of a leather purse being cinched, a terrified hardening of the upper lip, a fatal tensing of and lifting of the voice." In the fall begins Sunday school at Grace Evangelical Lutheran Church, Shillington, where father, the son of a Presbyterian minister, is a deacon. Of his immediate family, only he and father are regular churchgoers.

1939   Begins making unaccompanied visits to the Shillington movie house, two blocks from home. "The theatre ran three shows a week, for two days each, and was closed Sundays," he will remember. "Many weeks I went three times." Fascinated by Mickey Mouse, tells family and playmates that he hopes one day to work as a Disney animator, a notion he will entertain until his late teens. Keeps scrapbooks of syndicated comic strips printed in the Reading *Times* and *Eagle*, including *Popeye*, *Dick Tracy*, and *Toonerville Folks*, and copies the drawings to learn the artists' techniques. Enjoys comic books and, especially, Big Little Books—chunky ten-cent volumes, each two-page spread a captioned comic-strip panel opposite a page of narrative text—a large collection of which makes up most of his childhood library.

1942   Mother hires neighbor Clint Shilling, a professional artist and member of the town's founding family, to give Johnny private lessons in drawing and painting. Shilling is also a fine-art conservator at the Reading Public Museum and Art Gallery, where Johnny and mother will spend many Sundays viewing the permanent collection—mainly nineteenth-century oil landscapes—and exhibits of new art by regional talent. Also takes piano lessons, and though he masters elementary music theory and sight-reading, he seldom plays for his own pleasure.

1943   At Christmas, Aunt Mary Updike, a lover of literature who had once been Edmund Wilson's secretary at *The New Republic*, treats the Shillington Updikes to a subscription to *The New Yorker*. The magazine, with its witty and sophisticated covers and cartoons, its light verse, humor, fiction, and criticism, instantly captivates him: "It *knew* best, *was* best." New York and *The New Yorker* soon become, in his phrase, "the object of my fantasies and aspirations."

1944   On weekends takes the twenty-minute trolley ride to the Reading Public Library and brings home mysteries

(Agatha Christie, John Dickson Carr), humor books (P. G. Wodehouse and the writers he has enjoyed in *The New Yorker*—James Thurber, E. B. White, Robert Benchley), and sometimes science fiction. In September, enters Shillington High School as a seventh-grader. Father is his math teacher for the next three years; he is also coach of the school's swim team, keeper of the cash box at sports events, and something of the faculty clown, friendly, self-deprecating, and popular with the students.

1945   Begins contributing cartoons, light verse, and movie reviews to the *Chatterbox*, Shillington High School's mimeographed student weekly. (By the spring of 1950, the end of his senior year, he will make nearly three hundred signed contributions to the publication.) In late summer, family is presented the opportunity to repurchase the sandstone farmhouse in Plowville in which Grandma and Grandpa Hoyer once lived and mother was born and raised. Although the house, called Strawberry Hill, is smaller than the Shillington residence, it sits on eighty-three acres of arable land instead of a half-acre town lot. Built in 1812, it has no indoor plumbing, is heated by a fireplace and a coal-oil stove, and, for the first year or so, is without electricity. On October 31, all five family members move into Strawberry Hill, which will be the grown-ups' home for the rest of their lives. Updike will later depict the farm as a "wearying place of work, weeds, bugs, heat, mud, and wildlife" where mother led the others in imposing order—"renovating the old stone farmhouse, repairing the barn, planting rows of strawberries and asparagus and peas, mowing a lawn back into the shadow of the woods." Father buys his first car—a balky 1938 Buick, prone to emergency repairs—for his and his son's commute to and from Shillington High. To a thirteen-year-old boy with New York aspirations, the move seems "less an adventure than a deprivation," a step backward in personal and family fortune.

1946   He and father join the Robeson Evangelical Lutheran Church, known as Plow Church, in neighboring Mohnton. Not yet old enough to drive, resentful of the loss of the Shillington movie house and the trolley cars into Reading, he finds escape and solace through reading, writing, drawing, and listening to the radio, especially to Boston Red Sox games. ("Ted Williams had made a dent in my consciousness before the war," Updike will remember, "but it was the '46 Sox"—led to the American League pennant by Williams's phenomenal hitting—"that made me a passionate fan.") In June works briefly in a local lens factory, and then devotes the first of four summers to cultivating the farm's strawberry patch, partly to meet a 4-H Club requirement but also to supplement the family's income. During the evenings writes first extended piece of fiction, a murder mystery featuring a suave Spanish detective. In the fall, begins after-school ritual of smoking, talking, and playing pinball at Stephens' Luncheonette, a hangout for his circle of classmates and the rendezvous for his ride home with father.

1947   In fall takes Shillington High School class in drawing and painting from teacher Carleton Boyer.

1948   In May, exhibits a drawing in a juried show of student artwork at the Reading Public Museum and wins a Scholastic Art Award. In fall revises light verse printed in the *Chatterbox* and sends poems, two or three at a time, to *The New Yorker*. Submits, in regular weekly batches, pencil roughs for gag cartoons to *The New Yorker*, *Collier's*, and *The Saturday Evening Post*. In November "It Might Be Verse" appears in *Reflections*, a bimonthly poetry journal published in Hartwick, New York. It is the first of a handful of high-school and undergraduate acceptances by small-circulation magazines including *The American Courier* (Kansas City, Mo.), *American Weave* (Cleveland, Ohio), *Different* (Rogers, Ark.), and *The Florida Magazine of Verse*.

1949   In fall elected senior-class president. Writes most of the text and photo captions for *Hi-Life 1950*, the school yearbook. At mother's insistence, family visits the campuses of Harvard, Cornell, and Princeton universities, and he applies to all.

1950   In spring accepted by Cornell and Harvard and decides on the latter, which offers a full-tuition scholarship. In June graduates from Shillington High School as co-valedictorian. Types his collected poems, 1941–50, and has them professionally bound into a black hardcover volume, its gold-stamped spine reading *Up to Graduation*. Spends the first of three consecutive summers as copy boy for the Reading *Eagle*, fetching coffee for the Linotype operators and contributing jokes and verse to Jerry Kobrin's local-interest column, "Reading in Writing." In September arrives in Cambridge, Massachusetts, with few definite plans beyond joining the congregation of Faith Lutheran Church. Tells parents he is dismayed by the paucity of Harvard's studio-art offerings and thinks he might major in English literature: "I've never read, after all, and now is the time. Besides, what else is there?" Assigned a room in Hollis Hall, one of the oldest dormitories in Harvard Yard, and a roommate, Christopher "Kit" Lasch, the future cultural historian and social critic. His first semester is crowded with required courses that leave little time for cartooning, though he does pull together a portfolio in time for the midyear staff elections at *The Harvard Lampoon*.

1951   In February elected to the Literary Board of the *Lampoon*, an undergraduate humor monthly (nine issues per school year) that, as Updike will later comment, "had begun in the 1870s as an imitation of *Punch*" but by the 1950s "was an imitation of *The New Yorker*, which suited me fine." With the May issue he immediately establishes himself as the *Lampoon*'s most versatile and prolific staff member. (By the time he graduates, in June 1954, he will have contributed more than 50 poems, 30 prose pieces, and 150 cartoons and spot drawings, as well as 8 cover illustrations.) At the end of the term is elected "Narthex" for 1951–52, the least of the magazine's three named editorial positions. He and Lasch agree to continue as roommates and are assigned a suite in Lowell House for the next two years. During the summer writes opening chapters of "Willow," a novel inspired by his Shillington boyhood; at the start of his sophomore year, he shows his work-in-progress to Albert J. Guerard, the head of the college's writing department, who refers him to a sympathetic but tough-minded English instructor named Theodore Morrison. "Professor Morrison wavered between having me rewrite what I'd done or letting me go ahead with it," Updike reports to his parents. "But he read and talked with me for about an hour, [then] agreed to let me forge ahead." As Morrison's special student, he is required to write at least three thousand words of "Willow" every two weeks. His other classes include Harry Levin's yearlong Shakespeare course and a semester of medieval art. In the latter he meets Mary Entwistle Pennington (b. 1930), a ponytailed, tennis-sneakered Radcliffe senior majoring in fine arts, with whom he forms a romantic attachment. Raised mainly in Chicago, she is the daughter of the Rev. Leslie T. Pennington, a Unitarian minister, and Elizabeth Daniels Pennington, a former teacher of high-school Latin.

1952   In the winter studies Milton and, with Mary, takes Hyman Bloom's drawing class, Advanced Composition. In March abandons "Willow" to work on short stories with Professor Morrison. In June elected "Ibis" (second-in-charge) of the *Lampoon* for 1952–53. At the end of the school year, brings Mary home to Plowville to meet his family; she then returns to Radcliffe to graduate on June 15. After a final summer at the Reading *Eagle*, begins his junior year at Harvard. Continues his courtship of Mary, who lives with a roommate a ten-minute walk from Harvard Yard. Enrolls in Walter Jackson Bate's seminar on the history of literary criticism and takes classes in Spenser and in seventeenth-century English poetry. His writing instructor for the fall semester is Edgar F. Shannon Jr., a Tennyson scholar who challenges him to write in strict poetic forms. In November hears Adlai Stevenson campaign for the U.S. presidency in Boston and, raised a "reflexive Democrat," carries placards for him near Cambridge polling places on Election Day. After Christmas, travels to Chicago to meet the Pennington family and to present Mary with an engagement ring.

1953   In the spring continues working on rhymed and metered verse, now with Professor Morrison. In April is one of eight Harvard juniors named to Phi Beta Kappa. Elected president (editor-in-chief) of the *Lampoon* for 1953–54. On June 26, he and Mary are married at the First Parish Cambridge, the Unitarian church in Harvard Square, in a service performed by Mary's father. As a gift from one of the Rev. Pennington's parishioners, the newlyweds take a four-day honeymoon at a private beach house in Ipswich, Massachusetts, thirty miles north of Boston. For the rest of the summer they work at Sandy Island Camp, a YMCA family camp near Lakeport, New Hampshire, where he runs the office and she the camp store. In July, receives two letters from William Maxwell, an editor of fiction and poetry at *The New Yorker*, each rejecting a poem but encouraging him to send others. In September, the couple moves into an apartment at 79 Martin Street, north of

Harvard Square, and Updike starts his senior year. Later that month, Grandpa Hoyer dies at age ninety. Begins research for senior thesis, "Non-Horatian Elements in Robert Herrick's Imitations and Echoes of Horace," a yearlong project with advisor Kenneth Kempton. Takes courses in Anglo-Saxon and the Russian novel and writes short fiction for Albert J. Guerard. In December completes "Flick," a story about a former high-school basketball player struggling with young adulthood that Guerard thinks good enough for *The New Yorker*.

1954   Katharine S. White, fiction editor of *The New Yorker*, rejects "Flick," but Leo Hofeller, executive editor, suggests that Updike visit his office for a job interview. In April awarded a Frank Knox Memorial Fellowship, granting him a postgraduate year at one of several schools in the British Commonwealth; he chooses the Ruskin School of Drawing and Fine Art, Oxford University, which also agrees to take Mary as a part-time student. In June graduates *summa cum laude*, and he and Mary spend most of the summer at the Pennington family's summer cottage in South Duxbury, Vermont. On July 15, receives word that *The New Yorker* will publish his "Duet, with Muffled Brake Drums," a light-verse fantasy on the day that Rolls met Royce. ("From this poem's acceptance," Updike will later say, "I date my life as a professional writer.") By the end of the summer, Katharine S. White accepts four more poems and a short story, "Friends from Philadelphia." In August visits the *New Yorker* offices and meets William Maxwell but not the vacationing White and Hofeller. Later that week he and Mary sail from New York to Southampton aboard RMS *Caronia*, then settle into a basement flat at 213 Iffley Road, Oxford. There he rewrites "Flick," soon published in *The New Yorker* as "Ace in the Hole." In September signs an agreement granting the magazine first-reading rights in all his future writings.

1955   At the Ruskin School "paints onions and draws from the antique," and in the evenings reads Proust, Henry Green, and the Protestant theologians Kierkegaard and Karl Barth. Daughter, Elizabeth ("Liz") Pennington Updike, born April 1. In winter and spring, sells several poems and three stories to *The New Yorker*. On June 22, meets E. B. and Katharine S. White, who, traveling in England, make a special trip to Oxford to offer him a place on the staff of the magazine. Returns to New York aboard RMS *Britan-nic*. In late July rents a small temporary apartment at 126 Riverside Drive, at West Eighty-fifth Street, and on August 22 starts at *The New Yorker* as a writer for "The Talk of the Town." In compliance with the Reserve Forces Act of 1955, reports to the draft board; he is classified "4-F: Psoriasis." In September Grandma Hoyer dies at age eighty-three. On December 1, the Updikes move to larger apartment at 153 West Thirteenth Street, Greenwich Village.

1956   In January completes "Snowing in Greenwich Village," the first of more than a dozen short stories chronicling the increasingly troubled marriage of his characters Joan and Richard Maple. In April rereads "Willow" and again is moved to write a novel about his Shillington boyhood. Arriving early at *The New Yorker* every weekday morning, he drafts three pages of the book before turning to his current "Talk" assignment. At a lunch arranged by E. B. White, Cass Canfield, publisher at Harper & Bros., compliments him on his published stories and asks if, when the times comes, he might see his novel. By August, the end of his first year at the magazine, he is chafing in the harness of "The Talk of the Town." ("To concoct an anonymous fraction of it year after year loomed as fruitlessly selfless," he will remember. "It seemed unlikely I would ever get better at 'Talk' than I was at twenty-four.") By Christmas his novel, now called "Home," is almost complete.

1957   Second child, David Hoyer Updike, born January 19. One week later, Updike resolves to move his family to Ipswich, Massachusetts, and to continue writing for *The New Yorker* on a freelance basis. On February 9, during a weekend search for a suitable Ipswich rental, signs a one-year lease on "Little Violet," a two-bedroom lavender-shingled house near the corner of Heartbreak and Essex roads. Shortly after arriving in Ipswich on April 1, joins the congregation of Clifton Lutheran Church, in neighboring Marblehead. Introduced to the game of golf by his wife's aunt, he is soon devoting several hours a week to practicing his swing at Candlewood, the Ipswich public course. Plays kitchen-table poker every other Wednesday night with five to seven male neighbors, a ritual that will continue, in one kitchen or another, for nearly fifty years. With Mary takes up the recorder—she plays alto, he tenor—and joins three or four other musicians to form a long-lived, ever-expanding local recorder society, learning and eventually publicly performing works by Purcell, Handel, Pachelbel, and others. Finishes six-hundred-page draft of "Home," assembles slim collection of previously published poems, and gives Harper & Bros. the option on both. In late April, Cass Canfield accepts the poetry collection and assigns it to veteran editor Elizabeth Lawrence. In May, Canfield declines to publish "Home," thinking it "a very typical first novel"—a nostalgic childhood memoir that goes on far too long. Updike, stung by this criticism, conceives of a counter-novel—a brief and mildly futuristic "caricature of contemporary decadence," its protagonist a ninety-four-year-old man who leads a residents' revolt at an old-folks' home. He will finish a draft of the novel, "The Poorhouse Fair," by Christmas.

1958   Katharine S. White retires to Maine, and William Maxwell becomes Updike's fiction editor at *The New Yorker*. In January, Elizabeth Lawrence reports that Harpers is not convinced by the last third of "The Poorhouse Fair" and requests revisions. Updike withdraws the book and submits it to publisher Alfred A. Knopf, who accepts it as is. (The firm of Knopf will be his chief American publisher for the rest of his long career.) On March 2, receives advance copy of his poetry collection, *The Carpentered Hen and Other Tame Creatures*. Purchases a five-bedroom house, built in 1687, at 26 East Street, Ipswich, which will be his residence for the next twelve years. In May begins writing new novel, "Go Away," a high-school romance set in the Shillington and Plowville of 1947. Enjoys working with his Knopf editor, Stewart "Sandy" Richardson; also with the book designer Harry Ford, who gives "The Poorhouse Fair" a page and binding design that Updike will insist upon adapting for all his future Knopf titles. Begins ordering and revising short stories for his first collection, "The Same Door."

1959   In January publishes *The Poorhouse Fair*, which enjoys two weeks at number 16 on the New York Times Best Sellers list. Reads *On the Road* ("it's surprisingly good," he tells his parents) and writes a parody of Kerouac for *The New Yorker*. In February rereads the nearly completed first draft of "Go Away" and decides the book is "a mistake, a two-hundred-page and yearlong mistake, and would be best plowed under, leaving the material in the soil." In hopes of making up time lost on the aborted project, applies for—and in April is awarded—a Guggenheim Fellowship to underwrite a new novel, conceived as both a conservative answer to Kerouac and an expansion on themes first explored in "Ace in the Hole." Third child, Michael John Updike, born May 14. In August publishes *The Same Door: Short Stories*. ("An exciting brilliance pervades the sixteen pieces that make up this book," writes *The Saturday Review*. "All may be praised in superlatives without fear of fatuity.") In September finishes the first draft of his Guggenheim novel, "Rabbit, Run," and revises the manuscript through the end of the year. Now that daughter Liz is old enough for Sunday school, decides to leave the Lutheran church in Marblehead and, with his Unitarian wife, join the First Congregational Church in Ipswich, where the family can worship together. "A Gift from the City" included in *The Best American Short Stories 1959*.

1960   Delivers "Rabbit, Run" to Knopf on January 4. In winter spends five weeks with family in a rented house on Anguilla, in the British West Indies, a Caribbean holiday taken largely for the benefit of his psoriatic skin. There he writes several poems and five short stories, including "Pigeon Feathers" and "Home." In March rents a second-floor office in the block-long Caldwell Building, on South Main Street, Ipswich, where he will report six days a week through the summer of 1974. In April writes a memoir, "The Dogwood Tree," for Martin Levin's anthology *Five Boyhoods* (Doubleday, 1962), and a poem, "Seven Stanzas at Easter," for a religious arts festival at Clifton Lutheran Church. In May, *The Poorhouse Fair* awarded the Rosenthal Award of the American Academy of Arts and Letters "for a book of the previous year that is a considerable literary achievement." In July, in a conference room at Alfred A. Knopf, strikes obscenities from "Rabbit, Run" with his new editor, Judith Jones, at one elbow and a Knopf-appointed lawyer at the other. (Judith Jones will remain his Knopf editor for the rest of his life.) On September 26, attends Ted Williams's farewell game at Fenway Park and watches in fannish disbelief as his hero, in his final turn at bat, delivers one last home run. His account of the game, "Hub Fans Bid Kid Adieu," is published in *The New Yorker*, October 22. In November, *Rabbit, Run* published

to very strong reviews. ("The merit of the book," writes
Norman Mailer, "is in the dread Updike manages to convey" on behalf of Harry "Rabbit" Angstrom, "a young
man who is beginning to lose nothing less than his good
American soul.") The novel spends ten weeks on the New
York Times Best Sellers list, peaking at number 14. Fourth
child, Miranda Margaret Updike, born December 15.

1961   Newly fond of the Caribbean, spends a solitary week on
the beaches of Puerto Rico, St. John's, and St. Croix. (In
most of the following fifteen winters he will take a weeklong "hit of sun," often alone, on Antigua, Aruba, St.
Martin, Tortola, or, most frequently, St. Thomas.) Upon
return begins "An Old-Fashioned Romance," planned as a
short, lighthearted novel, set in the early 1950s, about a
love affair between a black Harvard undergraduate and his
white Radcliffe girlfriend. On March 11, "Translation," by
Linda Grace Hoyer, appears in *The New Yorker*. It is
mother's first published story; nine more will be accepted
by the magazine through 1983. In July *The New Yorker*
publishes "A & P," which will become Updike's most
widely anthologized story and a standard selection for
high-school literature textbooks. At the suggestion of editor William Shawn, begins to review books for *The New
Yorker*. (His first assignment, forty-six hundred words on
Dwight Macdonald's *Parodies: An Anthology*, appears in
the September 16 issue. Over the next forty-seven years, he
will contribute some 375 reviews and scores of unsigned
"Briefly Noted"s to the magazine's Books section.) In
September abandons "An Old-Fashioned Romance" and
begins "The Centaur," a novel designed as a contrasting
companion to *Rabbit, Run*, a study in adult duty and self-
sacrifice instead of youthful impulse and self-gratification.
As a favor to his friend and neighbor Bill Wasserman, editor of the weekly *Ipswich Chronicle*, begins a four-year
masquerade as "H.H.," pseudonymous reviewer of local
musical events. "Wife-wooing" included in *Prize Stories
1961: The O. Henry Awards*.

1962   In March publishes second collection, *Pigeon Feathers and
Other Stories*. ("Updike is not merely talented," writes
critic Granville Hicks, "he is bold, resourceful, and in-
tensely serious. We hear talk now and then of a breakthrough in fiction, the achievement of a new attitude and
hence a new method; something like that seems close at

hand in *Pigeon Feathers.*") The book spends six weeks on the New York Times Best Sellers list—an unusual distinction for a story collection—peaking at number 13. In April, delivers "The Centaur" to Knopf. In May begins research for a novel exploring the difficult presidency of Pennsylvania's James Buchanan (1857–61), but by Christmas will set the project aside. Teaches creative writing in Harvard's summer program, an experiment that confirms his distaste for the profession. In August, an affair with a woman of his Ipswich set precipitates a crisis that nearly ends both of their marriages. In November *The Magic Flute*, a prose adaptation of the Mozart opera with illustrations by Warren Chappell, published by Knopf Books for Young Readers. In late fall and winter, vacations with family in Antibes, France, and visits Naples and the ruins at Pompeii. "The Doctor's Wife" included in *Prize Stories 1962* and "Pigeon Feathers" in *The Best American Short Stories 1962*.

1963   In February publishes *The Centaur*, which spends ten weeks on the New York Times Best Sellers list, peaking at number 9. In April *The New Yorker* publishes "Giving Blood," a second Maples story. On May 1, in his Ipswich office, performs the story "Lifeguard," the poem "Earthworm," and other short pieces for freelance audio producer Laurence Lustig; the resulting LP, *John Updike Reading from His Works* (CMS Records, 1965), is the first of his many spoken-word recordings. Rewrites a section of the abandoned "Old-Fashioned Romance" as the long story "The Christian Roommates." Begins another long story, which, over the next eight months, develops into "Marry Me," a novel based closely on his adulterous affair. In September publishes second collection of verse, *Telephone Poles and Other Poems*.

1964   In January completes draft of "Marry Me," but with qualms both personal and artistic, sets the work aside. On March 10 accepts the National Book Award in Fiction for *The Centaur*; a citation by the judges—John Cheever, Philip Rahv, and Robie Macauley—calls the book a "brilliant account of a conflict of gifts between an inarticulate American father and his highly articulate son" that "readily takes on the risk of flamboyance in pursuing an acuteness of feeling." In April becomes, at age thirty-two, one of the youngest persons ever inducted into the National Institute of Arts and Letters. From May to August works on a short story about mother and Strawberry Hill that evolves into the novella "Of the Farm." In fall *The Ring*, a prose adaptation of Wagner's opera with illustrations by Warren Chappell, is published by Knopf Books for Young Readers, and *Olinger Stories*, a selection of Pennsylvania stories from *The Same Door* and *Pigeon Feathers*, is published by Vintage Books. ("If I had to give anybody one book of me," Updike tells an interviewer decades later, "it would be the Vintage *Olinger Stories*.") Is surprised by an invitation from the U.S. State Department to act as cultural ambassador to the Soviet Union, where *The Centaur* is popular in Russian translation. In late October, he and Mary spend ten days in Moscow and Leningrad with fellow-ambassador John Cheever; together they drink vodka with various members of the Writers Union, including Andrei Voznesensky and Yevgeny Yevtushenko. For the next five weeks the Updikes and their Soviet and State Department handlers travel to Kiev and Tbilisi, then to Bulgaria, Romania, and Czechoslovakia. Upon return in December writes "The Bulgarian Poetess," the first of twenty short stories concerning the life and times of Jewish American novelist Henry Bech, unprolific author of the Beat-era classic *Travel Light*, whose reputation grows as his literary powers decline.

1965   Throughout the winter revises "Of the Farm," delivering the manuscript on March 1. In May publishes *Assorted Prose*, a miscellany collecting "Talk" pieces, humorous sketches, and book reviews, anchored by "The Dogwood Tree," "Hub Fans," and "Grandmaster Nabokov," the first of many appreciations of Vladimir Nabokov, "the best writer of English prose currently holding American citizenship." On the afternoon of Sunday, June 13, the First Congregational Church of Ipswich, built 1846, is struck by lightning and burns to the ground; Updike, making what will prove a five-year commitment, joins the committee charged with overseeing the design and construction of a new church building. In November publishes *Of the Farm*. ("In this, his fourth novel," writes *The New York Times*, "Updike has achieved a sureness of touch, a suppleness of style, and a subtlety of vision that is gained by few writers of fiction.") *A Child's Calendar*, twelve poems with pencil illustrations by Nancy Ekholm Burkert, published by Knopf Books for Young Readers. In Paris *Le Centaure* wins the Prix du meilleur livre étranger for the year's best novel translated into French. Donates his literary manuscripts, 1953–65, to Harvard's Houghton Library. (In 2009, Harvard will purchase the remainder of his papers from his heirs posthumously.)

1966   In August, resumes work on his Buchanan novel, but soon abandons it for a panoramic novel of contemporary Ipswich and "the way we live now." In September publishes *The Music School*, his third collection of short stories. The book occasions a long photo-essay in *Life* magazine ("Can a Nice Novelist Finish First?," November 4) in which Updike tells an interviewer that "my subject is the American Protestant small-town middle class. I like middles. It is in middles where extremes clash, where ambiguity restlessly rules." In November, at the request of the visiting Yevtushenko, Updike and playwright Arthur Miller accompany the poet during the New York leg of his first American reading tour. "The Bulgarian Poetess" wins the O. Henry First Award and is featured in *Prize Stories 1966*.

1967   Ipswich novel, now called "Couples," develops into an ambitious (and sometimes satirically sociological) study of the death of traditional institutions and the rise of "post-Pill" paganism. During a family vacation on Martha's Vineyard, is interviewed for *The Paris Review*'s "Art of Fiction" series, a transcription of which he takes pains to revise into a definitive artistic credo. During the previous August on the Vineyard he had responded to a British journalist's questionnaire asking where he stood on the Vietnam War. His conservative answer, now published in the book *Authors Take Sides on Vietnam* (Simon & Schuster), is widely criticized in the liberal press and in his own social circle. ("I am for our intervention if it does some good," Updike wrote. "The crying need is for genuine elections whereby the South Vietnamese can express their will. If their will is for Communism, we should pick up our chips and leave. Until such a will is expressed . . . I do not see that we can abdicate our burdensome position in Vietnam.") "My undovishness," Updike will later write, "like my battered and vestigial but unsurrendered Christianity, constituted a refusal to give up, to deny and disown, my deepest and most fruitful self, my Shillington self—dimes for war stamps, nickels for the Sunday-school collection, and grown-ups maintaining order so that I might be free to play with my cartoons and Big Little Books." Is commissioned to write two short plays: "Three Texts from Early Ipswich," a pageant to be performed in celebration of the town's Seventeenth-Century Day, August 3, 1968, and an adaptation of the Grimms' fairy tale "The Fisherman and His Wife," to be performed, with music by Gunther Schuller, by the Opera Company of Boston in the spring of 1970. These happy experiments in theater will lead him to recast his Buchanan novel in the form of a stage play. "Marching through Boston," a Maples story, included in *Prize Stories 1967*.

1968 In February *The New Yorker* publishes "The Wait," a lengthy excerpt from "Marry Me." *Couples* appears on April 2; Wilfrid Sheed, reviewing it on the cover of *The New York Times Book Review*, calls it an "ingenious" vivisection of "an authentically decadent community," a "fiendish compendium of exurban manners . . . described with loving horror." On April 10, the book enters the New York Times Best Sellers list, where it remains for thirty-six consecutive weeks, usually in the number 2 position, just below Arthur Hailey's *Airport*. On April 26 a portrait labeled "Novelist John Updike" appears on the cover of *Time* under the headline "The Adulterous Society." David L. Wolper, who will later produce *Roots* and *The Thorn Birds*, options *Couples* for $360,000, but the film is never made. From April to August writes the long poem "Midpoint," employing the meters of Dante, Spenser, Whitman, and Pope "to take inventory of his life at the age of thirty-five." Resolves to spend the 1968–69 school year in London with his family, partly to escape the distractions of celebrity, partly to escape a "Vietnam-addled America distressing in its civil fury." In September takes up residence at 59 Cumberland Terrace, on Regent's Park, and contributes occasional "Notes of a Temporary Resident" to the *Times Literary Supplement*, *New Statesman*, and the BBC's *Listener* magazine. In the Reading Room of the British Museum toys with his Buchanan drama, but again sets the work aside. In the fall takes a trip alone to Egypt. "Your Lover Just Called," a Maples story, included in *Prize Stories 1968*.

1969 In February writes fourth Bech story, "Rich in Russia," and begins to see the outlines of a possible Bech collection. Spends most of April in Morocco with his family, while, in America, *Midpoint and Other Poems* is published. Returns from London and, from June through December, writes three more Bech episodes for the evolving quasi-novel "Bech: A Book." In September *Bottom's Dream*, a prose adaptation of Shakespeare's *Midsummer Night's Dream* with illustrations by Warren Chappell, published by Knopf Books for Young Readers.

1970   In winter researches the life and presidency of James Buchanan at the Historical Society of Pennsylvania, Philadelphia. On May 7, at Boston's Savoy Theatre, Schuller and Updike's children's opera, *The Fisherman and His Wife*, receives world première under the direction of Sarah Caldwell. In June publishes *Bech: A Book*, which spends eight weeks on the New York Times Best Sellers list, peaking at number 7. Working from literal translations supplied by Slavists, fashions English versions of ten poems by Yevtushenko for the Russian's bilingual collection *Stolen Apples* (Doubleday, 1971). In summer travels in Japan and South Korea with fifteen-year-old daughter Liz, and on July 1 delivers talk "Humor in Fiction" at PEN conference in Seoul. From June to November, as relief from the recalcitrant "pastness" of the Buchanan material, writes the first draft of "Rabbit Redux," a present-tense sequel to *Rabbit, Run*. In late spring purchases a new, larger house for family at 50 Labor-in-Vain Road, Ipswich. Sells the house at 26 East Street to Alexander Bernhard, a corporate lawyer in Boston, who, with his wife, Martha Ruggles Bernhard, becomes part of the Updikes' social set. In October, Jack Smight's production of *Rabbit, Run*, starring James Caan, released by Warner Bros. Pictures to uniformly bad reviews. ("*Rabbit, Run* wasn't released," Caan quips to Updike's amusement. "It escaped.") "Bech Takes Pot Luck" included in *Prize Stories 1970*.

1971   In March delivers Rabbit sequel, and devotes rest of the year to writing short fiction and to shaping a new story collection. In February *Enchantment*, fifteen autobiographical vignettes by Linda Grace Hoyer, published by Houghton Mifflin. In November publishes *Rabbit Redux*, which spends seventeen weeks on the New York Times Best Sellers list, peaking at number 4. (Richard Locke, in *The New York Times Book Review*, calls the novel "a great achievement . . . I can think of no stronger vindication of the claims of essentially realistic fiction than this extraordinary synthesis of the disparate elements of contemporary experience.") In December, in Ipswich, Updike breaks his leg while playing touch football; spends a week in the hospital and three months on crutches.

1972   In March visits Venezuela as a weeklong resident at the American Venezuelan Center, Caracas, and lectures to an unappreciative audience on *Doña Bárbara*'s relation to the American Western. ("What the Third World does not want to hear about," Updike learns, "is parallelisms with the U.S.") Father dies, April 16, at age seventy-two; he is buried in Plow Church Cemetery, Plowville. Updike returns one last time to the Buchanan play, which he finds impossible to cut to playable length and so expands. ("Exhaustiveness is a novelist's method," Updike will later remark, "and what we have here is a kind of novel conceived in the form of a play . . . a drama [to be] staged inside the reader's head.") Writes a long miscellaneous afterword to the work, and delivers the typescript before Christmas. In October publishes fourth collection, *Museums and Women and Other Stories*. (William H. Pritchard, in *The Hudson Review*, writes: "He is a religious writer; he is a comic realist; he knows what everything feels like, how everything works. He is putting together a body of work which in substantial intelligent creation will eventually be seen as second to none in our time.")

1973   In winter spends four weeks with Mary in Anglophone Africa—Ghana, Nigeria, Tanzania, Kenya, Ethiopia—courtesy of the Fulbright Board of Foreign Scholarships. Attends a Pan-African literary conference in Lagos, and repeatedly presents an apolitical paper, "The Cultural Situation of the American Writer," to the consternation of politicized African writers' groups. Upon return, records uneasy impressions of Africa, Venezuela, and South Korea in the story "Bech Third-Worlds It." In spring and summer, writes first draft of "A Month of Sundays," a comic reimagining of Hawthorne's *Scarlet Letter* narrated by the adulterous Rev. Tom Marshfield, a latter-day Arthur Dimmesdale. On June 12, at commencement exercises in Harvard Yard, reads autobiographical "Apologies to Harvard," the Phi Beta Kappa Poem for 1973. Writes a personal essay on golf for *The New York Times*, and is soon asked to contribute pieces about the game to *Golf Digest* and other sports publications. In the fall, at the request of Knopf Canada, makes publicity tour of Toronto, Calgary, and

Vancouver. Revises "A Month of Sundays" for delivery in the new year.

1974   In March, as a guest of the Australian Office of the Arts, delivers a speech, "Why Write?," at literary festivals in Sydney and Adelaide. Updike and Martha Ruggles Bernhard (b. 1937), their four-year acquaintance having become a deep attachment, decide to leave their spouses for each other. In June Updike moves from Labor-in-Vain Road to a studio apartment in Ipswich, and Alexander Bernhard moves out of the house on East Street. In summer publishes *Buchanan Dying*; the book receives few reviews, sells poorly, and soon goes out of print. In September, Updike leases apartment at 151 Beacon Street, in Back Bay, Boston, his "bachelor's accommodations" for the next twenty months. Throughout the fall, intermittently socializes with John Cheever, who, separated from his wife, is spending a year alone near Kenmore Square while teaching creative writing at Boston University. "Son" included in *The Best American Short Stories 1974*.

1975   In February publishes *A Month of Sundays*, which spends fifteen weeks on the New York Times Best Sellers list, peaking at number 6. In March, Updike assumes the remaining few weeks of Cheever's teaching obligation when Cheever, incapacitated by drink, resigns his position at Boston University. In April, at Berlitz in Central Square, Cambridge, begins a yearlong class in basic German, the language of his Pennsylvania forebears. In November publishes *Picked-Up Pieces*, collecting a decade's worth of speeches, essays, and humorous prose, the *Paris Review* interview, and some seventy book reviews. In November, undertakes experimental ultraviolet "light-box" treatments for psoriasis (PUVA therapy) at Mass General Hospital. "Nakedness," a Maples story, included in *Prize Stories 1975*.

1976   William Maxwell retires, and Roger Angell becomes Updike's fiction editor at *The New Yorker* for the rest of Updike's life. In winter, rereads the twelve-year-old manuscript of "Marry Me" and begins to revise it for publication. On the title page he labels the book a "romance," partly to highlight its Hawthorne-like allegorical scheme, partly to mark it as a thing apart from his other novels. In March, at Salem Court House, John and Mary Updike receive one of the first "no-fault" divorces granted by the Common-wealth of Massachusetts. In April and May, an abridged *Buchanan Dying* performed at Franklin and Marshall College, Lancaster, Pennsylvania. On May 21 is elevated from the 200-member National Institute of Arts and Letters to the 50-member American Academy of Arts and Letters. On May 11 purchases 58 West Main Street, a red clapboard house in Georgetown, Massachusetts, and moves out of his Boston apartment. On June 28 is joined in Georgetown by Martha and her three boys, John (age twelve), Jason (eleven), and Ted (five). In this, the summer of America's bicentennial, Updike, Shillington's favorite son, agrees to be Grand Marshal of his hometown's Fourth of July parade. In October *The New Yorker* publishes "Here Come the Maples," the concluding episode of the Maples series. In November *Marry Me: A Romance* published to polarized reviews. Though it spends six weeks on the New York Times Best Sellers list, peaking at number 7, many critics call it redundant, sentimental, a mere "pocket version" of *Couples*. On December 8, delivers "The Written Word," the Frank Nelson Doubleday Lecture for 1976, at the Smithsonian Institution, Washington, D.C. "Separating," a Maples story, is included in *Prize Stories 1976* and Updike is given the series' Special Award for Continuing Achievement. "The Man Who Loved Extinct Mammals" included in *The Best American Short Stories 1976*.

1977   In February, revised edition of *The Poorhouse Fair* (1959), with a new introduction by the author, published in hardcover by Knopf. In March an abridged *Buchanan Dying* receives eight staged readings at the Institute for Readers Theatre, San Diego, California. In April spends a week in Toledo and Madrid with mother and daughter Miranda. In May publishes fourth collection of poems, *Tossing and Turning*. Embarrassed by the reception of *Marry Me* and determined not to be typecast as chronicler of "the adulterous society," plans an ambitious departure—a Nabokovian flight of fancy set in an imaginary sub-Saharan country and narrated by an elegant Muslim dictator with an aversion to all things American. In September delivers his speech "The Cultural Situation of the American Writer" to a receptive conservative audience at the American Enterprise Institute, Washington, D.C. On September 30, marries Martha Ruggles Bernhard at Clifton Lutheran

Church, Marblehead. In October–November, the couple travels in Denmark, Sweden, and Norway at the invitation of Updike's Scandinavian publishers.

1978   Delivers African novel, "The Coup," on April 1. Arranges and revises his short stories of the last seven years, and writes "Atlantises" to round out the new collection. In November a thirty-minute film of "The Music School"—an actor's reading of the text accompanied by cinematic imagery—televised as part of PBS's "American Short Story" series. On August 9, Updike's son David, a Harvard undergraduate, publishes an autobiographical short story in *The New Yorker*; it will later be reprinted, with twelve other stories, in his collection *Out on the Marsh* (Godine, 1988). In the fall visits Jerusalem, Bethlehem, Tel Aviv, and Greece with Martha. In December, *The Coup* published to widespread media attention, including a front-page review in *The New York Times Book Review* and a long profile in *The New York Times Magazine*.

1979   On January 7, *The Coup* enters the New York Times Best Sellers list, where it remains for seventeen weeks, peaking at number 4. On March 12, Robert Geller's *Too Far to Go*, a two-hour made-for-television film based on the Maples stories, broadcast on NBC. Updike, who did not participate in the production, prepares a tie-in collection, *Too Far to Go: The Maples Stories*, published in paperback by Fawcett. In May delivers "Hawthorne's Religious Language," the annual Blashfield Address of the American Academy of Arts and Letters. When approached by James Forsht, editor of the U.S. edition of the French arts magazine *Réalités*, to write 650 words on a favorite painting, Updike responds with a series of nine such essays, his first sustained foray into art criticism. In June begins work on a third Rabbit novel, "Rabbit Is Rich." In October, *Problems and Other Stories* published. (In a front-page review, *The New York Times Book Review* calls *Problems* "a work of really awesome literary cunning. [It] won't be surpassed by any other collection of the next year, and perhaps not in the next ten.") Begins traveling to Europe with Martha every fall, usually for two weeks in Italy or France.

1980   In February completes the first draft of "Rabbit Is Rich." In June, after a reading at Case Western Reserve University, suffers crippling nausea; undergoes an emergency appendectomy at the Cleveland Clinic and is hospitalized for four days. In the fall visits London and the Orkney Islands with Martha. "Gesturing," a late Maples story, included in *The Best American Short Stories 1980*.

1981   In January delivers "Rabbit Is Rich." Returns to Venezuela for a second weeklong visit, during which he and Martha escape unscathed from a helicopter crash near Angel Falls. From June to December revises four previously uncollected Bech stories and writes three new ones to make "Bech Is Back," a second Bech book. On August 22, awarded the Edwin MacDowell Medal for outstanding contribution to American literature. In September publishes *Rabbit Is Rich*, which spends twenty-three weeks on the New York Times Best Sellers list, peaking at number 4. The BBC-TV arts magazine *Arena* and WGBH Boston coproduce "What Makes Rabbit Run?," an hour-long documentary featuring interviews with Updike at home, in Plowville, and in the offices of Alfred A. Knopf. "Still of Some Use" included in *The Best American Short Stories 1981*.

1982   *Rabbit Is Rich* awarded the Pulitzer Prize, the National Book Critics Circle Award, and the American Book Award in Fiction. In March, on Updike's fiftieth birthday, Knopf issues a revised edition of his first book, *The Carpentered Hen* (1958), with a new foreword by the author. In April "The Beloved," a long story of 1971 published only in excerpt in *The New Yorker*, printed by Lord John Press, Northridge, California, in an edition limited to four hundred signed copies. In May, moves to 675 Hale Street, in Beverly Farms, Massachusetts, his home for the rest of his life. On the second floor of the house an isolated suite of four small rooms, the former servants' quarters, becomes his new workspace. Spends the summer compiling and revising the contents of a third nonfiction collection. With Martha and her children becomes a parishioner at St. John's Episcopal Church, Beverly Farms. In October publishes *Bech Is Back*, which spends one week on the New York Times Best Sellers list at number 13. On October 18 *Time* magazine profiles Updike in a cover story titled "Going Great at Fifty." (This second *Time* cover painting, an oil portrait by Alex Katz, now hangs in the National Portrait Gallery, Washington, D.C.)

1983   From January to August drafts a novel about a modern-day devil who arrives in a Rhode Island seaport town to cultivate the powers of three young witches. On May 22 confirmed in the Episcopal Church by John B. Coburn, Bishop of Massachusetts. In September publishes *Hugging the Shore: Essays and Criticism*. ("With this latest volume," writes Michiko Kakutani in *The New York Times*, "Updike has established himself, in his 'improvised sub-career as a book reviewer,' as a major and enduring critical voice; indeed, as the preeminent critic of his generation.") Leon Wieseltier, literary editor of *The New Republic*, asks Updike to write about the Fairfield Porter retrospective at the Museum of Fine Arts, Boston, the first of several exhibitions he will review for that magazine. "The City" included in *Prize Stories 1983* and "Deaths of Distant Friends" in *The Best American Short Stories 1983*.

1984   With series editor Shannon Ravenel, selects the contents of *The Best American Short Stories 1984* (Houghton Mifflin, October). *Hugging the Shore* wins the National Book Critics Circle Award in Criticism. In March visits Kenya and Egypt with Martha and thirteen-year-old Ted. In May publishes *The Witches of Eastwick*, which spends twelve weeks on the New York Times Best Sellers list, peaking at number 5. In September "The Roommate," a two-hour adaptation of the story "The Christian Roommates," televised as part of PBS's "American Playhouse" series. When approached by a would-be biographer for permission to write his life, Updike begins to plan, not an autobiography, but a series of six memoirs "tracing the inner shape" of his experience. The first of these, on the world of his childhood and his early impressions of life, appears in the Christmas issue of *The New Yorker*.

1985   In February visits Arizona with Martha and is deeply attracted to its austere landscape. In March publishes fifth collection of poems, *Facing Nature*. In April travels with Martha to Switzerland and Germany. In May *Selected Stories*, a three-hour, two-cassette recording of six stories chosen and read by the author, released as part of the launch of Random House Audiobooks; Updike performs "A & P," "Pigeon Feathers," "The Family Meadow," "The Witnesses," "The Alligators," and "Separating." Composes two further memoirs, one on his psoriasis and the other on his stuttering. Writes "Majesty," a second variation on the themes of Hawthorne's *Scarlet Letter*, this time from the

perspective of a latter-day Roger Chillingworth. "The
Other" included in *Prize Stories 1985.*

1986   "Majesty" delivered to Knopf, whose executives, con-
cerned about confusion with a forthcoming biography of
Elizabeth II, propose a change of title to "Roger's Version."
In March travels with Martha and Ted in London, Oxford,
and the rural south of England. Upon return, collects and
revises his short stories of the last eight years. In late April
visits Prague, and in July writes "Bech in Czech," his first
Bech story in five years. In September publishes *Roger's
Version*, which spends fifteen weeks on the New York
Times Best Sellers list, peaking at number 4.

1987   Plans to cap his "*Scarlet Letter* series" with the comic novel
"S.," the confessions of Sarah Worth, a spiritual pilgrim who
leaves her husband and daughter in New England to join
the charismatic leader of an Arizona ashram. In April
publishes *Trust Me*, his sixth collection of stories. ("It is in
his short stories that we find Updike's most assured work,"
writes the *Washington Post.* "Almost without fail they give
pleasure, a quality not to be taken lightly.") On May 1 delivers "Howells as Anti-Novelist," keynote speech of Harvard's two-day celebration of William Dean Howells at
150. In June, George Miller's film *The Witches of Eastwick*,
starring Jack Nicholson, released by Warner Bros. Pictures. ("It is not a movie I would see twice," Updike tells
the agent responsible for the movie deal.) In August
spends five days in Helsinki at the request of his Finnish
publisher. In December elected chancellor of the American Academy of Arts and Letters for the three-year term
1988–90. "The Afterlife" included in *The Best American
Short Stories 1987.*

1988   Writes three further memoirs—on his social conservatism,
his Updike ancestry, and his sense of being a "self"—to
complete the manuscript of his book "Self-Consciousness."
In February an hour-long adaptation of "Pigeon Feathers"
televised as part of PBS's "American Playhouse" series. In
March publishes *S.*, which spends six weeks on the New
York Times Best Sellers list, peaking at number 10. In April,
during a visit to Northern Ohio University, in Ada, Ohio,
visits the Wilson Sporting Goods factory, the inspiration for
two short stories, "The Football Factory" and "Part of the

Process." At the invitation of Knopf's Judith Jones, collects his art writings for publication as a large-format illustrated art book. "Leaf Season" included in *Prize Stories 1988*.

1989   At New Year's begins work on a final Rabbit book, "Rabbit at Rest." In March *Self-Consciousness* published to strong reviews but modest sales. ("These memoirs," writes the *Chicago Tribune*, "take us inside Updike's mind in the way that biography almost never can.") In October publishes *Just Looking: Essays on Art*, and at the invitation of Robert Silvers, coeditor of *The New York Review of Books*, becomes a regular art critic for that magazine, contributing some fifty exhibition reviews over the next two decades. Mother dies of heart attack, October 10, at age eighty-five; she is buried beside her husband in Plow Church Cemetery. She leaves to her son the sandstone farmhouse and the land it stands on. She also leaves him her literary estate, including the page proof of *The Predator* (Ticknor & Fields, 1990), a second collection of autobiographical vignettes. Updike corrects proof and writes jacket copy, and his daughter Elizabeth provides line drawings as chapter openers. In a White House ceremony on November 17 receives the National Medal of Arts from President George H. W. Bush.

1990   In January delivers "Rabbit at Rest" and begins compiling a fourth collection of nonfiction prose. In the spring spends a week with Martha in Milan and visits the historic estate of Gabriele D'Annunzio. In September, takes the first of four golfing tours of the UK and Ireland with fellow-members of the Myopia Hunt Club, Hamilton, Massachusetts. In October publishes *Rabbit at Rest*, which spends seven weeks on the New York Times Best Sellers list, peaking at number 8.

1991   Rereads *Buchanan Dying* and, recalling his ordeal with that book, begins work on a comic novel that tells two mirroring stories: (a) an American professor of history remembers his untidy life during the mid-1970s and (b) interlards his reminiscence with pages from an unfinished project of that period, a life of President Buchanan. *Rabbit at Rest* awarded the Pulitzer Prize and the National Book Critics Circle Award in Fiction. In the fall visits London and Dublin with Martha. In November publishes *Odd*

Jobs, collecting nearly a thousand pages of literary journalism and other writings. "A Sandstone Farmhouse" included in *The Best American Short Stories 1991*.

1992   In February, at the invitation of his Brazilian publishers, travels in São Paulo, Ouro Prêto, Brasília, and Rio. (Brazil, Updike will later comment, "was a territory that lured me forward, into its luminous green depths, into its magical emptiness; it seemed one of the last earthly spaces that held room for the imagination.") On June 4 presented with an honorary Doctorate of Letters degree from Harvard University. In November, *Memories of the Ford Administration* published to mixed reviews and modest sales. "A Sandstone Farmhouse" wins the O. Henry First Award for best short story of the year and is featured in *Prize Stories 1992*.

1993   In June delivers novel "Brazil," a "magical-realist" retelling of the romance of Tristan and Iseult set in the slums of Rio and in the Brazilian backland. In April publishes *Collected Poems, 1953–1993*, gathering nearly all the poetry and light verse from his earlier volumes as well as more than seventy new and uncollected items. *Love Factories*, three uncollected short stories from 1988, printed by Eurographica, Helsinki, Finland, in an edition of 350 signed copies. In June he and Martha take a Harvard-sponsored cruise tracing the Mediterranean voyage of Homer's Odysseus. "Playing with Dynamite" included in *The Best American Short Stories 1993*.

1994   In January, *Brazil* published to mixed reviews and modest sales. "Grandparenting," a postscript to the Maples series, published in *The New Yorker*, February 21; the story is the capstone to a new collection of short fiction, delivered March 1. Revises, corrects, and expands the texts of the four Rabbit novels for a one-volume edition proposed by Everyman's Library; writes long introduction to the collection, "Rabbit Angstrom," and in July hand-delivers text of the book to Everyman's London office. Begins "In the Beauty of the Lilies," an ambitious novel tracing one American family's relationship with God—and with Hollywood's false idols—across four generations. In November publishes *The Afterlife and Other Stories*. ("Marvelously moving," writes *USA Today*. "These tales evoke a certain peace . . . and a wonder at what an astonishingly graceful writer Updike is.")

1995   In May *Rabbit at Rest* awarded the William Dean Howells Medal of the American Academy of Arts and Letters for the most distinguished American novel of the last five years. In July, *A Helpful Alphabet of Friendly Objects*, a volume of humorous verse with full-color photographs by son David, published by Knopf Books for Young Readers. *Rabbit Angstrom* published in London and New York by Everyman's Library. "The Black Room" included in *Prize Stories 1995*.

1996   In January publishes *In the Beauty of the Lilies*, which spends five weeks on the New York Times Best Sellers list, peaking at number 9. In September, *Golf Dreams*—a collection of essays, poems, and fiction about learning, playing, and loving the game—published by Knopf. Records selections from golf book for Random House Audiobooks, the last in a series of "read by the author" cassettes that began with *Selected Stories* (1985) and continued with performances of *Trust Me* and *The Afterlife*.

1997   In February is presented the Campion Award, an occasional prize given by *America* magazine to honor the lifework of a distinguished Christian man of letters. Takes the first of seven consecutive March holidays on Gasparilla Island, in southwest Florida. Revises "Bech in Czech" and spends most of the year writing four additional stories for a final Bech book, "Bech at Bay." In October publishes *Toward the End of Time*, a postapocalyptic novel of the year 2020, in which a dying New England investment banker lives not in the present but in a variety of simultaneous realities. (Margaret Atwood calls the book "a little corner of hell as meticulously painted as a Dutch interior.")

1998   In April *A Century of Arts and Letters*, the history of the American Academy of Arts and Letters "as told, decade by decade, by eleven members," published by Columbia University Press. (The volume was conceived and edited by Updike, who also provided a foreword and the chapter on the period 1938–47.) On May 2, receives the Harvard Arts Medal for lifetime contribution to literature. Spends four weeks in China and Hong Kong with Martha, September–October, while, in America, *Bech at Bay* is published to strong reviews. ("Like the other books about Henry Bech," writes Jonathan Yardley in the *Washington Post*, "this is modest in size but generous with its rewards.") With series editor Katrina Kenison, selects the contents of *The Best American Short Stories of the Century* (Houghton Mifflin, April 1999), representing his work with "Gesturing," from 1980. On November 18, awarded the National Book Foundation Medal for Distinguished Contribution to American Letters. "My Father on the Verge of Disgrace" included in *The Best American Short Stories 1998*.

1999 In January "His Oeuvre," a final Bech story, published in *The New Yorker*. After rereading *Hamlet* and related scholarship and criticism, writes "Gertrude and Claudius," a prose "prequel" to Shakespeare's play. In September publishes *More Matter*, a fifth collection of essays and reviews. In October begins a novella-length postscript to the Rabbit saga, in which Harry's survivors, ten years after the events of *Rabbit at Rest*, "fitfully entertain his memory." In November, a revised edition of *A Child's Calendar*, with new ink-and-watercolor illustrations by Trina Schart Hyman, published by Holiday House.

2000 In January publishes *Gertrude and Claudius*. ("Shakespeare's plays have had many offshoots," writes Peter Kemp in *The Times* of London. "*Gertrude and Claudius*, though, stands in a class of its own: a superlative homage from one imaginative veteran to another.") In February *A Child's Calendar* named a Caldecott Honor Book. On July 18, Cameron Mackintosh's West End musical *The Witches of Eastwick*, with book and lyrics by John Dempsey and music by Dana P. Rowe, begins a fifteen-month run at the Royal Theatre, Drury Lane. Having viewed and reviewed the Jackson Pollock retrospective at the Museum of Modern Art in November 1999, continues his research on the lives of Pollock and his wife, Lee Krasner, and is inspired to write "Seek My Face," a novel about the New York art world of the 1950s. In October spends three weeks in Japan with Martha. In November publishes *Licks of Love*, collecting twelve short stories and the novella "Rabbit Remembered."

2001 In March *The Complete Henry Bech*, an omnibus edition of the three Bech books and their postscript, "His Oeuvre," published by Everyman's Library, London. On April 17–19, visits Cincinnati for the series of readings and interviews documented by James Schiff in his book *Updike in Cincinnati* (Ohio University Press, 2007). In May, publishes seventh collection of verse, *Americana and Other Poems*. While visiting stepson Jason on September 11, witnesses the fall of the World Trade Center from a rooftop in Brooklyn Heights and records the horror as a "Talk of the Town" reporter. "Personal Archaeology" included in *The Best American Short Stories 2001*.

2002   In April the Updikes travel in Spain. With many of his early collections now out of print, revises short stories from 1953 to 1975 for republication in a definitive, omnibus edition. In November, *Seek My Face* published to mixed reviews.

2003   In January, *Karl Shapiro: Selected Poems*, edited with an introduction by Updike, published by The Library of America. The Updikes visit Arizona for the month of March and, upon their return home, decide to buy a winter home there. In April is presented the National Medal for the Humanities by President George W. Bush. In spring begins writing the novel "Villages," conceived as an account of the life and times of a representative American male of Updike's generation. In September he and Martha spend two weeks on the Danube and in Prague. In November publishes *The Early Stories: 1953–1975*, with an autobiographical foreword by the author. ("Updike's artistry . . . is deeply and wholly seen," writes *The Atlantic*. "One reads through the plenitude with delight, expectation, and at all times gratitude.")

2004   In January purchases a condominium in Tucson and, with Martha, spends the first of five consecutive Marches there. *The Early Stories* wins the PEN/Faulkner Award in Fiction. In October *Villages* published to mixed reviews. At the invitation of Knopf prepares a second collection of illustrated art writings on the model of *Just Looking*. "The Walk with Elizanne" included in *The Best American Short Stories 2004*.

2005   In winter and spring, drafts a "9/11" novel about an eighteen-year-old New Jersey boy, the son of an Irish American mother and an Egyptian father, who, as a truck driver for a Muslim-owned furniture retailer, is slowly drawn into a terrorist plot. In November publishes *Still Looking: Essays on American Art*, with pieces on Copley, Homer, Eakins, Stieglitz, Hopper, Pollock, Warhol, and others.

2006   For three weeks in January, travels in the Hindu south of

India with Martha. In June publishes *Terrorist*, which spends four weeks on the New York Times Best Sellers list—Updike's first appearance there in more than a decade—peaking at number 5. In September, a jury of Ann Beattie, Richard Ford, and Joyce Carol Oates gives Updike the Rea Award for his lifelong contribution to the art of the short story.

2007   In winter travels with Martha in Cambodia and Thailand. Devotes the rest of the year to writing "The Widows of Eastwick," a sequel to *Witches* (1984) and a meditation on youthful sins, abiding guilt, and the need for redemption. In May is awarded the Gold Medal in Fiction from American Academy of Arts and Letters. In October publishes *Due Considerations*, a sixth collection of essays and criticism.

2008   In January *The New Yorker* accepts what will prove to be his final short story, "The Full Glass." Updike submits it and seventeen other late stories to Knopf as the collection "My Father's Tears." In February travels with Martha in Egypt and Jordan. Everyman's Library offers to reprint, for the first time in hardcover, *Too Far to Go*; Updike revises the text, adds the late story "Grandparenting," and renames the volume *The Maples Stories*. On May 22, at the invitation of the National Endowment for the Humanities, presents "'The Clarity of Things': What Is American in American Art," the thirty-seventh annual Jefferson Lecture in the Humanities, at the Warner Theatre in Washington, D.C. In June The Library of America proposes a special edition of "Hub Fans Bid Kid Adieu" to commemorate the fiftieth anniversary of Ted Williams's last at-bat; Updike lightly revises the text and agrees to fashion a new preface and afterword for the book. In the summer begins research for, and writes opening chapters of, "The Last Epistle," a historical novel about the life of St. Paul. In September travels with Martha in Latvia, Lithuania, Estonia, Finland, St. Petersburg, and Moscow. In October, *The Widows of Eastwick* published, and Updike, though troubled by a persistent cough, undertakes two weeks of publicity appearances in New York City and on the West Coast. In November, believing he has pneumonia, is told by doctors at Massachusetts General Hospital that he is dying of stage IV lung cancer. In November and December, keeps a journal in verse of his hospital visits and prepares the manuscript of a final book, "Endpoint and Other Poems."

2009   On January 2, files his last piece for *The New Yorker*, a review of Blake Bailey's life of John Cheever. Selects readings for his funeral service, including his own devotional poems "Earthworm" and "Seven Stanzas at Easter." Dies in hospice, January 27, in Danvers, Massachusetts. Funeral, February 2, at St. John's Episcopal Church. Leaves four posthumous books in proof: *Endpoint* (April), *My Father's Tears* (June), *The Maples Stories* (August), and *Hub Fans Bid Kid Adieu* (June 2010). He is cremated, and his ashes are buried privately. In July 2010, his children place a memorial headstone, designed and carved by Michael Updike, near the graves of his parents and grandparents in Plow Church Cemetery, Plowville, Pennsylvania.

Note on the Texts

This volume presents texts of the three novels that John Updike published from April 1968, when he was thirty-five, to February 1975, when he was forty-two: *Couples* (1968), *Rabbit Redux* (1971), and *A Month of Sundays* (1975). It also presents, in an appendix, "Couples," a short story written in 1963, as it was privately printed, with an author's foreword, in 1976, as well as a note on *Rabbit Redux* included in a deluxe, limited edition of the novel printed in 1981.

COUPLES

Couples, Updike's fifth published novel, was composed from the fall of 1966 through the early summer of 1967. The novel had its germ in a short story, "Couples," completed in May 1963 (see note on the Appendix, below). *Couples*, like the other novels collected in the present volume, was written mainly in Updike's rented office in the Caldwell Building, on South Main Street in Ipswich, Massachusetts, where the author reported six days a week from March 1960 through the summer of 1974.

Couples was published in hardcover by Alfred A. Knopf, New York, on April 5, 1968. A British edition, offset from the Knopf pages, was published by Andre Deutsch Ltd., London, later the same year. The eleventh printing of the Knopf hardcover, dated June 2003, is the text used here; it was the last printing overseen by Updike during his lifetime.

RABBIT REDUX

Rabbit Redux was Updike's sixth published novel. In his introduction to *Rabbit Angstrom* (London and New York: Everyman's Library, 1995), a one-volume omnibus edition of *Rabbit, Run* (1960) and its sequels *Rabbit Redux* (1971), *Rabbit Is Rich* (1981), and *Rabbit at Rest* (1990), Updike writes:

"Unlike such estimable elders as Vonnegut, Vidal, and Mailer, I have little reformist tendency and instinct for social criticism. Perhaps the Lutheran creed of my boyhood imbued me with some of Luther's conservatism; perhaps growing up Democrat under Franklin Roosevelt inclined me to be unduly patriotic. In any case the rhetoric of social protest and revolt which roiled the Sixties alarmed and, even, disoriented me. The calls for civil rights, racial equality, sexual equality, freer sex, and peace in Vietnam were in themselves commendable and non-threatening; it was the savagery, between 1965 and 1973, of the domestic attack upon the good faith and common sense of our government, especially of that would-be Roosevelt Lyndon B. Johnson, that astonished me. The attack came, much of it, from the intellectual elite and their draft-vulnerable children. Civil disobedience was antithetical to my Fifties education, which had inculcated, on the professional level, an impassioned but cool aestheticism and implied, on the private, salvation through sensibility, which included an ironical detachment from the social issues fashionable in the Thirties. But the radicalizing Thirties had come round again, in psychedelic colors.

"I coped by moving, with my family, to England for a year, and reading in the British Museum about James Buchanan. Buchanan (1791–1868) was the only Pennsylvanian ever elected to the White House; the main triumph of his turbulent term (1857–61) was that, though elderly, he survived it, and left it to his successor, Abraham Lincoln, to start the Civil War. A pro-Southern Democrat who yet denied any state's constitutional right to secede, he embodied for me the drowned-out voice of careful, fussy reasonableness. For over a year, I read American history and tried unsuccessfully to shape this historical figure's dilemmas into a work of fiction. But my attempted pages showed me too earthbound a realist or too tame a visionary for the vigorous fakery of a historical novel.

"By the first month of 1970, back in the United States, I gave up the attempt. But then what to do? I owed my publisher a novel, and had not come up with one. From the start of our relationship, I had thought it a right and mutually profitable rhythm to offer Knopf a novel every other book. In the ten years since *Rabbit, Run* had ended on its ambiguous note, a number of people had asked me what happened to Harry. It came to me that he would have run around the block, returned to Mt. Judge and Janice, faced what music there was, and be now an all-too-settled working man—a Linotyper. For three summers I had worked as a copy boy in a small-city newspaper and had admired the men in green eyeshades as they perched at their square-keyed keyboards and called down a rain of brass matrices to become hot lead slugs, to become columns of type. It was the blue-collar equivalent of my sedentary, word-productive profession.

"He would be, my thirty-six-year-old Rabbit, one of those Middle Americans feeling overwhelmed and put upon by all the revolutions in the air; he would serve as a receptacle for my disquiet and resentments, which would sit more becomingly on him than on me. Rabbit to the rescue, and as before his creator was in a hurry. An examination of the manuscript reveals what I had forgotten, that I typed the first draft—the only novel of the four of which this is true. I began on February 7, 1970, finished that first draft on December 11, and had it typed up by Palm Sunday [April 4] 1971—which means that my publisher worked fast to get it out before the end of that year. If the novel achieved nothing else, it revived the word *redux*, which I had encountered in titles by Dryden and Trollope. From the Latin *reducere*, 'to bring back,' it is defined by Webster's as 'led back; specif., *Med.*, indicating return to health after disease.' People wanted to pronounce it 'raydoo,' as if it were French, but now I often see it in print, as a staple of journalese.

"Rabbit became too much a receptacle, perhaps, for every item in the headlines. A number of reviewers invited me to think so. But though I have had several occasions to reread the novel, few excisions suggested themselves to me. As a reader I am carried along the curve that I described in my flap copy: 'Rabbit is abandoned and mocked, his home is invaded, the world of his childhood decays into a mere sub-lunar void; still he clings to semblances of patriotism and paternity.' The novel is itself a moon shot: Janice's affair launches her husband, as he and his father witness the takeoff of Apollo 11 in the Phoenix Bar, into the extraterrestrial world of Jill and Skeeter. The eventual reunion of the married couple in the Safe Haven Motel is managed with the care and gingerly vocabulary of a spacecraft docking. It is the most violent and bizarre of these four novels, but, then, the Sixties were the most violent and bizarre of these decades. The possibly inordinate emphasis on sexual congress—an enthusiastic mixture of instruction manual and de Sadeian ballet—also partakes of the times.

"In *Rabbit, Run*, there is very little direct cultural and political reference, apart from the burst of news items that comes over Harry's car radio during his night of fleeing home. Of these, only the disappearance of the Dalai Lama from Tibet engages the fictional themes. In *Rabbit Redux*, the trip to the moon is the central metaphor. 'Trip' in Sixties parlance meant an inner journey of some strangeness; the little apple-green house in Penn Villas plays host to space invaders —a middle-class runaway and a black rhetorician. The long third chapter—longer still in the first draft—is a Sixties invention, a 'teach-in.' Rabbit tries to learn. Reading aloud the words of Frederick Douglass, he becomes black, and in a fashion seeks solidarity with Skeeter. African-Americans, Old World readers should be reminded, have an immigrant pedigree almost as long as that of Anglo-Americans; 'the Negro problem' is old in the New World. The United States is more than a tenth black; black music, black sorrow, black jubilation, black English, black style permeate the culture and have contributed much of what makes American music, especially, so globally potent. Yet the society continues racially divided, in the main, and Rabbit's reluctant crossing of the color line represents a tortured form of progress.

"The novel was meant to be symmetric with *Rabbit, Run*: this time, Janice leaves home and a young female dies on Harry's watch. Expatiation of the baby's death is the couple's joint quest throughout the series; Harry keeps looking for a daughter, and Janice strives for competence, for a redeemed opinion of herself. Nelson remains the wounded, helplessly indignant witness. He is ever shocked by 'the hardness of heart' that enables his father to live so egocentrically, as if enjoying divine favor.

"*Rabbit, Run*'s epigraph is an uncompleted thought by Pascal: 'The motions of Grace, the hardness of the heart; external circumstances.' In *Rabbit Redux*, external circumstances bear nightmarishly upon my skittish pilgrim; he achieves a measure of recognition that the rage and destructiveness boiling out of the television set belong to him. Many of the lessons of the Sixties became part of the status quo. Veterans became doves; bankers put on love beads. Among Harry's virtues, self-centered though he is, are the national curiosity, tolerance, and adaptability. America survives its chronic apocalypses. I did not know, though, when I abandoned to motel sleep the couple with a burnt-out house and a traumatized child, that they would wake to such prosperity."

Rabbit Redux was published in hardcover by Alfred A. Knopf, New York, on November 15, 1971. (Two excerpts from chapter 1 had appeared, in somewhat different form, in periodicals before publication: "Mom/Pop/Moon," in *The Atlantic Monthly* for August 1971, and "Rabbit's Evening Out," in *Esquire* for September 1971.) A special signed, slip-cased edition of the first printing, printed on special paper and specially bound, was issued by Knopf in an edition limited to 350 copies. A British trade edition, offset from the Knopf pages, was published by Andre Deutsch Ltd., London, in the spring of 1972. Deluxe, limited editions of *Rabbit Redux* were privately printed by the Franklin Press, Franklin Center, Pennsylvania, in 1981, and Easton Press, Norwalk, Connecticut, in 1993.

From late 1993 through mid-1994, Updike revised the texts of the four Rabbit novels for the omnibus edition *Rabbit Angstrom*, published simultaneously in New York and London by Everyman's Library on October 17, 1995. Updike wrote in the introduction to *Rabbit Angstrom* that "for this fresh printing, apt to be the last that I shall oversee, I have tried to smooth away such inconsistencies [in the series] as have come to my attention." He also wrote that "I have restored to *Redux* an omitted brief reappearance by Jack Eccles, who almost became the co-protagonist of Rabbit's first outing, and whose own 'outing' seemed to deserve a place in this full report."

(This episode, printed on pages 611–14 of the present volume, had previously appeared, as "An Encounter Left Out of *Rabbit Redux*," in *Pieces 2: A Journal of Short Fiction*, printed by Bits Press, of Cleveland, Ohio, in January 1980.) The texts of *Rabbit Angstrom* were reprinted, with a few additional revisions by the author, in a two-volume trade paperback set titled *The Rabbit Novels* (New York: Ballantine Books, 2003). As Updike advised his bibliographer Jack De Bellis that these were the "least incorrect" versions of the texts, the 2003 text of *Rabbit Redux*, from *The Rabbit Novels, Volume I: Rabbit, Run / Rabbit Redux*, is used here.

A MONTH OF SUNDAYS

The first draft of *A Month of Sundays*, Updike's seventh published novel, was composed in the spring and summer of 1973, and was revised throughout the winter of 1973–74. The novel was published in hardcover by Alfred A. Knopf, New York, on February 26, 1975. (An excerpt had appeared, as "A Month of Sundays," in *Playboy* for January 1975.) A special signed, slip-cased edition of the first printing, printed on special paper and specially bound, was issued by Knopf in an edition limited to 450 copies. A British trade edition, offset from the Knopf pages, was published by Andre Deutsch Ltd., London, in the fall of 1975.

The eighth printing of the Knopf hardcover edition, dated April 2006, is the text used here; it was the last printing issued during Updike's lifetime. A letter from Updike to Ken Schneider, his editor Judith Jones's assistant at Knopf, dated June 22, 2006, lists the following corrections to be made to later printings of *A Month of Sundays*, all of which have been made here: 793.12, finds [for "locates"]; 795.14, *libitum* [for "*libidum*"]; 798.4, Tom peeps. [inserted sentence]; 827.1, Peirce [for "Pierce"]; 837.35, X [for "*x*"]; 911.32, that, by [for "that by"]; 911.33, state from [for "state, from"]; 914.1, 8-iron and a relaxed little swing, picturing [for "8-iron, and with a relaxed little poke pictured"]; 914.5, Titleist. [for "Titlist."]; 914.22, de-Latinized [for "Latin"]; 914.27, we [for "us"]; 914.28, hunched over as [for "hunched over"]; 914.36, thirty [for "twenty"]; 916.23, up at [for "toward"]; 916.40, stroked the lag, [for "stroked it,"]; 917.4–5, fifteen-footer [for "fifteen-foot putt"]; 917.9, like many another miracle-worker I came to a sad end. [for "I lost."]; 918.2, rattle [for "rattle,"].

APPENDIX

The appendix presents three short texts by John Updike, two of them printed in 1976 and related to the novel *Couples*, the other printed in 1981 and related to *Rabbit Redux*.

In the spring of 1976, Updike prepared the typescript of *Couples: A Short Story* for printing as a 48-page, hand-sewn pamphlet by Halty Ferguson Publishing Co. (1971–82), a small press in Cambridge, Massachusetts, whose proprietors were William R. Ferguson (b. 1943), a letterpress printer and book designer, and his wife, Raquel Halty Ferguson (b. 1945), a professor of Spanish at Simmons College, in Boston, Massachusetts. The work consisted of two texts, "Couples," a freshly revised version of a previously unpublished short story that Updike had unsuccessfully submitted to *The New Yorker* in May 1963, and an autobiographical and critical foreword written specially for the pamphlet.

Couples: A Short Story was printed in an edition of 276 copies, all of which were signed by the author. Two hundred and fifty copies were numbered and sold by subscription; the remainder of the run, lettered A–Z, were not for sale.

The foreword to "Couples: A Short Story" was reprinted, under the rubric "On One's Own Oeuvre," as "A foreword to a limited edition of *Couples: A Short Story*, published by Halty Ferguson (Cambridge, Massachusetts) in 1976," in Updike's collection *Hugging the Shore: Essays and Criticism* (New York: Knopf, 1983). The text from *Hugging the Shore*, which was slightly revised from the Halty Ferguson printing, is used here.

The text of the short story "Couples" is reprinted, for the first time since its original printing, from copy "P" of the Halty Ferguson pamphlet.

"'Special Message' to readers of the Franklin Library's signed limited edition of *Rabbit Redux*" first appeared, as "A special message to subscribers from John Updike," in *Rabbit Redux*, by John Updike (Franklin Center, Pa.: Franklin Library, 1981). It was reprinted without changes, under the rubric "One's Own Oeuvre," as "A 'special message' to purchasers of the Franklin Library limited edition, in 1981, of *Rabbit Redux*," in Updike's collection *Hugging the Shore: Essays and Criticism* (New York: Knopf, 1983). The text from the Franklin Library printing is used here, under a title supplied by the editor of this volume.

This volume presents the texts of the original printings chosen for inclusion, but does not attempt to reproduce nontextual features of their typographical design. The texts are presented without change, except for the correction of typographical errors. Spelling, punctuation, even capitalization are often expressive features and are not altered, even when inconsistent or irregular. The following is a list of typographical errors corrected, cited by page and line number: 22.4, year-stints; 49.16, stroke; 80.30, hoardes; 100.12, It; 105.4–5,

Portugese; 105.5, boistrous; 109.4, Appleby's; 110.33, that that; 116.10, beside; 122.21, me,'; 126.4, explorer's; 148.22, octupi; 152.20, it known; 155.27, little-Smith's; 159.12, toothlesss?; 160.18, Okey-doke-doke; 170.31, collasped; 221.20, chose; 272.6, selectman; 290.40, Righty-right?; 375.22, Hanema's; 377.6, Whitman's; 379.29, Piet,; 386.1, "Angela.'; 399.34, is a; 401.8, little-Smith's; 404.34, me."; 405.32, feelers."; 410.29, horsehoe; 411.4, percieved; 412.3, gand-father; 414.3, then; 414.10, shadows.; 417.14, fom; 525.38, so not; 541.23, cause; 563.38, figertips; 570.40, "Almost".; 585.36, exclaims.; 603.8, next; 612.17, voice taken; 653.38, 'cage; 668.26, I keeps; 690.22, stared; 694.19, anymore;; 751.4, honey-blonde; 753.23–24, flyswatter; 768.6, honey-blonde; 814.5, blonde; 821.40, convenant; 826.25, alternate; 834.10, must a; 855.31, Bartok.; 867.23, Dow-Jones; 869.12, morcenary; 886.37, *alway.*; 889.15, poety; 904.20, Corrèges; 906.37, has just; 911.21, aquitted; 911.26, lie; 916.26, were; 916.32, *sent*; 934.4, *present*; 935.15, Columban; 959.30, blonde; 967.5, blonde.

Notes

In the notes below, the reference numbers denote page and line of this volume (the line count includes headings but not blank lines). No note is made for material that is sufficiently explained in context, nor are there notes for material included in standard desk-reference works such as Webster's Eleventh Collegiate, Biographical, and Geographical dictionaries or comparable internet resources such as Merriam-Webster's online dictionary. Foreign words and phrases are translated only if not translated in the text or if words are not evident English cognates. Quotations from Shakespeare are keyed to *The Riverside Shakespeare*, edited by G. Blakemore Evans (Boston: Houghton Mifflin, 1974). Quotations from the Bible are keyed to the King James Version. For further biographical information than is contained in the Chronology, see Updike's memoir "The Dogwood Tree: A Boyhood," collected in his miscellany *Assorted Prose* (New York: Knopf, 1965), and the six later memoirs collected in his book *Self-Consciousness* (New York: Knopf, 1989). *Updike*, by Adam Begley (New York: Harper, 2014), is a critical biography. *John Updike's Early Years*, by Jack De Bellis (Bethlehem, Pa.: Lehigh University Press, 2013), tells the story of Updike's life through age eighteen and relates it to the work. Selected print interviews, 1959–93, are collected in *Conversations with John Updike*, edited by James Plath (Jackson: University of Mississippi Press, 1994). In a sequel, *John Updike's Pennsylvania Interviews* (Bethlehem, Pa.: Lehigh University Press, 2016), Plath collects interviews and literary profiles from 1965 to 2009. For further bibliographical information than is contained in the Note on the Texts, see *John Updike: A Bibliography of Primary and Secondary Materials, 1948–2007*, by Jack De Bellis and Michael Broomfield (New Castle, Del.: Oak Knoll Press, 2007).

COUPLES

2.1 *To Mary*] Mary Updike (1930–2018), née Mary Entwistle Pennington, the author's first wife (1953–76) and mother of his four children.

2.2–9 There is a tendency . . . a living democracy.] From "The Effects of Space Exploration on Man's Condition and Stature" (1964), by the German-American Lutheran theologian Paul Tillich (1886–1965), in *The Future of Religions*, a posthumous collection of essays by and tributes to Tillich edited by Jerald C. Brauer (New York: Harper & Row, 1966).

2.12–15 We love the flesh; . . . heavy, gentle paws?] From "The Scythians" (1918), poem by Alexander Blok (1880–1921), in *An Anthology of Russian Literature in the Soviet Period, from Gorki to Pasternak*, edited and translated by Bernard Guilbert Guerney (New York: Vintage Books, 1960).

9.38–39 Jackie Kenneny's having a *ba*-by!"] On April 16, 1963, the White House announced that First Lady Jacqueline Kennedy was pregnant and was expected to give birth in the latter half of August. The baby, a son named Patrick Bouvier Kennedy, was born prematurely on August 7 at Otis Air Force Base on Cape Cod. He suffered from hyaline membrane disease, a pulmonary condition that was often fatal for premature newborns. To increase his chances of survival he was transported to Boston Children's Hospital and placed in a hyperbaric chamber, but he died the morning of August 9, thirty-nine hours after he was born.

12.20–21 Moses in the Nile . . . handmaids] See Exodus 2:1–10.

12.24–25 Words . . . Virgins pregnant through the ear.] According to certain Christian writers, including St. Augustine, Christ was conceived via God's words spoken into Mary's ear, which would allow her to become pregnant while remaining a virgin.

12.29 *breathes there a man so dead.*] From Walter Scott, *The Lay of the Last Minstrel* (1805), VI.i.1. The next lines, "Who never to himself hath said / This is my own, my native land!" are referred to at 13.24–25 and 14.29–30, respectively.

13.7–8 Chubby. *Huooff* . . . Twist!] From "The Twist" (1959), song written by Hank Ballard (1927–2003) that became a smash hit and launched a dance craze when recorded by Chubby Checker (b. 1941) in 1960.

14.3–4 in Dutch, *fokker, in de fuik lopen*] Breeder, fall into the trap.

14.30–31 Fairfox, Virginia] A pun on the name of the Virginia city of Fairfax.

16.16–17 northern peninsula . . . bridge had since been built.] Before the opening of the Mackinac Bridge in 1957, travel between the Upper and Lower Peninsulas of Michigan was possible only by ferries or other boats.

19.19–20 "All Hail the Power."] "All Hail the Power of Jesus' Name" (1779), well-known hymn with words by Edward Perronet (d. 1792) and sung to several tunes.

19.39 Grange] The Patrons of Husbandry, or the Grange, was founded in 1867 to advance the interests of farmers.

20.35 *jk, daar is je vader. Pas op, Piet, die hond bijt.*] Dutch: Look, there's your father. Watch out, Piet, the dog bites. *Naa kum*: variant of *nou kom*, "come on" or "keep up."

21.1–2 Dutch Reformed] Common name for the Christian Reformed Church, a North American Calvinist denomination founded by Dutch immigrants.

21.29   "We Are Climbing Jacob's Ladder."] A spiritual.

21.33–34   Children of light.] Christ's words in John 12:36: "While ye have light, believe in the light, that ye may be the children of light." The phrase "children of light" appears several times elsewhere in the New Testament.

22.38–39   palms spread across Jesus's path] On his journey to Jerusalem the week before his crucifixion, commemorated as Palm Sunday, on which parishioners are given palm fronds; see Matthew 21:8, Mark 11:8, Luke 19:36, and John 12:13. The "theft of the colt" of a donkey for him to ride on is mentioned in all the Gospel accounts except John.

23.4–5   accepts an expensive bottle of ointment and scorns the cost] Jesus approvingly allows himself to be anointed with expensive ointment in the story told in Matthew 26:6–13; Mark 14:3–9; Luke 7:36–50; and John 12:1–8.

23.6   overturn the counting tables of respectable bankers] See Matthew 21:12–13 and Mark 11:15, where Jesus overturns the tables of the money-changers in the temple.

23.10   "Lift Up Your Heads, Ye Mighty Gates"] Hymn with words (1642) by the German clergyman George Weissel (1590–1635), translated into English in 1855 by Catherine Winkworth (1827–1878).

24.30   MBTA] Massachusetts Bay Transportation Authority.

24.30   B.U.] Boston University.

29.24–25   "*Femme méchante*,"] French: Naughty woman.

30.33   tu *es confuse*,"] French: *you* are confused.

30.40   Jim Bishop] Journalist (1907–1987), author of *The Day Lincoln Was Shot* (1955), *The Day Christ Died* (1957), and *The Day Christ Was Born* (1960).

31.15–16   shocker about the Thresher?] USS *Thresher*, a nuclear submarine, sank off the coast of Cape Cod while conducting dive trials on April 10, resulting in the deaths of its entire crew.

31.25   *Che sarà sarà* . . . Dodo Day] In the Alfred Hitchcock film *The Man Who Knew Too Much* (1956), the actor and singer Doris Day (b. 1922) introduced the popular song "Que Será, Será (Whatever Will Be, Will Be)," music by Jay Livingston (1915–2001), words by Ray Evans (1915–2007); her recording was a hit single in the United States and abroad.

31.28   Kennedy'll up the stakes in Laos] The United States sent aid and military advisers to Laos in support of the Royal Lao government against pro-communist Pathet Lao rebels in the civil war that broke out after the country's independence in 1954. Weighing American options, President Kennedy rejected proposals for more extensive military intervention in the conflict and supported a peace agreement reached in Geneva in 1962, which established a coalition government involving the warring and neutral factions. The fighting soon resumed, however, and continued until a 1973 cease-fire accord. The Pathet Lao took over the country in 1975.

31.30   another Diem] Ngo Dinh Diem (1901–1963) was premier of the State of Vietnam, 1954–55, and president of the Republic of Vietnam, 1955–63. He was overthrown in a military coup on November 1, 1963, and killed the following day.

33.22–23   "Too much of water hast thou, poor Ophelia.] Laertes's words in Shakespeare's *Hamlet*, IV.vii.185, after receiving the news that his sister Ophelia has drowned.

33.27   "*Ecoutez.*"] French: Listen.

34.14   *Pacem in Terris*] Papal encyclical ("Peace on Earth," 1963).

34.17–18   the way U Whosie has bopped Tshombe in the Congo?"] In December 1962–January 1963, an offensive carried out by United Nations peacekeepers in the Congo crippled the secessionist movement of the province of Katenga, which had declared itself independent under the leadership of the businessman and politician Moïse Tshombe (1919–1969) in 1960. The UN secretary-general at the time was the Burmese diplomat U Thant (1909–1974).

34.35   a Schweitzer type,"] Albert Schweitzer (1875–1965), Alsatian-born theologian, physician, and musician who was well-known for his writing and for the hospital in Lambaréné (in present-day Gabon, Africa) where he spent most of his life working.

35.2   Why is Egypt merging with those other Arabs?] Gamal Abdel Nasser (1918–1970), the president of Egypt, 1956–70, was a vocal proponent of pan-Arab unity.

42.13   Lowell Thomas.] American journalist and broadcaster (1892–1981).

42.13   V-mail] Short for Victory Mail, a system used during World War II by which letters to military personnel were written on standardized sheets, censored, and transported in microfilm form.

44.28–29   Door Store . . . Design Research] Two Cambridge stores selling furniture, the latter specializing in contemporary design.

47.32   Seed. Among thorns. Fallen.] In the biblical Parable of the Sower (Matthew 13:3–9; Mark 4:1–9; Luke 8:4–8), the fates of several seeds meant for sowing are contrasted: the seedlings of those that had fallen among thorns were choked by the thorns.

52.8   Enovid] First oral contraceptive available for purchase in the United States.

52.35   Hitchcock chairs] Simple, mass-produced chairs designed in the early nineteenth century by Connecticut furniture manufacturer Lambert Hitchcock (1795–1892).

53.9–10   *Our Lady of the Flowers* and *Memoirs of a Woman of Pleasure*] *Our Lady of the Flowers* (1944), novel by the French poet, essayist, and novelist Jean Genet (1910–1986); *Memoirs of a Woman of Pleasure* (1748–49), original title of novel more commonly known as *Fanny Hill*, by the English writer John Cleland (1710–1789).

53.11   the Menningers] The American physician Charles Frederick Menninger (1862–1953) and his sons, Karl (1893–1990) and William (1899–1966), founded and operated a psychiatry clinic in Topeka, Kansas. Most prominent of the three men was Karl Menninger, whose books include *Man Against Himself* (1938), *Love Against Hate* (1942), and *The Vital Balance* (1963).

53.12   *Psycopathia Sexualis*] Pioneering study of sexual behavior by the German psychiatrist Richard Freiherr von Krafft-Ebing (1840–1902).

53.14–15   poems of Sappho as published by Peter Pauper] The 1942 English translation of Sappho's poetry by Peter Pauper Press, an illustrated edition of translations from many poets and translators.

53.16   works by Theodore Reik and Wilheim Reich] The Vienna-born psychoanalyst Theodor Reik (1888–1969), author of *Listening with the Third Ear* (1948), *The Psychology of Sex Relations* (1961), and many other books; the Austrian-born psychoanalyst Wilhelm Reich (1897–1957), whose books include *Character Analysis* (1933), *The Mass Psychology of Fascism* (1933), and *The Sexual Revolution* (1936).

58.40   Watertown arsenal.] Boston-area arsenal (1816–1967) that during the Cold War was the site of technological projects including the development of "Atomic Annie," a cannon capable of firing an atomic weapon.

59.17   Apollo Belvedere] Marble statue of the Greek god, thought to be a second-century Roman copy after a lost Greek bronze. In the eighteenth and nineteenth centuries it was held up as an aesthetic ideal.

61.31   Woods Hole] Woods Hole Oceanographic Institution in Cape Cod, Massachusetts.

64.40   Bob Cousy!"] Basketball player (b. 1928) who was one of the sport's first superstars, a point guard who played most of his career in the Boston area, in college at Holy Cross and then professionally for the Boston Celtics.

65.1   Goose Tatum] Basketball player and entertainer (1921–1967) who spent eleven years with the Harlem Globetrotters.

65.2   de whites ob dare eyes."] Cf. the order of William Prescott (1726–1795), American commander at the battle of Bunker Hill in 1775: "Do not fire until you see the whites of their eyes!"

68.21–22   *le doigt disloqué*."] French: the dislocated finger.

75.39   KENNEDY PRAISES STEEL RESTRAINT.] In April 1962 President Kennedy criticized United States Steel and other steel companies for a 6 percent price increase, which the companies then rolled back. The headline here refers to Kennedy's remarks on April 19, 1963, citing the steel industry's restraint in its recent modest price hikes and expressing the hope that the auto industry and other manufacturers would follow its example.

82.11 He was Ham] Ham was one of the biblical Noah's sons. His own son Canaan, because Ham had seen the drunken and naked Noah asleep in his tent, was cursed to be "a servant of servants . . . to his brethren." Ham has often been regarded as a black man because African peoples were listed among his descendants in Genesis 10:6–20 or because, according to a view first put forth in the fifteenth century, the descendants of Canaan were black while those of his uncles Shem and Japheth (Noah's other sons) were white.

94.34 *Madame Nhu*] Born Tran Le Xuan (1924–2011), the glamorous, influential, and outspoken wife of Ngo Dinh Nhu, the younger brother and chief political advisor of South Vietnamese president Ngo Dinh Diem (see note 170.24). She was official hostess of the government of Diem, who was unmarried.

95.32–33 ERHARD CERTAIN TO SUCCEED ADENAUER] The German politician Ludwig Erhard (1897–1977), a Christian Democrat, was economics minister in the government led from 1949 to 1963 by Konrad Adenauer (1876–1967), whom he succeeded as chancellor of West Germany, 1963–66.

97.29–30 Painter's life of Proust] The two-volume *Marcel Proust: A Biography* (1959, 1965) by the English writer George Duncan Painter (1914–2005).

104.5 *Barbe Bleue et Fatime*] Bluebeard and Fatima, husband and wife in the folktale of Bluebeard, best known in the version by French fabulist Charles Perrault (1628–1703). Bluebeard tries to murder Fatima after she opens a closet in his château against his express orders and discovers the corpses of his previous wives, but he is himself killed by her brothers.

104.35 Anzio and Guadalcanal] Anglo-American and German forces fought each other on the beachhead between the towns of Anzio and Nettuno, thirty miles southwest of Rome, January 22–May 23, 1944; Guadalcanal, in the Solomon Islands, was the site of a U.S. victory over the Japanese in February 1943 after six months of fighting.

108.7–9 *When all aloud . . . in the snow*] Shakespeare, *Love's Labors Lost*, V.ii.921–23.

108.12–14 I'll have a starling . . . still in motion] Shakespeare, *I Henry IV*, I.iii.224–26.

113.8 Rare Egyptian! Royal wench!] Shakespeare, *Antony and Cleopatra*, II.ii.218, 226.

116.30 *potage à la reine*] A creamy chicken soup.

118.20–21 Glenn Gould or Dinu Lipatti playing Bach or Schumann] The Canadian pianist Glenn Gould (1932–1982), known for his Bach interpretations, particularly his recordings of the *Goldberg Variations*; the Romanian pianist Dinu Lipatti (1917–1950), who recorded Schumann's piano concerto in 1948.

122.4–5   *après douze années très heureuses*] French: after twelve very happy years.

125.26   *Je regrette.*] French: I'm sorry.

129.26   "*wanton's bird.*"] Shakespeare, *Romeo and Juliet*, II.ii.177.

131.3   *Avec le coucou.*] French: With the imbecile.

131.17   *Ta poitrine, elle est magnifique.*] French: Your chest is magnificent.

132.23–24   Junior League] Charitable aid organization of upper-class young women founded in 1901 by a railroad magnate's daughter, Mary Harriman (1881–1934).

134.12   "Ripeness is all,"] Shakespeare, *King Lear*, V.ii.11.

134.28–29   *Trois soeurs est trop beaucoup.*] French: Three sisters is [*sic*] too much.

136.14–20   *Tu es comique . . . Tu es trop comique.*] French: You're funny. . . . You're too funny.

137.25   *mon petit chou*] Term of endearment in French, literally "my little cabbage."

137.33   *Tout le monde.*] French: Everybody.

138.9–10   "The mutable, rank-scented many."] Cf. Shakespeare, *Corialanus*, III.i.66.

139.8–9   now that the ecumenical council was adjourned] The Second Ecumenical Council of the Vatican, 1962–65, popularly known as Vatican II, had adjourned in December 1962 and would resume in September 1963.

139.30   World War II movie starring Brian Donlevy] *Wake Island* (1942), directed by John Farrow and starring tough-guy actor Brian Donlevy (1901–1972).

140.5   word games—Botticelli, Ghosts] Botticelli, guessing game in which a person thinks of a famous person at least as well-known as the Italian artist Sandro Botticelli, and then the other players try to identify the mystery person by asking yes-or-no questions; Ghosts, game where players must successively add a letter to a word fragment without forming a complete word.

140.8–9   UN military action in the Katanga province of the Congo] See note 34.17–18.

142.22–23   "that men should put an enemy . . . brains."] Shakespeare, *Othello*, II.iii.290–91.

145.2   Let copulation thrive."] *King Lear*, IV.vi.114.

147.26   vase of *mei ping* form] Chinese "plum blossom" vase with a small mouth, narrow neck, and wide shoulders.

148.33   *Et ma femme? Dort-elle?*] French: And my wife? Is she sleeping?

148.35   *La même.*] French: The same.

149.3   "Good night, sweet prince . . . angels, et cetera."] Horatio's lines after Hamlet dies in *Hamlet*, V.ii.199–200.

149.35   D'Annunzio] Gabriele D'Annunzio (1863–1938), Italian soldier, politician, and man of letters.

151.15–16   Let me not to the blah blah blah admit impediments] See the opening of Shakespeare's sonnet 116: "Let me not to the marriage of true minds / Admit impediments."

154.5   Little Golden Book] Series of original, inexpensive, cardboard-covered picture books for children, founded in 1942.

154.10   Ella] Jazz singer Ella Fitzgerald (1917–1996).

154.11–12   "These Foolish Things" . . . Around the World"] Jazz standards: "These Foolish Things (Remind Me of You)" (1936), music by Jack Strachey (1894–1972), words by Holt Marvell (pseud. Eric Maschwitz, 1901–1969); "You're the Top" (1934) by Cole Porter (1891–1964); and "I Can't Get Started" (1936), music by Vernon Duke (1903–1969), words by Ira Gershwin (1896–1983), whose opening lines are quoted at 155.2–3.

156.2–3   airplanes collided in Turkey] On February 1, 1963, a passenger plane collided with a Turkish air force aircraft over Ankara, killing 104 people.

156.3–4   coups transpired in Iraq and Togo] The Iraqi government of Abd al-Karim Qasim (1914–1963) was overthrown in a military coup, February 8–10, 1963, and was replaced by Ba'ath Party rule; the government of the first president of independent Togo, Sylvanus Olympio (1902–1963), was toppled and Olympio assassinated on January 13, 1963.

156.4   earthquakes in Libya] A severe earthquake struck northern Libya on February 21, 1963.

156.4–5   a stampede in the Canary Islands] On February 3, 1963, twenty-four people were killed after the partial collapse of a convent building in Tenerife, Canary Islands, leading to a stampede of people attempting to escape. The building had been crowded with people seeking shelter from a storm.

156.5–6   and in Ecuador a chapel collapsed . . . nuns] In a convent school in Biblián, Ecuador, on February 1, 1963.

157.21–22   "The horn, the horn . . . scorn,"] Shakespeare, *As You Like It*, IV.ii.17–18.

160.39   Idlewild] Former name of John F. Kennedy International Airport in New York City.

161.28   *merde*] French: shit.

162.6   get thee to a nunnery.] Hamlet to Ophelia in *Hamlet*, III.i.120.

165.6   Joan Baez] Folksinger and political activist (b. 1941).

166.38   Burl Ives] Folksinger and actor (1909–1995).

166.39   the late Pope John] John XXIII (Angelo Giuseppe Roncalli) had died on June 3, 1963.

166.40   Althea Gibson] Tennis player and golfer (1927–2003), a pioneering African American athlete who won eleven tennis championship titles in eight years.

169.5   "Terry and the Pirates,"] Comic strip, 1934–73, created by cartoonist Milton Caniff (1907–1988).

169.7   Yves Tanguy . . . Arshile Gorky."] French surrealist artist (1900–1955); Armenian artist (1904–1948) who immigrated to America in 1920.

169.9   Maxim,"] Russian writer Maxim Gorky (1868–1936), whose best-known play is *The Lower Depths* (1902).

170.24   No-go Diem,"] Ngo Dinh Diem, see note 31.30.

171.3   *Chacun à son goût*] French: To each his own.

172.2–3   Quang Duc had immolated himself] Protesting the South Vietnamese government's anti-Buddhist policies, the Vietnamese Buddhist monk Quang Duc (1897–1963) set himself on fire on June 11, 1963, triggering a wave of self-immolations by monks that were accompanied by street demonstrations and other forms of unrest leading up to the coup that toppled the Diem government on November 1, 1963.

172.3–4   Valentina Tereshkova had become the first woman in space] Tereshkova (b. 1937) was launched into space on the Vostok IV spacecraft on June 16, 1963.

172.4   John Profumo had resigned] English politician John Profumo (1915–2006), secretary of war in the Macmillan government, was discovered to be having an affair with nineteen-year-old Christine Keeler (1942–2017), who was also linked to a Soviet attaché in London. A government inquiry into the matter and its public notoriety led to Profumo's resignation on June 5, 1963, when he acknowledged that he had lied to Parliament about the affair.

172.4–5   the Lord's Prayer had been banned in the American public schools] On June 17, 1963, the Supreme Court handed down its decision in Abington School District *v.* Schempp, which ruled it unconstitutional for public schools to require devotional reading of the Bible, including the recitation of the Lord's Prayer.

173.22   *The Waves.*] Novel (1931) by the English novelist Virginia Woolf (1882–1941).

173.23   Cecil Beaton. Alec Guinness] English photographer (1904–1980) known for his celebrity portraits; English actor (1914–2000) whose films include *Kind Hearts and Coronets* (1949), *The Horse's Mouth* (1958), and *Our Man in Havana* (1959).

174.30–34   Abishag . . . knew her not."] See 1 Kings 1:1–4.

175.32   Dame May Whitty?"] English stage and film actor (1865–1948) who in her later career had roles in such films as *Night Must Fall* (1937), *The Lady Vanishes* (1938), and *Mrs. Miniver* (1942).

176.7   *en face*,"] French: on the opposing page.

176.16   Eliza Doolittle.] Young woman in George Bernard Shaw's comedy *Pygmalion* (1912), a flower-seller who is transformed into a proper lady under the tutelage of Professor Henry Higgins.

177.8–9   flower . . . flourished in the radioactive area?] Contrary to expectations, canna lilies were found growing amid the rubble of Hiroshima soon after the atomic bomb was dropped on the city.

177.13   "Devil's paintbrush,"] Wildflower (*Hieracium aurantiacum*) also known as orange hawkweed.

177.36   *Phineas Finn*,"] Novel (1867–68) by the English novelist Anthony Trollope (1815–1882).

178.1   Christine Keeler,"] See note 172.4.

184.12   *Where the Wild Things Are*] Popular children's picture book (1963) by Maurice Sendak (1928–2012).

188.35   Bovung] Dehydrated cow manure.

198.32–33   the Modern Library edition of *The Interpretation of Dreams*] Translation of Sigmund Freud's *Die Traumdeutung* (1899) by A. A. Brill published by the Modern Library in 1938.

200.13–14   the rich can't get through . . . shall be last.] Cf. Matthew 19:24 ("It is easier for a camel to go through the eye of a needle, than for a rich man to enter into the kingdom of God") and Matthew 20:16 ("So the last shall be first, and the first last: for many be called, but few chosen").

204.35–36   *Is het koud, Joop?*] Dutch: Is it cold, Joop?

214.6   Old Joe] Businessman and financier Joseph P. Kennedy Sr. (1888–1969), the father of President John F. Kennedy.

215.35–216.1   the Wednesday . . . first Russian ship was approaching the blockade.] During the Cuban Missile Crisis, October 16–28, 1962, the discovery of Soviet missile sites on Cuba led President Kennedy to order a naval "quarantine" of the island until the Soviets agreed to remove the missiles. The blockade went into effect on Wednesday, October 24, as Russian cargo ships were reported to be heading toward the blockade zone.

219.28–30   dirty movie?" . . . *Tom Jones*,"] Film adaptation (1963) starring Albert Finney (1936–2019) of the novel (1749) by Henry Fielding (1707–1754), recounting the amorous adventures of its eponymous hero.

221.10   Medgar Evers] Evers (1925–1963), the field secretary of the Mississippi NAACP, 1954–63, was fatally shot outside his house in Jackson by a white supremacist.

221.15   Birmingham Sunday-school children?] Ku Klux Klansmen bombed the Sixteenth Street Baptist Church in Birmingham, Alabama, on September 15, 1963, killing Denise McNair, eleven, Cynthia Wesley, fourteen, Carole Robertson, fourteen, and Addie Mae Collins, fourteen.

221.19   Massachusetts Fair Housing Bill] Anti-discrimination legislation expanding the provisions of the state's 1957 Fair Housing Practices Act to include single-family homes. It was signed into law on April 1, 1963.

224.20   Braque just died."] French artist Georges Braque died at eighty-one on August 31, 1963.

226.4–5   Delilah gazed upon the Samson she had shorn.] See Judges 16:4–30.

227.40   The serpent beguiled me.] Eve's words to Adam in Genesis 3:13, after eating the fruit of the Tree of Knowledge: "The serpent beguiled me, and I did eat."

228.10–11   *Che sarà, sarà*] "Whatever will be, will be," in a form of the maxim derived from Italian; see also note 31.25.

229.14   Almadén] A brand of cheap wine bottled in a large jug.

235.17   *Onvoldaan.*] Dutch: Unsatisfied.

237.36–37   Like two owls and two pussycats in a beautiful pea-green boat.] C.f. "The Owl and the Pussy-Cat" (1871), poem by English poet and artist Edward Lear (1812–1888).

242.26   Titan?] Family of rockets developed by the United States, including intercontinental ballistic missiles and the rockets used for unmanned and manned spaceflight missions in NASA's Gemini program.

243.26   like the Greenbergs] I.e., the Rosenbergs: Julius Rosenberg (1918–1953) and his wife Ethel Rosenberg (1915–1953), American spies for the Soviet Union who were convicted of espionage and executed on June 19, 1953.

243.27   traded to Russia for Gary Powers?] A U-2 spy plane piloted by Francis Gary Powers (1929–1977) for the Central Intelligence Agency was shot down over Sverdlovsk (Yekaterinburg) by a Soviet surface-to-air missile on May 1, 1960. Powers was captured and tried for espionage, and then released in a prisoner exchange on February 10, 1962.

248.27 Pablo Casals and Ruby Newman.] Spanish cellist, conductor, and composer Pablo Casals (1876–1973); Ruby Newman (1902–1973), Boston bandleader whose orchestra played society balls and had a long-standing engagement at the city's Ritz-Carlton Hotel.

260.36–37 saffron-robed monks protesting.] See note 172.2–3.

261.6–7 the new Salinger, with an endless title] *Raise High the Roof Beam, Carpenters and Seymour: An Introduction* (1963), book publication of two long stories by J. D. Salinger (1919–2010) that had appeared in *The New Yorker* in 1955 and 1959, respectively.

263.21–22 quintuplets like those born in South Dakota] The Fischer quintuplets, consisting of three female identical triplets, a boy, and a girl, were born in Aberdeen, South Dakota, on November 14, 1963.

267.9–10 her Greek beach] Jackie Kennedy vacationed in Greece during the first half of October 1962.

267.28–29 Cardinal Spellman] Francis Spellman (1889–1967), Roman Catholic archbishop of New York, 1939–67.

267.29 with his back] Kennedy suffered chronic back pain since his college years and underwent four spinal operations from 1944 to 1957.

267.36 *Dies, diei, diei, diem*] Latin: Day, in its nominative, genitive, dative, and accusative forms.

280.37 "Lady Be Good"] Title song for the musical (1924) by the British-born librettists Guy Bolton (1884–1979) and Fred Thompson (1884–1949), with music by George Gershwin (1898–1937) and lyrics by Ira Gershwin (1896–1983).

286.2 Oswald is an honorable man?] Cf. Mark Antony's eulogy for Caesar in *Julius Caesar*, III.ii.86–87: "But Brutus says he was ambitious / And Brutus is an honorable man."

286.7 Bob Taft] Robert A. Taft (1889–1953), Republican senator from Ohio, 1939–53, and an unsuccessful candidate for the Republican presidential nomination in 1940, 1948, and 1952.

286.14 *Merci pour votre mots très incisifs.*] French: Thanks for your very incisive words.

286.17 the Birchers'] Popular name for members of the John Birch Society, an extreme right-wing political organization founded in Indiana in 1958 by candy manufacturer Robert Welch (1899–1985) and named after John Birch (1918–1945), an American intelligence officer killed by the Chinese Communists at the end of World War II.

287.18 Huey Long.] American lawyer and populist Democratic politician (1893–1935) known as "The Kingfish," who was governor of Louisiana, 1928–32, and U.S. senator from 1932 to 1935, when he was assassinated.

292.36–37 "Stars Fell on Alabama."] Song (1934), music by Frank Perkins, words by Mitchell Parish (1900–1993); the recording by Doris Day is on her album *Day by Night* (1957), as are the songs that follow.

293.39 "Soft as the Starlight."] Song (1957) by Joe Lubin (1917–2001) and Jerome Lester Howard (1903–1952).

295.23 "Wrap Your Troubles in Dreams"] Song (1931) with music by Harry Barris (1905–1962), words by Ted Koehler (1894–1973) and Billy Moll (1905–1967).

296.11 AA] Alcoholics Anonymous.

297.21 *Une flamme éternelle.*] French: An eternal flame.

297.23 *Chérie, es-tu ivre?*] French: Dear, are you drunk?

297.40 "Close Your Eyes."] Song (1933) by Bernice Petkere (1901–2000).

298.16–17 Well done, thou good and faithful.] Cf. Matthew 25:21, in the Parable of the Talents.

303.2 "Stardust."] Song (1927) by Hoagy Carmichael (1899–1981), first recorded as an instrumental; Mitchell Parish added lyrics in 1929.

304.4 *La gauche efféminée.*] French: The effeminate left.

304.10 young widow . . . Madame Nhu] See notes 94.34 and 172.2–3; Nhu's husband was killed in the November coup.

304.32–33 "Under a Blanket of Blue."] Song (1933) with music by Jerry Livingston (1909–1987), words by Marty Symes (1904–1953) and Al J. Neiburg (1902–1978).

305.35–36 Upon what meat . . . grown so great?] *Julius Caesar*, I.ii.149–50.

311.7 "*but as grass.*"] Cf. Psalm 103:15.

317.24 Pope Paul being nearly trampled in Jerusalem.] Paul VI was engulfed by large crowds near the Damascus Gate in Jerusalem on January 5, 1964, at the beginning of a papal visit to the region, the first by a modern pope.

357.17 *Ulmis hollandicus*] Dutch elm.

359.21 Bread upon the waters.] From Ecclesiastes 11:1: "Cast thy bread upon the waters: for thou shalt find it after many days."

359.24–25 Loaves and fishes.] One of the miracles of Jesus, in which five loaves and two fish were multiplied to feed thousands; see Matthew 14:13–21, Mark 6:31–44, Luke 9:12–17, and John 6:1–14.

376.35 "A time to love, and a time to die."] Ecclesiastes 3:5.

378.14–15 Adam's naming of the beasts.] See Genesis 2:20.

390.23   old mousetrap play,"] The play-within-a-play staged in *Hamlet*, III.ii, which Hamlet uses to discern whether his uncle, now king of Denmark, murdered his father.

392.28–29   Dürer's praying hands] Drawing (1508) by the German artist Albrecht Dürer (1471–1528), now in the collection of the Albertina, Vienna.

394.38   *Gunsmoke.*] Long-running television Western, 1955–75, broadcast on CBS.

399.38   *La bel ange?*] French: The beautiful angel?

400.2   *tout le monde*] French: everybody.

400.17   *Pas d'offense*] French: No offense.

400.22   *Ton frère.*] French: Your brother.

401.4   *Je comprends.*] French: I understand.

402.12–13   The son of David will not come except to a generation that's wholly good or bad.] Talmud, Sanhedrin 98a.

409.25   McNamara. Rusk.] Robert McNamara (1916–2009), U.S. secretary of defense, 1961–68; Dean Rusk (1909–1994), U.S. secretary of state, 1961–69.

421.8–9   *How many miles must a man . . . the answer, my friends*] From "Blowin' in the Wind" (1963), song by Bob Dylan (b. 1941).

428.33   *Hayes-Bickford*] Boston-area franchise of greasy-spoon cafeterias.

432.31   peace to Laos] See note 31.28.

RABBIT REDUX

444.1–6   LIEUT. COL . . . *you.*] Dialogue between the commanders of the Soviet spacecrafts Soyuz 4 and Soyuz 5 as they executed the first docking in Earth orbit of two manned space vehicles, January 16, 1969.

451.10   half-dollars . . . out of circulation] Half-dollar coins with a portrait of John F. Kennedy, first minted in 1964, were often hoarded.

453.31–32   Big Little Books] Chunky ten-cent books, approximately 4 × 4½ inches and up to 2 inches thick, printed on pulp paper and bound in cardboard covers by Whitman Publishing Company, Racine, Wisconsin, from 1932 until the paper shortages of World War II. Adapted from episodic newspaper comic strips—*Mickey Mouse, Dick Tracy, Little Orphan Annie*—each page spread featured a black-and-white comics panel facing a page of narrative text.

454.1   MYBOYA MARTYRED] The Kenyan politician and government minister Tom Mboya (1930–1969), a leader in the country's independence movement, was fatally shot in Nairobi on July 5, 1969.

454.25   2001 SPACE OD'SEY] *2001: A Space Odyssey* (1969), film directed by Stanley Kubrick (1928–1999).

455.19   "They've left earth's orbit!"] The crew of the Apollo 11 moon mission left Earth's orbit a few hours after liftoff, July 16, 1969.

456.27–28   Tiny Tim.] Stage name of the American singer and ukulele player Herbert Butros Khaury (1932–1996), whose career peaked in the late 1960s.

457.16   Teresa] The actor and singer Teresa Martin (1948–2002), a regular on the third season (1970) of *Rowan & Martin's Laugh-In*, television variety show on NBC, 1968–73.

458.10   David Frost] *The David Frost Show*, syndicated television interview show, 1969–72, hosted by the English journalist and media personality David Frost (1939–2013).

461.11–12   on Carol Burnett . . . Gomer Pyle] *The Carol Burnett Show*, comedy and variety show on CBS television, 1967–78, hosted by Carol Burnett (b. 1933); the actor Jim Nabors (1930–2017) played the title role on the CBS television comedy *Gomer Pyle–USMC*, 1964–69.

461.25–26   Jack Armstrong . . . Jack Benny.] Radio programs: *Jack Armstrong, the All-American Boy*, adventure serial for young people broadcast on several networks, 1933–51; *The Jack Benny Program*, one of radio's earliest situation comedies, starring the American entertainer Jack Benny (1894–1974), broadcast on various networks and under various titles, 1932–55.

462.15   *que más sabe.*"] Rough Spanish homophonic equivalent ("who knows more") for "Kemosabe," a term of uncertain origin and meaning with which Tonto addresses the Lone Ranger.

462.33   the *William Tell* Overture] Overture to the opera (1829) by Italian composer Gioachino Rossini (1792–1868), accompanying the opening credits of the *Lone Ranger* television show.

462.35   "Indian Love Call."] Song from the 1924 operetta *Rose-Marie*, music by Rudolf Friml (1879–1972), words by Oscar Hammerstein II (1895–1960) and Otto Harbach (1873–1963).

465.31–32   *Der Schockelschtuhl*] Variant of German, der Schaukelstuhl: the rocking chair.

471.23   Banbury Cross] The English nursery rhyme "Ride a cock-horse to Banbury Cross."

475.34   Lord Fauntleroy blouse."] Ruffled and lace-trimmed blouse, modeled after clothing worn by the boy protagonist of *Little Lord Fauntleroy* (1886), best-selling novel by the English American writer Frances Hodgson Burnett (1849–1924).

476.19   *melopeta,*"] Melopita, a pie made with honey and a soft, ricotta-like cheese.

478.39–40   "*Yasou.*" . . . *spera,*"] Exchange of greetings in Greek: Hello and good evening.

480.18   Vitalis] A brand of hair tonic.

481.13   Albert F. Schweitzer] See note 34.35.

482.13   4-F.] Draft-board designation for those deemed unfit for military service.

482.18   He's silent majority,"] A supporter of American policy in Vietnam and more generally of traditional and conservative American values. The phrase became popular after President Nixon appealed to "the great silent majority of my fellow Americans" in a speech on November 3, 1969.

491.15   riots in York] Long-simmering racial tensions in York, Pennsylvania, erupted into several days of unrest, July 17–23, 1969, including the fatal shootings of a police officer and an African American woman visiting the city.

492.12–13   the big publicity-mad Norwegian . . . paper boat.] To test the hypothesis that ancient Egyptian sailors could have crossed the Atlantic on a vessel made of papyrus, the Norwegian anthropologist, adventurer, and writer Thor Heyerdahl (1914–2002) led a seven-man expedition to sail such a boat from Morocco to the Caribbean but had to abandon the voyage on June 18, 1969, after traveling 2,600 miles. A second attempt, made the following year, was successful.

501.27–28   rowboat landing in Florida . . . the Atlantic] The English adventurer and rower John Fairfax (1937–2012) completed a six-month solo journey by rowboat from the Canary Islands to Hollywood, Florida, on July 19, 1969.

510.9   beat Humphrey] Hubert Humphrey (1911–1978), vice president in the Johnson administration, was defeated by Nixon in the 1968 presidential election.

510.35–36   he dumped some girl . . . Massachusetts rivers.] On the night of July 18, 1969, Mary Jo Kopechne (1940–1969), a political campaign worker, left a party on Chappaquiddick Island off Martha's Vineyard, Massachusetts, with Massachusetts U.S. senator Edward Kennedy (1932–2009). She died after Kennedy drove his car off a wooden bridge into a tidal inlet. Kennedy survived the accident and did not report the incident to local police until after Kopechne's body had been found the next day. He pled guilty to leaving the scene of the accident and received a suspended sentence. Irregularities in the investigation contributed to suspicions of a cover-up, and questions about the incident followed Kennedy for the rest of his life.

511.15–17   old Joe . . . with Hitler when he was FDR's man in London.] Joseph P. Kennedy (see note 214.6) was U.S. ambassador to the United Kingdom, 1938–1940, and advocated a policy of appeasement toward Nazi Germany.

512.11   an old movie] *PT 109* (1963), film starring Cliff Robertson (1923–2011) about John F. Kennedy's wartime experience in the Navy.

512.29 this poor Polish girl, she comes from up near Williamsport] Mary Jo Kopechne (see note 510.35–36), born in Wilkes-Barre, Pennsylvania, grew up in New Jersey.

545.2 Wash is what Pilate said . . . go do] In Matthew 27:24, after Jesus is condemned to death, Pontius Pilate washes his hands and declares himself "innocent of the blood of this just person."

546.2 Br'er Rabbit] Trickster character in folklore popularized in *Uncle Remus, His Songs and Sayings: The Folklore of the Old Plantation* (1880) by Joel Chandler Harris (1848–1908).

547.5–7 tunes . . . "Summertime,"] "(Up a) Lazy River" (1931), song by the composer and pianist Hoagy Carmichael (1899–1981) and the clarinetist Sidney Arodin (1901–1948); "You're the Top" (1934), song by Cole Porter (1891–1964) from the musical *Anything Goes* (1934); "Thou Swell" (1927), song from the musical *A Connecticut Yankee* (1927), music by Richard Rodgers (1902–1979), words by Lorenz Hart (1895–1943); "Summertime" (1935), song from the opera *Porgy and Bess* (1935), music by George Gershwin (1898–1937), libretto by DuBose Heyward (1885–1940) and Ira Gershwin (1896–1983).

547.16–17 "My Funny Valentine," . . . Can't Get Started,"] "My Funny Valentine" (1937), song from the Rodgers and Hart musical *Babes in Arms*; "Smoke Gets in Your Eyes" (1933), song from the musical *Roberta*, music by Jerome Kern (1885–1945), words by Otto Harbach (1873–1963); "I Can't Get Started," see note 154.11–12.

548.13–15 begins to sing . . . time to die.] "Turn! Turn! Turn!," adaptation by folk singer Pete Seeger of Ecclesiastes 3:1–8, best known in the version recorded by The Byrds in 1965.

554.20–21 "Honeysuckle Rose"] Song (1928) with music by Fats Waller (1904–1943) and lyrics by Andy Razaf (1895–1973).

555.26 "Time After Time."] Song (1947), music by Jule Styne (1905–1994), words by Sammy Cahn (1913–1993).

556.5 seeing *Hair*."] Musical (1967), music by Galt MacDermot (1928–2018), libretto and lyrics by James Rado (b. 1932) and Gerome Ragni (1935–1991); its first Broadway run lasted for more than four years.

556.26 "There's a Small Hotel."] Song (1936) from the Rodgers and Hart musical *On Your Toes*.

561.18 TRUE GRIT.] Hollywood Western (1969) starring John Wayne, based on the novel (1968) by Charles Portis (b. 1933).

572.14 *Love is here to stay.*] From "Love Is Here to Stay" (1938), music by George Gershwin, words by Ira Gershwin, a song from the film *The Goldwyn Follies* (1938).

577.6–7 a piece of dirt . . . that thing in the Bible."] See Matthew 7:3–5, when Jesus asks: "Why beholdest thou the mote that is in thy brother's eye, but considerest not the beam that is in thine own eye?" The image also is given at Luke 6:41–42.

584.9 Brooks Robinson . . . McQueen] The Baltimore Orioles third baseman Brooks Robinson (b. 1937); the first baseman Orlando Cepeda (b. 1937), who played most of his Major League career with the San Francisco Giants; the actor Steve McQueen (1930–1980), starred in roles including films such as *The Great Escape* (1963) and *Bullitt* (1968).

584.11–12 singing . . . down"] From the first line of Bob Dylan's "Blowin' in the Wind" (see note 421.8–9).

587.30–31 "Farewell, Angelina, the sky is on fire,"] First line of "Farewell, Angelina," Bob Dylan song whose best-known version is the recording by folksinger Joan Baez (b. 1941) in 1965.

587.34–35 "All my tri-als, Lord, soon be o-over,"] From the folk song "All My Trials."

601.23–24 suppress the Whisky Rebellion in 1720 . . . 1799] The revolt in western Pennsylvania directed against federal excise taxes on spirits was suppressed in 1794.

604.5 Bessemer furnace] Furnace used in steel manufacturing employing the Bessemer process, developed in 1856, in which air is blown through molten pig iron to achieve a reduction in carbon, silicon, and manganese.

610.13 that Allen,"] Dick Allen (b. 1942), star player for the Philadelphia Phillies at the center of controversy during his time with the team, 1963–69, before he asked to be traded and was dealt to the St. Louis Cardinals. Pops claims to speak "without prejudice" because Allen is African American.

612.5 yet I live.] Cf. Galatians 2:20.

613.37–38 Pearls before swine . . . Gentiles.] See, respectively, Matthew 7:6 and 1 Corinthians 1:23.

614.23 PIG ATROCITIES STIR CAMDEN] Reports that three police officers had assaulted two sisters, aged twelve and fifteen, in Camden, New Jersey, on September 1, 1969, led to a confrontation between police and a large crowd the following night, in which a police officer and a teenaged girl were fatally shot.

614.32 BUTCH CASSDY & KID] *Butch Cassidy and the Sundance Kid* (1969), movie Western starring Paul Newman (1925–2008) and Robert Redford (b. 1936).

620.3–4 "*We've been raped,* . . . SOYUZ 5] Recorded during the docking of Soyuz 4 with Soyuz 5 (see note 444.1–6).

622.25 "That Old Rugged Cross"] "The Old Rugged Cross" (1912), hymn by the Methodist revival preacher George Bennard (1873–1958).

622.28 goof . . . purple hearts] Slang for street drugs: goof ball, a barbiturate; jolly bean, an amphetamine; red devil, a barbiturate; purple heart, half barbiturate and half amphetamine.

622.29 Panama Red] A type of marijuana.

623.4 "True Love," the old Crosby–Grace Kelly single.] Song (1956) by Cole Porter from the film *High Society*, in which it was performed by Bing Crosby (1903–1977) and Grace Kelly (1929–1982).

636.5 the slain Civil Rights leader] Medgar Evers (see note 221.10).

636.17 Robert Williams] Civil rights leader and activist (1925–1996) who chaired a North Carolina chapter of the NAACP and founded the Black Guard, an organization dedicated to the armed protection of the local African American community against racist violence. After white mobs attacked civil rights demonstrators in Monroe, North Carolina, on August 27, 1961, a white couple was detained inside his home for about two hours. Indicted on kidnapping charges as a result of the incident, Williams fled to Cuba and began broadcasting *Radio Free Dixie*, a weekly program that mixed political news and speeches with African American music. In 1965 Williams and his wife, Mabel, moved to Beijing, where he met with Mao Zedong and Zhou Enlai. The Williamses returned to the United States in 1969, settling in Michigan.

636.22–23 By many false prophets . . . Good Book] See Matthew 24:11, 14.

636.36 Strom Stormtrooper] Strom Thurmond (1902–2003), governor of South Carolina, 1947–51, senator from South Carolina, 1954–2003, and 1948 presidential nominee of the segregationist States' Rights Democratic Party.

636.36–37 Herod . . . all us black babies] A reference to the Massacre of the Innocents, mass slaughter of male babies ordered by Herod in Matthew 2:16.

637.40 *The Wretched of the Earth, Soul on Ice*] *The Wretched of the Earth* (1961), book by the Martinique-born political theorist and philosopher Frantz Fanon (1925–1961); *Soul on Ice* (1968), autobiography written in prison by Eldridge Cleaver (1935–1988), a leader of the Black Panther Party.

638.24–28 Government . . . intellectual elite.] From "China and Africa," a speech given in Beijing in 1959 by W.E.B. Du Bois (1868–1963). The next passage quoted is from Du Bois's *The World and Africa* (1947).

640.29 supercrackers like Yancy and Rhett] Prominent advocates of Southern secession: William Lowndes Yancey (1814–1863), who served as Confederate diplomatic commissioner in Britain and France, 1861–62, and Robert Barnwell Rhett (1800–1876), U.S. congressman, 1837–49, and U.S. senator, 1850–52.

640.36–39 dude called Ruffin . . . shot himself in the head when the South lost?] The Virginia planter Edmund Ruffin (1794–1865), an influential writer on agriculture, was a prominent defender of slavery and advocate of secession.

On June 17, 1865, Ruffin shot himself after writing in his diary of his "unmiti-gated hatred" for the "perfidious, malignant, & vile Yankee race."

642.1 Green pastures] The Pulitzer Prize–winning play (1930) and film (1936) *The Green Pastures* by Marc Connelly (1890–1980) was inspired by *Ol' Man Adam an' His Chillun* (1928), a retelling of biblical stories in purportedly black dialect by the white English professor Roark Bradford (1896–1943).

642.1 Forty acres and a mule] Widely used name for a program of land redis-tribution to people formerly enslaved based on General William T. Sherman's Special Field Order No. 15, issued January 16, 1865. The order, drafted in con-sultation with a group of African American religious leaders and approved by President Lincoln, granted a long swath of coastal territory from Charleston, South Carolina, to the St. John's River in Florida to families of former slaves and stipulated that "each family shall have a plot of not more than 40 acres of tillable ground." Sherman later proposed that the settlers could be lent mules by the Army. The order was revoked by President Andrew Johnson in the fall of 1865.

642.40–643.1 Freedman's Bureau was trashed] The Freedmen's Bureau, the federal agency established in 1865 to assist formerly enslaved people, was dis-banded in 1872.

643.3–4 Tilden was cheated out of the Presidency] The contested 1876 pres-idential election between Democrat Samuel Tilden (1814–1886) and Repub-lican Rutherford B. Hayes (1822–1893) was resolved via a compromise that awarded twenty disputed electoral votes to Hayes in exchange for the with-drawal of federal support for Republican state governments in the South, ef-fectively ending Reconstruction.

646.5–7 Everett Dirksen's funeral . . . Ho Chi Minh's ceremonies in Ha-noi] The Republican U.S. senator from Illinois Everett Dirksen (1896–1969) and the Vietnamese revolutionary and political leader Ho Chi Minh (1890–1969) died within a week of each other in early September 1969.

650.23 happy Rastus] Derogatory term for an African American man, based on cheerful black characters given the name in minstrel shows, fiction, and films.

650.30–31 free-soil convention in Kansas . . . no black faces here] After the proslavery faction won an overwhelming victory in the election of Kansas's first territorial legislature in March 1855, free-soil (or free-state) residents held a convention in Topeka, October 23–November 12, 1855, to draw up a consti-tution that, if ratified by a popular vote in the territory and then by the U.S. Congress, would allow Kansas to become a state. The convention's president, James Lane (1814–1866), later a Republican senator (1861–66), proposed that the new constitution exclude not only enslaved African Americans from the state but free "negroes and mulattoes" as well. The convention decided to submit the question of excluding free blacks to the voters as a separate clause in the ratification vote. On December 15, 1855, the free-state voters approved the constitution, 1,731–46, and the exclusionary clause, 1,287–458. Congress refused to accept the Topeka constitution.

651.15 *Slavery*] *Slavery: A Problem in American Institutional and Intellectual Life* (1957) by the historian Stanley M. Elkins (1925–2013).

651.18 a happening.] An artwork that blurred the boundaries between visual art and performance and often involved audience participation; such works were conceived and staged in the late 1950s and 1960s by artists including Allan Kaprow (1927–2006), who coined the term, John Cage (1912–1992), and figures associated with the Fluxus movement.

651.29–652.4 "*Think*," . . . *Thou hast what is thine.*"] From the conclusion of "A Letter on Slavery" (1848) by the Unitarian minister, author, and abolitionist Theodore Parker (1810–1860).

652.14–15 another . . . old William Lloyd] The speech quoted from is "No Compromise with Slavery" (1854) by the abolitionist William Lloyd Garrison (1805–1879).

654.11 People say to me Free Huey] Huey Newton (1942–1989), cofounder of the Black Panther Party, was arrested for the fatal shooting of Oakland police officer John Frey, Jr., on October 28, 1967. His arrest was regarded as politically motivated by his supporters, who adopted the rallying cry "Free Huey!" Newton was convicted of voluntary manslaughter in September 1968 and sentenced to two to fifteen years in prison. His conviction was overturned in May 1970 and, after two retrials ended in deadlocked juries, the charges were dismissed in December 1971.

655.2–7 "*I believe, my friends . . . our duty.*"] From W.E.B. Du Bois, *Black Reconstruction in America* (1935).

661.3 *Mod Squad*] Popular crime series on ABC television, 1968–73, featuring a trio of hip young undercover detectives.

664.25–26 *ao dai*] A fitted knee-length tunic worn by Vietnamese women.

665.15 Claymore] Directional mine used frequently during the Vietnam War.

666.33 *Samantha.*"] *Bewitched*, situation comedy on ABC television, 1964–72, whose main character, the suburban housewife Samantha Stevens, is a witch.

669.1–4 that cracker Fulldull or that Charlie McCarthy . . . Vietnam some sort of mistake] Arkansas Democrat J. William Fulbright (1905–1995) and Minnesota Democrat Eugene McCarthy (1916–2005) were two senators opposed to the Vietnam War. "Charlie McCarthy" refers to the most famous of the dummies used by the ventriloquist Edgar Bergen (1903–1978).

678.20–23 trial of the Chicago Eight . . . Bobby Seale] Bobby Seale (b. 1936), a cofounder of the Black Panther Party, was indicted in March 1969 along with seven white radicals for conspiring to incite riots during the 1968 Democratic National Convention in Chicago. After the trial began in September 1969, Seale repeatedly disrupted the proceedings to protest the refusal of the judge to grant a delay while his attorney recovered from surgery. Judge

Julius Hoffman (1895–1983) had Seale bound and gagged in the courtroom, then severed his case from the other defendants' and sentenced him to four years in prison for contempt of court. (The government chose not to retry him on the conspiracy charges, and his contempt conviction was overturned in 1972.) The other defendants were acquitted of the conspiracy charges against them, though several were convicted of lesser charges.

678.36–37   Jesus liberated the money-changers from the temple.] See Matthew 21:12–13.

678.38   The old Jesus brought a sword, right?] See Matthew 10:34, in which Jesus says, "I came not to send peace, but a sword."

679.1–2   John Kennel Badbreath and Leonard Birdbrain giving him fund-raising cocktail parties] The economist and diplomat John Kenneth Galbraith (1908–2006) was best known for *The Affluent Society* (1958), a book critical of midcentury America and its social and economic inequalities; the conductor and composer Leonard Bernstein (1918–1990) supported the Black Panthers by hosting a widely publicized fundraiser at his Park Avenue apartment in Manhattan on January 14, 1970.

679.22   SST] Supersonic transport, high-speed aircraft whose development became controversial because of concerns about sonic booms and possible damage to the ozone layer.

680.18   Agnew Dei] A merging of Agnus Dei (Latin, "lamb of God"), liturgical prayer used in several Christian denominations, with Spiro Agnew (1918–1996), vice president of the United States, 1969–73.

694.35   Arvin] ARVN, Army of the Republic of Viet Nam.

710.20   Wednesday's Moratorium Day] The Vietnam Moratorium to End the War in Vietnam (October 15, 1969) was a nationwide demonstration and teach-in, and was followed by a Moratorium March on Washington in November of that year.

728.17   APM] Anti-personnel mine.

742.4–5   Old Cushing up there in Boston] Richard James Cushing (1895–1970), archbishop of Boston, 1944–70.

760.3   *I Am Curious Yellow*] *I Am Curious (Yellow)* (1967), Swedish film directed by Vilgot Sjöman (1924–2006), initially banned in the United States because of its sexual content.

760.4   *Midnight Cowboy*] Film (1969) directed by John Schlesinger (1926–2003) about two hustlers in New York City, rated X on its release.

760.6   *Funny Girl*] Film (1968) directed by William Wyler (1902–1981) and starring Barbra Streisand (b. 1942), a movie biography of the comedian, singer, and actor Fanny Brice (1891–1951) that had originally been a Broadway musical.

760.15 Nick Arnstein] Professional gambler and criminal (1879–1965) who was Fanny Brice's second husband, an associate of organized crime boss Arnold Rothstein (1882–1928).

779.12 Datsun agency] Dealership for cars manufactured by the Japanese company Nissan; the name was discontinued in the 1980s.

A MONTH OF SUNDAYS

792.1 *For Judith Jones*] Jones (1924–2017) was Updike's editor at Alfred A. Knopf, Publisher, from 1960 until his death in 2009.

792.4–5 The principle of soul . . . principle of ambiguity.] From *History of Christian Thought* (1968) by the Protestant theologian Paul Tillich (1886–1965).

793.11–12 green and crowded land] Cf. "England's green and pleasant land" from the preface to *Milton: A Poem* (1804–10) by William Blake (1757–1827), widely known because of the English hymn "Jerusalem" (1916) by Hubert Parry (1848–1918), a musical setting of the poem.

793.19 doubt . . . Thomas] In John 20:24–29 the resurrected Jesus asks the skeptical apostle Thomas to thrust his hand into his wounds to satisfy Thomas's need for proof.

794.25 *Noli me tangere.*] Latin: Don't touch me, Jesus's words in the Vulgate to Mary Magdalene when he appears to her after the resurrection (John 20:17).

795.13–14 *ad libitum.*] Latin: optional.

795.29 *sanitas*] Latin: health.

796.10 one of Magritte's eerily outdoor paintings.] *Le faux miroir* ("The False Mirror," 1928) by René Magritte (1898–1967), Belgian painter and illustrator in the surrealist manner.

797.26 Chesterton somewhere says] In *Orthodoxy* (1908) by the English conservative Catholic writer G. K. Chesterton (1874–1936).

799.24–26 "With the help . . . sound feet"] From an 1847 journal entry by the Danish philosopher and theologian Søren Kierkegaard (1813–1855).

799.38 Jungian-Reichian] Offshoots of Freudian psychoanalytic theory and practice led respectively by the Swiss psychologist and writer Carl Jung (1875–1961) and Wilhelm Reich (see note 53.16).

799.39 Tillichic, Jasperian, Bultmannish] Referring to Paul Tillich (see note 792.4–5); the German philosopher Karl Jaspers (1883–1969), author of the three-volume *Philosophy* (1932) and works on the philosophy of religion; and the German biblical scholar and theologian Rudolf Bultmann (1884–1976), author of *Theology of the New Testament* (1948–53).

800.33 Shakti and Shiva.] Hindu deities: the goddess Shakti, also known as Parvati, and Shiva, one of the three primary Hindu gods.

800.35–36 "upon thy belly shalt thou go"] Genesis 3:14.

802.23 *Curo, curate, curare.*] The English word "curate" is derived from the Latin verb *curo*, to look after or to care for.

802.31–32 Remingtonesque work . . . prairie sunset] The American painter, sculptor, and illustrator Frederic Remington (1861–1909) is known for his Western subjects.

803.7–8 All men hate God, Melville says.] Cf. Herman Melville's letter to Nathaniel Hawthorne, June 1851: "I had rather be a fool with a heart, than Jupiter Olympus with his head. The Reason the mass of men fear God, and *at bottom dislike* him, is because they rather distrust His heart, and fancy Him all brain like a watch."

804.39–40 "He who is down," . . . "need fear no fall."] First line of hymn with words by the English writer John Bunyan (1628–1688), first published in his *Pilgrim's Progress*, part 2 (1684).

805.1 quoth the Psalmist] In Psalms 22:29.

805.12–14 ground of our being! . . . Tillichian pun] Paul Tillich equated God with the "ground of being" in *Systematic Theology* (1951–1963), *The Courage to Be* (1952), and elsewhere.

806.31 O. Henry and John Tunis and Admiral Byrd] O. Henry, pseudonym of William Sydney Porter (1862–1910), popular American writer of short stories known for their surprise endings; John R. Tunis (1889–1975), sportswriter and prolific writer of juvenile fiction with sports themes; Richard E. Byrd (1888–1957), polar explorer whose books about his experiences include *Little America* (1930), *Discovery* (1935), and *Alone* (1938).

806.38 *point de départ pour le croyant qui souffre*] French: point of departure for the suffering believer.

807.8 *Pensées!*] Collection of philosophical and theological observations by the French philosopher Blaise Pascal (1623–1662) first published posthumously in 1669–70.

807.9 John Dickson Carr] American writer (1906–1977) who also wrote under the name Carter Dickson; he was the author of many detective novels, including *Poison in Jest* (1932), *The Three Coffins* (1935), and *The Case of the Constant Suicides* (1941).

807.10 P. G. Wodehouse] British-born comic writer P. G. Wodehouse (1881–1875), the creator of Bertie Wooster and his butler, Jeeves.

807.11 Dorothy Sayers] English author (1893–1957) of detective novels including *The Unpleasantness at the Bellona Club* (1928), *Murder Must Advertise* (1933), and *Gaudy Night* (1936).

807.12 *Summa Theologica.*] Magnum opus (1266–73) of the scholastic philosopher and Dominican friar Thomas Aquinas (1225–1274).

807.15 a Barthian] Devotee of the thought of the influential Swiss Protestant theologian Karl Barth (1886–1986), author of the multivolume *Church Dogmatics* (1932–67).

807.17 Schleiermacher's and Ritschl's] The German philosopher Friedrich Schleiermacher (1768–1834), a pioneer of modern hermeneutics, including with regard to the Bible; the German Protestant theologian Albrecht Ritschl (1822–1889), author of *Justification and Reconciliation* (3 vols., 1870–74).

807.20–21 the Grand Inquisitor!] Central figure of a parable recounted by Ivan Karamazov to his brother Alyosha in Fyodor Dostoevsky's *The Brothers Karamazov* (1879–80).

807.22 *deus absconditus*!] Latin: hidden God, an important concept in Christian, and notably Lutheran, theology.

808.1–4 Robbe-Grillet . . . describe a chair] The French novelist, essayist, and filmmaker Alain Robbe-Grillet (1922–2008), author of *The Erasers* (1953), *The Voyeur* (1955), and *For a New Novel* (1963), was the leading theoretician of the *nouveau roman* or "new novel" movement, whose writers tended to focus on surface description and eschewed the conventional novelistic uses of plot and character.

808.27 *mors*!] Latin: death.

809.24–25 'A Mighty Fortress'] Hymn (c. 1527–29) written by Martin Luther.

810.8–10 *Sämtliche Orgelwerke . . . Dupré*] Complete Organ Works of Dietrich Buxtehude and Complete Organ Works of J. S. Bach annotated with fingerings by Marcel Dupré.

811.9 Uccello] Paolo Uccello (1397–1475), Florentine painter.

812.30–31 Biblical phrase . . . scales fell from my eyes.] See Acts 9:18; the phrase is used to describe the restoration of Paul's sight after being blinded on the road to Damascus.

816.35 equals 33] Christ's age when he was crucified.

817.11 *intellegere . . . esse.*] Latin: intelligence; being.

818.28 "*ux.*,"] Abbreviated form of Latin *uxor*: wife.

818.28 Chillingworth] Surname of Hester Prynne's husband in Nathaniel Hawthorne's *The Scarlet Letter* (1850).

825.20 Augustine and his *concupiscentia*] Augustine of Hippo (354–430) addressed the nature and implications of carnal lust (*concupiscentia carnis*) in his *Confessions* (397–400) and *On Marriage and Concupiscence* (419–21).

825.21   Bonaventura and his *gratia*] The Franciscan friar Bonaventure of Bagnoregio (Giovanni di Fidanza, ca. 1217–1274) explored the idea of divine grace (*gratia*) in works such as *Journey of the Mind to God*.

825.21   Anselm and his *librum arbitrium*] Free choice (*liberum arbitrium*) as fundamental to humanity was a key concept for the Christian theologian Anselm of Canterbury (1022–1109), who discussed this idea and related notions in the dialogue *On the Freedom of Choice* and other writings.

825.22   Aquinas and his *synderesis*] Also *synteresis*, concept in scholastic philosophy practiced by Aquinas and others that refers to the habituated knowledge in one's conscience of universally good moral actions.

825.22–23   Duns Scotus and his *pondus naturae*] The Scottish Franciscan theologian John Duns, known as Duns Scotus (ca. 1266–1308), described the human desire to move toward the perfection of God's vision as being akin to a "weight of nature" (*pondus naturae*).

825.23   Occam and his razor] The view of the English philosopher William of Ockham (1285–1349) that the simplest explanation is most likely the correct one is known as "Occam's razor."

825.24   Grotius and his *jus gentium*] International law or the "law of nations" (*jus gentium*) was of central concern to the Dutch jurist and philosopher Hugo Grotius (1583–1645).

825.30   Hume was exploding "ought" and "right"] One of the primary insights in the writings of the Scottish philosopher David Hume (1711–1776) is that moral judgments about what should be cannot be derived from things as they actually are.

825.31–32   Bentham . . . maximalization formulas.] The utilitarian philosophy of the English thinker Jeremy Bentham (1748–1832), in its belief that the good consisted of achieving the greatest happiness for the greatest number of people, sought the maximizing of pleasure and the diminishment of pain.

825.32–33   Spinoza, more *titillatio* than *hilaritas* . . . *conatus*] See the *Ethics* (1664–65, pub. 1677), of the Dutch Jewish philosopher Baruch Spinoza (1632–1677), Part III, Proposition 11, Scholium, in which he contrasts "the emotion of pleasure in reference to the body and mind together [referred to as] stimulation (*titillatio*) or merriment (*hilaritas*)" with "suffering (*dolor*) or melancholy (*melancholia*)." Spinoza uses the term *conatus* (striving) to characterize a force that compels things to continue to exist.

825.36–37   Kant . . . categorical imperatives and *Achtung*] The German philosopher Immanuel Kant (1724–1804) articulated the idea of the categorical imperative (in its first formulation in his *Groundwork of the Metaphysic of Morals* [1785], "Act only according to that maxim whereby you can, at the same time, will that it should become a universal law") as a fundamental element of his moral philosophy; he posits a feeling toward morality called *Achtung*, which has been translated as "reverence" and "respect."

826.6   "slave virtues" and "herd virtues."] Disdainful characterizations of historical and existing moral systems by the German philosopher Friedrich Nietzsche (1844–1900), opposed to what he deemed the genuine virtues of a "master morality."

826.36–37   British idealists, Green and Bradley] T. H. Green (1836–1882) and F. H. Bradley (1846–1924), two of the three most important philosophers in the British Idealism school.

827.1–2   Pierce, James, and Dewey] The American pragmatist philosophers Charles Sanders Peirce (1839–1914), William James (1842–1910), and John Dewey (1859–1952).

828.35   Marcion.] Second-century C.E. gnostic, founder of the Marcionite sect.

828.35   Flacius.] Matthias Flacius Illyricus (1520–1575), Lutheran theologian and church historian from Istria (in present-day Croatia).

830.8   *totaliter aliter*] Latin: wholly other.

830.32   McGovernism] Referring to the liberal antiwar politics of George McGovern (1922–2012), the senator from South Dakota who was the Democratic Party's unsuccessful candidate for president in 1972.

831.2   fidasustenative] Faith-sustaining.

831.17   Adonis . . . Venus] In a classical legend, the basis for numerous works of art and poetry (including the account in Ovid, *Metamorphosis*, book 10, and Shakespeare's poem *Venus and Adonis*), Venus falls in love with the exceptionally beautiful young man Adonis and, though warning that misfortune would befall him, fails to persuade him not to go off on a hunt, in which he is killed by a wild boar.

831.39   contract with Noah] See Genesis 9:8–17, in which God makes a covenant with Noah that there will not be a second flood to destroy humanity.

834.20   "second Osworld"?] Wordplay on the idea of a "second Oswald," a man impersonating Lee Harvey Oswald as part of a purported conspiracy to assassinate John F. Kennedy.

834.23   Dutch Schultz . . . Molly Bloom] The American racketeer and bootlegger born Arthur Flegenheimer (1902–1935), assassinated by other underworld figures; the wife of protagonist Leopold Bloom in James Joyce's *Ulysses* (1922), whose long monologue concludes the novel.

834.25   one of the Dead Sea Scrolls, by Andman Willsin] Wordplay on the name of the American literary critic Edmund Wilson (1895–1972), who wrote about the Dead Sea Scrolls in *The Scrolls of the Dead Sea* (1955) and scathingly criticized the genre of detective fiction in three essays published in *The New Yorker* in 1944 and 1945.

835.15–16   Pascal says man's glory is that he knows his misery.] In *Pensées*, 409: "la grandeur de l'homme est si visible qu'elle se tire même de sa misère."

837.24–26   The poor ye have . . . peace demonstration.] Cf. Jesus's words in Mark 14:7: "ye have the poor with you always" and Matthew 10:34, "I came not to send [bring] peace, but a sword."

838.16–17   It is easier for the camel . . . Judge not] See Matthew 19:24: "It is easier for a camel to go through the eye of a needle, than for a rich man to enter into the kingdom of God"; and Matthew 7:1: "Judge not, that ye be not judged."

838.23   New Left] Left-wing movements of the 1960s associated with the counterculture and student protest, most prominently Students for a Democratic Society (SDS).

839.24–25   Praetorius] German composer Michael Praetorius (1571?–1621), who set many Protestant hymns to music.

839.34   "A thousand ages in his sight—"] Cf. the hymn "Our God, Our Help in Ages Past" (1719), with words by the English hymnist Isaac Watts (1674–1748): "A thousand ages in thy sight / Are like an evening gone."

842.2   The agony of resurrection, a theme for Unamuno.] The Spanish writer and philosopher Miguel de Unamuno (1864–1936) was the author of, among other works, *The Agony of Christianity* (1925).

842.3   The agony of dried tubers. See Eliot, Tom.] Cf. T. S. Eliot's poem *The Waste Land* (1922), lines 5–7: "Winter kept us warm, covering / Earth in forgetful snow, feeding / A little life with dried tubers."

842.16–17   lo! to his wondering eyes did appear] Cf. the poem "A Visit from St. Nicholas" (1823) (also known as "'Twas the Night Before Christmas"), attributed to American professor and poet Clement Clark Moore (1779–1863): "When what to my wondering eyes did appear, / But a miniature sleigh and eight tiny rein-deer."

842.28–29   Heraclitean river . . . first stepped into it] Cf. "You could not step twice into the same river": well-known saying of the Greek pre-Socratic philosopher Heraclitus (c. 535–475 B.C.E.) as it is given in Plato, *Cratylus*, 402a.

843.17   *motor immotus.*] Latin: immovable mover, a Scholastic conception of God.

844.30   *à la* Latour,] As in the paintings of the French artist Georges de La Tour (1593–1652), which often feature striking images illuminated by candlelight and set against dark backgrounds.

846.25–26   her devils . . . residence in swine] A reference to the biblical story of the herd of Gadarene swine who are driven mad by demons and drown themselves (Matthew 8:28–34, Mark 5:1–20, and Luke 8:26–39).

849.2   Lazarene] Lazarus was raised from the dead by Jesus in John 11:1–44.

849.10–11 tower of Babel Barth says our merely human religiosity erects] See the conclusion of Barth's essay "The Righteousness of God" (1916).

849.35–36 Luther his beer . . . Bo tree?] Martin Luther was an enthusiastic beer drinker; the Buddha achieved enlightenment (in Japanese Zen Buddhism, *satori*) while meditating under a bodhi tree.

850.4 Gene Rostow] Eugene Rostow (1913–2002), lawyer and Yale University dean who advised the State Department and served as an undersecretary for political affairs in 1966.

851.5–6 pro-Caesar . . . Render unto him.] See Luke 20:25: "Then render unto Caesar the things that are Caesar's, and unto God the things that are God's."

851.7–8 Brutus and Cassius.] Roman conspirators in the assassination of Julius Caesar: the general and senator Gaius Cassius Longinus (d. 42 B.C.E.), the politician Marcus Junius Brutus (85–42 B.C.E.).

851.9 Somewhere Barth says,] At the end of Barth's 1919 lecture "The Christian's Place in Society," also known as the Tambach Lecture ("Denn was kann der Christ in der Gesellschaft anderes tun, als dem Tun Gottes aufmerksam zu folgen").

851.34 Tillich and Bultmann] See note 799.39.

852.12 *VOICI UNE SCÈNE. Où je ne suis pas.*] French: Here is a scene. Where I am not.

852.16 What is truth?] Pilate's question to Jesus, John 18:38.

852.34 *objets*] French: objects; here, knickknacks, bric-a-brac.

856.10 the Apologists] Early Christian theological writers, including Justin Martyr (ca. 100–165) and Tertullian (c. 155–ca. 240).

857.3–4 other side of the looking glass] The tales of Alice, the young heroine invented by the English writer and mathematician Lewis Carroll (pseud. Charles Lutwidge Dodgson, 1832–1898), are told in *Alice's Adventures in Wonderland* (1865) and its sequel *Through the Looking-Glass, and What Alice Found There* (1871).

857.7–8 denied her (no cock crew)] In all four Gospels, a cock crows after Peter's denials of Jesus early in the morning on the day of Jesus's crucifixion.

857.16 a novel by one of the Alcott sisters] Of the four Alcott sisters only Louisa May (1832–1888) was a novelist.

859.35–38 wedding at Cana . . . first miracle.] According to the Gospel of John, Jesus's first miracle was to turn water into wine at a wedding at Cana (the episode does not appear in the other Gospels). See John 2:1–11.

860.7–8 the multitude He had miraculously fed] See note 359.24–25.

860.32–34   as if Lazarus . . . withered under hypnosis.] See notes 849.2 and 846.25–26; in Matthew 21:18–22 and Mark 11:12–14, 11:20–25, Jesus curses a fig tree because it lacks any fruit to satisfy his hunger, causing it to wither.

861.12–13   "issue of blood for twelve years"] See Matthew 9:20–22, Mark 5:25–34, and Luke 8:43–48.

861.23–38   Do we not cry . . . His way.] See Luke 4:23–37.

862.19   Abbott and Costello] The American comedy duo Bud Abbott (1895–1974) and Lou Costello (1906–1959), veterans of burlesque and vaudeville who starred in thirty-six movies together.

862.20   W. C. Fieldish] In the style of the wisecracking American comic actor W. C. Fields (1880–1946).

862.21–23   graceful episode . . . in that fish's mouth a coin] Told in Matthew 17:24–27.

862.25   cosmic Tramp] The Tramp was a character portrayed by Charlie Chaplin (1889–1977) in films such as *The Gold Rush* (1925) and *Modern Times* (1936).

863.27–28   one of the infamous feasts of Baal-adoring Heliogabalus] According to a story told in the late Roman *Augustan History* about the emperor Marcus Aurelius Antoninus Augustus (ca. 204–222), later called Elagabalus or Heliogabalus (after the Roman sun god), a massive shower of flower petals was dropped from the ceiling of a banquet hall and smothered some of the feast's guests to death. Baal is the name of a Canaanite god worshipped by the Israelites in 1 Kings.

865.28   "Except a seed dieth,"] Cf. John 12:24.

866.35   The silence of this room *m'effraie*] Cf. Pascal, *Pensées*, 233: "Le silence éternel de ces espaces infinis m'effraie" ("The eternal silence of these infinite spaces frightens me").

867.4   Inbetweentimes] In Christian eschatology, the time between Christ's first and second comings.

867.13   keyboard of her gorgan] In Greek mythology, the sisters Stheno, Euryale, and Medusa were gorgons, creatures who would turn to stone anyone who looked at one of them directly.

867.14–15   *Venite* . . . *Sanctus*] Morning prayer service canticle, based on Psalm 95; liturgical passage ("Holy, holy, holy") sung, chanted, or spoken as prelude to the sacrament of communion.

867.16–18   "O Master . . . Where'er Ye Languish."] Hymn with words (1912) by the American Congregationalist minister and professor George E. Day (1815–1905), set to music (1738) by the English composer William Knapp (1698–1768); hymn with words (1897) by the American Congregationalist minister and social reformer Washington Gladden (1836–1918), set to music

(1842) by the German composer and musicologist Gottfried W. Fink (1783–1846); hymn with words (1816) by the Irish poet Thomas Moore (1779–1852), revised and complemented (1831) with additional words by the American church musician Thomas Hastings (1784–1872) and set to an adaptation of a traditional German melody.

868.8   Better, St. Paul said, to marry than to burn] In 1 Corinthians 7:9.

868.15   Colette] French novelist (1873–1954) who wrote candidly about sex and erotic relationships in books such as *Chéri* (1920) and the pseudonymously published "Claudine" tetralogy.

868.22   *consensus gentium*] Latin: agreement of the people.

869.36   had my being there] Cf. Acts 17:28: "For in him we live, and move, and have our being."

870.16   τέλος] Greek: telos, purpose or end.

870.25–26   my Jacob and Esau, my two sons] The biblical Jacob and Esau were the twin sons of Isaac.

870.35–36   Freud's . . . slip of the tips.] Sigmund Freud discussed the hidden significance of paraphaxes, or "slips of the tongue," in his 1901 book *The Psychopathology of Everyday Life.*

875.31   bridegroom cometh.] Matthew 25:6, from the parable of the wise and foolish virgins.

876.14   *les filles des villes*] French: city girls.

877.39–40   the ills that flesh is heir to.] Cf. Hamlet's soliloquy in *Hamlet*, III.i.61–62, "the thousand natural shocks / That flesh is heir to."

881.22–23   tartish Maria Schneider of *Last Tango*] The French actor Maria Schneider (1952–2011) was the female lead opposite Marlon Brando (1924–2004) in *Last Tango in Paris* (1972), film directed by Italian director Bernardo Bertolucci (1941–2018) and given an X rating in the United States for its sexual content.

882.9–10   like the freckled-faced blue-movie star . . . throats.] Linda Lovelace, the stage name of Linda Susan Boreman (1949–2002), was the star of the notorious and widely screened pornographic movie *Deep Throat* (1972).

883.32   νοῦς] Greek: nous, mind.

885.1–2   virile muckraking parsons of the first Roosevelt's reign] Adherents of the Social Gospel movement in American Protestantism during the late nineteenth and early twentieth centuries, including Washington Gladden (see note 867.16–18) and Walter Rauschenbusch (1861–1918).

885.37   the Charpentier] the French composer Gustave Charpentier (1860–1956).

886.37   *Rejoice in the Lord . . . Rejoice.*] Philippians 4:4.

887.29–30   Jesus Christ Superstar.] Stage musical (1970) and film (1973), music by Andrew Lloyd Webber (b. 1948), lyrics by Tim Rice (b. 1944).

888.12   *potens* was becoming *ens.*] Latin: ability; being.

888.23–24   talk . . . the truth with love, St. Paul prescribes] In Ephesians 4:14.

888.32–33   *intra cathedra*] Latin: within the office.

893.14   Friar Tuck] One of Robin Hood's Merry Men.

893.23   *vin*] French: wine.

894.22   *mignonette*] French: cutie.

895.21–22   Do you believe in God . . . Earth] Interrogative form used in baptism of the first line of the Apostles' Creed.

900.20   the Psalmist says] In Psalm 42:2.

900.21   we are told elsewhere] In Deuteronomy 32:2.

900.23–24   "He leadeth me . . . my soul"] Psalm 23:2–3.

900.35   *playas*] Spanish: beaches.

901.30–31   whom Jahweh appointed the apple of His eye] See Deuteronomy 32:10, in which God found Jacob "in a desert land, and in the waste howling wilderness; he led him about, he instructed him, he kept him as the apple of his eye."

904.6   chariot of fire] Phrase that appears in 2 Kings 2:11, 2 Kings 6:17, and in William Blake's preface to *Milton: A Poem* (see note 793.11–12).

904.20   Courrèges] Innovative French fashion designer André Courrèges (1923–2016), a contributor to women's fashion trends of the 1960s such as go-go boots and the miniskirt.

906.20   *glace vanille*] French: vanilla ice cream.

906.26–27   if Bebe Rebozo has a real name?] Charles Gregory Rebozo (1912–1998), known by his nickname Bebe, was a real estate developer, banker, and longtime close friend to Richard Nixon. His financial activities were scrutinized by government officials during the Watergate investigation and by journalists.

912.1–2   Boys' Town] Boys' orphanage and name for the organization founded in 1917 by the Catholic priest Edward Flanagan (1886–1948) that administers such facilities nationally.

912.29–31   "Let my bones . . . [Pusey translation].] From the opening of Augustine's *Confessions*, book 8, in its translation (1838) by Edward Bouverie Pusey (1800–1882).

914.5 Titleist] Sporting goods company specializing in golf equipment, clothing, and accessories.

914.11 lukewarm I spit thee out.] See Revelations 3:15–16: "I know thy works, that thou art neither cold nor hot: I would thou wert cold or hot. So then because thou art lukewarm, and neither cold nor hot, I will spue thee out of my mouth."

916.1–2 "*Unum baptisma in remissionem peccatorum,*"] From the Latin of the fourth-century Nicene Creed: "[I confess] one baptism for the remission of sins."

916.10 like old women gathering fuel in vacant lots] From the final lines of "Preludes" (1917) by the American poet T. S. Eliot (1888–1965): "The worlds revolve like ancient women / Gathering fuel in vacant lots."

916.11 "*Qui tollis peccata mundi,*" I consoled] From the Agnus Dei (see note 680.18): [Lamb of God,] who takes away the sins of the world, [have mercy upon us].

916.32 "*Pleni sunt coeli et terra gloria tua.*"] Latin: Heaven and earth are full of Thy glory, which is chanted or sung during the Sanctus (see note 867.14–15).

917.34 minion of the Babylonian mother of harlots] See Revelation 17 and its vision of the Whore of Babylon, who sits astride a seven-headed beast.

918.5 "*O salutaris hostia,*"] Eucharistic hymn ("O saving victim") by Thomas Aquinas.

920.7–9 Panovsky points out . . . its cathedrals.] Cf. *Scholasticism and Gothic Architecture* (1948, pub. 1951) by the German-born art historian Erwin Panofsky (1892–1968): "It was, however, in architecture that the habit of clarification [*manifestatio*] achieved its greatest triumphs. As High Scholasticism was governed by the principle of *manifestatio*, so was High Gothic architecture dominated . . . by what may be called the 'principle of transparency.'"

921.22 the hobgoblin of trivial minds.] Cf. Ralph Waldo Emerson, "Self-Reliance" (1841): "A foolish consistency is the hobgoblin of little minds, adored by little statesmen and philosophers and divines."

922.5–6 some kind of Stendhalian crystallization] In *De l'amour* (On Love, 1822), the French novelist Stendhal (pseud. Marie-Henri Beyle, 1783–1842) elaborated his concept of "crystallization" to describe "the process of the mind which discovers fresh perfections in its beloved at every turn of events."

924.2 *donum superadditum*] Latin: superadded gift, Christian theological term for the gratuitous gift of grace given to humans by God.

925.14 Pascal's notorious bet.] In *Pensées*, 233, Pascal asserts that belief in the existence or nonexistence of God should be regarded as a wager: "if you win, you win everything; if you lose, you lose nothing."

925.27–28   "potently . . . words of Luther] In *De Servo Arbitrio* (On the Bondage of the Will, 1525).

926.1–2   the Berrigans] Daniel Berrigan (1921–2016), American Jesuit priest, peace activist, and poet; his brother Philip Berrigan (1923–2002), Roman Catholic priest and antiwar activist.

926.8–9   the dismissal of St. Christopher] The feast day of St. Christopher, legendary third-century martyr long associated with the safety of travelers and with protection against sudden death, was removed in 1969 from the General Roman Calendar of the Roman Catholic Church.

928.30   Doré] The French artist Gustave Doré (1832–1883), whose many illustrations included those for editions of Dante's *Inferno* in 1857 and the Bible in 1866.

930.35–36   "Around the world in Eighty Days"] Title of the English translation of *Le tour du monde en quatre-vingts jours* (1874), adventure novel by the French writer Jules Verne (1828–1905).

932.21–22   Miguel de Unamuno . . . remarks] In *The Tragic Sense of Life* (1912).

933.20   Parousia] Christian theological term for the second coming of Christ.

934.2–4   *je m'effraie . . . Qui m'y a mis?*] "I take fright and am amazed to see myself here rather than there: there is no reason for me to be here rather than there, now rather than then. Who put me here?", Pascal's *Pensées*, 205, translated (1966) by A. J. Krailsheimer.

934.7–8   Bergson, that graceful fellow-traveller of our rough faith] The French Jewish philosopher Henri Bergson (1859–1941) wrote sympathetically about Christianity, especially about the Christian mystics, and considered conversion late in his life.

939.15   Bunyan tells us] See note 804.39–40.

939.26   Uranus to your Gaea,] One of the Titans in Greek mythology, a sky god; Gaea or Gaia, ancient Greek earth goddess.

940.8–9   *intelligens entis*] Latin: intelligent being.

940.31–32   become children . . . kingdom of God] Cf. Matthew 18:3.

941.22   true Lutheran experience] Martin Luther wrote candidly about his struggles with chronic constipation.

941.39   *esse est deus.*] Latin: being is God, a key concept put forth by the German mystic Meister Eckhart (ca. 1260–ca. 1327) in his *Opus tripartitum*.

943.4   bring to me a virgin lass as to a Minotaur] According to Greek legend, the Cretan king Minos demanded the sacrifice of Athenian youths every nine years to the Minotaur, a monster with a bull's head and a man's body who was kept in a labyrinth.

944.3–4   Meister Eckhardt . . . "the simple ground, the quiet desert"] See the discussion of Eckhart's thought in Paul Tillich's *A History of Christian Thought*, part 1, chapter 4, section N: "For the divinity [Eckhart] uses the terms of negative theology. He calls it the simple ground, the quiet desert."

APPENDIX

949.11   *The Centaur*] Updike's third novel, published in 1963.

950.5   Denis de Rougemont's theories of love] Put forth in *Love in the Western World* (1939; tr. 1956) by the Swiss philosopher and cultural historian Denis de Rougemont (1906–1985).

952.31   B & M] Boston & Maine Railroad.

958.20   the Grange] See note 19.39.

959.9   "Linda" to "Across the Alley from the Alamo."] Popular songs from 1946 written by, respectively, Jack Lawrence (1912–2009) and Joe Greene (1915–1986).

964.11   Simca] French automobile manufactured from 1934 to 1981.

964.27   like a de Latour, in the restaurant candlelight] See note 844.30.

973.35–36   Iphigenia is sacrificed] In Greek mythology, Agamemnon sacrifices his daughter Iphigenia so that his ships can sail to war against Troy.

974.1   "hardness of the heart"] The epigraph to Updike's novel *Rabbit, Run* (1960) reads as follows: "'The motions of Grace, the hardness of the heart; external circumstances.' —*Pascal, Pensée 507*."

974.5–6]   "timbered gables . . . plumped up like pillows."] See page 656 of the present volume.

THE LIBRARY OF AMERICA SERIES

Library of America fosters appreciation of America's literary heritage by publishing, and keeping permanently in print, authoritative editions of America's best and most significant writing. An independent nonprofit organization, it was founded in 1979 with seed funding from the National Endowment for the Humanities and the Ford Foundation.